JOSEPH WAMBAUGH

Four Complete Novels

JOSEPH WAMBAUGH

Four Complete Novels

The Blue Knight

The Black Marble

The New Centurions

The Choir Boys

AVENEL BOOKS · NEW YORK

This omnibus edition was previously published as separate volumes under the titles:

This edition is published by Avenel Books distributed by Crown Publishers, Inc. *The New Centurions* and *The Blue Knight* published by permission of Little, Brown & Company in arrangement with Atlantic Monthly Press. *The Choirboys* and *The Black Marble* published by arrangement with Delacorte Press, a Division of Dell Publishing Co., Inc.

Manufactured in the United States of America

h g f e d c b a

Library of Congress Cataloging in Publication Data

Wambaugh, Joseph.
Four complete novels.

Contents: The blue knight—The black marble—The new centurions—[etc.]
I. Title.
PS3573.A475A6 1982 813′.54 81-19092
ISBN 0-517-366479 AACR2

CONTENTS

The Blue Knight

TO MY PARENTS
AND TO
UPTON BIRNIE BRADY

I often remember the rookie days and those who had discovered the allure of the beat. Then I thought them just peculiar old men. Now I wish they were all still here and that they might approve of this book.

Wednesday, the first day

1

THE WHEEL HUMMED and Rollo mumbled Yiddish curses as he put rouge on the glistening bronze surface.

"There ain't a single blemish on this badge," he said.

"Sure there is, Rollo," I said. "Look closer. Between the *s* in *Los* and the big *A* in *Angeles*. I scratched it on the door of my locker."

"There ain't a single blemish on this badge," said Rollo, but he buffed, and in spite of his bitching I watched bronze change to gold, and chrome become silver. The blue enameled letters which said "Policeman," and "4207," jumped out at me.

"Okay, so now are you happy?" he sighed, leaning across the display case, handing me the badge.

"It's not too bad," I said, enjoying the heft of the heavy oval shield, polished to a luster that would reflect sunlight like a mirror.

"Business ain't bad enough, I got to humor a crazy old cop like you." Rollo scratched his scalp, and the hair, white and stiff, stood like ruffled chicken feathers.

"What's the matter, you old gonif, afraid some of your burglar friends will see a bluesuit in here and take their hot jewelry to some other crook?"

"Ho, ho! Bob Hope should watch out. When you get through sponging off the taxpayers you'll go after his job."

"Well, I've gotta go crush some crime. What do I owe you for the lousy badge polishing?"

"Don't make me laugh, I got a kidney infection. You been freeloading for twenty years, now all of a sudden you want to pay?"

"See you later, Rollo. I'm going over to Seymour's for breakfast. He appreciates me."

"Seymour too? I know Jews got to suffer in this world, but not all of us in one day."

"Good-bye, old shoe."

"Be careful, Bumper."

I strolled outside into the burning smog that hung over Main Street. I started to sweat as I stopped to admire Rollo's work. Most of the ridges had been rounded off long ago, and twenty years of rubbing gave it unbelievable brilliance. Turning the face of the shield to the white sun, I watched the gold and silver take the light. I pinned the badge to my shirt and looked at my reflection in the blue plastic that Rollo has over his front windows. The plastic was rippled and bubbled and my distorted reflection made me a freak. I looked at myself straight on, but still my stomach hung low and made me look like a blue kangaroo, and my ass was two nightsticks wide. My jowls hung to my chest in that awful reflection and my big rosy face and pink nose were a deep veiny blue like the color of my uniform which somehow didn't change colors in the reflection. It was ugly, but what made me keep looking was the shield. The four-inch oval on my chest glittered and twinkled so that after a second or two I couldn't even see the blue man behind it. I just stood there staring at that shield for maybe a full minute.

Seymour's delicatessen is only a half block from Rollo's jewelry store, but I decided to drive. My black-and-white was parked out front in Rollo's no parking zone because this downtown traffic is so miserable. If it weren't for those red curbs there'd be no place to park even a police car. I opened the white door and sat down carefully, the sunlight blasting through the windshield making the seat cushion hurt. I'd been driving the same black-and-white for six months and had worked a nice comfortable dip in the seat, so I rode cozy, like in a worn friendly saddle. It's really not too hard to loosen up seat springs with two hundred and seventy-five pounds.

I drove to Seymour's and when I pulled up in front I saw two guys across Fourth Street in the parking lot at the rear of the Pink Dragon. I watched for thirty seconds or so and it looked like they were setting something up, probably a narcotics buy. Even after twenty years I still get that thrill a cop gets at seeing things that are invisible to the square citizen. But what was the use? I could drive down Main Street anytime and see hugger-muggers, paddy hustlers, till-tappers, junkies, and then waste six or eight man-hours staking out on these small-timers and maybe end up with nothing. You only had time to grab the sure ones and just make mental notes of the rest.

The two in the parking lot interested me so I decided to watch them for a minute. They were dumb strung-out hypes. They should've made me by now. When I was younger I used to play the truth game. I hardly ever played it anymore. The object of the game is simple: I have to explain to an imaginary black-robed square (His Honor) how Officer William A. Morgan *knows* that those men are committing a criminal act. If the judge finds that I didn't have sufficient probable cause to stop, detain, and search my man, then I lose the game. Illegal search and seizure—case dismissed.

I usually beat the game whether it's imaginary or for real. My courtroom demeanor is very good, pretty articulate for an old-time copper, they say. And such a simple honest kisser. Big innocent blue eyes. Juries loved me. It's very hard to explain the "know." Some guys never master it. Let's see, I begin, I *know* they are setting up a buy because of . . . the clothing. That's a good start, the clothing. It's a suffocating day, Your Honor, and the tall one is wearing a long-sleeved shirt buttoned at the cuff. To hide his hype marks, of course. One of them is still wearing his "county shoes." That tells me he just got out of county jail, and the other one, yes, the other one—you only acquire that frantic pasty look in the joint: San Quentin, Folsom, maybe. He's been away a long time. And I would find out they'd just been in the Pink Dragon and no one but a whore, hype, pill-head, or other hustler would hang out in that dive. And I'd explain all this to my judge too, but I'd be a little more subtle, and then I'd be stopped. I could explain to my imaginary jurist but never to a real one about the instinct—the stage in this business when, like an animal, you can *feel* you've got one, and it can't be explained. You *feel* the truth, and you know. Try telling *that* to the judge, I thought. Try explaining *that*, sometime.

Just then a wino lurched across Main Street against the red light and a Lincoln jammed on the binders almost creaming him.

"Goddamnit, come over here," I yelled when he reached the sidewalk.

"Hi, Bumper," he croaked, holding the five-sizes-too-big pants around his bony hips, trying his best to look sober as he staggered sideways.

"You almost got killed, Noodles," I said.

"What's the difference?" he said, wiping the saliva from his chin with the grimy free hand. The other one gripped the pants so hard the big knuckles showed white through the dirt.

"I don't care about you but I don't want any wrecked Lincolns on my beat."

"Okay, Bumper."

"I'm gonna have to book you."

"I'm not that drunk, am I?"

"No, but you're dying."

"No crime in that." He coughed then and the spit that dribbled out the corner of his mouth was red and foamy.

"I'm booking you, Noodles," I said, mechanically filling in the boxes on the pad of drunk arrest reports that I carried in my hip pocket like I was still walking my beat instead of driving a black-and-white.

"Let's see, your real name is Ralph M. Milton, right?"

"Millard."

"Millard," I muttered, filling in the name. I must've busted Noodles a dozen times. I never used to forget names or faces.

"Let's see, eyes bloodshot, gait staggering, attitude stuporous, address transient. . . ."

"Got a cigarette?"

"I don't use them, Noodles," I said, tearing out the copies of the arrest report. "Wait a minute, the nightwatch left a half pack in the glove compartment. Go get them while I'm calling the wagon."

The wino shuffled to the radio car while I walked fifty feet down the street to a call box, unlocked it with my big brass key, and asked for the B-wagon to come to Fourth and Main. It would've been easier to use my car radio to call the wagon, but I walked a beat too many years to learn new habits.

That was something my body did to me, made me lose my foot beat and put me in a black-and-white. An ankle I broke years ago when I was a slick-sleeved rookie chasing a purse snatcher, finally decided it can't carry my big ass around anymore and swells up every time I'm on my feet a couple of hours. So I lost my foot beat and got a radio car. A one-man foot beat's the best job in this or any police department. It always amuses policemen to see the movies where the big hood or crooked politician yells, "I'll have you walking a beat, you dumb flatfoot," when really it's a sought-after job. You got to have whiskers to get a foot beat, and you have to be big and good. If only my legs would've held out. But even though I couldn't travel it too much on foot, it was still *my* beat, all of it. Everyone knew it all belonged to me more than anyone.

"Okay, Noodles, give this arrest report to the cops in the wagon and don't lose the copies."

"You're not coming with me?" He couldn't shake a cigarette from the pack with one trembling hand.

"No, you just lope on over to the corner and flag 'em down when they drive by. Tell 'em you want to climb aboard."

"First time I ever arrested myself," he coughed, as I lit a cigarette for him, and put the rest of the pack and the arrest report in his shirt pocket.

"See you later."

"I'll get six months. The judge warned me last time."

"I hope so, Noodles."

"I'll just start boozing again when they let me out. I'll just get scared and start again. You don't know what it's like to be scared at night when you're alone."

"How do you know, Noodles?"

"I'll just come back here and die in an alley. The cats and rats will eat me anyway, Bumper."

"Get your ass moving or you'll miss the wagon." I watched him stagger down Main for a minute and I yelled, "Don't you believe in miracles?"

He shook his head and I turned back to the guys in the parking lot again just as they disappeared inside the Pink Dragon. Someday, I thought, I'll kill that dragon and drink its blood.

I was too hungry to do police work, so I went into Seymour's. I usually like to eat breakfast right after rollcall and here it was ten o'clock and I was still screwing around.

Ruthie was bent over one of the tables scooping up a tip. She was very attractive from the rear and she must've caught me admiring her out of the corner of her eye. I suppose a blue man, dark blue in black leather, sets off signals in some people.

"Bumper," she said, wheeling around. "Where you been all week?"

"Hi, Ruthie," I said, always embarrassed by how glad she was to see me.

Seymour, a freckled redhead about my age, was putting together a pastrami sandwich behind the meat case. He heard Ruthie call my name and grinned.

"Well, look who's here. The finest cop money can buy."

"Just bring me a cold drink, you old shlimazel."

"Sure, champ." Seymour gave the pastrami to a take-out customer, made change, and put a cold beer and a frosted glass in front of me. He winked at the well-dressed man who sat at the counter to my left. The beer wasn't opened.

"Whadda you want me to do, bite the cap off?" I said, going along with his joke. No one on my beat had ever seen me drink on duty.

Seymour bent over, chuckling. He took the beer away and filled my glass with buttermilk.

"Where you been all week, Bumper?"

"Out there. Making the street safe for women and babies."

"Bumper's here!" he shouted to Henry in the back. That meant five scrambled eggs and twice the lox the paying customers get with an order. It also meant three onion bagels, toasted and oozing with butter and heaped with cream cheese. I don't eat breakfast at Seymour's more than once or twice a week, although I knew he'd feed me three free meals every day.

"Young Slagel told me he saw you directing traffic on Hill Street the other day," said Seymour.

"Yeah, the regular guy got stomach cramps just as I was driving by. I took over for him until his sergeant got somebody else."

"Directing traffic down there is a job for the young bucks," said Seymour, winking again at the businessman who was smiling at me and biting off large hunks of a Seymour's Special Corned Beef on Pumpernickel Sandwich.

"Meet any nice stuff down there, Bumper? An airline hostess, maybe? Or some of those office cuties?"

"I'm too old to interest them, Seymour. But let me tell you, watching all that young poon, I had to direct traffic like this." With that I stood up and did an imitation of waving at cars, bent forward with my legs and feet crossed.

Seymour fell backward and out came his high-pitched hoot of a laugh. This brought Ruthie over to see what happened.

"Show her, Bumper, please," Seymour gasped, wiping the tears away.

Ruthie waited with that promising smile of hers. She's every bit of forty-five, but firm, and golden blond, and very fair—as sexy a wench as I've ever seen. And the way she acted always made me know it was there for me, but I'd never taken it. She's one of the regular people on my beat and it's because of the way *they* feel about me, all of them, the people on my beat. Some of the smartest bluecoats I know have lots of broads but won't even cop a feel on their beats. Long ago I decided to admire her big buns from afar.

"I'm waiting, Bumper," she said, hands on those curvy hips.

"Another funny thing happened while I was directing traffic," I said, to change the subject. "There I was, blowing my whistle and waving at cars with one hand, and I had my other hand out palm up, and some little eighty-year-old lady comes up and drops a big fat letter on my palm. 'Could you please tell me the postage for this, Officer?' she says. Here I am with traffic backed up clear to Olive, both arms out and this letter on my palm. So, what the hell, I just put my feet together, arms out, and rock back and forth like a scale balancing, and say, 'That'll be twenty-one cents, ma'am, if you want it to go airmail.' 'Oh *thank* you, Officer,' she says."

Seymour hooted again and Ruthie laughed, but things quieted down when my food came, and I loosened my Sam Browne for the joy of eating. It annoyed me though when my belly pressed against the edge of the yellow Formica counter.

Seymour had a flurry of orders to go which he took care of and nobody bothered me for ten minutes or so except for Ruthie who wanted to make sure I had enough to eat, and that my eggs were fluffy enough, and also to rub a hip or something up against me so that I had trouble thinking about the third bagel.

The other counter customer finished his second cup of coffee and Seymour shuffled over.

"More coffee, Mister Parker?"

"No, I've had plenty."

I'd never seen this man before but I admired his clothes. He was stouter than me, soft fat, but his suit, not bought off the rack, hid most of it.

"You ever met Officer Bumper Morgan, Mister Parker?" asked Seymour.

We smiled, both too bloated and lazy to stand up and shake hands across two stools.

"I've heard of you, Officer," said Parker. "I recently opened a suite in the Roxman Building. Fine watches. Stop around anytime for a special discount." He put his card on the counter and pushed it halfway toward me. Seymour shoved it the rest of the way.

"Everyone around here's heard of Bumper," Seymour said proudly.

"I thought you'd be a bigger man, Officer," said Parker. "About six foot seven and three hundred pounds, from some of the stories I've heard."

"You just about got the weight right," said Seymour.

I was used to people saying I'm not as tall as they expected, or as I first appeared to be. A beat cop has to be big or he'll be fighting all the time. Sometimes a tough, feisty little cop resents it because he can't walk a foot beat, but the fact is that most people don't fear a little guy and a little guy'd just have to prove himself all the time, and sooner or later somebody'd take that nightstick off him and shove it up his ass. Of course I was in a radio car now, but as I said before, I was still a beat cop, more or less.

The problem with my size was that my frame was made for a guy six feet five or six instead of a guy barely six feet. My bones are big and heavy, especially my hands and feet. If I'd just have grown as tall as I was meant to, I wouldn't have the goddamn weight problem. My appetite was meant for a giant, and I finally convinced those police doctors who used to send "fat man letters" to my captain ordering me to cut down to two hundred and twenty pounds.

"Bumper's a one-man gang," said Seymour. "I tell you he's fought wars out there." Seymour waved at the street to indicate the "out there."

"Come on, Seymour," I said, but it was no use. This kind of talk shriveled my balls, but it did please me that a newcomer like Parker had heard of me. I wondered how special the "special discount" would be. My old watch was about finished.

"How long ago did you get this beat, Bumper?" asked Seymour, but didn't allow me to answer. "Well, it was almost twenty years. I know that, because when Bumper was a rookie, I was a young fella myself, working for my father right here. It was real bad then. We had B-girls and zoot-suiters and lots of crooks. In those days there was plenty of guys that would try the cop on the beat."

I looked over at Ruthie, who was smiling.

"Years ago, when Ruthie worked here the first time, Bumper saved her life when some guy jumped her at the bus stop on Second Street. He saved you, didn't he, Ruthie?"

"He sure did. He's my hero," she said, pouring me a cup of coffee.

"Bumper's always worked right here," Seymour continued. "On foot beats and now in a patrol car since he can't walk too good no more. His twenty-year anniversary is coming up, but we won't let him retire. What would it be like around here without the champ?"

Ruthie actually looked scared for a minute when Seymour said it, and this shook me.

"When is your twentieth year up, Bumper?" she asked.

"End of this month."

"You're not even considering pulling the pin, are you Bumper?" asked Seymour, who knew all the police lingo from feeding the beat cops for years.

"What do *you* think?" I asked, and Seymour seemed satisfied and started telling Parker a few more incidents from the Bumper Morgan legend. Ruthie kept watching me. Women are like cops, they sense things. When Seymour finally ran down, I promised to come back Friday for the Deluxe Businessman's Plate, said my good-byes, and left six bits for Ruthie which she didn't put in her tip dish under the counter. She looked me in the eye and dropped it right down her bra.

I'd forgotten about the heat and when it hit me I decided to drive straight for Elysian Park, sit on the grass, and smoke a cigar with my radio turned up loud enough so I wouldn't miss a call. I wanted to read about last night's Dodger game, so before getting in the car I walked down to the smoke shop. I picked up half a dozen fifty-cent cigars, and since the store recently changed hands and I didn't know the owner too well, I took a five out of my pocket.

"From you? Don't be silly, Officer Morgan," said the pencil-necked old man, and refused the money. I made a little small talk in way of payment, listened to a gripe or two about business, and left, forgetting to pick up a paper. I almost went back in, but I never make anyone bounce for two things in one day. I decided to get a late paper across the street from Frankie the dwarf. He had his Dodger's baseball cap tilted forward and pretended not to see me until I was almost behind him, then he turned fast and punched me in the thigh with a deformed little fist.

"Take that, you big slob. You might scare everybody else on the street, but I'll get a fat lock on you and break your kneecap."

"What's happening, Frankie?" I said, while he slipped a folded paper under my arm without me asking.

"No happenings, Killer. How you standing up under this heat?"

"Okay, I guess." I turned to the sports page while Frankie smoked a king-sized cigarette in a fancy silver holder half as long as his arm. His tiny face was pinched and ancient but he was only thirty years old.

A woman and a little boy about four years old were standing next to me, waiting for the red light to change.

"See that man," she said. "That's a policeman. He'll come and get you and put you in jail if you're bad." She gave me a sweet smile, very smug because she thought I was impressed with her good citizenship.

Frankie, who was only a half head taller than the kid, took a step toward them and said, "That's real clever, lady. Make him scared of the law. Then he'll grow up hating cops because *you* scared him to death."

"Easy, Frankie," I said, a little surprised.

The woman lifted the child and the second the light changed she ran from the angry dwarf.

"Sorry, Bumper," Frankie smiled. "Lord knows I'm not a cop lover."

"Thanks for the paper, old shoe," I said, keeping in the shade, nodding to several of the local characters and creeps who gave me a "Hi, Bumper."

I sauntered along toward Broadway to see what the crowds looked like today and to scare off any pickpockets that might be working the shoppers. I fired up one of those fifty-centers which are okay when I'm out of good hand-rolled custom-mades. As I rounded the corner on Broadway I saw six of the Krishna cult performing in their favorite place on the west sidewalk. They were all kids, the oldest being maybe twenty-five, boys and girls, shaved heads, a single long pigtail, bare feet with little bells on their ankles, pale orange saris, tambourines, flutes and guitars. They chanted and danced and put on a hell of a show there almost every day, and there was no way old Herman the Devil-drummer could compete with them. You could see his jaw flopping and knew he was screaming but you couldn't hear a word he said after they started *their* act.

Up until recently, this had been Herman's corner, and even before I came on the job Herman put in a ten-hour day right here passing out tracts and yelling about demons and damnation, collecting maybe twelve bucks a day from people who felt sorry for him. He used to be a lively guy, but now he looked old, bloodless, and dusty. His shiny black suit was threadbare and his frayed white collar was gray and dirty and he didn't seem to care anymore. I thought about trying to persuade him one more time to move down Broadway a few blocks where he wouldn't have to compete with these kids and all their color and music. But I knew it wouldn't do any good. Herman had been on his beat too long. I walked to my car thinking about him, poor old Devil-drummer.

As I was getting back in my saddle seat I got a burning pain in the gut and had to drop a couple acid eaters. I carried pockets full of white tablets. Acid eaters in the right pocket and bubble breakers in the left pocket. The acid eaters are just antacid pills and the bubble breakers are for gas and I'm cursed with both problems, more or less all the time. I sucked an acid eater and the fire died. Then I thought about Cassie because that sometimes settled my stomach. The decision to retire at twenty years had been made several weeks ago, and Cassie had lots of plans, but what she *didn't* know was that I'd decided last night to make Friday my last day on duty. Today, tomorrow, and Friday would be it. I could string my vacation days together and run them until the end of the month when my time was officially up.

Friday was also to be her last day at L.A. City College. She'd already prepared her final exams and had permission to leave school now, while a substitute instructor took over her classes. She had a good offer, a "wonderful opportunity" she called it, to join the faculty of an expensive girls' school in northern California, near San Francisco. They wanted her up there now, before they closed for the summer, so she could get an idea how things were done. She planned on leaving Monday, and at the end of the month when I retired, coming back to Los Angeles where we'd get married, then we'd go back to the apartment she'd have all fixed up and ready. But I'd decided to leave Friday and go with her. No sense fooling around any longer, I thought. It would be better to get it over with and I knew Cruz would be happy about it.

Cruz Segovia was my sergeant, and for twenty years he'd been the person closest to me. He was always afraid something would happen and he made me promise him I wouldn't blow this, the best deal of my life. And Cassie *was* the best deal, no doubt about it. A teacher, a divorced woman with no kids, a woman with real education, not just a couple college degrees. She was young-looking, forty-four years old, and had it all.

So I started making inquiries about what there was for a retired cop around the Bay area and damned if I didn't luck out and get steered into a good job with a large industrial security outfit that was owned by an ex-L.A.P.D. inspector I knew from the old days. I got the job of security chief at an electronics firm that has a solid government contract, and I'd have my own office and car, a secretary, *and* be making a hundred more a month than I was as a cop. The reason he picked me instead of one of the other applicants who were retired captains and inspectors is that he said he had enough administrators working for him and he wanted one real iron-nutted street cop. So this was maybe the first time I ever got rewarded for doing police work and I was pretty excited about starting something new and seeing if real police techniques and ideas couldn't do something for industrial security which was usually pretty pitiful at best.

The thirtieth of May, the day I'd officially retire, was also my fiftieth birthday. It was hard to believe I'd been around half a century, but it was harder to believe I'd lived in this world thirty years before I got my beat. I was sworn in as a cop on my thirtieth birthday, the second oldest guy in my academy class, the oldest being Cruz Segovia, who had tried three times to join the Department but couldn't pass the oral exam. It was probably because he was so shy and had such a heavy Spanish accent, being an El Paso Mexican. But his grammar was beautiful if you just bothered to listen past the accent, and finally he got an oral board that was smart enough to bother.

I was driving through Elysian Park as I was thinking these things and I spotted two motor cops in front of me, heading toward the police academy. The motor cop in front was a kid named Lefler, one of the hundred or so I've broken in. He'd recently transferred to Motors from Central and was riding tall in his new shiny boots, white helmet, and striped riding britches. His partner breaking him in on the motor beat was a leather-faced old fart named Crandall. He's the type that'll get hot at a traffic violator and screw up your public relations program by pulling up beside him and yelling, "Grab a piece of the curb, asshole."

Lefler's helmet was dazzling white and tilted forward, the short bill pulled down to his nose. I drove up beside him and yelled, "That's a gorgeous skid lid you got there, boy, but pull it up a little and lemme see those baby blues."

Lefler smiled and goosed his bike a little. He was even wearing expensive black leather gloves in this heat.

"Hi, Bumper," said Crandall, taking his hand from the bar for a minute. We rode slow side by side and I grinned at Lefler, who looked self-conscious.

"How's he doing, Crandall?" I asked. "I broke him in on the job. He's Bumper-ized."

"Not bad for a baby," Crandall shrugged.

"I see you took his training wheels off," I said, and Lefler giggled and goosed the Harley again.

I could see the edge of the horseshoe cleats on his heels and I knew his soles were probably studded with iron.

"Don't go walking around my beat with those boots on, kid," I yelled. "You'll be kicking up sparks and starting fires." I chuckled then as I remembered seeing a motor cop with two cups of coffee in his gloved hands go right on his ass one time because of those cleats.

I waved at Lefler and pulled away. Young hotdogs, I thought. I was glad I was older when I came on the job. But then, I knew I would never have been a motor officer. Writing traffic tickets was the one part of police work I didn't like. The only good thing about it was it gave you an excuse to stop some suspicious cars on the pretext of writing a ticket. More good arrests came from phony traffic stops than anything else. More policemen got blown up that way, too.

I decided, what the hell, I was too jumpy to lay around the park reading the paper. I'd been like a cat ever since I'd decided about Friday. I hardly slept last night. I headed back toward the beat.

I should be patrolling for the burglar, I thought. I really wanted him now that I only had a couple days left. He was a daytime hotel creeper and hitting maybe four to six hotel rooms in the best downtown hotels every time he went to work. The dicks talked to us at rollcall and said the M.O. run showed he preferred weekdays, especially Thursday and Friday, but a lot of jobs were showing up on Wednesdays. This guy would shim doors which isn't too hard to do in any hotel since they usually have the world's worst security, and he'd burgle the place whether the occupants were in or not. Of course he waited until they were in the shower or napping. I loved catching burglars. Most policemen call it fighting ghosts and give up trying to catch them, but I'd rather catch a hot prowl guy than a stickup man any day. And any burglar with balls enough to take a pad when the people are home is every bit as dangerous as a stickup man.

I decided I'd patrol the hotels by the Harbor Freeway. I had a theory this guy was using some sort of repairman disguise since he'd eluded all stakeouts so far, and I figured him for a repair or delivery truck. I envisioned him as an out-of-towner who used the convenient Harbor Freeway to come to his job. This burglar was doing ding-a-ling stuff on some of the jobs, cutting up clothing, usually women's or kids', tearing the crotch out of underwear, and on a recent job he stabbed the hell out of a big teddy bear that a little girl left on the bed covered up with a blanket. I was glad the people weren't in when he hit *that* time. He was kinky, but a clever burglar, a lucky burglar. I thought about patrolling around the hotels, but first I'd go see Glenda. She'd be rehearsing now, and I might never see her again. She was one of the people I owed a good-bye to.

I entered the side door of the run-down little theater. They mostly showed skin flicks now. They used to have a halfway decent burlesque house here, with some fair comics and good-looking girls. Glenda was something in those days. The "Gilded Girl" they called her. She'd come out in a gold sheath and peel to a golden G-string and gold pasties. She was tall and graceful, and a better-than-average dancer. She played some big-time clubs off and on, but she was thirty-eight years old now and after two or three husbands she was back down on Main Street competing with beaver movies between reels, and taxi dancing part-time down the street at the ballroom. She was maybe twenty pounds heavier, but she still looked good to me because I saw her like she used to be.

I stood there in the shadows backstage and got accustomed to the dark and the quiet. They didn't even have anyone on the door anymore. I guess even the weinie waggers and bustle rubbers gave up sneaking in the side door of this hole. The wallpaper was wet and rusty and curling off the walls like old scrolls. There were dirty costumes laying around on chairs. The popcorn machine, which they activated on weekend nights, was leaning against the wall, one leg broken.

"The cockroaches serve the popcorn in this joint. You don't want any, Bumper," said Glenda, who had stepped out of her dressing room and was watching me from the darkness.

"Hi, kid." I smiled and followed her voice through the dark to the dimly lit little dressing room.

She kissed me on the cheek like she always did, and I took off my hat and flopped down on the ragged overstuffed chair behind her makeup table.

"Hey, Saint Francis, where've all the birdies gone?" she said, tickling the bald spot on my crown. She always laid about a hundred old jokes on me every time we met.

Glenda was wearing net stockings with a hole in one leg and a sequined G-string. She was nude on top and didn't bother putting on a robe. I didn't blame her, it was so damn hot today, but she didn't usually go around like this in front of me and it made me a little nervous.

"Hot weather's here, baby," she said, sitting down and fixing her makeup. "When you going back on nights?"

Glenda knew my M.O. I work days in the winter, nightwatch in the summer when the Los Angeles sun starts turning the heavy bluesuit into sackcloth.

"I'll never go back on nights, Glenda," I said casually. "I'm retiring."

She turned around in her chair and those heavy white melons bounced once or twice. Her hair was long and blond. She always claimed she was a real blonde but I'd never know.

"You won't quit," she said. "You'll be here till they kick you out. Or till you die. Like me."

"We'll both leave here," I said, smiling because she was starting to look upset. "Some nice guy'll come along and . . ."

"Some nice guy took me out of here three times, Bumper. Trouble is I'm just not a nice girl. Too fucked up for any man. You're just kidding about retiring, aren't you?"

"How's Sissy?" I said, to change the subject.

Glenda answered by taking a package of snapshots out of her purse and handing them to me. I'm farsighted now and in the dimness I couldn't really see anything but the outline of a little girl holding a dog. I couldn't even say if the dog was real or stuffed.

"She's beautiful," I said, knowing she was. I'd last seen her several months ago when I drove Glenda home from work one night.

"Every dollar you ever gave me went into a bank account for her just like we agreed at first," said Glenda.

"I know that."

"I added to it on my own too."

"She'll have something someday."

"Bet your ass she will," said Glenda, lighting a cigarette.

I wondered how much I'd given Glenda over the past ten years. And I wondered how many really good arrests I'd made on information she gave me. She was one of my big secrets. The detectives had informants who they paid but the bluesuits weren't supposed to be involved in that kind of police work. Well, I had paid my informants too. But I didn't pay them from any Department money. I paid them from my pocket, and when I made the bust on the scam they gave me, I made it look like I lucked onto the arrest. Or I made up some other fanciful story for the arrest report. That way Glenda was protected and nobody could say Bumper Morgan was completely nuts for paying informants out of his own pocket. The first time, Glenda turned me a federal fugitive who was dating her and who carried a gun and pulled stickups. I tried to give her twenty bucks and she refused it, saying he was a no-good asshole and belonged in the joint and she was no snitch. I made her take it for Sissy who was a baby then, and who had no dad. Since then over the years I've probably laid a thousand on Glenda for Sissy. And I've probably made the best pinches of any cop in Central Division.

"She gonna be a blondie like momma?" I asked.

"Yeah," she smiled. "More blond than me though. And about ten times as smart. I think she's smarter already. I'm reading books like mad to keep up with her."

"Those private schools are tough," I nodded. "They teach them something."

"You notice this one, Bumper?" she smiled, coming over to me and sitting on the arm of the chair. She was smiling big and thinking about Sissy now. "The dog's pulling her hair. Look at the expression."

"Oh yeah," I said, seeing only a blur and feeling one of those heavy chi-chis resting on my shoulder. Hers were big and natural, not pumped full of plastic like so many these days.

"She's peeved in this one," said Glenda, leaning closer, and it was pressed against my cheek, and finally one tender doorbell went right in my ear.

"Damn it, Glenda!" I said, looking up.

"What?" she answered, moving back. She got it, and laughed her hard hoarse laugh. Then her laugh softened and she smiled and her big eyes went soft and I noticed the lashes were dark beneath the eyes and not from mascara. I thought Glenda was more attractive now than she ever was.

"I have a big feeling for you, Bumper," she said, and kissed me right on the mouth. "You and Sissy are the only ones. You're what's happening, baby."

Glenda was like Ruthie. She was one of the people who belonged to the beat. There were laws that I made for myself, but she was almost naked and to me she was still so beautiful.

"Now," she said, knowing I was about to explode. "Why not? You never have and I always wanted you to."

"Gotta get back to my car," I said, jumping up and crossing the room in three big steps. Then I mumbled something else about missing my radio calls, and Glenda told me to wait.

"You forgot your hat," she said, handing it to me.

"Thanks," I said, putting the lid on with one shaky hand. She held the other one and kissed my palm with a warm wet mouth.

"Don't think of leaving us, Bumper," she said and stared me in the eye.

"Here's a few bucks for Sissy," I said, fumbling in my pocket for a ten.

"I don't have any information this time," she said, shaking her head, but I tucked it inside her G-string and she grinned.

"It's for the kid."

There were some things I'd intended asking her about some gunsel I'd heard was hanging out in the skin houses and taxi-dance joints, but I couldn't trust myself alone with her for another minute. "See you later, kid," I said weakly.

"Bye, Bumper," she said as I picked my way through the darkness to the stage door. Aside from the fact that Cassie gave me all I could handle, there was another reason I tore myself away from her like that. Any cop knows you can't afford to get too tight with your informant. You try screwing a snitch and you'll be the one that ends up getting screwed.

2

After leaving Glenda it actually seemed cool on the street. Glenda never did anything like that before. Everyone was acting a little ding-a-ling when I mentioned my retirement. I didn't feel like climbing back inside that machine and listening to the noisy chatter on the radio.

It was still morning now and I was pretty happy, twirling my stick as I strolled along. I guess I *swaggered* along. Most beat officers swagger. People expect you to. It shows the hangtoughs you're not afraid, and people expect it. Also they expect an older cop to cock his hat a little so I always do that too.

I still wore the traditional eight-pointed hat and used a leather thong on my stick. The Department went to more modern round hats, like Air Force hats, and we all have to change over. I'd wear the eight-pointed police hat to the end, I thought. Then I thought about Friday as being the end and I started a fancy stick spin to keep my mind off it. I let the baton go bouncing off the sidewalk back up into my hand. Three shoe shine kids were watching me, two Mexican, one Negro. The baton trick impressed the hell out of them. I strung it out like a Yo-Yo, did some back twirls and dropped it back in the ring in one smooth motion.

"Want a choo chine, Bumper?" said one of the Mexican kids.

"Thanks pal, but I don't need one."

"It's free to you," he said, tagging along beside me for a minute.

"I'm buying juice today, pal," I said, flipping two quarters up in the air which one of them jumped up and caught. He ran to the orange juice parlor three doors away with the other two chasing him. The shoe shine boxes hung around their necks with ropes and thudded against their legs as they ran.

These little kids probably never saw a beat officer twirl a stick before. The Department ordered us to remove the leather thongs a couple years ago, but I never did and all the sergeants pretend not to notice as long as I borrow a regulation baton for inspections.

The stick is held in the ring now by a big rubber washer like the one that goes over the pipe in the back of your toilet. We've learned new ways to use the stick from some young Japanese cops who are karate and aikido experts. We use the blunt end of the stick more and I have to admit it beats hell out of the old caveman swing. I must've shattered six sticks over guys' heads, arms and legs in my time. Now I've learned from these Nisei kids how to swing that baton in a big arc and put my whole ass behind it. I could damn near drive it through a guy if I wanted to, and never hurt the stick. It's very graceful stuff too. I feel I can do twice as well in a brawl now. The only bad thing is, they convinced the Department brass that the leather thong was worthless. You see, these kids were never real beat men. Neither were the brass. They don't understand what the cop twirling his stick really means to people who see him stroll down a quiet street throwing that big shadow in an eight-pointed hat. Anyway, I'd never take off the leather thong. It made me sick to think of a toilet washer on a police weapon.

I stopped by the arcade and saw a big muscle-bound fruit hustler standing there. I just looked hard at him for a second, and he fell apart and slithered away. Then I saw two con guys leaning up against a wall flipping a quarter, hoping to get a square in a coin smack. I stared at them and they got nervous and skulked around to the parking lot and disappeared.

The arcade was almost deserted. I remember when the slime-balls used to be packed in there solid, asshole to belly button, waiting to look at the skin show in the viewer. That was a big thing then. The most daring thing around. The vice squad used to bust guys all the time for masturbating. There were pecker prints all over the walls in front of the viewer. Now you can walk in any bar or movie house down here and see live skin shows, or animal flicks, and I don't mean Walt Disney stuff. It's women and dogs, dykes and donkeys, dildos and whips, fags, chickens, and ducks. Sometimes it's hard to tell who or what is doing what to who or what.

Then I started thinking about the camera club that used to be next door to the arcade when nudity was still a big thing. It cost fifteen bucks to join and five bucks for every camera session. You got to take all the pictures of a naked girl you wanted, as long as you didn't get closer than two feet and as long as you didn't touch. Of course, most of the "photographers" didn't even have film in their cameras, but the management knew it and never bothered putting in real camera lights and nobody complained. It was really so innocent.

I was about to head back to my car when I noticed another junkie watching me. He was trying to decide whether to rabbit or freeze. He froze finally, his eyes roaming around too casually, hitting on everything but me, hoping he could melt into the jungle. I hardly ever bust hypes for marks anymore, and he looked too sick to be holding, but I thought I recognized him.

"Come here, man," I called and he came slinking my way like it was all over.

"Hello, Bumper."

"Well, hello, Wimpy," I said to the chalk-faced hype. "It took me a minute to recognize you. You're older."

"Went away for three years last time."

"How come so long?"

"Armed robbery. Went to Q behind armed robbery. Violence don't suit me. I shoulda stuck to boosting. San Quentin made me old, Bumper."

"Too bad, Wimpy. Yeah, now I remember. You did a few gas stations, right?"

He *was* old. His sandy hair was streaked with gray and it was patchy. And his teeth were rotting and loose in his mouth. It was starting to come back to me like it always does: Herman (Wimpy) Brown, a life-long hype and a pretty good snitch when he wanted to be. Couldn't be more than forty but he looked a lot older than me.

"I wish I hadn't never met that hangtough, Barty Mendez. Remember him, Bumper? A dope fiend shouldn't never do violent crime. You just ain't cut out for it. I coulda kept boosting cigarettes out of markets and made me a fair living for quite a while."

"How much you boosting now, Wimpy?" I said, giving him a light. He was clammy and covered with gooseflesh. If he knew anything he'd tell me. He wanted a taste so bad right now, he'd snitch on his mother.

"I don't boost anywhere near your beat, Bumper. I go out to the west side and lift maybe a couple dozen cartons of smokes a day outta those big markets. I don't do nothing down here except look for guys holding."

"You hang up your parole yet?"

"No, I ain't running from my parole officer. You can call in and check." He dragged hard on the cigarette but it wasn't doing much good.

"Let's see your arms, Wimpy," I said, taking one bony arm and pushing up the sleeve.

"You ain't gonna bust me on a chickenshit marks case, are you, Bumper?"

"I'm just curious," I said, noticing the inner elbows were fairly clean. I'd have to put on my glasses to see the marks and I never took my glasses to work. They stayed in my apartment.

"Few marks, Bumper, not too bad," he said, trying a black-toothed smile. "I shrink them with hemorrhoid ointment."

I bent the elbow and looked at the back of the forearm. "Damn, the whole Union Pacific could run on those tracks!" I didn't need glasses to see those swollen abscessed wounds.

"Don't bust me, Bumper," he whined. "I can work for you like I used to. I gave you some good things, remember? I turned the guy that juked that taxi dancer in the alley. The one that almost cut her tit off, remember?"

"Yeah, that's right," I said, as it came back to me. Wimpy *did* turn that one for me.

"Don't these P.O.'s ever look at your arms?" I asked, sliding the sleeves back down.

"Some're like cops, others're social workers. I always been lucky about drawing a square P.O. or one who really digs numbers, like how many guys he's rehabilitating. They don't want to *fail* you, you know? Nowadays they give you dope and call it something else and say you're cured. They show you statistics, but I think the ones they figure are clean are just dead, probably from an overdose."

"Make sure *you* don't O.D., Wimpy," I said, leading him away from the arcade so we could talk in private while I was walking him to the corner call box to run a make.

"I liked it inside when I was on the program, Bumper. Honest to God. C.R.C. is a good place. I knew guys with no priors who shot phony needle holes in their arms so they could go there instead of to Q. And I heard Tehachapi is even better. Good food, and you don't hardly work at all, and group therapy where you can shuck, and there's these trade schools there where you can jive around. I could do a nickel in those places and I wouldn't mind. In fact, last time I was sorta sorry they kicked me out after thirteen months. But three years in Q broke me, Bumper. You know you're really in the joint when you're in that place."

"Still think about geezing when you're inside?"

"Always think about that," he said, trying to smile again as we stopped next to the call box. There were people walking by but nobody close. "I need to geez bad now, Bumper. Real bad." He looked like he was going to cry.

"Well, don't flip. I might not bust you if you can do me some good. Start thinking real hard, while I run a make to see if you hung it up."

"My parole's good as gold," he said, already perking up now that he figured I wasn't going to book him for marks. "You and me could work good, Bumper. I always trusted you. You got a rep for protecting your informants. Nobody never got a rat jacket behind your busts. I know you got an army of snitches, but nobody never got a snitch jacket. You take care of your people."

"You won't get a jacket either, Wimpy. Work with me and nobody knows. Nobody."

Wimpy was sniffling and cotton-mouthed so I unlocked the call box and hurried up with the wants check. I gave the girl his name and birthdate, and lit his cigarette while we waited. He started looking around. He wasn't afraid to be caught informing, he was just looking for a connection: a peddler, a junkie, anybody that might be holding a cap. I'd blow my brains out first, I thought.

"You living at a halfway house?" I asked.

"Not now," he said. "You know, after being clean for three years I thought I could do it this time. Then I went and fixed the second day out and I was feeling so bad about it I went to a kick pad over on the east side and asked them to sign me in. They did and I was clean three more days, left the kick pad, scored some junk, and had a spike in my arm ever since."

"Ever fire when you were in the joint?" I asked, trying to keep the conversation going until the information came back.

"I never did. Never had the chance. I heard of a few guys. I once saw two guys make an outfit. They were expecting half a piece from somewheres. I don't know what they had planned, but they sure was making a fit."

"How?"

"They bust open this light bulb and one of them held the filament with a piece of cardboard and a rag and the other just kept heating it up with matches, and those suckers stretched that thing out until it was a pretty good eyedropper. They stuck a hole in it with a pin and attached a plastic spray bottle to it and it wasn't a bad fit. I'd a took a chance and stuck it in my arm if there was some dope in it."

"Probably break off in your vein."

"Worth the chance. I seen guys without a spike so strung out and hurting they cut their arm open with a razor and blow a mouthful of dope right in there."

He was puffing big on the smoke. His hands and arms were covered with the jailhouse tattoos made from pencil lead shavings which they mix with spit and jab into their arms with a million pinpricks. He probably did it when he was a youngster just coming up. Now he was an old head and had professional tattoos all over the places where he shoots junk, but nothing could hide those tracks.

"I used to be a boss booster at one time, Bumper. Not just a cigarette thief. I did department stores for good clothes and expensive perfume, even jewelry counters which are pretty tough to do. I wore two-hundred-dollar suits in the days when only rich guys wore suits that good."

"Work alone?"

"All alone, I swear. I didn't need nobody. I looked different then. I was good looking, honest I was. I even talked better. I used to read a lot of magazines and books. I could walk through these department stores and spot these young kids and temporary sales help and have them give me their money. *Give* me their money, I tell you."

"How'd you work that scam?"

"I'd tell them Mister Freeman, the retail manager, sent me to pick up their receipts. He didn't want too much in the registers, I'd say, and I'd stick out my money bag and they'd fill it up for Mister Freeman." Wimpy started to laugh and ended up wheezing and choking. He settled down after a minute.

"I sure owe plenty to Mister Freeman. I gotta repay that sucker if I ever meet him. I used that name in maybe fifty department stores. That was my real father's name. That's really *my* real name, but when I was a kid I took the name of this bastard my old lady married. I always played like my real old man would've did something for us if he'd been around, so this way he did. Old Mister Freeman must've gave me ten grand. Tax free. More than most old men ever give their kids, hey, Bumper?''

''More than mine, Wimpy,'' I smiled.

''I did real good on that till-tap. I looked so nice, carnation and all. I had another scam where I'd boost good stuff, expensive baby clothes, luggage, anything. Then I'd bring it back to the salesman in the store bag and tell him I didn't have my receipt but would they please give me back my money on account of little Bobby wouldn't be needing these things because he smothered in his crib last Tuesday. Or old Uncle Pete passed on just before he went on his last trip that he saved and dreamed about for forty-eight years and I couldn't bear to look at this luggage anymore. Honest, Bumper, they couldn't give me the bread fast enough. I even made *men* cry. I had one woman beg me to take ten bucks from her own purse to help with the baby's funeral. I took that ten bucks and bought a little ten-dollar bag of junk and all the time I was cutting open that balloon and cooking that stuff I thought, 'Oh you baby. You really are my baby.' I took that spike and dug a little grave in my flesh and when I shoved that thing in my arm and felt it going in, I said, 'Thank you, lady, thank you, thank you, this is the best funeral my baby could have.' Wimpy closed his eyes and lifted his face, smiling a little as he thought of his baby.

''Doesn't your P.O. ever give you a urinalysis or anything?'' I still couldn't get over an old head like him not having his arms or urine checked when he was on parole, even if he *was* paroled on a non-narcotics beef.

''Hasn't yet, Bumper. I ain't worried if he does. I always been lucky with P.O.'s. When they put me on the urine program I came up with the squeeze-bottle trick. I just got this square friend of mine, old Homer Allen, to keep me supplied with a fresh bottle of piss, and I kept that little plastic squeeze bottle full and hanging from a string inside my belt. My dumb little P.O. used to think he was sneaky and he'd catch me at my job or at home at night sometimes and ask for a urine sample and I'd just go to the john with him right behind me watching, and I'd reach in my fly and fill his little glass bottle full of Homer's piss. He thought he was real slick, but he never could catch me. He was such a square. I really liked him. I felt like a father to that kid.''

The girl came to the phone and read me Wimpy's record, telling me there were no wants.

''Well, you're not running,'' I said, hanging up the phone, closing the metal call box door, and hanging the brass key back on my belt.

''Told you, Bumper. I just saw my P.O. last week. I been reporting regular.''

''Okay, Wimpy, let's talk business,'' I said.

''I been thinking, Bumper, there's this dog motherfucker that did me bad one time. I wouldn't mind you popping him.''

''Okay,'' I said, giving him a chance to rationalize his snitching, which all informants have to do when they start out, or like Wimpy, when they haven't snitched for a long time.

''He deserves to march,'' said Wimpy. ''Everybody knows he's no good. He burned me on a buy one time. I bring him a guy to score some pot. It's not on consignment or nothing, and he sells the guy catnip and I told him I knew the guy good. The guy kicked my ass when he found out it was catnip.''

''Okay, let's do him,'' I said. ''But I ain't interested in some two- or three-lid punk.''

''I know, Bumper. He's a pretty big dealer. We'll set him up good. I'll tell him I got a guy with real bread and he should bring three kilos and meet me in a certain place and then maybe you just happen by or something when we're getting it out of the car and we both start to run but you go aftor him, naturally, and you get a three-key bust.''

''No good. I can't run anymore. We'll work out something else.''

''Any way you want, Bumper. I'll turn anybody for you. I'll roll over on anybody if you give me a break.''

''Except your best connection.''

''That's God you're talking about. But I think right this minute I'd even turn my connection for a fix.''

''Where's this pot dealer live? Near my beat?''

''Yeah, not far. East Sixth. We can take him at his hotel. That might be the best way. You can kick down the pad and let me get out the window. At heart he's just a punk. They call him Little Rudy. He makes roach holders out of chicken bones and folded-up matchbooks and all that punk-ass bullshit. Only thing is, don't let me get a jacket. See, he knows this boss dyke, a real mean bull dagger. Her pad's a shooting gallery for some of us. If she knows you finked, she'll sneak battery acid in your spoon and laugh while you mainline it home. She's a *dog* motherfucker.''

''Okay, Wimpy, when can you set it up?''

''Saturday, Bumper, we can do it Saturday.''

''No good,'' I said quickly, a gas pain slicing across my stomach. ''Friday's the latest for anything.''

''Christ, Bumper. He's out of town. I know for sure. I think he's gone to the border to score.''

''I can't wait past Friday. Think of somebody else then.''

''Shit, lemme think,'' he said, rapping his skinny fingers against his temple. ''Oh yeah, I got something. A guy in the Rainbow Hotel. A tall dude, maybe forty, forty-five, blondish hair. He's in the first apartment to the left on the second floor. I just heard last night he's a half-ass fence. Buys most anything you steal. Cheap, I hear. Pays less than a dime on the dollar. A righteous dog. He deserves to fall. I hear these dope fiends bring radios and stuff like that, usually in the early morning.''

''Okay, maybe I'll try him tomorrow,'' I said, not really very interested.

''Sure, he might have lots of loot in the pad. You could clean up all kinds of burglaries.''

''Okay, Wimpy, you can make it now. But I want to see you regular. At least three times a week.''

''Bumper, could you please loan me a little in advance?''

''You gotta be kidding, Wimpy! Pay a junkie in advance?''

''I'm in awful bad shape today, Bumper,'' he said with a cracked whispery voice, like a prayer. He looked as bad as any I'd ever seen. Then I remembered I'd never see him again. After Friday I'd never see any of them again. He couldn't do me any good and it was unbelievably stupid, but I gave him a ten which was just like folding up a sawbuck and sticking it in his arm. He'd be in the same shape twelve hours from now. He stared at the bill like he didn't believe it at first. I left him there and walked back to the car.

''We'll get that pothead for you,'' he said. ''He's sloppy. You'll find seeds between the carpet and the molding outside the door in the hall. I'll get you lots of probable cause to kick over the pad.''

''I know how to take down a dope pad, Wimpy,'' I said over my shoulder.

''Later, Bumper, see you later,'' he yelled, breaking into a coughing spasm.

3

I always try to learn something from the people on my beat, and as I drove away I tried to think if I learned anything from all Wimpy's chatter. I'd heard this kind of bullshit from a thousand hypes. Then I thought of the hemorrhoid ointment for shrinking hype marks. That was something new. I'd never heard that one before. I always try to teach the rookies to keep their mouths shut and learn to listen. They usually give more information than they get when they're interrogating somebody. Even a guy like Wimpy could teach you something if you just give him a chance.

I got back in my car and looked at my watch because I was starting to get hungry. Of course I'm always hungry, or rather, I always want to eat. But I don't eat between meals and I eat my meals at regular times unless the job prevents it. I believe in routine. If you have rules for little things, rules you make up yourself, and if you obey these rules, your life will be in order. I only alter routines when I have to.

One of the cats on the daywatch, a youngster named Wilson, drove by in his black-and-white but didn't notice me because he was eyeballing some hype that was hotfooting it across Broadway to reach the crowded Grand Central Market, probably to score. The doper was moving fast like a hype with some gold in his jeans. Wilson was a good young copper, but sometimes when I looked at him like this, in profile when he was looking somewhere else, that cowlick of his and that kid nose, and something else I couldn't put my finger on, made me think of someone. For a while it bothered me and then one night last week when I was thinking so hard about getting married, and about Cassie, it came to me—he reminded me of Billy a little bit, but I pushed it out of my mind because I don't think of dead children or any dead people, that's another rule of mine. But I *did* start thinking of Billy's mother and how bad my first marringe had been and whether it could have been good if Billy had lived, and I had to admit that it *could* have been good, and it would have lasted if Billy had lived.

Then I wondered how many bad marriages that started during the war years had turned out all right. But it wasn't just that, there was the other thing, the dying. I almost told Cruz Segovia about it one time when we used to be partners and we were working a lonely morning watch at three a.m., about how my parents died, and how my brother raised me and how he died, and how my son died, and how I admired Cruz because he had his wife and all those kids and gave himself away to them fearlessly. But I never told him, and when Esteban, his oldest son died in Vietnam, I watched Cruz with the others, and after the crushing grief he still gave himself away to them, completely. But I couldn't admire him for it anymore. I could marvel at it, but I couldn't admire it. I don't know what I felt about it after that.

Thinking all these foolish things made a gas bubble start, and I could imagine the bubble getting bigger and bigger. Then I took a bubble buster, chewed it up and swallowed it, made up my mind to start thinking about women or food or something good, raised up, farted, said ''Good morning, Your Honor,'' and felt a whole lot better.

4

It always made me feel good just to drive around *without* thinking, so I turned off my radio and did just that. Pretty soon, without looking at my watch, I knew it was time to eat. I couldn't decide whether to hit Chinatown or Little Tokyo today. I didn't want Mexican food, because I promised Cruz Segovia I'd come to his pad for dinner tonight and I'd get enough Mexican food to last me a week. His wife Socorro knew how I loved *chile relleno* and she'd fix a dozen just for me.

A few burgers sounded good and there's a place in Hollywood that has the greatest burgers in town. Every time I go to Hollywood I think about Myrna, a broad I used to fool around with a couple years ago. She was an unreal Hollywood type, but she had a good executive job in a network television studio and whenever we went anywhere she'd end up spending more bread than I would. She loved to waste money, but the thing she really had going as far as I was concerned is that she looked just like Madeleine Carroll whose pictures we had all over our barracks during the war. It wasn't just that Myrna had style and elegant, springy tits, it's that she really looked like a woman and acted like one, except that she was a stone pothead and liked to improvise *too* much sexually. I'm game for anything reasonable, but sometimes Myrna was a little too freaky about things, and she also insisted on turning me on, and finally I tried smoking pot one time with her, but I didn't feel good high like on fine scotch. On her coffee table she had at least half a key and that's a pound of pot and that's trouble. I could just picture me and her getting hauled off to jail in a nark ark. So it was a bummer, and I don't know if it's the overall depressant effect of pot or what, but I crashed afterwards, down, down, down, until I felt mean enough to kick the hell out of her. But then, come to think of it, I guess Myrna liked that best of all anyway. So, Madeleine Carroll or not, I finally shined her on and she gave up calling me after a couple weeks, probably having found herself a trained gorilla or something.

There was one thing about Myrna that I'd never forget—she was a great dancer, not a good dancer, a *great* dancer, because Myrna could completely stop thinking when she danced. I think that's the secret. She could dig hard rock and she was a real snake. When she moved on a dance floor, often as not, everyone would stop and watch. Of course they laughed at me—at first. Then they'd see there were *two* dancers out there. It's funny about dancing, it's like food or sex, it's something you do and you can just forget you *have* a brain. It's all body and deep in your guts, especially the hard rock. And hard rock's the best thing to happen to music. When Myrna and me were really moving, maybe at some kid place on the Sunset Strip, our bodies joined. It wasn't just a sex thing, but there *was* that too, it was like our bodies really made it together and you didn't even have to *think* anymore.

I used to always experiment by doing the funky chicken when we first started out. I know it's getting old now, but I'd do it and they'd all laugh, because of the way my belly jumped and swayed around. Then I'd always do it again right near the end of the song, and nobody laughed. They smiled, but nobody laughed, because they could see by then how graceful I really am, despite the way I'm built. Nobody's chicken was as funky as mine, so I always stood there flapping my elbows and bowing my knees just to test them. And despite the raw animal moves of Myrna, people also looked at *me*. They watched both of us dance. That's one thing I miss about Myrna.

I didn't feel like roaming so far from my beat today so I decided on beef teriyaki and headed for J-town. The Japanese have the commercial area around First and Second Streets between Los Angeles Street and Central Avenue. There are lots of colorful shops and restaurants and professional buildings. They also have their share of banks and lots of money to go in them. When I walked in the Geisha Doll on First Street, the lunch hour rush was just about over and the mama-san shuffled over with her little graceful steps like she was still twenty instead of sixty-five. She always wore a silk slit-skirted dress and she really didn't look too bad for an old girl. I always kidded her about a Japanese wearing a Chinese dress and she would laugh and say, "Make moah China ting in Tokyo than all China. And bettah, goddamn betcha." The place was plush and dark, lots of bamboo, beaded curtains, hanging lanterns.

"Boom-pah san, wheah you been hide?" she said as I stepped through the beads.

"Hello, Mother," I said, lifting her straight up under the arms and kissing her on the cheek. She only weighed about ninety pounds and seemed almost brittle, but once I didn't do this little trick and she got mad. She expected it and all the customers got a kick out of watching me perform. The cooks and all the pretty waitresses and Sumi, the hostess, dressed in a flaming orange kimono, expected it too. I saw Sumi tap a Japanese customer on the shoulder when I walked in.

I usually held the mama-san up like this for a good minute or so and snuggled her a little bit and joked around until everyone in the place was giggling, especially the mama-san, and then I put her down and let her tell anyone in shouting distance how "stlong is owah Boom-pah." My arms are good even though my legs are gone, but she was like a paper doll, no weight at all. She always said "*owah* Boom-pah," and I always took it to mean I belonged to J-town too and I liked the idea. Los Angeles policemen are very partial to Buddha heads because sometimes they seem like the only ones left in the world who really appreciate discipline, cleanliness, and hard work. I've even seen motor cops who'd hang a ticket on a one-legged leper, let a Nip go on a good traffic violation because they contribute practically nothing to the crime rate even though they're notoriously bad drivers. I've been noticing in recent years though that Orientals have been showing up as suspects on crime reports. If they degenerate like everyone else there'll be no *group* to look up to, just individuals.

"We have a nice table for you, Bumper," said Sumi with a smile that could almost make you forget food—almost. I started smelling things: tempura, rice wine, teriyaki steak. I have a sensitive nose and can pick out individual smells. It's really only *individual* things that count in this world. When you lump everything together you get goulash or chop suey or a greasy stew pot. I hated food like that.

"I think I'll sit at the *sushi* bar," I said to Sumi, who once confessed to me her real name was Gloria. People expected a geisha doll to have a Japanese name, so Gloria, a third generation American, obliged them. I agreed with her logic. There's no sense disappointing people.

There were two other men at the *sushi* bar, both Japanese, and Mako who worked the *sushi* bar smiled at me but looked a little grim at the challenge. He once told Mama that serving Boom-pah alone was like serving a *sushi* bar full of *sumos*. I couldn't help it, I loved those delicate little rice balls, molded by hand and wrapped in strips of pink salmon and octopus, abalone, tuna and shrimp. I loved the little hidden pockets of horseradish that surprised you and made your eyes water. And I loved a bowl of soup, especially soybean and seaweed, and to drink it from the bowl Japanese style. I put it away faster than Mako could lay it out and I guess I looked like a buffalo at the *sushi* bar. Much as I tried to control myself and use a little Japanese self-discipline, I kept throwing the chow down and emptying the little dishes while Mako grinned and sweated and put them up. I knew it was no way to behave at the *sushi* bar in a nice restaurant, this was for gourmets, the refined eaters of Japanese cuisine, and I attacked like a blue locust, but God, eating *sushi* is being in heaven. In fact, I'd settle for that, and become a Buddhist if heaven was a *sushi* bar.

There was only one thing that saved me from looking too bad to a Japanese—I could handle chopsticks like one of them. I first learned in Japan right after the war, and I've been coming to the Geisha Doll and every other restaurant here in J-town for twenty years so it was no wonder. Even without the bluesuit, they could look at me click those sticks and know I was no tourist passing through. Sometimes though, when I didn't think about it, I ate with both hands. I just couldn't devour it fast enough.

In cooler weather I always drank rice wine or hot sake with my meal, today, ice water. After I'd finished what two or three good-sized Japanese would consume, I quit and started drinking tea while Mama and Sumi made several trips over to make sure I had enough and to see that my tea was hot enough and to try to feed me some tempura, and the tender fried shrimp looked so good I ate a half dozen. If Sumi wasn't twenty years too young I'd have been awful tempted to try her too. But she was so delicate and beautiful and so *young,* I lost confidence even thinking about it. And then too, she was one of the people on my beat, and there's that thing, the way they think about me. Still, it always helped my appetite to eat in a place where there were pretty women. But until I was at least half full, I have to say I didn't notice women or anything else. The world disappears for me when I'm eating something I love.

The thing that always got to me about Mama was how much she thanked me for eating up half her kitchen. Naturally she would never let me pay for my food, but she always thanked me about ten times before I got out the door. Even for an Oriental she really overdid it. It made me feel guilty, and when I came here I sometimes wished I could violate the custom and pay her. But she'd fed cops before I came along and she'd feed them after, and that was the way things were. I didn't tell Mama that Friday was going to be my last day, and I didn't start thinking about it because with a barrel of *sushi* in my stomach I couldn't afford indigestion.

Sumi came over to me before I left and held the little teacup to my lips while I sipped it and she said, "Okay, Bumper, tell me an exciting cops-and-robbers story." She did this often, and I'm sure she was aware how she affected me up close there feeling her sweet breath, looking at those chocolate-brown eyes and soft skin.

"All right, my little lotus blossom," I said, like W. C. Fields, and she giggled. "One spine tingler, coming up."

Then I reverted to my normal voice and told her about the guy I stopped for blowing a red light at Second and San Pedro one day and how he'd been here a year from Japan and had a California license and all, but didn't speak English, or pretended not to so he could try to get out of the ticket. I decided to go ahead and hang one on him because he almost wiped out a guy in the crosswalk, and when I got it written he refused to sign it, telling me in pidgin, "Not gear-tee, not gear-tee," and I tried for five minutes to explain that the signature was just a promise to appear and he could have a jury trial if he wanted one and if he didn't sign I'd have to book him. He just kept shaking his head like he didn't savvy and finally I turned that ticket book over and drew a picture on the back. Then I drew the same picture for Sumi. It was a litile jail window with a stick figure hanging on the bars. He had a sad turned-down mouth and slant eyes. I'd showed him the picture and said, "You sign now, maybe?" and he wrote his name so fast and hard he broke my pencil lead.

Sumi laughed and repeated it in Japanese for Mama. When I left after tipping Mako they all thanked me again until I really *did* feel guilty. That was the only thing I didn't like about J-town. I wished to hell I could pay for my meal here, though I confess I never had that wish anywhere else.

Frankly, there was practically nothing to spend my money on. I ate three meals on my beat. I could buy booze, clothes, jewelry, and everything else you could think of at wholesale or less. In fact, somebody was always giving me something like that as a gift. I had my bread stop and a dairy that supplied me with gallons of free ice cream, milk, cottage cheese, all I wanted. My apartment was very nice and rent-free, even including utilities, because I helped the manager run the thirty-two units. At least he thought I helped him. He'd call me when he had a loud party or something, and I'd go up, join the party, and persuade them to quiet down a little, while I drank their booze and ate their canapés. Once in awhile I'd catch a peeping tom or something, and since the manager was such a mouse, he thought I was indispensable. Except for girlfriends and my informants it was always hard to find anything to spend my money on. Sometimes I actually went a week hardly spending a dime except for tips. I'm a big tipper, not like most policemen.

When it came to accepting things from people on my beat I did have one rule—no money. I felt that if I took money, which a lot of people tried to give me at Christmas time, I'd be getting bought. I never felt bought though if a guy gave me free meals or a case of booze, or a discounted sport coat, or if a dentist fixed my teeth at a special rate, or an optometrist bounced for a pair of sunglasses half price. These things weren't money, and I wasn't a hog about it. I never took more than

I could personally use, or which I could give to people like Cruz Segovia or Cassie, who recently complained that her apartment was beginning to look like a distillery. Also I never took anything from someone I might end up having to arrest. For instance, before we started really hating each other, Marvin Heywood, the owner of the Pink Dragon, tried to lay a couple cases of scotch on me, and I mean the best, but I turned him down. I'd known from the first day he opened that place it would be a hangout for slimeballs. Every day was like a San Quentin convention in that cesspool. And the more I thought of it, the more I got burned up thinking that after I retired nobody would roust the Dragon as hard as I always did. I caused Marvin a sixty-day liquor license suspension twice, and I probably cost him two thousand a month in lost business since some of the hoods were afraid to come there because of me.

I jumped in my car and decided to cruise by the Dragon for one last shot at it. When I parked out back, a hype in the doorway saw me and ran down the steps to tell everybody inside the heat was coming. I took my baton, wrapped the thong around my hand which they teach you not to do now, but which I've been doing for twenty years, and I walked down the concrete stairway to this cellar bar, and through the draped doorway. The front is framed by a pink dragon head. The front doorway is the mouth of the beast, the back door is under the tail. It always made me mad just to see the big dumb-looking dragon-mouth door. I went in the back door, up the dragon's ass, tapping my stick on the empty chairs and keeping my head on a swivel as I let my eyes get accustomed to the gloom. The pukepots were all sitting near the back. There were only about ten customers now in the early afternoon, and Marvin, all six feet six inches of him, was at the end of the bar grinning at a bad-looking bull dyke who was putting down a pretty well-built black stud in an arm wrestle.

Marvin was grinning, but he didn't mean it, he knew I was there. It curdled his blood to see me tapping on the furniture with my stick. That's why I did it. I always was as badge heavy and obnoxious as I could be when I was in there. I'd been in two brawls here and both times I knew Marvin was just wetting his shorts wishing he had the guts to jump in on me, but he thought better of it.

He weighed at least three hundred pounds and was damned tough. You had to be to own this joint, which catered to bookmakers, huggermugger whores, paddy hustlers, speed freaks, fruits and fruit hustlers, and ex-cons of both sexes and all ages. I'd never quite succeeded in provoking Marvin into attacking me, although it was common knowledge on the street that a shot fired at me one night from a passing car was some punk hired by Marvin. It was after that, even though nothing was ever proved, that I really began standing on the Dragon's tail. For a couple of months his business dropped to nothing with me living on his doorstep, and he sent two lawyers to my captain and the police commission to get me off his back. I relented as much as I had to, but I still gave him fits.

If I wasn't retiring there'd be hell to pay around here because once you get that twenty years' service in, you don't have to pussyfoot around so much. I mean no matter what kind of trouble you get into, nobody can ever take your pension away for any reason, even if they fire you. So if I were staying, I'd go right on. Screw the lawyers, screw the police commission. I'd land on that Dragon with both boondockers. And as I thought that, I looked down at my size thirteen triple E's. They were beat officer shoes, high top, laces with eyelets, ankle supporting, clumsy, round toes, beat officer shoes. A few years ago they were actually popular with young black guys, and almost came into style again. They called them "old man comforts" and they were soft and comfortable, but ugly as hell, I guess, to most people. I'd probably always wear them. I'd sunk my old man comforts in too many deserving asses to part with them now.

Finally Marvin got tired watching the arm wrestlers and pretending he didn't see me.

"Whadda you want, Morgan," he said. Even in the darkness I could see him getting red in the face, his big chin jutting.

"Just wondering how many scumbags were here today, Marvin," I said in a loud voice which caused four or five of them to look up. These days we're apt to get disciplinary action for making brutal remarks like that, even though these assholes would bust their guts laughing if I was courteous or even civil.

The bull dyke was the only righteous female in the place. In this dive you almost have to check everybody's plumbing to know whether it's interior or exterior. The two in dresses were drags, the others were fruit hustlers and flimflam guys. I recognized a sleazy bookmaker named Harold Wagner. One of the fruit hustlers was a youngster, maybe twenty-two or so. He was still young enough to be offended by my remark, especially since it was in front of the queen in the red mini who probably belonged to him. He mumbled something under his breath and Marvin told him to cool it since he didn't want to give me an excuse to make another bust in the place. The guy looked high on pot like most everyone these days.

"He your new playmate, Roxie?" I said to the red dress queen, whose real name I knew was John Jeffrey Alton.

"Yes," said the queen in a falsetto voice, and motioned to the kid to shut his mouth. He was a couple inches taller than me and big chested, probably shacking with Roxie now and they split what they get hustling. Roxie hustles the guys who want a queen, and the kid goes after the ones who want a jocker. This jocker would probably become a queen himself. I always felt sorry for queens because they're so frantic, searching, looking. Sometimes I twist them for information, but otherwise I leave them alone.

I was in a rotten mood thinking nobody would roust the Dragon after I was gone. They were all glaring at me now, especially Marvin with his mean gray eyes and knife mouth.

One young guy, too young to know better, leaned back in his chair and made a couple of oinks and said, "I smell pig."

I'd never seen him before. He looked like a college boy slumming. Maybe in some rah-rah campus crowd beer joint I'd just hee-haw and let him slide, but here in the Pink Dragon the beat cops rule by force and fear. If they stopped being afraid of me I was through, and the street would be a jungle which it is anyway, but at least now you can walk through it watching for occasional cobras and rabid dogs. I figured if it weren't for guys like me, there'd be no trails through the frigging forest.

"Oink, oink," he said again, with more confidence this time, since I hadn't responded. "I sure do smell pig."

"And what do pigs like best?" I smiled, slipping the stick back in my baton ring. "Pigs like to clean up garbage, and I see a pile." Still smiling I kicked the chair legs and he went down hard throwing a glass of beer on Roxie who forgot the falsetto and yelled, "Shithouse mouse!" in a pretty good baritone when the beer slid down his bra.

I had the guy in a wristlock before he knew what fell on him, and was on my way out the door, with him walking backwards, but not too fast in case someone else was ready.

"You bastard!" Marvin sputtered. "You assaulted my customer. You bastard! I'm calling my lawyer."

"Go right on, Marvin," I said, while the tall kid screamed and tippy-toed to the door because the upward thrust of the wristlock was making him go as high as he could. The smell of pot was hanging on his clothes but the euphoria wasn't dulling the pain of the wristlock. When you've got one that's really loaded you can't crank it on too hard because they don't react to pain, and you might break a wrist trying to make them flinch. This guy felt it though, and he was docile, ow, ow, owing all the way out. Marvin came around the bar and followed us to the door.

"There's witnesses!" he boomed. "This time there's witnesses to your dirty, filthy false arrest of my customer! What's the charge? What're you going to charge him with?"

"He's drunk, Marvin," I smiled, holding the wristlock with one hand, just in case Marvin was mad enough. I was up, high up, all alive, ready to fly.

"It's a lie. He's sober. He's sober as you."

"Why, Marvin," I said, "he's drunk in public view and unable to care for himself. I'm obliged to arrest him for his own protection. He *has* to be drunk to say what he did to me, don't you agree? And if you're not careful I might think you're trying to interfere with my arrest. You wouldn't like to try interfering with my arrest would you, Marvin?"

"We'll get you, Morgan," Marvin whispered helplessly. "We'll get your job one of these days."

"If you slimeballs could have my job I wouldn't want it," I said, let down because it was over.

The kid wasn't as loaded as I thought when I got him out of there into the sunshine and more or less fresh Los Angeles air.

"I'm not drunk," he repeated all the way to the Glass House, shaking his mop of blond hair out of his face since I had his hands cuffed behind his back. The Glass House is what the street people call our main police building because of all the windows.

"You *talked* your way into jail, boy," I said, lighting a cigar.

"You can't just put a sober man in jail for drunk because he calls you a pig," said the kid, and by the way he talked and looked, I figured him for an upper-middle-class student hanging out downtown with the scumbags for a perverse kick, and also because he was at heart a scumbag himself.

"More guys talk themselves into jail than get there any other way," I said.

"I demand an attorney," he said.

"Call one soon as you're booked."

"I'll bring those people to court. They'll testify I was sober. I'll sue you for false arrest."

"You wouldn't be getting a cherry, kid. Guys tried to sue me a dozen times. And you wouldn't get those assholes in the Dragon to give you the time of day if they had a crate full of alarm clocks."

"How can you book me for *drunk?* Are you prepared to swear before God that I was drunk?"

"There's no God down here on the beat, and anyway He'd never show His face in the Pink Dragon. The United States Supreme Court decisions don't work too well down here either. So you see, kid, I been forced to write my own laws, and you violated one in there. I just have to find you guilty of contempt of cop."

5

After I got the guy booked I didn't know what the hell to do. I had this empty feeling now that was making me depressed. I thought about the hotel burglar again, but I felt lazy. It was this empty feeling. I was in a black mood as I swung over toward Figueroa. I saw a mailbox handbook named Zoot Lafferty standing there near a public phone. He used to hang around Main and then Broadway and now Figueroa. If we could ever get him another block closer to the Harbor Freeway maybe we could push the bastard off the overpass sometime, I thought, in the mood for murder.

Lafferty always worked the businessmen in the area, taking the action and recording the bets inside a self-addressed stamped envelope. And he always hung around a mailbox and a public phone booth. If he saw someone that he figured was a vice cop, he'd run to the mailbox and deposit the letter. That way there'd be no evidence like betting markers or owe sheets the police could recover. He'd have the customers' bets the next day when the mail came, and in time for collection and payment. Like all handbooks though, he was scared of plainclothes vice cops but completely ignored uniformed policemen.

So one day when I was riding by, I slammed on the binders, jumped out of the black-and-white, and fell on Zoot's skinny ass before he could get to the mailbox. I caught him with the markers and they filed a felony bookmaking charge. I convicted him in Superior Court after I convinced the judge that I had a confidential reliable informant tell me all about Zoot's operation, which was true, and that I hid behind a bush just behind the phone booth and overheard the bets being taken over the phone, which was a lie. But I convinced the judge and that's all that matters. He had to pay a two-hundred-and-fifty-dollar fine and was given a year's probation, and that same day, he moved over here to Figueroa away from my beat where there are no bushes anywhere near his phone booth.

As I drove by Zoot, he waved at me and grinned and stood by the mailbox. I wondered if we could've got some help with the Post Office special agents to stop this flimflam, but it would've been awful hard and not worth the effort. You can't tamper with someone's mail very easy. Now, as I looked at his miserable face for the last time, my black mood got blacker and I thought, I'll bet no other uniformed cop ever takes the trouble to shag him after I'm gone.

Then I started thinking about bookmaking in general, and got even madder, because it was the kind of crime I couldn't do anything about. I saw the profits reaped from it all around me, and I saw the people involved in it, and knew some of them, and yet I couldn't do anything because they were so well organized and their weapons were so good and mine were so flimsy. The money was so unbelievably good that they could expand into semilegitimate businesses and drive out competition because they had the racket money to fall back on, and the legitimate businesses couldn't compete. And also they were tougher and ruthless and knew other ways to discourage competition. I always wanted to get one of them good, someone like Red Scalotta, a big book, whose fortune they say can't be guessed at. I thought all these things and how mad I get everytime I see a goddamn lovable Damon-Runyon-type bookmaker in a movie. I started thinking then about Angie Caputo, and got a dark kind of pleasure just picturing him and remembering how another old beat man, Sam Giraldi, had humbled him. Angie had never realized his potential as a hood after what Sam did to him.

Sam Giraldi is dead now. He died last year just fourteen months after he retired at twenty years' service. He was only forty-four when he had a fatal heart attack, which is particularly a policeman's disease. In a job like this, sitting on your ass for long periods of time and then moving in bursts of heart-cracking action, you can expect heart attacks. Especially since lots of us get so damned fat when we get older.

When he ruined Angie Caputo, Sam was thirty-seven years old but looked forty-seven in the face. He wasn't very tall, but had tremendous shoulders, a meaty face, and hands bigger than mine, all covered with heavy veins. He was a good handball player and his body was hard as a spring-loaded sap. He'd been a vice officer for years and then went back to uniform. Sam walked Alvarado when I walked downtown, and sometimes he'd drive over to my beat or I'd come over to his. We'd eat dinner together and talk shop or talk about baseball, which I like and which he was fanatic about. Sometimes, if we ate at his favorite delicatessen on Alvarado, I'd walk with him for a while and once or twice we made a pretty good pinch together like that.

It was on a wonderful summer night when a breeze was blowing off the water in MacArthur Park that I met Angie Caputo.

It seemed to be a sudden thing with Sam. It struck like a bullet, the look on his face, and he said, "See that guy? That's Angie Caputo, the pimp and book-maker's agent." And I said, "So what?" wondering what the hell was going on, because Sam looked like he was about to shoot the guy who was just coming out of a bar and getting ready to climb aboard a lavender Lincoln he had parked on Sixth Street. We got in Sam's car, getting ready to drive over to catch the eight o'clock show at the burlesque house out there on his beat.

"He hangs out further west, near Eighth Street," said Sam. "That's where he lives too. Not far from my pad, in fact. I been looking to see him for a few days now. I got it straight that he's the one that busted the jaw of Mister Rovitch that owns the cleaners where I get my uniforms done." Sam was talking in an unnaturally soft voice. He was a gentle guy and always talked low and quiet, but this was different.

"What'd he do that for?"

"Old guy was behind on interest payments to Harry Stapleton the loan shark. He had Angie do the job for him. Angie's a big man now. He don't have to do that kind of work no more, but he loves to do it sometimes. I hear he likes to use a pair of leather gloves with wrist pins in the palms."

"He get booked for it?"

Sam shook his head. "The old man swears three niggers mugged him."

"You sure it was Caputo?"

"I got a good snitch, Bumper."

And then Sam confessed to me that Caputo was from the same dirty town in Pennsylvania that he was from, and their families knew each other when they were kids, and they were even distant relatives. Then Sam turned the car around and drove back on Sixth Street and stopped at the corner.

"Get in, Angie," said Sam, as Caputo walked toward the car with a friendly smile.

"You busting me, Sam?" said Caputo, the smile widening, and I could hardly believe he was as old as Sam. His wavy hair was blue-black without a trace of gray, and his handsome profile was smooth, and his gray suit was beautiful. I turned around when Caputo held out a hand and smiled at me.

"Angie's my name," he said as we shook hands. "Where we going?"

"I understand you're the one that worked over the old man," said Sam in a much softer voice than before.

"You gotta be kidding, Sam. I got other things going. Your finks got the wrong boy for this one."

"I been looking for you."

"What for, Sam, you gonna bust me?"

"I can't bust you. I ain't been able to bust you since I knew you, even though I'd give my soul to do it."

"This guy's a comic," said Caputo, laughing as he lit a cigarette. "I can depend on old Sam to talk to me at least once a month about how he'd like to send me to the joint. He's a comic. Whadda you hear from the folks back in Aliquippa, Sam? How's Liz and Dolly? How's Dolly's kids?"

"Before this, you never really hurt nobody I knew personally," said Sam, still in the strange soft voice. "I knew the old man real good, you know."

"He one of your informers, Sam?" asked Caputo. "Too bad. Finks're hard to come by these days."

"Old guy like that. Bones might never heal."

"Okay, that's a shame. Now tell me where we're going. Is this some kind of roust? I wanna know."

''Here's where we're going. We're here,'' said Sam, driving the car under the ramp onto the lonely, dark, dirt road by the new freeway construction.

''What the fuck's going on?'' asked Caputo, for the first time not smiling.

''Stay in the car, Bumper,'' said Sam. ''I wanna talk with Angie alone.''

''Be careful, *fratello,*'' said Caputo. ''I ain't a punk you can scare. Be careful.''

''Don't say *fratello* to me,'' Sam whispered. ''You're a *dog's* brother. You beat old men. You beat women and live off them. You live off weak people's blood.''

''I'll have your job, you dumb dago,'' said Caputo, and I jumped out of the car when I heard the slapping thud of Sam's big fist and Caputo's cry of surprise. Sam was holding Caputo around the head and already I could see the blood as Sam hammered at his face. Then Caputo was on his back and he tried to hold off the blows of the big fist which drew back slowly and drove forward with speed and force. Caputo was hardly resisting now and didn't yell when Sam pulled out the heavy six-inch Smith and Wesson. Sam knelt on the arms of Caputo and cracked the gun muzzle through his teeth and into his mouth. Caputo's head kept jerking off the ground as he gagged on the gun muzzle twisting and digging in his throat but Sam pinned him there on the end of the barrel, whispering to him in Italian. Then Sam was on his feet and Caputo flopped on his stomach heaving bloody, pulpy tissue.

Sam and me drove back alone without talking. Sam was breathing hard and occasionally opened a window to spit a wad of phlegm. When Sam finally decided to talk he said, ''You don't have to worry, Bumper, Angie'll keep his mouth shut. He didn't even open it when I beat him, did he?''

''I'm not worried.''

''He won't say nothing,'' said Sam. ''And things'll be better on the street. They won't laugh at us and they won't be so bold. They'll be scared. And Angie'll never really be respected again. It'll be better out here on the street.''

''I'm just afraid he'll kill you, Sam.''

''He won't. He'll fear me. He'll be afraid that *I'll* kill *him*. And I will if he tries anything.''

''Christ, Sam, it's not worth getting so personally tied up to these assholes like this.''

''Look, Bumper, I worked bookmaking in Ad Vice and here in Central. I busted bookmakers and organized hoodlums for over eight years. I worked as much as six months on *one* bookmaker. Six months! I put together an investigation and gathered evidence that no gang lawyer could beat and I took back offices where I seized records that could prove, *prove* the guy was a millionaire book. And I convicted them and saw them get pitiful fines time after time and I *never* saw a bookmaker go to state prison even though it's a felony. Let somebody else work bookmaking I finally decided, and I came back to uniform. But Angie's different. I know him. All my life I knew him, and I live right up Serrano there, in the apartments. That's *my* neighborhood. I use that cleaners where the old man works. Sure he was my snitch but I liked him. I never paid him. He just told me things. He got a kid's a schoolteacher, the old man does. The books'll be scared now for a little while after what I done. They'll respect us for a little while.''

I had to agree with everything Sam said, but I'd never seen a guy worked over that bad before, not by a cop anyway. It bothered me. I worried about us, Sam and me, about what would happen if Caputo complained to the Department, but Sam was right. Caputo kept his mouth shut and I admit I was never sorry for what Sam did. When it was over I felt something and couldn't put my finger on it at first, and then one night laying in bed I figured it out. It was a feeling of something being *right*. For one of the few times on this job I saw an untouchable touched. I felt my thirst being slaked a little bit, and I was never sorry for what Sam did.

But Sam was dead now and I was retiring, and I was sure there weren't many other bluesuits in the division who could nail a bookmaker. I turned my car around and headed back toward Zoot Lafferty, still standing there in his pea green slack suit. I parked the black-and-white at the curb, got out, and very slow, with my sweaty uniform shirt sticking to my back, I walked over to Zoot who opened the package door on the red and blue mail box and stuck his arm inside. I stopped fifteen feet away and stared at him.

"Hello, Morgan," he said, with a crooked phony grin that told me he wished he'd have slunk off long before now. He was a pale, nervous guy, about forty-five years old, with a bald freckled skull.

"Hello, Zoot," I said, putting my baton back inside the ring, and measuring the distance between us.

"You got your rocks off once by busting me, Morgan. Why don't you go back over to your beat, and get outta my face? I moved clear over here to Figueroa to get away from you and your fucking beat, what more do you want?"

"How much action you got written down, Zoot?" I said, walking closer. "It'll inconvenience the shit out of you to let it go in the box, won't it?"

"Goddamnit, Morgan," said Zoot, blinking his eyes nervously, and scratching his scalp which looked loose and rubbery. "Why don't you quit rousting people. You're an old man, you know that? Why don't you just fuck off outta here and start acting like one."

When the slimeball said that, the blackness I felt turned blood red, and I sprinted those ten feet as he let the letter slide down inside the box. But he didn't get his hand out. I slammed the door hard and put my weight against it and the metal door bit into his wrist and he screamed.

"Zoot, it's time for you and me to have a talk." I had my hand on the mailbox package door, all my weight leaning hard, as he jerked for a second and then froze in pain, bug-eyed.

"Please, Morgan," he whispered, and I looked around, seeing there was a lot of car traffic but not many pedestrians.

"Zoot, before I retire I'd like to take a real good book, just one time. Not a sleazy little handbook like you but a real bookmaker, how about helping me?"

Tears began running down Zoot's cheeks and he showed his little yellow teeth and turned his face to the sun as he pulled another time on the arm. I pushed harder and he yelped loud, but there were noisy cars driving by.

"For God's sake, Morgan," he begged. "I don't know anything. Please let my arm out."

"I'll tell you what, Zoot. I'll settle for your phone spot. Who do you phone your action in to?"

"They phone *me*," he gasped, as I took a little weight off the door.

"You're a liar," I said, leaning again.

"Okay, okay, I'll give you the number," he said, and now he was blubbering outright and I got disgusted and then mad at him and at me and especially at the bookmaker I'd never have a chance to get, because he was too well protected and my weapons were too puny.

"I'll break your goddamn arm if you lie," I said, with my face right up to his. A young, pretty woman walked by just then, looked at Zoot's sweaty face and then at mine, and damn near ran across the street to get away from us.

"It's six-six-eight-two-seven-three-three," he sobbed.

"Repeat it."

"Six-six-eight-two-seven-three-three."

"One more time, and it better come out the same."

"Six-six-eight-two-seven-three-three. Oh, Christ!"

"How do you say it when you phone in the action?"

"Dandelion. I just say the word Dandelion and then I give the bets. I swear, Morgan."

"Wonder what Red Scalotta would say if he knew you gave me that information?" I smiled, and then I let him go when I saw by his eyes that I'd guessed right and he was involved with that particular bookmaker.

He pulled his arm out and sat down on the curb, holding it like it was broken and cursing under his breath as he wiped the tears away.

"How about talking with a vice cop about this?" I said, lighting a fresh cigar while he began rubbing his arm which was probably going numb.

"You're a psycho, Morgan!" he said looking up. "You're a real psycho if you think I'd fink on anybody."

"Look, Zoot, you talk to a vice cop like I say, and we'll protect you. You won't get a jacket. But if you don't, I'll personally see that Scalotta gets the word that you gave me the phone number and the code so we could stiff in a bet on the phone clerk. I'll let it be known that you're a paid snitch and when he finds out what you told me you know what? I bet he'll believe it. You ever see what some gunsel like Bernie Zolitch can do to a fink?"

"You're the most rottenest bastard I ever seen," said Zoot, standing up, very shaky, and white as paste.

"Look at it this way, Zoot, you cooperate just this once, we'll take one little pukepot sitting in some phone spot and that'll be all there is to it. We'll make sure we come up with a phony story about how we got the information like we always do to protect an informant, and nobody'll be the wiser. You can go back to your slimy little business and I give you my word I'll never roust you again. Not personally, that is. And you probably know I always keep my word. Course I can't guarantee you some *other* cop won't shag you sometime."

He hesitated for a second and then said, "I'll settle for *you* not rousting me no more, Morgan. Those vice cops I can live with."

"Let's take a ride. How's your arm feeling?"

"Fuck you, Morgan," he said, and I chuckled to myself and felt a little better about everything. We drove to Central Vice and I found the guy I wanted sitting in the office.

"Why aren't you out taking down some handbook, Charlie?" I said to the young vice cop who was leaning dangerously back in a swivel chair with his crepe-soled sneak shoes up on a desk doping the horses on a scratch sheet.

"Hi, Bumper," he grinned, and then recognized Zoot who he himself probably busted a time or two.

"Mr. Lafferty decide to give himself up?" said Charlie Bronski, a husky, square-faced guy with about five years on the Department. I broke him in when he was just out of the academy. I remembered him as a smart aggressive kid, but with humility. Just the kind I liked. You could teach that kind a little something. I wasn't ashamed to say he was Bumper-ized.

Charlie got up and put on a green striped, short-sleeved ivy-league shirt over the shoulder holster which he wore over a white T-shirt.

"Old Zoot here just decided to repent his evil ways, Charlie," I said, glancing at Zoot who looked as sad as anyone I'd ever seen.

"Let's get it over with, Morgan, for chrissake," said Zoot. "And you got to swear you'll keep it confidential."

"Swear, Charlie," I said.

"I swear," said Charlie. "What's this all about?"

"Zoot wants to trade a phone spot to us."

"For what?" asked Charlie.

"For nothing," said Zoot, very impatient. "Just because I'm a good fucking citizen. Now you want the information or not?"

"Okay," Charlie said, and I could tell he was trying to guess how I squeezed Zoot. Having worked with me for a few months, Charlie was familiar with my M.O. I'd always tried to teach him and other young cops that you can't be a varsity letterman when you deal with these barfbags. Or rather, you *could* be, and you'd probably be the one who became captain, or Chief of Police or something, but you can bet there'd always have to be the guys like me on the street to make you look good up there in that ivory tower by keeping the assholes from taking over the city.

"You wanna give us the relay, is that it?" said Charlie, and Zoot nodded, looking a little bit sick.

"*Is* it a relay spot? Are you sure?" asked Charlie.

"I'm not sure of a goddamn thing," Zoot blubbered, rubbing his arm again. "I only came 'cause I can't take this kind of heat. I can't take being rousted and hurt."

Charlie looked at me, and I thought that if this lifelong handbook, this ex-con and slimeball started crying, I'd flip. I was filled with loathing for a pukepot like Zoot, not because he snitched, hell, everybody snitches when the twist is good enough. It was this crybaby sniveling stuff that I couldn't take.

"Damn, Zoot!" I finally exploded. "You been a friggin' scammer all your life, fracturing every friggin' law you had nuts enough to crack, and you sit here now acting like a pious nun. If you wanna play your own tune you better damn well learn to dance to it, and right now you're gonna do the friggin' boogaloo, you goddamn hemorrhoid!"

I took a step toward Zoot's chair and he snapped up straight in his seat saying, "Okay, Morgan, okay. Whadda you want? For God's sake I'll tell you what you wanna know! You don't have to get tough!"

"Is the number you phone a relay?" repeated Charlie calmly.

"I think so," Zoot nodded. "Sounds like some goofy broad don't know nothing about the business. I been calling this same broad for six months now. She's probably just some stupid fucking housewife, sitting on a hot seat and taking them bets for somebody she don't even know."

"Usually record them on Formica," Charlie explained to me, "then somebody phones her several times a day and takes the action she wrote down. She can wipe the Formica in case the vice cops come busting down her door. She probably won't even know who pays her or where the phone calls come from."

"Fuck no, she ain't gonna know," said Zoot, looking at me. "This shit's too big, Morgan. It's too goddamn big. You ain't gonna bother nobody by rousting me. You don't understand, Morgan. People *want* us in business. What's a guy get for bookmaking? Even a big guy? A fucking fine. Who does time? You ever see a book get joint time?" said Zoot to Charlie, who shook his head. "Fuck no, you ain't and you ain't going to. Everybody bets with bookies for chrissake and those that don't, they like some other kind of vice. Give up, Morgan. You been a cop all these years and you don't know enough to give up fighting it. You can't save this rotten world."

"I ain't trying to, Zoot," I said. "I just love the friggin' battle!"

I went down the hall to the coffee room, figuring that Charlie should be alone with Zoot. Now that I had played the bad guy, he could play the good guy. An interrogation never works if it's not private, and Charlie was a good bullshitter. I had hopes he could get more out of Zoot because I had him loosened up. Anytime you get someone making speeches at you, you have a chance. If he's shaky about one thing, he might be about something else. I didn't think you could buy Zoot with money, he was too scared of everything. But being scared of us as well as the mob, he could be gotten to. Charlie could handle him.

Cruz Segovia was in the coffee room working on his log. I came in behind him. There was no one else in the room and Cruz was bent over the table writing in his log. He was so slim that even in his uniform he looked like a little boy bent over doing his homework. His face was still almost the same as when we were in the academy and except for his gray hair he hadn't changed much. He was barely five feet eight and sitting there he looked really small.

"*Qué pasó, compadre,*" I said, because he always said he wished I was Catholic and could have been the godfather for his last seven kids. His kids considered me their godfather anyway, and he called me *compadre*.

"*Orale, panzón,*" he said, like a pachuco, which he put on for me. He spoke beautiful Spanish and could also read and write Spanish which is rare for a Mexican. He was good with English too, but the barrios of El Paso Texas died hard, and Cruz had an accent when he spoke English.

"Where you been hiding out all day?" I said, putting a dime in the machine and getting Cruz a fresh cup, no cream and double sugar.

"You bastard," he said. "Where've *I* been hiding. Communication's been trying to get *you* all day! Don't you know that funny little box in your car is called a radio and you're supposed to listen for your calls and you're even supposed to handle them once in a while?"

"*Chale, chale.* Quit being a sergeant," I said. "Gimme some slack. I been bouncing in and out of that black-and-white machine so much I haven't heard anything."

"You'll be a beat cop all your life," he said, shaking his head. "You have no use at all for your radio, and if you didn't have your best friend for a sergeant, your big ass'd be fired."

"Yeah, but I got him," I grinned, poking him in the shoulder and making him swear.

"Seriously, Bumper," he said, and he didn't have to say "seriously" because his large black eyes always turned down when he was serious. "Seriously, the skipper asked me to ask you to pay a little more attention to the radio. He heard some of the younger officers complaining about always handling the calls in your district because you're off the radio walking around so much."

"Goddamn slick-sleeved rookies," I said, hot as hell, "they wouldn't know a snake in the grass if one jumped up and bit them on the dick. You seen these goddamn rookies nowadays, riding down the friggin' streets, ogling all the cunt, afraid to put on their hats because it might ruin their hair styles. Shit, I actually saw one of these pretty young fuzz sitting in his black-and-white spraying his hair! I swear, Cruz, most of these young cats wouldn't know their ass from a burnt biscuit."

"I know, Bumper," Cruz nodded with sympathy. "And the skipper knows a whole squad of these youngsters couldn't do half the police work you oldtimers do. That's why nobody says anything to you. But *hombre*, you have to handle some calls once in a while instead of walking that beat."

"I know," I said, looking at my coffee.

"Just stay on the air a little more."

"Okay, okay, you're the *macho*. You got the *huevos de oro*."

Cruz smiled now that he was through stepping on my meat. He was the only one that ever nagged me or told me what to do. When someone else had ideas along those lines, they'd hit Cruz with them, and if he thought I needed talking to, he'd do it. They figured I'd listen to Cruz.

"Don't forget, *loco,* you're coming to dinner tonight."

"Can you see me forgetting dinner at your pad?"

"You sure Cassie can't come with you?"

"She sure wishes she could. You know Friday's the last day for her at school and they're throwing a little party for her. She *has* to be there."

"I understand," said Cruz. "What day is she actually going up north? She decided yet?"

"Next week she'll be packed and gone."

"I don't know why you don't just take your vacation now and cut out with her. What's the sense of waiting till the end of the month? That vacation pay isn't worth being away from her for a few weeks, is it? She might come to her senses and ask herself why the hell she's marrying a mean old bastard like Bumper Morgan."

I wondered why I didn't tell Cruz that I'd decided to do just that. What the hell was the secret? Friday was going to be my last day. I never cared anything about the vacation pay. Was I really afraid to say it?

"Gonna be strange leaving everything," I muttered to my coffee cup.

"I'm glad for you, Bumper," said Cruz, running his slim fingers through his heavy gray hair. "If I didn't have all the kids I'd get the hell out too, I swear. I'm glad you're going."

Cruz and me had talked about it lots of times the last few years, ever since Cassie came along and it became inevitable that I'd marry her and probably pull the pin at twenty years instead of staying thirty like Cruz had to do. Now that it was here though, it seemed like we'd never discussed it at all. It was so damn strange.

"Cruz, I'm leaving Friday," I blurted. "I'm going to see Cassie and tell her I'll leave Friday. Why wait till the end of the month?"

"That's fine, *'mano!*" Cruz beamed, looking like he'd like to cut loose with a yelp, like he always did when he was drunk.

"I'll tell her today." Now I felt relieved, and drained the last of the coffee as I got up to leave. "And I don't give a damn if I loaf for a month. I'll just take it easy till I feel like starting my new job."

"That's right!" said Cruz, his eyes happy now. "Sit on that big fat *nalgas* for a year if you want to. They want *you* as security chief. They'll wait for you. And you have forty percent coming every month, and Cassie's got a good job, and you still have a good bank account don't you?"

"Hell yes," I answered, walking toward the door. "I never had to spend much money, with my beat and all."

"Shhh," Cruz grinned. "Haven't you heard? We're the new breed of professionals. We don't accept gratuities."

"Who said anything about gratuities? I only take tribute."

Cruz shook his head and said, "*Ahí te huacho*," which is anglicized slang meaning I'll be seeing, or rather, watching for you.

"*Ahí te huacho*," I answered.

After I left Cruz I went back to the vice squad office and found Zoot hanging his head, and Charlie downright happy, so I figured Charlie had done all right.

"I'd like to talk to you alone for a minute, Bumper," said Charlie, leading me into the next room and closing the door while Zoot sat there looking miserable.

"He told me lots more than he thinks he did," said Charlie. He was charged up like any good cop should be when he has something worthwhile.

"He thinks you're taking me off his back?" I asked.

"Yeah," Charlie smiled. "Play along. He thinks I'm going to save him from you. Just lay off him for a while, okay, Bumper? He told me he's planning on moving his territory out of the division to Alvarado in a couple of weeks but he has to stay around Figueroa for the time being. I told him I'd talk to you."

"Tell Zoot he doesn't have to worry about old Bumper any more," I said, getting another gas pain. I vowed to myself I'd lay off the soy sauce next time I ate in J-town.

"Yeah, he'll be a problem for the Rampart vice squad then," said Charlie not getting my meaning.

"Want me to take him back to Fig?"

"I'll take him," said Charlie. "I want to talk a little more."

"Do me a favor?"

"Sure, Bumper."

"You think there's any chance of something going down because of what Zoot told you?"

"There's a damn good chance. Zoot half-ass copped that he thinks the broad at the relay spot that takes his action is Reba McClain, and if it is we might be able to swing real good with her."

"How's that?"

"She's Red Scalotta's girlfriend. We took her down in another relay about six months ago and she got probation with a six months' jail sentence hanging. She's a meth head and an ex-con and stir crazy as hell. Kind of a sex thing. She's got a phobia about jails and bull dykes and all that. Real ding-a-ling, but a gorgeous little toadie. We were just talking last week about her and if we could shag her and catch her dirty we might get to Scalotta through her. She's a real shaky bitch. I think she'd turn her mama to stay on the street. You bringing in Zoot with that phone number was a godsend."

"Okay, then I'm really going to ask the favor."

"Sure."

"Take her today or tomorrow at the latest. If she gives you something good, like a back office, take it down on Friday."

"A back office! Jesus, I don't think she'll have that kind of information, Bumper. And hell, Friday is just two days away. Sometimes you stake out for weeks or months to take a back office. Jesus, that's where the book's records are kept. We'd have to get a search warrant and that takes lots of information beforehand. Why Friday?"

"I'm going on vacation. I want to be in on this one, Charlie. I never took a back office. I want it real bad, and it has to be before I go on vacation."

"I'd do it for you, Bumper, if I could, you know that, but Friday's only two days away!"

"Just do police work like I taught you, with balls and brains and some imagination. That's all I ask. Just try, okay?"

"Okay," Charlie said. "I'll give it a try."

Before I left I put on an act for Zoot so he'd think Charlie was his protector. I pretended I was mad at Charlie and Charlie pretended he was going to stop me from any future attempts to stuff Zoot down the goddamn mail chute.

6

After I got in my car I remembered the friendly ass bite Cruz gave me and I picked up the hand mike and said, "One-X-L-Forty-five, clear."

"One-X-L-Forty-five, handle this call," said the operator, and I grumbled and wrote the address down. "Meet One-L-Thirty, Ninth and Broadway."

"One-X-L-Forty-five, roger," I said disgustedly, and thought, that's what I get for clearing. Probably some huge crisis like taking a chickenshit theft report from some fatass stockbroker who got his wallet lifted while he was reading dirty magazines at the dirty bookstore on Broadway.

One-X-L-Thirty was a rookie sergeant named Grant who I didn't know very well. He wore one five-year hashmark showing he had between five and ten years on. I'd bet it was a whole lot closer to five. He had a ruddy, smooth face and a big vocabulary. I never heard him swear at any rollcall he conducted. I couldn't trust a policeman who didn't swear once in a while. You could hardly describe certain things you see and feelings you have in this job without some colorful language.

Grant was south of Ninth near Olympic, out of his car, pacing up and down as I drove up. I knew it was snobbish but I couldn't call a kid like him "Sergeant."

And I didn't want to be out and out rude so I didn't call these young sergeants by their last names. I didn't call them anything. It got awkward sometimes, and I had to say, "Hey pal," or "Listen bud" when I wanted to talk to one of them. Grant looked pretty nervous about something.

"What's up?" I asked, getting out of my car.

"We have a demonstration at the Army Induction Center."

"So?" I said, looking down the street at a group of about fifteen marchers picketing the building.

"A lot of draftees go in and out and there could be trouble. There're some pretty militant-looking types in that picket line."

"So what're we gonna do?"

"I just called you because I need someone to stand by and keep them under surveillance. I'm going to talk to the lieutenant about the advisability of calling a tactical alert. I'd like you to switch to frequency nine and keep me advised of any status change."

"Look, pal, this ain't no big thing. I mean, a tactical alert for fifteen ragtag flower sniffers?"

"You never know what it can turn into."

"Okay," and I sighed, even though I tried not to, "I'll sit right here."

"Might be a good idea to drive closer. Park across the street. Close enough to let them see you but far enough to keep them from trying to bait you."

"Okay, pal," I muttered, as Grant got in his car and sped toward the station to talk to Lieutenant Hilliard, who was a cool old head and wouldn't get in a flap over fifteen peace marchers.

I pulled out in the traffic and a guy in a blue Chevvy jumped on his brakes even though he was eighty feet back and going slow. People get black-and-white fever when they see a police car and they do idiotic things trying to be super careful. I've seen them concentrate so hard on one facet of safe driving, like giving an arm signal, that they bust right through a red light. That's black-and-white fever for you.

The marchers across Broadway caught my eye when two of them, a guy and a girl, were waving for me to come over. They seemed to be just jiving around but I thought I better go over for several reasons. First of all, there might really be something wrong. Second, if I didn't, it looked like hell for a big bad copper to be afraid to approach a group of demonstrators. And third, I had a theory that if enough force could be used fast enough in these confrontations there'd *be* no riot. I'd never seen real force used quick enough yet, and I thought, what the hell, now was my chance to test my theory since I was alone with no sergeants around.

These guys, at least a few of them, two black guys, and one white, bearded scuz in a dirty buckskin vest and yellow headband, looked radical enough to get violent with an overweight middle-aged cop like myself, but I firmly believed that if one of them made the mistake of putting his hands on me and I drove my stick three inches in his esophagus, the others would yell police brutality twice and slink away. Of course I wasn't sure, and I noticed that the recent arrivals swelled their numbers to twenty-three. Only five of them were girls. That many people could stomp me to applesauce without a doubt, but I wasn't really worried, mainly because even though they were fist shaking, most of them looked like middle-class white people just playing at revolution. If you have a few hungry-looking professionals like I figured the white guy in the headband to be, you could have trouble. Some of these could lend their guts to the others and set them off, but he was the only one I saw.

I drove around the block so I didn't have to make an illegal U-turn in front of them, made my illegal U-turn on Olympic, came back and parked in front of the marchers, who ignored me and kept marching and chanting, "Hell no, we won't go." And "Fuck Uncle Sam, and Auntie Spiro," and several other lewd remarks mostly directed at the President, the governor, and the mayor. A few years ago, if a guy yelled ''fuck'' in a public place in the presence of women or children, we'd have to drag his ass to jail.

''Hi, Officer, I love you,'' said one little female peace marcher, a cute blonde about seventeen, wearing two inches of false eyelashes that looked upside-down, and ironed-out shoulder-length hair.

''Hi, honey, I love you too,'' I smiled back, and leaned against the door of my car. I folded my arms and puffed a cigar until the two who had been waving at me decided to walk my way.

They were whispering now with another woman and finally the shorter girl, who was not exactly a girl, but a woman of about thirty-five, came right up. She was dressed like a teenager with a short yellow mini, violet panty hose, granny glasses, and white lipstick. Her legs were too damned fat and bumpy and she was wearing a theatrical smile with a cold arrogant look beneath it. Up close, she looked like one of the professionals and seemed to be a picket captain. Sometimes a woman, if she's the real thing, can be the detonator much quicker than a man can. This one seemed like the real thing, and I looked her in the eye and smiled while she toyed with a heavy peace medal hanging around her neck. Her eyes said, ''You're just a fat harmless cop, not worth my talents, but so far you're all we have here, and I don't know if an old bastard like you is even intelligent enough to know when he's being put down.''

That's what I saw in her eyes, and her phony smile, but she said nothing for a few more minutes. Then a car from one of the network stations rolled up and two men got out with a camera and mike.

The interest of the marchers picked up now that they were soon to be on tape, and the chanting grew louder, the gestures more fierce, and the old teenybopper in the yellow dress finally said, ''We called you over because you looked very forlorn. Where're the riot troops, or are you all we get today?''

''If you get *me*, baby, you ain't gonna want any more,'' I smiled through a puff of cigar smoke, pinning her eyeballs, admiring the fact that she didn't bat an eye even though I knew damn well she was expecting the businesslike professional clichés we're trained to give in these situations. I'd bet she was even surprised to see me slouching against my car like this, showing such little respect for this menacing group.

''You're not supposed to smoke in public, are you, Officer?'' She smiled, a little less arrogant now. She didn't know what the hell she had here, and was going to take her time about setting the bait.

''Maybe a real policeman ain't supposed to, but this uniform's just a shuck. I rented this ill-fitting clown suit to make an underground movie about this fat cop that steals apples and beats up flower children and old mini-skirted squatty-bodies with socks to match their varicose veins in front of the U.S. Army Induction Center.''

Then she lost her smile completely and stormed back to the guy in the headband who was also much older than he first appeared. They whispered and she looked at me as I puffed on the cigar and waved at some of the marchers who were putting me on, most of them just college-age kids having a good time. A couple of them sincerely seemed to like me even though they tossed a few insults to go along with the crowd.

Finally, the guy in the headband came my way shouting encouragement to the line of marchers who were going around and around in a long oval in front of the door, which was being guarded by two men in suits who were not policemen, but probably military personnel. The cameraman was shooting pictures now, and I hid my cigar and sucked in a few inches of gut when he photographed me. The babe in the yellow dress joined the group after passing out some Black Panther pins and she marched without once looking at me again.

"I hear you don't make like the other cops we've run into in these demonstrations," said the guy with the headband, suddenly standing in front of me and grinning. "The L.A.P.D. abandoning the oh so firm but courteous approach? Are you a new police riot technique? A caricature of a fat pig, a jolly jiveass old cop that we just can't get mad at? Is that it? They figure we couldn't use you for an Establishment symbol? Like you're too fucking comical looking, is that it?"

"Believe it or not, Tonto," I said, "I'm just the neighborhood cop. Not a secret weapon, nothing for lumpy legs to get tight-jawed about. I'm just your local policeman."

He twitched a little bit when I mentioned the broad so I guessed she might be his old lady. I figured they probably taught sociology 1A and 1B in one of the local junior colleges.

"Are you the only swine they're sending?" he asked, smiling not quite so much now which made me very happy. It's hard even for professionals like him to stay with a smirk when he's being rapped at where it hurts. He probably just *loves* everything about her, even the veiny old wheels. I decided, screw it, I was going to take the offensive with these assholes and see where it ended.

"Listen, Cochise," I said, the cigar between my teeth, "I'm the only old pig you're gonna see today. All the young piglets are staying in the pen. So why don't you and old purple pins just take your Che handbooks and cut out. Let these kids have their march with no problems. And take those two dudes with the naturals along with you." I pointed to the two black guys who were standing ten feet away watching us. "There ain't gonna be any more cops here, and there ain't gonna be any trouble."

"You *are* a bit refreshing," he said, trying to grin, but it was a crooked grin. "I was getting awfully sick of those unnatural pseudoprofessionals with their businesslike platitudes, pretending to look right through us when really they wanted to get us in the back room of some police station and beat our fucking heads in. I must say you're refreshing. You're truly a vicious fascist and don't pretend to be anything else."

Just then the mini-skirted broad walked up again. "Is he threatening you, John?" she said in a loud voice, looking over her shoulder, but the guys with the camera and mike were at the other end of the shouting line of marchers.

"Save it till they get to this end," I said, as I now estimated her age to be closer to forty. She was a few years older than he was and the mod camouflage looked downright comical. "Want some bubble gum, little girl?" I said.

"Shut your filthy mouth," he said, taking a step toward me. I was tight now, I wound myself up and was ready. "Stay frosty, Sitting Bull," I smiled. "Here, have a cigar." I offered one of my smokes, but he wheeled and walked away with old lumpy clicking along behind him.

The two black guys hadn't moved. They too were professionals, I was positive now, but they were a different kind. If anything went down, I planned to attack those two right away. They were the ones to worry about. They both wore black plastic jackets and one wore a black cossack hat. He never took his eyes off me. He'd be the very first one I'd go after, I thought. I kept that flaky look, grinning and waving at any kid who gave me the peace sign, but I was getting less and less sure I could handle the situation. There were a couple other guys in the group that might get froggy if someone leaped, and I've seen what only two guys can do if they get you down and put the boots to you, let alone nine or ten.

I hated to admit it but I was beginning to wish Grant would show up with a squad of bluecoats. Still, it was a quiet demonstration, as quiet as these things go, and there was probably nothing to worry about, I thought.

The march continued as it had for a few more minutes, with the young ones yelling slogans, and then headband and mini-skirt came back with six or eight people in tow. These kids were definitely collegiate, wearing flares or bleach-streaked Levis. Some of the boys had muttonchops and moustaches, most had collar-length hair, and two of them were pretty, suntanned girls. They looked friendly enough and I gave them a nod of the head when they stopped in front of me.

One particularly scurvy-looking slimeball walked up, smiled real friendly, and whispered, "You're a filthy, shit-eating pig."

I smiled back and whispered, "Your mother eats bacon."

"How can we start a riot with no riot squad," another said.

"Careful, Scott, he's not just a pig, he's a wild boar, you dig?" said the miniskirt who was standing behind the kids.

"Maybe *you* could use a little bore, sweetheart, maybe that's your trouble," I said, looking at the guy in the headband, and two of the kids chuckled.

"You seem to be the only Establishment representative we have at the moment, maybe you'd like to rap with us," said Scott, a tall kid with a scrubbed-looking face and a mop of blond hair. He had a cute little baby hanging on his arm and she seemed amused.

"Sure, just fire away," I said, still leaning back, acting relaxed as I puffed. I was actually beginning to *want* to rap with them. One time when I asked some young sergeant if I could take a shot at the "Policeman Bill" program and go talk to a class of high-school kids, he shined me on with a bunch of crap, and I realized then that they wanted those flat-stomached, clear-eyed, handsome young recruiting-poster cops for these jobs. I had my chance now and I liked the idea.

"What's your first name, Officer Morgan?" asked Scott, looking at my nameplate, "and what do you think of street demonstrations?"

Scott was smiling and I could hardly hear him over the yelling as the ring of marchers moved twenty feet closer to us to block the entrance more effectively after the fat bitch in yellow directed them to do it. Several kids mugged at the cameraman and waved "V" signs at him and me. One asshole, older than the others, flipped me the bone and then scowled into the camera.

"That's it, smile and say pig, you pukepot," I mumbled, noticing the two black cossacks were at the other end of the line of marchers talking to purple legs. Then I turned to Scott. "To answer your question, my name's Bumper Morgan and I don't mind demonstrations except that they take us cops away from our beats, and believe me we can't spare the time. Everybody loses when we're not on patrol."

"What do you patrol, the fucking barnyard?" said one little shitbird wearing shades and carrying a poster that showed a white army officer telephoning a black mother about her son being killed in Vietnam. She was shown in a corner of the poster and there was a big white cop clubbing her with an oversized baton.

"That poster doesn't make sense," I said. "It's awful damn lame. You might as well label it, 'Killed by the running dogs of imperialism!' I could do a lot better than that."

"Man, that's *exactly* what I told him," Scott laughed, and offered me a cigarette.

"No thanks," I said, as he and his baby doll lit one. "Now that one's sort of clever," I said, pointing to a sign which said "Today's pigs are tomorrow's pork-chops."

None of the other kids had anything to say yet, except the shithead with the poster, who yelled, "Like, what're we doing talking to this fucking fascist lackey?"

"Look," I said, "I ain't gonna lay down and play dead just because you can say 'fuck' pretty good. I mean nobody's shocked by that cheap shit anymore, so why don't we just talk quiet to each other. I wanna hear what you guys got to say."

"Good idea," said another kid, a black, with a wild natural, wire-rim glasses, and a tiger tooth necklace, who almost had to shout because of the noise. "Tell us why a man would want to be a cop. I mean really. I'm not putting you on, I want to know."

He was woofing me, because he winked at the blond kid, but I thought I'd *tell* them what I liked about it. What the hell, I liked having all these kids crowded around listening to me. Somebody then moved the marchers' line a little north again and I could almost talk in a normal voice.

"Well, I like to take lawbreakers off the street," I began.

"Just a minute," said the black kid, pushing his wire-rims up on his nose. "Please, Officer, no euphemisms. I'm from Watts." Then he purposely lapsed into a Negro drawl and said, "I been known' the PO-lice all mah life." The others laughed and he continued in his own voice. "Talk like a *real* cop and tell us like it is, without any bullshit. You know, use that favorite expression of L.A.P.D.—'asshole,' I believe it is." He smiled again after he said all this and so did I.

"What part of Watts you live in?" I asked.

"One-O-Three and Grape, baby," he answered.

"Okay, I'll talk plainer. I'm a cop because I love to throw assholes in jail, and if possible I like to send them to the joint."

"That's more like it," said the black kid. "Now you're lookin' so good and soundin' so fine."

The others applauded and grinned at each other.

"Isn't that kind of a depressing line of work?" asked Scott. "I mean, don't you like to do something *for* someone once in a while instead of *to* them?"

'I figure I do something *for* someone every time I make a good bust. I mean, you figure every real asshole you catch in a dead bang burglary or robbery's tore off probably a hundred people or so before you bring him down. I figure each time I make a pinch I save a hundred more, maybe even some lives. And I'll tell you, most victims are people who can't afford to be victims. People who can afford it have protection and insurance and aren't so vulnerable to all these scummy hemorrhoids. Know what I mean?"

Scott's little girlfriend was busting to throw in her two cents, but three guys popped off at once, and finally Scott's voice drowned out the others. "I'm a law student," he said, "and I intend to be your adversary someday in a courtroom. Tell me, do you really get satisfaction when you send a man away for ten years?"

"Listen, Scott," I said, "in the first place even Eichmann would stand a fifty-fifty chance of not doing ten years nowadays. You got to be a boss crook to pull that kind of time. In fact, you got to work at it to even *get* to state prison. Man, some of the cats I put away, I wouldn't give them ten years, I'd give them a goddamned lobotomy if I could."

I dropped my cigar because these kids had me charged up now. I figured they were starting to respect me a little and I even tried for a minute to hold in my gut but that was uncomfortable, and I gave it up.

"I saw a big article in some magazine a few years ago honoring these cops," I continued. " 'These are not pigs' the article said, and it showed one cop who'd delivered some babies, and one cop who'd rescued some people in a flood, and one cop who was a goddamn boy scout troop leader or something like that. You know, I delivered two babies myself. But we ain't being paid to be midwives or lifeguards or social workers. They got other people to do those jobs. Let's see somebody honor some copper because the guy made thirty good felony pinches a month for ten years and sent a couple hundred guys to San Quentin. Nobody ever gives an award to him. Even his sergeant ain't gonna appreciate that, but he'll get on his ass for not writing a traffic ticket every day because the goddamn city needs the revenue and there's no room in prisons anyway."

I should've been noticing things at about this time. I should've noticed that the guy in the headband and his old lady were staying away from me and so were the two black guys in the plastic jackets. In fact, all the ones I spotted were staying at the other end of the line of marchers who were quieting down and starting to get tired. I should've noticed that the boy, Scott, the other blond kid, and the tall black kid, were closer to me than the others, and so was the cute little twist hanging on Scott's arm and carrying a huge heavy-looking buckskin bag.

I noticed nothing, because for one of the few times in my life I wasn't being a cop. I was a big, funny-looking, blue-suited donkey and I thought I was home-run king belting them out over the fences. The reason was that I was somewhere I'd never been in my life. I was on a soapbox. Not a stage but a soapbox. A stage I could've handled. I can put on the act people want and expect, and I can still keep my eyes open and not get carried away with it, but this goddamned soapbox was something else. I was making speeches, one after another, about things that meant something to me, and all I could see was the loving gaze of my audience, and the sound of my own voice drowned out all the things that I should've been hearing and seeing.

"Maybe police departments should only recruit college graduates," Scott shrugged, coming a step closer.

"Yeah, they want us to solve crimes by these 'scientific methods,' whatever that means. And what do us cops do? We kiss ass and nod our heads and take federal funds to build computers and send cops to college and it all boils down to a cop with sharp eyes and an ability to talk to people who'll get the goddamn job done."

"Don't you think that in the age that's coming, policemen will be obsolete?" Scott's little girlfriend asked the question and she looked so wide-eyed I had to smile.

"I'm afraid not, honey," I said. "As long as there's people, there's gonna be lots of bad ones and greedy ones and weak ones."

"How can you feel that way about people and still care at all about helping them as you say you do when you arrest somebody?" she asked, shaking her head. She smiled sadly, like she felt sorry for me.

"Hell, baby, they ain't much but they're all we got. It's the only game in town!" I figured that was obvious to anybody and I started to wonder if they weren't still a little young. "By the way, are most of you social science and English majors?"

"Why do you say that?" asked the black kid, who was built like a ballplayer.

"The surveys say you are. I'm just asking. Just curious."

"I'm an engineering major," said the blond kid, who was now behind Scott, and then for the first time I was aware how close in on me these certain few were. I was becoming aware how polite they'd been to me. They were all activists and college people and no doubt had statistics and slogans and arguments to throw at me, yet I had it all my way. They just stood there nodding, smiling once in a while, and let me shoot my face off. I knew that something wasn't logical or right, but I was still intrigued with the sound of my own voice and so the fat blue maharishi said, "Anything else about police work you'd like to talk about?"

"Were you at Century City?" asked the little blonde.

"Yeah, I was there, and it wasn't anything like you read in the underground newspapers or on those edited TV tapes."

"It wasn't? I was there," said Scott.

"Well, I'm not gonna deny some people got hurt," I said, looking from one face to another for hostility. "There was the President of the United States to protect and there were thousands of war protestors out there and I guarantee you that was no bullshit about them having sharpened sticks and bags of shit and broken bottles and big rocks. I bet *I* could kill a guy with a rock."

"You didn't see any needless brutality?"

"What the hell's brutality?" I said. "Most of those bluecoats out there are just kids *your* age. When someone spits in his face, all the goddamn discipline in the world ain't gonna stop him or any normal kid from getting that other cat's teeth prints on his baton. There's times when you just *gotta* play a little catchup. You know what five thousand screaming people look like? Sure, we got some stick time in. Some scumbags, all they respect is force. You just gotta kick ass and collect names. Anybody with any balls woulda whaled on some of those pricks out there." Then I remembered the girl. "Sorry for the four-letter word, miss," I said as a reflex action.

"Prick is a five-letter word," she said, reminding me of the year I was living in.

Then suddenly, the blond kid behind Scott got hostile. "Why do we talk to a pig like this? He talks about helping people. What's he do besides beat their heads in, which he admits? What do you do in the ghettos of Watts for the black people?"

Then a middle-aged guy in a clergyman's collar and a black suit popped through the ring of young people. "I work in the eastside Chicano barrios," he announced. "What do you do for the Mexicans except exploit them?"

"What do *you* do?" I asked, getting uncomfortable at the sudden change of mood here, as several of the marchers joined the others and I was backed up against the car by fifteen or twenty people.

"I fight for the Chicanos. For brown power," said the clergyman.

"You ain't brown," I observed, growing more nervous.

"Inside I'm brown!"

"Take an enema," I mumbled, standing up straight, as I realized that things were wrong, all wrong.

Then I caught a glimpse of the black cossack hat to the left behind two girls who were crowding in to see what the yelling was all about, and I saw a hand flip a peace button at me, good and hard. It hit me in the face, the pin scratching me right under the left eye. The black guy looked at me very cool as I spun around, mad enough to charge right through the crowd.

"You try that again and I'll ding your bells, man," I said, loud enough for him to hear.

"Who?" he said, with a big grin through the moustache and goatee.

"Who, my ass," I said. "You ain't got feet that fit on a limb. I'm talking to *you*."

"You fat pig," he sneered and turned to the crowd. "He wants to arrest me! You pick out a black, that the way you do it, Mister PO-lice?"

"If anything goes down, I'm getting *you* first," I whispered, putting my left hand on the handle of my stick.

"He wants to arrest me," he repeated, louder now. "What's the charge? Being black? Don't I have any rights?"

"You're gonna get your rites," I muttered. "Your *last* rites."

"I should kill you," he said. "There's fifty braves here and we should kill you for all the brothers and sisters you pigs murdered."

"Get it on, sucker, anytime you're ready," I said with a show of bravado because I was really scared now.

I figured that many people let loose could turn me into a doormat in about three minutes. My breath was coming hard. I tried to keep my jaw from trembling and my brain working. They weren't going to get me down on the ground. Not without a gun in my hand. I decided it wouldn't be that easy to kick *my* brains in. I made up my mind to start shooting to save myself, and I decided I'd blow up the two Black Russians, Geronimo, and Purple Legs, not necessarily in that order.

Then a hand reached out and grabbed my necktie, but it was a breakaway tie, and I didn't go with it when the hand pulled it into the crowd. At about the same time the engineering major grabbed my badge, and I instinctively brought up my right hand, holding his hand on my chest, backing up until his elbow was straight. Then I brought my left fist up hard just above his elbow and he yelped and drew back. Several other people also drew back at the unmistakable scream of pain.

"Off the pig! Off the pig!" somebody yelled. "Rip him off!"

I pulled my baton out and felt the black-and-white behind me now and they were all screaming and threatening, even the full-of-shit padre.

I would've jumped in the car on the passenger side and locked the door but I couldn't. I felt the handle and it was locked, and the window was rolled up, and I was afraid that if I fooled around unlocking it, somebody might get his ass up and charge me.

Apparently the people inside the induction center didn't know a cop was about to get his ticket cancelled, because nobody came out. I could see the cameraman fighting to get through the crowd which was spilling out on the street and I had a crazy wish that he'd make it. That's the final vanity, I guess, but I kind of wanted him to film Bumper's Last Stand.

For a few seconds it could've gone either way and then the door to my car opened and hit me in the back, scaring the shit out of me.

"Get your butt in here, Bumper," said a familiar voice, which I obeyed. The second I closed the door something hit the window almost hard enough to break the glass and several people started kicking at the door and fender of my black-and-white.

"Give me the keys," said Stan Ludlow, who worked Intelligence Division. He was sitting behind the wheel, looking as dapper as always in a dark green suit and mint-colored necktie.

I gave him the keys from my belt and he drove away from the curb as I heard something else clunk off the fendor of the car. Four radio cars each containing three Metro officers pulled up at the induction center as we were leaving, and started dispelling the group.

"You're the ugliest rape victim I ever saw," said Stan, turning on Ninth Street and parking behind a plainclothes police car where his partner was waiting.

"What the hell you talking about?"

"Had, man. You just been had."

"I had a feeling something wasn't right," I said, getting sick because I was afraid to hear what I figured he was going to say. "Did they set me up?"

"Did they set you up? No, they didn't have to. You set yourself up! Christ, Bumper, you should know better than to make speeches to groups like that. What the hell made you do it?"

Stan had about fifteen years on the job and was a sergeant, but he was only about forty and except for his gray sideburns he looked lots younger. Still, I felt like a dumb little kid sitting there now. I felt like he was lots older and a damn sight wiser and took the assbite without looking at him.

"How'd you know I was speechmaking, Stan?"

"One of them is one of us," said Stan. "We had one of those guys wired with a mike. We listened to the whole thing, Bumper. We called for the Metro teams because we knew what was going to happen. Damn near didn't get to you quick enough though."

"Who were the leaders?" I was trying to save a grain or two of my pride. "The bitch in the yellow dress and the guru in the headband?"

"Hell no," said Stan, disgustedly. "Their names are John and Marie French. They're a couple of lames trying to groove with the kids. They're nothing. She's a self-proclaimed revolutionary from San Pedro and he's her husband. As a matter of fact he picked up our undercover man and drove him to the demonstration today when they were sent by the boss. French is mostly used as errand boy. He drives a VW bus and picks up everybody that needs a ride to all these peace marches. He's nothing. Why, did you have them figured for the leaders?"

"Sort of," I mumbled.

"You badmouthed them didn't you?"

"Sort of. What about the two in the Russian hats?"

"Nobody," said Stan. "They hang around all the time with their Panther buttons and get lots of pussy, but they're nobody. Just opportunists. Professional blacks."

"I guess the guy running the show was a tall nice-looking kid named Scott?" I said, as the lights slowly turned on.

"Yeah, Scott Hairston. He's from U.C.L.A. His sister Melba was the little blonde with the peachy ass who was hanging on his arm. She was the force behind subversive club chapters starting on her high school campus when she was still a bubblegummer. Their old man, Simon Hairston's an attorney and a slippery bastard, and his brother Josh is an old-time activist."

"So the bright-eyed little baby was a goddamn viper, huh? I guess they've passed me by, Stan."

Stan smiled sympathetically and lit my cigar for me. "Look, Bumper, these kids've been weaned on this bullshit. You're just a beginner. Don't feel too bad. But for God's sake, next time don't start chipping with them. No speeches, please!"

"I must've sounded like a boob," I said, and I could feel myself flushing clear to my toes.

"It's not that so much, Bumper, but that little bitch Melba put you on tape. She always solicits casual comments from cops. Sometimes she has a concealed hand mike with a wire running up her sleeve down to a box in her handbag. She carrying a big handbag today?"

I didn't have to answer. Stan saw it in the sick look on my face.

"They'll edit your remarks, Bumper. I heard some of them from the mike *our* guy was wearing. Christ, you talked about stick time and putting teeth marks on your baton and kicking ass and collecting names."

"But all that's not how I meant it, Stan."

"That's the way your comments'll be presented—out of context. It'll be printed that way in an underground newspaper or maybe even in a daily if Simon Hairston gets behind it."

"Oooooh," I said, tilting my hat over my eyes and slumping down in my seat.

"Don't have a coronary on me, Bumper," said Stan. "Everything's going to be all right."

"All right? I'll be the laughingstock of the Department!"

"Don't worry, Melba's tapes're going to disappear."

"The undercover man?"

Stan nodded.

"Bless him," I breathed. "Which one was he? Not the kid whose arm I almost broke?"

"No," Stan laughed, "the tall black kid. I'm only telling you because we're going to have to use him as a material witness in a few days anyway, and we'll have to disclose his identity. We got secret indictments on four guys who make pretty good explosives in the basement of a North Hollywood apartment building. He's been working for me since he joined the Department thirteen months ago. We have him enrolled in college. Nice kid. Hell of a basketball player. He can't wait to wear a bluesuit and work a radio car. He's sick of mingling with all these revolutionaries."

"How do you know he can get the tape?"

"He's been practically living in Melba's skivvies for at least six months now. He'll sleep with her tonight and that'll be it."

"Some job," I said.

"He doesn't mind that part of it," Stan chuckled. "He's anxious to see how all his friends react when they find out he's the heat. Says he's been using them as whipping boys and playing the outraged black man role for so long, they probably won't believe it till they actually see him in the blue uniform with that big hateful shield on his chest. And wait'll Melba finds out she's been balling a cop. You can bet she'll keep that a secret."

"Nobody's gonna hear about me then, huh, Stan?"

"I'll erase the tape, Bumper," said Stan, getting out of the car. "You know, in a way it worked out okay. Scott Hairston was expecting a hundred marchers in the next few hours. He didn't want trouble yet. You wrecked his game today."

"See you later, Stan," I said, trying to sound casual, like I wasn't totally humiliated. "Have a cigar, old shoe."

I was wrung out after that caper and even though it was getting late in the afternoon, I jumped on the Harbor Freeway and started driving south, as fast as traffic would permit, with some kind of half-baked idea about looking at the ocean. I was trying to do something which I usually do quite well, controlling my thoughts. It wouldn't do any good at all to stew over what happened, so I was trying to think about something else, maybe food, or Cassie, or how Glenda's jugs looked today—something good. But I was in a dark mood, and nothing good would come, so I decided to think of absolutely nothing which I can also do quite well.

I wheeled back to my beat and called the lieutenant, telling him about the ruckus at the induction center, leaving out all the details of course, and he told me the marchers dispersed very fast and there were only a few cars still at the scene. I knew there'd hardly be any mention of this one, a few TV shots on the six o'clock news and that'd be it. I hung up and got back in my car, hoping the cameraman hadn't caught me smoking the cigar. That's another silly rule, no smoking in public, as if a cop is a Buckingham Palace guard.

7

I drove around some more, cooling off, looking at my watch every few seconds, wanting this day to end. The noisy chatter on the radio was driving me nuts so I turned it off. Screw the radio, I thought, I never made a good pinch from a radio call. The good busts come from doing what I do best, walking and looking and talking to people.

I had a hell of an attack of indigestion going. I took four antacid tablets from the glove compartment and popped them all but I was still restless, squirming around on the seat. Cassie's three o'clock class would be finished now so I drove up Vermont to Los Angeles City College and parked out front in the red zone even though when I do that I always get a few digs from the kids or from teachers like, "You can do it but we get tickets for it." Today there was nobody in front and I didn't get any bullshit which I don't particularly mind anyway, since nobody including myself really likes authority symbols. I'm always one of the first to get my ass up when the brass tries to restrict my freedom with some idiotic rules.

I climbed the stairs leisurely, admiring the tits on some suntanned, athletic-looking, ponytailed gym teacher. She was in a hurry and took the stairs two at a time, still in her white shorts and sneakers and white jersey that showed all she had, and it was plenty. Some of the kids passing me in the halls made all the usual remarks, calling me Dick Tracy and Sheriff John, and there were a few giggles about Marlene somebody holding some pot and then Marlene squealed and giggled. We didn't used to get snickers about pot, and that reminded me of the only argument concerning pot that made any sense to me. Grass, like booze, breaks the chain and frees the beast, but does it so much easier and quicker. I've seen it thousands of times.

Cassie was in her office with the door opened talking to a stringy-haired bubblegummer in a micro-mini that showed her red-flowered pantygirdle when she sat down.

"Hi," said Cassie, when she saw me in the doorway. The girl looked at me and then back at Cassie, wondering what the fuzz was here for.

"We'll just be a minute," said Cassie, still smiling her clean white smile, and I nodded and walked down the hall to the water fountain thinking how damn good she looked in that orange dress. It was one of the twenty or so that I'd bought her since we met, and she finally agreed with me that she looked better in hot colors, even though she thought it was part of any man's M.O. to like his women in flaming oranges and reds.

Her hair was drawn back today and either way, back or down, her hair was beautiful. It was thick brown, streaked with silver, not gray, but real untouched silver, and her figure was damn good for a girl her age. She was tanned and looked more like a gym teacher than a French teacher. She always wore a size twelve and sometimes could wear a ten in certain full styles. I wondered if she still looked so good because she played tennis and golf or because she didn't have any kids when she was married, but then, Cruz's wife Socorro had a whole squad of kids and though she was a little overweight she still looked almost as good as Cassie. Some people just kept it all, I guess, which almost made me self-conscious being with this classy-looking woman when we went places together. I always felt like everyone was thinking, "He must have bread or she'd never be with him." But it was useless to question your luck, you just had to grab on when you had the chance, and I did. And then again, maybe I was one of those guys that's ugly in an attractive sort of way.

"Well?" said Cassie, and I turned my head and saw her standing in the doorway of her office, still smiling at me as I went over her with my eyes. The kid had left.

"That's the prettiest dress you have," I said, and I really meant it. At that moment she'd never looked better, even though some heavy wisps of hair were hanging on her cheeks and her lipstick was almost all gone.

"Why don't you admire my mind instead of my body once in a while like I do yours?" she grinned.

I followed her into the office and stepped close, intending to give her a kiss on the cheek. She surprised me by throwing her arms around my neck and kissing me long and hot, causing me to drop my hat on the floor and get pretty aroused even though we were standing in an open doorway and any minute a hundred people would walk past. When she finally stopped, she had the lazy dazzling look of a passionate woman.

"Shall we sweep everything off that damned desk?" she said in a husky voice, and for a minute or two I thought she would've. Then a bell rang and doors started opening and she laughed and sat down on her desk showing me some very shapely legs and you would never guess those wheels had been spinning for forty odd years. I plopped down in a leather chair, my mouth woolly dry from having that hot body up against me.

"Are you sure you won't come to the party tonight?" she said finally, lighting a cigarette.

"You know how I feel about it, Cassie," I said. "This is *your* night. Your friends and the students want to have you to themselves. I'll have you forever after that."

"Think you can handle me?" she asked, with a grin, and I knew from her grin she meant sexually. We had joked before about how I awoke this in her, which she said had been dormant since her husband left her seven years ago and maybe even before that, from what I knew of the poor crazy guy. He was a teacher like Cassie, but his field was chemistry.

We supposed that some of her nineteen-year-old students, as sex-obsessed as they are these days, might be making love more often than we did, but she didn't see how they could. She said it had never been like this with her, and she never knew it could be so good. Me, I've always appreciated how good it was. As long as I can remember, I've been horny.

"Come by the apartment at eleven," she said. "I'll make sure I'm home by then."

"That's pretty early to leave your friends."

"You don't think I'd sit around drinking with a bunch of educators when I could be learning at home with Officer Morgan, do you?"

"You mean I can teach a teacher?"

"You're one of the tops in your field."

"You have a class tomorrow morning," I reminded her.

"Be there at eleven."

"A lot of these teachers and students that don't have an early class tomorrow are gonna want to jive and woof a lot later than that. I think you ought to stay with them tonight, Cassie. They'd expect you to. You can't disappoint the people on your beat."

"Well, all right," she sighed. "But I won't even see you tomorrow night because I'll be dining with those two trustees. They want to give me one final look, and casually listen to my French to make sure I'm not going to corrupt the already corrupted debs at their institution. I suppose I can't run off and leave *them* either."

"It won't be long till I have you all to myself. Then *I'll* listen to your French and let you corrupt the hell out of me, okay?"

"Did you tell them you're retiring yet?" She asked the question easily, but looked me straight in the eye, waiting, and I got nervous.

"I've told Cruz," I said, "and I got a surprise for you."

"What?"

"I've decided that Friday's gonna be my last day. I'll start my vacation Saturday and finish my time while I'm on vacation. I'll be going with you."

Cassie didn't yell or jump up or look excited or anything, like I thought she would. She just went limp like her muscles relaxed suddenly, and she slipped off the desk and sat down on my lap where there isn't any too much room, and with her arms doubled around the top of my neck she started kissing me on the face and mouth and I saw her eyes were wet and soft like her lips, and next thing I know, I heard a lot of giggling. Eight or ten kids were standing in the hall watching us through the open door, but Cassie didn't seem to hear, or didn't care. I did though because I was sitting there in my bluesuit, being loved up and getting turned on in public.

"Cassie," I gasped, nodding toward the door, and she got up, and calmly shut the door on the kids like she was ready to start again.

I stood and picked up my hat from the floor. "Cassie, this is a school. I'm in uniform."

Cassie started laughing very hard and had to sit down in the chair I'd been in, leaning back, and holding her hands over her face as she laughed. I thought how sexy even her throat was, the throat usually being the first thing to show its age, but Cassie's was sleek.

"I wasn't going to rape you," she said at last, still chuckling between breaths.

"Well, it's just that you teachers are so permissive these days, I thought you might try to do me on the desk like you said."

"Oh, Bumper," she said finally, holding her arms out, and I came over and leaned down and she kissed me eight or ten warm times all over my face.

"I can't even begin to tell you how I feel now that you're really going to do it," she said. "When you said you actually *are* finishing up this Friday, and that you told Cruz Segovia, I just went to pieces. That was relief and joy you saw on my face when I closed the door, Bumper, not passion. Well, maybe a *little* of it was."

"We've been planning all along, Cassie, you act like it was really a shock to you."

"I've had nightmares about it. I've had fantasies awake and asleep of how after I'd gone, and got our apartment in San Francisco, you'd phone me one bitter night and tell me you weren't coming, that you just could never leave your beat."

"Cassie!"

"I haven't told you this before, Bumper, but it's been gnawing at me. Now that you've told Cruz, and it's only two more days, I know it's coming true."

"I'm not married to my goddamn job, Cassie," I said, thinking how little you know about a woman, even one as close as Cassie. "You should've seen what happened to me today. I was flimflammed by a soft-nutted little kid. He made a complete ass out of me. He made me look like a *square*."

Cassie looked interested and amused, the way she always does when I tell her about my job.

"What happened?" she asked, as I pulled out my last cigar and fired it up so I could keep calm when the humiliation swept over me.

"A demonstration at the Army Induction Center. A kid, a punk-ass kid, conned me and I started blabbing off about the job. Rapping real honest with him I was, and I find out later he's a professional revolutionary, probably a Red or something, and oh, I thought I was so goddamn hip to it. I been living too much on my beat, Cassie. Too much being the Man, I guess. Believing I could outsmart any bastard that skated by. Thinking the only ones I never could really get to were the organized ones, like the bookmakers and the big dope dealers. But *sometimes* I could do things that even hurt *them*. Now there's new ones that've come along. And they have organization. And I was like a baby, they handled me so easy."

"What the hell did you *do*, Bumper?"

"Talked. I talked to them straight about things. About thumping assholes that needed thumping. That kind of thing. I made *speeches*."

"Know what?" she said, putting her long-fingered hand on my knee. "Whatever happened out there, whatever you said, I'll bet wouldn't do you or the Department a damn bit of harm."

"Oh yeah, Cassie? You should've heard me talking about when the President was here and how we busted up the riot by busting up a skull or three. I was marvelous."

"Do you know a *gentle* way to break up riots?"

"No, but we're supposed to be professional enough not to talk to civilians the way we talk in police locker rooms."

"I'll take Officer Morgan over one of those terribly wholesome, terribly tiresome TV cops, and I don't think there's a gentle way to break up riots, so I think you should stop worrying about the whole thing. Just think, pretty soon you won't have any of these problems. You'll have a real position, an important one, and people working under you."

"I got to admit, it gets me pretty excited to think about it. I bet I can come up with ways to improve plant security that those guys never dreamed of."

"Of course you can."

"No matter what I do, you pump me up," I smiled. "That's why I wanted you for my girl in spite of all your shortcomings."

"Well, you're my Blue Knight. Do you know you're a knight? You joust and live off the land."

"Yeah, I guess you might say I live off my beat, all right. 'Course I don't do much jousting."

"Just *rousting?*"

"Yeah, I've rousted a couple thousand slimeballs in my time."

"So you're my Blue Knight."

"Wait a minute, kid," I said. "You're only getting a *former* knight if you get me."

"What do you mean, *'if'?*"

"It's okay to shuck about me being some kind of hero or something, but when I retire I'm just a has-been."

"Bumper," she said, and laughed a little, and kissed my hand like Glenda did. That was the second woman to kiss my hand today, I thought. "I'm not dazzled by authority symbols. It's really *you* that keeps me kissing your hands." She did it again and I've always thought that having a woman kiss your hands is just almost more than a man can take. "You're going to an important job. You'll be an executive. You have an awful lot to offer, especially to me. In fact, you have so much maybe I should share it."

"I can only handle one woman at a time, baby."

"Remember Nancy Vogler, from the English department?"

"Yeah, you want to share me with her?"

"Silly," she laughed. "Nancy and her husband were married twelve years and they didn't have any children. A couple of years ago they decided to take a boy into their home. He's eleven now."

"They adopted him?"

"No, not exactly. They're foster parents." Cassie's voice became serious. "She said being a foster parent is the most rewarding thing they've ever done. Nancy said they'd almost missed out on knowing what living is and didn't realize it until they got the boy."

Cassie seemed to be searching my face just then. Was she thinking about *my* boy? I'd only mentioned him once to her. Was there something she wanted to know?

"Bumper, after we get married and settled in our home, what would you say to *us* becoming foster parents? Not really adopting a child if you didn't want to, but being foster parents, sharing. You'd be someone for a boy to look up to and learn from."

"A kid! But I never thought about a family!"

"I've been thinking about this for a long time, and after seeing Nancy and hearing about their life, I think about how wonderful it would be for us. We're not old yet, but in ten or fifteen more years when we *are* getting old, there'd be someone else for both of us." She looked in my eyes and then down. "You may think I'm crazy, and I probably am, but I'd like you to give it some thought."

That hit me so hard I didn't know what to say, so I grinned a silly grin, kissed her on the cheek, said, "I'm end of watch in fifteen minutes. Bye, old shoe," and left.

She looked somehow younger and a little sad as she smiled and waved at me when I'd reached the stairway. When I got in my black-and-white I felt awful. I dropped two pills and headed east on Temple and cursed under my breath at every asshole that got in my way in this rush-hour traffic. I couldn't believe it. Leaving the Department after all these years and getting married was change enough, but a kid! Cassie had asked me about my ex-wife one time, just once, right after we started going together. I told her I was divorced and my son was dead and I didn't go into it any further. She never mentioned it again, never talked about kids in that way.

Damn, I thought, I guess every broad in the world should drop a foal at least once in her life or she'll never be happy. I pushed Cassie's idea out of my mind when I drove into the police building parking lot, down to the lower level where it was dark and fairly cool despite the early spring heat wave. I finished my log, gathered up my ticket books, and headed for the office to leave the log before I took off the uniform. I never wrote traffic tickets but they always issued me the ticket books. Since I made so many good felony pinches they pretty well kept their mouths shut about me not writing tickets, still, they always issued me the books and I always turned them back in just as full. That's the trouble with conformists, they'd never stop giving me those ticket books.

After putting the log in the daywatch basket I jived around with several of the young nightwatch coppers who wanted to know when I was changing to nights for the summer. They knew my M.O. too. Everybody knew it. I hated anyone getting my M.O. down too good like that. The most successful robbers and burglars are the ones who change their M.O.'s. They don't give you a chance to start sticking little colored pins in a map to plot their movements. That reminded me of a salty old cop named Nails Grogan who used to walk Hill Street.

About fifteen years ago, just for the hell of it, he started his own crime wave. He was teed off at some chickenshit lieutenant we had then, named Wall, who used to jump on our meat every night at rollcall because we weren't catching enough burglars. The way Wall figured this was that there were always so many little red pins on the pin maps for nighttime business burglaries, especially around Grogan's beat. Grogan always told me he didn't think Wall ever really read a burglary report and didn't know shit from gravy about what was going on. So a little at a time Nails started changing the pins every night before rollcall, taking the pins out of the area around his beat and sticking them in the east side. After a couple weeks of this, Wall told the rollcall what a hell of a job Grogan was doing with the burglary problem in his area, and restricted the ass chewing to guys that worked the eastside cars. I was the only one that knew what Grogan did and we got a big laugh out of it until Grogan went too far and pinned a full-blown crime wave on the east side, and Lieutenant Wall had the captain call out the Metro teams to catch the burglars. Finally the whole hoax was exposed when no one could find crime reports to go with all the little pins.

Wall was transferred to the morning watch, which is our graveyard shift, at the old Lincoln Heights jail. He retired from there a few years later. Nails Grogan never got made on that job, but Wall knew who screwed him, I'm sure. Nails was another guy that only lived a few years after he retired. He shot himself. I got a chill thinking about that, shook it off, and headed for the locker room where I took off the bluesuit and changed into my herringbone sport coat, gray slacks, and lemon yellow shirt, no tie. In this town you can usually get by without a tie anywhere you go.

Before I left, I plugged in my shaver and smoothed up a little bit. A couple of the guys were still in the locker room. One of them was an ambitious young bookworm named Wilson, who as usual was reading while sitting on the bench and slipping into his civvies. He was going to college three or four nights a week and always had a textbook tucked away in his police notebook. You'd see him in the coffee room or upstairs in the cafeteria going through it all the time. I'm something of a reader myself but I could never stand the thought of doing it because you had to.

"What're you reading?" I asked Wilson.

"Oh, just some criminal law," said Wilson, a thin youngster with a wide forehead and large blue eyes. He was a probationary policeman, less than a year on the job.

"Studying for sergeant already?" said Hawk, a cocky, square-shouldered kid about Wilson's age, who had two years on, and was going through his badge-heavy period.

"Just taking a few classes."

"You majoring in police science?" I asked.

"No, I'm majoring in government right now. I'm thinking about trying for law school." He didn't look right at me and I didn't think he would. This is something I've gotten used to from the younger cops, especially ones with some education, like Wilson. They don't know how to act when they're with old-timers like me. Some act salty like Hawk, trying to strut with an old beat cop, and it just looks silly. Others act more humble than they usually would, thinking an old lion like me would claw their ass for making an honest mistake out of greenness. Still others, like Wilson, pretty much act like themselves, but like most young people, they think an old fart that's never even made sergeant in twenty years must be nearly illiterate, so they generally restrict all conversation to the basics of police work to spare you, and they generally look embarrassed like Wilson did now, to admit to you that they read books. The generation gap is as bad in this job as it is in any other except for one thing: the hazards of the job shrink it pretty fast. After a few brushes with danger, a kid pretty much loses his innocence, which is what the generation gap is really all about—innocence.

"Answer me a law question," said Hawk, putting on some flared pants. We're too GI to permit mutton-chops or big moustaches or he'd surely have them. "If you commit suicide can you be prosecuted for murder?"

"Nobody ever has," Wilson smiled, as Hawk giggled and slipped on a watermelon-colored velvet shirt.

"That's only because of our permissive society," I said, and Wilson glanced at me and grinned.

"What's that book in your locker, Wilson?" I asked, nodding toward a big paperback on the top shelf.

"*Guns of August*."

"Oh yeah, I read that," I said. "I've read a hundred books about the First World War. Do you like it?"

"I do," he said, looking at me like he discovored the missing link. "I'm reading it for a history course."

"I read T. E. Lawrence's *Seven Pillars of Wisdom* when I was on my First World War kick. Every goddamn word. I had maps and books spread all over my pad. That little runt only weighed in at about a hundred thirty, but thirty pounds of that was brains and forty was balls. He was a boss warrior."

"A loner," Wilson nodded, really looking at me now.

"Right. That's what I dig about him. I would've liked him even better if he hadn't written it all so intimate for everyone to read. But then if he hadn't done that, I'd never have appreciated him. Maybe a guy like that finally gets tired of just enjoying it and *has* to tell it all to figure it all out and see if it means anything in the end."

"Maybe you should write your memoirs when you're through, Bumper," Wilson smiled. "You're as well known around here as Lawrence ever was in Arabia."

"Why don't you major in history?" I said. "If I went to college that'd be my meat. I think after a few courses in criminal law the rest of law school'd be a real drag, torts and contracts and all that bullshit. I could never plow though the dust and cobwebs."

"It's exciting if you like it," said Wilson, and Hawk looked a little ruffled that he was cut out of the conversation so he split.

"Maybe so," I said. "You must've had a few years of college when you came on the Department."

"Two years," Wilson nodded. "Now I'm halfway through my junior year. It takes forever when you're a full-time cop and a part-time student."

"You can tough it out," I said, lighting a cigar and sitting down on the bench, while part of my brain listened to the youngster and the other part was worrying about something else. I had the annoying feeling you get, that can sometimes be scary, that I'd been here with him before and we talked like this, or maybe it was somebody else, and then I thought, yes, that was it, maybe the cowlick in his hair reminded me of Billy, and I got an empty tremor in my stomach.

"How old're you, Wilson?"

"Twenty-six," he said, and a pain stabbed me and made me curse and rub my pot. Billy would've been twenty-six too!

"Hope your stomach holds out when you get my age. Were you in the service?"

"Army," he nodded.

"Vietnam?"

"Yeah," he nodded.

"Did you hate it?" I asked, expecting that all young people hated it.

"I didn't like the *war*. It scared hell out of me, but I didn't mind the *army* as much as I thought I would."

"That's sort of how I felt," I smiled. "I was in the Marine Corps for eight years."

"Korea?"

"No, I'm even older than that," I smiled. "I joined in forty-two, and got out in fifty, then came on the police department."

"You stayed in a long time," he said.

"Too long. The war scared me too, but sometimes peace is just as bad for a miliary man."

I didn't tell him the truth because it might tune him out, and the truth was that it *did* scare me, the war, but I didn't hate it. I didn't exactly like it, but I didn't hate it. It's fashionable to hate war, I know, and I wanted to hate it, but I never did.

"I swore when I left Vietnam I'd never fire another gun and here I am a cop. Figure that out," said Wilson.

I thought that was something, having him tell *me* that. Suddenly the age difference wasn't there. He was telling me things he probably told his young partners during lonely hours after two a.m. when you're fighting to keep awake or when you're "in the hole" trying to hide your radio car, in some alley where you can doze uncomfortably for an hour, but you never really rest. There's the fear of a sergeant catching you, or there's the radio. What if you *really* fall asleep and a hot call comes out and you miss it?

"Maybe you'll make twenty years without ever firing your gun on duty," I said.

"Have you had to shoot?"

"A few times," I nodded, and he let it drop like he should. It was only civilians who ask you, "What's it feel like to shoot someone?" and all that bullshit which is completely ridiculous, because if you do it in war or you do it as a cop, it doesn't feel like anything. If you do what has to be done, why *should* you feel anything? I never have. After the fear for your own life is past, and the adrenalin slows, nothing. But people generally can't stand truth. It makes a lousy story so I usually give them their clichés.

"You gonna stay on the job after you finish law school?"

"If I ever finish I might leave," he laughed. "But I can't really picture myself ever finishing."

"Maybe you won't want to leave by then. This is a pretty strange kind of job. It's . . . intense. Some guys wouldn't leave if they had a million bucks."

"How about you?"

"Oh, I'm pulling the pin," I said. "I'm almost gone. But the job gets to you. The way you see everyone so exposed and vulnerable. . . . And there's nothing like rolling up a good felon if you really got the instinct."

He looked at me for a moment and then said, "Rogers and I got a good two-eleven suspect last month. They cleared five holdups on this guy. He had a seven-point-six-five-millimeter pistol shoved down the back of his waistband when we stopped him for a traffic ticket. We got hinky because he was sweating and dry-mouthed when he talked to us. It's really something to get a guy like that, especially when you never know how close you came. I mean, he was just sitting there looking from Rogers to me, measuring, thinking about blowing us up. We realized it later, and it made the pinch that much more of a kick."

''That's part of it. You feel more alive. Hey, you talk like you're Bumper-ized and I didn't even break you in.''

''We worked together one night, remember?'' said Wilson. ''My first night out of the academy. I was more scared of you than I was the assholes on the street.''

''That's right, we *did* work together. I remember now,'' I lied.

''Well, I better get moving,'' said Wilson, and I was disappointed. ''Got to get to school. I've got two papers due next week and haven't started them.''

''Hang in there, Wilson. Hang tough,'' I said, as I locked my locker.

I walked to the parking lot and decided to tip a few at my neighborhood pub near Silverlake before going to Cruz's house. The proprietor was an old pal of mine who used to own a decent bar on my beat downtown before he bought this one. He was no longer on my beat of course, but he still bounced for drinks, I guess out of habit. Most bar owners don't pop for too many policemen, because they'll take advantage of it, policemen will, and there'll be so many at your watering hole you'll have to close the goddamn doors. Harry only popped for me and a few detectives he knew real well.

It was five o'clock when I parked my nineteen-fifty-one Ford in front of Harry's. I'd bought the car new and was still driving it. Almost twenty years and I only had a hundred and thirty thousand miles on her, and the same engine. I never went anywhere except at vacation time or sometimes when I'd take a trip to the river to fish. Since I met Cassie I've used the car more than I ever had before, but even with Cassie I seldom went far. We usually went to the movies in Hollywood, or to the Music Center to see light opera, or to the Bowl for a concert which was Cassie's favorite place to go, or to Dodger Stadium which was mine. Often we went out to the Strip to go dancing. Cassie was good. She had all the moves, but she couldn't get the hang of letting her body do it all. With Cassie the mind was always there. One thing I decided I wouldn't get rid of when I left L.A. was my Ford. I wanted to see just how long a car would live if you treated it right.

Harry was alone when I walked in the little knotty-pine tavern which had a pool table, a few sad booths, and a dozen bar stools. The neighborhood business was never very good. It was quiet and cool and dark in there and I was glad.

''Hi, Bumper,'' he said, drawing a draft beer in a frosted glass for me.

''Evening, Harry,'' I said, grabbing a handful of pretzels from one of the dishes he had on the bar. Harry's was one of the few joints left where you could actually get something free, like pretzels.

''How's business, Bumper?''

''Mine's always good, Harry,'' I said, which is what policemen always answer to that question.

''Anything exciting happen on your beat lately?'' Harry was about seventy, an ugly little goblin with bony shoulder blades who hopped around behind the bar like a sparrow.

''Let's see,'' I said, trying to think of some gossip. Since Harry used to own a bar downtown, he knew a lot of the people I knew. ''Yeah, remember Frog LaRue?''

''The little hype with the stooped-over walk?''

''That one.''

''Yeah,'' said Harry. ''I must've kicked that junkie out of my joint a million times after you said he was dealing dope. Never could figure out why he liked to set up deals in my bar.''

''He got his ass shot,'' I said.

''What'd he do, try to sell somebody powdered sugar in place of the stuff?''

''No, a narco cop nailed him.''

''Yeah? Why would anybody shoot Frog? He couldn't hurt nobody but himself.''

''Anybody can hurt somebody, Harry,'' I said. ''But in this case it was a mistake. Old Frog always kept a blade on the window sill in any hotel he stayed at. And the window'd be open even in the dead of winter. That was his M.O. If someone came to his door who he thought was cops, Frog'd slit the screen and throw his dope and his outfit right out the window. One night the narcs busted in the pad when they heard from a snitch that Frog was holding, and old Froggy dumped a spoon of junk out the window. He had to slit the screen to do it and when this narc came crashing through the door, his momentum carried him clear across this little room, practically onto Frog's bed. Frog was crouched there with the blade still in his hand. The partner coming through second had his gun drawn and that was it, he put two almost in the ten ring of the goddamn bull's-eye.'' I put my fist on my chest just to the right of the heart to show where they hit him.

''Hope the poor bastard didn't suffer.''

''Lived two days. He told about the knife bit to the detectives and swore how he never would've tried to stab a cop.''

''Poor bastard,'' said Harry.

''At least he died the way he lived. Armload of dope. I heard from one of the dicks that at the last they gave him a good stiff jolt of morphine. Said old Frog laying there with two big holes in his chest actually looked happy at the end.''

''Why in the hell don't the state just give dope to these poor bastards like Frog?'' said Harry, disgustedly.

''It's the high they crave, not just feeling healthy. They build up such a tolerance you'd have to keep increasing the dose and increasing it until you'd have to give them a fix that'd make a pussycat out of King Kong. And heroin substitutes don't work with a stone hype. He wants the *real* thing. Pretty soon you'd be giving him doses that'd kill him anyway.''

''What the hell, he'd be better off. Some of them probably wouldn't complain.''

''Got to agree with you there,'' I nodded. ''Damn straight.''

''Wish that bitch'd get here,'' Harry mumbled, checking the bar clock.

''Who's that?''

''Irma, the goofy barmaid I hired last week. You seen her yet?''

''Don't think so,'' I said, sipping the beer, so cold it hurt my teeth.

''Sexy little twist,'' said Harry, ''but a kook, you know? She'll steal your eyes out if you let her. But a good body. I'd like to break her open like a shotgun and horsefuck her.''

''Thought you told me you were getting too old for that,'' I said, licking the foam off my upper lip, and finishing the glass, which Harry hurried to refill.

''I am, God knows, but once in a while I get this terrible urge, know what I mean? Sometimes when I'm closing up and I'm alone with her. . . . I ain't stirred the old lady for a couple years, but I swear when I'm with Irma I get the urge like a young stallion. I'm not *that* old, you know. Not by a long shot. But you know how my health's always been. Lately there's been this prostate problem. Still, when I'm around this Irma I'm awful randy. I feel like I could screw anything from a burro to a cowboy boot.''

''I'll have to see this wench,'' I smiled.

''You won't take her away from me, will you, Bumper?''

I thought at first he was kidding and then I saw the desperate look on his face. ''No, of course not, Harry.''

''I really think I could make it with her, Bumper. I been depressed lately, especially with this prostate, but I could be a man again with Irma.''

''Sure, Harry.'' I'd noticed the change coming over him gradually for the past year. He sometimes forgot to pick up bar money, which was very unusual for him. He mixed up customers' names and sometimes told you things he'd told you the last time he saw you. Mostly that, repeating things. A few of the other regular customers mentioned it when we played pool out of earshot. Harry was getting senile and it was not only sad, it was scary. It made my skin crawl. I wondered how much longer he'd be able to run the joint. I laid a quarter on the bar, and sure enough, he absently picked it up. The first time I ever bought my own drink in Harry's place.

"My old lady can't last much longer, Bumper. I ever tell you that the doctors only give her a year?"

"Yeah, you told me."

"Guy my age can't be alone. This prostate thing, you know I got to stand there and coax for twenty minutes before I can take a leak. And you don't know how lovely it is to be able to sit down and take a nice easy crap. You know, Bumper, a nice easy crap is a thing of beauty."

"Yeah, I guess so."

"I could do all right with a dame like Irma. Make me young again, Irma could."

"Sure."

"You try to go it alone when you get old and you'll be rotting out a coffin liner before you know it. You got to have somebody to keep you alive. If you don't, you might die without even knowing it. Get what I mean?"

"Yeah."

It was so depressing being here with Harry that I decided to split, but one of the local cronies came in.

"Hello, Freddie," I said, as he squinted through six ounces of eyeglasses into the cool darkness.

"Hi, Bumper," said Freddie, recognizing my voice before he got close enough to make me through his half-inch horn-rims. Nobody could ever mistake his twangy voice which could get on your nerves after a bit. Freddie limped over and laid both arthritic hands on the bar knowing I'd bounce for a couple drinks.

"A cold one for Freddie," I said, suddenly afraid that Harry wouldn't even know him. But that was ridiculous, I thought, putting a dollar on the bar, Harry's deterioration was only beginning. I usually bought for the bar when there were enough people in there to make Harry a little coin, trouble is, there were seldom more than three or four customers in Harry's at any one time anymore. I guess everyone runs from a man when he starts to die.

"How's business, Bumper?" asked Freddie, holding the mug in both his hands, fingers like crooked twigs.

"My business's always good, Freddie."

Freddie snuffled and laughed. I stared at Freddie for a few seconds while he drank. My stomach was burning and Harry had me spooked. Freddie suddenly looked ancient too. Christ, he probably was at least sixty-five. I'd never thought about Freddie as an older guy, but suddenly he was. Little old men they were. I had nothing in common with them now.

"Girls keeping you busy lately, Bumper?" Harry winked. He didn't know about Cassie or that I stopped chasing around after I met her.

"Been slowing down a little in that department, Harry," I said.

"Keep at it, Bumper," said Harry, cocking his head to one side and nodding like a bird. "The art of fornication is something you lose if you don't practice it. The eye muscles relax, you get bifocals like Freddie. The love muscles relax, whatta you got?"

"Maybe he *is* getting old, Harry," said Freddie, dropping his empty glass on its side as he tried to hand it to Harry with those twisted hands.

"Old? You kidding?" I said.

"How about you, Freddie?" said Harry. "You ain't got arthritis of the cock, have you? When was the last time you had a piece of ass?"

"About the last time you did," said Freddie sharply.

"Shit, before my Flossie got sick, I used to tear off a chunk every night. Right up till when she got sick, and I was sixty-eight years old then."

"Haw!" said Freddie, spilling some beer over the gnarled fingers. "You ain't been able to do anything but lick it for the past twenty years."

"Yeah?" said Harry, nodding fast now, like a starving little bird at a feed tray. "You know what I did to Irma here one night? Know what?"

"What?"

"I laid her right over the table there. What do you think of that, wise guy?"

"Haw. Haw. Haw," said Freddie who had been a little bit fried when he came in and was really feeling it now.

"All you can do is read about it in those dirty books," said Harry. "Me, I don't read about it, I do it! I threw old Irma right over that bar there and poured her the salami for a half hour!"

"Haw. Haw. Haw," said Freddie. "It'd take you that long to find that shriveled up old cricket dick. Haw. Haw. Haw."

"What's the sense of starting a beef?" I muttered to both of them. I was getting a headache. "Gimme a couple aspirin, will you, Harry?" I said, and he shot the grinning Freddie a pissed-off look, and muttering under his breath, brought me a bottle of aspirin and a glass of water.

I shook out three pills and pushed the water away, swallowing the pills with a mouthful of beer. "One more beer," I said, "and then I gotta make it."

"Where you going, Bump? Out to hump?" Harry leered, and winked at Freddie, forgetting he was supposed to be mad as hell.

"Going to a friend's house for dinner."

"Nice slice of tail waiting, huh?" said Harry, nodding again.

"Not tonight. Just having a quiet dinner."

"Quiet dinner," said Freddie. "Haw. Haw. Haw."

"Screw you, Freddie," I said, getting mad for a second as he giggled in his beer. Then I thought, Jesus, I'm getting loony too.

The phone rang and Harry went to the back of the bar to answer it. In a few seconds he was bitching at somebody, and Freddie looked at me, shaking his head.

"Harry's going downhill real fast, Bumper."

"I know he is, so why get him pissed off?"

"I don't mean to," said Freddie. "I just lose my temper with him sometimes, he acts so damned nasty. I heard the doctors're just waiting for Flossie to die. Any day now."

I thought of how she was ten years ago, a fat, tough old broad, full of hell and jokes. She fixed such good cold-cut sandwiches I used to make a dinner out of them at least once a week.

"Harry can't make it without her," said Freddie. "Ever since she went away to the hospital last year he's been getting more and more childish, you noticed?"

I finished my beer and thought, I've *got* to get the hell out of here.

"It happens only to people like Harry and me. When you love somebody and need them so much especially when you're old, and then lose them, that's when it happens to you. It's the most godawful thing that ever could happen to you, when your mind rots like Harry's. Better your body goes like Flossie's. Flossie's the lucky one, you know. You're lucky too. You don't love nobody and you ain't married to nothing but that badge. Nothing can ever touch you, Bumper."

"Yeah, but how about when you get too old to do the job, Freddie? How about then?"

"Well, I never thought about that, Bumper." Freddie tipped the mug and dribbled on his chin. He licked some foam off one knotted knuckle. "Never thought about that, but I'd say you don't have to worry about it. You get a little older and charge around the way you do and somebody's bound to bump you off. It might sound cold, but what the hell, Bumper, look at *that* crazy old bastard." He waved a twisted claw toward Harry still yelling in the phone. "Screwing everything with his imagination and a piece of dead skin. Look at me. What the hell, dying on your beat wouldn't be the worst way to go, would it?"

"Know why I come to this place, Freddie? It's just the most cheerful goddamn drinking establishment in Los Angeles. Yeah, the conversation is stimulating and the atmosphere is very jolly and all."

Harry came back before I could get away from the bar. "Know who that was, Bumper?" he said, his eyes glassy and his cheeks pale. He had acne as a young man and now his putty-colored cheeks looked corroded.

"Who was it," I sighed, "Irma?"

"No, that was the hospital. I spent every cent I had, even with the hospital benefits, and now she's been put in a big ward with a million other old, dying people. And still I got to pay money for one thing or another. You know, when Flossie finally dies there ain't going to be nothing left to bury her. I had to cash in the insurance. How'll I bury old Flossie, Bumper?"

I started to say something to soothe Harry, but I heard sobbing and realized Freddie had started blubbering. Then in a second or two Harry started, so I threw five bucks on the bar for Freddie and Harry to get bombed on, and I got the hell away from those two without even saying good-bye. I've never understood how people can work in mental hospitals and old people's homes and places like that without going nuts. I felt about ready for the squirrel tank right now just being around those two guys for an hour.

8

Ten minutes later I was driving my Ford north on the Golden State Freeway and I started getting hungry for Socorro's enchiladas. I got to Eagle Rock at dusk and parked in front of the big old two-story house with the neat lawn and flower gardens on the sides. I was wondering if Socorro planted vegetables in the back this year, when I saw Cruz in the living room standing by the front window. He opened the door and stepped out on the porch, wearing a brown sport shirt and old brown slacks and his house slippers. Cruz didn't have to dress up for me, and I was glad to come here and see everyone comfortable, as though I belonged here, and in a way I did. Most bachelor cops have someplace like Cruz's house to go to once in a while. Naturally, you can get a little ding-a-ling if you live on the beat and don't ever spend some time with decent people. So you find a friend or a relative with a family and go there to get your supply of faith replenished.

I called Cruz my old roomie because when we first got out of the police academy twenty years ago, I moved into this big house with him and Socorro. Dolores was a baby, and Esteban a toddler. I took a room upstairs for over a year and helped them with their house payments until we were through paying for our uniforms and guns, and were both financially on our feet. That hadn't been a bad year and I'd never forget Socorro's cooking. She always said she'd rather cook for a man like me who appreciated her talent than a thin little guy like Cruz who never ate much and didn't really appreciate good food. Socorro was a slender girl then, twelve years younger than Cruz, nineteen years old, with two kids already, and the heavy Spanish accent of El Paso which is like that of Mexico itself. They'd had a pretty good life I guess, until Esteban insisted on joining the army and was killed two years ago. They weren't the same after that. They'd never be the same after that.

"How do you feel, *oso*?" said Cruz, as I climbed the concrete stairs to his porch. I grinned because Socorro had first started calling me "*oso*" way back in those days, and even now some of the policemen call me "bear" from Socorro's nickname.

"You hurting, Bumper?" Cruz asked. "I heard those kids gave you some trouble at the demonstration today."

"I'm okay," I answered. "What'd you hear?"

"Just that they pushed you around a little bit. *Hijo la—*. Why does a man your age get involved in that kind of stuff? Why don't you listen to me and just handle your radio calls and let those young coppers handle the militants and do the hotdog police work?"

"I answered a radio call. That's how it started. That's what I get for having that goddamn radio turned on."

"Come on in, you stubborn old bastard," Cruz grinned, holding the wood frame screen door open for me. Where could you see a wood frame screen door these days? It was an old house, but preserved. I loved it here. Cruz and me once sanded down all the woodwork in the living room, even the hardwood floor, and refinished it just as it had been when it was new.

"What're we having?" Cruz asked, brushing back his thick gray-black hair and nodding toward the kitchen.

"Well, let's see," I sniffed. I sniffed again a few times, and then took a great huge whiff. Actually I couldn't tell, because the chile and onion made it hard to differentiate, but I took a guess and pretended I knew.

"*Chile relleno, carnitas* and *cilantro* and onion. And . . . let's see . . . some enchiladas, some guacamole."

"I give up," Cruz shook his head. "The only thing you left out was rice and beans."

"Well, hell, Cruz, *arroz y frijoles*, that goes without saying."

"An animal's nose."

"Sukie in the kitchen?"

"Yeah, the kids're in the backyard, some of them."

I went through the big formal dining room to the kitchen and saw Socorro, her back to me, ladling out a huge wooden spoonful of rice into two of the bowls that sat on the drainboard. She was naturally a little the worse for wear after twenty years and nine kids, but her hair was as long and black and shiny rich as ever, and though she was twenty pounds heavier, she still was a strong, lively-looking girl with the whitest teeth I'd ever seen. I snuck up behind her and tickled her ribs.

"Ay!" she said, dropping the spoon. "Bumper!"

I gave her a hug from the back while Cruz chuckled and said, "You didn't surprise him, he smelled from the door and knew just what you fixed for him."

"He's not a man, this one," she smiled, "no man ever had a nose like that."

"Just what I told him," said Cruz.

"Sit down, Bumper," said Socorro, waving to the kitchen table, which, big and old as it was, looked lost in the huge kitchen. I'd seen this kitchen when there wasn't a pathway to walk through, the day after Chiristmas when all the kids were young and I'd brought them toys. Kids and toys literally covered every foot of linoleum and you couldn't even see the floor then.

"Beer, Bumper?" asked Cruz, and opened two cold ones without me answering. We still liked drinking them out of the bottle, both of us, and I almost finished mine without taking it away from my mouth. And Cruz, knowing my M.O. so well, uncapped another one.

"Cruz told me the news, Bumper. I was thrilled to hear it," said Socorro, slicing an onion, her eyes glistening from the fumes.

"About you retiring right away and going with Cassie when she leaves," said Cruz.

"That's good, Bumper," said Socorro. "There's no sense hanging around after Cassie leaves. I was worried about that."

"Sukie was afraid your *puta* would seduce you away from Cassie if she was up in San Francisco and you were down here."

"*Puta?*"

"The beat," said Cruz taking a gulp of the beer. "Socorro always calls it Bumper's *puta*."

"*Cuidao!*" said Socorro to Cruz. "The children are right outside the window." I could hear them laughing, and Nacho yelled something then, and the girls squealed.

"Since you're leaving, we can talk about her can't we, Bumper?" Cruz laughed. "That beat is a *puta* who seduced you all these years."

Then for the first time I noticed from his grin and his voice that Cruz had had a few before I got there. I looked at Socorro who nodded and said, "Yes, the old *borracho*'s been drinking since he got home from work. Wants to celebrate Bumper's last dinner as a bachelor, he says."

"Don't be too rough on him," I grinned. "He doesn't get drunk very often."

"Who's drunk?" said Cruz, indignantly.

"You're on your way, *pendejo*," said Socorro, and Cruz mumbled in Spanish, and I laughed and finished my beer.

"If it hadn't been for that *puta*, Bumper would've been a captain by now."

"Oh sure," I said, going to the refrigerator and drawing two more beers for Cruz and me. "Want one, Sukie?"

"No thanks," said Socorro, and Cruz burped a couple times.

"Think I'll go outside and see the kids," I said, and then I remembered the presents in the trunk of my car that I had bought Monday after Cruz invited me to dinner.

"Hey, you roughnecks," I said when I stepped out, and Nacho yelled, "Buuuum-per," and swung toward me from a rope looped over the limb of a big oak that covered most of the yard.

"You're getting about big enough to eat hay and pull a wagon, Nacho," I said. Then four of them ran toward me chattering about something, their eyes all sparkling because they knew damn well I'd never come for dinner without bringing them something.

"Where's Dolores?" I asked. She was my favorite now, the oldest after Esteban, and was a picture of what her mother had been. She was a college junior majoring in physics and engaged to a classmate of hers.

"Dolores is out with Gordon, where else?" said Ralph, a chubby ten-year-old, the baby of the family who was a terror, always raising some kind of hell and keeping everyone in an uproar.

"Where's Alice?"

"Over next door playing," said Ralph again, and the four of them, Nacho, Ralph, María, and Marta were all about to bust, and I was enjoying it even though it was a shame to make them go through this.

"Nacho," I said nonchalantly, "would you please take my car keys and get some things out of the trunk?"

"I'll help," shrieked Marta.

"I will," said María, jumping up and down, a little eleven-year-old dream in a pink dress and pink socks and black patent leather shoes. She was the prettiest and would be heartbreakingly beautiful someday.

"I'll go alone," said Nacho. "I don't need no help."

"The hell you will," said Ralph.

"You watch your language, Rafael," said María, and I had to turn around to keep from busting up at the way Ralph stuck his chubby little fanny out at her.

"Mama," said María. "Ralph did something dirty!"

"Snitch," said Ralph, running to the car with Nacho.

I strolled back into the kitchen still laughing, and Cruz and Socorro both were smiling at me because they knew how much I got a bang out of their kids.

"Take Bumper in the living room, Cruz," said Socorro. "Dinner won't be ready for twenty minutes."

"Come on, Bumper," said Cruz, taking four cold ones out of the refrigerator, and a beer opener. "I don't know why Mexican women get to be tyrants in their old age. They're so nice and obedient when they're young."

"Old age. Huh! Listen to the *viejo,* Bumper," she said, waving a wooden spoon in his direction, as we went in the living room and I flopped in Cruz's favorite chair because he insisted. He pushed the ottoman over and made me put my feet up.

"Damn, Cruz."

"Got to give you extra special treatment tonight, Bumper," he said, opening another beer for me. "You look dog tired, and this may be the last we have you for a long time."

"I'll only be living one hour away by air. You think Cassie and me aren't gonna come to L.A. once in a while? And you think you and Socorro and the kids aren't gonna come see us up there?"

"The whole platoon of us?" he laughed.

"We're gonna see each other plenty, that's for sure," I said, and fought against the down feeling that I was getting because I realized we probably would *not* be seeing each other very often at all.

"Yeah, Bumper," said Cruz, sitting across from me in the other old chair, almost as worn and comfortable as this one. "I was afraid that jealous bitch would never let you go."

"You mean my beat?"

"Right." He took several big gulps on the beer and I thought about how I was going to miss him.

"How come all the philosophizing tonight? Calling my beat a whore and all that?"

"I'm waxing poetic tonight."

"You also been tipping more than a little *cerveza.*"

Cruz winked and peeked toward the kitchen where we could hear Socorro banging around. He went to an old mahogany hutch that was just inside the dining room and took a half-empty bottle of mescal out of the bottom cabinet.

"That one have a worm in it?"

"If it did I drank it," he whispered. "Don't want Sukie to see me drinking it. I still have a little trouble with my liver and I'm not supposed to."

"Is that the stuff you bought in San Luis? That time on your vacation?"

"That's it, the end of it."

"You won't need any liver you drink that stuff."

"It's good, Bumper. Here, try a throatful or two."

"Better with salt and lemon."

"Pour it down. You're the big *macho*, damn it. Drink like one."

I took three fiery gulps and a few seconds after they hit bottom I regretted it, and had to drain my bottle of beer while Cruz chuckled and sipped slowly for his turn.

"Damn," I wheezed and then the fire fanned out and my guts uncoiled and I felt good. Then in a few minutes I felt better. That was the medicine my body needed.

"They don't always have salt and lemon lying around down in Mexico," said Cruz handing me back the mescal. "Real Mexicans just mix it with saliva."

"No wonder they're such tough little bastards," I wheezed, taking another gulp, but only one this time, and handing it back.

"How do you feel now, '*mano?*" Cruz giggled, and it made me start laughing, his silly little giggle that always started when he was half swacked.

"I feel about half as good as you," I said, and splashed some more beer into the burning pit that was my stomach. But it was a different fire entirely than the one made by the stomach acid, this was a friendly fire, and after it smoldered it felt great.

"Are you hungry?" asked Cruz.

"Ain't I always?"

"You are," he said, "you're hungry for almost everything. Always. I've often wished I was more like you."

"Like me?"

"Always feasting, on *everything*. Too bad it can't go on forever. But it can't. I'm damn glad you're getting out now."

"You're drunk."

"I am. But I know what I'm talking about, *'mano*. Cassie was sent to you. I prayed for that." Then Cruz reached in his pocket for the little leather pouch. In it was the string of black carved wooden beads he carried for luck. He squeezed the soft leather and put it away.

"Did those beads really come from Jerusalem?"

"They did, that's no baloney. I got them from a missionary priest for placing first in my school in El Paso. 'First prize in spelling to Cruz Guadalupe Segovia,' the priest said, as he stood in front of the whole school, and I died of happiness that day. I was thirteen, just barely. He got the beads in the Holy Land and they were blessed by Pius XI."

"How many kids did you beat out for the prize?"

"About six entered the contest. There were only seventy-five in the school altogether. I don't think the other five contestants spoke any English. They thought the contest would be in Spanish but it wasn't, so I won."

We both laughed at that. "I never won a thing, Cruz. You're way ahead of me." It was amazing to think of a real man like Cruz carrying those wooden beads. In this day and age!

Then the front door banged open and the living room was filled with seven yelling kids, only Dolores being absent that night, and Cruz shook his head and sat back quietly drinking his beer and Socorro came into the living room and tried to give me hell for buying all the presents, but you couldn't hear yourself over the noisy kids.

"Are these real big-league cleats?" asked Nacho as I adjusted the batting helmet for him and fixed the chin strap which I knew he'd throw away as soon as the other kids told him big leaguers don't wear chin straps.

"Look! Hot pants!" María squealed, holding them up against her adolescent body. They were sporty, blue denim with a bib, and patch pockets.

"Hot pants?" Cruz said. "Oh, no!"

"They even wear them to school, Papa. They do. Ask Bumper!"

"Ask Bumper," Cruz grumbled and drank some more beer.

The big kids were there then too, Linda, George, and Alice, all high school teenagers, and naturally I bought clothes for them. I got George a box of mod-colored long-sleeved shirts and from the look in his eyes I guess I couldn't have picked anything better.

After all the kids thanked me a dozen times, Socorro ordered them to put everything away and called us to dinner. We sat close together on different kinds of chairs at the huge rectangular oak table that weighed a ton. I know because I helped Cruz carry it in here twelve years ago when there was no telling how many kids were going to be sitting around it.

The youngest always said the prayers aloud. They crossed themselves and Ralph said grace, and they crossed themselves again and I was drooling because the *chiles rellenos* were on a huge platter right in front of me. The big *chiles* were stuffed with cheese and fried in a light fluffy batter, and before I could help myself, Alice was serving me and my plate was filled before any of those kids took a thing for themselves. Their mother and father never said anything to them, they just did things like that.

"You *do* have *cilantro,*" I said, salivating with a vengeance now. I knew I smelled that wonderful spice.

Marta, using her fingers, sprinkled a little extra *cilantro* over my *carnitas* when I said that, and I bit into a soft, handmade, flour tortilla crammed with *carnitas* and Socorro's own *chile* sauce.

"Well, Bumper?" said Cruz after I'd finished half a plateful which took about thirty-five seconds.

I moaned and rolled my eyeballs and everybody laughed because they knew that look so well.

"You see, Marta," said Socorro. "You wouldn't hate to cook so much if you could cook for somebody like Bumper who appreciates your work."

I grinned with a hog happy look, washing down some *chile relleno* and enchilada with three big swigs of cold beer. "Your mother is an artist!"

I finished three helpings of *carnitas,* the tender little chunks of pork which I covered with Socorro's *chile* and *cilantro* and onion. Then, after everyone was finished and there were nine pairs of brown eyes looking at me in wonder, I heaped the last three *chile rellenos* on my plate and rolled one up with the last flour tortilla and the last few bites of *carnitas* left in the bowl, and nine pairs of brown eyes got wider and rounder.

"*Por Dios,* I thought I made enough for twenty," said Socorro.

"You did, you did, Sukie," I said, enjoying being the whole show now, and finishing it in three big bites. "I'm just extra hungry tonight, and you made it extra good, and there's no sense leaving leftovers around to spoil." With that I ate half a *chile relleno* and swallowed some beer and looked around at all the eyes, and Nacho burped and groaned. We all busted up, Ralph especially, who fell off his chair onto the floor holding his stomach and laughing so hard I was afraid he'd get sick. It was a hell of a thing when you think of it, entertaining people by being a damn glutton, just to get attention.

After dinner we cleared the table and I got roped into a game of Scrabble with Alice and Marta and Nacho with the others kibitzing, and all the time I was swilling cold beer with an occasional shot of mescal that Cruz brought out in the open now. By nine o'clock when the kids had to go to bed I was pretty well lubricated.

They all kissed me good night except George and Nacho, who shook hands, and there were no arguments about going to bed, and fifteen minutes later it was still and quiet upstairs. I'd never seen Cruz or Socorro spank any of them. Of course the older ones spanked hell out of the younger ones, I'd seen that often enough. After all, everyone in this world needs a thumping once in a while.

We took the leaf out of the table and replaced the lace tablecloth and the three of us went into the living room. Cruz was pretty well bombed out, and after Socorro complained, he decided not to have another beer. I had a cold one in my right hand, and the last of the mescal in my left.

Cruz sat next to Socorro on the couch and he rubbed his face which was probably numb as hell. He gave her a kiss on the neck.

"Get out of here," she grumbled. "You smell like a stinking wino."

"How can I smell like a wino. I haven't had any wine," said Cruz.

"Remember how we used to sit like this after dinner back in the old days," I said, realizing how much the mescal affected me, because they were both starting to look a little fuzzy.

"Remember how little and skinny Sukie was," said Cruz, poking her arm.

"I'm going to let you have it in a minute," said Socorro, raising her hand which was a raw, worn-out looking hand for a girl her age. She wasn't quite forty years old.

"Sukie was the prettiest girl I'd ever seen," I said.

"I guess she was," said Cruz with a silly grin.

"And still is," I added. "And Cruz was the handsomest guy I ever saw outside of Tyrone Power or maybe Clark Gable."

"You really think Tyrone Power was better looking?" said Cruz, grinning again as Socorro shook her head, and to me he honestly didn't look a bit different now than he ever had, except for the gray hair. Damn him for staying young, I thought.

"Speaking of pretty girls," said Socorro, "let's hear about your new plans with Cassie."

"Well, like I told you, she was gonna go up north to an apartment and get squared away at school. Then after the end of May when Cruz and me have our twenty years, she'd fly back here and we'd get married. Now I've decided to cut it short. I'll work tomorrow and the next day and run my vacation days and days off together to the end of the month when I officially retire. That way I can leave with Cassie, probably Sunday morning or Monday and we'll swing through Las Vegas and get married on the way."

"Oh, Bumper, we wanted to be with you when you get married," said Socorro, looking disappointed.

"What the hell, at our age getting married ain't no big thing," I said.

"We love her, Bumper," said Socorro. "You're lucky, very lucky. She'll be perfect for you."

"What a looker." Cruz winked and tried to whistle, but he was too drunk.

Socorro shook her head and said, "*sinvergüenza*," and we both laughed at him.

"What're you going to do Friday?" asked Socorro. "Just go into rollcall and stand up and say you're retiring and this is your last day?"

"Nope, I'm just gonna fade away. I'm not telling a soul and I hope you haven't said anything to anyone, Cruz."

"Nothing," said Cruz, and he burped.

"I'm just cutting out like for my regular two days off, then I'm sending a registered letter to Personnel Division and one to the captain. I'll just sign all my retirement papers and mail them in. I can give my badge and I.D. card to Cruz before I leave and have him turn them in for me so I won't have to go back at all."

"You'll have to come back to L.A. for your retirement party," said Cruz. "We're sure as hell going to want to throw a retirement party for you."

"Thanks, Cruz, but I never liked retirement parties anyway. In fact I think they're miserable. I appreciate the thought but no party for me."

"Just think," said Socorro. "To be starting a new life! I wish Cruz could leave the job too."

"You said it," said Cruz, his eyes glassy though he sat up straight. "But with all our kids, I'm a thirty-year man. Thirty years, that's a lifetime. I'll be an old man when I pull the pin."

"Yeah, I guess I'm lucky," I said. "Remember when we were going through the academy, Cruz? We thought we were old men then, running with all those kids twenty-one and twenty-two years old. Here you were thirty-one, the oldest guy in the class, and I was close behind you. Remember Mendez always called us *elefante y ratoncito?*"

"The elephant and the mouse," Cruz giggled.

"The two old men of the class. Thirty years old and I thought I knew something then. Hell, you're still a baby at that age. We were both babies."

"We were babies, *'mano*," said Cruz. "But only because we hadn't been out there yet." Cruz waved his hand toward the streets. "You grow up fast out there and learn too much. It's no damn good for a man to learn as much as you learn out there. It ruins the way you think about things, and the way you feel. There're certain things you should believe and if you stay out there for twenty years you can't believe them anymore. That's not good."

"You still believe them, don't you, Cruz?" I asked, and Socorro looked at us like we were two raving drunks, which we probably were, but we understood, Cruz and me.

"I still believe them, Bumper, because I want to. And I have Sukie and the kids. I can come home, and then the other isn't real. You've had no one to go to. Thank God for Cassie."

"I've got to go fix school lunches. Excuse me, Bumper," said Socorro, and she gave us that shake of the head which meant, it's time to leave the drunken cops to their talk. But Cruz hardly ever got drunk, and she didn't really begrudge him, even though he had trouble with his liver.

"I never could tell you how glad we were when you first brought Cassie here for dinner, Bumper. Socorro and me, we stayed awake in bed that night and talked about it and how God must've sent her, even though you don't believe in God."

"I believe in the *gods*, you know that," I grinned, gulping the beer after I took the last sip of the mescal.

"There's only one God, goddamnit," said Cruz.

"Even your God has three faces, goddamnit," I said, and gave him a glance over the top of my beer bottle, making him laugh.

"Bumper, I'm trying to talk to you seriously." And his eyes turned down at the corners like always. I couldn't woof him anymore when his eyes did that.

"Okay."

"Cassie's the answer to a prayer."

"Why did you waste all your prayers on me?"

"Why do you think, *pendejo?* You're my brother, *mi hermano*."

That made me put the beer down, and I straightened up and looked at his big eyes. Cruz was struggling with the fog of the mescal and beer because he wanted to tell me something. I wondered how in hell he had ever made the Department physical. He was barely five-eight in his bare feet, and he was so damn skinny. He'd never gained a pound, but outside of Esteban, he had the finest-looking face you would ever see.

"I didn't know you thought that much about Cassie and me."

"Of course I did. After all, I prayed her here for you. Don't you see what you were heading for? You're fifty years old, Bumper. You and some of the other old beat cops've been the *machos* of the streets all these years, but Lord, I could just see you duking it out with some young stud or chasing somebody out there and all of a sudden just lying down on that street to die. You realize how many of our classmates had heart attacks already?"

"Part of being a policeman," I shrugged.

"Not to mention some asshole blowing you up," said Cruz. "You remember Driscoll? He had a heart attack just last month and he's not nearly as fat as you, and a few years younger, and I'll bet he never does anything harder than lift a pencil. Like you today, all alone, facing a mob, like a rookie! What the hell, Bumper, you think I want to be a pallbearer for a guy two hundred and eighty pounds?"

"Two seventy-five."

"When Cassie came, I said, 'Thank God, now Bumper's got a chance.' I worried though. I knew you were smart enough to see how much woman you had, but I was afraid that *puta* had too strong a grip on you."

"Was it *you* that kept getting me assigned to the north end districts all the time? Lieutenant Hilliard keep telling me it was a mistake every time I bitched about it."

"Yeah, I did it. I tried to get you away from your beat, but I gave up. You just kept coming back down anyway and that meant nobody was patrolling the north end, so I didn't accomplish anything. I can guess what it was to you, being *el campeón* out there, having people look at you the way they do on your beat."

"Yeah, well it isn't so much," I said, nervously fidgeting with the empty bottle.

"You know what happens to old cops who stay around the streets too long."

"What?" I said, and the enchilada caught me and bit into the inside of my gut.

"They get too old to do police work and they become *characters*. That's what I'd hate to see. You just becoming an old character, and maybe getting yourself hurt bad out there before you realize you're too old. Just too old."

"I'm not that old yet. Damn it, Cruz!"

"No, not for civilian life. You have lots of good years ahead of you. But for a warrior, it's time to quit, *'mano*. I was worried about her going up there and you coming along in a few weeks. I was afraid the *puta* would get you alone when Cassie wasn't there. I'm so damn glad you're leaving with Cassie."

"So am I, Cruz," I said, lowering my voice like I was afraid to let myself hear it. "You're right. I've half thought of these things. You're right. I think I'd blow my brains out if I ever got as lonely as some I've seen, like some of those people on my beat, homeless wandering people, that don't belong anywhere. . . ."

"That's it, Bumper. There's no place for a man alone, not really. You can get along without love when you're young and strong. Some guys can, guys like you. Me, I never could. And nobody can get along without it when he gets old. You shouldn't be afraid to love, *'mano*."

"Am I, Cruz?" I asked, chewing two tablets because a mailed fist was beating on my guts from the inside. "Is that why I feel so unsure of myself now that I'm leaving? Is that it?"

I could hear Socorro humming as she made lunches for the entire tribe. She would write each one's name on his lunch sack and put it in the refrigerator.

"Remember when we were together in the old days? You and me and Socorro and the two kids? And how you hardly ever spoke about your previous life even when you were drunk? You only said a little about your brother Clem who was dead, and your wife who'd left you. But you really told us more, much more about your brother. Sometimes you called him in your sleep. But mostly you called someone else."

I was rocking back now, holding my guts which were throbbing, and all the tablets in my pocket wouldn't help.

"You never told us about your boy. I always felt bad that you never told *me* about him, because of how close we are. You only told me about him in your sleep."

"What did I say?"

"You'd call 'Billy,' and you'd say things to him. Sometimes you'd cry, and I'd have to go in and pick up your covers and pillow from the floor and cover you up because you'd throw them clear off the bed."

"I never dreamed about him, never!"

"How else would I know, *'mano?*" he said softly. "We used to talk a lot about it, Socorro and me, and we used to worry about a man who'd loved a brother and a son like you had. We wondered if you'd be afraid to love again. It happens. But when you get old, you've got to. You've *got* to."

"But you're safe if you *don't*, Cruz!" I said, flinching from the pain. Cruz was looking at the floor, not used to talking to me like this, and he didn't notice my agony.

"You're safe, Bumper, in one way. But in the way that counts, you're in danger. Your soul is in danger if you don't love."

"Did you believe that when Esteban was killed? Did you?"

Cruz looked up at me, and his eyes got even softer than normal and turned way down at the corners because he was being most serious. His heavy lashes blinked twice and he sighed, "Yes. Even after Esteban, and even though he was the oldest and you always feel a little something extra for the firstborn. Even after Esteban was killed I felt this to be the truth. After the grief, I knew it was God's truth. I believed it, even then."

"I think I'll get a cup of coffee. I have a stomachache. Maybe something warm. . . ."

Cruz smiled, and leaned back in his chair. Socorro was finishing the last of the lunches and I chatted with her while we warmed up the coffee. The stomachache started to fade a little.

I drank the coffee and thought about what Cruz said which made sense, and yet, every time you get tied up to people something happens and that cord is cut, and I mean really cut with a bloody sword.

"Shall we go in and see how the old boy's doing?"

"Oh sure, Sukie," I said, putting my arm around her shoulder. Cruz was stretched out on the couch snoring.

"That's his drinking sleep. We'll never wake him up," she said. "Maybe I just better get his pillow and a blanket."

"He shouldn't be sleeping on the couch," I said. "It's drafty in this big living room." I went over to him and knelt down.

"What're you going to do?"

"Put him to bed," I said, picking him up in my arms.

"Bumper, you'll rupture yourself."

"He's light as a baby," I said, and he *was* surprisingly light. "Why the hell don't you make him eat more?" I said, following Socorro up the stairs.

"You know he doesn't like to eat. Let me help you, Bumper."

"Just lead the way, Mama. I can handle him just fine."

When we got in their bedroom I wasn't even breathing hard and I laid him on the bed, on the sheets. She had already pulled back the covers. Cruz was rattling and wheezing now and we both laughed.

"He snores awful," she said as I looked at the little squirt.

"He's the only *real* friend I ever made in twenty years. I know millions of people and I see them and eat with them and I'll miss things about all of them, but it won't be like something inside is gone, like with Cruz."

"Now you'll have Cassie. You'll be ten times closer with her." She held my hand then. Both her hands were tough and hard.

"You sound like your old man."

"We talk about you a lot."

"Good night," I said, kissing her on the cheek. "Cassie and me are coming by before we leave to say goodbye to all of you."

"Good night, Bumper."

"Good night, old shoe," I said to Cruz in a loud voice and he snorted and blew and I chuckled and descended the stairs. I let myself out after turning out the hall light and locking the door.

When I went to bed that night I started getting scared and didn't know why. I wished Cassie was with me. After I went to sleep I slept very well and didn't dream.

Thursday, the second day

9

THE NEXT MORNING I worked on my badge for five minutes, and my boondockers were glistening. I was kind of disappointed when Lieutenant Hilliard didn't have an inspection, I was looking so good. Cruz looked awful. He sat at the front table with Lieutenant Hilliard and did a bad job of reading off the crimes. Once or twice he looked at me and rolled his eyes which were really sad this morning because he was so hung over. After rollcall I got a chance to talk to him for a minute.

"You look a little *crudo*," I said, trying not to smile.

"What a bastard you are," he moaned.

"It wasn't the mescal. I think you swallowed the worm."

"A complete bastard."

"Can you meet me at noon? I wanna buy you lunch."

"Don't even talk about it," he groaned, and I had to laugh.

"Okay, but save me your lunch hour tomorrow. And pick out the best, most expensive place in town. Somewhere that doesn't bounce for bluecoats. That's where we're going for my last meal as a cop."

"You're actually going to *pay* for a meal on duty?"

"It'll be a first," I grinned, and he smiled but he acted like it hurt to grin.

"*Ahí te haucho*," I said, heading for the car.

"Don't forget you have court this afternoon, *'mano*," he said, always nagging me.

Before getting into my black-and-white I looked it over. It's always good to pull out the back seat before you leave, in case some innocent rookie on the night-watch let one of his sneaky prisoners stash his gun down there, or a condom full of heroin, or a goddamn hand grenade. It takes so long to make a policeman out of some of these kids, nothing would surprise me. But then I reminded myself what it was like to be twenty-two. They're right in the middle of growing up, these babies, and it's awful tough growing up in that bluecoat as twenty-two-year-old Establishment symbols. Still, it chills my nuts the way they stumble around like civilians for five years or so, and let people flimflam them. Someday, I thought, I'll probably find a dead midget jammed down there behind the friggin' seat.

As soon as I hit the bricks and started cruising I began thinking about the case I had this afternoon. It was a preliminary hearing on a guy named Landry and the dicks had filed on him for being an ex-con with a gun, and also filed one count of possession of marijuana. I didn't figure to have any problems with the case. I'd busted him in January after I'd gotten information on this gunsel from a snitch named Knobby Booker, who worked for me from time to time, and I went to a hotel room on East Sixth Street on some phony pretext I couldn't completely remember until I reread the arrest report. I busted Landry in his room while he was taking a nap in the middle of the afternoon. He had about two lids of pot in a sandwich bag in a drawer by his bed to give him guts when he pulled a robbery, and a fully loaded U.S. Army forty-five automatic under his mattress. He damned near went for it when I came through the door, and I almost blew him up when he started for it. In fact, it was a Mexican standoff for a few seconds, him with his hand an inch or so under the mattress, and me crouching and coming to the bed, my six-inch Smith aimed at his upper lip, and warning about what I was going to do if he didn't pull his hand out very very slow, and he did.

Landry had gotten out on five thousand dollars' bail which some old broad put up for him. He'd been a half-assed bit actor on TV and movies a few years back, and was somewhat of a gigolo with old women. He jumped bail and was rearrested in Denver and extradited, and the arrest was now four months old. I didn't remember all the details, but of course I would read the arrest report and be up on it before I testified. The main thing of course was to hold him to answer at the prelim without revealing my informant Knobby Booker, or without even letting anyone know I *had* an informant. It wasn't too hard if you knew how.

It was getting hot and smoggy and I was already starting to sweat in the armpits. I glanced over at an old billboard on Olive Street which said, "Don't start a boy on a life of crime by leaving your keys in the car," and I snorted and farted a couple of times in disgust. It's the goddamn do-gooder P.R. men, who dream up slogans like that to make everybody but the criminals feel guilty, who'll drive all *real* cops out of this business one of these days.

As I pulled to the curb opposite the Grand Central Market, a wino staggering down Broadway sucking on a short dog saw me, spun around, fell on his ass, dropped his bottle, and got up as though nothing happened. He started walking away from the short dog, which was rolling around on the sidewalk spilling sweet lucy all over the pavement.

"Pick up the dog, you jerk," I called to him. "I ain't gonna bust you."

"Thanks, Bumper," he said sheepishly and picked up the bottle. He waved, and hustled back down Broadway, a greasy black coat flapping around his skinny hips.

I tried to remember where I knew him from. Of course I knew him from the beat, but he wasn't just a wino face. There was something else. Then I saw through the gauntness and grime and recognized him and smiled because these days it always felt good to remember and prove to yourself that your memory is as sharp as ever.

They called him Beans. The real name I couldn't recall even though I'd had it printed up on a fancy certificate. He almost caused me to slug another policeman about ten years ago and I'd never come close to doing that before or since.

The policeman was Herb Slovin and he finally got his ass canned. Herb was fired for capping for a bail bondsman and had a nice thing going until they caught him. He was working vice and was telling everybody he busted to patronize Laswell Brothers Bail Bonds, and Slim Laswell was kicking back a few bucks to Herb for each one he sent. That's considered to be as bad as stealing, and the Department bounced his ass in a hurry after he was caught. He would've gone behind something else though if it hadn't been that. He was a hulking, cruel bastard and so horny he'd mount a cage if he thought there was a canary in there. I figured sooner or later he'd fall for broads or brutality.

It was Beans that almost caused me and Herb to tangle. Herb hated the drunk wagon. "Niggers and white garbage," he'd repeat over and over when something made him mad which was most of the time. And he called the wagon job "the N.H.I. detail." When you asked him what that stood for he'd say "No Humans Involved," and then he let out with that donkey bray of his. We were working the wagon one night and got a call on Beans because he was spread-eagled prone across San Pedro Street blocking two lanes of traffic, out cold. He'd puked and wet all over himself and didn't even wake up when we dragged him to the wagon and flipped him in on the floor. There was no problem. We both wore gloves like most wagon cops, and there were only two other winos inside. About ten minutes later when we were on East Sixth Street, we heard a ruckus in the back and had to stop the wagon and go back there and keep the other two winos from kicking hell out of Beans who woke up and was fighting mad for maybe the first time in his life. I'd busted him ten or twenty times for drunk and never had any trouble with him. You seldom have to hassle a stone wino like Beans.

They quieted down as soon as Herb opened the back door and threatened to tear their heads off, and I was just getting back in the wagon when Beans, sitting by the door, said, "Fuck you, you skin-headed jackass!" I cracked up laughing because Herb was bald, and with his long face and big yellow teeth and the way he brayed when he laughed, he *did* look like a skin-headed jackass.

Herb though, growled something, and snatched Beans right off the bench, out of the wagon into the street, and started belting him back and forth across the face with his big gloved hand. I realized from the thuds that they were sap gloves and Beans's face was already busted open and bleeding before I could pull Herb away and push him back, causing him to fall on his ass.

"You son of a bitch," he said, looking at me with a combination of surprise and blood red anger. He almost said it like a question he was so surprised.

"He's a wino, man," I answered, and that should've been enough for any cop, especially a veteran like Herb who had twelve years on the job at that time and knew that you don't beat up defenseless winos no matter what kind of trouble they give you. That was one of the first things we learned in the old days from the beat cops who broke us in. When a man takes a swing at you or actually hits you, you have the right to kick ass, that goes without saying. It doesn't have to be tit for tat, and if some asshole gives you tit, you tat his goddamn teeth down his throat. That way, you'll save some other cop from being slugged by the same pukepot if he learns his lesson from you.

But every real cop also knows you don't beat up winos. Even if they swing at you or actually hit you. Chances are it'll be a puny little swing and you can just handcuff him and throw him in jail. Cops know very well how many fellow policemen develop drinking problems themselves, and there's always the thought in the back of your mind that there on the sidewalk, but for the gods, sleeps old Bumper Morgan.

Anyway, Herb had violated a cop's code by beating up the wino and he knew it, which probably saved us a hell of a good go right there on East Sixth Street. And I'm not at all sure it might not've ended up by me getting my chubby face changed around by those sap gloves because Herb was an ex-wrestler and a very tough bastard.

"Don't you ever try that again," he said to me, as we put Beans back inside and locked the door.

"I won't, if you never beat up a drunk when you're working with me," I answered casually, but I was tense and coiled, ready to go, even thinking about unsnapping my holster because Herb looked damned dangerous at that moment, and you never know when an armed man might do something crazy. He was one of those creeps that carried an untraceable hideout gun and bragged how if he ever killed somebody he shouldn't have, he'd plant the gun on the corpse and claim self-defense. The mood was interrupted by a radio call just then, and I rogered it and we finished the night in silence. The next night Herb asked to go back to a radio car because him and me had a "personality conflict."

Shortly after that Herb went to vice and got fired, and I forgot all about that incident until about a year later on Main Street, when I ran into Beans again. That night I got into a battle with two guys I'd watched pull a pigeon drop on some old man. I'd stood inside a pawnshop and watched them through binoculars while they flimflammed him out of five hundred bucks.

They were bad young dudes, and the bigger of the two, a block-faced slob with an eighteen-inch neck was giving me a pretty good go, even though I'd already cracked two of his ribs with my stick. I couldn't finish him because the other one kept jumping on my back, kicking and biting, until I ran backward and slammed into a car and a brick wall, with him between me and the object. I did this twice and he kept hanging on and then somebody from the crowd of about twenty assholes who were gathered around enjoying the fight barreled in and tackled the little one and held him on the sidewalk until I could finish the big one by slapping him across the Adam's apple with the stick.

The other one gave up right then and I cuffed the two of them together and saw that my helper was old Beans the wino, sitting there throwing up, and bleeding from a cut eye where the little dude clawed him. I gave Beans a double sawbuck for that, and took him to a doctor, and I had the Captain's adjutant print up a beautiful certificate commending Beans for his good citizenship. Of course, I lied and said Beans was some respectable businessman who saw the fight and came to my aid. I couldn't tell them he was a down-and-out wino or they might not have done it. It was nicely framed and had Beans's real name on it, which I couldn't for the life of me remember now. I presented it to him the next time I found him bombed on East Sixth Street and he really seemed to like it.

As I remembered all this, I felt like calling him back and asking him if he still had it, but I figured he probably sold the frame for enough to buy a short dog, and used the certificate to plug the holes in his shoe. It's always best not to ask too many questions of people or to get to know them too well. You save yourself disappointment that way. Anyway, Beans was half a block away now, staggering down the street cradling the wine bottle under his greasy coat.

I took down my sunglasses which I keep stashed behind the visor in my car and settled down to cruise and watch the streets and relax even though I was too restless to really relax. I decided not to wait, but to cruise over to the school and see Cassie, who would be coming in early like she always did on Thursdays. She'd feel like I did, like everything she did these last days at school would be for the last time. But at least she knew she'd be doing similar things in another school.

I parked out front and got a few raspberries from the students for parking my black-and-white in the no parking zone, but I'd be damned if I'd walk clear from the faculty lot. Cassie wasn't in her office when I got there, but it was unlocked so I sat at her desk and waited.

The desk was exactly like the woman who manned it: smart and tidy, interesting and feminine. She had an odd-shaped ceramic ashtray on one side of the desk which she'd picked up in some junk store in west L.A. There was a small, delicately painted oriental vase that held a bunch of dying violets which Cassie would replace first thing after she arrived. Under the plastic cover on the desk blotter Cassie had a screwy selection of pictures of people she admired, mostly French poets. Cassie was long on poetry and tried to get me going on haiku for a while, but I finally convinced her I don't have the right kind of imagination for poetry. My reading is limited to history and to new ways of doing police work. I liked one poem Cassie showed me about wooly lambs and shepherds and wild killer dogs. I understood that one all right.

The door opened and Cassie and another teacher, a curvy little chicken in a hot pink mini, came giggling through the door.

"Oh!" said the young broad. "Who are you?" The blue uniform shocked her. I was sitting back in Cassie's comfortable leather-padded desk chair.

"I am the Pretty Good Shepherd," I said, puffing on my cigar and smiling at Cassie.

"Whatever that means," said Cassie, shaking her head, putting down a load of books, and kissing me on the cheek much to the surprise of her friend.

"You must be Cassie's fiancé," the friend laughed as it suddenly hit her. "I'm Maggie Carson."

"Pleased to meet you, Maggie. I'm Bumper Morgan," I said, always happy to meet a woman, especially a young one, who shakes hands, and with a firm friendly grip.

''I've heard about Cassie's policeman friend, but it surprised me, seeing that uniform so suddenly.''

''We've all got our skeletons rattling, Maggie,'' I said. ''Tell me, what've you done that makes you jump at the sight of the fuzz?''

''All right, Bumper,'' Cassie smiled. I was standing now, and she had me by the arm.

''I'll leave you two alone,'' said Maggie, with a sly wink, just as she'd seen and heard it in a thousand corny love movies.

''Nice kid,'' I said, after Maggie closed the door and I kissed Cassie four or five times.

''I missed you last night,'' said Cassie, standing there pressed up against me, smelling good and looking good in her yellow sleeveless dress. Her arms were red tan, her hair down, touching her shoulders.

''Your dinner date tonight still on?''

''Afraid so,'' she murmured.

''After tomorrow we'll have all the time we want together.''

''Think we'll ever have all the time we want?''

''You'll get sick of seeing me hanging around the pad.''

''Never happen. Besides, you'll be busy launching that new career.''

''I'm more worried about the other career.''

''Which one?''

''Being the kind of husband you think I'll be. I wonder if I'll be really good for you.''

''Bumper!'' she said, stepping back and looking to see if I meant it, and I tried a lopsided grin.

I kissed her then, as tenderly as I could, and held her. ''I didn't mean it the way it came out.''

''I know. I'm just a very insecure old dame.''

I could've kicked my ass for blurting out something that I knew would hurt her. It was like I wanted to hurt her a little for being the best thing that ever happened, for saving me from becoming a pitiful old man trying to do a young man's work, and doing brass balls police work was definitely a young man's work. I never could've been an inside man. Never a jailer, or a desk officer, or a supply man handing out weapons to guys doing the real police work. Cassie was saving me from that nightmare. I was getting out while I was still a man alive, with lots of good years ahead. And with somebody to care about. I got a vicious gas pain just then, and I wished I wasn't standing there with Cassie so I could pop a bubble breaker.

''I guess *I'm* the silly one,'' said Cassie.

''If you only knew how bad I want out, Cassie, you'd stop worrying.'' I patted her back like I was burping her when really I was wishing I could burp myself. I could feel the bubble getting bigger and floating up in my stomach.

''All right, Bumper Morgan,'' she said. ''Now what day are we actually leaving Los Angeles? I mean actually? As man and wife. We've got a million things to do.''

''Wait till tomorrow night, me proud beauty,'' I answered. ''Tomorrow night when we have some time to talk and to celebrate. Tomorrow night we make all the plans while having a wonderful dinner somewhere.''

''In my apartment.''

''Okay.''

''With some wonderful champagne.''

''I'll supply it.''

''Police discount?''

''Naturally. My last one.''

''And we celebrate tomorrow being the last day you'll ever have to put on that uniform and risk your neck for a lot of people who don't appreciate it.''

"Last day I risk my neck," I nodded. "But I never did risk it for anyone but myself. I had some fun these twenty years, Cassie."

"I know it."

"Even though sometimes it's a rotten job I wouldn't wish on anyone, still, I had good times. And any risks were for Bumper Morgan."

"Yes, love."

"So get your heart-shaped fanny in gear and get your day's work done. I still got almost two days of police work left to do." I stepped away from her and picked up my hat and cigar.

"Coming by this afternoon?"

"Tomorrow."

"Tonight," she said. "I'll get away before midnight. Come to my apartment at midnight."

"Let's get some sleep tonight, baby. Tomorrow's the last day for us both on our jobs. Let's make it a good one."

"I don't like my job as well since you charged into my life, do you know that?"

"Whadda you mean?"

"The academic life. I was one of the students who never left school. I loved waddling around with a gaggle of eggheads, and then *you* had to come along so, so . . . I don't know. And now nothing seems the same."

"Come on down, kid, I like your earthy side better."

"I want you to come tonight," she said, looking me dead in the eye.

"I'd rather be with you tonight than with anyone in the world, you know that, but I really ought to go by Abd's Harem and say good-bye to my friends there. And there're a few other places."

"You mustn't disappoint people," she smiled.

"You should try not to," I said, heating up from the way she looked me in the eye just then.

"It's getting tough to make love to you lately."

"A couple more days."

"See you tomorrow," she sighed. "I think I'll jump you here in my office when I get my hands on you."

"On duty?" I frowned, and put my hat on, tipping it at a jaunty angle because, let's face it, you feel pretty good when a woman like Cassie's quivering to get you in bed.

"Good-bye, Bumper," she smiled sadly.

"Later, kid. See you later."

As soon as I cleared after leaving Cassie I got a radio call.

"One-X-L-Forty-five, One-X-L-Forty-five," said the female communications operator, "see the man at the hotel, four-twenty-five South Main, about a possible d.b."

"One-X-L-Forty-five, roger," I said, thinking this will be my last dead body call.

An old one-legged guy with all the earmarks of a reformed alky was standing in the doorway of the fleabag hotel.

"You called?" I said, after parking the black-and-white in front and taking the stick from the holder on the door and slipping it through the ring on my belt.

"Yeah. I'm Poochie the elevator boy," said the old man. "I think a guy might be dead upstairs."

"What the hell made you think so?" I said sarcastically, as we started up the stairs and I smelled the d.b. from here. The floorboards were torn up and I could see the ground underneath.

The old guy hopped up the stairs pretty quick on his one crutch without ever stopping to rest. There were about twenty steps up to the second floor where the smell could drop you and would, except that most of the tenants were bums and winos whose senses, all of them, had been killed or numbed. I almost expected the second story to have a dirt floor, the place was so crummy.

"I ain't seen this guy in number two-twelve for oh, maybe a week," said Poochie, who had a face like an ax, with a toothless puckered mouth.

"Can't you smell him?"

"No," he said, looking at me with surprise. "Can you?"

"Never mind," I said, turning right in the hallway. "Don't bother telling me where two-twelve is, I could find it with my eyes closed. Get me some coffee."

"Cream and sugar?"

"No, I mean dry coffee, right out of the can. And a frying pan."

"Okay," he said, without asking dumb questions, conditioned by fifty years of being bossed around by cops. I held a handkerchief over my nose, and opened a window in the hallway which led out on the fire escape in the alley. I stuck my head out but it didn't help, I could still smell him.

After a long two minutes Poochie came hopping back on his crutch with a frying pan and the coffee.

"Hope there's a hot plate in here," I said, suddenly thinking there might not be, though lots of the transient hotels had them, especially in the rooms used by the semipermanent boarders.

"He's got one," nodded Poochie, handing me the passkey. The key turned but the door wouldn't budge.

"I coulda told you it wouldn't open. That's why I called you. Scared old man, Herky is. He keeps a bolt on the door whenever he's inside. I already tried to get in."

"Move back."

"Going to break it?"

"Got any other suggestions?" I said, the handkerchief over my face, breathing through my mouth.

"No, I think I can smell him now."

I booted the door right beside the lock and it crashed open, ripping the jamb loose. One rusty hinge tore free and the door dangled there by the bottom hinge.

"Yeah, he's dead," said Poochie, looking at Herky who had been dead for maybe five days, swollen and steamy in this unventilated room which not only had a hot plate, but a small gas heater that was raging on an eighty-five degree day.

"Can I look at him?" said Poochie, standing next to the bed, examining Herky's bloated stomach and rotting face. His eyelids were gone and the eyes stared silver and dull at the elevator boy who grinned toothlessly and clucked at the maggots on Herky's face and swollen sex organs.

I ran across the room and banged on the frame until I got the window open. Flies were crawling all over the glass, leaving wet tracks in the condensation. Then I ran to the hot plate, lit it, and threw the frying pan on the burner. I dumped the whole can of coffee on the frying pan, but the elevator boy was enjoying himself so much he didn't seem to mind my extravagance with his coffee. In a few minutes the coffee was burning, and a pungent smoky odor was filling the room, almost neutralizing the odor of Herky.

"You don't mind if I look at him?" asked Poochie again.

"Knock yourself out, pal," I answered, going for the door.

"Been dead a while hasn't he?"

"Little while longer and he'd have gone clear through the mattress."

I walked to the pay phone at the end of the hall on the second floor. "Come with me, pal," I called, figuring he'd roll old Herky soon as my back was turned. It's bad enough getting rolled when you're alive.

I put a dime in the pay phone and dialed operator. "Police department," I said, then waited for my dime to return as she rang the station. The dime didn't come. I looked hard at Poochie who turned away, very innocently.

"Someone stuffed the goddamn chute," I said. "Some asshole's gonna get my dime when he pulls the stuffing out later."

"Bunch of thieves around here, Officer," said Poochie, all puckered and a little chalkier than before.

I called the dicks and asked for one to come down and take the death report, then I hung up and lit a cigar, not that I really wanted one, but any smell would do at the moment.

"Is it true they explode like a bomb after a while?"

"What?"

"Stiffs. Like old Herky."

"Yeah, he'd've been all over your wallpaper pretty soon."

"Damn," said the elevator boy, grinning big and showing lots of gums, upper and lower. "Some of these guys like Herky got lots of dough hidden around," he said, winking at me.

"Yeah, well let's let him keep it. He's had it this long."

"Oh, I didn't mean we should take it."

"Course not."

"It's just that these coroner guys, they get to steal anything they find laying around."

"How long's old Herky been living here?" I asked, not bothering to find out his whole name. I'd let the detective worry about the report.

"Off and on, over five years I know of. All alone. Never even had no friends. Nobody. Just laid up there in that room sucking up the sneaky pete. Used to drink a gallon a day. I think he lived off his social security. Pay his rent, eat a little, drink a little. I never could do it myself. That's why I'm elevator boy. Can't make it on that social security."

"You ever talk to him?"

"Yeah, he never had nothing to say though. No family. Never been married. No relatives to speak of. Really alone, you know? I got me eight kids spread all over this damn country. I can go sponge off one of them ever' once in a while. Never gonna see old Poochie like that." He winked and tapped his chest with a bony thumb. "Guys like old Herky, they don't care about nobody and nobody cares about them. They check out of this world grabbing their throat and staring around a lonely hotel room. Those're the guys that swell up and pop all over your walls. Guys like old Herky." The elevator boy thought about old Herky popping, and he broke out in a snuffling croupy laugh because that was just funny as hell.

I hung around the lobby waiting for the detective to arrive and relieve me of caring for the body. While I was waiting I started examining both sides of the staircase walls. It was the old kind with a scalloped molding about seven feet up, and at the first landing there were dirty finger streaks below the molding while the rest of the wall on both sides was uniformly dirty, but unsmudged. I walked to the landing and reached up on the ledge, feeling a toilet-paper-wrapped bundle. I opened it and found a complete outfit: eyedropper, hypodermic needle, a piece of heavy thread, burned spoon, and razor blade.

I broke the eye dropper, bent the needle, and threw the hype kit in the trash can behind the rickety desk in the lobby.

"What's that?" asked the elevator boy.

"A fit."

"A hype's outfit?"

"Yeah."

"How'd you know it was there?"

"Elementary, my dear Poochie."

"That's pretty goddamn good."

The detective came in carrying a clipboard full of death reports. He was one of the newer ones, a young collegiate-looking type. I didn't know him. I talked to him for a few minutes and the elevator boy took him back to the body.

"Never catch old Poochie going it alone," he called to me with his gums showing. "Never gonna catch old Poochie busting like a balloon and plastered to your wallpaper."

"Good for you, Poochie," I nodded, taking a big breath out on the sidewalk, thinking I could still smell the dead body. I imagined that his odor was clinging to my clothes and I goosed the black-and-white, ripping off some rubber in my hurry to get away from that room.

I drove around for a while and started wondering what I should work on. I thought about the hotel burglar again and wondered if I could find Link Owens, a good little hotel creeper, who might be able to tell me something about this guy that'd been hitting us so hard. All hotel burglars know each other. Sometimes you see so many of them hanging around the lobbies of the better hotels, it looks like a thieves' convention. Then I got the code-two call to go to the station.

10

Code two means hurry up, and whenever policemen get that call to go to the station they start worrying about things. I've had a hundred partners tell me that: "What did I do wrong? Am I in trouble? Did something happen to the old lady? The kids?" I never had such thoughts, of course. A code-two call to go to the station just meant to me that they had some special shit detail they needed a man for, and mine happened to be the car they picked.

When I got to the watch commander's office, Lieutenant Hilliard was sitting at his desk reading the morning editorials, his millions of wrinkles deeper than usual, looking as mean as he always did when he read the cop-baiting letters to the editor and editorial cartoons which snipe at cops. He never stopped reading them though, and scowling all the way.

"Hi, Bumper," he said, glancing up. "One of the vice officers wants you in his office. Something about a bookmaker you turned for them?"

"Oh yeah, one of my snitches gave him some information yesterday. Guess Charlie Bronski needs to talk to me some more."

"Going to take down a bookie, Bumper?" Hilliard grinned. He was a hell of a copper in his day. He wore seven service stripes on his left forearm, each one signifying five years' service. His thin hands were knobby and covered with bulging blue veins. He had trouble with bone deterioration now, and walked with a cane.

"I'm a patrol officer. Can't be doing vice work. No time."

"If you've got something going with Bronski, go ahead and work on it. Vice caper or not, it's all police work. Besides, I've never seen many uniformed policemen tear off a bookmaker. That's about the only kind of pinch you've never made for me, Bumper."

"We'll see what we can do, Lieutenant," I smiled, and left him there, scowling at the editorials again, an old man that should've pulled the pin years ago. Now he'd been here too long. He couldn't leave or he'd die. And he couldn't do the work anymore, so he just sat and talked police work to other guys like him who believed police work meant throwing lots of bad guys in jail and that all your other duties were just incidental. The young officers were afraid to get close to the watch commander's office when he was in there. I've seen rookies call a sergeant out into the hall to have him approve a report so they wouldn't have to take it to Lieutenant Hilliard. He demanded excellence, especially on reports. Nobody's ever asked that of the young cops who were TV babies, not in all their lives. So he was generally avoided by the men he commanded.

Charlie Bronski was in his office with two other vice officers when I entered.

"What's up, Charlie?" I asked.

"We had some unbelievable luck, Bumper. We ran the phone number and it comes back to an apartment on Hobart near Eighth Street, and Red Scalotta hangs around Eighth Street quite a bit when he's not at his restaurant on Wilshire. I'm betting that phone number you squeezed out of Zoot goes right into Reba McClain's pad just like I hoped. She always stays close by Red, but never *too* close. Red's been married happily for thirty years and has a daughter in Stanford and a son in medical school. Salt of the earth, that asshole is."

"Gave nine thousand last year to two separate churches in Beverly Hills," said one of the other vice officers, who looked like a wild young head with his collar-length hair, and beard, and floppy hat with peace and pot buttons all over it. He wore a cruddy denim shirt cut off at the shoulders and looked like a typical Main Street fruit hustler.

"And God returns it a hundredfold," said the other vice officer, Nick Papalous, a melancholy-looking guy, with small white teeth. Nick had a big Zapata moustache, sideburns, and wore orange-flowered flares. I'd worked with Nick several times before he went to vice. He was a good cop for being so young.

"You seemed pretty hot on taking a book, Bumper, so I thought I'd see if you wanted to go with us. This isn't going to be a back office, but it might lead to one, thanks to your friend Zoot. What do you say, want to come?"

"Do I have to change to civvies?"

"Not if you don't want to. Nick and Fuzzy here are going to take the door down. You and me could stiff in the call from the pay phone at the corner. Your uniform wouldn't get in the way."

"Okay, let's go," I said, anxious for a little action, glad I didn't have to take the uniform off. "Never went on a vice raid before. Do we have to circumcise our watches and all that?"

"I'll do the door," Nick grinned. "Fuzzy'll watch out the window and keep an eyeball on you and Bumper down at the pay phone on the corner. When you get the bet stiffed, Fuzzy'll see your signal and give me the okay and down goes the door."

"Kind of touch kicking, ain't it, Nick, in those crepe-soled, sneak-and-peek shoes you guys wear?"

"Damn straight, Bumper," Nick smiled. "I could sure use those size-twelve boondockers of yours."

"Thirteens," I said.

"Wish I could take down the door," said Fuzzy. "Nothing I like better than John Wayne-ing a goddamn door."

"Tell Bumper why you can't, Fuzzy," Nick grinned.

"Got a sprained ankle and a pulled hamstring," said Fuzzy, taking a few limping steps to show me. "I was off duty for two weeks."

"Tell Bumper how it happened," said Nick, still grinning.

"Freakin' fruit," said Fuzzy, pulling off the wide-brimmed hat and throwing back his long blond hair. "We got a vice complaint about this fruit down at the main library, hangs around out back and really comes on strong with every young guy he sees."

"Fat mother," said Charlie. "Almost as heavy as you, Bumper. And strong."

"Damn!" said Fuzzy, shaking his head, looking serious even though Nick was still grinning. "You shoulda seen the arms on that animal! Anyway, I get picked to operate him, naturally."

"'Cause you're so pretty, Fuzzy," said Charlie.

"Yeah, anyway, I go out there, about two in the afternoon, and hang around a little bit, and sure enough, there he is standing by that scrub oak tree and I don't know which one's the freakin' tree for a couple minutes, he's so wide. And I swear I never saw a hornier fruit in my life 'cause I just walked up and said, 'Hi.' That's all, I swear."

"Come on, Fuzzy, you winked at him," said Charlie, winking at me.

"You asshole," said Fuzzy. "I swear I just said, 'Hi, Brucie,' or something like that, and this mother grabbed me. Grabbed me! In a bear hug! He pinned my arms! I was shocked, I tell you! Then he starts bouncing me up and down against his fat belly, saying, 'You're so cute. You're so cute. You're so cute.' "

Then Fuzzy stood up and started bouncing up and down with his arms up against his sides and his head bobbing. "Like this I was," said Fuzzy. "Like a goddamn rag doll bouncing, and I said, 'Y-y-y-you're u-u-u-under a-a-a-arrest,' and he stopped loving me and said, 'What?' and I said, 'YOU'RE UNDER ARREST, YOU FAT ZOMBIE!' And he threw me. Threw me! And I rolled down the hill and crashed into the concrete steps. And you know what happens then? My partner here lets him get away. He claims he couldn't catch the asshole and the guy couldn't run no faster than a pregnant alligator. My brave partner!"

"Fuzzy really wants that guy bad," Charlie grinned. "I tried to catch him, honest, Fuzzy." Then to me, "I think Fuzzy fell in love. He wanted the fat boy's phone number."

"Yuk!" said Fuzzy, getting a chill as he thought about it. "We got a warrant for that prick for battery on a police officer. Wait'll I get him. I'll get that prick in a choke hold and lobotomize him!"

"By the way, what's the signal you use for crashing in the pad?" I asked.

"We always give it this," said Charlie, pumping his closed fist up and down.

"Double time," I smiled. "Hey, that takes me back to my old infantry days." I felt good now, getting to do something a little different. Maybe I should've tried working vice, I thought, but no, I've had lots more action and lots more variety on my beat. That's where it's at. That's where it's really at.

"Reba must have some fine, fine pussy," said Fuzzy, puffing on a slim cigar and cocking his head at Charlie. I could tell by the smell it was a ten- or fifteen-center. I'd quit smoking first, I thought.

"She's been with Red a few years now," said Nick to Fuzzy. "Wait'll you meet her. Those mug shots don't do her justice. Good-looking snake."

"You cold-blooded vice cops don't care how good-looking a broad is," I said, needling Charlie. "All a broad is to you is a booking number. I'll bet when some fine-looking whore thinking you're a trick lays down and spreads her legs, you just drop that cold badge right on top of her."

"Right on her bare tummy," said Nick. "But I'll bet Reba has more than a nice tight pussy. A guy like Scalotta could have a million broads. She must give extra good head or something."

"That's what I need, a little skull," said Fuzzy, leaning back in a swivel chair, his soft-soled shoes propped up on a desk. He was a pink-faced kid above the beard, not a day over twenty-four, I'd guess.

"A *little* skull'd be the first you ever had, Fuzzy," said Nick.

"Ha!" said Fuzzy, the cigar clenched in his teeth. "I used to have this Chinese girlfriend that was a go-go dancer. . . ."

"Come on, Fuzzy," said Charlie, "let's not start those lies about all the puss you got when you worked Hollywood. Fuzzy's laid every toadie on Sunset Boulevard three times."

"I can tell you yellow is mellow," Fuzzy leered. "This chick wouldn't ball nobody but me. She used to wet her pants playing with the hair on my chest." Fuzzy stood up then, and flexed his bicep.

Nick, always a man of few words, said, ''Siddown, fruitbait.''

''Anyway, Reba ain't just a good head job,'' said Charlie. ''That's not why Scalotta keeps her. He's a leather freak and likes to savage a broad. Dresses her up in animal skins and whales the shit out of her.''

''I never really believed those rumors,'' said Nick.

''No shit?'' said Fuzzy, really interested now.

''We had a snitch tell us about it one time,'' said Charlie. ''The snitch said Red Scalotta digs dykes and whips and Reba's his favorite. The snitch told us it's the only way Red can get it up anymore.''

''He *is* an old guy,'' said Fuzzy seriously. ''At least fifty, I think.''

''Reba's a stone psycho, I tell you,'' said Charlie. ''Remember when we busted her, Nick? How she kept talking all the way to jail about the bull daggers and how they'd chase her around the goddamn jail cell before she could get bailed out.''

''That broad got dealt a bum hand,'' said Nick.

''Ain't got a full deck even now,'' Charlie agreed.

''She's scared of butches and yet she puts on dyke shows for Red Scalotta?'' said Fuzzy, his bearded baby face split by a grin as he pictured it.

''Let's get it over with,'' said Charlie. ''Then we can spend the rest of the day shooting pool in a nice cool beer bar, listening to Fuzzy's stories about all those Hollywood groupies.''

Nick and Fuzzy took one vice car and I rode with Charlie in another one. It's always possible there could be more than one in the pad, and they wanted room for prisoners.

''Groovy machine, Charlie,'' I said, looking over the vice car which was new and air-conditioned. It was gold with mags, a stick, and slicks on the back. The police radio was concealed inside,the glove compartment.

''It's not bad,'' said Charlie, ''especially the air conditioning. Ever see air conditioning in a police car, Bumper?''

''Not the ones I drive, Charlie,'' I said, firing up a cigar, and Charlie tore through the gears to show me the car had some life to it.

''Vice is lots of fun, Bumper, but you know, some of the best times were when I walked with you on your beat.''

''How long'd you work with me, Charlie, couple months?''

''About three months. Remember, we got that burglar that night? The guy that read the obituaries?''

''Oh yeah,'' I said, not remembering that it was Charlie who'd been with me. When they have you breaking in rookies, they all kind of merge in your memory, and you don't remember them very well as individuals.

''Remember? We were shaking this guy just outside the Indian beer bar near Third, and you noticed the obituary column folded up in his shirt pocket? Then you told me about how some burglars read the obituaries and then burgle the pads of the dead people after the funeral when chances are there's nobody going to be there for a while.''

''I remember,'' I said, blowing a cloud of smoke at the windshield, thinking how the widow or widower usually stays with a relative for a while. Rotten M.O., I can't stand grave robbing. Seems like your victim ought to have some kind of chance.

''We got a commendation for that pinch, Bumper.''

''We did? I can't remember.''

''Of course I got one only because I was with you. That guy burgled ten or fifteen pads like that. Remember? I was so green I couldn't understand why he carried a pair of socks in his back pocket and I asked you if many of these transient types carried a change of socks with them. Then you showed me the stretch marks in the socks from his fingers and explained how they wear them for gloves so's not to leave prints. You never put me down even when I asked something that dumb.''

''I always liked guys to ask questions,'' I said, beginning to wish Charlie'd shut up.

''Hey, Charlie,'' I said, to change the subject, ''if we take a good phone spot today, what're the chances it could lead to something big?''

''You mean like a back office?''

''Yeah.''

''Almost no chance at all. How come you're so damned anxious to take a back?''

''I don't know. I'm leaving the job soon and I never really took a big crook like Red Scalotta. I'd just like to nail one.''

''Christ, I never took anyone as big as Scalotta either. And what do you mean, you're leaving? Pulling the pin?''

''One of these days.''

''I just can't picture you retiring.''

''*You're* leaving after twenty years aren't you?''

''Yeah, but not *you*.''

''Let's forget about it,'' I said, and Charlie looked at me for a minute and then opened the glove compartment and turned to frequency six for two-way communication with the others.

''One-Victor-One to One-Victor-Two,'' said Charlie.

''One-Victor-Two, go,'' said Nick.

''One-Victor-One, I think it's best to park behind on the next street east, that's Harvard,'' said Charlie. ''If anybody happens to be looking they wouldn't see you go in through the parking area in the rear.''

''Okay, Charlie,'' said Nick, and in a few minutes we were there. Eighth Street is all commercial buildings with several bars and restaurants, and the residential north-south streets are lined with apartment buildings. We gave them a chance to get to the walkway on the second floor of the apartment house, and Charlie drove about two hundred feet south of Eighth on Harvard. We walked one block to the public telephone on the southwest corner at Hobart. After a couple of minutes, Fuzzy leaned over a wrought iron railing on the second floor and waved.

''Let's get it on, Bumper,'' said Charlie, dropping in a dime. Charlie hung up after a second. ''Busy.''

''Zoot give you the code and all that?''

''Twenty-eight for Dandelion is the code,'' Charlie nodded. ''This is a relay phone spot. If it was a relay call-back we might have some problems.''

''What's the difference?'' I asked, standing behind the phone booth so someone looking out of the apartment wouldn't see the bluesuit.

''A call-back is where the bettor or the handbook like Zoot calls the relay, that's like I'm going to do now. Then every fifteen minutes or so, the back office calls the relay and gets the bettor's number and calls the bettor himself. I think we'd have a poor chance with that kind of setup because back office clerks are sharper than some dummy sitting on the hot seat at a phone spot. Last time we took Reba McClain it was a regular relay spot where the bettor calls her and she writes the bets on a Formica board and then the back office calls every so often and she reads off the bets and wipes the Formica clean. It's better for us that way because we always try to get some physical evidence if we can move quick enough.''

''The Formica?''

''Yeah,'' Charlie nodded. ''Some guys kick in the door and throw something at the guy on the hot seat to distract him so he can't wipe the bets off. I've seen cops throw a tennis ball in the guy's face.''

''Why not a baseball?''

''That's not a bad idea. You'd make a good vice cop, Bumper.''

"Either way the person at the phone spot doesn't know the phone number or address of the back office?" I asked.

"Hell no. That's why I was telling you the chances are nil."

Charlie dropped the dime in again and again hung it up.

"Must be doing a good business," I said.

"Red Scalotta's relay spots always do real good," said Charlie. "I know personally of two Superior Court judges that bet with him."

"Probably some cops too," I said.

"Righteous," he nodded. "Everybody's got vices."

"Whadda you call that gimmick where the phone goes to another pad?"

"A tap out," said Charlie. "Sometimes you bust in an empty room and see nothing but a phone jack and a wire running out a window, and by the time you trace the wire down to the right apartment, the guy in the relay spot's long gone. Usually with a tap out, there's some kind of alarm hooked up so he knows when you crash in the decoy pad. Then there's a toggle relay, where a call can be laid off to another phone line. Like for instance the back office clerk dials the relay spot where the toggle switch is and he doesn't hang up. Then the bettor calls the relay and the back can take the action himself. All these gimmicks have disadvantages though. One of the main ones is that bettors don't like call-back setups. Most bettors are working stiffs and maybe on their coffee breaks they only have a few minutes to get in to their bookie, and they don't have ten or fifteen minutes to kill waiting for call-backs and all that crap. The regular relay spot with some guy or maybe some housewife earning a little extra bread by sitting on the hot seat is still the most convenient way for the book to operate."

"You get many broads at these phone spots?"

"We sure do. We get them in fronts and backs. That is, we get them in the relay phone spots as well as back offices. We hear Red Scalotta's organization pays a front clerk a hundred fifty a week and a back clerk three hundred a week. That's a good wage for a woman, considering it's tax free. A front clerk might have to go to jail once in a while but it ain't no big thing to her. The organization bails them out and pays all legal fees. Then they go right back to work. Hardly any judge is going to send someone to county jail for bookmaking, especially if she's female. And they'll never send anyone to state prison. I know a guy in the south end of town with over eighty bookmaking arrests. He's still in business."

"Sounds like a good business."

"It's a joke, Bumper. I don't know why I stay at it, I mean trying to nail them. We hear Red Scalotta's back offices gross from one to two million a year. And he probably has at least three backs going. That's a lot of bread even though he only nets eleven to sixteen percent of that. And when we take down these agents and convict them, they get a two-hundred-and-fifty-dollar fine. It's a sick joke."

"You ever get Red Scalotta himself?"

"Never. Red'll stay away from the back offices. He's got someone who takes care of everything. Once in a while we can take a front and on rare occasions a back and that's about all we can hope for. Well, let's try to duke our bet in again."

Charlie dropped in his dime and dialed the number. Then he looked excited and I knew someone answered.

"Hello," said Charlie, "this is twenty-eight for Dandelion. Give me number four in the second, five across. Give me a two-dollar, four-horse round robin in the second. The number two horse to the number four in the third to the number six in the fourth to number seven in the fifth."

Then Charlie stiffed in a few more bets for races at the local track, Hollywood Park, which is understood, unless you specify an Eastern track. Midway through the conversation, Charlie leaned out the phone booth and pumped his fist at Fuzzy, who disappeared inside the apartment building. Charlie motioned to me and I took off my hat and squeezed into the hot phone booth with him. He grinned and held the phone away from his ear, near mine.

I heard the crash over the phone, and the terrified woman scream and a second later Nick's voice came over the line and said, "Hello, sweetheart, would you care for a round robin or a three-horse parley today?"

Charlie chuckled and hung up the phone and we hopped back in the vice car and drove to the apartment house, parking in front.

When we got to the second floor, Fuzzy was smooth talking an irate landlady who was complaining about the fractured door which Nick was propping shut for privacy. A good-looking, dark-haired girl was sitting on the couch inside the apartment crying her eyes out.

"Hi, Reba," Charlie grinned as we walked in and looked around.

"Hello, Mister Bronski," she wailed, drenching the second of two handkerchiefs she held in her hands.

"The judge warned you last time, Reba," said Charlie. "This'll make your third bookmaking case. He told you you'd get those six months he suspended. You might even get a consecutive sentence on top of it."

"Please, Mister Bronski," she wailed, throwing herself face down on the couch and sobbing so hard the whole couch shook.

She was wearing a very smart jersey blouse and skirt, and a matching blue scarf was tied around her black hair. Her fair legs had a very light spattering of freckles on them. She was a fine-looking girl, very Irish.

Charlie took me in the frilly sweet-smelling bedroom where the phone was. Reba had smeared half the bets off a twelve-by-eighteen chalkboard, but the other bets were untouched. A wet cloth was on the floor where the board was dropped along with the phone.

"I'll bet she wet her pants again this time," said Charlie, still grinning as he examined the numbers and x's on the chalkboard which told the track, race, handicap position, and how much to win, place or show. The bettor's identification was written beside the bets. I noticed that K.L. placed one hell of a lot of bets, probably just before Charlie called.

"We're going to squeeze the shit out of her," Charlie whispered. "You think Zoot was shaky, wait'll you hear this broad. A real ding-a-ling."

"Go ahead," Nick was saying to someone on the phone when we came back in the living room. Fuzzy was nodding politely to the landlady and locking her out by closing the broken door and putting a chair in front of it.

"Right. Got it," said Nick, hanging up. A minute later the phone rang again.

"Hello," said Nick. "Right. Go ahead." Every few seconds he mumbled, "Yeah," as he wrote down bets. "Got it." He hung up.

"Nick's taking some bets mainly to fuck up Scalotta," Charlie explained to me. "Some of these guys might hit, or they might hear Reba got knocked over, and then they'll claim they placed their bet and there'll be no way to prove they didn't, so the book'll have to pay off or lose the customers. That's where we get most of our tips, from disgruntled bettors. It isn't too often a handbook like Zoot Lafferty comes dancing in, anxious to turn his bread and butter."

"Mister Bronski, can I talk to you?" Reba sobbed, as Nick and then Fuzzy answered the phone and took the bets.

"Let's go in the other room," said Charlie, and we followed Reba back into the bedroom where she sat down on the soft, king-sized bed and wiped away the wet mascara.

"I got no time for bullshit, Reba," said Charlie. "You're in no position to make deals. We got you by the curlies."

"I know, Mister Bronski," she said, taking deep breaths. "I ain't gonna bullshit you. I wanna work with you. I swear I'll do anything. But please don't let me get this third case. That Judge Bowers is a bastard. He told me if I violated my probation, he'd put me in. Please, Mister Bronski, you don't know what it's like there. I couldn't do six months. I couldn't even do six days. I'd kill myself."

"You want to work for me? What could you do?"

"Anything. I know a phone number. Two numbers. You could take two other places just like this one. I'll give you the numbers."

"How do you know them?"

"I ain't dumb, Mister Bronski. I listen and I learn things. When they're drunk or high they talk to me, just like all men."

"You mean Red Scalotta and his friends?"

"Please, Mister Bronski, I'll give you the numbers, but you can't take me to jail."

"That's not good enough, Reba," said Charlie, sitting down in a violet-colored satin chair next to a messy dressing table. He lit a cigarette as Reba glanced from Charlie to me, her forehead wrinkled, chewing her lip. "That's not near good enough," said Charlie.

"Whadda you want, Mister Bronski? I'll do anything you say."

"I want the back," said Charlie easily.

"What?"

"I want one of Red's back offices. That's all. Keep your phone spots. If we take too much right away it'll burn you and I want you to keep working for Red. But I want his back office. I think you can help me."

"Oh God, Mister Bronski. Oh Mother of God, I don't know about things like that, I swear. How would I know? I'm just answering phones here. How would I know?"

"You're Red's girlfriend."

"Red has other girlfriends!"

"You're his *special* girlfriend. And you're smart. You listen."

"I don't know things like that, Mister Bronski. I swear to God and His Mother. I'd tell you if I knew."

"Have a cigarette," said Charlie, and pushed one into Reba's trembling hand. I lit it for her and she glanced up like a trapped little rabbit, choked on the smoke, then took a deep breath, and inhaled down the right pipe. Charlie let her smoke for a few seconds. He had her ready to break, which is what you want, and you shouldn't wait, but she was obviously a ding-a-ling and you had to improvise when your subject is batty. He was letting her unwind, letting her get back a little confidence. Just for a minute.

"You wouldn't protect Red Scalotta if it meant your ass going to jail, would you, Reba?"

"Hell no, Mister Bronski, I wouldn't protect my mother if it meant that."

"Remember when I busted you before? Remember how we talked about those big hairy bull dykes you meet in jail? Remember how scared you were? Did any of them bother you?"

"Yes."

"Did you sleep in jail?"

"No, they bailed me out."

"What about after you get your six months, Reba? Then you have to sleep in jail. Did you see any dildoes in jail?"

"What's that?"

"Phony dicks."

"I hate those things," she shuddered.

"How would you like to wake up in the middle of the night with two big bull dykes working on you? And what's more, how would you feel if you really started *liking* it? It happens all the time to girls in jail. Pretty soon you're a stone butch, and then you might as well cut off that pretty hair, and strap down those big tits, because you're not a woman anymore. Then you can lay up in those butch pads with a bunch of bull daggers and a pack of smelly house cats and drop pills and shoot junk because you can't stand yourself."

"Why're you doing this to me, Mister Bronski?" said Reba, starting to sob again. She dropped the cigarette on the carpet and I picked it up and snuffed it. "Why do men like to hurt? You all hurt!"

"Does Red hurt you?" asked Charlie calmly, sweating a little as he lit another cigarette with the butt of the last one.

"Yes! He hurts!" she yelled, and Fuzzy stuck his head in the door to see what the shouting was about, but Charlie motioned him away while Reba sobbed.

"Does he make you do terrible things?" asked Charlie, and she was too hysterical to see he was talking to her like she was ten years old.

"Yes, the bastard! The freaky bastard. He hurts me! He likes to hurt! That fucking old freak!"

"I'll bet he makes you do things with bull daggers," said Charlie, glancing at me, and I realized I broke him in right. He wasn't a guy to only stick it in halfway.

"He *makes* me do it, Mister Bronski," said Reba. "I don't enjoy it, I swear I don't. I hate to do it with a woman. I wasn't raised like that. It's a terrible sin to do those things."

"I'll bet you don't like taking action for him either. You hate sitting on this hot seat answering the phones, don't you?"

"I *do* hate it, Mister Bronski. I *do* hate it. He's so goddamn cheap. He just won't give me money for anything. He makes me always work for it. I have to do those things with them two or three nights a week. And I have to sit here in this goddamn room and answer those goddamn phones and every minute I know some cop might be ready to break down the door and take me to jail. Oh, please help me, Mister Bronski."

"Stop protecting him then," said Charlie.

"He'll kill me, Mister Bronski," said Reba, and her pretty violet eyes were wide and round and her nostrils were flared, and you could smell the fear on her.

"He won't kill you, Reba," said Charlie soothingly. "You won't get a jacket. He'll never know you told me. We'll make it look like someone else told."

"No one else *knows*," she whispered, and her face was dead white.

"We'll work it out, Reba. Stop worrying, we know how to protect people that help us. We'll make it look like someone else set it up. I promise you, he'll never know you told."

"Tell me you swear to God you'll protect me."

"I swear to God I'll protect you."

"Tell me you swear to God I won't go to jail."

"We've got to book you, Reba. But you know Red'll bail you out in an hour. When your case comes up I'll personally go to Judge Bowers and you won't go to jail behind that probation violation."

"Are you a hundred percent sure?"

"I'm almost a hundred percent sure, Reba. Look, I'll talk for you myself. Judges are always ready to give people another chance, you know that."

"But that Judge Bowers is a bastard!"

"I'm a hundred percent sure, Reba. We can fix it."

"You got another cigarette?"

"Let's talk first. I can't waste any more time."

"If he finds out, I'm dead. My blood'll be on you."

"Where's the back?"

"I only know because I heard Red one night. It was after he'd had his dirty fun with me and a girl named Josie that he brought with him. She was as sick and filthy as Red. And he brought another guy with him, a Jew named Aaron something."

"Bald-headed guy, small, glasses and a gray moustache?"

''Yeah, that's him,'' said Reba.

''I know of him,'' said Charlie, and now he was squirming around on the velvet chair, because he had the scent, and I was starting to get it too, even though I didn't know who in the hell Aaron was.

''Anyway, this guy Aaron just watched Josie and me for a while and when Red got in bed with us, he told Aaron to go out in the living room and have a drink. Red was high as a kite that night, but at least he wasn't mean. He didn't hurt me. Can I please have that cigarette, Mister Bronski?''

''Here,'' said Charlie, and his hand wasn't quite as steady, which is okay, because that showed that good information could still excite him.

''Tastes good,'' said Reba, dragging hard on the cigarette. ''Afterwards, Red called a cab for Josie and sent her home, and him and Aaron started talking and I stayed in the bedroom. I was supposed to be asleep, but like I say, I'm not dumb, Mister Bronski, and I always listen and try to learn things.

''Aaron kept talking about the 'laundry,' and at first I didn't get it even though I knew that Red was getting ready to move out of his back offices. And even though I never saw it, or any other back office, I knew about them from talking to bookie agents and people in the business. Aaron was worrying about the door to the laundry and I figured there was something about the office door being too close to the laundry door, and Aaron tried to argue Red into putting another door in the back near an alley, but Red thought it would be too suspicious.

''That was all I heard, and then one day, when Red was taking me to his club for dinner, he said he had to stop by to pick up some cleaning and he parks by this place near Sixth and Kenmore, and he goes in a side door and comes out after a few minutes and says his suits weren't ready. Then I noticed the sign on the window. It was a Chinese laundry.'' Reba took two huge drags, blowing one through her nose as she drew on the second one.

''You're a smart girl, Reba,'' said Charlie.

''I ain't guaranteeing this is the right laundry, Mister Bronski. In fact, I ain't even sure the laundry they were talking about had anything to do with the back office. I just *think* it did.''

''I think you're right,'' said Charlie.

''You got to protect me, Mister Bronski. I got to live with him, and if he knows, I'll die. I'll die in a bad way, a *real* bad way, Mister Bronski. He told me once what he did to a girl that finked on him. It was thirty years ago, and he talked about it like it was yesterday, how she screamed and screamed. It was so awful it made me cry. You got to protect me!''

''I will, Reba. I promise. Do you know the address of the laundry?''

''I know,'' she nodded. ''There were some offices or something on the second floor, maybe like some business offices, and there was a third floor but nothing on the windows in the third floor.''

''Good girl, Reba,'' Charlie said, taking out his pad and pencil for the first time, now that he didn't have to worry about his writing breaking the flow of the interrogation.

''Charlie, give me your keys,'' I said. ''I better get back on patrol.''

''Okay, Bumper, glad you could come.'' Charlie flipped me the keys. ''Leave them under the visor. You know where we park?''

''Yeah, I'll see you later.''

''I'll let you know what happens, Bumper.''

''See you, Charlie. So long, kid,'' I said to Reba.

''Bye,'' she said, wiggling her fingers at me like a little girl.

11

It was okay driving back to the Glass House in the vice car because of the air conditioning. Some of the new black-and-whites had it, but I hadn't seen any yet. I turned on the radio and switched to a quiet music station and lit a cigar. I saw the temperature on the sign at a bank and it said eighty-two degrees. It felt hotter than that. It seemed awfully muggy.

After I crossed the Harbor Freeway I passed a large real estate office and smiled as I remembered how I cleaned them out of business machines one time. I had a snitch tell me that someone in the office bought several office machines from some burglar, but the snitch didn't know who bought them or even who the burglar was. I strolled in the office one day during their lunch hour when almost everyone was out and told them I was making security checks for a burglary prevention program the police department was sponsoring. A cute little office girl with a snappy fanny took me all around the place and I checked their doors and windows and she helped me write down the serial numbers of every machine in the place so that the police department would have a record if they were ever stolen. Then as soon as I got back to the station, I phoned Sacramento and gave them the numbers and found that thirteen of the nineteen machines had been stolen in various burglaries around the greater Los Angeles area. I went back with the burglary dicks and impounded them along with the office manager. IBM electric typewriters are just about the hottest thing going right now. Most of the machines are sold by the thieves to "legitimate" businessmen who, like everyone else, can't pass up a good buy.

It was getting close to lunch time and I parked the vice car at the police building and picked up my black-and-white, trying to decide where to have lunch. Olvera Street was out, because I'd had Mexican food with Cruz and Socorro last night. I thought about Chinatown, but I'd been there Tuesday, and I was just about ready to go to a good hamburger joint I know of when I thought about Odell Bacon. I hadn't had any bar-b-que for a while, so I headed south on Central Avenue to the Newton Street area and the more I thought about some bar-b-que the better it sounded and I started salivating.

I saw a Negro woman get off a bus and walk down a residential block from Central Avenue and I turned on that street for no reason, to get over to Avalon. Then I saw a black guy on the porch of a whitewashed frame house. He was watching the woman and almost got up from where he was sitting until he saw the black-and-white. Then he pretended to be looking at the sky and sat back, a little too cool, and I passed by and made a casual turn at the next block and then stomped down hard and gave her hell until I got to the first street north. Then I turned east again, south on Central, and finally made the whole block, deciding to come up the same street again. It was an old scam around here for purse snatchers to find a house where no one was home and sit on the stoop of the house near a bus stop, like they lived at the pad, and when a broad walked by, to run out, grab the purse, and then cut through the yard to the next street where a car would be stashed. Most black women around here don't carry purses. They carry their money in their bras out of necessity, so you don't see that scam used too much anymore, but I would've bet this guy was using it now. And this woman had a big brown leather purse. You just don't get suspicious of a guy when he approaches you from the porch of a house in your own neighborhood.

I saw the woman in mid-block and I saw the guy walking behind her pretty fast, I got overanxious and pushed a little too hard on the accelerator, instead of gliding along the curb, and the guy turned around, saw me, and cut to his right through some houses. I knew there'd be no sense going after him. He hadn't done anything yet, and besides, he'd lay up in some backyard like these guys always do and I'd never find him. I just went on to Odell Bacon's Bar-b-que, and when I passed the woman I glanced over and smiled, and she smiled back at me, a pleasant-looking old ewe. There were white sheep and black sheep and there were wild dogs and a few Pretty Good Shepherds. There'd be one sheep herder less after tomorrow, I thought.

I could smell the smoky meat a hundred yards away. They cooked it in three huge old-fashioned brick ovens. Odell and his brother Nate were both behind the counter when I walked in. They wore sparkling white cook's uniforms and hats and aprons even though they served the counter and watched the register and didn't have to do the cooking anymore. The place hadn't started to fill up for lunch yet. Only a few white people ate there, because they're afraid to come down here into what is considered the ghetto, and right now there were only a couple customers in the place and I was the only paddy. Everyone in South L.A. knew about Bacon's Bar-b-que though. It was the best soul food and bar-b-que restaurant in town.

"Hey, Bumper," said Nate, spotting me first. "What's happenin', man?" He was the youngest, about forty, coffee brown. He had well-muscled arms from working construction for years before he came in as Odell's partner.

"Nothin' to it, Nate," I grinned. "Hi, Odell."

"Aw right, Bumper," said Odell, and smiled big. He was a round-faced fat man. "I'm aw right. Where you been? Ain't seen you lately."

"Slowing down," I said. "Don't get around much these days."

"That'll be the day," Nate laughed. "When ol' Bumper can't git it on, it ain't worth gittin'."

"Some gumbo today, Bumper?" asked Odell.

"No, think I'll have me some ribs," I said, thinking the gumbo did sound good, but the generous way these guys made it, stuffed full of chicken and crab, it might spoil me for the bar-b-que and my system was braced for the tangy down-home sauce that was their specialty, the like of which I'd never had anywhere else.

"Guess who I saw yestiday, Bumper?" said Odell, as he boxed up some chicken and a hot plate of beef, French fries, and okra for a take-out customer.

"Who's that?"

"That ponk you tossed in jail that time, 'member? That guy that went upside ol' Nate's head over a argument about paying his bill, and you was just comin' through the door and you rattled his bones but good. 'Member?"

"Oh yeah, I remember. Sneed was his name. Smelled like dogshit."

"That's the one," Nate nodded. "Didn't want him as a customer no how. Dirty clothes, dirty body, dirty mouf."

"Lucky you didn't get gangrene when that prick hit you, Nate," I said.

"Ponk-ass bastard," said Nate, remembering the punch that put him out for almost five minutes. "He come in the other day. I recognized him right off, and I tol' him to git his ass out or I'd call Bumper. He musta 'membered the name, 'cause he got his ass out wif oney a few cuss words."

"He remembered me, huh?" I grinned as Odell set down a cold glass of water, and poured me a cup of coffee without asking. They knew of course that I didn't work Newton Street Station and they only bounced for the Newton Street patrol car in the area, but after that Sneed fight, they always fed *me* free too, and in fact, always tried to get me to come more often. But I didn't like to take advantage. Before that, I used to come and pay half price like any uniformed cop could do.

"Here come the noonday rush," said Nate, and I heard car doors slam and a dozen black people talking and laughing came in and took the large booths in the front. I figured them for teachers. There was a high school and two grade schools close by and the place was pretty full by the time Nate put my plate in front of me. Only it wasn't a plate, it was a platter. It was always the same. I'd ask for ribs, and I'd get ribs, a double portion, and a heap of beef, oozing with bar-b-que sauce, and some delicious fresh bread that was made next door, and an ice-cream scoop of whipped butter. I'd sop the bread in the bar-b-que and either Nate or Odell would ladle fresh hot bar-b-que on the platter all during the meal. With it I had a huge cold mound of delicious slaw, and only a few fries because there wasn't much room for anything else. There just was no fat on Odell's beef. He was too proud to permit it, because he was almost sixty years old and hadn't learned the ways of cutting corners and chiseling.

After I got over the first joy of remembering exactly how delicious the beef was, one of the waitresses started helping at the counter because Odell and Nate were swamped. She was a buxom girl, maybe thirty-five, a little bronzer than Nate, with a modest natural hairdo, which I like, not a way-out phony Afro. Her waist was very small for her size and the boobs soared out over a flat stomach. She knew I was admiring her and didn't seem to mind, and as always, a good-looking woman close by made the meal perfect.

"Her name's Trudy," said Odell, winking at me, when the waitress went to the far end of the counter. His wink and grin meant she was fair game and not married or anything. I used to date another of his waitresses once in a while, a plump, dusky girl named Wilma who was a thirty-two-year-old grandmother. She finally left Odell's and got married for the fourth time. I really enjoyed being with her. I taught her the swim and the jerk and the boogaloo when they first came out. I learned them from my Madeleine Carroll girlfriend.

"Thanks, Odell," I said. "Maybe next time I come in I'll take a table in her section."

"Anythin' funny happen lately, Bumper?" asked Nate after he passed some orders through to the kitchen.

"Not lately. . . . Let's see, did I ever tell you about the big dude I stopped for busting a stop sign out front of your place?"

"Naw, tell us," said Odell, stopping with a plate in his hand.

"Well, like I say, this guy blew the stop sign and I chased him and brought him down at Forty-first. He's a giant, six-feet-seven maybe, heavier than me. All muscle. I ran a make on him over the radio while I'm writing a ticket. Turns out there's a traffic warrant for his arrest."

"Damn," said Nate, all ears now. "You had to fight him?"

"When I tell him there's this warrant he says, 'Too bad, man. I just ain't going to jail.' Just that cool he said it. Then he steps back like he's ready."

"Goddamn," said Odell.

"So then it just comes to me, this idea. I walk over to the police car and pick up the radio and say in a loud voice, 'One-X-L-Forty-five requesting an ambulance at Forty-first and Avalon.' The big dude, he looks around and says, 'What's the ambulance for?' I say, 'That's for you, asshole, if you don't get in that car.'

"So he gets in the car and halfway to jail he starts chuckling, then pretty soon he really busts up. 'Man,' he says, 'you really flimflammed my ass. This is the first time I ever laughed my way to jail.' "

"Gud-damn, Bumper," said Odell. "You're somethin' else. Gud-damn." Then they both went off laughing to wait on customers.

I finished the rest of the meat, picked the bones, and sopped up the last of the bread, but I wasn't happy now. In fact, it was depressing there with a crowd of people and the waitresses rushing around and dishes clattering, so I said good-bye to Nate and Odell. Naturally, I couldn't tip them even though they personally served me, so I gave two bucks to Nate and said, "Give it to Trudy. Tell her it's an advance tip for the good service she's gonna give me next time when I take a table in her section."

"I'll tell her, Bumper," Nate grinned as I waved and burped and walked out the door.

As I was trying to read the temperature again over a savings and loan office, the time flashed on the marquee. It was one-thirty, which is the time afternoon court always convenes. It dawned on me that I'd forgotten I had to be at a preliminary hearing this afternoon!

I cursed and stomped on it, heading for the new municipal court annex on Sunset, near the Old Mission Plaza, and then I slowed down and thought, what the hell, this is the last time I'll ever go to court on duty. I may get called back to testify after I'm retired, but this'll be the last time *on duty* as a working cop, and I'd never been late to court in twenty years. So what the hell, I slowed down and cruised leisurely to the court building.

I passed one of the Indian bars on Main Street, and saw two drunken braves about to duke it out as they headed for the alley in back, pushing and yelling at each other. I knew lots of Payutes and Apaches and others from a dozen Southwest tribes, because so many of them ended up downtown here on my beat. But it was depressing being with them. They were so defeated, those that ended up on Main Street, and I was glad to see them in a fistfight once in a while. At least that proved they could strike back a little bit, at something, even if it was at another drunken tribal brother. Once they hit my beat they were usually finished, or maybe long before they arrived here. They'd become winos, and many of the women, fat five-dollar whores. You wanted to pick them up, shake them out, send them somewhere, in some direction, but there didn't seem to be anywhere an Indian wanted to go. They were hopeless, forlorn people. One old beat cop told me they could break your heart if you let them.

I saw a Gypsy family walking to a rusty old Pontiac in a parking lot near Third and Main. The mother was a stooped-over hag, filthy, with dangling earrings, a peasant blouse, and a full red skirt hanging lopsided below her knees. The man walked in front of her. He was four inches shorter and skinny, about my age. A very dark unshaven face turned my way, and I recognized him. He used to hang around downtown and work with a Gypsy dame on pigeon drops and once in a while a Jamaican switch. The broad was probably his old lady, but I couldn't remember the face just now. There were three kids following: a dirty, beautiful teenage girl dressed like her mother, a ragtag little boy of ten or so, and a curly-haired little doll of four who was dressed like mama also.

I wondered what kind of scam they were working on now, and I tried to think of his name and couldn't, and I wondered if he'd remember me. As late as I was for court, I pulled to the curb.

''Hey, just a minute,'' I called.

''What, what, what?'' said the man. ''Officer, what's the problem? What's the problem? Gypsy boy. I'm just a Gypsy boy. You know me don't you, Officer? I talked with you before, ain't I? We was just shopping, Officer. Me and my babies and my babies' mother.''

''Where're your packages?'' I asked, and he squinted from the bright sunshine and peered into the car from the passenger side. His family all stood like a row of quail, and watched me.

''We didn't see nothing we liked, Officer. We ain't got much money. Got to shop careful.'' He talked with his hands, hips, all his muscles, especially those dozen or so that moved the mobile face, in expressions of hope and despair and honesty. Oh, what honesty.

''What's your name?''

''Marcos. Ben Marcos.''

''Related to George Adams?''

''Sure. He was my cousin, God rest him.''

I laughed out loud then, because every Gypsy I'd ever talked to in twenty years claimed he was cousin to the late Gypsy king.

''I know you don't I, Officer?'' he asked, smiling then, because I had laughed, and I didn't want to leave because I enjoyed hearing the peculiar lilt to the Gypsy speech, and I enjoyed looking at his unwashed children who were exceptionally beautiful, and I wondered for the hundredth time whether a Gypsy could ever be honest after centuries of living under a code which praised deceit and trickery and theft from all but other Gypsies. Then I was sad because I'd always wanted to really know the Gypsies. That would be the hardest friendship I would ever make, but I had it on my list of things to accomplish before I die. I knew a clan leader named Frank Serna, and once I went to his home in Lincoln Heights and ate dinner with a houseful of his relatives, but of course they didn't talk about things they usually talked about, and I could tell by all the nervous jokes that having an outsider and especially a cop in the house was a very strange thing for the clan. Still, Frank asked me back, and when I had time I was going to work on breaking into the inner circle and making them trust me a little because there were Gypsy secrets I wanted to know. But I could never hope to do it without being a cop, because they'd only let me know them if they first thought I could do them some good, because all Gypsies lived in constant running warfare with cops. It was too late now, because I would *not* be a cop, and I would *never* get to learn the Gypsy secrets.

"We can go now, Officer?" said the Gypsy, holding his hands clasped together, in a prayerful gesture. "It's very hot for my babies' mama here in the sun."

I looked at the Gypsy woman then, looked at her face and she was *not* a hag, and not as old as I first thought. She stood much taller now and glared at me because her man was licking my boots and I saw that she had once been as pretty as her daughter, and I thought of how I had so often been accused of seeing good things in all women, even ones who were ugly to my partners, and I guessed it was true, that I exaggerated the beauty of all women I knew or ever saw. I wondered about that, and I was wallowing in depression now.

"Please, sir. Can we go now?" he said, the sweat running down the creases in his face, and on his unwashed neck.

"Go your way, Gypsy," I said, and dug out from the curb, and in a few minutes I was parked and walking in the court building.

12

"Been waiting for you, Bumper," said the robbery detective, a wrinkled old-timer named Miles. He had been a robbery detective even before I came on the job and was one of the last to still wear a wide-brimmed felt hat. They used to be called the "hat squad," and the wide felt hat was their trademark, but of course in recent years no one in Los Angeles wore hats like that. Miles was a stubborn old bastard though, he still wore his, and a wide-shouldered, too-big suit coat with two six-inch guns, one on each hip, because he was an old robbery detective and the hat squad legend demanded it and other policemen expected it.

"Sorry I'm late, Miles," I said.

"That's okay, the case just got sent out to Division Forty-two. Can you handle this by yourself? I got another prelim in Forty-three and a couple of rookie arresting officers for witnesses. If I ain't in there to tell this young D.A. how to put on his case, we might lose it."

"Sure, I'll handle it. Am I the only witness?"

"You and the hotel manager."

"Got the evidence?"

"Yeah, here it is." Miles pulled a large manila envelope out of his cheap plastic briefcase and I recognized the evidence tag I had stuck on there months ago when I made the arrest.

''The gun's in there and two clips.''

''Too bad you couldn't file a robbery.''

''Yeah, well like I explained to you right after that caper, we were lucky to get what we did.''

''You filed an eleven-five-thirty too, didn't you?''

''Oh yeah. Here's the pot, I almost forgot.'' Miles reached back in the briefcase and pulled out an analyzed-evidence envelope with my seal on it that contained the marijuana with the chemist's written analysis on the package.

''How many jobs you figure this guy for?''

''I think I told you four, didn t I?''

''Yeah.''

''Now we think he done six. Two in Rampart and four here in Central.''

''It's a shame you couldn't make him on at least one robbery.''

''You're telling me. I had him in a regular show-up and I had a few private mug-shot show-ups, and I talked and coaxed and damn near threatened my victims and witnesses and the closest I could ever come was one old broad that said he *looked* like the bandit.''

''Scumbag really did a good job with the makeup, huh?''

''Did a hell of a job,'' Miles nodded. ''Remember, he was an actor for a while and he did a hell of a good job with paint and putty. But shit, the M.O. was identical, the way he took mom and dad markets. Always asked for a case of some kind of beer they were short of and when they went in the back for the beer, boom, he pulled the forty-five automatic and took the place down.''

''He ever get violent?''

''Not in the jobs in Central. I found out later he pistol-whipped a guy in one of the Rampart jobs. Some seventy-year-old grocery clerk decided he was Wyatt Earp and tried to go for some fucked-up old thirty-two he had stashed under the counter. Landry really laid him open. Three times across the eyes with the forty-five. He blinded him. Old guy's still in the hospital.''

''His P.O. going to violate him?''

''This asshole has a rabbit's foot. He finished his parole two weeks before you busted him. Ain't that something else? Two weeks!''

''Well, I better get in there,'' I said. ''Some of these deputy D.A.'s get panicky when you're not holding their hands. You get a special D.A. for this one?''

''No. It's a dead bang case. You got him cold. Shouldn't be any search and seizure problems at all. And even though we know this guy's a good robber, we ain't got nothing on him today but some low-grade felonies, ex-con with a gun and possession of pot.''

''Can't we send him back to the joint with his record?''

''We're going to try. I'll stop in the courtroom soon as I can. If you finish before me, let me know if you held him to answer.''

''You got doubts I'll hold him?'' I grinned, and headed for the courtroom, feeling very strange as I had all day. The last time I wore a bluesuit into a courtroom, I thought.

This courtroom was almost empty. There were only three people in the audience, two older women, probably the kind that come downtown and watch criminal trials for fun, and a youngish guy in a business suit who was obviously a witness and looked disgusted as hell about being here. Since these courtrooms are for preliminary hearings only, there was no jury box, just the judge's bench and witness box, the counsel tables, the clerk's desk, and a small desk near the railing for the bailiff.

At least I'll be through hassling with this legal machinery, I thought, which cops tend to think is designed by a bunch of neurotics because it seems to go a hundred miles past the point where any sane man would've stopped. After a felony complaint is filed, the defendant is arraigned and then has a preliminary hearing which amounts to a trial. This takes the place of a grand jury indictment and it's held to see if there's good enough cause to bind him over to superior court for trial, and then he's arraigned again in superior court, and later has a trial. Except that in between there're a couple of hearings to set aside what you've done already. In capital cases there's a separate trial for guilt and another for penalty, so that's why celebrated California cases drag on for years until they cost so much that everybody gives up or lets the guy cop to a lesser included offense.

We have a very diligent bunch of young public defenders around here who, being on a monthly salary and not having to run from one good paying client to another, will drive you up a wall defending a chickenshit burglary like it was the Sacco-Vanzetti trial. The D.A.'s office has millions of very fine crimes to choose from and won't issue a felony complaint unless they're pretty damned sure they can get a conviction. But then, there aren't that many real felony convictions, because courts and prisons are so overcrowded. A misdemeanor plea is accepted lots of times even from guys with heavyweight priors.

All this would make Los Angeles a frustrating place to be a cop if it weren't for the fact that the West in general is not controlled by the political clubhouse, owing to the fact that our towns are so sprawling and young. This means that in my twenty years I could bust *any* deserving son of a bitch, and I never got bumrapped except once when I booked an obnoxious French diplomat for drunk driving after he bad-mouthed me. I later denied to my bosses that he told me of his diplomatic immunity.

But in spite of all the bitching by policemen there's one thing you can't deny: it's still the best system going, and even if it's rough on a cop, who the hell would want to walk a beat in Moscow or Madrid, or anywhere in between? We gripe for sympathy but most of us know that a cop's never going to be loved by people in general, and I say if you got to have lots of love, join the fire department.

I started listening a little bit to the preliminary hearing that was going on. The defendant was a tall, nice-looking guy named John Trafford, about twenty-seven years old, and his pretty woman, probably his wife, was in the courtroom. He kept turning and making courageous gestures in her direction which wasn't particularly impressing Judge Martha Redford, a tough, severe-looking old girl who I had always found to be a fair judge, both to the people and the defense. There was a fag testifying that this clean-cut-looking young chap had picked him up in a gay bar and gone to the fag's pad, where after an undescribed sex act the young defendant, who the fag called Tommy, had damn near cut his head off with a kitchen knife. And then he ransacked the fruit's pad and stole three hundred blood-soaked dollars which were found in his pocket by two uniformed coppers who shagged him downtown to Fifth and Main where he later illegally parked his car.

The defense counsel was badgering the fruit, an effeminate little man about forty years old, who owned a photography studio, and the fruit wasn't without sympathy for the defendant as he glanced nervously at his friend "Tommy," and I thought this was darkly humorous and typical. Weak people need people so much they'd forgive anything. I didn't think the defense counsel was succeeding too well in trying to minimize the thing as just another fruitroll, since the hospital record showed massive transfusions and a hundred or so sutures needed to close up the neck wounds of the fruit.

The young defendant turned around again and shot a long sad glance at pretty little mama who looked brave, and after Judge Redford held him to answer on the charges of attempted murder and robbery, his lawyer tried to con her into a bail reduction because the guy had never been busted before except once for wife beating.

Judge Redford looked at the defendant then, staring at his handsome face and calm eyes, and I could tell she wasn't listening to the deputy D.A. who was opposing the bail reduction and recounting the savagery of the cutting. She was just looking at the young dude and he was looking at her. His blond hair was neatly trimmed and he wore a subdued pin-striped suit.

Then she denied the motion for bail reduction, leaving the huge bail on this guy and I was sure she saw what I saw in his face. He was one to be reckoned with. You could see the confidence and intelligence in his icy expression. And power. There's real power you can feel when it's in a guy like this and it even gave me a chill. You can call him a psychopath or say that he's evil, but whatever he is, he's the deadly Enemy, and I wondered how many other times his acts ended in blood. Maybe it was him that ripped the black whore they dug out of a garbage pile on Seventh Street last month, I thought.

You've got to respect the power to harm in a guy like him, and you've got to be scared by it. It sure as hell scared Her Honor, and after she refused to lower the bail he smiled a charming boyish smile at her and she turned away. Then he looked at his teary wife again and smiled at her, and then he felt me watching and I caught his eye and felt *myself* smiling, and my look was saying: I know you. I know you very well. He looked at me calmly for a few seconds, then his eyes sort of glazed over and the deputy led him out of court. Now that I knew he hung around downtown, I thought, I'd be watching for that boy on my beat.

The judge left the bench and the deputy D.A., a youngster whose muttonchops and moustache didn't fit, started reading the complaint to get ready for my case.

Timothy Landry, my defendant, was led in by a deputy sheriff. A deputy public defender was handling the case since Landry was not employed, even though Miles figured he'd stolen ten thousand or so.

He was a craggy-looking guy, forty-four years old, with long, dyed black hair that was probably really gray, and a sallow face that on some guys never seems to get rosy again after they do some time in the joint. He had the look of an ex-con all over him. His bit movie parts were mostly westerns, a few years back, right after he got out of Folsom.

"Okay, Officer," said the young D.A., "where's the investigator?"

"He's busy in another court. I'm Morgan, the arresting officer. I'm handling the whole thing. Dead bang case. You shouldn't have any problems."

He probably had only a few months' experience. They stick these deputy D.A.'s in the preliminary hearings to give them instant courtroom experience handling several cases a day, and I figured this one hadn't been here more than a couple months. I'd never seen him before and I spent lots of time in court, because I made so many felony pinches.

"Where's the other witness?" asked the D.A., and for the first time I looked around the courtroom and spotted Homer Downey, who I'd almost forgotten was subpoenaed in this case. I didn't bother talking with him to make sure he knew what he'd be called on to testify to, because his part in it was so insignificant you almost didn't need him at all, except as probable cause for me going in the hotel room on an arrest warrant.

"Let's see," muttered the D.A. after he'd talked to Downey for a few minutes. He sat down at the counsel table reading the complaint and running his long fingers through his mop of brown hair. The public defender looked like a well-trimmed ivy-leaguer, and the D.A., who's theoretically the law and order guy, was mod. He even wore round granny glasses.

"Downey's the hotel manager?"

"Right," I said as the D.A. read my arrest report.

"On January thirty-first, you went to the Orchid Hotel at eight-two-seven East Sixth Street as part of your routine duties?"

"Right. I was making a check of the lobby to roust any winos that might've been hanging around. There were two sleeping it off in the lobby and I woke them up intending to book them when all of a sudden one of them runs up the stairs, and I suddenly felt I had more than a plain drunk so I ordered the other one to stay put and I chased the first one. He turned down the hall to the right on the third floor and I heard a door close and was almost positive he ran into room three-nineteen."

"Could you say if the man you chased was the defendant?"

"Couldn't say. He was tall and wore dark clothes. That fleabag joint is dark even in the daytime, and he was always one landing ahead of me."

"So what did you do?"

"I came back down the stairs, and found the first guy gone. I went to the manager, Homer Downey, and asked him who was living in room three-nineteen, and he showed me the name Timothy Landry on the register, and I used the pay telephone in the lobby and ran a warrant check through R and I and came up with a fifty-two dollar traffic warrant for Timothy Landry, eight-twenty-seven East Sixth Street. Then I asked the manager for his key in case Landry wouldn't open up and I went up to three-nineteen to serve the warrant on him."

"At this time you thought the guy that ran in the room was Landry?"

"Sure," I said, serious as hell.

I congratulated myself as the D.A. continued going over the complaint because that wasn't a bad story now that I went back over it again. I mean I felt I could've done better, but it wasn't bad. The truth was that a half hour before I went in Landry's room I'd promised Knobby Booker twenty bucks if he turned something good for me, and he told me he tricked with a whore the night before in the Orchid Hotel and that he knew her pretty good and she told him she just laid a guy across the hall and had seen a gun under his pillow while he was pouring her the pork.

With that information I'd gone in the hotel through the empty lobby to the manager's room and looked at his register, after which I'd gotten the passkey and gone straight to Landry's room where I went in and caught him with the gun and the pot. But there was no way I could tell the truth and accomplish two things: protecting Knobby, and convicting a no-good dangerous scumbag that should be back in the joint. I thought my story was very good.

"Okay, so then you knew there was a guy living in the room and he had a traffic warrant out for his arrest, and you had reason to believe he ran from you and was in fact hiding in his room?"

"Correct. So I took the passkey and went to the room and knocked twice and said, 'Police officer.' "

"You got a response?"

"Just like it says in my arrest report, counsel. A male voice said, 'What is it?' and I said, 'Police officer, are you Timothy Landry?' He said, 'Yeah, what do you want?' and I said, 'Open the door, I have a warrant for your arrest.' "

"Did you tell him what the warrant was for?"

"Right, I said a traffic warrant."

"What did he do?"

"Nothing. I heard the window open and knew there was a fire escape on that side of the building, and figuring he was going to escape, I used the passkey and opened the door."

"Where was he?"

"Sitting on the bed by the window, his hand under the mattress. I could see what appeared to be a blue steel gun barrel protruding a half inch from the mattress near his hand, and I drew my gun and made him stand up where I could see from the doorway that it *was* a gun. I handcuffed the defendant and at this time informed him he was under arrest. Then in plain view on the dresser I saw the waxed-paper sandwich bag with the pot in it. A few minutes later, Homer Downey came up the stairs, and joined me in the defendant's room and that was it."

"Beautiful probable cause," the D.A. smiled. "And real lucky police work."

"Real luck," I nodded seriously. "Fifty percent of good police work is just that, good luck."

"We shouldn't have a damn bit of trouble with Chimel or any other search and seizure cases. The contraband narcotics was in plain view, the gun was in plain view, and you got in the room legally attempting to serve a warrant. You announced your presence and demanded admittance. No problem with eight-forty-four of the penal code."

"Right."

"You only entered when you felt the man whom you held a warrant for was escaping?"

"I didn't hold the warrant," I reminded him. "I only knew about the existence of the warrant."

"Same thing. Afterwards, this guy jumped bail and was rearrested recently?"

"Right."

"Dead bang case."

"Right."

After the public defender was finished talking with Landry he surprised me by going to the rear of the courtroom and reading my arrest report and talking with Homer Downey, a twitchy little chipmunk who'd been manager of the Orchid for quite a few years. I'd spoken to Homer on maybe a half-dozen occasions, usually like in this case, to look at the register or to get the passkey.

After what seemed like an unreasonably long time, I leaned over to the D.A. sitting next to me at the counsel table. "Hey, I thought Homer was the people's witness. He's grinning at the P.D. like he's a witness for the defense."

"Don't worry about it," said the D.A. "Let him have his fun. That public defender's been doing this job for exactly two months. He's an eager beaver."

"'How long you been going it?"

"Four months," said the D.A., stroking his moustache, and we both laughed.

The P.D. came back to the counsel table and sat with Landry, who was dressed in an open-throat, big-collared, brown silk shirt, and tight chocolate pants. Then I saw an old skunk come in the courtroom. She had hair dyed like his, and baggy pantyhose and a short skirt that looked ridiculous on a woman her age, and I would've bet she was one of his girlfriends, maybe even the one he jumped bail on, who was ready to forgive. I was sure she was his baby when he turned around and her painted old kisser wrinkled in a smile. Landry looked straight ahead, and the bailiff in the court was not as relaxed as he usually was with an in-custody felony prisoner sitting at the counsel table. He too figured Landry for a bad son of a bitch, you could tell.

Landry smoothed his hair back twice and then seldom moved for the rest of the hearing.

Judge Redford took the bench again and we all quieted down and came to order.

"Is your true name Timothy G. Landry?" she asked the defendant, who was standing with the public defender.

"Yes, Your Honor."

Then she went into the monotonous reading of the rights even though they'd been read to Landry a hundred times by a hundred cops and a dozen other judges, and she explained the legal proceeding to him which *he* could have explained to *her*, and I looked at the clock, and finally, she tucked a wisp of straight gray hair behind her black horn-rimmed glasses and said, "Proceed."

She was a judge I always liked. I remembered once in a case where I'd busted three professional auto thieves in a hot Buick, she'd commended me in court. I'd stopped these guys cruising on North Broadway through Chinatown and I knew, *knew* something was wrong with them and something wrong with the car when I noticed the *rear* license plate was bug-spattered, but the license, the registration, the guy's driver's license, everything checked out. But I felt it and I knew. And then I looked at the identification tag, the metal tag on the door post with the spot-welded rivets, and I stuck my fingernail under it and one guy tried to split, and only stopped when I drew the six-inch and aimed at his back and yelled, "Freeze, asshole, or name your beneficiary."

Then I found that the tag was not spot-welded on, but was glued, and I pulled it off and later the detectives made the car as a Long Beach stolen. Judge Redford said it was good police work on my part.

The D.A. was ready to call his first witness, who was Homer Downey, and who the D.A. needed to verify the fact that he rented the room to Landry, in case Landry later at trial decided to say he was just spending the day in a friend's pad and didn't know how the gun and pot got in there. But the P.D. said, "Your Honor, I would move at this time to exclude all witnesses who are not presently being called upon to testify."

I expected that. P.D.'s always exclude all witnesses. I think it's the policy of their office. Sometimes it works pretty well for them, when witnesses are getting together on a story, but usually it's just a waste of time.

"Your Honor, I have only two witnesses," said the D.A., standing up. "Mr. Homer Downey and Officer Morgan the arresting officer, who is acting as my investigating officer. I would request that he be permitted to remain in the courtroom."

"The investigating officer will be permitted to remain, Mr. Jeffries," she said to the public defender. "That doesn't leave anyone we can exclude, does it?"

Jeffries, the public defender, blushed because he hadn't enough savvy to look over the reports to see how many witnesses there were, and the D.A. and I smiled, and the D.A. was getting ready to call old Homer when the P.D. said, "Your Honor, I ask that if the arresting officer is acting as the district attorney's investigating officer in this case, that he be instructed to testify first, even if it's out of order, and that the other witness be excluded."

The D.A. with his two months' extra courtroom experience chuckled out loud at that one. "I have no objection, Your Honor," he said.

"Let's get on with it, then," said the judge, who was getting impatient, and I thought maybe the air-conditioner wasn't working right because it was getting close in there.

She said, "Will the district attorney please have his other witness rise?"

After Downey was excluded and told to wait in the hall the D.A. finally said, "People call Officer Morgan," and I walked to the witness stand and the court clerk, a very pleasant woman about the judge's age, said, "Do you solemnly swear in the case now pending before this court to tell the truth, the whole truth, and nothing but the truth, so help you God?"

And I looked at her with my professional witness face and said, "Yes, I do."

That was something I'd never completely understood. In cases where I wasn't forced to embellish, I always said, "I do," and in cases where I was fabricating most of the probable cause, I always made it more emphatic and said, "*Yes*, I do." I couldn't really explain that. It wasn't that I felt guilty when I fabricated, because I didn't feel guilty, because if I hadn't fabricated, many many times, there were people who would have been victimized and suffered because I wouldn't have sent half the guys to the joint that I sent over the years. Like they say, most of the testimony by all witnesses in a criminal case is just lyin' and denyin'. In fact everyone expects the *defense* witnesses to "testilie" and would be surprised if they didn't.

"Take the stand and state your name, please," said the clerk.

"William A. Morgan, M-O-R-G-A-N."

"What is your occupation and assignment?" asked the D.A.

"I'm a police officer for the City of Los Angeles assigned to Central Division."

"Were you so employed on January thirty-first of this year?"

"Yes, sir."

"On that day did you have occasion to go to the address of eight-twenty-seven East Sixth Street?"

"Yes, sir."

"At about what time of the day or night was that?"

"About one-fifteen p.m."

"Will you explain your purpose for being at that location?"

"I was checking for drunks who often loiter and sleep in the lobby of the Orchid Hotel, and do damage to the furniture in the lobby."

"I see. Is this lobby open to the public?"

"Yes, it is."

"Had you made drunk arrests there in the past?"

"Yes, I had. Although usually, I just sent the drunks on their way, my purpose being mainly to protect the premises from damage."

"I see," said the D.A., and my baby blues were getting wider and rounder and I was polishing my halo. I worked hard on courtroom demeanor, and when I was a young cop, I used to practice in front of a mirror. I had been told lots of times that jurors had told deputy D.A.'s that the reason they convicted a defendant was that Officer Morgan was so *sincere* and honest-looking.

Then I explained how I chased the guy up the stairs and saw him run in room three-nineteen, and how naturally I was suspicious then, and I told how Homer showed me the register and I read Timothy Landry's name. I phoned R and I and gave them Landry's name and discovered there was a traffic warrant out for his arrest, and I believed he was the man who had run in three-nineteen. I wasn't worried about what Homer would say, because I *did* go to his door to get the passkey of course, and I *did* ask to see the register, and as far as Homer knew about the rest of it, it was the gospel.

When I got to the part about me knocking on the door and Landry answering and telling me he was Timothy Landry, I was afraid Landry was going to fly right out of his chair. That was his first indication I was embellishing the story a bit, and the part about the window opening could have been true, but the bastard snorted so loud when I said the gun was sticking out from under the mattress, that the P.D. had to poke him in the ribs and the judge shot him a sharp look.

I was sweating a little at that point because I was pissed off that a recent case made illegal the search of the premises pursuant to an arrest. Before this, I could've almost told the whole truth, because I would've been entitled to search the whole goddamn room which only made good sense. Who in the hell would waste four hours getting a search warrant when you didn't have anything definite to begin with, and couldn't get one issued in the first place?

So I told them how the green leafy substance resembling marijuana was in plain view on the dresser, and Landry rolled his eyes up and smacked his lips in disgust because I got the pot out of a shoe box stashed in the closet. The P.D. didn't bother taking me on *voir dire* for my opinion that the green leafy substance was pot, because I guessed he figured I'd made a thousand narcotics arrests, which I had.

In fact, the P.D. was so nice to me I should've been warned. The D.A. introduced the gun and the pot and the P.D. stipulated to the chemical analysis of the marijuana, and the D.A. introduced the gun as people's exhibit number one and the pot as people's number two. The P.D. never objected to anything on direct examination and my halo grew and grew until I must've looked like a bluesuited monk, with my bald spot and all. The P.D. never opened his mouth until the judge said, "Cross," and nodded toward him.

"Just a few questions, Officer Morgan," he smiled. He looked about twenty-five years old. He had a very friendly smile.

"Do you recall the name on the hotel register?"

"Objection, Your Honor," said the D.A. "What name, what are we . . ."

The judge waved the D.A. down, not bothering to sustain the objection as the P.D. said, "I'll rephrase the question, Your Honor. Officer, when you chased this man up the stairs and then returned to the manager's apartment did you look at the name on the register or did you ask Mr. Downey who lived there?"

"I asked for the register."

"Did you read the name?"

"Yes, sir."

"What was the name?"

"As I've testified, sir, it was the defendant's name, Timothy G. Landry."

"Did you then ask Mr. Downey the name of the man in three-nineteen?"

"I don't remember if I did or not. Probably not, since I read the name for myself."

"What was the warrant for, Officer? What violation?"

"It was a vehicle code violation, counsel. Twenty-one four-fifty-three-A, and failure to appear on that traffic violation."

"And it had his address on it?"

"Yes, sir."

"Did you make mention of the warrant number and the issuing court and the total bail and so forth on your police report?"

"Yes, sir, it's there in the report," I said, leaning forward just a little, just a hint. Leaning was a sincere gesture, I always felt.

Actually it was two hours after I arrested Landry that I discovered the traffic warrant. In fact, it was when I was getting ready to compose a plausible arrest report, and the discovery of a traffic warrant made me come up with this story.

"So you called into the office and found out that Timothy G. Landry of that address had a traffic warrant out for his arrest?"

"Yes, sir."

"Did you use Mr. Downey's phone?"

"No, sir, I used the pay phone in the hall."

"Why didn't you use Mr. Downey's phone? You could've saved a dime." The P.D. smiled again.

"If you dial operator and ask for the police you get your dime back anyway, counsel. I didn't want to bother Mr. Downey further, so I went out in the hall and used the pay phone."

"I see. Then you went back upstairs with the key Mr. Downey gave you?"

"Yes, sir."

"You knocked and announced yourself and made sure the voice inside was Timothy Landry, for whom you had knowledge that a warrant existed?"

"Yes, sir. The male voice said he was Timothy Landry. Or rather he said yes when I asked if he was Timothy Landry." I turned just a little toward the judge, nodding my head ever so slightly when I said this. Landry again rolled his eyeballs and slumped down in his seat at that one.

"Then when you heard the window opening and feared your traffic warrant suspect might escape down the fire escape, you forced entry?"

"I used the passkey."

"Yes, and you saw Mr. Landry on the edge of the bed as though getting ready to go out the window?"

"Yes, that's right."

"And you saw a metal object protruding from under the mattress?"

"I saw a blue metal object that I was sure was a gun barrel, counsel," I corrected him, gently.

"And you glanced to your right and there in plain view was the object marked people's two, the sandwich bag containing several grams of marijuana?"

"Yes, sir."

"I have no futher questions of this witness," said the P.D., and now I was starting to worry a little, because he just went over everything as though he were the D.A. on direct examination. He just made our case stronger by giving me a chance to tell it again.

What the hell? I thought, as the judge said, "You may step down."

I sat back at the counsel table and the D.A. shrugged at my questioning look.

"Call your next witness," said the judge, taking a sip of water, as the bailiff got Homer Downey from the hall. Homer slouched up to the stand, so skinny the crotch of his pants was around his knees. He wore a dirty white shirt for the occasion and a frayed necktie and the dandruff all over his thin brown hair was even visible from the counsel table. His complexion was as yellow and bumpy as cheese pizza.

He gave his name, the address of the Orchid Hotel, and said he had been managing the place for three years. Then the D.A. asked him if I contacted him on the day of the arrest and looked at his register and borrowed his passkey, and if some ten minutes later did he come to the defendant's room and see me with the defendant under arrest, and how long had the defendant lived there, and did he rent the room to the defendant and only the defendant, and did all the events testified to occur in the city and county of Los Angeles, and Homer was a fairly good talker and a good witness, also very sincere, and was finished in a few minutes.

When direct examination was finished the public defender stood up and started pacing like in the Perry Mason shows and the judge said, "Sit down, counsel," and he apologized and sat down like in a real courtroom, where witnesses are only approached by lawyers when permission is given by the judge and where theatrical stuff is out of the question.

"Mister Downey, when Officer Morgan came to your door on the day in question, you've testified that he asked to see your register, is that right?"

"Yes."

"Did he ask you who lived in three-nineteen?"

"Nope, just asked to see the register."

"Do you remember whose name appeared on the register?"

"Sure. His." Downey pointed at Landry, who stared back at him.

"By him, do you mean the defendant in this case? The man on my right?"

"Yes."

"And what's his name?"

"Timothy C. Landowne."

"Would you repeat that name, please, and spell it?"

My heart started beating hard then, and the sweat broke out and I said to myself, "Oh no, oh no!"

"Timothy C. Landowne. T-I-M . . ."

"Spell the last name please," the P.D. smiled and I got sick.

"Landowne. L-A-N-D-O-W-N-E."

"And the middle initial was C as in Charlie?"

"Yes, sir."

"Are you sure?"

"Sure I'm sure. He's been staying at the hotel for four, five months now. And he even stayed a couple months last year."

"Did you ever see the name Timothy G. Landry on any hotel records? That's L-A-N-D-R-Y?"

"No."

"Did you ever see the name anywhere?"

"No."

I could feel the D.A. next to me stiffen as he finally started to catch on.

"Did you at any time tell Officer Morgan that the man in three-nineteen was named Timothy G. Landry?"

"No, because that's not his name as far as I know, and I never heard that name before today."

"Thank you, Mister Downey," said the public defender, and I could feel Landry, grinning with his big shark teeth, and I was trying hard to come up with a story to get out of this. I knew at that moment, and admitted to myself finally and forever, that I should've been wearing my glasses before this, and could no longer do police work or anything else without them, and if I hadn't been so stupid and had my glasses on, I would've seen that the name on that register was a half-assed attempt at an alias on the part of Landry, and even though the traffic warrant was as good as gold and really belonged to him, I couldn't possibly have got the right information from R and I by giving the computer the wrong name. And the judge would be sure of that in a minute because the judge would have the defendant's make sheet. And even as I was thinking it she looked at me and whispered to the court clerk who handed her a copy of the make sheet and nowhere in his record did it show he used an alias of Landowne. So I was trapped, and then Homer nailed the coffin tight.

"What did the officer do after you gave him the key?"

"He went out the door and up the stairs."

"How do you know he went up the stairs?"

"The door was open just a crack. I put my slippers on in a hurry because I wanted to go up there too so's not to miss the action. I thought something might happen, you know, an arrest and all."

"You remember my talking to you just before this hearing and asking you a few questions, Mister Downey?"

"Yes, sir."

'Do you remember my asking you about the officer using the pay phone in the lobby to call the police station?"

"Yes, sir," he said, and I had a foul taste in my mouth and I was full of gas and had branding iron indigestion pains and no pills for them.

"Do you remember what you said about the phone?"

"Yes, sir, that it didn't work. It'd been out of order for a week and I'd called the phone company, and in fact I was mad because I thought maybe they came the night before when I was out because they promised to come, and I tried it that morning just before the officer came and it was still broke. Buzzed real crazy when you dropped a dime in."

"Did you drop a dime in that morning?"

"Yes, sir. I tried to use it to call the phone company and it didn't matter if I dialed or not, it made noises so I used my own phone."

"You could *not* call out on that phone?"

"Oh no, sir."

"I suppose the phone company would have a record of your request and when they finally fixed the phone?"

"Objection, Your Honor," said the D.A. weakly. "Calls for a conclusion."

"Sustained," said the judge, looking only at me now, and I looked at Homer just for something to do with my eyes.

"Did you go upstairs behind the officer?" asked the P.D. again, and now the D.A. had slumped in his chair and was tapping with a pencil, and I'd passed the point of nervous breathing and sweat. Now I was cold and thinking, thinking about how to get out of this and what I would say if they recalled me to the stand, if either of them recalled me, and I thought the defense might call me because I was *their* witness now, they owned me.

"I went upstairs a little bit after the officer."

"What did you see when you got up there?"

"The officer was standing outside Mister Landowne's room and like listening at the door. He had his hat in his hand and his ear was pressed up to the door."

"Did he appear to see you, or rather, to look in your direction?"

"No, he had his back to my end of the hall and I decided to peek from around the corner, because I didn't know what he was up to and maybe there'd be a big shoot-out or something, and I could run back down the stairs if something dangerous happened."

"Did you hear him knock on the door?"

"No, he didn't knock."

"Objection," said the D.A. "The witness was asked . . ."

"All right," said the judge, holding her hand up again as the D.A. sat back down.

"Did you ever *hear* the officer knock?" the judge asked the witness.

"No, sir," said Homer to the judge, and I heard a few snickers from the rear of the court, and I thanked the gods that there were only a few spectators and none of them were cops.

"Did the officer say anything while you were there observing?" asked the P.D.

"Nothing."

"How long did you watch him?"

"Two, three minutes, maybe longer. He knelt down and tried to peek in the keyhole, but I had them all plugged two years ago because of hotel creepers and peeping toms."

"Did you . . . strike that, did the officer say anything that you could hear while you were climbing the stairway?"

"I never heard him say nothing," said Homer, looking bewildered as hell, and noticing from my face that something was sure as hell wrong and I was very unhappy.

"Then what did he do?"

"Used the key. Opened the door."

"In what way? Quickly?"

"I would say careful. He like turned the key slow and careful, and then he pulled out his pistol and then he seemed to get the bolt turned, and he kicked open the door and jumped in the room with the gun out front."

"Could you hear any conversation then?"

"Oh yeah," he giggled, through gapped, brown-stained teeth. "The officer yelled something to Mister Landowne."

"What did he say? His *exact* words if you remember."

"He said, 'Freeze asshole, you move and you're wallpaper.' "

I heard all three spectators laugh at that one, but the judge didn't think it was funny and neither did the D.A., who looked almost as sick as I figured I looked.

"Did you go in the room?"

"Yes, sir, for a second."

"Did you see anything unusual about the room?"

"No. The officer told me to get out and go back to my room so I did."

"Did you notice if anything was on the dresser?"

"I didn't notice."

"Did you hear any other conversation between the officer and the defendant?"

"No."

"Nothing at all?"

"The officer warned him about something."

"What did he say?"

"It was about Mister Landowne not trying anything funny, something like that. I was walking out."

"What did he say?"

"Well, it's something else not exactly decent."

"We're grown up. What did he say?"

"He said, 'You get out of that chair and I'll shove this gun so far up your ass there'll be shit on the grips.' That's what he said. I'm sorry." Homer turned red and giggled nervously and shrugged at me.

"The defendant was sitting in a chair?"

"Yes."

"Was it his own gun the officer was talking about?"

"Objection," said the D.A.

"I'll rephrase that," said the P.D. "Was the officer holding his own gun in his hand at that time?"

"Yes, sir."

"Did you see the other gun at that time?"

"No, I never saw no other gun."

The P.D. hesitated for a long, deadly silent minute and chewed on the tip of his pencil, and I almost sighed out loud when he said, "I have no further questions," even though it was much too late to feel relieved.

"I have a question," said Judge Redford, and she pushed her glasses up over a hump on her thin nose and said, "Mister Downey, did you happen to go into the lobby any time that morning *before* the officer arrived?"

"No."

"You never went out or looked out into the lobby area?"

"Well, only when the officer drove up in front. I saw the police car parked in front, and I was curious and I started out the door and then I saw the officer climbing the front steps of the hotel and I went back inside to put a shirt and shoes on so's to look presentable in case he needed some help from me."

"Did you look into the lobby?"

"Well, yes, it's right in front of my door, ma'am."

"Who was in the lobby?"

"Why, nobody."

"Could you see the entire lobby? All the chairs? Everywhere in the lobby area?"

"Why sure. My front door opens right on the lobby and it's not very big."

"Think carefully. Did you see two men sleeping anywhere near the lobby area?"

"There was nobody there, Judge."

"And where was the officer when you were looking into the empty lobby?"

"Coming in the front door, ma'am. A couple seconds later he came to my door and asked about the room and looked at the register like I said."

My brain was burning up now like the rest of me, and I had an idiotic story ready when they recalled me about how I'd come in the lobby once and then got out and come in again when Homer saw me and thought it was the first entry. And I was prepared to swear the phone worked, because what the hell, anything was possible with telephone problems. And even if that bony-assed, dirty little sneak followed me up the stairs, maybe I could convince them I called to Landry *before* Downey got up there, and what the hell, Downey didn't know if the marijuana was on the dresser or in the closet, and I was trying to tell myself everything would be all right so I could keep the big-eyed honest look on my kisser because I needed it now if ever in my life.

I was waiting to be recalled and I was ready even though my right knee trembled and made me mad as hell, and then the judge said to the public defender and the D.A., "Will counsel please approach the bench?"

Then I knew it was all over and Landry was making noises and I could feel the shark grin as his head was turned toward me. I just stared straight ahead like a zombie and wondered if I'd walk out of this courtroom in handcuffs for perjury, because anybody in the world could see that dumb shit Homer Downey was telling the stone truth and didn't even know what the P.D. was doing to me.

When they came back to the table after talking with the judge, the D.A. smiled woodenly at me and whispered, "It was the name on the register. When the public defender realized that Homer didn't know Landry's real name, he asked him about the register. It was the register that opened it all up for him. She's going to dismiss the case. I don't know what to advise you, Officer. I've never had anything like this happen before. Maybe I should call my office and ask what to do if . . ."

"Would you care to offer a motion to dismiss, Mister Jeffries?" asked the judge to the public defender, who jumped to his feet and did just that, and then she dismissed the case, and I hardly heard Landry chuckling all over the place and I knew he was shaking hands with that baby-faced little python that defended him. Then Landry leaned over the public defender and said, "Thanks, stupid," to me, but the P.D. told him to cool it. Then the bailiff had his hand on my shoulder and said, "Judge Redford would like to see you in her chambers," and I saw the judge had left the bench and I walked like a toy soldier toward the open door. In a few seconds I was standing in the middle of this room, and facing a desk where the judge sat looking toward the wall which was lined with bookcases full of law books. She was taking deep breaths and thinking of what to say.

"Sit down," she said, finally, and I did. I dropped my hat on the floor and was afraid to stoop down to pick it up I was so dizzy.

"In all my years on the bench I've never had that happen. Not like that. I'd like to know why you did it."

"I want to tell you the truth," I said and my mouth was leathery. I had trouble forming the words. My lips popped from the dryness every time I opened my mouth. I had seen nervous suspects like that thousands of times when I had them good and dirty, and they knew I had them.

"Maybe I should advise you of your constitutional rights before you tell me anything," said the judge, and she took off her glasses and the bump on her nose was more prominent. She was a homely woman and looked smaller here in her office, but she looked stronger too, and aged.

"The hell with my rights!" I said suddenly. "I don't give a damn about my rights, I want to tell you the truth."

"But I intend to have the district attorney's office issue a perjury complaint against you. I'm going to have that hotel register brought in, and the phone company's repairman will be subpoenaed and so will Mister Downey of course, and I think you'll be convicted."

"Don't you even care about what I've got to say?" I was getting mad now as well as scared, and I could feel the tears coming to my eyes, and I hadn't felt anything like this since I couldn't remember when.

"What can you say? What can anyone say? I'm awfully disappointed. I'm sickened in fact." She rubbed her eyes at the corners for a second and I was busting and couldn't hold on.

"*You're* disappointed? *You're* sickened? What the hell do you think I'm feeling at this minute? I feel like you got a blowtorch on the inside of my guts and you won't turn it off and it'll never be turned off, that's what I feel, Your Honor. Now can I tell the God's truth? Will you at least let me tell it?"

"Go ahead," she said, and lit a cigarette and leaned back in the padded chair and watched me.

"Well, I have this snitch, Your Honor. And I've got to protect my informants, you know that. For his own personal safety, and so he can continue to give me information. And the way things are going in court nowadays with everyone so nervous about the defendant's rights, I'm afraid to even mention confidential informants like I used to, and I'm afraid to try to get a search warrant because the judges are so damn hinky they call damn near every informant a material witness, even when he's not. So in recent years I've started . . . exploring ways around."

"You've started lying."

"Yes, I've started lying! What the hell, I'd hardly ever convict any of these crooks if I didn't lie at least a little bit. You know what the search and seizure and arrest rules are like nowadays."

"Go on."

Then I told her how the arrest went down, exactly how it went down, and how I later got the idea about the traffic warrant when I found out he had one. And when I was finished, she smoked for a good two minutes and didn't say a word. Her cheeks were eroded and looked like they were hacked out of a rocky cliff. She was a strong old woman from another century as she sat there and showed me her profile and finally she said, "I've seen witnesses lie thousands of times. I guess every defendant lies to a greater or lesser degree and most defense witnesses stretch hell out of the truth, and of course I've seen police officers lie about probable cause. There's the old hackneyed story about feeling what appeared to be an offensive weapon like a knife in the defendant's pocket and reaching inside to retrieve the knife and finding it to be a stick of marijuana. That one's been told so many times by so many cops it makes judges want to vomit. And of course there's the furtive movement like the defendant is shoving something under the seat of the car. That's always good probable cause for a search, and likewise that's overdone. Sure, I've heard officers lie before, but nothing is black and white in this world and there are degrees of truth and untruth, and like many other judges who feel police officers cannot possibly protect the public these days, I've given officers the benefit of the doubt in probable cause situations. I never really believed a Los Angeles policeman would *completely* falsify his entire testimony as you've done today. That's why I feel sickened by it."

"I didn't falsify it all. He had the gun. It *was* under the mattress. He *had* the marijuana. I just lied about where I found it. Your Honor, he's an active bandit. The robbery dicks figure him for six robberies. He's beaten an old man and blinded him. He's . . ."

She held up her hand and said, "I didn't figure he was using that gun to stir his soup with, Officer Morgan. He has the look of a dangerous man about him."

"You could see it too!" I said. "Well . . ."

"Nothing," she interrupted. "That means nothing. The higher courts have given us difficult law, but by God, it's the law!"

"Your Honor," I said slowly. And then the tears filled my eyes and there was nothing I could do. "I'm not afraid of losing my pension. I've done nineteen years and over eleven months and I'm leaving the Department after tomorrow, and officially retiring in a few weeks, but I'm not afraid of losing the money. That's not why I'm asking, why I'm *begging* you to give me a chance. And it's not that I'm afraid to face a perjury charge and go to jail, because you can't be a crybaby in this world. But, Judge, there are people, policemen, and other people, people on my beat who think I'm something special. I'm one of the ones they really look up to, you know? I'm not just a character, I'm a hell of a cop!"

"I know you are," she said. "I've noticed you in my courtroom many times."

"You have?" Of course I'd been in her courtroom as a witness before, but I figured all bluecoats looked the same to blackrobes. "Don't get down on us, Judge Redford. Some coppers don't lie at all, and others only lie a little like you said. Only a few like me would do what I did."

"Why?"

"Because I care, Your Honor, goddamnit. Other cops put in their nine hours and go home to their families twenty miles from town and that's it, but guys like me, why I got nobody and I want nobody. I do my living on my beat. And I've got things inside me that make me do these things against my better judgment. That proves I'm dumber than the dumbest moron on my beat."

"You're not dumb. You're a clever witness. A very clever witness."

"I never lied that much before, Judge. I just thought I could get away with it. I just couldn't read that name right on that hotel register. If I could've read that name right on the register I never would've been able to pull off that traffic warrant story and I wouldn't've tried it. And I probably wouldn't be in this fix, and the reason I couldn't really see that name and only assumed it must've been Landry is because I'm fifty years old and far-sighted, and too stubborn to wear my glasses, and kidding myself that I'm thirty and doing a young man's job when I can't cut it anymore. I'm going out though, Judge. This clinches it if I ever had any doubts. Tomorrow's my last day. A knight. Yesterday somebody called me a Blue Knight. Why do people say such things? They make you think you're really something and so you got to win a battle every time out. Why should *I* care if Landry walks out of here? What's it to *me?* Why do they *call* you a knight?''

She looked at me then and put the cigarette out and I'd never in my life begged anyone for anything, and never licked anyone's boots. I was glad she was a woman because it wasn't quite so bad to be licking a woman's boots, not *quite* so bad, and my stomach wasn't only burning now, it was hurting in spasms, like a big fist was pounding inside in a jerky rhythm. I thought I'd double over from the pain in a few minutes.

''Officer Morgan, you fully agree don't you that we can call off the whole damn game and crawl back in primeval muck if the orderers, the enforcers of the law, begin to operate outside it? You understand that there could be no civilization, don't you? You know, don't you, that I as well as many other judges am terribly aware of the overwhelming numbers of criminals on those streets whom you policemen must protect us from? You cannot always do it and there are times when you are handcuffed by court decisions that presume the goodness of people past all logical presumption. But don't you think there are judges, and yes, even defense attorneys, who sympathize with you? Can't you see that you, you policemen of all people, must be more than you are? You must be patient and above all, honest. Can't you see if you go outside the law regardless of how absurd it seems, in the name of enforcing it, that we're all doomed? Can you see these things?''

''Yes. Yes, I know, but old Knobby Booker doesn't know. And if I had to name him as my snitch he might get a rat jacket and somebody might rip him off. . . .'' And now my voice was breaking and I could hardly see her because it was all over and I knew I'd be taken out of this courtroom and over to the county jail. ''When you're alone out there on that beat, Your Honor, and everyone knows you're the Man. . . . The way they look at you . . . and how it feels when they say, 'You're the champ, Bumper. You're a warlord. You're a Knight, a Blue Knight. . . .'' And then I could say no more and said no more that day to that woman.

The silence was buzzing in my ears and finally she said, ''Officer Morgan, I'm requesting that the deputy district attorney say nothing of your perjured testimony in his report to his office. I'm also going to request the public defender, the bailiff, the court reporter and the clerk, not to reveal what happened in there today. I want you to leave now so I can wonder if I've done the right thing. We'll never forget this, but we'll take no further action.''

I couldn't believe it. I sat for a second, paralyzed, and then I stood up and wiped my eyes and walked toward the door and stopped and didn't even think to thank her, and looked around, but she was turned in her chair and watching the book stacks again. When I walked through the courtroom, the public defender and the district attorney were talking quietly and both of them glanced at me. I could feel them look at me, but I went straight for the door, holding my stomach, and waiting for the cramps to subside so I could think.

I stepped into the hall and remembered vaguely that the gun and narcotics evidence were still in the courtroom, and then thought the hell with it, I had to get out in the car and drive with the breeze in my face before the blood surging through my skull blew the top of my head off.

I went straight for Elysian Park around the back side, got out of the car, filled my pockets with acid eaters from the glove compartment, and climbed the hill behind the reservoir. I could smell eucalyptus, and the dirt was dry and loose under my shoes. The hill was steeper than I thought and I was sweating pretty good after just a few minutes of walking. Then I saw two park peepers. One had binoculars to see the show better. They were watching the road down below where couples sit in their cars at any hour of the day or night under the trees and make love.

"Get outta my park, you barfbags," I said, and they turned around and saw me standing above them. They both were middle-aged guys. One of them, with fish-belly pale skin, wore orange checkered pants and a yellow turtleneck and had the binoculars up to his face. When I spoke he dropped them and bolted through the brush. The other guy looked indignant and started walking stiff-legged away like a cocky little terrier, but when I took a few steps toward him, cursing and growling, he started ruuning too, and I picked up the binoculars and threw them at him, but missed and they bounced off a tree and fell in the brush. Then I climbed the hill clear to the top and even though it was smoggy, the view was pretty good. By the time I flopped on the grass and took off my Sam Browne and my hat, the stomach cramps were all but gone. I fell asleep almost right away and slept an hour there on the cool grass.

13

When I woke up, the world tasted horrible and I popped an acid eater just to freshen my mouth. I laid there on my back for a while and looked up at a bluejay scampering around on a branch.

"Did you shit in my mouth?" I said, and then wondered what I'd been dreaming about because I was sweaty even though it was fairly cool here. A breeze blowing over me felt wonderful. I saw by my watch it was after four and I hated to get up but of course I had to. I sat up, tucked in my shirt, strapped on the Sam Browne and combed back my hair which was tough to do, it was so wild and wiry. And I thought, I'll be glad when it all falls out and then I won't have to screw around with it anymore. It was hell sometimes when even your hair wouldn't obey you. When you had no control over anything, even your goddamn hair. Maybe I should use hair spray, I thought, like these pretty young cops nowadays. Maybe while I still had some hair I should get those fifteen-dollar haircuts and ride around in a radio car all day, spraying my hair instead of booking these scumbags, and then I could stay out of trouble, then no judge could throw me in jail for perjury, and disgrace me, and ruin everything I've done for twenty years, and ruin everything they all think about me, all of them, the people on the beat.

One more day and it's over, thank Christ, I thought, and half stumbled down the hill to my car because I still wasn't completely awake.

"One-X-L-Forty-five, One-X-L-Forty-five, come in," said the communications operator, a few seconds after I started the car. She sounded exasperated as hell, so I guess she'd been trying to get me. Probably a major crisis, like a stolen bicycle, I thought.

"One-X-L-Forty-five, go," I said disgustedly into the mike.

"One-X-L-Forty-five, meet the plainclothes officer at the southeast corner of Beverly and Vermont in Rampart Division. This call has been approved by your watch commander."

I rogered the call and wondered what was going on and then despite how rotten I felt, how disgusted with everything and everybody, and mostly this miserable crummy job, despite all that, my heart started beating a little bit harder, and I got a sort of happy feeling bubbling around inside me because I knew it had to be Charlie Bronski. Charlie must have something, and next thing I knew I was driving huckety-buck over Temple, slicing through the heavy traffic and then bombing it down Vermont, and I spotted Charlie in a parking lot near a market. He was standing beside his car looking hot and tired and mad, but I knew he had something or he'd never call me out of my division like this.

''About time, Bumper,'' said Charlie. ''I been trying to reach you on the radio for half an hour. They told me you left court a long time ago.''

''Been out for investigation, Charlie. Too big to talk about.''

''Wonder what *that* means,'' Charlie smiled, with his broken-toothed, Slavic, hard-looking grin. ''I got something so good you won't believe it.''

''You busted Red Scalotta!''

''No, no, you're dreaming,'' he laughed. ''But I got the search warrant for the back that Reba told us about.''

''How'd you do it so fast?''

''I don't actually have it yet. I'll have it in fifteen minutes when Nick and Fuzzy and the Administrative Vice team get here. Nick just talked to me on the radio. Him and Fuzzy just left the Hall of Justice. They got the warrant and the Ad Vice team is on the way to assist.''

''How the hell did you do it, Charlie?'' I asked, and now I'd forgotten the judge, and the humiliation, and the misery, and Charlie and me were grinning at each other because we were both on the scent. And when a real cop gets on it, there's nothing else he can think about. Nothing.

''After we left Reba I couldn't wait to get started on this thing. We went to that laundry over near Sixth and Kenmore. Actually, it's a modern dry cleaning and laundry establishment. They do the work on the premises and it's pretty damned big. The building's on the corner and takes in the whole ground floor, and I even saw employees going up to the second floor where they have storage or something. I watched from across the street with binoculars and Fuzzy prowled around the back alley and found the door Reba said Aaron was talking about.''

''Who in the hell *is* Aaron, Charlie?''

''He's Scalotta's think man. Aaron Fishman. He's an accountant and a shrewd organizer and he's got everything it takes but guts, so he's a number two man to Scalotta. I never saw the guy, I only heard about him from Ad Vice and Intelligence. Soon as Reba described that little Jew I knew who she was talking about. He's Scalotta's link with the back offices. He protects Red's interests and hires the back clerks and keeps things moving. Dick Reemey at Intelligence says he doesn't think Red could operate without Aaron Fishman. Red's drifting away from the business more and more, getting in with the Hollywood crowd. Anyway, Fuzzy, who's a nosy bastard, went in the door to the laundry and found a stairway that was locked, and a door down. He went down and found a basement and an old vented furnace and a trash box, and he started sifting through and found a few adding machine tapes all ending in five's and zero's, and he even found a few charred pieces of owe sheets and a half-burned scratch sheet. I'll bet Aaron would set fire to his clerk if he knew he was that careless.''

Charlie chuckled for a minute and I lit a cigar and looked at my watch.

''Don't worry about the time, Bumper, the back office clerks don't leave until an hour or so past the last post. He's got to stay and figure his tops.''

''Tops ?''

''Top sheets. This shows each agent's code and lists his bettors and how much was won and lost.''

''Wonder how Zoot Lafferty did today?'' I laughed.

''Handbooks like Zoot get ten percent hot or cold, win or lose,'' said Charlie. ''Anyway, Fuzzy found a little evidence to corroborate Reba, and then came the most unbelievable tremendous piece of luck I ever had in this job. He's crawling around down there in the basement like a rat, picking up burned residue, and next thing he sees is a big ugly guy standing stone still in the dark corner of the basement. Fuzzy almost shit his pants and he didn't have a gun or anything because you don't really need weapons when you're working books. Next thing, this guy comes toward him like the creature from the black lagoon and Fuzzy said the door was behind the guy and just as he's thinking about rushing him with his head down and trying to bowl him over on his ass, the giant starts talking in a little-boy voice and says, 'Hello, my name is Bobby. Do you know how to fix electric trains?'

"And next thing Fuzzy knows this guy leads him to a little room in the back where there's a bed and a table and Fuzzy has to find a track break in a little electric train set that Bobby's got on his table, and all the time the guy's standing there, his head damn near touching the top of the doorway he's so big, and making sure Fuzzy fixes it."

"Well, what . . ."

"Lemme finish," Charlie laughed. "Anyway, Fuzzy gets the train fixed and the big ox starts banging Fuzzy on the back and shoulders out of sheer joy, almost knocking Fuzzy's bridgework loose, and Fuzzy finds out this moron is the cleanup man, evidently some retarded relative of the owner of the building, and he lives there in the basement and does the windows and floors and everything in the place.

"There're some offices on the second floor with a completely different stairway, Fuzzy discovers, and this locked door is the only way up to this part of the third floor except for the fire escape in back and the ladder's up and chained in place. This giant, Bobby, says that the third floor is all storage space for one of the offices on the second floor except for 'Miss Terry's place,' and then he starts telling Fuzzy how he likes Miss Terry and how she brings him pies and good things to eat every day, so Fuzzy starts pumping him and Bobby tells him how he hardly ever goes in Miss Terry's place, but he washes the windows once in a while and sometimes helps her with something. And with Fuzzy prodding, he tells about the wooden racks where all the little yellow cards are with the numbers. Those're the ABC professional-type markers of course, and he tells about the adding machine, two adding machines, in fact, and when Fuzzy shows him the burned National Daily Reporter, Bobby says, yeah, those are always there. In short, he completely describes an elite bookmaking office right up to the way papers are bundled and filed."

"You used this Bobby for your informant on the search warrant affidavit?"

"Yeah. I didn't have to mention anything about Reba. According to the affidavit, we got the warrant solely on the basis of this informant Bobby and our own corroborative findings."

"You'll have to use the poor guy in court?"

"He'll certainly have to be named," said Charlie.

"How old a guy is he?"

"I don't know, fifty, fifty-five."

"Think they'll hurt him?"

"Why should they? He doesn't even know what he's doing. They can see that. They just fucked up, that's all. Why should they hurt a dummy?"

"Because they're slimeballs."

"Well, you never know," Charlie shrugged. "They might. Anyway, we got the warrant, Bumper. By God, I kept my promise to you."

"Thanks, Charlie. Nobody could've done better. You got anybody staked on the place?"

"Milburn. He works in our office. We'll just end up busting the broad, Terry. According to the dummy she's the only one ever comes in there except once in a while a man comes in, he said. He couldn't remember what the man looked like. This is Thursday. Should be a lot of paper in that back office. If we get enough of the records we can hurt them, Bumper."

"A two-hundred-and-fifty-dollar fine?" I sniffed.

"If we get the right records we can put Internal Revenue on them. They can tax ten percent of gross for the year. And they can go back as far as five years. That hurts, Bumper. That hurts even a guy as big as Red Scalotta, but it's tough to pull it off."

''How're you going in?''

''We first decided to use Bobby. We can use subterfuge to get in if we can convince the court that we have information that this organization will attempt to destroy records. Hell, they all do that. Fuzzy thought about using Bobby to bang on the lower door to the inside stairway and call Terry and have Terry open the door which she can buzz open. We could tell Bobby it's a game or something, but Nick and Milburn voted us down. They thought when we charged through the door and up the steps through the office door and got Terry by the ass, old Bobby might decide to end the game. If he stopped playing I imagine he'd be no more dangerous than a brahma bull. Anyway, Nick and Milburn were afraid we'd have to hurt the dummy so they voted us down.''

''So how'll you do it?''

''We borrowed a black policewoman from Southwest Detectives. We got her in a blue dungaree apron suit like the black babes that work pressing downstairs. She's going to knock on the downstairs door and start yelling something unintelligible in a way-out suede dialect, and hope Terry buzzes her in. Then she's going to walk up the steps and blab something about a fire in the basement and get as close to Terry as she can, and we hope she can get right inside and get her down on the floor and sit on her because me and Nick'll be charging up that door right behind her. The Administrative Vice team'll follow in a few minutes and help us out since they're the experts on a back-office operation. You know, I only took one back office before so this'll be something for me too.''

''Where'll I be?''

''Well, we got to hide you with your bluesuit, naturally, so you can hang around out back, near the alley behind the solid wood fence on the west side. After we take the place I'll open the back window and call you and you can come on in and see the fruits of your labor with Zoot Lafferty.''

''What'll you do about getting by your star witness?''

''The dummy? Oh, Fuzzy got stuck with that job since he's Bobby's best pal,'' Charlie chuckled. ''Before any of us even get in position Fuzzy's going in to get Bobby and walk him down the street to the drugstore for an ice cream sundae.''

''One-Victor-One to Two, come in,'' said a voice over frequency six.

''That's Milburn at the back office,'' said Charlie, hurrying to the radio.

''Go, Lem,'' said Charlie over the mike.

''Listen, Charlie,'' said Milburn. ''A guy just went in that doorway outside. It's possible he could've turned left into the laundry, I couldn't tell, but I think he made a right to the office stairway.''

''What's he look like, Lem?'' asked Charlie.

''Caucasian, fifty-five to sixty, five-six, hundred fifty, bald, moustache, glasses. Dressed good. I think he parked one block north and walked down because I saw a white Cad circle the block twice and there was a bald guy driving and looking around like maybe for heat.''

''Okay, Lem, we'll be there pretty quick,'' said Charlie, hanging up the mike, red-faced and nodding at me without saying anything.

''Fishman,'' I said.

''Son of a bitch,'' said Charlie. ''Son of a bitch. He's there!''

Then Charlie got on the mike and called Nick and the others, having trouble keeping his voice low and modulated in his excitement, and it was affecting me and my heart started beating. Charlie told them to hurry it up and asked their estimated time of arrival.''

''Our E.T.A. is five minutes,'' said Nick over the radio.

''Jesus, Bumper, we got a chance to take the office and Aaron Fishman at the same time! That weaselly little cocksucker hasn't been busted since the depression days!''

I was still happy as hell for Charlie, but looking at it realistically, what the hell was there to scream about? They had an idiot for an informant, and I didn't want to throw cold water, but I knew damn well the search warrant stood a good chance of being traversed, especially if Bobby was brought into court as a material witness and they saw his I.Q. was less than par golf. And if it wasn't traversed, and they convicted the clerk and Fishman, what the hell would happen to them, a two-hundred-fifty-dollar fine? Fishman probably had four times that much in his pants pocket right now. And I wasn't any too thrilled about I.R.S. pulling off a big case and hitting them in the bankbook, but even if they did, what would it mean? That Scalotta couldn't buy a new whip every time he had parties with sick little girls like Reba? Or maybe Aaron Fishman would have to drive his Cad for two years without getting a new one? I couldn't see anything to get ecstatic about when I considered it all. In fact, I was feeling lower by the minute, and madder. I prayed Red Scalotta would show up there too and maybe try to resist arrest, even though my common sense told me nothing like that would ever happen, but if it did . . .

"There should be something there to destroy the important records," said Charlie, puffing on a cigarette and dancing around impatiently waiting for Nick and the others to drive up.

"You mean like flash paper? I've heard of that," I said.

"They sometimes use that, but mostly in fronts," said Charlie. "You touch a flame or a cigarette to it and it goes up in one big flash and leaves no residue. They also got this dissolving paper. You drop it in water and it dissolves with no residue you can put under a microscope. But sometimes in backs they have some type of small furnace they keep charged where they can throw the real important stuff. Where the hell is that Nick?"

"Right here, Charlie," I said, as the vice car sped across the parking lot. Nick and Fuzzy and the Negro policewoman were inside and another car was following with the two guys from Administrative Vice.

Everybody was wetting their pants when they found out Aaron Fishman was in there, and I marveled at vice officers, how they can get excited about something that is so disappointing, and depressing, and meaningless, when you thought about it. And then Charlie hurriedly explained to the Ad Vice guys what a uniformed cop was doing there, saying it started out as my caper. I knew one of the Ad Vice officers from when he used to work Central Patrol and we jawed and made plans for another five minutes, and finally piled into the cars.

We turned north on Catalina from Sixth Street before getting to Kenmore and then turned west and came down Kenmore from the north. The north side of Sixth Street is all apartment buildings and to the south is the Miracle Mile, Wilshire Boulevard. Sixth Street itself is mostly commercial buildings. Everybody parked to the north because the windows were painted on the top floor of the building on this side. It was the blind side, and after a few minutes everybody got ready when Fuzzy was seen through binoculars skipping down the sidewalk with Bobby, who even from this distance looked like Gargantua. With the giant gone the stronghold wasn't quite so impregnable.

In a few minutes they were all hustling down the sidewalk and I circled around the block on foot and came in behind the wooden fence and I was alone and sweating in the sunshine, wondering why the hell I wanted this so bad, and how the organization would get back on its feet, and another of Red's back offices would just take as much of the action as it could until a new back could be set up, and Aaron would get his new Cad in two years. And he and Red would be free to enjoy it all and maybe someone like me would be laying up in the county jail for perjury in the special tank where they keep policemen accused of crimes, because a policeman put in with the regular pukepots would live probably about one hour at best.

This job didn't make sense. How could I have told myself for twenty years that it made any sense at all? How could I charge around that beat, a big blue stupid clown, and pretend that anything made any sense at all? Judge Redford *should've* put me in jail, I thought. My brain was boiling in the sunshine, the sweat running in my eyes and burning. That would've been a consistent kind of lunacy at least. What the hell are we doing here like this?

Then suddenly I couldn't stand it there alone, my big ass only partly hidden by the fence, and I walked out in the alley and over to the fire escape of the old building. The iron ladder was chained up like an ancient fearsome drawbridge. A breach of fire regulation to chain it up, I thought, and I looked around for something to stand on, and spotted a trash can by the fence which I emptied and turned upside down under the ladder. And then in a minute I was dangling there like a fat sweaty baboon, tearing my pants on the concrete wall, scuffing my shoes, panting, and finally sobbing, because I couldn't get my ass up there on a window ledge where I could climb over the railing on the second floor.

I fell back once, clear to the alley below. I fell hard on my shoulder, and thought if I'd been able to read that hotel register I'd never have been humiliated like that, and I thought of how I was of no value whatever to this operation which was in itself of no value because if I couldn't catch Red Scalotta and Aaron Fishman by the rules, then they would put *me* in jail. And I sat on my ass there in the alley, panting, my hands red and sore and my shoulder hurting, and I thought then, if I go to the dungeon and Fishman goes free, then *I'm* the scumbag and *he's* the Blue Knight, and I wondered how he would look in my uniform.

Then I looked up at that ladder and vowed that I'd die here in this alley if I didn't climb that fire escape. I got back on the trash can and jumped up, grabbing the metal ladder and feeling it drop a little until the chain caught it. Then I shinnied up the wall again, gasping and sobbing out loud, the sweat like vinegar in my eyes, and got one foot up and had to stop and try to breathe in the heat. I almost let go and thought how that would make sense too if I fell head first now onto the garbage can and broke my fat neck. Then I took a huge breath and knew if I didn't make it now I never would make it, and I heaved my carcass up, up, and then I was sitting on the window ledge and surprisingly enough I still had my hat on and I hadn't lost my gun. I was perched there on the ledge in a pile of birdshit, and a fat gray pigeon sat on the fire escape railing over me. He cooed and looked at me gasping and grimacing and wondered if I was dangerous.

"Get outta here, you little prick," I whispered, when he crapped on my shoulder. I swung my hat at him and he squawked and flew away.

Then I dragged myself up carefully, keeping most of my weight on the window ledge, and I was on the railing and then I climbed over and was on the first landing of the fire escape where I had to rest for a minute because I was dizzy. I looked at my watch and saw that the policewoman should be about ready to try her flimflam now, so, dizzy or not, I climbed the second iron laddor.

It was steep and long to the third floor, one of those almost vertical iron ladders like on a ship, with round iron hand railings. I climbed as quietly as I could, taking long deep breaths. Then I was at the top and was glad I wouldn't have to make the steep descent back down. I should be walking out through the back office if everything went right. When Charlie opened the back door to call to me, I'd be standing right here watching the door instead of crouched in some alley. And if I heard any doors breaking, or any action at all, I'd kick in the back door here, and maybe *I'd* be the first one inside the place, and maybe I'd do something else that could land me in jail, but the way I felt this moment, maybe it would be worth it because twenty years didn't mean a goddamn thing when Scalotta and Fishman could wear *my* uniform and I could wear jail denims with striped patch pockets and lay up there in the cop's tank at the county jail.

Then I heard a crash and I knew the scam hadn't worked because this was a door breaking far away, way down below, which meant they'd had to break in that first door, run up those steps clear to the third floor and break in the other door, and then I found myself kicking on the back door which I didn't know was steel reinforced with a heavy bar across it. It wouldn't go, and at that moment I didn't know how sturdy they had made it and I thought it was a regular door and I was almost crying as I kicked it because I couldn't even take down a door anymore and I couldn't do *anything* anymore. But I kicked, and kicked, and finally I went to the window on the left and kicked right through it, cutting my leg. I broke out the glass with my hands and I lost my hat and cut my forehead on the glass and was raging and yelling something I couldn't remember when I stormed through that room and saw the terrified young woman and the trembling bald little man by the doorway, their arms full of boxes. They looked at me for a second and then the woman started screaming and the man went out the door, turned right and headed for the fire escape with me after him. He threw the bar off the steel door and was back out on the fire escape, a big cardboard box in his arms crammed with cards and papers, and he stopped on the landing and saw how steep that ladder was. He was holding tight to the heavy box and he turned his back to the ladder and gripped the box and was going to try to back down the iron stairs when I grabbed him with my bloody hands and he yelled at me as two pigeons flew in our faces with a whir and rattle of wings.

"Let me go!" he said, the little greenish sacs under his eyes bulging. "You ape, let me go!"

And then I don't know if I just let him go or if I put pressure against him. I honestly don't know, but it doesn't really make any difference, because pulling away from me like he was, and holding that box like Midas's gold, I knew exactly what would happen if I just suddenly did what he was asking.

So I don't know for sure if I shoved him or if I just released him, but as I said, the result would've been the same, and at this moment in my life it was the only thing that made the slightest bit of sense, the only thing I could do for any of it to make any sense at all. He would never wear my bluesuit, never, if I only did what he was asking. My heart was thumping like the pigeon's wing, and I just let go and dropped my bleeding hands to my sides.

He pitched backward then, and the weight of the box against his chest made him fall head first, clattering down the iron ladder like an anchor being dropped. He was screaming and the box had broken open and markers and papers were flying and sailing and tumbling through the air. It *did* sound like an anchor chain feeding out, the way he clattered down. On the landing below where he stopped, I saw his dentures on the first rung of the ladder not broken, and his glasses on the landing, broken, and the cardboard box on top of him so you could hardly see the little man doubled over beneath it. He was quiet for a second and then started whimpering, and finally sounded like a pigeon cooing.

"What happened, Bumper?" asked Charlie, running out on the fire escape, out of breath.

"Did you get all the right records, Charlie?"

"Oh my God, what happened?"

"He fell."

"Is he dead?"

"I don't think so, Charlie. He's making a lot of noises."

"I better call for an ambulance," said Charlie. "You better stay here."

"I intend to," I said, and stood there resting against the railing for five minutes watching Fishman. During this time, Nick and Charlie went down and unfolded him and mopped at his face and bald head, which was broken with huge lacerations.

Charlie and me left the others there and drove slowly in the wake of the screaming ambulance which was taking Fishman to Central Receiving Hospital.

"How bad is your leg cut?" asked Charlie, seeing the blood, a purple wine color when it soaks through a policeman's blue uniform.

"Not bad, Charlie," I said, dabbing at the cuts on my hands.

"Your face doesn't look bad. Little cut over your eye."

"I feel fine."

"There was a room across from the back office," said Charlie. "We found a gas-fed burn oven in there. It was fired up and vented through the roof. They would've got to it if you hadn't crashed through the window. I'm thankful you did it, Bumper. You saved everything for us."

"Glad I could help."

"Did Fishman try to fight you or anything?"

"He struggled a little. He just fell."

"I hope the little asshole dies. I'm thinking what he means to the organization and what he is, and I hope the little asshole dies, so help me God. You know, I thought you pushed him for a minute. I thought you did it and I was glad."

"He just fell, Charlie."

"Here we are, let's get you cleaned up," said Charlie, parking on the Sixth Street side of Central Receiving where a doctor was going into the ambulance that carried Fishman. The doctor came out in a few seconds and waved them on to General Hospital where there are better surgical facilities.

"How's he look, Doctor?" asked Charlie, as we walked through the emergency entrance.

"Not good," said the doctor.

"Think he'll die?" asked Charlie.

"I don't know. If he doesn't, he may wish he had."

The cut on my leg took a few stitches but the ones on my hands and face weren't bad and just took cleaning and a little germ killer. It was almost seven o'clock when I finished my reports telling how Fishman jerked out of my grasp and how I got cut.

When I left, Charlie was dictating his arrest report to a typist.

"Well, I'll be going now, Charlie," I said, and he stopped his dictation and stood up and walked with me a little way down the hall and looked for a second like he was going to shake hands with me.

"Thanks, Bumper, for everything. This is the best vice pinch I've ever been in on. We got more of their records than I could've dreamed of."

"Thanks for cutting me in on it, Charlie."

"It was *your* caper."

"Wonder how Fishman's doing?" I said, getting a sharp pain and feeling a bubble forming. I popped two tablets.

"Fuzzy called out there about a half hour ago. Couldn't find out much. I'll tell you one thing, I'll bet Red Scalotta has to get a new accountant and business advisor. I'll bet Fishman'll have trouble adding two-digit numbers after this."

"Well, maybe it worked out right."

"Right? It was more than that. For the first time in years I feel like maybe there *is* some justice in the world, and even though they fuck over you and rub it in your face and fuck over the law itself, well, now for the first time I feel like maybe there's other hands in it, and these hands'll give you some justice. I feel like the hand of God pushed that man down those stairs."

"The hand of God, huh? Yeah, well I'll be seeing you, Charlie. Hang in there, old shoe."

"See you, Bumper," said Charlie Bronski, his square face lit up, eyes crinkled, the broken tooth showing.

The locker room was empty when I got there, and after I sat down on the bench and started unlacing my boondockers, I suddenly realized how sore I was. Not the cuts from the glass, that was nothing. But my shoulder where I fell in that alley, and my arms and back from dangling there on that fire escape, when I couldn't do what any young cop could do—pull my ass up six feet in the air. And my hands were blistered and raw from hanging there and from clawing at the concrete wall trying to get that boost. Even my ass was sore, deep inside, the muscles of both cheeks, from kicking against that steel reinforced door and bouncing off it like a tennis ball, or maybe in my case like a lumpy medicine ball. I was very very sore all over.

In fifteen minutes I'd gotten into my sport coat and slacks, and combed my hair as best I could, which just means rearranging what resembles a bad wiring job, and slipped on my loafers, and was driving out of the parking lot in my Ford. The gas pains were gone, and no indigestion. Then I thought of Aaron Fishman again, folded over, his gouged head twisted under the puny little body with the big cardboard box on top. But I stopped that nonsense right there, and said, no, no, you won't haunt my sleep because it doesn't matter a bit that I made you fall. I was just the instrument of some force in this world that, when the time is right, screws over almost every man, good or bad, rich or poor, and usually does it just when the man can bear it least.

14

It was dark now, and the spring night, and the cool breeze, even the smog, all tasted good to me. I rolled the windows down to suck up the air, and jumped on the Hollywood Freeway, thinking how good it would be at Abd's Harem with a bunch of happy Arabs.

Hollywood was going pretty good for a Thursday night, Sunset and Hollywood Boulevards both being jammed with cars, mostly young people, teeny boppers who've literally taken over Hollywood at night. The place has lost the real glamour of the forties and early fifties. It's a kid's town now, and except for a million hippies, fruits and servicemen, that's about all you see around the Strip and the main thoroughfares. It's a very depressing place for that reason. The clubs are mostly bottomless skin houses and psychedelic joints, but there're still some places you can go, some excellent places to eat.

I'd come to know Yasser Hafiz and the others some ten or twelve years ago when I was walking my beat on Main Street. One night at about two a.m., I spotted a paddy hustler taking a guy up the back stairs of the Marlowe Hotel, a sleazy Main Street puke hole used by whores and fruits and paddy hustlers. I was alone because my partner, a piss-poor excuse for a cop named Syd Bacon, was laying up in a hotel room knocking a chunk off some bubble-assed taxi dancer he was going with. He was supposed to meet me back on the beat at one-thirty but never showed up.

I hurried around the front of the hotel that night and went up the other stairway and hid behind the deserted clerk's desk, and when the paddy hustler and his victim came that way down the hall, I jumped inside the small closet at the desk. I was just in time because the paddy hustler's two partners came out of a room two doors down and across the hall.

They were whispering, and one of them faded down the front stairway to watch the street. The second walked behind the desk, turned the lamp on and pretended to be reading a newspaper he carried with him. They were black of course. Paddy hustling was always a Negro flimflam and that's where the name came from, but lately I've seen white hustlers using this scam on other paddies.

"Say, brother," said the hustler who was with the paddy. I left the door open a crack and saw the paddy was a well-dressed young guy, bombed out of his skull, weaving around where he stood, trying hard to brush his thick black hair out of his eyes. He'd lost his necktie somewhere, and his white dress shirt was stained from booze and unbuttoned.

"Wha's happenin', blood?" said the desk clerk, putting down his paper.

"Alice in tonight?" said the first one, acting as the procurer. He was the bigger of the two, a very dark-skinned guy, tall and fairly young.

"Yeah, she's breathin' fire tonight," said the other one. He was young too. "Ain't had no man yet and that bitch is a nymphomaniac!"

"Really," said the procurer. "Really."

"Let's go, I'm ready," said the paddy, and I noticed his Middle East accent.

"Jist a minute, man," said his companion. "That whore is fine pussy, but she is a stone thief, man. You better leave the wallet with the desk clerk."

"Yeah, I kin put it in the safe," said the bored-looking guy behind the desk. "Never tell when that whore might talk you into a all-night ride and then rob your ass when you falls asleep."

"Right, brother," said the procurer.

The paddy shrugged and took out his wallet, putting it on the desk.

"Better leave the wristwatch and ring, too," warned the desk clerk.

"Thank you," the paddy nodded, obeying the desk clerk, who removed an envelope from under the counter, which he had put there for the valuables.

"Kin I have my five dollars now?" asked the first man. "And the clerk'll take the five for Alice and three for the room."

"All right," said the paddy, unsteadily counting out thirteen dollars for the two men.

"Now you go on in number two-thirty-seven there," said the desk clerk, pointing to the room where the first one had come out. "I'll buzz Alice's room and she be in there in 'bout five minutes. And baby, you better hold on 'cause she move like a steam drill."

The paddy smiled nervously and staggered down the hall, opening the door and disappearing inside.

"Ready, blood?" grinned the desk clerk.

"Le's go," said the big one, chuckling as the clerk turned off the lamp.

I'd come out of the closet without them seeing, and stood at the desk now, with my Smith pointed at the right eyeball of the desk clerk. "Want a room for the night, gentlemen?" I said. "Our accommodations ain't fancy, but it's clean and we can offer two very square meals a day."

The procurer was the first to recover, and he was trying to decide whether to run or try something more dangerous. Paddy hustlers didn't usually carry guns, but they often carried blades or crude saps of some kind. I aimed at *his* eyeball to quiet down his busy mind. "Freeze, or name your beneficiary," I said.

"Hey, Officer, wha's happenin'?" said the desk clerk with a big grin and showing lots of gold. "Where you come from?"

"Down the chimney. Now get your asses over there and spread-eagle on the wall!"

"Sheee-it, this is a humbug, we ain't done nothin'," said the procurer.

"Shit fuck," grumbled the desk clerk.

This was in the days when we still believed in wall searches, before so damn many policemen got shot or thumped by guys who practiced coming out of that spread-eagled position. I abandoned it a few days before the Department did, and I put hot suspects on their knees or bellies. But at this time I was still using the wall search.

"Move your legs back, desk clerk!" I said to the smaller one, who was being cute, barely leaning forward. He only shuffled his feet a few inches so I kicked him hard behind the right knee and he screamed and did what I told him. The scream brought the paddy out.

"Is something wrong?" asked the paddy who was half-undressed, trying to look sober as possible.

"I'm saving you from being flimflammed, asshole," I said. "Get your clothes on and come out here." He just stood there gaping. Then I yelled, "Get dressed, stupid!" my gun in my left hand still pointing at the spread-eagled paddy hustlers, and my handcuffs in my right hand getting ready to cuff the two hustlers together, and my eyes drilling the dipshit victim who stood there getting ready to ask more dumb questions. I didn't see or hear the third paddy hustler, a big bull of a kid, who'd crept up the front stairway when he heard the ruckus. If he'd been an experienced hustler instead of a youngster he'd have left the other two and gone his way. But being inexperienced, he was loyal to his partners, and just as I was getting ready to kick the paddy in the ass to get him moving, two hundred pounds falls on my back and I'm on the floor fighting for my gun and my life with all three hustlers.

"Git the gun, Tyrone!" yelled the desk clerk to the kid. "Jist git the *gun!*"

The procurer was cursing and hitting me in the face, head, and neck, anywhere he could, and the desk clerk was working on my ribs while I tried to protect myself with my left arm. All my thoughts were on the right arm, and hand, and the gun in the hand, which the kid was prying on with both his strong hands. For a few seconds everything was quiet, except for the moans and breathing and muffled swearing of the four of us, and then the kid was winning and almost had the gun worked loose when I heard a godawful Arab war cry and the paddy cracked the desk clerk over the head with a heavy metal ashtray.

Then the paddy was swinging it with both hands and I ducked my head, catching a glancing blow on the shoulder that made me yelp and which left a bruise as big as your fist. The fourth or fifth swing caught the procurer in the eyes and he was done, laying there holding his bleeding face and yelling, "YOW, YOW, YOW," like somebody cut his nuts off.

The kid lost his stomach at this point and said, "Aw right, aw right, aw right," raising his hands to surrender and scooting back on his ass with his hands in the air until he backed against the wall.

I was so sick and trembling I could've vomited and I was ready to kill all three of them, except that the desk clerk and the procurer looked half-dead already. The kid was untouched.

"Stand up," I said to the kid, and when he did, I put my gun in the holster, reached for my beavertail, and sapped him across the left collarbone. That started him yelling and bitching, and he didn't stop until we got him to the hospital, which made me completely disgusted. Up until then I had some respect for him because he was loyal to his friends and had enough guts to jump a cop who had a gun in his hand. But when he couldn't suffer in silence, he lost my respect. I figured this kind of crybaby'd probably make a complaint against me for police brutality or something, but he never did.

"What can I do, sir?" asked the paddy after I had the three hustlers halfway on their feet. I was trying to stay on mine as I leaned against the desk and covered them with the gun. This time I kept my eyes open.

"Go downstairs and put a dime in the pay phone and dial operator," I panted, still not sure how sober he was, even though he damn near decapitated all of us. "Ask for the police and tell them an officer needs assistance at the Marlowe Hotel, Fifth and Main."

"Marlowe Hotel," said the paddy. "Yes, sir."

I never found out what he said over the phone, but he must've laid it on pretty good because in three minutes I had patrol units, vice cops, felony cars, and even some dicks who rolled from the station. There were more cops than tenants at the

Marlowe and the street out front was lined with radio cars, their red lights glowing clear to Sixth Street.

The paddy turned out to be Yasser's oldest son, Abd, the one the Harem was named for, and that was how I got to know them. Abd stayed with me for several hours that night while I made my reports, and he seemed like a pretty good guy after he had a dozen cups of coffee and sobered up. He had a very bad recollection of the whole thing when we went to court against the paddy hustlers, and he ended up testifying to what I told him happened before we went in the courtroom. That part about saving my ass, he never did remember, and when I drove him home to Hollywood after work that night, in gratitude for what he did for me, he took me in the house, woke up his father, mother, uncle, and three of his brothers to introduce me and tell them that I saved him from being robbed and killed by three bandits. Of course he never told them the whole truth about how the thing went down in a whorehouse, but that was okay with me, and since he really thought *I* saved *him* instead of the other way around, and since he really enjoyed having been saved even though it didn't happen, and making me the family hero, what the hell, I let him tell it the way he believed it happened so as not to disappoint them.

It was about that time that Yasser and his clan had moved here from New York where they had a small restaurant. They had pooled every cent they could lay hands on to buy the joint in Hollywood, liquor license and all, and had it remodeled and ready to open. We sat in Yasser's kitchen that night, all of us, drinking *arak* and wine, and then beer, and we all got pretty zonked except Abd who was sick, and I picked out the name for the new restaurant.

It's a corny name, I know, but I was drunk when I picked it and I could've done better. But by then I was such a hero to them they wouldn't have changed it for anything. They insisted on me being a kind of permanent guest of Abd's Harem. I couldn't pay for a thing in there and that's why I didn't come as often as I wanted to.

I drove in the parking lot in back of Abd's Harem instead of having the parking lot attendant handle the Ford, and I came in through the kitchen.

"*Al-salām 'alaykum, Baba*," I said to Yasser Hafiz Hammad, a squat, completely bald old man with a heavy gray moustache, who had his back to me as he mixed up a huge metal bowlful of *kibbi* with clean powerful hands which he dipped often in ice water so the *kibbi* wouldn't stick to them.

"Bumper! *Wa-'alaykum al-salām*," he grinned through the great moustache. He hugged me with his arms, keeping his hands free, and kissed me on the mouth. That was something I couldn't get over about Arabs. They didn't usually kiss women in greeting, only men.

"Where the hell you keep yourself, Bumper?" he said, dipping a spoon in the raw *kibbi* for me to sample it. "We don't see you much no more."

"Delicious, *Baba*," I said.

"Yes, but is it ber-fect?"

"It's ber-fect, *Bubba*."

"You hungry, eh, Bumper?" he said, returning to the *kibbi* and making me some little round balls which he knew I'd eat raw. I liked raw *kibbi* every bit as good as baked, and *kibbi* with yogurt even better.

"You making *labaneeyee* tonight, *Baba*?"

"Sure, Bumper. Damn right. What else you want? *Sfeeha? Bamee?* Anything you want. We got lots of dish tonight. Bunch of Lebanese and Syrian guys in the banquet room. Ten entrées they order special. Son of a bitch, I cook all goddamn day. When I get rest, I coming out and have a goddamn glass of *arak* with you, okay?"

"Okay, *Baba*," I said, finishing the *kibbi* and watching Yasser work. He kneaded the ground lamb and cracked wheat and the onion and cinnamon and spices, after dipping his hands in the ice water to keep the mixture pliable. This *kibbi* was well stuffed with pine nuts and the meat was cooked in butter and braised. When Yasser got it all ready he spread the *kibbi* over the bottom of a metal pan and the *kibbi* stuffing over the top of that, and another layer of *kibbi* on top of that. He cut the whole pan into little diamond shapes and then baked it. Now I couldn't decide whether to have the *kibbi* with yogurt or the baked *kibbi*. What the hell, I'll have them both, I thought. I was pretty hungry now.

"Look, Bumper," said Yasser Hafiz, pointing to the little footballs of *kibbi* he'd been working on all day. He'd pressed hollows into the center and stuffed them with lamb stuffing and was cooking them in a yogurt sauce.

Yeah, I'll have both, I thought. I decided to go in and start on some appetizers. I was more than hungry all of a sudden and not quite so tired, and all I could think of was the wonderful food of Abd's Harem.

Inside, I spotted Ahmed right away, and he grinned and waved me to a table near the small dance area where one of his dancers could shove her belly in my face. Ahmed was tall for an Arab, about thirty years old, the youngest of Yasser's sons, and had lived in the States since he was a kid. He'd lost a lot of the Arab ways and didn't kiss me like his father and his uncles did, when the uncles were here helping wait tables or cooking on a busy weekend night.

"Glad you could come tonight, Bumper," said Ahmed with a hint of a New York accent, since his family had lived there several years before coming to Los Angeles. When he talked to the regular customers though, he put on a Middle East accent for show.

"Think I'll have some appetizers, Ahmed. I'm hungry tonight."

"Good, Bumper, good," said Ahmed, his dark eyes crinkling at the corners when he grinned, "We like to see you eat." He clapped his hands for a good-looking, red-haired waitress in a harem girl's outfit, and she came over to the table.

Abd's Harem was like all Middle East restaurants, but bigger than most. There were Saracen shields on the walls, and scimitars, and imitation Persian tapestries, and the booths and tables were dark and heavy, leather-padded, and studded with hammered bronzework. Soothing Arab music drifted through the place from several hidden speakers.

"Bring Bumper some lamb tongue, Barbara. What else would you like, Bumper?"

"A little *humos tahini,* Ahmed."

"Right. *Humos* too, Barbara."

Barbara smiled at me and said, "A drink, Bumper?"

"All right, I'll have *arak.*"

"If you'll excuse me, Bumper," said Ahmed, "I've got to take care of the banquet room for the next hour. Then I'll join you and we'll have a drink together."

"Go head on, kid," I nodded. "Looks like you're gonna have a nice crowd."

"Business is great, Bumper. Wait'll you see our new belly dancer."

I nodded and winked as Ahmed hurried toward the banquet room to take care of the roomful of Arabs. I could hear them from where I sat, proposing toasts and laughing. They seemed pretty well lubricated for so early in the evening.

The appetizers were already prepared and the waitress was back to my table in a few minutes with the little slices of lamb's tongue, boiled and pealed and seasoned with garlic and salt, and a good-sized dish of *humos,* which makes the greatest dip in the world. She gave me more *humos* than any of the paying customers get, and a large heap of the round flat pieces of warm Syrian bread covered with a napkin. I dipped into the *humos* right away with a large chunk of the Syrian bread and almost moaned out loud it was so delicious. I could taste the sesame seeds even though they were ground into the creamy blend of garbanzo beans, and I poured olive oil all over it, and dipped lots of oil up in my bread. I could also taste the clove and crushed garlic and almost forgot the lamb tongue I was enjoying the *humos* so much.

"Here's your *arak,* Bumper," said Barbara, bringing me the drink and another dish of *humos* a little smaller than the first. "Yasser says not to let you ruin your dinner with the tongue and *humos.*"

"No chance, kid," I said, after swallowing a huge mouthful of tongue and bread. I gulped some *arak* so I could talk. "Tell *Baba* I'm as hungry as a tribe of Bedouins and I'll eat out his whole kitchen if he's not careful."

"And as horny as a herd of goats?"

"Yeah, tell him that too," I chuckled. That was a standing joke between Yasser and Ahmed and me that all the girls had heard.

Now that the starvation phase was over I started to feel pain in my leg and shoulder. I poured some water into the clear *arak,* turning it milky. I glanced around to make sure no one could see and I loosened up my belt and smiled to myself as I smelled the food all through the place. I nibbled now, and tried not to be such a crude bastard, and I sipped my *arak,* getting three refills from Barbara who was a fast and good waitress. Then the pain started to go away.

I saw Ahmed running between kitchen, bar, and banquet room, and I thought that Yasser was lucky to have such good kids. All his sons had done well, and now the last one was staying in the business with him. The Arab music drifted slowly through the place and mingled with the food smell, and I was feeling damn warm now. In about an hour the band would be here, a three-piece Armenian group who played exotic music for the belly dancer that I was anxious to see. Ahmed really knew his dancers.

"Everything okay, Bumper?" Ahmed called in an Arab accent since other customers were around.

"Okay," I grinned, and he hurried past on one of his trips to the kitchen.

I was starting to sway with the sensual drums and I was feeling much better, admiring the rugs hanging on the walls, and other Arabian Nights decorations like water pipes that kids used now for smoking dope, and the swords up high enough on the walls so some drunk couldn't grab them and start his own dance. Abd's Harem was a very good place, I thought. Really an oasis in the middle of a tacky, noisy part of Hollywood which was generally so phony I couldn't stand it.

I noticed that Khalid, one of Yasser's brothers, was helping in the bar tonight. I figured as soon as he saw me I'd get another big hairy kiss.

"Ready, Bumper?" said Barbara, smiling pretty, and padding quietly up to my table with a huge tray on a food cart.

"Yeah, yeah," I said, looking at the dishes of baked *kibbi, kibbi* with yogurt, stuffed grape leaves and a small skewer of shish kebab.

"Yasser said to save room for dessert, Bumper," said Barbara as she left me there. I could think of nothing at times like these, except the table in front of me, and I waged a tough fight against myself to eat slowly and savor it, especially the grape leaves which were a surprise for me, because Yasser doesn't make them all the time. I could taste the mint, fragrant and tangy in the yogurt that I ladled over the grape leaves, pregnant with lamb and rice, succulent parsley. and spices. Yasser added just the right amount of lemon juice for my taste.

After a while, Barbara returned and smiled at me as I sat sipping my wine, at peace with the world.

"Some pastry, Bumper? *Baklawa?*"

"Oh no, Barbara," I said, holding my hand up weakly. "Too rich. No *baklawa,* no."

"All right," she laughed. "Yasser has something special for you. Did you save a little room?"

"Oh no," I said painfully, as she took away the cartload of empty plates.

Arabs are so friendly and hospitable, and they like so much to see me eat, I would've hated to do something horrible like upchucking all his hard work. My belly was bulging so much I had to move the chair back two inches, and my shirt was straining to pop open. I thought of Fatstuff in the old "Smilin' Jack" cartoon strip and remembered how I used to laugh at the poor bastard always popping his buttons, when I was young and slim.

A few minutes later Barbara came back with an oversized sherbet glass.

"*Moosh moosh!*" I said. "I haven't had *moosh moosh* for a year."

Barbara smiled and said, "Yasser says that Allah sent you tonight because Yasser made your favorite dessert today and thought about you."

"*Moosh moosh!*" I said as Barbara left me, and I scooped up a mouthful and let it lay there on my tongue, tasting the sweet apricot and lemon rind, and remembering how Yasser's wife, Yasmine, blended the apricot and lemon rind and sugar, and folded the apricot purée into the whipped cream before it was chilled. They all knew it was my very favorite. So I ended up having two more cups of *moosh moosh* and then I was really through. Barbara cleared the table for the last time and Ahmed and Yasser both joined me for ten minutes.

There's an Arab prayer which translates something like, "Give me a good digestion, Lord, and something to digest." It was the only prayer I ever heard that I thought made a lot of sense, and I thought that if I believed in God I wouldn't lay around begging from Him and mumbling a lot of phony promises. This particular Arab prayer said all I'd say to Him, and all I'd expect of Him, so even though I didn't believe, I said it before and after I ate dinner in Abd's Harem. Sometimes I even said it at other times. Sometimes even at home I said it.

When the Armenians arrived, I was happy to see the *oud* player was old Mr. Kamian. He didn't often play at Abd's Harem anymore. His grandsons Berge and George were with him, and anyone could see they were his grandsons, all three being tall, thin, with hawk noses and dark-rimmed blazing eyes. Berge would play the violin and George, the youngest, a boy not yet twenty, would play the *darbuka* drums. It was just a job to the two young ones. They were good musicians, but it was old Kamian I would hear as he plucked and stroked those *oud* strings with the quill of an eagle feather. It's a lute-like instrument and has no frets like a guitar. Yet the old man's fingers knew exactly where to dance on that *oud* neck, so fast it was hard to believe. It gave me goose bumps and made it hard to swallow when I saw that old man's slender, brittle-looking fingers dart over those twelve strings.

Once I was there in the afternoon when they were rehearsing new dancers, and old Kamian was telling Armenian tales to Berge's children. I sat there hidden behind a beaded curtain and heard Kamian tell about the fiery horses of Armenia, and pomegranates full of pearls and rubies, and about Hazaran-Bulbul, the magic nightingale of a thousand songs. He made me feel like a kid that day listening to him, and ever since, when I hear him play the *oud*, I could almost climb aboard one of those fiery horses.

Anothor time when I was here late at night listening to Mr. Kamian play, his oldest son Leon sat with me drinking scotch and told me the story of his father, how he was the only survivor of a large family which totaled, cousins and all, half of a village that was massacred by Turkish soldiers. Mr. Kamian was fifteen years old then, and his body was left in a big ditch with those of his parents, brothers, sisters, everyone in his entire world.

"The thing that saved him that day was the *smell* of death," said Leon, who spoke five languages, English with only a slight accent, and like all Armenians, loved to tell stories. "As he lay there, my father wanted to be dead with the others. It wasn't the sight or idea of death that made him drag himself up and out of that ditch, it was the smell of rotting bodies which at last was the only unbearable thing, and which drove him to the road and away from his village forever.

"For almost a year he wandered, his only possession an *oud* which he rescued from a plundered farmhouse. One night when he was huddling alone in the wilderness like Cain, feeling like the only human being left on earth, he became very angry that God would let this happen, and like the child he was, he *demanded* a sign from Him, and he waited and listened in the darkness, but he heard only the wind howling across the Russian steppes. Then he wondered how he could ever have believed in a God who would let this happen to Armenia, His tiny Christian island in a sea of Islam. There was no sign, so he strummed the *oud* and sang brave songs into the wind all that night.

"The very next night the boy was wandering through a village much like his had been, and of course he passed hundreds of starving refugees on the road. He took off from the road to find a place to sleep in the trees where someone wouldn't kill him just to steal the *oud*. There in the woods he saw a black sinister shape rising from the ground, and the first thing the boy thought was that it was a *dev*, one of those fearsome Armenian ogres his *nany* used to tell him about. He raised the flimsy *oud* like it was an ax and prepared to defend himself. Then the dark form took shape and spoke to him in Armenian from beneath a ragged cloak, 'Please, do you have something to eat?'

"The boy saw a child in the moonlight, covered with sores, stomach bloated, barely able to walk. Her teeth were loose, eyes and gums crusted, and a recently broken nose made it hard for her to breathe. He examined her face and saw that at no time could that face have been more than homely, but now it was truly awful. He spoke to her a few moments and found she was thirteen years old, a wandering refugee, and he remembered the proud and vain demand he had made of God the night before. He began to laugh then, and suddenly felt stronger. He couldn't stop laughing and the laughter filled him with strength. It alarmed the girl, and he saw it, and finally he said, "The God of Armenians has a sense of humor. How can you doubt someone with a sense of humor like His? You're to come with me, my little *dev*."

" 'What do you want of me, sir?' she asked, very frightened now.

" 'What do I want of you?' he answered softly. 'Look at you. What do you have to offer? Everything has been taken from you and everything has been done to you. What could anyone in the world possibly want of you now? Can you think of what it is, the thing I want?'

" 'No, sir.'

" 'There is only one thing left. To *love* you, of course. We're good for no more than this. Now come with me. We're going to find *our* Armenia.'

"She went with the half-starved, wild-eyed boy. They survived together and wandered to the Black Sea, somehow got passage, and crossed on foot through Europe, through the war and fighting, ever westward to the Atlantic, working, having children. Finally, in 1927, they and five children, having roamed half the world, arrived in New York, and from force of habit more than anything, kept wandering west, picking up jobs along the way until they reached the Pacific Ocean. Then my mother said, 'This is as far as we go. This ocean is too big.' And they stopped, had four more children, sixty-one grandchildren, and so far, ten great-grandchildren, more than forty with the Kamian name that would not die in the ditch in Armenia. Most of his sons and grandsons have done well, and he still likes to come here sometimes once a week and play his *oud* for a few people who understand."

So that was the story of old Kamian, and I didn't doubt any of it, because I've known a lot of tough bastards in my time that could've pulled off something like that, but the thing that amazed me, that I couldn't really understand, is how he could've taken the little girl with him that night. I mean he could've helped her, sure. But he purposely *gave* himself to her that night. After what he'd already been through, he up and *gave* himself to somebody! That was the most incredible thing about Mr. Kamian, that, and how the hell his fingers knew exactly where to go on that *oud* when there were no frets to guide them.

"You eat plenty, Bumper?" asked Yasser, who came to the table with Ahmed, and I responded by giving him a fatcat grin and pawing him on the hand, and whispering "*shukran*" in a way that you would know meant thanks without knowing Arabic.

"Maybe you'll convert me, feeding me like that. Maybe I'll become a Moslem," I added.

"What you do during Ramadan when you must fast?" laughed Yasser.

"You see how *big* Abd's kids?" said Yasser, lifting his apron to reach for his wallet, and laying some snapshots on me that I pretended I could see.

"Yeah, handsome kids," I said, hoping the old man wouldn't start showing me all his grandkids. He had about thirty of them, and like all Arabs, was crazy about children.

Ahmed spoke in Arabic that had to do with the banquet room, and Yasser seemed to remember something.

"Scoose me, Bumper," said the old boy, "I come back later, but I got things in the kitchen."

"Sure, *Baba*," I said, and Ahmed smiled as he watched his father strut back to the kitchen, the proud patriarch of a large family, and the head of a very good business, which Abd's Harem certainly was.

"How old is your father now?"

"Seventy-five," said Ahmed. "Looks good, doesn't he?"

"Damn good. Tell me, can he still eat like he used to, say ten, fifteen years ago?"

"He eats pretty well," Ahmed laughed. "But no, not like he used to. He used to eat like you, Bumper. It was a joy to watch him eat. He says food doesn't taste quite the same anymore."

I started getting gas pains, but didn't pop a tablet because it would be rude for Ahmed to see me do that after I'd just finished such a first-rate dinner.

"It'd be a terrible thing for your appetite to go," I said. "That'd be almost as bad as being castrated."

"Then I never want to get *that* old, Bumper," Ahmed laughed, with the strength and confidence of only thirty years on this earth. "Of course there's a third thing, remember, your digestion? Got to have that, too."

"Oh yeah," I said. "Got to have digestion or appetite ain't worth a damn."

Just then the lights dimmed, and a bluish spot danced around the small bandstand as the drums started first. Then I was amazed to see Laila Hammad run out to the floor, in a gold-and-white belly dancer's costume, and the music picked up as she stood there, chestnut hair hanging down over her boobs, fingers writhing, and working the *zils*, those little golden finger cymbals, hips swaying as George's hands beat a blood-heating rhythm on the *darbuka*. Ahmed grinned at me as I admired her strong golden thighs.

"How do you like our new dancer?"

"Laila's your dancer?"

"Wait'll you see her," said Ahmed, and it was true, she really was something. There was art to the dancing, not just lusty gyrations, and though I'm no judge of belly dancing, even I could see it.

"How old is she now?" I said to Ahmed, watching her mobile stomach, and the luxurious chestnut hair, which was all her own, and now hung down her back and then streamed over her wonderful-looking boobs.

"She's nineteen," said Ahmed, and I was very happy to see how good-looking she'd turned out.

Laila had worked as a waitress here for a few years, even when she was much too young to be doing it, but she always looked older, and her father, Khalil Hammad, was a cousin of Yasser's, who lingered for years with cancer, running up tremendous hospital bills before he finally died. Laila was a smart, hard-working girl, and helped support her three younger sisters. Ahmed once told me Laila never really knew her mother, an American broad who left them when they were little kids. I'd heard Laila was working in a bank the last couple years and doing okay.

You could really see the Arab blood in Laila now, in the sensual face, the nose a little too prominent but just suiting her, and in the wide full mouth, and glittering brown eyes. No wonder they were passionate people, I thought, with faces like that. Yes, Laila was a jewel, like a fine half-Arab mare with enough American blood to give good height and those terrific thighs. I wondered if Ahmed had anything going with her. Then Laila started "sprinkling salt" as the Arabs say. She revolved slowly on the ball of one bare foot, jerking a hip to each beat of the *darbuka*. And if there'd been a small bag of salt tied to the throbbing hip, she would've made a perfect ring of salt on the floor around her. It's a hot, graceful move, not hard at all. I do it myself to hard-rock music.

When Laila was finished with her dance and ran off the floor and the applause died down I said, "She's beautiful, Ahmed. Why don't you con her into marrying you?"

"Not interested," said Ahmed, shaking his head. He leaned over the table and took a sip of wine before speaking. "There's rumors, Bumper. Laila's supposed to be whoring."

"I can't believe that," I said, remembering her again as a teenage waitress who couldn't even put her lipstick on straight.

"She left her bank job over a year ago. Started belly dancing professionally. You never knew her when she was a real little tot. I remember when she was three years old and her aunts and uncles taught her to dance. She was the cutest thing you ever saw. She was a smart little girl."

"Where did you hear she was tricking?"

"In this business you hear all about the dancers," said Ahmed. "You know, she's one of the few belly dancers in town that's really an Arab, or rather, half-Arab. She's no cheapie, but she goes to bed with guys if they can pay the tariff. I hear she gets two hundred a night."

"Laila's had a pretty tough life, Ahmed," I said. "She had to raise little sisters. She never had time to be a kid herself."

"Look, I'm not blaming her, Bumper. What the hell, I'm an American. I'm not like the old folks who wait around on the morning after the wedding to make sure there's blood on the bridal sheets. But I have to admit that whoring bothers me. I'm just not that Americanized, I guess. I used to think maybe when Laila got old enough . . . well, it's too late now. I shouldn't have been so damn busy these last few years. I let her get away and now . . . it's just too late."

Ahmed ordered me another drink, then excused himself, saying he'd be back in a little while. I was starting to feel depressed all of a sudden. I wasn't sure if the talk about Laila set it off or what, but I thought about her selling her ass to these wealthy Hollywood creeps. Then I thought about Freddie and Harry, and Poochie and Herky, and Timothy G. for goddamn Landry, but that was *too* depressing to think about. Suddenly for no reason I thought about Esteban Segovia and how I used to worry that he really would become a priest like he wanted to be when he returned from Vietnam, instead of a dentist like I always wanted him to be. That dead boy was about Laila's age when he left. Babies. Nobody should die a baby.

All right, Bumper, I said to myself, let's settle down to some serious drinking. I called Barbara over and ordered a double scotch on the rocks even though I'd mixed my drinks too much and had already more than enough.

After my third scotch I heard a honey-dipped voice say, "Hi, Bumper."

"Laila!" I made a feeble attempt at getting up, as she sat down at my table, looking smooth and cool in a modest white dress, her hair tied back and hanging down one side, her face and arms the color of a golden olive.

"Ahmed told me you were here, Bumper," she smiled, and I lit her cigarette, liberated women be damned, and called Barbara over to get her a drink.

"Can I buy you a drink, kid?" I asked. "It's good to see you all grown up, a big girl and all, looking so damn gorgeous."

She ordered a bourbon and water and laughed at me, and I knew for sure I was pretty close to being wiped out. I decided to turn it off after I finished the scotch I held in my hand.

"I was grown up last time you saw me, Bumper," she said, grinning at my clownish attempts to act sober. "All men appreciate your womanhood better when they see your bare belly moving for them."

I thought about what Ahmed had told me, and though it didn't bother me like it did Ahmed, I was sorry she had to do it, or that she *thought* she had to do it.

"You mean that slick little belly was moving for ol' Bumper?" I said, trying to kid her like I used to, but my brain wasn't working right.

"Sure, for you. Aren't you the hero of this whole damned family?"

"Well how do you like dancing for a living?"

"It's as crummy as you'd expect."

"Why do you do it?"

"You ever try supporting two sisters on a bank teller's wage?"

"Bullshit," I said too loud, one elbow slipping out from under me. "Don't give me that crybaby stuff. A dish like you, why you could marry any rich guy you wanted."

"Wrong, Bumper. I could screw any rich guy I wanted. And get paid damn well for it."

"I wish you wouldn't talk like that, Laila."

"You old bear," she laughed, as I rubbed my face which had no feeling whatever. "I know Ahmed told you I'm a whore. It just shames the hell out of these Arabs. You know how subtle they are. Yasser hinted around the other day that maybe I should change my name now that I'm show biz. Hammad's too ordinary, he said. Maybe something more American. They're as subtle as a boot in the ass. How about Feinberg or Goldstein, Bumper? I'll bet they wouldn't mind if I called myself Laila Feinberg. That'd explain my being a whore to the other Arabs, wouldn't it? They could start a rumor that my mother was a Jew."

"What the hell're you telling *me* all this for?" I said, suddenly getting mad. "Go to a priest or a headshrinker, or go to the goddamn mosque and talk to the Prophet, why don't you? I had enough problems laid on me today. Now you?"

"Will you drive me home, Bumper? I do want to talk to you."

"How many more performances you got to go?" I asked, not sure I could stay upright in my chair if I had another drink.

"I'm through. Marsha's taking my next one for me. I've told Ahmed I'm getting cramps."

I found Ahmed and said good-bye while Laila waited for me in the parking lot. I tipped Barbara fifteen bucks, then I staggered into the kitchen, thanked Yasser, and kissed him on the big moustache while he hugged me and made me promise to come to his house in the next few weeks.

Laila was in the parking lot doing her best to ignore two well-dressed drunks in a black Lincoln. When they saw me staggering across the parking lot in their direction the driver stomped on it, laid a patch of rubber, and got the hell out.

"Lord, I don't blame them," Laila laughed. "You look wild and dangerous, Bumper. How'd you get those scratches on your face?"

"My Ford's right over there," I said, walking like Frankenstein's monster so I could stay on a straight course.

"The same old car? Oh, Bumper." She laughed like a kid and she put my arm around her and steered me to my Ford, but around to the passenger side. Then she patted my pockets, found my keys, got them, pushed me in, and closed the door behind me.

"Light-fingered broad," I mumbled. "You ever been a hugger-mugger?"

"What was that, Bumper?" she said, getting behind the wheal and cranking her up.

"Nothing, nothing," I mumbled, rubbing my face again.

I dozed while Laila drove. She turned the radio on and hummed, and she had a pretty good voice too. In fact, it put me to sleep, and she had to shake me awake when we got to her pad.

"I'm going to pour you some muddy Turkish coffee and we're going to talk," she said, helping me out of the Ford, and for a second the sidewalk came up in my eyes, but I closed them and stood there and everything righted itself.

"Ready to try the steps, Bumper?"

"As I'll ever be, kid."

"Let's get it on," she said, my arm around her wide shoulders, and she guided me up. She was a big strong girl. Ahmed was nuts, I thought. She'd make a hell of a wife for him or *any* young guy.

It took some doing but we reached the third floor of her apartment building, a very posh place, which was actually three L-shaped buildings scattered around two Olympic-sized pools. Mostly catered to swinging singles which reminded me of the younger sisters.

"The girls home?" I asked.

"I live alone during the school year, Bumper. Nadia lives in the dorm at U.S.C. She's a freshman. Dalal boards at Ramona Convent. She'll be going to college next year."

"Ramona Convent? I thought you were a Moslem."

"I'm nothing."

We got in the apartment and Laila guided me past the soft couch, which looked pretty good to sleep on, and dumped me in a straight-backed kitchen chair after taking off my sport coat and hanging it in a closet.

"You even wear a gun off duty?" she asked as she ladled out some coffee and ran some water from the tap.

"Yeah," I said, not knowing what she was talking about for a minute, I was so used to the gun. "This job makes you a coward. I don't even go out without it in this town anymore, except to Harry's bar or somewhere in the neighborhood."

"If I saw all the things you have, maybe I'd be afraid to go out without one too," she shrugged.

I didn't know I was dozing again until I smelled Laila there shaking me awake, a tiny cup of Turkish coffee thick and dark on a saucer in front of me. I smelled her sweetness and then I felt her cool hand again and then I saw her wide mouth smiling.

"Maybe I should spoon it down your throat till you get sober."

"I'm okay," I said, rubbing my face and head.

I drank the coffee as fast as I could even though it scalded my mouth and throat. Then she poured me another, and I excused myself, went to the head, took a leak, washed my face in cold water, and combed my hair. I was still bombed when I came back, but at least I wasn't a zombie.

Laila must've figured I was in good enough shape. "Let me turn on some music, Bumper, then we can talk."

"Okay." I finished the second cup almost as fast as the first and poured myself a third.

The soft stirring song of an Arab girl singer filled the room for a second and then Laila turned down the volume. It's a wailing kind of plaintive sound, almost like a chant at times, but it gets to you, at least it did to me, and I always conjured up mental pictures of the Temple of Karnak, and Giza, and the streets of Damascus, and a picture I once saw of a Bedouin on a pink granite cliff in the blinding sun looking out over the Valley of the Kings. I saw in his face that he knew more about history, even though he was probably illiterate, than I ever would, and I promised myself I'd go there to die when I got old. If I ever did *get* old, that is.

"I still like the old music," Laila smiled, nodding toward the stereo set. "Most people don't like it. I can put on something else if you want."

"Don't touch it," I said, and Laila looked in my eyes and seemed glad.

"I need your help, Bumper."

"Okay, what is it?"

"I want you to talk to my probation officer for me."

"You're on probation? What for?"

"Prostitution. The Hollywood vice cops got three of us in January. I pleaded guilty and was put on probation."

"Whadda you want me to do?"

"I wasn't given *summary* probation like my lousy thousand-dollar lawyer promised. I got a tough judge and I have to report to a P.O. for two years. I want to go somewhere and I need permission."

"Where you going?"

"Somewhere to have a baby. I want to go somewhere, have my baby, adopt it out, and come back."

She saw the 'Why me? Why in the hell me?' look in my eyes.

"Bumper, I need you for this. I don't want my sisters to know anything. Nothing, you hear? They'd only want to raise the baby and for God's sake, it's hard enough making it in this filthy world when you know who the hell your two parents are and have them to raise you. I've got a plan and you're the only one my whole damned tribe would listen to without question. They trust you completely. I want you to tell Yasser and Ahmed and all of them that you don't think I should be dancing for a living, and that you have a friend in New Orleans who has a good-paying office job for me. And then tell the same thing to my P.O. and convince her it's the truth. Then I'll disappear for seven or eight months and come back and tell everyone I didn't like the job or something. They'll all get mad as blazes but that'll be it."

"Where the hell you going?"

"What's it matter?" she shrugged. "Anywhere to have the kid and farm it out. To New Orleans. Wherever."

"You're not joining the coat hanger corps are you?"

"An abortion?" she laughed. "No, I figure when you make a mistake you should have the guts to at least see it through. I won't shove it down a garbage disposal. I was raised an Arab and I can't change."

"You got any money?"

"I've got thirteen thousand in a bank account. I'd like you to handle it for me and see that the girls have enough to get them through the summer while they're living here in my apartment. If everything goes right I'll be back for a New Year's Eve party with just you and me and the best bottle of scotch money can buy."

"Will you have enough to live on?" I asked, knowing where she got the thirteen thousand.

"I've got enough," she nodded.

"Listen, goddamn it, don't lie to me. I'm not gonna get involved if you're off somewhere selling your ass in a strange town with a foal kicking around in your belly."

"I wouldn't take any chances," she said, looking deep in my eyes again. "I swear it. I've got enough in another account to live damn well for the whole time I'll be gone. I'll show you my bankbooks. And I can afford to have the kid in a good hospital. A private room if I want it."

"Wow!" I said, getting up, light-headed and dizzy. I stood for a second and shuffled into the living room, dropping on the couch and laying back. I noticed that the red hose on Laila's crystal and gold narghile was uncoiled. Those pipes are fine decorator items but they never work right unless you stuff all the fittings with rags like Laila's was. I often smoked mint-flavored Turkish tobacco with Yasser. Laila smoked hashish. There was a black-and-white mosaic inlaid box setting next to the narghile. The lid was open and it was half full of hash, very high-grade, expensive, shoe-leather hash, pressed into dark flat sheets like the sole of your shoe.

Laila let me alone and cleared the kitchen table. What a hell of a time. First the decision to retire. And after I told Cassie, everything seemed right. And then Cassie wants a kid! And a goddamn pack of baby Bolsheviks make an ass out of me. Humiliate me! Then perjury, for chrissake. I felt like someone was putting out cigars on the inside of my belly, which was so hard and swollen I couldn't see my knees unless I sat up straight. But at least I got a back office, even if I did almost die in the pigeon shit.

''What a day,'' I said when Laila came in and sat down on the end of the couch.

''I'm sorry I asked you, Bumper.''

''No, no, don't say that. I'll do it. I'll help you.''

She didn't say anything, but she got up and came over and sat on the floor next to me, her eyes wet, and I'll be a son of a bitch if she didn't kiss my hand!

Laila got up then, and without saying anything, took my shoes off, and I let her lift my legs up and put them on the couch. I felt like a beached walrus laying there like that, but I was still swacked. In fact, I felt drunker now laying down, and I was afraid the room would start spinning, so I wanted to start talking. ''I had a miserable goddamn day.''

''Tell me about it, Bumper,'' said Laila, sitting there on the floor next to me and putting her cool hand on my hot forehead as I loosened my belt. I knew I was gone for the night. I was in no shape to get up, let alone drive home. I squirmed around until my sore shoulder was settled against a cushion.

''Your face and hands are cut and your body's hurting.''

''Guess I can sleep here, huh?''

''Of course. How'd you get hurt?''

''Slipped and fell off a fire escape. Whadda you think about me retiring, Laila?''

''Retiring? Don't be ridiculous. You're too full of hell.''

''I'm in my forties, goddamnit. No, I might as well level with you. I'll be fifty this month. Imagine that. When I was born Warren G. Harding was a new President!''

''You're too alive. Forget about it. It's too silly to think about.''

''I was sworn in on my thirtieth birthday, Laila. Know that?''

''Tell me about it,'' she said, stroking my cheek now, and I felt so damn comfortable I could've died.

''You weren't even born then. That's how long I been a cop.''

''Why'd you become a cop?''

''Oh, I don't know.''

''Well, what did you do *before* you became a cop?''

''I was in the Marine Corps over eight years.''

''Tell me about it.''

''I wanted to get away from the hometown, I guess. There was nobody left except a few cousins and one aunt. My brother Clem and me were raised by our grandmother, and after she died, Clem took care of me. He was a ripper, that bastard. Bigger than me, but didn't look anything like me. A handsome dog. Loved his food and drink and women. He owned his own gas station and just before Pearl Harbor, in November it was, he got killed when a truck tire blew up and he fell back into the grease pit. My brother Clem died in a filthy grease pit, killed by a goddamn tire! It was ridiculous. There was nobody else I gave a damn about so I joined the Corps. Guys actually *joined* in those days, believe it or not. I got wounded twice, once in Saipan and then in the knees at Iwo, and it almost kept me off the

Department. I had to flimflam the shit out of that police surgeon. You know what? I didn't hate war. I mean, why not admit it? I didn't hate it."

"Weren't you ever afraid?"

"Sure, but there's something about danger I like, and fighting was something I could do. I found that out right away and after the war I shipped over for another hitch and never did go back to Indiana. What the hell, I never had much there anyway. Billy was there with me and I had a job I liked."

"Who's Billy?"

"He was my son," I said, and I heard the air-conditioner going and I knew it was cool, because Laila looked so crisp and fresh, and yet my back was soaked and the sweat was pouring down my face and slipping beneath my collar.

"I never knew you were married, Bumper."

"It was a hundred years ago."

"Where's your wife?"

"I don't know. Missouri, I think. Or dead maybe. It's been so long. She was a girl I met in San Diego, a farm girl. Lots of them around out here on the coast during the war. They drifted out to find defense work, and some of them boozed it too much. Verna was a pale, skinny little thing. I was back in San Diego from my first trip over. I had my chest full of ribbons and had a cane because my first hit was in the thigh. That's one reason my legs aren't worth a shit today, I guess. I picked her up in a bar and slept with her that night and then I started coming by whenever I got liberty and next thing you know, before I ship out, she says she's knocked up. I had the feeling so many guys get, that they're gonna get bumped off, that their number's up, so we got drunk one night and I took her to a justice of the peace in Arizona and married her. She got an allotment and wrote me all the time and I didn't think too much about her till I got hit the second time and went home for good. And there she was, with my frail, sickly Billy. William's my real name, did you know that?"

"No, I didn't."

"So anyway, I screwed up, but just like you said, Laila, there was no sense anybody else suffering for it so I took Verna and Billy and we got a decent place to stay in Oceanside, and I thought, what the hell, this is a pretty fair life. So I reenlisted for another hitch and before long I was up for master sergeant. I could take Verna okay. I mean I gotta give her credit, after Billy came she quit boozing and kept a decent house. She was just a poor dumb farm girl but she treated me and Billy like champs, I have to admit. I was lucky and got to stay with Headquarters Company, Base, for five years, and Billy was to me, like . . . I don't know, standing on a granite cliff and watching all the world from the Beginning until Now, and for the first time there was a reason for it all. You understand?"

"Yes, I think so."

"You won't believe this, but when he was barely four years old he printed a valentine card for me. He could print and read at four years old, I swear it. He asked his mother how to make the words and then he composed it himself. It said, 'Dad. I love you. Love, Billy Morgan.' Just barely four years old. Can you believe that?"

"Yes, I believe you, Bumper."

"But like I said, he was a sickly boy like his mother, and even now when I tell you about him, I can't picture him. I put him away mentally, and it's not possible to picture how he looked, even if I try. You know, I read where only schizophrenics can control subconscious thought, and maybe I'm schizoid, I don't doubt it. But I can do it. Sometimes when I'm asleep and I see a shadow in a dream and the shadow is a little boy wearing glasses, or he has a cowlick sticking up in the back, I wake up. I sit straight up in my bed, wide awake. I *cannot* picture him either awake or asleep. You're smart to adopt out your kid, Laila."

"When did he die?"

"When he was just five. Right after his birthday, in fact. And it shouldn't have surprised me really. He was anemic and he had pneumonia twice as a baby, but still, it *was* a surprise, you know? Even though he was sick so long, it *was* a surprise, and after that, Verna seemed dead too. She told me a few weeks after we buried him that she was going home to Missouri and I thought it was a good idea so I gave her all the money I had and I never saw her again.

"After she left, I started drinking pretty good, and once, on weekend liberty, I came to L.A. and got so drunk I somehow ended up at El Toro Marine Base with a bunch of other drunken jarheads instead of at Camp Pendleton where I was stationed. The M.P.'s at the gate let the other drunks through, but of course my pass was wrong, so they stopped me. I was mean drunk then, and confused as hell, and I ended up swinging on the two M.P.'s.

"I can hardly remember late that night in the El Toro brig. All I really recall was two brig guards, one black guy and one white guy, wearing khaki pants and skivvy shirts, dragging me off the floor of the cell and taking me in the head where they worked me over with billies and then to the showers to wash off the blood. I remember holding onto the faucets with my head in the sink for protection, and the billies landing on my arms and ribs and kidneys and the back of my head. That was the first time my nose was ever broken."

Laila was still stroking my face and listening. Her hands felt cool and good.

"After that, they gave me a special courtmartial, and after all the M.P.'s testified, my defense counsel brought out a platoon or so of character witnesses, and even some civilians, wives of the marines who lived near Verna and Billy and me. They all talked about me, and Billy, and how extra smart and polite he was. Then the doctor who treated me in the brig testified as a defense witness that I was unbalanced at the time of the fight and not responsible for my actions, even though he had no psychiatric training. My defense counsel got away with it and when it was over I didn't get any brig time. I just got busted to buck sergeant.

"Is it hot in here, Laila?"

"No, Bumper," she said, stroking my cheek with the back of her fingers.

"Well, anyway, I took my discharge in the spring of nineteen-fifty and fooled around a year and finally joined the Los Angeles Police Department."

"Why did you do it, Bumper? The police force?"

"I don't know. I was good at fighting. I guess that's why. I thought about going back in the Corps when Korea broke out, and then I read something that said, 'Policemen are soldiers who act alone,' and I figured that was the only thing I hated about the military, that you couldn't act alone very much. And as a cop I could do it all myself, so I became a cop."

"You never heard from Verna?" asked Laila quietly, and suddenly I was cold and damp and getting chills laying there.

"About six years after I came on the job I got a letter from a lawyer in Joplin. I don't know how he found me. He said she'd filed for divorce and after that I got the final papers. I paid his fee and sent her about five hundred I'd saved, to get her started. I always hoped maybe she found some nice working stiff and went back to the farm life. She was one who couldn't make it by herself. She'd have to love somebody and then of course she'd have to suffer when something took them away from her, or maybe when they left on their own. She'd never learn you gotta suffer *alone* in this world. I never knew for sure what happened to her. I didn't try to find out because I'd probably just discover she was a wino and a streetwalking whore and I'd rather think otherwise."

"Bumper?"

"What?"

"Please take my bed tonight. Go in and shower and take my bed. You're dripping wet and you'll get sick if you stay here on the couch."

"I'll be okay. You should see some of the places I've slept. Just give me a blanket."

"Please."

She began trying to lift me and that almost made me laugh out loud. She was a strong girl, but no woman was about to raise Bumper Morgan, two hundred and seventy-five pounds anytime, and almost three hundred this night with all of me cold dead weight from the booze.

"Okay, okay," I grumbled, and found I wasn't too drunk when I stood up. I made my way to her bedroom, stripped, and jumped in the shower, turning it on cold at the end. When I was through I dried in her bath towel which smelled like woman, took the wet gauze bandage off my leg, and felt better than I had all day. I rinsed my mouth with toothpaste, examined my meat-red face and red-webbed eyes, and climbed in her bed naked, which is the only way to sleep, winter or summer.

The bed smelled like her too, or rather it smelled like woman, since all women are pretty much the same to me. They all smell and feel the same. It's the essence of womanhood, that's the thing I need.

I was dozing when Laila came in and tiptoed to the shower and it seemed like seconds later when she was sitting on the bed in a sheer white nightgown whispering to me. I smelled lilac, and then woman, and I came to with her velvet mouth all over my face.

"What the hell?" I mumbled, sitting up.

"I touched you tonight," said Laila. "You told me things. Maybe for the first time in years, Bumper, I've really touched another person!" She put her hand on my bare shoulder.

"Yeah, well that's enough touching for one night," I said, disgusted with myself for telling her all those personal things, and I took her hand off my shoulder. Now I'd have to fly back to L.A. in a couple of weeks to set this thing up with Laila and her family. Everyone was complicating my life lately.

"Bumper," she said, drawing her feet up under her and laughing pretty damn jolly for this time of night. "Bumper, you're wonderful. You're a wonderful old panda. A big blue-nosed panda. Do you know your nose is blue?"

"Yeah, it gets that way when I drink too much," I said, figuring she'd been smoking hash, able to see right through the nightie at her skin which was now exactly the color of apricots. "I had too many blood vessels busted too many times there on my nose."

"I want to get under the covers with you, Bumper."

"Look, kid," I said. "You don't owe me a goddamn thing. I'll be glad to help you flimflam your family."

"You've let me touch you, Bumper," she said, and the warm wide velvet mouth was on me again, my neck and cheek, and all that chestnut hair was covering me until I almost couldn't think about how ridiculous this was.

"Goddamnit," I said, holding her off. "This is a sickening thing you're doing. I knew you since you were a little girl. Damn it, kid, I'm an old bag of guts and you're still just a little girl to me. This is unnatural!"

"Don't call me kid. And don't try to stop me from having you."

"*Having* me? You're just impressed by cops. I'm a father symbol. Lots of young girls feel like that about cops."

"I hate cops," she answered, her boobs wobbling against my arms, which were getting tired. "It's you I want because you're more man than I've ever had my hands on."

"Yeah, I'm about six cubic yards," I said, very shaky.

"That's not what I meant," she said, her hands going over me, and she was kissing me again and I was doing everything I could to avoid the pleasures of a thousand and one nights.

"Listen, I couldn't if I wanted to," I groaned. "You're just too young, I just couldn't do it with a kid like you."

"Want to bet?"

"Don't, Laila."

"How can a man be so aware and be so square," she smiled, standing up and slipping off the nightie.

"It's just the bluesuit," I said with a voice gone hoarse and squeaky. "I probably look pretty sharp to you in my uniform."

Laila busted up then, falling on the bed and rolling on her stomach, laughing for a good minute. I smiled weakly, staring at her apricot ass and those thunder thighs, thinking it was over. But after she stopped laughing she smiled at me softer than ever, whispered in Arabic, and crept under the sheet.

Friday, the last day

15

I WOKE UP FRIDAY morning with a terrible hangover. Laila was sprawled half on top of me, a big smooth naked doe, which was the reason I woke up. After living so many years alone I don't like sleeping with anyone. Cassie, who I made love to maybe a hundred times, had never slept with me, not all night. We'd have to get twin beds, Cassie and me. I just can't stand to be too close to anybody for too long.

Laila didn't wake up and I took my clothes into the living room and dressed, leaving a note that said I'd get in touch in a week or so, to work out the details of handling her bank account and dumping a load of snow on Yasser and the family.

Before I left I crept back into the bedroom to look at her this last time. She was sprawled on her stomach, sleek and beautiful.

"*Salām*, Laila," I whispered. "A thousand *salāms*, little girl."

I very carefully made my way down the stairs of Laila's apartment house to my car parked in front, and I felt a little better when I got out on the road with the window down driving onto the Hollywood Freeway on a windy, not too smoggy day.

Then I thought for a few minutes about how it had been with Laila and I was ashamed because I always prided myself on being something more than the thousands of ugly old slimeballs you see in Hollywood with beautiful young babies like her. She did it because she was grateful and neurotic and confused and I took advantage. I'd always picked on someone my own size all my life, and now I was no better than any other horny old fart.

I went home and had a cold shower and a shave and I felt more or less human after some aspirin and three cups of coffee that started the heartburn going for the day. I wondered if after a few months of retirement my stomach might begin to rebuild itself, and who knows, maybe I'd have digestive peace.

I got to the Glass House a half hour early and by the time I shined my black high-top shoes, buffed the Sam Browne, hit the badge with some rouge and a cloth, I was sweating a little and feeling much improved. I put on a fresh uniform since the one from yesterday was covered with blood and birdshit. When I pinned on the gleaming shield and slid the scarred baton through the chrome ring on my Sam Browne I felt even better.

At rollcall Cruz was sitting as usual with the watch commander, Lieutenant Hilliard, at the table in front of the room, and Cruz glanced at me several times like he expected me to get up and make a grand announcement that this was my last day. Of course I didn't, and he looked a little disappointed. I hated to disappoint anyone, especially Cruz, but I wasn't going out with a trumpet blare. I really wanted Lieutenant Hilliard to hold an inspection this morning, my last one, and he did. He limped down the line and said my boondockers and my shield looked like a million bucks and he wished some of the young cops looked half as sharp. After inspection I drank a quart or so from the water fountain and I felt better yet.

I meant to speak to Cruz about our lunch date, but Lieutenant Hilliard was talking to him so I went out to the car, and decided to call him later. I fired up the black-and-white, put my baton in the holder on the door, tore off the paper on my writing pad, replaced the old hot sheet, checked the back seat for dead midgets, and drove out of the station. It was really unbelievable. The *last time*.

After hitting the bricks, I cleared over the air, even though I worried that I'd get a burglary report or some other chickenshit call before I could get something in my stomach. I couldn't stand the idea of anything heavy just now so I turned south on San Pedro and headed for the dairy, which was a very good place to go for hangover cures, at least it always was for me. It was more than a dairy, it was the plant and home office for a dairy that sold all over Southern California, and they made very good specialty products like cottage cheese and buttermilk and yogurt, all of which are wonderful for hangovers if you're not too far gone. I waved at the gate guard, got passed into the plant, and parked in front of the employee's store, which wasn't opened yet.

I saw one of the guys I knew behind the counter setting up the cash register and I knocked on the window.

''Hi, Bumper,'' he smiled, a young guy, with deep-set green eyes and a mop of black hair. ''What do you need?''

''Plasma, pal,'' I said, ''but I'll settle for yogurt.''

''Sure. Come on in, Bumper,'' he laughed, and I passed through, heading for the tall glass door to the cold room where the yogurt was kept. I took two yogurts from the shelf, and he gave me a plastic spoon when I put them on the counter.

''That all you're having, Bumper?'' he asked, as I shook my head and lifted the lid and spooned out a half pint of blueberry which I finished in three or four gulps and followed with a lime. And finally, what the hell, I thought, I grabbed another, French apple, and ate it while the guy counted his money and said something to me once or twice which I nodded at, and I smiled through a mouthful of cool creamy yogurt that was coating my stomach, soothing me, and making me well.

''Never saw anyone put away yogurt like that, Bumper,'' he said after I finished.

I couldn't remember this young guy's name, and wished like hell they wore their names on the gray work uniform because I always like to make a little small talk and call someone by name when he's feeding me. It's the least you can do.

''Could I have some buttermilk?'' I asked, after he threw the empty yogurt containers in a gleaming trash can behind the counter. The whole place sparkled, being a dairy, and it smelled clean, and was nice and cool.

''Why sure, Bumper,'' he said, leaving the counter and coming back with a pint of cold buttermilk. Most of the older guys around the dairy wouldn't bring me a pint container, and here I was dying of thirst from the booze. Rather than say anything I just tipped it up and poured it down, only swallowing three times to make him realize his mistake.

''Guess I should've brought you a quart, huh?'' he said after I put the milk carton down and licked my lips.

I smiled and shrugged and he went in the back, returning with a quart.

''Thanks, pal,'' I said. ''I'm pretty thirsty today.'' I tipped the quart up and let it flow thick and delicious into my mouth, and then I started swallowing, but not like before, more slowly. When I finished it I was really fit again. I was well. I could do anything now.

''Take a quart with you?'' he said. ''Would you like more yogurt or some cottage cheese?''

''No thanks,'' I said. I don't believe in being a hog like some cops I've worked with. ''Gotta get back to the streets. Friday mornings get pretty busy sometimes.''

I really should've talked a while. I knew I should, but I just didn't feel like it. It was the first time this guy ever served me so I said the thing that all policemen say when they're ninety percent sure what the answer will be.

"How much do I owe you?"

"Don't mention it," he said, shaking his head. "Come see us anytime, Bumper."

While driving out the main gate of the dairy, I fired up a fresh cigar which I knew couldn't possibly give me indigestion because my stomach was so well coated I could eat tin cans and not notice.

Then I realized that was the last time I'd ever make my dairy stop. Damn, I thought, everything I do today will be for the last time. Then I suddenly started hoping I'd get some routine calls like a burglary report or maybe a family dispute which I usually hated refereeing. I wouldn't even mind writing a traffic ticket today.

It would've been something, I thought, really something to have stayed on the job after my twenty years. You have your pension in the bag then, and you own your own mortgage, having bought and paid for them with twenty years' service. Regardless of what you ever do or don't do you have a forty percent pension the rest of your life, from the moment you leave the Department. Whether you're fired for pushing a slimeball down the fire escape, or whether you're booked for lying in court to put a scumbag where he ought to be, or whether you bust your stick over the hairy little skull of some college drat who's tearing at your badge and carrying a tape recorder at a demonstration, no matter what you do, they got to pay you that pension. If they have to, they'll mail those checks to you at San Quentin. Nobody can take your pension away. Knowing that might make police work even a little *more* fun, I thought. It might give you just a little more push, make you a little more aggressive. I would've liked to have done police work knowing that I owned my own mortgage.

As I was cruising I picked a voice out of the radio chatter. It was the girl with the cutest and sexiest voice I ever heard. She was on frequency thirteen today, and she had her own style of communicating. She didn't just come on the horn and answer with clipped phrases and impersonal "rogers." Her voice would rise and fall like a song, and getting even a traffic accident call from her, which patrol policemen hate worst because they're so tedious, was somehow not quite so bad. She must've been hot for some cop in unit Four-L-Nine because her voice came in soft and husky and sent a shiver through me when she said, "Foah-L-Ninah, rrrrrraj-ahh!"

Now that's the way to roger a call, I thought. I was driving nowhere at all, just touring the beat, looking at people I knew and ones I didn't know, trying not to think of all the things I'd never do out here. I was trading them for things I'd *rather* do, things any sane man would rather do, like be with Cassie and start my new career and live a civilized normal life. Funny I should think of it as *civilized*, that kind of life. That was one of the reasons I'd always wanted to go to North Africa to die.

I always figured kind of vaguely that if somebody didn't knock me off and I lasted say thirty years, I'd pull the pin then because I could never do my kind of police work past sixty. I really thought I could last that long though. I thought that if I cut down on the groceries and the drinking and the cigars, maybe I could last out here on the streets until I was sixty.Then I'd have learned almost all there was to learn here. I'd know all the secrets I always wanted to know and I'd hop a jet and go to the Valley of the Kings and look out there from a pink granite cliff and see where all civilization started, and maybe if I stayed there long enough and didn't get drunk and fall off a pyramid, or get stomped to death by a runaway camel, or ventilated by a Yankee-hating Arab, maybe if I lasted there long enough, I'd find out the last thing I wanted to know: whether *civilization* was worth the candle after all.

Then I thought of what Cruz would say if I ever got drunk enough to tell him about this. He'd say, " '*Mano*, let yourself love, and give yourself away. You'll get your answer. You don't need a sphinx or a pink granite cliff."

"Hi, Bumper," a voice yelled, and I turned from the glare of the morning sun and saw Percy opening his pawnshop.

''Hi, Percy,'' I yelled back, and slowed down to wave. He was a rare animal, an honest pawnbroker. He ran hypes and other thieves out of his shop if he even suspected they had something hot. And he always demanded good identification from a customer pawning something. He was an *honest* pawnbroker, a rare animal.

I remembered the time Percy gave me his traffic ticket to take care of because this was the first one he'd ever gotten. It was for jaywalking. He didn't own a car. He hated them and took a bus to the shop every day. I just couldn't disillusion old Percy by letting him know that I couldn't fix a ticket, so I took it and paid it for him. It's practically impossible to fix a ticket anymore in this town. You have to know the judge or the City Attorney. Lawyers take care of each other of course, but a cop can't fix a ticket. Anyway, I paid it and Percy thought I fixed it and wasn't disappointed. He thought I was a hell of a big man.

Another black-and-white cruised past me going south. The cop driving, a curly-haired kid named Nelson, waved, and I nodded back. He almost rear-ended a car stopped at the red light because he was looking at some chick in hot pants going into an office building. He was a typical young cop, I thought. Thinking of pussy instead of police work. And just like all these cats, Nelson loved talking about it. I think they all love talking about it these days more than they love doing it. That gave me a royal pain in the ass. I guess I've had more than my share in my time. I've had some good stuff for an ugly guy, but by Maggie's muff, I never talked about screwing a dame, not with anybody. In my day, a guy was unmanly if he did that. But your day is over after this day, I reminded myself, and swung south on Grand.

Then I heard a Central car get a report call at one of the big downtown hotels and I knew the hotel burglar had hit again. I'd give just about anything, I thought, to catch that guy today. That'd be like quitting after your last home run, like Ted Williams. A home run your last time up. That'd be something. I cruised around for twenty minutes and then drove to the hotel and parked behind the black-and-white that got the call. I sat there in my car smoking a cigar and waited another fifteen minutes until Clarence Evans came out. He was a fifteen-year cop, a tall stringbean who I used to play handball with before my ankles got so bad.

We had some good games. It's especially fun to play when you're working nightwatch and you get up to the academy about one a.m. after you finish work, and play three hard fast games and take a steam bath. Except Evans didn't like the steam bath, being so skinny. We always took a half case of beer with us and drank it up after we showered. He was one of the first Negroes I worked with as a partner when L.A.P.D. became completely integrated several years ago. He was a good copper and he liked working with me even though he knew I always preferred working alone. On nightwatch it's comforting sometimes to have someone riding shotgun or walking beside you. So I worked with him and lots of other guys even though I would've rather had a one-man beat or an ''L'' car that you work alone, ''L'' for lonesome. But I worked with him because I never could disappoint anyone that wanted to work with me that bad, and it made the handball playing more convenient.

Then I saw Clarence coming out of the hotel carrying his report notebook. He grinned at me, came walking light-footed over to my car, opened the door and sat down.

''What's happening, Bumper?''

''Just curious if the hotel creeper hit again, Clarence.''

''Took three rooms on the fifth floor and two on the fourth floor,'' he nodded.

''The people asleep?''

''In four of them. In the other one, they were down in the bar.''

''That means he hit before two a.m.''

''Right.''

''I can't figure this guy,'' I said, popping an antacid tablet. ''Usually he works in the daytime but sometimes in the early evening. Now he's hitting during the night when they're in and when they're not in. I never heard of a hotel burglar as squirrelly as this guy.''

''Maybe that's it,'' said Evans. ''A squirrel. Didn't he try to hurt a kid on one job?''

''A teddy bear. He stabbed hell out of a big teddy bear. It was all covered with a blanket and looked like a kid sleeping.''

''That cat's a squirrel,'' said Evans.

''That would explain why the other hotel burglars don't know anything,'' I said, puffing on the cigar and thinking. ''I never did think he was a pro, just a lucky amateur.''

''A lucky looney,'' said Evans. ''You talked to all your snitches?'' He knew my M.O. from working with me. He knew I had informants, but like everyone else he didn't know how many, or that I paid the good ones.

''I talked to just about everyone I know. I talked to a hotel burglar who told me he'd already been approached by three detectives and that he'd tell us if he knew anything, because this guy is bringing so much heat on all the hotels he'd like to see us get him.''

''Well, Bumper, if anybody lucks onto the guy I'm betting you will,'' said Evans, putting on his hat and getting out of the car.

''Police are baffled but an arrest is imminent,'' I winked, and started the car. It was going to be a very hot day.

I was given a report call at Pershing Square, an injury report. Probably some pensioner fell off his soapbox and was trying to figure how he could say there was a crack in the sidewalk and sue the city. I ignored the call for a few minutes and let her assign it to another unit. I didn't like to do that. I always believed you should handle the calls given to you, but damn it, I only had the rest of the day and that was it, and I thought about Oliver Horn and wondered why I hadn't thought about him before. I couldn't waste time on the report call so I let the other unit handle it and headed for the barbershop on Fourth Street.

Oliver was sitting on a chair on the sidewalk in front of the shop. His ever-present broom was across his lap, and he was dozing in the sunshine.

He was the last guy in the world you would ever want to die and come back looking like. Oliver was built like a walrus with one arm cut off above the elbow. It was done maybe forty years ago by probably the worst surgeon in the world. The skin just flapped over and hung there. He had orange hair and a big white belly covered with orange hair. He long ago gave up trying to keep his pants up, and usually they barely gripped him below the gut so that his belly button was always popping out at you. His shoelaces were untied and destroyed from stepping on them because it was too hard to tie them one-handed, and he had a huge lump on his chin. It looked like if you squeezed it, it'd break a window. But Oliver was surprisingly clever. He swept out the barbershop and two or three businesses on this part of Fourth Street, including a bar called Raymond's where quite a few ex-cons hung out. It was close to the big hotels and a good place to scam on the rich tourists. Oliver didn't miss anything and had given me some very good information over the years.

''You awake, Oliver?'' I asked.

He opened one blue-veined eyelid. ''Bumper, how's it wi'choo?''

''Okay, Oliver. Gonna be a hot one again today.''

''Yeah, I'm gettin' sticky. Let's go in the shop.''

''Don't have time. Listen, I was just wondering, you heard about this burglar that's been ripping us downtown here in all the big hotels for the past couple months?''

''No, ain't heard nothin'.''

"Well, this guy ain't no ordinary hotel thief. I mean he probably ain't none of the guys you ordinarily see around Raymond's, but he might be a guy that you would *sometimes* see there. What the hell, even a ding-a-ling has a drink once in a while, and Raymond's is convenient when you're getting ready to rape about ten rooms across the street."

"He a ding-a-ling?"

"Yeah."

"What's he look like?"

"I don't know."

"How can I find him then, Bumper?"

"I don't know, Oliver. I'm just having hunches now. I think the guy's done burglaries before. I mean he knows how to shim doors and all that. And like I say, he's a little dingy. I think he's gonna stab somebody before too long. He carries a blade. A *long* blade, because he went clear through a mattress with it."

"Why'd he stab a mattress?"

"He was trying to kill a teddy bear."

"You been drinkin', Bumper?"

I smiled, and then I wondered what the hell I was doing here because I didn't know enough about the burglar to give a snitch something to work with. I was grabbing at any straw in the wind so I could hit a home run before walking off the field for the last time. Absolutely pathetic and sickening, I thought, ashamed of myself.

"Here's five bucks," I said to Oliver. "Get yourself a steak."

"Jeez, Bumper," he said, "I ain't done nothin' for it."

"The guy carries a long-bladed knife and he's a psycho and lately he takes these hotels at any goddamn hour of the day or night. He just might go to Raymond's for a drink sometime. He just might use the rest room while you're cleaning up and maybe he'll be tempted to look at some of the stuff in his pockets to see what he stole. Or maybe he'll be sitting at the bar and he'll pull a pretty out of his pocket that he just snatched at the hotel, or maybe one of these sharp hotel burglars that hangs out at Raymond's will know something, or say something, and you're always around there. Maybe anything."

"Sure, Bumper, I'll call you right away I hear anything at all. Right away, Bumper. And you get any more clues you let me know, hey, Bumper?"

"Sure, Oliver, I'll get you a good one from my clues closet."

"Hey, that's aw right," Oliver hooted. He had no teeth in front, upper or lower. For a long time he had one upper tooth in front.

"Be seeing you, Oliver."

"Hey, Bumper, wait a minute, You ain't told me no funny cop stories in a long time. How 'bout a story?"

"I think you heard them all."

"Come on, Bumper."

"Well, let's see. I told you about the seventy-five-year-old nympho I busted over on Main that night?"

"Yeah, yeah," he hooted, "tell me that one again. That's a good one."

"I gotta go, Oliver, honest. But say, did I ever tell you about the time I caught the couple in the back seat up there in Elysian Park in one of those maker's acres?"

"No, tell me, Bumper."

"Well, I shined my light in there and here's these two down on the seat, the old boy throwing the knockwurst to his girlfriend, and this young partner I'm with says, 'What're you doing there?' And the guy gives the answer ninety percent of the guys do when you catch them in that position: 'Nothing, Officer.' "

"Yeah, yeah," said Oliver, his shaggy head bobbing.

"So I say to the guy, 'Well, if *you* ain't doing anything, move over there and hold my flashlight and lemme see what *I* can do.' "

"Whoooo, that's funny," said Oliver. "Whoooo, Bumper."

He was laughing so hard he hardly saw me go, and I left him there holding his big hard belly and laughing in the sunshine.

I thought about telling Oliver to call Central Detectives instead of me, because I wouldn't be here after today, but what the hell, then I'd have to tell him *why* I wouldn't be here, and I couldn't take another person telling me why I should or should not retire. If Oliver ever called, somebody'd tell him I was gone, and the information would eventually get to the dicks. So what the hell, I thought, pulling back into the traffic and breathing exhaust fumes. It would've been really something though, to get that burglar on this last day. Really something.

I looked at my watch and thought Cassie should be at school now, so I drove to City College and parked out front. I wondered why I didn't feel guilty about Laila. I guess I figured it wasn't really my fault.

Cassie was alone in the office when I got there. I closed the door, flipped my hat on a chair, walked over, and felt that same old amazement I've felt a thousand times over how well a woman fits in your arms, and how soft they feel.

"Thought about you all night," she said after I kissed her a dozen times or so. "Had a miserable evening. Couple of bores."

"You thought about me all night, huh?"

"Honestly, I did." She kissed me again. "I still have this awful feeling something's going to happen."

"Every guy that ever went into battle has that feeling."

"Is that what our marriage is going to be, a battle?"

"If it is, you'll win, baby. I'll surrender."

"Wait'll I get you tonight," she whispered. "You'll surrender all right."

"That green dress is gorgeous."

"But you still like hot colors better?"

"Of course."

"After we get married I'll wear nothing but reds and oranges and yellows. . . ."

"You ready to talk?"

"Sure, what is it?"

"Cruz gave me a talking-to—about you."

"Oh?"

"He thinks you're the greatest thing that ever happened to me."

"Go on," she smiled.

"Well . . ."

"Yes?"

"Damn it, I can't go on. Not in broad daylight with no drink in me. . . ."

"What did you talk about, silly?"

"About you. No, it was more about me. About things I need and things I'm afraid of. Twenty years he's my friend and suddenly I find out he's a damned intellectual."

"What do you need? What're you afraid of? I can't believe you've ever been afraid of anything."

"He knows me better than you know me."

"That makes me sad. I don't want anyone knowing you better than I do. Tell me what you talked about."

"I don't have time right now," I said, feeling a gas bubble forming. Then I lied and said, "I'm on the way to a call. I just had to stop for a minute. I'll tell you all about it tonight. I'll be at your pad at seven-thirty. We're going out to dinner, okay?"

"Okay."

"Then we'll curl up on your couch with a good bottle of wine."

"Sounds wonderful," she smiled, that clean, hot, female smile that made me kiss her.

''See you tonight,'' I whispered.

''Tonight,'' she gasped, and I realized I was crushing her. She stood in the doorway and watched me all the way down the stairs.

I got back in the car and dropped two of each kind of pill and grabbed a handful from the glove compartment and shoved them in my pants pockets for later.

As I drove back on the familiar streets of the beat I wondered why I couldn't talk to Cassie like I wanted. If you're going to marry someone you should be able to tell her almost anything about yourself that she has a right to know.

I pulled over at a phone booth then and called Cruz at the station. Lieutenant Hilliard answered and in a couple seconds I heard Cruz's soft voice, ''Sergeant Segovia?'' He said it like a question.

''Hello, Sergeant Segovia, this is future former Officer Morgan, what the hell you doing besides pushing a pencil and shuffling paper?''

''What're you doing besides ignoring your radio calls?''

''I'm just cruising around this miserable beat thinking how great it'll be not to have to do it anymore. You decided where you want me to take you for lunch?''

''You don't have to take me anywhere.''

''Look, goddamnit, we're going to some nice place, so if you won't pick it, I will.''

''Okay, take me to Seymour's.''

''On my beat? Oh, for chrissake. Look, you just meet me at Seymour's at eleven-thirty. Have a cup of coffee but don't eat a damn thing because we're going to a place I know in Beverly Hills.

''That's a long way from your beat, all right.''

''I'll pick you up at Seymour's.''

''Okay, *'mano, ahí te huacho.''*

I chuckled after I hung up at that Mexican slang because *watching* for me is exactly what Cruz always did when you stop and think about it. Most people say, ''I'll be seeing you,'' because that's what they do, but Cruz, he always watched for me. It felt good to have old sad-eye watching for me.

16

I got back in my car and cruised down Main Street, by the parking lot at the rear of the Pink Dragon. I was so sick of pushing this pile of iron around that I stopped to watch some guys in the parking lot.

There were three of them and they were up to something. I parked the car and backed up until the building hid me. I got out and walked to the corner of the building, took my hat off, and peeked around the corner and across the lot.

A skinny hype in a long-sleeved blue shirt was talking to another brown-shirted one. There was a third one with them, a little T-shirt who stood a few steps away. Suddenly Blue-shirt nodded to Brown-shirt, who walked up and gave something to little T-shirt, who gave Brown-shirt something back, and they all hustled off in different directions. Little T-shirt was walking toward me. He was looking back over his shoulder for cops, and walking right into me. I didn't feel like messing around with a narco bust but this was too easy. I stepped in the hotel doorway and when T-shirt walked past, squinting into the sun, I reached out, grabbed him by the arm, and jerked him inside. He was just a boy, scared as hell. I shoved him face forward into the wall, and grabbed the hip pocket of his denims.

''What've you got, boy? Bennies or reds? Or maybe you're an acid freak?''

''Hey, lemme go!'' he yelled.

I took the bennies out of his pocket. There were six rolls, five in a roll, held together by a rubber band. The day of ten-benny rolls was killed by inflation.

"How much did they make you pay, kid?" I asked, keeping a good grip on his arm. He didn't look so short up close, but he was skinny, with lots of brown hair, and young, too young to be downtown scoring pills in the middle of the morning.

"I paid seven dollars. But I won't ever do it again if you'll lemme go. Please lemme go."

"Put your hands behind you, kid," I said, unsnapping my handcuff case.

"What're you doing? Please don't put those on me. I won't hurt you or anything."

"I'm not afraid of you hurting me," I laughed, chewing on a wet cigar stump that I finally threw away. "It's just that my wheels are gone and my ass is too big to be chasing you all over these streets." I snapped on one cuff and brought his palms together behind his back and clicked on the other, taking them up snug.

"How much you say you paid for the pills?"

"Seven dollars. I won't never do it again if you'll lemme go, I swear." He was dancing around, nervous and scared, and he stepped on my right toe, scuffing up the shine.

"Careful, damn it."

"Oh, I'm sorry. Please lemme go. I didn't mean to step on you."

"Those cats charged you way too much for the pills," I said, as I led him to the radio car.

"I know you won't believe me but it's the first time I ever bought them. I don't know *what* the hell they cost."

"Sure it is."

"See, I knew you wouldn't believe me. You cops don't believe nobody."

"You know all about cops, do you?"

"I been arrested before. I know you cops. You all act the same."

"You must be a hell of a heavyweight desperado. Got a ten-page rap sheet, I bet. What've you been busted for?"

"Running away. Twice. And you don't have to put me down."

"How old are you?"

"Fourteen."

"In the car," I said, opening the front door. "And don't lean back on the cuffs or they'll tighten."

"You don't have to worry, I won't jump out," he said as I fastened the seat belt over his lap.

"I ain't worrying, kid."

"I got a name. It's Tilden," he said, his square chin jutting way out.

"Mine's Morgan."

'My first name's Tom."

"Mine's Bumper."

"Where're you taking me?"

"To Juvenile Narcotics."

"You gonna book me?"

"Of course."

"What could I expect," he said, nodding his head disgustedly. "How could I ever expect a cop to act like a human being."

"You shouldn't even expect a human being to act like a human being. You'll just get disappointed."

I turned the key and heard the click-click of a dead battery. Stone-cold dead without warning.

"Hang loose, kid," I said, getting out of the car.

"Where could *I* go?" he yelled, as I lifted the hood to see if someone had torn the wires out. That happens once in a while when you leave your black-and-white somewhere that you can't keep an eye on it. It looked okay though. I wondered if something was wrong with the alternator. A call box was less than fifty feet down the sidewalk so I moseyed to it, turning around several times to keep an eye on my little prisoner. I called in and asked for a garage man with a set of booster cables and was told to stand by for about twenty minutes and somebody'd get out to me. I thought about calling a sergeant since they carry booster cables in their cars, but I decided not to. What the hell, why be in a rush today? What was there to prove now? To anyone? To myself?

Then I started getting a little hungry because there was a small diner across the street and I could smell bacon and ham. The odor was blowing through the duct in the front of the place over the cooking stoves. The more I sniffed the hungrier I got, and I looked at my watch and thought, what the hell. I went back and unstrapped the kid.

"What's up? Where we going?"

"Across the street."

"What for? We taking a bus to your station or something?"

"No, we gotta wait for the garage man. We're going across the street so I can eat."

"You can't take me in there looking like this," said the kid, as I led him across the street. His naturally rosy cheeks were lobster-red now. "Take the handcuffs off."

"Not a chance. I could never catch a young antelope like you."

"I swear I won't run."

"I know you won't, with your hands cuffed behind you and me holding the chain."

"I'll die if you take me in there like a dog on a leash in front of all those people."

"Ain't nobody in there you know, kid. And anybody that might be in there's been in chains himself, probably. Nothing to be embarrassed about."

"I could sue you for this."

"Oh *could* you?" I said, holding the door and shoving him inside.

There were only three counter customers, two con guys, and a wino drinking coffee. They glanced up for a second and nobody even noticed the kid was cuffed. I pointed toward a table at the rear.

"Got no waitress this early, Bumper," said T-Bone, the proprietor, a huge Frenchman who wore a white chef's hat and a T-shirt, and white pants. I'd never seen him in anything else.

"We need a table, T-Bone," I said, pointing to the kid's handcuffs.

"Okay," said T-Bone. "What'll you have?"

"I'm not too hungry. Maybe a couple over-easy eggs and some bacon, and a few pieces of toast. And oh, maybe some hash browns. Glass of tomato juice. Some coffee. And whatever the kid wants."

"What'll you have, boy?" asked T-Bone, resting his huge hairy hands on the counter and grinning at the boy, with one gold and one silver front tooth. I wondered for the first time where in hell he got a silver crown like that. Funny I never thought of that before. T-Bone wasn't a man you talked to. He only used his voice when it was necessary. He just fed people with as few words as possible.

"How can I eat anything?" said the kid. "All chained up like a convict or something." His eyes were filling up and he looked awful young just then.

"I'm gonna unlock them," I said. "Now what the hell you want? T-Bone ain't got all day."

"I don't know what I want."

"Give him a couple fried eggs straight up, some bacon, and a glass of milk. You want hash browns, kid?"

"I guess so."

"Give him some orange juice too, and an order of toast. Make it a double order of toast. And some jam."

T-Bone nodded and scooped a handful of eggs from a bowl by the stove. He held four eggs in that big hand and cracked all four eggs one at a time without using the other hand. The kid was watching it.

"He's got some talent, hey, kid?"

"Yeah. You said you were taking these off."

"Get up and turn around," I said, and when he did I unlocked the right cuff and fastened it around the chrome leg of the table so he could sit there with one hand free.

"Is this what you call taking them off?" he said. "Now I'm like an organ grinder's monkey on a chain!"

"Where'd you ever see an organ grinder? There ain't been any grinders around here for years."

"I saw them on old TV movies. And that's what I look like."

"Okay, okay, quit chipping your teeth. You complain more than any kid I ever saw. You oughtta be glad to be getting some breakfast. I bet you didn't eat a thing at home this morning."

"I wasn't even *at* home this morning."

"Where'd you spend the night?"

He brushed back several locks of hair from his eyes with a dirty right hand. "I spent part of the night sleeping in one of those all-night movies till some creepy guy woke me up with his cruddy hand on my knee. Then I got the hell outta there. I slept for a little while in a chair in some hotel that was open just down the street."

"You run away from home?"

"No, I just didn't feel like sleeping at the pad last night. My sis wasn't home and I just didn't feel like sitting around by myself."

"You live with your sister?"

"Yeah."

"Where's your parents?"

"Ain't got none."

"How old's your sister?"

"Twenty-two."

"Just you and her, huh?"

"Naw, there's always somebody around. Right now it's a stud named Slim. Big Blue always got somebody around."

"That's what you call your sister? Big Blue?"

"She used to be a dancer, kind of. In a bar. Topless. She went by that name. Now she's getting too fat in the ass so she's hustling drinks at the Chinese Garden over on Western. You know the joint?"

"Yeah, I know it."

"Anyway, she always says soon as she loses thirty pounds she's going back to dancing which is a laugh because her ass is getting wider by the day. She likes to be called Big Blue so even *I* started calling her that. She got this phony dyed-black hair, see. It's almost blue."

"She oughtta wash your clothes for you once in a while. That shirt looks like a grease rag."

"That's 'cause I was working on a car with my next door neighbor yesterday. I didn't get a chance to change it." He looked offended by that crack. "I wear clothes clean as anybody. And I even wash them and iron them myself."

"That's the best way to be," I said, reaching over and unlocking the left cuff.

"You're taking them off?"

"Yeah. Go in the bathroom and wash your face and hands and arms. And your neck."

"You sure I won't go out the window?"

"Ain't no window in that john," I said. "And comb that mop outta your face so somebody can see what the hell you look like."

"Ain't got a comb."

"Here's mine," I said, giving him the pocket comb.

T-Bone handed me the glasses of juice, the coffee, and the milk while the kid was gone, and the bacon smell was all over the place now. I was wishing I'd asked for a double order of bacon even though I knew T-Bone would give me an extra big helping.

I was sipping the coffee when the kid came back in. He was looking a hundred percent better even though his neck was still dirty. At least his hair was slicked back and his face and arms up to the elbow were nice and clean. He wasn't a handsome kid, his face was too tough and craggy, but he had fine eyes, full of life, and he looked you right in your eye when he talked to you. That's what I liked best about him.

"There's your orange juice," I said.

"Here's your comb."

"Keep it. I don't even know why I carry it. I can't do anything with this patch of wires I got. I'll be glad when I get bald."

"Yeah, you couldn't look no worse if you was bald," he said, examining my hair.

"Drink your orange juice, kid."

We both drank our juice and T-Bone said, "Here, Bumper," and handed a tray across the counter, but before I could get up the kid was on his feet and grabbed the tray and laid everything out on the table like he knew what he was doing.

"Hey, you even know what side to put the knife and fork on," I said.

"Sure. I been a busboy. I done all kinds of work in my time."

"How old you say you are?"

"Fourteen. Well, almost fourteen. I'll be fourteen next October."

When he'd finished he sat down and started putting away the chow like he was as hungry as I thought he was. I threw one of my eggs on his plate when I saw two weren't going to do him, and I gave him a slice of my toast. He was a first-class eater. That was something else I liked about him.

When he was finishing the last of the toast and jam, I went to the door and looked across the street. A garage attendant was replacing my battery. He saw me and waved that it was okay. I waved back and went back inside to finish my coffee.

"You get enough to eat?" I asked.

"Yeah, thanks."

"You sure you don't want another side of bacon and a loaf or two of bread?"

"I don't get breakfasts like that too often," he grinned.

When we were getting ready to leave I tried to pay T-Bone.

"From you? No, Bumper."

"Well, for the kid's chow, then." I tried to make him take a few bucks.

"No, Bumper. You don't pay nothin'."

"Thanks, T-Bone. Be seeing you," I said, and he raised a huge hand covered with black hair, and smiled gold and silver. And I almost wanted to ask him about the silver crown because it was the last time I'd have a chance.

"You gonna put the bracelets back on?" asked the boy, as I lit a cigar and patted my stomach and took a deep sniff of morning smog.

"You promise you won't run?"

"I swear. I hate those damn things on my wrists. You feel so helpless, like a little baby."

"Okay, let's get in the car," I said, trotting across the street with him to get out of the way of the traffic.

"How many times you come downtown to score?" I asked before starting the car.

"I never been downtown alone before. I swear. And I didn't even hitchhike. I took a bus. I was even gonna take a bus back to Echo Park. I didn't wanna run into cops with the pills in my pocket."

"How long you been dropping bennies?"

"About three months. And I only tried them a couple times. A kid I know told me I could come down here and almost any guy hanging around could get them for me. I don't know why I did it."

"How many tubes you sniff a day?"

"I ain't a gluehead. It makes guys crazy. And I never sniffed paint, neither."

Then I started looking at this kid, really looking at him. Usually my brain records only necessary things about arrestees, but now I found myself looking really close and listening for lies. That's something else you can't tell the judge, that you'd bet your instinct against a polygraph. I *knew* this boy wasn't lying. But then, I seemed to be wrong about everything lately.

"I'm gonna book you and release you to your sister. That okay with you?"

"You ain't gonna send me to Juvenile Hall?"

"No. You wanna go there?"

"Christ, no. I gotta be free. I was scared you was gonna lock me up. Thanks. Thanks a lot. I just gotta be free. I couldn't stand being inside a place like that with everybody telling you what to do."

"If I ever see you downtown scoring pills again, I'll make sure you go to the Hall."

The kid took a deep breath. "You'll never see me again, I swear. Unless you come out around Echo Park."

"As a matter of fact, I don't live too far from there."

"Yeah? I got customers in Silverlake and all around Echo Park. Where do you live?"

"Not far from Bobby's drive-in. You know where that is? All the kids hang around there."

"Sure I do. I work with this old guy who's got this pickup truck and equipment. Why don't you let us do your yard? We do front and back, rake, trim, weed and everything for eight bucks."

"That's not too bad. How much you get yourself?"

'Four bucks. I do all the work. The old guy just flops in the shade somewhere till I'm through. But I need him because of the truck and stuff."

This kid had me so interested I suddenly realized we were just sitting there. I put the cigar in my teeth and turned the key. She fired right up and I pulled out in the traffic. But I couldn't get my mind off this boy.

"Whadda you do for fun? You play ball or anything?"

"No, I like swimming. I'm the best swimmer in my class, but I don't go out for the team."

"Why not?"

"I'm too busy with girls. Look." The boy took out his wallet and showed me his pictures. I glanced at them while turning on Pico, three shiny little faces that all looked the same to me.

"Pretty nice," I said, handing the pictures back.

"*Real* nice," said the kid with a wink.

"You look pretty athletic. Why don't you play baseball? That used to be my game."

"I like sports I can do by myself."

"Don't you have any buddies?"

"No, I'm more of a ladies' man."

"I know what you mean, but you can't go through this world by yourself. You should have some friends."

"I don't need nobody."

"What grade you in?"

"Eighth. I'll sure be glad to get the hell out of junior high. It's a ghoul school."

"How you gonna pass if you cut classes like this?"

"I don't ditch too often, and I'm pretty smart in school, believe it or not. I just felt rotten last night. Sometimes when you're alone a lot you get feeling rotten and you just wanna go out where there's some people. I figured, where am I gonna find lots of people? Downtown, right? So I came downtown. Then this morning I felt more rotten from sleeping in the creepy movie so I looked around and saw these two guys and asked them where I could get some bennies and they sold them to me. I really wanted to get high, but swear to God, I only dropped bennies a couple times before. And one lousy time I dropped a red devil and a rainbow with some guys at school, and that's all the dope I ever took. I don't really dig it, Officer. Sometimes I drink a little beer."

"I'm a beer man myself, and you can call me Bumper."

"Listen, Bumper, I meant it about doing your yard work. I'm a hell of a good worker. The old man ain't no good, but I just stick him away in a corner somewheres and you should see me go. You won't be sorry if you hire us."

"Well, I don't really have a yard myself. I live in this apartment building, but I kind of assist the manager and he's always letting the damn place go to hell. It's mostly planted in ivy and ice plant and junipers that he lets get pretty seedy-looking. Not too much lawn except little squares of grass in front of the downstairs apartments."

"You should see me pull weeds, Bumper. I'd have that ice plant looking alive and green in no time. And I know how to take care of junipers. You gotta trim them a little, kind of shape them. I can make a juniper look soft and trim as a virgin's puss. How about getting us the account? I could maybe give you a couple bucks kickback."

"Maybe I'll do that."

"Sure. When we get to the police station, I'll write out the old man's name and phone number for you. You just call him when you want us to come. One of these days I'm getting some business cards printed up. It impresses hell out of people when you drop a business card on them. I figure we'll double our business with a little advertising and some business cards."

"I wouldn't be surprised."

"This the place?" The kid looked up at the old brown brick station. I parked in the back.

"This is the place," I said. "Pretty damned dreary, huh?"

"It gives me the creepies."

"The office is upstairs," I said, leading him up and inside, where I found one of the Juvenile Narcotics officers eating lunch.

"Hi, Bumper," he said.

"What's happening, man," I answered, not able to think of his name. "Got a kid with some bennies. No big thing. I'll book him and pencil out a quick arrest report."

"Worthwhile for me talking to him?"

"Naw, just a little score. First time, he claims. I'll take care of it. When should I cite him back in?"

"Make it Tuesday. We're pretty well up to the ass in cite-ins."

"Okay," I said, and nodded to another plainclothes officer who came in and started talking to the first one.

"Stay put, kid," I said to the boy and went to the head. After I came out, I went to the soft drink machine and got myself a Coke and one for the boy. When I came back in he was looking at me kind of funny.

"Here's a Coke," I said, and we went in another office which was empty. I got a booking form and an arrest report and got ready to start writing.

He was still looking at me with a little smile on his face.

"What's wrong?" I said.

"Nothing."

"What're you grinning at?"

"Oh, was I grinning? I was just thinking about what those two cops out there said when you went to the john."

"What'd they say?"

"Oh, how you was some kind of cop."

"Yeah,"I mumbled as I put my initial on a couple of the bennies so I could recognize them if the case went to court. I knew it wouldn't though. I was going to request that the investigator just counsel and release him.

"You and your sister're gonna have to come in Tuesday morning and talk to an investigator."

"What for?"

"So he can decide if he ought to C-and-R you, or send you to court."

"What's C and R? Crush and rupture?"

"Hey, that's pretty good," I chuckled. He was a spunky little bastard. I was starting to feel kind of proud of him. "C and R means counsel and release. They almost always counsel and release a kid the first time he's busted instead of sending him to juvenile court."

"I told you I been busted twice for running away. This ain't my first fall."

"Don't worry about it. They're not gonna send you to court."

"How do you know?"

"They'll do what I ask."

"Those juvies said you was really some kind of cop. No wonder I got nailed so fast."

"You were no challenge," I said, putting the bennies in an evidence envelope and sealing it.

"I guess not. Don't forget to lemme give you the old guy's name and phone number for the yard work. Who you live with? Wife and kids?"

"I live alone."

"Yeah?"

"Yeah."

"I might be able to give you a special price on the yardwork. You know, you being a cop and all."

"Thanks, but you should charge your full price, son."

"You said baseball was your game, Bumper?"

"Yeah, that's right." I stopped writing for a minute because the boy seemed excited and was talking so much.

"You like the Dodgers?"

"Yeah, sure."

"I always wanted to learn about baseball. Maury Wills is a Dodger, ain't he?"

"Yeah."

"I'd like to go to a Dodger game sometime and see Maury Wills."

"You never been to a big league game?"

"Never been. Know what? There's this guy down the street. Old fat fart, maybe even older than you, and fatter even. He takes his kid to the school yard across the street all day Saturday and Sunday and hits fly balls to him. They go to a game practically ever week during baseball season."

"Yeah?"

"Yeah, and know what the best part of it is?"

"What?"

"All that exercise is really good for the old man. That kid's doing him a *favor* by playing ball with him."

"I better call your sister," I said, suddenly getting a gas bubble and a burning pain at the same time. I was also getting a little light-headed from the heat and because there were ideas trying to break through the front of my skull, but I thought it was better to leave them lay right now. The boy gave me the number and I dialed it.

"No answer, kid," I said, hanging up the phone.

"Christ, you gotta put me in Juvenile Hall if you don't find her?"

"Yeah, I do."

"You can't just drop me at the pad?"

"I can't."

"Damn. Call Ruby's Playhouse on Normandie. That joint opens early and Slim likes to hang out there sometimes. Damn, not the Hall!"

I got Ruby's Playhouse on the phone and asked for Sarah Tilden, which he said was her name.

"Big Blue," said the boy. "Ask for Big Blue."

"I wanna talk to Big Blue," I said, and then the bartender knew who I was talking about.

A slurred young voice said, "Yeah, who's this?"

"This is Officer Morgan, Los Angeles Police, Miss Tilden. I've arrested your brother downtown for possession of dangerous drugs. He had some pills on him. I'd like you to drive down to thirteen-thirty Georgia Street and pick him up. That's just south of Pico Boulevard and west of Figueroa." After I finished there was a silence on the line for a minute and then she said, "Well, that does it. Tell the little son of a bitch to get himself a lawyer. I'm through."

I let her go on with the griping a little longer and then I said, "Look, Miss Tilden, you'll have to come pick him up and then you'll have to come back here Tuesday morning and talk to an investigator. Maybe they can give you some advice."

"What happens if I don't come pick him up?" she said.

"I'd have to put him in Juvenile Hall and I don't think you'd want that. I don't think it would be good for him."

"Look, Officer," she said. "I wanna do what's right. But maybe you people could help me somehow. I'm a young woman, too goddamn young to be saddled with a kid his age. I can't raise a kid. It's too hard for me. I got a lousy job. Nobody should expect me to raise a kid brother. I been turned down for welfare even, how do you like that? If I was some nigger they'd gimme all the goddamn welfare I wanted. Look, maybe it would be best if you *did* put him in Juvenile Hall. Maybe it would be best for him. It's *him* I'm thinking of, you see. Or maybe you could put him in one of those foster homes. Not like a criminal, but someplace where somebody with lots of time can watch over him and see that he goes to school."

"Lady, I'm just the arresting officer and my job is to get him home right now. You can talk about all this crap to the juvenile investigator Tuesday morning, but I want you down here in fifteen minutes to take him home. You understand me?"

"Okay, okay, I understand you," she said. "Is it all right if I send a family friend?"

"Who is it?"

"It's Tommy's uncle. His name's Jake Pauley. He'll bring Tommy home."

"I guess it'll be okay."

After I hung up, the kid was looking at me with a lopsided smile. "How'd you like Big Blue?"

"Fine," I said, filling in the boxes on the arrest report. I was sorry I had called her in front of the kid, but I wasn't expecting all that bitching about coming to get him.

"She don't *want* me, does she?"

"She's sending your uncle to pick you up."

"I ain't got no uncle."

"Somebody named Jake Pauley."

"Hah! Old Jake baby? Hah! He's some uncle."

"Who's he? One of her friends?"

"They're friendly all right. She was shacked up with him before we moved in with Slim. I guess she's going back to Jake. Jesus, Slim'll cut Jake wide, deep, and often."

"You move around a lot, do you?"

"*Do* we? I been in seven different schools. Seven! But, I guess it's the same old story. You probably hear it all the time."

"Yeah, I hear it all the time."

I tried to get going on the report again and he let me write for a while but before I could finish he said, "Yeah, I been meaning to go to a Dodger game. I'd be willing to pay the way if I could get somebody with a little baseball savvy to go with me."

Now in addition to the gas and the indigestion, I had a headache, and I sat back with the booking slip finished and looked at him and let the thoughts come to the front of my skull, and of course it was clear as water that the gods conspire against men, because here was this boy. On my last day. Two days after Cassie first brought up the thing that's caused me a dozen indigestion attacks. And for a minute I was excited as hell and had to stand up and pace across the room and look out the window.

Here it is, I thought. Here's the thing that puts it all away for good. I fought an impulse to call Cassie and tell her about him, and another impulse to call his sister back and tell her not to bother sending Jake baby, and then I felt dizzy on top of the headache. I looked down at my shield and without willing it I reached down and touched it and my sweaty finger left a mark on the brass part which this morning had been polished to the luster of gold. The finger mark turned a tarnished orange before my eyes, and I thought about trading my gold and silver shield for a little tinny retirement badge that you can show to old men in bars to prove what you used to be, and which could never be polished to a luster that would reflect sunlight like a mirror.

Then the excitement I'd felt for a moment began to fade and was replaced with a kind of fear that grew and almost smothered me until I got hold of myself. This was too much. This was all *much* too much. Cassie was one terrible responsibility, but I needed her. Cruz told me. Socorro told me. The elevator boy in the death room of the hotel told me. The old blubbering drunks in Harry's bar told me. I needed her. Yes, maybe, but I didn't need this other kind of responsiblity. I didn't need *this* kind of cross. Not me. I walked into the other room where the juvenile officer was sitting.

"Listen, pal," I said. "This kid in here is waiting for his uncle. I explained the arrest to his sister and cited her back. I gotta meet a guy downtown and I'm late. How about taking care of him for me and I'll finish my reports later."

"Sure, Bumper. I'll take care of it," he said, and I wondered how calm I looked.

"Okay, kid, be seeing you," I said, passing through the room where the boy sat. "Hang in there, now."

"Where you going, Bumper?"

"Gotta hit the streets, kid," I said, trying to grin. "There's crime to crush."

"Yeah? Here's the phone number. I wrote it down on a piece of paper for you. Don't forget to call us."

"Yeah, well, I was thinking, my landlord is a cheap bastard. I don't think he'd ever go for eight bucks. I think you'd be better off not doing his place anyway. He probably wouldn't pay you on time or anything."

"That's okay. Give me your address, we'll come by and give you a special price. Remember, I can kick back a couple bucks."

"No, it wouldn't work out. See you around, huh?"

"How 'bout us getting together for a ball game, Bumper? I'll buy us a couple of box seats."

"I don't think so. I'm kind of giving up on the Dodgers."

"Wait a minute," he said, jumping to his feet. "We'll do your gardening for four dollars, Bumper. Imagine that! Four dollars! We'll work maybe three hours. You can't beat that."

"Sorry, kid," I said, scuttling for the door like a fat crab.

"Why did you ever mention it then? Why did you ever say 'maybe'?"

I can't help you, boy, I thought. I don't have what you need.

"Goddamn you!" he yelled after me, and his voice broke. "You're just a cop! Nothing but a goddamn cop!"

I got back in the car feeling like someone kicked me in the belly and I headed back downtown. I looked at my watch and groaned, wondering when this day would end.

At the corner of Pico and Figueroa I saw a blind man with a red-tipped cane getting ready to board a bus. Some do-gooder in a mod suit was grabbing the blind man's elbow and aiming him, and finally the blind man said something to the meddler and made his own way.

"That's telling him, Blinky," I said under my breath. "You got to do for yourself in this world or they'll beat you down. The gods are strong, lonesome bastards and *you* got to be too."

17

At eleven-fifteen I was parking in front of Seymour's to meet Cruz. His car was there but I looked in the window and he wasn't at the counter. I wondered where he could be. Then I looked down the block and saw three black-and-whites, two detective cars, and an ambulance.

Being off the air with the kid I hadn't heard a call come out, and I walked down there and made my way through a crowd of people that was forming on the sidewalk around the drugstore. Just like everybody else, I was curious.

"What's happening, Clarence?" I said to Evans, who was standing in front of the door.

"Didn't you hear, Bumper?" said Evans, and he was sweating and looked sick, his coffee-brown face working nervously every-which way, and he kept looking around everywhere but at me.

"Hear what?"

"There was a holdup. A cop walked in and got shot," said a humpbacked shine man in a sailor's hat, looking up at me with an idiotic smile.

My heart dropped and I felt the sick feeling all policemen get when you hear that another policeman was shot.

"Who?" I asked, worrying that it might've been that young bookworm, Wilson.

"It was a sergeant," said the hunchback.

I looked toward Seymour's then and I felt the blood rush to my head.

"Let me in there, Clarence," I said.

"Now, Bumper. No one's allowed in there and you can't do anything. . . ."

I shoved Evans aside and pushed on the swinging aluminum doors, which were bolted.

"Bumper, please," said Evans, but I pulled away from him and slammed my foot against the center of the two doors, driving the bolt out of the aluminum casing.

The doors flew open with a crash and I was inside and running through a checkstand toward the rear of the big drugstore. It seemed like the store was a mile long and I ran blind and light-headed, knocking a dozen hair spray cans off a shelf when I barreled around a row of display counters toward the popping flashbulbs and the dozen plainclothesmen who were huddled in groups at the back of the store.

The only uniformed officer was Lieutenant Hilliard and it seemed like I ran for fifteen minutes to cover the eighty feet to the pharmacy counter where Cruz Segovia lay dead.

"What the hell . . ." said a red-faced detective I could barely see through a watery mist as I knelt beside Cruz, who looked like a very young boy sprawled there on his back, his hat and gun on the floor beside him and a frothy blood puddle like a scarlet halo fanning out around him from a through-and-through head shot. There was one red glistening bullet hole to the left of his nose and one in his chest which was surrounded by wine-purple bloodstains on the blue uniform. His eyes were open and he was looking right at me. The corneas were not yet dull or cloudy and the eyes were turned down at the corners, those large eyes more serious and sad than ever I'd seen them, and I knelt beside him in his blood and whispered, " *'Mano! 'Mano! 'Mano!* Oh, Cruz!"

"Bumper, get the hell out of here," said the bald detective, grabbing my arm, and I looked up at him, seeing a very familiar face, but still I couldn't recognize him.

"Let him go, Leecher. We got enough pictures," said another plainclothesman, older, who was talking to Lieutenant Hilliard. He was one I should know too, I thought. It was so strange. I couldn't remember any of their names, except my lieutenant, who was in uniform.

Cruz looked at me so serious I couldn't bear it. And I reached in his pocket for the little leather pouch with the beads.

"You mustn't take anything from him," Lieutenant Hilliard said in my ear with his hand on my shoulder. "Only the coroner can do that, Bumper."

"His beads," I muttered. "He won them because he was the only one who could spell English words. I don't want them to know he carries beads like a nun."

"Okay, Bumper, okay," said Lieutenant Hilliard, patting my shoulder, and I took the pouch. Then I saw the box of cheap cigars spilled on the floor by his hand. And there was a ten-dollar bill there on the floor.

"Give me that blanket," I said to a young ambulance attendant who was standing there beside his stretcher, white in the face, smoking a cigarette.

He looked at me and then at the detectives.

"Give me that goddamn blanket!" I said, and he handed the folded-up blanket to me, which I covered Cruz with after I closed his eyes so he couldn't look at me like that. "*Ahí te huacho*," I whispered. "I'll be watching for you, *'mano*." Then I was on my feet and heading toward the door, gulping for breath.

"Bumper," Lieutenant Hilliard called, running painfully on his bad right leg and holding his hip.

I stopped before I got to the door.

"Will you go tell his wife?"

"He came in here to buy me a going-away present," I said, feeling a suffocating pressure in my chest.

"You were his best friend. You should tell her."

"He wanted to buy me a box of cigars," I said, grabbing him by the bony shoulder. "Damn him, I'd never smoke those cheap cigars. Damn him!"

"All right, Bumper. Go to the station. Don't try to work anymore today. You go on home. We'll take care of the notification. You take care of yourself."

I nodded and hurried out the door, looking at Clarence Evans but not understanding what he said to me. I got in the car and drove up Main Street, tearing my collar open to breathe, and thought about Cruz lying frail and naked and unprotected there in the morgue and thinking how they'd desecrate him, how they'd stick that turkey skewer in him for the liver temperature, and how they'd put a metal rod in the hole in his face for the bullet angle, and I was so damned glad I'd closed his eyes so he wouldn't be watching all that.

"You see, Cruz," I said, driving over Fourth Street with no idea where I was going. "You see? You almost had me convinced, but you were all wrong. I was right."

"You shouldn't be afraid to love, *'mano*," Cruz answered, and I slammed on my brakes when I heard him and I almost slid through the red light. Someone leaned on his horn and yelled at me.

"You're safe, Bumper, in one way," said Cruz in his gentle voice, "but in the way that counts, you're in danger. Your soul is in danger if you don't love."

I started when the light was green but I could hardly see.

"Did you believe that when Esteban was killed? Did you?"

"Yes, I knew it was the God's truth," he said, and his sad eyes turned down at the corners and this time I *did* blow a red light and I heard tires squeal and I turned right going the wrong way on Main Street and everyone was honking horns at me but I kept going to the next block and then turned left with the flow of traffic.

"Don't look at me with those goddamn turned-down eyes!" I yelled, my heart thudding like the pigeon's wing. "You're wrong, you foolish little man. Look at Socorro. Look at your children. Don't you see now, you're wrong? Damn those eyes!"

Then I pulled into an alley west of Broadway and got out of the car because I suddenly couldn't see at all now and I began to vomit. I threw it all up, all of it. Someone in a delivery truck stopped and said something but I waved him off and heaved and heaved it all away.

Then I got back in the car and the shock was wearing off. I drove to a pay phone and called Cassie before she left her office. I crowded in that phone booth doubled over by stomach cramps and I don't really know everything I said to her except that Cruz was dead and I wouldn't be going with her. Not now, not ever. And then there was lots of crying on the other end of the line and talking back and forth that didn't make any sense, and finally I heard myself say, "Yes, yes, Cassie. You go on. Yes, maybe I'll feel different later. Yes. Yes. Yes. Yes. You go on. Maybe I'll see you there in San Francisco. Maybe someday I'll feel different. Yes."

I was back in my car driving, and I knew I'd have to go to Socorro tonight and help her. I wanted to bury Cruz as soon as possible and I hoped she would want to. And now, gradually at first, and then more quickly, I felt as though a tremendous weight was lifted from my shoulders and there was no sense analyzing it, but there it was. I felt somehow light and free like when I first started on my beat. "There's nothing left now but the *puta*. But she's not a *puta, 'mano,* she's not!" I said, lying to both of us for the last time. "You couldn't tell a whore from a bewitching lady. I'll keep her as long as I can, Cruz, and when I can't keep her anymore she'll go to somebody that can. You can't blame her for that. That's the way the world is made." And Cruz didn't answer my lie and I didn't see his eyes. He was gone. He was like Herky now, nothing more.

I began thinking of all the wandering people: Indians, Gypsies, Armenians, the Bedouin on that cliff where I'd never go, and now I knew the Bedouin saw nothing more than sand out there in that valley.

And as I thought these things I turned to my left and I was staring into the mouth of the Pink Dragon. I passed the Dragon by and drove on toward the station, but the further I drove, the more the anger welled up in me, and the anger mixed with the freedom I felt, so that for a while I felt like the most vigorous and powerful man on earth, a real *macho*, Cruz would've said. I turned around and headed back to the Dragon. This was the day for the Dragon to die, I thought. I could make

Marvin fight me, and the others would help him. But no one could stand up to me and at last I'd destroy the Dragon.

Then I glanced down at my shield and saw that the smog had made the badge hideous. It was tarnished, and smeared with a drop of Cruz's blood. I stopped in front of Rollo's and went inside.

"Give it a fast buff, Rollo. I'm in a hurry."

"You know there ain't a single blemish on this badge," Rollo sighed.

"Just shine the goddamn badge."

He glanced up with his faded eyes, then at my trousers, at my wet bloody knees, and he bent silently over the wheel.

"There you are, Bumper," he said when he finished it.

I held the badge by the pin and hurried outside.

"Be careful, Bumper," he called. "Please be careful."

Passing by Rollo's store front I saw the distorted reflection in the folds of the plastic sun covering. I watched the reflection and had to laugh at the grotesque fat policeman who held the four-inch glittering shield in front of him as he lumbered to his car. The dark blue uniform was dripping sweat and the fat policeman opened the burning white door and squeezed his big stomach behind the wheel.

He settled in his saddle seat and jammed the nightstick under the seat cushion next to him, pointed forward.

Then he fastened his shield to his chest and urged the machine westward. The sun reflecting off the hood blinded him for a moment, but he flipped down the visor and drove west to the Pink Dragon.

"Now I'll kill the Dragon and drink its blood," said the comic blue policeman. "In the *front* door, down the Dragon's throat."

I laughed out loud at him because he was good for no more than this. He was disgusting and pathetic and he couldn't help himself. He needed no one. He sickened me. He only needed glory.

The Black Marble

For the sterling of Pasadena,
Beverly and John Tarr,
and
For Peter J. Monahan,
Sensitive soul,
Compassionate confessor,
Rhapsodical saloon keeper!

1

The *Batushka*

An explosion of chrysanthemums, candlelight, Oriental carpets, Byzantine eyes. Plumes of incense rising between two a cappella choirs, blown heavenward by chanting voices.

The man in the yellow rubber raincoat swayed unsteadily and raised his sturdy arms toward those marbling clouds of incense enveloping the Holy Virgin. Her eyes were sweet.

Other eyes were reproachful, severe. Byzantine eyes. A kaleidoscope of ikons, small and large: saints, holy men, madonnas. All around him the faces on the ikons stared with great, dark, unrelenting eyes.

From time to time the man in the yellow rubber raincoat would wobble against the burly woman standing next to him.

Finally she'd had enough. "*Zhopa!*" she muttered.

He answered her in English: "Yes, I'm terribly sorry."

Then both choirs burst forth with the tragic, timeless, Slavonic invocation: "Blessed art thou, Lord God of our Father . . . have *mercy* on us."

The man in the yellow rubber raincoat was overwhelmed by the enduring pathos in those Russian voices, and by the clouds of incense he breathed gratefully, and by the low gilded ceiling and the throngs of believers standing shoulder to shoulder. He kept looking about at the quixotic tapestry of ikons, and the huge ikonostasis screen. Great dark sad eyes. The ikon of the Virgin and Child nestled among apricot and butter and salmon carnations. The *batushka* raised the *pomazok* to brush the sign of the cross on the forehead of the first in a long queue of communicants.

The communicant was sleek and feline. Her gray coat was damp from the rain. It flared from a belted waist, and the fur cuffs and hem matched the fur in her hat. She wore calf-molded, gray leather boots. The man in the yellow rubber raincoat was overcome by her beauty when the *batushka* brushed a cross of holy oil on her forehead. She could have stepped from the stage of an opera by Glinka or Borodin: a maiden fallen from a troika in the forest. The man in the yellow rubber raincoat could almost imagine flakes of luminescent snow on the fur of her collar.

But it wasn't fur, not real fur anyway. And she wasn't Russian, and she certainly wasn't a maiden. She was third-generation Anglo-Irish, currently living with a second-generation Ukrainian, in church on Russian Christmas only to please his great-aunt, who was going to loan them fourteen thousand dollars unsecured for a Jaguar X-J-12, which she needed about as much as she needed those tight boots cutting off her circulation.

The room capacity was limited to three hundred. There were four hundred souls crowded into that modest cathedral for vesper service. Yet few residents of Los Angeles knew that this holy night, Thursday, January 6th, was the eve of Russian

Christmas. There was a far holier day to anticipate on Sunday. They *all* knew about that one. And this year, praise God, it would be celebrated in nearby Pasadena! Super Bowl XI.

The voices: "Blessed art thou . . . have *mercy* on us."

The man in the yellow rubber raincoat felt a bubble of sourness in his throat, swallowed it back, belched, and staggered sideways into the burly woman.

This time she wanted to make sure he understood. In accented English, she said, "Asshole!" And jolted him with a plump elbow to the ribs.

"Uh!" the man in the raincoat gasped, his wet cinnamon hair whipping across his eyes.

"Go home!" she whispered. "You damn dronk. Go home!" And she gave him another jab in the belly.

"Uh!" he belched. "Yes. I'm terribly sorry."

Then he turned, holding his stomach, and staggered toward the door, through the press of standing believers, out of this pewless teeming house of God.

When he got to the door, something clashed at his feet. A small boy said, "Hey," and grabbed his raincoat.

"Here," the boy said, handing the man a set of glinting handcuffs, one steel ratchet dangling open.

"Yes, I'm terribly sorry," the man in the yellow rubber raincoat said, taking the handcuffs and shoving them down inside the front of his belt.

One moment, candlelight and incense and color. The next, darkness cold and wet. But then, always just beyond, was black and cold and rainy night.

"Lord God, have mercy."

The man in the yellow rubber raincoat couldn't get the handcuffs tucked inside his belt. He didn't understand that the belt buckle had slid around to his hip. He groped and pulled at the belt, causing the handcuffs to fall down inside his underwear. The steel was cold, and he cried out as the open ratchet gouged his genitals.

The man in the yellow rubber raincoat struggled. He leaned against the wall of the cathedral, in the shadows, and thought about it. If he was logical and calm it should be very easy to extricate the handcuffs. But he was shivering in the rain. He lurked deeper in the shadows and stealthily withdrew the bottle of Stolichnaya from the pocket of his raincoat. He tipped it up, swaying, and in just seconds the silky flood of Russian vodka warmed him to the toes.

Now he stopped shivering. Now he could think. Except that he was reeling and had to sit. He plopped down on the front step of the cathedral. Right on the tip of the serrated edge of the steel ratchet, lined up directly with his scrotum.

A bent and withered usher inside the cathedral thought for a moment he heard a man scream. Impossible, he shrugged.

Now the man in the yellow rubber raincoat had totally lost the belt buckle. It was all the way around the back, as was the holster and bullet clip. The fly on the old loose poplins was pulled six inches off center. He groped and tugged. He pulled upward, which was the wrong way. The harder he pulled the harder the steel ratchet gouged deep into the wounded sac. He couldn't find the fly. It too had disappeared. He thought he had his pants on backward.

The bent and withered usher inside the cathedral cocked his head and looked toward the ikon of St. Isaac high on the wall. This time he was certain he heard a man scream.

Three women arrived late for Christmas vesper service. One was seventy-three years old, an immigrant and monarchist who had never stopped bemoaning immorality and anarchy in America, who dreamed of her bones' being buried in Russian soil. She crossed herself and threw her arms around her two daughters and shrieked in horror. There, by the old monastery garden, framed by the onion dome of the Holy Virgin Mary Russian Orthodox Cathedral, a howling dervish, a phantom with matted soppy hair, was twirling in the shadow of the golden cupola. His yellow rubber raincoat was spread wide. His dripping pants were torn down around his ankles. Both hands held his genitals. He moaned ghostlike, doing a lonely mad waltz in the rain.

Now, over the heartbreaklng Slavonic chorus, the bent and withered usher thought he heard a *woman* screaming. He cocked his head and offered a prayer to St. Isaac about the baffling indignities of advanced age.

The man in the yellow rubber raincoat was exhausted from the tremendous battle. His handcuffs were on the pavement, as was his four-inch Smith and Wesson .38 caliber revolver, as was a set of keys and a dirty handkerchief. Now he was sitting, bare buttocks in a rain puddle, pulling his underwear back up over his knees, realizing that his pants had not been on backward after all.

Five minutes later, he had all his equipment stuffed into the pockets of his raincoat along with the bottle of Stolichnaya. His fly zipper was torn completely off his baggy poplins and dangled between his legs. He stumbled thankfully back into the church.

''Have mercy on us . . . Holy God Immortal . . . Have mercy on us.''

He was once again hot and smothering in the damp press of communicants, watching a slender erect man at least eighty years of age, wearing a threadbare olive topcoat, drop to both knees before the ikon of the Virgin and Child. The old man bowed with grave reverence and stood unassisted before the *batushka,* aglow in the candlelight. The old man bent to the cross in the hand of the priest and kissed the golden bas-relief of the crucified Christ.

The *batushka* smiled in recognition. The old man was of the First Immigration, a brick mason from Rostov who had in years past donated his skill to his church. The man in the yellow rubber raincoat didn't know the brick mason. He saw instead a gallant old White Russian soldier, perhaps a Cossack colonel, now standing at attention before the *diakon* to receive the body of Christ as reverently as he may have stood before the czar himself before boarding a train for The Front.

It became too much for the man in the yellow rubber raincoat. He couldn't stifle the wet drunken sob. It escaped his mouth like the bark of a seal. The communicant in front of him was startled. He turned and looked at the flushed, tear-streaked face, the soppy strings of cinnamon hair flopping in his eyes.

''Yes, I'm terribly sorry,'' the man in the yellow rubber raincoat said in answer to the silent gaping communicant.

Now the man in the yellow rubber raincoat was himself kneeling before the holy ikon. He pressed his lips grimly, but to no avail. A great sob welled and he braked. The *batushka* looked up sharply.

Two altar boys assisting the *diakon* snickered and whispered to each other. The man in the yellow rubber raincoat had to be helped to his feet by two communicants. He turned and grinned foolishly at his benefactors and said, ''Yes, I'm terribly sorry.''

''Go on,'' the man behind him whispered. ''Go on, you're next.''

The man in the yellow rubber raincoat was swaying before the bearded *batushka,* who looked as though he'd rather give the drunk his fist than his blessing.

Then it simply became too much for the man in the yellow rubber raincoat. All of it: the holy Slavonic chants, the enveloping clouds of blessed incense, the myriads of candles and the rainbow sprays and burst of carnation and chrysanthemum, the gallant old soldier-brick mason, the omnipresent ikons, and those suffering reproachful Byzantine eyes. He slouched humbly before the priest. And then it all came. His brawny shoulders heaved and he bowed his head and let the scalding waters run. He wept.

His raincoat was open and with each shuddering heave of his shoulders the torn fragment of flyfront jumped and bounced between his knees, a sad rag of a puppet hopping gracelessly on a single wire.

It was unspeakably offensive in this holy place, on this holy day, yet so pathetic the old priest was touched.

"It's all right, my son," he said, and brushed the wand on the weeping man's forehead.

The man in the yellow rubber raincoat felt the warm oil trickle down between his eyes and he grabbed the hand of the bearded priest and said, "Father, I'm terribly sorry. I'm *so* sorry, *Batushka*."

"It's all right, my son. *S Rozhdeniem Khristovym*."

When he heard the ancient Christmas greeting, he kissed the hand of the *batushka*. Then he lunged past the communion basket and swayed toward the door, scarely able to breathe.

The bent and withered usher shook his head in disgust and threw open the door for the drunk in the yellow rubber raincoat. The rubber raincoat was old, a dirty canary yellow with a blue collar. The usher looked curiously at the raincoat. It was one of those long, high-visibility slickers worn by men who worked in auto traffic. The usher looked more closely. The raincoat bore an oval patch over the heart. As though for a badge!

"You *can't* be a policeman!" the usher sputtered.

"Yes, I'm terribly sorry," the man in the yellow rubber raincoat belched. Then he staggered into the night.

The last thing he heard before the rain struck his face was the eternal Slavonic chant: "Have mercy on us . . . Holy God Immortal . . . Have *mercy* on us."

2

La Buena Vida

Victoria's redolent warm puffs hinted of the pâté they had shared that night. Madeline Dills Whitfield lay awake listening to the rain. She snagged a lacquered Juliette fingernail on pearl satin sheets sliding closer to Victoria without waking her. Vickie whimpered in enviable sleep as Madeline waited for three Dalmanes and six ounces of Chivas Regal to release her.

Now their mouths were almost touching. Vickie's tongue flicked wet and Madeline ached to stroke the incredible arch of her neck. It was a marvelous neck, now carrying a faint scent of Bellodgia, a neck that lent great hauteur to her movements.

Hauteur. Madeline remembered last Monday afternoon when she and Vickie had strolled across the grounds of the Huntington Sheraton, that once-opulent old dowager of a hotel. That relic of the days when Pasadena was the cultural and social center of the entire Los Angeles area. When old bewhiskered Henry Huntington would don a homburg and waistcoat and ride from his San Marino mansion to Los Angeles in his own railroad car. On a private spur laid by Mexicans and Chinese to his very door.

It hurt to see her so seedy, time-ravaged and mutilated by a grotesque porte cochere of gray concrete, grafted onto the entrance of the hotel where Madeline's mother had been presented at a debutante ball in 1923. And it hurt more when she walked with Vickie by the Bell Tower, toward the hotel's Ship Room, where "Old" Pasadena society had enjoyed dance music virtually unchanged for thirty-five years.

Before she died, Madeline's mother said she was glad her husband had not lived to see the foreigners buy the dear grande dame. Old Pasadena feared the investors from the Far East would tear her down and cover the grounds with cherry trees and high-rise condos.

Madeline and Vickie had stopped in the lobby for a moment, and impulsively, Madeline had turned toward the creaky Picture Bridge which linked the old building with the homely new wing and overlooked the swimming pool where an Oriental waitress served cocktails. Madeline wanted a Scotch and water, but she paused on the footbridge and looked up at the rustic timbered roof, at the painted murals on the gables. The murals suggested pastoral early California. As it never was. Mexicans, Indians, Americans, padre, peasant, landowner: brothers all, in the ubiquitous vineyards and groves.

Then the too familiar empty thud in her chest. A rush of heat to her temples. The price for daring to wax nostalgic, for lingering on this Picture Bridge. Where she had so often stood as a girl and made wishes she had never been given reason to doubt would come true. Then she turned toward South Pasadena and saw the layers of mauve and azure gases heaving in from the west, and remembered that this lovely vapor blanket made the San Gabriel Valley air perhaps the deadliest in Southern California.

But it wasn't just the smog that was killing Old Pasadena. It was *la buena vida* of the past coupled with the frugality of the old social order. When white domestics would not work for the wages offered, there were others who would. The blacks were enticed to Pasadena in large numbers and they prospered and multiplied. And then more came and prospered less but still multiplied. Until a day when fourth-generation Old Pasadenans were troubled to discover that twenty-five percent of their school district was composed of children black and brown. And in another ten years they were shocked to discover that thirty-five percent of their public school children were black and brown. And then one day they were outraged and bewildered to discover that over fifty percent of the children in Pasadena public schools were black and brown! Then the white flight began in earnest.

A nine-thousand-square-foot mansion with guest house, tennis court, swimming pool, and two verdant acres of hundred-year-old twisted oak sold for one-fifth the price of what it would bring "over the hill," or "on the west side," on the beaten path of the *nouveau riche:* Beverly Hills, Holmby Hills, Bel-Air, Brentwood. Henceforth, Old Pasadena was under siege and near panic. Some were old enough to have children grown and need not fear ghetto busing. Others dropped all democratic pretext, and prep schools quickly became overcrowded. Others moved a few blocks away into the tiny bedroom community of San Marino which had its own public school district. All white.

Madeline Whitfield now needed that drink very badly. She and Vickie left the bridge and walked quickly down to poolside. Then she heard it. The man was unmistakably a Minnesota tourist in for the Super Bowl. Who else would be reeking of coconut oil, white-legged in Aloha print shorts, red socks, black-and-white patent-leather loafers? A hairy belly glistening oil in sunlight which any Californian knew was not hot enough to burn even this flabby outlander. But then he was probably using the pool and the sunshine as an excuse to get drunk at one o'clock in the afternoon. As if an excuse was needed during Rose Bowl and Super Bowl weeks in Pasadena.

The man's voice was bourbon thick. He said, "That bitch moves like a stallion!"

And Madeline Dills Whitfield, who had been forced into inactive, sustaining membership in the Pasadena Junior League three years before for being too old. Madeline Dills Whitfield, only twenty-five pounds past her prime, never considered pretty, but damn it, not homely. Four years divorced, childless, two-year analysand, three-year patient of a dermatologist (I *know* that middle-age fat is just excess adipose tissue, Doctor, but *why* did I have to grow a moustache!). Madeline Dills Whitfield, who dutifully spent more than she could afford in Beverly Hills high-fashion shops like Giorgio's—which boasted a billiard table, and a full-time bartender serving free drinks to patrons—where Pasadena matrons invariably shopped for clothing with exclusive labels but basic lines. Madeline Dills Whitfield, who cared enough to have her nails done at Ménage à Trois. (Also over the hill in Lotus Land—thirteen bucks, tip included, for a Juliette, forty-five to make hair look more natural, sixty-five bucks to look like you just got out of bed—and you better know the license number of your Mercedes because all the parking attendant has are Mercedes keys in *that* key box, lady.) Madeline Dills Whitfield, who had not seen male genitalia for five years, yet who was just peaking sexually at the age of forty-three, unsheathed a smile like a knife blade.

The kind of abandoned smile seldom seen on Pasadena Junior Leaguers, unless they were ignited by Bombay martinis at Annandale Country Club. A smile which would unquestionably be deemed provocative by the socially wed and nearly dead at the all-woman Town Club. Oh God, she dreaded the day she'd be old enough to *want* to join. Madeline Dills Whitfield unleashed a smile she had reserved for Mason Whitfield on those rare occasions he bedded her in the last dreadful years of their marriage.

A smile which carried a promise made instantly, consciously, irrevocably—to screw the patent-leather loafers right off this Minnesota greaseball.

A smile which was not even *seen* by the hairy stranger. Because he was admiring Vickie. Staring after *Vickie*.

The oily stranger turned again to his friend and said: "Look at the muscles in her legs. She moves like a stallion. I tell you!"

Then Madeline felt loneliness all right. And *real* fear. The kind that choked her awake in those first months after Mason had gone. The worst kind of fear, born of loneliness, which only became manageable when Vickie came.

Vickie. Madeline sat there with Vickie by the pool and drank three double Chivas with water-back, and controlled that fear and looked at the hairy stranger scornfully. She wasn't jealous, she was *proud*. Vickie belonged to *her,* and Madeline loved her obsessively.

The rain was steady. She wondered if she'd be awake the entire night. Probably, if she insisted on these tormenting thoughts. But as she lay in the dark and looked at Vickie's elegant jaw, she couldn't help admitting that she would have given a healthy chunk of a secretly unhealthy trust fund if that oily man had said drunkenly to Madeline: "You bitch, you carry yourself like a *stallion!*"

Madeline wryly wondered if, in the history of the old Huntington Hotel, any "sustaining" Junior Leaguer had sat by the Picture Bridge and yearned for a man to look at her thighs and arouse her with an antiquated, vulgar, erotic cliché. By comparing her to a male horse.

Victoria stirred in her sleep. Madeline touched her lovingly and risked awakening her by snuggling closer until her mouth was touching Vickie's ear.

"Sleep, love, sleep," Madeline whispered. She stroked that arched neck and said, "Sleep, my darling."

But Vickie opened her eyes: perfect ovals, blinking in momentary confusion. Madeline kissed each eye, marveling at the luster: wet chocolate irises, whites like lapis lazuli in the moonlight.

"Sleep, love, sleep."

Vickie sighed and turned just enough for Madeline to see how deep those eyes were set, how shaded by brows of silver white. Madeline wanted to touch her face and kiss that lovely ear.

Like most insomniacs, Madeline toyed masochistically with her devils in the night. Today's tennis exhibition at the Valley Hunt Club.

It is the oldest social club in the Los Angeles area. Where ladies still sit courtside and worry over comingout parties. Where Old Pasadena strives to nourish its moldering roots by presenting the family flowers at frantic and archaic debutante balls.

Madeline had been courtside at the Valley Hunt Club, ostensibly watching a listless college tennis exhibition while downing the third double Scotch and water of the afternoon. She had waited an appropriate time to order her fourth because of the presence of Edna Lofton, an obtrusive bitch Madeline had known since Kappa House days at the University of Southern California, when Edna was a smartass sorority viper.

Edna Lofton, another ''sustaining'' Junior Leaguer, also active with Madeline in the Junior Philharmonic and the Huntington Library Docents, seldom missed the opportunity to grin knowingly whenever Madeline ordered more than three or four afternoon cocktails at the club.

Like other ''younger'' Valley Hunt Club members, Edna had switched from Yves St. Laurent sunglasses to the latest from over the hill: oversized sunglasses with logograms engraved on the lower lens. In Edna's case it was a little white tennis racquet. It should have been a spider and a web, Madeline thought. Madeline herself had bought a pair in Beverly Hills at the Optique Boutique. She had wanted the tennis racquet too, but resisted because Edna had beaten her to it, so she settled for a white flower. Madeline thought the glasses chic and becoming, though the little speck was annoying when she looked at anything below eye level. The price tag annoyed her even more.

One day while shopping on Lake Avenue in Pasadena she had encountered something considerably below eye level: a barefoot black girl about seven years of age. The child stopped her skateboard. ''Lady?'' She was licking a green Popsicle, gawking at Madeline's ninety-dollar, double-gradient sunglasses.

''Yes, dear, what can I do for you?'' Madeline smiled.

The girl stopped licking and said, ''I was wonderin. How come you don't jist wipe the bird shit off them funny glasses?''

The following Sunday, Madeline's Mexican housekeeper, Yolanda, wore those glasses proudly to a picnic in Elysian Park.

Edna flipped up her sunglasses with the little tennis racquet on the lens, and said sweetly: ''Madeline, go easy, we're playing doubles later and may need you as a fourth.''

Madeline tried a sassy, nose-wrinkling grin. She stuck out her tongue at Edna, but given the pain and the fear and the Chivas Regal flush in her face, it didn't come off.

''Put your tongue in, dear,'' Edna purred. ''You look like the victim of a hanging.''

The second set was as dilatory as the first. Most of the spectators were of course U.S.C. rooters. Old Pasadena, if the money was still intact, seldom attended state-supported institutions like U.C.L.A. It was impossible to concentrate. She imagined Edna's vindictive gaze on her back.

Madeline was in tennis whites and hated it. She was considering trying tennis pants, but was fearful that the club would disapprove if she played in anything but a skirt. Actually she didn't want to play at all anymore. She had always hated the game, but without some exercise she'd probably look like a medicine ball. (Why the continual weight gain, Doctor? I don't drink *that* much. I haven't eaten a really full meal since my husband left me, I swear!)

Mason Whitfield. Stanford class of '48. Infantry officer in Korea. Decorated for typing a report in a tent near Seoul in freezing weather after the company clerk was evacuated with the clap. He had typed for six hours without gloves and was frostbitten. Mason returned to Pasadena wearing a Bronze Star and a Purple Heart.

Like his father before him, Mason had gone to Harvard for his LL.B. and joined a law firm in downtown Los Angeles. One of those giant firms where the lawyers in Probate don't even know the guys in Corporate. He managed to work ten years without ever setting foot in a courtroom. He made big bucks. He was a near-perfect,

Old Pasadena scion. He and Madeline prospered. But they didn't multiply. He had a flaw or two.

Madeline felt Edna's eyes on her back, and selfconsciously tucked a roll of cellulite under the tennis panty which was cutting into her flesh. Madeline just knew Edna was still telling the Filthy Story about Mason Whitfield, when he made a boozy revelation to the barman at the Hunt Club: "Wanna know why I left my wife? Zero sex appeal, that's why. And I just came back from a wonderful holiday in Acapulco. Wanna know what I like best about my secretary? The moustache doesn't scratch my balls as much as Madeline's did."

The secretary's name was Herbert.

Madeline was sure it was a rotten lie, because within a year Mason fired Herbert and married a San Marino widow without a moustache.

"Mrs. Whitfield? You probably don't remember me? We met at dinner? At the Cal Tech Athenaeum?"

Madeline looked up, blankly. She was feeling the Chivas Regal more than usual.

"Remember? I was with Dr. Harry Gray?"

He was a balding little man in a lumpy warm-up suit and dirty canvas Tretorns. He made every statement a question.

"Oh, yes," Madeline lied, "of course, you're . . ."

"Irwin Berg? Remember?"

"Oh, yes, Dr. Berg! Of course!"

Now she knew him. She had enjoyed talking with him at a Cal Tech dinner party to raise funds for foreign students. He was said to be an extraordinary astrophysicist and a candidate for Big Casino: a hot prospect for a Nobel Prize.

"May I buy you a drink?" His round, steel-rimmed eyeglasses were fogging and slipping over his perspiring nose.

"I'd *love* a drink," Madeline said. She was settling down, the last Scotch working nicely now. She leaned closer and whispered, "The barman probably couldn't make change for you anyway. Since I'm a member and you're a guest, I'll buy."

Then Madeline took the little scientist by the arm and walked him into the Hunt Room, where Edna Lofton was ordering a Virgin Mary, her muscular lacy bottom pressed against the mahogany.

Edna was laughing uproariously at one of Wendell Hargrove's dreadful jokes. Hargrove was a third-generation stockbroker and an "A" tennis player, which was the only thing keeping his fifty-year-old body intact, what with the fifth of booze he consumed at noon luncheons at the California Club in downtown Los Angeles. Were it not for his daily tennis, everyone knew that his fierce aging body could never withstand the massive bourbon dosage.

"Guess we won't need that fourth for mixed doubles, Madeline," Edna Lofton smiled. "Marcie's going to play again. So you can go ahead."

"Go ahead what?" Wendell Hargrove asked.

"Go ahead and have another double Scotch," Edna laughed. Then she added: "I might even have one."

But the damage was done. Madeline blushed painfully. Edna looked with curiosity at Madeline's companion and thrust out her hand: "Hi, I'm Edna Lofton."

"Oh? Pleased to meet you. I'm Irwin Berg."

Madeline said, "Dr. Berg's a guest of . . . who are you a guest of?"

"Mr. and Mrs. Bates. I met them at the Athenaeum. They're watching the match."

"You an M.D.?" Hargrove asked thickly and Madeline saw that he was well past any more tennis this day.

"Dr. Berg teaches at Cal Tech. He's an astrophysicist," Madeline offered, subtly eyeing the barman, who nodded and reached discreetly for the Chivas Regal.

"Really?" Edna said. "Don't get many astrophysicists in the Hunt Club."

Later that evening, Madeline, showered and dressed in a basic dark pantsuit, was standing alone at the dessert table deciding to pass the entrée in favor of some strudel and chocolate mousse when Edna Lofton got up from her table and crossed the dining room to talk to her.

"Is Dr. Goldberg with you, Madeline?" she asked, walking Madeline toward the empty drawing room

"Dr. Berg. No, he's not with me. Why?"

"He's sure a cute little fellow," Edna winked, batting her evening eyelashes.

"I suppose so," Madeline said cautiously.

"Play your cards right, Mad, and he might invite you to some of those *fun* Cal Tech science parties at the Athenaeum. A lot of *mature*, visiting professors must be awfully lonely for one of the few available *single ladies* they'd be proud to take just anywhere!"

"Edna . . ." Madeline sputtered, but too late. Edna Lofton had turned and was hurrying toward her guests in the dining room.

Madeline Dills Whitfield had stood alone in the empty drawing room and looked vacantly at the landscape painting as though she had never seen it before. She had seen it all her life. She suddenly longed for the paintings of hunters and hounds. In the *bar*.

A *single* lady. As though it was Madeline's fault. As though she had planned to be a single lady. She had never known *anyone* who had planned to be a single lady. Madeline Dills had never even lived away from her parents except for college terms at U.S.C., ten miles from Pasadena. Had never lived anywhere else except for six months in Europe with her parents when her father sold his interest in the orthopedic clinic and took a long vacation. She had never in her life given a *single* thought to being a single lady.

She was the daughter of Dr. Corey Dills and the wife of Mason Whitfield. She had willingly surrendered her Christian as well as her maiden name.

It had always been: "Mrs. Mason Whitfield is giving a tea Wednesday afternoon . . ."

Madeline Dills, by Dr. Corey Dills out of Mrs. Corey Dills. Edna Lofton, by Mr. Bradford Lofton out of Mrs. Bradford Lofton. They had to give up *both* names. Androgynous. *Mr*. Mason Whitfield and *Mrs*. Mason Whitfield. Hermaphroditic!

The stag ruled. It was her heritage and she accepted it. Which is perhaps why she didn't make a fuss during the divorce. Her family trust fund was much larger than his. *She* paid *him* for his share in the home and furnishings bought as community property. No alimony. She didn't need or want his money. Her mother was hale and hearty then. Madeline didn't make a fuss and Mason said he appreciated it. He said she was a perfect lady.

Now there was the new Mrs. Mason Whitfield living in San Marino. He hadn't the decency to give up his Annandale Country Club membership. So how does one address invitations? Mrs. Madeline Dills Whitfield? The return of her names was . . . awkward. As awkward as having *single* ladies at dinner parties. How does one seat them? And the clubs where *single* ladies were never meant to be? It wasn't awkward, it was *horrible*.

Thank God for Marian Milford's homosexual brother, Lace. He danced beautifully, had impeccable manners, and for ten years had eased dinner problems in Old Pasadena society by escorting half the widows and divorcées in town to social and charitable gatherings. Old Pasadena and San Marino had an exceedingly low divorce rate thanks to the continuity and tradition of society. And thanks to disapproving parents who structured wills and trusts which pauperized many a misbehaving daughter who opted to take the bit in her teeth like less constant, free-spirited sisters over the hill, on the west side.

The Dalmanes and Chivas were interacting. Madeline was about to drift asleep when Victoria sat up.

"Oh, no, Vickie!" Madeline groaned. "Not now. I'm dead!"

But Vickie yawned and stretched languorously and got out of bed. Madeline moaned, got up reeling, and stood naked in the moonlight, reviving when she threw open the French doors to the cold January air.

Suddenly she hoped that someone, anyone—man or woman—would see her through the rain and white oak trees and Canary Island pines. Perhaps someone higher up San Rafael, in a hillside mansion, a gardener, a maid, anyone. She was dizzy, yet she stood defiantly naked under a leering moon, convinced that if someone *could* see her through the wall of camellias that someone would be aroused by *her* naked body.

Then she looked down into the valley and saw that the rain had cleared the smog from the Rose Bowl. It would be an ugly carnival on Sunday when Super Bowl XI hit Pasadena, but she and Vickie would be across town winning the Beverly Hills Winter Show. She and Vickie would be basking in attention, glory, *celebrity*.

Vickie looked at Madeline for a moment, then turned and trotted over to an American Beauty. She squatted beside a puddle of fallen rose petals and emptied her bladder. Then she shook herself, scampered across the lawn, in through the French doors, and leaped up onto the bed.

The Dalmanes and Chivas turned Madeline's legs gelatinous. She closed the doors and threw herself into bed, hardly noticing the crumbs of mud and garden mulch on the pearly sheets.

"You're impossible, Vickie," she scolded. "Impossible!" Then she stroked Vickie's neck once, twice, and her hand fell limp.

Madeline had a wonderful dream that night. Vickie won best in show, easily earning the last of fifteen major points she needed to become a champion. And then she went on to Madison Square Garden to win. She became the unquestioned grand champion—the finest miniature schnauzer in America.

Vickie grunted uncomfortably for a moment. She growled and squirmed until she managed a puffy fart. Then another. Now she sighed happily and licked Madeline's face. Then she snuggled, and snored, and slept as deeply as her drugged mistress.

3

The Terrier King

The natural mascara around the eyes of the Dandie Dinmont was the blackest he had ever seen.

"Look at those saucers," he said, admiring their roundness. Then he turned to the girl, looked at her breasts and grinned. "Your saucers are beautiful too."

The girl feigned naïveté and said, "Not as pretty as the Dandie's, Mr. Skinner."

Then Philo Skinner turned his critical eye back to the Dandie Dinmont and startled the girl by flashing the straight razor so quickly in the face of the terrier. She was giad she hadn't gasped. He was mercurial, but with good cause. Philo Skinner was a top terrier man on the West Coast. In the past six years he had big wins at Madison Square Garden, Chicago International and Beverly Hills. With a Lakeland, a Kerry blue and a Dandie. The girl knew that if she could survive his temperamental eruptions, like the one earlier in the evening when she left a tassel 1 1/8 inches from the bottom of the ear leather in a Bedlington terrier (he measured it), and if she could get used to never being paid on time and having a few ''clerical errors'' in her paycheck (always errors which made her check *short*), and if she could repel his sporadic sexual advances, well, Philo Skinner was a champion dog handler. A *champion*. And she could learn.

''Don't ever let me see *you* trying this,'' Philo Skinner said, holding the Dandie firmly under the chin with the long fingers of his left hand while the straight razor in his right stripped the nose from the top to the tip. The Dandie's white topknot was electric from backcombing.

''I'd be scared to death to do that,'' the girl said. ''Those barber razors are scary.''

''Well, careless people can misuse a stripping knife as well. You ever hurt an animal here and you'll find your little fanny out in the street.''

He deliberately let his gaze drop to her little fanny, which was pointed up nicely through the gap in her white smock as she leaned across the grooming table.

''I'll be real careful always, Mr. Skinner,'' she said.

''Never use the knife when working under the eyes,'' he said, looking back to the patient little terrier. ''Roll the finger and thumb together the way the hair grows. See? How old are you, Pattie Mae?''

''I'm nineteen, Mr. Skinner,'' the girl said, marveling at those darting, tobacco-stained fingers.

He plucked the eyes clean, even to the lashes. He was so expert and quick the dog almost dozed through it.

''Can you guess how old *I* am, Pattie Mae?'' he asked, releasing the dog's chin and stroking the little animal behind the ears.

Oh, shit! She hated it when these old guys started that crap. It was impossible for her to guess the age of anybody over thirty let alone an old turkey like Mr. Skinner. His dyed black hair was all thin and scraggly. And he was all wrinkly around his droopy eyes and mouth. And those crappy gold chains around his neck and those Dacron leisure suits didn't fool nobody. Shit! Those nylon shirts open clear to his belly button, she could see the gray hairs all over his bony old chest! He could play all the Elton John tapes he wanted to, he was still just an old fart.

''I'd say you're about forty, Mr. Skinner,'' she lied.

''Not too good a guess, Pattie Mae,'' he grinned, teeth yellowed from three packs of Camels a day. ''I'm fifty-two years old.''

''Really!'' the girl said. ''I'd never . . .''

''You know, Pattie Mae, handlers are like jockeys. An owner can't show a dog in real competition any more than a horse owner can ride his horse. I'm a jockey and I can *ride,* baby. I can *ride*.''

''Uh-huh,'' the girl said, mesmerized by his fleet plucking gentle fingers.

''I'm glad you came to me to learn. I can teach you lots a things. You're talented. It takes much more talent to show *little* dogs. You like the terriers, don't you?''

''Yes, I love them, Mr. Skinner.''

Philo Skinner was still stripping. Fingers rolling, kneading, plucking, stripping. The dog sighed luxuriously. ''Be glad you don't handle poodles. All those fag handlers. No action for a young thing like you. It's tough enough to find some action when you're out on the road showing dogs. Lots a fag handlers.''

''Uh-huh,'' the girl said, sucking on a broken fingernail.

''Oh, you'll be a popular handler someday with the real men on the show tours. There's one woman handler, named Wilma. A punchboard. What the hell, she's a little dumpy, but when you been looking at dogs all day . . .''

''Uh-huh,'' the girl said, the joke wasted. ''You sure got the touch, Mr. Skinner!''

''Wanna strip the ears?'' He took her arm gently, nudging her in front of him at the grooming table.

"Okay, Mr. Skinner," she said, a bit edgy, wondering if tonight was the night. The other girls said he made his big move after you'd worked there about a month. She'd been working for Skinner Kennels three weeks.

Philo Skinner was standing behind the girl now, admiring how her bottom stretched the exotic orchid patches on the jeans. None of these young girls wore underpants anymore, he thought. Not a goddamn one of them! And they didn't bathe any too often either. This one had dust and lint in her scruffy brown hair and her dirty fingernails were bitten to the quick. But damn, she had tits like mangoes!

"Strip exactly one inch from the top to exactly one inch from the bottom. Understand?"

"Yes, sir," she said uneasily, feeling him press in behind her as he pretended to guide her hand to the tassel of the terrier's ear.

"The ears can't be clipped," he said and she smelled his tobacco-sour breath on her face. "It doesn't look natural. It has to be stripped to be natural."

He moved in very close, leaning on her leg. Oh, gross! The old fart had a hard-on!

"That's it, Pattie Mae," he whispered, rubbing it against her. "Strip all the hair away. Strip, Pattie Mae. *Strip!*"

The door opened and Philo Skinner leaped back, turning his body away from a squinting smock-clad woman dragging a reluctant Airedale through the door.

"Pattie Mae, why the hell're you still here?" she demanded, looking at Philo Skinner suspiciously. He adjusted his own white smock to hide the telltale bulge, and began fiddling with the cage dryer.

"Gotta be a goddamn electrician to keep things working around here," Philo Skinner grumbled. "Mavis, who the hell used this thing last, anyway?"

"I dunno," she said, still squinting from Philo to his new apprentice. "Pattie Mae, why you working so late?"

"Well, uh, Mr. Skinner said he needed . . ."

"Mavis, you know goddamn well we gotta get this Dandie ready. Christ, Pilkington's our best client these days. I gotta be free to devote the next couple days to the Beverly Hills Show, don't I? Christ, it's pouring outside!"

Philo Skinner was eminently thankful for the Thursday night rain, his excuse to turn to the window and let the tumescence subside. "Goddamn cold rainy night," he said gratefully.

"Well, since I don't really think Mr.. Skinner intends paying you time-and-a-half, I think you should go home now."

"Yes, Mrs. Skinner. I'll just put the Dandie to bed," the girl said, slipping the smock down over her breasts, braless under a jersey which said: "I love puppies and cuddly things."

Goddamn, Philo Skinner thought. Cuddly things. Goddamn. Then he looked at Mavis, fifty-one years old going on sixty. Skin like sizzling pancake batter. Two eye jobs already. Hair dyed the color of puppy shit, with enough spray to do a whole platoon of goddamn terriers. I love puppies and cuddly things. Oh, God! And then it swept him away: an overwhelming emptiness and yearning.

After the girl scurried out the door with the Dandie Dinmont, Mavis Skinner said, "Well, Philo, I hope this one stays a little longer than most. Think you can keep from running her off like all the others?"

Philo Skinner lit his sixty-third cigarette of that calendar day and sat on the grooming table and stared outside at the night rain. Emptiness, loss. Yearning for . . . for a chance. Just a goddamn *chance,* is all he asked.

"If I ever knew for sure what I suspect about you, Philo, it'd be sayonara, baby. I ain't Betsy or that other bitch you were married to. I won't put up with that shit."

Philo Skinner heard not a word. He dragged deeply on the Camel, exhaled up through his nose, back down into his tortured lungs, and stared at the rain. Yearning.

"It's been a rocky go, Philo. I mean it's been tougher being married to you for two years than it was to Milton for twenty-five years, I can tell you. I'll try to make it work, you know that. But I'm not gonna put up with any screwing around. You were thinking about nesting with that little bird, weren't you?"

And as he would look back on this moment for the rest of his life, Philo Skinner would always wonder precisely what event inspired him. Was it that pathetic fifty-two-year-old erection which died aborning? Was it Mavis' tongue, sharp as a grooming knife? Stripping away the little he had left the way you'd strip the loins of a schnauzer? Was it that he wanted to cry because Pattie Mae was only nineteen years old? He would always wonder.

"Philo, *were* you?"

But he was already through the door of the grooming room, heading for the kennel, heart thumping, hands and feet and armpits slimy. Philo switched on the light and stood in the center of the 175-foot concrete aisle which dissected the building. There were thirty floor-to-ceiling, chain-link dog pens on each side of the long aisle. Each four-by-eight-foot pen boasted running water, an easy-clean feeding trough, and a warm soft bed off the floor. In addition, each dog pen had a slit-rubber doggie door allowing easy access to outside dog runs twice the size of the inside pens, covered with gravel for the pleasure of the animal and to prevent splayed feet. The outside runs were protected by chain link, ten feet high—completely enclosed on top—not to keep dogs in but to keep thieves out. There were high-wattage security lights and a burglar alarm as well, to safeguard Skinner Kennels from prowling dognappers.

The inside lights woke several of the more nervous animals who whined when Philo walked to the pen containing Rutherford's bitch.

"Hello, honey," he whispered to the miniature schnauzer. The dog opened her eyes, wagged her stubby tail a few times and fell back asleep on her foam mattress.

Rutherford's bitch wasn't nearly right. Too cow-hocked. Way too throaty. But he knew one that was exactly right.

"Goddamn!" Philo whispered. Then he dropped his cigarette on the kennel floor, stepped on it and went back into the grooming room.

Philo arrived home that night, during the same hour that Madeline Dills Whitfield was being mercifully rendered unconscious by Chivas Regal and four Dalmanes, during the same hour that a drunken man in a yellow rubber raincoat was reeling through the door of his furnished apartment, dripping wet, eyes raw from vodka and incense and memories of other Russian Christmas Eves.

Philo made a telephone call to a man who owned a fashionable dress shop on Wilshire Boulevard. Who did other business more profitably.

"Hello, Arnold?" Philo whispered into the phone.

"Who's this?" an irritated voice answered.

"Philo Skinner."

"Why the hell you calling me at home? I told you to forget my home number. What I gotta do, get the fucking number changed?"

"Arnold, this is important."

"I told you, Philo, it's outta my hands. You owe almost eight dimes. You never shoulda got in so deep, but you did. So you gotta pay and you got two weeks more to do it. Now good night."

"Arnold, wait!" Philo begged. "I wanna pay you sooner. I wanna pay you Monday morning."

"Well that's different," the voice said, considerably more congenial.

"I can pay you all of it, Arnold. On Monday night. But you just gotta get me down on Minnesota in the Super Bowl."

"Good night, Philo."

"Wait! Wait, goddamnit!" Philo pleaded. "I been a good customer, Arnold. I been good. I been a friend!"

"Philo, you can't pay the eight K. Some guys are gonna be awful upset, and now you wanna get down some more?"

"Arnold, remember I told you Mavis has this property? It's an apartment building in Covina. Remember I told you? Well we sold it. We're netting eighty-five thousand! Christ, the escrow closes in ten days! Even if Minnesota loses Sunday and my markers go higher, I can pay *all* of it in ten days!"

There was silence on the line and the voice said: "Come see me tomorrow. *With* the escrow papers. Prove you got the property. You got, you sold it, you prove it, Philo."

"Arnold, please! Mavis can't know about this. Goddamit, it's technically *her* property from her first husband! I can't take a chance on Mavis finding out about the markers. *Trust* me! Please, Arnold!"

There was silence again and the voice said, "How much you wanna get down?"

"What's the best you can get me this late?"

"Six points."

"Okay, get me down for seven thousand."

"You're fucking *crazy,* Philo. Good night."

"Wait! Wait! Lay it off, you don't wanna cover it!"

"Philo, Minnesota is gonna *lose*. I tell you as a friend, Oakland's gonna win by ten at least."

"So what! I'm gonna have eighty-five thousand in ten days!"

Silence, and then: "Okay, and if you're wrong, your bill is gonna be fifteen thousand with our little store, counting the vigorish. That's outta my hands, Philo. You don't pay and it's *outta* my hands."

That night, while a tortured woman in a Pasadena mansion slept thanks to Scotch and drugs, and a tortured man in a furnished Hollywood apartment slept thanks to Russian vodka, Philo Skinner, cold sober and electrified, slept not at all.

Minnesota would *win*. Win, goddamnit! And then it would all be academic. There'd be no *need* to do it. He could maybe even laugh about it. To himself. But if Minnesota lost. If they lost . . . And then, the epiphany: He *knew* Minnesota would lose. He *wanted* Minnnesota to lose. And he was betting on them.

If Minnesota won he'd merely be covering his losses. His miserable life would be essentially unchanged. But if Minnesota lost . . . if they *lost,* he'd *have* to do it. And it would *work*. And he'd have eighty-five thousand dollars. Seventy thousand after paying his gambling losses. Seventy thousand tax-free dollars! But not from an escrow.

There was no escrow. There was no apartment house. He owned nothing but his business, and Skinner Kennels was hopelessly in the red. His house *might* net five thousand after the second mortgage was paid off. His four-year-old white El Dorado wasn't worth what he still owed on it.

The way out had come to him tonight, there in the grooming room, while Mavis was poor-mouthing him. Stripping, stripping it all away. But like most neophytes, Philo Skinner needed impetus to commit a serious crime.

Fear. He smoked, and sweated the length of his six-foot-three-inch frame. He listened to Mavis snore, and rain patter, and *welcomed* the rush of fear. That's what he *needed*. He even helped it along. He tried to imagine what they'd do to him if Minnesota lost. *When* Minnesota lost. If he phoned Arnold and told him it was a lie about owning an apartment house, that he couldn't pay.

Someone would come to the kennel when he was alone, at night. It wouldn't be Arnold of course. He tried to imagine the man. Two men, probably. Maybe one of them a big nigger. Philo Skinner had always feared black men. Maybe the other, some sleazy little kike friend of Arnold's. He would try to run but they'd corner him in the kennel. The dogs would bark wildly at the implacable strangers. They'd find Philo's grooming shears. The spook would want to castrate the honkie. The Jew would decide they should leave him in condition to sell and borrow and come up with the coin. The Jew would smile and say: "Let's *circumcise* this schmuck." Or maybe . . .

But it was enough. His side of the bed was soaked. He'd have to get up in a minute and change pajamas. His teeth and jaws ached from gnashing and clenching. This kind of sweat wasn't work sweat. It smelled entirely different. Now he had the impetus to do what he *wanted* to do. Philo Skinner learned what so many lawbreakers learn, and often admit, but not to judge and jury. It was a goddamn *thrill*. He was high! Philo Skinner drank moderately and despised the effect of drugs. He smoked grass and hash only to impress any young women he met in bars. Now, listening to the rain in the night, he was *flying*.

Fifty-two years of obeying every goddamn law on the books whether it made sense or not. Just this once he'd do it. And it wouldn't hurt anybody. Not very much, anyway. And not for very long. He'd never felt so alive.

Before he changed his sweaty pajamas, Philo Skinner lit his seventy-fourth cigarette of a very long day. He lay in the darkness, smiling. He was betting seven thousand dollars on the Minnesota Vikings. And they were going to lose. And then he would *have* to do it. And he would be rich. And free! He knew a former handler who had become a Mexican national and was doing all right as a partner in a Mexican hotel. Puerto Vallarta. Margaritas at sunset. White teeth. Brown bodies. *All* willing. Seventy thousand tax-free American dollars. Good-bye, Mavis. Good-bye to *all* the dogs.

He thought of the feisty Minnesota quarterback. Fran Tarkenton, I hope they break your fucking arm.

4

The Rabbit

Valnikov slept in the yellow rubber raincoat. He slept crossways on the daybed, one shoe on, one shoe off. He slept on his back, head tilted, face florid. His eyes were almost stuck shut from sour vomitus belches.

Valnikov snored and wheezed, and as usual, dreamed of the rabbit. He cried out in his sleep and awoke when the hunter cut the rabbit's throat, broke the rabbit's jaws, and began peeling the skin back over the rabbit's face. The tearing muscle hissed and jawbones crackled in the powerful hands.

"Lord God!" he sobbed and awoke himself.

It was hard to tell where he hurt most. His head felt like a huge festering sponge. His back felt hinged. If he tried to straighten, the crusted rusty hinges would scream.

He almost screamed when he stood. Now at least he knew what hurt most: the festering sponge. His head was mushy. Lord God, have mercy. He fell back on the bed, moaning. Then Misha said, "*Gavno*."

"Please, Misha," Valnikov pleaded. "Oh, my head!"

But Misha repeated, "*Gavno, gavno, gavno*."

Misha only knew one Russian word and it meant *shit*. In fact, it was the only *human* word he could say.

Valnikov glared with one blazing eye and saw that Misha was standing on Grisha's head. Misha twittered and chirped and sang for his master, who held his ears and cried: "Please, Misha, please. Noise *hurts*."

But Misha just tossed his lovely emerald head, preened, and said: "*Gavno*."

Shit.

Then Valnikov became aware that he was soaked by the perspiration from the oppressive rubber raincoat, and by the dream of the rabbit, which always brought night sweats.

Misha yelled: "*Gavno!*" like a challenge and through the agonizing mist of the vodka hangover Valnikov was amazed to see that Misha had just crapped on Grisha's head. As though he truly understood what the word meant! Well maybe he did. Who could say what a bird or a man understood.

It wasn't the shit, it was the noisy "*gavno*" which angered Grisha. The little rodent lunged at Misha, who squawked and flew to the trapeze at the top of the seven-foot cage. The furious little animal then sulked around the floor of the enormous cage until he found a comfortable place to settle down again. His head was covered with *gavno*.

The furnished bachelor apartment on Franklin Avenue was crisscrossed with clothesline which ran from the top of the giant animal cage to a nail pounded over the bathroom door frame. Three pairs of underwear and two pairs of socks were hung on that indoor clothesline, thanks to the endless queue of women at the apartment building's coin-operated clothes dryer.

There were unwashed glasses and dishes and empty vodka bottles on the formica table, on the plastic chairs, on the kitchen sink, in the kitchen sink.

Stacked higher than the dishes and glasses was a vast collection of recordings, in and out of album covers. The records were on the kitchen table, on the chairs, on the sink. And two were *in* the sink—which puzzled him this morning. At least they weren't damaged by water since he only washed dishes one at a time when necessary.

The tiny cluttered apartment boasted one great luxury, aside from the large record collection: a Micro Seike turntable and two Epicure speakers worth a thousand dollars each, capable of making the whole apartment house thump and vibrate.

Valnikov stood, stripped off the rubber raincoat and all of his wet outer clothing. He forced himself to march to the bathroom and showered in icy water, unaware for the moment that he had forgotten to remove his underwear and one sock.

His broad red face was bleeding in three places after he shaved. He spilled tea on his blue necktie when he drank, unable to hold the shaking glass of tea with both hands. Then he put the gerbil's food in Misha's dish and the parakeet's food in Grisha's dish. He was halfway out the door before he thought that he had possibly made a mistake. He returned and saw that he had.

He groaned, and shooed Misha away from the rodent's dish.

"Please, Misha, eat your own food."

His voice thundered in his ears, through the flaming mush of his brain, through the infected tissue.

"Oh, never mind," he said. "Go ahead and eat Grisha's food. Grisha, you eat Misha's food today."

He hobbled toward the door again, looking at his watch, listing from side to side. Then he realized that a burrowing rodent from southern Russia could never jump high enough to eat a parakeet's food in a feeding tray five feet above his head.

Valnikov managed to switch the food. Corn and barley for the gerbil, gravel and seed for the parakeet. Then he gave the little creatures water and looked at them.

"Are you two even slightly appreciative," he moaned, "of the pain this is giving me?"

Misha answered him. The parakeet had been swinging on his trapeze, his back to Valnikov. The emerald bird did a deliberate forward fall, gripping the tiny bar in his claws. When he was hanging upside down, staring directly into Valnikov's wet fiery eyes, Misha said: "*Gavno*."

Fifteen minutes later, Valnikov had parked his car and was weaving painfully toward the front door of Hollywood Police Station.

The caseload for business burglary was never too bad on Friday. Monday, after the channel-lock and pry-bar thieves had plundered during the two days businesses were closed, Valnikov would have his table littered with burglary reports. But today would be all right. Except for the merciless throbbing in his skull.

Two youngish homicide investigators the others called Frick and Frack were amusing themselves by telling ghoul stories to Irma Thebes, the foxy little investigator who worked the sex detail.

''Irma,'' Frick grinned, ''take a look at this suicide report.''

Irma grimaced, pretending she wasn't interested, but as always she read the report with abandon.

''Dude severed both wrists, then turned on the gas jets in his walk-up, then hit himself in the head three times with a hatchet. The third time he managed to pierce his skull.''

''That ain't nothing,'' Frack said, leaning over her desk. ''I had a broad last month cuts both wrists, then drinks D.D.T., then, get this, she tried to *choke* herself with a nylon stocking, using a wooden spoon for a tourniquet!''

''Awful, that's awful,'' Irma grimaced, dying for more.

Their unsmiling lieutenant, Woodenlips Mockett, interrupted by saying: ''How's that murder from over on La Brea? Any progress?''

''Naw, the victim ain't talking,'' Frick said, wanting to continue the game of Can You Top This for Irma Thebes.

''What is this, amateur night?'' Woodenlips Mockett snarled. ''You getting anywhere or not?'' Then he looked at Irma. ''I mean on the *murder case*.''

''Well no, Lieutenant,'' the young detective said. ''But that dude's a black militant and an ex-con. I think we find the guy done it we oughtta give him an ecology award.''

Dudley Knebel, a robbery detective, then said, ''Got a suspect? I got a victim who'll I.D. anybody I show him. Owns the burrito stand over on Western.''

''*That* dingaling!'' said a burglary dick they called Montezuma Montez. ''Him and his wife, Hamhocks Hilda, they'll pick your *partner* out of a lineup, give them a chance.''

''Hey, is it true about Hamhocks Hilda, the way she makes hamburgers?'' asked Frick.

''It *is* the gospel, Jack,'' Montezuma Montez answered, grinning. ''Captain Hooker *seen* it.''

''What's true?'' asked Woodenlips Mockett, nervously.

''Well, she's *always* pissed off at cops,'' Frick said. ''Cause she gets robbed, oh, two, three times a month. And we never catch nobody. So you order a hamburger, she takes the meat and mashes it right up between her legs, right up on her greasy old Brillo pad.''

''I don't believe that!'' cried Woodenlips Mockett, who had mooched two burgers from Hamhocks Hilda just the day before.

''I swear, Lieutenant,'' Frack said. ''When I busted her old man that time he went upside her head with a meat mallet, he told me what you gotta do is, you gotta always check the hamburger patty. See there's any little black curly hairs sticking out.''

''Well, that ain't no big thing,'' said Clarence Cromwell, one of two black detectives at Hollywood. ''She *cooks* it, don't she? Ain't so bad anyways, less he tuned Hilda's greasy old organ *jist* before she made your burger, Lieutenant.''

Woodenlips Mockett waited a decent interval before hurrying out of the office to check with Captain Hooker to see if the men were lying to him again.

Then a voice boomed through the slightly open door of the interrogation room. Nate Farmer, the other black detective unwillingly transferred to the sex detail from auto theft, was interviewing a rape victim who lacked credibility.

She too was black. So was the alleged suspect. Blacks robbed, raped and murdered other blacks, more often than not. Same with whites. Hoodlums rarely bothered to discriminate.

His voice thundered through the room: ''So he's been takin a piece for six months, and you been enjoyin it, and now all of a sudden you find your little belly gettin big and you're all of a sudden a *child* a seventeen, and your social worker says the county'll pay for your little whelp if you put your boyfriend in jail for rape? Well I ain't gonna go for it!''

''Last rape victim I handled turned out to be a call girl with twenty-two arrests,'' Irma Thebes observed.

''Didn't know she was raped till the check bounced, huh?'' said Frick.

A Cuban boy, eleven years of age, was sitting in the squad room listening wide-eyed to the raging black detective. The boy was a renowned Hollywood bicycle thief. They called him Earl Scheib Lopez, in honor of the auto painter who could paint any car for $49.95. Earl Scheib Lopez boasted that he could paint any hot bike for a buck and a quarter, in *ten* minutes, and had enough sniffable paint left to get three of his pals loaded.

Earl Scheib Lopez always had his jeans stuffed with coins and he was now playing nickel-dime blackjack with Fuzzy Spinks, of auto theft, who could tolerate the little bike bandit ever since the day he rolled over (for a fifty-buck snitch fee) on a Cuban gang who had hijacked a load of Ferraris, and Fuzzy got a leg up toward Investigator III. Earl Scheib Lopez used the fifty scoots to buy two cases of aerosol paint cans and there were three hundred bikes stolen in Hollywood in the next two weeks.

His latest arrest was for a bit of derring-do: On a whim, the little crook had jumped on a display bike in a department store downtown, ridden it through five screaming sales clerks, down the *escalator,* and out on the street making a getaway clear to Hollywood in twenty minutes. But he had underestimated his fame. The Central Division investigators had no trouble identifying the bike bandit: only Earl Scheib Lopez was *that* kind of swashbuckler.

But he wasn't swashbuckling now. He was playing blackjack very quietly with Fuzzy Spinks, who was baby-sitting him until they could release him to grandma, who was getting sick and tired of taking a bus to police stations and courtrooms for Earl Scheib Lopez. One day, after his third arrest in one month, she had made an extra bus trip. This one to the ''Glass House,'' Parker Center downtown, to the office of the chief of police. The old woman waited patiently for two hours to see the chief's adjutant and then explained through an interpreter in polite and formal Spanish that she had come to sign the necessary American documents—to put Earl Scheib Lopez in the gas chamber.

Fuzzy could see that the little thug was very anxiously listening to the mean-looking black detective yelling at his ''rape victim.''

''You ever pull any rapes yet, Earl?'' Fuzzy asked, peering at the boy over his bifocals, actually trying to get a peek at Earl's cards because the ante was up to thirty-five cents.

''No way!'' Earl said, staying on fourteen while Fuzzy busted.

''Yeah, well don't ever try it. These detectives here can look right up a broad's unit and check her lands and grooves. Just like the muzzle of a gun. Understand?''

''Yeah?'' Earl Scheib Lopez said, pretty damned impressed for once.

''They match em up with the marks on *your* rape tool, and you get twenty goddamn years. Get me?''

''Yes, *sir!*'' Earl Scheib Lopez said. He was showing a king of diamonds.

"You hitting?" the old cop asked hopefully, since he had to hit sixteen and was down to his last ninety cents.

"Damn it!" Max Haffenkamp, from residential burglary, slammed the phone down. "Hollywood's turned into a frigging ghetto! People're so evasive they won't even say hello, they think it's a cop."

"Tell em you found their welfare check," Clarence Cromwell said. "*Then* they'll talk to you honkies."

"Lord, I hope there's a gang killing tonight," said Frick. "I need some overtime, make my car payment."

"I'm losing weight, Irma," Frack leered, sucking in his chest. "Stomach like a washboard. You could wash your lace underwear on my tummy. Anytime."

Just then the rape victim stormed out of the interrogation room yelling: "Well if you won't bust that sucker, I'm goin to the F.B.I. cause I ain't his escape goat. And *you* nigger!" She aimed a skinny finger at Nate Farmer. "You I'm suin for defecation of character!"

All the yelling was interrupted when a radio voice came over the monitor. It was the police helicopter.

"This is Air Six," the radio voice said. "Anything for us?"

And then, as always, three or four ex-vice cops called out suggestions:

"Yeah, bomb the dopers on Sunset."

"Strafe the pimps on Hollywood Boulevard."

"Napalm the fruits on Selma Avenue."

And so forth.

Suddenly Frick threw his arrest reports to Frack. "Rape and murder. Rape and murder. I'm getting sick of it!" Frick cried.

"Humph," Clarence Cromwell snorted. "You the one doin all the rape and murder, chump. Killin time and screwin the city."

All conversations, bitching, and dramatic outcries were suddenly interrupted. It became breathlessly still.

Dora Simpson, the record clerk from downstairs, sashayed into the squad room, dropped some reports on the desk of Woodenlips Mockett, and wriggled out again.

"With those lungs, that girl could stay underwater for *days,*" Fuzzy Spinks sighed.

Dora Simpson had gone unnoticed during ten years of employment with the Los Angeles Police Department, until she transferred from Northeast Station to Hollywood Station. Then she had begun dating a retired plastic surgeon with a Pygmalion complex.

Dr. Henry Sprackle took a centimeter off the bridge of her nose and two off the tip. He implanted nearly a *pound* of foam in her sagging breasts and buttocks. He whacked away the loose flesh from under her chin and eyes and hacked off two and a half inches of belly fat.

Finally, he threw away her cat's-eye horn-rims and had her fitted with tinted contact lenses. He took her to Elizabeth Arden's for a Farrah Fawcett feather-cut and she was *almost* perfect. Then he took her to Frederick's of Hollywood and bought her ten pairs of crotchless black underwear and she *was* perfect.

Dora Simpson was born again, but no Baptist preacher had a hand in it. A former ugly duckling was now the object of many a wet dream at Hollywood Station, and indeed all over the Los Angeles Police Department. They said that Deputy Chief Digby Bates, the most notorious swain among the ranking brass, had offered the area commander *four* additional patrol officers if he would release Dora Simpson for a transfer.

Frick and Frack were insane over her. The two young cops had worked together six years, both in patrol and detectives, and they'd bedded the same station house groupies for so long they'd begun to have similar erotic fantasies. Most of them these days involved Dora Simpson because they thought of her as an android. She wasn't human. She was sculpted in the laboratory of Dr. Henry Sprackle.

All that jiggly stuffing in there! Imagine searching for the surgical scars! Would she do *anything* her master told her? It was wildly decadent and perverse. Frick said that as soon as his second divorce was final he was going to propose to her. Frack said that *he* was going to propose to Dr. Sprackle, since Dora Simpson as an android was not in a position to accept on her own behalf.

She was the station house celebrity for sure. Everyone called her Spareparts Simpson.

''Looks like you're going to a funeral, and it's yours,'' Clarence Cromwell said when Valnikov weaved through the maze of tables and coffee-drinking detectives with his second cup of tea.

The voices. The noise. The painful cacophony of two dozen detectives wearing out the only essential tools of an investigator: pencil and telephone.

''Light workload, Clarence?'' Valnikov asked.

''Nothin to it,'' Clarence Cromwell said. Broad-chested with a face as creased and shiny as old leather, he was a twenty-five-year cop who had also worked ''downtown'' in better days.

Covering for a high-rolling girlfriend who passed some bad checks had been Clarence's downfall and earned him a transfer (''There is *no such thing* as a disciplinary transfer in the Los Angeles Police Department. Of course, you understand that, Sergeant Cromwell? This is merely an adminstrative readjustment.'') back to where he started, Hollywood Station. But if one saw the glass half full, well, it wasn't as bad as 77th Street Station, which policed Watts, and was the armpit of detective duty. Hollywood dicks wasn't such bad duty, considering.

But poor Clarence Cromwell was withering on the vine. He wore a big moustache and a medium Afro and Italian suits. He was rushing resentfully into middle age, drinking too much, but not nearly like Valnikov. He was still wearing two shoulder holsters which thrilled the hell out of cop groupies but weren't much better than ballast these days. When Clarence had worked robbery-homicide downtown, those twin Colt magnums had blown away four bandits in six short happy years.

On the night following the last shoot-out, a Chinatown groupie sidled up to the still shaking detective at a bar and grabbed him by the crotch and said, ''I wanna see your *other* magnum, Clarence. Baby, you look like Sidney Poitier *wishes* he looked.''

Those were the days.

''You okay?'' Clarence Cromwell asked when he saw Valnikov's trembling hands.

''I'm all right, Clarence,'' Valnikov smiled, losing the thread of what the burglary report was all about.

''Got any bodies in jail today, Val?''

Valnikov looked at Clarence Cromwell and just shrugged pathetically. Clarence Cromwell lit a cigarette and looked at Valnikov's hands again.

Clarence Cromwell had been there many many times. Valnikov was one of four or five detectives Clarence Cromwell would bother with. First, because he knew Valnikov from robbery-homicide in better days. And secondly, because Valnikov was a veteran with more than twenty years service, most of it in the detective bureau. If there was anything Clarence Cromwell despised more than the police brass it was RE-cruits.

Clarence Cromwell looked around in disgust. Fuckin RE-cruits. Add up the total service of the whole burglary detail and there wouldn't be three hashmarks total. Except for himself and Valnikov. Fuzz-nutted kids. Like that little brother, Nate Farmer, always hollerin. Thinks he's some kind a black Kojak, or somethin. And those two kids Frick and Frack. All they ever thought about was their cocks. Homicide detectives, my ass.

Not detectives—"investigators." Now they were all "investigators." At least that's what the business cards said. That's what the brass decided they should be called nowadays. And they did "team policing." Whatever the hell that is. Nobody knew. Four "teams" of "investigators" working their little areas. Teams, my ass. This ain't no football game, Chief. Police work is a whole bunch of decisions you got to make your *own* self out on those streets. Except that every few years the brass had to come up with some new catchword to justify the budget. "Team policing." All it did was add a whole bunch of new chiefs to supervise fewer Indians. Some stations used to get by with one captain. Now they had to have *three*. And a whole fuckin sack full of lieutenants. They were about as useful as Woodenlips Mockett's balls. And Clarence knew *they* hadn't been used in years.

Clarence leafed through Valnikov's reports quickly and said, "You ain't got no bodies in jall. Get your ass on home, I'll cover for you. Shit, you're so full a Russian potata juice you're all swole up like a toad."

"That's real nice of you, Clarence." Valnikov tried to smile, but it hurt. *Hurt* to smile. "I'm okay."

Clarence Cromwell knew better. And it wasn't just the hangover. Valnikov was *not* okay. He was not anything like the detective who worked homicide downtown for fifteen years. That man was quiet and shy, but he was alert. This guy next to him was just some shipwreck victim. Clarence Cromwell pitied him, but he didn't know him.

Clarence looked around at the roar of activity, at the grinding paper mill. Papers everywhere. Take away my gun and car, but *please* don't take my pencils. Nobody noticed yet how extra bad Valnikov looked today: "Val, you got a comb?"

"A comb?" Valnikov looked at Clarence like he didn't understand the word. Like he didn't talk English anymore. "Yeah, Val, you know, a fuckin *comb*."

Clarence wondered if he could be using drugs. Naw, he thought, a lush like Val don't go smokin dope.

"Here's a comb, Val. I used to ride a old sorrel horse in Griffith Park, had neater lookin hair than you got. Go comb your hair, at least. You look like a Skid Row blood donor. What're they payin for a pint a blood these days, ten bucks for positive, twelve for negative?"

"Pardon?" Valnikov said.

"Gud-damn, man! Go in my locker and get yourself a clean necktie. Looks like you washed that one in vodka. Git your *shit* together, Val!"

But it was too late. Clarence Cromwell looked up and locked eyes with Captain Hooker, who nodded toward his office.

"There's jist one thing savin your ass, Val," Clarence Cromwell whispered before he stood up. "Me." Then he was gone toward the captain's office.

Valnikov just sat and stared blankly at his crime reports, and trembled, and thought he could hear the voices of a Slavonic choir. Far away. In the frozen Siberia of his mind.

Natalie Zimmerman was furious. She took long-legged strides back and forth, from wall to wall in Captain Hooker's private office. The giant strides were stretching the woolen skirt tight across her thighs.

Well now, old Nat's wheels ain't too bad, Clarence Cromwell thought, as he sat down. Ain't too bad at all.

"I do my job, Captain!" she said, voice shaking.

"I know you do, Natalie. You get straight upper-ten ratings, don't you?"

"Look, Captain, I wanna make Investigator Three."

"You will, I'm sure."

"Not if I work with that . . . with Valnikov. Because I'll get as bad as he is, you make me his partner!" She finally stopped pacing, flopped down in the chair next to Clarence Cromwell and brushed a wisp of frizzy buckskin-colored hair from her forehead.

Clarence Cromwell looked approvingly at Natalie Zimmerman's crossed legs and thought maybe this'll turn out to be a good idea. Might be what old Val needs.

"It's not forever, Natalie," Captain Hooker soothed. He was one of those scholarly looking kind of guys in three-button suits that always made Clarence Cromwell wonder how come they're cops. Hooker was hipless and had to wear suspenders to hold up his pants and gun-belt.

"Did you see him today, Captain?" Natalie pleaded, raising oversized glasses to rub the bridge of her nose. "The sucker's bombed. Let's face it!"

"He ain't bombed," Clarence offered. "He's jist hung over. Jist gotta have some tea, git his shit . . . uh, mind together."

"Why me, why me?" Natalie asked the lock of frizzy hair which usually hung on her forehead. She wore her Friz longer than most.

Captain Hooker studied her, nodding like a condescending headmaster. "You're the best female investigator I've got," Captain Hooker answered softly, hoping Natalie would lower her voice.

"That's great. You've only got two. How about Clarence here? Why can't he work with him? They're old buddies!"

"Uh, well, I, ar-uh, got my team to run," Clarence reminded her. Thinking: Uh-uh, *no* way, baby. I got my own drinkin problem. Me and Val together? Shit! Hose out the drunk tank, Barney, make room for the burglary detail!

"I've known Valnikov for twenty years," Captain Hooker said patiently. "He was only a two-year policeman then. He's always been a fine officer. And always a gentleman, I might add."

"Yeah, well that means this *gentleman's* got twenty-two years on the job, so he can go ahead and retire now and . . ."

"Valnikov is *still* a fine policeman," Captain Hooker said, raising his hand ever so slightly to quiet the passion of Natalie Zimmerman, who happened to catch Clarence Cromwell inspecting her bustline.

Clarence looked up innocently. The old bastard! It was no secret that Hooker did whatever Cromwell wanted. All Hooker was doing was biding his time. Three more months, he would have his thirty in, and would retire to a cushy teaching job in the Police Science Department at Cal State L.A. Everyone knew it. Just like everyone knew that Clarence Cromwell ran the goddamn detective division. Just because his bail bondsman buddy, No-Show Weems, had given him unlimited use of his 53-foot motor yacht with twin diesels and a flying bridge—an *idiot* like Cromwell who couldn't even drive a golf cart!—and Hipless Hooker just had to be the most fanatical deep-sea fisherman who ever lived. And Mrs. Hooker got seasick in the bathtub, so Hipless Hooker could sneak off unattended with Clarence Cromwell on that stinking boat practically every goddamn weekend, probably with some of Cromwell's old wino girlfriends. The evil old spook! He was looking at her tits again!

It was true that Clarence Cromwell had unlimited use of a $300,000 motor yacht. It was also true that Captain Hooker asked for Cromwell when he was kicked out of robbery-homicide because Hooker had heard about the magnificent boat. Hipless Hooker may have wondered why a well-heeled bail bondsman like No-Show Weems would be so generous with Clarence Cromwell, but he thought he shouldn't look a gift horse. He was absolutely right.

No-Show Weems was so called because even though he had thriving bail bond agencies all over Los Angeles County, every time the sweating fat man was asked how's business, he'd say: "Terrible. No show. No show. Nobody comes to court. Everybody jumps bail these days. No show. No show."

No-Show Weems had made the disastrous mistake of posting bail for the Moroni brothers, two bank robbers from San Pedro who had shot a bank guard during their last robbery and were awaiting trial, their combined bail set at two hundred thousand dollars. The D.A. had argued against lowering the ball, but the superior court judge had never forgotten Boys Town's Father Flanagan and believed, even before he became senile, that there is no such thing as a bad boy. No-Show Weems knew for sure that the Moroni brothers were bad boys. In fact, he knew it even before Sal Moroni got arrested for throwing a Sicilian cook out the window of an Italian restaurant for overcooking his scallopini.

The old cook swore vengeance after leaving the hospital with a brand-new hip joint, and decided to give the Moroni brothers a dose of Sicilian revenge. She had never heard of it in her country, but since all the American movies did it, Lucretia Pantuzzi, age sixty-eight, began limping up to their door in the middle of the night and leaving reeking bundles of putrid perch and rock cod in the Moroni mailbox. Take that, goatface! A little calling card from Lucretia Pantuzzi!

When the senile judge lowered bail, No-Show bit the bullet and posted it because the Moroni brothers had as an uncle a successful tuna fisherman who signed an agreement to make restitution if the Moroni boys jumped. But two weeks later the old fisherman had fallen from the stern of his trawler and drowned along with six porpoises, trapped in his own tuna nets. A save-the-porpoise environmentalist group threw a bash and offered several hearty toasts and hoorahs for more live porpoises and drowned dagos. The old fisherman's estate went into receivership and a legal battle ensued which tied up his assets.

Meanwhile, the Moroni brothers were getting sick and tired of finding stinking fish in their mailbox. It got so the bank robbers even hated to reach in the box for their welfare checks. And the fact is, they were just plain bored anyway. So they robbed a savings and loan office and cruised south with the migratory gray whales. All the way to Cabo San Lucas, on the tip of the Baja peninsula, in the country of Mexico.

One day Sal and Tony Moroni were lollygagging in the Mexican sunshine, drinking tequila and watching two drunken whores frolic in the surf. They saw a white motor cruiser on the horizon. The chartered cruiser powered ever closer to the beach, anchored some distance back of the surf line and lowered a rubber dinghy into the water. The dinghy had a big outboard engine and the guy in the boat made good time skimming over the swells to the beach.

When he got closer, the brothers saw he was wearing a red knitted cap pulled down almost to his eyes, and a red scarf tied across the lower part of his face. The dumb shit. It was seventy-two degrees on the beach. Then he got even closer. His hands and arms were dark. He was a nigger. A stupid nigger coming from the cool ocean to a warm beach in a red knitted hat and scarf. He looked so goddamn silly the whores joined the Moroni brothers and they all laughed like hell. Then he cut his engine and drifted in through the gentle surf right up to the beach. Dumb nigger probably coming ashore to buy some tequila for his boss on the yacht. He wasn't even looking at the naked whores, but it didn't matter. He looked so silly with his face all wrapped up that they laughed like hell.

And wept when the Moroni brothers, blindfolded and chained together with two sets of handcuffs, were sailing away at gunpoint in the little rubber dinghy.

They were blindfolded all the way, even after leaving the boat. They couldn't identify the boat, the skipper, or the nigger gunman. When they had to eat or use a toilet during the two-day voyage he would take off the handcuffs, but make them do it blindfolded. All they could say about him was that if they yelled or complained he'd put those two big magnums right in their ears and ask them if they saw the movie *Jaws*.

The police were given an anonymous phone tip and found the fugitives, minus handcuffs, gags, and blindfolds, locked in the trunk of an abandoned junkyard car near the Los Angeles County Jail parking lot.

The A.C.L.U. said that if their story were true their civil liberties had been horribly violated. The Mexican consulate said that if their story were true it was an international act of piracy. The L.A.P.D. bank squad said it was all bullshit, made up by the Moroni brothers who had always been poor sports anyway.

Actually, nobody *really* believed the outrageous tale. In fact the Moroni brothers got kidded so much in the slammer about the Scarlet Pimpernel and the Crimson Pirate that they stopped telling the story about the big nigger in the red mask. After a while even Sal Moroni stopped believing it really happened, and Tony had to kick the shit out of him to get his head straight.

And a few months later, No-Show Weems bought himself a 53-foot yacht much like the one the Moronis had seen on the horizon that day, and Clarence Cromwell got to use it just as much as he wanted.

Natalie Zimmerman knew part of the story of the motor yacht, but not all of it. Captain Hooker knew all he cared to know.

"Natalie," Hooker smiled unctuously. "Clarence here can tell you what a good policeman Valnikov was, all those years they worked together."

"I worked robbery, the bank detail," Clarence said, melodramatically closing his arm on the twin magnums. "Val was a heavyweight homicide dick, 'cept maybe for one or two other guys he was number one. He ain't always been a . . ."

"Drunk." Natalie finished the statement. Then quickly: "Captain, I've been put in a position to poor-mouth another officer like this and I don't like it a damn bit but . . ."

"Sometimes a fellow shouldn't work homicide that long," Captain Hooker offered.

"Yeah. I knew a old homicide guy," Clarence agreed. "Started floggin his . . . started masturbatin at a salesgirl in the May Company one day. Had to give the old sucker a psycho pension."

"To continue, Natalie," Hooker said hastily, "when Valnikov transferred in a month ago it was because of a . . . problem. He had some sort of scuffle with a doctor or something and . . ."

"A pathologist," Clarence said.

"Yes, a pathologist. During an autopsy."

"Wasn't nothin," Clarence assured her. "Jist a misunderstandin of some kind. Homicide dicks always get pissed off at those canoemakers at the morgue. Can't never give you enough evidence to make a good murder case, seems like."

"A misunderstanding," she smirked. "The kind you have in a saloon, for instance?"

Damn, this odd broad was one of the world's champion sneerers and smirkers, Clarence Cromwell thought.

"He had a drinking tendency," Hooker admitted. "And after this scuffle or whatever it was, his captain noted he'd been acting a little . . . well, distant for some time. Absent-minded. His reports are a little sloppy and incomplete. A little . . . oh, incoherent."

"He was always sort of a quiet guy, though," Clarence added.

"His captain thought a change of scenery would do him good. Clarence suggested I take him here at Hollywood and I agreed."

Attaboy, Clarence, Natalie thought, smirking.

"He went through a painful divorce a few years ago. Sometimes it makes a man take a drink, and what with . . ."

"Captain, I've been through *two* painful divorces," Natalie Zimmerman said, up again and pacing. "Look, sir, I'm thirty-nine years old. I've been a police officer eighteen years. I can't be expected to . . ."

"Yeah? You *that* old, Nat?" Clarence said.

". . . and I can't be expected to wet-nurse alcoholics."

"Wet-nurse. Hee hee," Clarence giggled. Looking at her tits.

"Nobody said he's an alcoholic," Hooker said. "We don't have alcoholics in the detective bureau!" *That* one made even Clarence Cromwell smirk.

"Look, Captain," she said. "I've been a good police officer. I worked my tail off to get my bachelor's degree and . . ."

"Her tail," Clarence said. "Hee hee." Looking at it admiringly.

"I don't think it's fair!" Natalie said, sneering at Clarence Cromwell, who was obviously behind all this.

The captain started getting gaseous and wished Clarence would just handle the whole matter so he could go shopping and buy himself a yachtsman cap. "Anyway, we . . . *I* think this aimless kind of behavior might diminish if he's not alone so much. He needs a partner. And not a partner who he'll let take charge. Because that's what he has a tendency to be—passive. He needs a *female* partner."

"Ah hah!" Natalie Zimmerman cried, smirking up at the frizzy lock on her forehead.

Now she understood. And with *that,* Natalie Zimmerman couldn't argue. She had been a cop too long to fight with *that* logic.

Natalie Zimmerman had been through it all, through all the humiliating chauvinism in a macho job where women couldn't advance past sergeant until recent years when they magnanimously promoted *one* woman to the rank of lieutenant. Where they used to start the women in the Lincoln Heights Jail until the sheriff's office took over that miserable job. Where Natalie Kelso had begun her police career at the age of twenty-one, still naïve enough to think she would be doing real police work like a real cop.

The Lincoln Heights Jail. Knee-deep in fingerprint ink, vomit, tears, blood. Memories. You've never smelled a stink until you smell the feet in those detention tanks.

"All right, Officer, bring in your next prisoner. Petty theft, huh? What is she, a drunken thief or a thieving drunk? Search her? Can't I just pat her down on the dry spots?" Mean Minnie from Main Street. She just loved to tease a rookie jailor by plucking shitballs from her jockey shorts—jockey shorts!—and flicking them in the rookie's hair when her back was turned.

"Oh, ma'am! Officer! You put me in the cell without money or cigarettes."

"Be glad you don't have any, lady. They'd kill you in that tank just to get them."

"Oh, ma'am! Officer! I found a body crab when I came in here, and it just died."

"Congratulations. You're lucky."

"But a thousand more just came to its funeral!"

"Oh, ma'am Officer! There's twenty people sleeping in my bed."

"How's that possible?"

"My bed's on the floor."

"But the fifth floor's *full* tonight. There *are* no more beds. Christ! What can *I* do! Take you home with me! Christ!"

A rookie jailor. Still green enough to shake hands with a pregnant Indian drunk from East Fifth Street. The woman had just blown her nose on that hand. *Never* shake hands. Never touch any of them unless you have to. *And don't let them ever touch you.*

Now the women were out on patrol with the men. Wearing men's uniforms, of course. A nasty gesture by the brass to humiliate them since the courts forced the brass to give the women parity. Now they were doing patrol work—the amazons, that is, who were as big and strong as men, as though size and strength were meaningful. But in the investigative divisions they still had them working mostly on juvenile cases, dealing with children and rape victims, doing paper work like glorified file clerks. No, she couldn't argue with Hipless Hooker's logic. If Valnikov were ever going to become an assertive cop, he'd sure as hell do it with a *female* partner. Every one of those *other* chauvinist bastards sure had, even a loanee from patrol she had trained three months ago. She was almost old enough to be the little asshole's mother.

"It ain't gonna be so bad workin with Valnikov," Clarence said, trying hard to come up with something positive for Natalie. Some talent Valnikov could offer. "Looky here," Clarence said. "He's smart. He talks Russian!"

"Wonderful," Natalie said, smirking up at her buckskin Friz. "If we get on the trail of some Communist spies, maybe I can use him."

Five minutes later, Valnikov was sitting in the chair next to Clarence Cromwell. The door was closed and Valnikov was so confused he thought Captain Hooker was telling him he was going to work juvenile with Natalie Zimmerman.

"But I like burglary, Cap," Valnikov said, trying to focus his watery blue eyes on Captain Hooker.

"What I'm saying, Val," Hooker said patiently, "is that I want Zimmerman here to work business burglary with *you*. You've got too much work in your district for one man. You should have a partner."

"Oh," Valnikov said, lips and throat parched. "Could you excuse me for a minute, Captain? I'd like to get a drink."

"Go ahead, Val," Hooker said, while Natalie Zimmerman sneered at her Friz.

Before Valnikov returned, she said, "One more question: Was he bombed or wasn't he, during his *problem* with the pathologist?"

"Argument over a homicide case." Hooker shrugged. "I don't even know the details. Insulted the doctor and got reported. He may have had liquor on his breath at the time. He just needed a transfer, I think."

"And now *we're* going to straighten him out?"

Valnikov scuttled back into the room, his cinnamon hair wet and stringy as though he'd made a half-hearted attempt to comb it. He wore Clarence Cromwell's green tie instead of his own dirty blue one. The tail of the tie hung three inches too low. It was a half inch off center and his collar button showed. He sat erect and made a vigorous attempt to focus his runny eyes.

"I see you're wearin my tie," Clarence nodded.

"Mai tai?" Valnikov said vacantly. "No, I don't care for exotic drinks."

Then Valnikov looked blankly at Captain Hooker, who laughed, thinking Valnikov had intentionally made a joke.

Natalie Zimmerman knew better. "Oh Jesus!" she said to her Friz.

In the squad room, Fuzzy Spinks had gone out in the field and Nate Farmer had taken over the blackjack game with Earl Scheib Lopez.

The black detective was glowering down at the eleven-year-old who was shaking so much he could hardly hold the cards.

"You think you're bad, Earl?" the detective whispered. "You ain't bad, Earl. Me, *I'm* bad! You hittin or stayin?"

"I'ma . . . I'ma . . . I'ma . . . h-h-h-hitting," Earl Scheib Lopez said, with a king showing and a jack in the hold. Then he said, "I b-b-b-b-busted," even before Nate Farmer gave him his card.

The big cop had won all of Fuzzy Spinks' money back and was into Earl for three of his own bucks while Earl's grandma sat at the table of the other kiddie cop, Irma Thebes, patiently trying to convince Montezuma, in formal Spanish, that *of course* Earl was old enough to be gassed at San Quentin.

5

The Big Sewer

Madeline Whitfield awakened that morning not knowing or caring that it was Russian Christmas. Nor did she care that in two days there would be a football game played within sight of her mansion, just down the hill in the arroyo, just near the base of the San Gabriel Mountains. Nor did she know that the most wistful, desperate dream of her life would be totally demolished by the arm of a left-handed quarterback.

To Madeline Whitfield the day was significant only because it was Friday. And that meant it was only two days from Sunday. And Sunday meant the Winter Show of 1977, sponsored by the elite Kennel Club of Beverly Hills, at the Los Angeles Memorial Sports Arena.

It was perhaps not as prestigious as the Summer Show, and certainly would not compare with Chicago International, or that jewel in the crown, the Westminster Kennel Club Show at Madison Square Garden. But it was an important show and for Madeline, crucial. There would be as many as five major points awarded, and Vickie with twelve needed only three more points to become a champion.

Madeline had agonized with Vickie's handler, Chester Biggs, whether or not to show her now in the Winter Show. Should they bring her in with a coat not quite prime and risk a loss to save the prime coat for New York in February? It was a decision which had to be made weeks in advance. Vickie had never lost yet, and Madeline was beside herself with anxiety. Finally, Chester made the decision by guessing who would judge. He guessed right. The judge was a shrewd old hand, one who could not be bought with expensive gratuities. A judge who knew his business, who would not penalize Vickie because her coat was now not quite prime, who would forgive, knowing that Vickie was being readied for Madison Square Garden and everlasting glory.

Madeline had overridden the vigorous objections of the dog handler by keeping Vickie at home these last crucial days before the show.

"Mrs. Whitfield, I've *got* to keep her for you," he had said. "Owners *don't* keep their dogs at home if they expect to win important dog shows!"

"But, Chester, I just can't bear parting with Vickie. She's never spent a night away from me since I got her."

"Mrs. Whitfield, do you want a pet or a *champion?* This dog is the finest miniature schnauzer bitch I've ever seen. She can win it *all,* do you understand? And I'm not talking about the best of breed, or best of terrier group. I'm talking about the best in show!"

"Chester, I'm sorry," Madeline Whitfield said. "You just . . . well, it's hard to say what Vickie means to me. She's like my child, silly as that sounds."

"It's not silly, Mrs. Whitfield. I've been a handler for a long time. I know how you feel about your Vickie. But you're so fortunate to possess a thing of rare beauty like Victoria Regina of Pasadena." He touched her hand in a gesture of understanding when he said it, thinking how that dumb name made him want to puke.

"And you're a generous woman who would want to share Victoria with dog lovers everywhere, like Norton Simon and Armand Hammer share their art. Vickie will never be as beautiful as she *can* be, never show her true perfection, if you don't let me keep her for you. You owe it to dog lovers and to Vickie and to yourself and . . ."

But to no avail. Victoria Regina of Pasadena would sleep between her mother's pearly sheets even the Saturday night before the big show. There was nothing Chester Biggs could do about it but come to the Whitfield home to groom and train the gorgeous little bitch and try to reason with the dowdy big bitch and try his best to win it all with this little schnauzer and build the reputation of his kennel to where even his stupid brother-in-law could run it and Chester Biggs could get his ass into real estate where he belonged.

Chester often said as much during the twelve months he was Vickie's handler. He had said it the night before the Santa Barbara Show last summer. He had said it in the bar of the hotel while drinking with three other dog handlers who discuss dog exhibitors the way thorough-bred trainers discuss horse owners. The conversation generally centered around the richest exhibitors, how much of a bonus had been laid on a handler for winning best of breed, how high the tariff would be if a client was *really* wealthy and competitive and you won him five major points.

Most handlers got only $35-40 a day per dog even when showing a tough breed like a German shepherd. Perhaps $100 a point as a winning bonus. You had to own a kennel to make enough to live on. Handling and showing a few dogs for rich clients simply wasn't enough, unless your client was a crazy Persian like the one who reportedly gave his New York handler a bonus of $10,000 for bringing him a win with his Great Pyrenees bitch.

There were some, like Buck Hickman, who found other ways to collect rich bonuses. Hickman had married a Beverly Hills client and now *he* was an exhibitor and hired his own handlers, and came to dog shows in blue blazers, his silver hair rinsed and back-combed and sprayed just like his dogs, with a rich man's winter suntan, as though born to the purple. That was a secret dream of many handlers who had rich lonely female clients. Women who doted and pampered and spent up to $40,000 a year to show their dogs. Reasonably young and willing dog handlers could hope. There was always a chance, since women exhibitors outnumbered men four to one.

When Chester Biggs sat in the bar that night in Santa Barbara, and talked about the potential of the great young schnauzer bitch who slept in the same bed as her lonely screwed-up owner in Pasadena, there was a handler present who paid more than passing attention, especially when he heard that the owner was rich and available. But he went back to more pressing problems, such as how to convince the cocktail waitress that they might be able to find a little action even in a town like Santa Barbara if she'd meet him when she got off work.

She'd almost laughed in his face because his gray roots were showing and he was tipping only fifty cents a round. "Some other time, high-roller," she finally told him.

Philo Skinner had sat there with yet another erection left to wilt. And at his age how many were *left?*

Madeline had a minor hangover from the Scotch and Dalmane. In the past she had experienced wretched ones from Scotch and Librium and Scotch and Valium. So far the Scotch and a small dose of Dalmane seemed the best way to sleep.

Victoria was certainly alive enough at eight a.m. She frisked in the kitchen, yapping and wiggling around Yolanda, the housekeeper, formerly a live-in with Madeline, now a day worker on Mondays and Fridays.

"Vee-kee," Yolanda grinned, showing golden Tijuana bridgework in front, a status symbol which, unfortunately, was as much a tip-off to Immigration officers as was the long shapeless hair, the cast-off clothes, the diffident bearing of the illegal aliens.

Vickie started leaping straight up, showing off, barking, begging for the liver tidbits she knew Yolanda would get from the refrigerator.

"Morning, Yolanda," Madeline groaned, shielding her eyes from the morning sun as she shuffled into the kitchen and collapsed at the table, tolerating Vickie's shrill and happy growls.

"Joo wan jus café, Meesus?"

"Please, Yolanda. And perhaps a little orange juice."

"Jas, Meesus," the plump young girl nodded, first giving Vickie another slice of boiled liver, humming with the Spanish music on the radio, too loud for Madeline, who nonetheless tolerated it as she tried to concentrate on the *Los Angeles Times*.

Madeline was distressed to read that one of the city's leading decorators was sick and tired of wicker and rattan and jungle plants and swore that it would be déclassé in six months. Madeline looked around at the white wicker chairs and rattan loveseat, and all the hanging fern which she had bought at great cost six months before when she saw a kitchen in the *Los Angeles Times* done by the same decorator. It was ever thus. She would finally get the courage or the impetus or the money to embrace a style about a month before it was déclassé, whether it be clothes or furniture or hairstyles.

Lord, she wished Yolanda would turn down that radio. The frequent commercials in machine-gun Spanish were unbearable right now. And Lord, she wished she could still afford to have Yolanda live in and take care of the house as it should be. As it was when Mason was here, before she had to close off three of the upstairs bedrooms, and the guest house, to conserve gas and keep the soaring maintenance costs in check. Many Old Pasadena scions lived on modest trusts and inheritances in mansions remodeled by Sears or Montgomery Ward. Lovely tiles which had been painted, fired, and glazed fifty years before by Spanish, Portuguese, and Mexican artisans now lay side by side with fifty-dollar sheets of formica. Many an eight-thousand-square-foot Colonial or Tudor mansion didn't have enough furniture left to fill a three-bedroom apartment. They settled for leaky gurgling toilets but kept their expensive club memberships, hence, their identities, intact.

One more year and the trust fund would be finished. As always, her stomach churned when she thought of it. *One* year. Who could have thought about such a possibility when she was Mrs. Mason Whitfield? Not even after the divorce. Her mother had always said the trust was constructed by Madeline's father to endure throughout his only child's lifetime. With "prudent" management, of course. Always, Madeline had thought of the trust anthropomorphically: at first a guardian angel, later a kindly uncle who would always *be* there. Except that when her father designed that trust he didn't consider something as imprudent as a breast cancer which spread to the bone and eventually devastated his widow, her property, her hospital insurance, her Medicare, *and* the trust fund which was to sustain Madeline Whitfield forever.

The medical bills had been truly unbelievable. That was the word. Until you'd been visited by a relentless cancer and all it entailed—chemotherapy, radiotherapy, *four* years of extensive hospitalization, outpatient nursing—the expense was not to be believed.

It was legally difficult, hence expensive, even to break the trust so that the money could be used. Lawyers had to be paid so that Madeline could pay doctors. She often thought bitterly that a physician like Dr. Corey Dills should have known how "imprudent" a raging disease could be, and how a healthy trust fund could decompose like the bones of Madeline's mother.

Toward the end, Madeline's lawyer tried to persuade her to apply, on her mother's behalf, for Medi-Cal. *Welfare*. A word used in Old Pasadena with words like *leftist* and *Socialist*. It was so unthinkable it would have killed the old woman swifter than the disease. The idea of it sent Madeline Whitfield off on the worst Scotch and sedative binge of her lifetime. She continued to pay for a private room and the best medical care possible until the very end. Mercifully, the old woman's bones mortified before the withering trust fund. But the trust was itself terminally afflicted. *One* more year.

There had been a few humiliating attempts to confront the inevitable. Madeline would never forget fearfully approaching the personnel desk of a women's shop on Lake Avenue.

"May I help you?" She was an overdressed woman with green eyelids.

"Yes, I . . . this is a résumé. I understand you have a position available. I'd like to apply."

"A position."

"Yes, as a saleslady. I happen to have a great deal of time on my hands lately and I . . . I'd like to keep busy."

"You'd like to apply as a part-time saleslady?"

"Yes. Or full time, perhaps. Actually, I have a great deal of time on my hands these days and . . . yes, full time."

The woman glanced at the résumé and looked up curiously.

"You live in the San Rafael district?"

"Yes."

"It's lovely up there," she smiled deferentially. "Some of our best customers live in those big lovely homes."

"Yes," Madeline said nervously.

"I see you have a master's degree in history, ma'am," the overdressed woman said, "And these character references, well, some of the most prominent members of the community!"

"Yes, do you think I might . . ."

"Tell me, Mrs. Whitfield, have you done this before? Sales, I mean? There's absolutely nothing here about work experience."

"I haven't been in sales, no, but I think I'd be suitable," Madeline said, face flaming.

"What kind of work have you done, ma'am?"

"Well, I was married, you see, and . . . well, I've been awfully busy over the past twenty years. Awfully busy running my home, and of course there was a great deal of charitable work, and so forth."

"Yes. Tell me, Mrs. Whitfield, have you ever . . . worked? I mean at a job?"

"Not exactly at a job, but . . ."

"Yes, well we have a store policy, ma'am. We, uh, only hire ladies with experience. Actually, ma'am, I wonder if you couldn't fill up this spare time in some other way. A lady of your background, I don't think you'd like being a salesperson. I certainly know what it's like to have free time on your hands. When my children grew up . . ."

"Yes, perhaps you're right," Madeline said, voice breaking. "One gets restless. Yes. Probably I should just increase my involvement in the Junior Philharmonic."

"Yes, that's what I'd recommend," the woman said.

"Yes, I think so. Yes," Madeline said, stumbling out of the office, forgetting her meticulously typed résumé.

Madeline looked at her watch and realized that she had to pull herself together. Chester would arrive in forty-five minutes to work with Vickie, and Madeline didn't want to be there for the session today. The anticipation was debilitating.

It was not good to let one's fantasies fly unchecked to New York and Madison Square Garden. To the prospect of owning a national champion.

The exclusive Beverly Hills Kennel Club had only twenty-three members. Well, there'd be twenty-four come this spring. How could they refuse to invite her to join? How could anyone in the dog world refuse her anything if . . . Westminster! Madison Square Garden! Lord!

Madeline scalded her lip with the coffee and decided to get dressed and assuage the tenseness by window-shopping on the west side, to stroll through the boutiques and shops like Theodore's. Not that she was young or brave or slim enough to shop there. Or *rich* enough, since their styles were faddish and you had to be ready to change each season. But it was fun to watch the platoons of voyeurs ogling the nubile young salesgirls who were pantyless and braless, and wore see-through cotton pants and T-shirts.

There was no such shopping in Old Pasadena. In Old Pasadena one shopped for "sensible" clothes, comfortable loafers with low stacked heels in colors to match wool-knit pants and jackets. Scottish plaid skirts would never be out of fashion, nor would cardigans and V-neck sweaters over cream-colored blouses. Sensible.

But if voyeurs went to shops like Theodore's to ogle the salesgirls, most Pasadena Junior Leaguers went there for similar reasons: They squandered money in overpriced west side restaurants, because of (Dare one admit it?) *movie stars*. "Last night at the Ma Maison, I dined next to Barbra Streisand . . ."

Though Old Pasadena deplored the libertine life-style over the hill—the star worship, the "A" tables at Chasen's, the parties upstairs at the Bistro. Though they would never *live* among them: the celebrities, the Jews, the *nouveau riche*—they were *insatiable* celebrity watchers. A proper Pasadena matron might never so much as glance toward the booth in the Palm Restaurant where Jack Nicholson was sitting, but her pulse was racing. And if, in the Polo Lounge, Warren Beatty said, "Pardon me, you dropped your napkin," to a Junior Leaguer from Old Pasadena, she would look at him blandly in *non*recognition, and say, "Thank you very much," grinding the Neil McCarthy salad thoroughly, with disciplined jaws that wanted to *tremble!*

A maître d' from the Huntington Sheraton Hotel commented wryly that Old Pasadena would dine and drink and dance from seven until midnight, and *grumble* if the check was more than twelve dollars per person. Yet they would gladly *tip* that much over the hill at Matteo's for an "A" table. A restaurateur could get rich off Old Pasadena, they said, if only he could bus in movie stars on Saturday night.

Madeline Dills Whitfield happened to pass the Brown Derby while driving in Beverly Hills that afternoon. She was fantasizing with delicious abandon. She and Vickie would be photographed at the Sign of the Dove in New York. (Did they let dogs in there? Well, *how* could they refuse a champion who had just won at Madison Square Garden?) There was a man with them at lunch. He was a well-known exhibitor from Long Island. He changed variously with her mood. Right now he looked like Paul Newman. Madeline would be pictured with Vickie in *Time* magazine, and the *Los Angeles Times* would do a feature article about the Pasadena dog who conquered New York. Madeline Dills Whitfield would be . . . well . . . *famous*.

In Old Pasadena, family, money, even power seldom got one's picture anywhere but the society page. It couldn't buy celebrity. In Old Pasadena, Madeline Whitfield would soon be as popular as a movie star.

She was so caught up in it she drove down Vine Street without rubbernecking. No matter, there were no movie stars lunching at the Derby at that moment. But if she had looked she might have noticed a gangly, middle-aged dog handler she'd often seen at shows. He was standing at Hollywood and Vine, thinking about a massage parlor on the Sunset Strip.

He was watching the door of the Brown Derby. He was about to commit a crime on a very holy day. But then, only two waiters in the Brown Derby and *nobody* in a Sunset Strip massage parlor knew it was a holy day, that it was Russian Christmas.

Like so many Big Moments in Philo's life, it all came down to a lost erection. Philo Skinner, ever the gambler, tossed a quarter in the air. Heads I drive to that massage parlor on the Strip and give my last fifty bucks to some pimply runaway bubblegummer with undeveloped tits to go down on me. Tails, I snatch the schnauzer from the Rolls-Royce and get *rich*. The blood was surging in his throat, his temples, his ruined chest. He sucked his twenty-ninth cigarette of the day, and flipped the quarter.

Heads. Later, maybe dejection, depression, regret, but now—relief. Thank God. He hadn't slept five minutes all night. He was suddenly horny as a billy goat.

But she wasn't a pimply runaway. The woman in the massage parlor was a forty-five-year-old professional with lurid eyebrows, who wasn't impressed with Philo's white-on-white leisure suit, and the imitation gold chain dangling on his bony chest.

"I already told you, honey," she said, all business, "I'll give you the standard massage, the businessman's special, or the super massage of the day. The prices are listed."

"Sweetie," Philo Skinner retorted, "I got a picture of General Grant in my pocket, but I'm not about to give him away without knowing *exactly* what I can expect."

"I'll give you the standard massage, the business man's . . ."

"What's wrong with you?"

"Nothing, Officer."

"Officer?"

"You sound like a cop."

"A cop."

"Last vice cop that tossed me in the slam looked about like you. Can't depend on cops being young and healthy-looking anymore. They dig up some ole bag a bones, give him a Lady Clairol dye job . . ."

"You miserable cunt!"

"Get outta my place of business!"

"Why you old pile a dog shit you got some nerve!"

"Get outta here!" she said, "before I call a *young* cop with a blue suit. I ain't goin for any a your vice cop entrapment."

Philo Skinner was outraged when he roared through the door onto Sunset Boulevard, as limp as linguini. Lady Clairol! With *her* lousy dye job? That old hound had a lot of room to talk!

And it was anger now, more than fear, even more that the *thrill* of it, which gave him the impetus. An amateur was about to make his irrevocable first step into crime.

Millie Muldoon Gharoujian always had lunch at the Brown Derby on Friday. Just as she always had dinner Thursday at Scandia and Wednesday at La Strada. Millie Muldoon Gharoujian was a creature of habit. It made it much easier to keep her life in order because she had a third-grade education and a 90 I.Q. In her younger days she had a body and bleach job like Harlow which got her out of the uniform of a waitress and into the bed of an Armenian junk dealer who obligingly departed for the Great Scrapyard after his second heart attack, leaving Millie to marry and divorce four young studs in succession and live a hell of a sexy life high up in Trousdale Estates overlooking all the glittering lights of Baghdad. She had owned at various times, in addition to the studs, a pet ocelot, a cheetah, a boa constrictor and a baby alligator named Archie who was accidentally flushed down the toilet. She also had less exotic creatures like a Siamese cat, a standard poodle, and a miniature schnauzer bitch with terrific bloodlines who liked to amuse herself by chewing the hell out of Archie the alligator, who got sick and tired of it and went bye-bye down the john.

The pup's name was Tutu and she later had shown well, twice winning best of breed, until her mistress got bored with dog shows because lots of the young studs around there were geldings. And because Millie got sick and tired of Tutu's handler always sniffing around like *he* was in heat. Millie Muldoon Gharoujian knew a fortune hunter when she saw one. Besides, the dog handler was at least fifty, about twenty years too old for her. Millie was seventy-six.

A lackluster cop named Leonard Leggett was the instrument whereby Archie and Tutu were linked again in the Great Chain of Life. For when Archie took a powder, and found himself tumbling pell-mell in a wild surging torrent right through Millie's new plumbing—while one of the studs in the round waterbed was going through Millie's *old* plumbing—Archie eventually escaped with his life through a pipe vent. Then Archie began an incredible odyssey overland, living on bugs and grasshoppers and french fries which, lucky for him, lay like hordes of dead locusts on the streets of Hollywood. At last, Archie followed his instincts to the Los Angeles sewers, coming to rest in the wonderful, cool, filthy muck below the streets. There was enough tasty fare for a whole battalion of alligators: pastrami sandwiches, beef dips, the ubiquitous soggy french fries, and tons of half-eaten Big Macs and ribs from Kentucky Colonel. And there was plenty of game: rats, snakes, turtles, puppies, human fetuses, a full-term baby or two. Some of it live, most of it dead, the flotsam and jetsam of Los Angeles. People got tired of things very easily in the city and it was adios, down the sewer.

But Archie found that peace and quiet were *boring*. In his dim reptile brain he perhaps remembered the bad old days when he was put upon by the schnauzer, and he became a tyrant in the sewers. He was soon five feet long, nose to tail, and still growing, rampaging around the sewers chewing the hell out of every hapless pet hamster or baby mouse that floated by on a Popsicle stick, right into the gaping maw of Archie the alligator. Then, one day, he made the mistake of chewing the hell out of the leg of Tyrone McGee, a sewer worker from Watts, who was sick and tired of being pushed around all his life and wasn't about to take any crap even from an alligator. Not in *his* sewer, he wasn't.

Tyrone McGee did what he had always done when bullies picked on him. He went and got his big brother. In this case, big brother was Leonard Leggett, the lack-luster cop, who reluctantly followed the bleeding sewer worker back down there in the dark and, shaking like a mouse on a Popsicle stick, dispatched Archie to the Big Sewer with three volleys from his Ithaca shotgun, giving Tyrone McGee a chance to grin malevolently at the belly-up sewer monster, and say, "Catch you later, alligator."

That same lackluster cop would make an insignificant bureaucratic decision which would decide the very destinies of four people: Madeline Whitfield, Philo Skinner, Natalie Zimmerman and A.M. Valnikov.

Millie's ex-dog handler, driven by anger for the massage parlor hussy, went for the Rolls-Royce three times. Each time a parking attendant came running by and Philo Skinner was forced to retreat to the safety of the street.

So, as destiny is often decided by tiny vagaries of fortune, the dog was not stolen from the car. If she had been taken from the car, it would have been, technically speaking, a burglary from auto, and would have been handled by the auto theft detail at Hollywood Station. (Policemen, ever the civil servants, have been known to get in screaming battles over who has to work on a crime report which will entail only a phone call, and a notation which reads: "No suspects. Investigation continued.") The parking lot attendant swore to Officer Leonard Leggett that no one got within a hundred feet of that Rolls-Royce, so it was correctly deduced by the lackluster cop that the dog got out of the car on her own. It was incorrectly deduced that the dog got lost. And since lost dogs don't require a written report, Leonard Leggett was about to go lethargically on his way. Except that Millie Muldoon Gharoujian came jiggling out of the Brown Derby with two studs young enough to be her grandsons. And with much more interest in the young studs than in the fact her schnauzer was gone, she said to Leonard Leggett, "Look, kiddo, I got more invested in that pooch than you *made* in the last five years. Now write me out a police report so I can get my insurance company to pay me a *little* dough anyway."

So Leonard Leggett, the lackluster cop, reluctantly penciled out a quick "unknown suspects" theft report to mollify Millie, and since thefts that take place on commercial property such as restaurants are routinely given to business burglary investigators, like Valnikov and Natalie Zimmerman . . . destiny.

The little terrier had spotted Philo Skinner on his first loping, crouching try for the Rolls-Royce. Philo was peeking up over the hood of a red Mark V when Tutu saw him. She hadn't seen her former handler in months and went wild with joy. Tutu had always loved Philo madly.

"Tutu! Hello, Tutu!" Philo whispered, squatting on the asphalt in his sweat-stained, white leisure suit.

Then he had to beat a skulking retreat when he saw another parking attendant coming his way.

After a few moments Philo came slinking back, sweat sticking in his lank dyed hair, all elbows and knees and bony shoulders, crouching behind a gray Mercedes 450 SEL, dizzy in the afternoon sun.

Then still another parking attendant with long floppy blond hair came hotfooting it across the parking lot and Philo began another gasping lope, his imitation gold medallion beating a bruise on his frail chest.

He was determined on the third try, pouring sweat, knees aching from all the squats, eyes raw from peeking over the shiny tops of Jaguars and Cadillacs like a movie Indian. His poor ragged lungs wheezed.

"Tutu! Come, Tutu!" he gasped. "Come to Philo!"

The little dog was berserk now, barking, growling, crying. Leaping up and grabbing the ledge of the open car window, holding herself against the glass, head and shoulders out the window, feet kicking and scratching, only to fall back inside.

Then Philo Skinner eyeballed another one of those tireless frigging kids slapping across the parking lot in his tennis shoes, and he was off again on his last scuttling painful retreat. He knew he was finished.

Five minutes later, Philo Skinner was sitting on the curb at Hollywood and Vine wheezing and creaking, wiping the sweat from his draining face with the sleeve of his ruined polyester jacket. He wanted to cry. He was thinking seriously about giving up this life of crime before it started, when he heard the shrill, ecstatic, *beautiful* bark.

She leaped on his back, nibbling, licking, yapping with purest joy.

"Tutu!" Philo cried.

Philo Skinner hugged the terrier against his heaving chest, and jaded Los Angeles motorists figured it was just another kinky Hollywood freako when they saw a man sitting on the curb kissing a little dog passionately on the mouth.

6

Siberia

"Uh, would you like to drive, Natalie?" Valnikov asked when they finally got their paper work arranged and began to make their calls on burglary victims.

"Hooker didn't even give me a chance to get my pending sex cases together," Natalie grumbled as she opened the passenger door of the stripped-down, tan Plymouth police car. "Just gave *my* sex cases to somebody else."

"We once had a terrible sex case," Valnikov said, sliding in behind the steering wheel. "Spring of 1953. Near the end of the war. The Reds sent in two whores with V.D. Almost wiped out our whole company. They say there's a new strain of V.D. going around now."

Natalie lit a cigarette and sneered at Valnikov's puny humor. But she saw nothing in those red and watery eyes. Nothing. Was he speaking without guile?

That was the thing about Valnikov. Nothing seemed to follow. In his short time in Hollywood Detectives he hadn't made any friends at all. His old crony, Clarence Cromwell, said he was just absentminded these days. You talked to him and he answered, but you never knew what kind of an answer you'd get from the turkey. They said he was bombed, swacked, bagged. By noon? She wasn't sure if it was booze. She wasn't sure of anything about him except that he was the non-sequitur king of the whole goddamn police department.

"How many calls do we have to make?" Natalie groused, settling on the well-worn passenger seat of the detective car.

"Oh, not too many," Valnikov said affably. His necktie was still askew and his cinnamon hair was fluffing up from the ridiculous combing he'd given it earlier.

"I never thought it would come to this," she sighed, thinking about the new assignment. "Maybe we can have a big day, huh? Maybe we can recover a stolen typewriter table and return it to the owner. Business burglary. Glorified furniture movers."

"I was a furniture mover for a year after I got out of the marines," Valnikov said pleasantly, blinking and wiping his watery eyes on the sleeve of his suitcoat. "Lot of Korean vets looking for jobs then. I was lucky to get a job on the police department. I have a brother, he couldn't find a job for eight months after World War II. He wasn't so lucky."

Natalie decided to get the partner-to-partner biographies over with. Ought to be able to dispense with his life history with about three questions. Then she could give hers: two divorces, one daughter away at college. The police department, because it's the best-paying job she could ever have, and she likes it well enough even though the brass does its best literally and figuratively to screw the policewomen every chance they get. And so forth.

She didn't smoke a cigarette, she *sighed* it. Sigh in the smoke angrily, sigh it out sadly, all the time pitying her luck. Why *me?* she asked her Friz.

"I'm divorced. I hear you are too. Live alone, huh?"

"Oh, no," he answered, driving exasperatingly slow through the noontime Hollywood traffic. "I live with Misha and Grisha."

"Your kids?"

"No. I don't live with my kid anymore. He lives with his mother in Chatsworth."

"Too bad. How old?"

"Forty-four."

Jesus Christ! She always had to look at the rummy to see if he was putting her on. He just drove aimlessly, blinking his sad patient eyes.

"My father used to be amazed by all the luxury in Hollywood in the old days. But it scared him because he was an immigrant."

"Is your father still alive?" Natalie said, not really giving a shit.

"No, my father died before my older brother was born."

"What did you say?"

"I said the Hollywood traffic scared him, but the Russian churches are mostly here in Hollywood."

Jesus Christ! The guy's brain is marinated! Shriveled! Sanforized! But she couldn't smell the booze on him. It must be dope. Jesus Christ! This rummy's a doper!

Natalie snuffed out her cigarette and tried to make it easier for him, as a test. "Valnikov, I wasn't asking how old . . . your father couldn't possibly die . . . never mind that. A moment ago I wasn't asking you how old *you* are. We were talking about . . . you said you live with Misha somebody . . . I thought it was your kid."

"Oh!" he smiled. "No, you asked if I lived alone. I said I live with Misha and Grisha. I think that's how you got confused."

"I got confused."

Then he turned right on Gramercy and began humming something she didn't recognize. He drove five miles an hour. He didn't speak. He hummed in a hoarse baritone.

"Valnikov."

"Yes?"

She was turned toward him now, looking and talking to him as carefully as she would to an axe murderer.

"How old are Misha and Grisha? No, wait. Who *are* Misha and Grisha? These people you live with?"

"Oh. Well, do you want me to answer the first question first?"

"The first question. Yes, answer the first question."

Valnikov took the longer tail on Clarence Cromwell's necktie and carefully wiped both eyes. The road was blurring.

"Pardon me," he said when he'd finished. "Well, let's see, Grisha is eight months old. I'm sure of that because I got him when he was a little baby. I fed him with an eyedropper. He used to squeak . . ."

"Valnikov . . ."

"And Misha, I'm just not sure about. I think Misha is older because he was full grown when I got him. Well, I just wouldn't like to say for sure."

"Valnikov," Natalie said, positive now that he was still swacked from the night before, wondering if she should make him drive right back to the station for a breathalyzer exam. They couldn't make her work with him if she could prove he was drunk on duty! "Valnikov, I was asking about . . . you said you have a son."

"Oh, yes. His name's Nick."

"And how is old is Nick?" It was a challenge now.

"My Nick is twenty. I never see him anymore."

"Why?"

"I think he doesn't like me. His mother doesn't like me."

"Valnikov?"

"Yes?"

"Do Misha and Grisha like you?"

"Of course! *They* like me a lot. I think Grisha likes me more. Misha only knows one word and I've tried hard to teach him lots of words. He just learned that word when I burned myself on the stove one night and I yelled *'Gavno!'* That means shit. Hard as I tried to teach him other words, he goes and picks up a bad one on his own. Just like a real kid would."

"Yeah. He talks and he's not a kid, right?"

"Of course not," Valnikov said, looking puzzled. "He's a parakeet. Green."

"Uh huh," said Natalie, her mind racing, wanting the day to end in a hurry so she could run to Hipless Hooker with as much of this bullshit as she could remember. He was a doper. He was loaded right now. Speed maybe. Or coke. This was perfect!

"And Grisha is . . ."

"Grisha's beautiful," Valnikov smiled.

"Wait a minute, wait a minute," Natalie said, raising her glasses and massaging the bridge of her nose. "I mean what . . . kind . . . of . . . *creature* is Grisha?"

"Oh, he's a gerbil," Valnikov said. "Didn't I say that?"

"You didn't, Valnikov. No, no, you really didn't!" Then she said, "What's a gerbil?"

"A little rodent, indigenous to southern Russia. I'm indigenous to northern Russia. At least my mother and father were indigenous."

Now she was excited with what she'd deduced. He had had no partners since his assignment to Hollywood Investigative Division. He'd been handling business burglary cases on his own, and keeping to himself. There was a damn good chance that nobody but she knew that he was a doper. Non sequitur, my ass. This dopey bastard couldn't string together one question and answer. They'd put him on the wall. Shake him down. Empty his pockets. Would they find Quaaludes? Or hash? That's it! He was fried on hash oil! He was hearing his own questions somewhere. Who knew from where?

Siberia. The questions today were coming from a frozen wasteland. The Siberia of his mind. This was a bad day. He knew last night of course that if he drank nearly a fifth of Stolichnaya, well, he would have a hard time today linking sentences together, understanding what people said to him. People would say things and he would hear them, but on these bad days it was very hard to put the picture in focus. There were little motes of light, the shimmering dots when a flashbulb pops. Like when they photograph a corpse. There would be a picture emerging there among the dots. He could almost get it, and if he did, well, then everything would start to make sense. But then someone would say something to him, talk to him like Natalie was talking to him now, and the shimmering sparkly picture would fade. The Great Secret would not be revealed. Not today. Stolichnaya. Too much vodka. But it was almost as bad other times too.

She was talking to him.

"I'm terribly sorry," Valnikov said, smiling that patient, watery-eyed, vacant smile. "What did you say?"

She had removed her glasses. She was pretty without her glasses, he thought. She was pretty with her glasses, he thought. It might be good to have a partner again. He forgot how long it had been. He truly wasn't sure right now if it was one month or one year.

"I asked," she said slowly, "if you were *sure* Misha and Grisha were boys? You refer to them in the masculine gender."

Now that, she thought, was the toughest question she had thrown at him all morning. Let's see how he handles it.

Valnikov's brow wrinkled, and he chewed his lip for a second and scratched the wild cinnamon hair curling over the frayed collar of a white dress shirt. His coat flapped open when he scratched his ribs. Jesus Christ! His inside coat pocket was repaired, not with thread, but with metal *staples*.

"I'm sure that Grisha is a boy," he answered finally. "I'm not really positive about Misha." He looked at her with grave blue eyes and thought that if you look very closely you can see a gerbil's dick, but not a parakeet's peter. But he couldn't say that to her.

"I see," Natalie said.

"Well now," Valnikov said cheerfully. "Shall we make our first call on a burglary victim?"

It was an interminable work day for Natalie Zimmerman. Hollywood had never looked seedier. Even the downtown area, "the sewer" as the cops called it, had never looked this bad to her. She had long since decided that Hollywood is a slum. At least parts of it. The "swells" of filmdom's Golden Age would be shocked: massage parlor girls flaunting their wares in doorways and windows. Dirty book stores. Clean book stores. More dirty book stores. Magazine stands, mostly dirty. Trolling homosexuals, both butch and queen. Jockers in leather and chains. Hustling black pimps. Listless whores, all colors. Paddy hustlers, pigeon droppers, pursepicks, muggers. Don't walk the Boulevard at night and expect to see Robert Redford, baby. Hoo-ray for Hol-lywood!

Business burglary. She despised it. A public relations job. Ought to hire the Rogers and Cowan Agency. "Unknown suspects broke into victim's place of business using a half-inch screwdriver. Property missing: IBM Selectric typewriters." Sell like hell. Every "honest" businessman in town will lay two hundred on a runny-nosed hype, no questions. Roll of stamps: same thing. Easy to peddle. Got to take a discount but what the hell. Took the office petty cash of course. Maybe took an adding machine if he was big and strong. Those goddamn IBMs are heavy. Same old bullshit, over and over. Why the masking tape? The scumbag dropped it. Uses it to tape the window when he breaks it out to reach inside. No falling glass. Watch out for scumbags who carry masking tape, dearie. They can also tape up your little mouth and eyeballs and then start operating *your* Selectric. (Why scare the shit out of the victim? Because she was so *miserable,* that's why.) Sixty-six thousand burglaries in this town last year, lady. No, that doesn't count car theft. That doesn't count robbery. That doesn't count half a dozen other kinds of larceny. That's just burglary. Just breaking and entering! How many detectives work burglary? Oh, in the whole damn city about two hundred, maybe. How's your math? Two hundred divided into sixty-five thousand is what? Not to mention the other larcenies the same dicks handle. And the arrestees they have to process. And the long days in court. *Solve* the crime! *Recover* your stolen property? How's your math, lady?

A dreary endless slogging death march. That's business burglary with Valnikov. Unknown suspects. Who ever saw a burglar? Like fighting ghosts. And Valnikov. A ghost himself.

Gas stations. A guy doesn't pay for his gas, peels out and beats the proprietor out of eight bucks. Who gets the crime reports? Business burglary. Trouble is there's *always* a suspect. The victims get his license number. Run the license, call the suspect. Where was your car Tuesday night at ten o'clock? Your son, Harvey? Uh huh. And how old is the little zit-faced, coke-snorting, hash-smoking son of a bitch? Seventeen? Yes, well he didn't pay for his gas at Seymour's Shell Station, corner of . . . Yes, that's right, little Hah-vey just didn't pay. (God, she hated transplanted New Yorkers.) No, no mistake. They took his license number. Yes, you take care of it with Seymour and we can close out our report. We won't arrest Hah-vey this time. Thank you very much.

A collection agency. Furniture movers. Paper shufflers. Business burglary. What a thrill. And this was only the *first* day! Why *me!*

But Valnikov didn't mind. He leisurely passed the time of day with every victim of every petty crime report they handled. Natalie was mad enough to spit. Especially, when they were an hour and a half past what should have been their lunch break and he gave twenty minutes to the sixty-five-year-old proprietor of a second-hand store on Western Avenue. She'd been burglarized three times in five weeks. Every time she picked up some decent merchandise, a hit-and-run window smash.

"Sergeant," the Filipino woman said, "I can't go on like this. I can't make enough to pay my utilities even. Do you think I could get a job with the police, maybe?" She brightened and said, "Maybe a crossing guard for school kids. I ain't too old, am I?"

"No, I don't think so. I see lots of old people," Valnikov said. "I can check. I can get an application sent to you."

Natalie was leaning against a ramshackle dress rack, smoking, bored stiff, when she heard the teapot whistle. She walked over to turn it off and saw a dish behind the hot-plate burner. There was a fork on the plate and what looked like corned beef hash. There was a half-empty can of dog food beside the hot plate.

The woman saw Natalie looking at it and scurried behind the counter, pushing everything back and covering it with a towel.

"My dog . . . my doggie's outside . . . I . . . well . . ."

"Yes, of course, Mrs. De la Cruz," Valnikov said, with his weary nod of the head. "I was telling Sergeant Zimmerman just this morning that every business person around here should have a watchdog. Wasn't I, Natalie?"

And Natalie had a dash of resentment to add to her frustration because a rummy like this saw something quicker than she did.

"I'll be very grateful if you could send me the application, Sergeant," she said to Valnikov, her dentures clicking. "I could dye my hair, pass for fifty-five, if there's an age limit."

"You just let me check on it for you, Mrs. De la Cruz," Valnikov said, patting her hand.

"I used to be an actress," she said to Natalie. "I can play any Asian. Trouble is, not too many good parts for Chinese, Japanese anymore. Lost my SAG card even. No Japanese parts."

Valnikov was reminded of something when she said "Chinese." There it was again. The sparkly flashbulbs. The picture almost formed. An Asian doctor. The morgue? He heard snatches of conversation. Chinese . . . Japanese . . . Japanese parts? Sony? Panasonic? Was her television on the blink?

"It's time to go, Valnikov," Natalie said, grabbing her partner's arm, as Mrs. De la Cruz looked questioningly at the confused detective.

"You won't forget to call me, Sergeant?"

"No ma'am, I won't," Valnikov said over his shoulder. "I think you'd make a super crossing guard."

"I'm getting hungry, what say we grab a bite," Natalie said after they got back in the car. She realized she had almost two hundred minutes left in this endless first day.

"Fine with me," Valnikov smiled. "Where would you like to go?"

"Well, I'd like to go to Sergio's Le Club, but I understand they're having another Save Harry Whatzisface party there today," she snorted. "Every guilt-ridden Hollywood liberal will be there. And that's just about all of them. Or we could . . ."

"Who's Harry Whatzisface?"

"The guy who played in *Deep Throat*. Don't you even read the entertainment section of the paper?"

"No."

"Hollywood folks stomping for our civil liberties and the creative freedom of all artists? You know, so Linda Lovelace can go down on Harry and Harry can go down on Linda and Big Brother can stop repressing us and King Kong can bugger Godzilla? Don't you read the paper?"

"Deep Throat was the guy in the Watergate case, wasn't he?" Valnikov answered.

"Valnikov, have you even seen a porno movie?"

"No, I haven't been to a movie in, oh . . . When was *Nicholas and Alexandra* out?"

"Several years."

"I haven't been to a movie in several years."

"What do you do with your time?"

"I listen to music. Or I go to a basketball game."

"Start the car and let's go eat, Valnikov."

"Oh, yes, sorry." He started the Plymouth, flicked on his turn signal, gave an arm signal, looked out the window craning his neck, then pulled into traffic at three miles per hour, while Natalie rolled her eyeballs. He turned on the blinker, made an arm signal, changed into the curb lane and stopped. "Did you decide where you want to eat?"

"Well, since we probably can't get an 'A' table at Chasen's and my favorite maître d' isn't at the Rangoon Racquet Club anymore, and since we're six days from payday and I've got about three goddamn dollars in my purse, what say we have a pizza?"

But he was wandering again. The sparkling lights were shimmering. He was trudging across the great trackless Steppes. A wasteland. The picture was dappled, formless. He saw . . . a rabbit in the snow.

"Would you say that again, please?" he mumbled.

"Pizza. Let's get a pizza." She couldn't keep her eyes off him. Couldn't wait to talk to Hipless Hooker. She was positive now that it wasn't speed. And it wasn't barbiturates. His pupils weren't dilated or contracted. No, he was spaced out on some sophisticated drug she wasn't familiar with. Some kind of dope that didn't take his pupils up or down.

Ten minutes later they were parked under a pepper tree near the observatory silently eating their pizzas. Still she watched him. He'd been raised by someone with table manners all right. It was rare to see a man eat anything with such delicacy, let alone a pizza. He chewed small bites thoroughly and dabbed at his lips with a paper napkin when there was nothing there. He was solicitous, asking whether she would like a bit more cream or sugar for her coffee. Whether her pizza was all right. Isn't it going to be a lovely day despite the smog? Then: "Were you married a long time, Natalie?"

"Which time, first or second?"

"Oh," he shrugged. "Let's say the second."

"What is this, a contest?"

"I was married sixteen years," he smiled, careful to swallow his food before speaking.

"Good. You win."

"Pardon me?"

"Never mind," she said, waving at the air. "I was married three years the first time and two years the second time. My daughter's from the first. My second didn't want me to be a cop and tried to make me quit. I stayed a cop. I have a twenty-one-year-old daughter away at college and I don't have a parakeet or a Goebbels."

"That's gerbil," he corrected her gently. "A soft *g* as in *gentle*. Goebbels was a Nazi who killed lots of Russians. My little gerbil is a Russian rodent. Would you like more cream for your coffee?"

"No, thank you."

"Would you like to see a movie?"

"What?"

"I gather you like movies. I asked if you'd like to see a movie."

"Now?"

"Of course not." Valnikov smiled, sipping at his tea.

It looked ridiculous! He was a hulking man with a broad Slavic forehead and he drank his tea like a grand duchess, for God's sake.

"What movie're you talking about?"

"Oh, whatever you like," he shrugged. "I don't know what's playing. You mentioned *Deep Throat*."

"*Deep Throat!* You're asking me to go with you to a porno movie!"

"Oh, I thought that's what you liked to see. You don't want to see *Deep Throat*?"

"I *saw* it. Twice. On dates with horny policemen who insisted. Jesus Christ, put a cigarette in your mouth, Valnikov!"

"Pardon?"

"Typical macho cop. A freebie cup of coffee, a cigarette, and a hard-on. I was starting to think you were a little strange. I guess you're normal enough."

"Pardon?" Now Valnikov had lost the thread again. It was unraveled and he hadn't the faintest idea why she was upset, why she was raising her voice.

"You've been working this division one month," she smirked. "We've hardly said more than a good morning before today. We've been partners for, oh, four hours. And you think you can dance me into a porno movie for a nooner?"

"Did I say something wrong?"

"Oh, Jesus Christ!" she sneered, shoving the paper cup into the bag. "Let's finish handling our calls."

Valnikov sipped the rest of the tea but his lunch was ruined. He knew for certain that he had offended her but didn't know why. He was troubled and didn't know what to say to make it right. The sparkling motes were swimming. He did the only thing he could. He started all over again. "Natalie, would you like to see a movie?"

She whirled in her seat, eyes narrowing behind the oversized glasses. She viciously brushed back a wisp of frizzy, buckskin hair.

"Do you mean *now?*"

"Oh, no. We're on duty. I meant tonight. Or tomorrow night. Or sometime. It doesn't matter. I haven't seen a movie in . . . I don't know how long."

"You don't know how long."

"No."

"Several years. Since *Nicholas and Alexandra.*"

"Yes, so I can wait. Maybe next month sometime?"

Oh, shit. She turned back and watched the foot traffic sliding by in the shimmering smog. She lit a cigarette. "Valnikov, do you want to take me to a porno? I mean a dirty movie? Is that it?"

"Well, I'd rather *not* see a dirty movie," he said, wiping his watery eyes on his shabby coatsleeve. "But if that's the kind of movie you like, I'm willing. I just thought maybe you were lonely and I felt sorry for you."

"How dare you!" Natalie screamed, in consummate frustration, making Valnikov hit the brakes, almost causing a van to rear-end them on McCadden Place. "How *dare* you say that to me! You don't even *know* me!"

"Did I say something wrong?"

"Wrong! You feel sorry for *me!* You want to take *me* to a porno house!"

"No, I've never even *been* to a porno house. I just gathered that's what *you'd* like. I mean, you said two policemen took you to this dirty movie so I thought maybe you liked it, and, well, if that would make you happy, I just thought . . ."

Natalie was going to scream when they got a radio call.

"Roger that, Natalie," he said, wondering why she was yelling.

"What . . . what . . ."

"We just got a call," he said. "Roger it, please."

"6-W-232 roger," she mumbled into the mike, and now she was looking dazed.

"Western and Romaine, see the vice officer. That was the call, Natalie. Wonder why they want a burglary team? Oh well, that's what makes our job interesting, eh?" He looked at her and smiled and blinked, his cinnamon hair blowing back from the gust of wind as he suddenly "speeded" up the detective car. Now they were going fifteen miles an hour.

The vice cop was about twenty-five years old. He wore his auburn hair in a huge Afro which he had done once a month at a beauty parlor on Sunset where he got a police discount. He was shirtless in a leather vest and wore five strands of beads around his neck. He recognized Natalie but didn't know Valnikov.

"You working burglary?" He leaned in the detective car window from the street side.

''Whaddaya got?'' she asked.

''Maybe something for you. There was a pawnshop burglary about three weeks ago. Down on Melrose, I think.''

''Western Avenue,'' Valnikov said.

''Yeah, that's right, on Western,'' the vice cop said, nodding his shaggy head. ''They ripped him off for some shotguns, one a double-barreled custom job with silver inlay . . .''

''Mother-of-pearl,'' Valnikov said.

''Mother-of-pearl?''

''Yes,'' Valnikov said.

''Was it your case?'' the vice cop asked.

''No, I just remember the report.''

''And you remember for sure it was mother-of-pearl?''

''Yes,'' Valnikov said, wiping his eyes.

''Okay, guess this ain't from that job.'' He held up a silver-inlaid, double-barreled twelve gauge, the walnut rubbed smooth from years of loving care. ''I'll just book it and let robbery try to make it on some other job. Just thought it might have been from that pawnshop burg, is all.''

''What's happening here anyway?'' Natalie asked. There was an ambulance in front and a crowd of onlookers from the surrounding homes. There were seven men being loaded into the black-and-whites. ''Somebody get shot?''

''No, but he might wish he had,'' said the vice cop.

''Catch the suspect?''

''Yeah, *he's* the suspect,'' the vice cop said, pointing to the blanket-covered man being bandaged by a paramedic as two policemen helped lift the gurney into the ambulance. ''Thought he was Jesse James. Decided to take down a crap game that floats in this apartment about every Wednesday. We been staking out next door since this morning, and damned if Jesse James here doesn't come crashing in the room just as we were about to make a little gambling bust. He leaps up on the table and fires his twelve gauge into the ceiling to get all the players' attention. I was next door alone, almost messed my pants. While I'm trying to call on the CC unit for some help, he gets carried away with scaring everybody. He's not satisfied that the players're shaking and begging so he fires *another* round to make them move a little quicker.''

''And that's just a double-barreled shotgun,'' Natalie observed.

''Yeah, and one by one, all the players noticed that too. They say the last thing old Jesse James says is 'Uh-oh.' And that may be the last thing he ever *does* say. They got through with him, his head squirms around like a water bed. Well, does your heart good once in a while to see justice done. Makes you think God ain't dead after all.''

When they were back on Vine Street stopped behind a fender-bender traffic accident, Natalie said, ''Did you really remember that Western Avenue pawnshop burglary?''

''Yes,'' Valnikov said.

''You must read hundreds of burglary reports.''

''Yes.''

''What was unusual about this one?''

''Nothing,'' he shrugged, at last his eyes starting to clear from the havoc of Russian vodka.

''Then how do you remember?''

''I always remember crime data. I don't know why. I've been a detective so long I just seem to remember.''

Memories. Twenty-two years a policeman. Fifteen of them working homicide downtown. Homicide. The first team. The varsity. Shootings, stabbings, rapes, mayhem. Torture murder, extortion murder, kidnap murder, sex murder. Domestic murder: husbands, wives, mothers, fathers. Who said a father never killed his seed? Valnikov knew better. But mothers were more innovative murderers of little children. Lots and lots of child murders. Whodunits, howdunits, whydunits. The Stinker Squad. Corpses. The faces of corpses: bewildered corpses, winking corpses, grieving corpses, laughing corpses, screaming corpses. There was no predicting the expression a corpse would wear to eternity. At times there were just chunks of corpses, slivers of corpses. Sometimes just heads. Remember Homer from Hollenbeck?

Sergeant Ambrose Schultz was the cutup of the Stinker Squad. He loved a good joke. They had been trying to help solve a headless whodunit in Hollenbeck Division for two months. Finally someone informed on a woman who poisoned her unfaithful boyfriend named Homer, and who beheaded the corpse *with a shovel*, which took an hour of relentless hacking but got rid of her tension. Then she preserved the lover's head in a crock of formaldehyde. (Why? they asked. You often discovered the who and the how but less often the why. Who can say why? Why anything?)

Homer's head was hanging around the squad room for a few days after they found it. The preserving fluid had long since leaked, and now Homer's head was putrefied, blackened, engorged.

Homer took with him to eternity the face of a gorilla.

One day Ambrose Schultz happened to notice that clerk typist, Lupe Rodriguez, had made her weekly trip to the panadería and bought four pounds of delicious stone-ground, corn tortillas, handmade in Boyle Heights by Mexican women squatting over brick firepits. Ambrose stole the tortillas out of Lupe's sack when she went to the john, and he left Homer's head inside. Lupe Rodriguez, a perennial dieter and incurable nibbler, was right in the middle of reading a sexy crime report when she reached down inside the sack to nibble. It was odd. The tortillas felt soggy. And *hairy?* They say her shrieks could be heard clear up in the chief's office. It was the best joke Ambrose Schultz pulled that year.

Until Ambrose happened to be handling a homosexual murder wherein one lover strangled the other one and whacked off his penis with a handsaw. Rodney, the demented survivor, said he kept Claude's ragged frontispiece in a fishbowl on his mantel to show his friends at a dinner party he gave after his lover had disappeared. The dinner party was not a success in that the first guest to examine the strange floating fish ran screaming to a telephone. Rodney couldn't understand it because he had spent a fortune on stuffed squab and party favors. He later told detectives he couldn't bear to part with that part of Claude just yet, and besides, he thought the penis in a pickle jar would be tacky, but in a fishbowl it would be a *great* conversation piece. The fishbowl and contents ended up in the care of Ambrose Schultz. Poor Lupe Rodriguez transferred to Personnel Division after *that* one. Memories.

"I said we've still got several victim contacts to make."

"Pardon me, Natalie?"

"I was talking to you."

"Sorry," he said, smiling pleasantly. "We have some more victims to contact, I think."

And that was the way the day went. Almost. The difference being that at 6:00 p.m. that day, when she should have been off-duty—when she should have been home in the bathtub, sipping a gin and tonic, listening to Engelbert Humperdinck sing his heart out—she was cowering on a napless carpet of a dingy apartment corridor, trying her best to keep her sphincter muscles tight and her bladder in control. (Oh God, I'm not wearing panties today!) For the first time in her entire police career she was on the verge of being shot to death. And it was all her fault. Not Valnikov's. *Hers.*

The call came at 4:20 p.m. It's never a call exactly, it's a scream. First the hotshot beeper over the radio. Then a shrill voice: "All units in the vicinity and

6-A-39! Officers need help, Lexington and Vermont! Shots fired! *Officers under sniper fire!*''

And then, heaven help any pedestrian or motorist within a hundred feet of a police car. Coffee cups splashing in the street. Dozing policemen jerking upright. Seat belts click and whir tight. Engines roar, transmissions scream. A hundred yards of burning rubber is smeared on Hollywood asphalt, curb, sidewalk. And, all too often, two police cars (one in compliance with regulations, using siren, another in a hurry to be first, *also* using his siren) collide at a blind intersection and never get to the call.

Probably the only Hollywood unit on the street which proceeded in its original direction was 6-W-232. Natalie was outraged.

''Valnikov, didn't you hear the hotshot call?''

''Yes, of course.''

''Aren't you going to roll on it?''

''Well, I hadn't planned to. We're over a mile away in heavy traffic. Besides, there'll be plenty of coverage.''

''Well that tears it!'' Natalie sneered. ''Are you a police officer or not!''

''Do you want me to go to the call? If you do . . .''

''Of *course* I do. Jesus Christ!''

''All right, Natalie,'' Valnikov shrugged. Then to please her, he stepped on the accelerator. They speeded up to twenty miles an hour. Natalie was beside herself.

''Put your frigging foot in the carburetor!'' she yelled.

''All right, Natalie. Calm yourself,'' he said.

Valnikov looked around cautiously, tightened his grip on the wheel, and speeded up to thirty miles an hour. Natalie gurgled and rolled her eyes.

Surprisingly, there were only four radio cars and one other plainclothes unit at the scene when they arrived. Still, it was bedlam. The radio cars were parked on the curbs, their doors wide open on the street side. Rush-hour traffic couldn't pass down the narrow street and was backed up for blocks. People were on their front lawns, and on balconies of nearby apartment buildings, and hiding behind palm trees. No one wanted to miss the police shooting somebody to death. Or being shot.

One young policeman, hatless, red-faced, was crouching behind his radio car screaming into the uncoiled hand mike. When he was finished he threw the mike into the car.

''Down! Get down!'' he screamed at Natalie as she jumped out of the detective car and ran toward the black-and-white, skirt hiked up over her knees, revolver in hand.

''What's going on?'' Natalie yelled, eyes ablaze.

Valnikov struggled to get free of his seat belt. He'd never pulled it so tight before. Natalie had startled him into it.

''A barricade suspect!'' the young bluesuit yelled. ''Upstairs in the back! He threatened to kill his wife and when she ran out the door he starts popping caps at her! She says he's got an army rifle and three handguns in there!''

''You call for SWAT?'' Natalie yelled. They were ten inches apart, screaming into each other's face.

''Yes!'' the young cop yelled, spraying her with saliva.

''Is there a sergeant here!'' Natalie sprayed him back.

''No!'' he screamed.

''Valnikov!'' Natalie screamed over her shoulder as he finally got out of the car and came toward them. ''Valnikov, you're in charge here!''

''Are you a sergeant?'' The young cop sprayed him wetter than Natalie had.

Valnikov couldn't seem to find his handkerchief but he remembered it was soiled from the flow of vodka-induced mucus that morning. He didn't want Natalie to see a dirty handkerchief so he wiped his face discreetly on his sleeve.

"Are you a sergeant!" the young bluecoat screamed again.

"Yes," Valnikov said, wishing everyone would stop yelling. Then he decided he'd better pin his badge to his coat pocket before a young policeman shot him dead.

"Whadda you want me to do, Sergeant!" the young cop yelled.

"Well," Valnikov began, as tactfully as possible, "I was wondering if you could stop spitting in my face? And, Natalie, I think you should wipe the moisture off your glasses. This is a dangerous situation and you've got to be able to see."

"SWAT's on the way, Sergeant!" the young cop screamed. "I've called for detectives and the watch commander! I've called for an ambulance in case we have any wounded! I've . . ."

Valnikov turned away, letting the spray strike his left cheek and then he did something Natalie thought extraordinary. He put his hand over the young policeman's mouth. A broad, strong hand. He clamped the lad's mouth shut and held on.

"Please, son," Valnikov said quietly. "I can't hear you because you're hollering so loud. When I let you talk again I want you to try to whisper. Now, whisper to me where the barricaded suspect is."

Natalie watched the young policeman's bulging eyes start to stabilize. His face was reddening, however, because he was having trouble breathing through his nose. He grabbed Valnikov's wrist and nodded. Valnikov released him.

"Thanks, Sergeant, I needed that," he said.

"Oh, Jesus Christ!" Natalie said to her Friz.

"Follow me, Sergeant!" the young cop said, and before Valnikov could grab him again, he was gone, duck-walking across the lawn toward the open door of the apartment building where another policeman crouched, fingering the trigger guard of a shotgun.

"I'm sorry we got involved in this, Natalie," Valnikov said reproachfully as he followed the cop across the lawn toward the ominous opening. Then they heard glass break, which caused everyone, Valnikov included, to fall flat on the pavement by the doorway.

"Son of a bitch aims a rifle out the window every minute or so!" said a craggy cop with a shotgun. "His wife says he's got a semiautomatic rifle and . . ."

"Where's the rest of the policemen?" Valnikov asked.

"Upstairs, second landing," said the craggy cop.

The young cop who screamed so much was crouched behind Valnikov, peeking up at that shattered broken window, his service revolver at the ready. Pointed right at Natalie's temple.

Natalie turned and found herself looking down the black hole of a four-inch Smith and Wesson. She could see the lands and grooves from a glint of sunshine.

"Oh, my God," she said and Valnikov quickly pushed the gun muzzle away. The young cop hadn't noticed a thing.

And then all hell broke loose. PLOOM! PLOOM! PLOOM! A whoosh of air. Windows shattered. A tire exploded.

"Who's shooting?"

"What the hell!"

"The bastard's got a cannon!"

So far, Valnikov noted, nothing unusual had happened. It was a typical barricaded-suspect situation. The kind that rates a small column in the second section of the morning paper, unless a cop gets killed. Then it's front page. So far it was ordinary. Everything screwed up.

A domestic scene. Probably caught his wife cheating. Or she caught him. Maybe the scrambled eggs were too slimy. I love you. I hate you. I love you so much I'm going to kill you. And he tries. He fails. I'm going to kill myself, then. But first of all I'm going to shoot up the goddamn street.

Actually, the berserk gunman yearned for the same things a ''sustaining'' Junior Leaguer in a Pasadena mansion did: attention, recognition, *celebrity*. He could only get it by playing a scene he'd seen in a thousand movies all his life: He was going out with guns blazing. Watch out, you coppers! Stanley Kravitz ain't going alone!

All of this was going incoherently through Valnikov's mind. Usually, he'd been called in when Stanley Kravitz lay dead, having tired of the game, having put his own rifle in his mouth and fired with his big toe. Valnikov had learned it's hard to fire with the big toe. Sometimes they missed and the side of their skulls cracked off but they lived. On an intravenous diet forever. Never again to complain about slimy scrambled eggs. *Looking* rather like slimy scrambled eggs. Sometimes, like this, Valnikov was there even *before* Stanley Kravitz fired with his big toe. But then a young cop with eyes like balloons would usually put one right in Stanley's ten ring, doing a better job on Stanley than he could have done on himself.

Before Valnikov moved up the stairs toward the upper landing where five policemen with shotguns and revolvers had fired twenty-three rounds through Stanley Kravitz' door, before he tried to quiet down five other policemen with balloon eyes, Valnikov turned to Natalie and said sadly, ''Why did you want to come here, Natalie? I *wish* you hadn't insisted on it.''

And then Stanley Kravitz (whose real name was William Allen Livingston) opened Act II with an M-14 and pinned everybody inside the building for two hours. And darkness fell.

A command post was set up. The SWAT truck arrived with spotlights. Deputy Chief Digby Bates hovered safely over the building in a helicopter, his teeth clenched in determination, face pressed to the glass, hoping the photographers below had enough light, and telephoto lenses on their Nikons.

It was ten minutes after dark that William Allen Livingston got sick and tired of the noisy police helicopter, and risked leaning out the window to fire up at the chopper. He shot a six-inch shard out of the bubble, causing Deputy Chief Digby Bates to forget about photographers with telephoto lenses and scream: ''Let's get the fuck OUT of here!'' spraying the pilot with saliva.

And then the situation got totally out of control, and twenty guns responded to the sniper by making a ruin of the side of the building where Livingston had barricaded himself. The police officers trapped inside heard Livingston speak for the first time. He played Act IV the way he'd been taught in Saturday matinees. He said, ''I'm coming out, coppers! With guns blazing!''

But before the barricaded suspect could get his guns blazing, a frenzied young cop on the stairwell screamed, ''The lights!'' And five bluecoats banged away with revolvers at the two wall sconces lighting the narrow hallway now that the sun had set.

Valnikov was momentarily deafened. Natalie was holding her ears. The uniformed cops fired eighteen rounds at the two lights. In the movies one would do. In real life, when adrenaline turns an arm to licorice, eighteen rounds won't do. They were covered with plaster dust. They could hardly breathe from the falling plaster and burning gunpowder. They missed the two lights completely. There was one hole in a lampshade.

They were reloading when Valnikov raised his voice for the first time. He shouted: ''Stop it! This is giving me a headache!''

''The lights, Sergeant!'' a young cop babbled.

''We're exposed to his fire!'' a tall cop added.

''He'll be coming out!'' a fat cop promised.

And then Natalie gasped because Valnikov stood, his gun in front of him at the ready, and advanced down the hallway toward the bullet-riddled door of William Allen Livingston, known to Valnikov as Stanley Kravitz, corpse-to-be.

Watching the door carefully, keeping as close to the wall as possible, covered with dust from the bullet-riddled walls and ceiling, Valnikov did something that no one had thought of.

He unscrewed the light bulb.

The hallway was immediately plunged into darkness. One policeman had a flashlight. He trained it on the door when Valnikov returned to his position.

Never one to avoid a cliché, William Allen Livingston yelled again. He said: "I'm coming out coppers and I'm taking some of you with me!"

"Wait a minute! Wait a minute!" Valnikov yelled back. "Let's talk about it. Let me come in and talk to you. I'm sure there's something we can . . ."

When the door flew open, Valnikov threw his heavy body across Natalie Zimmerman. William Allen Livingston lost several ounces of urine and defecation when the fusillade of .38 caliber and .00 buckshot devastated him, but, considering he was struck with twenty-seven lead projectiles, his total weight was increased considerably. The homicide detectives discovered later that the gun he died with was unloaded. He had obviously decided not to take anybody with him. But at least he got one wish. Even though he hadn't shot a cop and didn't rate any more than page thirteen, the siege was so grandiose that it was on the inside front page the next morning.

It made a hell of a flaming explosion, that last volley. One continuous roar in fact, which stayed with Natalie Zimmerman through it all, even while Valnikov, arms around her, led her down the back stairway, through the throngs of policemen, past the reporters, by the command post where Deputy Chief Digby Bates, wearing a flak jacket, was already preparing his statement, his good side facing the television camera crew across the street. Luckily, the detective car was not boxed in by the crowds of laughing, jeering, cheering, Hollywood onlookers who were having a whale of a good time.

There was a Good Humor man double parked beside their detective car selling frozen bananas. He'd busted two stoplights when he heard about the siege on the radio. Last time there was a big deal like this he'd been lucky enough to *be* there when a young rock singer leaped eight stories from the penthouse suite of a record company that wouldn't publish his music. The Good Humor man had strolled through the crowd and made thirty-two bucks selling ice cream and soda pop to all the folks with throats parched from yelling: "Jump, you chickenshit!"

Valnikov waited until the Good Humor man made a triple sale to a guy with two kids. One child sat on daddy's shoulders to see the body better when it was removed.

Natalie got in the car, lit a cigarette and smoked shakily. She couldn't keep her legs still. Nor her chin.

Finally Valnikov said, "Move that ice cream truck. I've got to get out."

"Fuck you, Jack," said the Good Humor man, not knowing Valnikov was a cop. "I'm selling ice cream."

Then Valnikov drew the revolver from his waist holster, pointed it at the astonished ice cream vendor who was holding an ice cream bar in one hand and a fistful of currency in the other.

"If you don't move that truck, I'll put a hole right through your Fudgsicle," Valnikov said.

While the ice cream truck clanked across a driveway with its driver yelling to the bluecoats that he'd found *another* madman with a gun, Valnikov was driving Natalie Zimmerman back toward Hollywood Station.

Finally she said, "Valnikov, where're we going?"

"We're going end-of-watch," he said. "We've had a very long day."

"We've got to go back! We were witnesses! We've got to give our statements!"

Valnikov shook his head and said persuasively: "There were so many policemen, nobody'll even remember us. Besides, what can we say? We didn't fire any shots. Our story isn't important or relevant. A man committed suicide. A dozen policemen witnessed it and helped him do it."

"But . . ."

"Somebody might find out we were at the scene and ask us some questions later. We didn't take part in the man's suicide. Why should we sit up all night while the shooting team interviews and reinterviews, and draws diagrams and takes pictures and . . . well, I think I'm too tired for all that nonsense so I'd just as soon go home, Natalie."

It was a very dark night in Hollywood. For a Friday, the car traffic was not particularly heavy. Of course Hollywood Boulevard and Sunset Boulevard were a mess thanks to the tourists, but Valnikov took the side streets. He drove, as always, ten miles an hour.

Natalie said, "Valnikov."

"Yes."

"I'm sorry I browbeat you into driving to that call."

"Browbeat me?"

"Well . . . we didn't . . . I didn't . . . well . . . you were . . ."

"Natalie, would you like to go to a movie? Not tonight, of course. Maybe next week? Or in two weeks? Maybe you could pick a first-run movie you'd like to see? I haven't been to a movie in . . . I don't know how long."

"Several years," she said, steadying her trembling knees as she smoked. "Since *Nicholas and Alexandra*."

Then they were on Wilcox, nearing the station. She knew the day-watch crew would be gone home except for the homicide team, there because of William Allen Livingston, deceased. Certainly Hipless Hooker would be gone to get ready for his goddamn voyage with Sinbad Cromwell tomorrow. Even if Captain Hooker were there she couldn't brace him with it tonight. Not now.

Of course, she couldn't go on working with a doper. But she couldn't help thinking of him leading her out through all that horror and chaos when her legs were shaking like . . . and she could not forget his heavy body shielding her from the Big Explosion. He had just thrown himself on her. And never mentioned it. She'd bet the dopey bastard didn't even know he did it. But she knew.

She couldn't tell Hooker tonight. She would have to think about it over the weekend. Tell him thoughtfully, carefully, that Valnikov was unfit for street duty. That perhaps they should make him submit to a search. A terrible, humiliating, degrading search, and find the drug, whatever it was making him behave so . . . so . . .

"Well, I think I'll go home and make myself a Christmas dinner," Valnikov said cheerfully, when they parked at Hollywood Station. "Would you please sign me out, Natalie?"

So . . . crazy!

"But Valnikov, it's January seventh!" Crazy! That's it! Crazy!

"My mother used to bake delicious sweets on Christmas," Valnikov smiled, shambling off in the darkness.

Merry Christmas, she thought. On January 7th. Crazy.

7

The Tragic Muse

On Saturday, January 8th, Madeline Whitfield did something she had never done before: She visited the Huntington Library on a crowded weekend day. She had to do something. It was impossible to sit at home and watch Chester doing his last-minute work with Vickie. She had been over the hill on Friday, prowling through the boutiques, so Beverly Hills was out. It wasn't ladies' day at the Country Club, so golf was out. She had old friends she could visit, but most of their children were home from prep school on weekends and it was . . . awkward. It was always awkward for a single woman. As repugnant as it sounded, she thought about going to the Valley Hunt Club to play some mixed doubles. But no, Saturday the men dominated the courts. A single woman. Discomfiture.

Or she could go to the Hunt Room and *drink*. She opted for the Huntington Library. If only she could have remained thirty-nine forever. If only the Junior League would raise the age limit for *active* members. There had always been something to occupy her there. Dozens of fund-raising projects for everything from planned parenthood to alcoholic rehabilitation.

The library grounds were overrun, not just by the regular crush of tourists and weekend visitors, but by two busloads of children on charter buses. Madeline had to park three blocks away and walk to the gates.

At least the "sustainers" of the Junior League could still be docents at the Huntington Library. Madeline adored taking tenth graders through the art gallery to point out the magnificent collection of French and English works of the seventeenth and eighteenth centuries. She loved to escort even younger children through on the rare occasions it was permitted, children from barrios and ghettos, seeing for the first time idyllic cherubic portraits of children from another time. *The Beckford Children* by Romney. *The Young Fortune Teller* by Reynolds. Children dressed and posed out of period by English artists copying the extravagant whimsical style of seventeenth-century Italians.

The boys and girls from the barrios and ghetto would look at the priceless works of art and follow Madeline through the former mansion of Henry and Arabella Huntington, past Houdon's great bronze, *Diana,* who always disappointed them because the naked woman wasn't built much better than the broad leading them, and what kinda jive-ass bullshit is this when that twat on the statue don't look like no twat I ever seen. And past *Venus,* by Giovanni Bologna (same complaint: nice ass, no twat). Through the main gallery where, voice trembling with emotion, Madeline would show the scruffy band of children the library's most famous painting, Gainsborough's *Blue Boy*.

"A ass-twitchin sissy if ever I seen one," said a young basketball star in a green and yellow apple hat.

Then to Madeline Whitfield's personal favorite, the greatest work of Reynolds and an eternal tribute to the leading actress of the English stage: *Mrs. Siddons as the Tragic Muse*. Madeline would explain to the children in great detail how Reynolds applied his paint to probe and penetrate and reveal the very *soul* of the great actress. Madeline would turn in three-quarter profile when she pointed out the dignity, the nobility in that famous face. Mrs. Siddons staring off with sad dreamy eyes, and pouting lips, and yes, children, some people have even said that if I turn like this, well (Madeline always blushed), that I bear a *slight* resemblance to the lady.

"I kin dig it," the stringbean in the apple hat nodded. "She do look somethin like that dumpy consti-pated broad in the pitcher."

But there'd be no docent tours for Madeline today.

Just a leisurely stroll about the grounds where Henry and Arabella Huntington once lived so sumptuously. Just to make this day pass. Just to avoid thinking about tomorrow, when Vickie would become a *champion*.

Madeline strolled first through the cactus garden where some 2500 species never failed to surprise her though she had come this way perhaps a thousand times. Spined cactus, spineless cactus, giant cactus, creeping cactus. Cactus which flowered at night. *Easter Echinopsis*, with night flowers like trumpets. *Living rock,* a spineless variety which protects through camouflage. *Milk barrel, Cow's horns*, the shaggy *Desert fans*, the massive *Golden barrel* as old as Madeline. The magnificent yuccas, over twenty feet tall.

There was no natural landscape on earth as quixotic as this. An alien landscape. As a child she imagined it as a garden on the moon.

It was *too* other-worldly today. She even passed the Japanese Gardens, wanting to avoid the exotic. She wanted to feel comfortable today. To belong. She headed for the Shakespeare Garden. Madeline needed the reassurance of Elizabethan flowers and the forest of azalea and camellia surrounding the north vista.

Here she felt safe. She'd played hide-and-seek through every path as a little girl, breaking the rules to pluck a pink camellia and pin it in her hair. She could run splashing in the Italian fountain in those days, able to see clear to Mount Baldy every day of the year. That was how she always wanted to remember Old Pasadena: a child doing cartwheels in the grass, surrounded by azalea and camellia, the mountaintops snowy and smog-free and as reassuring as Old Pasadena itself. Before the decline.

There was no place to sit today. Tourists occupied every bench. But there was an escape: Few tourists bothered to walk north by the orange and avocado groves. There wasn't much up there, just the mausoleum, the last vain act of Henry and Arabella Huntington.

Five Japanese tourists were there, taking pictures. She sat on the cool marble bench. It was always cool, the marble of the mausoleum, even in summer. She waited until the tourists left, then climbed the few steps and imagined the pinched dour face of Arabella Huntington, glaring at the world through bottle spectacles, swathed in black, hiding under a black hat anchored by a dozen glinting hatpins. Madeline could imagine Arabella walking these grounds. The incredible story went that she never wanted to see a gardener or servant as she walked, preferring to dream that all the beauty around her was manicured by God. When the hell did they work? As she slept? And there you lie, Arabella. And do you give a damn whether or not Victoria Regina of Pasadena is a champion tomorrow?

Then Madeline Whitfield sat on the mausoleum steps and wiped her eyes because those ghetto and barrio children didn't see a whit of beauty in Lawrence's *Pinkie*. Not a whit. And what would they say if they knew that she would not sleep this night with or without sixty milligrams of sedative, because of an honor to befall a *dog*. Well, it might just make *more* sense to those children than the Gainsborough or Reynolds or Romney she showed them.

They said that Constable's *Salisbury Cathedral* and *View on the Stour* was only the way some old dead white punk *wanted* things to look like, but you know nothin ain't *never* looked like that.

Would her dream for Vickie make any *less* sense to a group of ghetto schoolchildren than Constable's dream? Or Turner's? Or Arabella Huntington's?

Don't laugh at my dream, and I won't laugh at yours, Arabella.

On Saturday, January 8th, Philo Skinner spent a frantic, destructive, furtive day at his kennel grooming Tutu and working with her, trying desperately to prepare her in a single afternoon, having to run to the toilet every time the phone rang. No, Mavis, I *won't* be home early. No, goddamnit, there are no little birds here. Call every goddamn one of them. Call Pattie Mae's house if you think I have her here. Call every kid that ever worked for us. Call the fucking chief of police . . . No, wait, just don't call *anybody*. Jesus Christ! I am here *alone* catching up on the book work! And cleaning the shitty kennel because we can't afford Saturday help, and . . . no, don't come, I don't *need* any help. I'll see you tonight. What do I have to do, lay you to prove I wasn't screwing around this afternoon! Yeah, that's right, I *couidn't* do it twice in one day! Bang went the phone on the cradle. He needed an Alka-Seltzer. That cunt! Tongue like a stripping knife. Philo Skinner lit his forty-ninth cigarette of the day and began coughing.

They say the streets of Puerto Vallarta are cobblestone. And that you can see a flower-covered bridge where Richard used to sneak across at night to see Liz when he was still married to the other woman. They say a gringo can live down there like a sultan with a houseful of whores for $200 a month.

"How many months can I live like a sultan, Tutu, with seventy thousand bucks?"

The little dog wagged and whimpered every time he spoke to her.

"I'll tell you, Tutu," he said, trimming her leg furnishings. "Hold still, sweetheart, that's it. I'll tell you, sweetheart, a man can't *live* long enough to spend seventy thousand tax-free American greenbacks. That's how long."

Then he put down the shears and held Tutu's face in his tobacco-stained fingers and said, "I'd take you with me if I could, you know I would."

Then he broke out in a coughing spasm and went to the sink to spit up a massive wad of phlegm. The little schnauzer cried mournfully when he left her side even for a moment. Tutu was the only creature on the face of the earth who *loved* Philo Skinner.

On Saturday, January 8th, Valnikov got blind drunk on Stolichnaya vodka. And sat for the better part of the day and night in front of his stereo set listening to Feodor Chaliapin singing the farewell from *Boris Godunov*. When he got too drunk to understand the words he listened to the Osipov Balalaika Orchestra. When he got tired of that he did what he always did before falling unconscious. He listened to heartbreaking Russian Gypsy songs.

Then he lapsed into a deep drunken slumber and dreamed about the rabbit hopping through the snow. He knew there was no escaping the hunter. He knew the hunter would kill the rabbit and cut his throat, and break his jaws, and peel the face back away from the skull with the muscle hissing as it tore in the powerful hands of the hunter. As always, he sobbed while he dreamed.

8

The Cathedral

In many ways the Los Angeles Memorial Sports Arena was not unlike the Russian Orthodox cathedral on Sunday morning, January 9th. Thirty men were crawling all over the arena floor laying a thousand square yards of vivid red carpet and placing stanchions joined by yellow ribbon. Sprays of chrysanthemum and bouquets of carnation and Black Swan gladiolus were for this ceremony as well. Only the incense was lacking. The ikons were certainly there—by the *thousands*.

The ikons wore the faces of Alaskan malamutes, Belgian sheepdogs, Welsh terriers, dachshunds, beagles, Samoyeds, chow chows, pugs and Pekingese.

In addition to ikons there were medals and medallions with the faces of Pomeranians, Dobermans, boxers and Basenjis. Added to ikon and medallion were more secular objects, such as letter openers bearing the likenesses of Vizslas and Brittany spaniels. There were paintings, posters, plaques of bloodhounds, coonhounds, Akitas and bull mastiffs. There were T-shirts, pinup posters, glow-in-the-dark key chains, cups and plates bearing the faces of collies, poodles, St. Bernards.

The concessionaires were ready for action, all right. One tasteless concessionaire experimenting with plastic rosary beads actually sold several before the sponsors closed him down and banished him. That very day, there were two prayerful exhibitors with those beads, fingering the likeness of a plastic Italian greyhound.

There, in the cathedral of the West Coast dog world, before the light of dawn, with a thousand other souls, was a man infinitely more tense than any dog owner, or any member of the Oakland Raiders or Minnesota Vikings. Philo Skinner had already smoked 13 of what would be a record 105 cigarettes that day.

Philo had been one of the first in line during those brisk predawn hours. But within ten minutes of his arrival, the campers, vans, and motor homes were backed up in a queue of headlights which extended from the west side of the arena to Santa Barbara Avenue. Some of those dog handlers in the trucks chatted breezily on C.B.'s, some sat in the back of their vehicles and drank coffee, read the Sunday *Times*, readied themselves for what would be a long long day for hundreds of people and well over two thousand beasts.

When those vans, campers, and motor homes began roaring onto the floor of the vast arena, Philo Skinner was operating on instinct alone. By rote, he turned off the headlights and drove slowly to his favorite spot on the side of the arena where they showed the terriers. His hands were so slithery he dropped the steel-mesh exercise pens on the concrete floor. A handler next to him offered to help but Philo waved him away, lit a cigarette, sat down in a green canvas director's chair and watched the throngs arriving. There were squads of sleepy janitors who would be kept busy scooping up mountains of dog crap. But where the hell were the food concessionaires? Philo desperately needed some coffee. He was cold. Some judges were arriving already. He'd never been able to figure out why they got there so early. The freelance photographers who would be snapping pictures all day for the dog magazines were here. The dog owners *paid* to have their pictures taken and *paid* to have them put in the magazines.

The handlers and kennel workers were everywhere. All around him tables and cages were clanging against concrete. Then came the roar of engines as the trucks drove outside after delivering their animals.

Something was different today: a smattering of television sets for Super Bowl XI. Something Philo was counting on if his plan would work to its optimum.

Perhaps the exhibitors were present for something resembling a religious ritual, but the handlers weren't. Many were not about to miss the *other* ceremony taking place across town. In any event, there was not one healthy young giant from Minnesota or Oakland who was as tense, excited and prayerful as the long-legged asthmatic with dyed black hair who was trying to look dog show respectable in a three-button herringbone coat, gray woolen slacks and a paisley tie. Except for white patent-leather shoes, the real Philo Skinner clothing was underneath: the red silk underwear.

Oh, God, *why* didn't he bring another shirt? Philo Skinner, eyes dilated from it all, lungs rattling and creaking, was giving off an odor a whole can of aerosol spray couldn't hide. Philo Skinner had smelled his sweat and the sweat of other men, but the smell he was exuding was something else again: the smell of *fear*.

Somehow, sitting there in his director's chair, mildly paralyzed, Philo seemed more sensitive to the roar of action than he'd ever been. He was detached, drifting, numb, yet his mind was darting about like his dilated gaze. The handler two stations down had a Yorkshire with a touch-up. What would the handler say if Philo were to stroll down there and whisper in his ear, "Okay, dogmeat, lay fifty bucks on me or I'll tell the judge to suck his finger and run it across that bitch's withers. You little shitbag! Think you can pass off that dyed Yorkie? Maybe you can out there, but nothing gets past Philo Skinner! Not today! Philo Skinner's been in this racket thirty years. Philo Skinner's been there, baby!"

Better yet, let the Yorkie handler get in the ring, *then* whisper in his ear. "How would you like a suspension for that little dye job? Fuck the fifty bucks. Give me a *hundred,* you stinking little heap of dog shit! Think I don't know? I've *been* there. I'm Philo Skinner, Terrier King."

An exhibitor was sitting with his handler three stations down, frantically ripping through the show catalogue with a pencil, handicapping dog, handler, and judges with as much desperation as any horse player Philo had ever seen at Santa Anita. And here there was no money to be won by the dog owners, only great amounts to be *spent*.

"Hi, Mr. Skinner!" Pattie Mae yelled, clunking across the arena floor in a dead run, lucky she didn't break her dumb neck. Jesus Christ! She was wearing a worn-out cotton blouse, no bra, and a faded, wraparound skirt which barely wrapped around her terrific round ass, pantyless, no doubt. And platform clogs with ankle thongs! Seven goddamn inches high! He had told her not to wear jeans to her first show, to dress *conservatively*. Jesus Christ, she had a *daisy* in her lint-covered hair!

"Gosh, this is exciting, Mr. Skinner!" she said.

"Pattie Mae, take the van out to the parking lot and then come back. It's all unloaded."

"Where do I take it, Mr. . . ."

"Just drive the fucking thing out there and park it anywhere! Lock it up and come back here as soon as you can."

"Yes, Mr. Skinner," she said cautiously, looking at his dilated eyes, perhaps smelling him already.

He was still debilitated by the fear and tension. He lit another cigarette. Every handler around him was already set up. The handlers and their kennel employees were hard at work at the grooming tables. The dogs were being creamed with cholesterol, and the breeds with white coats were being cornstarched. The legs and beards and furnishings were being combed and brushed and trimmed. All around him was the whir of hair dryers, the buzz of electric clippers, the hiss of hair spray. (A no-no but everyone used it with impunity.) The incessant click of scissors and shears. The eleventh-hour show grooming being accomplished.

Then he began to smell the dog shit. The animals were nervous too, and the excrement was runny. Wonder what his own would smell like now? Lucky he hadn't eaten for a day and a half.

This was his *last* show, could that be part of it? The last contact with a way of life that hadn't been bad to him. If the truth be known, he loved dogs. Had always loved them, even as an urchin in a Tucson foster home where they ate pinto beans three times a day in the Depression. Even the stray dogs he secretly fed would eat the beans.

From dog shit to the fragrance of roses: white and red and yellow as buttercups. He loved the Santa Barbara Dog Show best. The flowers and grass and gentle loveliness. It reminded him of movies he'd seen. Like the Ascot Races in *My Fair Lady*. He used to dream of marrying a rich exhibitor and showing her terriers at the Santa Barbara show. Wearing a powder-blue blazer and white pants. Sipping from demitasse china. "Mr. Skinner."

"Huh?"

"Uh, Mr. Skinner, shouldn't we be setting up? I mean, we don't have that much time, do we?"

Jesus Christ, she at least could have washed the fucking lint out of her hair!

"Okay," he said, stepping on the cigarette. "Let's go to work and win a few points, Pattie Mae."

Madeline Whitfield glanced at the gangling dog handler with the crazed eyes who babbled ceaselessly to a nervous young girl grooming a Kerry blue. But her eyes passed over them as she strolled around the arena floor, trying to walk off the tension. Many dog exhibitors never saw their animals except at dog shows like these. They spent perhaps thousands of dollars on them and never saw them, because it was infinitely easier to win if the dogs stayed in the kennel with the handlers.

Madeline Whitfield of course was not that kind of dog owner. Not that she wanted to win less—in fact, she was searching for her favorite photographer, prepared to pay anything to get Vickie's photograph in one of a hundred dog magazines—she just didn't like to think of dogs living in a kennel like foster children.

Vickie had the love and care of a real child, and so far it hadn't harmed her chances to win. Madeline was proving that love and maternal care could compensate for the discipline of a kennel-reared champion.

Pattie Mae now had the cowering little whippet on the grooming table. His tail, curled between his legs against his stomach, looked from the side like a second penis. He was so delicate his legs were like fingers. The noose around the trembling animal's neck, attached to the metal arm on the grooming post, was perhaps the only thing keeping him from leaping off the steel table and running through the arena and out the open door. Which of course was what Philo Skinner felt like doing. His voice, almost drowned out by the noises around him, was pitched higher by the fear that possessed him.

"Squirrelly dog, Pattie Mae, that's a squirrelly goddamn dog."

"Yes, Mr. Skinner, I'll just starch his forelegs and . . ."

"Squirrelly! Just like his goddamn owner. I never shoulda said I'd bring him today. I should stick to terriers. He's six months away, training-wise. Look at him cringe. Jesus Christ! Put that dog back in the crate. He's got head trouble. Trouble in his goddamn head. Look at his eyes, Pattie Mae! Look at his eyes!"

But the girl couldn't help looking at Philo Skinner's eyes. They were the same as the whippet's: round, dilated, darting. Shit! The old fart was as scared as the poor little dog. And he smelled. Oh, gross! He *smelled!*

By 8:00 a.m. they'd already started judging the basset hounds in ring number one. The handlers and the low-slung little dogs were queued up tensely as Philo Skinner blundered past in a rush for the men's room. He had suddenly felt as though he'd been given an enema. He wasn't sure he'd make it. He realized he was going the wrong way, turned, and began a lanky loping dash toward the west rest room. He barely made the toilet in time to pass a pathetic little bubble which was all he had in him.

"Get me through the day!" Philo whispered to the god of gamblers and dog handlers. I've been decent to animals all my life! It's got to count for something! Jesus, no one could care for as many helpless unloved dogs as I have and not get *one* break in life. Gimme a break! Philo prayed in that canine cathedral that Sunday morning.

He was so frazzled and numb that when he left the rest room he actually bumped right into a grooming table and was staring eye to eye with an oversized standard poodle done in a continental clip. The enormous lion-colored mane and clipped hindquarters made him resemble a baboon. Philo Skinner was disoriented and giddy and felt for an insane moment that he *was* face to face with a yawning baboon. He tried to get hold of himself when the looming poodle roared in his face, but it was too late. He barely made it back to the toilet to squeeze yet another bubble past his inflamed and screaming hemorrhoids.

By the time Philo Skinner had returned to his grooming area, Pattie Mae had things pretty much under control. She had lost the daisy from her hair and the front of her see-through cotton blouse was covered with dog hair. But she was flush and beaming from the thrill of working her first show.

"Mr. Skinner!" she said when he arrived, looking wan and bleary eyed.

"Yeah, what's wrong?"

"Nothing!" she said, dabbing a little chalk on the beard of the drooling Dandie Dinmont. "It's just that I heard some handlers talking, and did you know that terriers have won three out of the last five Beverly Hills Winter Shows?"

"So what," Philo said, staring at the Dandie like he'd never seen him before.

"Well, jeez, it just shows how popular terriers are with the judges and everybody. I'm so glad I came to work for a kennel that mostly handles terriers and . . ."

"Got a lot a time, Pattie Mae," he said. "Dandies don't show for a while."

"Which ring?"

"Number eight."

It was amazing, he thought, how even now he could rattle off the data of his trade. He could hardly remember his telephone number at the moment, but he knew which ring each terrier breed would appear in and at what time. He was a dog man, for sure. He wondered absently if he'd miss this work just a little bit. He saw the whippet cowering in the corner of the exercise pen. He felt the obsessive need to talk.

"Got to match that dog, Pattie Mae. Match him if I decide to show him."

"Huh?"

"Stick a match up his ass!" he said testily.

"Oh, what for?"

"Jesus Christ, Pattie Mae, look at him! Do you want him to take a shit while I'm showing him in the goddamn ring?"

"How does a match make him . . ."

"Wouldn't *you* want to get rid of a match in *your* ass? Goddamnit, Pattie Mae, sometimes I think you're an idiot!"

But Philo's chastisement of his groomer was interrupted by a panting dog owner from Palo Alto, who was scurrying from one grooming table to the next, eyes more wild and demented than Philo Skinner's. She was over sixty years old, weighed two hundred and fifteen pounds, had a sable fur slung around her red splotchy neck, and wore a flowered hat which was tilted over her nose as she ran. Her voice had risen to a screech when she stopped before Pattie Mae and grabbed the girl desperately by the arm. She held a bichon frisé in her arms. Philo Skinner's expert eye spotted the tiny red spot of menstrual flow under the plumy white tail of the little bitch but Pattie Mae hadn't the faintest idea what was wrong when the puffing woman cried: "Honey, I need help desperately! Do you have a Tampax! Anybody! DOES ANYBODY HAVE A TAMPAX!"

Even before the astonished girl had a chance to reply, the mistress of the bichon frisé was off and running again.

"My gosh," Pattie Mae said to Philo Skinner. "A lady her age? Does she still . . ."

"Never mind, Pattie Mae, never mind. Let's move on to the Kerry blue," Philo said, shaking his head.

And so, with her plumy bottom pointed to the dome of the cathedral-arena, the bichon frisé went bobbing through the crowd in the arms of the owner she hardly knew and whom she was thinking of biting this very minute. A little animal, originally from the island of Tenerife, a darling of the courts, a breed that had led quite a happy life chasing little wooden balls and standing on front paws to the delight of royalty, only to be thrown rudely into the streets and sent rolling along the blood-drenched gutters with the heads of the courtesans. But the bichon frisé had endured. Three hundred years of grit and determination had come down to a search for a Tampax.

Philo Skinner was beginning to wonder. Would it be worth it all down there in Puerto Vallarta? On white sand, under white sun, in white-on-white linen suits? With brown girls, white in the tooth?

With Philo's brown fingers and blackened lungs. He coughed up a frightening gob of phlegm and spit it in a handkerchief which made Pattie Mae want to vomit. Oh, gross! Mr. Skinner, you make me sick! And you think you can fuck me? I'd rather be gangbanged by a pack of Dobermans! Oh, barf!

Then the female voice over the public address system, a voice which was to become familiar and incessant the entire day: "Janitor, ring four. Janitor, ring six. Janitor . . ."

Bring your pooper-scoopers, boys. The dogs are covering the red carpet in a sea of shit. "Janitor, ring ten. Janitor . . ."

Then a crowd of milling bystanders started screaming, and two people were knocked to the floor. A bull mastiff had suddenly gone insane with lust and leaped over his exercise pen, flattening a tiny Norwich terrier bitch. Lunging for all he was worth, the mastiff's huge pink erection overshot the target by a good eight inches. Two groomers were trying to rescue the Norwich, who was doing her damnedest to lift up high enough so the mastiff could get a better angle. If the hot little Norwich could have stood on a box she would have.

"Get that mastiff!" a handler screamed.

"It's not *my* mastiff! It's *your* slutty Norwich!" a groomer cried.

"If that brute hurts my little bitch . . . !" an exhibitor warned.

A matronly dog owner was strolling through with a white toy poodle, minding her own business, when the lust-crazed bull mastiff reacted after the sexy little Norwich was dragged away. He leaped on the woman and began humping her leg for all he was worth while she screamed and threw the fluffy poodle in the air like a soccer ball.

"Get the mastiff!" voices cried.

"Catch the poodle!" other voices cried.

"Knee him in the chest!" a voice from the grandstand advised.

"It always works on my husband!" another promised.

And now the whole west end of the grandstand was having a great time watching the frenzied mob battling the sex-mad mastiff. The woman was down on her back now amid a crowd of handlers wrestling the slobbering brute.

"Don't knee him with *both* knees now, dearie," a hot dog salesman giggled. "Or your next baby might look like J. Edgar Hoover."

The exhausted mastiff finally surrendered to his handler, who carried him out of the arena. This 180-pound champion would live to battle another day, but for now his eyes rolled and tongue lolled and he was carried in the arms of his panting, sweaty handler. The unsheathed pink erection draped futilely over his stomach made Philo Skinner shake his head and sympathize.

"I know how you feel, pal," Philo clucked.

"Is it always this exciting around here, Mr. Skinner?" Pattie Mae asked, blowing dry the Kerry, while Philo looked at his watch and lit another cigarette with the butt of the last.

"Taper the chest hair like I showed you. Damn it, Pattie Mae! You don't want a skirt on a goddamn Kerry blue!"

"Yes, Mr. Skinner."

At 10:00 a.m. Philo Skinner realized he would have to have his mind sufficiently under control to show his first dog in just thirty minutes.

At 10:30, Pattie Mae, her eyes bright with excitement said, "Mr. Skinner, you wanna bait the Kerry with a toy or a ball or some liver?"

"Liver," Philo said, snuffing a cigarette. "This Kerry always works best with liver. Wait a minute, I almost forgot. Check his teeth. That dumbass broad can't resist giving him chocolate cherries everytime she puts one in her own fat mouth."

"Yes, Mr. Skinner," Pattie Mae said, getting the tooth scaler, glancing at Philo from time to time, watching him wipe his sweaty hands on a handkerchief. Unbelievable! Like this was his first dog show!

Philo showed the Kerry like a sleepwalker. He'd always said he could do it in his sleep and he proved it.

"I guess you should always fold the excess lead, huh, Mr. Skinner?" Pattie Mae said as he adjusted his necktie, letting the Kerry smell the liver, preparing to queue up for the show ring.

"Huh?" The voices and sounds of the dog show were a roar in the ears of Philo Skinner. He wiped his forehead and hands again.

"I said, you always fold the excess show lead . . ."

"Yes yes yes. Fold the lead in your left hand, yes."

"By the way, Mr. Skinner, I was wondering, where did the schnauzer come from? Is it a new one of ours?"

"What?"

"The schnauzer bitch."

"The schnauzer bitch?"

"*That* one!" the girl said impatiently, pointing to Tutu, lying unhappily in a crate, looking hopefully at the love of her life, Philo Skinner.

"Oh, *that* schnauzer. Yes, I have a new client. Talked me into . . . into showing the bitch today, but she's not ready, just not ready."

"She's a gorgeous-looking bitch, Mr. Skinner. One of the best I ever seen. What's wrong? Can't she work properly? Gosh, her coat is perfect and . . ."

"Not ready, she's just not ready," Philo blurted. Then he lit his last cigarette before going in the ring. Jesus, this kid! He had to have some kind of plausible story for her. He had overlooked the fact that he'd have someone with him today. It was all so strange, like a dream, this crime business. As though there'd be no one but himself and the schnauzer and the target!

"Pattie Mae," Philo began thoughtfully, "sometimes you have to show fifteen dogs in a day. Sometimes overlapping occurs and you can't be in two rings at the same time. You could actually have to *miss* showing in one of the rings, and that client, that rich client could be sitting up there in the goddamn seats crying in her hankie and threatening to sue, or something. So today, since this is my last . . . since this is your *first* dog show I'm not showing many dogs so I brought along that schnauzer bitch as a favor to . . . it's time to go into the ring!"

"Yes, Mr. Skinner," the girl said quietly, looking into Philo's dilated eyes. "Is there anything I can do?"

"Always remember, Pattie Mae, you communicate with your fingers through the lead. You've got to have great fingers!" He said it as though he were going away and never coming back. "You've got to have great fingers!"

Philo almost panicked for a moment. He couldn't find the huge yellow sign with the red ring number. It was right in front of his face. He almost tripped over a Kerry blue. There was a long file of Kerry blues, yet for a moment he couldn't find the ring! He had to stop and commit a breach of etiquette. He had to smoke one last cigarette just seconds before going in.

A handler he'd never seen before turned and said loftily: "My bitch sneezes from cigarette smoke. Put it out, if you please!"

Philo Skinner had never had a fistfight in his entire life. Philo Skinner was so racked with asthma and incipient emphysema that even Pattie Mae could have beaten him up. Yet he suddenly shocked himself by stepping nose to nose with the other tall handler and saying, "Listen, buddy, if your bitch doesn't like cigarette smoke, then switch to cigars and divorce the cunt!"

Then Philo bumped past the florid handler and was in the ring. Out of the way, you creep! You fag! The *best* go in the ring first. The greenhorns go in last. Out of the fucking way for Philo Skinner, Terrier King!

Then he just toughed it out on instinct. He could hardly hear the applause of the terrier crowd. He concentrated on the Kerry. He wasn't aggressive enough. Maybe if he would growl a little. Christ, the dog was getting old. He had a good steely blue color, though. Where the fuck was Pattie Mae? Keep your goddamn hands off Tutu, you dumb little fucking hippie. Oh, shit, he wasn't even letting the Kerry set its own pace as they walked counterclockwise around the ring. Oh, shit! He was making the dog move too fast. Another prayer in the dog cathedral. Philo looked up at the steel-beamed ceiling: Let me get through this day and I'll never place another bet! Except maybe on jai alai if they have it in Puerto Vallarta. Do they bet on bullfights?

Pattie Mae meanwhile was fascinated by the miniature schnauzer, and Tutu was dying to get out of the cage and into an exercise pen. She was growling, wagging, hopping around her cage so much she bumped her head.

"Oh, poor thing!" Pattie Mae cried, opening the cage door. "Poor thing. You hurt your little head." And the girl scooped Tutu up into her arms and cuddled her against her face. "You're the prettiest schnauzer I ever seen!"

Then she put Tutu into an exercise pen and gave her a piece of liver which Tutu gobbled gratefully.

The milling throngs of people on the floor of the Sports Arena began flowing toward the food concessions as the morning wore on toward the lunch hour. Philo Skinner was in the ring doing the individual gaiting, "straight-down-and-back." He gaited the dog on his right to correct a slight tendency toward sidewinding. Then he gave an almost imperceptible tug on the lead to bring the head in from the outward line of travel. Even in a state of terror and panic, Philo Skinner was still a dog man.

When the judge trooped the line behind the terrier, Philo, never one to overhandle, reached down and ran his hand over the hindquarter subtly, ever subtly, because this Kerry showed very fine from behind. He noticed that the female handler on the left was staring at the judge. Dumb bitch, he thought. Bad form. Never stare at the judge even if you do have tits like searchlights.

Philo baited the dog subtly with the liver and the dog struck a noble pose. Goddamnit, he was going to get hold of himself and go out with a *win*.

Yet Philo was hardly aware of the burst of applause when his Kerry was named winner's dog, thereby moving closer to his owner's dream of best of breed, for which Philo was promised a $200 bonus.

Two hundred bucks. Best of breed. Shove it, Philo Skinner won't be needing it.

When he got back to the exercise pens, Pattie Mae was leaping up and down on her clogs.

"Wonderful, Mr. Skinner! You were wonderful!"

"Yeah, sure," he mumbled, hardly aware of her young tits jumping, of the look on her face which said: You don't even smell so bad no more, you old champion, you!

Then he saw the empty cage: "WHERE THE HELL IS THE SCHNAUZER BITCH?"

Pattie Mae almost fell on her ass as she whirled so fast in the seven-inch clogs.

"There, Mr. Skinner! I just put her in an exercise pen! She was getting squirrelly and I just . . . There, Mr. Skinner! She's right over there!"

And then Philo Skinner felt all his muscles go limp as he walked over to the wriggling, whining, leaping Tutu. He reached down and scratched her under the chin as the little dog licked and nibbled and whined for the embrace of her Philo.

"Tutu," Philo sighed. "Tutu, sweetheart!"

Then he turned to Pattie Mae, who was by now totally bewildered. "Pattie Mae, take a paper bag. Go out in the van and bring me that bottle of bourbon that's in the drawer under the hot plate in the back. Right away! Go!"

"Yes, Mr. Skinner," she said, and was off, in a clunking run across the arena. The man's a spaz! A total spaz!

"Tutu," Philo whispered. "We'll make it somehow. Somehow!"

Philo Skinner had learned something that all neophyte criminals learn: that it's pretty damn tough to pull your first job (and even your thirty-first) without something to bolster your courage. When Pattie Mae returned, Philo took the paper bag to the men's room, sat on the john and passed another pitiful but painful bubble, polishing off half a pint of bourbon faster than he had ever consumed spirits in his life.

After that, Philo Skinner felt a hell of a lot better about the whole business. The first thing he did was sidle up to Pattie Mae and bite her on the neck from behind.

"Mr. Skinner!"

"Hi, you foxy little kennel groupie, you!"

"Mr. Skinner!"

"Go over on Figueroa and buy me another pint of Jim Beam."

"I'm not old enough to buy liquor, Mr. Skinner. And you shouldn't be drinking . . . should you?"

"Not old enough . . . not old enough," Philo sighed. "Do you have any idea how long it's been since I wasn't *old* enough for something? I'm not *old* enough for social security, and I'm not *old* enough to get into the racetrack at a senior citizen's price, and I'm not *old* enough to ignore the fact that you are not wearing a bra as usual and no panties I bet, and you and me might just go out to dinner tomorrow night and how would you like to go somewhere where the tab for the evening is a hundred bucks? Huh! A *hundred* bucks?"

"Uh, Mr. Skinner, do you think you'd like some coffee? Lemme go get you some coffee, okay?"

"Too young to buy whiskey! Imagine that!"

"How about some coffee?"

"How about some pot?" He was buoyant. Up, down. up, down. Crime was like an elevator. "All you lint-covered, big-titted, flat-bellied chicks with flowers in your goddamn hair smoke grass. Jesus Christ, Pattie Mae, turn me on a little! Gimme a joint. I'll go smoke it in the crapper."

"I don't carry it with me, Mr. Skinner. Where would I carry it?" The girl was looking around nervously at the lone cop she'd seen roaming the arena.

"Not in a bra, that's for sure," Philo leered. "Not in panties either. So go out in your car and bring me back a joint. No, make it *two* joints."

"I don't know what's got into you, Mr. Skinner, but . . ."

"Go *do* it, Pattie Mae. Go out to your car, dig up under the dashboard or wherever the hell you little grasshoppers hide your stash and bring me back some pot! Hear me?"

"Okay, Mr. Skinner," she said. This would be her last show with this grungy old hound dog, that's for sure. Tomorrow she'd start making the rounds of the other kennels. Terrier King, my ass! This old geezer's brain was *thrashed!*

Philo Skinner decided he had half an hour before his next dog was due in the ring. Maybe longer because the show was running long. Philo went staggering around the arena floor, hands in his pockets, cigarette dangling from the corner of his tobacco-flecked lips, grinning, winking, leering at every female handler, exhibitor, or groomer, under the age of fifty. He was suddenly in a jovial *helpful* mood.

A buxom owner and a mousy woman handler were at a grooming table near the grandstand working on a Maltese terrier. Philo stood, hands in pockets, and shook his head.

The Maltese was rolled in oil and tissue paper and tied up with rubberbands so his long hair couldn't drag the ground and break off. But the Maltese terrier's coat wasn't the problem. His balls were. One was lost.

"What do you *mean?*" the frantic owner demanded, her diamond earrings dancing. "How can you *lose* it! My God, how can you *lose* a testicle!"

"Mrs. Dilfaunt, it happens all the time!" the harried handler explained, while two other dog groomers worked on a pair of bored spaniels who had been through it all too much to lose *their* balls.

"Happens all the time! To *lose* a testicle!"

"You're new to dog shows, Mrs. Dilfaunt," the handler tried to explain. "The dog is monorchid at the moment."

"Monorchid."

"Yes. He's tense, nervous. It's his first show. He's just sucked one testicle up, that's all. We've got to help him bring it down. The judges will reach under there and feel and there *has* to be two."

"My God!" the new owner screamed. "I pay a thousand bucks for a one-nutted dog!"

"I used to get the same way when I was tense," she suddenly heard a voice wheeze in her ear. Then she smelled sour tobacco breath and stale sweat and was staring into the heavy-lidded, boozy eyes of a gangly stranger with blue-black hair. "Tickle the end of my pecker, and I'll drop *my* nut every time!"

"Officer!" the woman screamed, as Philo went slinking off through the crowd. Giggling.

When Pattie Mae returned, she put her hand surreptitiously into Philo's coat pocket and said breathlessly: "One's Colombia Gold, the other's Maui wow-ee."

"Maui wow-ee!" Philo yelled, causing the cringing whippet to defecate for the third time.

And as crowds of the faithful trooped in and out of the Los Angeles Memorial Sports Arena, larger crowds, though not necessarily *more* faithful, began choking the inadequate roads into the Rose Bowl in Pasadena on a brisk, bright, perfect California football day. And if Philo Skinner had previously been ten times more tense than the entire offensive line of the Minnesota Vikings, he was okay at the moment. Okey-dokey. Philo left Pattie Mae with the animals, and went slinking around the outside rings to watch the working and sporting dogs. He had the two joints in his pocket.

He walked right up to a throng of nail-biting owners of golden retrievers and tried an experiment. He deliberately lit a joint with the butt of his Camel. Then he stood in their midst, hands in his pockets, chuckling to himself, smoking the joint right down to a roach. Once he tapped a man in a suede shooting jacket and said, "Your handler is standing the dog on a little hump of turf. He shouldn't face him downhill like that. That dog has a sloping top line and the downhill lie just emphasizes it."

The sport in the shooting jacket turned to Philo, looked him squarely in the face and said, "Sir, that dog is *perfect.*" Then he whirled and turned back to watch the judging with the rest of the nail-biters. Philo was grinning, the stick of Colombia Gold hanging out the side of his mouth. It went unnoticed. Goddamn, it was *fun* being an outlaw!

Philo smoked his Maui wow-ee while watching the German shepherds. He had never found a dog show so funny. The middle-aged handlers were really being put through it by a squinty woman judge who was every bit as tall as Philo but lots tougher. She looked as though she was enjoying their agony as much as Philo was. They couldn't satisfy her. Around and around the ring they ran. The tongues of the handlers were soon dangling longer than the shepherds'. Philo couldn't contain himself. "Atta girl, Granny!" he yelled. "Run their buns off!"

Then for the first time someone noticed. A teenaged boy in the crowd turned, looked at the emaciated dog handler, and said, "Hey, that guy's smoking grass!"

But too late. The outlaw was slithering away through the crowd, the joint cupped in his hand, still giggling.

When Philo was back in the arena heading toward his grooming area, he saw a tight little group of groomers and handlers kneeling on the floor next to a howling Great Dane.

"It's *your* fault," the exhibitor barked.

"It's *not* my fault, Mrs. Von Geldt. *You* had the dog all week!"

"It's *my* fault," a young groomer wailed. "I should have noticed."

"I'm changing kennels!" the exhibitor said.

"That's not helping matters. Just give me a chance . . ."

"Is there a doctor in the house!" the exhibitor screamed.

On a whim, Philo Skinner walked up and said, "I'm Doctor Skinner, what can I do for . . ."

Then he recognized the older dog handler kneeling behind the other one.

"Hello, Philo," the handler said. He was a well-known veteran on the circuit, so Philo's fun was cut short. "Anal glands impacted."

And then, loaded on bourbon and marijuana, certainly not feeling like going up a Great Dane's ass, Philo Skinner bent his gangling frame and squatted. He could never stand to see an animal suffer.

"I thought he had worms, the way he was sliding around on his bottom," the exhibitor cried.

"I think it happened today, Philo," the old handler said. "His eyes still look good."

"Yeah," Philo nodded, and without asking the leave of anyone, rancid Philo Skinner, smelling like thirty days in a dog run, probed the Dane's anus, and with thumb and forefinger—gently, ever so gently—pushed in until he was sure he was behind the glands. Then the dog yelped as Philo squeezed and pulled out and up and the secretion flowed through the anus. The secretion smelled worse than the armpits of Philo Skinner.

"Wash him off, he'll be okay," Philo said.

"Good hands, Philo," the old handler grinned. "You still got those good hands."

But Philo was up and loping sideways as though catching a Kenny Stabler pass. "*Great* hands!" Philo yelled. "Just like Fred Biletnikoff!"

After scoring his touchdown and washing his great hands, he returned to the tense group of people swabbing and toweling the anus of the Great Dane. The relieved exhibitor wearing an orchid carnation had her back to him. She caught a whiff of sweat and tobacco as a voice croaked: "Honey, if you ever need any help with *your* anal glands . . ."

Then he was off and running. It was a hell of a fun day. By God, Philo Skinner *would* miss the dog show circuit!

"Mr. Skinner," Pattie Mae said, shaking her head when he came reeling back to the grooming area. "I see you smoked the Gold."

"You know, Pattie Mae, tell the truth I never liked grass before. I just might switch." And with that he gave her a smack on the bottom. "Damn, I *knew* you didn't have any panties on!"

"Mr. Skinner, I just don't know how you're going to show the Dandie."

He looked at the dogs in the exercise pens. She'd groomed them beautifully. Philo Skinner knew he couldn't have done much better.

"You got good hands too, kid," he said seriously. "And Philo Skinner doesn't toss around compliments very often."

Then he sat in his director's chair and smoked and listened to the buzz of the crowd and the incessant voice on the public address system: "Janitor, ring nine. Janitor, ring four. Janitor . . ."

Endless. It was endless. The world was one big heap of shit. There were those that dropped it and those that cleaned it up. Well, Philo Skinner had scooped up his share of shit and now it was somebody else's turn. He started getting very depressed now and almost felt like crying. It was sad when you thought too much about it. The whole fucking world. Just one big mountain of shit.

Then he heard another crowd cheering. He looked blankly down to the next grooming area. A small television set was being adjusted by the handler there. Jesus Christ, he had forgotten for a minute. Jesus Christ, this goddamn dope boils your brain. The Super Bowl was about to begin! Philo Skinner's heart thumped in his throat. He lit his sixty-first cigarette.

By terrible coincidence they were showing the Dandies in ring number eight just five minutes before the kickoff of Super Bowl XI. Philo Skinner was standing like a zombie and peering through the hair of an English sheepdog on a grooming table trying to see the small television set.

''Mr. Skinner,'' Pattie Mae said, pulling on his arm. ''Mr. Skinner, it's time to show the Dandie.''

''Later,'' he mumbled, glued to the tube.

''Mr. Skinner! It's time!''

Then he turned his drug-dilated eyes to the frantic girl and said, ''Pattie Mae, what the hell! Now's as good a time as any. *You* show the Dandie.''

''Me! *Me* show the Dandie!''

''You.''

''Me!''

''Get hold a yourself. You've been to plenty a dog shows.''

''As a spectator!''

''Look, show the Dandie,'' Philo said, reeling from the effects of marijuana and bourbon. ''Show the dog or fuck the dog, I don't care *what* you do with the dog, but leave me alone.''

''Mr. Skinner, I'm quitting tomorrow morning. I'm not working for you anymore.''

''That's funny. Oh, God, that's funny,'' Philo croaked, then broke into a wheezy laughing fit that ended in an ounce of black phlegm being gagged into his handkerchief while Pattie Mae blanched. ''Listen,'' he gasped, still chuckling wheezily. ''*I* won't be working for me, come tomorrow.''

''What?''

''Never mind. Go show the goddamn Dandie. It's good experience for you.''

Mrs. Dexter Berryberry had been enjoying the dog show enormously up until that time. And here was the moment she'd been waiting for. She had bought tickets for seven members of her bridge club and they were all chatting excitedly in the grandstand waiting to see the Berryberry Dandie Dinmont do his stuff. Then Mrs. Berryberry began looking concerned. Where the hell was Philo Skinner? She counted one, two, *eight* Dandies. And the fourth one looked like her Pretty Pennie, but who the hell was that kid with the tits leading her Pretty Pennie?

Mrs. Dexter Berryberry wasn't there when her bridge club began the polite applause for Pretty Pennie of Hancock Park. She was hotfooting it down the stairs to the grooming area of Philo Skinner, searching the crowd for that slinky, teased-and-dyed, mangy bastard. She looked everywhere but in the small cluster of sports fans huddled around the television set.

Meanwhile Pattie Mae was knocking them dead in ring number eight. Perhaps not all of them, but certainly the sixty-year-old judge, Landon McWhorter, whose eyes started popping the moment the frazzled girl came bouncing into the ring. He stopped all the handlers once around, except for poor Pattie Mae, jogging along, turning her ankles on those seven-inch clogs. Old Landon grinned more with each bounce and hop, and made the girl do an L away from him, and if that wasn't enough, a T. He made her trot back and forth so much her wraparound skirt was unwrapping.

Unlike most judges he didn't stand his ground as she moved away, but followed along, making furious notes on his clipboard. His notes said: "Brisket flat and muscular. Hock shapely and well defined. Stifle magnificent!" And the dog wasn't bad either.

Mrs. Dexter Berryberry never saw Philo Skinner squatting on the floor in front of that television set smoking his sixty-eighth cigarette. When she returned to the grandstand, her bridge club stood and applauded her win. She accepted it graciously, thinking she must remember to give Philo a bonus for finding a little pigeon with tits big enough to bring old Landon McWhorter back to life.

At 1:20 p.m., early in the first quarter of Super Bowl XI, Philo Skinner, sobering up slightly, decided he'd had enough. He began rooting for the Minnesota Vikings! He only wanted to cover his gambling debts. He was a dog handler and a good one. His life wasn't so bad considering the alternatives. He swore he'd never bet on another horse or another football game if the Vikings could pull it off. So long, Puerto Vallarta! With his luck he'd die of Aztec Revenge anyway, first time he had a Bibb lettuce salad. Or he'd catch clap in some Mexican whorehouse and a swarm of vermin would penetrate his blood and go rushing madly to his brain and . . . Come on, you Vikings!

But at 1:26 p.m Errol Mann kicked a field goal for the Oakland Raiders.

"Mr. Skinner, we *won!*" Pattie Mae screamed, throwing her arms around his neck. For the first time, she kissed his cheek. "We *won*, Mr. Skinner! The Dandie *won!*"

"That's great, kid, that's really swell," Philo said. "How about going back and getting the bull terrier ready? He's next."

"Sure, Mr. Skinner. I'm so excited. We might win best of breed! My very first show!"

"Listen, honey, maybe you'd like to show the bull too."

"Would I? *Would* I?"

And she was off, running toward the grooming table, deciding to add just another touch of cornstarch.

At 1:42 p.m. the Oakland Raiders scored on a Kenny Stabler pass.

"My God," said Philo Skinner. The pile of butts at his feet had grown.

"Janitor, ring ten. Janitor, ring fifteen. Janitor . . ."

It was all turning to shit. He *would* be a criminal. As sure as there's shit in those shovels. It was Philo Skinner's destiny. He had no control over it. He had no choice in the matter. Fate had brought him here. And Philo Skinner found it as easy to accept a deterministic philosophy as had thousands of criminals before him. Dame Chance was guiding his destiny. His fate lay in the hands of that bearded, left-handed quarterback.

Eight minutes later, Oakland made it 17–0 and Philo Skinner nodded grimly. There was no point waiting any longer. Destiny had made the choice.

"Janitor, ring fifteen. Janitor, ring eight. Janitor . . ."

Pattie Mae didn't do so well with the Staffordshire bull terrier. This judge, a forty-six-year-old fireplug with tits three times bigger than Pattie Mae's, wasn't impressed.

"We didn't have a fair chance," Pattie Mae sobbed to a white-lipped Philo Skinner, who sat in his director's chair, drinking coffee, taking hold, preparing himself for the ordeal to come.

"Yeah, well that's the breaks. Don't worry about it."

"I tried so hard, but she wouldn't even look at us, Mr. Skinner."

"Don't worry about it, Pattie Mae," Philo Skinner said.

"The schnauzers will be going any minute in number seven, Mr. Skinner."

"Schnauzers?"

"Yes, schnauzers." The girl looked quizzically at Philo as she wiped her eyes with a tissue. Then she pointed at Tutu in the exercise pen.

"Yeah, well they're running late. Get her ready. I'll tell you about mini-schnauzers. Cheer up a little, okay."

"Sure," she sniffed.

Now he was once again Philo Skinner, Terrier King. He was still woozy from the drug and whiskey, but he was taking hold. There was no turning back now. That fucking Kenny Stabler couldn't miss with those passes. Was that Philo Skinner's fault? Was it *his* fault that Jim Marshall and Alan Page couldn't penetrate the Oakland offense and nail that whiskered son of a bitch? Jesus Christ, the Vikings were too old. Too *old!* The whole fucking world was too old! Is *that* Philo Skinner's fault?

"Okay, Pattie Mae, I'm going to give you a little bit on schnauzers while we get this little bitch ready."

"Great, Mr. Skinner," she sniffled, starting to recover from the loss. "By the way, where did she come from?"

"Whaddaya mean?" he said quickly.

"I mean, who owns her? How did we get her today? She's not one a our dogs is she? What's her name? Is she listed in the show catalogue?"

"Goddamn, Pattie Mae, you ask a lot of questions," said Philo, lighting a cigarette with steadying hands. "She's a beauty, isn't she? A little tiger. Schnauzers should never be cute. Growly and feisty, that's the sign of a winner. Know why?"

"Why, Mr. Skinner?"

"They were rat dogs in the old days. Tough little bastards. They could get chewed up by a whole goddamn platoon a rats and still come out on top. You ever wonder how we can strip them down like we do? Pluck them clean as a chicken and they don't feel a thing? The nerve endings aren't near the surface a the skin. That's why you can strip out these double-coated dogs. Strip the wiry jacket *and* the downy cotton. Try *that* with a poodle or Afghan. Just try it."

Philo's hands moved as gracefully as a blackjack dealer's. Touching, scissoring, trimming, combing. Pattie Mae almost forgot that he hadn't answered a single one of her questions.

"Sometimes you get a garbage coat on these schnauzers," Philo said, as he saw an almost microscopic lash protruding from the triangular shade of the schnauzer's shaggy eyebrows. "Sometimes they just grow a crummy jacket and all you can do is strip em out and wait till next time."

Tutu didn't move a muscle as Philo's scissors passed across her beautiful brown eyes. Tutu trusted Philo implicitly.

"Look at that eyeshade, Pattie Mae," Philo said, genuinely admiring the head of the little schnauzer. "You could almost shine that silver, put it in your little hope chest. You got a little hope chest, Pattie Mae?"

"What's a hope chest, Mr. Skinner?"

Jesus Christ. They're all so young. *Young!*

"Those goddamn Kerry blues give schnauzers lots a trouble in shows," Philo said, eyes darting toward the ring where he would *not* be showing this schnauzer. "People really like Kerry blues for some reason, but me, gimme a schnauzer any day. These are little working dogs, is what they are. Not some frigging pet. They reach. You got to learn how to use that lead, make these little tigers *reach*. Like a little Clydesdale horse. Look at the gorgeous furnishings on this bitch!"

"She's the best-looking schnauzer I ever seen, Mr. Skinner."

Second best around here, Philo thought. *Second* best. You'll see the first best later. About the time Fran Tarkenton is sitting on his ass in the locker room wondering what the hell happened. You'll see and even touch the *first* best and you won't even know it! Philo was feeling so much better he even took a peek down Pattie Mae's blouse when she leaned over the back of the schnauzer to comb her leg furnishings.

"She has such beautiful legs. As straight as posts," the girl said, admiring the sturdy silver furnishings, trimmed so that the little black toenails barely showed. "I like the schnauzer better too. More . . ."

"More balls," Philo Skinner said. "You like your dogs with balls and your men with balls. No sissies for you, right Pattie Mae? Real guys. Hey, Pattie Mae?"

"Sure, Mr. Skinner," the girl sighed, giving Philo the once-over. Six feet three, 145 pounds fully clothed. Hair like an ungroomed otter hound, dyed like a Kerry blue, chest like a cocker spaniel, legs like a whippet, droopy eyes like a beagle. At this moment smelling like one of those barrels of crap the honey dippers are scooping up in the show rings. A *real* guy, Mr. Skinner. Oh, *gross!*

"Janitor, ring number one. Janitor, ring number fourteen. Janitor . . ." The voice was chanting it now. "Janitor, ring number nine." It may as well have been in Latin. "Janitor, ring number twelve." Hail boxer, full of shit. Old age and shit! Philo wanted to cry. A church full of shit clear to the dome! A canine cathedral full of dog shit!

"Mr. Skinner, where did you say this schnauzer came from? What's her name? Who owns . . . ?"

"Here," Philo said, suddenly handing the scissors to the girl. "There's one hair protruding one-sixteenth of an inch from one of the furnishings. See if you can find it and trim it off. Old eagle-eye Skinner spotted it."

And when she took the scissors he let his hand fall against her left breast, the back of his bony knuckles sliding over the large nipple.

Eagle eye, my ass, she thought. Beagle eye, you mean. Beagle-eyed, smelly old fart. Ugh!

He *had* to come up with a story. She had already asked enough to get suspicious. "This little bitch, she, uh, well, I have this client. Oil. Scads of oil. Moved to Tulsa to be closer to her goddamn derricks. I ever tell you about how a savvy handler can give a rich client a champion, without too much trouble?"

"No," she said, looking over every inch of the schnauzer's furnishings for the elusive little hair he had referred to. Where *was* the dumb thing?

"Well, see, Pattie Mae, I can take a dog and pick some shows in Iowa or Oklahoma. Like once I took a Lakeland terrier on the Oregon circuit for a client. We entered five shows in five days and I earned all fifteen points and brought home a champion to mama. In a Lear Jet! Mama's *own* little Lear Jet. She slipped me a thousand bucks from her own little bank account, because daddy was a stingy old bastard. She also tried to slip me something else, I might add." With that, Philo gave Pattie Mae another pat on the fanny.

No pants, Philo thought, sighing.

Sickie! Pattie Mae thought, sighing.

"Anyway, Pattie Mae," Philo continued, "this broad that moved to Oklahoma, she called me and asked could I show her schnauzer. She's been keeping it with a sister-in-law in Malibu or somewhere. So I said okay, for an old client, and went out to Malibu, picked it up and here she is."

Then Philo Skinner stopped, lit a cigarette and stepped back from the grooming table. He held up Tutu's chin and said, "You know what? I still don't think she's ready. Her coat just isn't sharp enough. I don't wanna show this little bitch today."

"Mr. Skinner! I'm no expert, but . . ."

"Remember that!" Philo snapped.

"Yes, but I think this is the finest miniature schnauzer I ever seen! Why her coat looks prime to me, Mr. Skinner."

"To you, Pattie Mae, to *you*. Did you find that protruding hair in the furnishings?"

"Not yet," she said, bending lower, picking up the front paw of the patient Tutu, who panted and looked at Philo. Adoringly.

"Not *yet*," Philo scoffed. "And you think you know when a schnauzer is ready? Gimme those scissors."

And with that, Philo snatched the scissors from the girl's hand and clipped a nonexistent hair from the left front furnishing and said, "*That's* why you're here at Skinner Kennels. To learn. To learn from the Terrier King of the West Coast. This schnauzer is *not* ready and I'm looking out for the best interest of my client by deciding *not* to show her. Christ, there's a thousand other dog shows this little bitch can enter and win. *When* she's ready."

"You know best, Mr. Skinner."

"Believe it, baby," Philo said. Then he reached over and chucked the girl under the chin, once again letting his hand drop and slide across her nipple. "Hey, you did okay today. Who knows? You might win the terrier group with the Kerry."

The fate of the Minnesota Vikings was sealed at about the same moment the miniature schnauzers trotted into the ring that afternoon. Pattie Mae was standing by the ring next to Philo Skinner, who was watching every movement of a bitch called Victoria Regina of Pasadena.

"Look at her!" Philo said to Pattie Mae, whose feet were killing her and who was ready to call it a day.

"Beautiful!" he said. "No crossover in those feet. Tail not set too low. Great neck. Bet she stands thirteen and one half inches right on the nose. See, our schnauzer could never have beat *that* bitch. *That* is a champion."

"I guess so," the girl said, avoiding Philo's tobacco breath.

"I've never seen a finer mini-schnauzer," Philo mused. "Look how those first two schnauzers paddle. Schnauzers shouldn't paddle like toy poodles, for chrissake."

Then, pandemonium. Someone called the stick. Dog showing is a ladies' and gentlemen's sport.

"Son of a bitch! The stick!"

"That rotten bastard!"

"Prick bastard!"

"Kick his rotten ass, George. Challenge that dirty scum-sucking rotten little asshole."

"The stick!"

"What happened, Mr. Skinner?" Pattie Mae cried.

At one grooming station they were growling, snarling, lunging toward the ring. The people, that is. The dogs were quietly sitting, or trying to sleep through all the hullabaloo, nuzzling their balls, licking their twats, biting at imaginary itches brought about not by fleas but by the nervousness of the human beings which affected the dogs like poison ivy.

A siren could be heard faintly on Santa Barbara Avenue. The cops were chasing a drunk driver from Minnesota in a Hertz Rent-A-Car. He was careening around the Los Angeles Coliseum convinced that his Vikings were inside kicking the shit out of those pussies from Oakland. He was twelve miles and eighteen points away from the right stadium and the right score. The sirens set the dogs to howling, though Pattie Mae thought the dogs had joined the howling humans because they'd called the stick. Everyone took up the chant.

"He called the stick! The prick!"

Even Pattie Mae started yelling, "He called the stick, Mr. Skinner!" She was caught up in mob frenzy. "The dirty prick called the stick!"

"Pattie Mae, do you know what the stick is?" Philo asked.

"No."

"Calm down for chrissake and I'll tell you."

But it was hard to talk over all the noise.

The humans snarled and the sirens wailed, and some of the dogs in the ring began to howl and move their bowels.

"Janitor, ring number one. Janitor, ring number four. Are there any more janitors on lunch break? All janitors to the arena floor!"

"What's the stick, Mr. Skinner?" she asked when the animals and people stopped howling.

"See that third guy in the ring? The one with the phony dyed red hair?"

Yeah, phony hair, Pattie Mae thought.

"That guy with the phony dyed hair, he's an anesthesiologist from Laguna Beach. A one hundred percent, never deviating, pure-blooded, American Kennel Club registered, prick. He called the stick on that little schnauzer that Billie Jefferson's showing. See the little bitch? Third from the judge's right? Well, she might be a mite under twelve inches at the withers, and that prick, he can spot a schnauzer under twelve inches better than anybody I ever saw. He's called for the stick more than anyone. They used to walk them under a wicket, like a croquet wicket. Poor Billie. That little bitch isn't going to measure twelve inches. She'll be disqualified and Billie knows it. Poor bastard. Been a handler even longer than me. Hustling to make ends meet and some rich doctor from Laguna calls the stick on him. Poor bastard. Bet Billie'd like to put that fucking doctor under the wicket, play croquet on his goddamn phony dyed head. Poor old Blllie. Hard to make a living running a kennel, Pattie Mae."

"But if you love dogs, Mr. Skinner . . ."

"Love dogs," Philo said, and looked longingly toward ring number seven. His *last* dog show. "Yeah, I always loved them, true enough. Long as I can remember. When I was a scrawny hungry kid with not enough for me to eat, I always shared with some goddamn dog. Now I'm a scrawny hungry man and . . . aw, what the hell."

And for the first time, Pattie Mae looked at the old bastard with something other than apprehension or loathing. "You're not so scrawny, Mr. Skinner," the simple girl said. "You just smoke too much. And I'd lay off the Colombia Gold I was you, you're liable to lose some clients."

The little schnauzer measured 11 15/16 inches at the withers and was disqualified. The handler's groom at the next station vowed to cut the anesthesiologist's heart out with a stripping knife. And without any anesthetic, the cocksucker.

Then Philo Skinner, with an odd stare that frightened Pattie Mae, turned to her, and said: "Do you know how far people will go to win a show? In Madison Square Garden they cut the eyebrows and whiskers off a Scottie."

"They did! Oh, that's gross!" Pattie Mae grimaced.

"And they poisoned a collie. Poisoned him."

"Oh, my God!" Pattie Mae cried. She couldn't even bear to hear about people who didn't *brush* their animals. She sat for hours with her own Manchester terrier searching for fleas and ticks like a mother chimpanzee.

"I'd never hurt a dog," Philo Skinner announced. "Not for anything. Not ever. I'd rather kill a man than hurt a dog. Can you understand that?"

He was sweating again and starting to smell. The girl just looked at the staring, droopy, beagle eyes of her boss, and said, "Yes, Mr. Skinner."

The time was drawing close. Madeline Whitfield's bitch was certain to take a terrier group first. But she'd never get a chance to win best in show because Philo Skinnner had other plans.

Madeline Whitfield was ecstatic when Vickie won winners bitch. She was jumping around on the grandstand seats, banging friends and strangers on the arms and shoulders. Being congratulated, shaking hands, wiping tears from her eyes.

"Get the photographer!" Madeline cried. "Somebody get the photographer!"

Madeline Dills Whitfield was absolutely positive that this was her day. Victoria Regina of Pasadena was now a champion. She wasn't going to stop here, she was going to win best in show. Let them read *that* in the *Los Angeles Times* tomorrow with their all-bran cereal. Let them see who won Best in Winter Show, 1977! Madeline Whitfield couldn't quell the tears of joy. The more she was congratulated the more they flowed. Okay, Beverly Hills Kennel Club, are you ready to increase your membership to twenty-four? Not yet? Well, wait a few weeks. Wait until Victoria Regina of Pasadena wins Westminster! Wait until Madison Square Garden! Screw you, Junior League! She was never so happy in her entire life. All forty-three years had led her to this: her destiny. The pain, the sacrifice, had all been worth it. She was nearly a celebrity!

In thirty minutes she would be one of the most miserable, terrified women in Los Angeles. She would be infinitely more miserable than Fran Tarkenton, who was, at this very moment, caught by the television cameras, sitting on his helmet on the sidelines, wondering what the hell went wrong.

An exhibitor walked by the grooming station of Philo Skinner and said to a companion: "Our bitch is in season. She's not showing well."

Philo Skinner, who had never seen the woman in his life, said, "Yeah, you look a little nervous yourself. Checked *your* drawers lately?"

He was like that. Scared. Bold. Wild. Up again. Is this the way criminals were supposed to feel? It was as though all the conventions, all the regulations of the American Kennel Club had lost their meaning. These were the rules he lived by and they didn't mean a thing. He felt like taking off his Brooks Brothers coat and paisley necktie and yelling, "Janitor! Janitor! Come to Philo Skinner!" He wanted to throw it all into the steaming vats of dog shit. This is what it must be like to blow a safe, to steal a diamond, to rob a stagecoach! He didn't know it, but he was being propelled by the same megalomaniacal force as an eleven-year-old bike bandit named Earl Scheib Lopez. He was a goddamn swashbuckler!

He went to the exercise pens and picked up Tutu, who licked his hands and face as he carried her to her crate. He put her inside and for the first time in his life he did something which would cause great discomfort to an animal. An animal he loved. An animal which was going to let him live the rest of his days like the gentleman he always aspired to be.

"Pattie Mae, go over to the concession stand and get me some coffee. Black."

"Yes, Mr. Skinner," she said, and was off.

He took the syringe from the inside of the herringbone jacket. To be extra safe he removed it from the leather case and squeezed out a few drops.

Philo was still feeling some effects of the bourbon and marijuana. He hugged the little schnauzer to his face and kissed her whiskers. Tutu was delirious with joy because Philo was letting her lick his face. She growled, and licked and nibbled and told Philo how much she loved him.

"I wish I could take you with me, honey," Philo whispered.

Philo Skinner looked around. Most of the crowd was hovering around the ring. A few groomers were stationed at the grooming tables to watch over the animals not in the exercise pens. Nobody was paying the slightest attention to Philo Skinner.

"You and me, we could run on the beach in Mexico," Philo whispered. "If there was *any* way, you know I'd take you. I know you don't like that fat old bitch you live with, but she'll treat you okay. Oh, Christ, I'm sorry, Tutu . . ."

And he jammed the needle into her shoulder.

Tutu yelped and looked at Philo in disbelief. The tranquilizer worked at once, just as they said in the dog books. The dog's eyes filled with pain, then bewilderment. She looked at Philo Skinner like a stranger. She actually growled in confusion at the man she adored. Then she began panting and her eyes drooped and looked glazed over.

"You'll be okay, sweetheart," Philo whispered as he moved across the arena floor, bumping his way through the crowd, "You'll be okay in a little while, sweetheart. Philo's sorry." He forced himself to walk. *Walk* toward the grooming station of dog handler, Chester Biggs.

Philo Skinner had his hand under the chin of the little schnauzer, holding her head upright. Stroking the semiconscious animal under the chin, keeping his eyes riveted on his objective, hoping that he had assessed correctly, and that Chester Biggs, who often discussed sports with Philo Skinner, would be . . .

And he was! Chester Biggs was fifty feet away from his exercise pens, watching the degradation of the Minnesota Vikings. Gloating over the humiliation of the Minnesota team by the California team. But there was a dog groomer sitting by the exercise pens, reading a girlie magazine, watching over the eleven animals Chester Biggs was showing that day.

Chester, you should be getting your head together. Your schnauzer bitch could win best in show. If she was my bitch I wouldn't go to the crapper without her. You're a dumb fucking pile of dogmeat, Chester Biggs! You deserve to get ripped off, you dumb fucking pile of dogmeat! Dogs have been stolen before. Dogs were stolen at Madison Square Garden. But you aren't ever going to know about this one, Chester. Never!

The kennel boy, a sixteen-year-old, pimply strawberry blond with half an erection, was looking with disbelief at the enormous fluff of pubic hair on the girl in the skin magazine. He had never seen a real one. Are they *all* that hairy?

He never saw the sweaty, staring, gangling man with a listless schnauzer under his arm, skulking around the exercise pens and cages of Chester Biggs. He certainly never saw the man walk to the crate of Victoria Regina of Pasadena, and stand with his back to the kennel boy for no more than fifteen seconds. And he certainly never saw that Mr. Biggs' champion schnauzer now lay in her cage, eyes half closed and glazed, tongue lolling, panting heavily. The kennel boy couldn't take his eyes off the mound of fluff, tinted and back-combed like the topknot of a Bedlington terrier.

Philo Skinner, felon. From this moment on it was Puerto Vallarta or the slammer. He felt like he was on roller skates. He couldn't stop slipping and sliding and bumping into people as he made his way through the multitudes, toward his grooming station. He was trying to walk with grace and control, perhaps even stealth. Weren't crooks stealthy? Instead his always long, bent-kneed gait became a slinking lope. Philo Skinner was loping through the crowd, all elbows and knees. The schnauzer bitch in his arms was getting very upset and nervous.

"It's okay, baby, it's okay," Philo whispered, stroking Vickie under the throat.

Then he thudded into a handler going the other way with a toy poodle on a lead.

"Watch it, for chrissake!" the perspiring handler said.

Philo thought his goose was cooked. The poodle handler knows the schnauzer! The fag handler letting go with a falsetto shriek! Throw the little bitch in the sissy's face and run for it! Get across the Tijuana border with the three hundred bucks in your checking account before the nigger and Jew with the grooming shears arrive for the circumcision! Jesus!

But the poodle handler didn't even recognize Philo, let alone the bitch. How could he? The goddamn schnauzers were nearly identical. Get hold of yourself. For chrissake, you're Philo Skinner, Terrier King!

Thud! He crashed into a handler named Rosie Lutz, who, luckily for Philo, wore her hair like a Sealyham terrier and couldn't see Philo let alone Vickie. But Philo Skinner panicked. He was skidding and sliding on the slippery floor. He couldn't get traction. Jesus Christ, he couldn't get moving! It was like a bad dream! Does anybody have a skate key? Then he realized he was slipping and sliding in an enormous pile of nerve-runny dog crap, and the offender, a 200-pound St. Bernard, was being chastised by a woman who said: "Bad bad, Cyril! You embarrass mummy."

When he regained his footing, Philo Skinner threw caution to the winds. He stopped trying to be stealthy and just bolted through the crowd while Vickie growled fiercely. By the time he arrived at his grooming area, the little bitch had chewed a half-inch wound in the web of Philo Skinner's left hand without his even noticing it.

"Mr. Skinner, what's wrong!" Pattie Mae said, looking at Philo's white clammy face. "My gosh, the schnauzer's biting your hand!"

Philo looked down and saw Vickie, all spunk and grit, shaking Philo's bony hand around like her ancestors shook dead rats in the mountains of Bavaria. This might be a dog show, and maybe she was trained to let all sorts of strangers pinch and probe, knead and thump her withers and flanks and vagina and anus, and even go into her mouth, but she was an exceedingly intelligent and brave little dog, and sensed that this stranger was up to no good, smelling the fear on him. She wasn't about to let herself be mistreated by someone who smelled like this.

For the first time, Philo noticed her chesty growls. Then he saw the blood running down his wrist. Then and only then was Philo Skinner brought back to shattering reality. *Pain.*

Philo screamed, throwing Vickie four feet in the air, up and down into the arms of Pattie Mae, who caught her like a Kenny Stabler pitchout.

Vickie was howling for all she was worth now, and Philo was sliding around on his still greasy soles, holding his wounded hand by the wrist and making a hell of a commotion which attracted the attention of no more than fifty or sixty people.

"That man got bitten!" a bystander hollered.

"Help that man, he's hurt!" a groomer shouted.

"Is there a doctor in the house?" someone cried.

"Where's the injured animal?" A smallish man in a seersucker suit elbowed through the curious crowd.

"Right here, Doctor!" someone said.

"Oh. That's a man. I'm a veterinarian."

"Yow," Philo Skinner said, wiping his filthy handkerchief around the wound while the veterinarian retreated.

He was hoping the cops would be kind enough to handcuff him in front like they used to do in all the old movies and not in the back like he'd seen real-life cops do on the streets of Hollywood. He was already preparing his defense: I don't know what got into me, Officer. I'd like to plead guilty and go to jail for oh, a year or so, because I owe fifteen thousand, and there's this heartless kike and a nigger with a knife.

He looked around. There were no cops. In fact, there weren't too many people at all. Most had gotten tired of it. It wasn't much of a dog bite after all. Just some skinny guy making a big deal out of a little blood on his hand. What a bore. People went back to watching the various rings where the action was. Or to catch the locker room interviews of the victorious Raiders from Oakland.

"You okay, Philo?" the handler asked.

"Yeah."

"Better get a tetanus shot just to be sure."

"Yeah, thanks," said Philo Skinner as the handler went back to business.

Pattie Mae's nose was wrinkling. She kept backing up and finally bumped into the metal grooming table.

Then Philo smelled it. His shoes were a mess.

Vickie was trembling and whimpering in Pattie Mae's arms. The girl was stroking her, saying, "It's all right, sweetheart. It's all right."

Philo Skinner, criminal, suddenly wished he were a little dog and that a flower child would pick him up and cuddle him to her braless bosom telling him that everything would be all right. He figured Chester Biggs by now was leading a lynch mob across the arena floor. Philo was drenched in perspiration and stained by blood and dog shit. His hand was throbbing like his head. The whiskey he'd guzzled was rising up in his throat, causing his huge adam's apple to jerk around as he swallowed it back. The little schnauzer was staring at him with fear and fury in her eyes. There was only one thing Philo Skinner could do: He lit the seventy-second cigarette of the day. He stood and smoked. No blindfold, please. Bury me deep where the dogs can't dig. I'm Philo Skinner, Terrier King.

He was halfway through the cigarette when Pattie Mae said: "I just don't know what's wrong with the schnauzer, Mr. Skinner. She's acting so strange. Like she doesn't even know us. Gosh, this morning she was licking you and jumping around every time you came near her. What's wrong with her, Mr. Skinner? I think she's gone squirrelly or something."

"Squirrelly," he said. Smoking. Staring off in the distance. Wondering if convicts get to have pets. The Bird Man of Alcatraz. Maybe they'd make a movie about him, his cell full of terriers. It might not be so bad. A few years if he confessed. By then the gamblers would forget. Well, maybe he'd make something from the movie and he could pay them. Get out, start all over. The Dog Man of San Quentin . . .

"Mr. Skinner, you're so pale. I think you're going to faint from the shock of being bit! You better sit down. Do you think I should call a doctor? Sit down, Mr. Skinner."

Philo Skinner obeyed. He stepped woodenly over to his director's chair, sat, and smoked until the butt singed his calloused fingers. Pattie Mae put Vickie in Tutu's cage and said, "Mr. Skinner, since we're through for the day, do you think we could just load up and go home? Honest, I'm so tired I don't even want to stay for the end. I never thought I'd wanna leave early, but I'm so tired I just can't believe it. What a weird day!"

"A weird day."

"Can we go home, Mr. Skinner?"

"Go home."

"Yes, can we? Do you want me to go get the van?"

Philo Skinner looked around at the thinning crowd. The losers were already packing up to go. The bulk of the crowd would of course stay for the final judging, but a good many of the handlers who would not be part of it were folding up the exercise pens and grooming tables.

"Mr. Skinner, damn it, I think you're either in shock from that dog bite or you're tripping on that Colombia Gold. You wanna know the truth you're acting like a re-tard and I'm getting tired of it! Now you can fire me or not, but I'm going home! This is your last chance. Do you want me to get the van and help load up?"

"Get the van and help load up," Philo echoed, and Pattie Mae was off in an ankle-turning jog toward the parking lot.

When they were loading the dogs into the back of the van, Vickie began making a fuss. She started whimpering, and then she began to bark. It was a throaty, frightened bark at first. Then it got chesty and angry.

"Hush. You hush!" Pattie Mae said as they loaded the grooming table, exercise pens, and animals. "Hush now." And then: "Mr. Skinner, what's this schnauzer's name anyhow? You never did tell me. And I asked you ten times!"

"Name? Oh, that's Vic— Tu—" Jesus Christ, he'd almost forgotten he snatched Tutu too. Tutu too. Jesus! The schnauzer's name is Fred."

"Fred. A bitch named Fred?"

"How the hell should I know why they named a bitch Fred!" Philo was coming around, getting miserable and whiny again instead of catatonic. "It's probably short for Fredricka. Jesus Christ, I know lots of girls named Freddie. I know a guy named Shirley, for chrissake. Handles poodles. At least we call him Shirley, the stinking fag. Goddamnit, is it *my* fault they call her Fred? Let's get the hell outta here. I had enough dog shows to last a lifetime and I ain't woofing."

Fifteen minutes later he was saying good-bye to Pattie Mae in the parking lot.

"You did a great job today, honey," he said as she jumped out of the van and clonked over to her Volkswagen. "Here's a little thank you from Philo. Hope you didn't mean it about quitting. Think it over for a week."

A week. In a week he'd be following the sun and she could have Skinner Kennels, her and Mavis. Maybe before he left though he'd get one last chance to throw this little bitch his bone.

She looked at the five-dollar bill contemptuously. "I paid more than that for the grass you smoked up," she said. "Thanks a lot."

"Wait a minute, Pattie Mae," Philo whined. "I'm tapped right now. You just wait till your next paycheck. There's gonna be a little bonus in there from the boss. You won't be sorry. Just wait till next week. Meantime I'm gonna give you a call tomorrow night, talk about that dinner I promised you."

"Yeah, see you," she said, heading toward the beat-up Volkswagen.

"You wait till you get your check next week, sweetie!" Philo yelled. "Just wait."

Yeah. Wait till next week, he thought. I'll send you a fucking postcard with a dog on it. A chihuahua! Puerto Vallarta, get ready for Philo Skinner!

But Philo Skinner had one bit of unfinished business before the crime was consummated—the letter. He got it out of the glove compartment and checked it over. It was a lulu. Bits of newsprint glued to a piece of plain bond paper, just like in the movies. Only trouble is, he couldn't find names in the newspaper that worked out. He had smoked dozens of cigarettes and sat up until 3:00 a.m. trying to find something that had a *whit* in it. The goddamn L.A. *Times* should print something with a *whit* but they didn't. He found the *field* easy enough. Then he searched futilely for the word *bitch* in a family newspaper. Then he realized he had to cut one letter at a time.

Philo had worn rubber gloves when handling the extortion note. He was doing fine after he got past the *Mrs. Whitfield* except that he smoked a butt too far down as usual, and since the gloves had been soaked in rubbing alcohol which he used to swab a tick bite on a Lakeland terrier, he caught his hand on fire. Lucky for Philo Skinner the basin of foamy water was handy. For once Mavis' failure to clean up didn't rile him. The burning glove barely singed his fingers.

When he finally got the extortion note glued and trimmed and scrawled with crayon, it said:

> Mrs. Whitfield
> By now you know you do not have your bitch. Keep the bitch you have until you get orders from me. You will hear from me by phone. I will get your unlisted number by calling Biggs Kennels tomorrow and telling them I am your friend Richard. You will instruct them to give Richard your phone number. Do not say anything more to Biggs or to the police or you will not see your bitch alive.

The *Richard* was in honor of Richard Burton, whom Philo would do his best to imitate as a retired don in Puerto Vallarta. Wouldn't it be something if Richard Burton's villa was the one Philo finally settled in? Wouldn't *that* be something?

Everything was going just swell until he encountered the residue of the Super Bowl traffic pouring out of the inadequate access roads to the Rose Bowl in Pasadena. Philo almost got catatonic again when a Pasadena traffic policeman waved him to a stop when he entered the area of the Arroyo.

A cop! I'll come peaceably, Officer! I should have realized that crime doesn't pay!

"Can't you go around, buddy? Where you heading, Linda Vista?"

"Pardon?"

"I said, can't you go around? You trying to get up to Linda Vista?"

"Linda Vista."

"Well go around, buddy! Can't you see the traffic's backed up clear to the Bowl? Go around!"

And Philo went around, searching for the address in the dog show catalogue. He went around in a looping circle of ten miles. Philo Skinner ended up on the Ventura Freeway, got off, doubled back, got lost in Glendale, back on the freeway. He rechecked her address, looked at his street map of Pasadena, and was on and off the freeway three more times until he found the Mediterranean mansion.

Philo parked a hundred yards down the road near a score of Canary Island pine trees. Then, after looking in both directions, he moved along the stucco wall and past a wall of oleander, stopping every few seconds to listen for voices or footsteps. Nothing but birds, and sprinklers spraying vast lawns. Nothing but white oaks, pines and eucalyptus. Then he was at the iron gate. Philo stopped, looked both ways again, and broke into a lung-searing lope straight for the front door where he threw the letter. He scuttled back down the driveway, but after fifty yards he stopped. Philo coughed, gagged up a chunk of black phlegm and skulked back to the front door. He picked up the letter, glancing over his shoulder fearfully, and wiped the letter under sweaty armpits to remove fingerprints.

Two minutes later, looking as though he'd run a marathon, he was wheezing, creaking, gasping toward the waiting van where Vickie howled. She knew where she was. Her howls were heartbreaking even to Philo Skinner.

"Please shut up," he begged. "You'll be home in a few days. Please shut your trap. Philo won't hurt you."

Madeline was laughing and chatting with her friends and well-wishers, waiting in unbearable anticipation for the last stages of the competition.

"Mrs. Whitfield." Chester Biggs' face was gray.

"Yes, Chester."

"You better come. Vickie's sick."

Madeline Whitfield's nightmare began when she tore her panty hose and cut her leg stumbling down the steps of the grandstand. She didn't remember running with Chester Biggs, banging through the crowds, bumping the stands of concessionaires, almost knocking a photographer on the seat of her pants as she was snapping a Pomeranian bitch for a proud owner who would pay anything to get *her* picture in a dog magazine and to hell with the bitch. It's every girl for herself.

The schnauzer looked as though she were dying. Madeline gasped and picked her up from the grooming table against the advice of a veterinarian Biggs had found.

"Vickie, Vickie! Oh, Vickie!"

"I think this animal's been drugged," the veterinarian said. He put his hand on Madeline Whitfield's arm as she held the schnauzer against her face and cried, "Oh, Vickie! Vickie!"

"Ma'am, I think somebody's drugged your animal."

"That's impossible!" Chester Biggs said. "How could anybody drug Vickie? I've been right here. Right here all the . . ." Then he looked at the kennel boy with the skin magazine sticking out of the back pocket of his jeans. "That's impossible!" he repeated, thinking about the lawsuit she might slap on him. I'll kill that pimply little son of a bitch! thought Chester Biggs.

The schnauzer's eyes were glassy and heavy lidded. She was gasping for breath. Her tongue hung to the side frighteningly. Madeline hardly recognized her.

"The animal's a bit better than she was five minutes ago," the veterinarian said. "I think she's going to be all right."

The kennel boy was already retreating from Chester Biggs, who looked like an English bulldog as he walked toward the horny kid with the magazine, and said, "Come here, Junior, I want to *talk* to you."

Fifteen minutes later, the schnauzer was being rushed by Chester Biggs to Madeline's veterinarian in San Marino, who had been called from home and was in his office prepared to work on the bitch. Chester Biggs had one passing thought while speeding up the Pasadena Freeway. The schnauzer looked different. Almost as though the furnishings were . . . well, it must be her condition. She whined and squirmed around the floor of the crate.

Madeline Whitfield was sent home by the veterinarian, who suggested she see her doctor for a tranquilizer of her own. She wasn't in any condition to drive, and was taken home by the pimply kennel kid. He drove Madeline's Cadillac Fleetwood like it was a hearse, and spoke not a word.

The kid was wondering if he should take a bus clear out of the state. It wasn't *his* fault. It was that yawning fur on the broads in that magazine! But before the pimply kid went pushing, he saw the envelope on the doorstep. It had big newsprint letters stuck on it. It said: ''Urgent.''

''Mrs. Whitfield,'' he said, as Madeline fumbled with her keys and dropped them.

''Thank you. Thank you. Oh, I'm sorry.'' She started dropping keys again.

''Mrs. Whitfield, this letter must be for you. It says urgent.''

''Urgent.''

''Mrs. Whitfield, give me the keys. I'll open the door.''

Three minutes later the pimply kid was high stepping down the road, jumping in the bushes every time a car came by that might contain the murderous dog handler, Chester Biggs.

It took Madeline three minutes to get the letter opened. She was literally bouncing off the walls. There were a good number of chairs, couches, settees in this part of the mansion yet Madeline couldn't seem to find a place to sit. Finally she sat at the kitchen table. She was holding the envelope in her hand, but she was so numb she didn't know what to do. She might not have opened the envelope were it not for Philo Skinner's criminal training at Saturday matinees. The bizarre bits of newsprint brought her around enough to tear it open. She had to smoothe it out on the kitchen table. Two of the *b*'s had come unglued and were lying upside down on the table. Coincidentally, both *b*'s were in the word *bitch*. The first sentence read: ''By now you know you do not have your itch. Keep the itch you have until you get orders from me.''

Madeline began sobbing brokenly. She couldn't understand why someone would send an advertisement about *the itch* in newsprint. Madison Avenue! She was succumbing to hysteria and they wanted her to use their vaginal lotion! Oh, God!

Then the *Biggs Kennels* caught her eye. She got her sobbing under control and started reading from the beginning. She screamed and refused to answer the door when Chester Biggs arrived. It seemed as though he rang for fifteen minutes. Then a short time later the phone rang.

''Mrs. Whitfield!''

''Yes?''

''This is Chester, Mrs. Whitfield. I rang the bell for . . . You didn't answer.''

''No.''

''Mrs. Whitfield, I want to come up and see you.''

''How is she?'' Madeline said and she sounded calm to Chester Biggs.

''I'm *so* sorry, Mrs. Whitfield. She died. Vickie just died!''

There was silence on the line and he said, ''Mrs. Whitfield, I'd better come to see you. Right now. Are you all right? Do you want . . .''

''No, Chester,'' she said, staring at the extortion note, reading it word for word again as he spoke.

''Let me come see you, Mrs. Whitfield. I . . .''

''No, Chester, don't come. I'm all right,'' she said, wiping her runny nose, carefully placing the ugly letter back in the ugly envelope.

"He thinks it was a tranquilizer. Somebody didn't want Vickie to win. Some filthy devil wanted to win badly enough to . . . Maybe it was poison, I just don't know. There'll be an autopsy here and he'll send samples to a lab. I think I should call the police, don't you?"

"No!" she shouted in the mouthpiece causing Chester Biggs' ear to pop. When he stopped grimacing he said, "Why not, Mrs. Whitfield?"

"Vickie is mine. *Was* mine. It's not up to *you,* Chester. I don't want to call the police. If somebody wanted to win so badly as to give Vickie a drug, or poison, or whatever it was, so be it. She's not the first dog to be poisoned at a dog show and it's just pointless to cause more pain to ourselves by having policemen around."

"Whatever you say, Mrs. Whitfield, but sleep on it."

"I'll sleep on it."

"Maybe you'll feel different tomorrow."

"Perhaps, but I forbid you to call the police."

"Okay, Mrs. Whitfield. Well, you try to rest yourself."

"Chester."

"Yes."

"One thing. I was contacted at the show by someone who wants . . . wants a picture of Vickie for a magazine. His name is . . . Richard something. I forgot to give him my phone number, but he knows you're Vickie's handler. He may call you tomorrow. Give . . . give him my phone number." And then she began to weep. He didn't understand a word she said from then on.

"Okay, Mrs. Whitfield. I . . . well, good night, Mrs. Whitfield. I'm real sorry. The doctor's gonna keep Vickie here until you decide tomorrow how to, whether to bury Vickie or let him take care of it for you. Good night, Mrs. Whitfield."

"Wait!" she said.

"What is it, Mrs. Whitfield?"

"I *don't* want any autopsy. You bring Vickie home to me right now."

"Jesus, Mrs. Whitfield, don't do that. She's dead. She . . ."

"Chester, I want her home now. You bring her. I'll call a pet mortuary and arrange for the burial. I want you to bring her body home. Now."

It was nearly midnight before Madeline Whitfield summoned the courage to examine the cardboard carton Chester Biggs had placed on the dining room table.

When she touched the little body wrapped in the white towel, it wasn't as rigid and cold as she anticipated. And she saw almost at once that the dead schnauzer was not Victoria.

Tutu's heart and respiratory system had been overwhelmed by the drug at the end. She had died in pain, gasping for air. Her eyes drooped and the lower jaw jutted forward in the last spasm. With her whiskers and eyeshades soaked and plastered down, and with her lower jaw jutting, she looked like a little bull mastiff.

9

The Black Marble

Monday morning was very tough for Valnikov. It was even tougher for Captan Hooker, who, like Valnikov, had a devastating headache. But whereas Valnikov's headache came from a raging vodka hangover, Captain Hooker's came from problems with his troops. And it was those problems which possibly saved Valnikov's police career for the moment.

When Valnikov came shuffling into the squad room, Captain Hooker was sitting in his office with Clarence Cromwell and staring in disbelief at Montezuma Montez and Rocco Bambarella. Rocco was called Bullets Bambarella after a gas station holdup in which a robber fired eight shots at him and missed. They found an outline of 9 mm. bullet holes in the wall around Rocco Bambarella. It was only his slow reflexes that saved him. Any man with normal reaction time would have jumped left or right and been killed on the spot. Rocco Bambarella, who shot no worse than anyone else in combat situations, also emptied his gun, missed all six, but saved the day by throwing a full quart of 20w engine oil that coldcocked the bad guy and earned Rocco a commendation and something a policeman cherishes much more—a macho nickname. He was Bullets Bambarella forever.

Valnikov managed a smile and said, "Good morning, Natalie. Did you have a nice weekend?"

"Morning," she said, dropping her eyes nervously.

But Valnikov was in no condition to detect body language. He lumbered to his table and sat down, sorting through the mound of weekend burglary reports.

Natalie could hear them all hollering, especially Bullets, who said, "Look, Captain Hooker, I don't care if that Chinaman *does* sue Montezuma here . . ."

"Me!" the Chicano cop interrupted. "Why say Montezuma! I wasn't there with you!"

"You wasn't there with me?" said Bullets Bambarella in disbelief.

"Bullets, git your shit together!" Clarence Cromwell bellowed in total exasperation. "He *wasn't* there with you! You was there with two bluesuits! There was no other detective there!"

"He gave me the tip!" Bullets argued. "Montezuma, *you* gave me the information from *your* snitch . . ."

"*My* snitch! It was an anonymous call!"

"You're just protectin your snitch!" Bullets shot back.

"Please, please!" Captain Hooker begged, feeling the pain shooting across his forehead. Then he looked up at the aging black detective, standing just to the right of him. "Clarence, you're Bullets' supervisor. Can't *you* resolve this so we don't get another lawsuit? The commander said he's never heard of a detective division with so many lawsuits."

"You bring in these fuzz-nutted kids, you git lawsuits is what you git," Clarence snorted. "I told you, Bullets, you wanna play supercop, you and Montezuma and all these young hotdogs, you go work metro or surveillance or some fuckin glory job. You *don't* work divisional detectives!"

"Jesus, Clarence, lemme just explain my side," Bullets whined, since they all knew that Captain Hooker had spent the weekend on Clarence Cromwell's yacht and was unofficially only the bosun around here. "See, Clarence," Bullets explained, "I figured Montezuma gave me straight shit about this Chinaman runnin a printin press for bad checks in the back of his restaurant."

"Bad checks in the back of a Cantonese restaurant," Captain Hooker said vacantly, running his delicate fingers through his sparse gray hair. "Deputy Chief Lichtenwalter's *favorite* Cantonese restaurant."

"Well, anyways," Bullets continued, a bit more uneasy with this latest piece of intelligence. "I wanted to check it out so I called for a few reinforcements."

"Reinforcements," Captain Hooker said.

"And we was staked out in the back by the kitchen where they're throwin all these slimy duck skins out the door. Hit Butch Janowski right in the hat with one, he was hidin behind a trash can." Bullets stopped to laugh at the thought of Officer Butch Janowski getting a greasy duck skin right on his bean. Until he saw nobody else was even smiling. "And then we listen and we listen," he continued soberly.

"You don't work forgery detail," Captain Hooker reminded Bullets, who was starting to perspire.

"I know, Cap, but I thought, Jesus, a Chink printin hot checks there! Well, it sounded like a big caper. So I listen and I hear clickety-click-click."

"Clickety-click-click!" Captain Hooker said, pained.

"Sure!" Bullets explained. "You see, I figure it's a printin press printin up some bad checks. Clickety-click-click. So, bang!"

"Bang," said Captain Hooker.

"I just took positive police action and . . . and I booted the door and it fell right in on this Chink dishwasher, and he does a whoop-dee-doo into the sink and breaks a few . . . well, *several* dishes. And egg rolls and fortune cookies start flyin around and all, and uh, this old Chink that owns the place starts screamin and holdin his chest like he's havin a fit . . ."

"Or a heart attack," said Captain Hooker.

"Yeah, but it wasn't no heart attack, Boss," Bullets said. "It was more a fit, I would say."

"And his lawyer just hung up," Captain Hooker said very quietly, looking ever more like a pale Victorian headmaster. "And his lawyer says two million dollars."

"Two million bucks," said Bullets. "What's that mean?"

"It just means he's suing the city for two million dollars," said Captain Hooker, who startled everyone by suddenly standing and staring at Bullets with glittering eyes and shrieking: "BECAUSE YOU LITERALLY SCARED THE LIVING SHIT OUT OF THE OLD CHINAMAN!"

"Easy, Cap," said Clarence Cromwell, gently placing Captain Hooker back in his chair and squeezing his shoulders reassuringly. "Easy, Boss, it's gonna be okay. Easy does it."

"But I'm retiring in a matter of weeks!" Captain Hooker cried. "You *know* I can't take this kind of tension, Clarence!"

"Easy, Skipper, easy," said Clarence, massaging Captain Hooker's shoulders, which helped the headache a bit. And then Clarence said to Bullets: "I hear those old silky pajamas the Chinaman was wearing really *was* full a shit, Bullets. Butch Janowski told me."

"Hangin right to his knees," Bullets said proudly. Until he looked at Captain Hooker's demented stare again.

"Tell me, Bullets," said Clarence Cromwell, "what was the clickety-click-click sound if it wasn't a printin press makin bad checks?"

"It was a lunch break," the muscular young detective said sheepishly.

"A lunch break."

"All those Chinamen was eatin and clickin their chopsticks against their rice bowls. Jeez, it sounded *just like* a printin press makin bad . . ."

"Jam on outta here, Bullets," Clarence Cromwell warned, seeing the insane stare forming in Captain Hooker's eyes.

"Is it gonna be okay?" Bullets whined.

"You guys jist go back to work," Clarence Cromwell said, but he winked subtly, and Bullets breathed a sigh of relief and jammed on out of there.

Natalie Zimmerman thought it was her turn when Bullets Bambarella came out of Hipless Hooker's office glaring at Montezuma Montez, who was giving Bullets a screw-you-too look.

Bullets Bambarella suddenly said icily, "I hear you was at the weight machine the other day braggin how you could pick up the whole station."

"You heard that, huh?" said Montezuma just as icily.

"Bet you couldn't even shoulder press your own weight," said Bullets.

"You got five bucks?" said Montezuma Montez, getting the attention of all the boys and girls who loved macho contests.

"I got *ten* bucks that says *I* can shoulder press my weight," said Bullets.

"All that macaroni you eat? I oughtta make it fifteen bucks," Montezuma grinned at Dudley Knebel of the robbery detail.

"All those tortillas you eat? I oughtta make it *twenty* bucks," Bullets Bambarella grinned at Valnikov of the burglary detail, whose hangover was such that he didn't even know what the two young detectives were talking about.

So while half the squad room got up and followed the two buffaloes into the locker room, Natalie Zimmerman went to see Hipless Hooker and tell him what she had discovered on Friday.

She had gone sleepless last night, deciding to tell, not to tell, to tell. Finally, she knew she *had* to tell. She would have to tell even if he weren't her partner. Even if someone else were stuck with him and she was set free. Because he carried a badge. He carried a gun. He was a sergeant in the Los Angeles Police Department, assigned to Hollywood Investigative Division. And he was insane.

"You're next, Natalie," Clarence Cromwell said.

Goddamn! Clarence Cromwell was actually massaging Hooker's neck when she entered!

"What's your problem today, Natalie?" Captain Hooker sighed, and Natalie looked at Hipless Hooker relaxing under the hands of his sea captain, and she knew there'd be no chance. Still, she tried. "Captain, can I see you *privately?*"

"Oh, God, Natalie!" Captain Hooker said, not opening his eyes. "Do you have a problem too? Do you know how little time I have before I retire and how many problems are stacking up? A little to the left, Clarence."

"It's about Valnikov, Captain," Natalie said, glaring at Clarence Cromwell. "This little experiment of letting him work with a policewoman isn't going to work out. In fact . . ."

"Gud-damn, Natalie!" Clarence interrupted, stopping the massage of Hipless Hooker, who opened his eyes and sipped his coffee and dreamed of being back on Clarence's yacht, cruising into Avalon Harbor, catching fat sea bass and albacore. The Channel Islands. The serene Pacific. Maybe a sailfish. His wife hundreds of miles away in Van Nuys. Landlocked!

"Well, I gave it a try, Captain," Natalie said, "but it isn't going to work out and I have something important to tell you. About Valnikov."

"Yes, yes, what is it?" Hooker said, leafing through the papers on his desk.

"He's crazy," she said simply.

"Yes, what else?" Captain Hooker said absently.

"What else?"

"For God's sake, what's the problem?" Captain Hooker finally demanded.

"I just told you. He's crazy. Bats. Whacko. Do you understand? I'm not saying zany, balmy, or goofy. I'm saying he's psycho. A mental case. Bugs. Loony. A candidate for a pension, a gold retirement badge, and a canvas blazer with wraparound arms!"

"That is the dumbest gud-damn statement I ever heard you make, Natalie," Clarence Cromwell said, coming around and sitting on Hooker's desk, totally blocking him from view, letting Natalie know with whom she must deal in *this* room.

"Clarence, you don't really know Valnikov!"

"What the hell you mean? I worked downtown at robbery-homicide for years and . . ."

"You don't know him *now*. I tell you he's gone nuts. For *real*."

Captain Hooker was trying to listen, but he suddenly found a document on his desk which caused him great displeasure. "Bambarella!" he yelled, forgetting the door was closed, causing Clarence Cromwell to leap from the desk.

"Problem, Captain?"

"Bullets was driving one of our cars sixty miles an hour!"

"But, Skipper," Clarence reminded him. "The speed limit's fifty-five. That's only five miles over. Sixty miles an hour ain't too bad."

"In a subterranean garage?"

"Listen, Captain," Natalie Zimmerman said testily, "you just gotta hear me out on this Valnikov matter."

"Natalie, please!" Captain Hooker said. "Get to the point!"

"You only worked with him one day," Clarence Cromwell said. "He's a little quiet and standoffish, and you say he's gone round the bend. Okay, name *one* crazy thing he did."

"It's not that easy, Clarence. It's a combination of . . ."

"*One* thing," Clarence challenged. "Just one is all I ask."

"One thing?"

"*One* thing."

"Okay, one thing is he said he was going to make a Christmas dinner when we parted on Friday. I believe you'll notice that today is January tenth."

Clarence Cromwell chewed on that one for a moment, then he started giggling. "Well, I'll be gud-damned! Is *that* all it is? Jist sit yourself down and wait a minute, Natalie. I wanna check on somethin."

Natalie was greatly relieved to see Clarence Cromwell charge out the door. Now was her chance to get through to Hooker, if she could get him to stop reading the reports on his desk.

"Captain, there were *lots* of things. Little things. It's hard to get specific. You just put them all together and they spell nut. N-u-t."

"Yes," he said, looking up for a fleeting instant. "I know Valnikov is strange, that's why we put you with him. But, Natalie, really, can't you just work with him for a little while longer . . . God, look at this! Bambarella gets stopped by the security guard while he's speeding around the subterranean garage of an apartment house chasing some blonde in a convertible, and the security guard sees his shoulder holster and says are you a cop and Bambarella says, quote, no asshole, I'm a member of the cozy nostra! End quote. Oh, God! The cozy nostra!"

"Captain, you've got to listen to . . ."

But it was too late. His head was hurting too much. And Clarence Cromwell came flying through the door triumphantly. He slammed the door and said, "Natalie, do you know what last Friday was?"

"It was January seventh. What the hell do you mean?"

"I mean it was only January seventh to *you!* To him it was Christmas! It was Russian Christmas! *Now* how do you feel?"

"For heaven's sake," Captain Hooker said, actually smiling a little, another crisis averted. "Is *that* all it was! Natalie, why don't you just go to work now . . ."

"I don't give a goddamn if it *was* Russian Christmas. That wasn't the only thing."

"Yes, well, Natalie, this is very juvenile for an officer of your years and experience. I just . . . God, I've got a headache, Clarence!"

"I'll get you some aspirin, Cap," Clarence said, glaring at Natalie Zimmerman, who was looking at her Friz, pushing her oversized glasses back up on her nose. "I'll git you some aspirin, Captain, after Natalie goes back to work with her *partner,* Valnikov."

"Yes, yes," Captain Hooker said. "Look, I know you don't like burglary detail and you don't like Valnikov, but try to get along for a while. And if there's any evidence of, oh, bizarre behavior, report to me and we'll take further action. But do some investigating first, Natalie. Russian Christmas. God! Don't make rash accusations, please! I've got *enough* trouble!"

Clarence Cromwell started massaging the neck of the captain again, while he stared Natalie Zimmerman out of the office.

When Natalie returned to the squad room, Valnikov was sitting, drinking his third cup of tea. Why did he have to drink tea? Why couldn't he drink coffee like every other goddamn cop in the station? She plopped down in the chair beside him in utter frustration and looked at the tea bag on the saucer. She looked at Valnikov.

His eyes were red and watery. He wore the same necktie Clarence Cromwell had loaned him. He'd changed his suit from Friday. This one was gray, but even so, it looked just like the other. He *never* looked any different. Watery bloodshot eyes. A faint boozy smell early in the morning. Hair growing every which way, sometimes stuck down by a wet combing, sometimes springing up in a clump of cinnamon cowlicks. He was smiling amiably, that dumb patient smile. Natalie could think of only one thing at the moment. She said, "Valnikov, do you mind opening your suitcoat?"

"Pardon me, Natalie?"

"I said, would you please just unbutton your coat, and hold it open?"

"Of course," he shrugged. "If you're afraid that I forgot my gun, no, I'm very careful about such things."

She reached over and flipped open the coat. As she suspected, the inside pocket was repaired like the other suit, not with thread but metal staples.

"I figured."

"Figured?"

"That you'd do all your tailoring with the stapler here on your desk."

"I'm going to sew it. I've been meaning to do that, in fact."

"Doesn't matter," she sighed. "Except you couldn't pass through a scanner to get on an airplane. Not with all the metal you have holding your clothes together."

"Are we taking a flight somewhere?" asked the detective, blinking his watery eyes in confusion. "An extradition or something?"

I'm taking a flight, you dingaling, Natalie Zimmerman thought. I'm flying right over Hipless Hooker's head to the area commander, if I have to. And you're taking a flight right to the police department psychologist. Then she got a pang of remorse as she thought of his heavy body shielding her, keeping her from being hit by flying lead when William Allen Livingston exploded. But goddamnit, he's crazy!

"I've got all our reports logged, Natalie," Valnikov smiled, belatedly realizing she had been joking about the airplane. "I saw you had business with the captain so I got everything taken care of. We can go out in the field now if you like. We've just got one body in jail."

"Let's go see him, get it over with." She sighed.

"Okay, let's handle our case." He smiled.

You handle the case. I'll handle another case; she thought. And from that moment, as Valnikov was nearing what would be his most important case, Natalie Zimmerman decided that *her* case, the only case with which *she* would be concerned, was the case against Sergeant A. M. Valnikov. She was on her own investigation. And she would bring them irrefutable proof. The detective was not eccentric, not a "bit strange." The detective was mad.

Just before they got out the door, Clarence Cromwell came laughing out of Hipless Hooker's office and handed Natalie Zimmerman a burglary report. "Here's another one, jist came in, Nat! Somebody stole eighty-three pounds a bat guano from a store in your area!"

"So what's funny?"

"The captain asks me, he says, Clarence, we got a fertilizer store that big in Hollywood? I mean eighty-three *pounds* a bat guano? I say, no, Cap, it ain't no big company or nothin. It's jist some fly-by-night outfit!"

Clarence had to lean against the door, ready to collapse. Even Hipless Hooker had his head on his arms, laughing uproariously. They were in a good mood now from talking about the Channel Island voyage next weekend.

Valnikov didn't get it until Clarence turned and screamed: "Bat guano! Fly-by-night outfit! Git it?"

Then Valnikov got it, and while Natalie Zimmerman talked to her Friz, Valnikov chuckled politely.

The body they had in Central Jail belonged to Bernie Mitchell, better known all over Hollywood Station as "Itchy Mitch." So called, because he broke out in hives every time he got busted for a felony, which was, they said, only in the months with *r*'s in them. Itchy Mitch went to jail a lot all right, but since he only stole cars he seldom got more than a few months of county jail time. As a matter of fact, Itchy Mitch only decided to switch to burglary because he was afraid some judge might finally send him to state prison. He had been told that burglary, like auto theft, rarely drew a state prison term, unless you had lots of priors. Itchy Mitch had no prior arrests for burglary, so he decided he might be able to get busted four or five times without getting some judge mad at him.

He was making Natalie itch just looking at him across the table in the jail interrogation room. He was six feet two and weighed less than Natalie, who weighed in very nicely for five feet nine. He had a long fringe of brown hair and only fuzz on top. He was broken out in hives on his arms and neck and on his fuzzy skull. His filthy white dress shirt was torn open from all the scratching. He was sitting across the table from Valnikov and Natalie, looking from one to the other. Both hands were moving ceaselessly. Scratching.

Itchy Mitch scratched his neck, his sunken chest, his back as far up as he could reach, deep in both armpits, his legs. He wanted desperately to scratch his balls, but in deference to Natalie, he didn't. Then he started all over again: the neck, his chest, both armpits . . .

"Never shoulda got hooked up with the broad, Sergeant. Never shoulda," Itchy Mitch whined after they advised him of his constitutional rights, for perhaps the eighty-third time in his life.

"What broad?" Natalie asked mechanically, not really caring what broad. Valnikov had his case to work on, she had hers.

"Always a broad gets an honest man in trouble, Sergeant. Always a broad," said Itchy Mitch, scratching.

"Do you want to talk about the warehouse you were arrested in?" Valnikov asked.

"Shoulda stuck to being a used-car salesman, Sergeant," said Itchy Mitch, reaching clear down to his raw ankles. "Great job, great job. Then one day I'm sitting there looking at this limper. And I done it."

"Limper?" said Natalie, scratching.

"You know, a lemon, a dog. This lousy lemon we took in trade on a Buick. I'm sitting there thinking, who'd miss it? It's just growing hair. A bum stove and organ. Phony white shoes."

"I don't really get it, Mitch," said Valnikov, scratching.

"What?"

"Stove and organ? White shoes?"

"Radio and heater, Sergeant! And whitewalls!"

"Oh, well don't get mad, Mitch, I never worked auto theft detail," Valnikov apologized.

"So I drive it off to Arizona, but I never get there. I just picked the black marble. All my life I pick the black marble. Why me?" he demanded, reminding Valnikov of Natalie, the way he rolled his eyes back. "Why *me?*

"About the warehouse, Mitch," Natalie prodded, scratching.

"So I'm on my way to unload this limper in Arizona and I decide to stop at a carwash cause I got my girlfriend and I don't want her riding in no dirty car. Imagine that! Sadie's so cruddy I oughtta have *her* washed and polished and I'm worrying about mud on those phony whitewalls. Then up walks a spade, six feet thirteen or something, big moustache hanging down his mouth. I say who's this, Genghis Coon? He tells me who he is, all right. A cop! A goddamn detective, works that bad-cat auto theft detail. Puts the arm on me and I'm in the slammer and my boss won't believe I was just test driving it. All heart, my boss. That lemon wasn't worth five hundred bucks!"

"Uh, can you tell me what that's got to do with this burglary?" Valnikov asked.

"Huh? You don't get it?" Mitch said, scratching.

"I don't get it," said Valnikov, scratching.

"Sergeant, I had to get some money to pay the fine for the auto theft conviction! What the hell could I do? And I get caught inside the warehouse on my first try. That just goes to show I'm no burglar. Any kind a half-ass creeper could burgle a warehouse, for chrissake! Do they send burglars to state prison?"

"Not very often, Mitch," said Valnikov, making his last notes on Itchy Mitch's confession.

"That's *some* consolation," said Mitch to Natalie, who had an unbearable itch under her bra strap.

As they were escorting him back to the jailer, Itchy Mitch turned, scratching, and said: "One thing, Sergeant. You been around this world awhile. Tell me something."

"If I can, Mitch," said Valnikov, unbuttoning his collar and loosening his tie to get at an itch on his collarbone.

" Why do some people *always* have to pick the black marble?"

Unlike the violent Friday, Natalie Zimmerman found this Monday to be a typical detective's workday, which meant that ninety percent of the day was spent writing reports like a good bureaucrat. Just filing one count of second-degree burglary on Itchy Mitch took four hours, what with cooling their heels downtown in the district attorney's office, along with twenty other detectives. Valnikov was good at waiting. Natalie was miserable. She read the newspaper all the way through. She read every dumb magazine that was lying around, even the sports and girlie magazines one of the cretins had in his briefcase. She paced the halls, smoked, passed some time with another policewoman from Hollenbeck Division.

Whenever she'd return, Valnikov would just be sitting there like a dozing grizzly. He'd open his eyes from time to time for a pleasant nod of the head and a "Good morning" to any detectives who spoke to him, and go back into hibernation.

After the waiting room thinned out, when there were only two other detectives there, both of them nodding in their chairs, Valnikov began to whimper in his sleep. Natalie glanced up from her newspaper at her snoozing partner. He was sweating. Then he started whimpering so loudly he awakened another detective who looked at him and at Natalie and shrugged. Then Valnikov started to *sob*.

It was the rabbit. The wounded rabbit cringing in the snow. The snow, the land, stretchcd to eternity. Siberia. The hunter's veiny hands slashed the rabbit's throat and gutted him with two swipes of his blade glinting in the frosty sunlight. The rabbit's body jerked around on the log while the hunter pulled the guts out and broke its jaws and pulled on the face until the face was peeled back over the skull. The muscle and tissue hissed as it tore free in the powerful hands of the hunter.

"Valnikov!" She was shaking him.

"The rabbit!"

"What?"

"Natalie."

"Yes, you were sleeping. Having a nightmare or something."

"I was?" Both of the other detectives, strangers to Valnikov, were sitting straight in their chairs staring at him.

"Yes, you were . . . well, you were crying. Sort of."

"That's impossible," Valnikov said, reaching for his handkerchief with hands that trembled. "Impossible."

He wiped his face and was grateful when the receptionist said, "Valnikov and Zimmerman, Mr. Holman is available."

When they were back in their car, bound for Hollywood, Valnikov realized it was lunchtime. "Where would you like to eat today, Natalie?" he smiled.

"I don't care," she said.

It had been a quiet ride. That sobbing. He was crazy and had to be taken off the street, but God, that *sobbing* in his sleep. "Wherever you want to eat, Valnikov. It's up to you."

"Really?" he smiled. She hadn't been so kind to him since they'd been together. How long had it been? He had to stop and think for a moment. A week? Then he realized that it only seemed that long because Friday was the first day and the weekend intervened. The weekend. Lots of drinking this weekend. Stolichnaya. He had to watch that drinking. Some people might think he was an alcoholic.

"Where the hell are you going?" she asked as he suddenly wheeled off the outbound Hollywood Freeway and headed back toward downtown.

"You said we could eat anywhere today," Valnikov smiled. "If it's okay with you I'll take you somewhere a little different."

"Different?"

"You might like it," Valnikov said, looking a bit worried now. "Don't expect too much. It isn't much really. Just something I like to do for lunch from time to time."

"All right, Valnikov, all right," she sighed. "Anything's better than McDonald's. I can't look another Big Mac in the eye."

"Charlie Lightfoot," he murmured. They always said old Charlie Lightfoot was so cranky in the morning the only thing in the world he didn't hate was an Egg McMuffin. Charlie Lightfoot.

"Who's Charlie Lightfoot?" Natalie said.

"Why did you say that, Natalie?" He was stunned.

"Why did I say *what?*"

"I was just thinking about Charlie Lightfoot, and you said his name! That's amazing! Like a psychic . . ."

"Valnikov, you *said* his name!"

"No, I was just *thinking* about old Charlie Lightfoot and . . ."

"And you mumbled Charlie Lightfoot. Jesus Christ!"

"I did?"

Then he started looking alarmed. Like when she'd shaken him awake from his dream. A bull of a man like this. Frightened. She *had* to get evidence. For his own good as well as the police department's. It wasn't just for herself. "I sometimes mutter and mumble, too, when I'm thinking hard about something," she said. "It's no big thing."

"But I wasn't even thinking hard," he said, turning down Spring Street. "I just thought about old Charlie Lightfoot. He was my partner for years at homicide."

"Did you like it there, Valnikov?" she asked, offering him a cigarette as he drove ever cautiously through the heavy downtown traffic, blinking into the smog-filtered sunshine.

"I seldom smoke," he said. Then he thought about her question and said, "Well, I liked homicide work all right. I liked it okay. There's the prestige. You know, everybody thinks you're the varsity if you work homicide downtown. It was okay sometimes. Charlie Lightfoot was the best partner I ever had." Then he added, "Of course *we'll* be good partners, I'm sure, Natalie."

"Why did they . . . *you* decide to transfer to Hollywood dicks?" she asked suddenly.

"Well, I . . . I . . ." He didn't like that question. That was something that scared him lately. If he didn't like a question, if it troubled him, he couldn't quite get the handle. He wasn't even sure what she'd said. There was the murky picture again. All the sparkly shapes, something like a déjà vu experience. Something . . . something was there! If it would only take shape among the sparkly dots from the flashbulbs. If he could just see it once. And then it started to fade, as always. Come back. I almost had you that time!

Charlie Lightfoot. He had been a good partner. The best. A quiet man like Valnikov. Like Valnikov, years with a bad marriage. But a wife who hated him instead of one who drank and played. A child who drifted away. Strange, how they grow and drift and lose their respect for their fathers. The ancient inherited shame of fathers and sons. A good partner. The hardest single logistical task of police work. Find that partner. That good partner you can live with. Then keep him. Especially a homicide detective.

He hadn't answered her question about the transfer. Natalie was turned in her seat staring at him. She knew he had lost his direction. She knew he was somewhere else. Driving, just driving.

"Do you still see Charlie Lightfoot?" Natalie asked quietly. How do you make notes on this? What do you tell the captain? Did he have to go berserk before they'd believe her?

He was driving aimessly. He'd lost his sense of direction. His whole life in this city and he was lost.

"Tell me about Charlie Lightfoot," she said carefully.

He turned east on Fifth Street and looked at the sign as though he'd never been there. Then he said, "Charlie was old for his age. Twenty-six years on the job when he pulled the pin and went to Arizona. He bought a trailer there by the big river. Charlie was some kind of detective, though."

"What could he do, Valnikov? Tell me about him. What could he do that you admired?"

"Admired," Valnikov said. And now he was looking vague and confused, as confused as when he had awakened from the dream. He was starting to perspire. She noted that. She would remember when she went to the commander. When she described his symptoms to the department psychologist.

"Charlie could get through it all better than anyone," Valnikov said. "Better than me. Do you know how many calls you get from policemen? From the bluesuits and even from soft clothes guys? Do you know how many murders they discover that aren't murders at all?"

"No. How many?"

"Lots. A vice cop finds an encyclopedia salesman dead in a motel room when they're staked out on a whore. He's lying on his back across the bed. His head is down to the floor. There's a pile of blood under his head. The carpet can't soak it all up."

"A pile of blood," Natalie said quietly.

He turned south on Wall Street and unbuttoned his collar.

It's a pile of blood, all right. It's coagulating and you'd need a shovel to pick it up. There's a crimson stalactite growing from his nose to the shovelful of blood beneath him. The vice cop is jumpy and excited. He's discovered a murder victim. Should we call the press, Sergeant? Latent prints specialists? The captain?

No. No press. No prints men. No captain. No murder.

No murder? But, Sergeant. The blood! He's been beaten! Or shot! I didn't touch him. There must be a bullet wound!

No bullet wound. No shot. No murder. And then Chariie Lightfoot found the empty vial under the bed. He had probably told the doctor he needed his prescription refilled for his nerves. The prescription was one day old. His nerves wouldn't bother him anymore. He's swallowed, let's see, forty caps. That's almost two hundred milligrams, right? What did he wash it down with? Ah, yes. Here it is, Charlie. The glass is under the pillow.

But the blood! Sergeant, the blood . . .

. . . is from his nose. See the crimson stalactite? See it ooze and shine in the flashlight beam? There. It's coagulated from his nostril down to the shovelful of waxen blood on the floor. When he lost consciousness he fell back. His head's touching the floor. The blood begins draining, draining, draining. He's a white man but his face turns biack. The blood has no where to go. It's draining, draining. Finally the blood does what it must, it burst through his nose.

But, Sergeant! His face, all dark and swollen. I found him belly up. He looks like a . . . like a . . .

The encyclopedia salesman took with him to eternity the face of a turtle.

Are you sure. Sergeant? It's not a murder? The pile of blood?

No, son, it's the law of gravity.

"You were saying about the blood," said Natalie Zimmerman.

He had not spoken for two minutes but he thought he had explained the pile of blood. He went on to conclude his point about Charlie Lightfoot.

"Yes, so you see, Charlie could just cut through. It makes your job so much easier. They call you so needlessly, these policemen. Even the veterans. They just don't know. But Charlie knows. Knew."

"Knew what?" Natalie Zimmerman asked.

Charlie knew. How many murder themselves. God, how many!

First thing, you look for, Officer, did the victim commit suicide.

Suicide? You kidding, Sergeant? There's an old woman in there, stuffed in her closet. Her drawers are down around her ankles! She's been buggered and murdered! Should we call latent prints. Should we call the press? The captain?

No, Officer, it's a suicide.

A suicide! Wait a minute, I've been a cop twelve years!

Did you find it yet, Charlie?

Yes, here it is. She drank a can of Drāno. It unclogged her drain, all right.

But, but, look she's been sodomized. A rapist. A . . .

A bowel movement, Officer. She discovered pretty quick how fast that stuff unclogs the drain. Of course she wasn't really trying to unclog the drain, she was trying to go down the drain. All the way, and she did. But on the way she had to have a bowel movement. And she's sixty-five years old. And sixty-five-year-old ladies, even on the way down the drain, don't want to have bowel movements in their drawers. So she ran to the toilet but she never made it. And she fell sideways into the closet and that's blood and bile you see coming out her old rectum, all right. But nobody buggered her. And nobody killed her.

But, but, Sergeant Lightfoot. Sergeant Valnikov. I would have sworn. Her face! I would have sworn she was raped and strangled. Her cheeks are puffed up like . . . like . . .

The old woman with the unclogged drain took with her to eternity the face of a blowfish.

"Uh, where are we going, Valnikov?" Natalie asked nervously.

"Charlie Lightfoot used to hate one of the guys from latent prints," Valnikov said, turning on East Sixth Street, past the throngs of derelicts and winos. It was an aimless tour through Skid Row. Past the slave market where eight wretches sat on a bus bench, not waiting for a bus but talking to motorists who would stop. Wanna buy a slave, mister? No homo stuff. Just a day's work. Well, maybe half a day. Mow your lawn, paint your office. Haul your trash. No homo stuff for me, though. And no whips. None a that. Honest day's work. Fifteen dollars? Well, I don't know. Throw in two fifths a bourbon? You got yourself a deal, buddy!

"What guy from latent prints?" Natalie urged.

"This policeman. We called him Goremore. He used to like to fingerprint the corpses for us. Especially if he could find any excuse at all to use the bolt cutters."

"The bolt cutters."

"Goremore loved to cut their fingers off and put them in plastic bags and roll the fingerprints at his leisure back at the office, when he wasn't sitting around the crime lab trying to bring out the dates on buffalo nickels with etching acid. He used to love to go to the morgue and cut off those fingers. He used to say that he gave his wife a three-strand necklace of fingers for her birthday. Some people, some guys at the morgue, liked to joke around with Goremore. Once, on the Fourth of July, they stuck a tiny American flag on a toothpick into the penis of a cadaver. Goremore took a Polaroid of it. Carries it in his wallet to this day, I bet."

"Valnikov . . ."

Charlie was a good detective. Charlie once caught a stranger who wore rubber gloves when he tortured children. The only clue we ever had was one rubber glove from his fourth murder. When we caught him he had a schoolbook belonging to the little girl. It was a Braille reader, grade two. I'll never forget the title of that book. It was called *Happy Times*. Charlie couldn't get over it: a Braille reader called *Happy Times*.

"Valnikov, I think I've heard . . ."

"Charlie thought of turning the gloves inside out and sure enough they picked up a partial palm print on the *inside* of the rubber gloves. We got a conviction."

He was sweaty now and heading back westbound on the Skid Row street. Lines of bars, liquor stores, fleabag hotels, blood banks, the missions. The flotsam and jetsam which had not yet made it into the Big Sewer with Archie the Alligator.

"Where are you going, Valnikov? Do you know where you're driving?"

He stopped at a red light and wiped his face on his sleeve and said, "Of course. To lunch."

She knew he had no idea they'd been driving aimlessly for nearly half an hour. "Do you still see Charlie Lightfoot?"

"What? I told you when we started this conversation."

"*Told* me?"

"Charlie's dead. He died six months after he retired. I told you. Didn't I? By the Colorado River, they say. It was a hunting accident, they say. But Charlie was a fisherman. He was sitting on a log, they think. Cleaning his shotgun, they think. Somehow he had an accident. A load of twelve gauge square in the face. A hunting accident, they say."

Charlie Lightfoot took with him to eternity the face of a coral sponge.

"I don't think I care for any lunch today, Valnikov. Let's go back to Hollywood."

"No? Well, all right." And then he sat there at the intersection desperately looking around. She knew he was temporarily lost. Then he wiped his face again and said amiably, "Natalie, let's go to lunch. I have a surprise for you." He smiled with that big sincere dumb smile of his that she had come to know so well in just two days.

"Valnikov, I think I want to go back to the station."

"The station? We haven't even called on our burglary victims yet."

"Take me to the station, Valnikov. Please."

"All right," he said.

And that was it. She had made the decision. There was no tanglble proof that her partner was insane but she was certain that given an hour of conversation *anyone* could see. That was it. The die was cast. Except it wasn't. As always, fate can intervene. In this case, fate had been trucked into Skid Row in air-conditioned motor homes. Within those motor homes were two very pampered movie stars, reputed to be macho studs, who were portraying detectives on the trail of a whore who had gone underground in the Los Angeles skid row.

Every time the director tried to set up a scene the mob of derelicts sitting on the curb, sipping from short-dog wine bottles, started hooting and whistling and jeering: "Fake! Fake! Real cops don't do it that way! Fake! Fake!"

Finally, an assistant director got wise, bought ten fifths of Gallo burgundy from the nearest liquor store, passed it around the thirsty crowd, and they happily gave their blessing to the fake being perpetrated in their neighborhood.

While Valnikov and Natalie were trapped in the intersection trying to get through the maze of studio trucks and cars, vans and buses, they saw something which attracted their attention. There was a boy, fourteen years of age, wearing fifty-dollar, metal-studded jeans, and a T-shirt with the famous logo of a famous motion picture studio emblazoned across front and back, roaming around a group of semi-conscious winos in a vacant lot.

''Probably doing a little on-location casting,'' Natalie said. ''Why isn't the little germ in school.''

Actually, the little germ wasn't in school because his producer father hadn't been able to find one this semester which would take him. So poor Dad-o decided to employ Elliot Jr. for a few weeks helping out on his latest epic. To get rid of the little germ, the director promised him fifty bucks to make the location look more authentic.

The little germ took to his job with relish. In no time, he had the vacant lot strewn with bodies, and garbage, and whores. Of course, he promised each of the wretches a double sawbuck which would burn the hell out of the assistant director when he found out later, but no matter. Little Elliot, like big Elliot, wanted realism.

''The way these bums hang around these streets,'' Natalie muttered with disgust.

''Where can they go?'' Valnikov said. ''Beverly Hills? They've got nowhere to go.''

She looked quickly at him, because it was the first time she ever heard an edge to his voice. Then she followed his eyes to Elliot Jr., who was doing a little set decoration by spray-painting the side of a three-dollar-a-day hotel. On the side of the wall Elliot Jr. had spray-painted: ''Santa Claus butt fucks Rudolph the Red-nosed Reindeer.''

''Sweet,'' said Natalie. ''I'd like to spray-paint his goddamn head.''

''So would I,'' said Valnikov, who made a sudden southbound turn which threw Natalie against the dashboard. Then he wheeled to the curb, stood on the brakes and was out of the detective car before Natalie could pick up her oversized glasses.

By the time Natalie ran to the vacant lot, Valnikov had Elliot Jr. by the back of the neck with one hand and the spray can in his other. To the amazement of Natalie Zimmerman, and the dismay of Elliot Jr., and the delight of three winos who were not quite unconscious, Valnikov turned the spray can on Elliot's fifteen-dollar haircut and didn't release him until the can of silver paint sputtered and spit.

With Natalie behind the wheel, they raced three blocks before Elliot Jr., dripping paint, reached the wardrobe truck bawling for his father. For two weeks, Elliot Jr. would be the only fourteen-year-old in Beverly Hills with gray hair.

''Wow!'' cried a flushed Natalie Zimmerman when they were racing up Spring Street.

''Don't turn here, Natalie,'' said Valnikov. ''Keep going.''

''Wow, Valnikov!'' she cried. ''I hope nobody got our license number. Do you think the little germ knew you were a cop?''

''I don't think so,'' Valnikov shrugged.

Her glasses were askew and her buckskin Friz was hanging to her nose. She pushed them both up where they belonged and said, ''Do you know what you just did?''

''I painted his head,'' Valnikov said.

''You . . . I . . . I just lived my fantasy! Do you realize how seldom in a person's lifetime that happens? I had a fantasy. I mentioned it to you. And then *you* let me live it!''

''Why not?'' he said.

''Wow!''

"Natalie, do you still want to go to the station? Or should we handle our calls first, or what?"

She looked at him for a moment and said, "Let's handle some of our reports first. Let's make some calls. I don't think I have to go back to the station just yet."

Then they were headed back outbound on the Hollywood Freeway. Valnikov stole occasional bleary-eyed glances at the legs of Natalie Zimmerman. She was awfully attractive, he thought. Even with her goofy glasses and dopey hairdo, she was an attractive woman. Valnikov wondered if she might go to the movies with him now that he had sprayed the kid's hair silver.

While Valnikov was trying to get up the nerve to ask Natalie Zimmerman again to go to a movie, Madeline Dills Whitfield was sitting in her living room beside the telephone, drinking Scotch and water at noon.

The pet mortuary had already arrived and taken Tutu away.

"We were saddened to hear about your dear Victoria," the balding mortician said.

"Yes, yes, please, just give her a nice burial. Send the bill to me."

"But, Mrs. Whitfield, your dog handler, Mr. Biggs, said you'd probably want to select the casket and . . ."

"Something moderately priced," Madeline said, not trying to conceal the double Scotch. "Something moderate."

"We have some very nice, reasonably priced caskets that . . ."

"Yes, that'll do. Yes."

"As to a burial service, would you like . . ."

"No. No. No burial service. Bury her at once."

"But the grave site, Mrs. Whitfield. You should select her site, and we have to present the body of Victoria Reg . . ."

"Bury her at once, do you hear me! Today. Any grave plot win do. A moderately priced coffin. Take her away now and do it!"

"Yes, Mrs. Whitfield, yes. I understand perfectly. Yes, it'll be done at once. And for the billing, should we . . ."

"Send your bill to this address. Please, I'm not feeling well."

"You have our sympathy, Mrs. Whitfield, and be assured that Victoria Regina . . ."

"Yes, yes, yes."

And now she sat by the telephone, waiting. Finally she called the kennel of Chester Biggs.

"Chester?"

"Mrs. Whitfield?"

"Did that . . . that man phone? The man I mentioned yesterday? Richard?"

"Just a minute, Mrs. Whitfield."

An interminable wait and then, "Mrs. Whitfield, my wife said a man did call, and she gave him your number just as you instructed."

"How long ago?"

"She says an hour, Mrs. Whitfield."

"Thank you, Chester. Thank you. Good-bye."

An hour! Why hadn't he called? Why? Is he trying to make her suffer? Is that it? Are people who do such things sadists as well as common criminals? Do they delight in torturing their victims? Would he torture Vickie for his own perverted enjoyment? Is Vickie being whipped? Or burned? Oh God!

Madeline Whitfield spilled the glass of Scotch on the carpet and leaned across the arm of an old wingback chair, weeping.

At that moment, Victoria Regina of Pasadena was reluctantly taking a bite of boiled horsemeat from the tobacco-stained fingers of Philo Skinner, who had been trying to feed her for the last two hours.

"That's it, sweetie," Philo said soothingly. "Philo won't hurt you. Philo loves you. Philo loves all little terriers and you're *so* pretty."

He was at the end of the 175-foot aisle dividing the kennel. The last of thirty-two dog pens on each side of the long, low-roofed building had been reserved for Vickie who spent the first night of her life since weaning outside the bedroom of her mistress.

"Philo loves you, sweetie," he said, tempting the little schnauzer with a chunk of boiled liver. She approached him tentatively as he squatted outside the pen, handing the meat through the mesh.

"That's yum-yum," Philo said, as Vickie accepted her second nibble of meat and wrinkled her nose at the smell of Philo's endless cigarette chain. "You're going to be just fine, sweetheart," Philo said. "Here's another bite of yum-yum, and then Philo's going to call your mommy and your mommy's going to give Philo eighty-five dimes, and Philo's going to send you home wagging your tail. Okay, sweetie?"

After Philo was satisfied that Vickie was eating all right, he went to the office to make the call. Mavis had been hard to get rid of today.

"Philo, I know we're going broke around here, but I can't understand why you gave that Pattie Mae the day off. I mean we still have twenty-five dogs out there in those sixty dog runs, you know."

"Only twenty-five dogs," Philo sighed, trying hard to keep from laughing with joy. "Never been so bad, this business. Just trying to save a few bucks, my love."

"*You* save money?"

"Things are awful tough, my love. I can take care of twenty-five dogs easy."

"Sure isn't like you, Philo," she said suspiciously, "wanting to do all that work. You got something on your mind? Maybe you got Pattie Mae coming back here this afternoon and you don't want me here?"

"Oh, please, please, please!" Philo cried, lighting a cigarette with the butt of the last. "The last thing on my mind is pussy, goddamnit!" And at least *that* was the truth.

"Well, if I ever catch you, Philo, it's all over. You understand? You listening to me, Philo?"

Stripping, stripping, stripping. She never got tired of it. Well, two more days. Wednesday should be time enough. The Thursday flight to Puerto Vallarta would bring him in there just in time for a margarita at sunset.

She got the call at 2:50 p.m. He was speaking soft and had his voice muffled, like in the movies.

"This is Richard." Burton that is, get it? He was so excited he wanted to giggle insanely.

"Yes? Yes?"

"Have you told anyone? The police?"

"No one, I swear." Madeline, who had been getting desperately drunk, was now sweatily sober.

"I want eighty-five thousand dollars."

The number was so great, she was sure he said eighty-five hundred. She was expecting him to demand more than five thousand, so she wasn't too surprised. "Yes, yes," she said eagerly. I can get it by tomorrow. Perhaps by tonight if I . . ."

"Shut up and listen to me," Philo said excitedly, speaking with the mouthpiece wrapped in a paper towel. He was in a cocktall lounge, two blocks from Skinner

Kennels. The barroom was practically empty midday, but still he jumped at every sound the bartender made.

"Yes, I'm listening," she said.

"I want the money in tens and twenties and no more than two packages of fifties."

"How's Vickie? Is Vickie all right?"

"Listen to me, goddamnit, if you ever want to see your Vickie again."

Then Madeline started to cry and Philo Skinner realized he had to alter his technique. "Damn, lady, calm down. Listen, get hold a yourself. Your bitch is okay. She's fine. Cut it out, will ya?"

"Yes . . . I'm . . . I . . . yes . . . please . . . don't hurt her. *Please!*"

"*Hurt* her! Goddamnit, lady, I'm no criminal! What the hell's wrong with you? I never hurt a dog in my life. Get hold a yourself, lady."

"Yes . . . I'm sorry. All right. I'll get the eighty-five hundred and then where do I take it?"

The line was silent for a moment and Philo Skinner said: "That's eighty-five *thousand*, lady. Eighty-five *thousand!*"

"My God!" she cried. "That's impossible. Eighty-five *thousand?* I don't *have* eighty-five thousand dollars! I wouldn't know where to begin to *get* eighty-five thousand dollars. Please, sir. I beg you . . ."

"You lying bitch!" Philo screamed, then he caught himself and opened the phone booth door to peek at the bartender. "You lying bitch," he whispered. "I know about you. You're rich, goddamn you. Don't gimme that shit, you want your fucking schnauzer alive."

"Please, sir, please . . ." Then Philo had to wait while she wept again. "My God, sir . . . please . . . I beg you . . ."

Philo Skinner was starting to sweat in the phone booth. He lit a cigarette, still afraid to open the door. He began suffocating himself. His eyes were raw from the smoke by the time Madeline stopped crying and was able to talk.

"Lady, I know damn well how much you're worth. I saw your goddamn house. I know you're rich. Rich! I know you can get a measly eighty-five thousand. Now if you care for this bitch a yours, you'll do exactly like I say."

"Listen, listen to me," Madeline begged. "I'd give you anything. I swear. Anything! But you must believe me. I don't have eighty-five thousand dollars. This . . . this big house . . . there's no furniture upstairs. I keep it closed off. I had to refinance it last year. I live on a small trust fund. Please . . ."

"You cunt!" Philo screamed. "You rotten filthy lying cunt! You get the money and have it by noon tomorrow. I'm going to start working on this bitch a yours at noon tomorrow. I'm going to call you at six p.m. tonight and see what progress you made. You understand? And you better have something to tell me, hear? You hear?"

"Yes!" Madeline wailed. "Yes!"

"And one last thing, take care a that little schnauzer bitch you have with you. Keep your handler away from her so he doesn't see she's not your Victoria. I'll give you further instructions on what to do with her when I call you tonight."

Before Madeline could tell him the schnauzer was dead, he hung up.

Philo Skinner was still trembling with rage and frustration when he got back to the kennel. The cunt. The rotten miserable stingy lying *rich* cunt. Imagine, trying to flim-flam Philo Skinner like that. All these rich cunts were alike—stingy. Philo had pampered their goddamn dogs for twenty-five years and they were all alike. Spend twenty grand a year to show a single dog, and throw a Gainesburger to the dog handler. Well, this cunt wouldn't get away with that.

Philo Skinner sat down and began rehearsing his next telephone call. Imagine that, trying to flim-flam Philo Skinner, Terrier King!

Madeline was devastated when the terrifying extortionist hung up. It was a full hour before she could get up from the sofa where she lay, intermittently weeping and drinking.

She didn't pour a second drink. Instead, she began thinking. She surprised herself in that she began formulating a plan. She was filled with dread and overwhelming fear and yet she began to formulate a plan to deal with this extortionist. She found some strength she didn't know she had. The money was totally out of the question. She knew from her year-end audit that her net worth was around forty thousand dollars. That included the surrender value of her insurance policy, a second-trust deed, an inflated value on what was left of the antique furniture, her car, what little equity was left in the house after refinancing, and an arbitrary value placed on the small balance of the trust fund. Until now there was the dream, the fantasy, that after Vickie won Madison Square Garden, a man would rescue her, a widower with a substantial fortune. They would meet at The Sign of The Dove restaurant . . .

Immediate liquidation would take weeks! She would have to explain it to the extortionist when he called again. He'd *have* to listen to reason. Perhaps she could borrow nine thousand. Perhaps ten thousand, at the outside. There was Ariel Wentworth. Her husband was the chairman of the board of . . . which bank was it? Ariel might be able to help her get a loan. A very quick loan. Ten thousand dollars.

The alternative was the police. She was tempted to call them. She went to the phone three times. Each time, she returned to the first plan. The loan. She started to call Ariel. No, first she had to reason with the man who had Vickie. Make him see. Surely, he would see. He wasn't a monster. He said he'd never hurt an animal in his life. She rememberd him saying that. It was all she remembered, but he *did* say that. She drank no more that day. She sat in the living room waiting for six o'clock. Waiting for sundown. Waiting for the *call*.

The rest of the day for Natalie Zimmerman meant burglary investigation, pure and simple. Which meant public relations. An offer of sympathy to the victims who didn't really have any hope for the return of the merchandise. A few tips on how to prevent future breaking-and-entering, a crime report number for the sake of reporting the loss on a tax return or to an insurance company. Was the fingerprint man here yet? He said he didn't get any latent prints? No, they seldom leave prints, even if they *don't* use gloves. Sir, it's very very hard to get good lifts unless a surface is hard, smooth and clean. Yes, I know they get fingerprints in the movies from cotton handkerchiefs. Yes, I know that in the movies the detective caught a rapist by getting a fingerprint from . . . What? From a woman's tit? That's ridiculous!

A typical day for an investigator of business burglaries. They called on six victims and got not a single lead of any kind.

"No clues for the clues closet," Natalie Zimmerman smirked when they finished their fourth victim contact.

"Do you want to stop for some food?" Valnikov asked.

"I'm not hungry," she said. How could she be hungry? How could she get Captain Hooker away from Clarence Cromwell long enough to inform him about today? Valnikov was cracked. Over the edge. Just get him talking about his old homicide cases, Captain, if you don't believe me. Watch what happens to him when he starts talking about *that*.

But what if he doesn't always react the way he did today? A Braille reader. Charlie Lightfoot. Sobbing as he dreamed about some goddamn rabbit. What if he *could* fool Hooker, whose attention span on anything outside of that goddamn boat of Cromwell's was about three minutes? What if he doesn't always go whacko when you make him remember the bad old days?

"Valnikov?"

"Yes?"

"Let's just go stop somewhere, anywhere. Get a cup of coffee and a doughnut, or something."

"How about a deli on Fairfax? I could go for a nice onion bagel," Valnikov said pleasantly. His eyes were starting to clear up, the whites no longer laced with red webbing.

"Okay," she said, and then she said, "Valnikov, do you remember what we were talking about this morning?"

"What's that, Natalie?" he smiled.

She hesitated an instant, took a breath and bit the bullet: "We were talking about Charlie Lightfoot. About murder. Suicide. Dead bodies. Dead children. Your old job."

Corpses. There were stacks of corpses in the morgue. Corpses all around. In the autopsy rooms. In the coolers. In the halls. Tags on toes. Bulges under the sheets.

That one's a woman. Silicone. Look at the boobs. Like twin Everests. Ever rest, baby. What good did all that silicone do you? And that one. Under the sheet and stiff as a catfish. He's got more sticking out than we do alive, eh, Valnikov? And that one. The body's only four feet long. A boy or a girl? Is that the one came through on that West L.A. crime report? You know, the little girl, her mother used to trade for dope? You know the one? The one mom used to loan to the dyke? You know the one? The one the dyke started to sleep with when she was six years old, and then mom started battering when the dyke got tired of her? The one they used to photograph being screwed by the dyke's dope customers? The one mom used to take her empty spike (No heroin today, you little bitch, it's your fault. You could have kept her happy if you wanted to.) and ram the empty spike under her toenails and through her eardrums? You know the one?

Corpses in the morgue. A class of student nurses being taken through the morgue by an orderly who relishes their horror. Goremore is there cutting off fingers.

A little white around the gills, aren't you, girls? If you get tired, don't lay down on those *tables, girls.*

Of course he takes them right into an autopsy about to begin. One he knows about. This fellow loves *his work. He* loves *to take student nurses on tour. Look at that one. A ragpicker the cops found after three weeks in a boxcar.*

Goremore winks. Come closer, girls. Look. He's a black man but his face is white.

His face! His face is moving!

No, it's not moving, girls. It's covered with a swarm of maggots. The maggots are moving, girls. He's a maggot meal ticket.

Grab that girl! Goddamnit, Goremore, she fell on her head, you dumb shit!

And then Goremore says, Fuck it, I ain't no tour guide anyway, just as they jerk on the chin to see if the throat was cut, and the jaw rips loose. Half a pound of maggots sail in a heap and go plop on the tile floor. A second student nurse falls down beside the maggots. The fat and loggy maggots look at her curiously. But in their dim maggot brains they retreat and stay coiled, and writhing, and crawling on top of each other. Even maggots need maggots, after all.

The meal ticket took with him to eternity no face whatsoever.

And then, look out, Valnikov, here it comes! The sparkly flashes. It's the morgue, all right. There. It won't get away this time. Déjà vu. There's a picture *forming*. He's almost got it! It's a pathologist and a . . .

"Valnikov."

Oh, no, it's the *rabbit!* He's bounding through the snow!

"Valnikov. Valnikov!"

"Huh?"

"Valnikov, the stoplight went from red to green to red. Do you hear the horns?"

"Huh?"

Now Natalie Zimmerman was *frightened*. "Never mind, Valnikov. Don't tell me about Charlie Lightfoot. No murder. No dead bodies. Never mind, Valnikov, it's all right!"

"Huh?" Vainikov pulled into the traffic, ignoring the angry motorists behind him.

"What did you say, Natalie?"

"I said, tell me about burglary, Valnikov," she babbled. "Tell me about burglary. I wanna learn."

The picture was gone. Gone again. Valnikov was sweating and trembling.

"Burglary? Yes. As you know, I haven't been working burglary too long, Natalie, I'm an old homicide detective . . ."

"No homicide, Valnikov," said Natalie Zimmerman, her eyes big behind the big glasses. "Tell me about burglary. What have you learned about burglary? I wanna be a good burglary investigator."

"Oh," he said, wiping the sweat from his eyes. "Well, let's see, I've learned that a competent burglar can get through any hole or opening that's big enough for a human head. Isn't that interesting?"

"That's very interesting. Very interesting. Let's go get that coffee and bagel, Valnikov, then we'll be just about finished for the day and we can go to the station."

"All right," Valnikov smiled, the trembling almost stopped.

If only she had a tape recorder. It was going to be hard to explain it to Hipless Hooker. How can you explain it unless you were *there*. But if he didn't understand, she'd go to the area commander. She'd go, goddamnit!

The delicatessen was busy even at this hour. It was one of the oldest in Los Angeles.

One employee knew Valnikov, an old counterman. He had the whiskey voice and puffy eyes of a veteran alcoholic. Takes one to know one, Natalie thought, when he and Valnikov exchanged a warm greeting.

"Hello, Sergeant," the old man said with a wide peg-toothed grin.

Why did all the old people respond to Valnikov? What was his age? Only forty-four? Why did old people treat him like one of their own?

"Hi, Solly," Valnikov said, shaking hands with the counterman, who dried his wrinkled hands on his apron.

"I ain't seen you in I don't know how long, Sergeant," said the counterman. His hair was straight and white and combed back flat. "I was awful sorry about Sergeant Lightfoot. I heard nothing until recently. I was sorry."

"Yeah," said Valnikov. "This is my new partner. I work Hollywood Detectives now."

"A woman you work with?" said the counterman. "A pretty woman. You're lucky, Sergeant."

Then a fifty-year-old busboy came out of the kitchen carrying a metal tray loaded with sandwiches. He was dark, with a flat nose, and shiny black hair, blacker than Philo Skinner's dye job. He was short and squat, with no buttocks, wide hips and skinny legs. He was from the jungles of Sinaloa near Mazatlan, and was known as Indio.

Valnikov smiled at him and said, "Hello, Indio."

"*Sargento,*" the Indian grinned, and there it was: Tijuana bridgework. Gleaming.

"I've been dying for an onion bagel, Solly. What would you like, Natalie?"

"An onion bagel, please," she said.

"Coming up, Sergeant," the old man grinned. "With cream cheese?"

"Of course."

"Lox or herring?"

"Lox for me, Solly."

"That's right. It was Sergeant Lightfoot who liked herring."

"It was," said Valnikov.

Then Valnikov tried to light Natalie's cigarette. "How do you like the smell of this place, Natalie?"

"Smells fine," she said.

"I grew up in Russian Flats," he said. "Over near Boyle Heights. We were Russians and Jews and Mexicans in those days. I knew Solly's brother, owned a beer bar on Brooklyn Avenue in the old days."

"Is that so?" said Natalie Zimmerman.

"Do you know why the old Russians and Jews got along so well in Boyle Heights?'

"No."

"Because the Russians, like my parents, remembered how it was when they were fleeing the Bolsheviks. How the Jews gave them tea and bread. Not that the Jews were czarists, but they knew that some of the Whites were going to the magical place. To America. When I was a kid in Boyle Heights the Jewish kids used to think borscht was *their* food. Can you imagine?"

"Is that so," said Natalie Zimmerman, drinking her coffee and rehearsing the speech to Hipless Hooker. Look, Captain, if you won't listen to reason, there's always the area commander. I don't like to go over your head, but . . .

Then Solly gave Valnikov his tea. In a glass, Russian style. He remembered the old days too.

"I sure miss Sergeant Lightfoot," Solly said. "You know my grandson? The one I was worried always getting in trouble, that one?"

"Yes," Valnikov said.

"Well, a grand job in a grand place, he's got. A kettle wrench, is what."

"A kettle wrench?" said Natalie Zimmerman.

"A kettle wrench," Solly nodded. "You know, where they punch kettles."

"Oh?"

"He's a cowboy," Valnikov explained.

"Oh."

"The kettles are on a wrench," Solly explained.

"Oh."

"He was always a better boy after you and Sergeant Lightfoot arrested him," Solly said. "Excuse me. I got to go back in the kitchen. We got one dishwasher only today."

"Of course, Solly," Valnikov nodded.

Then another customer at the delicatessen counter said: "My bagel isn't toasted well enough. Take it back." He said it to Indio, who understood by his tone what the man meant. The man was older than the Indian, yet he wore a rainbow T-shirt, a bush coat, and pants carefully spattered with paint. In short, he was five years out of style and thought he was groovy. "Take this bagel back, it's not toasted well enough."

Indio picked up the plate and started for the kitchen.

The man said to his twenty-two-year-old female companion: "That's the trouble with these greaseballs. Let them work in delicatessens, whadda you expect?"

Natalie heard it and ignored it. Indio didn't understand it. Valnikov looked perturbed. In a few minutes Indio brought back the bagel and placed it before the aging hipster.

"It's still not toasted right," the man in the bush coat said. "What's the matter with you? You don't even speak English, do you? What are *you* doing working in a delicatessen anyway?"

Valnikov put down his glass of hot tea and walked over two stools to the man in the bush coat and said, "What's wrong with that bagel? Do you have a color chip to check your bagel with?"

The man looked up at the lumbering man with blazing watery eyes and mumbled something unintelligible to his little girlfriend, who was reading *Variety* and wondering how she got hooked up with this schmuck in the first place.

When Indio sheepishly picked up the dirty dishes and walked past Valnikov, the detective reached over and took the Indian's arm. "Solly," Valnikov said to the old man who spoke all the languages of Boyle Heights: English, Yiddish, Spanish. "Tell Indio for me that when Cortez came to the New World the Aztec emperor put a golden fingerbowl in front of him and the ignorant white man *drank* from it. Tell him that, will you?"

Natalie Zimmerman's mind was racing when they drove back to Hollywood Station. Captain, I have something . . . Captain, could you please excuse Sergeant Cromwell, this is *private*. Captain, if you don't listen to me I'm going to the area commander . . . Captain, sit down. I know you're retiring in a matter of weeks, but this is something you must deal with. Captain, Sergeant Valnikov is a raving lunatic!

Except at that very moment, Natalie Zimmerman's plans were being frustrated by none other than Bullets Bambarella, who was doing nothing more than being himself with an irate and very famous movie star who had come to Hollywood Detectives to complain about the arrest of his seventeen-year-old nephew on a narcotics charge.

"The kiddie cops ain't here," Bullets Bambarella said, hardly looking up from his *Playboy* magazine, which he had concealed inside the Los Angeles Police Department Manual that he was allegedly studying for promotion.

"Then I'd like to see the boss, whoever that is," said the famous movie star. He had curly dark hair and of course showed beautiful capped teeth. He wore a red-and-white shirtsuit, with the flap pocket bearing his initials. His flared pants bore chalk-white piping around medium bells. He wore kangaroo boots with five-inch heels. In short, he was conservatively dressed for Sunset Boulevard.

The teenage boy with him had dazzling real teeth, and wore a cotton safari shirt and faded jeans with belt loop legs that cost $130, hence were the most popular jeans in Baghdad. On the star's other arm, completing the trio, was a buxom woman with a red bandana over her dark blond hair. She fidgeted with sunglasses which, of course, were on top of her head.

"Well, whom can I talk with about this stupid arrest?" the movie star said to Bullets. "My nephew had a little angel dust. Big deal."

"You can talk to me, that's *whom,*" Bullets Bambarella sighed, closing the book.

"My nephew was arrested two hours ago and . . ."

"Yeah, you said that," Bullets yawned. "And I told you there ain't no kiddie cops here right now. And your nephew ain't here right now. So I guess there ain't much I can do for ya."

"Look, officer," said the famous movie star. "My nephew was arrested because he was holding this angel dust for somebody else and my business manager was supposed to take care of this and if he doesn't get here soon . . . Margo, take my car and go find that dumb shit."

Bullets watched the buxom lass and the movie star touch cheeks and kiss the air. Then she wriggled off to drive to the Sunset Strip and find the dumb shit.

"I've got an uncle who's a good friend of the district attorney and the chief of police," said the famous movie star.

"I got an uncle who's a notary public," Bullets Bambarella said. "How about givin me a break, fella. Come back later or something. Your nephew ain't here."

"Do you know who you're talking to?" said the young companion with dazzling teeth.

"No," said Bullets Bambarella, who was starting to get as pissed off as the famous movie star.

"I don't believe it," the lad said to the movie star. "Do you believe it? I don't believe it." Then he turned to Bullets and said, "Have you ever been to a movie?"

"Don't tell me," Bullets said. "He's an *actor*. I shoulda guessed."

"I'm not wasting any more time with you. Get me your commanding officer," the movie star said.

"He ain't here," said Bullets.

"Where is he?"

"Captain Hooker's off buying a yachting jacket," Bullets said.

"Is he a police captain or a sea captain?" the movie star snickered, causing his young companion to fall against him in a gush of giggles.

"You an actor too?" Bullets asked the young man.

"As a matter of fact he is," the movie star said.

Bullets examined the slender hips and torso of the young lad, who still had his hand on the movie star's arm. The lad had a large head and a small delicate face.

"Yeah, now I recognize ya," said Bullets. "You're one a Charlie's Angels, ain'tcha?"

Now the teenager was livid and looked as though he just might be crazy enough to attack Bullets Bambarella. "Bastard!" he said. "Ignorant bastard! I'll have your badge!"

Bullets then doubled his big fist and said, "Hey leading man, how'd you like me to make a character actor outta ya?"

"You bastard!" the young man screamed, causing Clarence Cromwell to get up and come out from the squad room.

"Bullets, gud-damn it, what're you do-in?" Clarence demanded.

"That bastard!" the young man shrieked while the movie star said, "Quiet down, Buddy, quiet down. Don't let him get your goat. Remember, Buddy, sticks and stones, sticks and stones . . ."

"Yeah and *keep* that in mind," Bullets said, picking up a nightstick.

"Who *are* these people?" Clarence demanded.

"I dunno. Claim they're actors. Look like a couple a interior *dick*-orators to me."

"I'll have his badge, I'll have his badge!" the young man sputtered.

"Everybody quiet down!" said Clarence Cromwell, finally recognizing the famous actor. "You too, Bullets!"

But it was too late. Bullets was having a good old time doing what he did best: causing a riot.

"Hey, Clarence, I just thought a somethin," Bullets giggled. Then he pointed to the movie star and said, "We oughtta book that man for burglary. Look at the age of his playmate. That's illegal entry!"

Captain Hooker came back in the station just in time to see the two actors raging at the reception desk, while Clarence Cromwell did his best to quiet everybody down. He'd had a long day and got the hell out because he recognized the famous actor immediately and started to get a headache thinking of the trouble this would cause him. Oh, God, is *he* the one nominated for an Academy Award?

When Natalie Zimmerman came back and hurried to Hipless Hooker's office, she saw no one but Bullets Bambarella waiting sulkily for Clarence Cromwell.

When Clarence finally came storming into the captain's office pointing a finger at Bullets Bambarella, Natalie knew that another day had passed.

She could hear Bullets through the open door saying, "But Clarence, you just can't please some people! Those two fruitcakes came in here and started pickin on me!"

"SHUT UP, BULLETS!" Clarence yelled as everyone signed out quietly and went home, including Natalie Zimmerman, who left talking to her Friz.

And Sergeant A.M. Valnikov had his police career extended for yet another day.

The phone call was late. It came at 6:45 p.m. Madeline Whitfield had drunk seven cups of coffee and had not had a Scotch since early afternoon. She was stunned at her reserve of strength. She was cold sober.

"This is Richard," the voice said. Philo Skinner still spoke through a paper towel. Now he was talking from a telephone booth in a service station some three blocks from Skinner Kennels.

"Yes. Yes! How's Vickie?"

"Vickie's fine. When do I get the money?"

"Please, you've got to listen to me, sir."

"When do I get the money?"

"Sir. I've been thinking all afternoon of ways to make you understand. I've got to be blunt and honest. Lots of people like me live in these Pasadena mansions with barely enough to . . ."

"When do I get the money, you lousy cunt!" Philo screamed into the mouthpiece. Then he got hold of himself, and looked around as though he could be heard by the passing cars in the early hours of night.

Madeline was determined to be reasonable and calm no matter how the man terrified her. "Sir, if you could come here and talk to me face to face, I could explain to you. I could show you my financial records. You'd understand how it is. Eighty-five thousand dollars! Why it's . . ."

"You rotten stingy cunt!" Philo Skinner was beside himself now. She could hardly understand him. "You want this bitch in one piece? You want this bitch alive? You . . . you . . . don't try to pull that shit on me, you rotten cunt!"

Madeline started to break, but only for a few seconds. The reserve of strength, where did it come from? A word from Edna Lofton at the Valley Hunt Club could set her off on a binge for three days, and yet, this very minute, with Vickie's life in the balance, she could deal with this madman, with this criminal. Madeline Whitfield had some *presence*. Madeline Whitfield was starting to have a little regard for herself.

"Please, listen to me," Madeline said. "Sir, I . . . I'm sure I can get some money for you. I'm sure I can borrow ten thousand dollars. Believe me when I tell you that I have just a little over five thousand of my own that I can get my hands on quickly. I can borrow ten. You'll have just over fifeen thousand dollars. I can get it for you by tomorrow. I can have it for you by the time the banks close tomorrow.I can . . ."

"Okay, now you listen to *me*." Philo had dropped the paper towel and was croaking into the mouthpiece. "I'm giving you until three o'clock tomorrow. When the banks close I'm calling you. You're going to tell me where I can pick up the eighty-five thousand . . ."

"Sir! Please believe me . . ."

"Shut up!" Philo screamed. "Shut your fucking mouth!"

When it was quiet Philo broke into a coughing spasm. Madeline heard the extortionist spit a wad of phlegm. Then he came back on the phone wheezing, and said, "If you don't have some good news for me, I'm cutting off one toe of your precious bitch and I'm sending it to you." Philo had seen that in a movie. "One toe at a time."

"Oh, please!" Madeline almost broke. Almost. She sat for a moment and took hold and said reasonably, "I'll do what I can, sir. I'll liquidate everything I can as quickly as possible. I'll talk to you tomorrow."

"If you even *think* about calling the cops . . ."

"I won't call them, sir. I give you my word. Don't hurt my Vickie. Please."

Philo was a nervous wreck when he got back to the kennel. He was late with the feeding. When he opened the door leading from the grooming room to the long rows of dog pens the animals went crazy.

Jesus. Only twenty-five animals. It wasn't his fault he had to resort to crime. He hadn't so much as cheated on his income tax before now. Well, maybe a little, but he was no criminal. What could a man do? With economic conditions like they were, what could a man do? It wasn't his fault.

Then Philo Skinner prepared the meal for the animals in his care. The bastards ate better than he did these days. That cunt. Lives in a fucking mansion over the Rose Bowl. The servants' quarters probably bigger than the house Philo lived in with all his brothers and sisters when he was a kid. I don't have the money, sir. The cunt! People like her made Philo Skinner what he was. Philo Skinner was a decent human being. Never hurt an animal in his life.

Then he remembered. That stingy miserable cunt got him so upset he forgot to give her instructions about Tutu. He wondered if there was some way he could get Tutu for himself. No, that was stupid. He couldn't risk that. A money drop was one thing. But a schnauzer drop? Tutu would have to go back with that horny cheap old cunt, Millie Muldoon Gharoujian. Too bad, Tutu. He would love to run on the beach in Puerto Vallarta, a rejuvenated man, Tutu by his side.

When Philo Skinner slept that night he had a dream. In the dream he was tiptoeing across a flower-covered rainbow bridge under a subtropical moon. In the dream Philo Skinner looked *just* like Richard Burton.

10

The Fiddler

Hipless Hooker came to work very late on Tuesday morning. He just knew there'd be another personnel complaint on his desk. He'd checked with his wife, who hated boats but *loved* movies, and discovered that the famous movie star he saw screaming at Bullets Bambarella last night had not been nominated for an Academy Award as he'd feared. At least that was *some* consolation. Maybe an actor who wasn't up for an Oscar couldn't cause him as much trouble as one who was. Hipless Hooker tried a glass of milk and it didn't help. He was sure the famous actor would be waiting for him with his attorney and that's why he came to work late.

When Hipless Hooker came in the door he headed straight for his office, tucking his chin under his lapel, hoping that no one would notice him. Natalie Zimmerman leaped up and ran across the squad room but Clarence Cromwell beat her to it. He went into Captain Hooker's office and slammed the door in her face.

''Did the movie star call the press last night, Clarence?'' Hooker asked, grimacing at the cup of coffee Clarence had for him.

''No coffee today, Skipper?''

''I've got terrible indigestion,'' Hooker groaned.

''I took care a both actors,'' Clarence grinned. ''Took them inside, bought them coffee, told them I was personally gonna kick Bullets' ass all over the station. And get this, when they left they was so happy they gave me two tickets to a preview movie at the Director's Guild!''

''You're amazing, Clarence!'' Captain Hooker cried.

''Captain? Got a few minutes?'' Natalie said, peeking in the door, her Friz hanging down over her big glasses.

"What's the problem, Natalie?" Clarence said gruffly.

"Captain, we've just *got* to talk about Valnikov!"

Then Natalie stood helplessly as both Clarence Cromwell and Hipless Hooker began moaning in unison. "Oooooohhhhh."

"Captain . . ." But she couldn't get a word in edgewise. So Natalie Zimmerman just stood there and sneered at her Friz until the men stopped groaning. When they were finished, Clarence Cromwell said, "Natalie, you said you was gonna work with the guy awhile and give it a fair try."

"Clarence, I gave it a fair . . ."

Then Hipless Hooker started groaning again. But this time it wasn't just *emotional* pain. He felt flame in his stomach that went right up his throat.

"Do you call a few days a fair chance, gud-damn it!" Clarence demanded.

"Oooooooooohhhhhhhh!" groaned Hipless Hooker.

They both stopped talking and looked at him.

"You okay, Skipper?" asked Clarence.

"My stomach!" Hipless Hooker cried. "Ooooooooohhhhhh!"

"Take it easy, Cap. Take it easy!" Clarence said. "Natalie, get me the spare keys. I'll run the boss over to the receiving hospital. What's it feel like, Cap? An ulcer?"

"I don't knooooooowwww!" cried Hipless Hooker. "It huuuuuuuurts!"

It started to hurt even worse when it turned out that Bullets Bambarella was the one who helped Captain Hooker out the door and half carried him to the car where Clarence Cromwell waited. "Please, Bullets," Hipless Hooker cried. "Don't get in any trouble while I'm gone!"

"Course not!" Bullets said. The very idea!

"I'm depending on you, son," said Hipless Hooker. "No trouble now. I'm depending on you."

"You can depend on me, Captain!" Bullets Bambarella promised. He was touched.

"Ooooooooohhhhhhhh!" Hipless Hooker said, when Bullets lifted him into Clarence Cromwell's car and they sped away to the hospital.

Natalie Zimmerman, like Philo Skinner, did not believe in the apathetic Gods. She believed that fate was conspiring against her in the Valnikov matter. Fate was protecting Sergeant A.M. Valnikov. It was getting spooky.

"Well, Natalie," he smiled, when she joined him at the burglary table. "We have a very light workload today."

She looked at him. His eyes were watery, as usual. He exuded a faint odor of booze, as usual. He wore another suit today, the cleaning tags still stapled to his inside pocket, as usual. The suitcoat hung open and the stapled repairs were visible, as usual. He was wearing a blue and white polka dot necktie, and his white shirt was more or less ironed. Frayed like the others, but ironed. So he was looking his best today for whatever reason.

The reason was Natalie Zimmerman. Valnikov had watched every move she made as she ran across the noisy crowded squad room. He watched as she smoked and paced in front of Captain Hooker's office until she was admitted. He watched her walking slowly back to the burglary table, her eyes rolled up in that odd way of hers. Valnikov thought she was pretty even with her dopey hairdo and her big dumb glasses.

Valnikov had deliberately cut his vodka consumption last night and he'd slept better as a result. He wasn't even positive that he'd dreamed about the rabbit, but he guessed he had. The sheets were sweat-soaked. Nevertheless, he felt pretty good today. He sipped his tea and smiled at her.

"I've gotta have another cup of coffee to get my clock started," Natalie sighed when she dropped herself into the chair beside him.

"Let me get it for you," Valnikov said, grabbing her coffee cup.

"Okay," she said. "Thanks."

''Sure,'' he said, wiping his eyes. It was the first time she'd let him do something for her. He wondered if it was the polka dot necktie and new shave lotion. He'd even combed his hair today. He thought he looked all right.

She thought he looked like hell. Pitiful. Why didn't he make it easy on her and just flip out in front of somebody? Like right now, in front of thirty witnesses? Fire off a round at the coffee maker because it was bitter or something. But he wouldn't even know. He drank tea. What kind of a cop drinks tea?

''All you people listen to this!'' said Lieutenant Woodenlips Mockett, who was totally ignored except by Valnikov, who was always respectful of authority. He put Natalie's coffee cup in front of her and gave Woodenlips his attention.

''Sergeant Ballew in patrol got a four-day suspension for an accidental discharge.''

''At his age they're all accidental,'' said Fuzzy Spinks of auto theft, who was older than Sergeant Ballew and knew what he was talking about.

''Sergeant Ballew accidently fired a round from the Ithaca and it went right through Deputy Chief Digby Bates' car.''

''Yeah?'' said Dudley Knebel of robbery, suddenly interested because he hated the chief's guts. ''Was Bates in the car?''

''Of course not!'' Woodenlips Mockett said. ''Ballew only got four days' suspension.''

''Only,'' Dudley Knebel said. ''That's a pretty tough bail schedule for one lousy shotgun round.''

''Yeah, now if the chief had been *in* the car . . .'' argued Max Haffenkamp of residential burglary.

''Then I'da gave Ballew four days' pay outta *my* pocket,'' Dudley Knebel said.

''You men don't take these things seriously enough,'' Woodenlips Mockett whined.

''Poor old Ballew,'' Fuzzy Spinks said. ''He got ten days' suspension last year for getting drunk and banging his girlfriend on duty.''

''On duty!'' Woodenlips Mockett cried. ''He should've been *fired* for that! Ten days is all he got?''

''Well, it's pretty tough when you figure the whole case was circumstantial,'' said Fuzzy. ''See, they stopped him on the way home for drunk driving.''

''Then it *wasn't* on duty,'' said Woodenlips Mockett.

''Well no,'' said Fuzzy Spinks, ''but it was only fifteen minutes past end-of-watch and his blood alcohol reading was .25 so they deduced it.''

''Did they *deduce* the girlfriend too?'' Woodenlips Mockett sneered. He sneered as well as Natalie Zimmerman any old day.

''Circumstantial evidence too,'' Fuzzy clucked, full of sympathy for poor old Sergeant Ballew. ''Before they shagged him for drunk driving he smashed into the telephone pole at Gower and Sunset. And when the lousy finks at the receiving hospital took Ballew's clothes off, they found a rubber.''

''A rubber!'' Nate Farmer of the sex detail was outraged. ''That don't prove nothin!''

''Poor old drunk still had it *on!*'' said Fuzzy Spinks.

''That's still just circumstantial evidence,'' said Nate Farmer. ''I suppose they checked the scummy thing for his girlfriend's fingerprints, huh?''

''Wouldn't put it past those squints at Internal Affairs,'' said Montezuma Montez.

Then Woodenlips Mockett gave up because he was the only one who didn't think Sergeant Ballew got railroaded on circumstantial evidence.

''I hear you're a golfer,'' Bullets suddenly said to Montezuma Montez.

''I play a little golf,'' said Montezuma without looking up.

''Sissy game,'' Bullets said. ''I never played golf in my life.''

''Too clumsy?'' said Montezuma Montez, putting down his pencil.

Bullets said, ''Any old man on crutches can play that game.''

''I'll bet you couldn't hit a golf ball fifty yards,'' said Montezuma Montez.

"Fifty yards," said Bullets. Now he *had* the wetback! "You heard him, Fuzzy. He said I couldn't hit a golf ball fifty yards!"

"If you never played before, I know you couldn't hit one fifty yards, Bullets," Fuzzy Spinks said, peeking over his bifocals. "Not on one swing anyway."

Then there was money flying all over the squad room. Bullets was covering all bets. Woodenlips Mockett was whining about gambling in a police station. Everyone was yelling and hollering but Bullets Bambarella covered thirty dollars. Five minutes later there were detective cars squealing out of Hollywood Station speeding to the Los Angeles Country Club where Investigator Nate Farmer could never hope to join, in that he was a black man, but where he could arrange for Bullets to hit a ball on the driving range because Nate's cousin was a caddy there.

While half the detective division at Hollywood Station was at the Los Angeles Country Club watching Bullets Bambarella make an ass out of himself by swinging a golf club like a baseball bat and digging up the largest chunk of ethnically restricted turf that anyone had seen in recent memory, and while the other half of the detective division, including Valnikov and Natalie Zimmerman, were handling their routine investigations, a "sustaining" Pasadena Junior Leaguer was doing some detective work of her own. And was surprising herself at how *well* she was doing it.

Madeline Whitfield had not slept but she had vowed over coffee that morning that she was not going to take a drink until Vickie came home to her. And she wasn't going to just wait until that man called.

She checked the lost and found in the morning *Times* and discovered that there were two schnauzers reported lost. The first belonged to a Redondo Beach phone number. The second was a San Gabriel number, close enough to Pasadena to make Madeline hope that this was the owner of the dead animal, and that there might be a connection which would lead her somewhere. Madeline Whitfield made phone calls, prepared to take copious notes. Except that the first missing schnauzer didn't even have cropped ears. The second was pregnant. Madeline Whitfield was thinking that she might have been too hasty in her temperance vow. She was thinking about a double Scotch when another thought intruded. She phoned the Pasadena Police, the Los Angeles County Sheriff's Office, and the Los Angeles Police Department, inquiring about lost or stolen schnauzers.

"But we don't keep reports on lost dogs," said a Los Angeles Police Department clerk who was almost as lethargic as Officer Leonard Leggett.

"Yes, yes, I understand that," said Madeline Whitfield. "But I'm wondering if someone reported a schnauzer *stolen*. You see, this is a very valuable dog. It's possibly a champion, very definitely show quality. Perhaps you have a report of a dog like this being *stolen?*"

"Just a minute, lady," the lethargic clerk said grumpily. Then when the clerk came back he said, "As a matter of fact we *did* get a hit on a stolen schnauzer."

"Yes?" Madeline said.

"Hollywood," the clerk said. "There was a schnauzer reported stolen in Hollywood Division on January eighth."

"Yes! Yes!" Madeline cried.

"Do you want the report number?" the clerk said. At 11:00 a.m. Woodenlips Mockett received a call at Hollywood Detectives.

"My name is Madeline Whitfield."

"Yes," Woodenlips Mockett said, wishing Captain Hooker would hurry up and get back from the hospital, because with Cromwell there holding his hand, and with the other lieutenant off sick, and with half the troops at some goddamn golf course watching Bullets Bambarella try to hit a golf ball, he was overworked. So far, he had had to make a pot of coffee and answer the phone twice.

"I'd like to inquire about a stolen schnauzer dog," the woman said. "I have a police report number."

"Where was the dog stolen, lady?' said Woodenlips Mockett. This kind of work was demeaning for a lieutenant. Demeaning!

"On Vine Street. The Brown Derby."

"Okay," Woodenlips Mockett sighed, "lemme check for you."

He found the theft report in the control folder belonging to Valnikov and Natalie Zimmerman. "Yeah, wh'adda you wanna know?" Woodenlips Mockett sighed. He intended to take an extra long lunch break to make up for all this work.

"I'd like to speak to the officer working on that case," said Madeline. "Is he there, please?"

"No. His name's Sergeant Valnikov. He'll be back late this afternoon."

"I'd like to talk to him if it's at all possible," Madeline said. "It's important."

"Where do you live?"

"Pasadena."

"Pasadena! Listen, lady, that's a little out of our jurisdiction. Gimme your number, I'll have him call you."

"Could you ask him to call me as soon as he can? I'll be here all day and I'm *most* anxious."

"Okay, gimme your number," Lieutenant Mockett sighed.

Ten minutes later, while driving on Hollywood Boulevard, Valnikov said, "Did you get that, Natalie?"

"Did I get what?" She was lost in a mad plan to go straight to Deputy Chief Digby Bates if she had to. God, what if Hipless Hooker was kept at the hospital? She'd *have* to go over Clarence Cromwell's head.

"We got a call to phone the station," said Valnikov, driving to the nearest call box on Sunset Boulevard.

A few minutes later Vaalnikov was talking on the field phone to Woodenlips, who was starting to calm down now that three teams of detectives had returned, gloating over all the money they'd won from Bullets Bambarella.

"Some broad in Pasadena gave me the number," the lieutenant said "She might know something about a case of yours. A dog snatching from the Brown Derby."

"Yes," Valnikov said. "I thought the dog probably ran away. It's a valuable dog according to the report and . . ."

"Yeah, yeah, that's the one,' said Woodenlips Mockett. "Call this broad, will you? Get her off my back. I got enough pressure right now."

Then Valnikov couldn't make out the rest because Bullets Bambarella was in the squad room yelling to Montezuma Montez:

"*You* a tennis player! Don't make me laugh!"

"Please, Bambarella," Lieutenant Mockett whined. "I can't hear myself talk. Did you get the message, Valnikov? Call this crazy dog about the goddamn lady!"

"That doesn't make much sense, Lieutenant," said Valnikov.

"Do you think *anything* makes sense around here!" Lieutenant Mockett cried. "How would *you* like to get stuck with all the work while Captain Hooker goes to the hospital for an ache in his tum tum? Huh?"

"Okay, Lieutenant," Valnikov said soothingly. "I'll call her. Don't let yourself get excited." Now now, Lieutenant. Now now.

When Valnikov returned to the detective car he found Natalie Zimmerman dashing off some confidential notes. Observations. About him.

"Natalie," he said, causing her to jump so suddenly her Friz bounced to the top of her head and down again.

"Yes?" she said.

"We got a strange call. Some woman in Pasadena wants us to call her about that dog that was stolen from the Brown Derby."

"What dog?"

"The theft report. You know? The one that came in yesterday morning?"

"Christ, Valnikov. You have time to read theft reports? I mean they give you so many burglary reports you can't even count them, you gotta *weigh* them. And you have time to read plain theft reports?"

"I read *all* our reports," he shrugged.

"And you remember them?"

"I can't help remembering," Valnikov said. "I just remember things about my job. They just . . . I just can't seem to get things out of my mind. Know what I mean?"

"Okay, big deal. We have a major crime about somebody stealing a dog?"

Valnikov shrugged again, and said, "I'll just run over to the gas station and use the phone. See what this is all about."

And while Natalie Zimmerman scribbled furiously, stopping every few seconds to blow her Friz off her glasses, Valnikov searched his pockets and found some small change to make a phone call which would profoundly affect the rest of his life.

"Hello, is this Mrs. Whitfield?" he said.

At first her heart stopped. No, it wasn't him. Richard's voice was high pitched. "Yes," she said. "This is Madeline Whitfield."

"This is Sergeant Valnikov, ma'am. Los Angeles Police Department. You called for me?"

"Oh, yes!" she said. "Sergeant, I live in Pasadena. I found . . . found a little schnauzer. The poor thing was dying. It died just after I found her. I . . . well, I looked in the *Times* and I phoned several police departments and I understand you're investigating a case about a stolen schnauzer?"

"Yes," Valnikov hesitated. "Actually, we haven't had time to contact the victim yet. To tell you the truth I just figured her schnauzer ran away or got lost. That's usually the case, and . . ."

"Can you tell me about the schnauzer, Sergeant?" Madeline Whitfield said quickly. "I know it's a bitch. Does your report describe her?"

"Well, not really, ma'am. Actually, I don't even know what a schnauzer looks like, to be honest."

"Does the report say that she's show quality? A champion perhaps?"

"Yes," Valnikov said. "The report does say she's valuable and has been in various dog shows."

Then the line was dead for a moment as Madeline tried to feign nonchalance. "Yes, show quality. That certainly sounds like the poor little schnauzer I found. Tell me, Sergeant, who is . . . *was* the owner?"

"Let's see, the report's in the car, ma'am. A woman in Trousdale Estates. That's in Beverly Hills."

"Could you give me her name and number, Sergeant?" Madeline said. "I'd like to ask her a few questions."

"I'd better have her phone you," said Valnikov. "We're not supposed to give out a victim's phone number. You understand. Did the dog have a collar?"

"No," said Madeline. "But perhaps the owner could describe the schnauzer. I happen to know a lot about this breed. I have a miniature schnauzer of my own."

"Okay, ma'am, I'll have the owner call you this afternoon. I'll be back in the station about four p.m. and . . ."

"No!" Madeline cried, and then she said calmly, "No, Sergeant. Please. Could you have her call me right away? This is urgent. I . . . I'm a dog owner myself and I know what this means. Please."

"I'll call her right away," said Valnikov.

"Thank you, Sergeant," said Madeline Whitfield.

"You're welcome."

Valnikov was almost out of change. He managed to scrape up enough for the second call. The phone rang seven times. He was about to hang up, when a young man answered.

"Yeah?"

"This is Sergeant Valnikov, Los Angeles Police Department."

"Yeah?"

"I'm investigating a theft of a dog. Is this the residence of Millie M. Gharoujian?"

"Just a minute." The line was quiet, then a muffled voice said, "Millie, it's for you. Some cop about Tutu."

"Hello," a husky voice breathed.

"Ma'am, this is Sergeant Valnikov, Los Ang—"

"Yeah, okay," said Millie. "You find Tutu?"

"Well, a lady in Pasadena thinks she might have your dog, ma'am. I'm sorry to say she found a champion class schnauzer that fits the description. But the poor dog died and . . ."

"Yeah, is it my Tutu?"

"I don't know, ma'am. She left her name and number if you'd care to call her."

"Look, pal. What's your name?"

"Valnikov, ma'am."

"Yeah. Listen, pal. I'm seventy-six years old."

"Yes, ma'am," said Valnikov.

"Well, you just interrupted the best . . . Look, I happen to be having a grand time and you have to interrupt it. Is *this* what I pay taxes for?"

"No, ma'am," said Valnikov.

"Okay, now look. My dog was snatched or ran off or whatever, last week. She's a three-year-old schnauzer that cost me upwards a twenty grand before I say, Millie, why you blowing all this dough on a goddamn dog? Get it?"

"Yes, ma'am."

"So look, I already made an insurance claim. If the dog's dead what the hell can I do about it, Sergeant?"

"I don't know, ma'am," said Valnikov. "Could you describe your dog? This lady seems terribly concerned and . . ."

"Jesus Christ!" Millie Muldoon Gharoujian cried. "I got two kids here that look like they were carved by Michelangelo and I'm supposed to worry about a *dog!*"

"She had no identification, I take it," said Valnikov.

"She had one white toenail on her left rear foot," Millie said gruffly. "My ex-dog handler, a jerk named Philo Skinner, used to paint that toenail black before the dog shows. Now please, Sergeant, I appreciate your dedication, but can I get back to *my* business with these boys? Don't you have any respect for senior citizens?"

"Yes, ma'am," said Valnikov. "Yes, ma'am."

"It took long enough," said Natalie Zimmerman when Valnikov returned to the detective car.

"Do you mind if we go back to the station? I have to call this lady from Pasadena again and I'm out of pocket change."

While Valnikov made his call at Hollywood Station, Natalie Zimmerman used the time to phone the hospital. She was told that Captain Hooker had just suffered an attack of stomach gas. He was with Sergeant Cromwell and was presumably resting easily. Natalie Zimmerman put in a call to the area commander, who was out to lunch. Then she returned to the burglary table where Valnikov was talking to Madeline Whitfield.

"That's right," Valnikov said into the phone. "The schnauzer had one white toenail on her left rear foot. What color are they normally? Black? Yes. Did you notice if the dog had one white toenail? You didn't notice. That's too bad. Where's the dead dog now? A what? A pet mortuary? Yes, I know where that is. Do they cremate them or bury them or what? They *embalm* them? Animals? Really? Well, the lady who reported the stolen schnauzer doesn't seem to care very much whether it's her dog or not. That's right. She really doesn't want to bother talking to you. I don't understand either. Yes, I'm a pet owner. I have a parakeet and a gerbil. A gerbil. No, it's a *gerbil*. Indigenous to southern Russia. For now I don't know what else I can do. Yes, that's all right, ma'am. Yes. Good-bye."

After he hung up, he looked at a totally frustrated Natalie Zimmerman.

"Would you like to go to lunch now?" he asked. "I have a surprise for you. A very unusual place to eat."

"What the hell!" she said to her Friz. "Let's go, Valnikov. I'll probably get botulism. Why do I *always* have to pick the black marble?"

He was driving the detective car along Pico Boulevard in a neighborhood she didn't know very well. He'd gone to Vermont and was now heading back west. The Cuban storefronts lined the street. There was Rosario's Boutique. Not like the boutiques in Beverly Hills. Rosario's was a storefront ten feet wide. The most expensive item cost $13.95 and Rosario's did not take credit cards. They passed a liquor store which carried a big window placard advertising *Silox Super-X, Cockroach Control Overnight. Guaranteed!* There was a storefront advertising *Consulto Espiritual,* in case you cared to know the mysteries of the past and future. The present was of not much interest to the spiritualist.

Then thriftshops and wooden buildings which should have been demolished. Vacant lots. Then another Cuban spiritualist who, incredibly enough, offered in addition to herbs and medicines—religion. The sign simply advertised: *Marta's religion*. Natalie Zimmerman thought that was honest enough.

Then past a huge primitive mural on the side of a building depicting dark Latin faces under Mexican sombreros, with eyes like Russian ikons, and letters emblazoned: TIERRA Y LIBERTAD! Leaving Valnikov uncertain as to whether the *tierra y libertad* was the dream of the Cubans of the neighborhood, or the Mexicans depicted thereon. No matter. All Latinos dreamed of *tierra y libertad* regardless of their homeland, and, like the Russians, had seen precious little of it in the course of history.

And then, between Mariposa and Normandie, the import stores which advertised Greek, Arab, Armenian, Persian, Turkish, Italian, Soviet imports. These stores were located strategically near St. Sophia's, the huge-domed cathedral for the Greek Orthodox of Los Angeles. Amidst the food stores there was an international record store which offered tapes and records to the ethnic shoppers.

When Valnikov pulled to the curb and parked, she heard and smelled the exotic.

"I buy my music there," Valnikov said, pointing to the record store from which balalaikas throbbed. Valnikov was beaming. They usually played bazouki because Greek customers far outnumbered Russian.

"Is this a restaurant?" Natalie asked, as Valnikov led her into the smallest of the stores. There were powerful odors of black and green olives, goat cheeses from five countries, oils and wines, pastries and breads, meats and spices from the nations of the Mediterranean. And in this particular store, some foods, some wines, some vodka from the north.

"Andrei Mikhailovich!" a man behind the counter thundered. He wore a meat-stained apron, and a tunic which marked him as a Molokan to those who knew.

"Iosif!" Valnikov grinned, and then a big man came out from the back room. He was wearing a blue sweater and spoke unaccented English. He was close to 280 pounds and stood well over six feet tall. His hair was nearly white but he had the same broad Slavic forehead as Valnikov, and the same kind of ingenuous grin which Natalie decided was more childlike than dumb.

He said, "Where you been for three weeks, you little jerk?" And he grabbed Valnikov, puckered, and kissed him smack on the mouth. They embraced and bobbed around for a few seconds. Dancing bears.

Then he gave Valnikov a crack on the shoulder and reached out with a sweep of an enormous arm, half crushing the astonished Natalie Zimmerman, and kissed *her* smack on the mouth. ''Hello, good-looking,'' he said. ''You smell like a cop to me. And that's a sexy smell!''

''You old devil,'' Valnikov chuckled.

The big man released Natalie Zimmerman and said, ''Now that we're acquainted, how about some borscht?''

''This is my brother, Alex,'' Valnikov said to Natalie, who was trying to keep her gun from falling out of her purse, her huge glasses from falling off her nose, and her bra from slipping up over her nipple, so quick and violent was the assault of the elder Valnikov. The Molokan butcher was shaking up and down in laughter as he cleavered through a lamb bone like it was salami.

''My partner, Natalie Zimmerman,'' said Valnikov.

''Ah-hah!'' said the elder Valnikov. ''I knew she was a cop, but she's not carrying a gun on her person, I can tell you that!''

Which propelled the Molokan butcher into a fit of bouncing laughter.

''We can't stay, Alex,'' Valnikov said. ''We haven't called on a single burglary victim today and . . .''

''Bull! You pop in here once a month and hardly ever come see your nephews and nieces and you can't stay! Bull!''

''How about some tea, Alex?'' Valnikov said sheepishly, as though the big man were his father, and indeed he could have been, thought Natalie Zimmerman. He was much older than Valnikov.

''Yeah, some tea *with* some lunch *here!*'' Alex Valnikov said.

''Honest, we gotta go,'' said Valnikov. ''How about something to take out? We can only stay a few minutes.''

''You know, you're a real pain in the ass, kid,'' said Alex Valnikov, shaking his head and opening the meat case while Natalie managed to slip the bra back down over the bruised nipple while the Molokan pretended not to notice. ''You're a real pain, boy. You must give me an hour of your time. In a whole year!''

''Well, I always mean to stop by,'' Valnikov apologized. ''But you know how busy cops are . . .''

''Sure. Save that for the dummies don't know any better. I know better.'' Then he turned to Natalie and his eyes, as blue as Valnikov's, creased, and he said, ''Now you met Valnikov the bashful. That's me.''

''I'm . . . overwhelmed,'' said Natalie while the Molokan whacked through another lamb shank.

''You didn't even come Thursday night,'' Alex Valnikov said. ''We were all expecting you to at least show up for church.''

''I went to church, Alex,'' Vainikov said, actually dropping his gaze before the chastisement. ''I went to the cathedral, that's why you didn't see me. I wouldn't miss on Christmas.''

''You'll have lunch with me then?''

''We'll have tea, Alex,'' Valnikov said. ''And if you can, maybe some lunch to take with us.''

''If I *can,*'' the elder Valnikov glowered. ''Listen to him. If I *can.*''

Valnikov was saved further scolding when an ancient crone with wrapped spindle legs came hobbling into the store. She looked first at the Molokan butcher then back toward Alex Valnikov. Then she recognized the detective.

''Sergeant Valnikov!'' she cried.

''Good afternoon, Mrs. Rosenfeldt,'' Valnikov said, running his fingers through his fluffy cinnamon hair.

''I've been wondering when you'd be back to your brother's store. We was talking about you just recently, ain't that true, Alex?''

''Every day, Mrs. Rosenfeldt,'' the elder Valnikov nodded.

"I was saying how we need a good cop in this neighborhood, like Alex's little brother. Wasn't I saying that, Alex?"

"You were, Mrs. Rosenfeldt," Alex said. "Every day."

"Come over here, Sergeant, let me tell you what's the latest mischief they're up to. Come over here."

"Yes, Mrs. Rosenfeldt," Valnikov said obediently, crossing by the meat counter while the Molokan swung the cleaver.

"Sergeant Valnikov," she whispered, pulling him down toward her face. She was toothless and smelled of fish. "It's Myer."

"Your husband," Valnikov whispered.

"Yes, they're at it again. I went to visit him in the rest home over in Boyle Heights. You know where that is?"

"I sure do, Mrs. Rosenfeldt," Valnikov nodded patiently, blinking his watery eyes.

"He's been taking up with a hussy there. Name's Ida Schwartz. You won't believe the sex goes on there. It's a disgrace. Of course, Myer's only a man. Him I don't blame. But Ida Schwartz? She should be in San Quentin, that woman."

"Yes, of course," Valnikov agreed. "How old is Mrs. Schwartz now? Eighty?"

"She's eighty-three, the stinking harlot!" Mrs. Rosenfeldt cried. "I don't blame Myer. A man is all he is. And there's just so much temptation a man can take."

"I understand, Mrs. Rosenfeldt," Valnikov nodded, gravely. His runny blue eyes were sad. Earl Scheib Lopez, 11 years old, and Ida Schwartz 83, San Quentin cellmates.

"Well, what can you do, Sergeant Valnikov?" the old woman demanded.

"It's very hard to put people in state prison," Valnikov explained. "Especially for . . ."

"Adultery!" she cried.

"Yes, especially for adultery. You see, it's not a crime."

"What is it coming to, this world, Sergeant?" Mrs. Rosenfeldt said.

"Now now, Mrs. Rosenfeldt," Valnikov said, leading her over to one of three folding chairs placed for the convenience of aged customers like Mrs. Rosenfeldt. "Just sit down, and my brother will fix you a nice cup of tea."

"Tea. That would be good, Sergeant," Mrs. Rosenfeldt said, with a gummy smile. A wet star slithered from her lashless eyes and followed a jagged course through the creases of her cheeks.

"Did I ever tell you about the samovar we had when I was a boy, Mrs. Rosenfeldt?" Valnikov said, sitting in a folding chair next to the fragile old woman. "Well, my parents carried that samovar and an ikon of St. Sergius and a picture of Nicholas the second across Siberia, all the way to Vladivostok. That's one-fourth of the world, Mrs. Rosenfeldt!"

"Imagine," the old lady said, forgetting about Myer banging that stinking harlot, Ida Schwartz.

"Finally they arrived at the sea, Mrs. Rosenfeldt. Can you imagine how it was then? All the Whites escaping with their families? And at last, with the help of other army officers, and mostly with the help of a fleeing nobleman my father had befriended, they crossed the great Pacific Ocean . . ."

"On a Canadian vessel!" she cackled triumphantly.

"That's right," Valnikov smiled, his sad runny eyes wet not from tears but Stolichnaya runoff. They'd be clearing at about 2:00 p.m. if he could judge by his vodka intake.

"They landed in Seattle!" Mrs. Rosenfeldt reminded him.

"Yes, that's right," Valnikov nodded.

"Is that true?" Natalie Zimmerman asked Alex Valnikov while Mrs. Rosenfeldt picked up the story of the Valnikov odyssey and told it to Valnikov.

"Sure," Alex Valnikov grinned. "They carried one other thing besides an ikon and samovar, and a picture of Nicholas Romanov. They carried *me*. I was two years old when we sailed from Vladivostok in 1922. And I was a one hundred percent, gum-chewing, Los Angeles teenager by the time that baby over there was born in the Depression. Mrs. Rosenfeldt's heard the story a hundred times or so, that's why she's doing the telling. Keeps her mind off her sex problems with Myer. Who died five years ago."

"You mean she doesn't accept that he's dead?"

"In a way she does," said Alex Valnikov, wrapping the cabbage rolls and pumpernickel. "Sometimes she seems to know for sure, then other times . . ."

"Does she come in every day?"

"Just about. And every time she sees my brother it sets her off to telling about how Ida Schwartz should be arrested. I imagine Ida Schwartz is dead by now too. We don't mind it. In fact Iosif looks forward to her stories."

The Molokan heard his name and grinned. One tooth was missing in front. Whack! went the cleaver.

"It's kind of a continuing soap opera," said Alex Valnikov. "My brother has a way with old people. Look at her. She's telling him about his own family who she never met. Have some tea." He served the tea in a glass. "Russian style," he explained.

"Tastes good," Natalie Zimmerman said, sipping the hot tea carefully.

The big man lowered his voice and said, "How long you been working with my brother?"

"Not long."

"What do you think?"

"What do you mean?"

"My brother drinks all the time. He didn't used to do that. Even after his divorce. My brother wasn't a drunk even after the divorce. Now my brother's a drunk. Do all the other cops talk about it?"

"No, I don't think so," Natalie Zimmerman said, putting her glass of hot tea on the meat counter. "Lots of veteran detectives are known to take a drink. I don't think he's known as a particularly heavy drinker."

"My brother started acting different a few months ago." Now he was whispering. "He had a partner, Charlie Lightfoot."

"I know about that," she nodded.

"About the time Charlie died, he started acting . . . different. Sort of absentminded. Sort of like his mind wanders. Then the *heavy* boozing started. Hell, we never see him anymore! I'm not his only family. We got a cousin lives in San Pedro and we got a cousin in Sylmar. Nobody sees him. We were a close family once. I worry about my brother. I got four kids that can make you stay up nights, all the crap they step in, but I worry most about my little brother."

"I don't think he's a real heavy drinker," Natalie Zimmerman lied, unable to look in the passionate blue eyes of Valnikov the elder. No, he's not a heavy drinker. Just a 14 karat alcoholic, is all. And a 21 karat dingaling to boot. And *I'm* the one fate elected to dispatch the clown with my terrible swift sword.

"Come get your tea, kld," Alex Valnikov said, and the detective got up, patted Mrs. Rosenfeldt's hand, and joined them.

"That's very sad," Natalie Zimmerman said, looking at the old woman who was now telling the Molokan butcher about Myer the whoremonger. That's what philanderers deserve. A cleaver. Whack!

"Well, we don't mind sadness," Alex Valnikov grinned. "Haven't you seen Russian plays? We're only happy when we're sad." He turned to his younger brother and said, "You changed your mind? Staying for some borscht, right?"

Valnikov smiled apologetically and sipped the tea from his glass and his elder brother sighed and handed the heavy paper bag to Natalie Zimmerman.

"It was nice to meet you, hon," the big man said. Then he leaned over and gave her a friendly hug which didn't roll up her bra this time.

"I'll be seeing you, Iosif," Valnikov said to the butcher, who by now was caught up in Mrs. Rosenfeldt's story of sex and depravity in the Jewish Home for the Aged.

"I see you, Andrei Mikhailovich!" the Molokan said, waving his cleaver.

Then Valnikov stopped at the door, where Natalie was taking money out of her purse to pay at the register.

"Don't be silly, honey," the elder Valnikov said. Then he turned to his brother and said, "You come for dinner. Soon. You and me haven't had a talk in a hell of a long time, boy."

"Bye, Alex. Thanks for the eats," Valnikov said, putting an arm around his brother. Then the bears danced for another moment and the elder Valnikov kissed him on the mouth. "You take *care,* Andrushka. You hear me?"

When they got back in the car, Valnikov took the wheel again and headed downtown. "Now comes the best part," he said to Natalie Zimmerman, who was lost in unhappy contemplation of black marbles.

He surprised her by parking at the Music Center. "Follow me," he said with that grin of his. She was sure now after meeting his brother. It was childlike. On Alex Valnikov the big grin didn't look so dumb.

She'd go along with anything on this, the last day. It was the least she could do before . . . before she went to see Hipless Hooker.

He parked on Hope Street and led her up the steps between the Dorothy Chandler Pavilion and the Mark Taper Forum. There were a few people roaming around, mostly coming from the restaurant on the Grand Avenue level. There were tourists taking pictures of the three neoclassical buildings which make up the Music Center complex, and of the enormous contemporary sculpture called *Peace on Earth*. Some decided it was a totem, no, a *pyramid* of bodies, animals and people, piled one on top of the other like a Hollywood orgy.

Valnikov led Natalie past the Mark Taper Forum with its quiet, asexual reflecting pool. It was windy and the snowcapped San Gabriels were visible from Bunker Hill today. Across the avenue was the county courthouse and a sculpted relief of a hopeful knight in chain mail brandishing the Magna Carta.

Then Valnikov beckoned Natalie toward a small cluster of people: tourists, downtown civil servants, pensioners, students, who were gathered around a young man with a full black beard and a war-surplus, navy peacoat, playing "Midnight in Moscow" for all he was worth. He was only worth a few bucks.

"They call him Horst," Valnikov whispered when they were sitting on the steps. "He's a fair musician. Plays here in the afternoons. I've heard he's a medical student."

The bearded young violinist had an old top hat upside down on the pavement. There were a few dollar bills and some change inside, but clearly, today's session was a bummer. Horst Vanderhoof was getting set to trip on home when he opened his eyes and saw that the small audience had grown by two.

"Charlie and I used to listen to him sometimes in the afternoons and have lunch like this. For a while, Charlie wanted to learn something about music."

Valnikov unwrapped a mound of hot cabbage rolls and set the paper plates, plastic forks, and paper napklns in front of Natalie on the concrete steps as though he were waiting on a table.

"Is your brother a caterer?" Natalie asked.

"The best," Valnikov smiled. "That's a big part of his business. He caters Russian weddings and parties. There's always an excuse for a celebration. If it isn't Pushkin's birthday it's Tolstoy's. Or it's the jubilee of the Bolshoi Ballet. Or the jubilee of the day somebody's cousin became an American citizen. Or somebody graduated from barber college. Anything."

"Cabbage rolls," she said. "I had a Polish grandmother made these."

"Oh, you're Polish!" said Valnikov, unwrapping the black bread and little cartons of whipped butter.

"I had a grandmother from Poland and I think a great-grandfather from Germany. Hell, I'm am American. What's that stuff?"

Valnikov held a paper plate stacked with golden pastries and said, "*Piroshki*. They're very light and filled with cheese or meat. My brother usually makes them both ways. And these others are fruit pastries."

"Looks good," Natalie said, as Valnikov presented the array of homemade Russian food.

"I think you'll like this black bread, Natalie," he said. "My mother used to make white bread only on Christmas or Easter. Sometime I'll bring some plastic containers and we'll get some borscht. My brother makes the best borscht you'll ever taste. The secret's in boiling the beef beforehand. And you add *dusha* last. That means soul. Oh, this is lamb, marinated and barbecued. He doesn't have it every day. We're lucky."

"It smells fantastic," Natalie Zimmerman said.

Then Valnikov noticed the music had stopped and he saw Horst packing up his violin case and emptying out the top hat. Most of the onlookers had strolled off.

"Wait, wait!" Valnikov yelled, putting down his plate scurrying up the steps toward the reflecting pool.

Then Natalie Zimmerman saw him reach in his pocket and give some money to Horst. The kid nodded, took off his top hat again, put down the violin case and opened it up.

When he returned, Valnikov said, "The best part is having music when you eat."

And then came the *pièce de résistance*. Valnikov drew from the bag a half bottle of Bulgarian wine which Alex had uncorked and capped.

"Wine too? I can't believe it!" Natalie Zimmerman said, as Valnikov chuckled and poured into styrofoam cups.

"There's a Russian toast which says, 'If we must die, let's do it with music.' " And then Horst burst forth with five bucks' worth of Rimsky-Korsakov. Horst could burst forth much better for a tenner, but Valnikov was satisfied.

Then Valnikov said, shyly, "Well, this is the surprise. How do you like it?"

And Natalie Zimmerman pushed terrible thoughts from her mind and concentrated on the wonderful food and the reflecting pool, and the clear sky and the mountains in the distance. She said, "This is the loveliest lunch I've ever had."

"*Na zdorovye!*" he grinnned happily, toasting her with the styrofoam cup.

Jesus, he had fine table manners. The poor doomed bastard. Jesus. Then for the first time, it occurred to her she had never called him by his first name. She didn't even *know* his first name! Sergeant A.M. Valnikov. Val.

"Andrei something, the butcher called you."

"Andrei Mikhailovich," he said, careful to swallow and dab his lips with the paper napkin before speaking.

"But what did your brother call you when he kissed you good-bye?"

"Silly, isn't it? Kissing like that. My brother never really escaped the old ways. He's still an *émigré* in his heart. He's saving to make a long vacation in Leningrad someday. I think this might be the year. Business is pretty good now."

"But what did he call you?"

"Andrushka," Valnikov said softly. "My mother always called me that."

"That's a nice name," Natalie Zimmerman said, looking at Horst the fiddler, who struggled a little, then got hot with Tchaikovsky.

"Do you mean it?"

"Sure. And what would be the Russian equivalent of my name? Of Natalie?"

Valnikov put down the cup and listened to the music for a moment. "The equivalent would be Natalia."

"Natalia," she said. "I've never liked Natalie."

"How about Natasha?" he said, looking deep in her eyes. "It's more endearing. Like Andrushka."

"Natasha," she said, pushing her drooping glasses up. "I like that better."

"Natasha," he whispered. Then he concentrated on buttering his black bread, but his Russian heart was advancing fifteen beats a minute.

While Natalie Zimmerman and Valnikov were having a memorable lunch, Madeline Whitfield and Philo Skinner were having a memorable phone conversation.

"It's Richard," Philo whispered into the mouthpiece. He was asphyxiating himself inside a smoky phone booth, in the heat of the afternoon, outside a motel five blocks from his business. It was the motel where he had dreamed of taking Pattie Mae to before she quit on him after the Sunday dog show. The miserable little cunt.

"Yes, I've been waiting for your call," said Madeline, fighting to keep her voice businesslike and unwavering.

"When do I get the money?" Philo croaked.

"You've got to control yourself, Richard, and let me talk," Madeline began. She'd rehearsed it and believed she could even deal with the threats and obscenities.

"Make it quick."

"I've been on the phone all day with my accountant and banker and . . ."

"You *told* someone about this!"

"No, no," she said quickly. "About needing money only. I just told them I had a pressing need for as much as I could possibly get. I even called an old classmate whose husband is chairman of the board of a savings and loan."

"What's the bottom line, lady?" Philo snarled.

"I will have, by noon tomorrow, twelve thousand dollars," Madeline said, and despite herself, her voice broke on the number.

"What did you say? WHAT DID YOU SAY?" Philo began hacking and gagging on the ubiquitous phlegm balls.

Madeline waited until the coughing stopped. When he came back he was wheezing: "Lady . . . lady . . ." Then he gasped and said, "You cunt!"

"Please, Richard," Madeline begged.

"You . . . you rotten cunt. Twelve thousand!"

"Listen to me," she said. "It's not only all I have in the world. It represents borrowed money. I'm looking for a *job*. I've never worked in my life. I'm not qualified for anything but I'm looking for a *job,* and this house was refinanced, and the money's all gone. My mother was sick for four years before she died! Do you know what round-the-clock nursing costs? Do you know what hospital bills are like? Please, Richard. Please!"

He didn't hear a complete sentence she uttered. Twelve thousand. It wouldn't even pay Arnold for the gambling losses. The kike and the nigger would be coming for him with the stripping knife. And he promised Arnold the money by Thursday, Plus three hundred interest for waiting past Monday. *Twelve* thousand?

"Twelve thousand," he said, then he felt it grow within him. Philo Skinner had spent much of his life being afraid. He was afraid right now of what the bookmakers would do to him, but he felt the fear being consumed by anger. Twelve thousand!

"I'm cutting off one of that bitch's toes right now. Stay on the line you cunt and you can hear her scream!"

"Noooooooo!" It was Madeline Whitfield who screamed.

"You wanna hear her scream, you cunt!" Philo yelled in the mouthpiece. "You lying, stingy *rich* cunt!"

''Can't we talk face to face, Richard?'' Madeline babbled. ''I swear I won't call the police. I'll come anywhere. Do anything you want. Oh, please don't hurt Vickie!''

''How's she gonna do in the next dog show, you cunt!''

''Please, please, please. I'll get more money. I swear! Give me one more day. One more.''

''I told you I want eighty-five thousand, you . . . you . . .''

''I'll get more! I can get more. If . . . if you let me have Vickie back. I can . . . I can send you five hundred a month until I pay it all. I'm going to get a—'' Madeline began weeping brokenly ''—job. Please.''

''I can't believe it!'' Philo said, dropping the paper towel he had wrapped over the mouthpiece. ''I can't believe it!'' He'd never seen anything like *this* in kidnapping movies. She wanted him to return the bitch and she'd pay the ransom on the installment plan? Ransom by credit card? ''Lady I'm gonna cut off a toe,'' Philo croaked weakly before another coughing spasm made him open the door of the phone booth and hack and wheeze and spit in the motel parking lot.

At which time the motel proprietor, Bessie Callahan, a woman Philo's age, with a surly red face and broken teeth, opened the screen door of the manager's office and yelled, ''Hey, fella, go and spit your goopers in the gutter, not on *my* property!''

''Fuck you too, you miserable cunt,'' Philo barked, which cost him yet another coughing spasm and another gooper on her sidewalk.

''What'd you call me, you scrawny coyote?'' Bessie Callahan challenged. ''If my husband was here he'd tie you in a knot, you filthy coyote!''

Then, wracked with pain and gasping for breath, and filled with consummate frustration and outrage and anger, Philo Skinner dropped the phone and stepped out of the phone booth, and for the first time in memory challenged someone to a fight. ''Step out here, you fat cunt,'' Philo gasped. ''Come out here and I'll punch your fat face in, you fat cunt!''

''Prick!'' yelled Bessie Callahan. ''Skinny prick! How *dare* you talk to a lady like this!''

And while a trembling Philo Skinner got control of himself, and lit his forty-seventh cigarette of the day, and picked up the phone only to find Madeline Whitfield hysterical because she thought the extortionist was cutting off Vickie's toe, Bessie Callahan had a little surprise for Philo Skinner.

''Control yourself, woman,'' he ordered Madeline Whitfield. ''Get yourself under control and listen to me, goddamnit!''

''Sir . . . sir . . . please don't, please!'' Madeline wailed.

''I'm calling you again at six o'clock tonight,'' Philo Skinner gasped. ''Have some good news for me then. I won't cut off any toes until we have *one* more talk. Understand? I won't cut off any toes. Yet.''

''Sir . . . sir . . . thank . . . thank you,'' Madeline sobbed.

''I'll be calling at six. Remember that! Six o'cl—'' But he never finished it. He thought he heard running water. Then the door of the phone booth burst open and Philo Skinner was drowning! He couldn't even scream. He swallowed his cigarette butt along with a mouthful of water. He breathed another mouthful into his lungs! He threw his hands out in front of him and fell down in the phone booth. Drowning.

Bessie Cailahan, like the sewer worker, Tyrone McGee, had been pushed around all her life, but not by alligators. And certainly not by filthy coyotes who used her telephone and spit goopers on her parking lot. At first she just intended to use the motel fire hose to wash up the wads of filthy goopers he'd deposited all over her sidewalk, but the more she thought of this coyote telling her he'd punch her in the face, and calling her a fat cunt—and heard the coyote screaming over the telephone, calling someone *else* a cunt—the more she decided he wasn't going to get away with it. How about some water for your filthy mouth, you chauvinist prick!

Bessie, her pale eyes bulging with the thrill of it, had Philo helpless on the floor of the phone booth before she knew what she was doing. Still, she kept the fire hose trained on his face. Philo flopped on his belly to breathe. He was finally able to scream but Bessie still wouldn't turn off the hose. Only when she realized what she was doing did she pull the nozzle lever stopping the powerful water jet and hightail it back to her apartment.

"I'll . . . I'll get you for this," Philo croaked, coughing water. The soggy cigarette came up in his throat. He swallowed it down but it came back up with his breakfast. Now Bessie had something else to hose away.

"I'm calling the cops, you coyote!" Bessie screamed through the latched screen door. "You can't attack a woman and get away with it. I am calling the cops!"

"Cops," Philo gasped. "Cops." He tried to get up but dropped to one knee, retching again. The second of his three polyester leisure suits, this one a cobalt blue, was absolutely drenched. Philo's shoes squished when he got to his feet staggering against the phone booth.

"The cops're coming, you coyote!" Bessie lied. "I hear the sirens. Now we'll see what they do to coyotes that pick on ladies."

"Cops," Philo muttered. Then he was off in a loping, squishy retreat to his El Dorado, which was parked in the alley.

Philo Skinner had driven two blocks before he realized there were no red lights in his rearview mirror. He pulled to the curb and leaned out the window. His tortured lungs were half full of water. He lay back against the leather Cadillac seats and pressed on his scrawny chest trying to give himself artificial respiration. Then he leaned over and out the passenger door, and moaned, hoping the water would trickle out his mouth.

An old pensioner was pushing home a shopping cart full of groceries when he saw a half-drowned man leaning out the El Dorado. The pensioner stopped the shopping cart and shuffled over to Philo, looking down at him curiously. The Cadillac was dry but the man was soaked and dripping.

"Looks like you run yourself through a car wash, sonny" the old man observed. "It's the *car* you're supposed to wash, not yourself."

"Ooooooooooohhhhhh," Philo Skinner moaned, sounding for all the world like Hipless Hooker with a bellyache.

"What's the matter, boy?" the old man said, sucking on a lipload of snuff.

"Ooooooooooohhhhhh," Philo answered.

"Well, I gotta go, sonny," the old snuff-dipper said. "I was you, next time I drive through the car wash, I'd call a lifeguard."

And while Philo Skinner was wishing he had the strength to start his Cadillac and run over the cackling snuff-dipper, Mavis Skinner was embarked on a little investigation of her own.

That goddamn Philo was acting awful strange lately. She'd bet he was playing around with some little bird at the kennel. Probably had that Pattie Mae coming in every day for some stud service. Probably buying her pretties with what little money the kennel took in. Well, Mavis Skinner wasn't going to put up with any little birds around *her* nest. She decided to pay Philo an unannounced visit.

She was disappointed not to find his car there. She unlocked the office and didn't find any little birds nesting. There was nothing unusual but an uncommonly bad stench coming from the dog pens. Philo hadn't been cleaning them like he said he was. The lazy asshole!

Then a station wagon pulled into the driveway. A man and a woman got out, leading a 110-pound German shepherd. They walked through the door in front of the animal, who carried his ears back and his tail tucked low. The enormous shepherd had an L-shaped scar over his right eye. His snout was crossed by another scar that drew a blue line from his eye to his scarred, curling lip. He had wary amber eyes. Mavis didn't like him one goddamn bit.

"Yes?" she said to the smiling couple who were dressed like a Hawaiian vacation.

"We'd like to board our Walter for two weeks," said the man. "We're going on a Caribbean cruise. The whole family." The thought of it made him grin wider.

"Well," Mavis said, studying the fearsome beast, "We specialize in terriers here."

"You only board terriers?"

"No, we board all breeds, but to tell the truth, sir, that looks like an attack dog to me."

Then the woman stopped smiling and said in a high voice, "Oh, Walter's rehabilitated."

"Rehabilitated?"

"He *used* to be a guard dog, but that was years ago. Why, he's a family pet. Our children ride him like a pony, and box his ears, and kiss him on the nose, and . . ."

"That dog's been mistreated," Mavis said, pointing at the scars. "I dunno . . ."

"Believe me," the man said, releasing Walter's lead, "this dog's perfectly gentle. We've adopted four animals from the S.P.C.A. Walter's our pride and joy. He's been tamed with love. He's a family pet."

But Walter hadn't *always* been a family pet and Mavis knew it by looking at him. He had been seized by court order five years before with thirteen other half-demented brutes, the property of another half-demented brute who owned a guard dog service and "trained" his animals with a three-foot length of ordinary garden hose, loaded with ordinary chunks of lead. Walter had a short unhappy career guarding industrial building sites before the court order brought him to the animal shelter and eventually to the home of the adopted parents who were determined to turn a snarling monster into a lap dog. And they did. He was seven years old now and it was the first time Walter had been away from his adopted family. It was the first time he was to be caged since his hateful formative time in guard dog service. Walter was indifferent to Mavis, but he didn't like cages. Not at all. The bad old days.

"We'll be glad to pay you a premium for taking Walter," the man said, "although he's perfectly safe to handle."

"A premium," she said. The magic word. Oh, what the hell.

So Walter had a new home temporarily. And it was to have a profound effect on Philo Skinner's future. Destiny.

When Horst was finished with a very mediocre "Dance of the Comedians" he cleared his throat and Valnikov started to reach in his pocket.

"Wait," Natalie said. "What's he want, more money?"

"It's okay, he's worth it," said Valnikov, but she put her hand on his arm and said, "We've had enough music. Don't spend any more money." Then she turned to the young man and said, "Thanks, kid, it was great."

The bearded young fiddler shrugged and began putting away his instrument.

"He ever play for free?" Natalie asked, devouring her fourth cabbage roll. The bread was incredible with the cabbage rolls and butter.

"Well, no, but it's all right."

"A pre-med student, huh? He's a future sawbones, all right. Get the money before the operation every time. Well, music or no music, it's been a memorable lunch."

"I'm so glad you enjoyed it, Natalie," Valnikov said, gathering up their paper and leftovers. "You know, it's almost end-of-watch. Time passed so fast today!"

Natalie Zimmerman was feeling even more miserable about everything during the drive to the station. Jesus, she *had* to do it. Nothing personal, Valnikov. You're a decent guy. Nothing personal. It's just that you're *nuts*. Turn around now and let Natalie Zimmerman split your skull with a cleaver. Whack! Let your *partner* do it to you. It's for the good of the police department, Captain. Valnikov is insane and anyone can see it if he spends more than an hour with the guy. But you see, sir, nobody spends any time with the poor slob. He's a loner. Not even his brother can get a handle on him. He's off and running, but if you corner him, sit him across the desk, get the doctor to start with the questions, you'll see it. He's on the verge of a breakdown. Hell, he's *already* broken down. He's . . . I don't know . . . he's limping along, Captain.

He can fool you sometimes. Because he's considerate, and thoughtful. Yes, you were right, he *is* a gentleman, and no, not many partners I ever had were gentlemen, and . . . God! She thought of Valnikov talking with the old people. No, she couldn't tell about spray-painting the little germ, because, God help her, she *loved* that. That's the point. A madman can infect people with his madness if you're with him long enough. You get a little crazy too. That's the point!

"That's the point," she said. Damn! Now he had *her* talking to herself.

"What's the point, Natalie?" Valnikov asked pleasantly, driving west on Fountain Avenue, into the sunset.

"Who knows," she muttered. "What's the point? Did you ever figure that out, Valnikov?" Now Natalie Zimmerman felt like crying because she didn't want to do it and she had to do it. "What's the point, Valnikov? All those things you talk about, all the killers you and Charlie Lightfoot hunted. All those murdered children. A Braille reading book. Was there any *point,* Valnikov?"

"There *is* no point, Natalie," Valnikov said matter-of-factly, both hands tightening on the steering wheel, driving as always, fifteen miles per hour. "There's no point and that's the point."

"What's the point?"

"That there's no point, Natalie. That's the point."

"Oh, Christ, Valnikov, let's go home."

"Okay, Natalie, we're home." And he wheeled into the police parking lot at Fountain and Wilcox.

Valnikov was just about ready to ask her to go to that movie when a man in a corduroy sport coat with leather elbow patches walked up to their car.

He was taller and younger than Valnikov. He looked like an overage jock, maybe a college football coach. He wore a button-down blue shirt and regimental necktie. He had lots of teeth.

"Jack!" Natalie said. "What're you doing here?"

"You've been wanting to see the musical at the Shubert? Well, guess who has tickets in the orchestra? That means an early dinner, so let's just go from here."

He threw his arm around her and kissed her cheek.

"Captain Packerton, meet my partner, Sergeant Valnikov," she said. "Uh, Captain Packerton commands West Valley Station."

"Pleased to meet you, Captain," said Valnikov, smiling with very sad eyes.

"Valnikov," Captain Packerton nodded, shaking hands perfunctorily. "Let's go, Natalie. Your partner can check you out."

"Jack, I've *got* to talk to Captain Hooker first. I can't leave just yet."

"Yes you can, Nat," Captain Packerton said, and this time he pulled her brazenly into him. "I've already talked to your lieutenant. He knows you have a hot date. Balinkov here will be glad to clean up your paper work, won't you, Balinkov?"

"Yes, Captain I'll be glad to," said Valnikov, gathering up the work folders and case envelopes which had fallen out of his cheap plastic briefcase. Then the burly detective turned his back and began trudging toward the station. The vent in his old suitcoat had split and his handcuffs were hanging out. The threadbare suit now looked as though he'd taken it out of a washer.

"Jack, I simply *must* talk to Captain Hooker. It's urgent."

"Yeah? What is it?"

"I can't talk about it. A personal problem."

"Yeah? Well, it's impossible anyway. He left with some black detective, I forget his name."

"Clarence Cromwell."

"Yeah, him. Something about a sale on fishing equipment at a discount store."

"Goddamnit!"

"Talk to him in the morning. Let's go to dinner and see the show. Then maybe to *your* place," he grinned.

He swept her along toward his car, which was parked in front of the station on Fountain Avenue. They passed Valnikov, who was shuffling along thinking that maybe he'd buy a bottle of Stolichnaya and pick up a hamburger and listen to some records tonight. Like any other night. Maybe he'd listen to the great Chaliapin sing the death scene from *Boris Godunov*.

"See you around, Balinkov," Captain Packerton said when they breezed by. He had his arm around Natalie's waist and she was having trouble matching his long strides.

She turned and looked at Valnikov, who smiled his dumb kid smile and waved his plastic briefcase, and lumbered into the station, watching the ground as he walked.

"Phone call came in for you, Val," Max Haffenkamp said when Valnikov sat heavily at the burglary table. Next to the empty chair belonging to Natalie Zimmerman.

"Thanks, Max," Valnikov said, looking at the number which seemed familiar. Of course. It was that Pasadena number he called today.

"Broad sounded like she mighta been crying," Max Haffenkamp said.

"Crying," Valnikov mumbled. A little vodka tonight. A little music. The death of *Boris Godunov*. Natalie seemed genuinely to like the music today. She could learn about music very quickly. She had a good mind and was a sympathetic person, you could tell. She and that Captain Packerton made a handsome couple. They were probably going to get married or something. Stolichnaya.

"She said the call was very important, Val," said Max Haffenkamp.

"Sure," Valnikov said. "I'll call her right away." He misdialed the number twice. He couldn't help thinking of how Natalie looked when she smiled. She had only smiled twice in the three days they'd been partners. She didn't smile much, but when she did . . .

"Hello?" the voice cried.

"This is Sergeant Valnikov, ma'am."

"Sergeant!"

"Yes."

"I have to see you at once!"

"At once?"

"Sergeant, I'm in trouble. Terrible trouble. I haven't been honest with you. Oh, God!"

"Trouble?"

"Sergeant, you have to come to my house. I lied to you. My schnauzer, my Vickie, was stolen from me Sunday at the dog show. And a man has been calling me. He wants a great amount of money to return Vickie. Please come!"

"How much does he want?"

"Eighty-five thousand dollars!" she cried.

"For a *dog?*"

"Yes," she cried. "It's insane. I mean I don't have it. If I had it I'd give it to him."

"You'd give him eighty-five thousand *dollars?*"

"Yes! Yes! But I don't have it! I don't . . ."

"One moment, please," said Valnikov. He opened his work folder to the theft report from the Brown Derby. It was getting confusing. "Ma'am," he said. "I have a theft report from a restaurant in Hollywood. You say your dog was stolen at a dog show?"

"Yes!"

"Where was the dog show?"

"The Sports Arena!"

"That's in Southwest Division, ma'am."

"I don't know about such things," she cried. "Please, I need help!"

"Yes," Valnikov said. "I'll get you some help, but first I have to know who to call. Let's see, your dog was stolen in Southwest. A man is extorting you by telephone at your home?"

"I thought about the F.B.I., Sergeant!"

"Yes, well they *do* get involved in kidnapping, ma'am. But I don't believe the Little Lindbergh Law applies to Scotties."

"Schnauzers."

"Not even to schnauzers, ma'am," Valnikov said patiently.

"I NEED HELP!" Madeline wailed.

'Let me call you right back, Mrs. Whitfield," said Valnikov. "Just stay calm and I'll call you right back."

When Valnikov did his best to explain the complicated problem of Madeline Whitfield to Woodenlips Mockett, the lieutenant started to get a stomachache like Captain Hooker's.

"Could you go over the whole thing one more time, Valnikov?" said Lieutenant Mockett, feeling the stomachache worsen. "Start with the dog theft at the Brown Derby."

And he did. Again. When Valnikov was finished with the story, Lieutenant Mockett showed his expertise at civil service. He could pass the buck with the best of them.

"It's simple. We don't have to handle it!" Lieutenant Mockett cried, and his woodenlips almost grinned in triumph.

"I realize, Lieutenant, that the dog theft took place at the Sports Arena," said Valnikov slowly.

"That's Southwest Division. They can handle it," said Lieutenant Mockett qulckly.

"And the extortion took place in Pasadena. At least the calls are *received* in Pasadena."

"Let Pasadena P.D. handle it," Lieutenant Mockett said quickly.

"Except that the jurisdiction from where the *original* crime emanates should handle the entire crime," said Valnikov.

"That's Southwest Detectives. That's Southwest!" Lieutenant Mockett cried. "The dog was snatched from the Sports Arena!"

"Yes, sir," Valnikov said, blinking patiently, "but this lady seems to believe that the dog they switched on her was definitely of championship caliber. And there's only one dog like that reported missing in the entire Los Angeles basin. And that's the dog that was stolen from the Brown Derby. So maybe Mrs. Whitfield is on to something. Maybe the extortionist *did* steal Mrs. Gharoujian's schnauzer as the *first* step in his extortion plan. If so, Hollywood Detectives would probably be the jurisdiction to follow through on the entire investigation. And that dog theft at the Brown Derby belongs to me."

Lieutenant Mockett was quiet for a minute as the psychosomatic stomachache worsened. Then he said, "You actually *want* to handle the case, Valnikov? A dognapping? Don't you have *enough* to do?"

"Well, I've been involved on the periphery and . . . well, the poor woman sounds so desperate."

"A dognapping. And you want to handle it," said Lieutenant Mockett, who could not understand why anyone under *any* circumstances would want to do work he didn't have to do. "You must be nuts, Valnikov."

And at last, someone agreed with Natalie Zimmerman, who was not present to hear it.

"Well, sir, I don't have anything else to do tonight."

"No overtime, Valnikov," Woodenlips Mockett warned. "The commander's been bitching about paying overtime. No overtime. That's out."

"I won't put in for overtime, Lieutenant," Valnikov promised.

"You won't put in for overtime?" cried Woodenlips Mockett. "You *must* be nuts, Valnikov!"

"Yes, sir," said Valnikov. "So if it's okay, I'll drive to Pasadena now and be present when the extortionist calls."

"I got a feeling we shouldn't get involved in this. It's always best never to get involved in cases unless you're absolutely sure you can't get out of it. I just wish I knew for sure the dead dog is the one stolen from Hollywood.'

"Tell you what, Lieutenant. I'll find out somehow. And if it turns out the dead dog isn't the one belonging to Mrs. Gharoujian, I'll turn the case over to Southwest Detectives."

"Okay, okay," Lieutenant Mockett said, holding his psychosomatic stomach. "Do you have an Alka-Seltzer? Does *anybody* have an Alka-Seltzer? Ooooohhhh!"

It was the first time Valnikov had ever driven on the Pasadena Freeway during rush hour. It was the oldest freeway and showed it, being too narrow to accommodate the flow of cars in 1977. The turnoff lanes were inadequate and a stalled car could stop traffic for miles. Valnikov passed time in bumper-to-bumper traffic and eye-burning air pollution by thinking about this day.

It was his best day in recent memory. He used to have some good days when he worked with Charlie Lightfoot. But today . . . today was the best day in years. He thought of Natalie's brown eyes smiling through those big glasses as she drank red wine. Was she drinking wine tonight? French wine out of crystal and not styrofoam? They were a good-looking couple, no doubt about it. *Na zdorovye,* Natalie. Still, it was harmless to dream. To pretend. It seemed as though he had lived alone all his life. He suddenly wanted to stop and buy some vodka. But only better-class liquor stores carried Russian vodka and he couldn't stomach American vodka. Then he thought of Madeline Whitfield. She didn't deserve that. She was a desperate woman in trouble and deserved a clearheaded policeman to help her. The vodka could come later.

He used his map book and found the house without much trouble. It was more beautiful than the old Spanish homes in the Los Feliz district. Valnikov admired the vast numbers of ancient oaks. The trees were all well over a century old. And camellias were everywhere. And eucalyptus and pine and azalea. Her driveway was circular and private. What would it be like to live in a house like this? Valnikov was certain a butler in livery would answer the door. He was excited. The Great Gatsby.

Madeline Whitfield answered the door. She'd touched up her makeup and combed her hair and hadn't had a drink, and she looked awful. Her eyes were swollen and raw from crying. She wore a white blouse and tartan woolen skirt. The blouse was stained by coffee. It was very hard to hold things steady in those hands.

"I'm Sergeant Valnikov," he said to the big woman. He guessed she was about his age. A little overweight but not bad-looking if it weren't for a rather heavy layer of hair under her nose.

"He said he'd call at six, Sergeant," she said with a great effort at control. "He's usually very punctual. Would you like some coffee while we wait?"

"No, thank you, ma'am," he said standing in the large foyer.

"Tea?"

"Yes, tea would be nice. Thank you."

"I'm ever so grateful to you, Sergeant," she said. "Please sit down and excuse me for a moment."

"I just hope we can help you," he said, looking at the quarry tile floor, done fifty years ago when craftsmen cared. And there was a beamed ceiling with something he'd never seen: ceiling boards painted by artisans in Moorish designs and Mexican colors, the most impressive residential ceiling he'd ever seen. The paint was kept vivid by nothing more than linseed oil. There was a sunken living room which was the style when great Southern California architects were having their heyday in Pasadena and Beverly Hills. The windows were too small, as was the style then, but were finished with mahogany frames and leaded glass. Privacy was more important than a view in 1927, but on the arroyo side, the windows had been enlarged over the years and there was a panoramic view of the Rose Bowl and the defunct Vista del Arroyo Hotel glowing pink and dusty gold in the setting sun. And in the foreground, the ominous old Suicide Bridge where many tormented souls had plunged to their deaths while looking at the lovely San Gabriels, and at the splendid old mansions dotting the hillside over the arroyo among the pines and camellias.

Madeline Whitfield returned, her face wet where she had been dabbing at her swollen eyes with a cold cloth. She carried a tray bearing English silver service given by a guest at her grandmother's wedding. There weren't many of the old things left. Not many at all.

"In here, please," she said and put the tray on the table in the library. It was a masculine heavy somber library, but sparsely furnished. She understood how impressive it must be to him.

"A grand old house, isn't it?"

"It certainly is," Valnikov said. He wished Natalie were here to see it.

"I have no help except for a girl who comes in two days a week for four hours a day."

No butler in livery? Not even an upstairs girl? No grounds-keeper?

She saw it and smiled and said, "I'm broke, Sergeant. Very nearly broke. I couldn't pay that monster if I wanted to. And I *do* want to. But I can't. That's why I have no choice but to ask the police to help me."

"I'm sorry about you being broke," he said. "And I'm sorry about your troubles. But I'm glad you called the police. I'll just have my tea plain, thank you."

"Behind lots and lots of these winding driveways and oak doors it's the same story, Sergeant," she said. "No romance of old money. Just people like me holding on."

"Yes, ma'am," he said, sipping his tea noiselessly.

The dusk was settling fast. It was twenty minutes until six. "Would you mind if I didn't turn the light on just yet?" she said. "I have a ripping headache. The dark soothes sometimes."

"I don't mind at all, Mrs. Whitfield," he said "I've noticed the same thing."

"What will I say when he calls?"

"I really don't know, Mrs. Whitfield," he said. "That's up to the extortionist. Just let him talk. The main thing is that you and I both pick up our phones together and that you stall for at least another day."

"Should I tell him the schnauzer is dead?"

"No, I don't think so."

"Why?"

"Let's not give *him* any information. Let him give *us* information."

"Should I promise him the eighty-five thousand tomorrow?"

"I don't think so," Valnikov said. "Just promise him you'll do better tomorrow. That you'll have some money soon. I've got to have time to work."

"Of course," she said. "I've been wracking my brain. I think I can get a few thousand more. I think I can raise seventeen thousand by tomorrow afternoon," she said.

"I wouldn't like you to pay anything, ma'am," Valnikov said. "But that decision's up to you."

"Vickie's like a child to me, Sergeant," she said. "Look around you. I live in this house alone. There's only Vickie."

"Alone. Yes. I can understand how you feel. Yes."

"How could that woman whose dog was stolen from the restaurant, how could she not care? Does she have a family living with her?"

"I rather doubt it, ma'am," said Valnikov, sipping. "She said she's seventy-six years old."

"And she doesn't care about her beautiful schnauzer? Does she have other pets?"

"You might say that, yes, ma'am," said Valnikov, blushing.

"At first Vickie was just to be a pet. I was lonely. And then people who knew, told me how exceptional she was. I began getting involved in showing her. I entered a whole new world of dog shows. The sport. The parties. The awards. Our picture was in the *Times*. Vickie opened up my life, you see."

"Yes, ma'am."

"And she *is* truly like my . . . it sounds foolish . . . like my child. That man said . . . said he'll cut off her toes. He may be doing it now."

"I don't think so, ma'am," said Valnikov.

"He sounds as though he would," she said and her voice broke. "He sounds so wicked. I can't help it. I have a dreadful premonition of this man holding Vickie on a table. With a knife!"

A knife. Valnikov was leaving her. Drifting. He was going after it! There it was! A little schnauzer dog. The big strong hands of the hunter. No! The *extortionist* with a knife. He was going to disembowel the little dog. The picture was there in the darkness. There was only moonlight now and he could almost see the doctor in the bloody smock cutting the rabbit's throat. He almost had it! Then a voice. Valnikov's own voice cried out and the rabbit bounded off through the snow and escaped.

The detective sat there trembling in the dark, on the damask wingback chair. He spilled some tea on his trousers. He didn't notice. Madeline Whitfield didn't notice either. She was lying across the sofa sobbing so hard she could scarcely breathe. Those pathetic sobs brought Valnikov back from Siberia.

"That's all right, Mrs. Whitfield," he said, when his own fear subsided. "Go on and cry. It's all right."

She cried for a long time. Whenever she tried to stop she would burst forth again. Valnikov sat quietly in dusky shadows, among leather-bound books and glossy old wood, in the lonely wingback chair. He watched the woman weeping on the sofa. It had been a long time since he'd heard such sounds of grief. Valnikov sat in brooding darkness and vowed he would find her little dog. Nothing would stop him.

Philo Skinner was not punctual. He didn't call until 6:15 p.m. He had gone home and changed into the last of his leisure suits. He couldn't explain why, but somehow he had a need to be well dressed when he consummated his crime. He didn't want to look like a bum even though no one would see him. He never wanted to look like a bum again. When he stripped off the soggy leisure suit he threw it in the trash can. Then he went back to the kennel to feed the dogs. It was getting harder to keep Mavis away from the kennel. By tomorrow she'd insist on coming in and might see the little schnauzer bitch. He had to get his money and return the dog tonight. Then it occurred to him: He hadn't yet given the rich broad her instructions on what to do with Tutu. Oh, well, Tutu was probably having a better time in the Pasadena mansion that she ever did with that stingy sex maniac, Millie Muldoon Gharoujian.

He wondered if old Millie still kept a couple of studs and a cobra, or mongoose, or whatever the hell. Once when Millie was still interested in dog shows he had come early and found the door open and there they were: a pile of bodies snoozing in Millie's water bed. The pile included Millie, two or three boys, a leopard or something, and incredibly enough, a goddamn baby alligator! Perverted old cunt!

Valnikov was on the phone extension in the library. Madeline was in the living room. The lights were on now and Madeline was shaky but controlled. After two rings, he nodded and they picked up the phones together. "Hello."

"It's Richard." He didn't bother with the paper towel anymore. And he'd returned to the cocktail lounge where he'd made the first call. Philo was getting bold. And desperate.

"Yes," she said.

"Do you have the money?"

"Not all of it."

"How much do you have?"

"Tomorrow I'll have more."

"How much do you have?"

"Tomorrow I'll have seventeen . . . no," she lied. "I'll have twenty thousand for you!"

"You cunt!" Philo screamed. "You owe me eighty-five thousand. You rotten cheap cunt!"

"Wait, please, Richard!" she said. It was much easier with Valnikov present. The extortionist didn't scare her so much anymore.

"Don't you please Richard me, you cunt," Philo wheezed. "You ain't gonna welsh on me. Not if you want your bitch allve. I'm sick a playing games with you. I been too nice to you, that's my problem. Well, no more Mr. Nice Guy!"

"Please, Richard, twenty thousand is a lot of money. I can get that much by this time tomorrow. That's a lot of money, Richard."

The line was quiet for a long moment. Twenty thousand. But he owed Arnold $15,200 as of today, and an extra hundred tomorrow! Puerto Vallarta *for life* on less than five thousand? Could she be telling the truth? But how *could* she be? That goddamn house she lived in? She had it, the cunt!

"I'm getting your bitch," he said. "And I'm calling you back in five minutes. And I'm going to cut her toe off while you listen to her scream. You ready for that?"

Madeline nearly dropped the receiver. She almost collapsed. But she looked at Valnikov, who just shook his head slowly at her. The husky detective stood like a rock, his cinnamon hair rumpled, his tie askew. A slouching man who might have never stood straight in his life. But he had a broad earthy strong face. And he sustained her by just shaking his head slowly, telling her not to break. She didn't.

"That won't help you at all, Richard," she said, her voice so controlled it surprised her. "If you hurt Vickie, she'll be worth nothing in a dog show. That's the only reason I bother, you know, to show her and win. Without a toe she's worth nothing. Injure her in any way and she's worth nothing.'' She held on, held on, closed her eyes. When she opened them, Valnikov was nodding. He seemed proud of her.

Philo was beside himself. He started yelling so loud that the bartender came over, banged on the door, and said, ''Hey fella, there's ladies in this joint! Watch your language.''

And Philo almost yelled something at the bartender, but he remembered what happened to him today in a phone booth when he popped off, so he bit his lip and kept quiet. When he came back on the line he said, ''You have *thirty*-five thousand for me at this time tomorrow night. *Thirty*-five and that's my last offer. You understand? I'm calling you at six o'clock tomorrow night and you're going to tell me you have the dough or I'm going to hurt that bitch. I never hurt an animal in my life, lady, but I swear I'll hurt your bitch if you don't have the dough for me by tomorrow night.''

''All right, Richard, I'll have it,'' she said. ''Goodbye.'' And she hung up the phone, walked back into the drawing room, threw herself on the couch and wept.

Valnikov sat quietly and watched her cry. He blinked patiently from time to time.

Finally, she said, ''I . . . I've been try . . . trying to get a . . . a job. I've never . . . never *worked*. This house . . . this . . . I'll have to be out in a year. I have . . . have enough in a trust fund to last till then. But I can't *get* it. I'd give it all to him. But I can't *get* it! It took a court order to get . . . get it for my mother's . . . her hospital expenses. Her funeral. I can't get . . .''

''Now now, Mrs. Whitfield,'' he sald, sighing deeply. His eyes were sad and red. ''Now now.''

''How does one find a *job*, Sergeant? Can . . . can you tell me? Where . . . what can I . . . what . . .''

''Now now, Mrs. Whitfield,'' Valnikov said softly.

Then he switched off the light and lumbered to the couch and sat down. He started patting her on the back. Now now, Mrs. Whitfield. Now now.

She didn't feel his hand at first, though it was a meaty hand. When she did, she sat up, but couldn't stop the tears.

Then Valnikov put his arm around her and it startled her. Still she couldn't stop weeping. Then Valnikov put both arms around her and she wept on his chest. He kept patting her back, rather solidly, as though he was trying to burp her. Then she relaxed and he began patting her softly. Then he was holding her, rocking her, patting her ever more gently and she was catching her breath.

Then she put both arms around Valnikov's neck and sat there crying in the darkness. Valnikov looked almost as sad as she. Now now, Mrs. Whitfield. Now now.

Then, instinctively, Valnikov began kissing Madeline Whitfield on the salty cheek. Now now. Now now. And she tightened her grip on his neck and let him.

Of course Valnikov could not have known that this woman had not felt a man's body in five years. He was only vaguely aware that he hadn't felt a woman's body since Thanksgiving weekend when he got drunk in a Chinatown bar and picked up a clerk typist from the police academy. Madeline turned her tear-drenched face to the detective and kissed his mouth. Valnikov responded. Then they were groping in the darkness on that damask sofa and she was saying, ''Sergeant, Sergeant!'' And he was replying, ''Mrs. Whitfield, Mrs. Whitfield!''

''Sergeant! Oh, Sergeant!'' she cried.

''Mrs. Whitfield,'' he cried. ''I'll find your doggie, I swear!''

''Sergeant!'' she cried, and unhooked his gun belt.

When he left her an hour later, he was filled with pity for this woman. She was sleeping soundly in her bed for the first time in days. He paused in the door to look at her naked body. She was a fine woman. He wished she could find someone from her station in life. She needed someone to care about. Something useful to do.

Valnikov went home and before he slept he renewed his vow to find this lonely woman's dog. Then he went to sleep and dreamed of the rabbit.

11

The Dog Lover

Valnikov felt very strange when he awakened Wednesday morning. At first, he didn't know what it was. He got up, boiled water for the tea, fed and watered Misha and Grisha, cleaned their cage. He brought the morning paper in, sat down to read. Then he looked around the bachelor apartment. Nothing had changed. He still had the same clotheslines strung from the animal cage to the nail he'd pounded into the top of the door frame. Several pair of underwear and socks still hung on the clothesline. There was still a pile of dirty dishes on the sink which he washed one plate at a time when he was hungry. There were still stacks of records and album covers strewn around the room. But something was different. Then it dawned on him. There was no empty bottle of Stolichnaya either on the kitchen table or on the walnut veneer coffee table. And that gave him the *big* clue as to what was totally different this morning: He had no hangover!

He had worked, and kept company with Madeline Whitfield until midnight. He had come home and gone to bed. He had not had a single glass of vodka. Remarkable! He got up, went into the bathroom, tossed two hand towels off the metal arm that dangled in front of the medicine cabinet. He examined his eyes. They were slightly red but *dry*. He looked well. He felt well. He celebrated by making himself two scrambled eggs and rye toast. He drank three cups of tea and had a glass of orange juice. Then he took a shower and ironed a clean shirt. He tied his tie carefully so the collar button didn't show. He put some tonic on his hair and combed it, careful to get a straight part.

He felt like a new man when he walked out that door. He couldn't wait to tell Natalie. They were going to catch a *criminal*.

When Valnikov got to the station, things were about to get tense. Bullets Bambarella had lost two weeks' pay in the last two days by making bets with Montezuma Montez. Aside from that, Bullets had had a lousy night with a cop groupie from downtown.

Bullets had Clarence Cromwell cornered at the burglary table when Valnikov got himself a cup of tea. Bullets was saying, ". . . so I take this broad home. You know her, Clarence?"

"Yeah, yeah, she works the D.A.'s office," Clarence sighed. All these young kids got woman troubles and who do they bring them to? Clarence Cromwell, that's who. "Bullets, do I look like the fuckin Ann Landers of Hollywood Detectives, or something?"

"But, Clarence, listen! She's a sicko. Some kinda fruitcake or somethin. She plays with her own clit when I'm lovin her up. Can you believe it? Then . . . get this . . . she starts suckin on her own big tit! I says to this freako, I says, 'Hey. Whadda you need *me* for?' She says, 'Come to think of it, dummy, I *don't*.' "

"Yeah, this is very interestin, Bullets. I mean, there ain't nothin I'd rather do than talk about your sex life but . . ."

"Then I done it!"

Suddenly the scowling black detective stiffened and said, "You done *what,* Bullets?"

"Nothin much. I just got mad. I just threw her in the swimmin pool, is all."

"Jesus! You had me scared for a minute. I can't be coverin for you anymore, Bullets!"

"I know, Clarence, and I just wanted you to know how it was."

"I don't think she can bitch too much, you just threw her in a swimming pool."

"Thanks for being so understandin, Clarence," Bullets breathed.

"Nothing but whackos in Hollywood anyway," said Montezuma Montez, overhearing Bullets' problems. "Over in East L.A. you pick up a Mexican chick, you buy a six-pack a beer and have a great old time in a drive-in movie. In Hollywood you pick up a broad you gotta spend thirty bucks on dinner. Then to satisfy her you gotta go down to Western Costume and rent a werewolf mask and spend the night whopping each other over the head with live kitty cats. I wanna transfer back to Hollenbeck," said Montezuma Montez.

But Bullets was ready for trouble. "Yeah, that's just like a spic to say that," Bullets sneered. "You get the wrong hole with those Mexican broads you end up with a blister on your joint, all the chili seeds they eat. I'll take a Hollywood girl any old time."

"Oh, yeah?" Montezuma said. "Well lemme tell you about this *Hollywood* lady I picked up the other night. Said her folks were from Venice. Not Venice, California. Venice, *Italy*. Had her little two-year-old spumoni sucker *in the car* when I picked her up at the tennis court," said Montezuma.

"That's a filthy lie," said Bullets Bambarella, and Clarence Cromwell finally said, "Will you two please shut up!"

"It's *gotta* be a lie, Clarence," Bullets argued. "You think a spic can play tennis?"

"Better than any dago I ever seen," said Montezuma Montez.

Then Bullets turned to Montezuma and said, "I never played tennis in my life and I could probably beat you."

"I could beat you left-handed," said Montezuma Montez.

"Gotcha covered, dummy!" Bullets yelled in triumph and suddenly Montezuma Montez was looking down at forty borrowed dollars, thinking he may have gone too far.

Then money was flying all over the squad room and Lieutenant Mockett was whining to no avail about illegal gambling, and four cars full of detectives went speeding to Hollywood High School for a bizarre one-set tennis match in stocking feet, suits, and ties, between two clumsy buffaloes, one of whom was playing with the wrong hand.

Natalie Zimmerman, wearing a new side-pleated skirt and matching cardigan jacket, came to work five minutes late, and was almost knocked to the floor by the thundering herd charging out of the station to the tennis match.

She was relieved to see that Hipless Hooker was also late. She was not going to fail today. She was going to grab him by the goddamn throat if she had to, the minute he came in the door. And then she was going to walk him into the office and put a chair in front of the door to keep out Clarence Cromwell. Then they were going to talk about Valnikov.

The reason she was late was that she had only gotten three hours' sleep, what with Captain Jack Packerton jumping on her every two hours or so to prove he still had it even though he'd just turned forty. She felt like telling him it would be the last all-nighter until he accepted impending middle age. And all the time he didn't know that Natalie Zimmerman had much the same fear because she had failed at orgasm the last *five* times.

What the hell, Jack, let's just live together. I've been divorced twice now and . . . Live together? Natalie, I'm a captain! Have you read the latest memorandum from Chief Digby Bates about moral rearmament? Do you know what would happen if a captain was found living in sin? Christ, I'd rather risk another divorce than face the alternative! Do you know that I stand a very good chance of being a deputy chief someday? What're you trying to do to my career? *Live* together? Without benefit of clergy? I WANNA BE A DEPUTY CHIEF!

And all she wanted to be was an Investigator III who wasn't lonely and who could have an occasional orgasm. Yet she was an Investigator II, and hadn't had one lately, and was working with a closet madman, and there was no help on the horizon.

She was telling all this silently to her Friz when Valnikov set a cup of coffee in front of her. He was looking all spruced up today for some reason. Just her luck. The day she vowed to expose him is the day he picks to get all gussied up and comb his hair. Well, it didn't matter whether he *looked* like a madman or not. He couldn't fool anybody if they just pushed the right buttons. Tell me about your dream, Valnikov. Is it Bugs Bunny? Peter Cottontail? Tell me about a rabbit that makes you cry. Jesus, he was smiling that big goofy kid smile.

"We have a real case to work on, Natalie." He said. "Would you care for a little cream or sugar?"

"No."

"I just finished telling Clarence about it."

And hearing his name, Clarence Cromwell came over and sat on Valnikov's table. "Mockett wants to know if you're putting in overtime for last night."

"No," said Valnikov.

"Okay, that'll keep him happy. I'm gonna have Max Haffenkamp handle your cases for today and maybe tomorrow. I might go out and help him. But that's *it*. We can't be makin no major crime outta this extortion."

"Extortion?" said Natalie.

"I'll tell you all about it," Valnikov said. "It's a pretty big one. Eighty-five thousand dollars."

"Yeah, but it's over a dog, Val. Keep that in mind. It's only a gud-damn pampered *dog*."

"I appreciate your handling my regular workload, Clarence," Valnikov said, and Natalie was shocked to see that even his blue eyes were clear this morning.

"One thing you gotta do first, Val," said Clarence. "Mockett says you make sure that dead dog is the one from the Brown Derby. Go to the pet mortuary and see if they haven't disposed of it yet. Have that broad from Trousdale . . . what's her name?"

"Millie Gharoujian."

"Yeah, you have her or somebody identify that dead dog. If it ain't from the Brown Derby, you turn the whole thing over to Southwest Detectives or Pasadena P.D. Them's orders from Mockett. First order he gave this month. We gotta humor him."

"Okay, Clarence," Valnikov said. "Let's go, Natalie."

"Wait a minute," she said, brushing her Friz out of her eyes. "Clarence, where's the captain? I have to talk to him and I'm not going anywhere until I do!"

"God-damn, Natalie!" Clarence sneered, standing up and putting his fists on his hips, the twin magnums dangling impotently beside his barrel chest.

"God-damn, what!" she sneered right back. A black General Patton!

"Is it that same thing you been complainin about the last three days, Natalie?"

"Yes it is," she said, looking involuntarily at Valnikov, who busied himself with a follow-up report, too polite to pry.

''Well, this is a hell of a time,'' Clarence snorted. ''You got an extortion to work on and you wanna go runnin to . . .''

He was interrupted when Natalie jumped to her feet. She jumped because Hipless Hooker came flying through the door and ran across the squad room. He was holding his stomach and was followed by a young woman in a yellow pantsuit, walking like a robot, wearing a neck brace.

''Clarence!'' Hipless Hooker cried, but Natalie Zimmerman beat Clarence to the captain's office.

''I just gotta talk to you today, Captain!'' Natalie cried.

''Not *now,* Natalie,'' Hooker whimpered. ''Clarence, this lady was waiting for me at the desk when I came in. She claims she was out on a date with Bullets Bambarella last night. She works for the district attorney's office. She wants to sue us for a half a million dollars!''

''Let's all go in and quiet down,'' said Clarence, smiling at the woman in the neck brace.

''Bullets told me about it, miss,'' Clarence said placatingly, ''but I didn't know he hurt you. He said he just pushed you into a swimmin pool.''

''He did!'' Hooker cried. ''But her apartment was two floors up!''

''I got a whiplash,'' the young woman said, ''and Bullets is *not* gonna get away with it.''

''Ooooooooooohhhhh, my stomach,'' Hooker suddenly moaned.

''And I was wearing a good wristwatch and my contact lenses at the time,'' the girl said, sitting down gingerly.

''Yeah, well I think we can clear this up,'' Clarence said as he closed the door in Natalie's face. ''You see, Bullets really *cares* about you a lot. He told me.''

It was starting to seem like a dream to Natalie Zimmerman. Destiny and Bullets Bambarella were conspiring to save Valnikov from his fate. And here they were driving up to the hill, high to the top of Trousdale Estates, overlooking Hollywood and Beverly Hills. Natalie Zimmerman was starting to believe she would never be rid of the man next to her, driving all of fifteen miles per hour.

''It's beautiful up here on top of the smog, isn't it?'' he said amiably, as she sat and smoked and thought about sex without orgasm. And the black marble.

''Yeah, beautiful.''

''Mrs. Gharoujian must be very rich.''

''Jesus!'' said Natalie, coming out of her funk when she saw the contemporary home of Millie Muldoon Gharoujian on the cul-de-sac overlooking all of Baghdad. There was a Silver Shadow Rolls-Royce in the driveway, and a chauffeur in a black cap. He was nineteen years old and had shoulder-length blond hair hanging from under his cap. He got out of the car when they pulled up to the gate.

Valnikov held his badge out the window and the chauffeur nodded and opened the gate. There was a granite fountain in the center of the circular drive. On it was a plaster sculpture of David. With an erection. A stream of water flowed from the erection. In the fountain, a boa constrictor writhed and rubbed his scales against the granite bowl and got a suntan, compliments of Millie Muldoon Gharoujian.

When Natalie pushed the doorbell, the chime played a chorus of ''Roll Out the Barrel.'' Then the door was opened by a houseboy with a 29 waist and 19-inch arms. The houseboy was eighteen years old and was a runner-up in a Mr. California contest.

''Mrs. Gharoujian is expecting you,'' he said, admitting them into the living room overlooking the cantilevered, clover-shaped swimming pool.

The living room was white. White sofas filled seventy square yards of room. White wall-to-wall carpet buried Natalie's heels. White slumpstone fireplace. White baby grand ingeniously built so that it could play as well as any upright player piano when Millie wasn't too tired to pump the white enamel foot pedals.

The white walls of the living room were covered with gilded antique mirrors and paintings of nudes, men and women. Over the fireplace was an enormous painting of a reclining Millie Gharoujian when she was thirty years old and still looked like Harlow. The painting was done in 1932.

Then the east wall, which was all mirrors, opened. Millie came briskly through the mirrored door. She had had five face lifts over the past twenty-five years, and in a huge silk kimono barely covering the breasts which hung like twin punching bags, she looked not a day over seventy-two. She was perspiring and red-faced and petulant.

"Sergeant, I told you on the phone, I already reported that schnauzer to my insurance company. It's a closed incident, far as I'm concerned. I appreciate you're a good cop and all that, but why don't you gimme a break? I got something in there hung like . . ."

"Yes, yes, yes!" Valnikov cried, not wanting Natalie to hear about Michelangelo penises. "But, Mrs. Gharoujian, if you could just come with us. The pet mortuary is only twenty minutes from here and we'd bring you right home as soon as you say if it's your Tutu or not. And . . ."

"Leave here? Now? Sergeant, you gotta be kidding! With what I got waiting for me on that water bed in there?"

"Uh, yes, I understand, ma'am," Valnikov said quickly, as Natalie moved a few feet to her left to try to see what Millie had on her water bed.

"Damn, you're a tough man, Sergeant," Millie sighed. Then she picked up a cigarette, put it into a ruby-studded holder, and said, "You married, Sergeant?"

"No ma'am," Valnikov said.

"Hmmm," said Millie. "Well, some other time maybe. Right now, I gotta get back to business."

"Is there anyone else here . . ."

"Anyone else here! You kidding! I got two kids in there with . . ."

"Yes, I mean anyone who could come with us and look at the dead schnauzer," said Valnikov. "It might save everyone a lot of trouble."

"Hey, Twinkles!" Millie yelled, and the houseboy returned from the kitchen with a plastic mixer full of banana daiquiris.

"Yes, Millie?"

She patted his buttocks and sighed, "If only you were Japanese, sweetie. Maybe we could get your eyes fixed. Listen, go with these cops, will ya? Have Buttons drive you in the Rolls. Look at this dead dog they wanna show you and see if it's Tutu or not. Then get your ass right back here. These two in the bedroom are already tired out." Then to Valnikov, "The youth of America ain't what it used to be, Sergeant. The President's Council on Physical Fitness oughtta listen to *me,* sometime. I could tell em."

"Yes, ma'am, and thank you," said Valnikov as he and Natalie followed Twinkles out the front door, getting a fair glimpse into Millie's boudoir. There was a huge hairy creature lying on the floor. Alive!

"There's a goat in there, Valnikov!" Natalie cried when they were outside.

"It's a baby llama," Twinkles said. "Millie's keeping it for a friend. And I'm getting sick and tired of cleaning llama shit all day, I can tell you." Twinkles peeled off his waistcoat and revealed a torso that actually split the shoulder seams of his starched white dress shirt. He rolled up the sleeves over bulging forearms with tendons like pencils. "We'll follow you in the Rolls," he said. "If it's Tutu, I'll know her."

There was a wake going on when they arrived at the pet mortuary. Three women and two men were weeping inconsolably and saying adieu to a raccoon who lay in state in a little walnut baby coffin. It had a fawn satin lining with black ruffles to match the tail stripe and mask on the eyes of the dead animal. The coffin had a double lid and the lower half was closed, revealing only the head and torso of the deceased. There was soft music drifting over the intercom, instrumental strings playing "My Buddy." The deceased had never looked better. His fur was brushed with lanolin. His black raccoon mask was touched up with shoe dye. His little raccoon hands were folded on his chest, as though in prayer, artfully kept in that position by driving a cobbler's needle clear through his chest and sewing them in place. In this prayerful pose the raccoon looked anything but dead. The raccoon could have been playing possum.

They were greeted by a balding man in a somber gray suit with a white carnation in his lapel.

"May I be of service?" he asked.

"Mr. Limpwood?"

"No, he's conducting a graveside service at the moment."

"I called him. I'm Sergeant Valnikov from the police department."

"Yes, he said to show you to the cemetery. He'll be finished shortly. It's a private graveside service for the immediate family."

Valnikov and Natalie walked outside and saw Mr. Limpwood consoling a tearful couple. He tried in vain to scratch the arched backs of the immediate family of Siamese cats. Then he walked jauntily along the cobbled path among tombstones and granite sculpture of all sizes and description which said things like: "Our beloved Duchess, lest we forget!" and "Farewell, Happy Oliver! Till we meet in the Great Beyond!"

He was dressed similarly to the other mortician, but was much shorter and more bald. He wore a white carnation. "May I be of service?"

Valnikov showed his badge and Mr. Limpwood registered disappointment. It was the best week since he'd been in business: fourteen dogs, ten cats, a chimpanzee, two ocelots, a piranha from Pomona (Not all freakos lived in Hollywood.) and a raccoon. There was a rumor that they might get an Arabian gelding, which had them all excited. (Eleven plots of ground to bury that baby. Eleven! And the embalming cost!) But these were just cops not customers.

"You know, Sergeant, I tried to call you this morning but you'd just left. I'm terribly sorry, but the deceased was buried last night. I thought we still had her set for burial this morning, but as you know, there was no bereaved, only dear Mrs. Whitfield, who kindly arranged for the burial, bless her heart."

"Where's she buried? Let's dig her up," said Valnikov.

"Dig her up? Sergeant! Exhume the body? I've never been asked . . ."

"I think that only applies to people bodies," said Valninov. "Is it that fresh grave over there? By the shovel?

"Yes, but I don't know! I don't want to be sued, Sergeant! In the event the deceased's next of kin is determined!"

"We can't determine anything until we look at the body," said Valnikov.

"Millie wants me back on time and she means business," said Twinkles suddenly, and Valnikov didn't doubt that at all. Then the giant kid strode over to the half-filled grave, stripped off his dress shirt, showing a black silk bodyshirt that Millie had bought him, and started swooping up earth like a steam shovel. He had the shallow grave uncovered in fifteen minutes.

"I don't want to be responsible," Mr. Limpwood cried. "I'm getting out of here." And he took off in a hurry while Twinkles pulled the box out of the ground with one hand. (It was a cheap pine box and not the walnut that Madeline paid for.)

The lad used the shovel blade and cracked it open easily. Then he grimaced. "Oh!" he said. "Oh, I don't think that's a schnauzer!"

"It's a schnauzer," Valnikov said, with little admiration for Mr. Limpwood's art. (When there's no bereaved, save a buck where you can.)

The young giant was unaccustomed to death in any form. "Tutu was so beautiful!" he said. "I don't know!"

"Mrs. Gharoujian said something about a white toenail on the rear foot. Do you remember that?"

"Do dead things look so . . ."

"Yes, they do," said Valnikov. "Now look at the back foot. You can just reach in there."

"I couldn't," the kid said, getting pale. "Is her body hard?"

"Rigor has come and gone," said Valnikov. "Let's see." And he reached in the coffin. "Yes. There *is* a whitish toenail. I think this might be Mrs. Gharoujian's Tutu."

"But the face!" the young man cried. Then he sat by the grave site and dropped his head. "I loved Tutu." His eyes were filling. "Millie never cared about her."

"Listen, son," Valnikov said, squatting beside the tearful body builder, "who would be able to positively identify this schnauzer by her markings? Who knew her best?"

"There are so many guys that come and go at Millie's," said the young man. "Everybody played with Tutu. So *many* guys."

"Mrs. Gharoujian mentioned her dog handler," said Valnikov. "Would he know her markings?"

"He might." The kid nodded, taking a look at the contorted mastiff face on the dead animal. "That *can't* be Tutu! Is *this* what death does to you?"

"Sometimes," said Valnikov. "What's the dog handler's name?"

"Philo Skinner," said the lad, looking in the grave. "She got tired of dog shows. Millie gets tired of everything. Maybe it *is* Tutu. I just can't say. I had no idea this is what it does! God, I'm sorry!"

"That's okay, son," said Valnikov patting the enormous shoulder of the young giant. "Thanks for your help, anyway."

"Maybe it *is* Tutu," the boy said softly, stealing his last glance into the pine coffin at the jutting mastiff jaw.

Tutu in her final agony took with her to eternity the face of J. Edgar Hoover.

When they got back to the waiting Rolls, Natalie said, "Buttons, give Twinkles a chance to get himself together. He'll be out in a minute."

"I ain't in no hurry to get back," the blond chauffeur shrugged. "No hurry at all."

And no wonder, Natalie Zimmerman thought, as she and Valinkov waved to Mr. Limpwood who was calling his lawyer to make sure somebody couldn't sue him for letting them dig up a stiff schnauzer. His lawyer wasn't in, so he looked at Valnikov's business card and called Hollywood Station just to make sure this was an authorized police investigation.

The phone was answered by Bullets Bambarella, who was back from the tennis match, dead broke, thinking he'd be eating grass in Griffith Park if this kept up.

"Good morning, Hollywood Investigation, Investigator Bambarella speaking, may I help you." Bullets gave the rote greeting sullenly, then he listened with only half his concentration. He was worried sick. He took a look at the captain's door. Thank God the groupie with the neck brace was gone. He knew he'd be facing Clarence Cromwell's wrath soon enough over this one. Jesus, Clarence, what I gotta do to make up? Marry the broad or what?

Then Bullets heard something which popped his eyes wide. "Just a second, Mr. Limpwood!" Bullets cried, punching the phone button and putting him on hold. Someone was in *lots* more trouble than he was! Bullets ran to the captain's door, knocked, and jerked it open.

"I ain't ready for you yet, Bullets," Clarence Cromwell said with murder in his eyes.

"But this is important, Clarence!" Bullets cried. "Captain! There's a guy on the phone. From a cemetery! Guess what Valnikov done! He dug up a grave! Some stiff named Schnozzle! And the mortician wants to talk to you right now!"

They said that Captain Hooker's moan set a new record for police department moaners. He was taken to the hospital with a gas attack severe enough to require an ambulance. Bullets Bambarella loyally accompanied his captain to the ambulance, saying, "Gee, Skipper, if you could just loosen up and fart you'd feel lots better."

"Ooooooohhh," said Hipless Hooker.

It didn't help when Clarence Cromwell phoned the hospital later that afternoon and tried to explain that it was only a dog's body. The medication they gave Hipless Hooker kept him belching and farting and off-duty all afternoon.

Which meant that Valnikov's career was secure another day.

"So what do you have in mind now, Valnikov?" said Natalie Zimmerman as they drove toward Pasadena on the freeway.

"I think we proceed on the assumption that the dead dog *is* Tutu."

"Where does that leave us?"

"With the responsibility to handle this case," said Valnikov. "It's *our* extortion. First thing to do is be there when he calls at three o'clock. What do you think?"

"I don't know what to think," Natalie sighed. "Maybe we should just turn the case over to Pasadena P.D."

"I feel a . . . responsibility," Valnikov said. "I want to help Mrs. Whitfield."

"It's only a dog, Valnikov."

"The extortionist calls her a bitch," Valnikov mused.

"Mrs. Whitfield?"

"No, the schnauzer. He always says the word bitch, never the word dog like you just did."

"So?"

"He's familiar with dogs. He uses the right terminology when he refers to Vickie. He knew Tutu would fool them long enough that he'd be home safe before they guessed. He's a dog lover."

"So?"

"Nothing. Something. I don't know. Another thing. He said, 'I've never hurt an animal in my life.' That was important to him."

"So?"

"I don't think we should let him know Tutu's dead. When we're out of possibilities, we can tell him he's killed Tutu. See how he acts."

"You think it was one of Millie's playmates?"

"That's what I'm thinking," Valnikov nodded. "If we could just get that woman's undivided attention for fifteen minutes."

"Impossible, what with the people, aardvarks and lizards in her bed."

"If we could get her thinking, I'll bet there're three or four guys who lived with her when she was involved in dog shows. I'll bet it's one of those guys."

"She's a chickenhawk!" Natalie sneered. "These kids come and go hourly through her zoo. Sunset Strip one week, Haight-Ashbury the next."

"Except that this one's in town. Only thing bothers me is the voice. That voice, even if he was an actor, that wasn't a youngster's voice. And Millie likes *boys*."

"So you think there were two."

"Or more," Valnikov nodded. "Would probably take two anyway. Millie's former friend takes Tutu from the restaurant. Maybe one or both take the dog into the show and switch schnauzers. Then the other one calls Mrs. Whitfield, the older man."

"A dog lover," Natalie sighed. Her police career had come to this.

"A dog lover," Valnikov said. "Yes. Not an ordinary thief. Not a burglar, certainly. Her address is in dog show catalogues, I'm sure. It wouldn't be hard to find. This is someone who was much more *comfortable* committing a theft in the presence of thousands of people at a dog show than he would be shimming her back door, or prowling her neighborhood. This wasn't an ordinary thief, or he'd have stolen the dog from *here*." And as he said it, Valnikov stopped by the iron gate overlooking the winding cobbled driveway into Madeline Whitfield's fifty-year-old Mediterranean mansion.

"Wow!" Natalie said. "I see why he picked her!"

"He picked the wrong victim," Valnikov said, wheeling into the driveway. "She's almost broke."

"How could you be broke and have a house like this? And squander money on a show dog?"

"That's what the extortionist can't understand," said Valnikov. "It's a long story."

Madeline Whitfield was on the steps when they got out of the detective car. She looked at Natalie curiously and smiled at Valnikov like an old friend.

"This is my partner, Sergeant Zimmerman," Valnikov said. "Mrs. Whitfield."

"Come in. I'm glad you came early. The waiting is hard."

"We're pretty sure the dead dog was the one belonging to Mrs. Gharoujian," said Valnikov. "I wish we knew for certain, though."

"Does that help you?" Madeline asked, and Natalie Zimmerman, a fair detective herself, noticed that Madeline Whitfield held Valnikov's arm all the way into the sitting room. And that when she said, "I'll get you some tea, Sergeant," she fluttered like a pigeon and *squeezed* his arm.

Natalie strolled around the room, admiring the view of the Rose Bowl. "How long did you stay here last night?"

"Pardon?"

"I said, how long did you stay here last night?"

"Uh, well, the extortionist called just after six."

"She lives all alone in this big house?"

"All alone," Valnikov nodded and his reddening face was not lost on Natalie Zimmerman.

"If she'd lose twenty-five pounds. And shave . . ." Natalie smirked.

"She's a fine lady," Valnikov said, a bit too quickly. "She's loving . . . of her Vickie. She's educated. She knows music. You should see her record collection."

"Really?" Natalie said. "I thought you were busy with an extortionist."

"I . . . uh, listened to a few records with her."

"Did she play? Music, I mean?"

"And she's very smart. After all, she's the one who first discovered that the dead dog was Mrs. Gharoujian's."

"Which we're not sure of at all," Natalie reminded him.

When Madeline returned, she said, "Sergeant Zimmerman, how would you like your tea?"

"Well, actually," Natalie said petulantly, "I'd prefer some coffee. Most *ordinary* cops drink coffee."

"Of course," she said. "It'll just take a minute." Then she poured for Valnikov and handed him the cup and saucer, and met his eyes, and smiled demurely, touching his arm before leaving for the kitchen again.

"Oh, horseshit!" Natalie said to her Friz.

"Pardon, Natalie?" said Valnikov.

"Nothing. Nothing at all," Natalie smirked. "It's not *my* business."

"What?"

"Nothing, for chrissake!"

"Sorry," said Valnikov, sipping. "Very good tea."

"Of course it's good tea. She probably has it imported from Bombay. From the plantation of a retired rajah, for chrissake."

"Sorry," said Valnikov, wondering why she had him apologizing.

"Did you ask *her* to go to the movies?" Natalie smirked.

"Why, no."

"Why not take her to see *Deep Throat?*"

"I told you I'd rather not see porno films, Natalie," Valnikov said. "But if you need an escort and you have to see it again, I'll be glad . . ."

Madeline's return interrupted Valnikov's offer and Natalie's impending outburst. Madeline put the coffee down and said nervously: "What should I tell him? Should I tell him I have the money?"

"I think it's time to say just that," Valnikov nodded while Natalie glared coldly at Madeline Whitfield, unable to fathom this overwhelming anger.

"I *do* have money for him, Sergeant. And as we discussed last night, it's *my* choice. I've decided today that if he'll promise to release Vickie unharmed, I'll give it all to him. I've managed to borrow and raise twenty thousand dollars!"

"That's stupid!" Natalie Zimmerman said.

"Please, Natalie," Valnikov said. "Natalie didn't mean that harshly, Mrs. Whitfield."

Now he was apologizing to this dowdy broad for his *partner's* manners! Him! A certified dingaling and a drunk apologizing to this Pasadena dog freak about Natalie's manners! Natalie was ranging from fury to contempt. For the both of them.

"I can understand that it might be hard for you to comprehend," Madeline said carefully to Natalie Zimmerman.

Don't patronize me, Dame Whitfield. Don't patronize Natalie Kelso Zimmerman or you'll be wearing a fat lip under that goddamn moustache!

"I can't understand *ever* giving in to kidnappers and extortionists," Natalie said. "For solid professional reasons *you* couldn't comprehend, Mrs. Whitfield. And I don't think many people, cops or civilians, could comprehend laying out twenty thousand in ransom for a *dog*."

"Sergeant Valnikov understands," Madeline said, looking at him with *that* look again while Natalie muttered to her Friz.

"I *do* understand, Mrs. Whitfield," Valnikov said, patting her hand. Now now. Keep your chin up, Mrs. Whitfield. Now now.

Natalie Zimmerman felt like screaming. Or getting sick. A *nut* who shouldn't even *be* a cop, and a woman maybe crazier, who's willing to shell out twenty grand for a pooch, and they're sitting here patty-caking and feeling smug and condescending toward the one who just can't understand. The *only* sane person in the goddamn house. What am I doing here! Why does everything happen to me? The black marble!

"What I'm hoping you might consider," Valnikov said, "is going along with a money drop. But trusting us to handle it for you. I want you to tell him you'll give him the money tomorrow. Tell him how much you have and that you'll be able to make the delivery tomorrow afternoon. Then we'll take over. We have helicopters and surveillance people who're expert at this sort of thing and . . ."

"I don't know. I think I'd just rather not risk it," Madeline said softly. "I *want* to let you catch him but . . ."

"I thought that if you trust me, personally, I could coordinate the operation," Valnikov said. "If you trust my judgment I'll promise not to let anything happen to scare him off and endanger Vickie. I won't risk Vickie's safety. If I'm positive we can take him, we'll take him. If not, we let the money go. What do you say? Do you trust me?"

She squeezed his forearm again, this time with both hands and whispered, "You *know* I do."

"Oh, *shit,*" Natalie muttered aloud.

"I give you my word I'm going to return Vickie to you. I promise," Valnikov said.

Then Madeline got tearful in spite of her best efforts, and Valnikov said, "Here, let me fix you some tea. Now now, Mrs. Whitfield. That's a brave girl. Now now."

"It's a dog."

"Pardon, Natalie?" Valnikov said.

"It's a dog," said Natalie Zimmerman to no one. To everyone. "It's a dog we're talking about."

"It's an extortion," Valnikov reminded her. "A felony."

"It's a *dog* you two are talking about," Natalie Zimmerman said stubbornly. "You two have *never* been talking about an extortion. You two are talking about a *dog*. I'm not running into a burning house to rescue a bowl of goldfish. And I'm not going to sit here and let you two make me so . . . make me forget that we're all talking about a *dog*. A dog! Do you hear me!"

But they didn't. Because Madeline Whitfield's tears had gotten the better of her and she was weeping on Valnikov's shoulder and Valnikov was patting her and saying, "Now now. I understand. You can be sure that I understand. Now now."

At which time Natalie Zimmerman got up and stalked out the front door to pace in the driveway and smoke, and watch the sun set pink and gold on the defunct hotel over the arroyo, over the picturesque Suicide Bridge.

Natalie felt a twinge of shame and then a rush of remorse as the anger ran out of her. Jesus, she couldn't even manage a little bile at a time like this? She was letting a brace of loonies make *her* ashamed for not being like them? Ever since she had been teamed with Valnikov, nothing made any sense. Before Valnikov, she knew who she was and where she was going. In that short time she'd seen a man shot to pieces, seen a kid's head painted silver, dug up a dog that was buried next to a goddamn koala bear, or a yak, or whatever the hell. And every time she tried to tell someone, another mental deficient, like Bullets Bambarella, would do something and they wouldn't listen to her. *Nobody* would listen to her. Now, Valnikov was talking about being a party to a money drop of twenty thousand dollars. For a *dog*. Explain *that* to the promotion board on your next oral exam, Natalie. Yes, sir, it just seemed like the thing to do at the time. Why did we willingly give the extortionist twenty thou? Because we didn't *have* eighty-five thou. If we had eighty-five thou like he demanded, we would have given him eighty-five thou. Because Valnikov and Mrs. Whitfield *understood* each other, that's why.

Natalie scraped her shoes and coughed and made some discreet noises before she went back inside. Just in case the two psychos were relieving each other's tensions on the floor. Like schnauzers. Like they probably did last night. I understand you, Mrs. Whitfield. Sure.

When she came back in the sitting room he had his suitcoat off and his tie loosened. Pretty chummy. Pretty goddamn chummy. Impulsively, she stepped back in the foyer and eavesdropped.

Valnikov was saying, "I've thought about it a lot and I truly believe a person can come out of something like this a stronger person."

"If I just get her back, Sergeant. If I just . . ."

"You will, I promise you," he said, taking her hand. "And about the other thing. Losing this house. Working. Listen, do you realize that in one year you could pick up enough college credits to get your state teaching credential?"

"Teaching credential?"

"Sure. With your fine education and sensitivity and intelligence, why you'd make a wonderful schoolteacher, Mrs. Whitfield. Just wonderful."

"It's true I've always enjoyed the children at the Huntington Library," she mused.

"That's the answer. Teaching," Valnikov said, her hand in both of his.

"Teaching. It *is* a possibility," she said eagerly. "Yes, it *is*! But . . . I wonder. Could I stay in this area? Would I be . . . embarrassed, moving, say, to a small apartment?"

"I think you should stay, Mrs. Whitfield," he said quietly. "From what you've told me, Old Pasadena isn't a place. It's a way of life. *Your* way of life. Maybe being a Russian I can identify in some ways. There's tradition here. Manners. Gentility. Order. Where else in Southern California are you going to find all that in these times? Old Pasadena is a *good* way of life for someone like you. My mother would have liked it. I think I'd like it too."

"If I'm interrupting anything I can go back outside," Natalie said to her Friz, causing them both to jump apart. Pretty chummy. Pretty goddamn chummy.

"Come on in, Natalie," Valnikov said. "It's almost time for him to call."

"You do the listening," Natalie said, sprawling on the settee, determined at least to demand overtime pay for all this.

"I think we should both listen," Valnikov said. "There's another extension in the bedroom."

Ah-hah, you son of a bitch! How do *you* know about the bedroom? Then remorse again. *Why* was she letting this lunatic liaison get her mad? Simple. Valnikov infected everyone. You're around him awhile, you start getting as nutty as he is. The hell with it. Now, she'd feel no guilt when she told them about his mental condition. None at all. Sorry Valnikov, but it's simply a matter of survival. Natalie Zimmerman's!

"Okay, I'll listen on the bedroom phone," Natalie smirked. "Unless *you'd* rather use the bedroom, Valnikov?"

Philo Skinner at that very moment was answering the extension in *his* bedroom. He held his hand over the receiver and whispered in desperation: "Arnold! You shouldn't call me at home!"

"That's exactly what I told *you,* Philo," the voice said. "Last week when you called me at home and talked me into letting you get down on the Vikings, and now it's Wednesday and I still ain't got my fifteen dimes."

"I *told* you the escrow money won't clear until Thursday, goddamnit!" Philo croaked. "I agreed to bump you a hundred a day. You want my blood?" You want my foreskin, you murderous fucking kike!

"I want your *balls*, Philo, you don't pay," he said.

Philo was right! The nigger with the knife!

"Why do you talk to me like this, Arnold?" Philo whined.

"Because it's Wednesday. And tomorrow's Thursday. And I carried you so far I need a head doctor, is why."

"So tomorrow I pay. Goddamnit, Arnold, I thought we were friends?"

"*Business* friends, Philo," the voice said. "Business friends. Tomorrow a man's coming to your house in the afternoon to close our transaction."

"Not my house, Arnold! Not my house!"

"The kennel, then," said the voice. "In the afternoon."

"Make it after two," Philo whined. "Make sure Mavis is gone. After two o'clock?"

"We are gonna close our transaction tomorrow afternoon, Philo, one way or the other."

"I know that, Arnold. I know!"

"Good night, Philo."

Phllo cut himself twice while shaving. He gave up and wiped the lather off his chin stubbles. He doused on half a can of baby powder but it couldn't dry the sweat pouring from his bony torso. Philo put on his polyester suit and a tapered orchid shirt. He hung his gold chains around his neck and teased his blue-black hair and started for the door.

But Mavis said, "Philo, I think I'll go to work with you tomorrow. I'm getting sick a soap operas all day. Maybe I'll do some bookwork."

"Christ, Mavis!" Philo said. "What kinda bookwork you think we got with twenty-five lousy dogs in the whole kennel? I told you there ain't enough work for even one kennel girl the way things are these days. Christ, I can't even keep busy with the grooming. Why you wanna hang around and go crazy too?"

"Just to be together, Philo. You're so jumpy lately. I know business is eating at you, but things'll work out. Business is funny."

"Yeah, well, I gotta run out get a few packs a cigarettes."

"Why you getting dressed up to buy cigarettes?"

"Christ, just cause I'm living like a bum don't mean I gotta dress like one. Get off my case, Mavis!"

"You been acting awful funny the last several days, Philo," Mavis said, turning down the television volume with a remote control. "If I didn't trust you I'd think you were maybe nesting with some little bird."

Then Philo lost his temper. "That does it! I'm going out to buy cigarettes. I'll be back within twenty minutes. You time me with a stopwatch. You and me been married six years. You tell me, can I run out of this house, drive somewhere, for five or ten minutes, meet some bird, take her to a motel, and come back here in twenty minutes? You tell me that's possible, you dumb shit!"

"I guess not," she said sweetly. "You couldn't even get a hard-on in half a day, come to think of it. In fact I ain't seen one in three months!"

Thank you, Mavis, he thought when he squealed out of the driveway in his El Dorado. It all comes down to an erection. I'll remember that in Puerto Vallarta when I'm screwing their serapes off, you miserable cunt!

The call was late. It came at 6:25 p.m.

"Hello."

"This is Richard. I want the money tonight. Get a pencil and paper. Here's the instruc—"

"I don't have the money tonight. I'll have it tomorrow."

"What!"

Very quickly she said, "I'll have the money tomorrow afternoon. I'll have it then but it's only twenty thousand dollars. I won't lie to you, that's how much I was able to borrow. I'll bring it wherever you say."

Twenty thousand dollars. He was stunned. Twenty thousand. Enough to pay off Arnold and five left over. Five thousand wouldn't begin to pay off his El Dorado! Five thousand wouldn't begin to pay his *delinquent* payments on the kennel! Five thousand wouldn't pay the balance of his income tax! (None of which he planned on paying anyway after he got the ransom.) Five grand! How long could he live in Puerto Vallarta on five grand? He was stunned.

It was fortunate that he had picked a remote telephone booth beside a service station that closed early on Wednesdays because he was screaming: "YOU CUNT! YOU WON'T GET AWAY WITH THIS! YOU WON'T! YOU CAN'T TREAT ME LIKE THIS! I WON'T LET YOU GET AWAY WITH THIS! YOU WAIT! I'M GOING TO CALL YOU BACK IN TEN MINUTES!"

Then, Philo Skinner, hardly aware of what he was doing, was speeding through alleys in his El Dorado, throwing up sparks in the night, clanging over holes in the asphalt and bumps in the pavement, roaring through backstreets toward Skinner

Kennels. Philo screeched to a stop in the parking lot, stumbled from the Cadillac, ran to the door with his jangling keys, and in a moment, was gasping and wheezing through the grooming room loping toward the kennel where twenty-five dogs went mad with joy, anger, or fear, depending upon their dispositions.

Philo unlocked the last dog pen but nearly lost Vickie, who went running toward the rubber doggie door and the gravel dog run outside, which was littered with defecation now that Philo Skinner was too busy being a criminal to clean up dog crap.

He grabbed her as she was almost through the doggie door and she growled but did not bite him, having gotten used to his rancid tobacco smell these past days. Then Philo ran to the office beside the grooming room, and throwing caution to the winds, picked up his own telephone.

Valnikov knew that Madeline's conversation had driven the extortionist to some desperate move, but he also knew that there was nothing to do but wait.

"Can't we trace the next call, Sergeant?" Madeline said fearfully. "He's going to do something terrible!"

"They can only trace calls easily in the movies," Valnikov said. "A phone trace is terribly complicated and has to be set up well in advance. We just have to wait."

They didn't have to wait long. She picked it up on the first ring. "Yes."

"Okay, you cunt," he snarled. "Now listen to this." And Philo Skinner held Vickie's mouth to the receiver and pinched the tender flesh around her vagina.

The little schnauzer yelped and began to whine.

"That's your Vickie, mommy. You recognize her voice, you cunt?" He had to drop the phone and cough until he spit a wad of phlegm in the wastepaper basket.

Madeline was trying to suppress a scream and it was only Valnikov's strong steady gaze and his reassuring nod that kept her from doing it.

"I . . . please . . . I don't know what Vickie sounds like . . . on the phone."

Which caused Natalie Zimmerman to put her phone down on the bed and walk downstairs to the drawing room, because she was absolutely certain now that she was the only sane person left in Los Angeles County. They were talking to the kidnapped dog.

"Listen, mommy, you miserable cunt!" And he pinched the animal brutally and Vickie yelped louder and began to cry.

"I take your word!" Madeline cried. "I believe you! I believe it's Vickie! Please don't!" And Valnikov couldn't hold her back this time. She began sobbing. But she was still holding the phone. Still listening and trying to answer.

"YOU LIED TO ME!" Philo shrieked. "Twenty thousand! You miserable cunt. It ain't enough. It ain't enough to get me *anywhere*. I'm going to do it. I swear to you I never hurt an animal in my life but I'm going to kill this bitch. NOW!"

Madeline said, "Wait! Wait! You've already killed once. Don't do it again. The little schnauzer you drugged. It's dead. Don't hurt another one!"

Then Philo gasped and had to cough and wheeze and catch his breath. And Valnikov listened.

"You're lying!" Philo finally said.

"I'm not," Madeline said. "The drug you gave her was too much. She died. There was nothing I could do."

"Dead?" Philo mumbled. Tutu was dead? The only creature in the world who loved Philo Skinner?

Valnikov was astonished. He motioned Natalie over to his phone. They stood together cheek to cheek and listened. The extortionist was crying!

"You rotten lying welsher," he sobbed. "You lied to me. You been lying to me all along. You been lying to me!"

"Please . . ." Madeline said. "Please!"

Philo Skinner threw the phone down on the desk, and still holding the whimpering schnauzer in his arms, ran crying into the grooming room and pinned Vickie on the metal table. The plucky little animal sensed danger and began to growl fiercely. When he removed one hand she bit him on the other and hung on. But Philo felt little pain, only rage. He reached for the instruments on the counter as Vickie snarled and chewed. He tried for the stripping knife. He couldn't reach it. He got his hand on the straight razor. Vickie growled in panic now, and still sobbing, Philo Skinner aped notorious kidnappers of recent history. Philo Skinner was a copycat.

He held Vickie's head on the metal table with his bleeding arm and sawed through the gristly flesh of her right ear. The gristle crackled when the razor sawed through. Vickie released her bite involuntarily and blood from Philo's hand ran down her throat as she screamed at the incredible pain. Philo didn't stop sawing until the razor was screeching across the stainless steel of the table. Then he looked down in horror at the bell-shaped schnauzer ear lying in blood.

Philo threw Vickie off the table and she hit the tile floor, still screaming, getting up, listing, staggering, falling to one side, instinctively trying to rub the devastating pain away on the slippery tile floor, leaving a trail of blood across the tile as she flopped like a fish on her bloody head. When she found herself in the corner of the room she rammed her head against the wall several times trying to escape. She let loose with a whine so loud and shrill that Philo had to hold his wounded hand over his left ear when he picked up the telephone. Then she balled up and tucked the amputation far beneath her as though she were ashamed of it.

Philo Skinner was panting and sobbing and gasping for air. "I . . . did it, you miserable woman!" he said. "I . . . you . . . you *made* me do it!"

"Vickie's dead. You killed Vickie," Madeline said, knowing it wasn't true, able to hear a dog screaming in the background.

"I cut off her ear!" Philo Skinner cried. "You *made* me do it! It's *your* fault!"

"Spare her *life!*" Madeline begged, and even Natalie Zimmerman was impressed. Madeline Whitfield was on her feet wiping her eyes. She was gaining control and the extortionist was going to pieces.

"Spare her *life,* Richard," Madeline repeated. "I'm going to take the twenty thousand dollars tomorrow. Tonight. Wherever you say. I don't care when. I'll pay it for Vickie's life. Where shall I take the money, Richard?"

Philo couldn't think. His hand hurt like hell. He was afraid for a moment that the tendon was severed, but he saw he had good finger movement. Vickie was still screaming piteously and Philo slammed the office door shut. Still she screamed.

"No, not tonight," he said. "Not tonight. Tomorrow. I'm going to call you tomorrow morning. Eleven o'clock. I'll tell you then. Bring the twenty thousand then."

"Yes, Richard," Madeline said, nodding at the mouthpiece. "Yes. I'll be here. I have the money. I'll do whatever you say. Yes."

When the phone went dead, Madeline sat down. She stared at Valnikov. Then at Natalie. Then at the phone.

Valnikov said, "We'll be here at nine a.m. with some other officers. Tomorrow he'll want the money. He'll decide that twenty thousand is better than nothing. In any case, you can observe the precautions we're going to take, and then you can decide whether or not to let us keep you under surveillance when you make the money drop. It'll be up to you. I promise." When he finished talking, Vainikov walked over and knelt in front of Madeline. "Do you understand me, Mrs. Whitfield?"

"Yes, Sergeant," she said.

"I'll be with you tomorrow morning. Don't be afraid."

"I'm not afraid," she answered bleakly.

"I know that." Valnikov patted her hand and said, "You're a very strong woman. Do you hear me?"

"Mrs. Whitfield," Natalie said. "If what we heard was . . . well, if he did what he said, then your dog is . . . mutilated. She's no longer a champion show dog. My God, Mrs. Whitfield! You don't want to give him the twenty thousand *now,* do you?"

"I want to give it to him even *more,*" Madeline Whitfield said. She looked evenly at Natalie. "I'd give him the eighty-five thousand if I had it. I'd give him anything. Now more than ever."

"Now more than ever," Natalie echoed.

"You don't understand," said Madeline Whitfield.

"I understand, Mrs. Whitfield," Valnikov said, patting her hand again and standing up. "I understand perfectly. Good night, Mrs. Whitfield."

Like Madeline Whitfield, Philo Skinner had to sit and stare for a while after hanging up the phone. But the worsening pain in his hand brought him around faster. He took off his bloodstained polyester jacket. The *last* of his polyester leisure suits would end up in the trash can this night. Vickie was no longer screaming. He opened the door to the grooming room. She was whimpering quietly in the corner.

Philo Skinner ran to the sink and began tearing out paper towels to wipe the grooming table and the floor. There was too much blood. He went to the closet and got the mop and pail. Then he cursed when he saw that he trailed his own blood to the closet and back. First things first, Philo! He went back to the sink and rolled up his sleeves and washed the blood from his hand. Vickie had really ripped him this time. He could close it with a butterfly bandage, though. No doctors. This one looked too much like a dog bite. No doctors. No explanations. He poured disinfectant over the wound and cried out in pain. His voice made Vickie whimper louder. He wrapped his hand in gauze for now. The butterfly bandage could come later.

He had the room cleaned in ten minutes. Except for the table. He hadn't touched the table yet because of the ear. Now it was time. He was dizzy. For one nightmarish second he imagined that it moved! That the frayed bleeding nerve ends made it twitch. He could hardly bear to look at it, but it was time. He got a paper towel. Then another. Then three more. With the padding between his fingers and the ear he reached for it. The ear slipped out of his grasp. It slapped on the table and splashed drops of blood.

"Oh," Philo said. "Oh."

Then he picked it up again. He held it away from his body like a poisonous snake. He ran for the toilet and threw it splashing into the bowl. He flushed the toilet and balled the paper towels up in a wad. The ear refused to go down in the Los Angeles sewers.

Philo looked in horror at the ear floating in the toilet bowl. Then it sank slowly. Then it bobbed up when the toilet gurgled.

"Oh!" Philo cried, holding his wounded hand to his mouth. "Oh!"

He ran back into the grooming room. He sloshed water on the bloody grooming table and washed it clean. He waited until the toilet filled. He ran back into the rest room and without looking in the bowl flushed the toilet. Then he staggered back in the grooming room and lit a cigarette. He washed his hands once, twice, three times in the deep sink. He washed them in water as hot as he could stand.

Then he felt a tingling around his skull, at about the hairline. The tingling wouldn't stop. He was wheezing and put the cigarette in the ashtray. His face started burning. He went back to the toilet. The ear was floating in the water.

Philo cried out and backed into the door, almost falling down. He flushed the toilet again and again. He stood over the toilet and watched it.

He watched it go down and disappear from sight while the toilet swooshed and gurgled. Then he watched it come back up.

It floated on the water like a dead bat.

"Oh," Philo said, then he started crying again. He was getting sick. He went back to the deep sink. He pulled out ten paper towels from the dispenser. He took the handful of towels and ran back to the toilet. He fished up the ear. He held it in front of him in horror, an arm's length from his body. He felt a bat crawling up his spine, clinging to his neck.

He loped out of the kennel, heading straight for the street. A car slammed on his brakes when he caught Philo in the headlight beams. The driver cursed and drove on. Philo ran shuddering to the sewer by the curb and threw Vickie's amputation down the black hole.

Philo was holding his arms and shivering when he came back inside the kennel. He couldn't stop shivering, but there was one task remaining. One more unbearable job to do. Philo looked fearfully at the bloody bundle in the corner. Philo had been unable to look there. Had been avoiding that corner, but now it was time.

He thought she would try to bite him for sure when he reached down beneath her. She didn't. The overwhelming pain from the razor had cut away her courage. Vickie whined and cried when he picked her up in his arms. Vickie's blood put stains on Philo's orchid shirt. She cried and licked Philo's tobacco-stained fingers.

As he bandaged her head, Philo Skinner was bawling louder than Vickie. Philo took her back to her dog pen and left more boiled liver than she could possibly eat even if she didn't vomit at the smell of food. He poured some warm milk in her bowl and even the smell of milk made her bilious. Still crying with her, Philo placed her gently in her bed and tried desperately to get her to accept a codeine pill in some ground beef. She retched when the food touched her whiskers. Then Philo started to retch. Philo Skinner slammed the chain-link gate and upchucked outside Vickie's pen. All twenty-five dogs began barking in joy, excitement, or fear, depending upon their dispositions, as their keeper crawled on all fours and vomited. Sick as a dog.

12

Charlie Lightfoot

It was eight o'clock by the time they were driving back to Hollywood Station.

"We've got a lot of work to do tomorrow morning before he calls," Valnikov said.

Natalie was riding silently, smoking, looking out at the headlights on the freeway.

"I think a phone trace for tomorrow would be useless even if we *could* arrange it," he said. "It's payday for him and he'll be careful. I think we should have three surveillance teams. If we can't get them from downtown our own guys'll have to do. We'll have a chopper standing by and one of our own people riding shotgun."

She shrugged without comment and Valnikov continued: "I just hope he's not too fancy with his money drop. I want to get him, but we can't endanger Vickie."

"Valnikov . . ."

"I *really* want to get this guy."

"Valnikov."

"Yes?"

"Vickie is a dog."

"Yes."

"I just have to keep saying that for my own benefit more than anyone's."

"You know, Natalie, I'm convinced the dead schnauzer is Tutu. And that's our only lead, really. I think that after we get the surveillance set up at Mrs. Whitfield's tomorrow we might call that kennel owner. What's his name? Skinner? If he knew Tutu that well, I'm going to ask him to come to the pet mortuary and make a positive identification. Then after that, I'm going to take him to Mrs. Gharoujian's if he's willing to come, and maybe between the two of them they'll have some idea which one of Mrs. Gharoujian's present or former house guests is capable of all this. You know Mrs. Gharoujian wouldn't bother with Tutu, so some of her boys must have worked with the animal. Some of her boys are very familiar with the world of dog shows. This man, Skinner, just might give us a lead as to which one."

Philo Skinner was late getting home. He came in the back door, wearing a grooming smock instead of the shirt and jacket he left with. He was relieved to see that Mavis was in the bedroom undressing for her bath. He got a windbreaker from the hall closet.

"That you, Philo?" Mavis yelled. "Twenty minutes, huh? Where you been, Philo?"

He zipped up the jacket and headed for the door again. The butterfly bandage hadn't closed the wound as well as he thought. The gauze was spotting red on the back of his hand. He banged noisily through the kitchen until he found the fifth of Canadian bourbon he'd bought for Christmas guests. It was still nearly full. Drinking was not a Philo Skinner vice. As he slammed out the kitchen door, Mavis yelled: "Philo? That you, Philo? You can't tell me you ain't nesting with some young bird! Philo!"

She opened the front door in time to see the Cadillac roaring out the driveway. Philo made a screeching right turn at the bottom of the street, driving back to the place he loved and hated. The only place he belonged: Skinner Kennels. Home of the Terrier King.

"How about stopping for dinner before we go back to the station, Natalie?" Valnikov said, impulsively.

"Dinner?"

"Sure. You have to eat. Why not let me buy you dinner? Any place you like."

"I can buy my own dinner," she said. Then she added: "Funny thing, I'm not even hungry. I haven't eaten in twenty-four hours and I'm not even hungry."

He drove silently for a moment and said, "Did you have a nice dinner last night? With your captain friend?"

"Yeah," she said, looking at him sharply. "Did you have a nice dinner with Mrs. Whitfield?"

"We didn't have dinner," Valnikov said, looking at Natalie in surprise as he took the Hollywood Freeway outbound, creeping into the slow lane.

"Didn't have time, huh?"

"Time?"

"Never mind."

They were quiet again until he said, "I know a Russian restaurant overlooking the Sunset Strip."

"The Strip," she scoffed. "They have an entertainment license?"

"Entertainment?"

"Sure. For the freak show while you eat."

"It's on the hill *over* the Strip. None of the Strip people come there. It's a family place. How about it, Natalie? Let's have a bite to eat. Their borscht is good. I guess I just don't feel like being alone tonight."

"Neither does Mrs. Whitfield, I'll bet," said Natalie.

"No."

"It's only a dog, Valnikov. Try to remember. It's only a dog."

"Yes."

"You feel sorry for her."

"Yes, very sorry."

"You feel sorry for lonely people."

"Yes."

"You think *I'm* lonely, is that it? You want to take me to dinner because I'm lonely."

"No."

"Because *you're* lonely."

"Yes."

"Okay, Valnikov, I just wanted to get it straight. Now let's go have some borscht. And I'll pay for my own."

"Swell!" he said, with a wide grin in the darkness, driving forty miles an hour for the first time.

"I have a daughter, Valnikov," she said. "My daughter goes to Colorado State and has a great old time. She majors in skiing and ski instructors, thanks to mom's monthly checks. But I *have* a daughter, and she loves me very much."

"That's swell, Natalie," Valnikov said. "I have a son, but I don't think he loves me at all. He turns down all my invitations and . . ."

"I also have a boyfriend, Jack Packerton. He'll probably be a deputy chief someday."

"Yes, I don't wonder," Valnikov said.

"What I'm saying is, I don't get dogs and people mixed up. I don't have a schnauzer or a parakeet or a gerbil. I don't want you to get me and Mrs. Whitfield mixed up. Not in *any* respect, do you understand?"

"Of course," he said. He couldn't seem to understand his partner even when he didn't have a hangover.

"I'm not at all like you and Mrs. Whitfield, Valnikov."

"Like me and Mrs. Whitfield?"

"Forget it," she said, brushing her hair off of her glasses. "I don't even understand myself anymore. I didn't get enough sleep last night I guess." (Failed orgasms on top of all this shit!) "I don't know what I'm babbling about, I guess. Or why. This crazy investigation is giving me a headache."

"You'll feel better after some borscht," Valnikov said, smiling again. "My mother always said that."

"After some borscht," Natalie sighed.

Valnikov turned off the freeway at Highland Avenue and drove out the Strip. He parked on the steep street in front of the restaurant, careful to cut his wheels in. Lose your car on this hill and it wouldn't stop until it squashed three cocaine peddlers, two pimps, and a Krishna chanter eating pumpkin seeds on Sunset Boulevard below.

Valnikov was disappointed that the proprietor wasn't in. He seldom got a chance to talk Russian these days and the Armenian waitress knew not a word. The restaurant wasn't doing much of a business on this chill Wednesday night. They took a seat by the window to look at the cascade of monster billboards on the Strip. An arabesque of color and blazing neon advertised famous rock stars Valnikov had never heard of.

"You know, Natalie," he smiled when they were seated. "I haven't had a vodka for two days."

''That must be a record,'' she said. ''I think you should have one tonight.''

''Well, would you like to join me?''

''Do you have any gin and tonic?'' Natalie said to the young waitress.

''Have you ever tasted Russian vodka?'' Valnikov said.

''What's the difference between Russian and American?'' Natalie shrugged.

''The whole world,'' Valnikov said. ''Will you try Russian? Just one?''

He looked at her with those serious, no *sad* blue eyes of his and his shy kid smile and she said, ''I'll try Russian. *Once*.'' When she said it she changed her mind immediately, but the tired waitress was gone.

''I'm so glad you came, Natalie,'' Valnikov said. ''I'm so *very* glad.''

The girl returned quickly with the two double shots. Valnikov beamed and raised his glass: *''Na vashe zdorovye!''* he said. ''To *your* health, Natalie.'' He downed the entire glass and closed his eyes blissfully.

Natalie was nothing if not plucky. She figured it would taste like American vodka, which always tasted to her as she imagined gasoline would taste. What the hell. Let him laugh his ass off when she did a backflip over the chair.

''Cheers,'' she said and downed the double shot. The heat flooded through her, and there was a not unpleasant taste from the bottom up, and then, ''Mellow!'' she cried. And it was. ''That's not like *any* vodka I've ever tasted.''

''It's Russian,'' Valnikov chuckled. ''There's a *world* of difference. It's east and west. It's Igor Stravinsky and Bob Dylan. It's . . . Russian. Want another?''

''What the hell,'' said Natalie Zimmerman.

''What the hell,'' she repeated after their second.

''What the hell,'' she giggled after the third. And then her nose was tingling and her fingers were getting numb.

''Na zdorovye,'' she said when they drank that one.

''Maybe you should sip it,'' Valnikov said. ''Some people put pepper in it.''

''It's so mellow!'' she cried. *''Na zdorovye!''* She was flushed and glowing. Her Friz was drooping.

''Want some borscht now, Natalie?'' Valnikov asked.

''Who needs borscht?'' she said. *''Na zdorovye!* I like this place. I might bring Jack here.''

''It's a nice quiet place,'' Valnikov said. ''Sometimes there's a gypsy violin. That's when I like it best.''

Natalie Zimmerman insisted on the fourth. She took Valnikov's word that the borscht was pretty good tonight. She let him ladle sour cream into it and she noted that it had a nice consistency going down. The black bread and butter also had a very nice texture, but she had to take his word on that, too. Because all she could really taste was the vodka, and she wasn't really tasting it. She was experiencing it.

''I don't think you should have another,'' Valnikov warned. ''Five double vodkas! That's a lot when you're not used to it.''

''I can buy my own, Valnikov,'' Natalie said with a toss of her buckskin Friz.

''Two more,'' Valnikov said to the waitress. ''Do you always drink so much?''

''Do *I* always drink . . . do *I* always . . . Valnikov, you're driving me crazy, do you know that?''

''I am?''

''I hardly drink at all!''

''Oh.''

''I'm a social drinker.''

''Sorry,'' he said.

''And I *hate* porno flicks.''

''Yes, of course,'' he said, dabbing at his lips with a napkin.

''And I never saw a man with such impeccable goddamn table manners. Why the hell don't you slurp your soup like Jack does!''

"Sorry, Natalie," Valnikov said, looking over his shoulder to see if her yelling was disturbing the other diners.

"Sorry. That sounds like you. Sorry. Quit being so considerate or you'll bore me too."

"Sor— Natalie, have a little more bread."

"I'd like a little more vodka."

"Oh, no. I wouldn't advise that."

"I'm thirty-goddamn-nine years old. I oughtta know how much I can drink."

"May I butter you some more bread, Natalie? This pumpernickel is very tasty, don't you think? It's so . . ."

"Russian," she said.

"Yes," he said. "Please try to eat some more. Lots more."

When the check came, Natalie Zimmerman was slightly more sober. At least she'd stopped yelling.

"Wasn't the pastry good?" he said, counting out a fifteen percent tip for the girl. Natalie was too drunk to object when he paid.

"Sure," Natalie said, lighting a cigarette with a match that missed the flame twice. Valnikov had given up trying to light them when she informed him that no cop should be lighting another cop's cigarettes, goddamnit!

"Will you have a little more tea before we go?" Valnikov said. It took lots more than five double vodkas to put him away. Maybe twice that many, and then— oblivion. A wasteland. Siberia.

"A little more tea," Natalie said, smoking, examining his face. Finally she said, "It's only a goddamn dog, Válnikov."

"I know," he said softly.

"It's *your* case. I'm just along for the ride."

"No, we're partners," he said.

"It's *your* case. I'm working on a case of my own," she blurted. Her words were slurred and her voice was getting loud again.

"What case is that?"

"The case of Sergeant A.M. Valnikov." She sighed the smoke out. "That's *my* case."

"I don't understand."

"Never mind," she said. "Tell me about your childhood."

"My childhood."

"Yeah, tell me about it. I told you about mine, didn't I? I got married in my childhood. To a dirt bag. Then I had a baby. Then I got rid of the dirt bag and became a cop to support my Becky. Then I married another dirt bag who didn't know he hated cops till he married one. Then I got rid of that dirt bag. And I did a hell of a good job raising a kid."

"I'm sure she's a fine girl," Valnikov said, sipping his tea.

"At least I don't think she's going to get herself knocked up like her mom did, because I don't think she'd take her skis off long enough to hop into bed with a guy. Can they do it on skis? God, I miss that kid. Do you ski?"

"No, I don't have any talents," he grinned. "My mother wasted money on piano lessons but I just didn't have the talent."

"You have talent," Natalie said, elbows on the table, her chin propped by both hands, her big glasses slipping down her nose.

"What talent?"

"You can catch felons," she said. "I just bet you caught lots and lots of felonious bastards when you worked homicide."

"I'll tell you a secret," he said. "My mother got me piano lessons but do you know what she *really* dreamed for me?"

"What's that?"

"She wanted me to be a ballet star."

This time the other diners *did* turn and look at the drunken broad with the big frizzy hairdo and the four-inch glasses who was doubled up in snuffling giggles and falling off her chair.

"A . . . a . . . ballet dancer!" she screamed. "You! Smokey the Bear in leotards!"

When she quieted down, Valnikov said, "My mother was always appalled by the lack of culture in America. To the day she died she couldn't believe that Americans found batting averages more important than ballet. But I was never quite . . . delicate enough to dance. And my big brother weighed two hundred pounds when he was thirteen years old, so it was hopeless."

"Did she teach you to eat the way you do?" Natalie asked.

"How do you mean?"

"I'll bet she was awfully big on table manners."

"*She* could dance, my mother!" Valnikov said. "Do you mind if I have just one more Stolichnaya?"

"Only if I can have one," Natalie said. She was still propping her chin in her hands, staring into Valnikov's blue eyes which were getting watery.

"Two," he said, holding up the vodka glass to the waitress.

"I just wish my mother could have seen the Moiseyev Dance Group. She could do all the national dances: Georgian, Crimean, Ukrainian. And remember, she never lived in a country called U.S.S.R. They'd fled before the Whites were really finished."

"They were from Leningrad?" Natalie said.

Valnikov nodded and said, "Petrograd, to them. Do you know that the city is filled with cottonwoods? Do you know that in late summer the flowers set seeds by the billions! It's extremely fine and silky. It fills the air. It piles up against the buildings like snowdrifts. You can imagine that it's snowing under a hot August sun. What a place!"

"You ever been there?"

"No. I'll go someday. When I save enough. My ex-wife's remarried. My child support officially stopped two years ago but I still send money. Nick doesn't return it so I guess he's using the money. I'll save enough one day, then I'll go there."

"Sounds like you could get a bad case of emphysema, all that milkweed blowing through the air," Natalie said, smiling at the waitress who set the last vodkas before them.

"Maybe," he said. "But, Natalie, the Paris of the North! Imagine a place with streets full of silky snowdrifts! In the hot August sun."

"I'm sure it's fantastic," she smiled, the warmest smile she had ever shown him, and it set his heart pounding. "*Na zdorovye!* That's melloooooow!"

"Ah, yes," he agreed when the vodka was flowing through him.

She looked at his dumb kid grin and said, "Why did you say your father died before your brother was born? That's impossible, you know."

"I didn't say that."

"Yes, you did. The first day we worked together. You've been . . . okay today. But sometimes you say things like that."

"Did I say that?"

"Does vodka drinking make you . . . *confused* the next day?"

"I don't think so."

"When did your father die?"

"In 1941. I wasn't quite eight years old."

"What did he do in this country?"

"Anything he could," Valnikov shrugged. "He never really learned much English. He had been a career soldier. He was a young captain in the czar's army."

"I see," Natalie said, feeling her speech getting thicker. "Do you think you meant his *spirit* died before your brother was born? Maybe during the Revolution when his whole world was going to hell?"

"I don't know. I don't remember saying that."

"Do you ever notice your mind wandering? Maybe find it tough to understand or answer questions?" Natalie's elbow slipped off the table and her face almost went in her plate.

"I think you've had enough vodka," Valnikov observed.

"You got *your* case to solve, I got mine," she said belligerently. "Let's go to my place."

"*Your* place!"

"No, on second thought, I can solve my place, I mean, case, better at your case, I mean place. Let's go to your place."

"My place?"

"You got any Russian vodka at your place?"

"Yes, but I don't think you should have any more."

"Okay, but I wanna go to *your* place. You gonna refuse a lady?"

Valnikov drove bleary-eyed down the hill to the Sunset Strip, careful not to run over any kids eating raisins and nuts. He spotted a flower child in bib overalls and rubber fishing boots. The flower child was doing what flower children so often do on the Strip—selling flowers. Little bunches of forget-me-nots and violets.

Valnikov weaved to the curb and jumped out of the car. When he came back he had a bunch of violets in his hand.

"Maybe you won't let me light your cigarettes, but you can't refuse me this," he said. "I'm not being chauvinistic or anything. Honest. It's just that Russians *love* to give flowers."

"Valnikov," she said, shaking her head and pressing the violets to her face. "You're a crazy crazy man, do you know that? I'll bet you *would* run into a burning house to save a bowl of goldfish."

When they were parked in front of Valnikov's furnished rooms on Franklin Avenue, he got thinking how the bachelor apartment looked. The daybed was, of course, unmade. The underwear and socks were still strung from the cage to the door. The pile of dishes in the kitchen. My God! Were the toilet and sink clean?

"Uh, Natalie, could you just sit here for a minute and finish your cigarette? Give me a couple minutes to straighten things out."

"You live upstairs, Valnikov?" she asked, a bit anxious about negotiating any stairway at this time. Now her fingers had feeling, but her toes were numb.

"Number twelve, right at the top of the stairs and turn left. Just give me two minutes, okay?"

"Two minutes," Natalie said, rubbing her nose which also had lost feeling. Stolichnaya. Siberia. Oblivion.

Valnikov didn't take the stairs any too gracefully himself. He had lots of trouble finding the lock. Then he was in and running through the apartment, grabbing underwear and socks and dirty dishes. He tossed the underwear and socks in the oven and the dirty dishes in the refrigerator. He picked up dozens of loose records off the floor and stacked them on the tired and shabby coffee table. He pulled up the cover on the daybed, smoothed hastily over the lumpy sheets, tossed the sleeping pillow under the daybed and arranged some throw-pillows for atmosphere. Then he saw that two of the pillows had tomato soup on them. He put them on the floor and kicked them under the daybed too. He heard Natalie climbing the stairs with no little effort. He dashed in the bathroom and inspected the toilet, shower, and sink. Okay except there was toothpaste smeared all over the sink. He grabbed a bath towel, did a quick wipe of the sink and ran into the kitchen, tossing the towel in the refrigerator with the dirty dishes. He was out of breath when she knocked.

Then he panicked for a second and ran to the seven-foot animal cage. Thank God! It didn't look too bad.

"*Gavno,*" said Misha to his master, who was indeed thinking about *gavno* on the cage floor.

Valnikov threw open the door and held the screen door for her. "Welcome, Natalie," he puffed. "I don't get too many visitors, I'm afraid. But welcome!"

Natalie weaved sideways as she crossed the room and sat on the only upholstered chair, cracking a loose record in three places.

"Oh, sorry!" Valnikov said, when she jumped up. He picked up the broken disc and said, "Mussorgsky. Not one of my favorites anyway."

"That's a lumpy-looking couch," she said.

"That's a daybed," said Valnikov. "Let me smooth it out."

"Why?" Natalie said suspiciously, missing the cigarette with her match again. "You think I'm going to lie on your *bed?*"

"No!" Valnikov cried.

At which time Natalie got up and sat on his daybed. "Lumpy," she complained.

"I can smooth it out," he said quickly.

"Not with *me* in it, pal," she said.

"Of course not!"

"For chrissake, Valnikov, sit down!"

"Would you like some tea?"

"I'd like some vodka. Russian vodka."

"How about some tea?"

"Well shove it, then! I can get vodka somewhere else!"

"I'll get you some vodka," said Valnikov, disappearing into the kitchen.

"How about some Gypsy music?" Natalie said, knocking the sparks from her cigarette all over his napless carpet. "Whoops!"

"Voice or violin!" Valnikov yelled from the kltchen.

"Both! Shoot the works!" Natalie said imperiously.

While she brushed off the sparks from his daybed, Valnikov poured the vodka and selected the records. First balalaika. Why not? Then some folk music. Happy music. Then . . . Gypsy.

When the first record played, Valnikov suddenly felt giddy and whimsical. He couldn't remember when he'd had so much fun! He was standing in the middle of the floor with a half-empty vodka glass in his hand.

The Russian baritone began with a lively song. Valnikov said, "It's called 'Kogda Ya Pyan.' " Then to her astonishment, Valnikov began a dance for her, translating the Russian lyric as he hopped and whirled.

First the Russian baritone, followed by Valnikov translating: "I shall drink and drink . . . and I am always drunk . . . there is nothing I am afraid of . . ."

"Sing it, Valnikov!" Natalie yelled, clapping her hands as Valnikov danced.

The Russian and Valnikov sang: "There is nothing I am afraid of!"

"Sing it, Valnikov!" Natalie ordered, spilling her vodka and pouring some more.

Valnikov danced with his vodka glass tight in his teeth, no hands. Then Valnikov fell down on the daybed next to Natalie.

He stripped off his suitcoat and unbuckled his gun belt. The gun and belt went flying into the overstuffed chair.

"Wait a minute, Valnikov," Natalie Zimmerman warned. "Keep the rest of our clothes *on!*"

But Valnikov wasn't even listening. He was up again. He loosened his tie and threw it off. He rolled up the sleeves of his white shirt. Like many burly men, Valnikov was light on his feet. He began dancing to the lively beat of "Kak U Duba Starovo."

"Dance, Valnikov!" Natalie giggled while she clapped. When the song ended he fell on the daybed again.

"That was terrific!" Natalie yelled. "*You're* terrific!"

"I am?"

"You're a terrific dancer!"

Then a Gypsy woman, who sounded like a man, began singing. Valnikov turned serious and poured more Stolichnaya for both of them. Gypsies. God help us. Gypsies.

"What is it, Valnikov?" she said.

"I don't know. I just get sad with the Gypsies."

"But why?"

"Because I'm supposed to, probably."

"You're a lousy American, Valnikov."

"Listen to this!"

A Gypsy baritone began singing "Starinye Vals," The Old Waltz.

"That's the most beautiful waltz I've ever heard," said Natalie Zimmerman.

"Do you waltz?" Valnikov asked.

"Yes."

He went to the turntable and moved the arm back to the beginning of "Starinye Vals." The Gypsy sang. Valnikov bowed and extended his arms. Natalie Zimmerman stood unsteadily and leaned toward him. He was a powerful leader. He led her gingerly around the debris in the tiny cluttered apartment while the Gypsy sang.

"The snowstorm howls behind the windows," Valnikov said, translating the lyric. "And no sound of the waltz is heard."

"Valnikov," she said, and pulled away from him, sitting down on the lumpy daybed. "What's happening to me!"

"And I was young." He translated the Gypsy's lyric.

"Valnikov!"

"And I *loved* you so much!" he said, translating the lyric.

"Do you have any more vodkka? I'd like some more vodka!"

"Of course," he said politely, and disappeared into the kitchen.

"Is the bathroom through this door, Valnikov?" she yelled while he was pouring the drinks.

"You can't miss it in this place," he said. "It's to the left."

She rinsed her face in cold water, dried, put on fresh lipstick and examined her watery eyes. My God, what's happening to me? Valnikov's a madman. But what's the matter with *me?* When she returned a Gypsy woman was singing as though her heart were breaking. Valnikov was dancing drunkenly in the middle of the floor.

"Valnikov, you're so funny," Natalie said while he swayed with the music. She was nearly as tall as he. "Stand up straight for once, why don't you?"

"I don't care about standing straight," he said, swaying to the music, eyes closed.

"You'd be almost six feet tall if you'd stand straight," Natalie said. "And you must weigh 220 pounds. You should be taller."

"I don't care if I'm six feet tall," Valnikov said, squatting on his haunches, trying some prisiadka kicks that put him temporarily on his ass.

"Valnikov!" Natalie shrieked. "This is hysterical!"

"The nightingales sang in the raspberry bushes!" Valnikov cried.

"What?" She poured his glass full of vodka as he got up, dancing.

"I said the nightingales sang in the raspberry bushes," Valnikov said. "Who but a Russian would write a lyric like that?"

And while a Gypsy baritone sang, Natalie smiled and said, "Is that what the song says?"

"The leaves of the poplars rustled," Valnikov translated.

"In the leafy forest young girls greeted the horsemen with song."

"That's what he's singing?" Natalie demanded.

Valnikov nodded and danced with his eyes closed.

He opened his eyes when the Gypsy stopped singing. Vanikov replayed the Old Waltz. She stood before him with her arms beckoning. He took her and they waltzed, careful to avoid the cage and coffee table.

"Tell me what the lyric says," she whispered.

"On a spring night an unknown voice sang the beautiful melody." Valnikov talked while the Gypsy sang.

"This is a *lovely* waltz," Natalie whispered, as they whirled slowly in the tiny apartment.

"*Gavno!*" said Misha, watching the dancers.

"And I was so young," Valnikov translated. "And I loved you so much!"

"I'm awful mad at you for laying Mrs. Whitfield last night, Valnikov," Natalie whispered as they waltzed.

"You are?" he said, light-headed, dizzy.

"Yes, I'm goddamn mad."

"Why, Natalie?"

"Because you're a police officer," she snapped. "It reflects badly on the whole police department, damn it. Screwing on duty!"

"I'm sorry, Natalie," he said. "That was a very unusual night for me."

"I forgive you," she said in his ear while the Gypsy sang. "What did that Gypsy say about nightingales, Valnikov?"

"That the nightingales sing in the raspberry bushes," Valnikov murmured against her cheek.

"Damn right they do," said Natalie Zimmerman, blowing her Friz out of her eyes. And suddenly kissing Valnikov's burning earlobe.

He was ecstatic. He never dared dream. "Natalie!" he cried.

Then she cried: "Andrushka!"

"What! *What* did you say!"

"Andrushka!" She kissed him and bit his ear.

The sound of her saying it nearly moved him to tears. "Natasha!" he cried.

He was the most tender and unselfish lover she had ever known. He kissed her body everywhere and endlessly. He caressed her everywhere and endlessly. He whispered to her in Russian and English. She didn't know if the words were his or the Gypsy's who sang to them through it all. Natalie Zimmerman had *four* orgasms, only one less than she *didn't* have all week with Captain Jack Packerton.

Every few moments she cried: "Andrushka!"

"Natasha!" he replied. "Oh, my Natasha!"

"Andrushka!"

At about the same moment that Natalie Zimmerman was having her fourth orgasm, Philo Skinner, who hadn't had one in three months, was sitting in the little office beside the grooming room, drinking Canadian bourbon by the light of a desk lamp, doodling on a note pad, staring at the telephone.

The whiskey was helping him to stop thinking about what he'd done. He wondered if she was able to sleep but he couldn't bring himself to go back in the kennel and look at her. He had arrived at a decision.

His Mexican tourist card had long since been arranged. There was a daily Mexicana Airlines flight at 3:00 p.m., a flight which would have him gliding over the subtropical paradise, over white beaches and warm ocean just after sunset, as he'd dreamed it. He wouldn't have seventy thousand dollars as he'd dreamed it, but he wouldn't have five thousand either. He was going to have *twenty* thousand. He was going to stiff Arnold and take the bundle and run. He smiled grimly and hoped the other bookmakers cut *Arnold's* balls off. Let the kike and nigger come looking for Philo tomorrow afternoon. At about that time he'd be high over the Gulf of California. Drinking margaritas.

Of course he could never come back to his country. That made him sad. But then, never is a long time. Maybe Arnold would die, the bloodsucker. Philo Skinner might be back one day. He'd take that twenty K and run it up ten times that much in two years. There were investments to be made in a country like Mexico, and he could outsmart any greaseball that ever lived. Philo Skinner would probably *own* half of Puerto Vallarta before long.

Then as Philo drained the paper cup and started to pour some more bourbon he had a terrifying notion. Christ, what if she had second thoughts? What if she decided a one-eared dog was worth nothing to her? What if all that talk about Vickie being like a kid to her was *just* talk? What if she was really a celebrity-hungry cunt like most of them, who didn't really give a schnauzer's shit about their animals as long as Philo made them win? Twenty thousand for a maimed animal? Why did he tell her he mutilated the schnauzer? Why *did* he mutilate the schnauzer? He'd never hurt an animal in his life!

Before he'd made a conscious choice, Philo had the phone in his hand and was dialing the number he knew so well.

She lay awake in the moonlight, on satin sheets damp with tears. She sensed who it was. Their conversation was grimly subdued this time. They were both exhausted.

"Hello."

"It's Richard."

"I know."

"Get dressed if you're not. Get the money."

"All right."

"How big is the bundle?"

"Not large." It was surprising what a small bundle twenty thousand dollars made.

"Can you put it in a shopping bag?"

"Yes, easily," she said.

"Okay, put it in a shopping bag. No, a plastic bag. Do you have any plastic trash bags?"

"Yes, I think so."

"Put it in the plastic bag. Wrap the bag good and tape it shut. Make a neat bundle."

"Yes."

"Drive . . . let's see . . . drive east on the Suicide Bridge. Drive slow."

"Yes."

"When you get to the east end of the bridge, toss the bundle out the passenger side of the car. Carefully. So it falls in the street."

"Yes."

"There shouldn't be a single car on that bridge at this hour. Don't most of you people in that area use the freeway instead of the old Suicide Bridge?"

"Yes. There won't be anyone on the bridge."

"If there is, if you see another car's lights, don't drop the money. Go home and wait for my call. Understand?"

"Yes. When will you bring Vickie home?"

"I won't *bring* Vickie home. You'll get a call from me tomorrow at noon. I'll pick a safe place for Vickie near your home. Maybe a church or a public building. I'll tie her up there and I'll call you and tell you where."

"How is she?" Madeline stifled a sob, remembering the horror of that last call.

"She's all right," Philo said bleakly. "That wasn't my fault. I never hurt an animal before. That was *your* fault."

"Yes. I'll do as you say. Shall I go now?"

"Wait exactly thirty minutes. In thirty minutes you better be driving east on the Suicide Bridge. And there better not be any cops around."

"There won't be."

Then Philo lied and said, ''Because if there are . . . if there are, my friend is ordered to cut the schnauzer's head off.''

''Oh, my God,'' Madeline said.

Then Philo told the truth and said, ''Do you know *why* I decided on the Suicide Bridge?''

''No.''

''Because,'' he said, ''if there *are* any cops waiting for me, I'm going to *jump* off that bridge.''

''There won't be, I swear.''

''I'll be dead and so will your Vickie.''

''Yes, I understand.''

''This is *not* the way I planned it, lady. I'm not stupid enough to plan it like this. I'm desperate, do you believe me?''

''I believe you,'' she said.

''So we're going to just *do* it. In thirty minutes. And trust each other. I get the money, you get Vickie. Or I jump. Right now, lady, I want you to believe that it don't make much difference to me.''

There was a range light burning in the kitchen, otherwise the cluttered apartment was dark. They lay in Valnikov's daybed with only a coverlet over them. She had her face on his hairy keg of a chest listening to his heart. He had a heavy slow heartbeat now. He wouldn't stop caressing her. Her head, her shoulders, her neck, her arms. Natalie Zimmerman was purring like a cat. In fact, Misha and Grisha were getting nervous just listening to her.

''Andrushka?'' she said.

''Yes, Natasha?''

''It's been a good night.''

''The best of my entire life,'' he said.

''Andrushka?'' she said.

''Yes?''

''Nothing. I just love the sound of the name.''

They were silent for a moment and he said, ''Natasha?''

''Yes?''

''Nothing. I just love Natasha.''

Suddenly it troubled her. She said, ''The name? You mean you love the *name*.''

But he was silent. So she said, ''This is just a crazy night. We're just drunk and having a hell of a good time and . . . this is just a crazy night that's resulted from a crazy day and the craziest investigation of my life and . . . well, you mean you love the *name* Natasha.''

His silence troubled her more. It made her remember the case *she* was working on. Reporting his madness was now out of the question. In fact, it was past changing her burglary assignment. She was going to demand a transfer from Hollywood Detectives immediately. She didn't want to be there when somebody *else* discovered the truth about Valnikov. But mental aberration wasn't incurable. It wasn't irreversible, for God's sake! And though she had to get away from him, there was no denying how much she liked him. You *had* to like anybody born and raised in Los Angeles, twenty-two years a cop, who was as corny and old-fashioned as he was. And so crazy. And that, she reasoned, was probably what brought on the orgasmic bursts. Some perverse streak in her she wasn't aware of. Making love to a madman.

''So it's been the best night of your entire life,'' she said.

''Yes,'' he said, still stroking, caressing, as he listened to the Gypsy violin and stared at the darkened ceiling.

''Tell me more about your entire life,'' she said.

''How can I tell you about my entire life?'' he chuckled.

"Tell me about your old neighborhood."

"Boyle Heights? Well, it was Russian and Jewish and Mexican, and old. It's a very old neighborhood. Now of course it's almost all Mexican."

"Were you a happy kid?" she asked, propping herself up on an elbow, looking at his eyes, wet in the darkness.

"Sure I was happy," he said. "Of course it was tough after my father died, but Alex was much older and he supported us just fine."

"Did you go to church?"

"Of *course* we went to church," Valnikov smiled. "Our lives centered around the church. Our *batushka* was there. Our professor was there. We went to services and to Sunday School and to Russian school all there in the church. All of us had to learn to read and write the language from our professor."

"The Russian language?"

"The *only* language as far as our mothers were concerned. They were monarchists, you see. They truly believed they were going back one day. Every single one of them dreamed of at least having their bones sent back someday when the Bolsheviks were overthrown. Do you have any idea how impractical they were, those immigrants? How they dreamed? How mystical they were?"

"But you kids were happy?"

"Of course we were happy. It got a little tough *after* World War Two when it wasn't fashionable to be a Russian anymore. In fact, when I graduated from high school it was very unfashionable. We were in the Korean War, and kids used to call us Communists and Reds. The new immigrants from the second immigration had it worse. They actually *were* Soviets and got it from all sides. If you didn't go to church even the old Russian people called you a Bolshevik. The American kids didn't know the difference. We were *all* Bolsheviks, even though every single house of the first immigration had a picture of Nicholas Romanov displayed as reverently as an ikon. You could depend on it. Nicholas, then the Virgin, then *Khristos*."

"Did you think in Russian?"

"Only until the fifth grade or so. Then I started to think in English. My Russian got terrible. But my mother lived long enough to hear Khrushchev on television and she said her Andrushka would always speak Russian better than that ignorant Ukrainian. She used to say that when that peasant farted you could hear it from Moscow to Malibu." Valnikov stopped to laugh and wipe his eyes at the memory.

Natalie Zimmerman got up suddenly and walked naked to the kitchen and he heard her pouring something. He thought it was water but she returned with a tumbler full of vodka.

"Here," she said.

"I don't want any more."

"Please have some more. I'd like to talk."

"But I don't need vodka to talk."

"You might."

"But I'm trying to cut down on my drinking."

"Do it tomorrow. Tonight drink for me. I'll help you."

Valnikov pulled himself up on the daybed and let her prop a pillow behind him. Then Natalie slipped under the sheet again next to him.

"Drink," she said. And he drank.

"I want to hear more about your old partner."

"Charlie Lightfoot?"

"Yes. Why was he such a good homicide detective?"

Valnikov drank now without prompting. "Good? He was good. He could cut through it all."

"Yes?"

"Like the old black woman they found decomposing in her bed. The neighbors called to complain about the bad smell coming from her little cottage." Valnikov stopped to drink again. "And the officer that got there discovered the glass was smashed out of a side window. And then he discovered a pane broken out of the back door. And then he discovered a burnt match on the back porch. And another in the kitchen. And another in the hall. And another . . ." He drank more vodka. Ah, what does Natalie call it? Mellow. Yes. "And another and another. Burnt matches leading all over the house and finally into her bedroom, where the trail stopped. And there she was. Charlie used to keep the crime lab photo. You see, the patrol officers had called the crime lab and latent prints and photo lab and their watch commander. Her hair was white and electric. It fanned out electric around her skull. She was so decomposed her eyes were silver sockets and her lips were mostly gone showing all her teeth clear up past where there should have been tissue and wasn't. Charlie took one look and said, No murder. No murder! they yelled. No murder? The house has been broken into. A burglar broke in and murdered her in her bed! I'll bet they'll find a knife wound! the patrol officers yelled. Maybe she was strangled. Oh, everyone was raising hell over this one."

"And *was* it murder?" Natalie asked while Valnikov sipped at the glass.

"No murder," Valnikov said. "Charlie got all the bluesuits together and showed them how it happened. The burglar came to the house at night. He broke out the pane in the back door. The glass is on the floor inside. He starts lighting matches, going around the house, pleased as punch, wondering how he's going to cart all this stuff away. Maybe there's a bad smell coming from the bedroom. Maybe he's got a cold and doesn't smell it. Anyway, the trail of matches tells us that he goes in there last. He's maybe singing to himself. She's got a TV set, a nice transistor radio, some money in a kitchen jar. He's going to make enough to buy some dope. He lights the very last match at the foot of the bed. Then he sees the corpse I described to you. The bedroom window is busted from the inside out. He yells and goes through the glass head first. He's still running . . ." Valnikov was shaking the daybed with his laughter. "She was ninety years old and died a natural death, the autopsy showed. He's still running . . ."

Valnikov, incredibly enough, almost had the tumbler emptied. *He* wouldn't die a natural death, she thought. Not if he continued to drink like that. Which of course she wasn't helping.

"Why did Charlie Lightfoot shoot himself?" she said suddenly.

Valnikov drained the glass. "They said it was a hunting accident."

"Charlie Lightfoot was no hunter," she reminded him.

Valnikov said, "He never should have retired. He had his work, at least."

"Did he like his work?"

"He was old. He was very old for his age. He thought the world was draining into a sump hole. The Big Sewer is how he referred to everything. Gone down the Big Sewer, Charlie would say about a dead body. He was an atheist, Charlie was. And human beings were nothing more than . . . than something to rush down the Big Sewer."

"He was your friend. He liked you, didn't he?"

"He did," Valnikov nodded. "Except toward the end. He didn't care about anyone, especially not himself. I think I started drinking on duty then. I'd been a policeman twenty-one years, and even as a detective I never drank on duty. When all the other dicks had martinis and bourbon for lunch, I never drank on duty. We both started drinking a lot then. On duty, off duty." Valnikov sighed. "When Charlie pulled the pin and went to be a mountain man I knew it wouldn't work out. We were both in the habit of daytime drinking then. We'd had the worst time either of us ever had then."

"The worst time?"

"*Five* child murders in a month! Nobody ever had to handle that many so quickly. And we were only supposed to assist divisional detectives on their unsolved murders, on their whodunits."

"Did you get the killer?"

"Killers!" Valnikov cried suddenly. "That's just it. They were unrelated killings. Five in a row, all under ten years old. Three by their mothers, one by a father, one by a mother *with* a father. They weren't whodunits. The divisional detectives should have been able to see the marks of old torture. Five in a row we had. That was too *many*."

He dropped the water tumbler. It didn't spill. It was empty. "Here, let me get you some more," Natalie Zimmerman said. And she was up and hurrying to the kitchen again. Let old Natalie help you. Sure. Let Natalie do the torturing. God, Valnikov could make you hate yourself. He had that way about him. She poured the glass half full of Russian vodka. Have a shot of oblivion, Valnikov. Kiss your liver good-bye. Compliments of your good old partner, Natalie Zimmerman. Let your partner turn your head into *piroshki*.

When she handed him the vodka his hands were shaking. He drank with both hands. He was perspiring and his teeth were chattering. She pulled a blanket up over them and got under the covers.

"What made you get in the fight with the doctor?"

"Doctor?"

"They kicked you out of homicide. They transferred you to Hollywood Detectives, didn't they? Was it drinking? There was some problem. At an autopsy."

"Doctor," he mumbled. And there it was! The sparkly dots beginning to shape into . . . a doctor! There was an Asian doctor. No, a Caucasian doctor. *Two* doctors.

"What is it, Valnikov?" she demanded.

He drank vodka. It spilled down his chin onto the curly cinnamon hair on his chest. "Sometimes I get a picture," he said, staring off in the darkness at the picture forming. Siberia. Snow again. "The picture just gets . . . away."

"Does it come every day?" Natalie Zimmerman was sitting up in the daybed, white flesh in the darkness.

"Every day," Valnikov said. "If I could just get it once. It's like . . . déjà vu," he said.

"It's déjà vu. But the most . . . intense kind of déjà vu. I . . . I know that if I could just get it clear and see it..."

"Does it come at night? In a dream?"

There it went. The sparkling dots were swimming and losing form.

"Do you dream about a rabbit?" she pressed.

Now it was coming back. Now, by God! The rabbit was hopping through the snow.

"The rabbit!"

"Do you dream about a rabbit?"

"Yes!" he cried.

"Take it easy," Natalie said. "Drink a little vodka."

Valnikov drained the water tumbler. She didn't know anyone could drink that much and stay conscious.

"What's the last autopsy you remember? It must have been the one where you got in trouble."

"Last autopsy?" he said, watching the dots lose their shimmer. Watching the phantoms retreat in the darkness.

"How many autopsies have you attended?"

He looked at her and said, "Hundreds, I guess. I don't know."

"And the *last* one. Who was dead?"

"The last one," he muttered.

Was that the one with the pretty teenager who had died of a barbiturate overdose? Yes. No.

How about this one, Valnikov? This little chippy and her boyfriends, they have a pill-popping party and she . . . get this . . . she dies of an overdose. Look.

The man plunges the turkey skewer into her flawless young belly. The steel dart squeaks when it goes in.

Get this: The liver temperature says she was dead all the time the boys were gangfucking her last night. Imagine that? They banged a corpse! Know what one doper says when they told him that? He says, well, she always was a dead piece a ass. I didn't notice no difference. Isn't that a scream?

A scream.

The little boy used to scream, Sergeant.

Then why didn't you call the police, damn you!

But I didn't want to get involved.

Involved! How long did you hear these screams in the night? How long?

Three weeks, the neighbor answers fearfully.

Three weeks! Three weeks! If there's a hell, lady, you'll burn there! If there's a hell!

There is no hell, Charlie Lightfoot says. There's no heaven either. There's just the Big Sewer.

Tutu was there. Charlie Lightfoot was there. The rabbit was there.

"The rabbit!" Valnikov cried out. He had been drifting asleep and Natalie Zimmerman, who by now decided that it was very dangerous playing Dr. Jung, decided to let him.

He sat up straight in bed, dripping sweat and cried: "The rabbit!"

"What's the rabbit doing, Valnikov?"

"The hunter's gutting him," Valnikov cried. "With a big knife. A butcher knife with a white handle like bone!"

"Try to remember, what did the hunter do then?"

And it came. For the first time in the months that it had been tormenting him it started to come. The picture was forming on the ceiling, among the sparks and motes and shimmering dots. "He's gutting it like a fish! He's reaching inside the throat that he's slashed open. It's like holding a fish by the gills. He just reached clear inside and the little fish body jerks upward. He jerks the little body up with his strong hands."

"The fish? The fish?" Natalie demanded.

"The rabbit!" Valnikov cried. "The neck is limp and the little head is thrown back because he's got it under the throat. *In* the throat. He's got the jaws. His big hand is clear inside. The little head is thrown back on the . . ."

"On what?"

"On the wooden pedestal. The light . . ."

"What kind of light?"

"Sunlight!" he cried. "And snow. The doctor must have caught the rabbit in the snow!"

"And then what?"

"It changes," Valnikov said. "The picture changes but I still see it. I . . . I had to keep looking at the little arms and hands to remember it's still a rabbit. Because the face was all swollen and deformed from the beatings . . ."

"Yes? Yes?"

'He starts skinning it then. He tears the face right back over the skull. The face is pulled inside out, the little swollen deformed face. The hair is fine because it's so young. The hair goes inside out too!" Valnikov sobbed.

"Yes," Natalie said. "What then?"

"I have to keep looking at the arms and hands to . . . to remember it's a rabbit! I think it's a *fish* he treats it so brutally."

"The hunter?"

"Yes. He says the anus is still open. After death!" Valnikov was crying now.

"Yes. Go on."

"I know what that means. I've investigated hundreds, *hundreds*. I just had four others. This is too *many!*"

"What does it mean? The anus being open?"

"Sodomy after death," Valnikov cried. "I thought it was *only* the mother! I *believed* the father because he seemed so pathetic. He said he'd been away. He cried so much I believed him. But there was semen in the anus. The neighbors didn't want to get involved. He screamed in the night. Five in a row. That's too *many!*"

"Was Charlie Lightfoot there?"

"Huh?"

"In the dream? Is Charlie Lightfoot there when the . . . rabbit is skinned?"

"No, Charlie was dead. Charlie had been dead for a month."

"Did you attack the hunter in the dream?"

"I wanted to," Valnikov said. "I wanted to. I wanted to kill him with his own knife with the bone handle. There were granules under the tongue. He said maybe it's some toxic substance. He had a swab right there. He could swab out the granules for the lab. But he just . . . just took the bone handled knife and sliced off the little tongue! I wanted to kill him then," Valnikov said. Then he started crying again.

"What happened?" Natalie said. She was crying too.

"He said, 'Are you crazy? What's wrong with you?' I said, 'You could use the swab! You don't have to treat it so brutally. You don't have to. Hasn't it had enough? Isn't the torture, isn't a gaping anus enough! Look at him! You've turned his face inside out like a surgical glove! Isn't that enough! His face is like a doctor's glove hanging inside out!' "

The little rabbit took with him to eternity a face like a rubber glove.

"He said, 'I *thought* you looked drunk! I smell the booze on your breath!' I said, 'I'd like to punch your face in.' He said, 'You're drunk, I'm going to report you to your commander.' And I . . . I looked around. I'd been there hundreds of times. Hundreds. I saw an orderly helping an Asian pathologist on another one. They weren't paying any attention. They were cutting through yellow fat with a bone-handled knife. They were cutting a skull off with a power saw. The orderly was pulling out the intestines in a big heap and piling them on the knees. There was an enormous brain tied with a blue string. You'd never believe it could fit inside a skull it was so big. The orderly was putting a piece of meat in a jar. He was eating a jelly roll."

"Did you hit the doctor?"

"No." Valnikov sighed again and again. "I just realized at last that . . . that Charlie Lightfoot was right. I stopped going to church. It's nothing more than a Big Sewer and it's nothing more than gutted fish in the end. Or a . . ."

"A rabbit." Natalie said.

"Yes.Or a . . ."

"A schnauzer," Natalie said.

"I just realized that there's nothing more than the Big Sewer. Anything else is . . ."

"Is what you make of it," Natalie said. "What *we* make of it." She held him in her arms. He was wet and cold and shivering.

"I don't want to be like Charlie Lightfoot," Valnikov said, burying his face in her naked breasts.

Natalie rocked him and said, "You're *not* like Charlie Lightfoot. You're not *anything* like Charlie Lightfoot."

"I'm afraid," he said.

"Hush," she whispered, kissing his head. "You're not anything at all like Charlie Lightfoot. Hush, Andrushka," she whispered. "Go to sleep and dream of . . . of those Russian nightingales singing in the raspberry bushes."

She rocked him and was covered by his sweat. She threw off the clammy sheet and drew up the warm blankets. He was so devastated by the vodka and the tears that he fell unconscious almost at once, his face pressed against her. Natalie Zimmerman still rocked him and caressed his burning body until she fell asleep.

13

Suicide Bridge

Valnikov didn't dream of nightingales singing in the raspberry bushes. And he didn't dream about a rabbit. He dreamed he was walzing with Natalie Zimmerman. In the squad room of Hollywood Detectives. Hipless Hooker yelled about a tummyache and Clarence Cromwell said they were crazy but he didn't care. They danced to the "Starinye Vais."

And while Valnikov dreamed his fantasy, Philo Skinner *lived* his. He was sitting in his El Dorado, west of Suicide Bridge, in the darkness. He was terrified that a cop would come by, but in a Cadillac El Dorado he hoped he could reassure a cop. Walting for a girlfriend, Officer. Please don't pry. She's a married lady and you know how it is. Only in the middle of the night, Officer. Gotta take it when we can. When the old boy's asleep. Hah-hah!

He saw her Fleetwood right on schedule. His heart was banging in his ears. She drove past his El Dorado without looking. She started across Suicide Bridge. He saw headlights in the distance, but the headlights turned toward the freeway. Madeline began crossing the bridge, toward the ghostly looming old hotel. Her brake lights went on when she reached the east end of the bridge. Philo started his engine but kept his lights out. Madeline's brake lights went out and her Fleetwood continued to Orange Grove Avenue, which two weeks ago was jammed with Rose Parade flower floats. Then she was gone.

Philo Skinner drove drunkenly, dangerously, recklessly, east over the bridge. He panicked when he reached the end of the bridge. It wasn't there. No, it *was* there! It was in the gutter! He slammed on the brakes and leaped out of the Cadillac. He twisted his ankle and fell, tearing the knee out of the polyester trousers. He picked the bundle up. It was small. Could twenty thousand dollars be contained in such a small package? He ran back to the car. He jammed it in low gear and sped toward Orange Grove Avenue.

Philo broke into a coughing spasm on the freeway. His eyes filled and clouded and he was gagging on an enormous wad of phlegm. He desperately groped for the electric window buttons until he had every window in the car open. He didn't realize for a moment he was hyperventilating. When he realized it he hacked the phlegm from his ragged lungs and spit out the window. It blew back with a smack on the side of his El Dorado. He deliberately exhaled until he was able to breathe again. He was wheezing and creaking, but he was able to breathe at last. He tore open the plastic as he drove. He switched on the map light. He looked at the thrilling pictures of Ulysses S. Grant and Benjamin Franklin. Hundreds of pictures. He spent the night in the kennel office caressing them, fondling them, caressing them again and again. Philo Skinner made noises that were half laugh, half cry. He was sick and exhausted but now he wanted to live. He hid the money in the supply closet and slept curled up on the grooming table. He dreamed of a white sand beach and a puppy frolicking in the surf. The puppy, of course, looked like Tutu.

14

The Assassin

Natalie was awakened at dawn by Misha expressing his opinion of it all: ''*Gavno*'' the bird cried. ''*Gavno. Gavno.*''

Then she heard the shower turning off, and Valnikov, wearing an old flannel bathrobe, tried to tiptoe quietly to the kitchen. She sat up in bed.

''Oh, sorry. Did I wake you?'' He was drying his hair. ''I wanted to get your breakfast before you had to get up.''

''What time is it?'' she asked, pulling back a taped window shade to peer out at the street lights.''

''Five thirty.''

''Five thirty!''

''We'll have to get an early start. I've already called Clarence Cromwell at home. He'll meet us in the office at seven so we can get started. He's going to arrange for the helicopter and the surveillance cars. I hope we don't have to use our own guys, but if we do, I think Fuzzy Spinks might be a good man on point. What do you think?''

Think? Think? Who could think anything about the past days. My God, she'd lost her ability to think or she wouldn't be lying here! With a pathetic tormented crazy man and a bird that yelled shit in a foreign language and a goddamn Russian rat that kept trying to keep the bird off his head. What a night! What a week! *She'd* be the one they retired. Give old Natalie Zimmerman a medical pension and a party and six months in Camarillo State Hospital with a live-in psychiatrist.

''How do you like your eggs?'' Valnikov smiled. ''I'm a pretty good cook.''

''Please, Valnikov,'' she said, sitting up and wrapping the sheet around her. ''Please don't.''

''Don't what, Natasha?''

''Don't cook for me. Don't do anything for me. And *don't* call me Natasha.''

''Sorry,'' he said.

''And don't say you're sorry. I'm sorry for *you*.''

''For me?''

''Never mind. Let me shower and get dressed. We'll have some coffee.''

''You wouldn't like tea?'' he said ''In a glass?''

''I'll have coffee. In a cup.''

''Coffee, sure.'' Valnikov said, losing his buoyancy, shuffling into the kitchen to look for the coffeepot. He hoped he had some coffee. He hoped he could come to understand Natalie Zimmerman.

Twenty minutes later they were both dressed and sitting at the tiny kltchen table. He drank tea from a glass. She drank coffee from a cup. East and West.

His hair was carefully parted and combed, but still a cinnamon cowlick popped up at the crown. She watched him sip his tea. Noiselessly, just as his mother had taught him.

''Do you have a hangover?'' she asked, breaking the silence.

''A little.'' His sad blue eyes were watery and bloodshot. His necktie was off center. Another cowlick popped up as he sipped the tea. He looked ridiculous.

"Valnikov."

"Yes, Natash. . . Natalie?"

"Do you ever think of retiring? After all, you have twenty-two years service. You could retire now with almost half your pay. You're still young. You could find an . . . easier job to make up the difference. Do you ever think about retiring?"

"I think about it sometimes," he said. "I think about it, but I'm forty-four years old and I don't know anything but police work."

"I'll bet your brother'd take you in business with him. He's crazy about you, your brother."

"I don't want to work for Alex," Valnikov smiled. "He's too much like a father. Besides I'd just get in his way. I don't know his business. But I did think about something."

"Yes?"

"Well, I know something about music. Not so much about pop or rock, but do you know there aren't many good record stores with imported records? Not in a good location. I think that if someone opened a foreign music store in a good location, like here in Hollywood . . ."

"Holly-weird. Ugh!"

"Yes, it's not the greatest place to live anymore, but to do business with Russians, and Greeks, Armenians, Persians, Arabs, and so forth, well, they *like* Hollywood. It still represents the magic of America. The Good Life."

"Do you have any money for a business?"

"I have a few thousand saved," he said, pouring some more coffee for Natalie. He was pleased that she didn't seem angry anymore. Maybe it's when she just wakes up, he thought. "And I could go to my brother for a loan. And I guess I could borrow some from a bank. I could start on a shoestring. After all, I'd have my police pension to live on."

"Are you going to do it?"

"Well, I never had any reason to make a move before now."

"Before now."

"Yes," he said, blinking his sad eyes, wiping them with a napkin. "Sorry. Too much vodka always does this to me."

"I noticed," she said. Then, "Tell me, Valnikov, did you ever feel like you always pick the black marble?"

"The black marble?"

"Yeah, remember Itchy Mitch?" she said, scratching under her bra strap. "The black marble."

"No, I don't think I ever felt like that," he said.

"You don't expect much, do you?"

"I don't know, Natash . . . Natalie," he said.

"Why did your wife leave you?"

"Oh, she said I bored her stiff. She said I was . . . well, you said it too. Out of date."

"I didn't mean it like that, Valnikov."

"It's all right. I am."

"Not like that. Not like she meant it."

"Well, she liked to go out a lot. And I thought we should stay home with our son more. And besides, I couldn't afford to take her to the Polo Lounge for lunch and Chasen's for dinner and . . ."

"You don't see the kid?"

"No," he sighed, standing up, getting more hot water for his tea. "I don't know, maybe I bored him too. He got in lots of trouble. Three arrests for smoking pot before he was fourteen. And twice they let him go because his dad was a cop. He finally said he hated cops. *All* cops. Well, I don't know."

"How old is he now?"

"He's twenty. Just twenty."

"He's young," Natalie said. "Kids change when they grow up."

"Yes," he sighed. "They change."

"Tell me," she said, lighting a cigarette. "When your wife and boy left, when Charlie died, when you were working those homicide cases, when the drinking was very bad and you were having those bad dreams, tell me, did you ever say to yourself, why do I *always* pick the black marble? Haven't you *ever* said that?"

"I don't think so," he said.

"Why?"

"Why?"

"Yes, I wanna know why."

"I don't know," he shrugged. "My mother always said . . . you see, my mother and father, the people from the first immigration, they didn't come to America *for* the Good Life. America was the *end* of the Good Life for them. Until the day she died she never stopped talking about her home in Petrograd. That's why I guess I seem so . . . old-fashioned, maybe. Even though I was born and raised in Los Angeles, I heard so much about the suffering of Mother Russia and the sorrow of life, and . . . well, I never expected much, I guess. I don't know." Valnikov sipped his tea and dabbed at imagined moisture on his lip and said, "Maybe my father . . . I didn't know him well, of course, but maybe before he died, maybe when he was here in Los Angeles during the Depression trying for jobs he couldn't get, never speaking this foreign tongue, maybe my father wondered about the black marble. I'll bet he did. I'll bet that when his entire world had been destroyed he said to himself: Mikhail Ivanovich, why do you always have to pick the black marble?"

"Valnikov."

"Yes, Natalie."

"I'm asking for a transfer."

"From the burglary detail?"

"From Hollywood Detectives."

"Oh? Is it because . . ."

"Look, Valnikov, I don't know what happened last night. I don't understand anything anymore, so help me. I mean, I'm running around looking for a one-eared dog like it's the Patty Hearst kidnapping. I mean I'm calling myself by another name, even."

"Natasha," he smiled.

"Don't call me that. This isn't a goddamn Chekhov play."

"Sorry."

"Valnikov, doesn't it seem that things have become a bit too much for you? The dreams?"

"I didn't dream about the rabbit last night." He wanted to tell her what he dreamed about.

"Yes, but it seems you've been undergoing a kind of . . . mental breakdown. You *must* know you haven't been yourself for quite a while now. For several months from everything I can understand. I mean the incident in the morgue? When you threatened the doctor? I mean, you have some *problems* to cope with."

"I can cope with them . . . now."

"Oh, please don't say that to me, Valnikov. Last night was last night! I don't understand last night. If our . . . *talking* last night was helpful, I'm very glad. So help me, I am. Look, do you know what I've planned for next month? Jack Packerton and I are flying to Honolulu. Then we're going to Kauai where we're renting a bungalow in Hanalei Bay. It's supposed to be a paradise."

"A paradise," Valnikov said.

"Jack's going to be a deputy chief on this department."

"Yes, you said that before."

"Yeah, well what I'm saying is, I've got a routine. My life's in *order*. Yours is a mess. Do you understand?"

"I guess so," he said.

"Hell, Jack's been wanting to get married for the past six months. I wanna just live with him but he has this phobia. Deputy Chief Digby Bates gets tight-jawed when unmarried officers live together. Did you read the moral rearmament bulletin from that Jesus Freak?"

"No," Valnikov said.

"Anyway, that's where *my* head is. I don't want to be always picking the black marble!"

"Well," Valnikov sighed, dabbing at this lips, "I guess we'd better get going. Clarence Cromwell's going to wonder where we are."

"Yeah, let's get it on," Natalie Zimmerman mumbled miserably.

Valnikov fed and watered Misha and Grisha before they left. Then he went into the bedroom and strapped on his gun belt and got his suitcoat with the stapled pockets. Natalie could hear his heavy sighs from the other room. She watched the little creatures in the big cage.

"Whadda you think of it?" she said to the parakeet knowing what his answer would be.

He did a forward fall, looked at her while hanging upside down, and said, "*Gavno*."

Clarence Cromwell was on his second cup of coffee when they arrived.

"Glad you could finally make it," he growled, "after you git me outta bed at some ungodly hour!" Then he looked at Natalie and noticed she wore the same clothes as the day before. She never did that. And her Friz was a little unfrizzed. And she came in *with* Valnikov. Clarence hadn't been a detective twenty years without being observant.

Natalie saw him grinning at them. The evil old spook!

"Are we getting the chopper?" Valnikov asked, gathering his paper work from the report box while Natalie headed for the coffee.

"Got it," Clarence said. "Okay on the surveillance teams too. Gonna have quite a show. Hope the dognapper shows up."

"The extortionist," Valnikov said.

"Yeah. Hope he shows up."

Then the phone rang and Cromwell grabbed it. "Yeah," he said. Then to Valnikov, "For you."

"Valnikov," he said, picking up his extension and punching the first line.

"Sergeant, this is Madeline Whitfield," she said, very tentatively.

"Mrs. Whitfield!" Valnikov said. "What happened? Did he call?"

"He called. Last night. At about two a.m. I . . . Sergeant, I'm sorry. I took him the money. He told me to drop it off on the bridge by my home. I did it. I assume he picked it up. I went back at daybreak and it was gone. I haven't slept a minute. I guess he got it. I . . ."

"Do you have Vickie?" Valnikov said and got Natalie's attention at once. He held his hand over the phone and said, "She dropped the money on him during the night."

"No," she said, her voice cracking. "He said he'll call me today. He promised he'll release her today. I just have to wait. I'm sorry, Sergeant. Well . . . I wanted . . . I know I probably did the wrong thing. I *wanted* to do it your way. Well . . . she's all there is in my life. Well . . ."

"Don't cry, Mrs. Whitfield," Valnikov said softly. "I do understand. I don't blame you for anything. I do understand. Don't cry. Now now, it's going to be all right, I promise you. There'll be someone here all day who can get in touch with me. You call the moment you hear from him. Yes. Don't cry. I promise you it'll be all right."

When he hung up, Clarence took a drink of coffee and said, "I'll cancel the chopper and the surveillance teams."

"She doesn't have Vickie yet," Valnikov said. "Why didn't I think of that? Why didn't I anticipate that he might call during the night?"

"Because this guy doesn't do anything orderly," Natalie said. "He's erratic and messy and crazy and you can't figure him because of it. Don't worry about it. It's not your fault. You've done all you can do."

Valnikov was on his feet. "It's almost eight o'clock," he said. "I'm still going to contact Mrs. Gharoujian's dog handler. That man Skinner. I'm going to have a talk with him about all the guys who lived with Mrs. Gharoujian when he was showing Tutu. He's the only hope there is now. He's got to come up with a few names for us."

"Valnikov, it's over, forget it!" Natalie said. "She chose to pay the money. He'll probably release the dog like he said. Or maybe the dog's dead. In either case, you've done all . . ."

"I'm going to Skinner Kennels," he said, looking through the phone book.

"Well, sit down awhile at least," Clarence Cromwell said. "It ain't even opened yet, if it keeps regular business hours. Sit down and drink your tea and relax a little bit. This ain't the Patty Hearst kidnapping."

Which caused Natalie Zimmerman to say, "*That* is maybe the first time I ever agreed with *anything* you ever said, Clarence."

As the other detectives straggled in for the day, and as Natalie Zimmerman did their routine paper work and filing of crime reports, Valnikov drank tea and made secret notes and drew pictures of a schnauzer and a bird.

Natalie glanced over at the pad and recognized the dog. "What's that, your parakeet?" she asked.

He almost told her it was a Russian nightingale in a raspberry bush, but he looked up with sorrowful runny eyes and said, "Yeah, my parakeet."

Captain Hooker arrived rather early. He had a paper bag in his arms. It contained three bottles of Maalox. He figured that would keep his stomach quiet for a couple of days at least. But he was wrong.

First of all, Bullets Bambarella usually had a Twinkie with his morning coffee but couldn't afford one now, so he was grumpy. He had exactly two dollars and fifty cents to last until payday thanks to the bets he'd lost to the smirking Mexican, Montezuma Montez. Bullets was looking for trouble, right off the bat.

"How about lendin me ten bucks till payday, Clarence?" he whispered to the grizzled black detective.

"What for? You got some other bet you wanna lose to Montezuma?" Clarence snorted.

"Listen, Clarence, you ever hear of a good Mexican heavyweight? There *ain't* any. I think we could go up to the academy, get some boxing gloves and . . ."

"I don't want any of my men boxing," said Woodenlips Mockett, overhearing it. "Somebody'll get hurt."

"I could lick him, Clarence," Bullets whined. "You could make some money bettin on me!"

When Bullets had gone back to the residential burglary table Clarence said, "Humph! Young coppers around here, they jist wear me down is what they do. I see them smart-walkin all over the Chinatown barrooms these days. Their gud-damn guns hangin out so all the girls know they're cops. Shee-it. They probably drink High-waiian punch on the rocks. They jist wear me down."

Then Frick said to Frack, "Who smells so good, you or Irma?" And he bit the giggling policewoman on the shoulder.

''Me,'' said Frack, ''and I don't know how to control it, neither.''

Then Bullets interrupted them with an important announcement: ''Italian food is the best in the world. Italians are gourmets. Mexicans eat horsemeat tacos.''

''Bullets, is your mind gone, along with your paycheck?'' said Clarence.

''I just heard that Montezuma is making enchiladas for the detective party next week,'' said Bullets.

''So what's it to you?'' said Montezuma Montez, and all the telephone calls stopped as the squad room got ready for a fight.

''I won't have my men boxing,'' Woodenlips Mockett whined to Clarence Cromwell.

''Well, I don't wanna go to no party where I gotta eat horsemeat enchiladas,'' said Bullets glaring at Montezuma Montez.

Frick and Frack were now grinning back and forth from Bullets to Montezuma. There were secret bets coming out under the tables. ''They're gonna fight, Clarence! You stop them!'' Woodenlips Mockett cried.

Then Bullets said, ''Italians are gourmets. Chefs. You probably never heard of eggplant parmesan.''

''I heard of it,'' Montezuma said.

''Put my eggplant and your enchilada side by side, your enchilada's gonna taste like horseshit.''

''I'm somewhat of a gourmet if I do say so,'' said Dudley Knebel. ''I'd like to try them both.''

''So would I,'' said Irma Thebes.

''Could you be a fair judge, Dudley?'' Bullets challenged.

''Perfectly,'' said Dudley Knebel.

''Me too,'' said Irma.

''I think I could go for it too,'' said Nate Farmer. ''But I think we should be able to write our opinions secret, so no hard feelins later.''

''I'll read the findings,'' said Max Haffenkamp, ''and just say which dish the judges picked.''

''Okay,'' said Bullets. ''Clarence, will you loan me twenty bucks?''

''I'll take five a that,'' said Frick.

''I'll take five,'' said Frack.

''Who wants *thirty* bucks?'' said Bullets. ''Payable on payday?''

''Covered!'' said Montezuma.

''Well, that does it!'' said Clarence Cromwell with utter, lip-curling contempt. ''You don't have to worry about a fistfight no more, Lieutenant. It's down to a fuckin bake-off!''

Captain Hooker came out of the office, heading for the hot plate. He was going to pour some water into his powdered chocolate.

''Everything going smoothly, Clarence?'' he said, mixing the brew.

''Fine, Skipper,'' said Clarence.

Dudley Knebel said, ''Oh, Captain. You know that market they robbed three times this month? The one on the Boulevard? Well, the commander called and suggests we stake it out this Thursday. Maybe the computers told him.''

''Now if the computer could just *do* the stakeout . . .'' Clarence grumbled.

''Clarence will coordinate it for you,'' Hipless Hooker said. He didn't have time for any of this. He had to go buy a new pair of deck shoes, the kind real yachtsmen wear.

''Yeah, but Captain,'' Dudley Knebel persisted, ''the commander says we should put an undercover cop behind the counter. You know, dressed like one a the clerks? Because they pistol-whipped the last three clerks and he figures a cop should be there.''

''Great,'' Clarence Cromwell snorted. ''Let a cop get pistol-whipped instead of a clerk.''

''Yes, yes,'' Hipless Hooker said impatiently. ''Well, just pick someone to masquerade as the clerk. Police work entails some risks once in a while ''

"Yes, sir," said Knebel. "But the crooks been in there three times. They *know* all the clerks. The commander said to put in a guy who actually resembles the oldest clerk and let the poor clerk work another part of the store."

"Well for heaven's sake, can't you find an officer who resembles the old clerk?"

"Yes, sir," said Dudley Knebel. "The commander says that you look just like him."

Captain Hooker had to go home that morning with a dreadful tummyache. Which in no way affected Valnikov's police career this time. Valnikov's destiny was in other hands.

At 9:15 a.m. Valnikov finished drawing his eighth nightingale in a raspberry bush. By now Natalie guessed that he was not drawing parakeets.

Valnikov jumped up and said, "Clarence, I'm going to that kennel and talk to Mr. Skinner. I just can't sit around. If Mrs. Whitfield calls, get me on the radio or call me at the kennel. I wrote the number down on my note pad." Then without looking at her he said softly, "Natalie, maybe you wouldn't mind staying and doing our paper work this morning? I won't be . . . needing you."

"I wouldn't mind," she said, not looking at him either. And all the non-looks and averted eyes were not lost on Clarence Cromwell, who just shook his head and said, "Gud-damn! Don't *nothin* ever work out right for *nobody* in this guddamn world!"

"What?" Woodenlips Mockett said.

"Nothin," Clarence Cromwell grumbled. "Nothin, guddamnit!"

Philo Skinner had not been able to sleep for a day and a half. Nor had he shaved. He was wearing a pair of brushed denims and a striped turtleneck sweater. He hung his new imitation gold chain outside the sweater. He had bought the clothes this morning the moment the stores opened. He had a battered suitcase, which usually stored dog powders and lotions, packed with new clothing. He wasn't even going home. He also packed a hair dryer which had dried a thousand dogs but never a human head. He couldn't find another thing he cared to take. He was sure he could outfit himself in a fancy Puerto Vallarta hotel cheaper than here. That peso devaluation was going to make his twenty thousand look pretty good. Pretty damn good! He glanced in the mirror and his spirits fell for a moment. He looked terrible: eyes baggy and sunken, cheeks hollow and gray and bristling. Hands gray and scaly. The tension had taken a great toll on the Terrier King.

He had thought about driving the El Dorado across the border and trying to sell it in Tijuana to some Mexican crook. He quickly dismissed that idea, having heard about gringos being robbed and murdered down there these days. Just his luck to have them discover he was carrying twenty K and cut his throat.

He couldn't stop trembling, more from exhaustion than excitement. Mavis said yesterday she would be in this afternoon. Well, let her come. He wanted to leave her a note but couldn't think of anything sarcastic enough. He parked the El Dorado in the rear of the kennel, out of sight. He didn't want any new customers today.

Only one thing left: the schnauzer. Philo had to take the bitch and drop her someplace and phone the Whitfield broad. Then he was going to the airport. They'd find the car in a few days. They'd probably find out he took a Puerto Vallarta flight. So what? A guy with lots of debts bugs out. Happens all the time. There was absolutely no connection with the dog snatching so there'd never be a cop looking for him. And Mavis could find some other sap to work the kennel, to slave like a goddamn sled dog. Of course Arnold might find out Philo had booked a flight to Puerto Vallarta. So what? That was a long way from here. Arnold was a two-bit bookmaker. The kike and the nigger with the knife wouldn't dare try anything on the Mexican Gold Coast. They don't put up with crooks down there.

Let Arnold try. Philo'd have the *Federales* on him. Dig a grave, smoke a cigarette, and adios, Arnold, you fucking vampire.

Then he heard a car door slam. The door of the detective car slammed shut on the dream of Philo Skinner. He looked out and didn't see a detective. He saw a burly man with wild cinnamon hair and a slouchy walk, coming right for the front door.

He knew who it was at once, this brawny stranger! He was the nigger and the kike! It was Arnold's gunsel. Arnold crossed him up, that slimy bloodsucker. He said a man would come that *afternoon,* not morning! Philo peeked through the shade and the man got closer.

This gorilla wouldn't listen to reason! They *never* do in the movies. He'd just start tearing the place apart looking for money. He'd find the flight bag with the twenty K. *After* he cut Philo's throat! Then Philo tried to calm himself. No, it's just a customer, that's all it is. Just someone who wants Philo to take care of his fucking Irish setter for a couple weeks. That's all it is. The man was at the door now. He was knocking. Philo peeked through the blind and looked for a telltale bulge under his arm. The suit hugged his husky torso pretty well. There was no bulge. Philo was imagining things. Jesus! He had to keep his mind together. He'd be on that plane in a few hours. Then the man knocked again. Still Philo peeked. Go away, asshole. Take your fucking Irish setter and . . . Then the man pulled open his jacket to get a notebook. Philo saw it. It was on his belt. A gun! It *is* one of Arnold's gunsels! He *won't* cut Philo's throat! He'll shoot his balls off!

Philo Skinner knocked the metal grooming table clear across the room when he ran for the office. The table clashed to the tile floor and knocked bottles smashing against the wall. Philo grabbed the suitcase and the flight bag with the money. He slipped on the shampoo, which was all over the floor, and fell hard, cutting his hands before he got to the kennel door.

Valnikov heard the commotion and tried the door. It was locked. He heard the dogs barking and howling and heard someone running in the kennel. He thought that he had stumbled into a burglary in progress! Someone was ransacking Skinner Kennels! Then he heard another crashing sound as Philo Skinner slammed into the steel-reinforced back door, double keyed on *both* sides. Security, Philo. There's lots of thieves in this world. And you just caught one, Mavis. Thanks for *everything!* You cunt!

"YOU CUNT!" Philo screamed, and twenty-five animals went mad. A Welsh terrier began barking. A Great Dane started bellowing. A malamute howled like a wolf. Then other voices joined the chorus. Mavis couldn't have heard Philo's hysterical obscenity if she were in the grooming room.

Neither could Valnikov. All he heard was a burglar trapped inside, trying to get out. Perhaps more than one burglar. He drew his revolver and kicked the door beside the lock. The jamb splintered but it didn't open. He backed up, took a step and kicked again and the door fell off the hinges and crashed on the overturned grooming table. The clashing crashing splintering sound made Philo and the dogs howl all the louder.

Philo dropped his suitcase but clung to the flight bag. He ran desperately back, back toward the grooming room. There was only one potential weapon in the kennel, and it was 100 feet back down the narrow aisle between the pens full of bellowing beasts.

Philo Skinner was holding his chest, fighting back a coughing spasm. He felt a ball of phlegm as big as a fist ripping free from his lungs and rising in his throat. Yet he couldn't make a sound. Arnold's enforcer was creeping through the grooming room. Philo could hear his quiet steps on the broken glass. Philo held his breath as much as possible. The wheezing sounded deafening to him even in the din from the frightened animals. Philo removed a small fire extinguisher from the wall and backed into the shadows, into an alcove near the side door leading to the fenced exterior aisle on the periphery of the dog runs. Philo almost kicked over a mop and pail of water. The chunk of black phlegm was rising, rising, choking him. Please! Just a few seconds more!

Then Valnikov cautiously opened the door to the kennel. The dogs in the near cages saw this stranger with a gun. A Doberman started going berserk slashing at the chain link with his teeth. Philo Skinner backed against a concrete wall, saw the gun of Arnold's enforcer, and thought he would strangle before the bullets tore through his tortured lungs.

Valnikov saw a T-shaped aisle at the far end of the kennel where Philo had dropped his suitcase. Valnikov started to move toward the suitcase when Philo's survival instincts took over. Valnikov saw a blur from the corner of his right eye. He turned but not fast enough. The fire extinguisher caught him on his broad forehead, over his right eye. Philo had swung with all his strength. It was enough. Valnikov fell back heavily against the first dog pen and went down on the concrete floor. He dropped his gun, but instinctively fell on top of it.

Philo Skinner was stopped by the chunk of poison in his throat. He started to gag and cough and gag some more. He leaned against the wall and gagged it out. A hunk of phlegm like a black golf ball splattered on the concrete floor. Valnikov was groaning and flopping on the floor like a beached baby whale.

Both men were acutely aware of their danger and both tried to recover first. It was Philo who at last caught some life-saving oxygen in those creaking lungs. He took as many sweet breaths as he dared and leaped forward. He picked up the fire extinguisher. He raised it over his head and Valnikov was just able to raise his left arm in time. It cracked down on his forearm and Valnikov cried out.

The dogs were by now frothing and screaming and running in circles, sensing a death struggle in their midst. The Doberman was past madness. His foam white lips and gums were bleeding from gnawing on the chain-link dog pen. Without knowing why, the Doberman lusted to be part of the kill. He was not an attack dog, but smelling blood and seeing the frenzied thrashing of two men at his feet, he wanted to kill without reason.

Philo wheezed and gulped and raised the fire extinguisher again. Valnikov held up the wounded arm but the fire extinguisher crashed into the arm *and* his head, near the temple. The cowlicks immediately became matted with blood as the vessels burst. Blood was running down Valnikov's face and neck. He bellowed like the Great Dane and rolled over on his stomach, on top of the gun. He groped under his stomach for the gun when Philo attacked again. Philo missed Valnikov's head this time but the fire extinguisher smashed into Valnikov's right shoulder and his fingers became paralyzed for a moment. He couldn't pick up the gun.

Philo had now fallen on top of Arnold's assassin. He couldn't move the heavy man, but he punched at the broad head weakly with his bony fists. He thrashed and whimpered and pulled on the assassin's bloody hair but there was no moving a man who weighed more than a St. Bernard. Philo then reached under Valnikov, under his belly. Valnikov's half-paralyzed fingers and Philo's tobacco-stained fingers fought over the revolver.

Philo was whining and whimpering louder than any dog in the kennel. Then he started growling like the Doberman. He buried his stained teeth in Valnikov's shoulder, but the bulky flesh was too hard. Philo bit Valnikov on the bloody neck. Still he couldn't get the gun.

Then Philo fell on his stomach and put both hands beneath the detective and with all his strength moved the body. Philo reached under and jerked backward and rolled over against the door to the grooming room. The gun was in his hand.

Valnikov and Philo lay prone for a moment staring at each other across four feet of bloody concrete floor. The dogs were running in drooling circles. A Sealyham terrier was lying on her back kicking her feet. She was crazier than the Doberman by now.

Valnikov was shaking his head like a wounded bull, moaning in pain as the initial shock decreased. He thought he was going to die. He watched the burglar's eyes.

Philo knew he had hurt the assassin. Still, he was infinitely stronger than Philo even in this condition. Philo Skinner had never considered that he might have to kill a man. He kept the gun pointed at the assassin's bloody face. He wasn't absolutely certain whether you had to cock this revolver but he guessed you didn't. He was trying to get up the strength and courage to do what he had to do. But he had never in his life hurt an animal. How could he kill a man?

"You . . . you . . . turn around." Philo stopped to cough and spit on the floor but he never took his eyes off Arnold's assassin. "Crawl on your stomach. Crawl . . . back. Back! Crawl back or I'll kill you."

Valnikov hesitated for a second. Then, on his stomach, his suitcoat torn in three places, he began wriggling back along the floor.

"Back!" Philo commanded. "Crawl back! Further! Further!"

Valnikov inched back, wiping blood from his face, never taking his eyes off the burglar.

When Valnikov was lying beside an empty animal pen on the west side of the kennel, Philo said, "Stop." Only then did Philo Skinner struggle to his feet and walk carefully along the pens to his right, just avoiding the Doberman who was desperately trying to get his nose through the mesh and grab Philo's skinny thigh.

Philo stood over Valnikov and said, "Put your face down on the concrete." Valnikov did, and waited for the bullet to crack through the back of his skull. He wanted to roll quickly to the right, to die fighting for his life, but the pain had weakened him. Pain, more than anything, made him obey when he was sure it was the end. He thought of something to take with him to eternity. He thought of nightingales singing in a raspberry bush.

But Philo said, "Don't move or I'll kill you." And he heard Philo fumbling with a set of keys. Then Philo turned the lock on the door of the empty dog pen. He pulled the door open. "Now crawl in there on your stomach," Philo wheezed. "Stay on your stomach. Don't try to get up or you're dead."

Still Valnikov had not spoken a word. He began crawling. He pushed a large feeding dish out of his way. He crawled past a mound of feces. A very *large* mound. He heard a low rumbling just beyond the doggie door leading to the gravel dog run outside.

Philo, standing in the doorway of the pen, didn't hear the rumble that Valnikov could hear at floor level. Philo couldn't hear anything in that howling, barking, growling, whining, yapping canine bedlam.

And then, Philo Skinner, who had been beaten up by every half-assed bully all through his miserable childhood, Philo Skinner, who had been punched around by half the redneck squirts in his army platoon before his medical discharge for asthma, Philo Skinner, who for the first time in his life had bested another human being in a physical encounter, couldn't resist a victorious howl or two. Like a wild dog standing over his helpless prey.

"Tell your boss," Philo croaked triumphantly. "Tell that bloodsucker that Philo Skinner said adios! Tell him next time to try it himself, he wants to take Philo Skinner!"

Philo was enjoying him so much he did not see the maniacal amber eye on the other side of the slit in the rubber doggie door. Valnikov saw that frightful eye. Valnikov heard the rumbling, which at floor level sounded like an earthquake beginning, or a cyclone on the horizon.

Walter, the German shepherd, didn't like being away from his adopted family. Walter didn't like the pen they had put him in, the first time he had been caged since those bad old days as an attack dog. Walter didn't even like the delicious horsemeat and liver that Mavis had tried to feed him yesterday. But most of all Walter didn't like *guns*.

In fact, Walter had been trained by his former owner to hate guns. And to rip into tiny pieces of hamburger any human being who *dared* to point a gun at him. Walter's former owner taught all his doggies very special tricks with his lead-filled rubber hose. The tricks made his guard dogs very popular with his clients. Walter's former owner, who loved his work as much as his animals hated theirs, wore special equipment for his demonstrations. The special equipment included a steel-mesh apron. Strapped outside the apron was a Little League groin cup, covered with sponge rubber. Something a crazed animal could get his teeth into.

The potential clients invariably laughed like hell when they saw that *these* dogs weren't so stupid as to let someone "feed them the arm" like most attack dogs. Walter and his thirteen wretched pals were taught to feint for their master's padded forearm and then dive straight for the Little League cup and tear it off the apron. One of Walter's chums was so crazed by the "training" that he once tried to *eat* the groin cup. The clients laughed like hell at the demonstration. These dogs would attack a burglar right where he *lived*.

Philo Skinner was enjoying this moment of triumph too much to see anything. He was so busy gloating over the fallen assassin, he didn't notice the huge mound of feces in the "empty" pen. He didn't see the amber eye of the cyclone. He never heard the roar.

The roar.

Valnikov covered his face when the cyclone roared over him. The black-and-tan cyclone bashed Philo into the steel post holding the seven-foot gate of the pen. Philo's head striking the post hardly bothered him. What did bother him was that this cyclone had him pinned up against the chainlink wall trying to chew his groin into hamburger.

Valnikov struggled to his knees and crawled away from the snarling slashing frenzied beast, while every dog in the kennel increased the roar by several decibels, totally drowning out Philo Skinner's screaming. The dog lost his first grip and settled on the extremely sensitive flesh on the very top of the inner thigh of Philo Skinner. The dog plunged his teeth into this tender meat just as the first two explosions erupted his flanks. The dog jerked his head around and snapped at his own flesh like a shark, amber eyes wide with the same surprise Valnikov had shown, the shock of unbelievable pain. Philo was backed against one side of the pen and Valnikov the other. Both watched the shepherd thrashing and then Philo pointed the gun and an explosion splattered through the shoulder of the dog and he fell on his back kicking his feet.

Philo Skinner looked down at the blood spreading over his crotch and he screamed like a woman. Valnikov at last felt the full effects of the concussion and started to get dizzy and very sick. Valnikov was crawling on his stomach getting sicker and sicker when he saw in amazement that the dog had gotten his feet under him and was coiled again. The last thing Valnikov saw of the dog in life was the look on his face. The look of consummate hate and outrage as he made his last pain-wracked leap at the terror-filled face of Philo Skinner.

Philo was coughing and spitting when he fed his arm to Walter and fired three rounds into the chest of the monster, and this time the echoing explosions drowned out the animal din.

Then Valnikov was swallowing back the vomit and kneeling on all fours watching the shrieking dog handler try to throw the body off himself. Valnikov didn't know that Philo had fired all six rounds, and made a lunge for the gun while Philo fought with the dead animal.

Philo didn't know that he had fired all six rounds and the gun clicked impotently three times in the face of Valnikov as he lunged forward. Then the three of them rolled on the floor, through blood and feces. Two wounded, weak, desperate men with a dead dog between. Two bodies thrashed and punched and kicked and rolled in slow motion. Walter lay dead, pressed between them, a shepherd sandwich.

Philo hacked at Valnikov with the gun, hitting him once on the shoulder, but Valnikov slid free and Philo only hit the dead dog with the next blow. Philo whimpered and sobbed and threw the gun at Valnikov, striking him in the chest. Then Philo got to his knees and crawled for the open gate. He grabbed the metal post, pulled himself upright and was one step out of the cage when Valnikov grabbed his legs in a bear hug and held on.

"You bastard!" Philo shrieked. "Let me go!"

The dogs answered with ear-splitting howls.

Valnikov gradually pulled himself to his knees, trying not to vomit, holding Philo around the legs.

Philo held on to the gate post and yelled "YOU BASTARD!" as Valnikov, with nearly a hundred pounds more weight, locked around Philo's bloody hips and pulled him back into the pen.

"BAST—" Philo sobbed and grabbed the cage gate while falling, and it clanged shut as the two sick and wounded men fell on their backs next to Walter.

Philo looked at the locked gate and started crying. Valnikov looked at the locked gate and started throwing up. Walter looked at the locked gate with dead eyes.

When Valnikov stopped vomiting, the concussion played a trick on him. His head started falling on one shoulder, then the other. It felt like his head had ballast attached, or that his thick neck had lost its strength. He couldn't keep his head straight.

Philo Skinner looked at him and got to his feet. The gate in front of him went clear to the ceiling. He thought about crawling through the doggie door but the outside dog run was completely fenced up to eight feet, and then the chain link had been stretched over the top. Skinner Kennels has the best of security for your pet. Thanks, Mavis.

There was only one thing to do. The side walls of chain-link fence in each dog run stopped one foot short of the ten-foot ceiling. But there were eleven dog pens between Philo and the aisle to freedom. Eleven dog pens full of terriers. There were seven dog pens the other way. Full of huge beasts like Walter. Philo Skinner, Terrier King, started the climb the long way.

He was wheezing and gasping and slippery with sweat and blood when he reached the top of the first chain-link wall. He took as large a breath as possible without coughing, and heaved his lanky frame up on the top bar and hung scrambling down the side. He fell to his knees when he dropped. He looked at his crotch. It was throbbing but the spreading stain had stopped. Oh, please, God, let me have a cock when I look, Philo prayed. I'll *need* it in Puerto Vallarta. Please God!

While Philo scrambled up the next wall of fencing, Valnikov concentrated on staying conscious. He lay face to face with the shepherd and tried to think of other things. He was clammy over his whole body and knew he had to lie still for a moment if there was any possibility of avoiding unconsciousness. He stared into the dead eyes of Walter. Courage had not been enough. Three bullets weren't enough to overcome that bravery and rage, but six had done the trick. Walter's death mask was frozen in a look of . . . what was it? The snarl had been replaced and he looked lonely and hopeless. He had probably sensed it was futile at the end. Valnikov found that look of despair truly unbearable.

Walter took with him to eternity the lonely hopeless face of Charlie Lightfoot.

Then Valnikov tried to sit up. He was careful and tentative. He used the chain link to support him. He looked up at the burglar, moaning and scrambling over the second bar of steel. The burglar dropped down heavily into the next animal pen and fell on top of a whining Kerry blue terrier. Now there were two dog pens separating them.

Three minutes later, both men were trying the wall of chain-link fencing. Valnikov was not so dizzy now, but still feared falling unconscious from a height of nine feet.

Philo Skinner was so exhausted he wasn't thinking of anything but breathing. One breath at a time, Philo. One breath at a time through raw crusty lips.

The pursuit through the dog pens lasted one hour. Panting, moaning, crying out. Up nine feet of fence, balancing precariously on the top until the feet were over the side, scrambling for toeholds, flesh tearing, sliding down into the next pen, falling in little piles of terrier feces.

The sick and wounded pursuer was never able to gain on the sick and wounded quarry during the funeral chase. They watched each other wordlessly through two walls of steel mesh and by unspoken agreement took their rests together. Usually it was Valnikov who signaled the rest break was over, by heaving his heavy bulk upright, and stretching his broad bleeding fingers over the steel mesh and hoisting himself up. Sweat scorched their eyeballs and flowed painfully into the numerous wounds on their tortured bodies.

When Philo was two cages from the aisle he had a horrible siege of giddiness. He had to sit down, right in a puddle of yellow diarrhetic Dandie Dinmont dog shit, brought about by the hysterical hour the animals had endured. But dog shit was the least of Philo's worries. He stared in disbelief as the bullish assassin didn't seize the opportunity to rest himself. Philo watched in horror as the assassin went up the next wall of steel, like a giant crab, two inches at a time. Philo watched in terror as the bloody assassin, his clothes in rags, hung for a second on the bar nine feet over the concrete floor.

"Fall, you bastard. Break your fucking neck!" Philo croaked, but the giant crab gripped the side of the chain link and scuttled down the other side. Now there was only one wall of fencing between them.

The assassin staggered over to that fence and stared Philo straight in the eyes. Then he tried to climb. But he couldn't. He fell to his knees and groaned almost as painfully as Philo Skinner. Then an astonishing thing happened while a terrified Yorkshire terrier crawled over to the assassin and curled up in a gesture of total submission. The astonishing thing was that when the assassin tried to nudge the terrier out of his way his tattered coat sleeve caught on something on his belt. The assassin reached back to pull the coat free and a pair of handcuffs clattered to the floor.

Handcuffs? On a hired thug? Philo Skinner wiped the sweat from his face with what was left of his turtleneck sweater. His imitation gold chain hung clear to his bloody crotch and he jerked it off his neck and tossed it aside. A hired killer with handcuffs?

"Who . . . who are you?" Philo croaked.

"Who . . . who are *you?*" Valnikov gasped.

"I . . . I asked you first," Philo croaked.

"I . . . I'm . . . Valnikov, Los . . . Los Angeles Police Department. And you . . . you're under arrest!" Valnikov gasped.

"You . . . you . . . you aren't gonna *kill* me?" Philo wheezed.

"I'm . . . I'm going to . . . *arrest* you!" Valnikov panted.

And then Philo realized. A cop! Somehow they'd solved it already. Somehow he'd left a clue for them. They'd traced that last call he was dumb enough to make from the kennel when he was desperate. When he'd cut the bitch's ear off and wasn't thinking clearly anymore.

"I never hurt any animal in my life!" Philo whined. "That cunt made me do it!"

"Made . . . made you do what?" Valnikov panted.

"Cut . . . cut the ear off!" Philo cried. "I'll give the money back! I never hurt an animal in my life!"

Then Valnikov wiped his sweaty face with his sleeve and stood up, holding on to the chain link. He tried to get his head clear. He followed Philo's eyes to the last pen, the one beyond Philo Skinner. To the little schnauzer curled up in a corner, trembling and whining softly. A little schnauzer with her head wrapped in gauze bandage.

"You! *You* stole the dog!" Valnikov cried.

"Well, what . . . what did you think?" Philo said.

"That you were a . . . a burglar!" Valnikov said.

"You what?" Philo got even more pale and pulled himself painfully to his feet. "Why . . . why'd you come here?"

"To ask . . . to ask about Mrs. Gharoujian's Tutu. I . . . I hoped you might be able to tell me if someone . . . if one of her boyfriends could have . . ."

"How did you *know* the dead schnauzer was Millie's Tutu?" Philo cried.

"I *didn't* know for sure." Valnikov panted. "I was here to ask you to look at it."

"NOOOOOOOO!" Philo howled, and some of the dogs who had been quieting down started howling again with Philo Skinner.

And while Philo was busy howling, Valnikov took the opportunity to begin scaling the cage that separated them. Philo finally stopped howling when he saw the detective halfway up the steel mesh, and then he yelped and turned and began a desperate climb up the penultimate fence of steel.

Philo was cursing and whining at the top, seemingly without the strength to pull his bony body over the bar. Then he heard the detective's heavy body thud to the floor below him. Valnikov grunted, slipped in feces and fell, his head thudding on the concrete.

Then Philo was over, down into the last dog pen. Into Vickie's pen. The little schnauzer squirmed deeper into the corner, as far as she could get from Philo Skinner. She was trembling so hard her toenails were wearing down on the concrete floor.

Valnikov was on his back, groaning. He didn't know he'd been unconscious until he looked up and saw Philo Skinner, with one last effort, pulling himself up the nine feet to the last bar. Valnikov was on his feet then and climbing. Both men were sobbing, more from exhaustion than the pain, which was anesthetized by the fatigue. Valnikov somehow reached the top of the horizontal steel bar when Philo Skinner reached his.

Philo Skinner looked over at the detective perched like himself nine feet over the floor and he cried, "You didn't even *know* I did it! You came to have me look at Tutu! Why does everything happen to me! *YAAAAAAAAAAA!*"

And after Philo Skinner's primal scream, he let go and fell scrambling down the steel mesh to the floor. He was in the aisle. He had made it. He was free.

Valnikov fell, landing on one knee. He heard something pop and cried out in pain, but he crawled across the cage and pulled himself upright. He was standing face to face with Philo Skinner between the last strands of steel.

Then the whimpering beside him made him look down at the mutilated schnauzer. "You . . . you're under arrest," Valnikov gasped.

"You . . . you catch me first," Philo wheezed, picking up the suitcase, shocked to discover that he couldn't lift it with one hand now.

"Don't . . . don't," Valnikov said, feeling himself getting dizzy again. "Give up, Skinner. Give up."

Philo almost vomited again when he looked at his blood-stained crotch. Please let it be there, God! Oh, please! He found that he could pick up the lightweight suitcase if he used both hands. The last thing he said to Valnikov was: "You tell them . . . tell them that Philo Skinner never . . . never hurt an animal in his *life!*"

Then while Valnikov tried to scale the last wall of steel mesh, he heard Philo in the doorway grunting and wheezing as he picked up the flight bag, dragging the suitcase with one hand. He heard glass breaking as Philo made his way through the debris in the grooming room.

Valnikov was sick and reeling from vertigo when he reached the top bar. He knew he had one surge left, only one. He yelled and felt like the blood would burst from his nose as he pulled his heavy body up, up, until his bloody fingers gripped. He kicked and lunged and got his toe hooked over the top. He couldn't rest. He had to keep the momentum of the last surge. It helped to yell, with the bellowing dogs, and then he was balancing on the top. But there was nothing left. He couldn't climb down, he couldn't hang and drop, he just had to risk it. He let his feet fall and followed with the rest of his bulk and dropped stiff-legged, sending a shock through his skull. Then he fell on his back and lay there.

The dogs seemed quieter now, and then he heard the engine of the El Dorado grinding. Philo Skinner in his panic had flooded the engine. Valnikov looked at Vickie still huddled in panic and terror. Poor thing, he thought. Poor tortured little . . .

"Now now, Vickie," he said. "Now now. You're going *home*."

Philo Skinner sobbed in desperation, turned off the key, and forced himself to sit while the carburetor drained. He looked at his face in the rearview mirror and couldn't believe what he saw. He'd seen starved scabby mongrels that looked better. The mucus clotted in his windpipe and he gagged.

Valnikov staggered down the long aisle between the animals, determined not to faint, forgetting for a moment who he was pursuing and why. He reached the door before Philo tried again. If Philo had turned and seen the detective, with his trousers flapping in shreds, one coat sleeve totally gone and the other hanging from the elbow, the detective with his face grimy and caked with blood and dog food, Philo might have panicked and flooded the El Dorado again. But he didn't even see his pursuer staggering toward his Cadillac. He looked at the ignition and turned it. The engine roared.

Philo screamed with joy and squealed away, never seeing the relentless bloody crab falling on his face in the parking lot of Philo Skinner, Terrier King.

15

Paradise

Philo Skinner was halfway to the airport before he had even a remote idea of what he was doing. It wasn't the incredible exhaustion, nor the horror, nor the pain that revived him. It was the smell. The smell of stale sweat, the smell of blood and fear. Mostly it was the smell of dog shit. Philo Skinner had excrement in his hair, on his pants, on his bare chest. It was mashed into the hair of his armpits where the clothing was torn away. It was even in his pockets!

Philo turned off the San Diego Freeway and drove aimlessly for twenty minutes in an area he didn't know. Then he found a public park. He circled the park several times until he found a rest room. He parked the car in the shade of an elm tree and when there were no passersby in sight, he got out of the car and hobbled across the green expanse toward the park rest room, dragging both suitcase and flight bag.

Five minutes later, Philo Skinner was standing stark naked in the rest room, bathing himself with paper towels and harsh hand soap in one of two rusty sinks. He cried out often and sobbed in relief when he got all the dried blood off his wounded genitalia and saw it was still there. But it would be out of action a long

long time. The foreskin was ripped and already swollen purple. His testicles were still intact, but his upper thighs on both sides were mangled and still bleeding. He knew he needed suturing. Philo Skinner had doctored many injured dogs in his time and had a very good idea of what dog bites could do. His hands were a bloody mess, as were his knees and chest. One eye was blue and green and swollen shut and he knew he would need more sutures behind his ear where he could hardly stem the flow of blood.

Philo urinated in the sink and cried out in pain. Then he opened the suitcase and used two of his brand-new thirty-dollar body shirts as *diapers*. He couldn't afford to arouse suspicion by bleeding all over the seats in the airport lounge. He tied both shirts around him like loincloths, put on the new pants and cursed because he had bought them so stylishly tight. Like everything else it had seemed like a good idea at the time. He put on the jacket of his new leisure suit and planned to keep it buttoned since both new shirts were wrapping his groin. This left him without shirt, socks and shoes, as there was no way he could use his time and waning energy to clean the blood and feces from his imitation alligators.

Fifteen minutes later, a clerk in a men's store just off the San Diego Freeway was surprised to see a man who looked like he just played goalie without a mask stroll into the store barefoot and shirtless. The customer was easy to please, and didn't even care that the patent-leather shoes failed to coordinate with the leisure suit.

The clerk noticed that the man's flesh was gray where he wasn't bruised, and that a trickle of blood leaked down behind his ear. Philo noticed too and bought a dozen handkerchiefs which he jammed in his pockets. He paid in cash and limped out of the store, pausing in the doorway to double up in pain. Then he went next door to a liquor store and bought four packs of Camels which he figured would see him through the next twelve hours.

At 2:00 p.m. Philo Skinner was limping up to the Mexicana Airlines desk at Los Angeles International. He dabbed often at the flow of blood behind his ear. It would stop temporarily and then start leaking. He felt soppy between his legs and knew he was bleeding again down there. Philo Skinner knew he was *hurt*.

When he put the flight bag through the x-ray he panicked for a second. Did he leave his ballpoint pen in there? Was there any metal in there which might cause them to open it? He was ready to faint when he got through the x-ray check. A woman in a uniform handed him his flight bag.

Each step was agony now. Philo was limping to his terminal when he spotted a skycap carrying some bags toward the front.

"Hey, pal," Philo croaked. "If you'll run quick and get a wheelchair and help me to my gate, I'll give you twenty bucks."

The skycap looked at Philo's battered, sweaty, gray face and said, "Man, you're hurtin. You better let me git you a doctor!"

"Hey, I just had a little traffic accident, that's all," Philo wheezed. "I been checked and I'm okay. Look, get that wheelchair and it's worth *thirty* bucks."

"Okay," the skycap said. "Be back in five minutes."

Philo sat and waited and watched passengers being checked for guns and bombs and wished *he* had a gun or bomb. He'd come this far. He had a feeling he wasn't going to make it. He'd rather be dead than go to prison. He felt so sick he thought he might die. He wanted to die in Puerto Vallarta. To die with his dream. In paradise.

"Ready, mister?" the skycap said and Philo opened his eyes. The skycap was standing there with a wheelchair.

"Yeah," Philo said. "Could you do me one more favor? Light me a cigarette. I ain't got a match."

The skycap wheeled Philo, smoking and coughing, through the terminal to his gate. The skycap was reluctant to leave Philo.

"Hey, you sure you oughtta be takin this flight?" the skycap said. "They ain't gonna let you on this flight, bad as you look. Not if you can't make it on your own."

"I'll make it," Philo said, giving the skycap two twenties. "Keep the change," Philo said. It was the biggest tip he ever gave in his life.

"Anything else I can do, mister?"

"One more thing, pal," Philo croaked. "Use a couple bucks a that tip and bring me a drink. Straight whiskey. Put it in a paper cup or something so you can get it here."

"You got it, mister," said the skycap, who was gone and back in five minutes.

Just a moment before the public address system announced that the 3:00 p.m. Mexicana Airlines flight was boarding, Philo Skinner had stemmed the blood behind his ear. He had dabbed at his face with what was left of his dozen handkerchiefs. The sweat would alert them to his condition more than the swollen battered face. He put on his bubble sunglasses and looked down, frightened to see a tiny bloodstain starting on the crotch of his polyester pants. Why had he picked a cream-colored suit? Why couldn't he have picked red? Why couldn't he have done a lot of things?

Why did he always have to pick the black marble?

When he hobbled toward the Mexicana jet, he said, as casually as possible to a young man who looked like a student on holiday, "Hey, pal, how bout letting me just lean on your arm when we board this plane? See, I had this car accident and I'm not feeling too good."

The stewardess assigning the seats said, "Are you all right, señor?"

The handkerchief, wiping his face every few seconds, couldn't keep it dry. The pain was so terrifying that the sweat poured with every step. "I'll be okay, soon as you fix me a margarita," Philo grinned. "I had a car accident this morning but the doc says I'm fine. Just bring that margarita as soon as you can."

"I'm sorry, señor, but we are out of margarita mix."

"No margarita?" Philo croaked, limping down the aisle to his seat in first class.

"I can feex you a nice Bloody Mary," she smiled.

"Blood," said Philo. "Just a bourbon and water."

"Right after takeoff, señor," she said.

"Right after takeoff," said Philo Skinner, his mouth as dry as a tomb.

Valnikov was never fully unconscious. He was never fully conscious either. He saw Clarence Cromwell in the hospital room. And Hipless Hooker. He didn't see Natalie. They were talking to him. He couldn't understand everything they said. Clarence kept grinning and patting Valnikov gently on the arm and saying, "They don't make em like this no more. Fuckin kids with peanut balls think they're cops!"

Then Hipless Hooker left, but Clarence stayed.

"Did you get Skinner, Clarence?" Valnikov said, coming out of the sedative mist. He had been in some trackless wasteland, it seemed. But at least it wasn't Siberia.

"We'll get him, Val," Clarence said. "Don't you worry, we gonna git that sucker. The little dog's back with her momma at least. She called about you, maybe ten times. Wants to send you flowers and visit you and have the chief give you a medal or a ticker-tape parade or somethin. Last time she called she said for me to say to you that Vickie's gonna be okay and that she's gonna be okay too. Whatever that means."

"I think she *will* be okay," Valnikov nodded. "Did Natalie call?"

"She, uh, she sends her . . . wishes for uh . . . you to get well. I called your brother, but the doc says no visitors till tomorrow. I figured I ain't exactly a visitor and I knew you'd wanna know what's goin on when you came around."

"Do I have a phone in here, Clarence?"

"Course you got a phone, fool!" Clarence grinned. "You think I'm gonna let them put a ace detective in a room without a phone?"

"Dial Natalie for me, will you?"

"I don't know her number."

"Sure you do. You have all our phone numbers in your little notebook. The one in your coat pocket."

"Oh, yeah," Clarence said glumly, taking out the notebook.

While he dialed, Valnikov touched his head. It was swathed in a bandage that covered his left ear. Some hair stuck out on top. He had some pain in his knee, and his shoulder and ribs hurt, but he didn't really feel as much pain as he expected.

"Natalie?" said Clarence, scowling. "This is me, Clarence. Jist a minute."

He handed the phone to Valnikov, who took it and said, "Natalie?"

"Valnikov!" she said, "I was worried! How *are* you? They said for us not to visit you until tomorrow! I would've come!"

"I know you would, Natalie," Valnikov smiled. "How are *you?*"

"We heard you have a concussion. And there was gunfire! A dead dog. Did you shoot him?"

"No, Skinner did. Natalie, are you . . . well, when do you leave for Hawaii?"

"Valnikov," she said softly, then the phone was quiet. In the background Valnikov heard the voice of Captain Jack Packerton saying, "Who's that, Natalie? Who're you talking to?"

"My partner," she said. Then to Valnikov: "We moved up our plans. We're going tomorrow. We had our reservations changed. It was tough to do, but we were told that in two weeks there might be too much rain in that part of Kauai. Rain would ruin our vacation."

"Yes, of course," Valnikov said.

"Clarence Cromwell fixed it so I could leave tomorrow."

"Yes, he's a good man to work for," said Valnikov.

"I wouldn't have gone without checking on you though. I was going to stop tomorrow to see you. Our flight isn't until tomorrow afternoon."

"Yes, that's the best time to fly," said Valnikov.

"Well, I better let you rest. You take care, huh? Would you like to have visitors tomorrow? I could bring some books or . . ."

"No, I don't think so, Natalie. I think I'll just rest tomorrow. You have a good time in Hawaii, okay?"

"Okay, Valnikov. Be seeing you."

"Be seeing you," he said, handing the phone to Clarence, who hung it up.

Clarence said, "Hey, guess what? I decided I'm gettin sick and tired a sittin around on my ass runnin that division. I wanna do some detective work again. I was hopin you and me might team up a few days a week. Couple a real ball-bustin cops! How bout that!"

"Great, Clarence," Valnikov mumbled. "Sounds great."

"Okay, you git some sleep now, hear? I'll come see you tomorrow. Doc says he's on'y gonna keep you maybe a day or so. Git some sleep, hear?"

"What time is it?"

"Ten o'clock," Clarence said.

"Night or morning?"

"Night. This is still Thursday. All you lost is an afternoon."

"That's all I lost," said Valnikov.

Philo Skinner didn't come soaring in over white beaches and crashing surf at sunset. It was after dark when they touched down, but it wouldn't have mattered anyway. Philo Skinner was slumped in his seat, with his head on a bloody pillow, trying to keep from vomiting. He was burning with fever and making all the first-class passengers around him sick by coughing up endless phlegm balls and spitting into a towel.

The stewardess had not noticed the serious condition of the gray feverish man until they had passed the point of no return. She advised the pilot, who came back to talk to him.

Philo nodded in answer to most of the questions. "I got in a car accident yesterday. Been in the hospital but I'm okay. I'm okay, goddamnit!"

At one point, while Philo slept fitfully, moaning in pain, the stewardess gently removed the flight bag from his lap and put it on the floor under him. The battered man had not released his death grip on the flight bag since boarding. She was afraid of it. Some sophisticated explosives could get by the detector. She opened the flight bag and then closed it quickly and took it forward to the captain, who asked that a radio message be relayed to Los Angeles. The captain believed they had a wounded bank robber aboard.

There was an ambulance waiting when the plane touched down. At about the same time that Valnikov lay staring at the ceiling in the police ward at Central Receiving Hospital, Philo Skinner was being admitted to the Hospital Seguro Social. Philo had not seen the beach and surf nor even the sunshine in Puerto Vallarta. Philo's fever was more than 104 degrees, though they measured it in centigrade and only translated it to Fahrenheit when he demanded to know. Philo Skinner requested that someone from the American consulate be brought to him immediately.

Philo had been asleep for hours but was awakened by a throbbing in his penis. The throbbing became warm, then white hot. He cried out and a young man walked in. The man was in street clothes. He was short and slender, had a small moustache and black hair bright and shiny under the white light.

"I am Doctor Rivera," he said in nearly unaccented English.

"It hurts," Philo sobbed. "Down here." He had to reach with his right arm since the other contained an intravenous needle. He patted the bandages between his legs. "Is it . . . Oh, please! Is it . . . ?"

"Still there?" the doctor smiled. "It is still there, Mr. Skinner. But you have been mauled pretty badly. You won't be having much of a sex life for a while, but yes, it is all still there."

"Thank God," Philo sobbed. "Doctor, I hurt!"

"You are urinating," the doctor said. "I had to put a catheter in you. You are a sick man, Mr. Skinner."

"Where's my . . . my flight bag?" Philo croaked.

"Mexicana Airlines has seized your flight bag, Mr. Skinner," the young doctor said. "There is a receipt for almost twenty thousand dollars from Mexicana Airlines. They have seized your flight bag pending an investigation with the American authorities."

"Oh, God!" Philo cried.

"Tell me, Mr. Skinner," the young doctor said, curiously, "are you a bank robber or what?"

"Oh, God!" Philo cried.

"You may as well satisfy my curiosity," the doctor shrugged. "I am sure the Los Angeles Police or the F.B.I. or someone is after you. A man with animal bites and multiple contusions and lacerations? A man with a bag full of money? We have a little . . . how do you say . . . lottery going on. Some of the doctors and nurses think you are a bank robber. But I don't think banks employ police dogs in Los Angeles. I went to Loma Linda University and I never saw a police dog in a Los Angeles bank."

"Oh, God, a *lottery!*" Philo cried. He who lives by the bookmaker . . .

"I think you are a safe . . . how do you say?"

"Cracker," Philo croaked.

"Yes, a safecracker. I think that you were cracking a safe and a watchman turned a dog loose on you and . . . tell me, Mr. Skinner, did you kill someone? A watchman maybe?"

Then while Philo was looking around the little hospital room at the Friday morning sky over Puerto Vallarta, at the smiling young doctor with eyes as brown as a dog's, with eyes as oval and brown as . . .

"I killed Tutu," Philo said.

"You what?"

"I KILLED TUTU!" Philo wailed, hollow-eyed and frightful. "And I cut Vickie's ear off! And I shot . . . I shot . . ." But Philo couldn't continue. His tears were scalding. Philo Skinner's long bony frame was heaving and shaking the bed. Philo Skinner only stopped crying when he broke into a coughing spasm that almost strangled him.

A nurse came running in and the doctor said something in Spanish.

"Lean forward, a little, Mr. Skinner," the doctor said. "Here, spit the phlegm in this tray."

When Philo lay back on the pillow he could hardly see them through the tears. The nurse wiped his eyes and his mouth and said something in Spanish to the doctor.

The doctor's oval eyes were round and electric now. Nobody was going to win *this* lottery! A mass murderer!

"Do you want to tell me about it, Mr. Skinner?" the doctor said. "You killed *how* many? And you cut off an ear?" The doctor couldn't wait to tell the staff. The skinny gringo was another Charles Manson!

"Please, Doctor," Philo sobbed. "I don't wanna die here. I don't wanna die in this foreign country."

"You are not going to die, Mr. Skinner."

"I don't wanna *live* in a foreign country!" Philo cried.

"You are full of infection and you have lost blood and I believe you have a fairly serious lung disorder, but . . ."

"I wanna go home!" Philo wailed. "Call the Los Angeles cops, Doctor. Tell them to get me home."

"Yes, but about all those you killed, can you tell me . . ."

"I'm an American," Philo Skinner sobbed. "I wanna go *home!*"

16

Byzantine Eyes

On Friday, Valnikov got out of bed before noon and walked unsteadily around the room. Then he phoned his brother and told him to go to the apartment and bring him some clothes.

At 1:30 p.m. Alex Valnikov had come and gone, and his younger brother was walking around the ward in poplin slacks and an old sport shirt.

At 2:00 p.m. a nurse complained to a doctor that Sergeant Valnikov was checking out of the hospital whether they liked it or not.

At 2:30 p.m. Hipless Hooker called Valnikov's room and ordered him to listen to his doctor.

At 2:30 p.m. Sergeant Valnikov informed Hipless Hooker politely that he had just retired from the Los Angeles Police Department and that Captain Hooker could start processing his retirement papers.

At 5:30 p.m., just after a blazing winter sunset in Los Angeles, Valnikov was sitting on the steps by the reflecting pool at the Los Angeles Music Center, listening to Horst, the fiddler, play Rimsky-Korsakov. Fifteen bucks' worth.

Horst was getting tired. There was no one left at this time of day except this guy with the turban bandage who wanted Russian music. Horst asked him what happened to his head, but the guy just said, ''An accident.''

Horst was happy to take the guy's bread, but the fifteen bucks' worth had just about run out and Horst had exhausted his Russian repertoire and didn't want to start over again.

Valnikov sat with his back to Hope Street. He listened to a Gypsy violin and stared at the melancholy tableau of a fiddler, and beyond, in the dusk, the courthouse and the knight in chain mail with his hopeful document wrested from King John.

Then Valnikov heard a familiar voice: ''They tell me it's raining in Kauai.''

Valnikov turned and cried: ''Natalie!''

''Sit down, don't get up,'' she said. ''Oh, he hurt you! Oh!''

''Hurt? Hurt?'' Valnikov cried, with the biggest dumbest smile she'd ever seen on him. ''I'm fine! I'm swell!''

Then Natalie walked over to Horst, the fiddler, and said, ''Your motor still running, Horst?''

''Huh?''

''We got any music left for the loot he's laid on you?''

''This is it, lady, I gotta go home.''

Natalie Zimmerman took a twenty out of her purse and said, ''Rev it up Horst. Until this is gone.''

''Okay, lady,'' Horst grinned. ''Whadda ya wanna hear?''

''Gypsy,'' she said. ''Russian Gypsy.''

''Jesus, more Russian? Does it have to be *Russian?*''

''*If* you want the grease for your crank,'' she said, brushing her Friz out of her eyes.

''How about 'Ochi Chornyia'?'' Horst suggested. ''You know, 'Dark Eyes'?''

''Okay, Horst, give us a shot of 'Dark Eyes,' '' she said, going back to Valnikov, who was standing on the steps, looking like a quiz show contestant.

''Sit down and rest yourself,'' Natalie said, forcing him down on the steps. ''You shouldn't even *be* here. I heard you walked out of the hospital. I heard you retired. Was that for real?''

''I've had enough,'' he said. ''But you? You're *not* going to Hawaii?''

''Waste of money,'' she said. ''I think I'd rather invest my savings in a music store or something.''

As Horst burst into twenty bucks' worth of ''Ochi Chornyia,'' Natalie moved close to Valnikov and said, ''Do you know the lyrics to this one?''

''I can speak them to you,'' he said. ''I'm not in very good voice but . . .''

Then Natalie moved even closer. He looked at her big goofy glasses, at her brown eyes behind them, and translated from the Russian. ''Dark eyes, passionate eyes, fiery and beautiful eyes. How I love you . . .''

''Yes,'' she whispered. ''Go on.''

''The rest of the song is sad, like all Gypsy songs,'' he said joyfully.

''Then don't tell it to me,'' she said. ''We'll settle for that part.''

''You have eyes like the Virgin on the ikon,'' he said. ''The Byzantine eyes. The *sweet* Byzantine eyes!''

She put her head on his shoulder and those Byzantine eyes started to fill up while Horst played and eavesdropped.

''I thought I'd picked the black marble,'' Valnikov said.

"I don't wanna be like Charlie Lightfoot," Natalie said.

"You're not *anything* like Charlie Lightfoot," Valnikov said.

"Andrushka!" Natalie said, and it melted him.

He kissed her gently. She kissed him passionately. Then they lay back across the steps while Horst pretended to look elsewhere.

They faced Hope Street and kissed to a Gypsy violin.

"Andrushka!" she cried.

"Natasha!" he cried.

Then Horst got awfully nervous and started looking around. It was dark now, thank goodness. Good thing there weren't any bystanders around. Still, there was a lot of light from the reflecting pool.

"Hey, lady, I can't afford to get in trouble with the management around here," said Horst.

Natalie broke the kiss to say, "Keep it in gear, Horst."

Horst thought of the twenty scoots and kept playing. But finally they were getting *too* playful.

"Hey!" he said, stopping the music. "Why don't you two go to a motel or something? I'll refund part of your money."

Valnikov didn't even hear him. Valnikov was hearing nightingales singing in the raspberry bush. Natalie didn't break their kiss but she felt for her purse. She pulled out her service revolver and put it on the step beside her. Then she broke the kiss.

"How would you like a hole in your fiddle, Horst?"

"My God, lady! My God!" Horst cried. "That's a gun! Hey, lady! I don't want any trouble! Hey, lady!"

"Then you better crank it on, kid," Natalie said, tapping the revolver, biting on Valnikov's lower lip until they were lost in another interminable kiss.

Horst was so scared he could hardly finger the violin. His fingers were so sweaty they were slipping off the strings. Every time he thought about picking up his top hat full of money, and the violin case, and folding chair, and running like hell, he'd look at the gun lying there beside the two lustcrazed maniacs.

"Hey, lady!" Horst cried, playing an off-key "Ochi Chornyia." "Gimme a break!"

Then he looked in the shadows and saw their hands roving, caressing. Heard the kisses and moaning.

"Oh, Andrushka!"

"My Natasha!"

"You two oughtta be ashamed!" Horst whined, still playing. "A cop might come along and think I'm involved in this." Then he looked at the gun. "In fact I wish a cop *would* come along!"

"Andrushka!" Natalie cried.

"Natasha!"

"And they say *my* generation's going to hell," Horst whimpered.

Horst stole one last glance at the gun, gleaming malevolently by the light from the reflecting pool. Horst suddenly felt he might wet his pants. Why is there *never* a cop in this town when you need one? Horst looked at the madman with her. Christ, his head was all swathed in a bandage turban. He probably just had a lobotomy. No sense even *trying* to talk to him. And the female thug with the gun was obviously *more* dangerous.

So there was nothing to do but play "Ochi Chornyia" until they either shot him dead or let him go. Horst locked his knees and concentrated on controlling his bladder and played his violin gamely.

All he *ever* wanted to do was become a doctor and help people. And maybe make twenty grand a year on unreported fees he didn't have to claim on his income tax so he could buy a Porsche Turbo. And maybe pad the Medicare statements here and there to make enough to buy a ski boat with a 454 Chevy engine. Jesus, he was a humanitarian!

His bladder was about to explode. Horst groaned and looked at the night sky and concentrated on one brave star which had penetrated the smog. Horst whined aloud to that hopeful star. Horst asked the timeless, universal, unanswerable question. ''Why do I *always* have to pick the black marble?''

The lovers never heard him. They heard a Gypsy violin, and Russian nightingales and their hammering hearts.

''Andrushka!''

''My Natasha!''

''Oh, Andrushka!''

The New Centurions

FOR DEE
And of course
FOR ALL THE CENTURIONS

Early Summer 1960

1

The Runner

LYING PROSTRATE, Serge Duran gaped at Augustus Plebesly who was racing inexorably around the track. That's a ridiculous name, thought Serge—Augustus Plebesly. It's a ridiculous name for a puny runt who can run like a goddamn antelope.

Plebesly ran abreast of, and was matching strides with, the feared P.T. instructor, Officer Randolph. If Randolph took up the challenge he'd never stop. Twenty laps. Twenty-five. Until there was nothing left but forty-nine sweat-suit-covered corpses and forty-nine puddles of puke. Serge had already vomited once and knew another was coming up.

"Get up, Duran!" a voice thundered from above. Serge's eyes focused on the massive blur standing over him.

"Get up! Get up!" roared Officer Randolph, who had halted the wretched weary group of cadets.

Serge staggered to his feet and limped after his classmates as Officer Randolph ran ahead to catch Plebesly. Porfirio Rodriguez dropped back and patted Serge on the shoulder. "Don't give up, Sergio," Rodriguez panted. "Stay with 'em, man."

Serge ignored him and lurched forward in anguish. That's just like a Texas Chicano, he thought. Afraid I'll disgrace him in front of the *gabachos*. If I wasn't a Mexican he'd let me lay until the crabgrass was growing out my ears.

If he could only remember how many laps they had run. Twenty was their record before today, and today was hot, ninety-five degrees at least. And sultry. It was only their fourth week in the police academy. They weren't in shape yet. Randolph wouldn't dare run them more than twenty laps today. Serge leaned forward and concentrated on placing one foot in front of the other.

After another half-lap the burning in his chest was no longer bearable. He tasted something strange and choked in panic; he was going to faint. But luckily, Roy Fehler picked that exact moment to fall on his face, causing the collapse of eight other police cadets. Serge gave silent thanks to Fehler who was bleeding from the nose. The class had lost its momentum and a minor mutiny occurred as one cadet after another dropped to his knees and retched. Only Plebesly and a few others remained standing.

"You want to be Los Angeles policemen!" shouted Randolph. "You aren't fit to *wash* police cars! And I guarantee you one thing, if you aren't on your feet in five seconds, you'll never ride in one!"

One by one the sullen cadets got to their feet and soon all were standing except Fehler who was unsuccessfully trying to stop the nosebleed by lying on his back, his handsome face tilted up to the white sun. Fehler's pale crew cut was streaked with dust and blood. Officer Randolph strode over to him.

"Okay, Fehler, go take a shower and report to the sergeant. We'll get you to Central Receiving Hospital for an X ray."

Serge glanced fearfully at Plebesly who was doing some knee bends to keep loose. Oh no, Serge thought; look tired, Plebesly! Be human! You stupid ass, you'll antagonize Randolph!

Serge saw Officer Randolph regarding Plebesly, but the instructor only said, "Okay, you weaklings. That's enough running for today. Get on your back and we'll do some sit-ups."

With relief the class began the less painful session of calisthenics and self-defense. Serge wished he wasn't so big. He'd like to get paired up with Plebesly so he could crush the little bastard when they were practicing the police holds.

After several minutes of sit-ups, leg-ups, and push-ups, Randolph shouted, "Okay, onesies on twosies! Let's go!"

The class formed a circle and Serge was again teamed with Andrews, the man who marched next to him in formation. Andrews was big, even bigger than Serge, and infinitely harder and stronger. Like Plebesly, Andrews seemed bent on doing his very best, and he had almost choked Serge into unconsciousness the day before when they were practicing the bar strangle. When Serge recovered, he blindly grabbed Andrews by the shirt front and whispered a violent threat that he couldn't clearly remember when his rage subsided. To his surprise, Andrews apologizd, a frightened look on the broad flat face as he realized that Serge had been hurt. He apologized three times that same day and beamed when Serge finally assured him there were no hard feelings. He's just an overgrown Plebesly, Serge thought. These dedicated types are all alike. They're so damn serious you can't hate them like you should.

"Okay, switch around," shouted Randolph. "Twosies on onesies this time."

Each man changed with his partner. This time Andrews played the role of suspect and it was Serge's job to control him.

"Okay, let's try the come-along again," shouted Randolph. "And do it right, this time. Ready? One!"

Serge took Andrews' wide hand at the count of one but realized that the come-along hold had vanished in the intellectual darkness that fifteen or more laps temporarily brought about.

"Two!" shouted Randolph.

"Is this the come-along, Andrews?" whispered Serge, as he saw Randolph helping another cadet who was even more confused.

Andrews responded by twisting his own hand into the come-along position and wincing so that Randolph would think that Serge had him writhing in agony, hence, a "proper" come-along. When Randolph passed he nodded in satisfaction at the pain Serge was inflicting.

"I'm not hurting you, am I?" Serge whispered.

"No, I'm okay," smiled Andrews, baring his large gapped teeth.

You just can't hate these serious ones, Serge thought, and looked around the sweating ring of gray-clad cadets for Plebesly. You had to admire the control the squirt had over his slim little body. On their first physical qualification test Plebesly had done twenty-five perfect chins, a hundred sit-ups in eighty-five seconds, and threatened to break the academy record for running the obstacle course. It was that which Serge feared most. The obstacle course with the dreaded wall that defeated him at first glance.

It was inexpicable that he should fear that wall. He was an athlete, at least he had been, six years ago at Chino High School. He had lettered in football three years, a lineman, but quick, and well-coordinated for his size. And his size was inexplicable, six feet three, large-boned, slightly freckled, with light brown hair and eyes—so that it was a family joke that he could not possibly be a Mexican boy, at least not of the Duran family who were especially small and dark—and if his mother had not been from the old country and not disposed to offcolor *chistes* they might have teased her with remarks about the blond *gabacho* giant who owned the small grocery store where for years she bought *harina* and *maíz* for the tortillas which she made by hand. His mother had never put store-bought tortillas on the family table. And suddenly he wondered why he was thinking about his mother now, and what good it did to ever think of the dead.

"All right, sit down," shouted Randolph, who didn't have to repeat the command.

The class of forty-eight cadets, minus Roy Fehler, slumped to the grass happy in the knowledge that there was only relaxation ahead, unless you were chosen as Randolph's demonstration victim.

Serge was still tense. Randolph often chose the big men to demonstrate the holds on. The instructor was himself a medium-sized man, but muscular, and hard as a gun barrel. He invariably hurt you when applying the holds. It seemed to be part of the game to toss the cadet a little harder than necessary, or to make him cry out from a hand, arm, or leg hold. The class got a nervous laugh from the torture, but Serge vowed that the next time Randolph used him for a onesies on twosies demonstration, he was not going to stand for any rougher than necessary treatment. However he hadn't decided what to do about it. He wanted this job. Being a cop would be a fairly interesting way to make four hundred and eighty-nine dollars a month. He relaxed as Randolph chose Augustus Plebesly for his victim.

"Okay, you already learned the bar strangle," said Randolph. "It's a good hold when you apply it right. When you apply it wrong, it's not worth a damn. Now I'm going to show you a variation of that strangle."

Randolph took a position behind Plebesly, reached around his throat with a massive forearm, and hooked the small neck in the crook of his arm. "I'm now applying pressure to the carotid artery," Randolph announced. "My forearm and bicep are choking off the oxygen flow to his brain. He would pass out very quickly if I applied pressure." As he said it, he *did* apply pressure, and Plebesly's large blue eyes fluttered twice and bulged in terror. Randolph relaxed his hold, grinned, and slapped Plebesly on the back to indicate he was through with him.

"Okay, ones on twos," shouted Randolph. "We only got a few minutes left. Let's go! I want you to practice this one."

As each number one man got his arm around the waiting throat of number two, Randolph shouted, "Lift the elbow. You have to get his chin up. If he keeps his chin down, he'll beat you. Make him lift that chin and then put it on him. Easy, though. And just for a second."

Serge knew that Andrews would be very careful about hurting him after the outburst the other day. He could see that Andrews was trying not to, the big arm around his neck flexed only a little, and yet the pain was unbelievable. Serge instinctively grabbed Andrews' arm.

"Sorry, Duran," said Andrews with a worried look.

"'s allright," Serge gasped. "That's a hell of a hold!"

When it was twos on ones, Serge lifted Andrews' chin. He had never hurt Andrews in any of the prior P.T. sessions. He didn't think Andrews could be hurt. He squeezed the throat in the crook, pulling his wrist toward him, and held it several seconds. Andrews' hands did not come up as his had. He must be applying it wrong, he thought.

Serge raised the elbow and increased the pressure.

"Am I doing it right?" asked Serge trying to see Andrews' upturned face.

"Let him go, Duran!" screamed Randolph. Serge jumped back, startled, and released Andrews who thudded to the ground red-faced, eyes half open and glazed.

"For chrissake, Duran," said Randolph, raising the massive torso of Andrews in his arms.

"I didn't mean to," Serge sputtered.

"I told you guys, easy!" said Randolph, as Andrews lurched to his feet "You can cause brain damage with that hold. You stop the oxygen flow to the brain for too long a period and you're really going to hurt somebody, maybe kill them."

"I'm sorry, Andrews," said Serge, vastly relieved when the big man gave him a weak smile. "Why didn't you tap my arm or kick me or something? I didn't know I was hurting you."

"I wanted you to get the hold right," said Andrews, "and after a few seconds, I just blacked out."

"You be damn careful with that hold," shouted Randolph. "I don't want nobody hurt before you even graduate from the academy. But maybe you'll learn something from this. When you guys leave here, you're going out where there's guys that aren't afraid of that badge and gun. In fact, they might try to stick that badge up your ass to say they did it, and that big oval shield would sure hurt coming out. This particular hold might save you. If you get it on right you can put anybody out, and it just might rescue your ass someday. Okay, ones on twos again!"

"Your turn to get even," said Serge to Andrews who was massaging the side of his throat and swallowing painfully.

"I'll be careful," said Andrews, putting his huge arm around Serge's neck. "Let's just pretend I'm choking you," said Andrews.

"That's okay by me," said Serge.

Officer Randolph moved from one pair of cadets to another, adjusting the choke hold, raising elbows, turning wrists, straightening torsos, until he had had enough. "Okay, sit down, you guys. We're just wasting our time today."

The class collapsed on the grass like a huge gray many-legged insect and each cadet waited for an outburst from Randolph who was pacing in a tight circle, formidable in his yellow polo shirt, blue shorts, and black high-topped gym shoes.

Serge was bigger than Randolph, Andrews much bigger. Yet they all seemed small beside him. It was the sweat suits, he thought, the ill-fitting baggy pants and gray sweat shirts always sweat-soaked and ugly. And it was the haircuts. The cadets wore short military style haircuts which made all the young men look smaller and younger.

"It's hard to put everything into the self-defense session," said Randolph, finally breaking silence, still pacing, arms folded as he watched the grass. "It's damn hot and I run you hard. Maybe sometimes I run you too hard. Well, I got my own theory on physical training for policemen and it's time I explained it to you."

That's very thoughtful, you bastard, thought Serge, rubbing his side, which still ached from the twenty laps around the track. He was just beginning to be able to take large breaths without coughing or without his lungs hurting.

"Most of you guys don't know what it's like to fight another guy," said Randolph. "I'm sure you all had your scraps in high school, maybe a scuffle or two somewhere else. A couple of you are Korean vets and think you seen it all, and Wilson here has been in the Golden Gloves. But none of you really knows what it's like to fight another man no holds barred and win. You're going to have to be ready to do it anytime. And you have to win. I'm going to show you something. Plebesly, come here!"

Serge smiled as Plebesly sprang to his feet and trotted into the center of the circle. The round blue eyes showed no fatigue and stared patiently at the instructor apparently ready for a painful, elbow-wrenching arm hold or any other punishiment Officer Randolph cared to offer.

"Come closer, Plebesly," said Randolph, gripping the little man by the shoulder and whispering in his ear for several seconds.

Serge leaned back on his elbows, happy in the knowledge that Randolph was evidently going to use the remainder of the P.T. class for his demonstration. Serge's stomach muscles loosened and a sunny wave of relaxation swept over him. It was getting so he was having dreams of running the track. Suddenly he saw Randolph staring at him.

"You, Duran, and you, Andrews, come up here!"

Serge fought a momentary surge of anger, but then dejectedly plodded into the circle, remembering that the last time he had failed to master a complicated hold, he was given three laps around the track. He wanted to be a policeman, but he would not run that track again for anyone. Not this day. Not now.

"I picked Duran and Andrews because they're big," said Randolph. "Now, I want you two to put Plebesly's hands behind his back and handcuff him. Just simulate the cuffing, but get him in the cuffing position. He's the suspect, you two are the policemen. Okay, go ahead."

Serge looked at Andrews for a plan to take the retreating Plebesly, who backed in a circle, hands at his sides, away from the two big men. Just like the Corps, thought Serge. Always the games. First in boot camp, then in I.T.R. at Camp Pendleton. The Korean War had been over a year when he joined, and yet they talked about the gooks like they would be waiting to swarm over their ship the first moment they landed in Pacific waters.

Andrews made a lunge for Plebesly, who almost slithered away but was caught by the sleeve of his sweat shirt. Serge jumped on Plebesly's back and the little man went down under Serge's two hundred and fifteen pounds. But then he wriggled and twisted, and suddenly Serge was under Plebesly and Andrews was on Plebesly's back forcing the combined weight of himself and Plebesly on Serge's aching ribs.

"Pull him away, Andrews," Serge wheezed. "Get a wristlock!"

Serge pushed himself up but Plebesly had locked his arms and legs around Serge's body from the rear and hung there leechlike with enough weight to topple Serge over backward on the clinging Plebesly who gasped but would not let go. Andrews managed to pry the little man's fingers loose, but the sinewy legs held on and by now Serge was beaten and sat there with the implacable monkey clinging to his torso.

"Get a choke hold on him, damn it," Serge muttered.

"I'm trying. I'm too tired," Andrews whispered, as Plebesly buried his face deeper into Serge's dripping back.

"Okay, that's enough," Randolph commanded. Plebesly instantly released Serge, bounded to his feet and trotted to his place in the grassy circle.

Serge stood up and for a second the earth tilted. Then he dropped to the ground next to Andrews.

"The reason for all that was to prove a point," shouted Randolph to the sprawling broken circle of cadets. "I told Plebesly to resist. That's all. Just to resist and not let them pin his arms. You'll notice he didn't fight back. He just resisted. And Andrews and Duran are both twice his size. They would never have got their man handcuffed. They would have lost him eventually. The point is that they were expending twice the energy to overcome his resistance and they couldn't do it. Now, every one of you guys is going to run into this kind of problem lots of times. Maybe your man is going to decide you aren't going to handcuff him. Or maybe he'll even fight back. You saw the trouble little Plebesly gave the two big guys, and he wasn't even fighting back. What I'm trying to do is tell you that these fights out there in the streets are just endurance contests. The guy who can *endure* usually wins. That's why I'm running your asses off. When you leave here you'll have endurance. Now, if I can teach you an armlock and that choke hold, maybe that will be enough. You all saw what the choke can do. The trouble is getting the choke on the guy when he's struggling and fighting back. I can't teach you self-defense in thirteen weeks.

"All that Hollywood crap is just that—crap. You try throwing that haymaker at somebody's chin and you'll probably hit the top of his head and break your hand. Never use your fists. If someone uses his fists you use your stick and try to break a wrist or knee like we teach you. If he uses a knife you use a gun and cancel his ticket then and there. But if you find yourself without a stick and the situation doesn't permit deadly force, well then you better be able to out-endure the son of a bitch. That's why you see these newspaper pictures of six cops subduing one guy. *Any* guy or even any woman can wear out several policemen just by resisting. It's goddamn hard to take a man who doesn't want to be taken. But try explaining it to the jury or the neighbors who read in the papers how an arrestee was hurt by two or three cops twice his size. They'll want to know why you resorted to beating the guy's head in. Why didn't you just put a fancy judo hold on him and flip him on his ass. In the movies it's nothing.

"And while I'm on the subject, there's something else the movies have done for us—they created a legend about winging your man, shooting from the hip and all that bullshit. Well I'm not your shooting instructor but it all ties in with self-defense. You guys have been here long enough to know how hard it is to hit a still target, let alone a moving one. Those of you who make your twenty years will miss that goddamn paper man every time you come up here for your monthly pistol qualification. And he's only a paper man. He don't shoot back. The light's good and the adrenalin hasn't turned your arm into a licorice stick like it does in combat. And yet when you blow some asshole up and were lucky to even hit him you'll hear a member of the coroner's jury say, 'Why didn't you shoot to wound him? Did you have to kill him? Why didn't you shoot the gun out of his hand!' "

Randolph's face was crimson and two wide sweat streams ran down either side of his neck. When he was in uniform he wore three service stripes on his sleeve indicating at least fifteen years with the Department. Yet Serge could hardly believe he was more than thirty. He hadn't a gray hair and his physique was flawless.

"What I want you guys to take from my class is this: it's a bitch to subdue a man with a gun or a stick or a sap, let alone with your hands. Just keep yourself in half-assed condition and you'll *out-endure* him. Take the bastard any way you can. If you can use these two or three holds I teach you, then use them. If you can't, hit him with a brick or anything else. Just subdue your man and you'll be in one piece the day your twentieth anniversary rolls around and you sign those retirement papers. That's why I run your asses off."

2

Stress

"I don't know why I'm so nervous," said Gus Plebesly. "We've been told about the stress interview. It's just to shake us up."

"Relax, Gus," said Wilson, who leaned against the wall, smoking, careful not to drop ashes on the khaki cadet uniform.

Gus admired the luster of Wilson's black shoes. Wilson had been a marine. He knew how to spit-shine shoes, and he could drill troops and call cadence. He was Gus's squad leader and had many of the qualities which Gus believed men could only gain in military service. Gus wished he were a veteran and had been places, then perhaps he would have confidence. He should have. He was the number one man in his class in physical training, but at this moment he wasn't sure he would be able to speak during the stress interview. He had waited in dread so many times in high school when he had to give an oral report. In college he had once consumed almost a half pint of gin diluted with soda pop before he could give a three-minute speech in a public speaking class. And he had gotten away with it. He wished he could do it now. But these men were police officers. Professionals. They would detect the alcohol in his eyes, speech, or gait. He couldn't fool them with so cheap a trick.

"You sure look nervous," said Wilson, offering Gus a cigarette from the pack he kept in his sock, GI fashion.

"Thanks a lot, Wilson," Gus mumbled, refusing the cigarette.

"Look, these guys are just going to try to psyche you," said Wilson. "I talked to a guy who graduated in April. They just pick on you in these stress interviews. You know, about your P.T. or your shooting, or maybe your academic standing. But hell, Plebesly, you're okay in everything and tops in P.T. What can they say?"

"I don't know. Nothing, I guess."

"Take me," said Wilson. "My shooting is so shitty I might as well throw my gun at the goddamn target. They'll probably rip me apart. Tell me how they're going to wash me out if I don't come to the pistol range during the lunch hour and practice extra. That kind of bullshit. But I'm not worried. You realize how bad they need cops in this town? And in the next five, six years it's going to get lots worse. All those guys that came on right after the war will have their twenty years. I tell you we'll all be captains before we finish our tours with the Department."

Gus studied Wilson, a short man, even a hair shorter than Gus. He must have stretched to meet the minimum five feet eight inches, Gus thought, but husky, big biceps and a fighter's shoulders, with a broken nose. He had wrestled Wilson in the self-defense classes and had found Wilson surprisingly easy to take down and control. Wilson was much stronger, but Gus was more agile and could persevere.

Gus understood what Officer Randolph had told them, and he believed that if he could outlast his opponents he needn't be afraid. He was surprised at how well it had worked so far in training. But what would a man like Wilson, an ex-fighter, do to him in a real fight? Gus had never hit a man, not with a fist, not with anything. What would happen to his splendid endurance when a man like Wilson buried a heavy fist in his stomach or crashed one to his jaw? He had been a varsity sprinter in high school, but had always avoided contact sports. He had never been an aggressive person. What in the hell had made him think he could be a policeman? Sure the pay was pretty good, what with the security and pension. He could never hope to do as well in the bank. He had hated that dreary low paying job and had almost laughed when the operations officer had assured him that in five more years he could expect to make what he, the operations officer, was making, which was less than a starting Los Angeles policeman. And so he had come this far. Eight weeks and they hadn't found him out yet. But they might at this stress interview.

"Only one thing worries me," said Wilson. "Know what that is?"

"What?" asked Gus, wiping his wet palms on the legs of the khaki uniform.

"Skeletons. I hear they sometimes rattle the bones in the stress interview. You know how they say the background investigation of all cadets goes on for weeks after we enter the academy."

"Yes?"

"Well, I hear they sometimes use the stress interview to tell a guy he's been washed out. You know, like, 'The background investigator discovered you were once a member of the Nazi Bund of Milwaukee. You're washed out, kid.' That kind of bullshit."

"I guess I don't have to worry about my background," Gus smiled feebly. "I've lived in Azusa my whole life."

"Come on, Plebesly, don't tell me there isn't something you've done. Every guy in this class has something in his background. Some little thing that he wouldn't want the Department to find out. I saw the faces that day when the instructor said, 'Mosley, report to the lieutenant.' And Mosley never came back to class. And then Ratcliffe left the same way. They found out something about them and they were washed out. Just like that, they disappeared. You ever read *Nineteen Eighty-Four*?''

''No, but I know about it,'' said Gus.

''It's the same principle here. They know none of us has told them everything. We all got a secret. Maybe they can stress it out of us. But just keep cool, and don't tell them anything. You'll be okay.''

Gus's heart sank when the door to the captain's office opened and Cadet Roy Fehler strode out, tall, straight, and as confident as always. Gus envied him his assurance and hardly heard Fehler say, ''Next man.''

Then Wilson was shoving him toward the door and he looked at his reflection in the mirror on the cigarette machine and the milky blue eyes were his, but he hardly recognized the thin white face. The sparse sandy hair seemed familiar but the narrow white lips were not his, and he was through the door and facing the three inquisitors who looked at him from behind a conference table. He recognized Lieutenant Hartley and Sergeant Jacobs. He knew the third man must be the commander, Captain Smithson, who had addressed them the first day in the academy.

''Sit down, Plebesly,'' said unsmiling Lieutenant Hartley.

The three men whispered for a moment and reviewed a sheaf of papers before them. The lieutenant, a florid bald man with plum-colored lips, suddenly grinned broadly and said, ''Well, so far you're doing fine here at the academy, Plebesly. You might work on your shooting a bit, but in the classroom you're excellent and on the P.T. field you're tops.''

Gus became aware that the captain and Sergeant Jacobs were also smiling, but he suspected trickery when the captain said, ''What shall we talk about? Would you like to tell us about yourself?''

''Yes sir,'' said Gus, trying to adjust to the unexpected friendliness.

''Well, go ahead then, Plebesly,'' said Sergeant Jacobs with an amused look. ''Tell us all about yourself. We're listening.''

''Tell us about your college training,'' said Captain Smithson after several silent seconds. ''Your personnel folder says you attended junior college for two years. Were you an athlete?''

''No sir,'' croaked Gus. ''I mean I tried out for track. I didn't have time, though.''

''I'll bet you were a sprinter,'' smiled the lieutenant.

''Yes sir, and I tried hurdles,'' said Gus, trying to smile back. ''I had to work and carry fifteen units, sir. I had to quit track.''

''What was your major?'' asked Captain Smithson.

''Business administration,'' said Gus, wishing he had added ''sir,'' and thinking that a veteran like Wilson would never fail to throw a sir into every sentence, but he was not accustomed to this quasi-military situation.

''What kind of work did you do before coming on the Department?'' asked Captain Smithson, leafing through the folder. ''Post Office, wasn't it?''

''No sir. Bank. I worked at a bank. Four years. Ever since high school.''

''What made you want to be a policeman?'' asked the captain, touching the gaunt tanned cheek with a pencil.

''The pay and the security,'' Gus answered, and then quickly, ''and it's a good career, a profession. And I like it so far.''

''Poicemen don't make very good pay,'' said Sergeant Jacobs.

''It's the most I ever made, sir,'' said Gus, deciding to be truthful. ''I never made anywhere near four eighty-nine a month before, sir. And I have two children and one on the way.''

''You're only twenty-two years old,'' Sergeant Jacobs whistled. ''What a family you're making.''

''We were married right after high school.''

''Do you intend to finish college?'' asked Lieutenant Hartley.

''Oh, yes sir,'' said Gus. ''I'm going to switch my major to police science, sir.''

"Business administration is a good field of study," said Captain Smithson. "If you like it, stay with it. The Department can find good use for business administration majors."

"Yes sir," said Gus.

"That's all, Plebesly," said Captain Smithson. "Keep working on your shooting. It could be better. And send in the next cadet, please."

3

The Scholar

Roy Fehler had to admit it pleased him when he overheard two of his classmates mention his name in a whispered conversation during a smoking break after class. He heard the cadet mutter "intellectual," reverently, he thought, just after he recorded the highest score in the report writing class conducted by Officer Willis. He found the academic portion of recruit training unchallenging and if it weren't for some difficulties on the pistol range and his lack of endurance on the P.T. field, he would probably be the top cadet in his class and win the Smith & Wesson always awarded to the top cadet at graduation. It would be a tragedy, he thought, if someone like Plebesly won the revolver merely because he could run faster or shoot better than Roy.

He was anxious for Sergeant Harris to come in the classroom for their three hours of criminal law. It was the most stimulating part of recruit training even though Harris was only an adequate teacher. Roy had bought a copy of Fricke's *California Criminal Law,* and had read it twice in the past two weeks. He had challenged Harris on several points of law and believed that Harris had become more alert of late for fear of being embarrassed by a knowledgeable recruit. The classroom quieted abruptly.

Sergeant Harris strode to the front of the class, spread his notes on the lectern and lit the first of the several cigarettes he would smoke during his lecture. He had a face like porous concrete, but Roy thought he wore his uniform well. The tailored blue wool seemed particularly attractive on tall slim men, and Roy wondered how he would look when he had the blue uniform and black Sam Browne.

"We're going to continue with search and seizure of evidence," said Harris, scratching the bald spot at the crown of his rust-colored hair.

"By the way, Fehler," said Sergeant Harris, "you were right yesterday about the uncorroborated testimony of an accomplice being sufficient to prove the corpus delicti. But it isn't enough to convict."

"No, of course not," said Roy, nodding his thanks to Harris for the acknowledgment. He wasn't sure whether Harris appreciated the significance of a few well-placed brain-teasing questions. It was the student who brought a class to life. He had learned this from Professor Raymond who had encouraged him to specialize in criminology when he was drifting aimlessly in the social sciences unable to find a specialty which really interested him. And it was Professor Raymond who begged him not to drop out of college, because he had added so much to the three classes he had taken from the kindly round little man with the burning brown eyes. But he was tired of college; even the independent study with Professor Raymond had begun to bore him. It had come to him suddenly one sleepless night when the presence of Dorothy and her pregnancy was oppressing him that he ought to leave college and join the police department for a year, two years, until he learned something of crime and criminals that might not be available to the criminologist.

The next day he applied at City Hall wondering if he should phone his father or wait until he was actually sworn in, as he would be in about three months, if he passed all the tests and survived the character investigation which he knew would pose no problem. His father was terribly disappointed and his older brother Carl had reminded him that his education had already cost the family business in excess of nine thousand dollars, especially since he could not wait until he finished college to marry, and that in any event, a criminologist would be of little use to a restaurant supply business. Roy had told Carl that he would pay back every cent, and he certainly intended to, but it was difficult living on the policeman's beginning salary which was not the advertised four hundred and eighty-nine dollars a month—not when they deducted for your pension, Police Relief, the Police Protective League, the Police Credit Union which loaned the money for the uniforms, income tax, and the medical plan. But he vowed he'd pay Carl and his father every cent. And he'd finish college and be a criminologist eventually, never making the money his brother Carl would make, but being infinitely happier.

"Yesterday we talked about the famous cases like Cahan, Rochin, and others," said Sergeant Harris. "And we talked about Mapp versus Ohio which any rookie would know was illegal search and seizure, and I mentioned how it sometimes seems to policemen that the court is lying in wait for bad cases like Mapp versus Ohio so they can restrict police power a little more. Now that you're policemen, or almost policemen, you're going to become very interested in the decisions handed down by the courts in the area of search and seizure. You're going to be upset, confused, and generally pissed off most of the time, and you're going to hear locker room bitching about the fact that most landmark decisions are five to four, and how can a working cop be expected to make a sudden decision in the heat of combat and then be second-guessed by the Vestal Virgins of the Potomac, and all that other crap. But in my opinion, that kind of talk is self-defeating. We're only concerned with the U.S. and California supreme courts and a couple of appellate courts. So don't worry about some of these freakish decisions that an individual judge hands down. Even if it's your case and it's one you wanted to win. Chances are the defendant will be busted again before long and we'll get another crack at him. And the judge's decision ends right there on the bench. It's not going to have a goddamn thing to do with the next case you try.

"Now I know I got you guys pretty confused yesterday with the problems of search incident to a lawful arrest. We know we can search when?" Sergeant Harris waved a burning cigarette vaguely toward the rear of the room.

Roy didn't bother to turn toward the voice which answered, "When you have a search warrant, or when you have consent, or incident to a lawful arrest." The voice Roy knew belonged to Samuel Isenberg, the only other cadet whom Roy felt might challenge him scholastically.

"Right," said Sergeant Harris, blowing a cloud of smoke through his nose. "Half you people will never get a search warrant in your entire careers. Most of the two hundred thousand arrests we make in a year are made on the basis of reasonable cause to believe a felony has been committed, or because a crime has been committed in the officer's presence. You're going to stumble onto crimes and criminals and bang! You've got to move, not take six hours to get a search warrant. It's for that reason that we're not going to talk about this kind of search. I've saved the other kind of search until today because to me it's the most challenging—that's search incident to a lawful arrest. If the court ever takes this kind of search away from us we'll be nearly out of business."

Isenberg raised his hand, and Sergeant Harris nodded while taking an incredible puff on the cigarette. What was a fairly good-sized butt was now scorching his fingers. He snuffed it out as Isenberg said, ''Would you repeat, sir, about the search of the premises ninety-five feet from the defendant's house?''

''I was afraid of that.'' Harris smiled, shrugged, and lit another cigarette. ''I shouldn't bring up those cases. I did what I criticize other officers for doing, bitching about controversial cases and prophesying doom. Okay. I just said that it hasn't yet been defined what *under the defendant's control* means in terms of search of the premises incident to the arrest. The court has deemed in its infinite wisdom that an arrest ninety-five feet away from the house did not give oficers the right to go into the house and search under the theory of the defendant having control of the premises. Also, I mentioned that in another case a person sixty feet away was deemed to have control of a car in question. And then I mentioned a third case in which officers arrested some bookmakers in their car a half block away and the court held the search of the car and premises was reasonable.

''But don't worry about that kind of crap. I shouldn't have mentioned it anyway because I'm basically an optimist. I always see the glass half full not half empty. Some policemen predict that the courts will eventually strip us of all our right to search incident to arrest, but that would cripple us. I don't think it will happen. I feel that one of these days the Chief Sorcerer in Washington and his eight little apprentices will get themselves together and all this will be straightened out.''

The class tittered and Roy felt himself becoming irked. Harris just couldn't resist criticizing the Supreme Court, thought Roy. He hadn't heard any instructor discuss the law without taking a few shots at the Court. Harris seemed reasonable but he probably felt obligated to do it too. So far, all of the cases Roy had read, that were so bitterly opposed by the instructors, seemed to him just and intelligent. They were based on libertarian principles and it seemed to him unfair to say such thoughtful decisions were unrealistic.

''Okay you guys, quit leading me off on tangents. We're supposed to be talking about searches incident to a lawful arrest. How about this one: Two officers observe a cab double-parked in front of a hotel. The fare, a man, gets out of the front seat. A woman comes out of the hotel and gets in the rear seat. Another man not with the woman walks up and gets in the back seat with the woman. Two policemen observe the action and decide to investigate. They approach and order the occupants out of the cab. They observe the man remove his hand from the juncture of the seat and back cushion. The officers remove the rear cushion and find three marijuana cigarettes. The man was convicted. Was the decision affirmed or denied by the appellate court? Anyone want to make a guess?''

''Denied,'' said Guminski, a thin, wiry-haired man of about thirty, whom Roy guessed to be the oldest cadet in the class.

''See. You guys are already thinking like cops,'' Harris chuckled. ''You're ready to believe the courts are screwing us every time. Well you're wrong. The conviction was affirmed. But there was something I failed to mention that contributed to the decision. What do you think it might be?''

Roy raised his hand and when Harris nodded, Roy asked, ''What time of day was it?''

''Good,'' said Sergeant Harris. ''You might've guessed, it was an unusual hour. About 3:00 A.M. Now on what grounds could they search the cab?''

''Incident to a lawful arrest,'' said Roy, without raising his hand or waiting for Harris to nod.

''Who were they arresting?'' asked Harris.

Roy was sorry he had responded so quickly. He realized he was being trapped. ''Not the defendant or the woman,'' he said slowly, while his mind worked furiously. ''The cabdriver!''

The class burst out laughing but was silenced by a wave of Harris' nicotine-stained left hand. Harris bared his large brownish teeth in a grin and said, ''Go ahead, Fehler, what's your reasoning?''

"They could arrest the cabbie for double-parking," said Roy. "That's a violation, and then search incident to the lawful arrest."

"Not bad," said Harris. "I like to see you people thinking even when you're wrong."

Hugh Franklin, the broad-shouldered recruit who sat next to Roy at the alphabetically arranged tables, chuckled louder than Roy felt was necessary. Franklin did not like him, Roy was certain. Franklin was an all-American jock strapper. A high school letterman according to the conversations they had the first few days in the academy. Then three years in the navy, where he played baseball and toured the Orient, thoroughly enjoying himself, and now to the police department, when he couldn't make it in Class D professional baseball.

"Why is Fehler wrong?" Harris asked the class, and Roy became annoyed that the entire class should be asked to attack his answer. Why didn't Harris just give the reason instead of asking everyone to comment? Could it be that Harris was trying to embarrass him? Perhaps he didn't like having a recruit in the class who took the trouble to do independent study in criminal law and not just blindly accept the legal interpretations which evolve from the police point of view.

"Yes, Isenberg," said Harris, and this time Roy turned around so that he would not miss Isenberg's annoying manner of answering questions.

"I doubt that the search of the cab could be justified incident to the arrest of the driver for double-parking," said Isenberg carefully, his dark-lidded black eyes moving from Harris to Roy and back to the instructor. "It's true the driver committed a traffic violation and could be cited, and a traffic ticket is technically an arrest, but how could you search the cab for contraband? That has nothing to do with a traffic violation, does it?"

"Are you asking me?" said Harris.

"No sir, that's my answer." Isenberg smiled shyly, and Roy felt disgust for Isenberg's pretense at humility. He felt the same toward Plebesly and the diffidence he showed when someone expressed admiration for his athletic prowess. He believed them both to be conceited men. Isenberg was another one, he knew, who was just discharged from the army. He wondered how many men joined the Department because they were simply looking for a job and how many like himself had more serious motives.

"Was the search incident to the arrest of anyone?" asked Harris.

"No. I don't think so," said Isenberg, clearing his throat nervously. "I don't think anyone was under arrest at the time the officer found the contraband. The officer could detain and interrogate people under unusual circumstances at night according to Giske versus Sanders, and I don't think there was anything unreasonable in ordering them out of the cab. The officers had a justifiable suspicion that something unusual was going on. When the defendant reached behind the seat I think that might be construed as a furtive action." Isenberg's voice trailed off and several recruits including Roy raised their hands.

Harris looked at no one but Roy. "Go ahead, Fehler," he said.

"I don't think the officers had the right to order them out of the cab. And when were they arrested, after they found the narcotics? What if they would have got out of the cab and just walked away? Would the officers have the right to stop them?"

"How about that, Isenberg?" asked Harris, lighting a fresh cigarette with a battered silver lighter. "Could the officers stop them from walking away, before the contraband was found?"

"Uh, yes, I think so," said Isenberg looking at Roy, who interrupted him.

"Were they under arrest then?" asked Roy. "They must have been under arrest if the officers could stop them from walking away. And if they were under arrest what was their crime? The marijuana wasn't found for several seconds after they had them already under arrest."

Roy smiled indulgently to show Isenberg and Harris there were no hard feelings at having proved Isenberg wrong.

"The point is, they were not under arrest, Fehler," said Isenberg, addressing Roy directly for the first time. "We have the right to stop and interrogate. The person is obliged to identify himself and explain what's going on. And we can resort to any means to make him submit. Yet we haven't arrested him for any crime. If he explains what's going on and it's reasonable, we release him. I think that's what Giske versus Sanders meant. So in this case, the officers stopped, interrogated, and recovered the marijuana during their investigation. Then and only then were the suspects placed under arrest."

Roy knew from Harris' pleased expression that Isenberg was correct.

"How could you prove someone else hadn't dumped the marijuana behind the seat?" asked Roy, unable to dull the sharp edge on his voice.

"I should've mentioned that the cabbie testified to cleaning out the back of the cab earlier in the evening because of a sick passenger who threw up back there," said Harris. "And no one had been in the back seat until the woman and the defendant got in."

"That certainly makes a difference," said Roy, appealing to Harris for some concession to his interpretation.

"Well, that wasn't the issue I was concerned with," said Harris. "It was the question of searching prior to an actual arrest that I wanted someone to bring out of this case, and Isenberg did it beautifuly. You all understand, don't you?"

"Yes sir," said Roy, "but the case would certainly have been reversed if the cabbie hadn't testified to cleaning out the back that same evening. That was certainly an important point, sir."

"Yes, Fehler," Sergeant Harris sighed. "You were partly right. I should've mentioned that, Fehler."

August 1960

4

Huero

SERGE GAVE his shoes a quick buff, threw the shoe brush in his locker, and slammed the metal door. He was late for roll call. It was two minutes after four o'clock. Damn the traffic, he thought. How can I put up with this traffic and smog for twenty years? He paused before the full-length mirror, alone in the locker room. His brass buttons and Sam Browne needed polish. His blue woolen uniform was so lint covered it looked hairy. He cursed as he realized there might be an inspection tonight.

Serge picked up his notebook, the packet of traffic citations and a map book of city streets. He shoved his shiny new five-cell flashlight into the deep pocket of his uniform pants, grabbed his baton, and put his hat on, since his hands were too full to carry it. The other night watch officers were talking noisily as he entered the roll call room. The watch commander's desk was unoccupied. Serge was relieved to see that he too was late and by the time he arrived five minutes later, Serge had dabbed most of the lint from his uniform with a piece of two-inch-wide masking tape which he carried in his notebook for such emergencies.

"After those new uniforms are cleaned a few times you won't have so much trouble with lint," said Perkins, the desk officer, a nineteen-year policeman now on light duty while recovering from a serious heart attack.

"Oh, yeah," Serge nodded, self-conscious of his brand new, never cleaned blue uniform, announcing that he was one of the rookies just graduated last week from the academy. He and two members of his class had been assigned to Hollenbeck. It wasn't hard to see how they had been selected, he thought. The other officers were Chacon and Medina. He had heard in the academy that most officers with Spanish surnames ended up in Hollenbeck Division but he had hoped he might be an exception. Not everyone recognized Duran as a Spanish name. He had been mistaken for German and even Irish, especially by people who couldn't believe a Mexican could be fair, freckled, and speak without a trace of a Spanish accent. The Negro officers were not all assigned to the Negro areas; he was irked that the Chicanos were all stuck here in Hollenbeck. He could see the need for Spanish-speaking officers here, but nobody had even bothered to see if he could speak Spanish. It was just "Duran to Hollenbeck," another victim of a system.

"Ramirez," said Lieutenant Jethro, settling his long sagging body in the desk chair and opening the time book.

"Here."

"Anderson."

"Here."

"You're working Four-A-Five."

"Bradbury."

"Here."

"Gonsalvez."

"Here."

"Four-A-Eleven."

Serge answered when his name was called along with his partner for the night, Galloway, whom he had not worked with since arriving in the division. He was scheduled off tomorrow, Sunday, after working six days, and wished he weren't. Every night was a new adventure and he smiled as he reaalized he would probably be glad for days off soon enough. He tired of everything quickly. Still, this was a more interesting job than most. He couldn't honestly think of one he'd like better. Of course, when he finished college, he might find something better. And then he had to smile again at himself. He had enrolled in two night classes at East Los Angeles Junior College. Six units. Only a hundred and eighteen to go, and here I sit dreaming about finishing college, he thought.

"Okay, here's the crimes," said the lieutenant, after calling the roll. Perkins took the lineup board downstairs to the teletype machine to be forwarded to Communications, so that Communications downtown would know which cars were working in Hollenbeck. The policemen opened their notebooks to a fresh page, and got ready to write.

Lieutenant Jethro was a loose-skinned, sallow man with a hard mouth and very cold eyes. Serge had learned however that he was the division's best-liked supervisor. The men considered him fair.

"Had a robbery at twenty-nine twenty-two Brooklyn Avenue," he read mechanically. "At Big G restaurant. Today, 9:30 A.M. Suspect: male, Mexican, twenty-three to twenty-five years, five-five to five-six, hundred sixty to hundred seventy pounds, black hair, brown eyes, medium complexion, wearing a dark shirt and dark pants, carried a hand gun, got eighty-five dollars from the cash register and took victim's wallet and I.D. . . . Goddamn it, that's a shitty description!" said Lieutenant Jethro suddenly. "This is what we were talking about last night at roll call training. What the hell good does a description like that do you?"

"Maybe that's all they could get out of the guy, Lieutenant," said Milton, the burly baiter of supervisors who always took the last seat of the last table in the roll call room, and whose four service stripes, indicating twenty years service, entitled him to a constant barrage of sarcasm directed at the sergeants. He was usually pretty quiet around the lieutenant though, Serge thought.

"Bullshit, Milt," said Jethro. "This poor bastard Hector Lopez has been hit a half dozen times this year. I'm always seeing his name on robbery, burglary, or till tap reports. He's become a professional victim, and he usually gives an outstanding description of the suspect. It's just that some officer—in this case, it was a day watch officer—was in a big hurry and didn't try to get a decent description. This is a good example of a worthless piece of paper that can't be any use to the detectives. That description could fit twenty percent of the guys on the street right now."

"It only takes a few minutes extra to get a decent description the dicks can work with," Jethro continued. "How did the guy comb his hair? Did he have a moustache? Glasses? Tattoos? A distinctive walk? How about his teeth? His clothes? There's dozens of little things about clothes that might be important. How did he talk? Did he have a gravel voice? Did he have a Spanish accent? How about that gun? This report says handgun. What the hell does that tell you? I know goddamn well Lopez knows the difference between an automatic and a revolver. And was it chrome plated or blue steel?" Jethro dropped the papers disgustedly into the folder. "We had lots of crimes last night, but none of the suspect descriptions are worth a shit so I'm not going to read them." He closed the folders and sat back in his chair on the ten-inch platform, looking down at the policemen of the night watch. "Anything you guys want to talk about before we have an inspection?" he asked.

A groan went up at the mention of the word inspection, and Serge rubbed the toes of each shoe on the back of his calves, irritated once more at the Los Angeles traffic which prevented him from arriving at the station early enough to shine them.

Jethro's colorless eyes glinted merrily around the room for a moment. "If no one can think of something to say, we might as well get started with the inspection. We'll have more time to look a little harder."

"Wait a minute, Lieutenant," said Milton, a wet stump of cigar between his little teeth. "Give me a second, I'll think of something."

"Yeah, Milt, I don't blame you for wanting to stall me," said Jethro. "It looks like you shined those shoes with a Hershey bar."

The men chuckled and Milton beamed and puffed from the end seat at the last row of tables in the rear of the squad room. On his first night in Hollenbeck, Milton had informed Serge that the last row of tables belonged to *los veteranos* and that rookies generally sat toward the front of the room. Serge hadn't worked with Milton yet, and was looking forward to it. He was loud and overbearing but the men told him he could learn a lot from Milton if Milton felt like teaching him.

"One thing before inspection," said Jethro. "Who's working Forty-three tonight? You, Galloway?"

Serge's partner nodded.

"Who's working with you, one of the new men? Duran, right? You two check those pin maps before you go out. They're killing us on Brooklyn Avenue about midnight. We've had three window smashes this week and two last week. All about the same time, and they're grabbing quite a bit of loot."

Serge looked at the walls which were lined with identical street maps of Hollenbeck Division. Each map bore different colored pins, some to indicate burglaries, the multicolored pins indicating whether they occurred on morning, day, or night watch. Other maps showed where robberies were occurring. Still others showed locations of car thefts and thefts from vehicles.

"Let's fall in for inspection," said Lieutenant Jethro.

This was Serge's first inspection since leaving the academy. He wondered where fourteen men could line up in the crowded room. He saw quickly that they formed one rank along the side wall in front of the pin maps. The tall men fell in toward the front of the room so Serge headed for the front, standing next to Bressler, who was the only officer taller than himself.

"Okay, you're supposed to be at attention," said the Lieutenant quietly to a policeman in the center of the rank who was muttering about something.

"At close interval, dress right, dress!"

The policemen, hands on right hips, elbows touching the man to the right, dressed the rank perfunctorily and Jethro didn't bother to check the line.

"Ready, front!"

When Jethro inspected him, Serge stared at the top of the lieutenant's head as he had been taught in boot camp six years ago when he was eighteen, just graduated from high school, broken-hearted that the Korean War ended before he could get in it and win several pounds of medals which he could pin to the beautiful Marine Corps dress blue uniform which they didn't issue you and he never got around to buying because he grew up quickly under the stunning realities of Marine Corps boot camp.

Jethro paused a few extra seconds in front of Ruben Gonsalvez, a jovial dark-skinned Mexican who, Serge guessed, was a veteran of at least ten years with the Department.

"You're getting rounder every day, Ruben," said Jethro in his toneless unsmiling voice.

"Yes, Lieutenant," answered Gonsalvez and Serge did not yet dare to look down the line.

''You been eating at Manuel's again, I see,'' said Jethro, and with peripheral vision Serge could see the lieutenant touching Gonsalvez's necktie.

''Yes, sir,'' said Gonsalvez. ''The top stains above the tie bar are *chile verde*. The other ones are *menudo*.''

This time Serge turned a fraction of an inch and detected no expression on Jethro or Gonsalvez.

''How about you, Milt? When you changing the oil on your necktie?'' said Jethro, moving down the line to the white-haired veteran who stood so straight he looked like a tall man but standing next to him Serge guessed he wasn't five feet ten.

''Right after inspection, Lieutenant,'' said Milton, and Serge sneaked a glance at Jethro, who shook his head sadly and moved to the end of the rank.

''Night watch. One pace forward . . . No, as you were,'' said Jethro, shuffling to the front of the roll call room. ''I'm afraid to inspect you from the rear. Some of you'll probably have bananas or girlie magazines hanging out of your back pockets. Dis-missed!''

So this is how it is, thought Serge, gathering up his equipment, looking for Galloway to whom he had never been introduced. He was afraid the division would be GI and he wasn't sure how long he could take military discipline. This was okay. He could tolerate this much discipline indefinitely, he thought.

Galloway walked up and offered his hand. ''Duran?''

''Yeah,'' said Serge, shaking hands with the freckled young man.

''What do your friends call you?'' asked Galloway and Serge smiled as he recognized the hackneyed opening line that policemen use on suspects to determine street names which were usually much more valuable to know than true names.

''Serge. How about you?''

''Pete.''

''Okay, Pete, what do you want to do tonight?'' asked Serge, hoping that Galloway would let him drive. This was his sixth night and he hadn't driven yet.

''You're just out of the last class, aren't you?'' asked Galloway.

''Yeah,'' said Serge, disappointed.

''You familiar with the city?''

''No, I lived in Chino before coming on the job.''

''Guess you better keep books then. I'll drive, okay?''

''You're the boss,'' Serge said cheerfully.

''No, we're equals,'' said Galloway. ''Partners.''

It was satisfying to be able to get settled in the radio car without asking a dozen inane questions or fumbling around with your equipment. Serge felt he could handle the passenger officer's routine duties as well as possible by now. Serge put his flashlight and hat in the back seat along with his baton which was thrust under the back cushion for easy access. He was surprised to see Galloway slide the baton under the back cushion in the front seat, lancelike, right next to him.

''I like my stick closer to me,'' said Galloway. ''It's my blue blanket.''

''Four-A-Forty-three, night watch, clear,'' said Serge into the hand mike as Galloway started the engine of the Plymouth, and backed out of the parking space and onto First Street, the setting sun forcing Serge to put on his sunglasses as he wrote their names on the daily log.

''What did you do before coming on the job?'' asked Galloway.

''Marine Corps for four years,'' said Serge, writing his serial number on the log.

''How do you like police work so far?'' asked Galloway.

''Fine,'' Serge answered, writing carefully as the car bounced over a rut in the street.

''It's a good job,'' said Galloway. ''I'm starting my fourth year next month. Can't complain so far.''

The sandy hair and freckles made Galloway look like a high school kid, Serge thought. With four years on the job he has to be at least twenty-five.

"This your first Saturday night?"

"Yeah."

"Quite a difference on weekends. Maybe we'll see a little action."

"Hope so."

"Done anything exciting yet?"

"Nothing," said Serge. "Took some burglary reports. Wrote a few tickets. Booked a couple drunks and a few traffic warrants. Haven't even made a felony arrest yet."

"We'll try to get you a felony tonight." Galloway offered Serge a cigarette and he accepted.

"Thanks. I was going to ask you to stop so I could get some," said Serge, lighting Galloway's with his Zippo that used to have a brass globe and anchor affixed to it. There was now just a naked metallic ring on the lighter where he had pried the Marine Corps emblem off in Okinawa after a salty pfc with a year and a half in the corps had kidded him about only gung-ho recruits carrying P.X. Zippos with big fat emblems on them.

Serge smiled as he remembered how badly the young marines wanted to be salts. How they had scrubbed and bleached their new dungarees and put sea dips in the caps. He hadn't completely gotten over it, he thought, remembering how his new blue uniform made him uneasy tonight when Perkins mentioned the lint.

The incessant chattering on the police radio was still giving Serge trouble. He knew it would be some time before he was able to pick his car number, Four-A-Forty-three, from the jumble of voices that crowded the police frequencies. He was starting to recognize some of the voices of the Communications operators. One sounded like an old maid schoolmarm, another like a youngish Marilyn Monroe, and a third had a trace of a Southern accent.

"We got a call," said Galloway.

"What?"

"Tell her to repeat," said Galloway.

"Four-A-Forty-three, repeat, please," said Serge, his pencil poised over the pad which was affixed to a metal shelf in front of the hot sheet.

"Four-A-Forty-three," said the schoolmarm, "one-two-seven South Chicago, see the woman, four-five-nine report."

"Four-A-Forty-three, roger," said Serge. And to Galloway, "Sorry. I can't pick our calls out of all that noise, yet."

"Takes a little time," said Galloway, turning around in a gas station parking lot, heading east toward Chicago Street.

"Where you living?" asked Galloway, as Serge took a deep puff on the cigarette to finish it before they arrived.

"Alhambra. I got an apartment over there."

"Guess Chino's too far to drive, huh?"

"Yeah."

"Married?"

"No," said Serge.

"Got parents in Chino?"

"No, they're both dead. Got an older brother there. And a sister in Pomona."

"Oh," said Galloway, looking at him like he was a war orphan.

"I have a nice little apartment, and the apartment house is crawling with broads," said Serge, so his baby faced partner would stop being embarrassed at prying.

"Really?" Galloway grinned. "Must be nice being a bachelor. I got hooked at nineteen, so I wouldn't know."

After turning north on Chicago Street, Galloway gave Serge a puzzled look as Serge craned his neck to catch the house numbers on the east side of the street.

"One twenty-seven will be on the west," said Galloway. "Even numbers are always on the east and south."

"All over the city?"

"All over," Galloway laughed. "Hasn't anybody told you that yet?"

"Not yet. I've been checking both sides of the street on every call. Pretty dumb."

"Sometimes the senior officer forgets to mention the obvious. As long as you're willing to admit you know nothing, you'll learn fast enough. Some guys hate to show they don't know anything."

Serge was out of the car while Galloway was still applying the emergency brake. He removed his stick from the back seat and slid it in through the baton holder on the left side of his Sam Browne. He noticed that Galloway left his baton in the car, but he guessed he should adhere to the rules very closely for a while, and the rule was carry your batons.

The house was a one-story faded pink frame. Most of the houses in East Los Angeles seemed faded. This was an old part of the city. The streets were narrow and Serge noticed many aged people.

"Come in, come in, gentlemen," said the snuffling puckered old woman in an olive-drab dress and bandaged legs, as they stepped on the tiny porch one at a time, shouldering their way through a forest of potted ferns and flowers.

"Step right in, right in," she smiled and Serge was surprised to see a mouthful of what he was sure were real teeth. She should have been toothless. A fleshy goiter dropped from her neck.

"It's not so often we see the policemen these days," she smiled. "We used to know all the police at the Boyle Heights station. I used to know some officers' names, but already they're retired I guess."

Serge smiled at the Molly Goldberg accent, but he noticed Galloway was nodding soberly at the old woman as he sat in the ancient creaking rocker in front of a brightly painted unused fireplace. Serge smelled fish and flowers, mustiness and perfume, and bread in the oven. He removed his cap and sat on the lumpy napless sofa with a cheap oriental tapestry thrown over the back to dull the thrust of the broken springs he felt against his back.

"I'm Mrs. Waxman," said the old woman. "I been right here in this house for thirty-eight years."

"Is that a fact?" said Galloway.

"Would you like something? A cup of coffee, maybe. Or a cupcake?"

"No thank you," said Galloway. Serge shook his head and smiled.

"I used to walk down the police station some summer evenings and chat with the desk officer. There was a Jewish boy worked there named Sergeant Muellstein. You ever know him?"

"No," said Galloway.

"Brooklyn Avenue was really something then. You should have seen Boyle Heights. Some of the finest families in Los Angeles was living here. Then the Mexicans started moving in and all the people ran out and went to the west side. Just the old Jews like me are left with the Mexicans now. What do you think of the church down the street?"

"Which church?" asked Galloway.

"Hah! You don't have to say. I understand you got a job to do." The old woman smiled knowingly at Galloway and winked at Serge.

"They dare to call the place a synagogue," she croaked. "Could you imagine it?"

Serge glanced through the window at the light-studded Star of David atop the First Hebrew Christian Synagogue at the residential corner of Chicago Street and Michigan Avenue.

"You see what's right across the street?" said the old woman.

"What?" asked Serge.

"The United Mexican Baptist Church," said the old woman, with a triumphant nod of her chalk-white head. "I knew it was going to happen. I told them in the forties when they all started moving."

"Told who?" asked Serge, listening intently. "We could have lived with the Mexicans. An Orthodox Jew is like a Catholic Mexican. We could have lived. Now look what we got. Reform Jews was bad enough. Now, Christian Jews? Don't make me laugh. And Mexican Baptisters? You see, everything is out of whack now. Now there's just a few of us old ones left. I don't even go out of my yard, no more."

"I guess you called us because of Mrs. Horwitz," said Galloway, adding to Serge's confusion.

"Yes, it's the same old story. There ain't nobody can get along with the woman," said Mrs. Waxman. "She tells everybody her husband has a better shop than my Morris. Hah! My Morris is a watchmaker. Do you understand? A real watchmaker! A craftsman, not some junk repairman!" The old woman stood up, gesturing angrily at the center of the room as a trickle of saliva ran uncontrolled from the corner of her wrinkled mouth.

"Now, now, Mrs. Waxman," said Galloway, helping her back to the chair. "I'm going right over to Mrs. Horwitz and tell her to stop spreading those stories. If she doesn't, why I'll threaten to put her in jail."

"Would you? Would you do that?" asked the old woman. "But don't arrest her, mind you. Just give her a pretty good scare."

"We're going over there right now," said Galloway, putting on his cap and standing up.

"Serves her right, serves her right," said Mrs. Waxman, beaming at the two young men.

"Good-bye, Mrs. Waxman," said Galloway.

"Bye," Serge mumbled, hoping that Galloway had not noticed how long it took him to catch on to the old woman's senility.

"She's a regular," Galloway explained, starting the car and lighting a cigarette. "I guess I been there a dozen times. The old Jews always say 'Boyle Heights,' never Hollenbeck or East L.A. This *was* the Jewish community before the Chicanos moved in."

"Doesn't she have a family?" asked Serge, marking the call in the log.

"No. Another abandoned old lady," said Galloway. "I'd rather some asshole shoot me in the street tonight than end up old and alone like her."

"Where's Mrs. Horwitz live?"

"Who knows? West side probably, where all the Jews with money went. Or maybe she's dead."

Serge borrowed another of Galloway's cigarettes and relaxed as Galloway patrolled slowly in the late summer dusk. He stopped in front of a liquor store and asked Serge what brand he smoked and entered the store without asking for money. Serge knew that this meant the liquor store was Galloway's cigarette stop, or rather it belonged to the car, Four-A-Forty-three. He had accepted the minor gratuity when each partner he had worked with offered it. Only one, a serious, alert young policeman named Kilton, had stopped at a place where Serge had to pay for cigarettes.

Galloway came back after repaying the liquor store proprietor with a few minutes of small talk and flipped the cigarettes into Serge's lap.

"How about some coffee?" asked Galloway.

"Sounds good."

Galloway made a U-turn and drove to a small sidewalk restaurant on Fourth Street. He parked in the empty parking lot, turned up the police radio and got out leaving the door to the car open so they could hear the radio.

"Hi, baby face," said the bleached blonde working the counter, who spoiled her eyes by drawing her eyebrows at a ridiculous angle.

If there was one thing most Mexicans had it was good heads of hair, thought Serge. Why had this one destroyed hers with chemicals?

"Afternoon, Sylvia," said Galloway. "Meet my partner, Serge Duran."

"Qué tal, huero?" said Sylvia, pouring two steaming cups of coffee which Galloway did not offer to pay for.

"Hi," said Serge, sipping the burning coffee and hoping the remark would pass.

"Huero?" said Galloway. "You a Chicano, Serge?"

"What do you think, *pendejo?"* Sylvia laughed raucously, showing a gold-capped eyetooth. "With a name like Duran?"

"I'll be damned," said Galloway. "You sure look like a paddy."

"He's a real *huero,* baby," said Sylvia with a flirtatious smile at Serge. "He's almost as fair as you."

"Can't we talk about something else?" asked Serge, irritated more at himself for being embarrassed than at these two grinning fools. He told himself he was not ashamed of being Mexican, it was simply less complicated to be an Anglo. And an Anglo he had been for the past five years. He had only returned to Chino a few times after his mother died and one of those times was for a fourteen-day leave with his brother when they buried her. He had tired of the dreary little town in five days and returned to the base, selling his unused leave to the Marine Corps when he was discharged.

"Well, it's good to have a partner who can speak Spanish," said Galloway. "We can use you around here."

"What makes you think I can speak Spanish?" asked Serge, very careful to maintain the narrow cordiality in his voice.

Sylvia looked at Serge strangely, stopped smiling, and returned to the sink where she began washing a small pile of cups and glasses.

"You one of those Chicanos who can't speak Spanish?" Galloway laughed. "We got another one like that, Montez. They transfer him to Hollenbeck and he can't speak Spanish any better than me."

"I don't need it. I get along well enough in English," said Serge.

"Better than me, I hope," smiled Galloway. "If you can't *spell* better than me we'll be in lots of trouble when we make our reports."

Serge gulped down the coffee and waited anxiously as Galloway tried in vain to get Sylvia talking again. She smiled at his jokes but remained at the sink and looked coldly at Serge. "Bye-bye, baby face," she said, as they thanked her for the free coffee and left.

"It's too bad you don't speak Spanish real good," said Galloway as the sun dropped through the smoggy glow in the west. "With a paddy-looking guy like you we could overhear lots of good information. Our arrestees would never guess you could understand them and we could learn all kind of things."

"How often you pick up a sitting duck?" asked Serge, to change the subject, checking a license plate against the numbers on the hot sheet.

"Ducks? Oh, I get one a week maybe. There's plenty of hot cars sitting around Hollenbeck."

"How about rollers?" asked Serge. "How many hot cars do you get rolling?"

"Hot rollers? Oh, maybe one a month, I average. They're just teen-age joyriders usually. Are you just half Mexican?"

Bullshit, thought Serge, taking a large puff on the cigarette, deciding that Galloway would not be denied.

"No, I'm all Mexican. But we just didn't talk Spanish at home."

"Your parents didn't talk it?"

"My father died when I was young. My mother talked half English and half Spanish. We always answered in English. I left home when I got out of high school and went in the Marine Corps for four years. I just got out eight months ago. I've been away from the language and I've forgotten it. I never knew very much Spanish to begin with.''

''Too bad,' Galloway murmured and seemed satisfied.

Serge slumped in the seat staring blankly at the old houses of Boyle Heights and fought a mild wave of depression. Only two of the other policemen he had worked with had forced him to explain his Spanish name. Damn curious people, he thought. He asked nothing of people, nothing, not even of his brother, Angel, who had tried in every way possible to get him to settle in Chino after leaving the corps, and to go into his gas station with him. Serge told him he didn't plan to work very hard at anything and his brother had to put in thirteen hours every day in the grimy gas station in Chino. He could have done that. Maybe marry some fertile Mexican girl and have nine kids and learn to live on tortillas and beans because that's all you could afford when things were lean in the *barrio*. Well here he was working in another Chicano *barrio* he thought with a crooked smile. But he'd be out of here as soon as he finished his year's probationary period. Hollywood Division appealed to him, or perhaps West Los Angeles. He could rent an apartment near the ocean. The rent would be high, but maybe he could share the cost with another policeman or two. He had heard stories of the aspiring actresses who languish all over the westside streets.

''You ever worked the west side?'' he asked Galloway suddenly.

''No, I just worked Newton Street and here at Hollenbeck,'' Galloway answered.

''I hear there're lots of girls in Hollywood and West L.A.,'' said Serge.

''I guess so,'' said Galloway and the leer looked ridiculous with the freckles.

''You hear a lot of pussy stories from policemen. I've been wondering how true they are.''

''A lot of them are true,'' said Galloway. ''It seems to me that policemen do pretty well because for one thing girls trust you right off. I mean a girl isn't going to be afraid to meet a guy after work when she sees him sitting in a black and white police car in a big blue uniform. She knows you're not a rapist or a nut or something. At least she can be pretty sure. That means something in this town. And she can also be pretty sure you're a fairly clean-cut individual. And then some girls are attracted by the job itself. It's more than the uniform, it's the authority or something. We got a half dozen cop chasers in every division. You'll get to know some of them. All the policemen know them. They try their damnedest to lay every guy at the station. Some are actually pretty good-looking. You met Lupe, yet?''

''Who's she?'' asked Serge.

''She's one of Hollenbeck's cop chasers. Drives a Lincoln convertible. You'll run into her before long. Good lay, I heard.'' Galloway leered again through the freckles and Serge had to laugh aloud.

''I'm looking forward to meeting her,'' said Serge.

''There's probably lots of stuff in Hollywood. I never worked those fancy silk stocking divisions so I wouldn't know. But I'd be willing to bet there's more here on the east side than anywhere.''

''Let's drive around the division, do you mind?'' asked Serge.

''No, where do you want to go?''

''Let's tour the streets, all around Boyle Heights.''

''One fifty-cent tour of Hollenbeck Division coming up,'' said Galloway.

Serge stopped looking for a traffic violator and he didn't check the hot sheet even once for the sitting duck he craved. He smoked and watched people and houses. All the houses were old, most of the people were Mexican. Most of the streets were too narrow, and Serge guessed they were designed decades before anyone dreamed that Los Angeles would be a city on wheels. And when they did realize it, the east side was too old and too poor and the streets stayed too narrow, and the houses got older. Serge felt his stomach tighten and his face grew unaccountably warm as he saw the secondhand stores. *Ropa usada,* the signs said. And the *panadería* filled with sweet breads, cookies and cakes, usually a bit too oily for him. And the scores of restaurants with painted windows announcing that *menudo* was served on Saturdays and Sundays and Serge wondered how anyone could eat the tripe and hominy and thin red broth. Especially he wondered how he had been able to eat it as a child, but he guessed it was because they had been hungry. He thought of his brother Angel and his sister Aurora and how they would squeeze half a lemon in the *menudo,* sprinkle in oregano and slosh corn tortillas in the broth faster than his mother could make them. His father had been a tubercular whom he barely remembered as a smiling man with bony wrists, lying in bed all the time, coughing and smelling bad from the sickness. He only produced three children and little else in this world and Serge couldn't at the moment think of another family on his street with only three children except the Kulaskis and they were Anglos, at least to the Chicanos they were Anglos, but now he thought how humorous it was to have considered these Polacks as Anglo. He also wondered if it was true that the large quantity of corn the Mexicans consumed by eating tortillas three times a day produced the fine teeth. It was Mexican folklore that this was the case and it was certainly true that he and most of his boyhood friends had teeth like alligators. Serge had been to a dentist for the first time while in the Marine Corps where he had two molars filled.

Night was falling faster now that summer had almost gone and as he watched and listened a strange but oddly familar feeling swept over him. First it was a tremor in the stomach and then up around the chest and his face felt warm; he was filled with anxious longing, or was it, could it be, nostalgia? It was all he could do to keep from laughing aloud as he thought it must be nostalgia, for this was Chino on a grand scale. He was watching the same people who were doing the same things they had done in Chino, and he thought how strange that part of a man could yearn for the place of his youth even when he despised it, and what produced it, and what it produced. But at least it was the only innocent years he had ever known and there had been his mother. He guessed it was really her that he yearned for and the safety she represented. We all must long for that, he thought.

Serge watched the garish lighted madness on the San Bernardino Freeway as Galloway drove south on Soto back to Boyle Heights. There was a minor accident on the freeway below and a flare pattern had traffic backed up as far as he could see. A man held what looked like a bloody handkerchief to his face and talked to a traffic officer in a white hat who held a flashlight under his arm as he wrote in his notebook. No one really wants to grow up and go out in all this, he thought, looking down at the thousands of crawling headlights and the squatty white tow truck which was removing the debris. That must be what you long for—childhood—not for the people or the place. Those poor stupid Chicanos, he thought. Pitiful bastards.

"Getting hungry, partner?" asked Galloway.

"Anytime," said Serge, deciding to leave Chino five years in the past where it belonged.

"We don't have many eating spots in Hollenbeck," said Galloway. "And the few we do have aren't fit to eat in."

Serge had already been a policeman long enough to learn that "eating spot" meant more than restaurant, it meant restaurant that served free food to policemen. He still felt uncomfortable about accepting the free meals especially since they had been warned about gratuities in the police academy. It seemed however that the sergeants looked the other way when it came to free cigarettes, food, newspapers and coffee.

"I don't mind paying for dinner," said Serge.

"You don't have anything against paying half price, do you? We have a place in our area that pops for half."

"I don't mind at all," Serge smiled.

"We actually do have a place that bounces for everything. It's called El Soberano, that means the sovereign. We call it El Sobaco. You know what that means, don't you ?"

"No," Serge lied.

"That means the armpit. It's a real scuzzy joint. A beer joint that serves food. Real ptomaine tavern."

"Serves greasy tacos, I bet." Serge smiled wryly, knowing what the place would look like. "Everybody drinking and dancing I bet, and every night some guy gets jealous of his girl friend and you get a call there to break up a fight."

"You described it perfect," said Galloway. "I don't know about the food though. For all I know, they might drive a sick bull out on the floor at dinner time and everybody slices a steak with their blades."

"Let's hit the half-price joint," said Serge.

"Tell her to repeat!" Galloway commanded.

"What?"

"The radio. We just got another call."

"Son of a bitch. Sorry, partner, I've got to start listening to that jumble of noise." He pressed the red mike button. "Four-A-Forty-three, repeat."

"Four-A-Forty-three, Four-A-Forty-three," said the shrill voice, who had replaced the schoolmarm, "Three-three-seven South Mott, see the woman, four-five-nine suspect there now. Code two."

"Four-A-Forty-three, roger," said Serge.

Galloway stepped down unexpectedly on the accelerator and Serge bounced off the back cushion. "Sorry," Galloway grinned. "Sometimes I'm a leadfoot. I can't help stomping down on a four-five-nine call. Love to catch those burglars."

Serge was glad to see his partner's blue eyes shining happily. He hoped the thrills of the job would not wear off too soon on himself. They obviously hadn't on Galloway. It was reassuring. Everything in the world seemed to grow so dull so quickly.

Galloway slowed at a red light, looked both ways carelessly and roared across First Street as a westbound station wagon squealed and blasted its horn.

"Jesus," Serge whispered aloud.

"Sorry," said Galloway sheepishly, slowing down but only a little. Two blocks farther, he streaked through a partially blind intersection with a posted stop sign and Serge closed his eyes but heard no squealing tires.

"I dont have to tell you you shouldn't drive like this, do I?" said Galloway. "At least not while you're on probation. You can't afford to catch any heat from the sergeants while you're on probation." Galloway made a grinding right turn and another left at the next block.

"If I obeyed all the goddamn rules of the road like they tell us to, we'd never get there quick enough to catch anyone. And I figure it's my ass if we get in an accident, so what the hell."

How about my ass, you dumb ass, Serge thought, one hand braced on the dashboard, the other gripping the top of the back cushion. He had never envisioned hurtling down busy streets at these speeds. Galloway was a fearless and stupidly lucky driver.

Serge realized that he could not afford to get a quick reputation of troublemaker. New rookies should be all ears and short on mouth, but this was too much. He was going to demand that Galloway slow down. He made the decision just as his sweaty left hand lost its grip on the cushion.

"This is the street," said Galloway. "It's about mid-block." He turned off his headlights and glided noiselessly to the curb, several houses from where the address should have been. "Don't close your door," said Galloway, slipping out of the car and padding along the curb while Serge was still unfastening his seat belt.

Serge got out and followed Galloway, who wore ripple-soled shoes and his key ring tucked in his back pocket. Serge now saw the reason as his own new leather-soled shoes skidded and crunched noisily on the pavement. He tucked the jingling key ring in the back pocket and walked as softly as he could.

It was a dark residential street and he lost Galloway in the gloom, cursing as he forgot the address they were sent to. He broke into a slow run when Galloway, standing in the darkness of a driveway, startled him.

''It's okay, he's long gone,'' said Galloway.

''Got a description?'' asked Serge, noticing the side door of the leaning stucco house was standing open and seeing the tiny dark woman in a straight cotton dress standing near Galloway.

''He's been gone ten minutes,'' said Galloway. ''She doesn't have a phone and couldn't find a neighbor at home. She made the call at the drugstore.''

''She saw him?''

''Came home and found the pad ransacked. She must've surprised the burglar, because she heard someone run through the back bedroom and go out the window. A car took off down the alley a second later. She didn't see the suspect, the car or anything.''

Two more radio cars suddenly glided down the street, one from each direction.

''Go broadcast a code four,'' said Galloway. ''Just say the four-five-nine occurred ten minutes ago and the suspect left in a vehicle and was not seen. When you're finished come in the house and we'll take a report.''

Serge held up four fingers to the policemen in the other cars indicating a code four, that no assistance was needed. As he returned to the house from making the broadcast, he decided that this payday he would invest in a pair of ripple soles or get these leather soles replaced with rubber.

He heard the sobbing as he approached the open side door and Galloway's voice coming from the front of the small house.

Serge did not go into the living room for a moment. He stood and looked around the kitchen, smelling the cilantro and onion, and seeing jalapeño chili peppers on the tile drainboard. He remembered as he saw the package of corn tortillas that his mother would never have any but homemade tortillas in her house. There was an eight-inch-high madonna on the refrigerator and school pictures of five smiling children, and he knew without examining her closely that the madonna would be Our Lady of Guadalupe in pink gown and blue veil. He wondered where the other favorite saint of the Mexicans was hiding. But Martin de Porres was not in the kitchen, and Serge entered the living room, which was small and scantily furnished with outdated blond furniture.

''We bought that TV set so recently,'' said the woman, who had stopped weeping and was staring at the dazzling white wall where the freshly cut two-foot antenna wire lay coiled on the floor.

''Anything else missing?'' asked Galloway.

''I'll look,'' she sighed. ''We only made six payments on it. I guess we got to pay for it even though it's gone.''

''I wouldn't,'' said Galloway. ''Call the store. Tell them it's stolen.''

''We bought it at Frank's Appliance Store. He's not a rich man. He can't afford to take our loss.''

''Do you have theft insurance?'' asked Galloway.

''Just fire. We was going to get theft. We was just talking about it because of so many burglaries around here.''

They followed her into the bedroom and Serge saw him—Blessed Martin de Porres, the black holy man in his white robe and black cloak and black hands which said to the Chicano, ''Look at my face, not brown but black and yet even for me Nuestro Señor delivers miracles.'' Serge wondered if they still made Mexican movies about Martin de Porres and Pancho Villa and other folk heroes. Mexicans are great believers he thought. Lousy Catholics, really. Not devout churchgoers like Italians and Irish. The Aztec blood diluted the orthodox Spanish Catholicism. He thought of the various signals he had seen Mexicans make to their particular version of the Christian deity as they genuflected on both knees in the crumbling stucco church in Chino. Some made the sign of the Cross in the conventional Mexican fashion, completing the sign with a kiss on the thumbnail. Others made the sign three times with three kisses, others six times or more. Some made a small cross with the thumb on the forehead, then touched the breast and both shoulders, then returned to the lips for another cross, breast and shoulders again, and another small cross on the lips followed by ten signs on the head, breast and shoulders. He loved to watch them then, particularly during the Forty Hours when the Blessed Sacrament was exposed, and he being an altar boy was obliged to sit or kneel at the foot of the altar for four hours until relieved by Mando Rentería, an emaciated altar boy two years younger than he who was never on time for Mass or anything else. Serge used to watch them and he recalled that no matter what sign they made to whatever strange idol they worshiped who was certainly not the traditional Christ, they touched their knees to the floor when they genuflected and did not fake a genuflection as he had seen so many Anglos do in much finer churches in the short time he still bothered to attend Mass after his mother died. And they had looked at the mute stone figures on the altar with consummate veneration. And whether or not they attended Mass every Sunday, you knew that they were communicating with a spirit when they prayed.

He remembered Father McCarthy, the pastor of the parish, when he had overheard him say to Sister Mary Immaculate, the principal of the school, "They are not good Catholics, but they are so respectful and they believe so well." Serge, then a novice altar boy, was in the sacristy to get his white surplice which he had forgotten to bring home. His mother had sent him back to get it because she insisted on washing and starching the surplice every time he served a Mass even though it was completely unnecessary and this would wear it out much too soon and then she would have to make him another one. Serge knew who Father McCarthy meant when he said "they" to the tall craggy-faced Irish nun who cracked Serge's hands unmercifully with a ruler during the first five years of grammar school when he would talk in class or daydream. Then she had changed abruptly the last three years when he was a gangling altar boy tripping over his cassock that was one of Father McCarthy's cut-down cassocks because he was so tall for a Mexican boy, and she doted over him because he learned his Latin so quickly and pronounced it "so wondrously well." But it was easy, because in those days he still spoke a little Spanish and the Latin did not seem really so strange, not nearly so strange as English seemed those first years of grammar school. And now that he had all but forgotten Spanish it was hard to believe that he once spoke no English.

"Ayeeee," she wailed suddenly, opening the closet in the ransacked bedroom. "The money, it's gone."

"You had money?" said Galloway to the angular, dark little woman, who stared in disbelief at Galloway and then at the closet.

"It was more than sixty dollars," she cried. "*Dios mío!* I put it in there. It was sitting right there." Suddenly she began rummaging through the already ransacked bedroom. "Maybe the thief dropped it," she said, and Serge knew that she might destroy any fingerprints on the chest of drawers and the other smooth-surfaced objects in the bedroom, but he had also learned enough by now to know there were probably no prints anyway as most competent burglars used socks on their hands, or gloves, or wiped their prints. He knew that Galloway knew she might destroy evidence, but Galloway motioned him into the living room.

"Let her blow off steam," Galloway whispered. "The only good place for prints is the window ledge anyway. She's not going to touch that."

Serge nodded, took off his hat and sat down. After a few moments, the furious rustling sounds in the bedroom subsided and the utter silence that followed made Serge wish very much that she would hurry and tell them what was missing so they could make their report and leave.

"You're going to find out before too long that we're the only ones that see the victims," said Galloway. "The judges and probation officers and social workers and everybody else think mainly about the suspect and how they can help him stop whatever he specializes in doing to his victims, but you and me are the only ones who see what he does to his victims—right after it's done. And this is only a little burglary."

She should pray to Our Lady of Guadalupe or Blessed Martin, thought Serge. Or maybe to Pancho Villa. That would be just as useful. Oh, they're great believers, these Chicanos, he thought.

5

The Centurions

"Here comes Lafitte," said the tall policeman. "Three minutes till roll call but he'll be on time. Watch him."

Gus watched Lafitte grin at the tall policeman, and open his locker with one hand, while the other unbuttoned the yellow sport shirt. When Gus looked up again after giving his shoes a last touch with the shine rag, Lafitte was fully dressed in his uniform and was fastening the Sam Browne.

"I'll bet it takes you longer to get into your jammies at night than it does to throw on that blue suit, eh Lafitte?" said the tall policeman.

"Your pay doesn't start till 3:00 P.M.," Lafitte answered. "No sense giving the Department any extra minutes. It all adds up in a year."

Gus stole a glance at Lafitte's brass buttons on his shirt pocket flaps and epaulets and saw the tiny holes in the center of the star on the buttons. This proved the buttons had seen a good deal of polishing, he thought. A hole was worn in the middle. He looked at his own brass buttons and saw they were not a lustrous gold like Lafitte's. If he had been in the service he would have learned a good deal about such things, he thought. On the opposite side of the metal lockers was the roll call room, lockers, rows of benches, tables, and the watch commander's desk at the front, all crammed into one thirty by fifty foot room. Gus was told that the old station would be replaced in a few years by a new station, but it thrilled him just as it was. This was his first night in University Division. He was not a cadet now; the academy was finished and he could not believe it was Gus Plebesly inside this tallored blue woolen shirt which bore the glistening oval shield. He took a place at the second row of tables from the rear of the room. This seemed safe enough. The rear table was almost filled with older officers, and no one sat at the front one. The second row from the rear should be safe enough, he thought. There were twenty-two policemen at this early night watch roll call and he felt reassured when he saw Griggs and Patzloff, two of his academy classmates, who had also been sent to University Division from the academy.

Griggs and Patzloff were talking quietly and Gus debated about moving across the room to their table but he decided it might attract too much attention, and anyway, it was one minute to roll call. The doors at the rear of the room swung open and a man in civilian clothes entered, and a burly, bald policeman at the rear table shouted, "Salone, why ain't you suited up?"

"Light duty," said Salone. "I'm working the desk tonight. No roll call."

"Son of a bitch," said the burly policeman, "too sick to ride around with me in a radio car? What the hell's wrong with you?"

"Gum infection."

"You don't sit on your gums, Salone," said the burly policeman. "Son of a bitch. Now I guess I'll get stuck with one of these slick-sleeved little RE-cruits."

Everyone laughed and Gus's face turned hot and he pretended he didn't hear the remark. Then he realized why the burly policeman had said "slick-sleeved." He glanced over his shoulder and saw the rows of white service stripes on the lower sleeves of the policemen at the rear table, one stripe for each five years' service, and he understood the epithet. The doors swung open and two sergeants entered carrying manila folders and a large square board from which the car plan would be read.

"Three-A-Five, Hill and Matthews," said the pipe-smoking sergeant with the receding hairline.

"Here."

"Here."

"Three-A-Nine, Carson and Lafitte."

"Here."

"Here," said Lafitte, and Gus recognized the voice.

"Three-A-Eleven, Ball and Gladstone."

"Here," said one of the two Negro policemen in the room.

"Here," said the other Negro.

Gus was afraid he would be put with the burly policeman and was glad to hear him answer "Here" when he was assigned with someone else.

Finally the sergeant said, "Three-A-Ninety-nine, Kilvinsky and Plebesly."

"Here," said Kilvinsky and Gus turned, smiling nervously at the tall silver-haired policeman in the back row who smiled back at him.

"Here, sir," said Gus, and then cursed himself for saying "sir." He was out of the academy now. "Sirs" were reserved for lieutenants and higher.

"We have three new officers with us," said the pipe-smoking sergeant. "Glad to have you men. I'm Sergeant Bridget and this ruddy Irishman on my right is Sergeant O'Toole. Looks just like the big Irish cop you see in all the old B movies, doesn't he?"

Sergeant O'Toole grinned broadly and nodded to the new officers.

"Before we read the crimes, I want to talk about the supervisor's meeting today," said Sergeant Bridget as he thumbed through one of the manila folders.

Gus gazed around the room at the several maps of University Division which were covered with multicolored pins that he thought must signify certain crimes or arrests. Soon he would know all the little things and he would be one of them. Or would he be one of them? His forehead and armpits began to perspire and he thought, I will not think that. It's self-defeating and neurotic to think like that. I'm just as good as any of them. I was tops in my class in physical training. What right do I have to degrade myself. I promised myself I'd stop doing that.

"One thing the captain talked about at the supervisor's meeting was the time and mileage check," said Bridget. "He wanted us to remind you guys to broadcast your time and mileage *every* time you transport a female in a police car—for any reason. Some bitch in Newton Division beefed a policeman last week. Says he took her in a park and tried to lay her. It was easy to prove she lied because the policeman gave his mileage to Communications at ten minutes past eleven when he left her pad and he gave his mileage again at eleven twenty-three when he arrived at the Main Jail. His mileage and the time check proved he couldn't have driven her up in Elysian Park like she claimed."

"Hey Sarge," said a lean swarthy policeman near the front. "If the Newton Street policeman who she accused is Harry Ferndale, she's probably telling the truth. He's so horny he'd plow a dead alligator or even a live one if somebody'd hold the tail."

"Damn it, Leoni," grinned Sergeant Bridget as the others chuckled, "we got some new men here tonight. You roll call pop-offs ought to be trying to set some kind of example, at least on their first night. This is serious shit I'm reading. The next thing the captain wanted us to bring up is that some Seventy-seventh Street officer in traffic court was asked by the defendant's lawyer what drew his attention to the defendant's vehicle to cite it for an illegal turn, and the officer said because the defendant was driving with his arm around a well-known Negro prostitute."

The roll call room burst into laughter and Bridget held up a hand to quiet them. "I know that's funny and all that, but number one, you can prejudice a case by implying that you were trying to suppress prostitution, not enforce traffic laws. And number two, this little remark got back to the guy's old lady and he's beefing the policeman. An investigation started already."

"Is it true?" asked Matthews.

"Yeah, he was with a whore I guess."

"Then let the asshole beef," said Matthews, and Gus realized that they used "asshole" as much here in the divisions as the instructors did in the academy and he guessed it was the favorite epithet of policemen, at least Los Angeles policemen.

"Anyway, the captain says no more of it," Bridget continued, "and another thing the old man says is that you guys are not at *any* time to push cars with your police vehicle. Snider on the day watch was giving a poor stranded motorist a push and he jumped the bumper and busted the guy's taillights and dented his deck lid and the prick is threatening to sue the city if his car isn't fixed. So no more pushing."

"How about on the freeway, or when a stalled car has a street bottled up?" asked Leoni.

"Okay, you and I know there are exceptions to everything in this business, but in almost all cases no pushing, okay?"

"Has the captain ever done police work out in the street?" asked Matthews. "I bet he had some cushy office job since he's been on the Department."

"Let's not get personal, Mike," smiled Bridget. "The next thing is these preliminary investigations in burglary and robbery cases. Now, you guys aren't detectives, but you aren't mere report writers either. You're supposed to conduct a preliminary investigation out there, not just fill in a bunch of blanks on a crime report." Bridget paused and lit the long-stemmed pipe he had been toying with. "We all know that we seldom get good latent prints from a gun because of the broken surface, but Jesus Christ, a couple weeks ago an officer of this division didn't bother worrying about prints on a gun a suspect dropped at the scene of a liquor store robbery! And the dicks had a damned good suspect in custody the next day but the dumb ass liquor store owner was some idiot who claimed he was new in the business in this part of town and he couldn't tell Negroes apart. There wouldn't have been any case at all because the officer handled the suspect's gun and ruined any prints there might have been, except for one thing—it was an automatic. Lucky for the officer, because he might've got a couple days suspension for screwing up the case like that."

"Were the prints on the clip?" asked Lafitte.

"No, the officer screwed those up when he took the clip out, but there were prints on the cartridges. They got part of the friction ridges on the center portion of the suspect's right thumb on several of the shells where he'd pushed them in the clip. The officer claimed the liquor store owner had handled the gun first so the officer decided all possibility of getting prints was destroyed. I'd like to know how the hell he knew that. It doesn't matter who handles the gun, you should still treat it like it's printable and notify the latent prints specialists."

"Tell them about the rags," said Sergeant O'Toole without looking up.

"Oh yeah. In another job recently, an officer had to be reminded by a sergeant at the scene to book the rags the suspect used to bind the victim. And the suspect had brought the rags with him! Christ, they could have laundry marks or they could be matched up with other rags that the dicks might later find in the suspect's pad or on some other job. I know you guys know most of this shit, but some of you are getting awful careless. Okay, that's all the bitching I have for you, I guess. Any questions on the supervisor's meeting?"

"Yeah, you ever talk about the good things we do?" asked Matthews.

"Glad you asked that, Mike," said Sergeant Bridget, his teeth clenched on the black pipe stem. "As a matter of fact the lieutenant wrote you a little commendation for the hot roller you got the other night. Come on up and sign it."

"In eighteen years I guess I got a hundred of these things," grumbled Matthews, striding heavy-footed to the front of the room, "but I still get the same goddamn skinny paycheck every two weeks."

"You're getting almost six bills a month, Mike. Quit your kicking," said Bridget, then turning to the others said, "Mike went in pursuit and brought down a hot car driven by a damn good burglar and he likes a little 'at-a-boy' once in a while just like the rest of us, despite his bitching. You new men are going to find out that if you have a yen for lots of thanks and praise, you picked the wrong profession. Want to read the crimes, William, me boy?" he said to Sergeant O'Toole.

"Lots of crimes in the division last night, but not too many good descriptions," said O'Toole with a trace of a New York accent. "Got one happy moment on the crime sheet though. Cornelius Arps, the Western Avenue pimp, got cut by one of his whores and he EX-pired at 3:00 A.M. in General Hospital."

A loud cheer went up in the room. It startled Gus.

"Which whore did it?" shouted Leoni.

"One calls herself Tammy Randolph. Anybody know her?"

"She worked usually around Twenty-first and Western," said Kilvinsky, and Gus turned for another appraisal of his partner who looked more like a doctor than what he imagined a policeman should look like. The older ones, he noticed, looked hard around the mouth and their eyes seemed to watch things not just look at things, but to watch as though they were waiting for something, but that might be his imagination, he thought.

"How'd she do him?" asked Lafitte.

"You'll never believe this," said O'Toole, "but the old canoe maker at the autopsy today claimed that she punctured the aorta with a three and a half inch blade! She hit him so hard in the side with this little pocket knife that it severed a rib and punctured the aorta. Now how could a broad do that?"

"You never saw Tammy Randolph," said Kilvinsky quietly. "A hundred and ninety pounds of fighting whore. She's the one that beat hell out of the vice officer last summer, remember?"

"Oh, is that the same bitch?" asked Bridget. "Well, she atoned for it by juking Cornelius Arps."

"Why didn't you get the lieutenant to write her an at-a-boy like he did me?" asked Matthews as the men laughed.

"Here's a suspect wanted for attempted murder and two-eleven," said O'Toole. "Name is Calvin Tubbs, male, Negro, born 6-12-35, five ten, one eighty-five, black hair, brown eyes, medium complexion, wears his hair marcelled, full moustache, drives a 1959 Ford convertible, white over maroon, license John Victor David one seven three. Hangs out here in University at Normandie and Adams, and at Western and Adams. Robbed a bread truck driver and shot him for the hell of it. They made him on six other jobs—all bread trucks. He's bought and paid for, you can render that asshole."

"Really raping those bread trucks and buses, ain't they?" said Matthews.

"You know it," said O'Toole, glancing over the bifocals. "For the benefit of you new men, we should tell you it's not safe to ride a bus in this part of town. Armed bandits rob a bus almost every day and sometimes rob the passengers too. So if you have a flat tire on your way to work, call a cab. And the bread truck drivers or anybody else that's a street vendor gets hit regular, too. I know one bread truck driver that was held up twenty-one times in one year."

"That guy's a professional victim," said Leoni.

"He can probably run a show-up better than the robbery dicks," said Matthews.

Gus glanced over at the two Negro officers who sat together near the front, but they laughed when the others did and showed no sign of discomfort. Gus knew that all the "down heres" referred to the Negro divisions and he wondered if all the cracks about the crimes affected them personally. He decided they must be used to it.

"Had kind of an interesting homicide the other night," O'Toole continued in his monotone. "Family beef. Some dude told his old lady she was a bum lay and she shot him twice and he fell off the porch and broke his leg and she ran inside, got a kitchen knife and came back and started cutting where the jagged bone stuck out. Almost got the leg all the way off by the time the first radio car got there. They tell me they couldn't even take a regular blood test. There was no blood left in the guy's veins. Had to take it from the spleen."

"Wonder if she *was* a bum lay," said Leoni.

"By the way," said Sergeant Bridget, "any of you guys know an old lady named Alice Hockington? Lives on Twenty-eighth near Hoover?"

No one answered and Sergeant Bridget said, "She called last night and said a car came by on a prowler call last week. Who was it?"

"Why do you want to know?" asked a bass voice from the last table.

"Goddamn suspicious cops," Bridget said, shaking his head. "Well screw you guys then. I was just going to tell you the old girl died and left ten thousand dollars to the nice policemen who chased a prowler away. Now, who wants to cop out?"

"That was me, Sarge," said Leoni.

"Bullshit," said Matthews, "that was me and Cavanaugh."

The others laughed and Bridget said, "Anyway, the old girl called last night. She didn't really die, but she's thinking about it. She said she wanted that handsome tall young policeman with the black moustache (that sounds like you, Lafitte) to come by every afternoon and check for the evening newspaper. If it's still on her porch at five o'clock it means she's dead and she wants you to bust the door in if that happens. Because of her dog, she said."

"She afraid he'll starve or she afraid he won't starve?" asked Lafitte.

"The sympathy of these guys really is touching," said Bridget.

"Can I go on with the crimes or am I boring you guys," said O'Toole. "Attempt rape, last night, 11:10 P.M., three-six-nine West Thirty-seventh Place. Suspect awoke victim by placing hand over her mouth, said, 'Don't move. I love you and I want to prove it.' Fondled victim's private parts while he held a two-inch blue steel revolver in the air for her to see. Suspect wore a blue suit . . ."

"Bluesuit?" asked Lafitte. "Sounds like a policeman."

"Suspect wore blue suit and light colored shirt," O'Toole continued. "Was male, Negro, twenty-eight to thirty, six foot two, hundred ninety, black, brown, medium complexion."

"Sounds exactly like Gladstone. I think we can solve this one," Lafitte said.

"Victim screamed and suspect jumped out window and was seen getting into a late model yellow vehicle parked on Hoover."

"What kind of car you got, Gladstone?" asked Lafitte and the big Negro policeman turned and grinned, "She wouldn't have screamed if it'd been me."

"The hell she wouldn't," said Matthews. "I seen Glad in the academy showers one time. That would be assault with a deadly weapon."

"Assault with a friendly weapon," said Gladstone.

"Let's go to work," said Sergeant Bridget, and Gus was glad there was no inspection because he didn't think his buttons would pass and he wondered how often they had inspections here in the divisions. Not very often, he guessed, from the uniforms he saw around him, which were certainly not up to academy standards. He guessed things would be relaxed out here. Soon, he would be relaxed too. He would be part of it.

Gus stood with his notebook a few steps from Kilvinsky and smiled when Kilvinsky turned around.

"Gus Plebesly," said Gus, shaking Kilvinsky's wide, smooth hand.

"Andy's the first name," said Kilvinsky looking down at Gus with an easy grin. Gus guessed he might be six feet four.

"Guess you're stuck with me tonight," said Gus.

"All month. And I don't mind."

"Whatever you say is okay with me."

"That goes without saying."

"Oh, yes sir."

"You don't have to sir me," Kilvinsky laughed. "My gray hair only means that I've been around a long time. We're partners. You have a notebook?"

"Yes."

"Okay, you keep books for the first week or so. After you learn to take a report and get to know the streets a little bit, I'll let you drive. All new policemen love to drive."

"Anything. Anything is okay with me."

"Guess I'm ready, Gus. Let's go downstairs," said Kilvinsky, and they walked side by side through the double doors and down the turning stairway of old University station.

"See those pictures, partner?" said Kilvinsky pointing to the glass-covered portraits of University policemen who had been killed on duty. "Those guys aren't heroes. Those guys just screwed up and they're dead. Pretty soon you'll get comfortable and relaxed out there, just like the rest of us. But don't get too comfortable. Remember the guys in the pictures."

"I don't feel like I'll ever get comfortable," Gus said.

"You will, partner. You will," said Kilvinsky. "Let's find our black and white and go to work."

The inadequate parking lot was teeming with blue uniforms as the night watch relieved the day watch at 3:45 P.M. The sun was still very hot and ties could remain off until later in the evening. Gus wondered at the heavy long-sleeved blue uniforms. His arms were sweating and the wool was harsh.

"I'm not used to wearing such heavy clothes in the heat," he smiled to Kilvinsky, as he wiped his forehead with a handkerchief.

"You'll get used to it," said Kilvinsky, sitting carefully on the sun-heated vinyl seat and releasing the seat lock to slide back and make room for his long legs.

Gus placed the new hot sheet in the holder and wrote 3-A-99 on the notebook pad so that he would not forget who they were. That seemed odd, he thought. He was now 3-A-99. He felt his heart race and he knew he was more excited than he should be. He hoped it was just that—excitement. There was nothing yet to fear.

"The passenger officer handles the radio, Gus."

"Okay."

"You won't hear our calls at first. That radio will just be an incoherent mess of conversation for a while. In a week or so you'll start to hear our calls."

"Okay."

"Ready for a night of romance, intrigue and adventure on the streets of the asphalt jungle?" asked Kilvinsky dramatically.

"Sure," Gus smiled.

''Okay, kid,'' Kilvinsky laughed. ''You a little thrilled?''

''Yes.''

''Good. That's the way you should be.''

As Kilvinsky drove from the station parking lot he turned west on Jefferson and Gus flipped down the visor and squinted into the sun. The radio car smelled faintly of vomit.

''Want a tour of the division?'' asked Kilvinsky.

''Sure.''

''Almost all the citizens here are Negroes. Some whites. Some Mexicans. Mostly Negroes. Lots of crime when you have lots of Negroes. We work Ninety-nine. Our area is *all* black. Close to Newton. Ours are eastside Negroes. When they got some money they move west of Figueroa and Vermont and maybe west of Western. Then they call themselves westside Negroes and expect to be treated differently. I treat everyone the same, white or black. I'm civil to all people, courteous to none. I think courtesy implies servility. Policemen don't have to be servile or apologize to anyone for doing their job. This is a philosophy lesson I throw in free to every rookie I break in. Old-timers like me love to hear themselves talk. You'll get used to radio car philosophers.''

''How much time do you have on the Department?'' asked Gus, looking at the three service stripes on Kilvinsky's sleeve which meant at least fifteen years. But he had a youthful face if it weren't for the silver hair and the glasses. Gus guessed he was in good condition. He had a powerful-looking body.

''Twenty years this December,'' said Kilvinsky.

''You retiring?''

''Haven't decided.''

They rode silently for several minutes and Gus looked at the city and realized he knew nothing about Negroes. He enjoyed the names on the churches. On a corner he saw a one-story, white-washed frame building with a handmade sign which said, ''Lion of Judah and Kingdom of Christ Church,'' and on the same block was the ''Sacred Defender Baptist Church'' and in a moment he saw the ''Hearty Welcome Missionary Baptist Church'' and on and on he read the signs on the scores of churches and hoped he could remember them to tell Vickie when he got home tonight. He thought the churches were wonderful.

''Sure is hot,'' said Gus, wiping his forehead with the back of his hand.

''You don't have to wear your lid in the car, you know,'' said Kilvinsky. ''Only when you get out.''

''Oh,'' said Gus, taking off the hat quickly. ''I forgot I had it on.''

Kilvinsky smiled and hummed softly as he patrolled the streets, letting Gus sightsee and Gus watched how slowly he drove and how deliberately. He would remember that. Kilvinsky patrolled at fifteen miles an hour.

''Guess I'll get used to the heavy uniform,'' said Gus, pushing the sleeve from his sticky arms.

''Chief Parker doesn't go for short sleeves,'' said Kilvinsky.

''Why not?''

''Doesn't like hairy arms and tattoos. Long sleeves are more dignified.''

''He spoke to our graduating class,'' said Gus, remembering the eloquence of the chief and the perfect Engish which had deeply impressed Vickie who sat proudly in the audience that day.

''He's one of a vanishing kind,'' said Kilvinsky.

''I've heard he's strict.''

''He's a Calvinist. Know what that is?''

''A puritan?''

''He professes to be Roman Catholic, but I say he's a Calvinist. He won't compromise on matters of principle. He's despised by lots of people.''

''He is?'' said Gus, reading the signs on the store windows.

"He knows evil when he sees it. He recognizes the weakness of people. He has a passion for order and the rule of law. He can be relentless," said Kilvinsky.

"You sound as if you kind of admire him."

"I love him. When he's gone, nothing will be the same."

What a strange man Kilvinsky is, Gus thought. He talked absently and if it weren't for the boyish grin, Gus would have been uncomfortable with him. Then Gus watched a young Negro strutting across Jefferson Boulevard and he studied the swaying, limber shoulder movement, bent-elbowed free swinging arms, and the rubber-kneed big stepping bounce and as Kilvinsky remarked, "He's walkin' smart," Gus realized how profoundly ignorant he was about Negroes and he was anxious to learn about them, and about all people. If he could just learn and grow he would know something about people after a few years in this job. He thought of the squirming muscle in the long brown arms of the young man who was now blocks behind him. He wondered how he would fare if the two of them were face to face in a police-suspect confrontation when he had no partner and he could not use his sidearm and the young Negro was not impressed with his glittering golden shield and suit of blue. He cursed himself again for the insidious fear and he vowed he would master it but he always made this vow and still the fear came or rather the promise of fear, the nervous growling stomach, the clammy hands, the leathery mouth, but enough, enough to make him suspect that when the time came he would not behave like a policeman.

What if a man the size of Kilvinsky resisted arrest? Gus thought. How could I possibly handle him? There were things he wanted to ask, but was ashamed to ask Kilvinsky. Things he might ask a smaller man, after he got to know him, if he ever did get to really know him. He had never had many friends and at this moment he doubted that he could find any among these uniformed men who made him feel like a small boy. Maybe it had all been a mistake, he thought. Maybe he could never be one of them. They seemed so forceful and confident. They had seen things. But maybe it was just bravado. Maybe it was that.

But what would happen if someone's life, maybe Kilvinsky's life, depended on his conquest of fear which he had never been able to conquer? Those four years of marriage while he worked in a bank had not prepared him to cope with that. And why hadn't he the courage to talk to Vickie about things like this, and then he thought of the times he had lain beside her in the darkness, particularly after lovemaking, and he had thought of these things and prayed to have the courage to talk to Vickie about it, but he hadn't, and no one knew that *he* knew that he was a coward. But what would it ever have mattered that he was a coward if he had stayed in the bank where he belonged? Why could he do well in wrestling and physical training, but turn sick and impotent when the other man was not playing a game? Once in P.T. when he was wrestling with Walmsley he had applied the wristlock too firmly as Officer Randolph had shown them. Walmsley became angry and when Gus saw his eyes, the fear came, his strength deserted him and Walmsley easily took him down. He did it viciously and Gus did not resist even though he knew he was stronger and twice as agile as Walmsley. But that was all part of being a coward, that inability to control your body. Is the hate the thing I fear? Is that it? A face full of hate?

"Come on granny, let the clutch out," Kilvinsky said as a female driver in front of them crept toward the signal causing them to stop instead of making the yellow light.

"One-seven-three west Fifty-fourth Street," said Kilvinsky, tapping on the writing pad between them.

"What?" asked Gus.

"We got a call. One-seven-three west Fifty-fourth Street. Write it down."

"Oh. Sorry, I can't make any sense out of the radio yet."

"Roger the call," said Kilvinsky.

"Three-A-Ninety-nine, roger," said Gus into the hand mike.

"You'll start picking our calls out of all that chatter pretty soon," said Kilvinsky. "Takes a while. You'll get it."

"What kind of call was it?"

"Unknown trouble call. That means the person who called isn't sure what the problem is, or it means he wasn't coherent or the operator couldn't understand him, or it could mean anything. I don't like those calls. You don't know what the hell you have until you get there."

Gus nervously looked at the storefronts. He saw two Negroes with high shiny pompadours and colorful one-piece jump suits park a red Cadillac convertible in front of a window which said, "Big Red's Process Parlor," and below it in yellow letters Gus read, "Process, do-it yourself process, Quo Vadis, and other styles."

"What do you call the hairdos on those two men?" asked Gus.

"Those two pimps? That style is just called a process, some call it a marcel. Old-time policemen might refer to it as gassed hair, but for police reports most of us just use the word 'process.' Costs them a lot of money to keep a nice process like that, but then, pimps have lots of money. And a process is as important to them as a Cadillac. No self-respecting pimp would be caught without both of them."

Gus wished the sun would drop, then it might cool off. He loved summer nights when the days were hot and paper-dry like this one. He noticed the crescent and star over the white two-story stucco building on the corner. Two men in close-cropped hair and black suits with maroon neckties stood in front of the wide doors with their hands behind their backs and glared at the police car as they continued south.

"That a church?" asked Gus to Kilvinsky, who never looked toward the building or the men.

"That's the Muslim temple. Do you know about Muslims?"

"I've read a little in the papers, that's all."

"They're a fanatical sect that's sprung up recently all over the country. A lot of them are ex-cons. They're all cop haters."

"They look so clean-cut," said Gus, glancing over his shoulder at the two men whose faces were turned in the direction of the police car.

"They're just part of what's happening in the country," said Kilvinsky. "Nobody knows what's happening yet, except a few people like the chief. It may take ten years to figure it all out."

"What *is* happening?" asked Gus.

"It's a long story," Kilvinsky said. "And I'm not sure myself. And besides, here's the pad."

Gus turned and saw the one-seven-three over the mailbox of the green stucco house with a trash-littered front yard.

Gus almost didn't see the trembling old Negro in khaki work clothes huddled on an ancient wicker chair on the dilapidated porch of the house.

"Glad yo'all could come officahs," he said, standing, quivering, with sporadic looks toward the door standing ajar.

"What's the problem?" asked Kilvinsky, climbing the three stairs to the porch, his cap placed precisely straight on the silver mane.

"An jist came home and ah saw a man in the house. Ah don' know him. He jist was sittin' there starin' at me and ah got scairt and run out heah and ovah nex' do' and ah use mah neighbah's phone and while I was waitin' ah look back inside an' theah he sits jist rockin', an' Lord, ah think he's a crazy man. He don' say nothin' jist sits an' rocks."

Gus reached involuntarily for the baton and fingered the grooved handle, waiting for Kilvinsky to decide their first move and he was embarrassed by his relief when he understood, when Kilvinsky winked and said, "Wait here, partner, in case he tries to go out the back door. There's a fence back there so he'd have to come back through the front.''

Gus waited with the old man and in a few minutes he heard Kilvinsky shout, ''Alright you son of a bitch, get out of here and don't come back!'' And he heard the back door slam. Then Kilvinsky opened the screen and said, ''Okay, Mister, come on in. He's gone.''

Gus followed the gnarled old man, who removed the crumpled hat when he crossed the threshold.

''He sho' is gone, officahs,'' said the old man, but the trembling had not stopped.

''I told him not to come back,'' said Kilvinsky. ''I don't think you'll be seeing him again around this neighborhood.''

''God bless yo'all,'' said the old man, shuffling toward the back door and locking it.

''How long's it been since you had a drink?'' asked Kilvinsky.

''Oh, couple days now,'' said the old man, smiling a black-toothed smile. ''Check's due in the mail any day now.''

''Well, just fix yourself a cup of tea and try to get some sleep. You'll feel lots better tomorrow.''

''Ah thanks yo'all,'' said the old man as they walked down the cracked concrete sidewalk to the car. Kilvinsky didn't say anything as he drove off and Gus said finally, ''Those d.t.'s must be hell, huh?''

''Must be hell,'' Kilvinsky nodded.

''We got a coffee spot down the street,'' said Kilvinsky. ''It's so bad you could pour it in your battery when she dies, but it's free and so are the doughnuts.''

''Sounds good to me,'' said Gus.

Kilvinsky parked in the littered coffee shop parking lot and Gus went inside to get the coffee. He left his cap in the car and felt like a veteran, hatless, striding into the coffee shop where he watched a wizened, alcoholic-looking man who was listlessly pouring coffee for three Negro counter customers.

''Coffee?'' he said to Gus, coming toward him with two paper cups in his hand.

''Please.''

''Cream?''

''Only in one,'' said Gus, as the counterman drew the coffee from the urns and placed the cups on the counter as Gus self-consciously tried to decide the most diplomatic way to order doughnuts which were free. You didn't wish to be presumptuous even though you wanted a doughnut. It would be so much simpler if they just paid for the coffee and doughnuts, he thought, but then that would counter the tradition and if you did something like that the word might be passed that you were a troublemaker. The man solved his dilemma by saying, ''Doughnuts?''

''Please,'' said Gus, relieved.

''Chocolate or plain? I'm out of glazed.''

''Two plain,'' said Gus, realizing that Kilvinsky had not stated his preference.

''Tops for the cups?''

''No, I can manage,'' said Gus and a moment later discovered that this chain of coffee shops made the hottest coffee in Los Angeles.

''It's sure hot,'' he smiled weakly, in case Kilvinsky had seen him spill coffee on himself. His forehead perspired from the sudden flash of pain.

''Wait till you're on the morning watch,'' said Kilvinsky. ''Some chilly winter night about 1:00 A.M. this coffee will light a fire in you and see you through the night.''

The sun was dropping on the horizon but it was still hot and Gus thought a Coke would have been better than a cup of coffee but he had already noticed that policemen were coffee drinkers and he guessed he may as well get used to it because he was going to be one of them, come what may.

Gus sipped the steaming coffee a full three minutes after it sat on the roof of the police car and found that he still could not stand the temperature; he waited and watched Kilvinsky out of the corner of his eye and saw him taking great gulps as he smoked a cigarette and adjusted the radio until it was barely audible, still much too low for Gus, but then, Gus knew he could not pick their calls out of that chaotic garble of voices anyway, so if Kilvinsky could hear it, it was enough.

Gus saw a stooped ragpicker in filthy denim trousers and a torn, grimy, checkered shirt several sizes too large, and a GI helmet liner with a hole on the side through which a snarled handful of the ragpicker's gray hair protruded. He pushed a shopping cart stolidly down the sidewalk, ignoring six or seven Negro children who taunted him, and until he was very close Gus could not guess what his race was but guessed he was white because of the long gray hair. Then he saw that he was indeed a white man, but covered with crusty layers of filth. The ragpicker stopped near crevices and crannies between and behind the rows of one-story business buildings. He probed in trash cans and behind clumps of weeds in vacant lots until he discovered his prizes and the shopping cart was already filled with empty bottles which the children grabbed at. They shrieked in delight when the ragpicker made ineffectual swipes at their darting hands with his hairy paws too broad and massive for the emaciated body.

''Maybe he was wearing that helmet on some Pacific island when it got that hole blown in it,'' said Gus.

''It'd be nice to think so,'' said Kilvinsky. ''Adds a little glamour to the old ragpicker. You should keep an eye on those guys, though. They steal plenty. We watched one pushing his little cart along Vermont on Christmas Eve clouting presents out of cars that were parked at the curb. Had a pile of bottles and other trash on top and a cartload of stolen Christmas presents beneath.''

Kilvinsky started the car and resumed his slow patrol and Gus felt much more at ease after the coffee and doughnut which domesticized the strange feeling he had here in the city. He was so provincial, he thought, even though he grew up in Azusa, and made frequent trips to Los Angeles.

Kilvinsky drove slowly enough for Gus to read the signs in the windows of the drugstores and neighborhood markets, which advertised hair straighteners, skin brighteners, scalp conditioner, pressing oil, waxes and pomades. Kilvinsky pointed to a large crudely lettered whitewashed warning on a board fence which said, ''Bab bog,'' and Gus noticed the professional lettering on the pool hall window which said, ''Billard Parler.'' Kilvinsky parked in front of the pool hall, telling Gus he had something to show him.

The pool hall, which Gus supposed would be empty at the dinner hour, was teeming with men and a few women, all Negro except for two of the three women who slouched at a table near the small room at the rear of the building. Gus noticed one of the women, a middle-aged woman with hair like flames, scurried into the back room as soon as she spotted them. The pool players ignored them and continued the nine ball contests.

''Probably a little dice game going in the back,'' said Kilvinsky as Gus eagerly studied everything about the place, the floor caked with grime, six threadbare pool tables, two dozen men sitting or standing against the walls, the blaring record player being overseen by a pudgy cigar chewer in a blue silk undershirt, the smell of stale sweat and beer, for which there was no license, cigarette smoke, and through it all a good barbecue smell. Gus knew by the smell that whatever else they were doing in the back room, somebody was cooking, and that seemed very strange somehow. The three women were all fiftyish and very alcoholic-looking, the Negro being the slimmest and cleanest-looking of the three although she too was foul enough, Gus thought.

"A shine parlor or pool hall down here is the last stop for a white whore," said Kilvinsky following Gus's eyes. "There's what I brought you in here to see." Kilvinsky pointed at a sign high on the wall over the door which led to the back room. The sign read, "No liquor or narcotics allowed."

Gus was relieved to get back in the air, and he inhaled deeply. Kilvinsky resumed patrol and Gus was already starting to know the voices of the female Communications operators, particularly the one with the deep young voice on frequency thirteen, who would occasionally whisper "Hi" into the mike or "roger" in coy response to the policemen's voices he could not hear. It had been a surprise to him that the radios were two-way radios and not three-way, but it was just as well, he thought, because the jumble of women's voices was hard enough to understand without more voices from all the radio cars being thrown in.

"I'll wait till dark to show you Western Avenue," said Kilvinsky and now Gus could definitely feel the refreshing coolness of approaching night although it was far from dark.

"What's on Western Avenue?"

"Whores. Of course there're whores all over this part of town, but Western is the whore center of the city. They're all over the street."

"Don't we arrest them?"

"*We* don't. What would we arrest them for? Walking the street? Just *being* whores? No crime in that. Vice officers arrest them when they tail them to their trick pad, or when they operate the girl undercover and get an offer of prostitution."

"I wonder what working vice would be like?" Gus mused aloud.

"You might get a chance to find out someday," Kilvinsky said. "You're kind of small and . . . oh, a little more docile than the average pushy cop. I think you'd be a good undercover operator. You don't look like a policeman."

Gus thought of being here in the streets in plainclothes, perhaps without a partner, and he was glad such assignments were voluntary. He watched a very dark-skinned homosexual mincing across Vernon Avenue when the light turned green.

"Hope we don't lose our masquerading laws," said Kilvinsky.

"What's that?"

"City ordinance against a man dressing up like a woman or vice versa. Keeps the fruits from going around full drag and causing all sorts of police problems. I got a feeling though that that's another law on the way out. Better write that address down."

"What address?"

"We just got a call."

"We did? Where?" asked Gus, turning the radio louder and readying his pencil.

"Three-A-Ninety-nine, repeat," said Kilvinsky.

"Three-A-Ninety-nine, Three-A-Ninety-nine, a forgery suspect there now, at Forty-one-thirty-two south Broadway, see the man at that location, code two."

"Three-A-Ninety-nine, roger," said Gus, rubbing his palms on his thighs impatiently, and wondering why Kilvinsky didn't drive a bit faster. After all, it was a code two call.

They were only three blocks from the call but when they arrived another car was already parked in the front of the market and Kilvinsky double-parked until Leoni walked out of the store and over to their car.

"Suspect's a female wino," said Leoni, leaning in the window on Gus's side. "Guy offered her ten bucks to try and pass a hundred and thirty dollar payroll check. Probably a phony, but it looks pretty good. Check writer was used. The bitch said the guy was middle-aged, red shirt, average size. She just met him in a gin mill."

"Negro?" asked Kilvinsky.

"What else?"

"We'll take a look around," Kilvinsky said.

Kilvinsky circled the block once, studying people and cars. Gus wondered what they were supposed to be looking for because there were less than ten men in the immediate area who were middle-sized and none of them had on a red shirt, but on his second pass around the block, Kilvinsky turned sharply into a drugstore parking lot and zoomed across the alley toward a man who was walking toward the sidewalk. Kilvinsky jammed on the brakes and was on his feet before Gus was certain he was stopping.

''Just a minute,'' said Kilvinsky to the man who continued walking. ''Hold it, there.''

The man turned and looked quizzically at the two policemen. He wore a brown checkered shirt and a black felt stingy brim with a fat yellow feather. He was neither middle-aged nor of average size, but rather he was in his early thirties, Gus guessed, and was tall and portly.

''What you want?'' asked the man and Gus noticed the deep scar which followed the cheek line and was at first not apparent.

''Your identification, please,'' said Kilvinsky.

''What for?''

''I'll explain in a minute, but let me see your I.D. first. Something just happened.''

''Oh,'' sneered the man, ''and I'm suspicious, huh? I'm black so that makes me suspicious, huh? Black man is just ol' Joe Lunchmeat to you, huh?''

''Look around you,'' Kilvinsky said, taking a giant stride forward, ''you see anybody that ain't black except my partner and me? Now I picked you cause I got a motherfuckin' good reason. Break out that I.D. cause we ain't got time for shuckin'.''

''Okay, Officer,'' said the man, ''I ain't got nothin' to hide, it just that the PO-lice is always fuckin' over me ever' time I goes outside and I'm a workin' man. I works ever' day.''

Kilvinsky examined the social security card and Gus thought how Kilvinsky had talked to the man. His rage was profound and with his size it had cowed the Negro, and Kilvinsky had talked like a Negro, exactly like a Negro, Gus thought.

''This I.D. ain't shit, man,'' said Kilvinsky. ''Got something with your thumb print or a picture on it? Got a driver's license maybe?''

''What I need a drivin' license fo'? I ain't drivin'.''

''What you been busted for?''

''Gamblin', traffic tickets, suspicious, a time or two.''

''Forgery?''

''No, man.''

''Flim flam?''

''No, man. I gambles a little bit, I ain't no criminal, no jive.''

''Yeah, you jivin',' said Kilvinsky. ''Your mouth is dry; you're lickin' your lips.''

''Sheee-it, man, when the bluesuits stops me, I always gets nervous.''

''Your heart is hammerin',' said Kilvinsky, placing a hand on the man's chest. ''What's your real name?''

''Gandy. Woodrow Gandy. Just like it say on that card,'' said the man who now was obviously nervous. He shuffled his feet and could not control the darting pink tongue which moistened brown lips every few seconds.

''Hop in the car, Gandy,'' said Kilvinsky. ''There's an old drunk across the street. I want her to take a look at you.''

''Ohooo man, this is a roust!'' said Gandy as Kilvinsky patted him down. ''This is a humbug and a roust!''

Gus noticed that Gandy knew which side of the police car to sit in, and Gus sat behind Kilvinsky and reached across locking the door on Gandy's side.

They drove back to the bank and found Leoni sitting in his radio car with a frazzled bleary-eyed Negro woman about forty who peeked out the window of Leoni's car toward Gandy when Kilvinsky pulled along-side.

"That's him. That the nigger that got me in all this trouble!" she shrieked, and then to Gandy she said. "Yeah, you, you bastard, standin' there finger poppin' and talkin' so smart to ever'one and tell me how easy I could earn ten dollars and how smart you was and all, you black son of a bitch. That's the one, Officer, I done told you I would be yo' witness and I means it, no jive. I tol' you he had a big flappy mouf like Cheetah. He the one all right. If I'm lyin', I'm flyin'."

Gandy turned away from the drunken woman and Gus was embarrassed by her words, but Gandy seemed completely unconcerned and Gus was astonished at how they degraded one another. He guessed they learned from the white man.

It was after nine o'clock when they finally got Gandy in the booking office of University jail. It was an antiquated jail and looked like a dungeon. Gus wondered what the cells were like. He wondered why they didn't take Gandy's shoelaces like they do in movies, but he remembered hearing a policeman in the academy saying that you can't stop a man from committing suicide who really wants to and then he described the death of the prisoner who tied strips of a pillowcase around his neck and then to the barred door. The man did a backflip, breaking his neck, and the officer quipped that deaths in jail caused tons of paper work and were very inconsiderate on the part of the deceased. Of course everybody laughed as policemen always did at grim humor and attempts at humor.

Over the booking officer's desk was a sign which read, "Support your local police. Be a snitch," and a toy spear perhaps three feet long decorated with African symbols and colorful feathers. It had a rubber blade and a sign over it said, "Search your prisoners thoroughly." Gus wondered if the Negro policemen were offended by this and for the first time in his life he was becoming acutely aware of Negroes in general, and he guessed he would become even more so because he would now spend most of his waking hours here among them. He wasn't sorry, he was interested, but he was also afraid of them. But then, he would probably be almost as fearful of any people no matter where he was stationed, and then he thought, what if Gandy had resisted arrest and what if Kilvinsky were not with him. Could he have handled a man like Gandy?

As the booking officer typed, Gus thought of Gus, Jr., three years old, and how chesty he was. Gus knew he would be a big husky boy. Already he could throw a man-sized basketball halfway across the living room and this was their favorite toy even though they broke one of Vickie's new decanters with it. Gus clearly remembered his own father's rough and tumble play although he never saw him again after the divorce, and how they had played. He remembered the moustache with wisps of gray among the brown and the big dry hard hands which tossed him confidently and surely into the air until he could hardly breathe for the laughter. He described this to his mother once when he was twelve, and old enough to see how miserably sad it made her. He never mentioned his father again and tried to be more helpful to his mother than ever because he was four years older than John and was his mother's little man she said. Gus guessed he was fiercely proud of the fact that he had worked since he was a small boy to help support the three of them. Now the pride was gone and it was a genuine hardship to set aside fifty dollars a month for her and John, now that he and Vickie were married and he had his own family.

"Ready to go, pard?" asked Kilvinsky.

"Oh, sure."

"Daydreaming?"

"Yeah."

"Let's go eat now, and do the arrest report later."

"Okay," said Gus, brightening at the thought. "You aren't too mad to eat, are you?"

"Mad?"

"For a minute I thought you were going to eat that suspect alive."

"I wasn't mad," said Kilvinsky, looking at Gus in surprise as they walked to the car. "That was just my act. Change the words once in a while, but I use the same tune. Don't they teach you about interrogation at the academy anymore?"

"I thought you were blowing your top."

"Hell, no. I just figured he was the type who only respected naked strength, not civility. You can't use that technique on everybody. In fact, if you try it on some guys you might find yourself on your back looking up. But I figured he'd quiet down if I talked his language, so I did. You have to size up each suspect fast and make up your mind how you're going to talk to him."

"Oh," said Gus. "But how did you know he was the suspect? He didn't look like her description. His shirt wasn't even red."

"How did I know," Kilvinsky murmured. "Let's see. You haven't been to court yet, have you?"

"No."

"Well, you'll have to start answering the question, 'How did you know?' I don't honestly know how I knew. But I knew. At least I was pretty sure. The shirt wasn't red, but it wasn't green either. It was a color that could be called red by a fuzzy-eyed drunk. It was a rusty brown. And Gandy was standing a little too casually there in the parking lot. He was too cool and he gave me too much of an 'I got nothing to hide' look when I was driving by and eyeballing everybody that could possibly be the guy. And when I came back around he had moved to the other side of the lot. He was still moving when I turned the corner but when he sees us he stops to show us he's not walking away. He's got nothing to hide. I know this means nothing by itself, but these are some of the little things. I just *knew,* I tell you."

"Instinct?"

"I think so. But I wouldn't say that in court."

"Will you have trouble in court with this case?"

"Oh no. This isn't a search and seizure case. If we had a search and seizure case going, that feeling and those little things he did wouldn't be enough. We'd lose. Unless we stretched the truth."

"Do you stretch the truth sometimes?"

"I don't. I don't care enough about people in general to get emotionally involved. I don't give a shit if I busted Jack the Ripper and lost him on an unreasonable search. As long as the asshole stays off *my* property, I don't worry about it. Some policemen become avenging angels. They have a real animal who's hurt a lot of people and they decide they have to convict him even if it means lying in court, but I say it's not worth it. The public isn't worth your risking a perjury rap. And he'll be back on the street before long anyway. Stay frosty. Relax. That's the way to do this job. You can beat it then. You take your forty percent after twenty years, and your family, if you still have one, and you make it. Go to Oregon or Montana."

"Do you have a family?"

"I'm single now. This job isn't conducive to stable family relationships, the marriage counselors say. I think we're near the top in suicide rate."

"I hope I can do this job," Gus blurted, surprised at the desperate tone in his own voice.

"Police work is seventy percent common sense. That's about what makes a policeman, common sense, and the ability to make a quick decision. You've got to cultivate those abilities or get out. You'll learn to appreciate this in your fellow policemen. Pretty soon, you won't be able to feel the same way about your friends in the lodge or church or in your neighborhood because they won't measure up to policemen in these ways. You'll be able to come up with a quick solution for *any* kind of strange situation because you have to do it every day, and you'll get mad as hell at your old friends if they can't.''

Gus noticed that now that night had come, the streets were filling with people, black people, and the building fronts shone forth. It seemed that every block had at least one bar or liquor store and all the liquor store proprietors were white men. It seemed to Gus that now you didn't notice the churches, only the bars and liquor stores and places where crowds of people were standing around. He saw boisterous crowds around hamburger stands, liquor stores, certain porches of certain apartment houses, parking lots, shine stands, record stores, and a suspicious place whose windows advertised that this was a ''Social Club.'' Gus noticed the peephole in the door and he wished that he could be inside there unnoticed, and his curiosity was stronger than his fear.

''How about some soul food, brother?'' asked Kilvinsky with a Negro accent as he parked in front of the neat lunch counter on Normandie.

''I'll try anything,'' Gus smiled.

''Fat Jack makes the best gumbo in town. Lots of shrimp and crab meat and chicken and okra, easy on the rice and lots of down home flavor. Real Looos-iana gumbo.''

''You from the South?''

''No, I just appreciate the cooking,'' Kilvinsky said, and held the door as they entered the restaurant. Soon they were served the huge bowl of gumbo and Gus liked the way Fat Jack said, ''They was full of shrimps tonight.'' He poured some hot sauce on the gumbo as Kilvinsky did even though it was tangy enough, but it was delicious, even the chopped-up chicken necks and the crab claws which had to be picked and sucked clean. Kilvinsky poured more ladles of hot sauce over the spicy gruel and ate half a pan of corn bread. But it was spoiled a little because they each left a quarter tip for the waitress and that was all, and Gus felt guilty to accept a gratuity and he wondered how he would explain it to a sergeant. He wondered if Fat Jack and the waitresses called them freeloaders behind their backs.

At 11:00 P.M. while cruising the dark residential streets north of Slauson Avenue, Kilvinsky said, ''You ready to go work the whore wagon?''

''The what?''

''I asked the sergeant if we could take the wagon out tonight to roust the whores and he said it'd be okay if the air was quiet and I haven't heard a radio call in University Division for a half hour, so let's go in and get the wagon. I think you might find it educational.''

''There don't seem to be too many whores around,'' said Gus. ''There were those two at Vernon and Broadway you pointed out and one on Fifty-eighth, but . . .''

''Wait till you see Western Avenue.''

After arriving at the station Kilvinsky pointed to the blue panel truck in the station parking lot with the white ''Los Angeles Police Department'' on the side. The back end was windowless and two benches were attached to each wall of the truck. A heavy steel screen separated the passengers from the front of the cab.

''Let's go tell the boss we're gong out in the wagon,'' said Kilvinsky, and after another fifteen-minute delay while Kilvinsky joked with Candy the policewoman at the desk, they were in the wagon which rumbled down Jefferson Boulevard like a blue rhino. Gus thought he would hate to be sitting on the wooden bench in the back of this hard-riding wagon.

Kilvinsky turned north on Western Avenue and they had not driven two blocks on Western until he found himself counting the sauntering, wriggling, garishly dressed women who strolled down the sidewalks mostly *with* the traffic so that the cars would pull conveniently to the curb. The bars and restaurants on and near

Western were bulging with people and there was a formidable fleet of Cadillac convertibles parked in the lot of "Blue Dot McAfee's Casbah."

"Pimping is profitable," said Kilvinsky, pointing to the Cadillacs. "There's too much money in pussy. I suspect that's why it's not legalized in many countries. Too much profit and no overhead. The pimps would control the economy in no time."

"Christ, it looks like it's legal *here!*" said Gus, taking in the colorful figures on both sides of Western who were leaning in the windows of parked cars, standing in groups or sitting on the low walls in front of the residences. Gus noticed that the prostitutes looked with concern at the blue wagon as it rumbled north toward Adams Boulevard.

"I believe in giving them one pass down Western to show the wagon's out. If they stay on the street we pick them up. Sure a lot of money in wigs out there, huh?"

"God, yes." said Gus, looking at an incredibly buxom prostitute standing alone on the corner of Twenty-seventh. He was astounded at how attractive some of them were and he noticed that they all carried purses.

"They've got purses," Gus said.

"Oh, yeah," Kilvinsky smiled. "Just for show. High skinny heels and purses, short skirts or tight pants. Uniform of the day. But don't worry, they don't carry any bread in those purses. All women in these parts carry their money in their bras."

When they got to Washington Boulevard, Kilvinsky turned around.

"There were twenty-eight whores on the Avenue," said Gus. "And I think I missed counting some right at first!"

"The people around here have got to stop it," said Kilvinsky, lighting a cigarette and inserting it in a plastic cigarette holder. "Soon as they bitch loud enough the judges will give the girls some time and they'll go underground again. I know a whore with seventy-three prior arrests. Most time she ever did was six months on two separate occasions. This whore wagon is completely illegal by the way."

"What do we do with them? Where do we take them? I was wondering about that."

"For a ride, that's all. We pick them up and ride them around for an hour or so and take them to the station and run a make to see if they have any traffic warrants and let them go from the station. It's illegal as hell. We'll be stopped from doing it one of these days, but right now it works. The girls hate to be picked up in the wagon. Stop-gap measure. Let's take those two."

Gus saw no one at first and then saw a movement in the shadows near the phone booth at the corner of Twenty-first Street and two girls in blue dresses walked west on Twenty-first. They ignored Kilvinsky's, "Evening ladies," until both policemen were out of the cab and Kilvinsky was holding the back door of the wagon open.

"Shit, fuck, Kilvinsky, you always picks on me," said the younger of the two, a yellow girl in an auburn wig who, Gus supposed, was even younger than himself.

"Who's the baby?" asked the other, pointing at Gus and appearing resigned to climbing the high step into the back of the panel. She hiked the flesh-tight blue satin dress up to her hips to make the step. "Give me a lift, baby," she said to Gus but didn't hold out her hand. "Grab a handful of mah big ass and push."

Kilvinsky chewed on the cigarette holder and eyed Gus with frank amusement, and Gus saw her firm pantiless buttocks like a dark melon with a sliver removed. He held her around the waist and boosted her up as she shrieked with laughter and Kilvinsky chuckled softly as he locked the double doors and they climbed back in the cab.

The next girl they picked up at Adams, and there were not so many now that everyone knew the wagon was out, but they picked up three more at Twenty-seventh, one of whom cursed Kilvinsky viciously because someone had made her ride in the wagon only last night and it wasn't her turn again, she said.

Once the prostitutes were in the wagon, they chattered and laughed pleasantly enough. It seemed to Gus that a few of them might be enjoying the respite from the street and Kilvinsky assured him that there was truth in this when Gus asked him, because their work was very dangerous and demanding, what with robbers and sadists prowling for prostitutes. The pimps provided little protection except from other pimps who were constantly trying to enlarge their own stables.

The tall policeman who had talked to Lafitte in the locker room was standing with his partner at Twenty-eighth beside the open door of the radio car talking to two prostitutes. The tall one motioned them to the curb.

"Got two for you, Andy," said the tall policeman.

"Yeah, you should make sergeant for this, you blue-eyed devil," said the umber-colored girl, with a natural hairdo, and a severe short-skirted black dress.

"She doesn't like you, Bethel," said Kilvinsky to the tall policeman.

"He don't know how to talk to a woman," said the girl. "Nobody likes this funky devil."

"I don't see any women," said Bethel, "just two whores."

"Yo' wife's a whore, bastard," spat the girl, leaning forward at the waist. "She fucks fo' peanuts. I gets two hundred dollars every day fo' fuckin' you pitiful paddy motherfuckers. Yo' wife's the real whore."

"Get in the wagon, bitch," said Bethel, shoving the girl across the sidewalk and Gus grabbed her to keep her from falling.

"We goin' to fix you whiteys, one day," said the girl, sobbing. "You devil! I never feel you blue-eyed devils, do you hear? I feel nothin'! You paddy motherfuckers never make me feel nothin' with yo' needle dicks. You ain't gonna git away wif pushin' me aroun', hear me?"

"Okay, Alice, hop in, will you," said Kilvinsky, holding the girl's arm as she yielded and climbed into the wagon.

"That there suckah don't evah talk right to nobody," said a voice inside the blackness of the wagon. "He think people is dogs or somethin'. We is motherfuckin' ladies."

"I haven't met you yet," said Bethel, offering his hand to Gus who shook it, looking up at the large brown eyes of Bethel.

"This is quite an experience," said Gus haltingly.

"It's a garbage truck," said Bethel. "But this ain't too bad, really. You ought to work Newton Division ..."

"We've got to get going, Bethel," said Kilvinsky.

"One thing, Plebesly," said Bethel, "at least working around here you never run into nobody smarter than you."

"Do I have to get in the wagon, too?" asked the second girl and for the first time Gus noticed she was white. She had a high-styled black wig and her eyes were dark. She had a fine sun tan but she was definitely a white woman and Gus thought she was exceptionally pretty.

"Your old man is Eddie Simms, ain't that right, nigger?" Bethel whispered to the girl, whom he held by the upper arm. "You give all your money to a nigger, don't you? You'd do just anything for that slick-haired boy, wouldn't you? That makes you a nigger too, don't it, nigger?"

"Get in the wagon, Rose," said Kilvinsky taking her arm, but Bethel gave her a push and she dropped her purse and fell heavily into Kilvinsky, who cursed and lifted her into the wagon with one large hand while Gus picked up the purse.

"When you get more time on the job you'll learn not to manhandle another officer's prisoner," said Kilvinsky to Bethel as they got back in the wagon.

Bethel faced Kilvinsky for a moment, but said nothing, turned, got back in his car, and was roaring halfway up Western before Kilvinsky ever started the motor.

"Got lots of problems, that kid," said Kilvinsky. "Only two years on the Department and already he's got lots of problems."

"Hey," said a voice from the back of the wagon as they bounced and jogged across Jefferson and began an aimless ride to harass the prostitutes. "Yo'all need some pillas back here. This is terrible bumpy."

"Your pillow is built in, baby," said Kilvinsky and several girls laughed.

"Hey silver hair. How 'bout lettin' us out ovah on Vermont or somewhere," said another voice. "I jist got to make me some coin tonight."

"Kilvinsky got soul," said another voice. "He git us some scotch if we ask him pretty. You got soul, don't you, Mr. Kilvinsky?"

"Baby, Ah gots more soul than Ah kin control," said Kilvinsky and the girls burst into laughter.

"He sho' kin talk that trash," said a throaty voice that sounded like the girl who had cursed Bethel.

Kilvinsky parked in front of a liquor store and shouted over his shoulder, "Get your money ready and tell me what you want." Then to Gus, "Stay in the wagon. I'll be back."

Kilvinsky went around to the back and opened the door.

"Dollar each," said one of the girls and Gus heard the rustle of clothing and paper and the clink of coins.

"Two quarts of milk and a fifth of scotch. That okay?" asked one of the girls and several voices muttered, "Uh huh."

"Give me enough for paper cups," said Kilvinsky, "I'm not going to use my own money."

"Baby, if you'd turn in that bluesuit, you wouldn't have to worry 'bout money," said the one called Alice. "I'd keep you forever, you beautiful blue-eyed devil."

The girls laughed loudly as Kilvinsky closed the wagon and entered the liquor store, returning with a shopping bag in a few minutes.

He handed the bag in the door and was back in the cab and moving when Gus heard the liquor being poured.

"Change is in the bag," said Kilvinsky.

"Gud-dam," muttered one of the prostitutes. "Scotch and milk is the best motherfuckin' drink in the world. Want a drink, Kilvinsky?"

"You know we can't drink on duty."

"I know somethin' we can do on duty," said another one. "And yo' sergeant won't smell it on yo' breath. Less'n you want to get down on yo' knees and French me."

The girls screamed in laughter and Kilvinsky said, "I'm too damn old for you young girls."

"You ever change yo' mind, let me know," said Alice, "a foxy little whore like me could make you young again."

Kilvinsky drove aimlessly for more than a half hour while Gus listened as the prostitutes laughed and talked shop, each girl trying to top the last one with her account of the "weird tricks" she had encountered.

"Hell," said one prostitute, "I had one pick me up right here on Twenty-eighth and Western one night and take me clear to Beverly Heels for a hundred bucks and that bastard had me cut the head of a live chicken right there in some plushy apartment and then squish the chicken aroun' in the sink while the water was runnin' and he stood there and comed like a dog."

"Lord! Why did you do it, girl?" asked another.

"Shee-it, I didn't know what the suckah wanted till he got me in that place and handed me the butcher knife. Then I was so scared I jist did it so he wouldn' git mad. Ol' funky bastard, he was. Didn' think he could even git a stiff one."

"How 'bout that freak that lives up there in Van Nuys that likes to French inside a coffin. He sho' is a crazy motherfucker," said a shrill voice.

"That milk bath guy picked Wilma up one night, didn't he Wilma?" said another.

"Yeah, but he ain't nothin' too weird. Ah don' mind him, 'cept he lives too far away, way up in North Hollywood in one of them pads on a mountain. He jist gives you a bath in a tub full of milk. He pays damn good."

"He don' do nothin' else?"

"Oh, he Frenches you a little, but not too much."

"Shit, they almost all Frenches you anymore. People is gettin' so goddamn weird all they evah wants to do is eat pussy."

"That right, girl. I was sayin' that the other day (pour me a little scotch, honey) people jist French or git Frenched anymore. I can't remember when a trick wanted to fuck me for his ten dollars."

"Yeah, but these is all white tricks. Black men still likes to fuck."

"Shee-it, I wouldn' know 'bout that. You take black tricks, baby?"

"Sometimes, don't you?"

"Nevah. Nevah. My ol' man tol' me any who' dum 'nuff to take black tricks deserves it if she gits her ass robbed or cut. Ah never fucked a niggah in my life fo' money. An' ah never fucked a white man fo' free."

"Amen. Give me another shot of that scotch, baby, ah wants to tell you 'bout this here rich bitch from Hollywood that picked me up one night an' she wanted to give me a hunderd an' fifty dollars to go home an' let her eat mah pussy an' her husband is sittin' right there in the car with her an' she tells me he jist likes to watch."

Gus listened to tale after tale, each more bizarre than the last and when the voices were slurring, Kilvinsky said, "Let's head for the station and let them go a few blocks away. They're too drunk to take them in the station. The sergeant would want us to book them for being drunk and then they might tell him where they got the booze."

As the wagon bounced toward the station, the night drawing to a close, Gus found himself more relaxed than he had been for days. As for a physical confrontation, why, it might never happen and if it did, he would probably do well enough. He was feeling a lot better now. He hoped Vickie would be awake. He had so much to tell her.

"You're going to learn things down here, Gus," said Kilvinsky. "Every day down here is like ten days in a white division. It's the intensity down here, not just the high crime rate. You'll be a veteran after a year. It's the thousands of little things. Like the fact that you shouldn't use a pay phone. The coin chutes of all the public phones around here are stuffed so you can't get any coins back. Then once every few days the thief comes along and pulls the stuffing out with a piece of wire and gets the three dollars worth of coins that've collected there. And other things. Kid's bikes. They're all stolen, or they all have stolen parts on them, so don't ask questions to any kid about his bike or you'll be tied up all night with bike reports. Little things, see, like New Year's Eve down here sounds like the battle of Midway. All these people seem to have guns. New Year's Eve will terrify you when you realize how many of them have guns and what's going to happen someday if this Civil Rights push ever breaks into armed rebellion. But the time passes fast down here, because these people keep us eternally busy and that's important to me. I only have a short time to go for my pension and I'm interested in time."

"I'm not sorry I'm here," said Gus.

"It's all happening here, partner. Big things. This Civil Rights business and the Black Muslims and all are just the start of it. Authority is being challenged and the Negroes are at the front, but they're just a small part of it. You're going to have an impossible job in the next five years or I miss my guess."

Kilvinsky steered around an automobile wheel which was lying in the center of the residential street, but he rolled over another which lay on the other side of the street, unobserved, until they were on it. The exhausted blue van bounced painfully on its axle and a chorus of laughter was interrupted by an explosion of curses.

"Goddamn! Take it easy, Kilvinsky! You ain't drivin' no fuckin' cattle truck," said Alice.

"It's the great myth," said Kilvinsky to Gus, ignoring the voices behind them, "the myth whatever it happens to be that breaks civil authority. I wonder if a couple of centurions might've sat around like you and me one hot dry evening talking about the myth of Christianity that was defeating them. They would've been afraid, I bet, but the new myth was loaded with 'don'ts', so one kind of authority was just being substituted for another. Civilization was never in jeopardy. But today the 'don'ts' are dying or being murdered in the name of freedom and we policemen can't save them. Once the people become accustomed to the death of a 'don't,' well then, the other 'don'ts' die much easier. Usually all the vice laws die first because people are generally vice-ridden anyway. Then the ordinary misdemeanors and some felonies become unenforceable until freedom prevails. Then later the freed people have to organize an army of their own to find order because they learn that freedom is horrifying and ugly and only small doses of it can be tolerated." Kilvinsky laughed self-consciously, a laugh that ended when he put the battered cigarette holder in his mouth and chewed on it quietly for several seconds. "I warned you us old coppers are big bullshitters, didn't I, Gus?"

6

The Swamper

"How about driving to a gamewell phone? I got to call the desk about something," said Whitey Duncan, and Roy sighed, turning the radio car right on Adams toward Hooper where he thought there was a call box.

"Go to Twenty-third and Hooper," said Duncan. "That's one of the few call boxes that works in this lousy division. Nothing works. The people don't work, the call boxes don't work, nothing works."

Some of the policemen don't work, thought Roy, and wondered how they could have possibly assigned him with Duncan five nights in a row. Granted, August was a time when the car plan was short due to vacations, but Roy thought that was a feeble reason and inexcusable supervisory technique to give a rookie officer to a partner like Duncan. After his second night with Whitey he had even subtly suggested to Sergeant Coffin that he would like to work with an aggressive younger officer, but Coffin had cut him off abruptly as though a new officer had no right to ask for a specific car or partner. Roy felt that he was being penalized for speaking up by being inflicted with Duncan for five days.

"I'll be right back, kid," said Whitey, leaving his hat in the radio car as he strolled to the call box, unsnapped the gamewell key from the ring hanging on his Sam Browne, and opened the box which was attached to the far side of a telephone pole out of Roy's line of sight. Roy could only see some white hair, a round blue stomach and shiny black shoe protruding from the vertical line of the pole.

Roy was told that Whitey had been a foot policeman in Central Division for almost twenty years and that he could never get used to working in a radio car. That was probably why he insisted on calling the station a half dozen times a night to talk to his friend, Sam Tucker, the desk officer.

After a few moments, Whitey swaggered back to the car and settled back, lighting his third cigar of the evening.

"You sure like to use that call box," said Roy with a forced smile, trying to conceal the anger brought about by the boredom of working with a useless partner like Whitey when he was brand-new and eager to learn.

"Got to ring in. Let the desk know where you're at."

"Your radio tells them that, Whitey. Policemen have radios in their cars nowadays."

"I'm not used to it," said Whitey. "Like to ring in on the call box. Besides, I like to talk to my old buddy, Sam Tucker. Good man, old Sammy."

"How come you always call in on the same box?"

"Habit, boy. When you get to be old Whitey's age, you start doing everything the same."

It was true, Roy thought. Unless an urgent call intervened, they would eat at precisely ten o'clock every night at one of three greasy spoon restaurants that served Whitey free meals. Then, fifteen minutes would be spent at the station for Whitey's bowel movement. Then back out for the remainder of the watch, which would be broken by two or three stops at certain liquor stores for free cigars and of course the recurrent messages to Sam Tucker from the call box at Twenty-third and Hooper.

"How about driving through the produce market?" said Whitey. "I never took you in there yet, did I?"

"Whatever you say," Roy sighed.

Whitey directed Roy through bustling narrow streets blocked by a maze of trucks and milling swampers who were just coming to work. "Over there," said Whitey. "That's old Foo Foo's place. He has the best bananas in the market. Park right there, kid. Then we'll get some avocados. They're a quarter apiece, right now. You like avocados? Then maybe a lug of peaches. I know a guy on the other side of the market, he has the best peaches. Never a bruise." Whitey lumbered out of the car, and put on his hat at a jaunty beat officer's angle, grabbed his baton, probably from force of habit, and began twirling it expertly in his left hand as he approached the gaunt Chinese who was sweating in a pair of khaki shorts and an undershirt as he threw huge bunches of bananas onto a produce truck. The Chinese bared his gold and silver bridgework when Whitey approached and Roy lit a cigarette and watched in revulsion as Whitey put his baton in the ring on his belt and helped Foo Foo toss bananas onto the truck.

Professional policeman, Roy thought viciously, as he remembered the suave, silver-haired captain who had lectured them in the academy about the new professionalism. But it seemed the fat cop stealing apples died hard. Look at the old bastard, thought Roy, throwing bananas in full uniform while all the other swampers are laughing their heads off. Why doesn't he retire from the Department, and then he could swamp bananas full time. I hope a tarantula bites him on his fat ass, Roy thought.

How they could have sent him to Newton Street Station, Roy could not understand. What was the sense of giving them three choices of divisions if they were then ignored and sent arbitrarily from the academy to a station twenty miles from home. He lived almost in the valley. They could have sent him to one of the valley divisions or Highland Park or even Central which was his third choice, but Newton Street he had not counted on. It was the poorest of the Negro divisions and the drabness of the area was depressing. This was the "east side" and he already had learned that as soon as the newly emigrated Negroes could afford it, they moved to the "west side," somewhere west of Figueroa Street. But the fact that the majority of the people here were Negro was the one thing that appealed to Roy. When he left the Department to be a criminologist he intended to have a thorough understanding of the ghetto. He hoped to learn all that was necessary in a year or so, and then transfer north, perhaps to Van Nuys or North Hollywood.

When they finally left the produce market, the back seat of the radio car was filled with bananas, avocados and peaches, as well as a basket of tomatoes which Whitey had scrounged as an afterthought.

"You know you got a right to half of these," said Whitey as they loaded the produce into his private car in the station parking lot.

"I told you I didn't want any."

"Partners got to share and share alike. You got a right to half of it. How about the avocados? Why don't you take the avocados?"

"Son of a bitch," Roy blurted, "I don't want it! Look here, I'm just out of the academy. I've got eight months more to do on my probationary period. They can fire me on a whim anytime between now and then. No civil service protection for a probationer, you know. I can't be taking gratuities. At least not things like this. Free meals—cigarettes—coffee—that stuff seems to be traditional, but what if the sergeant saw us in the produce market tonight? I could lose my job!"

"Sorry, kid," said Whitey with a hurt expression. "I didn't know you felt that way. I'd take all the heat if we'd got caught, you should know that."

"Yeah? What would I use as an excuse? That you put a gun to my head and forced me to go with you on that shopping tour?"

Whitey completed the transfer of fruit without further comment and didn't speak again until they were back patrolling their district, then he said, "Hey, partner, drive to a call box, I got to ring in again."

"What the hell for?" said Roy, not caring what Whitey thought anymore. "What's going on? You got a bunch of broads leaving messages at the desk for you or something?"

"I just talk to old Sam Tucker," said Whitey with a deep sigh. "The old bastard gets lonesome there at the desk. We was academy classmates, you know. Twenty-six years this October. It's tough on him being colored and working a nigger division like this. Some nights he feels pretty low when they bring in some black bastard that killed an old lady or some other shitty thing like that, and these policemen shoot off their mouth in the coffee room about niggers and such. Sam hears it and it bothers him, so he gets feeling low. Course, he's too old to be a cop anyway. He was thirty-one when he came on the job. He ought to pull the pin and leave this crappy place."

"How old were you when you came on, Whitey?"

"Twenty-nine. Hey, drive to the call box on Twenty-third. You know that's my favorite box."

"I ought to know by now," said Roy.

Roy parked at the curb and waited hopelessly while Whitey went to the call box and talked to Sam Tucker for ten minutes.

Police professionalism would come only after the old breed was gone, Roy thought. That didn't really trouble him though, because he had no intention of making a career of police work. That reminded him he had better get busy and register for the coming semester if he hoped to keep on schedule and complete his degree as planned. He wondered how anyone could want to do this kind of work for a career. Now that the training phase was over, he was part of a system he would master, learn from, and leave behind.

He glanced in the car mirror. The sun had given him a fine color. Dorothy said she'd never seen him so tan, and whether it was the uniform or his fitness she obviously found him more desirable and wanted him to make love to her often. But it may have been only because she was pregnant with their first baby and she knew that soon there would be none of it for a while. And he did it, though the enormous mound of life almost revolted him and he pretended to enjoy it as much as he did when she was lithe with a satin stomach that would probably bear stretch scars forever now that she was pregnant. That was her fault. They had decided not to have children for five years, but she had made a mistake. The news had staggered him. All his plans had to be changed. She could no longer work as a senior steno at Rhem Electronics, and she had been making an excellent wage. He would have to stay with the Department an extra year or so to save money. He would not ask his father or Carl for assistance, not even for a loan now that they all knew he would never enter the family firm.

Trying to please them was the reason he changed his major three times until he took abnormal psychology with Professor Raymond, and learned from the flabby little scholar who he was. The kindly man, who had been like a father, had almost wept when Roy told him he was leaving college to join the Los Angeles Police Department for a year or two. They had sat in Professor Raymond's office until midnight while the little man coaxed and urged and swore at Roy's stubbornness and at last gave in when Roy convinced him he was tired and probably would fail every class next semester if he remained, that a year or two away from the books but in close touch with life would give him the impetus to return and take his bachelor's and master's degrees. And who knows, if he were the scholar that Professor Raymond believed he could be, he might even keep right on while he had the momentum and get his Ph.D.

"We might be colleagues someday, Roy," said the professor fervently shaking Roy's dry hand in both his moist soft ones. "Keep in touch with me, Roy."

And he had meant to. He wanted to talk with someone as sensitive as the professor about the things he had learned so far. He talked with Dorothy, of course. But she was so involved in the mysteries of childbirth that he doubted that she listened when he brought home the tales of the bizarre situations he encountered as a policeman and what they meant to a behaviorist.

While waiting for Whitey, Roy tilted the car mirror down and examined his badge and brass buttons. He was tall and slim but his shoulders were broad enough to make the tailored blue shirt becoming. His Sam Browne glistened and his shoes were as good as he could get them without the fanatical spit shine that some of the others employed. He kept the badge lustrous with a treated cloth and some jeweler's rouge. He decided that when his hair grew out he would never cut it short again. He had heard that a butch haircut sometimes grows out wavier than before.

"You're absolutely beautiful," said Whitey, jerking open the door and flopping into the seat with a fatuous grin at Roy.

"I dropped some cigarette ash on my shirt," said Roy, tilting the mirror to its former position. "I was just brushing it off."

"Let's go do some police work," said Whitey, rubbing his hands together.

"Why bother? We only have three more hours until end of watch," said Roy. "What the hell did Tucker tell you to make you so happy?"

"Nothing. I just feel good. It's a nice summer night. I just feel like working. Let's catch a burglar. Anybody show you yet how to patrol for burglars?"

"Thirteen-A-Forty-three, Thirteen-A-Forty-three," said the operator and Whitey turned up the volume, "see the woman, landlord-tenant dispute, forty-nine, thirty-nine south Avalon."

"Thirteen-A-Forty-three, roger," said Whitey into the hand mike. Then to Roy, "Well, instead of catching crooks, let's go pacify the natives."

Roy parked in front of the house on Avalon which was easy to find because of the porch light and the fragile white-haired Negro woman standing on the porch watching the street. She was perhaps sixty and smiled timidly when Roy and Whitey climbed the ten steps.

"This is it, Mr. PO-lice," she said, opening the battered screen door. "Won't you please come in?"

Roy removed his hat upon entering and became annoyed when Whitey failed to remove his also. It seemed that everything Whitey did irritated him.

"Won't you sit down?" she smiled, and Roy admired the tidy house she kept which looked old and clean and orderly like her.

"No, thanks, ma'am," said Whitey. "What can we do for you?"

"I got these here people that lives in the back. I don't know what to do. I hopes you can help me. They don't pay the rent on time never. And now they's two months behind and I needs the money terrible bad. I only lives on a little social security, you see, and I just got to have the rent."

"I appreciate your problem, ma'am, I sure do," said Whitey. "I once owned a duplex myself. I had some tenants that wouldn't pay and I had a heck of a time. Mine had five kids that like to've torn the place down. Yours have any kids?"

"They does. Six. And they tears up my property terrible."

"It's rough," said Whitey, shaking his head.

"What can I do, sir? Can you help me? I begged them to pay me."

"Sure wish we could," said Whitey, "but you see this is a civil matter and we only deal in criminal matters. You'd have to get the county marshal to serve them with a notice to quit and then you'd have to sue them for unlawful detainer. That's what they call it and that would take time and you'd have to pay a lawyer."

"I don't have no money for a lawyer, Mr. PO-lice," said the old woman, her thin hand touching Whitey beseechingly on the arm.

"I appreciate that, ma'am," said Whitey, "I sure do. By the way, is that corn bread I smell?"

"It sho' is, sir. Would you like some?"

"Would I?" said Whitey, removing his hat and leading the old woman to the kitchen. "I'm a country-raised boy. I grew up in Arkansas on corn bread."

"Would you like some?" she smiled to Roy.

"No, thank you," he said.

"Some coffee? It's fresh."

"No ma'am, thank you."

"I don't know when I had such good corn bread," said Whitey. "Soon's I finish I'm going back and talk to your tenants for you. They in the little cottage in the rear?"

"Yes, sir. That's where they is. I sure would appreciate that and I'm going to tell our councilman what a fine PO-lice force we have. You always so good to me no matter what I calls for. You from Newton Street Station, ain't you?"

"Yes, ma'am, you just tell the councilman that you liked the service of old Whitey from Newton Street. You can even call the station and tell my sergeant if you want to."

"Why I'll do that, I surely will, Mr. Whitey. Can I get you some more corn bread?"

"No, no thank you," said Whitey, wiping his entire face with the linen napkin the old woman got for him. "We'll have a little talk with them and I bet they get your rent to you real quick."

"Thank you very much," the old woman called, as Roy followed Whitey and his flashlight beam down the narrow walkway to the rear of the property. Roy's frustration had subsided in his pity for the plight of the old woman and his admiration of her neat little house. There weren't enough like her in the ghetto, he thought.

"It's too damned bad that people would take advantage of a nice old woman like that," said Roy as they approached the rear cottage.

"How do you know they did?" asked Whitey.

"What do you mean? You heard her."

"I heard one side of a landlord-tenant dispute," said Whitey. "Now I got to hear the other side. You're the judge in all these dispute calls we get. Never make a decision till both sides present their cases."

This time Roy bit his lip to enforce his silence. The absurdity of this man was beyond belief. A child could see the old woman had a just grievance and he knew before the door opened that the cottage would be a filthy hovel where miserable children lived in squalor with deadbeat parents.

A coffee-colored woman in her late twenties opened the door when Whitey tapped.

"Mrs. Carson said she was going to call the PO-lice," said the woman with a tired smile. "Come in, Officers."

Roy followed Whitey into the little house which had a bedroom in the back, a small kitchen, and a living room filled by the six children who were gathered around an ancient television with a dying picture tube.

"Honey," she called, and a man padded into the room from the back, wearing frayed khaki trousers and a faded blue short-sleeved shirt which revealed oversized arms and battered hard-working hands.

"I just didn't think she'd really call the law," he said with an embarrassed smile at the officers, as Roy wondered how the cottage could be kept this clean with so many small children.

"We're two weeks behind in our rent," he drawled. "We never been behind befo' 'cept oncet and that was fo' three days. That ol' lady is mighty hard."

"She says you're over two months behind," said Roy.

"Looky here," said the man, going to the kitchen cupboard and returning with several slips of paper. "Here's last month's receipt and the month befo' and the one befo' that, clear back to January when we fust came here from Arkansas."

"You from Arkansas?" said Whitey. "Whereabouts? I'm from Arkansas too."

"Wait a minute, Whitey," said Roy, then turned back to the man. "Why would Mrs. Carson say you were behind in your rent? She said you never pay her on time and she's told you how she needs the money and that your kids have destroyed her property. Why would she say that?"

"Officer," said the man, "Mrs. Carson is a very hard lady. She owns most of this side of Avalon from Fo'ty-ninth Street on down to the co'ner."

"Have your children ever destroyed her property?" asked Roy weakly.

"Look at my house, Officer," said the woman. "Do it look like we the kind of folks that would let a chil' tear up a house? Once James there broke her basement window chucking a rock at a tin can. But she added that on our rent payment and we paid fo' it."

"How do you like California?" asked Whitey.

"Oh, we likes it fine," smiled the man. "Soon's we can save a little we wants to maybe buy a small house and get away from Mrs. Carson."

"Well, we got to be going now," said Whitey. "Sure sorry you're having troubles with your landlady. I want to wish you good luck here in California, and listen, if you ever happen to make any down-home Arkansas meals and have some left over you just call Newton Street Station and let me know, will you?"

"Why, we'll do that, sir," said the woman. "Who'll we ask fo'?"

"Just say old Whitey. And you might tell the sergeant old Whitey gave you good service. We need a pat on the back once in a while."

"Thank you, Officer," said the man. "It's surely a comfort to meet such fine *po*-licemen here."

"So long, kids," shouted Whitey to the six beaming brown faces which by now were gazing reverently at the policemen. They all waved good-byes as Roy followed the fat blue swaggering figure back down the narrow walkway to the car.

While Whitey was lighting a cigar Roy asked, "How did you know the old lady was lying? You probably answered calls there before, right?"

"Never did," said Whitey. "Goddamn cigars. Wonder if good cigars draw better than cheap ones?"

"Well how did you know then? You must've suspected she was lying."

"I never said she was lying. I don't say it now. There's two sides to every beef. Experience'll teach you that. You got to listen to the first guy like he's giving you the gospel and then go to the second guy and do the same thing. You just got to be patient, use horse sense and this job is easy."

Handling a rent dispute doesn't make you a policeman, Roy thought. There's more to police work than that.

"You ready to teach me how to catch a burglar now?" asked Roy, knowing the satirical edge on his voice was apparent.

"Okay, but first I got to make sure you can handle a simple landlord-tenant beef. First thing you already learned, don't take no sides. Next thing, a landlord-tenant beef or anything else could involve a psycho, or a crook with something in the pad he don't want you to see, or somebody that's so pissed off at his landlord or tenant that he's ready to climb the ass of anybody that comes through the door."

"So?"

"So be careful. Walk into any pad like a policeman not an insurance man. Stick your flashlight in your back pocket if there's light on in the pad, and keep your lid on your head. Then you got two hands ready to use. You start strolling in these pads with a light in one hand and a hat in the other you might find you need a third hand quick some night and you'll be a real courteous corpse with your hat in your hand."

"I didn't think the old lady was very dangerous."

"I had a senile old lady stick a pair of scissors right through the web of my hand one time," said Whitey. "You do what you want, I just give the tips for what they're worth. Hey, kid, how about letting me call in. Head for my call box, will you?"

Roy watched Whitey at the call box and fumed. Patronizing stupid bastard, he thought. Roy realized he had a lot to learn, but he wanted to learn it from a real policeman, not from an overweight old windbag who was a caricature of a police officer. The incessant chatter of the police radio subsided for a moment and Roy heard a dull clink of glass.

Then the realization struck him and he smiled. How foolish not to have guessed it before! He couldn't help grinning when Whitey returned to the car.

"Let's go to work, kid," said Whitey, as he got back in.

"Sure thing, partner," said Roy. "But first, I think I'll call in. I want to leave a message with the desk."

"Wait a minute!" said Whitey. "Let's drive to the station. You can tell him personally."

"No, it'll just take a minute, I can use this call box," said Roy.

"No! Wait a minute! The box is screwed up. Just before I hung up, it started buzzing. Almost busted my eardrum. It ain't working right!"

"Well, I'll just try it," said Roy, and moved as though to get out of the car.

"Wait, please!" said Whitey, grabbing Roy's elbow. "Let's go in right now. I got to take a shit terrible bad. Take me to the station right now and you can give your message to Sam."

"Why, Whitey," Roy grinned triumphantly, and with Whitey's perspiring face this close, the fresh whiskey odor was overpowering, "you always crap fifteen minutes after we eat dinner. You told me your guts start rumbling right after your evening meal. What's the matter?"

"It's my age," said Whitey, staring sadly at the floorboard as Roy gunned the engine and drove into the traffic lane, "when you get my age you can't depend on nothing, not even your guts, especially not your guts."

August 1961

7

Guerra!

THEY WERE told by the Gang Squad detective that the war had actually started six weeks ago when the Junior Falcons jumped a seventeen-year-old member of *Los Gavilanes* named Felix Orozco who had made the consummate and final mistake of running out of gas in Falcon territory in a striped nineteen forty-eight Chevrolet that the Falcons knew belonged to a *Gavilán*. Felix was beaten to death with his own tire iron which he had used to break the wrist of the first Falcon who had come at him with a sharpened screwdriver. The girl friend of Felix Orozco, thirteen-year-old Connie Madrid, was not killed by the Junior Falcons but her face was badly ripped by a whistling slash of the car antenna that was broken off the car by El Pablo of the Junior Falcons who, it was believed by the detectives, was the one responsible for flogging Felix Orozco with the limber piece of steel as he lay, already dead probably, from countless kicks to the head and face.

Connie had been a less than cooperative witness and now after two hearing postponements in juvenile court, it was believed by the homicide team that she would probably deny in court that she saw anything.

Since the death of Felix, there had been seven cases of gang reprisals involving *Los Gavilanes* and the Junior Falcons, but on one occasion a member of the Easystreeters, named Ramon Garcia, was mistaken for a Junior Falcon and the Easystreeters announced against *Los Gavilanes*. Then, *Los Rojos,* who had no love for the Junior Falcons but who hated the Easystreeters, saw the opportunity once and for all to join a powerful ally and destroy the hated Easystreeters. Hollenbeck Division was plunged into a war that produced at least one gang incident every night, and made Serge more than ever want to transfer to Hollywood Division.

He had been getting used to Hollenbeck. It was a small division, and after a year, he was getting to know people. It helped being familiar with the regulars and when you saw someone like Marcial Tapia—who had been a burglar for over twenty years—when you saw him driving a pickup truck in the Flats (when he lived his entire life in Lincoln Heights) and the Flats was an area of commercial buildings, factories, and businesses, which were closed on weekends and it was five o'clock Sunday afternoon and all the businesses were closed—well then, you had better stop Marcial Tapia and check the contents of the truck bed which was covered with three barrels of trash and refuse. Serge had done this just three weeks before and found seven new portable television sets, an adding machine, and two typewriters beneath the pile of rubble. He had received a commendation for the arrest of Tapia, his second commendation since becoming a policeman. He had made an excellent arrest report detailing the probable cause for the arrest and search, telling how Tapia had committed a traffic violation which had caused him to stop the truck, and how he had observed the rabbit ear antenna protruding from the pile of trash. He also told how Tapia had appeared exceptionally nervous and evasive when questioned about the telltale antenna, and how when it was all added up he, being a reasonable and prudent man, with a year's experience as a police officer, believed there was something being concealed in the truck and this was how he told it in court, and it was, of course, all bullshit. He had stopped Tapia only because he recognized him and knew his background and suspected what he was doing in the commercial area of the Flats on a Sunday afternoon.

It infuriated him that he had to lie, at least it used to infuriate him, but it soon came easy enough to him when he saw that if he stuck strictly to the truth he would probably lose more than half of his arrests which involved probable cause to stop and search, because the courts were not reasonable and prudent in their assessment of what was reasonable and prudent. So Serge had decided irrevocably several months ago that he would never lose another case that hinged on a word, innuendo, or interpretation of an action by a black-robed idealist who had never done police work. It wasn't that he was trying to protect the victims, he believed that if you did not enjoy taking an asshole off the street, even if it's only for a little while, then you are in the wrong business.

"Why so quiet?" asked Milton, as he propped his elbow on the seat cushion and puffed his foul cigar, looking utterly content because they had just finished an enormous plate of chile verde, rice, and frijoles at a Mexican restaurant where Milton had been eating for eighteen years. He could eat his chile as hot as any Mexican after working Hollenbeck so long, and Raul Muñoz, the owner, challenged Milton by serving them his special chile "not for gringo tastes." Milton had consumed the chile with a bland expression saying it was tasty but not hot enough. Serge however had drunk three strawberry sodas with his meal and had his water refilled twice. That had not quenched the fire and he had ordered a large glass of milk finally. His stomach was just now becoming normal.

"What the hell. You never ate real Mexican food before?" asked Milton as Serge drove slowly through the dark summer night, enjoying the cool breeze which made the long-sleeved blue woolen uniform shirt bearable.

"I never ate that kind of green chile," said Serge, "you think it's safe to light a cigarette?"

"I think if I ever get married again, I'll marry a *Mexicana* who can make that kind of chile verde that bites back," Milton sighed, blowing cigar smoke out the window.

Serge was Milton's regular partner this month and so far he could tolerate the overweight blustering old policeman. He thought that Milton liked him, even though he always called him a "damn rookie" and sometimes treated him as though he had been on the Department fifteen days rather than fifteen months. But then, he once heard Milton call Simon a damn rookie and Simon had eight years on the Department.

"Four-A-Eleven," said the Communications operator, "at eighteen-thirteen Brooklyn, see the woman, A.D.W. report."

Serge waited for Milton to roger the call, which of course was his job as passenger officer, but the old glutton was too comfortable, with one fat leg crossed over the other, a hand on his belly and a pleading look at Serge.

"Four-A-Eleven, roger," said Serge and Milton nodded his gratitude at not having to move just yet.

"I think I'll trade you in for a police dog," said Serge, seeing by his watch that it was 9:45. Only three hours to go. It had been a quick evening, though uneventful for a Saturday night.

"At least you can catch a number for me," said Serge to Milton, who had closed his eyes and leaned his head against the door post.

''Okay, Sergio, my boy, if you're going to nag me,'' said Milton, pronouncing it Ser-jee-oh instead of with a soft throaty g in two syllables as it was meant to be pronounced.

Milton shined the spotlight at the housefronts trying to read a number. Serge did not like to be called Sergio no matter how it was said. It was a name from his childhood and childhood was so far in the past that he could hardly remember. He had not seen his brother Angel nor his sister Aurora since Aurora's birthday dinner at Angel's house when he had brought presents to Aurora and all his nephews and nieces. He had been scolded by Aurora and Angel's wife Yolanda for coming by so seldom. But since his mother was gone he had little reason to return to Chino and he relized that when the memory of his mother would begin to fade, his visits would probably be no more than twice a year. But so far, his memories of her were still very vivid and it was difficult to understand because he had never thought of her so frequently when she lived. In fact, when he left her at eighteen to join the Marine Corps, he had intended never to live at home again, but to leave the bleak little neighborhood and go perhaps to Los Angeles. He had not at that time considered being a policeman. Then he thought of how she, like all Mexican mothers, called her sons *mi hijo* and said it like one word which made it more intimate than ''my son'' in English.

''Must be the gray house,'' said Milton. ''That one. The one with the balcony. Jesus Christ, those timbers are rotten. I wouldn't walk on that balcony.''

''With your weight I wouldn't walk on the First Street bridge,'' said Serge.

''Goddamn rookies, no respect for senior partners anymore,'' said Milton as Serge parked the radio car.

The house sat on the edge of an alley and north of the alley was a commercial building, windowless on the south wall. The builder of the edifice had made the error of plastering the building with a coat of soft irresistible yellow paint. Serge guessed that the wall had not remained inviolate for two days after it was completed. This was a gang neighborhood, a Mexican gang neighborhood, and Mexican gang members were obsessed with a compulsion to make their mark on the world. Serge stopped for a moment, taking the last puff on his cigarette while Milton got his notebook and flashlight. Serge read the writing on the wall in black and red paint from spray cans which all gang members carried in their cars in case they would spot a windfall like this creamy yellow irresistible blank wall. There was a heart in red, three feet in diameter, which bore the names of ''Ruben and Isabel'' folowed by ''*mi vida*'' and there was the huge declaration of an Easystreeter which said ''*El Wimpy de los Easystreeters,*'' and another one which said ''Ruben *de los Easystreeters*,'' but Ruben would not be outdone by Wimpy and the legend below his name said ''*de los Easystreeters y del mundo*,'' and Serge smiled wryly as he thought of Ruben who claimed the world as his domain because Serge had yet to meet a gang member who had ever been outside Los Angeles County. There were other names of Junior Easystreeters and Peewee Easystreeters, dozens of them, and declarations of love and ferocity and the claims that this was the land of the Easystreeters. Of course at the bottom of the wall was the inevitable ''*CON SAFOS,*'' the crucial gang incantation not to be found in any Spanish dictionary, which declared that none of the writing on this wall can ever be altered or despoiled by anything later written by the enemy.

As Serge read, the disgust welled in him but it was interrupted by a blast of horns and a caravan of cars moving down State Street decorated with strings of pink and white paper carnations announcing a Mexican wedding. The men in the cars wore white dinner jackets and the girls chiffon dresses of blue. The bride of course wore white and a white veil which she wore pulled back as she kissed her new husband who Serge guessed could not be more than eighteen. The car directly behind the bride and groom's blasted the horn louder than the rest to sound approval at the prolonged kiss.

"In a few months we'll be called in to handle their family disputes," said Serge grinding the cigarette out on the sidewalk.

"Think it'll take that long before he starts kicking the hell out of her?" asked Milton.

"No, probably not," said Serge as they walked to the house.

"That's why I told the lieutenant if he had to stick me with a rookie, to give me that half-breed Mexican Sergio Duran," said Milton slapping Serge on the shoulder. "You may be short on experience, Sergio my boy, but you're as cynical as any twenty-year cop on the Department."

Serge did not correct Milton who had referred to him on another occasion as his half-caste partner. He had never claimed to be only half-Mexican, but the idea had spread somehow and Serge merely acquiesced by his silence when some overly inquisitive partner asked him if it were true his mother had been an Anglo which would certainly explain why he didn't speak Spanish and why he was such a big man and so fair. At first it had bothered him for someone to think his mother was other than what she had been, but damn it, it was better this way he told himself. Otherwise, he would have been constantly plagued like Ruben Gonsalvez and the other Chicano cops with hundreds of duties involving translation. And it was true, it was utterly true that he no longer spoke the language. Certainly he understood things that were said, but he had to concentrate fully to understand a conversation and it was not worth the effort to him. And he forgot the words. He could not answer even if he did understand a little. So it was better this way. Even with a name like Sergio Duran you could not be expected to speak Spanish if your mother was not Mexican.

"Hope this goddamn balcony doesn't cave in while we're in the pad," said Milton, flipping the remains of his wet cigar in the alley as they knocked on the screen door.

Two little boys came to the door and held it open silently.

"Is Mama home?" asked Milton, tapping the shorter one under the chin.

"Our father is a policeman too," said the taller one, who was very thin and dirty. His eyes were as black as his hair and he was obviously excited at having the policemen in his house.

"He is?" said Serge, wondering if it were true. "You mean he's a guard of some kind?"

"He's a policeman," said the boy, nodding for emphasis. "He's a *capitán de policía*. I swear it."

"Where?" asked Serge. "Not here in Los Angeles?"

"In Juárez, Mexico," answered the boy. "Where we come from."

Milton chuckled, and when Serge turned he reddened as he saw Milton was laughing at him, not at the boy.

That was something he hadn't yet mastered completely, the capacity to mentally challenge anything, *anything* that people told you because it was usually erroneous, exaggerated, rationalized or downright deceptive.

"Go get Mama," said Milton, and the shorter child obeyed immediately. The taller one stood staring at Serge in wonder.

The boy reminded Serge of someone, he couldn't remember who. The same hollow eyes of opaque blackness, bony arms, and a buttonless shirt that had never been completely clean. A boy in the old life perhaps, or one of the Korean children who shined their shoes and swept the barracks. No, it was one from the old life, a childhood friend had eyes like that, but he couldn't remember which one. Why should he try? The memory failure was further proof the cord was irreparably severed, the operation a success.

The child stared at the shiny black Sam Browne belt, the key ring with the huge brass key which unlocked police call boxes, and the chrome-plated whistle which Serge had bought to replace the plastic one the Department supplied. While Serge glanced up the stairs toward the woman who was answering the child they had sent, he felt a light touch on the key ring. When he looked down the child was still staring, but his hands were at his sides.

"Here kid," said Milton, removing the whistle from his key ring. "Take it outside and blow your brains out. But I want it back when I leave, hear me?"

The boy smiled and took the whistle from Milton. Before he stepped from the house, the shrill screams of the whistle pierced the summer night.

"Christ, he'll have the whole neighborhood complaining," said Serge, moving toward the door to call the boy.

"Let him," said Milton, grabbing Serge's arm.

"You gave it to him," Serge shrugged. "It's your whistle."

"Yep," said Milton.

"He'll probably steal the goddamn thing," said Serge, disgustedly.

"You're probably right. That's what I like about you, kid, you're a realist."

It was an old two-story house and Serge guessed it housed a family on each floor. They were standing in a living room which had two twin beds shoved into a far corner. The kitchen was in the rear of the house and another room which he could not see into. It was probably another bedroom. It was a very large old house, very large for one family. At least it was very large for one family on welfare, as he guessed this one was, for there were no man signs around the house, only children's and women's things.

"Up here, please," said the woman, who stood at the top of the staircase in the darkness. She was pregnant and carried a baby in her arms who was not more than a year old.

"The light over the steps is out. I'm sorry," she said, as they used their flashlights to light the creaking, precarious steps.

"In here, please," she said entering the room to the left of the landing.

It looked very much like the room downstairs, a combination living room and bedroom where at least two children slept. There was a half-dead portable television on a low end table and three girls and the boy they had sent upstairs were sitting in front of it watching a grotesque cowboy whose elongated head sat atop an enormous avocado body.

"That TV needs repair," said Milton.

"Oh yes," she smiled. "I'm going to get it fixed soon."

"You know Jesse's TV Shop on First Street?" asked Milton.

"I think so," she nodded, "near the bank?"

"Yeah. Take it to him. He's honest. He's been around here at least twenty years that I know of."

"I will, thank you," she said, giving the fat baby to the oldest girl, a child of about ten, who was sitting on the end of the blanket-covered couch.

"What's the problem?" asked Serge.

"My oldest boy got beat up today," said the woman. "He's in the bedroom. When I told him I called the cops, he went in there and won't come out. His head is bleeding and he won't let me take him to General Hospital or nothing. Could you please talk to him or something?"

"We can't talk if he won't open the door," said Serge.

"He'll open it," said the woman. Her huge stomach was tearing the shapeless black dress at the seams. She shuffled barefoot to the closed door at the rear of a cluttered hallway.

"Nacho," she called. "Nacho! Open the door! He's stubborn," she said turning to the two policemen. "Ignacio, you open it!"

Serge wondered when was the last time Nacho had been kicked in the ass by his mother. Never, probably. If there had ever been a real father living in the pad, he probably didn't care enough to do the job. He would never have dared to defy his own mother like this, Serge thought. And she had raised them without a father.

And the house was always spotless, not like this filth. And she had worked and he was glad because if they had given away welfare in those days like they did today, they probably would have accepted it because who could refuse money.

"Come on, Nacho, open the door and let's stop playing around," said Milton. "And hurry up! We're not going to stand around all night."

The lock turned and a chunky shirtless boy of about sixteen opened the door, turned his back, and walked across the room to a wicker chair where he had apparently been sitting. He held a grimy washcloth to his head, the webs of his fingers crusty with blood and car grease.

"What happened to you?" asked Milton, entering the room and turning up a table lamp to examine the boy's head.

"I fell," he said, with a surly look at Milton and another at Serge. The look he gave his mother infuriated Serge who shook a cigarette from his pack and lit it.

"Look, we don't care whether your head gets infected or not," said Milton. "And we don't care if you want to be stupid and get in gang beefs and die like a stupid *vato* in the street. That's your business. But you think about it, because we're only going to give you about two minutes to decide whether you want to let us take you to the hospital and get your head sewed up and tell us what happened, or whether you want to go to bed like that and wake up with gangrene of the superego which usually only takes three hours to kill you. I can see that wound is already getting green flakes all over it. That's a sure sign."

The boy looked at Milton's expressionless beefy face for a moment. "All right, you might as well take me to the hospital," he said, snatching a soiled T-shirt from the bedpost.

"What happened? *Los Rojos* get you?" asked Milton, turning sideways to get down the narrow creaking stairway with Nacho.

"Will you bring him home?" asked the woman.

"We'll take him to Lincoln Heights Receiving Hospital," said Serge. "You'll have to bring him home."

"I don't got a car," said the woman. "And I got the kids here. Maybe I can get Ralph next door to take me. Can you wait a minute?"

"We'll bring him home after he's fixed up," said Milton.

It was that kind of thing that made Serge damn mad at Milton at least once every working night. It was not their responsibility to bring people home from the hospital, or jail, or anywhere else they took them. Police cars made one-way trips. It was Saturday night and there were lots more interesting things to do than nurse-maid this kid. It would never have occurred to Milton to ask him what *he* wanted to do, thought Serge. Serge would need ten more years as a cop before he rated simple consideration from Milton. Besides, that was the trouble with people like these, someone was always doing for them what they should do for themselves.

"We'll have him back in less than an hour," said Milton to the panting woman who rested her big belly against the precarious banister and apparently decided not to descend the entire stairway.

When Serge turned to go he noticed that above the doorway in the living room of the downstairs family were two eight-by-four-inch holy cards. One was Our Lady of Guadalupe and the other Blessed Martin de Porres. In the center was another card, a bit larger, which contained a green and gold horseshoe covered with glitter and a border of four-leaf clovers.

Nacho had mastered the stride of the Mexican gang member and Serge was looking at him as they crossed the front yard. He didn't see the car cruising slowly down the street, lights out, until it was close. At first he thought it was another radio car on early prowler patrol and then he saw it was a green metal-flaked Chevrolet. Four or five heads barely showed above the window ledges which told Serge automatically that the seats were dropped and that it was probably a gang car.

"Who are those low riders?" Serge asked, turning to Nacho, who was gaping in terror at the car. The car stopped near Nacho's alley and for the first time the low riders seemed to notice the radio car which was partially hidden from view behind a junk-laden van parked in front.

Nacho bolted for the house at the same moment that Serge realized these were *Los Rojos* who had attacked the boy and were probably returning to be more thorough.

Nacho's little brother gave a happy blast on the police whistle.

"*La jura!*" said a voice from the car, apparently seeing the policemen step from the shadows into the light from the open doorway. The driver turned on the lights and the car lurched forward and stalled as Serge ran toward it, ignoring Milton who shouted, "Duran, get your ass back here!"

Serge had a half-formed thought of jerking the cursing driver out of the car as he ground the starter desperately, but when Serge was ten feet from the car he heard a pop, and an orange fiery blossom flashed from the interior of the car. Serge froze as he instinctively knew what it was before his mind fully comprehended, and the Chevy started, faltered, and roared east on Brooklyn Avenue.

"The keys!" Milton roared, standing beside the open driver's door of the radio car. "Throw the keys!"

Serge obeyed immediately although still stunned by the realization that they had fired at him point-blank. He barely jumped in the passenger seat when Milton squealed from the curb and the flashing red light and siren brought Serge back to reality.

"Four-A-Eleven in pursuit!" Serge yelled into the open microphone, and began shouting the streets they were passing as the Communications operator cleared the frequency of conversation so that all units could be informed that Four-A-Eleven was pursuing a 1948 Chevrolet eastbound on Marengo.

"Four-A-Eleven, your location!" shouted the Communications operator.

Serge turned the radio as loud as it would go and rolled up the window but could still hardly hear Milton and the operator over the din of the siren and the roaring engine as Milton gained on the careening low riders who narrowly missed a head-on collision with a left turner.

"Four-A-Eleven approaching Soto Street, still eastbound on Marengo," Serge shouted, and then realized his seat belt was not fastened.

"Four-A-Eleven your location! Come in Four-A-Eleven!" shouted the Communications operator as Serge fumbled with the seat belt, cursed, and dropped the mike.

"They're bailing out!" Milton shouted and Serge looked up to see the Chevrolet skidding to a stop in the middle of Soto Street as all four doors were flung open.

"The one in the right rear fired the shot. Get him!" Milton yelled as Serge was running in the street before the radio car finished the jolting sliding stop.

Several passing cars slammed on brakes as Serge chased the *Rojo* in the brown hat and yellow Pendleton shirt down Soto and east on Wabash. Serge was utterly unaware that he had run two blocks at top speed when suddenly the air scorched his lungs and his legs turned weak, but they were still running through the darkness. He had lost his baton and his hat, and the flashlight fluttering in his swinging left hand lighted nothing but empty sidewalk in front of him. Then his man was gone. Serge stopped and scanned the street frantically. The street was quiet and badly lit. He heard nothing but his outraged thudding heart and the sawing breaths that frightened him. He heard a barking dog close to his left, and another, and a crash in the rear yard of a run-down yellow frame house behind him. He turned off the flashlight, picked a yard farther west and crept between two houses. When he reached the rear of the house he stopped, listened, and crouched down. The first dog, two doors away, had stopped barking, but the other in the next yard was snarling and yelping as though he was bumping against a taut chain. The lights were going on and Serge waited. He jerked his gun out as the figure appeared from the yard gracefully with a light leap over the wooden fence. He was there in the driveway silhouetted against the whitewashed background of the two-car garage like the paper man on the pistol range, and Serge was struck with the thought that he was no doubt a juvenile and should not be shot under any circumstances but defense of your life. Yet he decided quite calmly that this *Rojo* was not getting another shot at Serge Duran, and he cocked the gun which did not startle the dark figure who was twelve feet away, but the flashlight did, and there he was in the intense beam of the five cell. Serge had already taken up the slack of the fleshy padding of the right index finger and this *Rojo* would never know that only a microscopic layer of human flesh over unyielding finger bone kept the hammer from failing as Serge exerted perhaps a pound of pull on the trigger of the cocked revolver which was pointed at the stomach of the boy.

''Freeze,'' Serge breathed, watching the hands of the boy and deciding that if they moved, if they moved at all . . .

''Don't! Don't,'' said the boy, who stared at the beam, but stood motionless, one foot turned to the side, as in a clumsy stop-action camera shot. ''Oh, don't,'' he said and Serge realized he was creeping forward in a duck walk, the gun extended in front of him. He also realized how much pressure he was exerting on the trigger and he always wondered why the hammer had not fallen.

''Just move,'' Serge whispered, as he circled the quivering boy and moved in behind him, the flaslight under his arm as he patted the *Rojo* down for the gun that had made the orange flash.

''I don't got a weapon,'' said the boy.

''Shut your mouth,'' said Serge teeth clenched, and as he found no gun his stomach began to loosen a bit and the breathing evened.

Serge handcuffed the boy carefully behind his back, tightening the iron until the boy winced. He uncocked and holstered the gun and his hand shook so badly that for a second he almost considered holstering the gun still cocked because he was afraid the hammer might slip while he uncocked it.

''Let's go,'' he said, finally, shoving the boy ahead of him.

When they got to the front street, Serge saw several people on the porches, and two police cars were driving slowly from opposite directions, spotlights flashing, undoubtedly looking for him.

Serge shoved the boy into the street and when the beam of the first spotlight hit them the radio car accelerated and jerked to a stop in front of them.

Ruben Gonsalvez was the passenger officer, and he ran around the car throwing open the door on the near side.

''This the one who fired at you?'' he asked.

''You prove it, *puto,*'' the boy said, grinning now in the presence of the other officers and the three or four onlookers who were standing on porches, as dogs for three blocks howled and barked at the siren of the help car which had raced code three to their aid.

Serge grasped the boy by the neck, bent his head and shoved him in the back seat, crawling in beside him and forcing him to the right side of the car.

''Tough now that you got your friends, ain't you, *pinchi jura,*'' said the boy and Serge tightened the iron again until the boy sobbed, ''You dirty motherfucking cop.''

''Shut your mouth,'' said Serge.

''*Chinga tu madre!*'' said the boy.

''I should have killed you.''

''*Tu madre!*''

And then Serge realized he was squeezing the hard rubber grips of the Smith & Wesson. He was pressing the trigger guard and he remembered the way he felt when he had the boy in his sights, the black shadow who had almost ended him at age twenty-four when his entire life was ahead, for reasons not he nor this little *vato* could understand. He had not known he was capable of this kind of terrifying rage. But to be almost murdered. It was utterly absurd.

"*Tu madre,*" the boy repeated, and the fury crept over Serge again. It wasn't the same in Spanish, he thought. It was so much filthier, almost unbearable, that this gutter animal would dare to mention her like that . . .

"You don't like that, do you, gringo?" said the boy, baring his white teeth in the darkness. "You understand some Spanish, huh? You don't like me talking about your moth . . ."

And Serge was choking him, down, down, to the floor he took him, screaming silently, staring into the exposed whites of swollen horrified eyes, and Serge through the irresistible shroud of smothering fury probed for the little bones in front of the throat, which if broken . . . and then Gonsalvez was holding Serge across the forehead and bending him backward in a bow. Then he was lying flat on his back in the street and Gonsalvez was kneeling beside him, panting and babbling incoherently in Spanish and English, patting him on the shoulder but keeping a firm grip on one arm.

"Easy, easy easy," said Gonsalvez. "*Hombre,* Jesus Christ! Sergio, *no es nada,* man. You're okay, now. Relax, *hombre. Hijo la* . . ."

Serge turned his back to the radio car and supported himself against it. He had never wept, he thought, never in his life, not when she died, not ever. And he did not weep now, as he shakily accepted the cigarette which Gonsalvez had lit for him.

"Nobody saw nothing, Sergio," said Gonsalvez, as Serge sucked dully on the cigarette, filled with a hopeless sickness which he did not want to analyze now, hoping he could maintain control of himself because he was more afraid than he had ever been in his life, and he knew vaguely it was things in himself he feared.

"Good thing those people on the porch went in the pad," Gonsalvez whispered. "Nobody saw nothing."

"I'm going to sue you, motherfucker," said the raspy sobbing voice inside the car. "I'm going to get you."

Gonsalvez tightened his grip on Serge's arm. "Don't listen to that *cabrone*. I think he's going to have bruises on his neck. If he does, he got them when you arrested him in the backyard. He fought with you and you grabbed him by the neck during the fight, got it?"

Serge nodded, not caring about anything but the slight pleasure the cigarette was giving him as he breathed only smoke, exhaling a cloud through his nose as he sucked in another fiery puff.

When Serge sat in the detective squad room at two o'clock that morning, he appreciated Milton as he never had before. He came now to understand how little he had known about the blustering, red-faced old policeman who, after a whispered conversation with Gonsalvez, took charge of the young prisoner, reported verbally to the sergeant and the detectives, and generally left Serge to sit in the detective squad room, smoke, and go through the motions of participating in the writing of reports. The night watch detectives and juvenile officers were all kept overtime interrogating suspects and witnesses. Four radio cars were assigned to search the streets, yards, sidewalks and sewers in the route of the pursuit from the point of inception to the dark driveway where Serge made his arrest. But as of two o'clock the boy's gun had not been found.

"Want some more coffee?" asked Milton, placing a mug of black coffee on the table where Serge sat listlessly penciling out a statement on the shooting that would be retyped on the arrest report.

"They find the gun yet?" asked Serge.

Milton shook his head, taking a sip from his own cup. ''The way I figure it, the kid you chased had the gun with him and dumped it when he was in those yards. You realize the thousands of places a gun could be concealed in one junky little yard? And he was probably in several yards jumping fences. He could've thrown it on the roof of one of the houses. He could've pulled up a little grass and buried it. He could've thrown it as far as he could over to the next street. He could've got rid of it during the pursuit, too. The guys couldn't possibly check every inch of evey yard, every ivy patch, every roof of every building, and every parked car along the route where he could've thrown it.''

''Sounds like you think they won't find it?''

''You should be ready for the possibility,'' Milton shrugged. ''Without the gun, we've got no case. These con wise little mothers are sticking together pretty damn good on their stories. There was no gun, they say.''

''You saw the muzzle flash,'' said Serge.

''Sure, I did. But we got to prove it was a gun.''

''How about that kid Ignacio? He saw it.''

''He saw nothing. At least he says he saw nothing. He claims he was running for the house when he heard the loud crack. Sounded like a backfire, he says.''

''How about his mother. She was on the porch.''

''Says she saw nothing. She don't want to get involved with these gang wars. You can understand her position.''

''I can only understand that little killer has to be taken off the street.''

''I know how you feel, kid,'' said Milton, putting his hand on Serge's shoulder and pulling a chair close. ''And listen, that kid didn't mention anything that happened later, you know what I mean. At least not yet, he didn't. I noticed some marks on his neck, but he's pretty dark-complected. They don't show up.''

Serge looked into the blackness of the cup and swallowed a gulp of the bitter burning coffee.

''Once a guy swung a blade at me,'' said Milton quietly. ''It wasn't too many years ago. Almost opened up this big pile of guts.'' Milton patted the bulging belly. ''He had a honed, eight-inch blade and he really tried to hit me. Something made me move. I never saw it coming. I was just making a pinch on this guy for holding a little weed, that's all. Something made me move. Maybe I heard it, I don't know. When he missed me, I jumped back, fell on my ass and pulled my gun just as he was getting ready to try again. He dropped the knife and kind of smiled, you know, like, 'This time you win, copper.' I put the gun away, took out the baton and broke two of his ribs and they had to put thirteen stitches in his head. I know I'd have killed him if my partner didn't stop me. I never done that before or since. I mean I never let go before. But I was having personal problems at the time, a divorce and all, and this bastard had tried to render me, and I just let go, that's all. I never had no regrets at what I did to him, understand? I was sick at what I did to myself. I mean, he dragged me down to the jungle floor and made me an animal too, that's what I hated. But I thought about it for a few days and I decided that I had just acted like a regular man and not like a cop. A policeman isn't supposed to be afraid or shocked or mad when some bastard tries to make a canoe out of him with a switchblade. So I just did what any guy might've. But that don't mean I couldn't handle it a little better if it ever happened again. And I'll tell you one thing, he only got a hundred and twenty days for almost murdering me, and that didn't bother him, but I'll bet he learned something from what I did to him and he might think twice before trying to knife another cop. This is a brutal business you're in, kid. So don't stew over things. And if you learn something about yourself that you'd be better off not knowing, well, just slide along, it'll work out.''

Serge nodded at Milton to acknowledge what his partner was trying to do. He drained the coffee cup and lit another cigarette as one of the detectives came in the squad room carrying a flashlight and a yellow legal tablet. The detective took off his coat and crossed the room to Milton and Serge.

"We're going to sack up these four dudes now," said the detective, a youthful curly-haired sergeant, whose name Serge couldn't remember. "Three of them are seventeen and they're going to Georgia Street, but I'll tell you for sure they'll be out Monday. We got no case."

"How old is the one that shot at my partner?" asked Milton.

"Primitivo Chavez? He's an adult. Eighteen years old. He'll go to Central jail, but we'll have to kick him out in forty-eight hours unless we can turn up that gun."

"How about the bullet?" asked Serge.

"From where you were standing and from where those guys were sitting in that low rider Chevy, I'm guessing that the trajectory of the bullet would be at least forty-five degrees out the window of the car. It would've hit you in the face if it'd been aimed right, but since it didn't I'm thinking it went approximately between the houses you guys were in and the next one west. That's separated by the other one by about a half acre of vacant lot. In other words, I think the goddamn bullet didn't hit a thing and probably right now is sitting on the freeway out near General Hospital. Sorry, guys, you don't want to nail these four assholes any more than I do. We figure the one cat, Jesus Martinez, is involved in an unsolved gang killing in Highland Park where a kid got blown up. We can't prove that one either."

"How about the paraffin test, Sam," said Milton. "Can't that show if a guy's fired a gun?"

"Not worth a shit, Milton," said the detective. "Only in the movie whodunits. A guy can have nitrates on his hands from a thousand other ways. The paraffin test is no good."

"Maybe a witness or maybe the gun will turn up tomorrow," said Milton.

"Maybe it will," said the detective doubtfully. "I'm glad I'm not a juvenile officer. They only call us in when these assholes start shooting each other. I'd hate to handle them every day for all their ordinary burglaries and robberies and stuff. I'll stick to adult investigation. At least they get a *little* time when I convict them."

"What kind of records they got?" asked Milton.

"About what you'd expect: lots of burglaries, A.D.W.'s, joy riding galore, robberies, narco and a scattered rape here and there. The Chavez kid's been sent to Youth Authority camp once. The others never have been sent to camp. This is Chavez' first bust as an adult. He only turned eighteen last month. At least he'll get a taste of the men's jail for a few days."

"That'll just give him something to talk about when he goes back to the neighborhood," said Milton.

"I guess so," sighed the detective. "He'll already have all the status in the world for getting away with shooting at Duran. I've been trying to learn something from all these little gang hoods you guys bring in. Want to hear something? Follow me." The detective led the way to a locked door which when opened revealed a small closet filled with sound and recording equipment. The detective turned on the switch to the recorder and Serge recognized the insolent thin voice of Primitivo Chavez.

"I never shot nobody, man. Why should I?"

"Why not?" said the detective's voice.

"That's a better question," said the boy.

"It would be smart to tell the truth, Primo. The truth always makes you feel better and clears the way for a new start."

"New start? I like my old start. How about a smoke?"

The tape spun silently for a moment and Serge heard the flicker and spurt of a match and then the detective's steady voice again.

"We'll find the gun, Primo, it's only a matter of time."

The boy laughed a thin snuffling laugh and Serge felt his heart thump as he remembered how he felt when he had the skinny throat.

"You ain't never going to find no gun," said the boy. "I ain't worried about that."

"You hid it pretty good, I bet," said the detective. "You got some brains, I imagine."

"I didn't say I had a gun. I just said you ain't never going to find no gun."

"Read that," the detective suddenly commanded.

"What's that?" asked the boy, suspiciously.

"Just a news magazine. Just something I found laying around. Read it for me, *ése*."

"What for, man? What kind of games you playing?"

"Just my own little experiment. Something I do with all gang members."

"You trying to prove something?"

"Maybe."

"Well prove it with somebody else."

"How far you go in school, Primo?"

"Twelfth grade. I quit in twelfth grade."

"Yeah? Well you can read pretty good, then. Just open the magazine and read anything."

Serge heard the rustle of pages and then a moment of silence followed by, "Look man, I don't got time for kid games. *Véte a la chingada*."

"You can't read can you, Primo? And they passed you clear through to the twelfth grade hoping that being in the twelfth grade would make you a twelfth grader and then they made it tough when they realized they couldn't give an illiterate a diploma. These do-gooders really fucked you up, didn't they Primo."

"What're you talking about, man? I'd rather talk about this shooting you say I did than all this other shit."

"How far you been in your life, Primo?"

"How far?"

"Yeah, how far. You live in the housing projects down by the animal shelter, right?"

"Dogtown, man. You can call it Dogtown, we ain't ashamed of that."

"Okay, Dogtown. What's the farthest you ever been from Dogtown? Ever been to Lincoln Heights?"

"Lincoln Heights? Sure, I been there."

"How many times? Three?"

"Three, four, I don't know. Hey, I had enough of this kind of talk. I don't know what the hell you want, *Ya estuvo*."

"Have another cigarette," said the detective. "And take a few for later."

"Okay, for cigarettes I can put up with this bullshit."

"Lincoln Heights is maybe two miles from Dogtown. You ever been farther?"

The tape was silent once again and then the boy said, "I been to El Serreno. How far is that?"

"About a mile farther."

"So I seen enough."

"Ever see the ocean?"

"No."

"How about a lake or river?"

"I seen a river, the goddamnn L.A. River runs right by Dogtown, don't it?"

"Yeah, sometimes there's eight inches of water in the channel."

"Who cares about that shit anyway. I got everything I want in Dogtown. I don't want to go nowhere."

The tape was silent once more and the boy said, "Wait a minute. I been somewhere far. A hundred miles, maybe."

"Where was that?"

"In camp. The last time I got busted for burglary they sent me away to camp for four months. I was fucking glad to get back to Dogtown."

The detective smiled and turned off the recorder. "Primitivo Chavez is a typical teen-age gang member. I'd say."

"What're you trying to prove, Sam?" asked Milton. "You going to rehabilitate him?"

"Not me," the detective smiled. "Nobody could do it now. You could give Primo two million bucks and he'd never leave Dogtown and the gang and the fun of cutting down one of the Easystreeters—or a cop, maybe. Primo is too old. He's molded. He's lost."

"He deserves to be," said Milton bitterly. "That little son of a bitch'll die by the sword."

8

Classrooms

"I've already explained to you twice that your signature on this traffic citation is merely a promise to appear. You are not admitting guilt. Understand?" said Rantlee, with a glance at the group of onlookers that suddenly formed.

"Well, I still ain't signin' nothin'," said the tow truck driver, slouched back against his white truck, brown muscular arms folded across his chest. He raised his face to the setting sun at the conclusion of a sentence and cast triumphant looks at the bystanders who now numbered about twenty, and Gus wondered if now were the time to saunter to the radio car and put in a call for assistance.

Why wait until it started? They could be killed quickly by a mob. But should he wait a few more minutes? Would it seem cowardly to put in a call for backup units at this moment, because the truck driver was merely arguing, putting up a bluff for the onlookers? He would probably sign the ticket in a moment or so.

"If you refuse to sign, we have no choice but to arrest you," said Rantlee. "If you sign, it's like putting up a bond. Your word is the bond and we can let you go. You have the right to a trial, a jury trial if you want one."

"That's what I'm going to ask for, too. A jury trial."

"Fine. Now, please sign the ticket."

"I'm goin' to make you spend all day in court on your day off."

"Fine!"

"You jist like to drive around givin' tickets to Negroes,don't you?"

"Look around, Mister," said Rantlee, his face crimson now. "There ain't nobody on the streets around here, *but* Negroes. Now why do you suppose I picked on you and not somebody else?"

"Any nigger would do, wouldn't it? I jist happened to be the one you picked."

"You just happened to be the one that ran the red light. Now, are you going to sign this ticket?"

"You specially likes to pick on wildcat tow truckers, don't you? Always chasin' us away from accident scenes so the truckers that contract with the PO-lice Department can git the tow."

"Lock up your truck if you're not going to sign. Let's get going to the station."

"You don't even got my real name on that ticket. My name ain't Wilfred Sentley."

"That's what your license says."

"My real name is Wilfred 3X, whitey. Gave to me by the prophet himself."

"That's fine. But for our purposes, you can sign your slave name to this ticket. Just sign Wilfred Sentley."

"You jist love workin' down here, don't you? You jist soil your shorts I bet, when you think about comin' here every day and fuckin' all the black people you can."

"Yeah, get it up in there real tight, whitey," said a voice at the rear of the crowd of teen-agers, "so it feels real good when you come."

This brought peals of laughter from the high school crowd who had run across from the hot dog stand on the opposite corner.

"Yes, I just love working down here," said Rantlee in a toneless voice, but his red face betrayed him and he stopped. "Lock your truck," he said finally.

"See how they treats black people, brothers and sisters," the man shouted, turning to the crowd on the sidewalk which had doubled in the last minute and now blocked access to the police car, and Gus's jaw was trembling so that he clamped his teeth shut tight. It's gone too far, thought Gus.

"See how they is?" shouted the man, and several children in the front of the crowd joined a tall belligerent drunk in his early twenties who lurched into the street from the Easy Time Shine Parlor and announced that he could kill any motherfuckin' white cop that ever lived with his two black hands, which brought a whoop and cheer from the younger children who urged him on.

Rantlee pushed through the crowd suddenly and Gus knew he was going to the radio, and for an agonizing moment Gus was alone in the center of the ring of faces, some of which he told himself, would surely help him. If anything happened someone would help him. He told himself it was not hate he saw in every face because his imagination was rampant now and the fear subsided only slightly when Rantlee pushed his way back through the crowd.

"Okay, there're five cars on the way," Rantlee said to Gus and turned to the truck driver. "Now, you sign or if you want to start something, we got enough help that'll be here in two minutes to take care of you and anybody else that decides to be froggy and leap."

"You got your quota to write, don't you?" the man sneered.

"No, we used to have a quota, now I can write every goddamn ticket I want to," Rantlee said, and held the pencil up to the driver's face. "And this is your last chance to sign, 'cause when the first police car gets here, you go to jail, whether you sign or not."

The man took a step forward and stared in the young policeman's gray eyes for a long moment. Gus saw that he was as tall as Rantlee and just as well built. Then Gus looked at the three young men in black Russian peasant hats and white tunics who whispered together on the curb, watching Gus. He knew it would be them that he would have to contend with if anything happened.

"Your day is comin'," said the driver, ripping the pencil from Rantlee's hand and scrawling his name across the face of the citation. "You ain't goin' to be top dog much longer."

While Rantlee tore the white violator's copy from the ticket book, the driver let Rantlee's pencil fall to the ground and Rantlee pretended not to notice. He gave the ticket to the driver who snatched it from the policeman's hand and was still talking to the dispersing crowd when Gus and Rantlee were back in the car, pulling slowly from the curb while several young Negroes grudgingly stepped from their path. They both ignored a loud thump and knew that one of the ones in the peasant caps had kicked their fender, to the delight of the children.

They stopped for a few seconds and Gus locked his door while a boy in a yellow shirt in a last show of bravado sauntered out of the path of the bumper. Gus recoiled when he turned to the right and saw a brown face only a few inches from his, but it was only a boy of about nine years and he studied Gus while Rantlee impatiently revved the engine. Gus saw only childlike curiosity in the face and all but the three in the peasant caps were now walking away. Gus smiled at the little face and the black eyes which never left his.

"Hello, young man," said Gus, but his voice was weak.

"Why do you like to shoot black people?" asked the boy.

"Who told you that? That's not . . .." The lurching police car threw him back in his seat and Rantlee was roaring south on Broadway and west on Fifty-fourth Street back to their area. Gus turned and saw the little boy still standing in the street looking after the speeding radio car.

"They never used to gather like that," said Rantlee lighting a cigarette. "Three years ago when I first came on the job, I used to like working down here because Negroes understood our job almost as well as we did and crowds never used to gather like that. Not nowadays. They gather for any excuse. They're getting ready for something. I shouldn't let them bait me. I shouldn't argue at all. But the pressure is starting to get to me. Were you very scared?"

"Yeah," said Gus, wondering how obvious it was that he was paralyzed out there, like he had been on only a few other occasions in the past year. One of these days, he was going to have to take direct forceful action when he was paralyzed like that. Then he'd know about himself. So far, something always intervened. He had escaped his fate, but one of these days, he'd know.

"I wasn't a bit scared," said Rantlee.

"You weren't?"

"No, but somebody shit on my seat," he grinned, smoking the cigarette and they both laughed the hearty laugh of tension relieved.

"Crowd like that could do you in two minutes," said Rantlee, blowing a plume of smoke out the window, and Gus thought that he hadn't shown the slightest fear to the onlookers. Rantlee was only twenty-four years old and looked younger with his auburn hair and rosy complexion.

"Think we ought to cancel the assistance you called for?" asked Gus. "We don't need them now."

"Sure, go ahead," said Rantlee and eyed Gus curiously as Gus said, "Three-A-Ninety-one, cancel the assistance to Fifty-first and south Broadway, crowd has dispersed." Gus received no reply and Rantlee grinned wider and Gus for the first time noticed that the radio was dead. Then he saw the mike cord dangling impotently and he realized that someone had jerked the wire out while they had been surrounded.

"You were bluffing them when you told him help was coming."

"Was I ever!" said Rantlee, and Gus was very glad to be driving toward the radio shop and after that to the Crenshaw area which was the "silk stocking" part of University Division, where large numbers of whites still resided. The Negroes there were "westside Negroes" and the sixty-thousand-dollar homes in Baldwin Hills overlooked the large department stores, where you would not be surrounded by a hostile ring of black faces.

On the side of a stucco apartment building facing the Harbor Freeway, Gus saw sprayed in letters four feet high "Oncle Remus is an Oncle Tom," and then Rantlee was on the freeway speeding north. In a few moments the tall palms which line the freeway in south central Los Angeles were replaced by the civic center buildings and they were downtown driving leisurely toward the police building radio shop to have the mike replaced.

Gus admired the beautiful women who always seemed to be plentiful on the downtown streets and he felt a faint rumble of heat and hoped Vickie would still be awake tonight. Despite the precautions, Vickie was not the same lover she had been, but he guessed it was only natural. Then he felt the creeping guilt which he had been experiencing periodically since Billy was born and he knew it was ridiculous to blame himself, but yet any intelligent man would have seen to it that a twenty-three-year-old girl did not give birth to three children in less than five years of marriage, especially when the girl was not really mature, depending on her man for all but the most basic decisions, when she believed her man was a strong man, and oh, what a laugh that was.

Since he had admitted to himself that marriage had been a mistake, it had somehow become easier. Once you face something you can live with it, he thought. How could he have known at age eighteen what things were all about? He still didn't know but at least he now knew life was more than a ceaseless yearning for sex and romantic love. Vickie had been a pretty girl with a fine body and he had had to settle for plain girls all his life, even in his senior year in high school when he could not find a date for the Christmas formal, ending up with Mildred Greer, his next door neighbor, who was only sixteen and built like a shot-putter. She had embarrassed him by wearing a pink chiffon that would have been old-fashioned ten years before. So it was not his fault entirely that he had married Vickie when they were much too young and knew nothing except each other's bodies. What else mattered at age eighteen?

"You see that guy with the mop of blond hair?" asked Rantlee.

"Which guy?"

"The one in the green T-shirt. You see him make us and run through the parking lot?"

"No."

"Funny, how many people get black and white fever and start moving fast in the opposite direction. You can't go after them all. You think about them though. They make you hinky. What's their secret? You always wonder."

"I know what you mean," said Gus and then wondered how a pretty girl like Vickie could be so dependent and weak. He had always thought that attractive people should naturally have a certain amount of confidence. He always thought that if he had been a big man that he would not have been so afraid of people, so unable to converse freely with anyone but intimate friends. The intimate friends were few in number, and at this moment other than his boyhood friend, Bill Halleran, he could think of no one he really wanted to be with. Except Kilvinsky. But Kilvinsky was so much older and he had no family now that his ex-wife was remarried. Every time Kilvinsky came to his house for dinner he played with Gus's children and then became morose, so that even Vickie noticed it. As much as he liked Kilvinsky, whom he felt was a teacher and more than a friend, he didn't really see him much after Kilvinsky had decided to transfer to Communications Division which he said was out to pasture for old cops. Last month he had retired suddenly and was gone to Oregon where Gus pictured him in an extra-large khaki shirt and khaki trousers, his silver hair matted down from the baseball cap he always wore when he fished.

The fishing trip to the Colorado River that he had taken with Kilvinsky and three other policemen had been a wonderful trip and now he could think of Kilvinsky like he had been at the river, chewing on the battered cigarette holder while he all but ignored the burning cigarette it held, casting and reeling in the line with ease, showing that the wide hard hands were nimble and quick, not merely strong. Once when Kilvinsky had been to their house for dinner, right after they bought the three-bedroom house and were still short on furniture, Kilvinsky had taken little John into the almost bare living room and tossed him in the air with his big sure hands until John and even Gus who watched were laughing so hard they could hardly breathe. And, inevitably, Kilvinsky became gloomy after the children went to bed. Once when Gus asked him about his family he said they were now living in New Jersey and Gus realized he must not question him further. All of the other policeman friends were "on duty" friends. Why couldn't he like anyone else the way he liked Kilvinsky, he wondered.

"I gotta transfer out of University," said Rantlee.

"Why?"

"Niggers are driving me crazy. Sometimes I think I'll kill one someday when he does what that bastard in the tow truck did. If someone would've made the first move those savages would've cut off our heads and shrunk them. Before I came on this job I wouldn't even use the word nigger. It embarrassed me. Now it's the most used word in my vocabulary. It says everything I feel. I've never used it in front of one yet but I probably will sooner or later and he'll beef me and I'll get suspended."

"Remember Kilvinsky?" asked Gus. "He always used to say that the black people were only the spearhead of a bigger attack on authority and law that was surely coming in the next ten years. He always said not to make the mistake of thinking your enemy was the Negro. It wasn't that simple, he said."

"It's strange as hell what happens to you," said Rantlee. "I'm finding myself agreeing with every right wing son of a bitch I ever read about. I wasn't brought up that way. My father's a flaming liberal and we're getting so we hate to see each other anymore because a big argument starts. I'm even getting to become sympathetic with some of these rabid anticommunist causes. Yet at the same time I admire the Reds for their efficiency. They can keep order, for chrissake. They know just how far you can let people go before you pull the chain. It's all mixed up, Plebesly. I haven't figured things out yet." Rantlee ran his hand through his wavy hair and tapped on the window ledge as he talked and then turned right on First Street. Gus thought he wouldn't mind working Central Division because downtown Los Angeles seemed exciting with the lights and the rush of people, but it was also sordid if you looked closely at the people who inhabit the downtown streets. At least most of them were white and you didn't have the feeling of being in an enemy camp.

"Maybe I'm wrong in blaming it all on the Negroes," said Rantlee. "Maybe it's a combination of causes, but by God the Negroes are a big part of it."

Gus hadn't yet finished his coffee when their radio was repaired and he hurried to the radio shop bathroom and on the way out noticed in the mirror that his always thin straw-colored hair was now falling out badly. He guessed he'd be bald at thirty, but what did it matter anyway he thought wryly. He noticed also that his uniform was becoming shiny which was the mark of a veteran but it was also fraying at the collar and the cuffs. He dreaded the thought of buying another because they were outrageously expensive. The uniform dealers kept the price up all over Los Angeles and you had to pay it.

Rantlee seemed in better spirits as they drove back down the Harbor Freeway to their beat.

"Hear about the shooting in Newton Street?"

"No," said Gus.

"They got a policeman on the fire for shooting a guy that works in a liquor store on Olympic. Officer rolls up to the store answering a silent alarm, and just as he's getting ready to peek in the window to see if it's for real or phony, the proprietor comes running out and starts screaming and pointing toward the alley across the street. One officer runs in the alley and the other circles the block and picks a spot where he thinks anybody back there would come out, and in a few minutes he hears running footsteps and hides behind the corner of an apartment house with his gun out and ready, and in a few seconds a guy comes busting around the corner with a Mauser in his hand and the officer yells freeze and the guy whirls around and the officer naturally lets go and puts five right in the ten ring." Rantlee placed his clenched fist against his chest to indicate the tight pattern of the bullets.

"So what's wrong with the shooting?" asked Gus.

"The guy was an employee in the store who was chasing the suspect with his boss's gun."

"The officer couldn't have known. I don't see any real problem. It's unfortunate, but . . ."

"The guy was black and some of the black newspapers are playing it up, you know, how innocent people are killed every day by the storm troops in occupied south central Los Angeles. And how the Jew proprietor in the ghetto sends his black lackeys to do the jobs he hasn't got the guts to do. Odd how the Jews can support the blacks who hate them so much."

"I guess they haven't forgotten how they suffered themselves," said Gus.

"That's a kind thought," said Rantlee. "But I think it's because they make so goddamn much money off these poor ignorant black people from their stores and rents. They sure as hell don't live among them. Jesus Christ, now I'm a Jew hater. I tell you, Plebesly, I'm transferring to the valley or West L.A. or somewhere. These niggers are driving me crazy."

They were barely back to their area when Gus logged the family dispute call on Main Street.

"Oh, no," Rantlee groaned. "Back on the goddamn east side." And Gus noticed that Rantlee, who was not a particularly slow driver, headed for the call at a snail's pace. In a few minutes they were parked in front of an ancient two-story house which was tall and narrow and gray. It seemed to be used by four families and they knew which door to knock on by the shouts which could be heard from the street. Rantlee kicked three times against the base of the door to be heard over the din of voices inside.

A sagging square-shouldered woman of about forty opened the door. She held a plump brown baby in one arm and in the other she held a bowl of gray baby food and a spoon. The baby food was all over the infant's face and his diaper was as gray as the siding of the house.

"Come in, Officers," she nodded. "I'm the one who called."

"Yeah, that's right, you punk ass bitch, call the law," said the watery-eyed man in a dirty undershirt. "But while they're here, tell them how you drinks away the welfare check and how I has to support these here kids and three of them ain't even mine. Tell them."

"Okay, okay," said Rantlee, holding up his hands for silence and Gus noticed that the four children sprawled on the sagging couch watched the TV set with little or no interest in the fight or the officers' arrival.

"You some husban'," she spat. "You know, when he drunk, Officer, he jist climbs on me and starts ruttin'. Don't make no diff'ence if the chirrun is here or not. That the kind of man he is."

"That is a gud-dam lie," said the man, and Gus saw they were both half drunk. The man must have been fifty but his shoulders were blocklike and his biceps heavily veined. "I'm goin' tell you like it is," he said to Rantlee. "You a man and I'm a man and I works ever' day."

Rantlee turned to Gus and winked and Gus wondered how many black men he had heard preface a remark to him with, "You a man and I'm a man," fearful that the white law did not truly believe it. They knew how policemen could be impressed by the fact that they worked and did not draw welfare. He wondered how many black men he had heard saying, "I works ever' day," to the white law, and well they might, Gus thought, because he had seen how it *did* work, how a policeman could be talked out of issuing a traffic ticket to a black man with a workman's helmet, or a lunch bucket, or a floor polisher, or some other proof of toil. Gus realized that policemen expected so little of Negroes that a job alone and clean children were unalterable proof that this was a decent man as opposed to the ones with dirty children, who were probably the enemy.

"We didn't come to referee a brawl," said Rantlee. "Why don't we quiet down and talk. You come in here, sir, and talk to me. You talk to my partner, ma'am." Rantlee walked the man into the kitchen to separate them which was of course what Gus knew he would do.

Gus listened to the woman, hardly hearing her, because he had heard similar stories so many times and after they had told the officers their problems, the problems would diminish. Then they could probably talk the man into taking a walk for a while and coming home when things had cooled off and that was the whole secret of handling disputes.

"That man is a righteous dog, Officer," said the woman, shoving a spoonful of food into the pink little mouth of the greedy baby who would only be silenced by the spoon. "That man is terrible jealous and he drink all the time and he don't really work. He live on my county check and he jist lay up here and don't never give nothin' to me 'cept chirrun. I jist wants you to take him out of here."

"You legally married?" asked Gus.

"No, we's common law."

"How long you been together?"

"Ten years and that is too long. Last week, when I cashed my check and bought some groc'ries and came home, why that man snatched the change right outten my hand and went out and laid up wif some woman fo' two days and come back here wif not a cent and I takes him back and then tonight that nigger hits me wif his fist 'cause I ain't got no mo' money fo' him to drink up. An' that's as true as this baby here."

"Well, we'll try to talk him into leaving for a while."

"I wants him outten this house fo' good!"

"We'll talk to him."

"I'm tryin' to raise my chirruns right 'cause I sees all these chirruns nowadays jist jumpin' rope and smokin' dope."

A loud burst of staccato raps startled Gus and the woman stepped to the door and opened it for a furious, very dark, middle-aged man in a tattered flannel bathrobe.

"H'lo Harvey," she said.

"I'm gittin gud-dam sick of the noise in this apartment," said the man.

"He hit me agin, Harvey."

"You goin' to have to git out if you can't git along. I got other tenants in this house."

"What do you want?" shouted the woman's husband who crossed the living room in three angry strides. "We got our rent paid up. You got no right in here."

"This is my house. I got all the right I need," said the man in the bathrobe.

"You git yo' raggedy ass outa my apartment before I throws you out," said the man in the undershirt and Gus saw that the landlord was not as fierce as he seemed and he took a step backward even though Rantlee stepped between them.

"That's enough," said Rantlee.

"Why don't you take him out, Officers," said the landlord, wilting before the glare of the smaller man in the undershirt.

"Yeah, so you kin come sniffin' roun' here after my woman. That would tickle you wouldn' it?"

"Why don't you go back to your apartment, sir," said Rantlee to the landlord, "until we get things settled."

"Don't worry, Officers," said the man in the undershirt, drilling the landlord with his watery black eyes, the blue black lips forming a deliberate sneer, "I wouldn't hurt that. That's pussy."

Nobody can manage an insult like them, Gus thought. And he looked with awe at the rough black face, and how the nostrils had flared, and the eyes and mouth and nostrils had joined to create the quintessence of contempt. "I wouldn' even touch that wif a angry hand. That ain't no man. That's jist pussy!"

They can teach me, thought Gus. There is no other people like them. There was fear, but he could learn things here. And where could he go where there would not be fear?

9

Spade Bit

It was Wednesday and Roy Fehler hurried to the station because he was sure he would be on the transfer list. Most of his academy classmates had their transfers by now and he had been requesting North Hollywood or Highland Park for five months. When he did not find his name on the transfer he was bitterly disappointed and now he knew he must intensify his efforts in college to complete his degree so he could quit this thankless job. And it was thankless, they all knew it. They all talked about it often enough. If you want gratitude for your work, be a fireman they always said.

He had done his best for the past year. He had brought compassion to all his dealings with the Negro. He had learned from them, and hoped he had taught them something. It was time to move on now. He had wanted to work on the other side of town. There was still so much to learn about people yet they left him here at Newton Street. They had forgotten him. He'd increase his unit load next semester, and to hell with concentrating his efforts on being a good police officer. What had it gotten him? He had earned only six units in the past two semesters and had gotten only C's because he read law and police science textbooks when he should have been working on course assignments. At this rate it would take years to finish his degree. Even Professor Raymond seldom wrote anymore. Everyone had forgotten him.

Roy examined his lean body in the full-length mirror and thought the uniform still fit as well as the day he left the academy. He hadn't been exercising but he watched what he ate and thought he still wore the blue suit well.

He was a few minutes late for roll call and muttered "Here" when Lieutenant Bilkins called his name, but he didn't hear Bilkins read the daily crimes and wanted suspects even though he mechanically wrote the information in his notebook just as all the others did. Sam Tucker came straggling in ten minutes after roll call, still adjusting his tie clip with his heavily veined blue-black hands as he sat down at the bench in front of the first row of tables.

"If we could get old Sam to quit counting his money, we could get him here on time," said Bilkins, glancing down at the grizzled Negro officer with his blank narrow eyes.

"Today's rent day, Lieutenant," said Tucker. "Got to stop by my tenants' and collect my share of their welfare checks before they blow it on booze."

"Just like you Jew landlords," sniffed Bilkins, "bleed the ghetto black man, keep him down in the east side."

"You don't think I'd let them live in West L.A. with me, do you?" said Tucker with a perfectly sober expression which brought a burst of laughter from the already sleepy morning watch officers.

"For you guys who don't know, Sam owns half of Newton Division," said Bilkins. "Police work is a hobby with him. That's why Sam's always late the first Wednesday of every month. If we could stop him from counting his money we could get him here on time. And if we could break all the mirrors in the joint, we could get Fehler here on time."

Roy cursed himself for flushing deeply as the roll call boomed with the chuckles of his fellow officers. That was unfair as hell, he thought. And it wasn't that funny. He knew he was a bit vain, but so was everyone.

"By the way, Fehler, you and Light keep an eyeball out for the hot prowl suspect in your district. The prick hit again last night and I think it's only a matter of time till he hurts somebody."

"Did he leave his calling card again?" asked Light, Roy's partner this month, a round-shouldered, two-year Negro policeman, slightly taller than Roy and a difficult man for Roy to understand. He couldn't seem to develop rapport with Light even though he went out of his way as he always did with Negroes.

"He dropped his calling card right on the fucking kitchen table this time," said Bilkins dryly, running a big hand over his bald head and puffing on a badly scarred pipe. "For you new guys that don't know what we're talking about, this cat burglar has hit about fifteen times in the past two months in Ninety-nine's district. He never woke nobody in any of his jobs except once when he woke a guy who had just got home and wasn't sleeping too sound yet. He slugged the guy in the chops with a metal ashtray and bailed out the window, glass and all. His calling card is a pile of shit, his shit, which he dumps in some conspicuous place."

"Why would he do that?" asked Blanden, a curly-haired young policeman with large round eyes, who was new and aggressive, too aggressive for a rookie, Roy thought. And then Roy thought the act of defecation was clearly what Konrad Lorenz called "a triumph reaction," the swelling and flapping of the geese. It was utterly explainable, thought Roy, simply a biological response. He could tell them about it.

"Who knows?" Bilkins shrugged. "Lots of burglars do it. It's a fairly common M.O. Probably to show their contempt for the squares and the law and everything, I guess. Anyway, he's a shitter and wouldn't it be nice if somebody would wake up some night and grab a shotgun and catch the bastard squatting on their kitchen table just squeezing out a big one, and baloooey, he'd be shitting out a new hole."

"Is there any description on this guy yet?" asked Roy, still smarting from Bilkins' gratuitous remark about the mirror, but man enough he thought, to overlook immaturity in a superior.

"Nothing new. Male, Negro, thirty to thirty-five, medium-sized, processed hair, that's it."

"He sounds like a real sweetheart," said Tucker.

"His mother should've washed him out with a douche bag," said Bilkins. "Okay, I been inspecting you for the last three minutes and you all look good except Whitey Duncan who's got dried barbecue sauce all over his tie."

"Do I?" said Whitey, looking toward the tie which was ridiculously short hanging over a belly which Roy thought had swelled three inches in the past year. Thank heavens he didn't have to work with Whitey anymore.

"I saw Whitey this afternoon down at Sister Maybelle's Barbeque Junction on Central Avenue," said Sam Tucker, grinning at Whitey affectionately. "He comes to work two hours early on payday and runs down to Sister Maybelle's for an early supper."

"Why the hell would Whitey need money to eat?" shouted a voice in the back of the room and the men chuckled.

"Who said that?" said Bilkins. "We don't accept gratuities or free meals. Who the hell said that?" Then to Tucker, "What do you think Whitey's up to, Sam? Think he's got the hots for Maybelle?"

"I think he's trying to pass, Lieutenant," Tucker answered. "He was sitting there amongst ten or fifteen black faces and he had barbecue sauce from his eyebrows to his chin. Shit, you couldn't even see that pudgy pink face. I think he's trying to pass. Everybody wants to be black, nowadays."

Bilkins puffed and blew gray clouds and the fathomless eyes roved the roll call room. He seemed satisfied that they were all in good spirits and Roy knew he would never send them out in the morning watch until they were laughing or otherwise cheerful. He had overheard Bilkins telling a young sergeant that no man who did police work from midnight to 9:00 A.M. should be subject to any kind of GI discipline. Roy wondered if Bilkins wasn't too soft on the men because Bilkins' watch was never the high producer in arrests or traffic citations or anything else, except perhaps in good cheer which was a commodity of doubtful value in police work. Police work is serious business, Roy thought. Clowns should join a circus.

"Want to drive or keep score?" asked Light after roll call and Roy realized Light must want to drive because he had driven last night and knew it was Roy's turn to drive tonight. He asked, therefore he must be hoping for another night at the wheel. Roy knew that Light was self-conscious because Roy was such an excellent report writer and that when working with Roy, Light hated to keep the log and make the reports as the passenger officer must do.

"I'll keep books if you want to drive," said Roy.

"Suit yourself," said Light, holding a cigarette between his teeth and Roy often thought he was one of the darkest Negroes he had ever seen. It was hard to see where his hairline began, he was so dark.

"You want to drive, don't you?"

"Up to you."

"You want to or don't you?"

"Okay I'll drive," said Light and Roy was starting the night out annoyed. If a man had a deficiency why in the hell didn't he admit the deficiency instead of running away from it? He hoped he had helped Light recognize some of his defense mechanisms with his blunt frankness. Light would be a much happier young man if he could come to know himself just a little better, thought Roy. He always thought of Light as his junior even though he was twenty-five, two years older than Roy. It was probably his college training, he thought, which brought him of age sooner than most.

As Roy was crossing the parking lot to the radio car, he saw a new Buick stop in the green parking zone in front of the station. A large-busted young woman jumped from the car and hurried into the station. Probably a policeman's girl friend he thought. She was not particularly attractive, but down here any white girl attracted attention, and several other policemen turned to watch. Roy felt a sudden longing for his freedom, for the carefree liberty of his early college days before he met Dorothy. How could he ever have thought they could be compatible? Dorothy, a receptionist in an insurance office, barely a high school graduate, having got her diploma only after a math class was waived by an understanding principal. He had known her too long. Childhood sweethearts are the stuff of movie mags. Romantic nonsense, he thought bitterly, and it had never been anything but bickering and misery since Dorothy became pregnant with Becky. But, God, how he loved Becky. She had flaxen hair and pale blue eyes like his side of the family, and she was incredibly intelligent. Even their pediatrician had admitted she was an extraordinary child. It was ironic, he thought, that her conception had shown him irrevocably the mistake he had made in marrying Dorothy, in marrying anyone so young, when he still had the promise of a splendid life to come. Yet, almost from the moment of birth Becky had shown him still another life, and he felt something utterly unique which he recognized as love. For the first time in his life he loved without question or reason, and when he held his daughter in his arms and saw himself in her violet irises, he wondered if he could ever leave Dorothy because he worshiped this soft creature. He was drawn to the tranquility she could produce in him instantly, at almost any moment, when he pressed the tiny white cheek to his own.

"Want some coffee?" asked Light as they cleared from the station, but at that moment the Communications operator gave them a call to Seventh Street and Central. Roy heard the call and heard Light and wrote the address of the call as well as the time the call was received. He did all this mechanically now and never for a moment stopped thinking of Becky. It was becoming too easy, this job, he thought. He could make the necessary moves while only ten percent of his mind was functioning as a policeman.

"There he is," said Light as he made a U-turn in the intersection at Seventh Street. "Looks like a ragpicker."

"He is," said Roy in disgust as he shined his spotlight on the supine figure, sleeping on the sidewalk. The front of his trousers was soaked with urine and a sinuous trickle flowed down the sidewalk. Roy could smell the vomit and the excrement while still twenty feet away. The drunk had lost one torn and dismal shoe in his travels and a ragged felt hat, three sizes too big, lay crushed beneath his face. His hands clawed at the concrete and his bare foot dug in when Light struck him on the sole of the other foot with his baton, but then he became absolutely still as though he had grabbed for the softness and security of his bed, and having found it, relaxed and returned to the slumber of the consummate alcoholic.

"Goddamn Winos," said Light, striking the man more sharply on the sole of the shoe. "He's got piss, puke, and lord knows what, all over him. I ain't about to carry him."

"Neither am I," said Roy.

"Come on, wino. Goddamn," said Light, stooping down and placing the knuckles of his thick brown index fingers into the hollow behind the ears of the wino. Roy knew how strong Light was, and cringed when his partner applied the painful pressure to the mastoids. The wino screamed and grabbed Light's wrists and came up vertically from the ground clinging to the powerful forearms of the policeman. Roy was surprised to see the man was a light-skinned Negro. The race of the ragpicker was almost indistinguishable.

"Don't hurt me," said the wino. "Don't, don't, don't, don't."

"We don't want to hurt you, man," said Light, "but we ain't carrying your smelly ass. Let's walk." Light released the man who collapsed softly to the sidewalk and then tumbled back lightly on a fragile elbow and Roy thought when they're this far gone with malnutrition, when they bear the wounds of rats and even alley cats that have nibbled at the pungent flesh as they lay for hours in ghastly places, when they're like this, it's impossible to estimate how close to death they are.

"You got gloves on?" asked Light, bending down and touching the wino's hand. Roy shined the flashlight beam in the lap of the man and Light recoiled in horror.

"His hand. Damn, I touched it."

"What is it?"

"Look at that hand!"

Roy thought at first that the wino was wearing a glove which had been turned inside out and was hanging inside out by the fingertips. Then he saw it was the flesh of the right hand which was hanging from all five fingers. The pink muscle and tendon of the hand were exposed and Roy thought for a minute that some terrible accident had torn his flesh off, but he saw the other hand was beginning to shed the flesh so he concluded the man was deteriorating like a corpse. He was long dead and didn't know it. Roy walked to the radio car and opened the door.

"I hate like hell to go to all the trouble of absentee booking a drunk at the General Hospital prison ward," said Roy, "but I'm afraid this guy's about dead."

"No choice," Light shrugged. "I imagine the police been keeping him alive for twenty years now, though. Think we're doing him a favor each time? It would've been over long ago if some policeman would just've let him lay."

"Yeah, but we got a radio call," said Roy. "Somebody reported him lying here. We couldn't ride off and leave him."

"I know. We got to protect our own asses."

"You wouldn't leave him anyway, would you?"

"They'll dry him out and give him ninety days and he'll be right back here, come Thanksgiving. Eventually he'll die right here in the street. Does it matter when?"

"You wouldn't leave him," Roy smiled uneasily. "You're not that cold, Light. He's a human being. He's not a dog."

"That right?" said Light to the wino who stared dumbly at Roy, his blue-lidded eyes crusty yellow at the corners.

"You really a man?" asked Light, tapping the wino gently on the sole of his shoe with the baton. "You sure you ain't a dog?"

"Yeah, I'm a dog," croaked the wino and the policemen looked at each other in amazement that he could speak. "I'm a dog. I'm a dog. Bow wow, you motherfuckers."

"I'll be damned," grinned Light, "maybe you're worth saving after all."

Roy found the absentee booking of a prisoner at General Hospital to be a complicated procedure which necessitated a stop at Central Receiving Hospital and then a trip to Lincoln Heights Jail with the prisoner's property which in this case was the handful of rags that would be burned, and the presentation of the jail clinic with the treatment slips and finally the completion of paper work at the prison ward of the General Hospital. He was exhausted at three-thirty when Light was driving back to their division and they stopped at the doughnut shop at Slauson and Broadway for some bad but very hot coffee and free doughnuts. The Communications operator gave them a family dispute call. Light cursed and threw his empty paper cup in the trash can at the rear of the doughnut shop.

"A family dispute at four in the morning. Son of a bitch."

"I felt like taking it easy for a while too," Roy nodded. "I'm getting hungry, and not for these goddamn doughnuts. I feel like some real food."

"We usually wait till seven o'clock," said Light, starting the car while Roy gulped down the last of his coffee.

"I know we do," said Roy. "That's the trouble with this goddamn morning watch. I eat breakfast at seven o'clock in the morning. Then I go home and go to bed and when I get up in the late afternoon, I can't stand anything heavy so I eat breakfast again, and then maybe around eleven just before I come to work I grab a couple eggs. Jesus, I'm eating breakfast three times a day!"

Light settled the family dispute the easiest way by taking the husband's identification and calling into R and I where he found there were two traffic warrants out for his arrest. As they were taking him out of the house, his wife, who had called them to complain of his beating her, begged them not to arrest her man. When they put him in the radio car she cursed the policemen and said, "I'll get bail money somehow. I'll get you out, baby."

It was almost five o'clock when they got their prisoner booked and drove back to their beat.

"Want some coffee?" asked Light.

"I've got indigestion."

"Me too. I get it every morning about this time. Too damned late to go to the hole."

Roy was glad. He hated "going to the hole" which meant hiding your car in some bleak alley or concealed parking lot, sleeping the fitful frantic half-awake sleep of the morning watch policeman, more nerve-racking than restful. He never objected when Light did it though. He just sat there awake, dozing, mostly awake, and thought about his future and his daughter Becky who was inextricably tied to any dream of the future.

It was 8:30 A.M. and Roy was sleepy. The morning sun was scorching his raw eyeballs when they got the silent robbery alarm call to the telephone company just as they were heading for the station to go home.

"Thirteen-A-Forty-one, roger," said Roy and rolled up his window so that the siren would not drown out the radio broadcasting, but they were close and Light did not turn on the siren.

"Think it's a false alarm?" asked Roy nervously as Light made a sweeping right turn through a narrow gap in the busy early morning commuter traffic. Suddenly Roy was wide awake.

"Probably is," Light muttered. "Some new cashier probably set off the silent alarm and didn't know she did it. But that place has been knocked over two or three times and it's usually early in the morning. Last time the bandit fired a shot at a clerk."

"Can't get too much money early in the morning," said Roy. "Not many people come in this early to pay bills."

"Hoods around here will bum you down for ten bucks," said Light, and he turned sharply toward the curb and Roy saw that they had arrived. Light parked fifty feet from the entrance to the building where the lobby was already filling with people paying their utility bills. All of the customers were Negro as were many of the employees.

Roy saw the two men at the cashier's counter turn and look toward him as he came through the front door. Light had gone to cover the side door and now Roy took a step toward the men. They turned before he got very far into the lobby and were almost to the door when he realized they were the only two in the place who could possibly be robbery suspects. The other customers were either women or couples, some with children.

He thought of the embarrassment it would cause them if it was a false alarm, how there was so much talk these days that black men could not proceed about their business in the ghetto without being molested by white policemen, and he had seen what he considered overly aggressive police tactics. Yet he knew he must challenge them and for his own protection should be ready because they had after all received a silent robbery alarm call. He decided to let them reach the sidewalk and then to talk to them. Nobody behind the cashier's windows had signaled him. It was undoubtedly a false alarm, but he must talk to them.

"Freeze!" said Light, who had approached from behind him noiselessly and was standing with his gun leveled at the middle of the back of the man in the black leather jacket and green stingy brim who was preparing to shove the swinging door. "Don't touch that door, brother," said Light.

"What is this?" said the man closest to Roy, who started to place his left hand in his trouser pocket.

"You freeze, man, or your ass is gone," Light whispered and the man raised the mobile hand sharply.

"What the fuck is this?" the man in the brown sweater said and Roy thought he was almost as dark as Light but not nearly as hard looking. At the present moment Light looked deadly.

Roy heard four car doors slam and three uniformed officers responding to the hot shot call came running toward the front door while another came in the side door Light had entered.

"Search them," said Light as the men were pushed outside, and Light walked across the floor to the cashier's cage with Roy.

"Who pushed the button?" Light called to the gathering circle of employees, most of whom were unaware that something unusual was happening until the policemen rushed through the door.

"I did," said a tiny blond woman who stood three windows away from where the two men had been doing business.

"Were they trying to rob the place or not?" asked Light impatiently.

"Well, no," said the woman. "But I recognized the one in the hat. He's the one who robbed us with a gun last June. He robbed my window. I'd know him anywhere. When I saw him this morning, I just pushed the button to get you here quick. Maybe I just should have phoned."

"No, I guess it's okay to use the silent button in cases like that," Light grinned. "Just don't push the button when you want us here to arrest a drunk out front."

"Oh no, Officer. I know that button is for emergencies."

"What were they doing?" asked Light to the pretty Mexican girl who worked the counter where the men were standing.

"Just paying a bill," said the girl. "Nothing else."

"You sure about that guy?" Light asked the timorous blond.

"I'm positive, sir," said the woman.

"Good work, then," said Light. "What's your name? The robbery detectives will probably be calling you in a little while."

"Phyllis Trent."

"Thanks, ma'am," said Light and he walked long-legged across the lobby while Roy followed.

"Want us to take them?" asked the day watch officer who had the two men handcuffed and standing next to his radio car.

"Damn right," said Light. "We're morning watch. Man, we want to go home. That guy have anything in that left front pocket? He sure wanted to get in there."

"Yeah, a couple joints, wrapped in a rubber band, and a little loose pot in his shirt pocket in a sandwich bag."

"Yeah? How about that. I thought it was a gun. If that asshole had decided to go for it quick, I'd have figured it was a gun for sure. He'd be crossing the river Jordan about now."

"The river Styx," smiled the day watch officer, opening the door for the man in the black leather jacket, handcuffed now.

As they were driving to the station, Roy thought several times he should let the whole incident pass, but he sensed Light was unhappy with the way he had handled the situation in the lobby. Finally Roy said, "How did you tumble to them being suspects, Light? Did one of the employees give you a sign?"

"No," said Light, chewing on the filter of a cigarette, as they sped north on Central Avenue. "They were the only likely-looking pair in the place, didn't you think?"

"Yes, but for all we knew it was a false alarm."

"Why didn't you stop them before I came up, Fehler? They were almost out the door. And why didn't you have your gun ready?"

"We didn't know for sure they were suspects," Roy repeated, feeling the anger well up.

"Fehler, they were, in fact, suspects, and if old stingy brim had brought his iron with him this trip, you'd be laying back there on that floor, you know that?"

"Goddamn it, I'm not a rookie, Light. I didn't think the situation warranted me drawing a gun, so I didn't."

"Let's clear the air, Fehler, we got a whole month to work together. Tell me something truthfully, if they'd been white would you've been quicker to take positive action?"

"What do you mean?"

"I mean that you're so goddamn careful not to offend black people in any way that I think you risk your goddamn life and *mine* so's not to look like a big blond storm trooper standing there frisking a black man in a public place in front of all those black people. What do you think of that?"

"You know what's wrong with you, Light? You're ashamed of your people," blurted Roy, and it was out before he could retract it.

"What the hell do you mean?" asked Light and Roy cursed himself but it was too late now and the words he was repressing had to be released.

"Alright Light, I know your problem and I'm going to tell you what it is. You're too damned tough on your people. You don't have to be cruel to them. Don't you see, Light? You feel guilty because you're trying so hard to pull yourself from that kind of degrading ghetto environment. You feel shame and guilt for them."

"I'll be damned," said Light, looking at Roy as if for the first time. "I always knew you were a little strange, Fehler, but I didn't know you were a social worker."

"I'm your friend, Light," said Roy. "That's why I'm telling you."

"Yeah, well listen, friend, I don't look at a lot of these people as black or white or even as people. They're assholes. And when some of these kids grow up they'll probably be assholes too, even though I feel sorry as hell for them right now."

"Yes, I understand," said Roy, nodding tolerantly, "there's a tendency of the oppressed to embrace the ideals of the oppressor. Don't you see that's what happened to you?"

"I'm not oppressed, Fehler. Why do white liberals have to look at every Negro as an oppressed black man?"

"I don't consider myself a liberal."

"People like you are worse than the Klan. Your paternalism makes you worse than the other kind. Quit looking at these people as Negroes or problems. I worked a silk stocking division out on the west side when I first came out of the academy and I never thought of a Caucasian asshole in terms of race. An asshole is an asshole, they're just a little darker here. But not to you. He's a Negro and needs a special kind of protective handling."

"Wait a minute," said Roy. "You don't understand."

"The hell I don't," snapped Light, who had now pulled to the curb at Washington and Central and turned in the seat to face Roy squarely. "You been here over a year now, haven't you? You know the amount of crime in the Negro divisions. Yet the D.A. won't hardly file a felony assault if it's a Negro victim and suspect involved. You know what the detectives say, 'Forty stitches or a gunshot is a felony. Anything less is a misdemeanor.' Negroes are expected to act that way. White liberals have said, 'That's alright, Mister Black man,' and they're always careful to say *Mister*. 'That's alright, you have been oppressed and therefore you are not entirely responsible for your actions. We guilty whites are responsible,' and what does the black man do then? Why, he takes full advantage of his tolerant white brother's misplaced kindness, just like the white would do if the positions were reversed because people in general are just plain assholes unless they got a spade bit in their mouths. Remember, Fehler, people need spades, not spurs."

Roy felt the blood rush to his face and he cursed his stammer as he struggled to master the situation. Light's outburst had been so unwarranted, so sudden . . . "Light, don't get excited, we're not communicating. We're not . . ."

"I'm not excited," said Light, deliberately now. "It's just that sometimes I've been close to busting since I started working with you. Remember the kid at Jefferson High School last week? The robbery report, remember?"

"Yes, what about it?"

"I wanted to tell you this then. I was choking on my frustration the way you patronized that little bastard. I went to high school right here in southeast L.A. I saw that same kind of shakedown every day. The blacks were the majority and the white kids were terrorized. 'Gimme a dime, motherfucker. Gimme a dime or I'll cut yo' ass.' Then we gave whitey a punch in the mouth whether or not we got the dime. And these were *poor* white kids. Poor as us, sometimes from mixed marriages and shack jobs. You didn't want to book that kid. You wanted to apply your double standard because he was a downtrodden black boy and the victim was white."

"You don't understand," said Roy bleakly. "Negroes hate the whites because they know they're faceless nonhuman creatures in the eyes of the whites."

"Yeah, yeah, I know that's what intellectuals say. You know, Fehler, you're not the only cop that's read a book or two."

"I never said I was, goddamn it," said Roy.

"I tell you Fehler, those white boys in my school were without faces to *us*. What do you think of that? And we terrorized those poor bastards. The few I ever got to know didn't hate us, they were afraid of us, because of our numerical superiority. Get off your knees when you're talking to Negroes, Fehler. We're just like whites. Assholes, most of us. Just like whites. Make the Negro answer to the law for his crimes just like a white man. Don't take away his manhood by coddling him. Don't make him a domestic animal. All men are the same. Just keep him on a mean spade bit with a long shank. When he gets too spirited, jerk those reins, man!"

August 1962

10

The Lotus Eaters

SERGE LISTENED to the dreary monotone of Sergeant Burke who was conducting roll call training. He looked around the roll call room at Milton and Gonsalvez and the new faces, all of whom he knew by now since his return to Hollenbeck. He remembered how Burke's roll call training used to bore him and still did. But he was no longer annoyed by it.

The five months from January to June which he had spent in Hollywood Division was by now a grotesque candy-striped memory which seemed to have never happened. Though he had to admit it had been educational. Everyone in Hollywood is a phony, a fruit, or a flimflam man, a partner had warned him. At first the glamour and hilarity fascinated him and he slept with some of the most beautiful girls he would ever see, satin blondes, silky redheads, dark ones he avoided, for those were all he had in Hollenbeck Division. They were not all aspiring actresses, these lovely girls who are drawn to Hollywood from everywhere, but they all yearned for something. He never bothered to find out what. As long as they yearned for him for a few hours, or pretended to, that was all he asked of them.

And then it all began to depress him, especially the intense look of the revelers when he got to know them. He shared an apartment with two other policemen and he could never go to bed before three o'clock because the blue light would be burning, indicating that one of them had been lucky and please give them some more time. They were very lucky, his roommates, who were equally handsome, wholesome-looking, and accomplished handlers of women. He had learned from them, and by being a roommate had been satisfied with the chaff when the chaff was a pale trembling creature who was all lips and breasts and eyes. It didn't even matter if she ate bennies frantically and babbled of the prospective modeling job which would thrust her into the centerfold of *Playboy*. And there was another who, in the middle of the heated preliminaries of lovemaking said, "Serge, baby, I realize you're a cop and all, but I know you're no square and you wouldn't mind if I smoked a little pot first, would you? It makes it all so much better. You should try it. We'll be so much better lovers." He thought about letting her do it, but the bennies were only a misdemeanor and marijuana was a felony, and he was afraid to be here while she did it, and besides, she had annihilated his ego and desire with her need for euphoria. When she disappeared into the bedroom for the marijuana, he put on his shoes and coat and crept out the door, an ache in his loins.

There were lots of other girls, waitresses and office girls, some of whom were ordinary, but then there was Esther, who was the most beautiful girl he had ever met. Esther who had called the police to complain about the peepers who were a constant annoyance to her, but her apartment was on the ground floor and she dressed with her drapes open because she "just loved the cooling breezes." She seemed genuinely surprised when Serge suggested she draw her drapes at night or move to an upstairs apartment. It had started out passionately between them but she was totally unique, with her moist lips and face and hands. Her eyes too were moist as was most of her torso, particularly the ample breasts. A fine layer of not unpleasant perspiration covered her during the lovemaking so that sleeping with Esther was like a steam and rub, except it was not as therapeutic—because even though a night-long bout with Esther left him exhausted, he did not feel cleansed from the inside out as he did when he left the steam room at the police academy. Perhaps Esther could not open his pores. Her heat was not purgative.

Her style of love had begun strangely enough, but then a few of her more bizarre improvisations began to repel him slightly. One bawdy Saturday, he had become drunk in her apartment, and she had become drunk too except she drank only a fourth as much as he. She made frequent trips to the bedroom which he did not question. Then that evening when he was preparing to take her and she was more than ready, they had tumbled and clawed their way to the bed and suddenly the things she was whispering through the drunken mist became coherent. It wasn't her usual string of obscenities and he listened stunned to what she suggested. Then it was not passion but frenzy he saw in the moist eyes and she stepped half naked to the closet and dragged out various accouterments, some of which he understood and others he did not. She told him that the young couple next door, Phil and Nora, whom he had decided were a pleasant pair, were ready for a "fabulously exciting evening." If he would only say the word they would be there in a minute and it could begin.

When he left Esther's apartment a moment later she was uttering a stream of grotesque curses that made him shiver with nausea.

A few nights later Serge was asked by his partner, Harry Edmonds, why he was so quiet and although he answered that there was nothing wrong, he was deeply aware that he was unhappy in Hollywood where life was ethereal and complicated. The most routine call became impossible in this place. Burglary reports would often turn into therapy sessions with unhappy neurotics who had to be subjected to a crude psychoanalysis to determine the true deflated value of a wristwatch or fur coat stolen by a Hollywood burglar who often as not turned out to be as neurotic as his victim.

At ten minutes past nine, that night, Serge and Edmonds received a call to an apartment on Wilcox not far from Hollywood station.

"This is a pretty swinging apartment house," said Edmonds, a young policeman with sideburns a bit too long and a moustache that Serge thought ridiculous on him.

"You got calls here before?" asked Serge.

"Yeah, the manager's a woman. A dyke, I think. She only rents to broads far as I can see. There's always some beef here. Usually between the manager and some boyfriend of one of the female tenants. If the girls want to have girl parties, she never bitches."

Serge carried his eight by eleven notebook under his arm and tapped on the manager's door with his flashlight.

"You call?" he asked the lean, sweater-clad woman who held a bloody towel in one hand and a cigarette in the other.

"Come in," she said. "The girl you want to talk to is in here."

Serge and Edmonds followed the woman through a colorful green-gold and blue living room into the kitchen. Serge thought the black sweater and close-fitting pants very becoming. Although her hair was short it was silver-tipped and styled attractively. He guessed her age at thirty-five and wondered if Edmonds was right that she was a lesbian. Nothing in Hollywood could surprise him anymore, he thought.

The quivering brunette was seated at the kitchen table holding a second towel, ice-filled, to the left side of her face. Her right eye was swollen shut and her lower lip was turning blue but was not badly cut. Serge guessed the blood must have been from her nose which was not bleeding now and didn't look broken. It wasn't a particularly good-looking nose at best, he thought, and he looked at her crossed legs which were nicely shaped, but both knees were scraped. The torn hose hung from her left leg and had fallen down around the shoe, but she seemed too miserable to care.

"Her boyfriend did it," said the manager, who waved them to the wrought iron leather-padded chairs which surrounded the oval table.

Serge opened his notebook, leafing past the burglary and robbery reports and removed a miscelaneous crime report.

"Lover's quarrel?" he asked.

The brunette swallowed and the tear-filled eyes over-flowed into the blood-stained towel.

Serge lit a cigarette, leaned back and waited for her to stop, realizing vaguely that this might not be *complete* melodrama since the injuries were real and probably quite painful.

"What's your name?" he asked, finally, as he realized it was ten o'clock and their favorite restaurant preferred that they eat before ten-thirty when the paying customers needed most of the counter space.

"Lola St. John," she sobbed.

"This is the second time that bastard beat you, isn't it, honey?" asked the manager. "Give the officers the same name you were using when you made the last report."

"Rachel Sebastian," she said, dabbing at the tender lip and examining the towel.

Serge erased the Lola St. John and wrote the other name across the top.

"You prosecute him last time he beat you?" Serge asked. "Or did you drop the charges?"

"I had him arrested."

"Then you dropped the charges and refused to prosecute?"

"I love him," she muttered, touching the lip with a pink tongue tip. An exquisite jewel formed at the corner of each eye, gumming with mascara.

"Before we go to a lot of trouble, are you going to go through with the prosecution this time?"

"This time I had it. I will. I swear by all that's holy."

Serge glanced at Edmonds and began filling in the boxes on the crime report. "How old are you?"

"Twenty-eight."

That was the third lie. Or was it the fourth? Sometime he meant to count the lies at the completion of a report.

"Occupation?"

"Actress."

"What else you do? When you're between acting jobs, I mean."

"I'm sometimes night manager and hostess at Frederick's Restaurant in Culver City."

Serge knew the place. He wrote "carhop" in the space for victim's occupation.

The manager uncoiled and crossed the kitchen to the refrigerator. She refilled a clean towel with ice cubes and returned to the battered woman.

"That son of a bitch is no good. I won't have him back here, honey. I want you for a tenant and all, but that man cannot come in this building."

"Don't worry, Terry, he won't," she said, accepting the towel, which was pressed to her jaw.

"Has he beat you on only one prior occasion?" asked Serge, beginning the narrative of the report, wishing he had sharpened the pencil at the station.

"Well, actually, I had him arrested another time," she said. "I'm just a sucker for a big good-looking guy, I guess." She smiled and fluttered the unclosed eye at Serge and he guessed she was signaling that he was big enough to suit her.

"What name were you using that time?" asked Serge, thinking she was probably blousy at best, but the legs were good and the stomach was still pretty flat.

"That time I was using Constance Deville, I believe. I was under contract to Universal under that name. Wait a minute, that was in sixty-one. I don't think . . . Christ, it's hard to think. That man of mine knocked something loose. Let's see."

"Were you drinking tonight?" asked Edmonds.

"It started in a bar," she nodded. "I think I was using my real name, then," she added thoughtfully.

"What's your real name?" asked Serge.

"God my head hurts," she moaned. "Felicia Randall."

"You want to see your own doctor?" asked Serge, not mentioning that free emergency care was available to crime victims because he did not want to take this woman to the hospital and bring her back.

"I don't think I need a doct . . . Wait a minute, did I say Felicia Randall? Christ almighty! That's not my *real* name. I was born and raised Dolores Miller. Until I was sixteen, I was Dolores Miller. Christ almighty! I almost forgot my real name! I almost forgot who I was," she said, looking at each of them in wonder.

Later that month, while patroling Hollywood Boulevard at about 3:00 A.M. with a sleepy-eyed partner named Reeves, Serge had taken a good look at the people who walk the streets of the glamour capital at this hour. Mostly homosexuals of course, and he was getting to recognize some of them after seeing them night after night as they preyed on the servicemen. There were lots of other hustlers who in turn preyed on the homosexuals, not for lust but for money which they got one way or the other. This accounted for a good number of beatings, robberies and killings and until the hour of sunrise when his watch ended, Serge was forced to arbitrate the affairs of these wretched men and he was still revolted with all of it a week later when he returned to Alhambra and rented his old apartment. He talked with Captain Sanders of Hollenbeck Division who agreed to arrange a transfer back to Hollenbeck because he said he remembered Serge as an excellent young officer.

Burke was winding up the roll call training which nobody ever listened to and Serge did not at this moment even know the subject of the lesson. He decided he would drive tonight. He didn't feel like making reports so he'd do the driving. Milton always let him do exactly as he wished. He liked working with Milton and he even liked Burke's slow deliberate ways. There were worse supervisors. It was good to be back in the old station.

Serge was even beginning to lose his dislike for the area. It was not Hollywood, rather it was the opposite of glamorous. It was dull and old and poor with tall narrow houses like gravestones and the smell of the Vernon slaughterhouses remained. It was the place where the immigrants came upon their arrival from Mexico. It was the place where the second and third generation remained, who could not afford to improve their lot. He knew now of the many Russian Molokan families, the men with beards and tunics and the women with covered heads, who lived between Lorena and Indiana Streets after Russian flats had been changed to a low-priced housing project. There was a sizable number of Chinese here in Boyle Heights and Chinese restaurants had Spanish menus. There were many Japanese, and the older women still carried sun parasols. There were the old Jews of course, few now, and sometimes nine old Jews had to scour Brooklyn Avenue and finally hire a drunken Mexican for a minyan of ten to start prayers in temple. These old ones would soon all be dead, the synagogues closed, and Boyle Heights would be changed without them. There were Arab street hawkers selling clothing and rugs. There were even gypsies who lived near North Broadway where many Italians still lived, and there was the Indian church on Hancock Street, the congregation being mostly Pima and Navajo. There were many Negroes in the housing projects of Ramona Gardens and Aliso Village whom the Mexicans only tolerated, and there were the Mexican Americans themselves who made up eighty percent of the population of Hollenbeck Division. There were few white Anglo-Protestant families here unless they were very poor.

There were few phonies in the Hollenbeck area, Serge thought as he slowed on Brooklyn Avenue to park in front of Milton's favorite restaurant. Almost everyone is exactly as he seems. It was very comforting to work in a place where almost everyone is exactly as he seems.

11

The Veteran

"Two years ago tonight I came to University," said Gus. "Fresh out of the academy. It doesn't seem possible. Time has passed."

"You're about due for a transfer, aren't you?" asked Craig.

"Overdue. I'm expecting to be on the next transfer."

"Where you want to go?"

"I don't care."

"Another black division?"

"No, I'd like a change. Little further north, maybe."

"I'm glad I came here. I can learn fast down here," said Craig.

"Be careful you don't learn too fast," said Gus and dropped the Plymouth into low as he slowed for the red light because he was getting tired driving. It had been a very quiet evening and policemen toyed with the cars out of boredom after several hours of slow monotonous patrol. It was only nine-thirty. They shouldn't have eaten so early, Gus thought. The rest of the night would drag.

"Have you ever been in a shooting?" asked Craig.

"No."

"How about a real knockdown fight?"

"I haven't," said Gus. "Not a real fight. A few belligerent bastards, but not a real fight."

"You've been lucky."

"I have," said Gus, and for a second it started coming over him again, but he had learned how to subdue it. He was seldom afraid for no reason anymore. The times when he was afraid he had good reason to be. He had worked with an old-time policeman one night who had told him that in twenty-three years he had never had a real fight or fired his gun in the line of duty, or even been close to death except in a few traffic chases and he didn't think a policeman had to become involved in such things unless he went out of his way to become involved. The thought was comforting except that this policeman had spent his career in West Valley and Van Nuys Division which was the next thing to being retired, and he had only been in University for a few months, a disciplinary transfer. Still, Gus thought, after two years he had escaped the confrontation he feared. But did he really fear so much now, he wondered? The blue suit and badge, and the endless decisions and arbitration of other people's problems (when he didn't really know the answers but on the street at midnight there was no one else to find an answer except him and therefore he had made the choices for others and on a few occasions lives had depended on his decisions), yes, these decisions, and the blue suit and the badge had given him confidence he never dreamed he might possess. Though there were still agonizing self-doubts, his life had been deeply touched by this and he was as happy as he ever expected to be.

If he could transfer to a quiet white division, he would probably be happier if he were not troubled by guilt at being there. But if he could be satisfied that he had the necessary courage and had nothing further to prove to himself, why then he could transfer to Highland Park, and be closer to home and finally content. But that of course was bullshit because if police work had taught him anything it had taught him that happiness is for fools and children to dream of. Reasonable contentment was a more likely goal.

He began thinking of Vickie's widening hips and how twenty pounds even on a pretty girl like Vickie could make such a difference so that sometimes he was unsure whether their infrequent lovemaking was because she was so terribly frightened of another pregnancy, for which he couldn't blame her, or was it because she was growing less and less attractive. It wasn't just the bulkiness which had transformed a sleek body that was made for a bed, it wasn't just that, it was the breakdown of personality which he could only blame on a youthful hasty marriage and three children which were too much for a weak-willed girl of less than average intelligence who had always depended upon others, who now leaned so heavily on him.

He guessed he would be up all night with the baby if her cold weren't any better, and he felt a tiny surge of purgative anger but he knew he had no right to be angry with Vickie who was the prettiest girl who had ever shown an interest in him. After all, he was certainly not a trophy to cherish. He glanced in the rearview mirror and saw that his sandy hair was very thin now and he had been forced to reassess his guess; he knew he would be bald long before he was thirty and he already had tiny wrinkles at the corners of his eyes. He laughed at himself for his disappointment in Vickie for getting fat. But that wasn't it, he thought. That wasn't it at all. It was her.

"Gus, do you think policemen are in a better position to understand criminality than, say, penologists or parole officers or other behavioral scientists?"

"My God," Gus laughed. "What kind of question is that? Is that a test question?"

"As a matter of fact it is," said Craig. "I'm taking psych at Long Beach State and my professor has quite a background in criminology. He thinks policemen are arrogant and clannish and distrust other experts, and believe they're the only ones who really understand crime."

"That's a fair assessment," said Gus. He reminded himself that this would be the last semester he could afford to rest because he would get out of the habit of going to school. If he ever wanted the degree he would have to get back in classes next semester without fail.

"Do you agree with that?" asked Craig.

"I think so."

"Well I've only been out of the academy a few months but I don't think policemen are clannish. I've still got all my old friends."

"I still have mine," said Gus. "But you'll see after a year or so that you feel a little different about them. They don't know, you see. And criminologists don't know. Police see a hundred percent of criminality. We see noncriminals and real criminals who're involved in crime. We see witnesses to crimes and victims of crimes and we see them during and immediately after crimes occur. We see the perpetrators during and right after and we see victims sometimes before the crimes occur and we know they're going to be victims, and we see perpetrators before and we know they're going to be perpetrators. We can't do a damned thing about it even though we know through our experience. We *know*. Tell that to your professor and he'll think *you* need a psychologist. Your professor sees them in a test tube and in an institution and he thinks these are criminals, these unfortunate unloved losers he's studying, but what he doesn't realize is that so many thousands of the winners out here are involved in crime just as deeply as his unloved losers. If he really knew how much crime occurs he wouldn't be so damned smug. Policemen are snobs, but we're not smug because this kind of knowledge doesn't make you self-satisfied, it just scares you."

"I never heard you talk so much, Gus," said Craig, looking at Gus with new interest, and Gus felt an urge to talk about these things because he never talked about them very much except to Kilvinsky when he was here. He had learned all these things from Kilvinsky anyway, and then his experience had shown Kilvinsky was right.

"You can't exaggerate the closeness of our dealings with people," said Gus. "We see them when nobody else sees them, when they're being born and dying and fornicating and drunk." Now Gus knew it was Kilvinsky talking and he was using Kilvinsky's very words; it made him feel a little like Kilvinsky was still here when he used the big man's words and that was a good feeling. "We see people when they're taking anything of value from other people and when they're without shame or very much ashamed and we learn secrets that their husbands and wives don't even know, secrets that they even try to keep from themselves, and what the hell, when you learn these things about people who aren't institutionalized, people who're out here where you can see them function every day, well then, you really *know*. Of course you get clannish and associate with others who know. It's only natural."

"I like to hear you talk, Gus," said Craig. "You're usually so quiet I thought maybe you didn't like me. You know, us rookies worry about everything."

"I know," said Gus, moved by Craig's frank boyishness.

"It's valuable to hear an experienced officer talk about things," said Craig, and it was very hard for Gus to control a smile when he thought of Craig thinking of him as a veteran.

"While I'm philosophizing, you want a definition of police brutality?" asked Gus.

"Okay."

"Police brutality means to act as an ordinary prudent person, without a policeman's self-discipline, would surely act under the stresses of police work."

"Is that one of the Chief's quotes?"

"No, Kilvinsky said that."

"Is he the guy who wrote the book on police supervision?"

"No, Kilvinsky was a great philosopher."

"Never heard of him."

"On punishment Kilvinsky said, 'We don't want to punish offenders by putting them in institutions, we only want to separate ourselves from them when their pattern of deviation becomes immutably written in pain and blood.' Kilvinsky was drinking a little when he said that. He was usually much more earthy."

"You knew him?"

"I studied under him. He also said, 'I don't care if you supply the asshole with dames and dope for the rest of his life as long as we keep him in the joint.' In fact, Kilvinsky would have out-liberaled the most ardent liberal when it came to prison reforms. He thought they should be very agreeable places. He thought it was stupid and useless and cruel to try to punish *or* to try to rehabilitate most people with 'the pattern' as he called it. He had it pretty well doped out to where his penal institutions would save society untold money and grief."

"Three-A-Thirteen, Three-A-Thirteen," said the operator. "See the man, family dispute, twenty-six, thirty-five south Hobart."

"Well, it's fun to talk on a quiet night," said Gus, "but duty calls."

Craig rogered the call as Gus turned the car north and then east toward Hobart.

"I wish I had had this Kilvinsky for a professor," said Craig. "I think I'd have liked him."

"You'd have loved him," said Gus.

When Gus stepped out of the radio car he realized how unusually quiet a night it had been for a Thursday. He listened for a moment but the street lined on both sides with one-story private residences was absolutely still. Thursday, in preparation for weekend activity, was usually a fairly busy night and then he realized that welfare checks would arrive in the next few days. With no money the people were quiet this Thursday.

"I think it's the house in the rear," said Craig, shining his flashlight to the right of the darkened pink stucco front house. Gus saw the lighted porch and followed Craig down the walk to the rear house where a shirtless Negro stepped out of the shadows with a baseball bat in his hand and Gus had his revolver unsnapped, in his hand, crouching instinctively before he realized why. The man threw the ball bat to the ground.

"Don't shoot. I called you. I'm the one that called. Don't shoot."

"Jesus Christ," said Gus, seeing the Negro lurch drunkenly to his left, waving his big hands to the officers as he held them high overhead.

"You could get killed like that, jumping out with a club," said Craig, snapping his holster.

Gus could not find the pocket in the holster and had to use both shaking hands to put the gun away, and could not speak, did not dare to speak because Craig would see, anyone would see how unreasonably frightened he had been. He was humiliated to see that Craig was merely startled and was already asking questions of the drunken Negro while his own heart was hammering blood into his ears so that he couldn't make out the conversation until the Negro said, "I hit the motherfucker with the bat. He layin' back there. I think I done killed him and I wants to pay the price."

"Show us," Craig commanded, and Gus followed the two of them to the rear of the cottage which was pink like the front house, but a frame building not stucco, and Gus sucked deeply at the air to still his beating heart. In the rear yard they found the lanky Negro with a head like a bloody bullet lying on his face and beating the ground with a bony fist as he moaned softly.

"Guess I didn' kill him," said the drunken Negro. "Sho' thought he was dead."

"Can you get up?" asked Craig, already obviously accustomed to bloody scenes, knowing that most people can shed a great deal of blood and unless wounds are of certain types, people can usually function quite well with them.

"Hurts," said the man on the ground and rolled over on one elbow. Gus saw that he too was drunk and he grinned foolishly at the officers and said, "Take me to the hospital and git me sewed up will you, Officer?"

"Shall I call an ambulance?" asked Craig.

"Doesn't really need one," said Gus, his voice steady now, "but you may as well. He'd get blood all over the radio car."

"Don't want to press no cha'ges Officer," said the bloody man. "Jist want sewed up."

What if I'd shot him, thought Gus while Craig's voice echoed through the narrow walkway and was followed by a static explosion. A female voice blared out and Craig adjusted the volume and repeated his request for an ambulance. Someday I'll become scared like that and I *will* kill someone and I'll cover it up neatly just as I could have covered up this one because a man leaped out of the darkness with an upraised club. But Craig was only startled; he didn't even clear the holster and there I was crouched with three pounds of pressure on the trigger and thank God, I didn't cock the gun unconsciously or I'd have killed him sure. As it was, the hammer was moving back double action, moving, and God, what if Craig hadn't been in front of me, I know I'd have killed him. His body had reacted independent of his mind. He'd have to think about that later. This could be the thing that might save him if *real* danger came. If it ever comes I hope it comes suddenly, he thought, without warning like a man leaping out of darkness. Then my body might save me, he thought.

As his heart pounded more slowly, Gus remembered that he had put off his running program for a week and he must not do that, because if you lose momentum you'll stop. He decided to go to the academy and run tonight after he got off duty. It would be a beautiful night and of course there would be no one else on the track except possibly Seymour, the leathery old motor officer who was a hulking man with a huge stomach, wide hips, and a face like eroded clay from riding the motorcycle more than twenty years. Sometimes Gus would find Seymour out there lumbering around the police academy track at 3:00 A.M. blowing and steaming. After his shower, when he was dressed in the blue uniform, riding breeches, black boots and white helmet, why then Seymour looked formidable again and not nearly as fat. He rode the motor lightly and could do wonders with the heavy machine. He had been a friend of Kilvinsky and how Gus had enjoyed the nocturnal runs when Kilvinsky was with him, and how they would rest on the turf. He had loved listening to Kilvinsky and Seymour discussing the old times on the police department when things were simple, when good and evil were definitive. He remembered how he would pretend to be as tired as Kilvinsky when they had covered their fifteen laps, gone to the steam room and then the showers, but actually he could have run fifteen more without exhausting himself. It was a beautiful night tonight. It would be good to get on the cool grass and run and run. He would try to run five miles tonight, five hard fast miles, and then he would not need a steam bath. He would shower, go home, and sleep into the afternoon tomorrow if it were not too hot to sleep, if the children would let him sleep, and if Vickie would not need him to help her replace a light bulb that was simply too high to reach after she became dizzy standing on a chair. Or to help her shop because it was impossible to shop nowadays alone even if you could leave the children with your neighbor because the markets were horribly confusing and you couldn't find anything, and sometimes you just wanted to scream, especially when you thought of returning to a house with three children and oh, God, Gus, what if I'm pregnant again? I'm five days overdue. Yes I'm sure, I'm sure.

"Ambulance on the way," said Craig, clicking back down the walkway and Gus made a mental note to suggest to Craig that he get rubber-soled shoes or at least to remove the cleat from his heels because even working uniformed patrol, it paid to walk quietly a good part of the time. It was hard enough to do with a jingling key ring and creaking Sam Browne and jostling baton.

"Why did you hit him?" asked Craig, and by now the bloody man was sitting up and wailing as the pain was apparently penetrating the drunken euphoria.

"Ah tol' him I was goin' to do it nex' time he messed wif Tillie. Las' time I came home early I catched them in bed sleepin' an' drunk on mah whiskey an' there they was comf'table wif Tillie's bare ass right up there nex' to him and that thing still there inside her an' I reached ovah an' pulled it out and I woke him up an' tol' him if he evah did that again why I would whop him up side the head and I came home early tonight and I catched them agin an' I did it."

"I had it comin', Charlie," said the bloody man. "You right. You right."

Gus heard the wail of the ambulance siren in the distance and looked at his watch. By the time they finished the arrest report it would be end-of-watch and he could go to the academy and run and run.

"Don' you worry, Charlie, I won't have you arrested," said the bloody man. "You the bes' friend I evah had."

"I'm afraid Charlie has to go to jail, friend," said Craig, helping the bloody man to his feet.

"I won' sign no complaint," warned the bloody man and then winced as he stood erect and touched his head tenderly.

"Doesn't matter if you do or not," said Gus. "This is a felony and we're going to put him in jail just in case you up and die on us in the next few days."

"Don' you worry, Charlie," said the bloody man. "I ain't goin' to die on you."

"You can talk to the detectives tomorrow about refusing to prosecute," said Gus as they all walked to the front. "But tonight, your friend is going to jail."

The winking piercing red siren light announced the arrival of the ambulance even though the driver had killed the siren. Gus flashed his light to show the driver the house and the ambulance slid in at the curb and the attendant jumped out. He took the arm of the bloody man as the driver opened the door.

"Don' you worry now, Charlie, I won' persecute you," said the bloody man. "An' Ah'll take good care of Tillie too while you in jail. Don' you worry none 'bout her neither. Hear?"

12

Enema

Roy's heart thumped as the telephone rang in the receiver which he held pressed to his ear. The door to the vice squad office was locked and he knew the rest of the night watch teams would not be straggling into the office for at least a half hour. He decided to call Dorothy from a police department phone to save the long distance charge. It was hard enough trying to make rent payments in two places and support himself after he sent his monthly payment to Dorothy. Then there was his car payment and it was becoming apparent he would soon have to sell the Thunderbird and settle for a lower priced car when this was one of the few luxuries he had left.

He was almost glad she wasn't home and was about to hang up when he heard the unmistakable pitch of Dorothy's unmistakable voice which so often made a simple greeting sound like a question.

"Hello?"

"Hello, Dorothy, hope I didn't disturb you."

"Roy? I was in the shower."

"Oh, I'm sorry, I'll call back."

"No, it's alright. I'm in my bathrobe. What is it?"

"Is it the gold robe I got you for your last birthday?"

"We were already separated on my last birthday, Roy. It was the year before you got me a gold robe and this isn't it."

"Oh. How's Becky?"

"You just saw her last week, Roy. She's still the same."

"Goddamnit, Dorothy, can't you even spare me an occasional kind word."

"Yes, Roy, but please don't let's get started again on the same old thing. The divorce will be final in just eighty-nine days and that's it. We're not coming back to you."

Roy swallowed hard and the tears rushed to his eyes. He didn't speak for several seconds until he was sure he had control.

"Roy?"

"Yes, Dorothy."

"Roy, this is useless."

"God, I'll do anything you say, Dorothy. Please come home. Don't go through with it."

"We've been over this again and again."

"I'm terribly lonely."

"A handsome man like you? A golden-haired, blue-eyed Apollo like Roy Fehler? You didn't have any trouble finding companionship while we were together."

"Christ, Dorothy, it only happened once or twice. I've told you all about it."

"I know, Roy. It wasn't that. You weren't particularly unfaithful as far as men go. But I just stopped caring. I just don't care for you anymore, can't you understand that?"

"Please give her to me, Dorothy," Roy sobbed brokenly, and then the dam burst and he began crying in the mouthpiece, turning toward the door fearful that one of the other vice officers would come in early, and humiliated that he was doing this and letting Dorothy hear it.

"Roy, Roy, don't do that. I know how you're suffering without Becky."

"Give her to me, Dorothy," Roy sniffed, wiping his face on the sleeve of his orange checkered sport shirt which he wore hanging out of his belt to cover the gun and handcuffs.

"Roy, I'm her mother."

"I'll pay you anything, Dorothy. My father has some money set aside for me in his will. Carl once hinted to me that if I ever changed my mind about going in the family store, I could maybe get my hands on it. I'll get it. I'll give it to you. Anything, Dorothy."

"I'm not selling my baby, Roy! When the hell are you going to grow up?"

"I'll move back with Mom and Dad. Mom could take care of Becky while I work. I've already talked to Mom. Please, Dorothy, you don't know how I love her. I love her so much more than you do."

The line was dead for a moment and Roy was coldly afraid she had hung up, then she said, "Maybe you do, Roy. Maybe in your own way you do. But I don't think you love her for herself. It's something else you see in her. But it doesn't matter who loves her more. The point is that a child, especially a little girl, needs a mother."

"There's *my* mother . . ."

"Goddamnit Roy, will you shut up and stop thinking about yourself for just once in your life? I'm trying to tell you Becky needs a mother, a real mother, and I happen to be that mother. Now my lawyer's told you and I've told you that you can have more than adequate visitation rights. You can have whatever is reasonable. I'll be very liberal in that regard. I don't think I've been unfair in my child support demands. And surely, the dollar a year alimony isn't too difficult to manage."

Roy heaved three deep breaths and the sting of his humiliation swept over him. He was thankful he had finally decided to make his final plea by telephone because he feared this might happen. He had been so distraught through the divorce that he could hardly control simple emotions anymore.

"You're very generous, Dorothy," he said, finally.

"I wish you everything good, so help me God I do."

"Thank you."

"Can I give you some advice, Roy? I think I know you better than anyone."

"Why not? I'm vulnerable to anything right now. Tell me to drop dead, I'll probably do it."

"No you won't Roy. You'll be all right. Listen, get on course and go somewhere. You studied criminology after switching your major two or three times. You said you'd only be a policeman for a year or so and it's already more than two years and you're nowhere near your degree. But that's okay if being a policeman is what you want. But I don't think it is. You've never really liked it."

"It's better than working for a living."

"Please don't joke now, Roy. This is the last free advice I'll ever be giving you. Get on course. Even if it's going back to your dad's store. You could do a lot worse. I don't think you'll be a successful policeman. You always seemed unhappy with some aspect of the job or other."

"Maybe I'd be miserable at anything."

"Maybe so, Roy. Maybe so. Anyway, do what you think is best, and I'm sure I'll be seeing you often when you come to get Becky."

"You can bet on that."

"Good-bye, Roy."

Roy sat at the cluttered table in the vice office and smoked, even though he had a severe case of indigestion and suspected an incipient ulcer. He finished the first cigarette and used the smoldering coal to light another. He knew the fire in his stomach would worsen and that was alright too. He thought for an instant about the new untested Smith & Wesson two-inch which rested lightly on his hip and had made him so acutely aware that for the first time in his police career he was working a plainclothes assignment. For the first time he realized how badly he wanted that assignment, and how, when the watch commander had asked him if he would care for a loan to the vice squad for thirty days, he had jumped at it. He began feeling a little better and decided it was foolish and melodramatic to think of the Smith & Wesson as he had for that moment. Things were not that bad yet. He still had hope.

The lock turned and the door swung open in one motion and Roy did not recognize the balding loudly dressed man who came in with a gun belt slung over his shoulder and a paper sack in his hand.

"Hello," said Roy, standing up and hoping the evidence of tears was no longer in his face.

"Hi," said the man, extending his hand. "You must be a new man."

"I'm Roy Fehler. I'm on loan to vice for the month. This is only my third night here."

"Oh? I'm Frank Gant. I been on days off since Monday. I heard we were borrowing someone from patrol." He had a massive hand and shook hands violently. "I didn't think anyone was here. Usually the first night watch guy that arrives unlocks the door."

"Sorry," said Roy. "I'll unlock the door next time."

"Oh that's okay. You met the rest of the crew?"

"Yeah. You were the only one I didn't meet."

"Saved the best till last," Gant smiled, putting the paper sack on top of a metal file cabinet.

"My lunch," he said, pointing to the sack. "You brown bagging it?"

"No, I've bought my lunch the last two nights."

"Might as well brown bag it," said Gant. "You'll find there are lots of disadvantages to working vice. When you take off that blue suit you lose your eating spots. We have to pay for our meals or else brown bag it. I brown bag it. Working vice is expensive enough."

"Guess I'll do the same. I can't stand to spend too much money these days."

"You'll be expected to spend some," said Gant, sitting down at the table and opening the log to make the entry for August third. "They give us a few bucks a week to operate on, and we usually blow that the first night. From then on, you use your own dough if you want to operate. Me, I try not to spend too much. I got five kids."

"I'm with you," said Roy.

"They give you any money yet?"

"We operated a bar last night for liquor law violations," said Roy. "I chitted for two dollars, but really I spent five. I lost three on the deal."

"That's the way vice is," Gant sighed. "It's a damn good job and if you like to work you'll love it here, but the bastards won't give us enough money to work on."

"I'd like to work vice as a regular assignment. Maybe this is a good chance to show what I can do."

"It is," said Gant, opening a bulging manila folder and removing some forms which Roy had already come to recoginze as vice complaints. "How long you been in Central, Roy? I don't believe I ever saw you before."

"Just a few months. I came from Newton."

"Down in the jungle, huh? Bet you're glad to get away from there."

"I wanted a change."

"Any change is for the better when you get away from there. I used to work Newton, but that was before the Civil Rights push. Now that they been promised nigger heaven it's not the same working down there. I'll never go back."

"It's a very complicated problem," said Roy, lighting another cigarette as he rubbed his burning stomach and blew a gray plume of smoke through his nose.

"We got some splibs in Central too, but not too many. Just over on the east side and in the projects mostly, and a few others scattered around. Too much business and industry in the downtown area for them to swarm in."

"I'd like to help you with the paper work," said Roy, becoming irritated and uncomfortable as he always did when anyone talked about Negroes like this.

"No, that's okay. These are old vice complaints that there's a follow-up due on. You wouldn't know what to write. Why don't you look through the whore book. It's good to get to know the regulars. Or read over some of the arrest reports to see how vice pinches are made. You made a whore pinch yet?"

"No, we tailed a couple last night but we lost them. We've been mostly operating the bars. We got a bartender for serving a drunk, but that's the only pinch we made in two nights."

"Well Gant's back so we'll go to work now."

"You're not a sergeant are you?" asked Roy, realizing that he still wasn't sure who all were working vice officers and who were supervisors. The whole atmosphere was very informal and different from patrol.

"Hell no," Gant laughed. "I should be, but I can't pass the damned exam. Been failing that son of a bitch for fourteen years. I'm just a policeman like you."

"Not too sure of the chain of command around here," Roy smiled.

"How much time you got on?"

"Almost three years," said Roy and then was afraid Gant would pin him down to months because two years and three months was certainly not "almost three years."

"Different on vice, isn't it? Calling your sergeant by his first name and all that. Far cry from patrol, huh? This is a close group. Vice work has to be. It's intimate work. You'll be in close and up tight with all kinds of people. You'll see every kind of depravity you ever imagined and some you can't even imagine when you see it. They only let a guy work eighteen months of this shit. Too goddamned sordid, that and the kind of life you lead. Hanging around in bars all night, boozing and playing around with broads. You married?"

"No," said Roy, and was struck with a spasm of indigestion that made him rub his stomach again.

"The whores don't tempt nobody, at least they shouldn't after you been around them awhile and get to know them. But there's a lot of pretty sexy toadies that hang around in some of these bars, lonely broads on the make, you know, just amateurs, freebies, and we're always hanging around too. It gets kind of tempting. Only thing Sergeant Jacovitch demands of us troops is that we don't play around on company time. If we meet something nice, we should make a date for our night off. Jake says if he catches us fooling around in some gin mill with a babe, she better be a professional whore or he'll bounce us off the squad."

"I'm going through a divorce right now. I'm not really thinking too much about women." Roy said it, and hoped Gant would ask him when the divorce was final or make some other comment about Roy's problem because he had a sudden urge to talk to someone, anyone, about it, and perhaps Gant had also been through it. So many policemen had.

"You know the division pretty well, Roy?" asked Gant, disappointing him.

"Pretty well."

"Well, you can study that pin map on the wall," said Gant, waving aimlessly at the wall as he made an entry on a work sheet which Roy knew would later be typed onto the vice complaint.

"What will we work tonight, whores?"

"Whores, yeah. We got to get some pinches. Haven't been doing too much lately. Maybe some fruits. We work fruits when we need some bookings. They're the easiest."

Roy heard voices and Phillips, a swarthy young man with unruly hair and a bristling moustache, walked through the door.

"Hello everybody," he announced, throwing a binocular case on the table, and carrying a set of walkie-talkies under his arm.

"What're the CC units for?" asked Gant. "Some kind of big deal tonight?"

"Maybe," said Phillips nodding to Roy. "Just before we went home last night we got a call from Ziggy's bull dagger informant that The Cave was going to have some lewd movies going tonight. We might try to operate the place."

"Hell, Mickey the bartender knows every goddamn one of us. How we going to operate it? I made so damn many pinches in there, they'd know me if I came in a gorilla suit."

"A gorilla suit would be normal dress in that ding-a-ling joint," said Phillips.

"You know The Cave?" asked Gant to Roy.

"That fruit joint on Main?" asked Roy, remembering a fight call he had received there on his first night in Central Division.

"Yeah, but it's not just fruits. There's lesbians, sadists, masochists, hypes, whores, flim flammers, paddy hustlers, hugger muggers, ex-cons of all descriptions, and anybody else with a kink of some kind or other. Who in the hell's going to operate for us, Phillips?"

"Guess?" said Phillips, grinning at Roy.

"Oh yeah," said Gant. "Nobody around the streets knows you yet."

"I was there in uniform once," said Roy, not relishing the idea of going alone into The Cave.

"In uniform you're just a faceless blue man," said Gant. "Nobody will recognize you now that you're in plainclothes. You know, Phillips, I think old Roy here will do alright in there."

"Yeah, those fruits'll go for that blond hair," said Phillips with a chuckle.

The other night watch team came in. Simeone and Ranatti were neighbors as well as partners and drove to work together. Sergeant Jacovitch came in last and Roy, still an outsider not accustomed to the vice squad routine, read arrest reports while the others sat around the long table in the cluttered office doing their paper work. They were all young men, not much older than himself except for Gant and Sergeant Jacovitch, who were approaching middle age. They all dressed nearly alike with bright-colored cotton shirts hanging outside their pants, and comfortable cotton trousers which it didn't matter if they soiled or tore while climbing a tree or crawling along a darkened hedge as Roy had done the night before when they had followed a whore and a trick to the trick pad, but had lost them when they entered the dingy apartment house because they were spotted by a tall Negro with processed hair who was undoubtedly a lookout. Roy noticed they all wore soft-soled shoes, crepe or ripple soles, so they could creep and peek and pry and Roy was not completely certain that he would like to receive an eighteen-month assignment to vice because he respected the privacy of others. He believed that this undercover surveillance smacked of fascism and he believed that people, damn it, were trustworthy and there were very few bad ones despite what cynical policemen said. Then he remembered Dorothy's admonition that he had never really liked this job, but what the hell, he thought, vice work should be fascinating. At least for a month.

''Bring your arrest reports in here, Roy,'' called Jacovitch, who slid his chair to the side. ''Might as well sit in here and listen to all the bullshit while you're reading the lies on those arrest reports.''

''What lies?'' asked Ranatti, a handsome, liquid-eyed young man who wore an upside-down shoulder holster over a T-shirt. His outer shirt, a long-sleeved navy blue cotton was hung carefully over the back of his chair and he checked it often to make sure the tail was not dragging the floor.

''The Sarge thinks we exaggerate sometimes on our arrest reports,'' said Simeone to Roy. He was younger looking than Ranatti, rosy cheeked, and had slightly protruding ears.

''I wouldn't say that,'' said Jacovitch. ''But I've tried a dozen operators on Ruby Shannon and you guys are the only ones ever did any good.''

''What're you beefing about Jake, we got a case on her didn't we?'' Ranatti beamed.

''Yeah,'' said Jacovitch, with a wary glance first at Ranatti, then at Simeone. ''But she told me you zoomed her. You know the lieutenant doesn't want any hummer pinches.''

''Aw, it was no hummer, Jake,'' said Simeone, ''she just went for old Rosso here.'' He jerked a finger toward the grinning Ranatti.

''Sure seems funny,'' said Jacovitch. ''She can usually smell a cop a block away, and Ranatti fooled her. Shit, he looks like he's fresh off the beat.''

''No, look, Jake,'' said Ranatti. ''We really hooked her legal, honest we did. I operated her in my own inimitable style. You know, played a slick young pool room dago, and she went for it. Never dreamt I was the heat.''

''Another thing, it's unusual for Ruby to go on a six-forty-seven A,'' said Jacovitch. ''She groped you, huh, Rosso?''

''Honest to God, she honked my horn,'' said Ranatti, raising a rather stubby right hand heavenward. ''Gave it two toots with a thumb and forefinger before I laid the iron on her wrists.''

''I don't trust either of you bastards,'' said Jacovitch to the grinning young men. ''Lieutenant Francis and me were cruising the whore spots last week and we stopped and talked to Ruby at Fifth and Stanford. She mentioned the cute little Eye-talian cop that booked her on a hummer. She claims she laid a hand on your knee and you pinched her for lewd conduct right then.''

''Look, boss, I'm lewd from the knee on up. Don't you believe those Latin lover stories?''

They all chuckled and Jacovitch turned to Roy. ''What I'm trying to tell these guys is to lay off the hummers. We got a lieutenant that's very explicit about nice legal pinches. If the whore doesn't say the right words to you for a violation or if she doesn't grope you lewdly, there's no basis for a legal bust.''

''What if she shakes you down for a gun, Jake?'' asked Simeone, lighting a fat cigar that looked comical in the puffy young lips. ''If she does that, I say she ought to get busted for lewd conduct. You can embellish your report a bit.''

''Goddamn, Sim, no embellishment. That's what I'm trying to get through to you. Look, I'm not the whole show, I'm just one of the clowns. The boss says we do police work straight arrow.''

''Okay, Jake, but vice is a different kind of police work,'' said Gant, joining in the conversation for the first time.

''Look,'' said Jacovitch in exasperation. ''Do you really want to roust these whores? If you do, you got to make what amounts to a false arrest report and then perjure yourself to convict her. It's not worth it. There'll always be whores. Why risk your job for a lousy misdemeanor? And while I'm on the subject, the boss is a little hinky about some of these tails you been pulling where you tail the whore to the trick pad and hear her offer the guy a French for ten bucks.''

''So?'' said Simeone, not smiling now. ''We made one like that last week. Something wrong with it?''

''The lieutenant told me he drove by one of the apartment houses where a team made a bust like that. He didn't say it was you, Sim, but he did say that the goddamn place had a windowless concrete wall on the side where the offer was supposed to be heard by the officers.''

''Goddamn it,'' said Gant, standing up suddenly, and striding across the room to his lunch sack, where he removed another cigar. ''What does that fucking boy-lieutenant think this is, a college debating class with all the fucking rules laid down. I never bitched about him before, Jake, but do you know one night he asked me if I'd been drinking? Can you beat it? Ask a vice officer if he's been drinking. I said fuck, yes, Lieutenant, what the hell do you think I should do when I'm operating a bar. Then he asked me if we always pay for our booze and whether we accept sandwiches from bar owners who know we're heat. He wants a bunch of goody goody teetotalers with their lunch money pinned to their underwear. I'm quitting the squad if this prick gets any worse.''

''Take it easy. Jesus,'' said Jacovitch, looking fearfully toward the door. ''He's our boss. We got to have a little loyalty.''

''That guy's blossoming out, Jake,'' said Simeone. ''He's trying to be the youngest captain on the job. You got to watch the blossomers, they'll use their troops for manure.''

Jacovitch looked helplessly at Roy and Roy was certain he would be admonished later by Jacovitch to keep silent about the bitching in the vice squad. He was a poor example of a supervisor if he let it die like this, thought Roy. He should never have let it go this far, but now that it had, he should set them straight. The lieutenant was the officer in charge, and if Roy were in charge, by God, he would hope his sergeant did not permit the men to insult him.

''Let's talk about something else, you mutineers,'' Jacovitch announced nervously, jerking his glasses off and wiping them although they seemed to Roy perfectly clean.

''Did you guys hear how many marines Hollywood vice busted last weekend?'' asked Simeone, and Roy thought Jacovitch looked obviously relieved that the conversation had shifted.

''What's happening in Hollywood?'' asked Gant.

''What always happens?'' said Simeone. ''The joint is lousy with faggots. I hear they got twenty marines in fruit pinches last weekend. They're going to notify the general at Camp Pendleton.''

''That pisses me off,'' said Gant. ''I was in the corps, but things were different in those days. Even marines are different now.''

''Yeah, I hear there're so many fruit marines being busted, the jarheads at Camp Pendleton are afraid to be seen eating a banana,'' said Ranatti. ''They eat it sideways now like an ear of corn.''

''Anybody had a chance to work on the vice complaint at the Regent Arms?'' asked Jacovitch.

''Maybe we could use our loaner here for that one,'' said Ranatti, nodding at Roy. ''I think operating that joint is the only way. We prowled it. I got a ladder up to the balcony on the second floor and saw the room where those two whores are tricking, but I couldn't get close enough to the window.''

"Trouble is, they're damn particular who they take," said Simeone. "I think one or maybe two bellboys are working with them and sending up the tricks. Maybe Roy here could check in and we could set something up."

"Roy's too young," said Gant. "We need an old guy like me, but I been around so long one of those whores would probably recognize me. How about you, Jake? You're old enough and prosperous looking. We'll make you an out of town sport and set something up."

"Might be alright," said Jacovitch, running his fingers through his thinning black hair. "But the boss doesn't like the sergeants to operate too much. I'll see what he thinks."

"The Clarke Apartments is expanding their operations too," said Ranatti. "Apartments six, seven, and eight all have hot beds in them now. Sim and me were staked out there last night for less than an hour and we must've seen these three whores take twelve or thirteen tricks in there one after another. The trick checks in at the desk each time too, so the place is making a fortune."

"One hot bed can make you plenty," Jacovitch nodded.

"These three are really busy. They don't even bother changing sheets," said Ranatti.

"That used to be a square place," said Gant. "I used to take a date there after work whenever I'd get lucky. Too bad they had to get involved in prostitution. Nice old guy runs the joint."

"Too much money in vice," said Jacovitch looking at each of them. "It can corrupt anybody."

"Hey, you guys hear what Harwell did in the restroom at the Garthwaite Theater?" asked Simeone.

"Harwell's a day watch vice officer," said Jacovitch to Roy. "He's about as psycho as Simeone and Ranatti. We all got our crosses to bear."

"What did he do this time?" asked Gant, completing his scribbled notes on a page of yellow legal-size paper.

"He was working the restroom on the vice complaint from the manager, and he spots a brand-new glory hole between the walls of the toilets, so he plops his big ass down on the last stool without dropping his pants and he just sits there smoking his big cigar and pretty soon some fruit comes in and goes straight to the glory hole and sticks his joint through at old Harwell. Lopez was watching from the trap behind the air conditioning on the east wall and he could see real good since we had the manager take the doors off all the johns to discourage the fruits. He said when the guy's joint came poking through the hole, why old Harwell tapped the ashes off that big cigar and blew on the coal till it was glowing red then ground it right into the head of the guy's dick. Says the fruit was screaming on the floor when they left."

"That bastard's psycho," Jacovitch murmured. "This is his second tour on vice. I had my doubts about him. Bastard's psycho."

"You ever hear about the glory hole in Bloomfield's Department Store in the ladies dressing room?" asked Ranatti. "Where the wienie wagger shoved it through at the old babe changing clothes and she stuck a hatpin clear through it and the son of a bitch was pinned right there when the cops arrived."

"I heard that one for years," said Phillips. "I think some cop dreamed that one up for a good locker room story."

"Well, the one about Harwell is true," said Simeone. "Lopez told me. Said they got the hell out right away. Harwell wanted to book the fruit. Can you imagine, after he damn near burned his dick off, he wants to put him in jail? Lopez told him, 'Let's get the hell out of here and the fruit'll never know it was a cop that did it.' "

"Bastard's going to get fired someday," Jacovitch grumbled.

"Look, you got to keep your sense of humor working this job," Ranatti grinned. "You'd go nuts if you didn't."

"I'd like to've seen that," said Gant. "Was the fruit a white guy?"

"Pretty close," said Simeone. "He was Italian."

"You asshole," said Ranatti.

"You guys remember this is trash night," said Jacovitch.

"What a pain in the ass," said Simeone. "I forgot. Jesus Christ, I wore decent clothes tonight."

"Trash night is the night we help the day watch," said Jacovitch to Roy. "We've agreed to rummage through the garbage cans real late at night on the night before the weekly trash pickup. The day watch gives us the addresses of the places they suspect are bookie joints and we check their trash cans."

"I can tell all my friends I'm a G-man," Ranatti muttered. "G for garbage."

"It worked pretty good so far," said Jacovitch to Roy. "We've found betting markers in garbage cans in three places. That gave day watch something to work on."

"And I go home smelling like a garbage dump," said Ranatti.

"One night we were rummaging in the cans back of Red Cat Sam's restaurant," said Simeone, grinning at Jacovitch, "and we find a big hog's head. Goddamn hog had a head like a lion. Old Red Cat's a splib, specializes in soul food. Anyway, we brought the head back for Jake, here. We stuck it in his wall locker and went home. Next night we come to work early to make sure we see him open it and that's the goddamn night this new lieutenant gets transferred in, unbeknownst to us. And they gave Jake's locker to him. He opened that door and didn't say a goddamn thing. Nothing! Nobody said nothing. We just all pretended like we were doing our paper work or something, and didn't say nothing!"

"He told me later that he thought this was an initiation for the new commander," said Jacovitch, lighting a cigarette and coughing hoarsely. "Maybe that's why he's made it so tough on us."

"Let's not talk about him anymore. I get depressed," said Gant. "You guys ready to go to work?"

"Wait a minute before you go," said Jacovitch. "We got something pretty big cooking tonight. We're going to take The Cave at 1:00 A.M. I know you guys've probably heard rumors because it's impossible to keep a secret in this outfit. Anyway, we got some good scam from a reliable snitch that The Cave is having a lewd movie show tonight. I can't understand it unless Frippo the owner is just plain desperate for business. Anyway, the word is out and the goddamn place is going to be packed tonight. Do you know anything about The Cave, Roy?"

"A little," Roy nodded.

"We been hitting them pretty hard lately," said Jacovitch. "One more good bust and I think we can get his liquor license. Tonight should be it. You guys drop whatever you're doing and meet me here at about midnight. We're borrowing about a dozen uniformed policemen from patrol and two teams from Administrative Vice are going to assist. The movie show is supposed to start about one and we're going to have Roy inside. As soon as the movie starts, Roy, you casually walk to the restroom. We already heard from the snitch that nobody's going to get in or out the front door after it starts. Stick a cigarette out the window and wave it around. We'll be sitting outside where we can see that window. Then we'll use the key and come in the front door."

"You have a key to the place?" asked Roy.

"Yeah," Ranatti grinned. "That's it in the corner." He pointed to a four-foot metal post with a heavy steel plate welded on the end and handles affixed to each side so that four men could swing it.

"It should come off with no problems," Jacovitch said. "I don't think you'll have any trouble, but if you should, like if something screwy should happen—if you're made as a vice officer, if you're in any danger at all—you just pick up a barstool or a beer mug or anything and toss it through the front window. Then we'll be right in. But you won't have any trouble.''

''Do I just sit there and have a drink?'' asked Roy.

''Yeah. Order beer and drink out of the bottle,'' said Ranatti. ''You don't dare drink out of a glass in the slimy place. Hey, Sim, is Dawn LaVere still hustling out of The Cave?''

''I saw her out front last week,'' Simeone nodded.

''Watch for that bitch, Roy. She's the smartest whore I ever saw. She can spot a cop quick. If she suspects you're vice she'll start her act. Sit next to you, put a hand around your waist and pat you down for a gun and handcuffs while she's tucking a big tit under your armpit to keep you busy. She'll feel your key ring or get her hands on it if she can to see if you got call box keys or handcuff keys. And she'll feel for two wallets because she knows most policemen carry one wallet with their money and another one for their badge. I'd advise you to leave your badge and gun and everything with Gant before you go in.''

''I don't know about that,'' said Jacovitch. ''He'd better be armed. I don't want him getting hurt.''

''A gun can screw up the deal, Jake,'' Ranatti protested. ''He might as well get used to taking a few chances. We all got to if we want to work vice.''

''I don't know. I'll think about it,'' said Jacovitch.

''Another thing, don't let old Dawn kiss you,'' giggled Ranatti. ''She loves to snuggle around with guys she's hustling. Real affectionate whore, but she's got VD and TB.''

''Runny at both ends,'' Simeone nodded. ''All the time.''

''She gobbles about twenty joints a night,'' said Ranatti. ''Dawn once told me she don't even screw anymore. Most guys would rather have head jobs and that's a lot easier for her. She don't even have to undress.''

''She a dyke?'' asked Gant.

''Oh yeah,'' said Ranatti. ''She lives over on Alvarado with some big fat bull dagger. Told me one time she can't stand to lay a man anymore.''

''A vice officer hears all the girls' problems,'' said Phillips to Roy. ''We get to know all these assholes so well.''

''Want Roy to work with me?'' asked Gant to Jacovitch.

''I want the four of you to work together tonight,'' said Jacovitch. ''I don't want you guys getting hung up on something and not be ready to go on The Cave when it's time. You four go out together. You can take two cars, but decide what you're going to do till midnight and do it together. Phillips'll work with me.''

''Let's go down on Sixth and see if Roy can operate a streetwalker,'' said Gant to Ranatti and Simeone who were already taking their small flashlights out of the drawer of a filing cabinet.

''Trash night and I'm wearing a brand-new shirt,'' Ranatti grumbled, buttoning the shirt gingerly. Roy noticed it fitted well and the shoulder holster was completely concealed. He wondered if he should invest in a shoulder holster. He decided to wait. He was only working vice this month and it might be a long time before he was given a permanent plainclothes assignment. Surely though, someone would want him soon. Felony car, vice, someone would want him. He was sure it was evident to everyone that he was an exceptionally good policeman but police work was temporary and he knew he should be thinking about what courses he would be taking this semester. He seemed to have lost his drive in that direction. Maybe, he thought, I'll take a vacation this semester.

They took two cars. Gant was driving a two-tone green Chevrolet which the vice officers had done their best to camouflage by putting oversized tires on the back. Someone had hung a fuzzy object from the mirror and Gant told Roy that Simeone was responsible for the college decals plastered all over the rear window. Still,

Roy thought, it looked like a stripped down, low priced, plainclothes police car. The Department, according to Gant, was very tight with expenditures of funds for undercover operation.

Gant drove Roy to the parking lot where he had his private car.

''Listen Roy,'' said Gant. ''We'll be in the vacant lot behind the yellow apartment building north of Sixth just off Towne Avenue. You make a pass by there and see where we are. Then you cruise a few blocks down on Sixth and you should see a hustler or two even this early in the evening. If you get her, bring her back to the meeting place.''

''Okay,'' said Roy.

''You sure you learned last night what you need for a whore pinch?'' asked Gant.

''Offer of sex for money,'' said Roy. ''Seems simple enough.''

''Okay, Roy, go ahead,'' said Gant. ''If you see a whore you suspect is a man dressed up as a woman, don't hit on him. Pass him by and try another one. We don't operate fruits alone. They're the most dangerous unpredictable bastards in the world. You just hit on women—*real* women.''

''Okay,'' Roy said, getting anxious to start. It was a dark night, and being out here on the city streets in plainclothes was like being out here for the very first time. It was eerie and exciting. His heart began thudding.

''Go ahead, kid,'' said Gant. ''Take it easy though.''

Roy noticed that his hands became extremely clammy and the steering wheel slippery as he turned east on Sixth Street. It wasn't that he was alone, because he was not really alone with Gant and Ranatti and Simeone staked out just a few blocks away. But he was for the first time out in the streets minus the security of the badge and blue suit, and though he knew this street fairly well, it seemed altogether strange. A vice officer loses the comfort of the big brass shield, he thought. He acquires an identity. Without the blue suit he becomes a mere man who must function as a street dweller. His confidence was waning. Was it more than nervousness? He put a hand on his chest and measured the thuds. Was it fear?

Roy saw a streetwalker at Fifth and Stanford. She was an emaciated Negro with straight legs and Roy guessed she was an addict with her look of yearning. She smiled as he drove slowly by.

''Hello blondie,'' she said, walking up to Roy's car on the passenger side and peering in.

''Hello there,'' Roy said, forced a smile, and cursed silently at his quivering voice.

''Haven't I seen you around?'' she asked, still smiling an uninviting bad-toothed smile as she glanced around the car, probing, and Roy guessed that she suspected immediately.

''I've never been here before,'' Roy answered. ''A friend told me about this place. Said I could have a good time.''

''What do you do for a living, baby?'' she smiled.

''Insurance man.''

''That's funny, you look just like a cop to me,'' she said, drilling him with her eyes.

''A cop?'' he laughed brokenly. ''Not me.''

''You look exactly like a young cop,'' she said unblinkingly while he withered.

''Look, you're making me nervous with this cop talk,'' said Roy. ''Can I get a good time around here, or not?''

''Maybe you could,'' she said. ''What do you have in mind?''

Roy remembered last night's admonishment by Jacovitch about entrapment and he knew she was trying to lead him into making the offer himself.

''Don't you know?'' he said, trying a coy smile but uncertain how it looked.

''Give me a card, baby, I might want to buy some insurance sometime.''

''Card?''

"A business card. Give me a business card."

"Look, I'm a married man. I don't want you to know my name. What're you trying to do, blackmail me?" said Roy, congratulating himself on his quick thinking and making a note to borrow some cards from an insurance office for any future operations.

"Okay," she smiled easily. "Tear your name off the card or scratch it out with that pen in your shirt pocket. Just let me see that you have a card."

"I don't have any with me," said Roy. "Come on, let's get down to business."

"Uh huh," she said, "let's do that. And my business is minding my own business. Any insurance man that ain't got a million cards in his wallet is a mighty poor insurance man."

"So I'm a poor insurance man. What the hell," said Roy hopelessly as she turned to walk away.

"You ain't even a good vice cop," she sneered over her shoulder.

"Bitch," said Roy.

"Paddy, blue-eyed motherfucker," said the prostitute.

Roy turned right on the next street, drove south to Seventh then back up to Sixth where he parked his car a half block away with the lights out and watched the prostitute talking to a tall Negro in a gray felt hat who nodded and walked quickly down the block to a fat prostitute in a green satin dress whom Roy hadn't seen before. She ran inside the building and talked with two women in the doorway who were just coming out. Roy drove to the meeting place where he found Gant sitting in the back seat of Ranatti and Simeone's car.

"Might as well go somewhere else," said Roy. "I'm burned."

"What happened?" asked Gant.

"A skinny whore in a brown dress recognized me from working uniform in this area," Roy lied. "I saw her look at me and run and tell all the whores on the block. It's no use, I'm burned here."

"Let's go over to the park and bust a quick fruit or two," said Ranatti. "We haven't made a fruit pinch for a few days."

After leaving his private car in the station parking lot Roy rejoined Gant in the vice car and they drove toward the park. Roy was disappointed that he had so far been unable to make a vice arrest, but he decided he'd operate successfully in The Cave later tonight and it now occurred to him that he had no idea how to arrest a homosexual.

"What're the elements of a fruit pinch?" asked Roy.

"That's easier than a whore bust," said Gant, driving casually through the early evening traffic. "If he makes a lewd offer in a public place, that's it. Or if he gropes you. But as far as I'm concerned you don't have to let a man grab your joint. If it looks like he's making a move to honk you, just grab his hand and he's busted. We'll say on the arrest report he touched your privates. I don't give a shit what Jacovitch says about legal arrests and embellishing arrest reports, I don't let nobody touch my tool unless she's wearing a dress and I know for sure there's a female body under the dress."

"Seems like you could just settle for the verbal offer," said Roy.

"Yeah, you could. But some faggots are real aggressive. You say hello and bang, they got you by the dork. I don't expect you to submit to that crap. Just operating fruits is bad enough. But maybe we won't have to operate them. Maybe we can catch them in the trap."

"I heard lots of talk about *the trap*. What is it?" asked Roy, feeling a bit uncomfortable about the prospect of working fruits.

"That's what we call a vantage point," said Gant, accelerating up the hill on Sixth Street past Central Receiving Hospital. "There's lots of places where fruits hang out, like public restrooms. Well, some of these places install vents covered with heavy mesh screen or something like that, where we can peek through into the restroom area. Most of the places take the doors off the shithouses for us too. Then we sit in *the trap*, as we call it, and peek through into the restroom. Of course there's legal technicalities like probable cause and exploratory searches involved here, but I'll tell you about that when we make the arrest report—if we catch any. Sometimes we use the CC units and let one guy sit in the trap with a radio and if he sees some fruit action in the john, he whispers to us over the radio and in we come. Let me warn you about fruits. I don't know what you're expecting, but I can tell you that a fruit can look like anything. He can be a big manly guy with a wife and kids and a good job, he can be a professional man, or a priest, or even a cop. We've caught people from every walk of life in these traps. All kinds of people got kinks, and in my opinion, any guy with this particular kind of kink that has to indulge it occasionally will sooner or later look for a public restroom or some other sleazy fruit hangout. It's part of the cruddy thrill I guess. I talked to a million fruits in my time and lots of them cop out to needing a little action in a place like this once in a while even when they can have their kicks in private with a discreet boyfriend. I don't know why, I just know they do it. So the thing is, you might run into a pretty square kind of fruit in here. Like I said, a respectable married guy or something, and when he finds out you're the law, that son of a bitch might come uncorked. Suddenly be pictures a big scandal where Mama and the kiddies and all his friends read on the front page of the *Times* that old Herbie is really a cocksucker. That's what's going on in his sweaty brain. And you be careful, because if you was taking him for murder he wouldn't be near as panicky or dangerous. This prick might literally try to kill you to get away. I say don't get yourself hurt for a lousy misdemeanor pinch that ain't worth a goddamn in court anyway. You know what the average fruit gets? About a fifty-dollar fine and that's it. He'd have to have a bunch of priors to draw any jail time. But these fruits don't know all this and if they don't know it they don't think of it when you're arresting them. All they're thinking about is getting away from you. And they're fucked up in the head anyway or they wouldn't be there in the first place, so you just be careful working fruits."

"I will," said Roy, feeling his heart race again. He hadn't bargained for the dangers of vice work. When he first learned he was going to vice he vaguely pictured girls and drinking. He thought of how he had never actually been in a fight in the two years he had been a policeman. He had to assist a partner wrestle a man to the ground a few times where the handcuffs were applied without too much trouble. But he had never actually struck a man, nor had anyone ever struck him. And a vice officer carried no baton. "Do you carry a sap?" Roy asked.

"You bet," said Gant, lifting his shirt and showing Roy the huge black beaver-tail sap he carried inside his waistband.

"Maybe I ought to buy one," said Roy.

"I think you ought to have one," Gant nodded. "Vice officers get in some good ones and that onesies on twosies wristlock they teach you in the academy never seems to work when you're squirming around on some piss-covered restroom floor with some bloody sweaty fruit, or maybe battling some hugger mugger's pimp in some dark hotel lobby when your partner doesn't know where the hell you are."

"This job doesn't sound too good after all," Roy smiled weakly.

"I'm just telling the worst that can happen," said Gant. "They're the things that happen to young hot dogs like Ranatti and Simeone. But you stick with the old salts like me and nothing's going to happen. We won't make as many pinches as those guys but we'll go home in one piece every night."

Gant parked the vice car a half block from the park and walked to the hedgerow on the south side of the duck pond where they found Ranatti and Simeone sprawled on the grass smoking and throwing pieces of popcorn to a hissing black gander who accepted the tribute but scorned them for their charity.

"Nobody appreciates something for nothing," said Ranatti, pointing his cigarette at the ferocious gander who tired of the popcorn and waddled to the water's edge.

"We going to operate, or work the trap?" asked Gant.

"Whatever you want," Simeone shrugged.

"What do you want to do, Roy?" asked Gant.

"Hell, I'm too new to know," said Roy. "If we operate that means we walk around and pose as fruits?"

"Just be available," said Simeone. "You don't have to swish around or play with your coins in your pants pocket or anything. Just hang around and talk to the fruits that hit on you. Usually one or two of us operate out around the trees and the other two wait somewhere. If you get an offer you bring the fruit to the waiting place. Tell him you got a car nearby or a pad, or tell him anything. Just get him to us, then we all take him. One man never takes a fruit alone."

"I already told him that," said Gant.

"Or, if you're squeamish about playing fruit, and I don't blame you if you are," said Ranatti, "'cause I never could stand to operate them—well, then we can go to the trap. Then you only watch them in a lewd act. You don't have to actually mingle with them like when you operate."

"Let's do that," said Roy.

"You two want inside or outside?" asked Simeone to Gant.

"Outside. What do you think?"

"What did you ask him for?" said Ranatti.

"He respects his elders," said Gant as they began strolling through the park. It was a warm summer evening, and a slight breeze cooled Roy's face as it came off the pond. Many of the ducks were asleep, and aside from the steady flow of nearby traffic it was quiet and restful here.

"It's a beautiful place," said Roy.

"The park?" said Ranatti. "Oh, yeah. But it's full of faggots and thieves and assholes in general. No decent people dare hang around here after dark."

"Except us vice officers," said Simeone.

"He said decent people," Gant reminded him.

"Once in a while some squares that're new in town might come around here after dark with the family, but they soon see what's happening. They used to lock up the johns at night, but some brainy park administrator decided to leave them open. The open restrooms draw fruits like flies."

"Fruit flies," said Simeone.

"We used to only have a hundred fruits a night around here. Now we got a thousand. Maybe we can get the restrooms closed again."

"That's it over there," said Gant to Roy, pointing at the large stucco outbuilding squatting near a clump of elm that rustled in the wind which had grown stronger.

"Roy, you and me'll wait behind those trees over there," said Gant. "When they come out of the trap we'll see them and run over and help them."

"One time," said Simeone, "there were only two of us here and we caught eight fruits in there. One was gobbling another's joint, and the other six were standing around fondling anything they could find."

"A real circle jerk," said Ranatti. "We snuck out of the trap and didn't know what the hell to do with eight of them. Finally Sim spots a pile of roofing tiles at the corner of the tool shed and he sticks his head in and yells, 'All you fruits are under arrest.' Then he slams the door shut and backs off to the pile of tiles and starts heaving them at the door every time one of them tries to get out. He was really enjoying it, I think. I ran to the call box on the corner and put out a help call and when the black and whites got here we still had all eight fruits trapped in the crapper. But the wall of the building looked like a machine gun squad had strafed it."

"See what I told you before about sticking with me and staying out of trouble," said Gant, walking toward the clump of trees where they would wait. "Why don't you go in with them for a while, Roy? You might as well see what it's all about."

Ranatti removed his key ring from his pocket and unlocked the padlock on a massive tool shed which was attached to the side of the building. Roy entered the shed and was followed by Ranatti who held the door for him and closed it behind them. It was deep and black in the shed except for a patch of light six feet up on the wall near the roof of the shed. Ranatti took Roy's elbow and guided him through the darkness and pointed to a step and a three-foot platform leading up to the patch of light. Roy stepped up and looked through the heavy gauge sheets of wire mesh into the interior of the restroom. The room was about thirty by twenty feet, Roy thought. He envisioned the dimension might be a question by the defense if he ever had to go to court on an arrest he made here. There were four urinals and four stools behind them separated by metal walls. Roy noticed there were no doors on the front of the stalls and several peepholes were drilled in the metal walls which separated the toilets.

They waited silently for several minutes and then Roy heard feet shuffling on the concrete walk leading toward the front door. An old stooped tramp slouched in toting a bundle which he opened when he got inside. The tramp took four wine bottles from the dirty sack and drained the half mouthful of wine which remained in each of them. Then he put the bottles back into the bundle and Roy wondered what value they could have. The old man wobbled over to the last stool where he removed his filthy coat, lunged sideways against the wall, righted himself, and took the floppy hat from his tremendous shaggy head. The tramp dropped his pants and sat down in one motion and a tremendous gaseous explosion echoed through the restroom.

"Oh Christ," Simeone whispered. "Just our luck."

The stench filled the room instantly.

"Jesus Christ," said Ranatti, "this place smells like a shithouse."

"Were you expecting a flowershop?" asked Simeone.

"This is a degrading job," Roy muttered and went to the door for some fresh air.

"Well, the old thief's got enough asswipe stashed to last a week," said Simeone in a loud voice.

Roy looked back into the restroom and saw the tramp still sitting on the toilet, slumped against the side wall snoring loudly. A huge wad of toilet paper protruded from the top of his ragged undershirt.

"Hey!" Simeone called. "Wake up you old ragpicker. Wake up!"

The tramp stirred, blinked twice and closed his eyes again.

"Hey, he's not sleeping real sound yet," said Ranatti. "Hey! Old man! Wake up! Get your ass up and out of here!"

This time the tramp stirred, grunted and opened his eyes with a snap of his head.

"Get the hell out of here, you old crud!" said Simeone.

"Who said that?" asked the tramp, leaning forward on the toilet trying to peek around the wall of the toilet stall.

"It's me. God!" said Ranatti. "Get the hell out of here."

"Wise son of a bitch, huh?" said the tramp. "Jus' wait a minute."

As the tramp was struggling back into his pants, Roy heard footsteps and a pale, nervous-looking man with a receding hairline and green-tinted glasses entered the restroom.

"A fruit," Ranatti whispered in Roy's ear.

The man looked in each toilet stall and seeing only the uninteresting tramp in the last stall, walked to the urinal on the far side of the room.

The tramp did not buckle his belt but merely tied the leather around his waist. He slammed the floppy hat back on his head and picked up the bundle. Then he saw the man standing at the last urinal. The tramp put down the bundle.

"Hello God," said the tramp.

"Beg your pardon?" said the man, still standing at the urinal.

"Ain't you God?" asked the tramp. "Didn't you tell me to get the hell out of here? Well I might not look like much, but no son of a bitch tells me to get my ass out of a public shithouse, you son of a bitch." The tramp put down his bundle deliberately while the terrified man re-zipped his trousers. As the man skidded toward the door across the slippery floor of the restroom the tramp threw a wine bottle that crashed on the doorjamb and showered the man with glass fragments. The tramp hobbled to the door and looked after his fleeing enemy, then returned to his bundle and hefted it to his shoulder. With a toothless triumphant grin he staggered from the restroom.

"Sometimes you get a chance to do good things for people in this job," said Simeone lighting a cigarette, making Roy wish he would not smoke in the stifling dark enclosure of the shed.

It was perhaps five minutes when another step was heard. A tall, muscular man of about thirty entered, walked to the sink and ran a comb deliberately through his wavy brown hair without glancing to his left. Then he examined the wide collar of a green sport shirt worn beneath a lightweight well-fitting lime sweater. Then he walked to each toilet stall and looked inside. He then walked to the urinal which had been occupied by the pale man, unzipped his trousers and stood there not urinating. Ranatti nodded in the darkness to Roy but Roy did not believe he could be a fruit. The man stood at the urinal for almost five minutes craning his neck occasionally toward the door when a sound was heard outside. Twice Roy thought someone would enter and he now knew of course what the man was waiting for, and he shivered in the back of his neck and decided when another one came in he did not want to watch, was not curious enough to watch because already he felt slightly nauseated. He always had the idea that fruits were all swishes, hence identifiable, and it sickened him to see this average-looking man in here, and he did not want to watch. Then an old man entered. Roy didn't see him until he was through the door and stepping lightly to the urinal at the opposite end of the line. The old man was perhaps seventy, dressed nattily in a blue pinstripe with natural shoulders and matching vest, and a blue silk tie over a pale blue shirt. His hair was pearl white and styled. His hands were lightly veined and he picked nervously at invisible lint on the impeccable suit. He looked at the tall man at the other urinal and smiled and the light glinted off his silver collar pin and Roy was struck with a wave of revulsion not imperceptible like before, but gut wrenching as the old man, still holding his hands near his groin out of Roy's line of sight, hopped along the urinals until he was standing next to the tall man. He laughed softly and so did the tall man who said, "You're too old." Roy whispered incredulously to Ranatti, "He's an old man! My God, he's an old man!"

"What the hell," Ranatti whispered dryly, "fruits grow old too."

The old man left after being repulsed another time. He stopped in the doorway but finally left in dejection.

"He didn't really do anything lewd," Simeone whispered to Roy. "He just stood next to him at the urinal. No touching or anything. He didn't even jerk off. No good for an arrest."

Roy thought the hell with it he had seen enough and decided to join Gant on the cool clean grass in the invigorating air when he heard voices and feet scraping and decided to see who or what would enter. He heard a man say something in rapid Spanish and a child answered. The only thing Roy understood was "Sí Papá." Then Roy heard the man walking away from the doorway and he heard other children's voices talking Spanish. A boy of about six skipped in the restroom not looking at the tall man and ran to a toilet where he turned his back to the watchers, dropped his short pants to the floor revealing his plump brown behind, and urinated in the toilet while he hummed a child's song. Roy smiled for a moment, but then he remembered the tall man. He saw the tall man's hand moving frantically in the area of his crotch and then he stepped away from the urinal and masturbated as he faced the boy but hurriedly returned to the urinal when a child's shrill laugh pierced the silence from the outside. The boy adjusted his pants and ran from the restroom still humming, and Roy heard him shout, ''Carlos! Carlos!'' to a child who answered from a long way across the park. The child never saw the tall man who now grunted while he stood at the old place and his hand moved more frantically than before.

''See? Our job *is* worth doing,'' Simeone grinned viciously. ''Let's take that bastard.''

As the three men broke from the shed door, Simeone whistled and Gant came running from the clump of swaying elms. Roy saw a man and three children across the expanse of darkness strolling across the grass carrying shopping bags. They were almost out of the park.

Simeone led the way into the restroom with his badge in his hand. The man looked at the four vice officers and fumbled with the zipper of his trousers.

''You like kids?'' Simeone grinned. ''I'll bet you got some little bubblegummers of your own. Want to bet, Rosso?'' he said and turned to Ranatti.

''What is this?'' asked the man, his face white, jaw twitching.

''Answer me!'' Simeone commanded. ''You got kids? And a wife?''

''I'm getting out of here,'' said the man, walking toward Simeone who shoved him back against the wall of the restroom.

''No need for that,'' said Gant, standing on the threshold.

''I'm not getting rough,'' said Simeone. ''I just want to know if he's got a wife and kids. They almost always do. Do you, man?''

''Yes, of course. But why are you arresting me? Lord, I didn't do anything,'' he said as Simeone handcuffed his hands behind his back.

''Always handcuff fruits,'' Simeone smiled to Roy. ''Always. No exceptions.''

As they were leaving the park, Roy walked behind with Gant.

''How do you like working fruits, kid?'' asked Gant.

''Not too good,'' Roy answered.

''Look over there,'' said Gant, pointing toward the pond where a slender young man in tight coffee-colored pants and a lacy orange shirt was mincing along the edge of the water.

''That's what I thought all fruits looked like,'' said Roy.

The young man stopped every thirty feet or so, genuflected, crossed himself, and prayed silently. Roy counted six genuflections before he reached the street where he disappeared in the pedestrian traffic.

''Some of them are pretty pitiful. That one's trying to resist,'' Gant shrugged, offering Roy a cigarette which he accepted. ''They're the most promiscuous creatures that ever walked the earth. They're so goddamned unsatisfied they're always seeking. Now you see why we try to work whores, and gambling, and bars as much as possible. And remember, you can get the shit kicked out of you working fruits. On top of all the rest of the crap you got to put up with, it's dangerous as hell.''

Roy's mind drifted back then, back to college. He had been reminded of someone. Of course! he thought suddenly, as he remembered the mannerisms of Professor Raymond. It had never occurred to him before! Professor Raymond was a fruit!

''Can we work whores tomorrow night?'' asked Roy.

''Sure, kid,'' Gant laughed.

At midnight, Roy was getting tired of sitting in the vice office watching Gant do his paper work as he talked baseball with Phillips and Sergeant Jacovitch. Ranatti and Simeone had not returned since taking the fruit to jail, but Roy heard Jacovitch mention their names during a phone conversation and he cursed when he hung up and muttered something to Gant while Roy glanced over vice reports in the other room.

Ranatti and Simeone rushed in just after midnight. "Ready to raid The Cave?" Ranatti grinned.

"I got a call, Rosso," said Jacovitch quietly. "Some whore called and asked for the sergeant. Said her name was Rosie Redfield and that you guys tore the wiring out of her car and flattened her tires."

"Us?" said Ranatti.

"She named you," said Jacovitch soberly to the young men who did not seem overly surprised.

"That's the whore that thinks she owns Sixth and Alvarado," said Simeone. "We told you about her, Jake. We busted her three times last month and she got her cases consolidated and got summary probation. We've done everything to try to get her to hustle someplace else. Hell, we got two vice complaints about her hustling on that corner."

"Did you know where she parked her car?" asked Jacovitch.

"Yeah, we know," Ranatti admitted. "Did she say she saw us fucking up her car?"

"No, if she did, I'd have to take a personnel complaint against you. You realize that, don't you? There'd be an investigation. She just suspects it was you."

"This ain't no game we're playing out there," said Simeone. "We've done our best to get rid of that bitch. She's not just a whore, she's a booster and a hugger mugger and everything else. She's a rotten bitch and works for Silver Shapiro and he's a rotten pimp and extortionist and God knows what all."

"I'm not even going to ask you if you did it," said Jacovitch, "but I'm warning you guys for the last time about this kind of stuff. You got to stay strictly within the law and Department regulations."

"You know what, Jake?" asked Ranatti, sitting heavily in a chair, and propping a crepe-soled shoe on a typewriter table. "If we did just that, we wouldn't convict one asshole a week. The goddamn streets wouldn't be safe even for us."

It was five minutes till one when Roy parked his private car at Fourth and Broadway and walked toward Main in the direction of The Cave. It was a warm evening, but he shivered as he stood waiting for a green light. He knew the rest of the squad was ready and already in position and he knew there was no particular danger in this, but he was unarmed and felt terribly alone and vulnerable. He walked timorously through the oval doorway of The Cave and stood for a moment adjusting his eyes to the blackness, bumping his head on a plaster stalactite which hung down next to the second entryway. The spacious interior was jammed with people and he shouldered his way to the bar, already beginning to perspire, and found a space to stand between a leering red-haired homosexual and a Negro prostitute who looked him over and apparently did not find him as interesting as the balding man to her left who nervously rubbed his shoulder against her large loose breasts.

Roy started to order a whiskey and soda, remembered Ranatti, and asked for a bottle of beer instead. He ignored the glass, wiped the mouth of the bottle with his hand and drank from the bottle.

Roy saw several booths and tables occupied by lesbians, the butches fondling the femmes, kissing shoulders and arms. Homosexual male couples filled a good part of the room but when one couple tried to dance, mannish female waitresses ordered them to sit, pointing at the "No Dancing" sign. There were prostitutes of all descriptions some of whom were plainly men masquerading as women, but the Negro next to him was certainly a woman, he thought, as she shook a shoulder strap free so the bald man could see more of the vast brown orbs.

Roy saw a group of leather jackets behind a latticework partition which seemed to be drawing a group of onlookers and he squeezed past several people milling in the aisles and beating the tables with glasses to the strident sounds of an outrageous red jukebox. When he got to the latticework he peered through and saw two young men, long sideburned twins with chain belts, arm wrestling on a swaying table with a burning candle at each side of the table to scorch the back of the loser's hand. Two men watched fascinated from a booth to Roy's right. One was collegiate-looking and blond. The other was equally clean-cut, with thick dark hair. They looked as out of place as Roy felt he must look, but when the curling hair on one wrestler's hand began sizzling in the flame of the candle, the young blond man squeezed the thigh of the other, who responded with an excited gasp, and as the candle burned flesh, he held the ear of his blond friend and twisted it violently. No one but Roy seemed to notice, as the onlookers worshiped the searing flame.

Roy returned to the bar and ordered a second beer and a third. It was almost one-thirty and he thought the information had been false when suddenly the jukebox was unplugged and the crowd became silent.

''Lock the door,'' shouted the bartender, a hairy giant, who announced to the crowd, ''The show starts now. Nobody leaves till it's over.''

Roy watched the butch waitress switch on the movie projector which was placed on a table near the latticework that divided the two sections of the room. The white wall was the projection screen and the crowd burst into laughter as a silent Woody Woodpecker cartoon flashed on the wall.

Roy was trying to figure it all out when Woody Woodpecker was suddenly replaced by two oiled naked men who were wrestling on a filthy mat in a ramshackle gymnasium. A cheer went up from the leather jackets across the floor, but after a few moments the scene shifted abruptly to two naked women, one young and reasonably attractive, the other puffy and middle-aged. They nibbled and kissed and fondled on an unmade bed for a few moments while the lesbian tables whistled, but the scene shifted another time to a backyard where a woman in a puckered bathing suit orally copulated a fat man in khaki shorts and most of the crowd laughed but no one cheered. Then it was back to the naked male wrestlers which brought some more groans and catcalls from the leather jackets. When the film slipped off the sprocket and the picture jumped out of focus in a crucial scene in the lewd wrestling match, Roy was surprised to see the bald man, who had previously been interested in the Negro prostitute, jerk off his brown loafer and begin banging on the bar shouting, ''Fix it! Hurry up, fix the goddamn thing!'' After that, he left the prostitute and joined the leather jackets in the other room.

They were still working on the film when Roy sidled along the bar toward the men's restroom. He walked unnoticed tbrough a doorway and found himself in a dimly lit corridor and saw a sign marked ''Women?'' on the left and ''Men?'' on the right. He entered the men's restroom, smelled marijuana unmistakably, and found a leather jacket just coming from the toilet by the open window.

Roy pretended to wash his hands while the young man, in Levis, cleated boots, and leather jacket, fumbled drunkenly with the chain around his waist. He had an enormous head with unkempt hair and a ragged light brown moustache.

Roy stalled for a moment and fidgeted with a paper towel but could not get to the window for the signal.

Finally the leather jacket looked at him. ''I'm not interested right now, blondie,'' he leered. ''See me later. Give me your phone number.''

''Go to hell,'' Roy said, infuriated, forgetting the window for a moment.

''Oh, you got a little spunk? I like that,'' said the leather jacket and he put his fists on his hips and looked even thicker through the chest and back. ''Maybe you could interest me after all,'' he grinned lasciviously.

''Stay right there,'' warned Roy to the advancing barrel-chested sadist, who began uncoiling the chain around his waist.

Roy then, at that moment, for the first time in his life knew real fear, hopeless fear, which debilitated, overwhelmed, flashed and froze him. He was panic-stricken and never clearly knew how he had done it, but he knew later that he kicked the assailant once, just as the chain writhed and slid around his fist. The leather jacket screamed and fell to the floor holding his groin with one hand but grabbed Roy's leg with the other and as Roy pulled frantically the whiskered face pressed on his leg and Roy felt the teeth, but jerked free as the teeth closed on his calf. He heard a tearing noise and saw a patch of his trousers hanging from the whiskered mouth, and then Roy leaped over him into the toilet area and thought wildly that the other leather jackets had heard the scream. Roy hurled a metal wastebasket through the glass and scrambled out the window, dropping five feet to a concrete walk where he was struck by the beam of a flashlight in the hand of a uniformed policeman.

"You the vice officer we're waiting for?" the officer whispered.

"Yeah, let's go," Roy said and ran for the front of The Cave where he saw a dozen blue uniforms already approaching. The vice car zoomed up in the front of the bar and Gant and Ranatti alighted carrying "the key" and they slammed it into the double doors of The Cave as Roy shuffled across the sidewalk and sat on the fender of the vice car and felt like he would vomit.

Roy stepped back away from the entrance and decided he was too sick to go back into that foul steamy place and he watched the door finally fall from the hinges and the wagon pulled up in front. Now there were at least fifteen bluesuits and they formed a sweeping V and Roy was panting from his heart-cracking effort, thinking now he would vomit, and he watched the vast blue wedge of bodies insert itself into the opening of The Cave. Soon the blue line disappeared inside and the others came squirming, running, tumbling out. The drunks were thrown into the wagon expertly by two big policemen wearing black gloves. The others were shoved into various directions, and Roy, holding a handkerchief over his mouth, watched them as they spilled into the street, all gray and brown and faceless now as the lights over the entrance were turned off and the garish colors and frivolity were extinguished. Roy wondered when they would stop coming but after five minutes they still flowed out into the street, noisy and perspiring. Roy thought he could smell them, and they flowed swiftly up and down the street when they hit the sidewalk, those who were not being booked. Soon Roy saw two policemen helping the leather-covered bear out the door and he was still holding his groin. Roy was about to tell them to book that one, but he saw he was being put in the wagon anyway so he remained silent and continued watching in sickened fascination until the street was quiet and the cathartic blue wedge of policemen withdrew from the mouth of The Cave. The wagon drove off as Ranatti and Simeone and Gant had the owner and two barmaids in custody and were nailing the broken front door closed and padlocking it.

"What's the matter, kid?" asked Gant walking up to Roy who still had the handkerchief held to his mouth.

"I had a little scuffle in there."

"You did?" said Gant, putting a hand on each of Roy's shoulders.

"I'm sick," said Roy.

"Did you get hurt?" asked Gant, his eyes wide as he examined Roy's face.

"I'm just sick," said Roy, shaking his head. "I just saw the asshole of the world get a blue enema."

"Yeah? Well get used to it, kid," said Gant. "Everything you seen in there will be legal before long."

"Let's get out of here," Simeone called from behind the wheel of the vice car. He pointed at a crawling yellow street cleaner which was inching down Main Street. Roy and Gant squeezed in the car with the arrestees and Simeone and Ranatti.

Roy leaned out the window as they drove away and saw the street cleaner squirt a stream of water over the street and curb around The Cave. The machine hissed and roared and Roy watched the filth being washed away.

August 1963

13

The Madonna

SERGE WONDERED if any of his academy classmates had plainclothes assignments yet. Probably Fehler or Isenberg and a few of the others had made it to vice or to a felony squad. But not many of them, he guessed. He had been astonished when Sergeant Farrell asked him if he would like to work felony cars this month and then if he worked out it might be a permanent assignment.

This was his second week in F-Cars. He had never realized how much more comfortable it could be to do police work in a business suit rather than the heavy woolen uniforms and unwieldy Sam Browne belt. He wore a four-inch lightweight Colt which he had just bought last payday after seeing how heavy the six-inch Smith rides on your hip in a plainclothes holster.

He suspected that Milton had recommended him to Sergeant Farrell for the F-Car. Milton and Farrell were friends and Farrell seemed to like and respect the old man. However he got here, it was fine to get out of the black and white car for a while. Not that the street people did not know them, two men in business suits, in a low priced, four-door Plymouth—two men who drove slowly and watched streets and people. But at least they were inconspicuous enough to avoid being troubled by the endless numbers of people who need a policeman to solve an endless number of problems that a policeman is not qualified to solve, but must make an attempt to solve, because he is an easily accessible member of the establishment and traditionally vulnerable to criticism. Serge happily blew three smoke rings which would have been perfect except that the breeze took them, the breeze which was pleasant because it had been a very hot summer and the nights were not as cool as Los Angeles nights usually are.

Serge's partner, Harry Ralston, seemed to sense his contentment.

"Think you're going to like F-Cars?" he grinned, turning toward Serge who was slumped in the seat, admiring an exceptionaly voluptuous girl in a clinging white cotton dress.

"I'm going to like it," Serge smiled.

"I know how you feel. It's great to get out of uniform, ain't it?"

"Great."

"I was in uniform eight years," said Ralston. "I was really ready. Got five years in felony cars now, and I still like it. Beats uniform patrol."

"I've got a lot to learn," said Serge.

"You'll learn. It's different from patrol. You're already learning that, I think."

Serge nodded, dropping the cigarette out the window, a luxury he never could have allowed himself in a black and white car where some citizen with an ax to grind might take his car number and report him to his sergeant for the vehicle code violation of dropping the lighted substance from a car.

"Ready for code seven?" asked Ralston, looking at his watch. "It's not nine o'clock yet, but I'm hungry as hell."

"I can eat," said Serge, picking up the mike. "Four-Frank-One requesting code seven at Brooklyn and Mott."

"Four-Frank-One, okay seven," said the Communications operator and Serge checked his watch to be sure and clear over the radio when their forty-five minutes were up. It irritated him that the Department made them work an eight hour and forty-five minute shift. Since the forty-five minutes was his own time, he made sure he used every minute of it.

"Hello, Mr. Rosales," said Ralston, as they took the booth on the far wall nearest the kitchen. It was noisy and hot from the stoves in this particular booth, but Ralston loved to be near the kitchen smells. He was a man who lived to eat, Serge thought, and his incredible appetite belied his lankiness.

"Good evening, señores," smiled the old man, coming from behind the counter where three customers sat. He wiped the table which needed no wiping. He poured two glasses of water for them after swiping at the inside of Ralston's already sparkling glass with a dazzling white towel he carried over a sloping shoulder. The old man wore a full moustache which exactly suited him, Serge thought.

"What will you have, señores?" asked Mr. Rosales, giving them each a hand-printed menu that misspelled the dishes in Spanish on the right side as well as in English on the left side. They can live here all their lives and never learn English, thought Serge. They never learn Spanish either. Just a strange anglicized version of both, which the educated, old country Mexicans scoff at.

"I'll have *huevos rancheros,*" said Ralston, with an accent that made Serge wince in spite of himself.

The old man seemed to love it however, when Ralston tried Spanish. "And you, señor?"

"I guess I'll have *chile relleno,*" said Serge with a pronunciation that was every bit as anglicized as Ralston's. All of the officers knew by now that he spoke no Spanish and understood only a few words.

"Smell the onions and green chile," said Ralston while Mr. Rosales' pudgy little wife was preparing the food in the back room which had been converted into an inadequately ventilated kitchen.

"How can you tell it's green chile?" asked Serge, feeling jovial tonight. "Maybe it's red chile or maybe it's not chile at all."

"My nose never fails," said Ralston, touching the side of his nostril. "You should quit smoking and your sense of smell would become acute like mine."

Serge thought that a beer would do good with the *chile relleno* and he wondered if Ralston knew Serge better, would he order a beer with his dinner? They were working plainclothes now, and a beer with dinner wouldn't hurt. Vice officers of course drank freely, and detectives were legendary lushes, so why not F-Car officers? he thought. But he realized that he was drinking too much beer lately and was going to have to trim off ten pounds before his next physical or the doctor would surely send his captain "a fat man letter." He hadn't had much beer in Hollywood where martinis were his drink. It had been very easy to get to enjoy martinis. He had been drunk a good deal of his off-duty time. But that was all part of his education, he thought. The body should not be mistreated, at least not badly. He was considering cutting down his smoking to a pack a day and had again begun playing handball at the academy. There was something about being back in Hollenbeck that restored his health.

He looked more than casually at the girl who brought their dinners, holding the burning dishes with two colorful pot holders, the drops of perspiration shining on her bronze cheekbones and on the too long upper lip. She wore her hair braided, close to the head like an Indian and Serge guessed she was not more than seventeen. Her hands were ghostly white from the flour and they reminded him of his mother's hands. He wondered how long she had been this side of the border.

"Thank you," he said, smiling as she set the plate in front of him. She smiled back, a clean smile, and Serge noticed she wore only a little lipstick. The heavy eyelashes and perfect brows were not man-made.

"Gracias, señorita," said Ralston, leering at the plate of *huevos rancheros* and ignoring the girl who placed it in front of him.

"De nada, señor," she smiled again.

"Cute kid," said Serge, toying with the rice and refried beans which were still too hot to eat.

Ralston nodded with enthusiasm, and dumped another ladle of homemade chile sauce on the eggs, the rice, everything. Then he sloshed his large flour tortilla around through all of it and took an enormous bite.

Mr. Rosales whispered to the girl and she returned to the table just as Serge's food was becoming cool enough to eat and Ralston's was half gone.

"Joo wan'," she said. "Joo weesh . . ." She stopped and turned to Mr. Rosales who nodded his approval.

"Coffee," he urged her. "Coff—ee."

"I don' talk *inglés* good," she laughed to Serge who was thinnking how smooth and slim she looked, yet how strong. Her breasts were round and the extra weight womanhood brings could only improve her.

"I'll have some more coffee," Serge smiled.

"Sí café, por favor," said Ralston, a forkful of frijoles poised at his mobile lip.

When the girl disappeared into the kitchen Mr. Rosales came over to the table. "Everything is alright?" he smiled through the great moustache.

"Dee-licious," Ralston murmured.

"Who's the little girl?" asked Serge, sipping at the last of his water which Mr. Rosales hurried to refill.

"She is the daughter of my *compadre*. She just got here from Guadalajara last Monday. I swore to my *compadre* many years ago that if I ever made good in this country I would send for his oldest girl, my godchild, and educate her like an American. He said it would be better to educate a boy and I agreed, but he never had a boy. Not to this day. Eleven girls."

Serge laughed and said, "She looks like she'll do."

"Yes, Mariana is very smart," he nodded enthusiastically. "And she was just eighteen. I am sending her to night school next month to learn English and then we shall see what she wants to do."

"She'll probably find some young guy and get married before you have anything to say about it," said Ralston, punctuating his pronouncement with a repressed belch.

"Maybe so," Mr. Rosales sighed. "You know, it is so much better here than in Mexico that the people do not care to make themselves a great success. Just to be here is so much more than they ever dreamed, that it is enough. They become content to work in a car wash or a sewing factory. But I think that she is a smart girl and will do better."

The girl made three trips to their table during the remainder of the meal, but didn't try English again.

Ralston caught Serge watching her because he said, "She's legal, you know. Eighteen."

"You're kidding. I wouldn't raid a nursery."

"Some baby," said Ralston and Serge hoped he wouldn't light one of his cheap cigars. When they were in the car with the windows open they weren't so bad.

''She looks like a young Dolores Del Rio to me,'' said Ralston, blowing two heavy palls of smoke over the table.

She did not resemble Dolores Del Rio, Serge thought. But she had the thing that made Del Rio the beloved woman of Mexico, an object of veneration by millions of Mexicans who had seldom if ever seen her in a movie—she too had the madonna look.

''What's your last name?'' asked Serge, as she made her last trip to the table with a coffee refill. He knew it was customary for policemen who had received a free meal to tip a quarter, but he slipped seventy-five cents under a plate.

''Mande, señor?'' she said turning to Mr. Rosales who was busy with a counter customer.

''Your last name,'' said Ralston carefully. ''Mariana *qué?''*

''Ah,'' she smiled. ''Mariana Paloma,'' and then she turned from Serge's steady gaze and took some of the plates to the kitchen.

''Paloma,'' said Serge. ''A dove. It fits.''

''I eat here once a week,'' said Ralston eyeing Serge curiously. ''We don't want to burn the place up with too many free meals.''

''Don't worry,'' said Serge quickly, getting the implication. ''This is your eating spot. I'll never come here unless I'm working with you.''

''The girl is your business,'' said Ralston. ''You can come off duty if you want, but I'd hate for someone to burn up the eating spot I cultivated for years. He used to charge me half price and now it's free.''

''Don't worry,'' Serge repeated. ''And that girl doesn't interest me like that, for God's sake. I've got enough female problems without a kid that can't speak English.''

''You single guys,'' Ralston sighed. ''I should have those problems. You got one lined up tonight after work?''

''I got one,'' Serge answered without enthusiasm.

''She got a friend?''

''Not that I know of,'' Serge smiled.

''What's she look like?'' Ralston leered, now that the hunger drive was apparently slaked.

''A honey blonde. All ass,'' Serge answered, and that about described Margie who lived in the upstairs rear of his apartment building. The landlady had already warned him about being more discreet when he left Margie's apartment in the morning.

''A real honey blonde, huh?'' Ralston murmured.

''What's real?'' asked Serge, and then thought, she's real enough in her own way, and it doesn't matter if the glistening honey is the fruit of the hairdresser's art because everything of beauty in the world has been tinted or somehow transformed by a clever artisan. You can always discover how it's done if you look closely enough. But who wants to look? During those times when he needed her, Margie was plenty real, he thought.

''What's a bachelor do besides lay everything in sight?'' asked Ralston. ''You happy being alone?''

''I don't even want a roommate to share expenses. I like being alone.'' Serge was the first to get up and turned to look for the girl who was out of sight in the kitchen.

''Buenas noches, Señor Rosales,'' Ralston called.

''Andale pues,'' shouted Mr. Rosales, over the din of a too loud mariachi record which someone had played on the jukebox.

''You watch TV a lot?'' asked Ralston when they were back in the car. ''I'm asking about single life because me and the old lady aren't getting along very good at all right now and who knows what might happen.''

''Oh?'' said Serge hoping Ralston would not bore him with a long account of his marital problems which so many other partners had done during the long hours on patrol when the night was quiet because it was a week night, when the people were between paydays and welfare checks, and were not drinking. "Well, I read a lot, novels mostly. I play handball at least three or four times a week at the academy. I go to movies and watch a little TV. I got to a lot of Dodger games. There isn't all the carousing you think." And then he remembered Hollywood again. "At least not anymore. That can get old, too."

"Maybe I'll be finding out," said Ralston, driving toward Hollenbeck Park.

Serge took the flashlight from under the seat and placed it on the seat beside him. He turned the volume of the radio up slightly, hoping it would dissuade Ralston from trying to compete with it, but Serge felt certain he was going to hear a domestic tirade.

"Four-Frank-One, clear," said Serge into the mike.

"Maybe you can entice little Dolores Del Rio to your pad if you play your cards right," said Ralston as the Communications operator acknowledged they were clear. Ralston began a slow halfhearted residential burglar patrol in the area east of the park which had been hard hit by a cat burglar the past few weeks. They had already decided that after midnight, they would prowl the streets on foot which seemed to be the only effective way to catch the cat.

"I told you that babies don't interest me," said Serge.

"Maybe she's got a cousin or a fat aunt or something. I'm ready for some action. My old lady shut me off. I could grow a long moustache for her like that actor that plays in all the Mexican movies, what's his name?"

"Pedro Armendariz," said Serge without thinking.

"Yeah, that guy. It seems like he's on every marquee around here, him and Dolores."

"They were even the big stars when I was a kid," said Serge gazing at the cloudless sky which was only slightly smoggy tonight.

"Yeah? You went to Mexican movies? I thought you don't speak Spanish."

"I understood a little when I was a kid," Serge answered, sitting up in the seat. "Anybody could understand those simple pictures. All guns and guitars."

Ralston quieted down and the radio droned on and he relaxed again. He found himself thinking of the little dove and he wondered if she would be as satisfying as Elenita who was the first girl he ever had, the dusky fifteen-year-old daughter of a bracero who was well worn by the time she seduced Serge when he himself was fifteen. He had returned to her every Friday night for a year and sometimes she would have him, but sometimes there would be older boys already there and he would go away to avoid trouble. Elenita was everybody's girl but he liked to pretend she was his girl until one June afternoon when the gossip blazed through the school that Elenita had been taken from school because she was pregnant. Several boys, mostly the members of the football squad, began to talk in frightened whispers. Then came the rumor a few days later that Elenita was also found to have been syphilitic and the frightened whispers became frantic. Serge had terrible fantasies of elephantine pus-filled genitals and he prayed and lit three candles every other day until he felt the danger period had passed even though he never knew for sure if it had, or even whether poor Elenita was really so afflicted. He could ill afford thirty cents for candles in those days when the part-time gas pumping job only netted nine dollars a week which he had to give to his mother.

Then he felt guilty for thinking about the girl Mariana like this because eighteen years, despite what the law said, did not make you an adult. He was twenty-six now and wondered if another ten years would do the job for him. If he could continue to profit from all the lies and cruelty and violence this job had shown him, maybe he could grow up sooner. If he could quit seeing a saint in the tawny face of a perfectly healthy little animal like Mariana he would be so much closer to maturity. Maybe that's the part of being a Chicano I can't shake off, Serge thought, the superstitious longing—brown magic—The Sorceress of Guadelupe—

or Guadalajara—a simple bastard yearning for the Madonna in a miserable Mexican restaurant.

14

The Operator

"No wonder Plebesly gets more whore offers than anybody else on the squad. Look at him. Does this boy look like a cop?" roared Bonelli, stocky, middle-aged and balding, with dark whiskers which when they were two days old were dirty gray. They always seemed at least two days old, and whenever Sergeant Anderson objected, Bonelli just reminded him that this was Wilshire vice squad and not a goddamned military academy and he was only trying to look like the rest of the assholes out on the street so he could fit in better as an undercover operator. He always addressed Anderson by his first name which was Mike and so did the others because it was customary in a vice squad to be more intimate with your supervisors, but Gus did not like or trust Anderson and neither did the others. He was on the lieutenant's list and would probably someday be a captain at least, but the lanky young man with the blond sparse moustache was a natural disciplinarian and would be better, they all concluded, in a patrol function which was more GI than a vice squad.

"One whore Gus got last week never did believe he was a cop," laughed Bonelli, throwing his feet up on the table in the vice office and spilling some cigar ashes on a report which Sergeant Anderson was writing. Anderson's lips tightened under the pale moustache, but he said nothing, got up and went to his own desk to work.

"I remember that one, Sal," said Petrie to Bonelli. "Old Salvatore had to save Gus from that whore. She thought he was a PO-lice impersonator when he finally badged her."

They all laughed at Petrie's affected Negro dialect, even Hunter, the slim Negro officer who was the only Negro on the night watch. He laughed heartily, but Gus laughed nervously partly because they were roasting him but partly because he could never get used to Negro jokes in front of a Negro even though he had been a vice officer for three months now and should be accustomed to the merciless chiding which went on ritually every night before they went out to the streets. Each of them subjected the other to cracks which stopped at neither race, religion, or physical defects.

Yet the six policemen and Sergeant Handle, who was one of *them*, went to Bonelli's apartment at least once a week after work and played pool and drank a case of beer at least. Or sometimes they went to Sergeant Handle's house and played poker all night. Once when they had gone to Hunter's apartment which was here in Wilshire Division in the racially mixed neighborhood near Pico and La Brea, Bonelli had made a whispered remark to Hunter that he had been kicked in the shoulder by a whore while making a lewd conduct arrest and that at his age arthritis might set in. Bonelli couldn't pull the sleeve of his outrageous Hawaiian shirt over the hairy shoulder to show Hunter because the shoulder was too large, and finally, Bonelli said, "Anyway, the bruise is the color of your ass." When Hunter's lithe mahogany-colored wife Marie, who had entered the room unnoticed, said, "What, red?" with a perfectly sober expression, Gus began to enjoy the camaraderie which was not affected or strained and did not pretend that being policemen made them brothers or more than brothers.

But they did have a secret which seemed to unite them more closely than normal friendship and that was the knowledge that they *knew* things, basic things about strength and weakness, courage and fear, good and evil, especially good and evil. Even though arguments would rage especially when Bonelli was drunk, they all agreed on very fundamental things and usually did not discuss these things because any policeman who had common sense and had been a policeman long enough would surely learn the truth and it was useless to talk about it. They mostly talked about their work and women, and either fishing, golf, or baseball, depending upon whether Farrell or Schulmann or Hunter was controlling the conversation. But when Petrie was working they talked about movies, since Petrie had an uncle who was a director, and Petrie was starstruck even though he had been a policeman five years.

There were a few more cracks made about Gus's meek appearance and how none of the whores could believe he was a policeman which made him the best whore operator on the watch, but then they began talking about other things because Gus never joked back and it was not as much fun as picking on Bonelli who had a caustic tongue and was quick at repartee.

"Hey Marty," said Farrell to Hunter who was trying to pencil out a follow-up to a vice complaint. He held his forehead in a smooth brown hand while the pencil moved jerkily and stopped often while Hunter laughed at something Bonelli said. It was obvious that Hunter would rather work with Bonelli than any of the others, but Sergeant Anderson figured the deployment carefully so that certain men were working on certain nights because he had fixed opinions on supervision and deployment. He informed them that he was very close to his degree in government and he had twelve units in psychology and only *he* was in a position to know who should work with whom, and Bonelli had whispered gruffly, "How did this cunt get on the vice squad?"

"Hey, Marty," Farrell repeated, until Hunter looked up. "How come you people are always complaining that there aren't enough blacks in this job or that group or something and then when we *do* use enough you still bitch. Listen to this article in the *Times,* 'The NAACP sought a class action on behalf of all the men on death's row because it contends a disproportionate number of them are Negroes.' "

"People are never satisfied," said Hunter.

"By the way Marty, you getting your share of that white liberal pussy that's floating around the *ghetto* these days?" asked Bernbaum.

"Marty's going to pass the sergeant's exam this time, ain't you, Marty," said Bonelli. "He'll get forty points on his own and they'll give him forty more for being black."

"And when we get to be on top, first thing I'm going to do is go after your woman, Sal," said Hunter, glancing up from his report.

"Oh, Christ, Marty, do me a favor, go after Elsie right now, will you? That bitch does nothing but talk about marriage anymore and me with three divorces behind me. I need another wife like . . ."

"Do any of you have any rubbers?" asked Sergeant Anderson, suddenly walking into the working area of the vice office separated from his desk by a row of lockers.

"No, if we think a broad is bad enough for rubbers, we generally get a head job," said Farrell, his close-set blue eyes examining Anderson with humor.

"I was referring to the use of rubbers for evidence containers," said Anderson coldly. "We still use them to pour drinks into, don't we?"

"We got a box in the locker, Mike," said Bonelli, and they became quiet when they saw he disliked Farrell's joke. "Working a bar tonight?"

"We've had a complaint about The Cellar for two weeks now. I thought we'd try to take it."

"They serving after hours?" asked Farrell.

"If you could take time out from your joke writing and look at the vice complaints you'd see that the bartender at The Cellar lives in an apartment upstairs and that after two o'clock he sometimes invites customers up to the pad where he continues to operate a bar. After hours."

"We'll try it for you tonight, Mike," said Bonelli with his conciliatory tone, but Gus thought that the heavily browed brown eyes were not conciliatory. They fixed Anderson with a bland expression.

"I want to work it myself," said Anderson. "I'll meet you and Plebesly at Third and Western at eleven and we'll decide then whether to go together or separate."

"I can't go at all," said Bonelli. "I made too many pinches around there. The bartender knows me."

"Might be a good idea for you to go in with one of us," said Bernbaum, scratching his wiry brush of red hair with a pencil. "We could have a drink and leave. They wouldn't suspect the joint was full of cops. They'd probably be satisfied that everything was cool after us two left."

"I think there's a couple of whores working in there," said Hunter. "Me and Bonelli were in there one night and there was an ugly little brunette and another old bat that sure looked like hookers."

"Alright, we'll all meet at Andre's Restaurant at eleven and talk it over," said Anderson going back to his desk. "And another thing, the streetwalkers are getting pretty thick out there on Sunday and Monday nights, I hear. They must know those are the vice squad's nights off so some of you are going to start working Sundays."

"You guys see those magazines the day watch picked up at a trick pad?" asked Bernbaum, and the conversation again picked up now that Anderson was finished.

"I seen enough of that garbage to last me a lifetime," said Bonelli.

"No, these weren't regular nudie mags," said Bernbaum. "These were pinup mags, but somebody had taken about a hundred Polaroid pictures of guys' dicks and cut them out and stuck them on the girls in the magazines."

"Psychos. The world is full of psychos," said Farrell.

"By the way, are we working fruits tonight, Marty?" asked Petrie.

"Lord, no. We busted enough last week to last all month."

"Think I'll go on days for a while," said Bernbaum. "I'd like to work books. Get me away from all these slimes you have to bust at night."

"Well I'll guarantee you, bookmakers are assholes," said Bonelli. "They're mostly Jews, ain't they?"

"Oh yeah, the Mafia's all Jews too," said Bernbaum. "I think there's a few Italian bookmakers up on Eighth Street last I heard."

Gus felt Bonelli look at him when Bernbaum said it and he knew Bonelli was thinking about Lou Scalise, the bookmaking agent and collector for the loan sharks whom Bonelli hated with a hatred that now made Gus's palms sweat as he thought of it.

"Incidentally, Petrie," said Marty Hunter, slamming the logbook, "the next time we take a fighter, how about using the sap on *him,* not on *me*. Last night we take Biff's Cocktail Lounge for serving a drunk and when we try to bust the drunk he starts a fight and *I* get sapped by my partner."

"Bullshit, Marty. I just grazed your elbow with the sap."

"Anytime more than one policeman jumps a suspect the policeman ends up getting hurt," said Farrell. "I remember the night we had that fairy lumberjack." They laughed and Farrell looked appealingly to Bonelli. "Yeah the guy was a lumberman from Oregon. And he's a suck*or* not a suck*ee*. Comes to L.A. and wears eye shadow. Anyway, he's swishing around Lafayette Park and gropes Bonelli, remember, Sal?"

"I'll never forget that asshole."

"Anyway, there were five of us in the park that night and for fifteen minutes we all battle that puke. He threw me in the pond and threw Steve in there twice.

We thumped the shit out of each other with saps and it finally ended when Sal held his head underwater for a few minutes. He never did get sapped or even hurt and every one of us policemen had to get patched up."

"Funny thing," said Bernbaum, "when Sal had him about half drowned and he was panicky and all, know what he does? He yells, 'Help, police!' Imagine that, with five policemen all over him, he yells that."

"He know you were policemen?" asked Gus.

"Sure he knew," said Farrell. "He said to Bonelli, 'Ain't no cop in the world can take me.' He didn't figure on five, though."

"I had a guy yell that one time when I was in full uniform," said Bernbaum. "Funny what people say when you're wrestling them off to jail."

"Garbage," said Bonelli. "Garbage."

"You handle these assholes, you got to wash your hands *before* you take a leak," said Hunter.

"Remember the time the swish kissed you, Ben?" said Farrell to Bernbaum, and the ruddy-faced young policeman winced in disgust.

"Walked into a bar where we got a complaint some fruits were dancing," said Hunter, "and this little blond swish flits right up to Ben as we were sitting at the bar and plants a smack right on his kisser and then he dances away into the dark. Ben goes to the head and washes his mouth with hand soap and we leave without even working the joint."

"I heard enough. I'm going to take a crap and then we're going to work," said Bonelli standing up, scratching his stomach and lumbering toward the toilet across the hall.

"You say you're going in there to give birth to a sergeant?" said Farrell, winking at Petrie who shook his head and whispered, "Anderson doesn't appreciate your humor."

When Bonelli returned, he and Gus gathered their binoculars and small flashlights and batons which they would put under the seat of the vice car in case of emergency. After reassuring Anderson they wouldn't forget to meet him they went to their car without deciding what they were going to do.

"Want to work complaints, or whores?" asked Bonelli.

"We got some crappy three eighteens," said Gus. "One about the floating card game in the hotel sounds like fun, but it only goes on Saturdays."

"Yeah, let's work whores," said Bonelli.

"Tail or operate?"

"Feel like operating?"

"I don't mind. I'll get my car," said Gus.

"Got enough gas? That cheap prick Anderson won't break loose with any more operating money till next week. You'd think it was his bread and not the city's."

"I've got gas," said Gus. "I'll take a sweep around Washington and La Brea and meet you in the back of the drive-in in fifteen minutes. Sooner, if I get a whore."

"Get a whore. We need the pinches. This's been a slim month."

Gus drove down West Boulevard to Washington and over Washington toward La Brea, but he hadn't gotten two blocks on Washington until he spotted two prostitutes. He was preparing to swing in toward the curb when he saw one was Margaret Pearl whom he had arrested almost three months ago when he first came to the vice squad and she would surely recognize him so he drove past. Already the pulse beat was advancing.

Gus remembered how it had been when he had first come to vice, or rather, he did not remember clearly. Those first nights and those first few arrests were difficult to envision coherently. There was a red cloud of fear enveloping his memory of those nights and that was something else he could not understand. Why did he see or rather feel a red mist about his memories when he was very much afraid? Why were all such memories red-tinged? Was it blood or fire or what? He had been so thoroughly frightened that the prostitutes had come to his car with their offers without questioning his identity. They hadn't dreamed he was a cop, and he had been a vastly successful vice operator. Now that he had some confidence and was no longer so afraid except of things he should be afraid of, he was having to work much harder to get an offer. He was being turned down occasionally by girls who suspected he might be a policeman. Still, he could get twice the girls that any of the others could, only because he looked less like a policeman than any of them. Bonelli had told him it was not just his size. He was actually as tall and heavy as Marty Hunter. It was his diffidence, and Bonelli said that was a shame because the meek would inherit this miserable earth and Gus was too nice a guy to get stuck with it.

Gus hoped he would spot a white whore tonight. He had only arrested a few white whores and these were in bars on Vermont. He had never gotten a white streetwalker, although there were some of them here in this Negro half of Wilshire Division, but there weren't many. He thought Wilshire Division was a good division to work because of the variety. He could leave this Negro section and drive to the northwest boundaries of the division and be on the Miracle Mile and Restaurant Row. There was great variety in a few square miles. He was glad they had transferred him here, and almost immediately he had been marked as a future vice officer by his watch commander Lieutenant Goskin who had finally recommended him when the opening came. Gus wondered how many of his academy classmates were working plainclothes assignments yet. It was good, and it would be very good when the nauseating fear at last disappeared, the fear of being on the streets alone without the security of the blue uniform and badge. There was not too much else to really fear because if you were careful you would never have to fight anyone alone. If you were careful, you would always have Bonelli with you and Bonelli was as powerful and reassuring as Kilvinsky, but of course he did not have Kilvinsky's intellect.

Gus reminded himself that he had not answered Kilvinsky's last letter and he would do that tomorrow. It had worried him. Kilvinsky did not talk of the fishing and the lake and the peaceful mountains anymore. He talked of his children and his ex-wife and Kilvinsky had never talked of them when he had been here. He told of how his youngest son had written him and how his answer to the boy had been returned unopened and how he and his ex-wife had promised themselves years ago that it would be better if the boy forgot him, but he didn't say why. Gus knew that he had never gone East to visit them at his wife's home, and Gus never knew why, and he thought he would give a great deal to learn Kilvinsky's secrets. The latest letters indicated that Kilvinsky wanted to tell someone, wanted to tell Gus, and Gus decided to ask the big man to come to Los Angeles for a visit before the summer ended. Lord, it would be good to see his friend, Gus thought.

Then Gus realized he also had to send a check to his mother and John because it was less painful than going to see them and hearing how they could no longer make it on seventy-five a month from him even with the welfare check, because things were so dear today and poor John can't work, what with his slipped disc which Gus knew was an excuse for workman's compensation and a free ride from Gus. He was ashamed of his disgust as he thought of those weaklings and then he thought of Vickie. He wondered why his mother and his brother and his wife were all weaklings and depended so completely on him, and anger made him feel better as always, purged him. He saw a chubby Negro prostitute wiggling down Washington Boulevard toward Cloverdale. He pulled to the curb beside her and feigned the nervous smile which used to come so naturally.

''Hi baby,'' said the prostitute looking in the window of his car as Gus went through his act of looking around as though fearful of seeing police.

''Hello,'' said Gus. ''Want a ride?''

"I ain't out here to ride, baby," said the prostitute watching him closely. "At least I ain't out here to ride no cars."

"Well I'm ready for anything," said Gus, careful not to use any of the forbidden words of entrapment, even though Sal often argued with him that it is obviously impossible to entrap a whore, and he should only worry about entrapment later while writing the report because following the rules of the game was crazy. But Gus had answered that the rules made it all *civilized*.

"Look, Officer," said the girl suddenly, "why don't you go on up to the academy and play yourself a nice game of handball?"

"What?" said Gus blandly, as she examined his eyes.

"Jist a joke, baby," she said finally. "We got to be careful of vice officers."

"Vice officers? Where?" said Gus gunning his motor. "Maybe we better forget all about this."

"Don't git nervous, honey," she said, getting in the car and moving over to him. "I'll give you such a nice French that you goin' to be glad you came down here tonight and don't worry none about the vice, I got them all paid off. They never bother me."

"Where should I drive?" asked Gus.

"Down La Brea there. The Notel Motel. They got electric beds that vibrate and mirrors on the walls and ceilings and I got my own room reserved and it ain't goin' to cost you nothin' extra. It's all yours for fifteen dollars."

"That sounds about right," said Gus turning around and bouncing into the drive-in parking lot where Bonelli waited and Sal smiled through the heavy whiskers when he saw the prostitute.

"Hi baby, how's tricks?" said Bonelli opening the door for her.

"Tricks was fine, Mr. Bonelli, till I hit on this one," said the girl looking at Gus in disbelief. "I would a swore he was a trick. He really a cop?"

Gus showed the prostitute his badge and got back in the car.

"He looks too motherfuckin' peaceable to be a cop," said the prostitute in disgust as Gus drove out of the lot for another try before they made the long drive to Lincoln Heights jail.

Gus swept the block twice and then made a wider arc and finally decided to drive north on La Brea toward Venice where he had seen prostitutes the last few nights, and then he saw three Cadillacs parked side by side in the motel parking lot. He recognized a prostitute standing outside the purple Cadillac talking to Eddie Parsons and Big Dog Hanley and another Negro pimp he didn't recognize. Gus remembered the time they had arrested Big Dog when Gus had just arrived in Wilshire Division last year and was still working uniform patrol. They had stopped Big Dog for an unsafe lane change and while Gus was writing the ticket, his partner Drew Watson, an aggressive and inquisitive policeman, had spotted the pearl handle of a .22 revolver protruding from under the seat. He had retrieved it and arrested Big Dog, taking him to the detectives who, since Big Dog was a pimp, and had a five-page rap sheet, decided to book him for robbery, impound his car, and book his roll of flash-money as evidence. When they counted out the bills which came to eight hundred dollars and told Big Dog they were booking the money, he broke down and wept, begging the detective not to book his money because it had been done to him before and it took months to get it back and it was *his* money so please don't book it. That surprised Gus in that Big Dog was at once the most insolent and arrogant of all the pimps and here he was begging for his roll and crying. Then Gus realized that without the roll and the Cadillac, he was nothing, and Big Dog knew it and realized that the other pimps and prostitutes knew it, and he would lose everything. It would be taken away by pimps with a bankroll who commanded respect.

Then Gus saw the white prostitute at Venice and La Brea. He accelerated but she had already reached a red Cadillac hardtop and she was alone and getting in the driver's side when Gus slowed and double-parked next to her. He smiled his carefully rehearsed smile which had seldom failed so far.

"Looking for me, sweetie?" asked the girl, and up close she did not look nearly as good although the tight silver pants and black jersey fit well. Gus could see even in this light that the swirling blond hair was a wig and the makeup was garish.

"I think you're the one I've been looking for," Gus smiled.

"Pull up in front of me and park," said the girl. "Then walk on back here and let's talk."

Gus pulled in at the curb and turned his lights out, slipped the holstered two-inch Smith & Wesson under the seat, got out, and walked back to the Cadillac and up to the driver's side.

"Looking for action, sweetie?" asked the girl with a smile that Gus thought was rehearsed as carefully as his. "Sure am," he shot back with his own version of a smile.

"How much you willing to spend?" she said coyly and reached out the window with a long clawed finger and ran it seductively over his torso while she felt for a gun and he smiled to himself because he had left the gun in the car.

She seemed satisfied not feeling a gun or other evidence that he was a policeman and she apparently saw little use in wasting more time. "How about a nice ten dollar fuck?" she said.

"You don't mince words," said Gus, pulling out the badge he had in his back pocket. "You're under arrest."

"Oh crap," moaned the girl. "Man, I just got out of jail. Oh no," she wailed.

"Let's go," said Gus, opening the door of the Cadillac. "Alright, lemme get my purse," she spat, but turned the key and cramped the wheel hard to the left as the Cadillac lurched forward and Gus, not knowing why, leaped on the side of the car and in only seconds he was clinging to the back of the seat and standing on nothing as the powerful car sped east on Venice. He reached desperately across her for the keys, but she drove her little fist into his face and he slid back and tasted the blood from his nose. His eye caught the speedometer registering sixty and quickly seventy and his lower body was swept backward in a rush of wind and he clung to the seat as the cursing prostitute swerved the Cadillac across three lanes attempting to hurl him to his death and now for the first time he was conscious of exactly what he was doing and he prayed to God the body would not fail him now and it would just cling—that was all—just cling.

There were other cars on Venice. Gus knew this from the blasting horns and squeal of tires but he kept his eyes closed and clung as she beat at his hands with a purse and then with a high-heeled shoe as the Cadillac swerved and skidded on Venice Boulevard. Gus tried to remember a simple prayer from his boyhood because he knew there would be a jarring flaming crash but he couldn't remember the prayer and suddenly there was a giddy sliding turn and he knew this was the end and now he would be hurtled through space like a bullet, but then the car righted itself and was speeding back westbound on Venice the way it had come and Gus thought if he could reach his gun, if he dared release the grip of one hand, he would take her with him to the grave and then he remembered the gun was in his car and he thought if he could crank the wheel now at eighty miles an hour he could flip the Cadillac and that would be as good as the gun. He wanted to, but the body would not obey and would only cling stubbornly to the back cushion of the seat. Then the prostitute began pushing the door open as she cut the wheel back and forth and the force hurtled his feet straight back and Gus found his voice, but it was a whisper and she was shrieking curses and the car tape deck had somehow been turned as loudly as it would go and the music from the car stereo and roar of the wind and screams of the prostitute were deafening and he shouted in her ear, "Please, please, let me go! I won't arrest you if you'll let me go. Slow down and let me jump!"

She answered by cutting the wheel recklessly to the right and saying, "Die, you dirty little motherfucker."

Gus saw La Brea coming up and the traffic was moderate when she slashed through the red light at ninety miles an hour and Gus heard the unmistakable screech and crash but still they flew and he knew another car had crashed in the intersection and then all lanes were blocked east and west just west of La Brea as a stream of fire trucks lumbered north at the next intersection. The prostitute slammed on her brakes and turned left on a dark residential street, but made the turn much too sharply and the Cadillac slid and righted and careened to the right and up over a lawn taking out twenty feet of picket fence which hurtled in clattering fragments over the hood of the car and cracked the windshield of the Cadillac which sliced across lawns and through hedges with the prostitute riding the burning brakes and the lawns hurtling by were coming slower and slower and Gus guessed the car was going only thirty miles an hour when he let go but he hit the grass with a shock and his body coiled and rolled without command but he was still rolling when he crashed into a parked car and sat there for a long moment as the earth moved up and down. Then he was on his feet as the lights were being turned on all over the block and the neighborhood dogs had gone mad and the Cadillac was now almost out of sight.

Gus then started to run as the people poured from the houses. He was almost at La Brea when he began to feel the pain in his hip and his arm and several other places and he wondered why he was running, but right now it was the only thing that made sense. So he ran faster and faster and then he was at his car and driving, but his legs, although they would run, would not be still enough to maneuver the car, and twice he had to stop and rub them before reaching the station. He drove his car to the rear of the station and went in the back door and down to the bathroom where he examined his gray face which was badly scratched and bruised from the blows. When he washed away the blood it didn't look bad but his left knee was mushy and the sweat dried cold on his chest and back. Then he noticed the terrible smell and his stomach turned as he realized what it was and he hurried to the locker thankful that he kept a sport coat and slacks in case he tore his clothing prowling or in case an assignment demanded a dressier appearance. He crept back down to the restroom and cleansed his legs and buttocks, sobbing breathlessly in shame and fear and relief.

After he was washed, he put on the clean slacks and rolled the trousers and soiled underwear into a ball and threw the stinking bundle outside in the trash can at the rear of the station. He got back in the car and drove to the drive-in where he knew Bonelli would be frantic because he had been gone almost an hour and he was still uncertain if he could carry off the lie when he drove to the rear of the restaurant. He found Bonelli with two radio cars who had begun a search for Gus. He told the lie which he had formulated while the tears choked him as he drove to the restaurant. He had to lie because if they knew they had a policeman who was so stupid he would jump on the side of a car, why they would kick him off the squad, and rightly so, for such an officer certainly would need more seasoning—if not a psychiatrist. So he told them an elaborate lie about a prostitute who had hit him in the face with a shoe and had leaped from his car and how he had chased her through alleys on foot for a half hour and finally lost her. Bonelli had told him it was dangerous to go off alone away from your car but he was so damned glad to see Gus was alright that he dropped it at that not even noticing the clothes change, and they drove to the Main Jail. Several times Gus thought he would break down and weep and in fact he twice stifled a sob. But he did not break down and after an hour or so his legs and hands stopped shaking completely. But he could not eat and when they stopped later for a hamburger he had almost gotten sick at the sight of food.

''You look awful,'' said Bonelli, after he had eaten and they were cruising down Wilshire Boulevard. Gus was looking out the window at the street and the cars and people, feeling not elated at being still alive but darkly depressed. He wished for a moment that the car had overturned during that bowel-searing moment when she had skidded and he knew they were doing ninety.

''I guess that hassle with the whore was a little too much for me,'' Gus said.

''How far you say you chased that whore?'' asked Bonelli with a look of disbelief.

''Several blocks I guess. Why?''

''I happen to know you run like a cougar. How come you couldn't catch her?''

''Well, the truth is, she kicked me in the balls, Sal. I was ashamed to tell you. I was lying in the alley for twenty minutes.''

''Well, why in the hell didn't you say you caught a nut shot for chrissake? No wonder you been looking sick all night. I'm taking you home.''

''No. No, I don't want to go home,'' said Gus and thought he would analyze later why he preferred being at work even now when he was despairing of everything.

''Suit yourself, but I want you to really go through that whore mug book tomorrow night and keep looking till you find that bitch. We're going to get a warrant for battery on a police oficer.''

''I told you, Sal, she was a new one. I never saw her before.''

''We'll find the cunt,'' said Bonelli and seemed content with Gus's explanation. Gus felt better now and his stomach hardly hurt at all. He sat back and wondered where he would get the money for his mother this payday because the furniture payment was due, but he decided not to worry about it because thinking about his mother and John always made his stomach tighten up and he had enough of that tonight.

At eleven o'clock, Sal said, ''Guess we better go see the boy leader, huh?''

''Okay,'' Gus mumbled, unaware that he had been dozing.

''You sure you don't want to go home?''

''I feel fine.''

They met Anderson at the restaurant looking sour and impatient as he sipped a cup of creamy coffee and tapped on a table with a teaspoon.

''You're late,'' he muttered as they sat down.

''Yeah,'' said Bonelli.

''I took a booth so we wouldn't be overheard,'' said Anderson, worrying the tip of the sparse moustache with the handle of the teaspoon.

''Yeah, can't be too careful when you're in this business,'' said Bonelli, and Anderson glanced sharply at the stony brown eyes looking for irony.

''The others aren't coming. Hunter and his partner got a couple whores and the others took a game.''

''Dice?''

''Cards,'' said Anderson and Gus became irritated as he always did when Anderson referred to Hunter and *his partner* or *the others* when there were only eight of them altogether and he should know their names well enough by now.

''The three of us working the bar?'' asked Bonelli.

''Not you. They know you so you stay outside. I've got a good place picked out for surveillance across the street in an apartment house parking lot. You be there when we bring out an arrestee, or if we get invited to the apartment for after-hour drinking like I hope, we may just have a drink and leave and call for reinforcements.''

''Don't forget to pour the drink in the rubber,'' said Sal.

''Of course,'' said Anderson.

''Don't pour too much. Those rubbers break if you pour too much booze in.''

''I can manage,'' said Anderson.

''Especially *that* rubber. Don't pour too much in.''

''Why?''

''I used that one on my girl friend Bertha last night. It ain't brand-new anymore.''

Anderson looked at Bonelli for a second and then chortled self-consciously.

"He thinks I'm joking," said Bonelli to Gus.

"Great kidders," said Anderson. "Let's get going. I'm anxious to do police work."

Bonelli shrugged to Gus as they followed Anderson to his car and drove behind him to within a block of The Cellar where they decided Anderson and Gus would go in separately at five-minute intervals. They might find an excuse to get together once inside, but they were going to act like strangers.

Once inside, Gus wasn't interested in arrests or police work or anything but the drink in front of him when he sat at the leather-padded bar. He drank two whiskeys with soda and ordered a third, but the peace-giving warmth started before he had finished the second and he wondered if his was the type of personality that was conducive to alcoholism. He guessed it was, and that was one reason he seldom drank, but it was mainly that he hated the taste except for whiskey and soda which he could tolerate. Tonight they were good, and his hand began to beat time to the blaring jukebox and for the first time he looked around the bar. It was a good noisy crowd for a week night. The bar was crowded as were the booths and the tables were almost all occupied. After his third drink he noticed Sergeant Anderson sitting alone at a tiny round table, sipping a cocktail and staring hard at Gus before getting up and going to the jukebox.

Gus followed and fumbled in his pocket for a quarter as he approached the glowing machine which fiickered green and blue light across the intense face of Anderson.

"Good crowd," said Gus, pretending to pick out a recording. Gus noticed that his mouth was getting numb and he was lightheaded and the music made his heart beat fast. He finished the drink in his hand.

"Better take it easy on the drinking," whispered Anderson. "You'll have to be sober if we're going to operate this place." Anderson punched a selection and pretended to search for another.

"You operate better if you look like one of the boozers," said Gus, and surprised himself because he never contradicted sergeants, least of all Anderson whom he feared.

"Make your drink last," said Anderson. "But don't overdo it that way either or they'll suspect you're vice."

"Okay," said Gus. "Shall we sit together?"

"Not yet," said Anderson. "There're two women at the table directly in front of me. I think they're hustlers, but I'm not sure. It wouldn't hurt to try for a prostitution offer. If we get it, we could always try to use them to duke us into the upstairs drinking. Then we could bust them when we bust the after-hours place."

"Good plan," said Gus, belching wetly.

"Don't talk so loud for crying out loud."

"Sorry," said Gus, belching again.

"You go back to the bar and watch me. If I'm not doing well with the women you stroll over to their table and hit on them. If you score, I'll invite myself over again."

"Okay," said Gus and Anderson punched the last record on the jukebox and the buzz of voices in the bar threatened to drown out the jukebox until Gus's ears popped and he knew most of the buzz was in his head and he thought of the speeding Cadillac, became frightened, and forced it from his mind.

"Go back to your table now," whispered Anderson. "We've been standing here too long."

"Shouldn't I play a record? That's what I came here for," said Gus, pointing to the glowing machine.

"Oh yes," said Anderson. "Play something first."

"Okay," said Gus, belching again.

"You better take it easy with the booze," said Anderson, as he strode back to his table.

Gus found the blurred record labels too hard to read and just punched the first three buttons on the machine. He liked the hard rock that was now being played and he found his fingers snapping and his shoulders swaying as he returned to the bar and had another whiskey and soda which he drank furtively hoping Anderson would not see. Then he ordered another and picked his way through the crowd to the two women at the table who did indeed look like prostitutes, he thought.

The younger of the two, a slightly bulging silver-tipped brunette in a gold sheath, smiled at Gus immediately as he stood, tapping a foot to the music, in front of their table. He sipped his drink and gave them both a leer which he knew they would respond to, and he glanced at Anderson who glared morosely over his drink and he almost laughed because he hadn't felt so happy in months and he knew he was getting drunk. But his sensibility had become actually more acute, he thought, and he saw things in perspective and God life, was good. He leered from the younger one to the bleached fat one who was fifty-five if she was a day, and the fat one blinked at Gus through alcoholic blue eyes and Gus guessed she was not a true professional hooker, but just a companion for the younger. She would probably join in if the opportunity arose, but who in hell would pay money for the hag?

"All alone?" slurred the older one, as Gus stood before them, growing hilarious now, as he bounced and swayed to the music which was building to a crescendo of drums and electric guitar.

"Nobody's alone as long as there's music and drink and love," said Gus, toasting each of them with the whiskey and soda and then pouring it down as he thought how damned eloquent that was, and if he could only remember it later.

"Well, sit down and tell me more, you cute little thing," said the old blonde pointing to the empty chair.

"May I buy you girls a drink?" asked Gus, leaning both elbows on the table and thinking how the younger one really wasn't too bad except for her bad nose which was bent to the right and her fuzzy eyebrows which began and ended nowhere, but she had enormous breasts and he stared at them frankly and then hurled a lewd smile in her face as he snapped his fingers for the waitress who was giving Anderson another drink.

Both women ordered manhattans and he had whiskey and soda and noticed Anderson looked angrier than usual. Anderson finished two drinks while the fat blonde told a long obscene joke about a little Jew and a blue-eyed camel and Gus roared even though he failed to get the punch line, and when he calmed himself the old blonde said, "We didn't even get introduced. I'm Fluffy Largo. This is Poppy La Farge."

"My name is Lance Jeffrey Savage," said Gus, standing shakily and bowing to both giggling women.

"Ain't he the cutest little shit?" said Fluffy to Poppy.

"Where do you work, Lance?" asked Poppy letting her hand rest against her forearm as she dipped her torso forward revealing a half inch more cleavage.

"I work at a cantaloupe factory," said Gus staring at Poppy's breasts. "I mean a dress factory," he added looking up to see if they caught it.

"Cantaloupes," said Fluffy and burst into a high whooping laugh that ended in a snort.

Damn good, thought Gus. That was damn good. And he wondered how he could so easily think of such spectacularly funny things tonight, and then he looked over at Anderson who was paying for another drink and Gus said to the women, "Hey, see that guy over there?"

"Yeah, the bastard tried to pick us up a minute ago," said Fluffy, scratching her vast belly and pulling up a slipping bra strap which had dropped below the shoulder onto the flabby pink bicep.

"I know him," said Gus. "Let's invite him over."

"You know him?" asked Poppy. "He looks like a cop to me."

"Hah, hah, hah," said Gus. "A cop. I knew that sucker for five years. He used to own a string of gas stations. His old lady divorced him though and now he's down to three. Always has plenty of bread on him, though."

"Don't you have any bread, Lance?" asked Fluffy suddenly.

"Just seventy-five bucks," said Gus. "That enough?"

"Well," Fluffy smiled. "We expect to show you a good time after this joint closes and naturally, all good things are expensive."

"What kind of dresses you like, Fluffy?" asked Gus expansively. "I carry samples in my car and I want to see you dolls in some fine goods."

"Really?" said Poppy with a huge grin. "Do you have any size fourteens?"

"I got 'em baby," said Gus.

"You got a twenty-two and a half?" asked Fluffy. "This old green rag is falling apart."

"I got 'em Fluffy," said Gus and now he was annoyed because he had absolutely no feeling in his lower jaw, mouth and tongue.

"Listen, Lance," said Poppy, pulling her chair next to his. "We usually don't sleep with nobody for less than a hundred a night each. But maybe for those dresses, I could let you have it for oh, fifty bucks, and maybe we could talk Fluffy into a twenty-five dollar ride. What do you say, Fluff? He's a damned nice guy."

"He's a cute little shit," said Fluffy. "I'll do it."

"Okay, dolls," said Gus, holding up three fingers to the waitress, even though he sensed Anderson was glaring at him through the smoky darkness.

"Why don't we get started now?" asked Poppy. "It's almost one o'clock."

"Not yet," said Gus. "I hear they swing after hours in this joint. What say we try to get in upstairs after two? After a few drinks and a little fun, we can head for the motel."

"George charges a lot for drinks upstairs," said Poppy. "You only got seventy-five bucks and we need it worse than George."

"Listen," Gus muttered, pitying for a moment a drowning fly who thrashed in a ringed puddle on the cluttered table. "I got a plan. Let's invite that guy I know over here and we'll take him with us upstairs to George's place after the bar closes. And we'll all drink off his money. He's loaded. And then after we drink for a while the three of us'll ditch him and head for the pad. I hate to go to bed yet, I'm having too much fun."

"You don't know what fun is, you cute little shit," said Fluffy, squeezing Gus's thigh with a pudgy pink hand and lurching forward heavily into Gus as she tried to kiss him on the cheek with a mouth that looked like a deflated tire tube.

"Cut that out, Fluff," said Poppy. "Crissake, you get thrown in jail for drunk and what're we going to do?"

"She isn't drunk," said Gus drunkenly, as his elbow slipped off the table from the weight of Fluffy's heavy body.

"We better get out of here and head for the motel right now," said Poppy. "You two are going to fuck up the whole deal if you get busted like a couple common winos."

"Just a minute," said Gus, waving a hand toward where he thought Anderson would be.

"We don't want that guy," said Poppy.

"Shut up, Poppy," said Gus.

"Shut up, Poppy," said Fluffy. "The more, the fuckin' merrier."

"This is the last time I take you with me, Fluffy," said Poppy, taking a big swallow of the cocktail.

"You wanted me?" asked Anderson, and Gus looked up at the red-eyed sergeant standing over him.

''Sure, sure,'' mumbled Gus. ''Sit down . . . Chauncey. Girls, this is Chauncey Dunghill, my old friend. Chauncey, meet Fluffy and Poppy, my new friends.'' Gus held his whiskey up in a toast to the three of them and swallowed a gulp he could hardly taste.

''Pleased to meet you,'' said Anderson stiffly and Gus squinted at the sergeant and remembered that Bonelli had told him that Anderson could not operate bars because he got high on two drinks being a teetotaler except when duty called. Gus smiled and leaned over the table seeing the peculiar angle of Anderson's eyes.

''Ol' Chaunce has to catch up with us,'' said Gus, ''if he wants to come with us to George's private bar for a few belts after two.''

''Shit,'' said Poppy.

''Private bar?'' said Anderson with a crafty look at Gus, toying with his sparse moustache.

''Sure, these girls are taking us upstairs. They know this guy George and he's got a swinging after-hours joint and you can come as long as you buy all the drinks, right, girls?''

''Tha's right,'' said Fluffy and kissed Gus on the cheek with a jarring collision and Gus winced in spite of the drink in him and wondered about the diseases prostitutes' mouths must carry. He furtively spilled a little whiskey on his hand and dabbed it on the spot to kill the germs.

''You buying drinks, Chauncey?'' asked Fluffy with a challenge in her voice as she looked at Anderson like a boxer eyeing an opponent.

''Four drinks,'' said Anderson to the waitress.

''Two for you,'' said Gus.

''What?''

''You got to catch up.''

''Well?'' said the bored waitress, hesitating.

''You catch up or we don't take you upstairs,'' said Gus.

''Bring me two daiquiris,'' said Anderson and glared at Gus who giggled all through the joke about the Jew and the blue-eyed camel which Fluffy repeated for Anderson.

''Chug-a-lug the drink,'' Gus commanded to Anderson when the daiquiris arrived.

''I'll drink as I please,'' said Anderson.

''Chug-a-lug, mudder-fug,'' commanded Fluffy, and the purple pouches under her eyes bulged ominously. Gus cheered as Anderson put the first drink away and smiled weakly at Poppy who was now smoking and nursing her drink.

Gus leered in earnest at her bulging breasts and told Fluffy a joke about a one-titted stripper who couldn't twirl a tassle, but he forgot how it ended and he stopped in the middle. Fluffy whooped and snorted and said it was the funniest joke she ever heard.

When Anderson finished his second drink, he signaled for five more and now grinned gaily at Poppy, asking her if she had ever been a dancer because she had wonderful legs.

''Chug-a-lug,'' said Anderson when the drinks arrived.

''Mudder-fug,'' said Fluffy, and exploded in cackles, bumping heads painfully with Gus.

''This is all right,'' said Anderson, after his glass was drained, and he picked up his next. ''I'm catching up, Poppy.''

''Something's goin' to happen,'' Poppy whined. ''You can't get drunk in this business, Fluffy.''

''I'm not drunk. Lance's drunk,'' said Fluffy. ''Chauncey's drunk too.''

''You're a beautiful girl and I really mean it, Poppy,'' sald Anderson, and Gus roared, ''Oooooh, stop it, Chauncey, you're killing me,'' and then Gus giggled in a prolonged burst of hilarity which threatened to suffocate him. When he recovered he saw that everyone on that side of the bar was laughing at him and that made him laugh harder and he only stopped when Fluffy grabbed him in a bulging embrace, called him a cute little shit, and kissed him on the open mouth. She probably went around the world tonight, he thought, cringing in horror. He took a hurried drink, swishing it around in his mouth and held up his hand for another.

"You had enough to drink," said Anderson with a surly slurred voice.

"Speak for yourself, Chauncey," said Gus trying not to think of how prostitutes used their mouths, as he became nauseous.

"We all had enough to drink," said Poppy. "I know something's going to go wrong."

"You're really a lovely girl, Poppy," said Anderson as he spilled half his drink on her gold purse.

"Bunch of fuckin' drunks," said Poppy.

"I'm sorry, Poppy," said Anderson. "Really I am."

Anderson finished his drink and ordered another round even though Poppy had not touched her last one, and finally Anderson drank his and Poppy's two manhattans when Fluffy dared him to. Gus had a headache and still felt nauseous as he remembered hearing a whore in the wagon saying she once gave twenty-two head jobs in one night, and he looked at Fluffy's mouth which had actually touched the inside of his. He sloshed more of the drink around in his mouth and pushed Fluffy away each time she leaned over and squeezed his thigh and now he found he was becoming angry at everything while only moments ago he was happy. He glared at Anderson's sparse moustache and thought what a miserable son of a bitch he was.

"I'm not feeling too good, Poppy," said Anderson who had been patting her hand and telling her that business was bad and he only made fifty thousand last year as she looked as though she didn't believe him.

"Let's all get out of here," said Poppy. "Can you still walk, Fluffy?"

"I can dance," growled Fluffy, whose head seemed to be sinking lower into the mass of her body.

"I'm getting sick," said Anderson.

"Kiss the son of a bitch," whispered Gus suddenly into Fluffy's ear.

"What?" asked Fluffy, swiping at an indomitable drop of moisture which clung to the ball of her nose.

"Grab that bastard like you did me around the arms and give him a big sloppy kiss and make sure you stick your old tongue right in there."

"But I don't even like the shithead," Fluffy whispered.

"I'll give you an extra five bucks later," whispered Gus.

"Okay," said Fluffy, leaning over the table and knocking an empty glass on the floor as she pinned the arms of the surprised Anderson and ground her mouth against his until he could manage the leverage to plop her back in the chair.

"Why did you do that?" Anderson gasped.

" 'Cause I love you, you shithead," said Fluffy and when the waitress passed with a tray of beers for the adjoining table, Fluffy grabbed a beer from the tray and stuck her chin in the foam and said, "Look at me, I'm a billy goat." Anderson paid for the beer and tipped the angry waitress two dollars.

"Come on, Fluffy," said Poppy after the waitress left, "let's go to the restroom and wash your goddamn face and then we're getting Lance and going to the motel right now. Understand, Lance?"

"Sure, sure, Poppy, whatever you say," said Gus, grinning at the outraged Anderson and feeling happy again.

When they were gone Anderson lurched forward, almost fell to the floor and looked painfully at Gus. "Plebesly, we're too goddamn drunk to do our job. Do you realize that?"

"We're not drunk, Sergeant. You're drunk," said Gus.

"I'm getting sick, Plebesly," pleaded Anderson.

''Know what Fluffy told me, Sergeant?'' said Gus. ''She told me she worked in a whorehouse all day and blew twenty-two guys.''

''She did?'' said Anderson, holding his hand to his mouth.

''She said she gives around the world or straight French 'cause it's too much trouble to screw and she'll go right up the old poop chute if a guy wants it.''

''Don't tell me that, Plebesly,'' said Anderson. ''I'm sick, Plebesly.''

''I'm sorry she kissed you, Sergeant,'' said Gus, ''I'm sorry 'cause those spermatozoas are probably swarming down your friggin' throat right this minute and swishing their tails against your friggin' tonsils.''

Anderson cursed and stumbled sideways, heading for the exit. His handcuffs fell out and clashed to the floor. Gus stooped carefully, retrieved the handcuffs and weaved his way through the tables after Anderson. Even on the sidewalk outside Gus could hear Poppy's curse when she found the table empty. Then Gus crossed the street, carefully following the wavy white line to the opposite curb. It seemed like a mile to the darkened parking lot where he found Anderson vomiting beside his car and Bonelli looking at Gus with affection.

''What happened in there?'' asked Bonelli.

''We drank with two whores.''

''Didn't they hit on you? Didn't you get an offer?''

''Yes, but there's too much between us now. I couldn't bear to arrest them.''

''You drank Anderson under the table, kid,'' Bonelli grinned.

''Under the friggin' table. I really did, Sal,'' Gus squeaked.

''How do you feel?''

''I'm getting sick.''

''Come on,'' said Bonelli, throwing a big hairy arm around Gus's shoulder and patting him on the cheek. ''Let's go get you some coffee, son.''

15

Conception

The transfer to Seventy-seventh Street station had been a demoralizing blow. Now, after his fourth week in the division Roy could still not believe they would do this to him. He knew that most of his academy class had been transferred to three divisions but he hoped he might escape the third one. After all, he was well liked in Central Division and he had already worked Newton Street and didn't dream they would make him work another black division. But then again, he should have expected it. Everything the Department did was senseless and illogical and none of the command officers cared in the least about intangibles like morale as long as they were efficient, icily efficient, and as long as the public knew and appreciated their efficiency. But Christ, Roy thought, Seventy-seventh Division! Fifty-ninth Place and Avalon, Slauson and Broadway, Ninety-second and Beach, One Hundred and Third, all of Watts for that matter! It was Newton Street magnified ten times, it was violence and crime, and every night he was wading through blood.

The stores, the offices, even the churches looked like fortresses with bars and grates and chains protecting doors and windows and he had even seen private uniformed guards in churches during services. It was impossible.

''Let's go to work,'' said Lieutenant Feeney to the night watch oficers. Feeney was a laconic twenty-year man with a melancholy face who seemed to Roy a decent watch commander, but he had to be because in this hellish division a rigid disciplinarian would drive the men to mutiny.

Roy put on his cap, jammed the flashlight in the sap pocket and picked up his books. He hadn't heard a single thing that was said at roll call. He was getting worse about that lately. Someday he'd miss something important. They must occasionally say something important, he thought.

Roy did not walk down the stairs with Rolfe, his partner. The laughter and voices of the others angered him for no apparent reason. The uniform clung wetly on this hot evening and chafed and hung like an oppressive blue pall. Roy dragged himself to the radio car and was glad it was Rolfe's turn to drive tonight. He hadn't the energy. It would be a sultry night as well as hot.

Roy wrote his name mechanically in the log and wrote Rolfe's name on the line below. He made a few other notations, then slammed the notebook as Rolfe drove out of the station parking lot and Roy turned the windwing so that what breeze there was cooled him a little.

"Anything special you want to do tonight?" asked Rolfe, a young, usually smiling ex-sailor who had been a policeman just one year and who still had a bubbling exuberance for police work that Roy found annoying.

"Nothing special," said Roy, closing the windwing when he lit a cigarette which tasted bad.

"Let's drive by Fifty-ninth and Avalon," said Rolfe. "We haven't been giving the pill pushers too much attention lately."

"Okay," Roy sighed, thinking that only one more night and then he was off for three. And then he began thinking of Alice, the buxom nurse who for six months he watched leaving the apartment house across the street from his, but whom he never tried before last week because he was keeping well satisfied by fair and fragile Jenny, the steno who only lived across the hall. Jenny was so available and so convenient and so eager for love at any hour, sometimes too eager. She insisted on lovemaking when he was exhausted from an overtime shift and any sane person should have been long asleep. He would stumble into his apartment and close the door quietly and before he could even get into his pajamas she would be in his bedroom, having heard him enter and having used the key he never should have given her. He would turn around suddenly when he felt her presence in the silent room and she would burst into a fit of giggling because she had scared hell out of him. She would be in her nightgown, not a well-shaped girl, far too thin, but very pretty and insatiable in her lust. He knew there were other men too despite what Jenny said, but he didn't give a damn because she was too much for him anyway, and besides, now that he had met Alice, milky, scrubbed and starched Alice, and had luxuriated in her yielding softness one fortunate night last week, now he was going to have to discourage Jenny.

"Looks like a good crowd this evening," said Rolfe. Roy wished he would be quiet when he was thinking about Alice and her splendid gourd-shaped breasts which in themselves provided him with hours of excitement and wonder. If Jenny was two feverish eyes, Alice was two peace-giving breasts. He wondered if there lived a woman whom he could think of as a whole person. He didn't think of Dorothy at all anymore. But then he realized he never thought of anyone as a whole person anymore. Carl was a mouth, an open mouth that criticized incessantly. His father was a pair of eyes, not devouring him like Jenny's, but entreating him, mournful eyes that wanted him to submit to the suffocation of his and Carl's tyranny.

"If only I could add an S to the Fehler and Son sign," his father had pleaded. "Oh Roy, I'd pay a fortune for that privilege." And then he had come to think of his mother as only a pair of hands, clasped hands, moist hands, talking hands which cajoled, "Roy, Roy, we never see you anymore and when are you leaving that city and coming home where you belong, Roy?"

Then he thought of Becky, and he felt his heart race. He could think of her as a whole person. She was scampering about now and she seemed so happy to see him when he came. He would never let a week pass without seeing her and to hell with Dorothy and her fat-assed henpecked fiancé, because he would never let a weekend pass without seeing Becky. Never. He would bring her presents, spend whatever he wished, and they could go to hell.

The evening dragged even though many radio calls were being given to Seventy-seventh cars. He was afraid to ask for code seven for fear they'd get a call. His stomach was rumbling. He should have eaten lunch today.

"Ask for seven," said Rolfe.

"Twelve-A-Five requesting code seven at the station," said Roy, wishing that he had packed something better than a cheese sandwich in his lunch. It was too close to payday to be buying dinner. He wished there were more eating spots on Seventy-seventh Street. He had long since decided that free food was not unprofessional. Everyone accepted meals and the restaurant proprietors did not seem to mind. They wanted policemen in the place or they wouldn't do it. But he and Rolfe had no eating spot in their district that would even feed them at a discount.

"Twelve-A-Five, continue patrol," said the operator, "and handle this call: See the woman, unknown trouble, eleven-o-four, east Ninety-second Street, code two."

Roy rogered the call and turned to Rolfe, "Shit! I'm starving."

"I hate unknown trouble calls," said Rolfe. "They always make me nervous. I like to know what to expect."

"This goddamned jungle," said Roy, flipping his cigarette out the window. "You don't get off on time, you miss your meals, fifteen radio calls a night. I've got to get a transfer."

"Do you really feel that way?" asked Rolfe, turning to Roy with a surprised look. "I like it here. The time passes fast. We're so busy that it's time to go home when I feel like I just came to work. All this action is pretty exciting to me."

"You'll get over that crap," said Roy. "Turn left here. This is Ninety-second."

There was a woman in a clean white turban standing in the front yard of the house next to eleven-o-four. Rolfe parked and she waved nervously as they got out of the car.

"Evening," said Rolfe as they approached the woman, putting on their caps.

"I'm the one that called Mr. PO-lice," she whispered. "They's a lady in that house that is terrible drunk all the time. She got a new baby, one of them preemeys, jist a tiny bug of a chil', and she always drunk, 'specially when her man at work, and he at work tonight."

"She bothering you?" asked Roy.

"It the baby, Mr. PO-lice," said the woman, her arms folded over the ample stomach, as she glanced several times at the house. "She dropped that chil' on the ground last week. I seed her, but my husband say it ain't none our business, but tonight she was staggerin' around' that front porch wif the chil' again and she almost fell right off the porch and I tol' my husband I was calling the PO-lice and tha's what I done."

"Okay, we'll go have a talk with her," said Roy, walking toward the one-story frame house with a rotting picket fence.

Roy walked carefully up the dangerous porch steps and stood by habit to one side of the doorway as Rolfe stood to the other side and knocked. They heard the shuffling of feet and a crash and then they knocked again. After more than a minute a woman with oily ringlets opened the door and stared at the policemen with watery little eyes.

"What you want?" she asked, weaving from side to side as she held tightly to the doorknob for support.

"We were told you might be having some trouble," said Rolfe with his young easy smile. "Mind if we come in? We're here to help you."

"I know how the PO-lices helps," said the woman, bumping the doorway with her wide shoulder during a sudden lurch sideways.

"Look, lady," said Roy, "We were told your baby might be in some danger. How about showing us that the baby's okay and we'll be on our way."

"Get off my porch," said the woman as she prepared to close the door, and Roy shrugged at Rolfe because they couldn't force their way in with no more cause than her being drunk. Roy decided to stop and buy a hamburger to go with the cheese sandwich that he had begun to crave. Then the baby shrieked. It was not a petulant baby scream of anger or discomfort, but it was a full-blown scream of pain or terror and Rolfe was through the door before the shriek died. Pushing past the drunken woman he bounded across the small living room into the kitchen. Roy was just entering the house when Rolfe emerged from the kitchen carrying the incredibly tiny nightgown-clad baby in his arms.

"She laid the baby on the kitchen table next to her ashtray," said Rolfe, awkwardly rocking the moaning brown-skinned infant. "It got hold of the burning cigarette. Hand's burned, and the stomach too. Look at the hole in the nightgown. Poor thing." Rolfe glared at the angry woman over his shoulder as he cradled the baby in one big arm away from the mother who looked on the verge of drunken decision.

"Give me my chil'," she said stepping toward Rolfe.

"Just a minute, lady," said Roy, grabbing her by a surprisingly hard bicep. "Partner, I think we've got enough to book her for child endangering. Lady, you're under ar . . ." She drove an elbow into the side of Roy's neck and his head struck the edge of the door with a painful shock and he heard Rolfe shout as she lunged for him and Roy stared transfixed as he saw the fragile, screaming baby being pulled by the woman who had the left arm and Rolfe who had the right leg in one hand while his other hand clawed the air in horror and helplessness.

"Let it go, Rolfe," Roy shouted, as the woman jerked backward viciously and Rolfe followed her, unwilling to surrender the wailing infant completely.

Finally Rolfe released the child, and Roy shuddered as the woman fell heavily back into a chair holding the baby by one leg across her lap.

"Let her keep it, Rolfe!" Roy shouted, still unable to decide what to do because they would surely kill it, but Rolfe had pounced on the woman who was digging and punching at his face, still holding the baby in a death grip, first by the leg, then by the arm when Rolfe pulled a hand free. Roy leaped forward when she grabbed the now silent baby by the throat.

"My God, my God," Roy whispered, as he tore the fingers free one at a time while Rolfe pinned the woman's other arm and she cursed and spat and he had the last finger twisted free and was lifting the trembling little body in one hand when the woman's head snapped forward and her teeth closed first on Roy's hand and he shouted in sudden pain. She released him and bit at the child as Rolfe grabbed the woman's neck, and tried to force the head back, but the large white teeth flashed and snapped again and again at the baby, and then the baby shrieked once more, long and loud. Roy pulled the infant and the nightgown ripped away in the woman's mouth and Roy did not look at the baby, but ran to the bedroom with it and put it on the bed and came back to help Rolfe handcuff her.

It was after midnight when they got the woman booked and the baby admitted to the hospital. It was too late to eat now and Roy could not eat anyway and he told himself for the tenth time to stop thinking about what the baby's body looked like there on the shockingly white table in the emergency ward. Rolfe had also been unusually silent for the past hour or so.

"Someone else tried to bite me once," Roy said suddenly as he puffed on a cigarette and leaned back in the car as Rolfe was driving them to the station to complete the reports. "It wasn't like this at all. It was a man and he was white, and there was no excuse at all. I was trying to get away from him. It was in a restroom."

Rolfe looked at him curiously and Roy said, "I was working vice. He was trying to devour me. People are cannibals I guess. They just eat each other. Sometimes they don't even have the decency to kill you before they eat you."

"Hey, there's a waitress I know pretty good down at a restaurant at a Hundred-fifteenth and Western. I go there after work for coffee all the time. How about us stopping there for a few minutes before we go to the station? We could at least drink some coffee and unwind. And who knows, maybe we'll get hungry. I think she'd bounce for a free meal if the boss isn't there."

"Why not?" said Roy, thinking the coffee sounded good and it would be a pleasure to drive through the west side of the division for a change, which was only part Negro and relatively peaceful. Roy hoped he could work Ninety-one next month and get as far west and south as the division went. He had to get away from black faces. He was starting to change toward them and he knew it was wrong. But still it was happening.

They were only two blocks from the restaurant and Roy was already feeling reassured at seeing the predominantly white faces driving and walking by when Rolfe said, "Fehler, did you look in that liquor store we just passed?"

"No, why?" asked Roy.

"There was nobody behind the counter," said Rolfe.

"So he went in the back room," said Roy. "Look, do you want to play cops and robbers or do we get some coffee?"

"I'm just going to have a look," said Rolfe, making a U-turn and driving north again while Roy shook his head and vowed to ask for an older, more settled partner next month.

Rolfe parked across the street from the store and they watched the interior for a second. They saw a sandy-haired man in a yellow sport shirt run from the back room to the cash register where he punched several keys, and then they saw him clearly shove the gun inside his belt.

"Officers need help, One one three and Western!" Rolfe whispered into the radio, and then he was out of the car, hatless, flashlight in hand, running low to the north side of the building. He evidently remembered Roy who was just getting around the front of the car because he stooped, turned, and pointed to the rear door indicating that he would take the rear and then he disappeared in the shadows streaking for the darkness of the rear alley.

Roy debated a moment where he should place himself, thought of lying across the hood of a car that was parked directly in front of the store and was probably the suspect's car, but changed his mind and decided to get behind the corner of the building at the southwest corner where he could have a clear line of fire if the man came out the front. He began trembling, wondered for a moment if he could shoot a man, and decided not to think about that.

Then he saw that one of the cars in the bar parking lot next door was occupied by a man and woman who sat in the front seat apparently oblivious to the policemen's presence. Roy saw that they would be directly in the line of fire of the gunman if he would shoot at Roy hiding behind the corner of the building. His conscience nagged and his hand trembled more, and he thought if I leave here to run across the vacant lot and tell them to get the hell out, he might come out the door and I'll be caught out of position. But Jesus Christ, be might kill them and I'd never be able to forget . . . Then he decided, and made a dash to the yellow Plymouth thinking: Stupid bastard, probably sitting there playing with her tits and doesn't even know they might get killed. Roy was beside the car and he saw the girl look at him wide-eyed as he held his revolver at his side. The man opened the door quickly.

"Get that car the hell out of here," said Roy and he never forgot the foolish grin and the look of patent unconcern on the face of the little freckled man who leveled the sawed-off shotgun. Then the yellow and red flame crashed into him and he flew back across the sidewalk. He slid off the curb into the gutter where he lay on his side weeping because he could not get up and he had to get up because he could see the slimy intestines wet in the moonlight flopping out of his lower stomach in a pile. They began touching the street and Roy strained to turn over. He heard footsteps and a man said, "Goddamnit Harry, get in!" and another male voice said, "I didn't even know they was out here!" Then the car started and roared across the sidewalk and off the curb and it sounded like more footsteps farther away. He heard Rolfe shouting, "Stop! Stop!" and heard four or five shots and tires squeal. Then he remembered that the intestines were lying on the street and he was filled with horror because they were lying there in the filthy street getting dirty and he began to cry. He squirmed a little to get on his back and get them bunched up because if he could just shovel them back inside and brush the dirt off them he knew he'd be alright because they were oh so dirty now. But he couldn't lift them. His left arm wouldn't move and it hurt so much to try to reach across the bubbling hole with his right arm so he began to cry again, and thought: Oh, if only it would rain. Oh, why can't it rain in August, and suddenly as he cried, he was deafened by thunder and the lightning flashed and clattered and the rain poured down on him. He thanked God and cried tears of joy because the rain was washing all the dirt off the heap of guts that was hanging out. He watched them shine wet red in the rain, clean and red, as all the filth was flushed away and he was still crying happily when Rolfe leaned over him. There were other policemen there and none of them were wet from the rain. He couldn't understand that.

Roy could not have said how long he had been in the police ward of Central Receiving Hospital. Could not at this moment say if it was days or weeks. It was always the same: blinds drawn, the hum of the air conditioning, the patter of soft-soled footsteps, whispers, needles and tubes which were endlessly inserted and withdrawn, but now he guessed perhaps three weeks had passed. He wouldn't ask Tony who sat there reading a magazine by the inadequate night light with a grin on his effeminate face.

"Tony," said Roy, and the little male nurse put the magazine on the table and walked to the bed.

"Hello Roy," Tony smiled. "Woke up, huh?"

"How long I been sleeping?"

"Not too long, two, three hours, maybe," said Tony. "You were restless tonight. I thought I'd sit in here, I figured you'd wake up."

"It hurts tonight," said Roy, sliding the cover back to look at the hole covered with light gauze. It no longer bubbled and sickened him but it could not be sutured because of its size and had to heal on its own. It had already begun to shrink a little.

"It looks good tonight, Roy," Tony smiled. "Pretty soon no more I.V.'s, you'll be eating real food."

"It hurts like hell."

"Dr. Zelko says you're doing wonderfully, Roy. I'll bet you're out of here in two more months. And back to work in six. Light duty of course. Maybe you can work the desk for a while."

"I need something for the pain tonight."

"I can't. I've had specific orders about that. Dr. Zelko says we were giving you too many injections."

"Screw Dr. Zelko! I need something. Do you know what adhesions are? Your goddamn guts tighten up and come together like they were glued. Do you know what that's like?"

"Now, now," said Tony, wiping Roy's forehead with a towel.

"Look how my leg's swollen. There's a nerve that's damaged. Ask Dr. Zelko. I need something. That nerve keeps me in terrible pain."

"I'm sorry, Roy," said Tony, his smooth little face contorted with concern. "I wish I could do more for you. You're our number one patient . . ."

"Shove it!" said Roy and Tony walked back to his chair, sat down, and continued reading.

Roy stared at the holes in the acoustical ceiling and counted rows but he soon tired of that. When the pain was really bad and they wouldn't give him his medication he sometimes thought of Becky and that helped a little. He thought that Dorothy had been here once with Becky but he couldn't be sure. He was about to ask Tony, but Tony was his night nurse and he wouldn't know if they had visited him. His father and mother had been here several times and Carl had come at least once in the beginning. He remembered that. He had opened his eyes one afternoon and seen Carl and his parents, and the wound started hurting again and his cries of anguish had sent them out and brought the delicious indescribable injection that was all he lived for now. Some policemen had come, but he couldn't say just who. He thought he remembered Rolfe, and Captain James, and he thought he saw Whitey Duncan once through a sheet of fire. Now he was getting frightened because his stomach was clenching like a painful fist as though it didn't belong to him and acted on its own in defiance of the waves of anguish that were punishing it.

"What do I look like?" asked Roy suddenly.

"Pardon, Roy?" said Tony, jumping to his feet.

"Get me a mirror. Hurry up."

"What for, Roy?" Tony smiled, opening the drawer of the table in the corner of the private room.

"Have you ever had a really bad stomachache?" asked Roy. "One that made you sick clear through?"

"Yes," said Tony, bringing the smaller mirror over to Roy's bed.

"Well it was nothing. Nothing, do you understand?"

"I can't give you anything," said Tony, holding the mirror up for Roy.

"Who's that?" said Roy, and the fear swelled and pounded and swelled in him as he looked at the thin gray face with the dark-rimmed eyes and the thousands of greasy globules of sweat that roughened the texture of the face that stared at him in horror.

"You don't look bad at all, now. We thought we were going to lose you for the longest time. Now we know you're going to be alright."

"I've got to have some medication, Tony. I'll give you twenty dollars. Fifty. I'll give you fifty dollars."

"Please, Roy," said Tony returning to his chair.

"If I only had my gun," Roy sobbed.

"Don't talk like that, Roy."

"I'd blow my brains out. But first I'd kill you, you little cocksucker."

"You're a cruel man. And I don't have to stand for your insults. I've done everything I could for you. We all have. We've done everything to save you."

"I'm sorry I called you that. You can't help it if you're a fruit. I'm sorry. Please get some medication. I'll give you a hundred dollars."

"I'm going out. You ring if you really need me."

"Don't go. I'm afraid to be alone with it. Stay here. I'm sorry. Please."

"Alright. Forget it," Tony grumbled, sitting down.

"Dr. Zelko has terrible eyes," said Roy.

"What do you mean?" Tony sighed, putting down the magazine.

"There's hardly any iris. Just two round black little balls like two slugs of double ought buckshot. I can't bear his eyes."

"Is that the kind of buckshot that hit you, Roy?"

"No. I'd be stinking up a cofffin now if it had been double ought buck. It was number seven and a half birdshot. You ever hunt?"

"No."

"He hit me from less than two feet away. Some hit my Sam Browne but I got most of it. He was such a silly-looking man. That's why I didn't bring the gun up. He was so silly-looking I just couldn't believe it. And he was a white man. And that sawed-off shotgun was so silly-looking and monstrous I couldn't believe that either. Maybe if he'd been a regular-looking man and had a regular handgun I could've brought my gun up, but I just held it there at my side and he looked so damned silly when he fired."

"I don't want to hear it. Stop talking about it, Roy."

"You asked me. You asked about the buckshot, didn't you?"

"I'm sorry I did. I'd just better go out for a while and maybe you can sleep."

"Go ahead!" Roy sobbed. "All of you can leave me. Look at what you've done to me though. Look at my body. You made me a freak, all you bastards. I got a huge open hole in my belly and you put another one in me and now I can wake up and find a pile of shit on my chest."

"You had to have a colostomy, Roy."

"Yeah? How would you like to have an asshole in your stomach? How would you like to wake up and look at a bag of shit on your chest?"

"I always clean it up as soon as I see it. Now you try to . . ."

"Yeah," he cried, weeping openly now, "you made me a freak. I got a bloody pussy that won't close and an asshole in front that I can't control and they're both right here on my stomach where I've got to look at them. I'm a goddamn freak." Then Roy wept and the pain worsened but he wept more and the pain made him weep harder and harder until he gasped and tried to stop so that he could control the inexorable pain that he prayed would kill him instantly in one huge crashing red and yellow ball of fire.

Tony wiped his face and was about to speak when Roy's sobbing subsided and he gasped, "I . . . I've got to . . . to turn over. It's killing me like this. Please, help me. Help me get on my stomach for a little while."

"Sure, Roy," said Tony, gently lifting him and then letting the bed down flat and taking the pillow away as Roy rested on the throbbing burning wound and sobbed spasmodically and blew his nose in the tissue Tony gave him.

Roy lay like this for perhaps five minutes and then he could bear it no more and turned, but Tony had stepped out into the corridor. He thought the hell with it he'd turn himself over and maybe the effort would kill him and that would be fine. He raised up on an elbow, feeling the sweat streaming over his rib cage and then moved as quickly as he could and fell on his back again. He felt the sweat flowing freely over his entire body. He felt something else and pulled the Scotch tape loose and glanced at the wound and screamed.

"What is it?" said Tony, running in the room.

"Look at it!" said Roy, staring at the fibrous bloody clump which protruded from the wound.

"What the hell?" said Tony, looking toward the hall and then back at Roy with confusion in his eyes.

Roy gaped at the wound and then at Tony and seeing the worried little face on the nurse began to giggle.

"I'll get a doctor, Roy," said Tony.

"Wait a minute," said Roy, laughing harder now. "I don't need a doctor. Oh Christ, this is too funny." Roy gasped and stopped laughing when another spasm struck him but even the pain could not completely destroy the humor of it. "Do you know what that mess is, Tony? That's the goddamn wadding!"

"The what?"

"The wadding of the shotgun shell! It finally worked itself out. Look close. There's even some shot mixed in there. Two little pieces of shot. Oh Christ, that's funny. Oh, Christ. Go make the announcement to the staff that there was a happy event in the police ward. Tell them that Dr. Zelko's monster strained his new pussy and gave birth to a three-ounce pile of bloody wadding. And it had eyes like Dr. Zelko! Oh Christ, that's funny."

"I'll get a doctor, Roy. We'll clean that up."

"Don't try taking my baby away, you goddamn faggot! I once saw a nigger try to eat her baby when I did that to her. Oh Christ, this is too funny," Roy gasped, wiping the tears away.

August 1964

16

The Saint

SERGE STRETCHED and yawned, then put his feet on the desk in the deserted juvenile office at Hollenbeck station. He smoked and wondered when his partner Stan Blackburn would return. Stan had asked Serge to wait in the office while he did some "personal business" which Serge knew to be a woman whose divorce was not final, who had three children that were old enough to get him into trouble when the romance finally ended. An officer would get at least a suspension for conduct unbecoming, when an adulterous affair was brought to the Department's attention. Serge wondered if he would tomcat around—if—he married.

Serge had accepted the assignment as a juvenile officer only because he was assured he would not be transferred to Georgia Street Station but could remain here in Hollenbeck and work the night watch J-Car. He decided that the juvenile background would look good in his record when he went up for promotion. But first he would have to pass the written exam and it would be extremely doubtful that he would manage that since he couldn't imagine himself knuckling down to a rigid study program. He hadn't been able to make himself study even in his college classes and he smiled as he recalled the brave ambition of a few years ago to work diligently for the degree and advance quickly in his profession. After several false starts, he was now a government major at Cal State and had only accumulated thirty-three units.

But he enjoyed his work here at Hollenbeck and he made more than enough money to support himself. He had a surprisingly sound savings program and he couldn't see any farther than perhaps detective sergeant here at Hollenbeck. That would be enough, he thought. At the end of his twenty years he would be forty-three years old and able to draw forty percent of his salary the rest of his life which would certainly not be lived here in Los Angeles, or anywhere near Los Angeles. He thought of San Diego. It was pleasant down there, but not in the city, some suburb perhaps. There should be a woman and children somewhere in his plans, he knew. It could not be avoided indefinitely. And it was true that he was more and more becoming restless and sentimental. The home and hearth television stories were starting to interest him slightly.

He had been seeing a great deal of Paula. No other girl had ever stirred this much interest in him. She was not a beauty, but she was attractive and her clear gray eyes held your attention unless she was wearing tight-fitting clothes and then she became extremely interesting. He knew she would marry him. She had hinted often enough that she wanted a family. He told her you'd better get started because you're now twenty-two, and she asked him if he'd like to sire her a couple of kids. When he said, "My pleasure," she said they'd have to be legitimate.

Paula had other assets. Her father, Dr. Thomas Adams, was a successful dentist in Alhambra, and would probably bestow a small piece of property on a lucky son-in-law since Paula was his only child and overly indulged. Paula had taken apartment number twelve in his building, formerly occupied by a steno named Maureen Ball, and Serge had hardly noticed the change in women and had begun dating Paula without a break in stride. He knew that some evening, after a good dinner and more than a few martinis, he would probably go through the formality of asking her, and tell her to go ahead and inform the family to prepare the marriage feast because, what the hell, he couldn't go on aimlessly forever.

At eight-thirty the sun had fallen and it was cool enough to take a ride around Hollenbeck. Serge was wishing Stan Blackburn would come back and he was trying to decide whether to resume reading the treatise on the California constitution for the summer school class he wished he hadn't taken, or whether to read a novel which he had brought to work tonight because he knew he would be waiting in the office for several hours.

Blackburn came whistling through the door just as Serge made the decision of the novel over the California constitution. Blackburn had a simpering smile on his face and the evidence of his personal business was easy to see.

"Better wipe the lipstick off your shirt front," said Serge.

"Wonder how it got way down there," said Blackburn with a knowing wink at his mark of conquest.

Serge had seen her once when Blackburn had parked in the alley next to her duplex, and gone inside for a moment. Serge wouldn't have bothered with her even without the dangers of an estranged husband, and children who might report to Daddy.

Blackburn ran a comb through his thinning gray hair, straightened his tie, and dabbed at the lipstick stain on his white shirt.

"Ready to go to work?" asked Serge, swinging his feet off the desk.

"I don't know. I'm kind of tired," Blackburn chuckled.

"Let's go, Casanova," said Serge, shaking his head. "I guess I better drive so you can rest and restore yourself."

Serge decided to drive south on Soto and east toward the new Pomona freeway right-of-way. Sometimes in the late afternoon if it wasn't too hot, he liked to watch the workmen scurrying about to complete another vast Los Angeles complex of steel and concrete, obsolete before it is finished, guaranteed to be strangled by cars one hour after its opening. One thing the freeway had done, it had broken up *Los Gavilanes*. The doctrine of eminent domain had succeeded in gang busting where the police, probation department, and juvenile court had failed—*Los Gavilanes* had dissolved when the state bought the property and the parents of *Los Gavilanes* scattered through East Los Angeles.

Serge decided to drive through the concrete paths at Hollenbeck Park to check for juvenile gang activity. They hadn't made an arrest for a week, mostly because of Blackburn's time-consuming romantic meetings and Serge hoped they might spot something tonight. He liked to do just enough work to keep the sergeant off his back, although nothing had yet been said about their lack of accomplishment this week.

As Serge drove toward the boathouse, a figure disappeared in the bushes and they heard a hollow clunk as a bottle hastily dropped, struck a rock.

"See who that was?" asked Serge as Blackburn lazily ran the spotlight over the bushes.

"Looked like one of the Pee Wees. Bimbo Zaragoza, I think."

"Drinking a little wine, I guess."

"Yeah, that's not like him. He's a glue head."

"Any port in a storm."

"Port. Hah, that's pretty good."

"Think we can drive down below and catch him?"

"No, he's clear across the lake by now." Blackburn leaned back and closed his eyes.

"We better make a pinch tonight," said Serge.

"Nothing to worry about," said Blackburn, eyes still closed as he took the wrappers off two sticks of gum and shoved them in his mouth.

As Serge came out of the park onto Boyle Street he saw two more Pee Wees but Bimbo was not with them. The smaller one he recognized as Mario Vega, the other he couldn't recall.

"Who's the big one?" he asked.

Blackburn opened one eye and shined the light on the two boys who grinned and began walking toward Whittier Boulevard.

"Ape man, they called him. I forget his real name."

As they passed the boys, Serge snorted at the exaggerated cholo walk of ape man: toes turned out, heels digging in, arms swinging freely, this was the trademark of the gang member. This and the curious deliberate ritual chewing on imaginary chewing gum. One wore Levis, the other khakis slit at the bottoms at the seams to "hang tough" over the black polished shoes. Both wore Pendleton shirts buttoned at the cuff to hide the puncture marks which, if they had them, would bring the status of the addict. And both wore navy watch caps as they wear in youth camp, and this showed they were ex-cons whether or not they actually were.

Serge caught a few words of the conversation when they drove slowly past the boys, mostly muffled Spanish obscenities. Then he thought of the books which talked of the formalism of Spanish insults in which acts are only implied. Not so in familiar informal Mexican, he thought. A Mexican insult or vulgarism could surpass in color even the English equivalent. The Chicanos had given life to the Spanish obscenity.

Serge had decided that Blackburn was asleep when at ten past ten the Communications operator said, "All Hollenbeck units, and Four-A-Forty-three, a four-eighty-four suspect just left twenty-three eleven Brooklyn Avenue running eastbound on Brooklyn and south on Soto. Suspect is male, Mexican, thirty-five to forty, five feet eight to ten, a hundred sixty to a hundred and seventy, black hair, wearing a dirty short-sleeved red turtleneck shirt, khaki pants, carrying a plaster statue."

Serge and Blackburn were on Brooklyn approaching St. Louis when the call came out. They passed the scene of the theft and Serge saw the radio car parked in front, the dome light on and an officer sitting inside. The other officer was in the store talking with the proprietor.

Serge double-parked for a moment beside the radio car, and read "Luz del Día Religious Store" on the window.

"What did he get?" he called to the officer who was a new rookie that Serge didn't know.

"A religious statue, sir," said the young officer, probably thinking they were worthy of the "sir" since they were plainclothesmen. Serge was glad to see that his drowsing partner at least opened his eyes when he talked to the rookie. He hated to disillusion the young ones too quickly.

Serge turned south on Soto and began glancing around for the thief. He turned east on First and north on Matthews and spotted the red turtleneck lurching down the street. The witness had given an excellent description he thought, but she didn't say he was drunk.

"Here he comes," said Serge.

"Who?"

"The four-eighty-four suspect from the religious store. This has to be him. Look."

"Yeah, that must be him," said Blackburn, lighting up the weaving drunk with the spotlight. The drunk threw his hands in front of his face.

Serge stopped a few feet in front of the man and they both got out.

"Where's the statue?" asked Blackburn.

"I ain't got nothing, sir," said the man, watery-eyed and bloated. His turtleneck was purple with the stains of a hundred pints of wine.

"I know this guy," said Blackburn. "Let's see, Eddie . . . Eddie something."

"Eduardo Onofre Esquer," said the man, swaying precariously. "I 'member you, sir. You bosted me lots of times for drunk."

"Yeah. Eddie was one of the Brooklyn Avenue winos for years. Where you been, Eddie?"

"I got a jeer last time, sir. I been in the county for a jeer."

"A year? For drunk?"

"Not for drunk. Petty theft, sir. I was choplifting a couple pairs of woman's stocking to sell for a drink."

"And now you're doing the same damn thing," said Blackburn. "You know petty theft with a prior is a felony. You're going to go for a felony this time."

"Please sir," sobbed Eddie. "Don' bost me this time."

"Get in, Eddie," said Serge. "Show us where you threw it."

"Please don' bost me," said Eddie, as Serge started the car and drove east on Michigan.

"Which way, Eddie?" asked Serge.

"I didn' throw it, sir. I set it down at the church when I saw what it was."

Blackburn's spotlight lighted up the white robe and black cowl and black face of Martin de Porres on the steps in front of the drab gray building on Breed Street.

"When I saw what it was, I put it there on the steps of the church."

"That ain't no church," said Blackburn. "That's a synagogue."

"Anyway, I put it there for the priest to find," said Eddie. "Please don' bost me, sir. I'll go straight home to my room if you give me a break. I won' steal no more. I swear on my mother."

"What do you say, partner?" asked Serge, grinning.

"What the hell. We're juvenile officers, ain't we?" said Blackburn. "Eddie's no juvenile."

"Go home, Eddie," said Serge, reaching over the seat and unlocking the rear door of the car.

"Thank you, sir," said Eddie. "Thank you. I'm going home." Eddie stumbled over the curb, righted himself and staggered down the sidewalk toward home as Serge retrieved the statue from the steps of the synagogue.

"Thank you, sir," Eddie shouted over his shoulder. "I didn' know what I was taking. I swear to God I wouldn' steal a saint."

"You about ready to eat?" asked Blackburn, after they left black Martin at the religious store, telling the proprietor they found him undamaged on the sidewalk two blocks away, and that perhaps the thief had a conscience and could not steal Martin de Porres. The proprietor said, "*Quizás, quizás. Quién sabe?* We like to think of a thief with a soul."

Blackburn offered the old man a cigarette and said, "We've got to believe there are good ones, eh señor? Young men like my *compañero* here, they don't need anything, but when they get a little older like you and me they need some faith, eh?"

And the old man nodded, puffed on the cigarette and said, "It is very true, señor."

"Ready to eat?" Serge asked Blackburn.

Blackburn was silent for a minute, then said, "Take me to the station, will you, Serge?"

"What for?"

"I want to make a call. You go eat, and pick me up later."

Now what the hell's going on? Serge thought. This guy had more personal problems than any partner he ever had.

"I'm going to call my wife," said Blackburn.

"You're separated, aren't you?" asked Serge, and was then sorry he said it because innocent remarks like that could leave an opening for a lurid confession of marital problems.

"Yeah, but I'm going to call her and ask her if I can come home. What am I doing living in a bachelor pad? I'm forty-two years old. I'm going to tell her we can make it if we have faith."

That's just swell, Serge thought. Black Martin worked his magic on the horny old bastard.

Serge dropped Blackburn at the station and drove back to Brooklyn deciding he'd have some Mexican food. Some *carnitas* sounded good and there were a couple of places on Brooklyn that gave policemen half price and made *carnitas* Michoacán style.

Then he thought of Mr. Rosales' place. He hadn't been there in a few months and there was always Mariana who looked better and better each time he stopped. One of these days he might ask her out to a movie. Then he realized he hadn't dated a Mexican girl since high school.

He didn't see Mariana when he first entered the restaurant. He had been coming in once or twice a month, but had missed the last few months—because of a thirty-day vacation and a waitress that Blackburn was trying to seduce at a downtown drive-in who was unaccountably interested in the old boy and was supplying them with hot dogs, hamburgers and occasional pastramis courtesy of the boss who did not know she was doing it.

"Ah, señor Duran," said Mr. Rosales, waving Serge to a booth. "We have not seen you. How are you? Have you been sick?"

"Vacation, Mr. Rosales," said Serge. "Am I too late to eat?"

"No, of course not. Some *carnitas?* I have a new cook from Guanajuato. She can make delicious *barbacoa* and *birria*."

"Maybe just a couple of tacos, Mr. Rosales. And coffee."

"Tacos. *Con todo?*"

"Yes, lots of chile."

"Right away, señor Duran," said Mr. Rosales, going to the kitchen, and Serge waited but it was not Mariana who returned with the coffee, it was another girl, older, thinner, inexperienced as a waitress, who spilled a little coffee while pouring.

Serge drank the coffee and smoked until she brought him the tacos. He was not as hungry as he thought, even though the new cook made them just as good as the last one. Every bit of fat was trimmed off the tiny chunks of pork and the onions were grated with care, with cilantro sprinkled over the meat. The chile sauce, Serge thought, was the best he ever tasted, but still he was not as hungry as he thought.

Midway through the first taco, he caught Mr. Rosales' eye and the little man hurried to his table. "More café?" he asked.

"No, this is fine. I was just wondering, where's Mariana? New job?"

"No," he laughed. "Business is so good I have two waitresses now. I have sent her to the market. We ran out of milk tonight. She will be back soon."

"How's her English? Improving?"

"You will be surprised. She is a very smart one. She talks much better than I do."

"Your English is beautiful, Mr. Rosales."

"Thank you. And your Spanish, señor? I have never heard you speaking Spanish. I thought you were Anglo until I learned your name. You are half Anglo, perhaps? Or a real Spaniard?"

"Here she comes," said Serge, relieved to have Mariana interrupt the conversation. She was carrying two large bags and closed the door with her foot, not seeing Serge who took a grocery bag from her hand.

"Señor Duran!" she said, her black eyes glowing. "How good it is to see joo."

"How good it is to hear you speak such beautiful English," Serge smiled, and nodded to Mr. Rosales, as he helped her take the milk to the kitchen.

Serge returned to the table and ate heartily while Mariana put on an apron and came to his table with a fresh pot of coffee.

"Two more tacos, Mariana," he said, noting with approval that she had gained a few pounds and was now rounding into womanhood.

"Joo are hungry tonight, señor Duran? We have missed you."

"I'm hungry tonight, Mariana," he said. "I've missed you too."

She smiled and returned to the kitchen and he was surprised that he could have forgotten that clean white smile. Now that he saw it again, he thought it astonishing that he could have forgotten. It was still too thin and delicate a face. The forehead was ample, the upper lip still a bit long, the black eyes heavy-lashed and full of life. It was still the madonna face. He knew the tiny fire of longing still lived in spite of what the world had told him, and that flame was glowing red hot at this moment. He thought he'd let it smolder for a while because it was not unpleasant.

When Mariana brought the second plate of tacos, he brushed against her fingers. "Let me hear you speak English," he said.

"What do joo wish me to say?" she laughed, self-consciously.

"First of all, stop calling me señor. You know my name, don't you?"

"I know it."

"What is it?"

"Sergio."

"Serge."

"I cannot say that word. The end is too harsh and difficult. But Sergio is soft and easy to say. Try it jurself."

"Ser-hee-oh."

"Ay, that sounds berry comic. Can you no' say Sergio?" she laughed. "Sergio. Two sounds. No more. No' three sounds."

"Of course," he smiled. "My mother called me Sergio."

"Joo see," she laughed. "I knew that joo could say it. But why don' joo ever talk Spanish?"

"I've forgotten," he smiled, and thought, you couldn't help smiling at her. She was a delightful little child. "You're a dove," he said.

"What is a dove?"

"*Una paloma.*"

"But that is my name. Mariana Paloma."

"It fits. You're a little dove."

"I am no' so little. It is that joo are a big man."

"Did you ever see a man so big in your country?"

"No' many," she said.

"How old are you, Mariana, nineteen?"

"Jas."

"Say yes."

"Jes."

"Y-y-yes."

"J-j-jes."

They both laughed and Serge said, "Would you like me to teach you to say yes? Yes is easy to say."

"I wish to learn all English words," she answered, and Serge felt ashamed because her eyes were innocent, and she didn't understand. Then he thought, for

God's sake, there are plenty of girls even if Paula wasn't enough which she most certainly was. What would it prove to take a simple child like this? Had he lived so long alone that self-gratification had become the only purpose for living?

Still he said, "You don't work Sundays, do you?"

"No."

"Would you like to go somewhere with me? To dinner? Or to a theater? Have you ever seen a real play? With music?"

"Joo want me to go with joo? *De veras?*"

"If Mr. Rosales will let you."

"He will let me go anywhere with joo. He thinks joo are a good man. Joo mean it?"

"I mean it. Where shall we go?"

"To a lake. Can we go to a lake? In the afternoon? I will bring food. I have never seen a lake in this country."

"Okay, a picnic," he laughed. "We call it a picnic when people bring food and go to a lake."

"That is another hard word," she said.

Serge thought several times on Saturday of calling Mr. Rosales' restaurant and calling off the outing. He never was aware of having any particular respect for himself. He realized that he was always one who wanted only to get along, to do things the easiest, least painful way, and if he could have a woman, a book, or a movie, and get drunk at least once a month, he thought that he had mastered life. But now there was the lust for the girl and it was not that he was Don Quixote, he thought, but it was a totally unnecessary bit of cruelty to take a child like her who had seen or done nothing in a short difficult life, and to whom he must seem something special with a one-year-old Corvette and expensive gaudy sports coats which Paula bought for him. He was degenerating, he thought. In three years he'd be thirty. What would he be then?

In order to sleep Saturday night, he made a solemn promise to himself that under no circumstances would he engage in a cheap seduction of a girl who was the ward of a kindly old man who had done him no harm. And besides, he grinned wryly, if Mr. Rosales found out, there would be no more free meals for the Hollenbeck policemen. Free meals were harder to come by than women—even if she were truly the Virgin of Guadalajara.

He picked her up at the restaurant because that Sunday she had to work two hours from ten until noon when the afternoon girl came on. Mr. Rosales seemed very glad to see him and she had a shopping bag full of food which she called her "chopping sack." Mr. Rosales waved to them as they drove away from the restaurant and Serge checked his tank because he intended to drive all the way to Lake Arrowhead. If she wanted a lake, he'd give her the best, he thought, complete with lakeside homes that should open those gleaming black eyes as wide as silver pesos.

"I didn't know if joo would come," she smiled.

"Why do you say that?"

"Joo are always joking with señor Rosales and with the other girl and me. I thought maybe it was a joke."

"You were ready, weren't you?"

"I still thought it was maybe a joke. But I went to a berry early Mass and prepared the food."

"What kind of food? Mexican?"

"*Claro*. I am *Mexicana?* No?"

"You are," he laughed. "You are *muy Mexicana*."

"And joo are completely an American. I cannot believe that joo could have a name like Sergio Duran."

"Sometimes I can't believe it either, little dove."

''I like that name,'' she smiled, and Serge thought she's not a wilting flower, this one. She carries her face uplifted and looks right in your eye, even when she's blushing because you've made her terribly self-conscious.

''And I like your red dress. And I like your hair down, long like that.''

''A waitress cannot wear her hair like this. Sometimes I think I chould cut the hair like American girls.''

''Never do that!'' he said. ''You're not an American girl. Do you want to be one?''

''Only sometimes,'' she said, looking at him seriously, and then they were silent for a while but it was not an uncomfortable silence. Occasionally she would ask him about a town they passed or an unusual building. She amazed him by noticing and knowing the names of several species of flowers that were used to decorate portions of the San Bernardino Freeway. And she knew them in English.

She surprised him again when she said, ''I love the flowers and plants so much, señor Rosales was telling me I chould perhaps study botany instead of language.''

''Study?'' he said in amazement. ''Where?''

''I am starting college in Se'tember,'' she smiled. ''My teacher at my English class says that my reading of English is good and that I will speak also berry good after I begin to study in college.''

''College!'' he said ''But little girls from Mexico don't come here and go to college. It's wonderful! I'm very glad.''

''Thank joo,'' she smiled. ''I am happy that joo are pleased with me. My teacher says that I may do well even though I have no' too much ed-joocation because I read and write so good in Spanish. My mother was also a berry good reader and had a good ed-joocation before she married my poor father who had none.''

''Is your mother alive?''

''No, not for three years.''

''Your father is?''

''Oh jes, he is a big strong man. Always berry alive. But not so much as before Mamá died. I have ten junger sisters. I will earn money and I will send for them one by one unless they marry before I earn money.''

''You're an ambitious girl.''

''What means this?''

''You have great strength and desire to succeed.''

''It is nothing.''

''So you'll study botany, eh?''

''I will study English and Spanish,'' she said. ''I can be a teacher in perhaps four jeers or a translator in less time working for the courthouse if I work hard. Botany is just a foolish thought. Could joo see me as an edjoocated woman?''

''I can't see you as a woman at all,'' he said, even as he studied her ripe young body. ''You're just a little dove to me.''

''Ah, Sergio,'' she laughed, ''joo get such things from the books. I used to watch joo, before we became friends, when I would serve the food to joo and jour *compañero,* the other policeman. Joo would carry books in the coat pocket and read while eating. There is not a place in the real life for little doves. Joo must be strong and work berry hard. Still, I like to hear joo say that I am a dove.''

''You're only nineteen years old,'' he said.

''A Mexican girl is a woman long before. I am a woman, Sergio.''

They drove again in silence and Serge deeply enjoyed her enjoyment of the passing miles, and vineyards, and towns, which he scarcely noticed.

Mariana was as impressed with the lake as he knew she would be. He rented a motorboat, and for an hour showed her the lakeside Arrowhead homes. He knew she was speechless at such wealth.

''But there are so many!'' she exclaimed. ''There must be so many rich ones.''

''They're many,'' he said. ''And I'll never be one of them.''

"But that is not important," she said, leaning an inch closer to him as he steered the boat out into open water. The bright sunlight reflecting off the water hurt his eyes and he put his sunglasses on. She looked a deeper bronze, and the wind caught her deep brown hair and swept it back at least twelve inches from the nape of her exposed neck. It was four o'clock and the sun was still hot when they finished the lunch on a rocky hill on the far side of the lake which Serge had discovered another time with another girl who liked picnics and making love in open places.

"I thought you were bringing Mexican food," said Serge, finishing his fifth piece of tender chicken and washing it down with strawberry soda which was kept chilled by a plastic bucket of ice in the bottom of the shopping bag.

"I heard that Americans take *pollo frito* on a picnic," she laughed. "I was told that all Americans expected it."

"It's delicious," he sighed, thinking he hadn't had strawberry soda lately. He wondered again why strawberry is by far the favorite flavor of Mexicans, and any Good Humor man in East Los Angeles carries an extra box of strawberry sundaes and Popsicles.

"Señora Rosales wanted me to bring *chicharrones* and beer for joo, but I didn't, because I thought joo would like the other better."

"I loved your lunch, Mariana," he smiled, wondering how long it had been since he tasted the rich crispy pork rinds. Then he realized he had never tasted *chicharrones* with beer because when his mother made them he was too young to drink beer. He found himself suddenly yearning for some *chicharrones* and a cold glass of beer. You always want what you don't have at the moment, he thought.

He watched Mariana as she cleaned up the picnic things, putting the paper plates in an extra shopping bag she brought. In a few minutes he would not have known anyone had eaten there. She was a totally efficient girl, he thought, and she looked dazzling in the red dress and black sandals. She had lovely toes and feet, brown and smooth like the rest of her. He got a sharp pain in the lower part of his chest as he thought about the rest of her and remembered the vow of abstinence he had made to the person he was growing to respect the least in all the world.

When she finished she sat next to him and drew her knees up and put her hands on her knees and her chin on her hands.

"Joo want to know something?" she asked gazing at the water.

"What?"

"I never have seen a lake. Not here. Not in Mexico. Only in movies. This is my first real lake to see."

"Do you like it?" he asked, feeling his palms become a little moist. The pain returned to his chest as his mouth turned dry.

"Joo have given me a fine day, Sergio," she said looking at him with heaviness in her voice.

"So you've enjoyed it?"

"Jas."

"Not jas," he laughed. "Yes."

"Jes," she smiled.

"Like this. Y-y-yes. Here, put your chin forward just a little bit." He held her chin in his fingers and tugged lightly. But her whole face came forward to him.

"Yes," he said, and his fingers trembled. "I told you I'd teach you to say yes."

"Yes," she said.

"You said it."

"Yes, Sergio, oh, yes, yes," she breathed.

"Fly away, little dove," he said not knowing the strange hollow voice. "Please fly away," he said, and yet he held her shoulders fearing she would.

"Yes, Sergio, yes."

"You're making a mistake, little dove," he whispered, but her lip touched his cheek.

''I say yes, Sergio. For you, yes. *Para tí,* yes, yes.''

17

Kiddy Cops

Lucy was merely attractive, but her eyes were alert and missed nothing and devoured you when you were talking to her. Yet you were never uncomfortable because of it. Instead, you succumbed to being devoured and you liked it. Yes, you liked it. Gus took his gaze from the road and examined her long legs, crossed at the ankle, hose sheer, pale and subtle. She sat relaxed much like a male partner and smoked and watched the street as Gus cruised, much like a male partner would, but it was nothing like working with a male partner. With some of the other policewomen there was no difference, except you had to be more careful and not get involved in things where there was the slightest element of danger. Not if you could help it, because a policewoman was still a woman, nothing more, and you were responsible for her safety, being the male half of the team. With some policewoman partners it was almost like being with a man, but not with Lucy. Gus wondered why he liked being devoured by those brown eyes which crinkled at the corners. He was normally shriveled by eyes which looked too hard.

''Think you're going to stay with police work, Lucy?'' asked Gus, turning on Main Street thinking she would probably enjoy touring the skid row streets. Most new policewomen did.

''I love it, Gus,'' she said. ''It's a fascinating job. Especially here in Juvenile Division. I don't think working the women's jail would've been nearly as good.''

''I don't think so either. I can't picture you in there pushing those bull daggers around.''

''I can't either,'' she grimaced, ''but I guess sooner or later I'll get assigned there.''

''Maybe not,'' said Gus. ''You're a good juvenile officer, you know. For just being a few weeks out of the academy I'd say you're exceptional. They may keep you in Juvenile.''

''Oh sure, I'm indispensable,'' she laughed.

''You're smart and quick and you're the first policewoman I ever enjoyed working with. Most policemen don't like working with women.'' He pretended to watch the road very closely as he said it because he felt the brown eyes. He hadn't meant to say this. It was only 7:00 P.M., not dark yet, and he didn't want to blush and let her see it. But then, she would probably even see it in the dark with those eyes.

''That's a fine compliment, Gus,'' said Lucy. ''You've been a patient teacher.''

''Oh, I don't know it all myself yet,'' said Gus, working hard at not blushing by thinking of other things as he talked, like where they would eat, and that they should walk through the Main Street bus depot and look for runaway juveniles because Sunday night was a slow night, or maybe they should cruise through Elysian Park and look for the kids who would surely be there on a Sunday drinking beer on the grass. Lieutenant Dilford loved them to make arrests for minors' possession of alcohol and Dilford treated it like patrol watch commanders treated good felony arrests.

''You've been working Juvenile about six months, haven't you?'' asked Lucy.

''About five months now. I've still got lots to learn.''

''Where did you work before that, Central Vice?''

"Wilshire Vice."

"I can't picture you as a vice officer," she laughed. "When I worked Lincoln Heights Jail on weekend assignments, the vice officers would be in and out all night. I can't picture you as a vice officer."

"I know. I don't look man enough to be a vice officer, do I?"

"Oh, I didn't mean that, Gus," she said, uncrossing her ankles and drilling him with her brown eyes. When they were working they darkened her face which was smooth and milky. "I didn't mean that at all. In fact, I didn't like them because they were loud and talked to policewomen like they talked to their whores. I didn't think all that bravado made them more manly. I think that being quiet and gentle and having some humility is very manly, but I didn't see many vice officers like that."

"Well, they have to construct some kind of defense against all the sordid things they see," said Gus, elated because she as much as admitted that she was fond of him and saw things in him. Then he became disgusted and thought viciously, you simpering little bastard. He thought of Vickie who was recovering from an appendectomy and he hoped she would sleep tonight, and he swore that he would stop this childish flirtation before it went any further because Lucy would soon see it even though she was not a self-conscious person and did not notice such things. But when she did, finally, she would probably say, that's not what I meant, that's not what I meant at all. Simpering little bastard, he thought again, and peeked in the rearview mirror at his sandy receding hair which was hardly noticeable. In a few years he would be completely bald and he wondered if he would still be dreaming of a bright, pale, brown-eyed girl who would smile in pity or perhaps revulsion if she knew the thoughts he had about her.

"What time should we check out the unfit home?" asked Lucy, and Gus was glad she had changed the subject. He couldn't help smiling at the man walking up Hill Street who turned his head to look at Lucy as they passed. He remembered how men used to turn like that to look at Vickie when they were first married, before she got so heavy. He thought of how he and Lucy must look, two young people, he in a suit and tie and white shirt and her in a modest green dress which fit so well. They might be going to dinner, or to the Bowl for a concert, or to the Sports Arena. Of course, all the street people recognized the plain four-door Plymouth as a police car, and knew the man and woman were juvenile officers, but to anyone else they might just be lovers.

"What time, Gus?"

"It's twenty after seven."

"No," she laughed. "What time do we check out the unfit home the lieutenant mentioned?'

"Oh, let's do it now. Sorry, I was dreaming."

"How's your wife recovering from her appendectomy?" asked Lucy. Gus hated to talk about Vickie to her, but she always asked things about his family as partners did, often in the early morning hours when things were quiet and partners talked.

"She's getting along all right."

"How's your little one? He's talking, isn't he?"

"Chattering," Gus smiled, and he never hesitated to talk about his children to her because she wanted to hear, he was sure of it.

"They look so beautiful in the pictures. I'd love to see them some time."

"I'd like you to," said Gus.

"I hope it's quiet tonight."

"Why? The night passes slow when it's quiet."

"Yes, but I can get you talking then," she laughed. "I learn more about being a cop in the late hours when I get you talking."

"You mean when I tell you all the things Kilvinsky taught me?" he smiled.

"Yes, but I bet you're a better teacher than your friend Kilvinsky was."

"Oh, no. Kilvinsky was the best," said Gus, his face burning again. "That reminds me, I've got to write him. He hasn't been answering my letters lately and I'm worried. Ever since he took the trip East to see his ex-wife and children."

"Are you sure he came back?"

"Yes. I got one letter right after he came back, but it didn't say anything."

"Isn't it strange that he never visited his own children before that?"

"He must've had a reason," said Gus.

"I don't think you could abandon your children like that."

"He didn't abandon them," said Gus quickly. "Kilvinsky wouldn't do that. He's just a mysterious man, that's all. He must've had good reasons."

"If your wife ever left you, you wouldn't abandon your children, Gus, not you. Not for any reason."

"Well, I can't judge him," said Gus, glad darkness was settling on downtown as he stopped for a light.

"He's not the father you are, I bet," said Lucy and she was watching him again.

"Oh, you're wrong," said Gus. "Kilvinsky would be a good father. He'd be as good a father as anyone could want. He could tell you things, and when he talked you knew he was right. Things seemed all in place when he explained them."

"It's getting dark."

"Let's go handle the unfit home," said Gus, growing uneasy at the deprecating talk about Kilvinsky.

"Okay, it was on West Temple, wasn't it?"

"It might be a phony call."

"Anonymous?"

"Yeah, a woman called the watch commander and said a neighbor in apartment twenty-three had a cruddy pad and left a little kid alone all the time."

"I haven't been in a real unfit home yet," said Lucy. "They've all turned out to be false alarms."

"Remember how to tell a real unfit?" smiled Gus.

"Sure. If you stomp your foot and the roaches are so tame they don't run, then you know it's a real unfit."

"Right," Gus grinned. "And if we could bottle the smell we'd win every case in court."

Gus drove through the Second Street tunnel and over the Harbor Freeway and turned north, then west on Temple, the setting sun glowing dirty pink on the horizon. It had been a smoggy day.

"I bet it's the white apartment building," said Lucy pointing toward the three-story stucco with an imitation stone facade.

"Eighteen thirteen. That's it," said Gus parking in front and wondering if he had enough money to buy a decent dinner tonight. With anyone else he ate hamburgers or brown bagged it, but Lucy ate well and liked a hot dinner. He went along with her, pretending this was what he wanted too, even though he had less than five dollars to last until payday, and less than a half tank of gas in his car. Monday night he had an argument with Vickie over the check to his mother which had shrunk to forty-five dollars a month because John was in the army, thank God.

The argument was so violent it made him sick. Lucy had noticed his depression the next evening. And now he thought of how he had blurted it out to Lucy that night, and how kind she had been and how ashamed he had been and still was that he had told her. Yet it had lifted his spirits. And come to think of it, she hadn't asked to eat in a real restaurant since that night, and she had insisted on buying the coffee or Cokes more often than she should.

It was built to wear only for a time, like so many southern California apartment houses. Gus parked in front and they climbed the twenty-four steps to the second floor. Gus noticed that the metal railing, which only vaguely resembled wrought iron, was loose. He drew his hand back and guessed that someday a drunk would stagger from his apartment door and hit the railing and plunge twenty feet to the concrete below, but being drunk, he would probably receive only abrasions. Apartment twenty-three was in the back. The drapes were drawn and the door was closed, and this alone made Gus suspect there was no one home, because in all the other occupied apartments the doors were open. All had outside screen doors and the people were trying to catch the evening breeze because it had been a hot smoggy day.

Gus knocked and rang the tinny chime and knocked again. Finally, Lucy shrugged and they turned to go and Gus was glad because he didn't feel like working; he felt like driving through Elysian Park pretending to look for juvenile drinkers and just look at Lucy and talk to her perhaps on the upper road on the east side near the reservoir which looked like black ice in the moonlight.

"You the cops?" whispered a woman who suddenly appeared inside the dusty screen door of apartment number twenty-one.

"Yes. Did you call?" asked Gus.

"I'm the one," said the woman. "I called but I said I didn't want nobody to know I called. They aren't home now, but the kid's in there."

"What seems to be the problem?" asked Gus.

"Well, come on in. It looks like I'm going to get involved anyway," she muttered holding the screen and licking the absurdly made-up lips which were drawn on halfway to her nose. In fact, all her makeup had a theatrical exaggeration designed for an audience that must be far far away.

"I talked to some Lieutenant Whatzizname and told him that place isn't fit for pigs most of the time and the kid gets left alone and I never see him outside hardly. Last night he was screaming and screaming and I think the old man was beating him 'cause the old lady was screaming too."

"Do you know the people in that apartment?" asked Gus.

"Lord, no. They're trash," said the woman, uncoiling a wiry wisp of blond hair with gray roots. "They only been living here a month and they go out almost every night and sometimes they have a babysitter, a cousin or something, staying with their kid. And sometimes they got nobody staying with him. I learned long time ago to mind my own business but today it was so damn hot they had the door open and I happened to walk by and the place looks like a slit trench and I know what a slit trench is because I like war novels. There was dog crap from this dirty little terrier they got, and food and other crud all over the floor and then when they left the kid today I just said what the hell, I'll call and remain anonymous but now it looks like I can't be anonymous, huh?"

"How old is the child?" asked Gus.

"Three. A little boy. He hardly never comes outside. The old man's a souse. The mother seems okay. Just a dirty little mouse, you know what I mean. A souse and a mouse. I think the old man pushes her around when he's drunk, but it don't matter much to her probably, because she's usually drunk when he is. Fine neighbors. This place had class a few years ago. I'm moving."

"How old are they? The parents?"

"Young people. Not thirty I don't think. Dirty people though."

"You sure the little boy's in there alone? Right now?"

"I saw them leave, Officer. I'm sure. He's in there. He's a quiet little guy. Never hear a peep out of him. He's in there."

"What apartment is the landlady in? We'll need a passkey."

"Martha went to the movies tonight. She told me she was going. I never thought about the key." The woman shook her head and tugged at the frayed waistband of the olive stretch pants that were never meant to be stretched so much.

"We can't just break the door down on this information."

"Why not? The kid's only three and he's in there alone."

"No," said Gus, shaking his head. "He could be in there and maybe they took him when you weren't looking. Maybe a lot of things. We'll just have to come back later when they're home and try to get invited inside to take a look around."

"Goddamn," said the woman. "The one time in my life I call a cop and try to do a decent thing and look what happens."

"Let me go try the door," said Gus. "Maybe it's open."

"The one time I call the cops," said the woman to Lucy as Gus stepped outside and walked down the walkway to number twenty-three. He opened the screen and turned the knob and the door slid open.

"Lucy," he called, and stepped inside the stifling apartment, looking carefully for the "dirty little terrier" that might suddenly grab him by the ankle. He stepped around a moist stinking brown heap in the center of the floor and decided the dog must be large for a terrier. Then he heard the pat pat on the vinyl tile floor and the gaunt gray dog appeared from the bathroom, looked at Gus, wagged his stumpy tail, yawned, and returned to the bathroom. Gus glanced in the empty bedroom and pointed to the pile in the floor when Lucy entered and she walked around it and followed him into the living room.

"Dirty people," said the woman, who had followed Lucy inside.

"This certainly isn't bad by unfit home standards," explained Gus. "It has to be really dangerous. Broken windows, leaky stove. Clothes hanging over an open flame. Knee-deep in defecation, not just a pile in the floor. And garbage laying around. Clogged toilet. I've seen places where the wall seems to move and then you realize that it's a solid sheet of roaches. This isn't bad. And there's no child in that bedroom."

"He's here I tell you!"

"Look for yourself," said Gus, and stood aside as the woman bounced into the bedroom. Her cheeks shook with every step, she walked so heavily.

It was now quite dark and Lucy switched on the hall light and walked toward the small bathroom.

"He's got to be here," said the woman. "I watched them leave."

"Gus!" said Lucy, and he came to the bathroom door as she switched on the light and he saw the little boy on the floor by the bathtub curled up with the dog on a pile of bath towels. The boy was asleep and even before Lucy turned on the light Gus saw the absurd purple rings around his eyes and the swollen mouth cracked and raw from a recent beating. The boy slobbered and wheezed and Gus guessed the nose was broken. The coagulation had the nostrils blocked and Gus saw the way the hand was bent.

"Dirty people," whispered the woman, and then began crying at once, and Lucy took her out without Gus saying anything. Lucy was back in a moment and neither of them spoke as Lucy lifted him in her arms and took him to the bedroom where he didn't awaken until she had him dressed. Gus marveled at her strength and how she gently managed the broken wrist and never woke him until they were starting out of the apartment.

The boy saw Gus first when he awoke and the swollen eyes stared for a second and then through pain or terror the fearful moaning started which never ceased for the hour they were with the boy.

"We'll be back," said Gus to the woman who stood sobbing in the doorway of her apartment. Gus tried to take the boy when they started down the stairway, but when he touched the boy he recoiled and uttered a shriek. Lucy said, "It's okay, Gus, he's afraid of you. There, there, darling." And she patted him as Gus shined his light on the stairway for her. In a few moments they were driving to Central Receiving Hospital and each time Gus got too near the little boy, the moan became a terrible cry so he let Lucy handle him.

"He doesn't even look three years old," said Gus when they parked in the hospital parking lot. "He's so little."

Gus waited in the hallway while they worked on the boy and when a second doctor was called in to look at the arm, Gus peered through the door and saw the first doctor, a floppy-haired young man, nod to the second doctor and point to the little boy whose battered face, green and blue and purple in the naked light, looked as though it had been painted by a surrealist gone mad. "Dig the crazy clownface," said the first doctor with a bitter smile.

Lucy came out in fifteen minutes and said, "Gus, his rectum was stitched up!"

"His rectum?"

"It had been stitched up! Oh Christ, Gus, I know it's usually the father in these sex things, but Christ, I can't believe it."

"Was it a professional stitching job?"

"Yes. A doctor did it. Why wouldn't the doctor notify the police? Why?"

"There are doctors," said Gus.

"He's afraid of men, Gus. He was just as much afraid of the doctor as he was of you. The nurse and I had to pet him and talk to him so the doctor could get near him." Lucy looked for a moment like she would cry but instead she lit a cigarette and walked with Gus to the phone and waited until he phoned the watch commander.

"He's a bright child," said Lucy, as Gus waited for the lieutenant to come to the phone. "When the nurse asked him who did that to his rectum, he said, 'Daddy did it 'cause I'm a bad boy.' Oh Christ, Gus . . ."

It was eleven o'clock before they completed their reports on the boy who was admitted to General Hospital. The parents hadn't returned home yet and Lieutenant Dilford had another team staked out on the apartment. Gus and Lucy resumed patrol.

"There's no sense thinking about it," said Gus when Lucy was silent for a half hour.

"I know," she said, forcing a smile and Gus thought of her comforting the child and thought how beautiful she had looked then.

"My gosh, it's almost eleven," said Gus. "You hungry?"

"No."

"But can you eat?"

"You eat. I'll have coffee."

"Let's both have coffee," said Gus, driving to a restaurant on Sunset Boulevard where there were booths for two and anyone who noticed them would think they were lovers or perhaps a young married couple. Gus thought of how he was wrinkling at the corners of his mouth much like his mother. He smiled, because on second thought no one would believe he was a *young* lover.

When they were seated in the booth in the bright spacious restaurant Gus noticed the rusty smear on the shoulder of her dress and he thought again of how she had been with the child, of how strong she was in every way and how capable. He wondered what it would be like to live your life with someone whom you did not have to take care of and he wondered what it would be like to have someone take care of you occasionally, or at least pretend to. The anger started to build when he thought of Vickie and his mother and at least the army could take care of his brother for a few years. Gus vowed that if his mother let John freeload off her when he returned from the service that she would do it on her county check because he would refuse to give her another cent. As soon as he thought this he knew it was a lie because he too was basically a weakling, his only strength being that he could earn a living. When it came down to it he would go on giving them money because he was too much of a weakling to do otherwise. How much easier would life be, he wondered, being married to a strong girl like Lucy.

"You've got blood on your dress," said Gus, nodding to the smear on her shoulder and he was immediately sorry he said it because he should be trying to cheer her up.

"I don't care," she said, not bothering to look at it, and something had been building up in him. At that moment he almost blurted something. If those steady eyes had been on him instead of on the table he probably would have blurted it but he didn't, and was glad he didn't, because she probably would have looked at him sadly and said, "But that's not what I meant at all."

Gus noticed the three teen-age girls in the large booth across from them gossiping in shrill voices and smoking compulsively as they tried in vain to handle the two little boys who kept slipping unnoticed to the floor and scampering down the aisle between the booths.

One of the girls with a proud bulging belly smiled often at the children of her adolescent girl friends, who had no doubt long since found the mystery of motherhood to be quite different from what had been anticipated. All three girls had ugly hairdos, high, teased, and bleached, and Gus thought that Vickie had been a mother that young. Then the guilt, which he knew was foolish, began to come again, but he forgot it when one of the young mothers grabbed the red-haired tot and cracked him across the face as she whispered, "Sit down and behave you little son of a bitch."

Their coffee was half drunk when Lucy said, "Have you been thinking about the little boy, Gus?"

"Not at all," said Gus.

"Isn't it hard not to?"

"No it's not. Not after you get the hang of it. And you should learn that as soon as you can, Lucy."

"What should I think about?"

"Your own problems. That's what I've been doing. Worrying about my own petty problems."

"Tell me about *your* problems, Gus," said Lucy. "Give me something else to worry about."

"Well, we haven't made a juvenile arrest for three days. The boss is going to be getting on us. That's something to worry about."

"Do you *really* like juvenile work, Gus? I mean all things considered do you like being a kiddy cop?"

"I do, Lucy. It's not easy to explain, but it's like, well, especially with the little ones, I like the job because *we* protect them. Take the boy tonight. His father will be arrested and maybe the D.A. will be able to show that he did those things to the boy and maybe he won't. The boy will be a very bad witness or I miss my guess. Maybe the mother will tell the truth, but that's doubtful. And by the time the lawyers, headshrinkers, and criminologists have their say, nothing much will happen to him. But at least we got the boy out of there. I'm sure juvenile court won't give him back to them. Maybe we've saved his life. I like to think that we protect the children. To tell you the truth, if the door'd been locked I would've broken it down. I'd just about made up my mind. We're the only ones who can save the little kids from their parents."

"Wouldn't you like to take a man like that and make him confess?" said Lucy, smashing her cigarette butt in the ashtray.

"I used to think I could torture the truth out of people," Gus smiled, "but after I was a policeman for a while and saw and arrested some of the really bad ones, I found that I didn't even want to touch them or be with them. I'd never make the grade in a medieval dungeon."

"I had a very proper and square upbringing," said Lucy, sipping her coffee as Gus stared at a place on her white collarbone where the brown hair touched it and caressed it when she moved her head even slightly. He was disgusted because his heart was racing and his hands were clammy. So he stopped staring at that tender patch of flesh. "My dad teaches high school, like I told you, and Mother would have trouble believing that a parent would even let his child go around without freshly washed drawers. They're good people, you know? How can good people conceive of the existence of really bad people? I was going to be a social worker until I found what L.A.P.D. was paying policewomen. How could I ever be a social worker now that I've caught the scent of evil? People aren't basically good after all, are they?''

''But maybe they're not bad, either.''

''But they're not good, damn it. All my professors told me they were good! And people lie. God, how they lie. I can't get over how people lie.''

''That was the single most difficult thing for me to learn,'' Gus said. ''I believed people for my first year or so on the job. No matter what anybody said. I wouldn't even listen to Kilvinsky. All my life I beieved what people told me was the truth, and I was a lousy policeman until I got over that mistake. Now I know they'll lie when the truth would help. They'll lie when their lives depend on the truth.''

''What a rotten way to make a living,'' said Lucy.

''Not for a man. For a woman, maybe. But you'll find someone and get married. You won't be doing this all your life.'' Gus avoided her eyes when he said it.

''I'll be sure not to marry a policeman. That would mean I couldn't escape it.''

''Cops are terrible husbands anyway,'' Gus smiled. ''Divorce rate is sky high.''

''You're a cop and you're not a terrible husband.''

''How do you know?'' he said, and then was caught and trapped by the brown eyes.

''I know you. Better than I've ever known anyone.''

''Well,'' said Gus, ''I don't know . . . well . . .'' and then he gave up and succumbed to the unblinking eyes, a happy gray rabbit surrendering to the benevolent lethal embrace of the fox and he decided that wherever the conversation went from here he would go with it willingly. Now his heart hammered joyfully.

''You're a good policeman,'' she said. ''You know how things are and yet you're gentle and compassionate, especially with kids. That's a rare thing you know. How can you know what people are and still treat them like they were good?''

''People are weak. I guess I'm resigned to handling weak people. I guess I know them because I'm so weak myself.''

''You're the strongest man I've ever known, and the gentlest.''

''Lucy, I want to buy you a drink after work tonight. We'll just have time for one before the bars close. Will you stop at Marty's Lounge with me?''

''I don't think so.''

''Oh, I don't mean anything by it,'' said Gus, cursing himself for saying such a silly thing, because he meant everything by it and of course she knew he meant everything by it.

''This will be our last night together,'' said Lucy.

''What do you mean?''

''The lieutenant asked me tonight if I'd like to be loaned to Harbor Juvenile starting tomorrow and if it worked out maybe it could be permanent. I told him I'd like to think about it. I've decided.''

''But that's too far to drive! You live in Glendale.''

''I'm a single girl who lives in an apartment. I can move.''

''But you like police work! The Harbor will be too dull. You'll miss the action you get around here.''

''Was it terrible growing up without a father, Gus?'' she asked suddenly.

''Yes, but . . .''

''Could you ever do that to your children?''

''What?''

''Could you ever make them grow up without a father, or with a weekend father, twice a month?''

He wanted to say "yes" to the eyes that he knew wanted him to say "yes," but he faltered. He often thought later that if he hadn't faltered he might have said "yes," and where would things have gone if he had merely said "yes." But he did not say "yes," he said nothing for several seconds, and her mouth smiled and she said, "Of course you couldn't. And that's the kind of man I want to marry me and give me babies. I should've found you about three kids ago. Now how about taking me to the station? I'm going to ask the lieutenant if I can go home. I have a rotten headache."

There must be something he could say but the more he thought, the less sense all this made. His brain was whirling when he parked in the station lot and while Lucy was putting her things away he decided that now, this moment, he would meet her in the parking lot at her car and he would tell her something. They would work out something because if he didn't do it now, right now, he never would. And his very life, no, his soul was on the line.

"Oh, Plebesly," said Lieutenant Dilford, stepping out of his office and beckoning to Gus.

"Yes, sir?" said Gus, entering the watch commander's office.

"Sit down for a second, Gus. I've got some bad news for you. Your wife called."

"What happened?" asked Gus, leaping to his feet. "The kids? Did something happen?"

"No, no. Your wife and kids are okay. Sit down, Gus."

"My mother?" asked Gus, ashamed at his relief that it was his mother, not his children.

"It's your friend Andy Kilvinsky, Gus. I knew him well when I worked University years ago. Your wife said that she was called tonight by a lawyer up in Oregon. Kilvinsky left you a few thousand dollars. He's dead, Gus. He shot himself."

Gus heard the lieutenant's voice droning monotonously for several seconds before he got up and walked to the front door, and the lieutenant was nodding and saying something as though he approved. But Gus did not know what he was saying as he walked weak-legged down the stairway to his car in the parking lot. He was out of the parking lot and on his way home before he started to cry and he thought of Kilvinsky and cried for him. His head bent in anguish and he thought incoherently of the little boy tonight and of all fatherless children. He could no longer see the road. Then he thought of himself and his grief and shame and anger. The tears came like lava. He pulled to the curb and the tears scalded him and his body was convulsed by shuddering sobs for all the silent misery of life. He no longer knew for whom he wept and he was past caring. He wept alone.

18

The Huckster

"I'm sure glad they sent me to Seventy-seventh Street," said Dugan, the ruddy-faced little rookie who had been Roy's partner for a week. "I've learned a hell of a lot from working a Negro division. And I've had good partners breaking me in."

"Seventy-seventh Street is as good a place to work as any," said Roy, thinking how glad he'd be when the sun dropped below the elevated Harbor freeway. The streets would begin to cool and the uniform would become bearable.

"You been here quite a while now, haven't you, Roy?"

"About fifteen months. You're busy in this division. There's always something happening so you're busy. There's no time to sit and think, and time passes. That's why I like it."

"You ever work in a white division?"

"Central," Roy nodded.

"Is it the same as a black division?"

"It's slower. Not as much crime so it's slower. Time passes slower. But it's the same. People are all murderous bastards, they're just a little darker down here."

"How long have you been back to work, Roy? If you don't mind talking about it. As soon as I transferred in, I heard right away about how you were shot. Not many guys have ever survived a shotgun blast in the stomach. I guess."

"Not many."

"I guess you hate to talk about it."

"I don't hate to but I'm tired talking about it. I talked about it for the past five months when I was working light duty on the desk. I told the story a thousand times to every curious policeman who wanted to see how I screwed up and got myself shot like that. I'm just tired telling it. You don't mind."

"Oh, hell no, Roy. I understand completely. You *are* feeling okay, now, aren't you. I mean I'll be glad to drive *and* keep books any night you want to take it easy."

"I'm okay, Dugan," Roy laughed. "I played three hard games of handball last week. I'm doing fine, physically."

"I figure I'm lucky to have an experienced partner who's been around and done everything. But I ask too many questions sometimes. I have a big Irish mouth that I can't control sometimes."

"Okay, partner," Roy smiled.

"Anytime you want me to shut up just say the word."

"Okay, partner."

"Twelve-A-Nine, Twelve-A-Nine, see the woman, four five nine report, eighty-three twenty-nine south Vermont, apartment B as in boy."

"Twelve-A-Nine, roger," said Dugan, and Roy turned into the orange and purple smog-streaked sunset and drove leisurely to the call.

"I used to think most burglaries happened at night," said Dugan. "When I was a civilian, I mean. I guess the biggest portion happen during the day when people aren't home."

"That's right," said Roy.

"Most burglars wouldn't go in an occupied pad at night, would they?"

"Too dangerous," said Roy, lighting a cigarette, which tasted better than the last, now that it was cooling off.

"I'd sure like to nail a good burglar one of these nights. Maybe we'll get one tonight."

"Maybe," Roy answered, turning south on Vermont Avenue from Florence.

"I'm going to continue my education," said Dugan. "I picked up a few units since getting out of the navy but now I'm going to get serious and go after a degree in police science. You going to school, Roy?"

"No."

"You ever go?"

"I used to."

"Got quite a ways to go for your degree?"

"Twenty units maybe."

"Is that all? That's terrific. You going to sign up this semester?"

"Too late."

"You *are* going to finish?"

"Of course I am," said Roy and his stomach began to burn from a sudden wave of indigestion and a shudder of nausea followed. Indigestion brought nausea now.

His stomach would never be reliable again he supposed, and this bright-eyed rookie was upsetting his stomach with his prying, and his exasperating innocence.

That would change, Roy thought. Not abruptly, but gradually. Life would steal his innocence a bit at a time like an owl steals chicks until the nest is empty and awesome in its loneliness.

''That looks like the pad, partner,'' said Dugan, putting on his cap and opening the door before Roy stopped the car.

''Wait'll I stop, Dugan,'' said Roy. ''I don't want you breaking a leg. This is only a report call.''

''Oh, sorry,'' Dugan smiled, reddening.

It was an upstairs apartment at the rear. Dugan tapped on the door lightly with the butt of his flashlight as Roy usually did, and as he probably had seen Roy do. Roy also noticed that Dugan had switched to Roy's brand of cigarettes and had bought a new three-cell, big-headed flashlight like Roy's even though his five-cell was only a few weeks old. I always wanted a son, Roy thought, sardonically, as he watched Dugan knock and step carefully to the side of the door as Roy had taught him to do on any call no matter how routine, at any time. And he always had his right hand free, carrying the report notebook and the flashlight in the left. He kept his hat on when they entered a house until they were absolutely sure what they had and only then did they sit down and remove the hats and relax. But Roy never relaxed anymore even when he wanted to relax, even as he concentrated on relaxation, because he must if his stomach would ever heal. He could not afford an ulcer now, could never afford one. He wanted so to relax. But now Dorothy was hounding him to let her new fat middle-aged husband adopt Becky. He had told her he'd see them both dead first and Dorothy had been trying to reach him through his mother whom Dorothy had always found an intercessor. And he was thinking of Becky and how she said ''Daddy'' and how incredibly beautiful and golden she was. The apartment door was opened by a girl who was not beautiful and golden but Roy thought immediately that she was attractive. She was dark-brown-skinned, too dark he thought, even though her eyes were light brown and flecked with black specks that reminded him of the flecks in his daughter's eyes. Roy guessed she was his age or older and he thought the natural African hairdo was attractive on black women even though he despised it on the men. At least she didn't go in for dangling bone or iron earrings and other pretentious Africana. Just the hairdo. That was alright, he thought. It was natural.

She waved them in and pointed carelessly to the ransacked apartment. Roy saw that the molding had been pried from the door with a quarter-inch screwdriver which was then used to easily shim the door.

''These wafer locks aren't worth anything,'' said Roy, touching the lock with his flashlight.

''Now you tell me,'' she smiled and shook her head sadly. ''They cleaned me out. They really did.''

She was surprisingly tall, he noticed, as she stood next to him, not having to tilt her face very much to look in his eyes. He guessed she was five feet nine. And she was shapely.

''Did you touch anything?'' asked Dugan.

''No.''

''Let's see if we can find some nice smooth items that prints can be lifted from,'' said Dugan, putting his notebook down and prowling around the apartment.

''This happened while you were at work?'' asked Roy, sitting on a high stool at the kitchen bar.

''Yes.''

''Where do you work?''

''I'm a dental technician. I work downtown.''

''Live alone?''

"Yes."

"What all is missing?"

"Color TV set. A wristwatch, Polaroid camera. Clothes. Just about everything I own that's worth a damn."

"That's a shame," said Roy, thinking that she was *very* shapely and thinking that he had never tried a black woman and had not tried any woman since recovering from the wound, except for Velma, the overweight beautician whom he had met through his mother's neighbor Mrs. Smedley. Velma hadn't been interesting enough to attract him more than once every two or three weeks and he wondered if the buckshot hadn't done something to diminish his sex drive, and if it did, what the hell, it would be natural for him to lose the full appreciation of one of the few pleasures life seemed to hold for every poor son of a bitch it finally murdered.

"Is there much of a chance of getting the TV back?" she asked.

"Do you know the serial number?"

"Afraid not," she said.

"Not too much chance then."

"Do most burglaries go unsolved?"

"In a way they do. I mean they're not officially cleared. The stolen property is never recovered because burglars sell it real fast to fences or in pawnshops or just to no-questions-asked-people they meet on the street. The burglars usually get caught sooner or later and sometimes the detectives know they're good for lots and lots of jobs, maybe dozens or hundreds, but they usually don't get the property back."

"So the guilty get caught sooner or later, but it doesn't help their victims, is that it?"

"That's about it."

"Bastards," she whispered.

Why doesn't she move, Roy thought. Why doesn't she move farther west to the periphery of the black district. Even if she can't get completely away from it she could move to the salt and pepper periphery where there's less crime. But what the hell, he thought. Some white burglar with a kink would probably strangle her in her bed some night. You can't get away from evil. It leaps all barriers, racial or otherwise.

"It'll take a long time to replace all your losses," said Roy.

"You bet," she said, turning away because there were tears glistening, dampening the heavy fringe of real eyelash. "Want some coffee?"

"Sure," said Roy, glad that Dugan was still rummaging in the bedroom. As he watched her going from the stove to a cupboard he thought: maybe I could go for a little of that. Maybe all of the simple animal pleasures aren't gone for me.

"I'm going to fortify my coffee," she said, handing him a gold-rimmed cup and saucer, cream pitcher, and sugar bowl. She returned to the cupboard, brought out a fifth of unopened Canadian bourbon, cracked the seal, and poured a liberal shot into the coffee.

"I never drink alone," she said, "but tonight I think I'll get loaded. I feel rotten!"

Roy's eyes roved from the girl to the bottle and back and then to the bottle and he told himself that he was not in any danger yet. He only drank because he enjoyed it, because he needed to relax and if the drinking was not good for his stomach, the therapeutic value of a whiskey tranquilizer more than made up for its ill effects. At least he was not interested in drugs. It could have happened in the hospital. It happened to lots of people with long-term painful injuries who were kept on medication. He could get through his shift without a drink, he knew. But he wasn't harming anyone. A few ounces of whiskey always sharpened his wits and not a partner had ever suspected, least of all not little Dugan.

"If I weren't on duty, I'd join you," said Roy.

"Too bad," she said, not looking at him as she took a sip, grimaced, and took a larger one.

"If I were off duty I wouldn't let you drink alone," he said, and watched the glance she gave him and then she turned away and sipped the coffee again and did not answer.

"Might as well get the report started," said Dugan, coming back into the living room. "There's a jewelry box and a few other things in there that might have latent fingerprints on them. I've stacked them in the corner. The print man will be out tonight or tomorrow to dust the dresser and those items."

"I won't be here tomorrow. I work during the day."

"Maybe he can come tonight if he's not too busy," said Dugan.

"He'll come tonight. I'll make sure. I'll tell him you're a special friend of mine," said Roy, and she looked at him again and he saw no sign.

"Well, might as well get started on this report, ma'am," said Dugan. "Can I have your name?"

"Laura Hunt," she said, and this time Roy thought he saw in her eyes a sign.

As they were driving back to the station, Roy began to get jittery. It was not happening as often lately, he told himself. It was not nearly as bad now that he was back in the radio car. Those months of working the desk had been bad, though. He had periodic pain and his nerves were bothering him. He kept a bottle in the trunk of his car and made frequent trips to the parking lot. He worried that Lieutenant Crow, the watch commander, suspected something, but he had never been questioned. He never overdid it. He only drank enough to relax or to assuage the pain or to fight the depression. Only two times did he overdo it, unable to complete his tour of duty. He feigned sickness on those occasions, an attack of nausea he had said, and had gone to the lonely apartment, being careful to keep the speedometer needle pegged at thirty-five miles an hour and concentrating on the elusive white line in the highway. It was much better now that he was in the radio car again. Everything was better. And being back in the old apartment was good for him.

The months of living with his parents had been as damaging to his emotions as anything else. And Carl—with his fat little children and his impeccable wife Marjorie and his new car and his goddamn belly hanging over his belt even though he wasn't thirty years old—Carl was unbearable: "We can still find a spot for you, Roy. Of course, you couldn't expect to start as an *equal* partner, but eventually . . . after all, it *is* the family business and you *are* my brother . . . I always thought you could be a businessman if you just made up your mind to grow up and now I hope your brush with death has made you come to your senses and realize where you belong and abandon your whims you remember Roy when I was a child I wanted to be a policeman too and a fireman but I outgrew them and you've admitted that you don't really like your job and if you don't you can never expect to be a really successful policeman if there is such a thing and Roy you must realize by now that you're never going to get your degree in criminology. Roy, you haven't the desire to hit the books again and I don't blame you because why in the hell would you want to be a criminologist anyway and oh you don't want to be one anymore well Roy that's the best news I've heard from you in some time well we can make a place for you in the business and someday soon it can be changed to Fehler and Sons and someday Roy it will be Fehler Brothers and God knows Dad and Mom would be so pleased and I'll do everything I can to bring you along and make you the kind of businessman worthy of the family name and you know it will be different than working for a boss who is an impersonal taskmaster because I know your faults and weaknesses Roy. God knows we all have them and I'll make allowances because after all you *are* my brother."

When Roy had at last decided to come back to duty and move to the apartment again it had been Carl who was the most bewildered by it all. Christ, I need to relax, Roy thought, looking at Dugan who was driving slowly checking license numbers against the hot sheet. Dugan checked thousands of license numbers against the hot sheet.

"Drive to Eighty-second and Hoover," said Roy.

"Okay, Roy. What for?"

"I want to use the call box."

"To call the station? I thought we were going in with the burglary report anyway."

"I want to call R & I. And I don't want to go in just yet. Let's patrol for a while."

"Okay. There's a call box just down the street."

"Doesn't work."

"Sure it does. I just used it the other night."

"Look, Dugan. Take me to Eighty-second and Hoover. You know that's the call box I always use. It works all the time and I like to use it."

"Okay, Roy," Dugan laughed. "I guess I'll start developing habits too when I get a little more experience."

Roy's heart thumped as he stood behind the opened metal door of the call box and drank hopefully. He might only have to make one call to R & I tonight, he thought grimly. He'd have to be extremely careful with a rookie like Dugan. His throat and stomach were still burning but he drank again and again. He was very nervous tonight. Sometimes it happened like this. His hands would become clammy and he would feel light-headed and he had to relax. He screwed the lid back on the bourbon and replaced the bottle in the call box. Then he stood for a moment sucking and chewing on three breath mints and an enormous wad of chewing gum. He returned to the car where Dugan was impatiently tapping on the steering wheel.

"Let's go to the station now, Dugan my lad," said Roy, already more relaxed, knowing the depression would dissolve.

"Now? Okay, Roy. But I thought you said later."

"Got to go to the can," Roy grinned, lighting a cigarette and whistling a themeless tune as Dugan accelerated.

While Dugan was in the report room getting a DR number for his burglary report, Roy started, wavered, and started again for the parking lot. He debated with himself as he stood by the door of his yellow Chevrolet, but then he realized that another drink could not possibly do more than relax him a bit more and completely defeat the towering specter of depression that was the hardest thing to combat unassisted. He looked around, and seeing no one in the dark parking lot, unlocked the Chevrolet, removed the pint from the glove compartment and took a large fiery mouthful. He capped the bottle, hesitated, uncapped it and took another, then one more, and put the bottle away.

Dugan was ready when he walked back in the station.

"Ready to go, Roy?" Dugan smiled.

"Let's go, my boy," Roy chuckled, but before they had patrolled for half an hour, Roy had to call R & I from the call box at Eighty-second and Hoover.

At 11:00 P.M. Roy was feeling marvelous and he began thinking about the girl. He thought of her bottle too and wondered if she were feeling as fine as he was. He also thought of her smooth lithe body.

"That was a pretty nice-looking girl, that Laura Hunt," said Roy.

"Who?" asked Dugan.

"That broad. The burglary report. You know."

"Oh, yeah, pretty nice," said Dugan. "Wish I could write a ticket. I haven't got a mover yet this month. Trouble is, I haven't learned to spot them yet. Unless a guy blasts right through a red light three seconds late or something obvious like that."

"She was put together," said Roy. "I liked that, didn't you?"

"Yeah. Do you know a good spot to sit? Some good spot where we could get a sure ticket?"

''An apple orchard, huh? Yeah, drive down Broadway, I'll show you an apple orchard, a stop sign that people have to stop for. We'll get you six tickets if you want them.''

''Just one will do. I think I should try to write one mover a day. What do you think?''

''One every other day is enough to keep the boss happy. We got more to do than write tickets in this goddamn division. Hadn't you noticed?''

''Yes,'' laughed Dugan, ''I guess we're busy with more serious things down here.''

''How old are you, Dugan?''

''Twenty-one, why?''

''Just wondering.''

''I look young, don't I?''

''About eighteen. I knew you had to be twenty-one to get on the job, but you look about eighteen.''

''I know. How old are you, Roy?''

''Twenty-six.''

''Is that all? I thought you were older. I guess because I'm a rookie, everyone seems much older.''

''Before we get that ticket, drive down Vermont.''

''Any place in particular?''

''To the apartment. Where we took the burglary report.''

''Any special reason?'' asked Dugan, looking at Roy warily, exposing large portions of the whites of his large, slightly protruding eyes, and the eyes shining in the darkness made Roy laugh.

''I'm going to do a little pubic relations, Dugan my boy. I mean public relations.''

Dugan drove silently and when they reached the apartment building he turned off on the first side street and shut his lights off.

''I'm still on probation, Roy. I don't want to get in trouble.''

''Don't worry,'' Roy chuckled, dropping his flashlight on the street as he got out of the car.

''What should I do?''

''Wait right here, what else? I'm just going to try to set something up for later. I'll be back in two minutes for heaven's sake.''

''Oh, that's good. It's just that I'm on probation,'' said Dugan as Roy strode unsteadily to the front of the building and almost laughed aloud as he stumbled on the first step.

''Hello,'' he grinned, before she had a chance to speak, while the door chime still echoed through the breezeway. ''I'm almost off duty and I wondered if you were really going to get drunk. I plan to, and one sad drunk always seeks out another, doesn't he?''

''I'm not really surprised to see you,'' she said, holding a white robe at the bosom, not looking particularly friendly or unfriendly.

''I really *am* sad,'' he said, still standing in the doorway. ''The only sadder face I've seen lately is yours. The way you were tonight. I thought we could have a few drinks and sympathize with each other.''

''I have a head start on you,'' she said, unsmiling, pointing to the fifth on the breakfast bar that was no longer full.

''I can catch up,'' said Roy.

''I have to get up early and go to work tomorrow.''

''I won't stay long. Just a drink or two and a friendly pair of eyes is all I need.''

''Can't you find the drink and eyes at home?''

''Only the drink. My place is as lonely as this one.''

''What time do you get off?''

''Before one. I'll be here before one.''

"That's late as hell."

"Please."

"Alright,". she said, and smiled a little for the first time and closed the door softly, as he crept down the stairway, holding the handrail in a tight grip.

"We got a call," said Dugan. "I was about to come and get you."

"What is it?"

"Go to the station, code two. Wonder what's up?"

"Who knows?" said Roy, lighting a cigarette, and opening a fresh stick of gum in case he would be talking to a sergeant at the station.

Sergeant Schumann was waiting in the parking lot when they arrived, along with two other radio car teams. Roy walked carefully when they parked their car and joined the others.

"Okay, everyone's here, I guess," said Schumann, a young sergeant with an imperious manner who annoyed Roy.

"What's up?" asked Roy, knowing that Schumann would make an adventure out of an assignment to write parking tickets.

"We're going to tour Watts," said Schumann. "We've gotten several letters in the last week from Councilman Gibbs' office and a couple from citizens groups complaining about the drunken loafers on the streets in Watts. We're going to clean them up tonight."

"You better rent a couple semi's then," said Betterton, a cigar-smoking veteran, "one little B wagon ain't going to hold the drunks that hang out on one corner."

Schumann cleared his throat and smiled self-consciously as the policemen laughed, all except Benson, a Negro who did not laugh, Roy noticed.

"Well, we're going to make some arrests, anyway," said Schumann. "You men know all the spots around a Hundred and Third and down around Imperial and maybe Ninety-second and Beach. Fehler, you and your partner take the wagon. You other men, take your cars. That'll make six policemen so you shouldn't have any trouble. Stick together. Fill the wagon first, then scoop up a few in your radio cars and bring them in. Not here, take them to Central Jail. I'll make sure it's okay at Central. That's all. Good hunting."

"Oh, sweet Jesus," Betterton groaned, as they walked to their cars. "Good hunting. Did you hear that? Oh, sweet Jesus. I'm glad I retire in a couple years. This is the new breed? Good hunting, men. Oh, Jesus."

"Want me to drive the wagon, Roy," asked Dugan eagerly.

"Of course. You're driving the car tonight, aren't you? You drive the wagon."

"You don't need a chauffeur's license, do you?"

"It's just a beat-up panel truck, Dugan," said Roy as they walked to the rear parking lot. Then Roy stopped, saying, "I just thought of something. I want to get a fresh pack of cigarettes from my car. Get the wagon and meet me in front of the station."

Roy could hear Dugan racing the engine of the wagon as he fumbled in the darkness for his car keys and at last was forced to use the flashlight, but this side of the parking lot was still and quiet and he knew he was worrying unnecessarily. He wouldn't do it if he weren't feeling a little depressed again. Finally he unlocked the car, held the button on the door post in so the overhead light stayed out as he opened the bottle one-handed, expertly, and sat with his legs out of the car ready to jump out in case he heard footsteps. He finished the pint in four or five swallows and felt in the glove compartment for the other but couldn't find it, and he realized there was no other. He had finished it this morning. Funny, he chuckled silently, that's pretty funny. Then he locked the car and walked woodenly to the wagon which Dugan was revving in front of the station. He chewed the mints as he walked and lit a cigarette he didn't really want.

"Might be kind of fun working a drunk wagon," said Dugan, "I've never done it before."

''Oh yeah,'' said Roy. ''Soon as a drunk pukes on you or rubs his shit-covered pants against your uniform, let me know how you like it.''

''Never thought of that,'' said Dugan. ''Do you think I should get my gloves? I bought some.''

''Leave them. We'll just hold the door open and let the other guys throw the drunks in.''

The rattling bumping panel truck was making Roy slightly sick as he leaned his head out the window. The summer breeze felt good. He began to doze and awakened with a start when Dugan drove over the curb into the parking lot at Ninety-second and Beach and the arrests began.

''Maybe we'll find somebody with a little marijuana or something,'' said Dugan, jumping out of the wagon as Roy looked sleepily at the throng of Negroes, who had been drinking in the parked cars, shooting dice against the back wall of the liquor store, standing, sitting, reclining in discarded chairs, or on milk crates, or on hoods and bumpers of ancient cars which always seemed to be available in any vacant lot or field in Watts. There were even several women among them in the darkness and Roy wondered what the hell was the attraction in these loitering places amid the rubble and broken glass. But then he remembered what some of the houses were like inside and he guessed the smell outdoors was certainly an improvement, although it wasn't any too good because in the loitering places were always packs of prowling hungry dogs and lots of animal and human excrement and lots of winos with all the smells they brought with them. Roy walked carefully to the rear of the wagon and slid the steel bolt back and opened the double doors. He staggered as he stepped back and this annoyed him. Got to watch that, he thought, and then the thought of a drunken policeman loading drunks in the drunk wagon struck him as particularly funny. He began giggling and had to sit in the wagon for a few minutes until he could control his mirth.

They arrested four drunks, one of whom was a ragpicker, lying almost unnoticed against the wall behind three overflowing trash cans. He held a half-eaten brown apple in one bony yellow hand and they had to carry him and flip him into the wagon onto the floor. The other drunks sitting on the benches on each side of the wagon didn't seem to notice the foul bundle at their feet.

They patrolled One Hundred and Third and then drove down Wilmington. In less than a half hour the wagon was filled with sixteen men and each radio car held three more. Betterton waved to Roy and sped ahead toward the Harbor Freeway and downtown as the slower wagon rumbled and clunked along.

''Mustn't be too comfortable back there,'' said Dugan, ''maybe I should drive slower.''

''They can't feel anything,'' said Roy, and this struck him as very amusing. ''Don't take the freeway,'' said Roy. ''Let's go on the surface streets. But first go up Hoover.''

''What for?''

''I want to call the station.''

''We can go by the station, Roy,'' said Dugan.

''I want to call in. No sense going in. It's out of the way.''

''Well, your favorite call box is out of the way, Roy. I think you can use another call box.''

''Do as I ask you, please,'' said Roy deliberately. ''I always use the same call box.''

''I think I know why. I'm not completely stupid. I'm not driving to that call box.''

''Do as I say, goddamnit!''

''Alright, but I don't want to work with you anymore. I'm afraid to work with you, Roy.''

"Fine. Go tell Schumann tomorrow that you and me have a personality conflict. Or I'll tell him. Or tell him whatever you want."

"I won't tell him the truth. Don't worry about that. I'm no fink."

"Truth? What the hell is the truth? If you've got that figured out, let *me* know, not Schumann."

Roy sat silently as Dugan drove obediently to the call box and parked in the usual place. Roy went to the box and tried to put his car key in the lock, then he tried his house key, and finally used the call box key. This was very funny too and restored his good humor. He opened it and drank until he finished. He threw it behind the hedge as he always did after his last call of the evening, and he laughed loud as he walked back to the wagon when he wondered what the resident there thought when he found an empty half-pint in his flower garden each morning.

"Drive up Central Avenue," said Roy. "I want to drive through Newton and see if I see any of the guys I used to know." He was talking slightly slurred now. But as long as he knew it he'd be alright. He was always very careful. He put three fresh sticks of gum in his mouth and smoked as Dugan drove silently.

"This was a good division to work," said Roy, looking at the hundreds of Negroes still on the streets at this hour. "People never go home in Newton Street. You can find thousands of people on the corners at five in the morning. I learned a lot here. I used to have a partner named Whitey Duncan. He taught me a lot. He came to see me when I was hurt. When not many other guys came, he came to see me. Four or five times Whitey came and brought me magazines and cigarettes. He died a few months ago. He was a goddamn drunk and died of cirrhosis of the liver just like a goddamn drunk. Poor old drunk. He liked people too. Really liked them. That's the worst kind of drunk to be. That'll kill you fast. Poor old fat bastard."

Roy began dozing again and checked his watch. After they got rid of the drunks and got back to the station it would be end of watch and he could change clothes and go see her. He didn't really still want her so much physically, but she had eyes he could talk to, and he wanted to talk. Then Roy saw the huge crowd at Twenty-second and Central.

"There's a place you can always get a load of drunks," said Roy, noticing that his face was becoming numb.

Dugan stopped for the pedestrians and Roy had a hilarious thought.

"Hey, Dugan, you know what this wagon reminds me of? An Italian huckster that used to peddle vegetables on our street when I was a kid. His panel truck was just like this one, smaller maybe, but it was blue and closed in like this one and he'd bang on the side and yell, 'Ap-ple, ra-dish, coo-cumbers for sale!' " Roy began laughing uproariously and Dugan's worried look made him laugh even harder. "Turn left quick and drive through the parking lot where all those assholes are standing around shuckin' and jivin'. Drive through there!"

"What for, Roy? Damn it, you're drunk!"

Roy reached across the cab and turned the wheel sharply to the left, still chuckling.

"Okay, let go," said Dugan, "I'll drive through, but I promise you I'm not working with you tomorrow night or ever!"

Roy waited until Dugan was halfway through the parking lot, parting the worried throngs of loiterers before him, moving slowly toward the other driveway and the street. Some of the more drunken ones scurried away from the wagon. Roy leaned out the window and slapped the side of the blue panel truck three times and shouted, "Nig-gers, nig-gers, niggers for sale!"

August 1965

19

The Queue

IT WAS BAD on Wednesday. The Hollenbeck policemen listened in disbelief to their police radios which broadcast a steady flow of help and assistance calls put out by the officers from Seventy-seventh Street Station.

"The riot is starting," said Blackburn as he and Serge patrolled nervously in the juvenile car but could not concentrate on anything but what was happening in the southeast part of the city.

"I don't think it'll be a real riot," said Serge.

"I tell you it's starting," said Blackburn, and Serge wondered if he could be right as he listened to the frantic operators sending cars from several divisions into Seventy-seventh Street where crowds apparently were forming at One Hundred Sixteenth Street and Avalon Boulevard. By ten o'clock a command post had been set up at Imperial and Avalon and a perimeter patrol was activated. It was obvious to Serge as he listened that there were insufficient police units to cope with a deteriorating situation.

"I tell you it's starting," said Blackburn. "It's L.A.'s turn. Burn, burn, burn. Let's get the hell to a restaurant and eat because we ain't going home tonight I tell you."

"I'm ready to eat," said Serge. "But I'm not going to worry too much yet."

"I tell you they're ready to rip loose," said Blackburn, and Serge could not determine if his partner was glad of it or not. Perhaps he's glad, thought Serge. After all, his life has been rather uneventful since his wife sued him for divorce and he was afraid to be caught in any more adulterous situations until the case was decided.

"Where do we want to eat?" asked Serge.

"Let's go to Rosales' place. We ain't ate there in a couple weeks. At least I haven't. Is it still on with you and the little waitress?"

"I see her once in a while," said Serge.

"Sure don't blame you," said Blackburn. "She's turned out real nice. Wish I could see somebody. Anybody. Doesn't she have a cousin?"

"Nope."

"I can't see my own women. My goddamn wife got my notebook with every goddamn number in it. I'm afraid she's got the places staked out. I wish I had one she didn't know about."

"Can't you wait until your divorce goes to trial?"

"Wait? Goddamn. You know I'm a man that needs my pussy. I ain't had a goddamn thing for almost three months. By the way, your little girl friend ain't working as much as she used to, is she?"

"She's going to college," said Serge. "She still works some. I think she'll be working tonight."

"What's with your other girl friend? That blonde that picked you up that night at the station. It still on with her?"

"Paula? It's more or less on, I guess."

"Bet she wants to marry you, right? That's what all these cunts want. Don't do it, I'm telling you. You got the life now, boy. Don't change it."

Serge could never control his heartbeat when he was near her and that was the thing that most annoyed him. When they left their car parked at the curb and entered the restaurant only minutes before Mr. Rosales put up the closed sign, his heart galloped, and Mr. Rosales nodded his gray head and waved them to a booth. He had thought for months that Mr. Rosales had guessed how it was with him and Mariana, but there had been no indication, and at last, he decided it was only the tattered remnants of his conscience fluttering in the hot wind of his passion. He made it a point not to meet her more than once a week, sometimes less, and he always brought her home early and feigned perfect innocence even though they had just spent several hours in a tiny motel room which the management kept for Hollenbeck policemen who only had to show a badge in lieu of payment. He thought at first that it would be only a short time before the inevitable melodrama would begin and she would wail and weep that she couldn't go on like this in a cheap motel and that her tears would destroy the pleasure—but it hadn't happened yet. When he was making love to Mariana it was the same no matter where, and it seemed to be so with her also. She had never complained and there were never any serious promises made by either of them. He was glad it was so, and yet he waited anxiously for the melodrama. Surely it would come.

And making love with Mariana was something to analyze, he thought, but he had as yet been unable to understand how she alone had made it so different. It wasn't only because he had been her first, because he had felt like this with that dark-eyed little daughter of the bracero when he was fifteen, and he was certainly not the first with that one, and sometimes he was not the first on any given evening with that one. It was not only that he had been first, it was that he was purged each time when it was over. Her heat burned him from the inside out and he was at peace. She opened his pores and drained the impurities. That was why he kept coming back for more although it was difficult enough to single-handedly match the sexual prowess of Paula who was suspecting there was another girl and was demanding more and more of him until the ultimatum and melodrama was certainly overdue with Paula also. Paula had almost exploded in tears two nights before when they were watching an inane television movie and he had commented on the aging spinster in the story who was unhappily pursuing a fat little stockbroker who was not able to break the stranglehold of a domineering wife.

"Show a little pity!" she almost shouted when he snorted at the miserable woman. "Where's your compassion? She's scared to death of being alone. She needs love, damn it. Can't you see that she has no love?"

He decided to be careful after that, very careful about what he said because the end was very near. He would have to decide whether to marry Paula or not. And if he didn't, he decided he would probably never marry because the prospects would never again be this good.

He thought this as they waited for Mariana to come from the kitchen and take their order, but she didn't come. Mr. Rosales himself came to the table with coffee and a writing pad and Serge said, "Where is she?" and watched closely but detected nothing in the eyes or manner of the proprietor who said, "I thought she should study tonight. I told her to stay home and study. She does so well with her studies. I do not want her to become too tired or upset because of overwork or anything else." He glanced at Serge when he said "anything else," and it was not a malicious glance, but now Serge was positive the old man knew how it was, but Christ, anyone with any intelligence would know that he wasn't taking her out several times a month this past year just to hold her hand. Christ, he was almost twenty-nine years old and she was twenty. What the hell did anybody expect?

Serge toyed with his food, and Blackburn as usual devoured everything in sight and without much urging finished most of what Serge didn't eat.

"Worried about the riot?" asked Blackburn. "Don't blame you. Makes me a little queasy to think that they might do here what they did in the East."

"It'll never be like that here," said Serge. "We're not going to tolerate the bullshit as long as they did back East."

"Yeah, we're the best Department in the country," said Blackburn. "That's what our press notices say. But I want to know how a few hundred bluesuits are going to turn back a black ocean of people."

"It won't be like that, I'm sure it won't."

They were all held over in Hollenbeck that night. But at 3:00 A.M. they were permitted to secure, and Blackburn only shrugged when Serge told him that it was evidently quelled and that tomorrow things would be normal.

But on Thursday things were not normal and at 7:05 P.M. a crowd of two thousand again gathered at One Hundred Sixteenth and Avalon and units from Central, University, Newton and Hollenbeck were rushed to the trouble spot. At 10:00 P.M. Serge and Blackburn had given up all pretense of patrolling and sat in the station parking lot listening to the police radio in disbelief as did four of the uniformed officers who were preparing to leave for the Watts area.

Shots were fired at a police vehicle at Imperial Highway and Parmelee, and an hour later Serge heard a sergeant being denied a request for tear gas.

"I guess they don't think the sergeant knows what the fuck is going on out there," said Blackburn. "I guess they think he should reason with them instead of using gas on them."

The word came again a few hours past midnight that they would not be sent to Watts and Serge and Blackburn were given permission to secure. Serge had called Mariana at the restaurant at ten-thirty and she had agreed to meet him in front of the Rosales house whenever he could get there. She often studied until late in the morning and Serge would come by when the Rosales family was asleep. He would park across the street in the shade of an elm and she would come out to the car and it would always be better than he remembered. He could not seem to hold the moment in his mind. Not the moment with Mariana. He could not remember the catharsis of her lovemaking. He could only remember that it was like bathing in a warm pool in the darkness and he felt refreshed and never at any time did he think it was not good for *him*. For *her*, he wondered.

He almost didn't stop because it was fifteen past two, but the light was burning and so he stopped, knowing that if she were awake she would hear. In a moment he saw her tiptoe out the front door wearing the soft blue robe and filmy pink nightgown he had come to know so well even though he had never seen it in the light. But he knew the feel of it well and his mouth became dry as he held a hand over the dome light and opened the door for her.

"I thought you would not come," she said when he stopped kissing her for a moment.

"I had to come. You know I can't stay away very long."

"It is the same with me, Sergio, but wait. Wait!" she said, pushing his hands away.

"What is it, little dove?"

"We should talk, Sergio. It is exactly one year since we went to the mountain and I saw my first lake. Do you remember?"

This is it, he thought almost triumphantly. I knew it would come. And though he dreaded the weeping, he was glad it would be finally ended. The waiting.

"I remember the mountain and the lake."

"I regret nothing, Sergio. You should know that."

"But?" he said, lighting a cigarette, preparing for an embarrassing scene. Paula will be next, he thought. After Mariana.

"But it is so much better if it should stop now while we both feel what we feel for each other."

"You're not pregnant, are you?" Serge said suddenly as the thought struck him that this was what she was preparing to tell him.

"Poor Sergio," she smiled sadly. "No, *querido*, I am not. I have learned all the ways of prevention well even though they shame me. Poor Sergio. And what if I was? Do you think I would go away with your baby in my stomach? To Guadalajara perhaps? And live my poor life out raising your child and yearning only for your arms? I have told you before, Sergio, you read too many books. I have my own life to live. It is as important to me as yours is to you."

"What the hell is this? What are you driving at?" He couldn't see her eyes in the darkness and he didn't like any of this. She had never talked like this before and it was unnerving him. He wanted to turn on the light to be sure it was her.

"I cannot pretend I can get over you easy, Sergio. I cannot pretend I do not love you enough to live like this. But it would not be forever. Sooner or later, you would marry your other one and please do not tell me there is not another one."

"I won't, but . . ."

"Please, Sergio, let me finish. If you can be a whole man by marrying your other one, then do it. Do something, Sergio. Find out what you must do. And I say this: if you find it is my kind of life you want to share, then come to this house. Come on a Sunday in the afternoon like you did the first time when we went to the lake in the mountain. Tell señor Rosales what you wish to say to me, because he is my father here. Then if he approves, come to me and say it. And then it will be announced in the church and we will not touch each other as we have done, until the night of the marriage. And I will marry you in a white dress, Sergio. But I will not wait for you forever."

Serge groped for the light switch, but she grabbed his hand and when he reached for her desperately she pulled away.

"Why do you talk like this with such a strange voice? My God, Mariana, what've I done?"

"Nothing, Sergio. You have done absolutely nothing. But it has been a year. I was a Catholic before. But since we had our love, I have not been to confession or Communion."

"So, that's it," he nodded. "The goddamn religion's got you all confused. Do you feel sinful when we make love? Is that it?"

"It is not only that, Sergio, but it is partly that. I went to confession last Saturday. I am again a child of God. But it is not only that. I want you, Sergio, but only if you are a complete man. I want Sergio Duran, a *complete* man. Do you understand?"

"Mariana," he said in bleak frustration, but when he reached for her she opened the door and was gliding barefoot across the shadowy street. "Mariana!"

"You must never return, Sergio," she whispered, her voice breaking for an instant, "unless you come as I have said." He squinted through the darkness and saw her standing for a moment straight and still, the long blue robe fluttering against her calves. Her chin was uplifted as always, and he felt the pain in his chest grow sharper and thought for one horrible moment that he was being ripped in two and only part of him sat there mute before this ghostly apparition whom he had thought he knew and understood.

"And if you come, I will wear white. Do you hear me? I will wear white, Sergio!

On Friday, the thirteenth of August, Serge was awakened at noon by Sergeant Latham who shouted something in the phone as Serge sat up in bed and tried to make his brain function.

"Are you awake, Serge?" asked Latham.

"Yeah, yeah," he said, finally. "Now I am. What the hell did you say?"

"I said that you've got to come in right away. All the juvenile officers are being sent to Seventy-seventh Street Station. Do you have a uniform?"

"Yeah, Christ, I think so. I got it here somewhere."

"Are you sure you're awake?"

"Yeah, I'm awake."

"Okay, dig your blue suit out of mothballs and put it on. Take your baton, flashlight and helmet. Don't wear a necktie and don't bother taking your soft hat. You're going into combat, man."

"What's happening now?" asked Serge, his heart already beginning to advance its rhythm.

"Bad. It's bad. Just get the hell down to Seventy-seventh. I'll be there myself as soon as I get all our people there."

Serge cursed as he cut his face twice while shaving. His light-brown eyes were watery, the irises trapped in a web of scarlet. The toothpaste and mouthwash did not cleanse his mouth of the vile taste which the pint of scotch had left there. He had drunk and read until an hour past daybreak after Mariana had left him there babbling to himself in the darkness and he hadn't yet thought it all out. How could he have been so wrong about his little dove who was in fact a hunting hawk, strong and independent. Was he the predator or the prey? She didn't need him the way he had gleefully imagined. When the hell would he be right about someone or something? And now, with a brain-cracking headache and a stomach twisted with anxiety and seething alcohol, and perhaps two hours sleep, he was going into he knew not what, where he might need every bit of physical strength and mental alertness to save his very life.

When this insanity in the streets was over and things returned to normal he would marry Paula, he thought. He would accept as much of her father's dowry as was offered and play house and live as comfortably as he possibly could. He would stay away from Mariana because it was only her youth and virginity that had attracted him in the first place as it would have attracted any reasonably degenerate hedonist. Now he could see that stewing over that had been stupidly romantic because it appeared that she had taken more than he had. He doubted whether she were feeling as miserable as he was at this very moment and he suddenly thought, let them shoot me, let some black son of a bitch shoot me. I'm not capable of finding peace. Maybe there's no such thing. Maybe it exists only in books.

Serge found that he could not buckle the Sam Browne and had to let it out a notch. He had been drinking more lately and was not playing handball as much since he was trying to handle two women. The waistband of the blue woolen trousers was hard to button and he had to suck in his stomach to fasten both buttons. He still looked slim enough in the tight-fitting heavy woolen uniform, he thought, and decided to concentrate on such trivialities as his growing stomach because he could not afford at this moment to be caught in a swamp of depression. He was going into something that no policeman in this city had ever before been asked to face and his death wish might be happily granted by some fanatic. He knew himself well enough to know that he was definitely afraid to die and therefore probably did not really want to.

Serge saw the smoke before he was five miles from Watts and realized then what policemen had been saying for two days, that this conflagration would not remain on One Hundred and Sixteenth Street or even on One Hundred and Third, but that it would spread through the entire southern metropolitan area. The uniform was unbearable in the heat and even the sunglasses didn't stop the sun from cutting his eyes and boiling his brain. He looked at the helmet beside him on the seat and dreaded putting it on. He stayed on the Harbor Freeway to Florence Avenue then south on Broadway to Seventy-seventh Station which was as chaotic as he expected, with scores of police cars going and coming and newsmen roaming aimlessly about looking for escorts into the perimeter, and the scream of sirens from ambulances, fire trucks and radio cars. He parked on the street as close as he could get to the station and was waved wildly to the watch commander's office by the desk officer who was talking into two telephones, looking like he was feeling about as miserable as Serge. The watch commander's office was jammed with policemen and reporters who were being asked to remain outside by a perspiring sergeant with a face like a dried apple. The only one who seemed to have some idea of what was happening was a balding lieutenant with four service stripes on his sleeve. He sat calmly at a desk and puffed on a brown hooked pipe.

"I'm Duran from Hollenbeck Juvenile," said Serge.

"Okay, boy, what're your initials?" asked the lieutenant.

"S," said Serge.

"Serial number?"

"One o five eight three."

"Hollenbeck Juvenile, you say?"

"Yes."

"Okay, you'll be known as Twelve-Adam-Forty-five. You'll team up with Jenkins from Harbor and Peters from Central. They should be out in the parking lot."

"Three-man cars?"

"You'll wish it was six," said the lieutenant, making an entry in a logbook. "Pick up two boxes of thirty-eight ammo from the sergeant out by the jail. Make sure there's one shotgun in your car and an extra box of shotgun rounds. What division are you from, boy?" said the lieutenant to the small policeman in an oversized helmet who came in behind him. Serge then recognized him as Gus Plebesly from his academy class. He hadn't seen Plebesly in perhaps a year, but he didn't stop. Plebesly's eyes were round and blue as ever. Serge wondered if he looked as frightened as Plebesly.

"You drive," said Serge. "I don't know the division."

"Neither do I," said Jenkins. He had a bobbing Adam's apple and blinked his eyes often. Serge could see that he was not the only one who wished he were somewhere else.

"Do you know Peters?" asked Serge.

"Just met him," said Jenkins. "He ran inside to take a crap."

"Let's let him drive," said Serge.

"Suits me. You want the shotgun?"

"You can have it."

"I'd rather have my blanket and teddy bear right now," said Jenkins.

"This him?" asked Serge, pointing at the tall, loose-jointed man striding toward them. He seemed too long for his uniform pants which stopped three inches above the shoes, and the shirt cuffs were too short. He was pretty well built and Serge was glad. Jenkins didn't seem too impressive and they'd probably need lots of muscle before this tour of duty ended.

Serge and Peters shook hands and Serge said, "We've elected you driver, okay?"

"Okay," said Peters, who had two service stripes on his sleeve, making him senior officer in the car. "Either of you guys know the division?"

"Neither of us," said Jenkins.

"That makes it unanimous," said Peters. "Let's go before I talk myself into another bowel movement. I got eleven years on this job but I never saw what I saw here last night. Either of you here last night?"

"Not me," said Serge.

"I was on station defense at Harbor Station," said Jenkins, shaking his head.

"Well pucker up your asshole and get a good grip on the seat because I'm telling you you aren't going to believe this is America. I saw this in Korea, sure, but this is America."

"Cut it out, or you'll be loosening up *my* bowels," said Jenkins, laughing nervously.

"You'll be able to shit through a screen door without hitting the wire, before too long," said Peters.

Before driving three blocks south on Broadway, which was lined on both sides by roving crowds, a two-pound chunk of concrete crashed through the rear window of the car and thudded against the back of the front seat cushion. A cheer went up from forty or more people who were spilling from the corner of Eighty-first and Broadway as the Communications operator screamed: "Officer needs help, Manchester and Broadway! Officer needs assistance, One O Three and Grape! Officer needs assistance Avalon and Imperial!" And then it became difficult to become greatly concerned by the urgent calls that burst over the radio every few seconds, because when you sped toward one call another came out in the opposite direction. It seemed to Serge they were chasing in a mad S-shape configuration through Watts and back toward Manchester never accomplishing anything but making their car a target for rioters who pelted it three times with rocks and once with a bottle. It was incredible, and when Serge looked at the unbelieving stare of Jenkins he realized what he must look like. Nothing was said during the first forty-five minutes of chaotic driving through the littered streets which were filled with surging chanting crowds and careening fire engines. Thousands of felonies were being committed with impunity and the three of them stared and only once or twice did Peters slow the car down as a group of looters were busy at work smashing windows. Jenkins aimed the shotgun out the window, and as soon as the groups of Negroes broke from the path of the riot gun, Peters would accelerate and drive to another location.

"What the hell are we doing?" asked Serge finally, at the end of the first hour in which few words were spoken. Each man seemed to be mastering his fear and incredulity at the bedlam in the streets and at the few, very few police cars they actually saw in the area.

"We're staying out of trouble until the National Guard gets here, that's what," said Peters. "This is nothing yet. Wait till tonight. You ain't seen nothing yet."

"Maybe we should do something," said Jenkins. "We're just driving around."

"Well, let's stop at a Hundred and Third," said Peters angrily. "I'll let you two out and you can try and stop five hundred niggers from carrying away the stores. You want to go down there? How about up on Central Avenue? Want to get out of the car up there? You saw it. How about on Broadway? We can clear the intersection at Manchester. There's not much looting there. They're only chunking rocks at every black and white that drives by. I'll let you boys clear the intersection there with your shotgun. But just watch out they don't stick that gun up your ass and fire all five rounds."

"Want to take a rest and let me drive?" asked Serge quietly.

"Sure, you can drive if you want to. Just wait till it gets dark. You'll get action soon enough."

When Serge took the wheel he checked his watch and saw it was ten minutes until 6:00 P.M. The sun was still high enough to intensify the heat that hung over the city from the fires which seemed to be surrounding them on the south and east but which Peters had avoided. Roving bands of Negroes, men, women and children, screamed and jeered and looted as they drove past. It was utterly useless, Serge thought, to attempt to answer calls on the radio which were being repeated by babbling female Communications operators, some of whom were choked with sobs and impossible to understand.

It was apparent that most of the activity was in Watts proper, and Serge headed for One Hundred and Third Street feeling an overwhelming desire to create some order. He had never felt he was a leader but if he could only gather a few pliable men like Jenkins who seemed willing to obey, and Peters who would submit to more apparent courage, Serge felt he *could* do something. Someone had to do something. They passed another careening police car every five minutes or so, manned by three helmeted officers who all seemed as disorganized and bewildered as themselves. If they were not pulled together soon, it could not be stopped at all, Serge thought. He sped south on Central Avenue and east to Watts substation where he found what he craved more than he had ever craved for a woman—a semblance of order.

"Let's join that group," said Serge, pointing to a squad of ten men who were milling around the entrance of the hotel two doors from the station. Serge saw there was a sergeant talking to them and his stomach uncoiled a little. Now he could abandon the wild scheme he was formulating which called for a grouping of men which he was somehow going to accomplish through sheer bravado because goddammit, someone had to do something. But they had a sergeant, and he could follow. He was glad.

"Need some help?" asked Jenkins as they joined the group.

The sergeant turned and Serge saw a two-inch gash on his left cheekbone caked with dust and coagulation but there was no fear in his eyes. His sleeves were rolled up to the elbow, showing massive forearms and on closer examination Serge saw fury in the green eyes of the sergeant. He looked like he could do something.

"See what's left of those stores on the south side?" said the sergeant, whose voice was raspy, Serge thought, from screaming orders in the face of this black hurricane which must be repelled.

"See those fucking stores that aren't burning?" the sergeant repeated. "Well they're full of looters. I just drove past and lost every window in my fucking car before I reached Compton Avenue. I think there's about sixty looters or more in those three fucking stores on the south and I think there's at least a hundred in the back because they drove a truck right through the fucking rear walls and they're carrying the places away."

"What the hell can we do about it?" asked Peters, as Serge watched the building on the north side three blocks east burning to the ground while the firemen waited near the station apparently unable to go in because of sniper fire.

"I'm not ordering nobody to do nothing," said the sergeant, and Serge saw he was much older than he first appeared, but he was not afraid and he was a sergeant. "If you want to come with me, let's go in those stores and clean them out. Nobody's challenged these motherfuckers here today. I tell you nobody's stood up to them. They been having it their own way."

"It might be ten to one in there," said Peters, and Serge felt his stomach writhing again, and deliberately starting to coil.

"Well I'm going in," said the sergeant. "You guys can suit yourselves."

They all followed dumbly, even Peters, and the sergeant started out at a walk, but soon they found themselves trotting and they would have run blindly if the sergeant had, but he was smart enough to keep the pace at a reasonably ordered trot to conserve energy. They advanced on the stores and a dozen looters struggled with the removal of heavy appliances through the shattered front windows and didn't even notice them coming.

The sergeant shattered his baton on the first swing at a looter, and the others watched for an instant as he dove through the store window, kicking a sweat-soaked shirtless teen-ager who was straining at the foot of a king-sized bed which he and another boy were attempting to carry away headboard and all. Then the ten policemen were among them swinging batons and shouting. As Serge was pushed to the glass-littered floor of the store by a huge mulatto in a bloody undershirt he saw perhaps ten men run in the rear door of the store hurling bottles as they ran, and Serge, as he lay in the litter of broken glass which was lacerating his hands, wondered about the volume of alcohoic beverage bottles which seemed to supply the mighty arsenal of missiles that seemed to be at the fingertips of every Negro in Watts. In that insane moment he thought that Mexicans do not drink so much and there wouldn't be this many bottles lying around Hollenbeck. Then a shot rang out and the mulatto who was by now on his feet began running and Jenkins shouldered the riot gun and fired four rounds toward the rear of the store. When Serge looked up, deafened from the explosions twelve inches from his ear, he saw the black reinforcements, all ten lying on the floor, but then one stood up and then another and another, and within a few seconds nine of them were streaking across the devastated parking lot. The looters in the street were shouting and dropping their booty and running.

''I must have shot high,'' said Jenkins and Serge saw the pellet pattern seven feet up on the rear wall. They heard screaming and saw a white-haired toothless Negro clutching his ankle which was bleeding freely. He tried to rise. fell, and crawled to a mutilated queen-sized gilded bed. He crawled under it and curled his feet under him.

''They're gone,'' said the sergeant in wonder. ''One minute they were crawling over us like ants and now they're gone!''

''I didn't mean to shoot,'' said Jenkins. ''One of them fired first. I saw the flash and I heard it. I just started shooting back.''

''Don't worry about it,'' said the sergeant. ''Goddamn! They're gone. Why the hell didn't we start shooting two nights ago? Goddamn! It really works!''

In ten minutes they were on their way to General Hospital and the moans of the old Negro were getting on Serge's nerves. He looked at Peters who was sitting against the door of the car, his helmet on the seat beside him, his thinning hair plastered down with sweat as he stared at the radio which had increased in intensity as they sped northbound on the Harbor Freeway. The sky was black now on three sides as the fires were leaping over farther north.

''We'll be there in a minute,'' said Serge. ''Can't you stop groaning for a while?''

''Lord, it hurts,'' said the old man who rocked and squeezed the knee six inches above the wet wound which Jenkins seemed unwilling to look at.

''We'll be there in a minute,'' said Serge, and he was glad it was Jenkins who had shot him, because Jenkins was his partner and now they would book him at the prison ward of General Hospital and that meant they could leave the streets for an hour or two. He felt the need to escape and order his thinking which had begun to worry him because blind fury could certainly get him killed out there.

''Must have hit him with one pellet,'' said Peters dully. ''Five rounds. Sixty pellets of double ought buck and one looter gets hit in the ankle by one little pellet. But I'll bet before this night's over some cop will get it from a single shot from a handgun fired at two hundred yards by some asshole that never shot a gun before. Some cop'll get it tonight. Maybe more than just one.''

How did I get stuck with someone like him? Serge thought. I needed two strong partners today and look what I got.

Jenkins held the elbow of the scrawny old man as he limped into the hospital and up the elevator to the prison ward. After booking the prisoner they stopped at the emergency entrance where Serge had his cut hands treated and after they were washed he saw that the cuts were very superficial and a few Band-Aids did the trick. At nine o'clock they were driving slowly south on the Harbor Freeway and the Communications operators were reciting the calls perfunctorily—calls which, before this madness, would have sent a dozen police cars speeding from all directions but now had become as routine as a family dispute call. ''Officer needs help! Four Nine and Central!'' said the operator. ''Officer needs help, Vernon and Central! Officer needs assistance, Vernon and Avalon! Officer needs assistance, One one five and Avalon! Looting, Vernon and Broadway! Looting, Five eight and Hoover! Looters, Four three and Main!'' Then another operator would cut in and recite her list of emergencies which they had given up trying to assign to specific cars because it was obvious now to everyone that there weren't enough cars to even protect each other, let alone quell the looting and burning and sniping.

Serge blundered into a sniper's line of fire on Central Avenue, which was badly burned. They had to park across from a flaming two-story brick building and hide behind their car because two fire trucks had come in behind them and blocked the street and had then been abandoned when the sniping started. The sniping, for all but the combat veterans of Korea and World War II, was a terrible new experience. As Serge hid for forty minutes behind his car and fired a few wild shots at the windows of a sinister yellow apartment building where someone said the snipers were hiding, he thought this the most frightening part of all. He wondered if a police force could cope with snipers and remain a police force. He began thinking that something was going on here in this riot, something monumental for all the nation, perhaps an end of something. But he had better keep his wits about him and concentrate on that yellow building. Then the word was passed by a grimy young policeman in a torn uniform who crawled to their position on his stomach that the National Guard had arrived.

At five past midnight they responded to a help call at a furniture store on south Broadway where three officers had an unknown number of looters trapped inside. One officer swore that when a lookout had ducked inside after the police car drove up, he had seen a rifle in the looter's hands, and another policeman who worked this area said that the office of this particular furniture store contained a small arsenal because the owner was a nervous white man who had been robbed a dozen times.

Serge, without thinking, ordered Peters and one of the policemen from the other teams to the rear of the store where a blue-clad white helmeted figure was already crouched in the shadows, his shotgun leveled at the back door. They went without question, and then Serge realized he was giving commands and thought wryly, at last you are a leader of men and will probably get a slug in your big ass for your trouble. He looked around and several blocks south on Broadway he saw an overturned car still smoldering and the incessant crackling of pistol fire echoed through the night, but for five hundred yards in each direction it was surprisingly quiet. He felt that if he could do something in this gutted skeleton of a furniture store, then a vestige of sanity would be preserved and then he thought that that in itself was insane thinking.

"Well, what's next, Captain?" said the wrinkled grinning policeman who knelt next to him behind the cover of Serge's radio car. Jenkins had the riot gun resting across the deck lid of the car pointed at the store front with its gaping jagged opening where plate glass used to be.

"I guess I *am* giving orders," Serge smiled. "You can do what you want, of course, but somebody ought to take charge. And I make the biggest target."

"That's a good enough reason," said the policeman. "What do you want to do?"

"How many you think are in there?"

"A dozen, maybe."

"Maybe we should wait for more help."

"We've had them trapped for twenty minutes, and we put in maybe five requests for help. You guys are the only ones we've seen. I'd say offhand there isn't any help around right now."

"I think we ought to arrest everyone in that store," said Serge. "We've been racing around all night getting shot at and clubbing people and mostly chasing them from one store to another and one street to another. I think we ought to arrest everyone in that store right now."

"Good idea," said the wrinkled policeman. "I haven't actually made a pinch all night. I just been acting like a goddamn infantryman, crawling and running and sniping. This is Los Angeles not Iwo Jima."

"Let's book these assholes," Jenkins said angrily.

Serge stood up and ran in a crouch to a telephone pole a few feet to the side of the storefront.

"You people in there," Serge shouted, "come out with your hands on top of your head!" He waited for thirty seconds and looked toward Jenkins. He shook his head and pointed to the barrel of the riot gun.

"You people come out or we're going to kill every goddamn one of you," Serge shouted. "Come out! Now!"

Serge waited another silent half minute and felt the fury returning. He had only momentary seizures of anger tonight. Mostly it was fear, but occasionally the anger would prevail.

"Jenkins, give them a volley," Serge commanded. "This time aim low enough to hit somebody." Then Serge leveled his revolver on the store front and fired three rounds into the blackness and the flaming explosions of the riot gun split the immediate silence. He heard nothing for several seconds until the ringing echo ceased and then he heard a wail, shrill and ghostly. It sounded like an infant. Then a man cursed and shouted, "We comin' out. Don't shoot us. We comin' out."

The first looter to appear was about eight years old. He wept freely, his hands held high in the air, his dirty red short pants hanging to the knees, and the loose sole of his left shoe flip-flopped on the pavement as he crossed the sidewalk and stood wailing now in the beam of Jenkins' spotlight.

A woman, apparently the child's mother, came next holding one hand high while the other dragged along a hysterical girl of ten who babbled and held a hand over her eyes to ward off the white beam of light. The next two out were men, and one of them, an old one, was still repeating, "We comin', don't shoot," and the other had his hands clasped on top of his head staring sullenly into the beam of light. He muttered obscenities every few seconds.

"How many more in there?" Serge demanded.

"Oney one," said the old man. "God, they's oney one, Mabel Simms is in there, but I think you done killed her."

"Where's the one with the rifle?" asked Serge.

"They ain't no rifle," said the old man. "We was jist tryin' to git a few things before it was too late. Ain't none of us stole a thing these three days and ever'body else had all these new things and we jist decided to git us somethin'. We jist live across the street, Officer."

"There was a man with a rifle ducked in that fucking doorway when we drove up," said the wrinkled policeman. "Where is he?"

"That was me, Mister PO-liceman," said the old man. "It wan't no rifle. It was a shovel. I was jist bustin' all the glass out the window so my grandkids wouldn't git cut goin' in. I never stole in all my life befo' I swear."

"I'll take a look," said the wrinkled policeman, entering the blackened store carefully, and Jenkins followed, the twin beams of their flashlights crisscrossing in the darkness for more than three minutes. They came out of the store one on each side of an immense black woman whose ringlets hung in her eyes. She murmured, "Jesus, Jesus, Jesus." They half-carried her out to where the others were as she let out an awesome shriek of despair.

"Where's she hit?" asked Serge.

"I don't think she's hit," said the wrinkled policeman as he released her and let her bulk slide to the pavement where she pounded her hands on the concrete and moaned.

"Kin I look at her?" asked the old man. "I been knowin' her for ten years. She live next do' to me."

"Go ahead," said Serge, and watched while the old man labored to get the big woman sitting upright. He supported her with great effort and patted her shoulder while he talked too low for Serge to hear.

"She ain't hurt," said the old man. "She jist scared to death like the rest of us."

Like all of us, Serge thought, and then he thought that this was a very fitting end to the military campaign of Serge Duran, leader of men. It was about as he should have expected. Reality was always the opposite of what he at first anticipated. He knew this for certain now, therefore it was about as he should have expected.

"You going to book them?" asked the wrinkled policeman.

"You can have them," said Serge.

"Don't fight over us, you honky motherfuckers," said the surly muscled man whose hands were unclasped now and hung loosely at his sides.

"You get those hands on top of your head, or I'll open your belly," said the wrinkled policeman, as he stepped forward and jammed the muzzle of the shotgun in the man's stomach. Serge saw the finger tighten on the trigger when the Negro instinctively touched the barrel, but then the Negro looked in the wrinkled policeman's eyes and removed his hand as though the barrel was on fire. He clasped the hands on top of his head.

"Why didn't you try to pull it away?" the wrinkled policeman whispered. "I was going to make you let go."

"You can have them," said Serge. "We're leaving."

"We'll take this one," said the wrinkled policeman. "The rest of you people get your asses home and stay there."

Jenkins and Peters agreed that they should go to Seventy-seventh Station because they might get relieved since they had been on duty now twelve hours. It did seem that things had quieted down a bit even though Watts substation was under some type of sniper siege, but there were apparently enough units there, so Serge drove to the station and thought he had not died like the heroes of his novels, even though he was at least as neurotic and confused as any of them. He suddenly remembered that last month during a two-day stretch of staying in the apartment and reading, he had read a book on T. E. Lawrence and maybe the romantic heroism of books had triggered his irresistible urge to surround and capture the furniture store which had ended in low comedy. Mariana said he read too many books. But it wasn't just that. It was that things were breaking apart. He was accustomed to the feeling lately that *he* was breaking apart, but now everything was fragmented—not in two reasonably neat sections but in jagged chaotic slivers and chunks, and he was one of society's orderers, as trite as it sounded. Even though he had never felt particularly idealistic before, now, surrounded by darkness and fire and noise and chaos, he, suddenly given the opportunity, had to create a tiny bit of order in that gutted store on south Broadway. But what good had it done? It had ended as all his attempts to do a worthy thing invariably ended. That was why marriage to Paula, and getting drunk occasionally and spending Paula's father's money seemed a most appropriate life for Serge Duran.

To the surprise of all three of them, they were relieved when they reached the station. They muttered a brief good-bye to each other and hurried to their cars before someone changed his mind and made them stay for the rest of the night. Serge drove home by the Harbor Freeway and the skies were still glowing red but it was apparent that the National Guard was making a difference. There were far fewer fires and after reaching Jefferson he turned around and saw no more fires. Instead of going straight to the apartment he stopped at an all night hamburger stand in Boyle Heights and for the first time in thirteen hours, now that he was back in Hollenbeck Division, he felt safe.

The night man knew Serge as a juvenile officer in plainclothes and he shook his head when Serge walked inside and sat down in the deserted diner.

"What's it like down there?" asked the night man.

"It's still pretty bad," said Serge running his fingers through his hair, sticky and matted from the helmet and soot and sweat. His hands were filthy, but there was no restroom for the customers and he decided to just have a cup of coffee and go home.

"I almost didn't know you in the uniform," said the night man. "You're always wearing a suit."

"We're all in uniform today," said Serge.

"I can understand," said the night man, and Serge thought his sparse moustache made him look like Cantinflas although he was a tall man.

"Good coffee," said Serge, and so was the cigarette, and his stomach unwound for the last time that night as the hot coffee splashed into it.

"I don't know why the boss wants me here," said the night man. "There have been few customers. Everyone's staying at home because of the *mallate*. But I shouldn't use that word. Nigger is a terrible word and *mallate* means the same thing but is even worse."

"Yes."

"I don't think the blacks would try to burn the east side. They don't get along with us Mexicans, but they respect us. They know we'd kill them if they tried to burn our homes. They don't fear the Anglo. No one fears the Anglo. Your people are growing weak."

"I wouldn't be surprised," said Serge.

"I've noticed that here in this country, the Mexican is forced to live close to black people because he's poor. When I first came here the Mexicans wanted to get away from the black who is exactly unlike a Mexican, and to live near the Anglo who is more nearly the same. But the things that've been happening, the softness of the Anglo, the way you tell the world you're sorry for feeding them, and the way you take away the Negro's self-respect by giving everything to him, I'm starting to think that the Mexican should avoid the Anglo. I can tell you these things? I won't offend you? I talk so much tonight. I'm sick to my heart because of the riot."

"I'm not an easily offended Anglo," said Serge. "You can talk to me like I was a Mexican."

"Some police officers who work in the *barrios* seem *muy Mexicano* to me," smiled the night man. "You, señor, even look a little *Mexicano,* mostly around the eyes, I think."

"You think so?"

"I meant that as a compliment."

"I know."

"When I came to this country twelve years ago, I thought it was bad that the Mexicans lived mostly in the east side here where the old ways were kept. I even thought we should not teach our children *la lengua* because they should completely learn to be Americans. I've looked closely and I believe that the Anglos in this place accept us almost like other Anglos. I used to feel very proud to be accepted like an Anglo because I know of the bad treatment of Mexicans not too long ago. But as I watched you grow weak and fearful that you wouldn't have the love of the world, then I thought: look, Armando—*Mira, hombre, los gabachos* are nothing to envy. You wouldn't be one of them if you could. If a man tried to burn your house or hold a knife at your belly you kill him and no matter his color. If he broke your laws you would prove to him that it's painful to do such a thing. Even a child learns that the burning coal hurts if you get close. Don't the gringos teach this to their children?"

"Not all of us."

"I agree. You seem to say, touch it six or five times and maybe it burns and maybe not. Then he grows to be a man and runs through your streets and it's not all his fault because he never learned the hot coal burns. I think I'm glad to live in your country, but only as a Mexican. Forgive me, señor, but I wouldn't be a gringo. And if your people continue to grow weak and corrupt I'll leave your comforts and return to Mexico because I don't wish to see your great nation fall."

"Maybe I'll go with you," said Serge. "Got any room down there?"

"In Mexico there's room for all," smiled the night man, carrying a fresh coffeepot to the counter. "Would you like me to tell you of Mexico? It always makes me glad to talk of Yucatán."

"I'd like that," said Serge. "Are you from Yucatán?"

"Yes. It's far, far. You know of the place?"

"Tell me about it. But first, can I use your bathroom? I've got to wash. And can you fix me something to eat?"

"Certainly, señor. Go through that door. What would you like to eat. Ham? Eggs? Bacon?"

"We're going to talk about Mexico. I should eat Mexican food. How about *menudo*? You'd be surprised how long it's been since I ate *menudo*."

"I have *menudo,*" laughed the night man. "It's not excellent, but it passes."

"Do you have corn tortillas?"

"Of course."

"How about lemon? And oregano?"

"I have them, señor. You know about *menudo*. Now I'm ashamed to give you my poor *menudo*."

Serge saw that it was after four but he wasn't the least bit sleepy and he felt suddenly exhilarated yet relaxed. But mostly he was hungry. He laughed in the mirror at the grimy sweat-stained face and thought, God, how I'm hungry for *menudo*.

Suddenly Serge popped his head out the door, his hands still covered with suds. "Tell me, señor, have you traveled a lot in Mexico?"

"I know the country. *De veras*. I know my Mexico."

"Have you been to Guadalajara?"

"It's a beautiful city. I know it well. The people are wonderful, but all the people of Mexico are wonderful and will treat you very good."

"Will you tell me about Guadalajara too? I want to know about that city."

"A pleasure, señor," chuckled the night man. "To have someone to talk to at this lonely hour is a pleasure, especially someone who wants to hear about my country. I'd give you free *menudo* even if you were not a policeman."

It was seven o'clock when Serge was driving home, so full of *menudo* and tortillas he hoped he wouldn't get a stomachache. He wished he had some *yerba buena* like his mother used to fix. It never failed to help a stomachache and he couldn't afford to be ill because in exactly six hours he would have to get up and be ready for another night. The news on the car radio indicated that looting and burning was expected to resume heavily today.

Serge took Mission Road instead of the freeway and there on North Mission Road he saw something that made him brake sharply and slow to fifteen miles per hour and stare. Eight or ten men, one woman, and two small boys, were lined up at the door of a restaurant which was not yet open. They carried pots and pans of all shapes, but each pot was ample in size and Serge realized they were waiting for the restaurant to open so they could buy a pot of *menudo* and take it home because they were sick or someone in the house was sick from drinking too much on Friday night. There was not a Mexican who did not believe with all his soul that *menudo* cured hangovers and because they believed, it did in fact cure the hangover, and even though his stomach felt like a goatskin bag pumped full of the stuff, he would have stopped and bought some more to keep for later if he had a pot. Then he looked at his helmet, but the liner was too grimy from oil and soot to carry *menudo* in, and he accelerated the Corvette and headed for his bed.

He felt he would sleep better than he had in weeks even though he had seen the beginning of the end of things, because now that they had a taste of anarchy, and saw how easy it is to defeat the civil authority, there would be more and it would be the white revolutionary who would do it. This was the beginning, and the Anglos were neither strong enough nor realistic enough to stop it. They doubted everything, especially themselves. Perhaps they had lost the capacity to believe. They could never believe in the miracle in a pot of *menudo*.

As he looked in the rearview mirror, the queue of forlorn Mexicans with their *menudo* pots had disappeared, but in a few moments, their spirits would be soaring he thought, because the *menudo* would make them well.

"They are not good Catholics," Father McCarthy had said, "but they are so respectful and they believe so well." *Andale pues*, Serge thought. To bed.

20

The Chase

"Good thing they're too fucking dumb to make fire bombs out of wine bottles," said Silverson and Gus cringed as a rock skidded over the already dented deck lid and slammed against the already cracked rear window. A glass fragment struck the Negro policeman whose name Gus had already forgotten, or perhaps it was buried there among the ruins of his rational mind which had been annihilated by terror.

"Shoot that motherfucker that . . ." screamed Silverson to Gus, but then sped away from the mob before finishing the sentence.

"Yeah, those Coke bottles aren't breaking," said the Negro policeman. "If that last one would've broke, we'd have a lap full of flaming gasoline right now."

They had been out only thirty minutes, Gus thought. He knew it was only thirty because it was now five till eight and still it wasn't dark and it had been seven-twenty-five when they drove from the parking lot at Seventy-seventh Station because it was written here on his log. He could see it. It had only been thirty minutes ago. So how could they survive twelve hours of this? They had been told they would be relieved in twelve hours, but of course they would all be dead.

"Friday the thireenth," muttered Silverson, slowing down now that they had run the gauntlet on Eighty-sixth Street where a mob of fifty young Negroes appeared from nowhere and a cocktail had bounced off the door but failed to burst. This happened after someone had cracked the side window with a rock. Now Gus stared at another rock which was lying on the floor at his feet and he thought, we've only been out thirty minutes. Isn't that incredible.

"Some organization we got," said Silverson, turning back east toward Watts where most of the radio calls seemed to be emanating at the moment. "I never worked this crummy division in my life. I don't know my ass from pork sausage."

"I never worked down here either," said the Negro policeman. "How about you, Plebesly? It is Plebesly, isn't it?"

"No, I don't know the streets," said Gus, holding the shotgun tightly against his belly and wondering if the paralysis would fade because he was sure he could not get out of the car, but then he supposed that if they succeeded in breaking a fire bomb inside, his instinct would get him out. Then he thought of himself on fire.

"They just tell you here's a box of thirty-eights and a shotgun and point out two other guys and say take a car and go out there. It's ridiculous," said Silverson. "None of us ever worked down here before. Hell, man, I worked Highland Park for twelve years. I don't know my ass from sliced salami down here."

"Some guys got called down here last night," said the soft-spoken Negro policeman. "I work Wilshire, but I didn't get called down here last night."

"The whole goddamn Department's here tonight," said Silverson. "Where in the hell's Central Avenue? There was an assistance call on Central Avenue."

"Don't worry about it," said the Negro policeman. "There'll be another one any minute."

"Look at that!" said Silverson, and aimed the radio car down the wrong side of San Pedro Street as he accelerated toward a market where a band of eight or ten men were systematically carrying out boxes of groceries.

"Those brazen assholes," said the Negro policeman and he was out and running toward the storefront after the already fleeing looters as soon as Silverson parked. To his surprise, Gus's body functioned and his arm opened the door and his legs carried him, unsteadily, but still carried him, at a straight-legged lope toward the storefront. The Negro policeman had a tall very black man by the shirt front and palmed him across the face with his gloved hands which were probably sap gloves because the man spun backward and fell through the yawning hole in the plate glass, screaming as his arm was raked and bloodied by the jagged edge.

The others scattered through back and side doors and in a few seconds only the three policemen and the bleeding looter stood in the gutted store.

"Lemme go," pleaded the looter to the Negro policeman. "We're both black. You're just like me"

"I'm not nothin' like you, bastard," said the Negro policeman, showing great strength by lifting the looter one-handed. "I am nothing whatever like you."

A peaceful hour passed while they took their looter to the station and engaged in what had to pass for booking, but which required only a skeleton of an arrest report and no booking slip at all. This hour passed much too quickly for Gus who found that hot coffee knotted his stomach even more. Before he could believe it they were back on the streets, only now, night had come. The small arms fire was crackling through the darkness. He had fooled them for five years, thought Gus. He had almost fooled himself, but tonight they would know, and he would know. He wondered if it would be as he always feared, himself trembling like a rabbit before the deadly eye at the last moment. This is how he always thought it would be at the instant when the great fear came, whatever that fear was, which irrevocably paralyzed his disciplined body and brought the final mutiny of body against mind.

"Listen to that gunfire," said Silverson as they were back on Broadway and the sky glowed from a dozen fires. He had to take several detours on their patrol to nowhere in particular, because of the fire engines blocking streets.

"This is crazy," said the Negro policeman, who Gus knew by now was named Clancy.

It is the natural tendency of things toward chaos, Gus thought. It's a very basic natural law Kilvinsky always said, and only the order makers could temporarily halt its march, but eventually there will certainly be darkness and chaos, Kilvinsky had said.

"Look at that asshole," said Clancy, and shined his spotlight on a lone looter who was reaching though a window of a liquor store feeling for a quart of clear liquid that rested there, miraculously whole among the broken glass. "We ought to give that bastard some sidewalk surgery. Wonder how he'd like a lobotomy by Dr. Smith and Dr. Wesson?"

Clancy was carrying the shotgun now and as Silverson stopped the car Clancy fired a blast into the air behind the man who did not turn but continued his probing, and when he reached the bottle he turned a scowling brown face to the naked light, and walked slowly away from the store with his prize.

"Son of a bitch, we're whipped," said Silverson and drove away from the lonely snarling figure who continued his inexorable pace in the darkness.

For another hour it was the same: speeding to calls only to arrive in time to chase fleeting shapes in the darkness as the Communications operators continued a barrage of help and assistance and looting calls until all calls were routine and they wisely decided that the main order of business would be protecting each other and surviving the night uninjured.

But at 11:00 P.M. as they were scattering a group intent on burning a large food market on Santa Barbara Avenue, Silverson said, "Let's catch a couple of these assholes. Can you run, Plebesly?"

"I can run," said Gus grimly, and he knew, somehow knew he could run. In fact, he had to run, and this time when Silverson squealed into the curb and fleeting shadows faded into darker shadow there was another shadow pursuing fleeter than the rest. The last looter hadn't gotten a hundred feet from the store when Gus overtook him and slammed the heel of his hand in the back of the looter's head. He heard him fall and grind along the sidewalk, and from the shouts he knew that Clancy and Silverson had grabbed him. Gus pursued the next shadow and within a minute he was streaking down Forty-seventh Street through the residential darkness after the second shadow and another shadow a half block ahead. Despite the Sam Browne and the strangeness of a helmet, and the baton clacking against the metal of his belt, he felt unencumbered, and swift, and free. He ran like he ran in the academy, like he still ran at least twice a week during his workouts, and he was doing the thing he did best in all the world. Suddenly he knew that none of them could stand up to him. And though he was afraid, he knew he would endure and his spirit ignited as the sweat boiled him and the warm wind fed the fire as he ran and ran.

He caught the second shadow near Avalon and saw that the man was huge with a triangular neck that sloped from ear to shoulder but he was easy to sidestep when he made two or three halfhearted lunges toward Gus and then collapsed in a gasping heap without being struck by the baton that Gus held ready. He handcuffed the looter to the bumper bracket of a recently wrecked car that was squatting at the curb where the man fell.

Gus looked up and the third shadow hadn't made another three hundred feet but jogged painfully toward Avalon Boulevard, looking often over his shoulder and Gus was running again, easy striding, loose, letting his body run as the mind rested, which is the only way to run successfully. The shadow was getting larger and larger and was in the blue glow of the street lamp when Gus was on him. The looter's eyes binked back in disbelief at the oncoming policeman. Gus was panting but bounded forward still strong when the exhausted man turned and stumbled toward a pile of litter beside a smoldering building and came up with a piece of two by four. He held it in both hands like a ball bat.

He was perhaps twenty, six feet two, and fierce. Gus was afraid, and though his mind told him to use his gun because that was the only sensible thing to do, he reached instead for his baton and circled the man who sucked and rattled at the air and Gus was sure he would cave in. But still the man held the two by four as Gus circled him. Drops of sweat plinked on the concrete sidewalk at his feet and his white shirt was completely transparent now and clung to him.

"Drop that," said Gus. "I don't want to hit you."

The looter continued to back away and the heavy wood wavered as more eye white showed than a moment before.

"Drop that or I'll smash you," said Gus. "I'm stronger than you."

The board slid from the looter's hands and clunked to the pavement and he caved and lay there gasping while Gus wondered what to do with him. He wished he had taken Silverson's handcuffs, but it had happened so fast. His body had just started the chase and left his mind behind, but now his mind had caught up with the body and was all together.

Then he saw a black and white roaring down Avalon. He stepped into the street and waved it down and in a few minutes he was back on Santa Barbara and reunited with Silverson and Clancy who were astonished by his feat. They took all three looters to the station where Silverson told the jailer how his ''little partner'' had caught the three looters, but Gus still found that his stomach rebelled at coffee and would accept only water, and forty-five minutes later when they went back on the streets he was still trembling and perspiring badly and told himself, what did you expect? That it would now all vanish like in a war movie? That you who feared everything for a lifetime now would dramatically know no fear? He completed the night as he had begun it, quivering, at moments near panic, but there was a difference: he knew the body would not fail him even if the mind would bolt and run with graceful antelope leaps until it vanished. The body would remain and function. It was his destiny to endure, and knowing it he would never truly panic. And this, he thought, would be a splendid discovery in any coward's life.

21

The Golden Knight

What the hell's going on? Roy thought, standing in the middle of the intersection of Manchester and Broadway gaping at the crowd of two hundred on the northeast corner and wondering if they would break in the bank. The sun was still bright and hot. Then he heard a crash and saw that the group of one hundred on the northwest corner had broken in the windows of the storefronts and were beginning to loot. What the hell's happening, thought Roy, and gained little solace from the faces of the policemen near him who seemed as bewildered as he. Then they smashed the windows at the southwest corner and Roy thought, my God, a hundred more gathered and I didn't even see them! Suddenly only the southeastern side of the intersection was clear and most of the policemen were retreating to this side of the street except one stocky policeman who charged a pocket of six or eight Negroes with their arms full of men's clothing who were strolling to a double-parked Buick. The policeman struck the first man in the back with the point of the baton and brought the second one to his knees with a skillful slashing blow across the leg, and then the policeman was hit full in the face with a milk crate thrown from the crowd and he was being kicked by eighteen or twenty men and women. Roy joined a squad of six rescuers who ran across Manchester. They dragged him away and were pelted by a hail of stones and bottles one of which struck Roy on the elbow and caused him to cry out.

''Where do the rocks come from?'' asked a gray-haired, beefy policeman with a torn uniform shirt. ''How in the hell do they find so many rocks lying around in a city street?''

After they got the injured man to a radio car, the dozen officers returned to the intersection through which all vehicle traffic had been diverted. Officers and mob watched each other amid the screams and taunts and laughter and blaring radios. Roy never knew who fired the first shot, but the gunfire erupted. He fell to his stomach and began to tremble and crawled into the doorway of a pawnshop holding both arms over his stomach. Then he thought of removing the white helmet and holding it over his stomach, but he realized how futile it would be. He saw three or four more radio cars roaring into the chaotic intersection as the crowds panicked and broke into and away from the confused policemen who were shouting conflicting orders to each other. No one knew where the gunfire was coming from.

Roy stayed in the doorway and protected his stomach as the rumors came of snipers on every roof and that they were firing from the crowd and then several policemen began firing at a house on the residential street just south of Manchester. Soon the house was riddled with shotgun and revolver fire, but Roy never saw the outcome because a frantic policeman waved them north again and when he ran a hundred yards he saw a dead Negro blocking the sidewalk, shot through the neck, and another dead in the middle of the street. This can't be true, Roy thought. It's broad daylight. This is America. Los Angeles. And then he fell to his stomach again because he saw the brick hurtling end over end toward him and it shattered the plate glass window behind him. A cheer went up from thirty Negroes who had appeared in the alley to the left and a young policeman ran up to Roy as he was getting up. The young policeman said, "The one in the red shirt threw the brick," and he aimed coolly at the running Negroes and fired the riot gun. The blast took two of the men down. The man in red held his leg screaming and another in a brown shirt limped to his feet and was pulled into a mob of cursing looters where he disappeared as the looters scurried away from the young policeman with the riot gun. Then Roy heard two small pops and saw a tiny flash in the midst of the retreating crowd and the car window next to Roy shattered.

"Show yourself, you bastard," the young policeman shouted to the invisible sniper and then turned his back on them and walked slowly away. "This isn't real," he muttered to Roy. "Is it?"

Then Roy saw something extraordinary: a young black with a full beard and a black beret and silk undershirt and huge natural under the beret, a fiercely militant-looking young man, stepped in front of a mob of fifty and told them to go home and that the police were not their enemies, and other things equally provocative. He had to be removed from the area in a car under guard when the mob turned on him and kicked him unconscious in less than a minute, before the policemen could drive them off.

The sirens shrieked and two ambulances and a police car containing six policemen drove up. Roy saw there was a sergeant with them. He was young and almost everyone ignored him as he tried in vain to create order at least among the squad of policemen, but it took almost an hour to get the dead and wounded to the hospital and the temporary morgue. The Watts riot had begun in earnest this Friday afternoon.

Roy was ordered by the sergeant to arrest a wounded man in a red shirt, and he was teamed with two other policemen. They took the man to the prison ward of the County Hospital in a radio car with a windshield and rear window completely destroyed by rocks. The paint on the white door was scorched from a fire bomb and Roy was glad to be taking the long drive to the hospital. He hoped his new parters would not be too anxious to return to the streets.

It was after dark when they were driving again toward Seventy-seventh Street Station and by now Roy and his partners knew each other. Each had started the afternoon with different partners until the chaos at Manchester and Broadway, but what the hell did it matter, they decided, who was working with whom. They made a pact to stay one with the other and to provide mutual protection, not to stray far from each other, because they had only one shotgun, Roy's, and it was not reassuring at all, not on this night, but at least it was something.

"It's not nine o'clock yet," said Barkley, a ten-year policeman from Harbor Division with a face like a bruised tomato who had, for their first two hours together, mumbled over and over that "it was unbelievable, all so unbelievable," until he was asked to please shut up by Winslow, a fifteen-year policeman from West Los Angeles Division who was the driver and a slow careful driver he was, Roy thought. Roy was thankful he had a veteran driving.

Roy sat alone in the back seat cradling the shotgun, a box of shotgun shells on the seat next to him. He had not fired the gun yet, but he had made the decision to fire at anyone who threw a rock or fire bomb at them, and at anyone who shot or aimed a gun at them or looked like he was aiming a gun at them. They were shooting looters. Everyone knew it. He decided he would not shoot looters, but he was glad some of the others were doing it. They had seen a semblance of order begin in the bursts of initial gunfire. Only deadly force could destroy this thing and he was glad they were shooting looters, but he decided he would not shoot looters. And he would try not to shoot anyone. And he would shoot no one in the stomach.

In one of my rare displays of humanity I will blow their heads off, he thought. Under no circumstance will I shoot a man in the stomach.

"Where you want to go, Fehler?" asked Winslow, rolling a cigar from side to side in his wide mouth. "You know the area best."

"Sounds like Central Avenue and Broadway and a Hundred and Third are getting hit the hardest," said Barkley.

"Let's try Central Avenue," said Roy, and at 9:10 P.M. when they were only two blocks from Central Avenue the fire department requested assistanee because they were being fired on in a six-block stretch of Central Avenue.

Roy felt the heat when they were still a half block from Central and Winslow parked as close to the inferno as he could get. Roy was perspiring freely and by the time they jogged the five hundred feet to the first besieged fire truck they were all sweating and the night air was scorching Roy's lungs and the pop pop pop of gunfire was coming from several directions. Roy began to develop a fierce stomachache, one which could not be relieved by a bowel movement, and a ricochet pinged off the concrete sidewalk. The three policemen dived for the fire truck and huddled next to a filthy, yellow-helmeted, wide-eyed fireman.

It was not Central Avenue, Roy thought. It was not even possible that the signpost which pointed Forty-sixth Street east and west and Central Avenue north and south could be right. He had worked Newton Street. He had patrolled these streets with dozens of other partners, with partners now dead even, like Whitey Duncan. This street was a vivid part of his learning. He had been educated in southeast Los Angeles and Central Avenue had been a valuable schoolroom but this hissing inferno was not Central Avenue. Then Roy for the first time noticed the two cars overturned and burning. He suddenly could not remember what kind of buildings had been there on Forty-seventh and Forty-sixth that were now sheets of flame two hundred feet high. If this had happened a year ago I would certainly not believe it, he thought. I would simply believe that it was a fantastic seizure of d.t.'s and I would take another drink. Then he thought of Laura, and he was astonished that now, even now, as he lay by the big wheel of the fire engine and the sounds of gunfire and sirens and growling flames were all around him, even now, he could get the empty ache within him that would be filled warmly when he thought of holding her, and how she stroked his hair as no one, not Dorothy, not his mother, no woman, had done. He had guessed he loved her when the yearning for drink began to wane, and he knew it when, three months after their affair began, he realized that she aroused the same feeling within him that Becky did, who was now talking clearly and was assuredly a brilliant child—not simply beautiful, but stunning. Roy ached again as he thought of Becky, ethereal, bright, and golden—and Laura, dusky and real, altogether real, who had begun to put him together, Laura, who was five months younger than he, but who seemed years older, who used pity and compassion and love and anger until he stopped drinking after he was suspended sixty days for being found drunk on duty, and who lived with him and kept him for those sixty days in her apartment, and who said nothing, but only watched him with those tawny tragic eyes when he began to resemble a man again and decided to return to his own apartment. She said nothing about that since, and he still came to her three or four nights a week because he still needed her badly. She watched him, always watched him with those liquid eyes. With Laura the sex made it perfect but was far, far from all of it, and that was another reason he knew he loved her. He had been on the verge of a decision about her for weeks and even months and he began to tremble as he thought that if it weren't for the ache and the warmth which always came when he thought of Becky or Laura, if it weren't for this feeling he could evoke in himself, then now, now in the blood and hate and fear and chaos, he would turn the riot gun around and look in the great black eye of the twelve gauge and jerk the trigger. Then he guessed he was far from healthy yet, despite Laura's reassurance, or he wouldn't think such thoughts. Suicide was madness, he had always been taught to believe, but what was this around him, if not madness? He began to get light-headed and decided to stop thinking so hard. His palms were dripping wet and leaving tiny drops of moisture on the receiver of the shotgun. Then he worried about the moisture rusting the piece. He wiped the receiver with his sleeve until he realized what he was doing and laughed aloud.

"You guys come with me!" shouted a sergeant, crouching as he ran past the fire engine. "We got to clean these snipers out and get the firemen working before the whole goddamn city burns down."

But though they walked along Central Avenue in groups of three for over an hour they never saw a sniper but only heard, and they chased and occasionally shot at shadowy figures who scurried in and out of gutted storefronts that were not in flames. Roy did not shoot because the conditions had not been met. Still, he was glad the others were shooting. When Central Avenue reached the point that it was burning more or less quietly and there was little left to steal, Winslow suggested they go elsewhere, but first they should stop at a restaurant and eat. When they asked which restaurant he had in mind, he waved an arm and they followed him to the car and found that the two remaining unbroken windows had been smashed out in their absence and the upholstery had been cut, but not the tires strangely enough, so Winslow drove to a restaurant on Florence Avenue that he said he had noticed earlier. They walked through a gigantic hole in the wall of the cafe where a car must have smashed through. Roy guessed the car had probably been driven by some terrified white man passing through the riot area who had been attacked by the mobs that were stopping traffic and beating whites earlier in the day when they owned the streets before the shooting started. Then again it could have been a looter's car which the police had chased until he crashed though the restaurant in spectacular fashion. What difference did it make? Roy thought.

"Shine your flashlight over here," said Winslow, removing six hamburger patties from the refrigerator which was not running. "They're still cold. It's okay," said Winslow. "See if you can find the buns in that drawer, Fehler. I think the mustard and stuff is behind you there on the little table."

"The gas still works," said Barkley, propping his flashlight on the counter with the beam directed on the griddle. "I'm a pretty good cook. Want me to get them started?"

"Go head on, brother," said Winslow in an affected Negro accent, as he squeezed a head of lettuce he found on the floor, peeling away the outer leaves and dropping them in a cardboard box. They ate and drank several bottles of soda pop which were not cold enough, but it wasn't at all bad there in the darkness and it was after midnight when they finished and sat smoking, looking at each other as the ceaseless crackling small arms fire and ubiquitous smell of smoke reminded them that they had to go back. Finally it was Barkley who said, "Might as well get back out there. But I wish they hadn't broke our windows out. You know, the one thing that scares me most is that a cocktail will come flying in the car and bust, and fry us. If we only had windows we could roll them up."

Roy was more impressed with Winslow as the night wore on. He drove through Watts and west and north through the rest of the gutted city as though he were on routine patrol. He seemed to be listening carefully to the garbled endless, breathless calls that were blaring out at them over the radio. Finally one of the operators with a girlish voice began sobbing hysterically as she was jabbering a string of twelve emergency calls to "any unit in the vicinity," and she and all of them must realize by now that there were no units in certain vicinities, and if there were they were hard pressed to save their own asses and to hell with anything else. But at 2:00 A.M. Winslow stopped the car on Normandie Avenue which was exceptionally dark except for a building burning in the distance and they watched a gang of perhaps thirty looters ransacking a clothing store and Winslow said, "There's too many of them for us to handle, wouldn't you say?"

"They might have guns," said Barkley.

"See the car out front, the green Lincoln?" said Winslow. "I'm going after them when they leave. We'll get some of them at least. It's about time we threw some looters in jail."

Three men got in the car and even from a half block away in the darkness, Roy could see that the back seat of the Lincoln was filled with suits and dresses. The Lincoln pulled away from the curb and Winslow said, "Dirty motherfuckers," and the radio car roared forward. Winslow turned on his headlights and red lights and they passed the clothing store and crossed Fifty-first Street at eighty miles per hour and the chase was on.

The driver of the Lincoln was a good driver but his brakes were not good and the police car had tremendous brakes and could corner better. Winslow ate up the ground which separated them and didn't listen to Barkley who was shouting directions at him. Roy sat silently in the rear seat and wished they had seat belts in the back seat too. He could see that Winslow was oblivious of both of them and would catch that Lincoln if it killed all of them and then they were going northbound on Vermont. Roy did not look at the speedometer but knew they were traveling in excess of one hundred and this was of course absolutely insane because there were thousands of looters, thousands! But Winslow wanted *these* looters and Barkley shouted, "Soldiers!" and Roy saw a National Guard roadblock two blocks north and the Lincoln's driver, a hundred feet ahead, saw it too and burned out the rest of his brakes trying to turn left before reaching the roadblock. A National Guardsman began firing a machine gun and Winslow jammed on his brakes when they saw the muzzle flashes and heard the clug-a-clug-a-clug-a-clug and saw the tracers explode on the asphalt closer to them than to the Lincoln. Roy was horrified to see that the Lincoln did not crash as he was sure it would. The driver made the turn and was speeding west on a narrow dark residential street and Winslow doggedly made the turn and Roy wondered if he could lean out the window and fire the riot gun, or perhaps his revolver because that Lincoln had to be stopped before Winslow killed them all. He was surprised to discover how badly he wanted to live now, and he saw Laura's face for an instant and was thrown against the door handle when Winslow made an impossible right turn and picked up two hundred feet on the Lincoln.

Winslow, trying to conserve power, wasn't using his siren and Roy had lost count of the other cars they had almost hit, but he was thankful that at this hour in this part of the city, there were few civilian autos on the street and Barkley uttered a joyful whoop when the Lincoln bounced over the curb turning left again, and slammed against a parked car. The Lincoln was still skidding in a tight circle when the three looters were leaping out, and Winslow, jaw set, was driving across the sidewalk at the fleeing driver, a slim Negro who was running down the middle of the sidewalk with an occasional terrified glance over his shoulder at the approaching headlights. Roy realized that Winslow was going to run him down as he drove the radio car down the residential sidewalk taking corners off fences and running over shrubbery with the radio car that was too wide for the sidewalk. They were less than thirty feet from the looter when he turned the last time and his mouth opened in a soundless shriek as he dived over a chain link fence. Winslow skidded past him, cursed, and leaped out of the car. Roy and Barkley were out in a second but

Winslow, amazingly agile for his size and age, was already over the fence and crashing through the rear yard. Roy heard four shots and then two more as he threw the riot gun over the fence and scrambled after it, ripping his trousers, but in a moment Winslow came walking back reloading his revolver.

"He got away," said Winslow. "The motherfucking nigger got away. I'd give a thousand dollars for one more shot at him."

When they got back in the car Winslow circled the block and returned to the looter's green Lincoln which sat awkwardly in the middle of the street, steam hissing from the broken radiator.

Winslow stepped slowly from the radio car and asked Roy for the riot gun. Roy gave him the gun and shrugged at Barkley as Winslow stepped to the car and fired two flaming blasts at the rear tires. Then he stepped to the front of the car and smashed out the headlights with the butt of the gun and then broke the windshield. Then he circled the car, his shotgun ready like it was a dangerous wounded thing that might yet attack, and he slammed the gun butt into both side windows. Roy looked toward the houses on both sides of the street, but all were dark. The residents of southeast Los Angeles, who had always known how to mind their own business, were not curious at any sounds they heard *this* night.

"That's enough, Winslow," Barkley shouted. "Let's get the hell out of here."

But Winslow opened the car door and Roy could not see what he was doing. In a second he emerged with a large piece of fabric and Roy watched him in the beam of the headlights as he put his pocket knife away. He removed the gas cap and shoved the piece of material into the tank and dripped gasoline on the street beneath the tank.

"Winslow, are you nuts?" shouted Barkley. "Let's get the hell out of here!"

But Winslow ignored him and made his trickle of gasoline extend a safe distance from the Lincoln and then he shoved the soaked piece of cloth back into the tank except for two feet of it which hung to the ground. He ran to the mouth of the gasoline stream and lit it and there was a small smothered explosion almost instantly and the car was burning well as Winslow got back in the radio car and drove away in the relaxed careful manner of before.

"How can you fight them without getting just like them?" said Winslow finally to his silent partners. "I'm just a nigger now, and you know what? I feel pretty good."

Things became a little quieter after three, and at 4:00 A.M. they drove to Seventy-seventh Station, and after working a fifteen-hour watch, Roy was relieved. He was too tired to change into his civilian clothes, and was certainly too tired to drive to his apartment. And even if he weren't, he would not go home tonight. There was only one place in the world he would go tonight. It was exactly four-thirty when he parked in front of Laura's apartment. He could not hear the pop of gunfire now. This part of Vermont had been untouched by fire and almost untouched by looting. It was very dark and still. He only knocked twice when she opened the door.

"Roy! What time is it?" she asked, in a yellow nightgown and robe, and already he felt the pleasurable ache.

"I'm sorry to come so late. I had to, Laura."

"Well, come in. You look like you're about to fall on your face."

Roy entered and she switched on a lamp and held his arms as she watched him in her unique way. "You're a mess. You're really a filthy mess. Take your uniform off and I'll fill the bath. Are you hungry?"

Roy shook his head as he walked into the familiar comfortable bedroom and unhooked the Sam Browne, letting it fall to the floor. Then, remembering how tidy Laura was, he pushed it with his foot into the corner by the closet and sat heavily in a padded, hot pink and white bedroom chair. He took his shoes off and sat for a minute wanting a cigarette but too tired to light one.

''Want a drink, Roy?'' asked Laura, leaving the bathroom as the tub filled with a sound of rushing restorative water.

''I don't need a drink, Laura. Not even tonight.''

''One drink won't hurt you. Not anymore.''

''I don't want one.''

''Okay, baby,'' she said, picking up his shoes and putting them in the bottom of the closet.

''What the hell would I do without you?''

''I haven't seen you for four days. I guess you've been busy.''

''I was going to come Wednesday night. That's when this thing started, but we had to work overtime. And yesterday too. And then tonight, Laura, tonight was the worst, but I had to come tonight. I couldn't stay away any longer.''

''I'm very sorry about all this, Roy,'' she said, pulling off his damp black socks, as he thanked her silently for helping him.

''Sorry about what?''

''About the riot.''

''Why? Did you start it?''

''I'm black.''

''You're not black and I'm not white. We're lovers.''

''I'm a Negro, Roy. Isn't that why you moved back home in your apartment? You knew I wanted you to stay with me.''

''I think I'm too tired to talk about that, Laura,'' said Roy, standing up and kissing her and then he took off the dusty shirt which was sticking to him. She hung up the shirt and the trousers and he left his shorts and T-shirt on the bathroom floor. He glanced at the concave scar on his abdomen and stepped into the steaming suds-filled tub. Never had a bath felt better. He leaned back with his eyes closed and set his mind free and dozed for a moment, then felt her presence. She was sitting on the floor beside the tub watching him.

''Thank you, Laura,'' he said, loving the flecks in the light brown eyes, and the smooth brown skin and the graceful fingers she laid against his shoulder.

''What do you suppose I see in you?'' she smiled, caressing his neck. ''It must be the attraction of opposites, don't you think? Your golden hair and golden body. You're just the most beautiful man I know. Think that's it?''

''That's just gold plate,'' said Roy. ''There's nothing but pot metal underneath.''

''There's plenty underneath.''

''If there's anything, you put it there. There was nothing when you found me last year.''

''*I* was nothing,'' she corrected him.

''You're everything. You're beauty and love and kindness, but mostly you're order. I need order right now, Laura. I'm very scared, you know. There's chaos out there.''

''I know.''

''I haven't been this afraid since you dried me out and taught me not to be afraid. God, you should see what chaos looks like, Laura.''

''I know. I know,'' she said, still stroking his neck.

''I can't stay away from you anymore,'' he said, staring at the faucet which dripped sporadically into the suds. ''I didn't have the guts to stay with you, Laura. I need peace and tranquility and I knew we'd face hatred together and I didn't have the guts. But now that I've been back in that lonely apartment I don't have the guts to be away from you and now that I've been in that darkness and madness tonight, I could never make it without you and . . .''

''Don't talk anymore, Roy,'' she said getting up. ''Wait until tomorrow. See how you feel tomorrow.''

''No,'' he said, grabbing her arm with a wet, soapy hand. ''You can't depend on tomorrow. I tell you the way it is out there, you mustn't depend on tomorrow.

I live for you now. You can never get rid of me now. Never.'' Roy pulled her down and kissed her on the mouth and then kissed the palm of her hand, and she stroked his neck with the other hand, saying, ''Baby, baby,'' as she always did and which never failed to soothe him.

They were still awake, lying naked on their backs with only a sheet over them when the sun rose in Los Angeles.

''You should go to sleep.'' she whispered. ''You've got to go back to the street tonight.''

''It won't be bad now,'' he said.

''Yes. Maybe the National Guard will have things under control.''

''It doesn't matter if they don't. It still won't be bad now. My vacation begins September first. It'll surely be over by then. Do you mind gettiing married in Las Vegas? We can do it without waiting.''

''We don't have to get married. It doesn't matter if we're married.''

''I still have a conventional bone or two in my body, I guess. Do it for me.''

''Alright. For you.''

''Weren't you brought up to respect the institution of marriage?''

''My daddy was a Baptist preacher,'' she laughed.

''Well then it's settled. I was brought up a Lutheran, but we never went to church very much except when appearances demanded it, so I think we'll raise our children as Baptists.''

''I'm nothing now. Not a Baptist. Nothing.''

''You're everything.''

''Do we have a right to have children?''

''You're goddamn right we do.''

''The golden knight and his dark lady,'' she said. ''But we'll suffer, you and me. I promise you. You don't know what a holy war is.''

''We'll win.''

''I've never seen you so happy.''

''I've never been so happy.''

''Do you want to know why I loved you from the first?''

''Why?''

''You weren't like other white men that flirted with me and that asked me out on dates to their apartments or maybe to some out of the way pretty nice place where lots of mixed couples go. I never really could trust a white man because I could see that they saw something in me that they wanted, but it wasn't me.''

''What was it?''

''I don't know. Just lust maybe, for a little brown animal. Primitive vitality of a Negro, that sort of thing.''

''My, you're intellectual tonight.''

''It's morning.''

''This morning then.''

''Then there were white liberals who would've taken me to a governor's ball, but I think with people like that almost any Negro would do. I don't trust those people either.''

''Then there was me.''

''Then there was you.''

''Old Roy the wino.''

''Not anymore.''

''Because I borrowed some of your guts.''

''You're such a humble man that I get annoyed with you.''

''I used to be arrogant and conceited.''

''I can't believe that.''

''Neither can I anymore. But it's true.''

"You were different than any white man I ever met. You needed something from me, but it was something one human being could give another and it had nothing to do with my being Negro. You always looked at me as a woman and a person, do you know that?"

"Guess I'm just not the lusty type."

"You're very lusty," she laughed. "You're a marvelous lusty lover and right now you're too silly to talk to."

"Where'll we go for a honeymoon?"

"Do we have to have one of those too?"

"Of course," said Roy. "I'm conventional, remember?"

"San Francisco is a fine city. Have you ever been there?"

"No, let's go to San Francisco."

"It's also a very tolerant city. You've got to consider things like that now."

"It's so quiet," said Roy. "For a while last night when I was most afraid I thought the sound of the fire would never stop. I thought I'd always hear the fire roaring in my ears."

22

Reunion

"I hear we're going back to almost normal deployment starting tomorrow," said Roy. It pleased him to say it because he and Laura had decided that as soon as the riot was completely finished and he could do it, he would ask for some special days off and they would go to San Francisco for a week after being married in Las Vegas where they might stay for a few days, but then again they might go from Vegas to Tahoe for a night . . . "Sure will be nice to get off the twelve-hour shifts," said Roy in a burst of exuberance at the thought of doing it, and now that he and Laura were going to do it all his doubts dissolved.

"I've had enough of it," said Serge Duran as he made a lazy U-turn on Crenshaw where they were on perimeter patrol and Roy liked the solid way Duran drove, in fact he liked Duran whom he had only seen a dozen times during these five years and whom he never bothered to get to know. But they had been together only two hours tonight and he liked him and was glad that when the perimeter patrols were set that Duran had told the sergeant, "Let me work with my two classmates Fehler and Plebesly." And Gus Plebesly seemed like a very decent sort and Roy hoped he might become good friends with both these men. He became acutely aware that he had no real friends among policemen, had never made any, but he was going to change that, he was changing lots of things.

"Now that the riot's just about done, it's hard to believe it happened," said Gus, and Roy thought that Plebesly had aged more than five years. He remembered Plebesly as a timid man, perhaps the smallest in their class but he seemed taller now and solider. Of course he remembered Plebesly's inhuman stamina and smiled as he thought of how his endurance had been a threat to their P.T. instructor, Officer Randolph.

"It's not hard to believe it happened when you drive down Central Avenue or a Hundred and Third Street," said Serge. "Were you down there on Friday night, Roy?"

"I was there," said Roy.

"I think we were there too," said Gus, "but I was too scared to know for sure."

"Likewise, brother," said Roy.

"But I was so scared I can hardly remember most of the things that happened," said Gus, and Roy saw that the shy grin was the same, and so was the deprecatory manner that used to annoy Roy because he was too stupid in those days to see that it was thoroughly genuine.

"I was thinking the same thing just today," said Serge. "Friday night is already becoming a kind of mist in my mind. I can't remember big chunks of it. Except the fear, of course."

"You feel that way too, Serge?" said Gus. "How about you, Roy?"

"Sure, Gus," said Roy. "I was scared to death."

"Be damned," said Gus and was silent and Roy guessed that Gus felt reassured. It was comforting to talk with a policeman who, like himself, was obviously filled with doubts, and he pitied Gus now and felt the tug of friendship.

"Did you ever finish college, Roy?" asked Serge. "I remember talking to you in the academy about your degree in criminology. You were pretty close to it then."

"I never got any closer, Serge," laughed Roy and was surprised to discover no irony in the laugh and he guessed he was finally making peace with Roy Fehler.

"I never built up too many units myself," said Serge, nodding his understanding. "Sorry now that I didn't, with our first sergeant exam coming up. How about you, Gus? You go to school?"

"Off and on," said Gus. "I hope to have my bachelor's in business administration in about a year."

"Good for you, Gus," said Roy. "We'll be working for you one of these days."

"Oh, no," said Gus, apologetically. "I haven't really studied for the sergeant's exam, and besides, I freeze in test situations. I know I'll fail miserably."

"You'll be a great sergeant, Gus," said Serge, and he seemed to mean it. Roy felt drawn to both of them and he wanted them to know about his coming marriage—wanted them to know about Laura, about a white policeman with a black wife and whether they thought he was mad, because he was sure they were compassionate men. But even if they thought him a fool and proved it by polite embarrassment it wouldn't change a thing.

"It's getting dark, thank goodness," said Gus. "It was so smoggy and hot today. I'd sure like to go for a swim. I've got a neighbor with a pool. Maybe I'll ask him tomorrow."

"How about tonight?" said Serge. "After we get off I've got a pool in my apartment building. We might as well take advantage of it because I'm moving in a few weeks."

"Where you moving?" asked Gus.

"My girl and I have a pad picked out to buy. It'll be lawn mowing and weed pulling instead of moonlight swims, I guess."

"You're getting married?" asked Roy. "I'm getting married as soon as I can get a week off."

"You're tumbling too?" smiled Serge. "That's reassuring."

"I thought you were already married, Roy," said Gus.

"I was when we were in the academy. I was divorced not long after that."

"Have kids, Roy?" asked Gus.

"A little girl," said Roy, and then he thought of her last Sunday when he had brought her to Laura's apartment. He thought of how Laura had played with her and made Becky love her.

"You didn't go sour on marriage?" asked Serge.

"Nothing wrong with marriage," said Roy. "It gives you children and Gus can tell you what children give you."

"Couldn't make it without them," said Gus.

"How long you been married, Gus?" asked Serge.

"Nine years. All my ife."

''How old are you?''

''Twenty-seven.''

''What's your girl's name, Serge?'' asked Roy as he had an idea.

''Mariana.''

''How about having that swim tomorrow?'' said Roy. ''Maybe Gus and his wife and Laura and I could come over to your place and meet your fiancée and we could have a swim and a few beers before we go to work tomorrow afternoon.'' It was done, he thought. It would be the first test.

''Okay,'' said Serge, with enthusiasm. ''Can you make it, Gus?''

''Well, my wife hasn't been feeling well lately, but maybe she'd like to come over even if she won't swim. I'd sure like to come.''

''That's fine. I'll be expecting you,'' said Serge. ''How about ten o'clock in the morning?'

''Fine.'' said Gus, and Roy thought this would be the best way for him to see. To just bring her and see. The hell with apologies and warnings. Let them see her, lots of her, long-legged and shapely and incomparable in a bathing suit. Then he'd know how it would be, what he could expect.

''Would it be too much . . .'' Gus hesitated. ''I mean, I hate to ask you . . . If your landlady wouldn't like it, or if maybe you don't want a bunch of noisy kids around . . . I could understand . . .''

''You want to bring your kids?'' Serge smiled.

''I would.''

''Bring them,'' said Serge. ''Mariana loves kids. She wants six or eight.''

''Thanks,'' said Gus. ''My kids will be thrilled. That's a beautiful name your fiancée has—Mariana.''

''Mariana Paloma,'' said Serge.

''That's Spanish, isn't it?'' asked Gus.

''She's Mexican,'' said Serge. ''From Guadalajara.''

''Come to think of it, isn't Duran a Spanish name?''

''I'm Mexican too,'' said Serge.

''I'll be damned. That never occurred to me,'' said Roy, looking at Serge for some Mexican features and finding none, except perhaps something about the shape of his eyes.

''Are you of Mexican descent on both sides?'' asked Gus. ''You don't look it.''

''One hundred percent,'' Serge laughed. ''I guess I'm probably more Mexican than anyone I know.''

''You speak Spanish then?'' asked Gus.

''Hardly at all,'' Serge answered. ''When I was a boy I did, but I've forgotten. I guess I'll learn again though. I went to Mariana's home Sunday afternoon, and after I got the blessing of Mr. Rosales, her *padrino,* I went to her and tried to ask her in Spanish. I think it ended up more in English than Spanish. I must've been a hell of a sight, a big stammering clown with an armload of white roses.''

''I'll bet you were just smashing,'' Roy grinned, wondering if he looked as contented as Serge.

''Mariana's informed me we'll talk only Spanish in our house until my Spanish is at least as good as her English.''

''That's very nice,'' said Gus, and Roy wondered if she had required courting in the old Mexican manner. He wondered if Serge had known her a long time before he kissed her. I'm getting corny, Roy smiled to himself.

''Usually Mexican men dominate their women,'' said Serge, ''until they get old and then Mama is the boss and the old boys pay for their tyranny. But I'm afraid Mariana and I are starting out the other way around.''

''Nothing wrong with a strong woman,'' said Roy. ''A policeman needs one.''

''Yes,'' said Gus, gazing at the blazing sunset. ''Not many guys can do this job alone.''

"Well, we're *veteranos*, now," said Serge. "Five years. We can sew a hash mark on our sleeves. I thought we were going to have a class reunion after five years."

"That would've been nice," said Gus. "We can have a small reunion party tomorrow afternoon. If they bring us all back to the command post maybe we can work together again tomorrow night."

"I really think we'll be going back to our divisions tomorrow," said Serge. "This riot is over."

"I wonder how long the experts will screw around with their cause theories?" said Roy.

"This is just the beginning," said Serge. "They'll appoint commissions, and intellectuals who know two or three Negroes will demonstrate their expertise in race relations and this will be only the begininng. Negroes are no better and no worse than whites. I think they'll do whatever they can get away with and whatever is expected of them, and from now on there'll be lots of Negroes living up to their angry black man press notices."

"Do you think blacks are the same as whites?" asked Roy to Gus, who was still watching the sunset.

"Yes," said Gus absently. "I learned it five years ago from my first partner who was the best policeman I ever knew. Kilvinsky used to say that most people are like plankton that can't fight the currents but only drift with the waves and tides, and some are like benthos which can do it but have to crawl along the slimy ocean floor to do it. And then others are like nekton which can actually fight the currents but don't have to crawl on the bottom to do it but it's so hard on the nekton that they must be very strong. I guess he figured the best of us were like the nekton. Anyway, he always said that in the big dark sea, the shape or shade of the poor suffering little things didn't matter at all."

"Sounds like he was a philosopher," Roy smiled.

"Sometimes I think I made a mistake becoming a cop," said Serge. "I look back over these five years and the frustrations have been bad but I guess there's nothing I'd rather do."

"I saw an editorial today that said it was just deplorable that so many people had been shot and killed in the riot," said Gus. "The guy said, 'We must assume that police can shoot to *wound*. Therefore it follows that the police must be intentionally killing all these people.'"

"That's a screwed-up syllogism," said Serge. "But you can't blame the ignorant bastards. They've seen a thousand movies that prove you can wing a guy or shoot a gun out of his hands. What the hell, you can't blame them."

"Just a pile of plankton dumped in a sea of concrete, eh, Gus?" said Roy.

"I guess I don't really regret the job," said Gus. "I guess I think I know something that most people don't."

"All we can do is try to protect ourselves," said Roy. "We sure as hell can't change them."

"And we can't save them," said Gus. "Nor ourselves. Poor bastards."

"Hey, this conversation is getting too damned depressing," said Roy suddenly. "The riot's over. Better days are coming. We're having a swimming party tomorrow. Let's cheer up."

"Okay, let's try to catch a crook," said Serge. "A good felony pinch always lifts my spirits. You used to work this area, didn't you Gus?"

"Sure," said Gus, straightening up and smiling. "Drive west toward Crenshaw. I know where there's some dropoff spots for hot rollers. Maybe we can pick up a car thief."

Roy was the first to see the woman waving to them from the car parked near the phone booth on Rodeo Road.

"I think we got a citizen's call," said Roy.

"That's okay, I was getting tired driving around anyway," said Serge. "Maybe she has an insurmountable problem we can surmount."

"It got dark fast tonight," Gus observed. "A couple of minutes ago I was enjoying the sunset and now, bang, it's dark."

Serge parked beside the woman who squirmed out of the Volkswagen awkwardly and shuffled over to their car in her bedroom slippers and bathrobe which fought to conceal her expansive largeness.

"I was just going to the phone booth to call the cops," she puffed, and before he was out of the car Roy smelled the alcoholic breath and examined the red face and weedy dyed red hair.

"What's the problem, ma'am?" said Gus.

"My old man is nuts. He's been drinking and not going to work lately and not supporting me and my kids and beating hell out of me whenever he feels like it and tonight he's completely nuts and he kicked me right in the side. The bastard. I think he broke a rib." The woman writhed inside the bathrobe and touched her ribs.

"You live far from here?" asked Serge.

"Just down the street on Coliseum," said the woman. "How about coming home and throwing him out for me?"

"He your legal husband?" asked Serge.

"Yeah, but he's nuts."

"Okay, we'll follow you home and have a talk with him."

"You can't talk to him," the woman insisted, getting back inside the Volkswagen. "The bastard's crazy tonight."

"Okay, we'll follow you home," said Roy.

"Breaks the monotony, anyway," said Gus, as they drove behind the little car and Roy put the shotgun down on the floor in the back and wondered if they should lock it in the front when they went in the woman's residence or would it be alright here on the floor if the car doors were locked. He decided to leave it on the floor.

"Is this neighborhood mostly white?" asked Serge to Gus.

"It's mixed," said Gus. "It's mixed clear out to La Cienega and up into Hollywood."

"If this town has a ghetto it's the biggest goddamn ghetto in the world," said Serge. "Some ghetto. Look up there in Baldwin Hills."

"Fancy pads," said Gus. "That's a mixed neighborhood too."

"I think the broad in the VW is the best pinch we'll see tonight," said Roy. "She almost creamed that Ford when she turned."

"She's loaded," said Serge. "Tell you what, if she smashes into somebody we'll just take off like we don't know her. I figured she was too drunk to drive when she waddled out of that car and lit my cigarette with her breath."

"Must be that apartment house," said Gus, flashing the spotlight on the number over the door as Serge pulled in behind the Volkswagen which she parked four feet from the curb.

"Three-Z-Ninety-one, citizen's call, forty-one twenty-three, Coliseum Drive," said Gus into the mike.

"Don't forget to lock your door," said Roy. "I left the shotgun on the floor."

"I'm not going in," said the woman. "I'm afraid of him. He said he'd kill me if I called the cops on him."

"Your kids in there?" asked Serge.

"No," she breathed. "They ran next door when we started fighting. I guess I should tell you there's a gun in there and he's nuts as hell tonight."

"Where's the gun?" asked Gus.

"Bedroom closet," said the woman. "When you take him you can take that too."

"We don't know if we're taking anybody yet," said Roy. "We're going to talk to him first."

Serge started up the steps first as she said, "Number twelve. We live in number twelve."

They passed through a landscaped archway and into a court surrounded by apartments. There was a calm lighted swimming pool to their left and a sun deck with Ping-Pong tables to the right. Roy was surprised at the size of the apartment building after passing through the deceiving archway.

"Very nice," said Gus, obviously admiring the swimming pool.

"Twelve must be this way," said Roy, walking toward the tile staircase surrounded by face-high ferns. Roy thought he could still smell the woman's alcohoic breath when a frail chalky man in a damp undershirt stepped from behind a dwarfed twisted tree and lunged toward Roy who turned on the stairway. The man pointed the cheap .22 revolver at Roy's stomach and fired once and as Roy sat down on the stairway in amazement the sounds of shouts and gunfire and a deathless scream echoed through the vast patio. Then Roy realized he was lying at the foot of the staircase alone and it was quiet for a moment. Then he was aware that it was his stomach.

"Oh, not there," said Roy and he clamped his teeth on his tongue and fought the burst of hysteria. The shock. It can kill. The shock!

Then he pulled the shirt open and unbuckled the Sam Browne and looked at the tiny bubbling cavity in the pit of his stomach. He knew he could not survive another one. Not there. Not in the guts. He had no guts left!

Roy unclamped his teeth and had to swallow many times because of the blood from his ripped tongue. It didn't hurt so much this time, he thought, and he was astonished at his lucidity. He saw that Serge and Gus were kneeling beside him, ashen-faced. Serge crossed himself and kissed his thumbnail.

It was *much* easier this time. By God, it was! The pain was diminishing and an insidious warmth crept over him. But no, it was all wrong. It shouldn't happen now. Then he panicked as he realized that it shouldn't happen now because he was starting to know. Oh, please, not now, he thought. I'm starting to know.

"Know, know," said Roy. "Know, know, know, know." His voice sounded to him hollow and rhythmic like the tolling of a bell. And then he could no longer speak.

"*Santa María,*" said Serge taking his hand. "*Santa María* . . . where's the goddamn ambulance? *Ay, Dios mío* . . . Gus, he's cold. *Sóbale las manos* . . ."

Then Roy heard Gus sob, "He's gone, Serge. Poor Roy, poor poor man. He's gone."

Then Roy heard Serge say, "We should cover him. Did you hear him? He was saying no to death. No, no, no, he said. *Santa María!*"

I am not dead, Roy thought. It is monstrous to say I am dead. And then he saw Becky walking primly through a grassy field and she looked so grownup he said Rebecca when he called her name and she came smiling to her father, the sun glistening off her hair, more golden than his had ever been.

"*Dios te salve María, llena de gracia, el Señor es contigo* . . ." said Serge.

"I'll cover him. I'll get a blanket from somebody," said Gus. "Please, somebody, give me a blanket."

Now Roy released himself to the billowy white sheets of darkness and the last thing he ever heard was Sergio Durán saying, "*Santa María,*" again and again.

The Choir Boys

For loyal friends
Irving Feffer, attorney at law
Sgt. Richard Kalk, LAPD
and
For the Choirboys
May your songs comfort and cheer

Prologue

THE THIRD MARINES were bleeding and dying for three nameless hills north of Khe Sanh in 1967. The North Vietnamese Army divisions were fighting around the DMZ and the marines had found several NVA command posts and crude field hospitals in the cave-pocked hills. The caves ran clear to the Laotian border and patrols were sent out to drop grenades down their air shafts and to flush the NVA out of the ground holes called spider traps.

On a night after the biggest battles were decided a squad of marines was ambushed by NVA and shot to pieces. Just two hours after the sun went down two marines huddled together in a cave that had formerly been an NVA hospital. It was deserted now except for broken beds made from bamboo and fragments of lumber. It was dank and musty and the two marines whispered frantically, trying to decide how to get back to their company. They were bewildered, couldn't comprehend what had happened so suddenly.

The tall marine, a fire team leader, wished desperately that his automatic rifleman had survived, or at least his other rifleman. His companion, a short and frail rifleman, was a new replacement who hadn't the sense to grab the M-14. He crouched trembling like a dog waiting for a command to move.

Then they heard the voices in the darkness. Many voices. The two marines crawled back, back into the cave, pressed against a wall as the NVA killing patrol searched for survivors of the ambush.

Both marines felt their dungarees suck at them as they wiped the sweat from their eyes and clamped their jaws to keep their teeth quiet. The short marine was whimpering.

Then an NVA rifleman said something to a comrade and cautiously entered the cave flashing a light into the cold wet interior.

The marines ground their faces into the slimy soil until they heard some nervous laughter and another soldier walk in as the light was switched off. The tall marine dared to peek from their nest and clearly saw the soldier silhouetted against the mouth of the cave. He was carrying a clump of Chinese stick grenades and a flame thrower. He scuttled toward them.

The soldier stumbled, muttered something and stood looking down a tunnel to his right, fingering the flame thrower while the two marines lay behind him almost at his feet. They could smell his sweat and a powerful odor of fish sauce and raw garlic. Then the soldier turned and walked back toward the cave opening where the voices got louder. Several soldiers propped their weapons against the clattering rocks and sat down for a break.

And as the short marine felt the panic deepen and believed that he could no longer control the sobs he was smothering, the tall marine suddenly started suffocating, or thought he was. He ripped at the collar of his jacket, panting. Only the soldiers' voices outside saved them.

It was the tall stronger one who began to cry. The walls and darkness closed in. He began to hyperventilate and couldn't get enough air. At first he wept almost imperceptibly, but then convulsively, and voices or not, the short marine was sure the NVA could not help but hear him. Desperately, instinctively, there in the darkness he took the tall marine in his arms and patted his shoulder and whispered: "Now now now. Hush now. I'm right here. You're *not* alone."

Gradually the tall marine began to quiet down and breathe regularly and when the patrol moved on five minutes later he was totally in control. He led the short marine back to their battered company. They were nineteen years old. They were children.

1

Territorial Imperative

THE MAN most deserving of credit for keeping the MacArthur Park killing out of the newspapers before it brought discredit to the Los Angeles Police Department was Commander Hector Moss. It was perhaps Commander Moss' finest hour.

The blond commander was so exultant this afternoon he didn't mind that Deputy Chief Adrian Lynch was keeping him waiting the allotted time. Chief Lynch kept all callers waiting precisely three minutes before coming to the phone, unless his secretary told him it was an assistant chief or the chief of police himself or one of the commissioners or a city councilman or anyone at City Hall who reported directly to the mayor.

Moss despised Lynch for having a do-nothing job and a specially ordered oversized desk. Moss knew for a fact that Deputy Chief Lynch had secret plans to increase his personal staff by two: one policewoman and one civilian, both of whom were busty young women. Commander Moss knew this because his adjutant, Lieutenant Dewey Treadwell, had sneaked into Lynch's office and searched his file basket when a janitor left the door open. Of course Lieutenant Treadwell could not receive a specifically worded commendation for his assignment but he did receive an ambiguously worded "attaboy" from Moss.

But there was another assignment which Treadwell had failed to carry out, and Commander Moss' stomach soured as he remembered it. It had to do with Moss' IQ score of 107. Throughout his twenty-one year career his IQ had meant nothing to his rise to the rank of commander. Indeed, he had not even known what his score was. He had been a state college honors student in police science and reasoned that no one with an ordinary IQ could manage this. But with the retirement of a senior deputy chief it had been called to Moss' attention by none other than Deputy Chief Lynch who didn't think the promotion board would consider a man for such a high police post who possessed an IQ of only 107. Lynch's own IQ was 140.

Commander Moss was livid. He took Lieutenant Treadwell to a Chinatown bar one Friday after work and forced the teetotaler to down five cocktails, promising his personal patronage for the rest of Treadwell's career if he could carry off a most delicate assignment. The ever ambitious, thirty year old lieutenant agreed to slip into Personnel Division that night and change Commander Moss' IQ score from 107 to 141.

Commander Moss downed his fourth Singapore sling and said, "Treadwell, I know I can depend on you."

But instantly the lieutenant's ambition gave way to fear. He stammered, "If anything ever . . . well, look, sir, the watch commander of Personnel is a former detective. He might start sniffing around. They have ways in the crime lab to tell if documents have been tampered with!"

"Don't talk crime lab to me, Treadwell," Moss replied. "Have you ever worked the Detective Bureau?"

"No, sir."

"You listen to me, Treadwell. You're an office pogue. You never been anything *but* an office pogue. You don't have the slightest idea what goes on in a working police division. But you keep your mouth shut and do what you're told and I'll see to it that you're a captain someday and you can have your own station to play with. You don't and I'll have you in uniform on the nightwatch in Watts. Understand me, Treadwell?"

"Oh, yes, sir!"

"Now drink your Pink Lady," Commander Moss commanded. (It was Hector Moss who had persuaded the chief of police that the traditional police rank of "inspector" was no longer viable in an era of violence when policemen are called upon to employ counterinsurgency tactics. Thanks to Moss all officers formerly of the inspector rank could now call themselves "commander." Moss had "Commander and Mrs. Hector Moss" painted on his home mailbox. Commander Moss had been a PFC in the army.)

Lieutenant Treadwell tried desperately every night for three weeks to sneak into Personnel Division. Each morning he reported a "Sorry, sir, negative" to Commander Moss. Lieutenant Dewey Treadwell lost ten pounds in those three weeks. He slept no more than four hours a night and then only fitfully. He was impotent. On the twenty-first night of his mission he was almost caught by a janitor. Lieutenant Treadwell was defeated and admitted it to Commander Moss on a black Wednesday morning.

The commander listened to his adjutant's excuses for a moment and said, "Did you get a good look at the janitor's face, Lieutenant?"

"Yes, sir. No . . . I don't know, sir. Why?"

"Because that boogie might live in Watts. And you'll need some friends there. BECAUSE THAT'S WHERE I'M SENDING YOU ON THE NEXT TRANSFER, YOU INCOMPETENT FUCKING PANSY!"

Commander Moss did not send Lieutenant Treadwell to Watts. He decided a spineless jellyfish was preferable to a smart aleck like Lieutenant Wirtz who worked for Deputy Chief Lynch. What he *did* was to go into Personnel Division in broad daylight, rip the commendation he wrote for Treadwell out of the file, draw a black *X* through it with a felt tipped pen, seal it in an envelope and leave it in Lieutenant Treadwell's incoming basket without comment.

Lieutenant Treadwell, after his hair started falling out in tufts, earned his way back into Commander Moss' good graces by authoring that portion of the Los Angeles Police Department manual which reads:

> SIDEBURNS: Sideburns shall not extend below the bottom of the outer ear opening (the top of the earlobe) and shall end in a clean-shaven horizontal iline. The flare (terminal portion of the sideburn) shall not exceed the width of the main portion of the sideburn by more than one-fourth of the unflared width.
>
> MOUSTACHES: A short and neatly trimmed moustache of natural color may be worn. Moustaches shall not extend below the vermilion border of the upper lip or the corners of the mouth and may not extend to the side more than one-quarter inch beyond the corners of the mouth.

It took Lieutenant Treadwell thirteen weeks to compose the regulations. He was toasted and congratulated at a staff meeting. He beamed proudly. The regulations were perfect. No one could understand them.

As Commander Moss cooled his heels on the telephone waiting for Deputy Chief Adrian Lynch, the deputy chief was watching the second hand on his watch sweep past the normal three minute interval he reserved for most callers. Chief Lynch couldn't decide whether to give Moss a four minute wait or have his secretary say he would call back. Of course he couldn't be obviously rude. That bastard Moss had the ear of the chief of police and every other idiot who didn't know him well. Lynch hated those phony golden locks which Moss probably tinted. The asshole was at least forty-five years old and still looked like a Boy Scout. Not a wrinkle on that smirking kisser.

Lynch punched the phone button viciously and chirped, "Good morning, Deputy Chief Lynch speaking. May I help you?"

"It's I, Chief. Hec Moss," said the commander, and Chief Lynch grimaced and thought, It's I. Oh shit!

"Yeah Hec."

"Chief, it's about the MacArthur Park orgy."

"Goddamnit, don't call it that!"

"Sorry sir. I meant the choir practice."

"Don't call it that either. That's all we need for the papers to pick it up.'

"Yes sir," Moss said. And then more slyly, "I'm very cognizant of bad press, sir. After all, I squelched the thing and assuaged the victim's family."

Oh shit! thought Lynch. *Assuaged*. "Yes, Hec," said the chief wearily.

"Well sir, I was wondering, just to lock the thing up so to speak, I was wondering if we shouldn't have the chief order quick trial boards for every officer who was at the orgy. Fire them all."

"Don't . . . say . . . *orgy*. And don't . . . say . . . *choir practice!*"

"Sorry sir."

"That's not very good thinking, Hec." The chief tilted back in his chair, lifted his wing tips to the desk top, raised up his rust colored hairpiece and scratched his freckled rubbery scalp. "I don't think we should consider firing them."

"They deserve it, sir."

"They deserve more than that, Hec. The bastards deserve to be in jail as accessories to a killing. I'd personally like to see every one of them in Folsom Prison. *But* they might make a fuss. They might bring in some lawyers to the trial board. They might notify the press if we have a mass dismissal. In short, they might hurl a pail of defecation into the air conditioning."

Chief Lynch waited for a chuckle from Moss, got none and thought again about Moss' low IQ. "Anyway, Hec," he continued, "we have a real good case only against the one who did the shooting and I think we're stuck with that. We'll give the others a trial board and a six month suspension, but we'll take care of it quietly. Maybe we can scare some of them into resigning."

"Some goddamn shrink at General Hospital's saying that killer's nuts."

"What do you expect from General Hospital? What're they good for anyway but treating the lame and lazy on the welfare rolls? What do you plan to do about that dumbass detective who examined the officer the night of the shooting and ordered him taken to the psychiatric ward?"

"Ten days off?"

"Should get twenty."

"Afraid he might complain to the press."

"Guess you're right," Chief Lynch conceded grudgingly.

"Well, hope you're happy with our office, Chief!"

"You did a fine job, Hec," Deputy Chief Lynch said. "But I wish you'd talk to your secretary. I've had reports she didn't say 'good morning' twice last week when my adjutant called."

"Won't happen again, Chief."

"Bye bye, Hec."

Deputy Chief Lynch wouldn't stand for a violation of the Los Angeles Police Department order concerning phone answering. After all, he had written the order. Officers had to answer thus:

"Good morning [afternoon or evening], Wilshire Watch Commander's Office, Officer Fernwood speaking. May I help you?"

If any word was left out of this standard greeting, the officer could be subject to disciplinary action.

It was said that once when a desk officer at Newton Street Station had uttered the entire phrase before giving the caller a chance to speak, the caller, a cardiac victim, fell unconscious before completing the address where the ambulance should be sent and died twenty minutes later.

Deputy Chief Lynch was a man to reckon with because he had thought of the most printable slogan in the history of the department. It was the slogan for a simple plan to spread out the staff officers geographically, giving them line control over everything in a given area. But if the plan were to be newsworthy, it needed a word or words to make it sound sophisticated, military and *dramatic*.

It came to Deputy Chief Lynch in a dream one night after he saw *Command Decision* on "The Late Show."

"Territorial Imperative!" he screamed in his sleep, terrifying his wife.

"But what's it mean, sir?" his adjutant asked the next day.

"That's the beauty of it, stupid. It means whatever you want it to mean," Chief Lynch answered testily.

"I see! Brilliant, sir!" cried the adjutant.

One often read in the Los Angeles newspapers that the chief of police was shuffling his officers around in the interest of "Territorial Imperative."

2

The Body Count

Deputy Chief Adrian Lynch could sit for hours and stare at stacks of paper and suck on an unlit pipe and look overworked. This alone would not have made him a success however if he had not been the driving force behind Team Policing and the Basic Car Plan which everyone knew were the pet projects of the Big Chief.

"Team Policing" was nothing more than the deployment as often as possible of the same men in a given radio car district, making these men responsible not only for uniform patrol in that district but for helping the detectives with their follow-up investigation. The detectives (now called "investigators") resented the encroachment of younger patrol officers in the investigative work. The patrol officers in turn resented a phase of the Basic Car Plan which in reality was the plan itself. It was the Basic Car Plan Meeting. It was resented by everybody.

This meeting usually took place at a school or auditorium in the district patrolled by the given car. It was more or less a glorified coffee klatch to which doughnuts were added as an enticement. They were picked up free, compliments of a large doughnut chain. Police administrators could swear that crime had dropped because two dozen lonely old ladies had coffee and doughnuts with two charming, well groomed, young uniformed policemen who couldn't wait to get rid of the old ladies so they could get off duty and meet some young ladies.

When Deputy Chief Lynch was still a commander he had had the foresight to transfer to his office an enterprising young policeman who had been a second lieutenant in Vietnam and was an absolute master of the body count. Officer

Weishart made sure that all Basic Car meetings in divisions commanded by Lynch would take place in school buildings adjacent to crowded playgrounds. Officer Weishart supplied not only coffee and doughnuts for the pensioners in the neighborhood but cookies and punch for the children. He enticed hundreds of kids from the streets to set foot inside the auditorium wherein they would be duly logged. *Each* time they came and went. If anyone had ever bothered to audit Officer Weishart's statistics he would have discovered that to accommodate the mobs reported, the grammar school auditorium would have had to be the size of the Los Angeles Coliseum.

But Team Policing and the Basic Car Plan had created lots and lots of new jobs for officers of staff rank. Therefore lieutenants made captain, captains made commander and commanders made deputy chief, and everyone had all the time they needed to think up new things for the working cops to do aside from catching crooks, which most of the new captains, commanders and deputy chiefs knew nothing about.

If Deputy Chief Lynch had an Achilles' heel which might someday preclude his elevation to chief of police it was his lubricious lusting after his secretary, Theda Gunther, the wife of Lieutenant Harry Gunther, who every time he turned around found himself transferred farther and farther from his Eagle Rock home, which allowed his wife more and more time with Deputy Chief Lynch who wished there was a police station for Lieutenant Gunther even farther from downtown than West Valley Station.

If the body count at the Basic Car Plan meetings was Chief Lynch's greatest accomplishment as a police officer his most thrilling by far was fornicating with Theda Gunther on top of the desk of that goddamn religious fanatic, Assistant Chief Buster Llewellyn.

They had gotten drunk in Chinatown the night Lynch suggested it, and there had almost been a slight scandal when they staggered into the police building at 2:00 A.M.

It had been a mad coupling for both of them what with the possibility of being caught in such a hallowed spot. Theda Gunther ripped off Deputy Chief Lynch's hairpiece in the throes of orgasm, and he, instinctively grabbing for the three hundred dollar toupee, had a premature withdrawal, leaving evidence all over the irreplaceable hand tooled blotter with Llewellyn's religious slogans engraved on all four corners.

Lynch feared that Llewellyn might immediately recognize the night deposit for what it was. He might send the blotter to the crime lab and seek the assistance of some smartass like his adjutant, a surly former detective. Chief Lynch didn't know *what* a former detective might be able to uncover.

When the case of the MacArthur Park killing came to his attention Deputy Chief Lynch listened to all the details, including the stories of lurid fantastic orgies involving officers and station house groupies. He became angrier than anyone had ever seen him. He wanted to jail the officers. Due to his accident on Llewellyn's desk he had become a nervous wreck. For three weeks Theda Gunther as usual rubbed her hot curvy body all over him when they passed in the office but he was as flaccid as linguini. She eventually got huffy and stopped calling him old donkey dick.

Of course Chief Lynch wasn't the only one affected by the killing. Wilshire Station Captain Stanley Drobeck was fuming because he had to write a thirty page report to the chief of police about the MacArthur Park incident with all available information on the drinking, the degenerates and the dead body. This on top of the Captain Cunkle scandal which itself took ten pages to describe.

Captain Drobeck felt that a station captain truly had the hot seat in the police department. All the big chief did was make speeches and hog headlines. It was the captains who were deluged by paper work, who made the decisions and who were *there*. It certainly wasn't the big chief and it wasn't Deputy Chief Adrian Lynch, who, Drobeck knew, spent the entire day trying to seduce his secretary, Theda

Gunther, whose lieutenant husband was not likely ever to get transferred any closer to downtown and had taken to riding a motorbike to save gas.

Captain Drobeck despised libertines, like Deputy Chief Lynch and Captain Cunkle of Wilshire Detectives, who had been the cause of his latest and largest internal discipline matter before the MacArthur Park killing.

Cunkle was a loathsome veteran detective who had somehow managed to pass his promotion exams without more than a high school education and had conned his way past the promotion boards. When former Inspector Moss convinced the chief he should change the designation of ''inspector'' to ''commander'' it was Cunkle who said that the public associated the title of ''inspector'' with a police officer and that ''commander'' was purely a military term and that he wanted to be a cop not a soldier.

It had been Captain Drobeck's recent pleasure to recommend ten days' suspension for a single, male, twenty-five year old policeman who had been found to be living with a single, female, twenty-three year old bank teller. The charge was conduct unbecoming an officer, or CUBO, called ''cue-bow'' by the policemen. He had recommended twenty days for a policewoman in the same circumstances in that a female officer should be even more above reproach than a male.

When Captain Cunkle was finally caught by a private detective in a motel with Hester Billings, the wife of a prominent attorney, Captain Drobeck made the following recommendation to Deputy Chief Lynch:

> Despite the risk of being accused by the rank-and-file officers of applying a double standard if this confidential investigation leaks, I am recommending that you take no action against Captain Wesley Cunkle, who, as you know, was caught in a compromising position with a female person not his wife. The enclosed photos were taken by a well-known private investigator, himself a former police officer, thoroughly unscrupulous, but reportedly discreet. The negatives will be destroyed if the demand of his employer, the female person's husband, is met.
>
> The demand is: a quick divorce without alimony and with custody of the children for Mr.——.
>
> There is some complication in that Captain Cunkle is, as you know, to be elevated to the rank of commander on the next transfer list. If he is not promoted, the field policemen may lose confidence in their leaders and get wind of this scandal despite our efforts to keep it stonewalled.
>
> Respectfully,

Chief Lynch read the correspondence and looked at the photos of Captain Cunkle naked on his knees on the floor of a motel his eyes glazed by martinis and lust. Then the chief looked at Mrs. Billings spread-eagled on the bed unaware of Private Investigator Slim Scully snapping his Nikon for all he was worth.

''What do you think, sir?'' asked Captain Drobeck who personally delivered the confidential reports and series of photos to the chief.

''Damn, she's got a hairy box!'' Chief Lynch whistled.

At the same moment that Captain Drobeck was making his recommendation to Deputy Chief Lynch concerning the secret matter of Captain Cunkle, an early nightwatch rollcall was being conducted at 77th Street Station. An alcoholic twenty-five year policeman named Aaron Mobley said to the sergeant in charge of the roll-call, ''Goddamnit, I don't mind how much pussy Cunkle eats, but why does a working copper get a suspension for the same thing a captain does?''

''Come on,'' said the florid sergeant. ''We been yakking about this for two days. I'd rather *do* it than talk about it. Let's read off the crimes.''

Finally, Ruben Wilkie, a twenty-six year cop who was the partner of Aaron Mobley, had the last word: "He gobbles one beaver and gets promoted. I've ate close to three hundred bearded clams in my time and never even got a commendation!"

But perhaps the *very* last word on the subject was uttered by Police Commissioner Howie Morton. The police commissioners were political appointees, titular department heads, who knew little about police work but were generally harmless since the true power rested with the chief. Police Commissioner Morton was a white Anglo. The board always had at least one black, one Mexican-American, one Jew and, of late, one woman. It had never had a Persian, a Filipino or a Navajo and never would until those ethnic groups acquired a political base in Los Angeles.

Police Commissioner Morton was able to learn about the supersecret Captain Cunkle scandal because he had a distant cousin, a garage mechanic at Southwest Station, who overheard the janitors saying they were sick of hearing about it. Commissioner Morton persuaded a sergeant who worked Internal Affairs Division to obtain the photos for him. The last word on the Commander Cunkle scandal was hence uttered by Police Commissioner Morton. He looked at the photos and whistled. "Damn, she's got a hairy box!"

3

Cue-Bow

Commander Hector Moss was popular at functions wherein people with causes wanted a member of the police department to beat up verbally.

Commander Moss, the perennial toastmaster, always wore handcuffs on the front of his belt. When he stood before a DAR meeting and had the ladies agog with his wavy blond hair and stories of crime and violence, the coat would be pulled open and the handcuffs would appear. Sometimes the right side of his coat slipped open to show a chrome plated Smith and Wesson Combat Masterpiece tugging down at the alligator belt, custom made to support the weight of the heavy gun. Commander Moss had been in various administrative jobs since being promoted to sergeant sixteen years ago. The gun had never been fired. The ammunition was so old it is doubtful it *could* fire. Commander Moss got the stories of crime and violence from police reports which crossed his desk each day. Commander Moss was an excellent storyteller.

The MacArthur Park killing had in truth been a godsend. Hector Moss thrived on crisis and longed to prove his rapport with the media. Besides, he desperately needed something to relieve the boredom of sitting and poring through the house organ, called *The Beat Magazine*, making sure that as always there was nothing in it more cerebral than who had a baby and who died and that there was at least one picture of some vacationing motor cop in Mexico grinning at a dead fish.

There had never been a controversial article in that magazine to stir up or reflect the opinion of the street cops. He often said that if someone ever organized those ignorant bastards, look out. Commander Moss was like a slaver who lived in fear of native footsteps on the decks in the night.

At this hour, on a hot August afternoon with the officers involved in the killing being sweated in the interrogation rooms of Internal Affairs Division, Commander Moss decided on a technique he believed was essential for dealing with any reporters who might belatedly get onto the story of the dead body in MacArthur Park. He didn't wait to be phoned by the enemies who worked for what he considered a loathsome left wing rag. He phoned his favorite reporter with the other paper, after he made sure the reporter had heard something about the case from a different source.

"I wanted you to know about it as soon as I had the full story," said Commander Moss, smiling at the telephone. "It appears an off-duty officer had an accident with a gun in MacArthur Park at about two A.M. I hope you can soft-pedal it for the sake of the seven thousand fine boys and girls in this department. Yes, it was a tragedy all right. A young man is dead. Yes. One officer's relieved from duty pending an investigation. Yes, yes, there is *some* evidence of drinking. I don't know, could've dropped the gun and it went off. I just don't know yet. Been a policeman almost five years. Vietnam vet. Right. Yes, there's some evidence the officer was with friends. To level with you, Pete, there's a strong possibility some policemen bought a sixpack of beer and stopped in the park on the way home to unwind and talk. Yes, that's Conduct Unbecoming an Officer. We call it cue-bow. Choir practice? No, don't believe I know that term. Choir practice? No, never heard of it."

When the reporter hung up, Commander Moss sat back and put his feet up on his desk, which was actually two square inches larger than Chief Lynch's specially ordered desk, and said to his secretary, "I know that wasn't the first choir practice in that park. I'd love to know about some of the *other* ones."

4

Sergeant Nick Yanov

Actually there were dozens of choir practices in MacArthur Park attended faithfully by ten policemen who worked out of Wilshire Police Station but chose MacArthur Park as the choir practice site because it was in Rampart Station's territory. They believed that one does not shit in one's own nest.

The first choir practice in MacArthur Park took place in the early spring when the nights became warm enough. Most of the choirboys were unencumbered. That was by design of Harold Bloomguard who was really the driving force behind the inception of the MacArthur Park choir practice. Harold always maintained that they shouldn't have married men in the group because they would quite likely have to go home early, and early dropouts were the death of any good choir practice.

"The songs must go on!" was the way Harold always put it.

Of course no one ever really sang at choir practice. Their "songs" were of a different genus but served much the same purpose as rousing choral work. It was called by various names at other police departments. It was merely an off-duty meeting, usually in a secluded hideaway, for policemen who, having just finished their tour of duty, were too tense or stimulated or electrified to go to a silent sleeping house and lie down like ordinary people while nerve ends sparked. One hadn't always enough money to go to a policemen's bar. Still one felt the need to uncoil and have a drink and talk with others who had been on the streets that night. To reassure oneself.

Sergeant Nick Yanov could have been a charter member during those five months when the MacArthur Park choir practices were being held. He was invited by Harold Bloomguard one evening after a 3:00 P.M. nightwatch rollcall at which the uniformed policemen had a surprise visit from Captain Stanley Drobeck. The station commander wore a silk suit with a belt in the back, and black and white patent leather shoes. When Captain Drobeck entered the assembly room he caused Lieutenant Alvin Finque, who was conducting the rollcall, to jump unconsciously to attention which embarrassed the blue uniformed patrol officers. Since police service is not nearly as GI as military service, the only time one stands at attention is during inspection or formal ceremonies.

Lieutenant Finque blushed and sat back down. He blinked and said ''Hi Skipper'' to Captain Drobeck.

''Whoever made the pinch on the burglar in Seven-A-One's area deserves a good smoke!'' the captain announced, as he threw four fifteen-cent cigars out into the audience of twenty-eight nightwatch officers and, smiling with self-satisfaction, strode out the door. His hair was freshly rinsed and was blue white that day.

Only three nightwatch officers were old enough to smoke a cigar without looking silly. One was Herbert ''Spermwhale'' Whalen and he had caught the burglar. He was a MacArthur Park choirboy.

Like all old veterans, Spermwhale sat in the back row and insisted on wearing his hat. Cocked to the side, of course. Spermwhale picked up one of the cigars from the floor, examined the brand, sat on it and loosed an enormous fart which moved out every policeman nearby. Then he tossed the cigar back on the floor. Another choirboy, Spencer Van Moot of 7-A-33, picked it up gingerly with two fingers, stripped off the cellophane and said, ''It'll be okay after it dries out.''

Lieutenant Finque had just replaced Lieutenant Grimsley whose transfer was mysteriously precipitated by Spermwhale Whalen. Lieutenant Finque was of medium height with straight hair which was parted and combed straight back much as his father had done when his father was still in style in 1939, the year of Lieutenant Finque's birth. The lieutenant was unsure in his new rank but rarely if ever heeded the advice he always asked for from Sergeant Nick Yanov, the hipless chesty field sergeant, who had to shave twice a day to control his whiskers.

Sergeant Yanov was an eleven year officer, and at age thirty-four actually had less supervisory experience than Lieutenant Finque. But he had the distinction of being the only person of supervisory rank ever to be invited to a MacArthur Park choir practice, which he wisely declined.

Sergeant Yanov's only immediate passion in life, like many officers at Wilshire Station, was some night to drag Officer Reba Hadley away from the nightwatch desk and into the basement and rip her tight blue uniform blouse and skirt from her tantalizing young body and literally screw the badge right off her. Which was perhaps symbolically linked with Yanov's avowed belief that superior officers like Lieutenant Finque had been screwing him mercilessly for the past eleven years.

Lieutenant Finque had a different passion. He wanted to be the first watch commander in Wilshire Division history to catch every single member of his watch out of his car with his hat off or drinking free coffee or failing to answer a telephone properly.

When things quieted down from Spermwhale's contribution to rollcall, Lieutenant Finque said, ''Fellows, we have some rollcall material to give you on diplomatic immunity in misdemeanor cases. In case you should have the occasion to run into a consul or ambassador in the course of your duties, does everyone know the difference between a consul and an ambassador?''

''An ambassador is a Nash,'' said Harold Bloomguard of 7-A-29. ''Don't see too many these days.''

''I heard those consulate cocksuckers just wipe their ass with their parking tickets in New York,'' offered Roscoe Rules of 7-A-85.

''If you work for the UN you can do no wrong in the first place,'' said Spencer Van Moot of 7-A-33.

''Well, I hope you all read the material,'' Lieutenant Finque said jauntily as the drops of acid formed. He was never sure if they were being insubordinate.

''Finque's rollcalls are about as exciting as a parking ticket,'' whispered Francis Tanaguchi of 7-A-77 to his partner, Calvin Potts.

''And to think I left a sick bed to come to work today,'' Calvin groaned.

"Your girl wasn't feeling well?" Francis asked.

"On to more important things, men," Lieutenant Finque said, as Sergeant Nick Yanov, who sat on his left on the platform in front of the assembly, looked at the ceiling and drummed nervously on the table with his fingers. "I hope you men have been trying to sell whistles. The nightwatch has been doing pretty badly compared to the daywatch."

This announcement caused Sergeant Yanov to lean back in his chair and start rubbing his eyes with the heels of both hands so that he would not have to see the eye rolling, lip curling, head shaking, feet shuffling, which was utterly lost on Lieutenant Finque who had given birth to the whistle selling campaign.

It had been a master stroke which actually was suggested by an eighty year old spinster who attended every single Basic Car Plan meeting. Since Lieutenant Finque was pretty sure the old woman was senile and would not remember she had thought of it, he adopted the idea as his own and the uniformed patrol force of Wilshire Station found themselves being forced to sell black plastic whistles for fifty cents to women they contacted on their calls. The object was that if a woman were ever accosted on the street by thugs she should pull out her whistle and blow it.

The proceeds from the whistle sales went to the station's Youth Services Fund and quickly earned several thousand dollars. Lieutenant Finque was hoping the idea would earn him a written commendation from Deputy Chief Lynch, which wouldn't look bad in his personnel package.

Spermwhale Whalen had sold the most whistles on the nightwatch, six in fact. But actually he had bought them himself and given them to his favorite streetwalking whores with the instruction that if they ever had a slow evening and felt like giving away a free blowjob to a old pal just to pucker on the whistle when 7-A-1 came cruising by.

There was not a recorded case of a radio car in the vast and crowded district ever hearing a distress whistle, but it was said that the whistle saved the property of one woman on LaCienega Boulevard when a purse snatcher almost fell to the sidewalk in a giggling fit at the sight of a sixty year old matron in a chinchilla coat blowing a little plastic whistle until her face looked like a rotten strawberry.

"One last order of business before we have inspection and hit the streets," the lieutenant said. "The detectives would like the cars in the area to keep an eye on Wilbur's Tavern on Sixth Street. They have reports that the owner is beating up barmaids who're too intimidated to make a report. He apparently only hires girls willing to orally copulate him. And if they start to object after a time, he beats them up and threatens them. Seven-A-Twenty-nine, how about stopping in there once every couple days?"

"Right, Lieutenant," said Harold Bloomguard who looked at his grinning partner, Sam Niles.

Minutes after rollcall, 7-A-29 was speeding to the station call but was beaten by ten other nightwatch policemen swarming all over the tavern checking out the barmaids.

5

7-A-85: Roscoe Rules and Dean Pratt

Probably the most choir practices were called by Harold Bloomguard of 7-A-29. Probably the least choir practices were called by 7-A-85. Roscoe Rules just didn't seem to need them as much.

One choir practice however was hastily called by Dean Pratt of 7-A-85, five months before the choir practice killing. It was on the night Roscoe Rules became a legend in his own time.

Henry Rules was nicknamed "Roscoe" by Harold Bloomguard at another midnight choir practice when Rules, who had just seen an old Bogart movie on television, finished telling the others of a recent arrest: "This black ass, abba dabba motherfucker looked like he was gonna rabbit, so I drew down and zonked him across the gourd with my roscoe."

For a moment drunken Harold Bloomguard looked at his partner Sam Niles in disbelief. Rules had not said "gun" or "piece" or ".39" but had actually said "roscoe."

"Oh, lizard shit!" cried Bloomguard. "Roscoe! Roscoe! Did you hear that?"

"You mean your 'gat,' Rules?" roared Sam Niles, who was also drunk, and he rolled over on his blanket in the grass, spilling half a gallon of wine worth about three dollars.

From then on, to all the choirboys, Henry Rules became known as "Roscoe" Rules. The only one to call him "Henry" occasionally was his partner Dean Pratt who was afraid of him.

Roscoe Rules was a five year policeman. He had long arms and veiny hands. He was tall and hard and strong. And mean. No one who talked as mean as Roscoe Rules could have survived twenty-nine years on this earth without *being* mean. His parents had been struggling farmers in Idaho, then in the San Joaquin Valley of California, where they acquired a little property before each died in early middle age.

"Roscoe Rules handed out towels in the showers at Auschwitz," the policemen said.

"Roscoe Rules was a Manson family reject—too nasty."

"Roscoe Rules believes in feeding stray puppies and kittens—to his piranha."

And so forth.

If there was one thing Roscoe Rules wished, after having seen all of the world he cared to see, it was that there was a word as dirty as "nigger" to apply to all mankind. Since he had little imagination he had to settle for "asshole." But he realized that all Los Angeles policemen and most American policemen used that as the best of all possible words.

Caivin Potts, the only black choirboy, agreed wholeheartedly with Roscoe when he drunkenly expressed his dilemma one night at choir practice in the park.

"That's the only thing I like about you, Roscoe," Calvin said. "You don't just hate brothers. You hate *everyone*. Even more than I do. Without prejudice or bias."

"Gimme a word then," Roscoe said. He was reeling and vomitous, looking over his shoulder for Harold Bloomguard who at 150 pounds would fight anyone who was cruel to the MacArthur Park ducks.

"Gimme a word," Roscoe repeated and furtively chucked a large jagged rock at a fuzzy duckling who swam too close, just missing the baby who went squawking to its mother.

Everyone went through the ordinary police repertoire for Roscoe Rules.

"How about fartsuckers?"

"Not rotten enough."

"Slimeballs?"

"That's getting old."

"Scumbags?"

"Naw."

"Cumbuckets?"

"Too long."

"Hemorrhoids?"

"Everybody uses that."

"Scrotums?"

"Not bad, but too long."

"Scrotes, then," said Willie Wright who was now drunk enough to use unwholesome language.

"That's it!" Roscoe Rules shouted. "Scrotes! That's what all people are: ignorant filthy disgusting ugly worthless scrotes. I like that! Scrotes!"

"A man's philosophy expressed in a word," said Baxter Slate of 7-A-1. "Hear! Hear!" He held up his fifth of Sneaky Pete, drained it in three gulps, suddenly felt the special effects of the port and barbiturates he secretly popped, fell over and moaned.

There was however one thing which endeared Roscoe Rules to all the other choirboys: he was, next to Spencer Van Moot of 7-A-33, the greatest promoter any of them had ever seen. Roscoe could, when he cared to, arrange food and drink for the most voluptuous tastes—all of it free—for the other choirboys, who called him an insufferable prick.

At first the only thing Roscoe didn't like about his partner Dean Pratt was his styled red hair. But he soon came to hate his partner for his drunken crying jags at choir practice. There was another thing about Dean Pratt which *all* the choirboys despised and that was that the twenty-five year old bachelor's brain became temporarily but totally destroyed by less than ten ounces of any alcoholic drink. Then it was impossible to make the grinning redhead understand *anything*. Any question, statement, piece of smalltalk would be met by an idiotic frustrating maddening double beseechment:

"I don't get it. I don't get it." Or, "Whaddaya trying to say? Whaddaya trying to say?" Or, most frequently heard, "Whaddaya mean? Whaddaya mean?"

And so, Dean Pratt eventually became known as Whaddayamean Dean. The first few sessions of the MacArthur Park choirboys found Roscoe Rule, Calvin Potts or Spermwhale Whalen eventually grabbing the lanky redhead by the front of his Bugs Bunny sweatshirt and shaking him in rage with Dean in drunken tears babbling, "I don't get it. I don't get it. Whaddaya mean? Whaddaya *mean?*"

Yet Whaddayamean Dean became the first policeman Roscoe Rules ever took home to meet his family. Roscoe, one of three choirboys who were married, lived on a one acre piece of ground east of Chino, California, some sixty miles from Wilshire Station. Even the few friends Roscoe had made these past four years would not drive that far to be sociable. Roscoe loved it there and made the daily trek gladly. His children could grow up in a rural setting as he had. Of course they would not have to work nearly as hard. His two boys, eight and nine, only had to hoe and weed and water his corn, onions, carrots, squash and melons. Then after cleaning the animals' stalls, picking the infectious dung and hay from the horse's hooves and treating the swaybacked pony for ringbone, they could have the rest of the day for playing. After they studied for a minimum of one and a half hours on weekdays and two on Saturdays and Sundays. And after they took turns pitching and catching a baseball for forty-five minutes on weekends.

Roscoe Rules had convinced both his sons that they would be allstar players their first season in Little League. And they were. And he had convinced them that if they didn't get straight A's through elementary school they would get what the recalcitrant pony got when it misbehaved.

Roscoe's two sons hated riding as much as the pony hated being ridden, but when the pony wouldn't ride, Roscoe would snare the pony's front feet, loop his rope around the corral fence and deftly jerk the animal's legs back toward his hindquarters, catching the beast when it fell with a straight right between the eyes. He wore his old sap gloves with the lead filled palm and padded knuckles (which a sob sister sergeant had caught him beating up a drunk with and which he had been ordered to get rid of). That jerking rope, that punch and the bone bruising force of crashing to earth never failed to tame the pony who would obey for several weeks until the stupid creature forgot and became stubborn. Then he would require "gentling" again. Roscoe Rules believed that animals and people were basically alike: they were all scrotes.

Roscoe was very proud of the clean healthy life he had provided for his sons away from the city. He counted the years, months and weeks until he could retire with a twenty year service pension to his little ranch east of Chino and live out his days with his wife Clara (a secret drinker), and raise grandchildren in the same American tradition and perhaps buy them ponies and make ballplayers out of them. And give them all the advantages he had provided for his own children.

Roscoe was, like most policemen, conservative politically by virtue of his inescapable police cynicism but more so because of his misanthropy which had its roots in childhood. He had served in Vietnam and had almost made the Army his career until an LAPD recruiting poster had forced him to compare the benefits of police work to military service.

Roscoe was not a religious man. He scowled at American Legion benedictions. He scoffed at his Presbyterian wife and forbade her to make weaklings of their children by taking them to Sunday school. He said that instead of turning the other cheek you should sap the motherfuckers to their knees then choke them out until they were "doing the chicken" on the ground and then step over their twitching, jerking, unconscious bodies and kneedrop them with the full weight of your body down through the spear of the knee into the kidney. And that if Jesus Christ didn't have the balls to treat his enemies like that he was just another faggot Jew. Roscoe Rules wasn't raising his sons to be faggots.

But Roscoe Rules had a sense of humor. He carried in his wallet two photographs from his Army days which were getting cracked and faded despite the plastic envelopes he kept them in. One showed a Vietnamese girl of twelve or thirteen trying gamely to earn five American dollars by copulating an emaciated oxen which Roscoe and several other American cowboys had lassoed and tied thrashing on its back in a bamboo corral.

The second photo, which everyone at Wilshire Station had seen, was of Roscoe holding the severed head of a Vietcong by the hair as Roscoe leered into the camera, tongue lolling, neck twisted to one side. The photo had "Igor and friend" printed across the bottom. The thought of the photo was to trigger Roscoe's finest hour as a member of the Los Angeles Police Department.

Whaddayamean Dean hated being the partner of someone as mean as Roscoe Rules. He knew his own physical limitations and rarely talked tough on the street unless he was absolutely sure that the other person was terrified of police, in which case he allowed himself the luxury of tossing around a few "assholes," or "scrotes" to please Roscoe.

"Know why niggers survive serious wounds, partner?" Roscoe Rules asked Whaddayamean Dean.

"No, why, Henry?" asked Whaddayamean Dean, using the given name abhorred by the other choirboys.

"They're too dumb to go into shock."

Whaddayamean Dean giggled and snuffled and looked up from his driving at the browless blue eyes of Roscoe Rules, and at his freckled hands which would nervously grab at the crotch, especially when the conversation turned to women. Roscoe was one of those policemen who would sit bored in a radio car in the dark and quiet hours and talk of his incredible sexual encounters in Vietnam or Tijuana and knead and squeeze his genitals until his partners got nauseated.

Working with Roscoe Rules was many things but it was never dull. He was what is known in LAPD jargon as a "Four-fifteen personality," 415 being the California penal code section which defines disturbing the peace. Indeed, Roscoe Rules had turned many bloodless family fights or landlord-tenant disputes into minor riots by his presence. He had been transferred around the department more than any member of his academy class, had been the subject of many complaints of excessive force from citizens and even from a few police supervisors, who generally do not challenge the techniques of policemen like Roscoe Rules. Not if they respond promptly to radio calls, write one moving traffic violation a day and stop at least three people daily for field interrogations.

During their first week as partners, Roscoe started a small riot. It was in 7-A-77's area, but Calvin Potts and Francis Tanaguchi were handling a call in 7-A-29's area, while Harold Bloomguard and Sam Niles were handling a call in 7-A-1's area, while Spermwhale Whalen and Baxter Slate were parked in an alley near Crenshaw Boulevard, Spermwhale receiving a listless headjob from an aging black prostitute whom he had known from his days at old University Station.

The call had originated as a neighbor dispute, and by the time Roscoe and Whaddayamean Dean arrived, what had been a potentially dangerous situation in an unhappily mixed apartment house on Cloverdale had pretty well petered out to the name calling, face saving phase. There were two tired men involved: a black and a Mexican who did not really want to fight for the honor of their bickering wives or anything else.

"Took a report here one time," Roscoe observed as they climbed the stairway at nine o'clock that night. "Some abba dabba made a report that one a her cubs was missing. Had so fucking many milksuckers running around she forgot the police department summer camp was taking care a the little prick for a week. That's what kind a people we run our kiddie camps for. Didn't know he was gone till she had a head count!"

Whaddayamean Dean shivered as he saw a team of roaches charge on a chunk of slimy red hamburger which lay rotting on the landing.

There was a sign on the manager's door which said: "No loiterers in this building. Due to lady tenants being kidnapped, molested and robbed the LAPD will arrest loiterers."

On the second landing they passed a staggering wine reeking black woman who ignored them. She was barefoot, wore pinned black slacks and an extra large dirty blouse which hung outside. The blouse was hiked in the back because of the lopsided hump which bent her double and reduced a woman who was meant to be of average height to a misshapen dwarf.

Roscoe tapped the hump as he passed, winked mischievously at Whaddayamean Dean and said to the stuporous woman, "I got a *hunch* you're for me, baby!"

Roscoe was still giggling when they found the remnants of the once smoldering neighbor dispute. The rival factions were almost evenly divided. Two sets of neighbors, including husbands, wives, teenage and preteen children, backed the play of each injured party. Mexicans backed Mexicans, blacks backed blacks. There had been twenty-two people screaming and threatening at the height of the dispute. Now there were just the husbands of the aggrieved women. The black man had a trickle of blood running from the corner of his mouth where the Mexican had accidentally bumped him when they were pushing and shoving, preparatory to doing battle.

The black man, a squatty hod carrier with enormous shoulders and a wild full natural hairdo, looked relieved by the presence of the bluesuits and shouted angrily, "You made me bleed, motherfucker! You gonna pay. I'm gonna kick ass for this!"

"Anytime, man, anytime," said the Mexican, a slightly shorter man, a member of the same hod carrier's local, who had been on many jobs with the black man and was almost a friend.

The Mexican, like the black man, was dressed in dirty work pants and was shirtless to unnerve his opponent. He did not have such an intimidating physique in terms of musculature, but his chest, back and rib cage were crisscrossed with many scars: some like coiled rope, some like purple zippers, from old gang wars in East Los Angeles where he had fought his way through the elaborate gang hierarchy to emerge as a seasoned *veterano* covered with battle wounds and glory. But then the Mexican had gotten married, fathered seven children, lost his taste for street war and in truth had not faced a foe for many years.

"What started the beef?" Roscoe Rules asked, deciding to talk to the Mexican.

The Mexican shrugged, touched his hand nervously to the drooping Zapata moustache, lowered his eyes and turned his scarred back to the two policemen.

The black hod carrier's wife spoke first. "The problem is, Officer, that this broad and her daughter always has to hang clothes on the same day that I'm hanging mine. And that ain't no big thang, cept they got no respect and just throws other folks' clothes on the ground like pigs. And I has to put another quarter in the machine and wash my clothes all over agin."

"That's a lie," said the husky Mexican woman, throwing her long sweaty brown hair back over her shoulder. "Her and her daughter are the ones that don't have no respect. Animals, that's what they are."

"Go back to Mexico, bitch," the black woman said.

"I was born here, nigger. Go back to Africa," the Mexican woman said, and Whaddayamean Dean stepped between them as the black woman lunged forward, bumping Whaddayamean Dean into Roscoe, who fell against the black man, who accidentally stepped on Roscoe's plain toed, ripple soled police shoes, which he had spit shined every day for the eight months he owned them.

"Goddamn it!" Roscoe yelled, holding his arms out between the two women, eyeballs white with disgust. "I heard enough!" he thundered, arms still extended, knees slightly bent, face twisted in agony like Samson straining at the pillars.

Then Roscoe dropped his hands to his hips and walked in slow circles. Finally he paused, looked at the people like a sad but patient uncle, nodded and said, "I heard enough!"

"Looky here, Officer," said the black man, "I don't mean no disrespect but I heard enough a you sayin you heard enough. You're makin me nervous."

Roscoe walked over to Whaddayamean Dean, pulled him aside and whispered, "This spade's the troublemaker far as I can see. I think he's got a leaky seabag. Dingaling. Psycho. You can't even talk to him. Look what the motherfucker did to my shoe!"

"I think we can quiet them down," Whaddayamean Dean said as Roscoe stood on one foot like a blue flamingo, rubbing his toe hopelessly on the calf of his left leg.

"Can I talk to you?" Whaddayamean Dean asked the Mexican, walking him to the other end of the hall while Roscoe Rules hustled the silent black thirty feet down the stairway.

"I don't want no more trouble, outta you," Roscoe whispered when he got the hod carrier to a private place.

"I ain't gonna give you no trouble, Officer," the black man said, looking up at the mirthless blue eyes of Roscoe Rules which were difficult to see because like most hotdogs he wore his cap tipped forward until the brim almost touched his nose.

"Don't argue with me, man!" Roscoe said. His nostrils splayed as he sensed the fear on the man who stood hangdog before him.

"What's your name?" Roscoe then demanded.

"Charles ar-uh Henderson," the hod carrier answered, and then added impatiently. "Look, I wanna go back inside with my family. I'm tired a all this and I just wanna go to bed. I worked hard . . ."

But Roscoe became enraged at the latent impudence and snarled, "Look here, Charles ar-uh Henderson, don't you be telling me what you're gonna do. I'll tell you when you can go back inside and maybe you won't be going back inside at all. Maybe you're gonna be going to the slam tonight!"

"What for? I ain't done nothin. What right you got . . ."

"Right? Right?" Roscoe snarled, spraying the hod carrier with saliva. "Man, one more word and I'm gonna book your ass! I'll personally lock you in the slammer! I'll set your hair on fire!"

Whaddayamean Dean called down to Roscoe and suggested that they switch hod carriers. As soon as they had, he tried in vain to calm the outraged black man.

A few minutes later he heard Roscoe offer some advice to the Mexican hod carrier: "If that loudmouth bitch was my old lady I'd kick her in the cunt."

Twenty years ago the Mexican had broken a full bottle of beer over the head of a man for merely smiling at his woman. Twenty years ago, when she was a lithe young girl with a smooth sensuous belly, he would have shot to death any man, cop or not, who would dare to refer to her as a bitch.

Roscoe Rules knew nothing of *machismo* and did not even sense the slight almost imperceptible flickering of the left eyelid of the Mexican. Nor did he notice that those burning black eyes were no longer pointed somewhere between the shield and necktie of Roscoe Rules, but were fixed on his face, at the browless blue eyes of the tall policeman.

"Now you two act like men and shake hands so we can leave," Roscoe ordered.

"Huh?" the Mexican said incredulously, and even the black hod carrier looked up in disbelief.

"I said shake hands. Let's be men about this. The fight's over and you'll feel better if you shake hands."

"I'm forty-two years old," the Mexican said softly, the eyelid flickering more noticeably. "Almost old enough to be your father. I ain't shaking hands like no kid on a playground."

"You'll do what I say or sleep in the slammer," Roscoe said, remembering how in school everyone felt better and even drank beer after a good fight.

"What charge?" demanded the Mexican, his breathing erratic now. "What fuckin charge?"

"You both been drinking," Roscoe said, losing confidence in his constituted authority, but infuriated by the insolence which was quickly undermining what he thought was a controlled situation.

Roscoe, like most black-glove cops, believed implicitly that if you ever backed down even for a moment in dealing with assholes and scrotes the entire structure of American law enforcement would crash to the ground in a mushroom cloud of dust.

"We ain't drunk," the Mexican said. "I had a can of beer when I got home from work. One goddamn can!" He spoke in accented Cholo English: staccato, clipped, just as he did when he was a respected gang member.

Then Roscoe Rules pushed him back into an alcove away from the eyes of those down the hall who had made their own peace by now and were preparing to go back into their apartments to fix dinner. Roscoe pulled his baton from the ring and hated this sullen Mexican and the glowering black man and even Whaddayamean Dean whose nervousness enraged Roscoe because if you ever let these scrotes think you were afraid . . .

Then Roscoe looked around, guessing there were a dozen people between them and the radio car, and started to realize that this was not the time or place. But the Mexican made Roscoe Rules forget that it was the wrong time and place when he looked at the tall policeman with the harder crueler larger body and said, "I never let a man talk to me like this. You better book me or you better let me go but don't you talk to me like this anymore or . . . or . . ."

"Or? Or?" Roscoe said, his hairless brows throbbing as he touched the small man on the chest with the tip of his stick. "You Mexicans're all alike. Think you're tough, huh? Bantam-weight champ a this garbage dump, huh? I oughtta tear that oily moustache off your face."

Then the flickering eyelid was still and the eyes glazed over. "Go ahead," the Mexican barely whispered.

And Roscoe Rules did. A second later the Mexican was standing there with a one inch piece of his right moustache and the skin surrounding it in Roscoe Rules' left hand. The raw flesh began to spot at once with pinpoints of blood.

Then the Mexican screamed and kicked Roscoe Rules in the balls.

Suddenly Whaddayamean Dean found himself trying to get the Mexican's neck in the crook of his arm, to squeeze off the oxygen to the brain, which would make him lose consciousness and flop convulsively on the ground, thus "doing the chicken."

The Mexican's erstwhile black enemy was experiencing a deep sense of guilt and outrage at the Mexican's plight.

"You honky motherfucker!" the black hod carrier yelled when he finally exploded. He tossed a straight right at Whaddayamean Dean which caught him on the left temple and knocked him free of the Mexican and over the kneeling body of Roscoe Rules who was hoping desperately he wouldn't puke from the kick in the balls.

Roscoe aimed a spunky blow at the black hod carrier's leg with his unauthorized, thirty-four ounce sap which pulled his pants down when he wasn't careful to keep his Sam Browne buckled tightly.

Hit em in the shins. They can't take that, thought Roscoe, swinging the sap weakly, relying on folklore to save him now that he could not stand up.

But the hod carrier did not seem to feel the sap bouncing off his legs as he and the Mexican took turns punching Whaddayamean Dean silly.

The redhead had lost his baton and gun and was bouncing back and forth between the two men. "Partner! Partnerrrr!" Whaddayamean Dean yelled, but Roscoe Rules could only kneel there, look up in hatred and wish he could shoot the nigger, the spick and his puny partner.

Then Roscoe fell over on his back, nursing his rapidly swelling testicles, spitting foam like a mad dog.

It ended abruptly. There had been men, women and children screaming, encouraging, cursing gleefully. There had been bodies thudding off the walls, doors slamming. Then silence.

Roscoe Rules and Whaddayamean Dean Pratt were alone in the hallway. Both on the floor, uniforms half torn off, batons, hats, flashlights, guns and notebooks scattered. Whaddayamean Dean lay moaning, draped across an overturned trash can. Roscoe Rules felt his strength returning as he struggled to his feet, keeping his balls in both hands for fear if he dropped them they'd burst like ripe tomatoes.

Roscoe was finished for the evening. He was content to limp down the stairs to sit in the radio car and wait for the arrival of other units after his partner staggered to the car and put out the "officers need help" call. Roscoe could not return with Whaddayamean Dean when he went back into the building with some sixteen policemen and began breaking down doors in a vain search for the two hod carriers who had escaped and were not arrested for two weeks.

"Give em a few licks for me, partner," Roscoe had whispered to his partner as he shuffled slowly to the ambulance, walking bowlegged, holding the enflamed swollen testicles in both hands as though he had a double handful of heavy bullion or precious gems. Which indeed he did as far as he was concerned. He thought at that moment that he might lose them forever and nothing ever seemed as precious. He refused to release the handful of damaged flesh even to step up into the ambulance, and just stood there, bowlegged, holding himself while two ambulance attendants lifted him up in a seated carry.

Before they closed the ambulance door, he called weakly to his battered partner, "Give em one for me, Dean! One for your partner! And get em in a wristlock! Bend em down! Make em bite their own balls! Then play catch-up with your stick! Then kneedrop them! Puncture their kidneys! Rupture their spleens! Make em do the chicken!"

Five people went to jail that night for various charges ranging from resisting officers to plain drunk. The black man was picked up two weeks later at the Hod Carriers Local. After five court continuances he spent ten days in jail which he was permitted to serve on weekends because of his work and large family. The

Mexican hod carrier who also had a large family was given a longer jail term because of his youthful record of violence. All but fifteen days were suspended.

Both men were heroes with their families and neighbors for some time to come, and the Mexican, who had been experiencing a diminished sex drive, discovered after his release from jail that he was like a young stallion. His wife said she never had it so good.

After Roscoe Rules recovered from the beating at the hands of the hod carriers he was anxious to get back to the streets and make the citizenry of Wilshire Division pay for his wounds and humiliation. There was no shame in the injuries themselves. On the contrary, Roscoe wore his scars as proudly as the Mexican wore the mementoes of his youthful gang fights. What humiliated Roscoe was that they got punched and stomped two on two. When he told the story to other officers the number of assailants grew in number until even Whaddayamean Dean wasn't sure just how many people had a piece of him. Roscoe never did know. The entire experience was blurred in his mind what with vomiting and painful fearful days in the hospital when he erroneously thought his manhood would be forever compromised. He admitted to his partner that he had no clear recollection of what had happened and even after his total recovery referred to the experience grimly as The Day My Balls Blew Up.

But from then on, Roscoe was more cautious than before. If a suspect even looked as though he might be anxious to cause trouble he would find himself wearing Roscoe's unauthorized sap in his hair. During his one month convalescence Roscoe was unable to raise what Harold Bloomguard called a "diamond cutter" or even a "blue veiner" due to the shooting pains in his groin. His wife told a sympathetic neighbor she never had it so good.

But Roscoe never lost his sense of humor. While he was off duty recuperating he invited Whaddayamean Dean to his ranch east of Chino for a down home pit barbecue.

"Not like that nigger slop you see in all these greasy spoons in town," he promised, but a real barbecue, worthy of the Middle American farmers Roscoe had sprung from.

When Whaddayamean Dean asked Roscoe if he planned to return to the Midwest when he retired from police work, Roscoe said, fuck no, that those redneck maggots like to read their Bibles over you while they screwed you in the ass. Once when waxing philosophical he admitted that he had only truly been happy in Vietnam, and that if he hadn't been dumb enough to knock up his old lady and get married young he'd have loved to have gone to Africa and hired out as a mercenary.

"Imagine getting paid to kill niggers," he mused.

Then he proved that he hadn't lost his sense of humor when his eight year old son Clyde came crying into the yard where Roscoe and Whaddayamean Dean sat drinking beer from the cans and working on a radio controlled airplane which Roscoe Rules had bought for his son's birthday two years ago and not let him play with because he wasn't old enough. Roscoe loved to sit in the yard and terrorize the pony by divebombing it with the roaring little airplane. It was a Messerschmitt with authentic German insignia and an added touch of a swastika on the tail.

"Daddy!" said his son Clyde. "Look at Pookie!"

"What's wrong with him, son?" asked Roscoe solicitously as the boy held the little box turtle in his hands. The creature's head drooped, obviously near death from some reptile malady.

"It's a goner, get rid of it," Roscoe said without touching the turtle.

"No, Daddy!" cried the boy. "He'll be okay! Pookie's gonna be okay!"

"Give him here," Roscoe said, winking at Whaddayamean Dean. "I'll see what I can do."

Then he snatched the little turtle from the child's hand and with the cutting pliers he was using to repair the gas engine of the Messerschmitt, snipped the head of the box turtle off at the base of the shell, the feet kicking frantically in death.

"Now we can use him for a paperweight," Roscoe said.

He told the story all over Wilshire Station the next day, claiming it proved he was the meanest, baaaaadest motherfucker that ever wore a blue suit in Wilshire Station, while Whaddayamean Dean unknowingly used exactly the phrase which had been used by Roscoe's last five partners. He whispered that Roscoe was an insufferable prick.

Roscoe Rules continued pretty much as before despite his Waterloo at the hands of the hod carriers. He asked to return to 7-A-85 so he could be in the south end of Wilshire Division in the thick of the action. And since Roscoe arrested so many drunk drivers and wrote such an incredible number of traffic tickets he was still the darling of those police supervisors who believe that writing one moving traffic violation a day is tangible proof of good police work.

Roscoe also arrested more drunk drivers than most traffic cars. Of course, he also went to court more than any traffic car because he booked the "borderline" drunk drivers. In fact, he wrote the "borderline" tickets.

"All I see and some I don't see," as Roscoe put it.

On the night that Roscoe Rules was to become a legend he and Whaddayamean Dean had been trying to catch a drunk driver by staking out a bar on West Jefferson frequented by hard drinking blacks who wasted no time with fancy drinks, but nightly consumed gallons of Scotch, gin and beer. Roscoe had hoped to find a drunk sleeping in his car in the parking lot at the rear and wake him gently, telling him that he had better go home and sleep it off. Then they would wait down the street in the darkness and arrest the grateful motorist for drunk driving as he passed by.

Some policemen become legends by virtue of accumulated felony arrests which propel them into the category of instinctive policemen, who doglike smell or sense when something is wrong: when a suspect is lying, when a turn of the head or clicking of eyeballs means more than just another case of black and white fever. When one *knows* which cars to stop, which pedestrian to talk to, most importantly, which one to *believe,* since most policemen eventually conclude that in addition to being hopelessly weak the human race is composed of an incredible collection of liars who will lie even when the truth would save them, and more often than not haven't the faintest idea of what the truth really is.

But there are other ways to become police legends, that is, by a single action or reaction which is so outrageous that within twenty-four hours it is the subject of every rollcall in the city. Roscoe Rules was about to become that kind of legend.

That fateful night started pretty much as every other night with Roscoe driving and discussing the merits of fast cars, hotshot chase driving, devastating weapons and ammunition, and even women, since his wounded testicles were once more intact and functioning. As he talked, Roscoe as always unconsciously squeezed, kneaded and pulled at himself.

The salmon smoggy sun had dropped suddenly that evening. They were driving through their district at dusk, looking for traffic tickets which Roscoe believed in writing at the beginning of the watch. Often, a motorist could blow a red light at eight miles an hour during the busy late hours and Roscoe would ignore him or not even see him *if* he had already written his ticket for the night.

They passed a construction crew building a new elementary school in a black neighborhood near Washington Boulevard, and Roscoe yelled "Building new cages, huh?" to a white man in a hard hat who grinned and raised a hammer.

"The air's quiet," Roscoe remarked, lighting a Marlboro. "Not too many radio calls in Wilshire, but I got a feeling it's gonna be a busy Thursday night. Animals got their welfare checks today. Should be lots a action."

A battered Texas Chevrolet driven by a grim looking white man with faded eyes pulled up next to them at a red light. The woman passenger, gaunt and weak, had difficulty rolling down the window. She was holding a baby in her arms, and one of the four blond children in the back seat helped her.

''Suh,'' she said, ''kin you tell us where the Gen'ral Hospital is?''

''Sure,'' Roscoe answered. ''Just go straight on this street to the Harbor Freeway and turn right. Keep going ten miles. You can't miss it.''

''Thank ye,'' she smiled, and again battled the window which was jammed in the bent frame.

Whaddayamean Dean looked at his partner quizzically and Roscoe explained, ''Fuck this white trash. They're worse'n niggers, coming here and making us pay for their little milksuckers. General Hospital, my ass. Wonder what they'll say when they find themselves looking at the ocean?''

Roscoe then spotted a black man in a business suit walking on Western Avenue with a young white woman in a green tallored jacket and skirt. She was obviously not one of the white prostitutes who worked the area so Roscoe kept his voice low when he drove by, looked in their direction and said, ''Price of pork what it is, and a spade can still buy a white pig for ten dollars?''

''You know, I never drove in a pursuit,'' Whaddayamean Dean observed as he saw an LAPD traffic car zooming past them to overtake a speeder on Olympic Boulevard.

''Remember one thing, babe,'' Roscoe said, his voice dropping an octave as it always did when he assumed the role of training officer, ''don't never try to overtake a fast car on the outside when you're going in a turn. Most cars'll flip on a piece of spit. Hit him on the inner rear fender and he'll eat the windshield. I once saw a freeway car drive a motherfucker right into an abutment by doing that. Sucker's car blew up like a howitzer shell. Took four pricks off the welfare rolls *permanent*. And you gotta know when your engine's gonna flame out. These hogs probably only top out at a hundred ten so you push it very long you'll probably throw a bearing, drop a rod and blow the engine. That's embarrassing in a good pursuit. Makes you feel stupid.

''In addition to knowing your car you gotta know all your equipment,'' Roscoe continued, ''like that peashooter you're carrying. I wish I could talk you into buying a magnum and carrying some good, gut ripping hollow points in it. I want a gun that'll stop some scrote when I need him stopped. After the prick's dead I'll worry about the ammunition being department approved. I ever tell you about that abba dabba burglar my partner shot when I used to work the Watts car? Ripping off a gas station when he set off the silent alarm. We were carrying those peashooters like you got. That sucker could run the hundred in ten flat till my partner shot him, and then he ran it in nine-nine. So I made a vow to get rid a this worthless ammo and get me some killing stuff. I made a study of velocity and shock.''

And then they got their *first* bloody call of the night. ''Seven-A-Eighty-five. A possible jumper, Wilshire and Mariposa,'' said the communications operator. ''Handle the call code three.''

Roscoe preferred working an extra car, called an 'X-car,'' because instead of saying ''Seven-X-Eighty-five'' or ''Seven-X-ray-Eighty-five,'' he could improvise by saying, ''Seven-Exceptional-Eighty-five,'' or ''Seven-Exciting-Eighty-five.''

Roscoe was falling in love with the voice of the radio operator on frequency ten whom he had never seen. So Roscoe picked up the mike, pushed the button to send, made three kissing sounds and said, ''This is Seven-Ay-ya-Eighty-five. I say Seven-a-for-Atomic-Eighty-five, rrrrrajah on the call.''

Then he released the button, turned to Whaddayamean Dean and said, ''That'll make her wet her pants.''

And the radio operator, who was a fat, fifty-nine year old housewife with six children older than Roscoe Rules, turned to the operator on her left and said, ''That guy on Seven-A-Eighty-five sounds like an insufferable prick.''

A janitor named Homer Tilden had placed the jumper call when a twenty-two year old receptionist named Melissa Monroe returned to the office some three hours after the building closed and demanded to be let in on the pretext of having left an important document there.

"I never shoulda let her in, it's my fault, all my fault," the plump black janitor later sobbed to detectives.

Then the janitor pictured the pert smiling girl with the jazz age bob, who always yelled "Night, Mr. Tilden!" when she left at night, and he burst into tears like a child.

When Roscoe Rules and Dean Pratt arrived, red lights flashing and siren screaming, there was already a small group of morbid onlookers who had come across from the Ambassador Hotel. Homer Tilden led the two policemen to the elevator and up to the twenty-first floor where the young woman sat on the window ledge of her own office, feet dangling, looking down curiously at the crowd gathering. In the distance the wail of a fire department emergency vehicle trapped by Wilshire Boulevard night traffic three blocks west.

"Don't come near me," the girl said calmly, her hair blowing wispily around her tiny ears as the two policemen ran from the elevator and burst into the office.

"Go downstairs," Roscoe said to Homer Tilden who was holding his chest and panting as though he had run the twenty-one stories instead of taking the elevator.

"Maybe I . . ."

"Go downstairs!" Roscoe repeated. "There's gonna be other people coming."

And as the janitor obeyed, Roscoe Rules began to imagine a picture and write-up in tomorrow's *Los Angeles Times* if he could save the beautiful jumper. She was a fox and would surely rate an inside front page photo, along with her savior.

"Look, miss," Roscoe said and stepped forward. But the girl moved inches closer to her destiny, and Roscoe froze in his tracks.

"Maybe we better back off, partner," Dean whispered, looking for the moment far younger than his twenty-five years, his freckles swimming in streams of sweat.

"We don't back off nothing," Roscoe whispered back. "She's a dingaling, and there's ways to handle them." Then to the girl Roscoe said, "Nothing's as bad as that. Come on in. Let's jaw about it."

He said it fliply with a grin and stepped forward, stopping when the girl moved forward another two inches and now teetered on the very edge, framed against the faded smoggy night sky of the Miracle Mile.

"Oh no!" Dean said. "No, miss! Don't go any closer! Come on, partner, let's go downstairs and give this lady a chance to think!"

But as Roscoe Rules saw a *Times* write-up and perhaps a police department medal of valor slipping through his fingers, he decided to try a different approach. He had seen Charles Laughton or someone do it successfully on an old TV movie. You could shame a jumper into surrendering.

"All right then, goddamnit!" Roscoe shouted to the girl. "You got your audience. It's your life. If it ain't worth a shit to you, it ain't worth a shit to us. Go ahead, girl. We can't stay here all night babying you. We got other things to do. Go ahead, girl! Jump!"

And she did. Without a word or a tear she looked at Roscoe Rules and Dean Pratt and in fact never took her large violet eyes off them as she let herself slip from the ledge and fell at thirty-two feet per second squared, legs first, with a scream that was lost in a woosh of air and rustling skirt which had blown up over her face.

What was left of Melissa Monroe was being covered by a sheet when Dean Pratt stumbled by on his way to the radio car.

"Let me make the reports, partner," Roscoe Rules said, and for the very first time Dean heard Roscoe's voice quiver with uncertainty.

Then Whaddayamean Dean looked at Melissa Monroe and said later it was as though God in Heaven was displeased with dessert and had hauled off and threw it at the Ambassador Hotel but missed and splattered the sidewalk on Wilshire Boulevard. Skull and body had exploded. Organs and brain littered the pavement.

She was white and yellow and pink, covered with lumpy red sauce and syrup. Melissa Monroe had been turned into a raspberry sundae.

Dean Pratt was very quiet for the rest of this bloodiest of all nights of his life. He thought they were finished when at the station Roscoe Rules finished writing his 15.7 report: that indispensable police document which handily covers all those police situations which do not conveniently fit into a category such as robbery, burglary or vehicle theft.

''Remember, partner,'' Roscoe warned as they sat alone in the station coffee room, ''as soon as the janitor left, she just jumped. Nothing was said by nobody. She just jumped!''

Dean Pratt nodded and sipped at a soft drink, longing for a water tumbler of straight bourbon as he had never longed for anything in his life. He hoped there might be some downers left in the bottom of his closet at home where his girlfriend left a small cache. He was terrified by barbiturates since drug use was an irrevocable firing offense. But he wanted to get loaded and sleep.

At 11:00 P.M. Roscoe Rules dragged his partner out of the coffee room and said, ''Come on, partner, let's go do some police work.''

''Huh?''

''Come on, goddamnit, let's hit the bricks.'' Roscoe grinned. ''We ain't through yet. We still got forty-five minutes.''

''Jesus Christ,'' said Dean.

''Come on!'' Roscoe commanded, his grin vanishing. He took Whaddayamean Dean very firmly by the arm and walked him out to the radio car.

''Don't go cuntish on me!'' Roscoe snarled when he drove away from the station. ''As far as I'm concerned we handled that call just right. If that whacko bitch wanted to take gas, fuck it, it ain't our fault.''

When Dean didn't answer Roscoe became angrier. His hairless brows puckered and whitened. ''Fuck it! Who cares if *all* these rotten motherfuckers take gas. They're all shit sucking, miserable scrotes anyways. What the fuck's a life anyway, less it's yours?''

Still Dean did not answer and Roscoe unconsciously pulled at his crotch and raged on. ''You bust a good felony and you tell him to throw up his hands. He don't do it and there's no witnesses, I say put him *down*. Understand? Shoot em down like birds that shit on your roof. Remember that nigger and spick The Night My Balls Blew Up? I'm gonna get them someday. And I'll worship the ground they're laid under. You'd like to blow em down, wouldn't you?''

''I guess so,'' Dean nodded.

''One nigger plus one spick equals a Mexi-coon!'' Roscoe shouted. ''That's my hard charging partner! One a these nights we'll get a couple a scrotes who wanna go the hard way. We'll show some a these so called cops with their withered nuts how a couple a honest to God hard chargers do it! We'll perform a little retroactive birth control and blow the motherfuckers right outta their shoes with my magnum and your little peashooter!''

''I guess so, Roscoe,'' Dean mumbled.

Roscoe was unconsciously pushing the radio car eighty miles an hour on the Santa Monica Freeway, heading nowhere, feeling the rush of cool wind, stroking himself while Whaddayamean Dean watched the speedometer.

And then they received the last radio call of the night.

''Seven-A-Eighty-five, Seven-Adam-Eight-five, assist the traffic unit, Venice and Hauser. Code two.''

''Seven-A-Eighty-five, roger,'' Dean responded, banging the mike back in the holder, disgustedly jotting the location on the notebook pad.

''Shit fuck!'' said Roscoe Rules, an expression he seldom used anymore since a former partner convinced him that it made him sound like a Central Avenue nigger.

''I've had enough for one night,'' Dean grumbled. ''I was ready for code seven.''

"Coulda used some chow myself," said Roscoe. "Don't the scrotes at communications have another car they can pick on? Shit fuck! Give her the handcuffs, partner."

Dean Pratt, as Roscoe Rules had taught him, opened the bracelet of his handcuffs, holding it next to the hand mike, and squeezed the bracelet through five or six times, making a ratchet sound very like a large zipper being ripped open and closed. Roscoe was convinced that the sound would be magnified in the operator's radio headset.

"Sounds like the jolly green giant opening his fly, don't it, partner?"

Whaddayamean Dean nodded, suddenly a bit carsick. He hadn't had a thing to eat for almost twenty-four hours. He had been in court all day and had come straight to work after testifying. And Roscoe Rules sitting there pulling on his dork wasn't doing anything to settle his queasiness.

"I ever tell you about that slopehead we used to gang-bang in Nam, partner?" Roscoe asked, in a downright jovial mood since this would be their last call.

Even if it was a quickie he intended to make it an "end-of-watcher," by "milking" the time out and failing to clear when they were finished.

"Don't think you told me that one," Dean sighed, by now deciding that he would rather have four fingers of bourbon than a hamburger.

"This little gook was about fourteen, but retarded. Had the brain of a chicken and nearsighted to boot. We got a translator to tell her that fucking was good for her eyes. She was ugly as a busted blister. Just a little better than jacking off. Best part wasn't the pussy, it was cleaning her up ahead a time. We used to get these fifty cent rice paddy whores like her and throw them in this big wooden tub and eight or ten of us would get hot water and GI brushes and scrub the stink off them. Goddamn, that was fun! We'd lather them up and scrub every inch. Shit, we'd take our clothes off and fall in the water and drink beer and wash those bitches. Seems kinda weird but it was more fun washing them than gang fucking them."

Dean nodded and leaned back while Roscoe drove west on Venice Boulevard and dreamed of thin young yellow bodies in soapy water. He had had many a lay but never had a more exciting sexual experience than scrubbing and lathering the rice paddy whores. Even now he got a blue veiner every time he held a bar of soap.

"Shit fuck!" Dean observed. "There it is!"

And there it was! Traffic was snarled six blocks in every direction. Fifty people were milling around like ghouls, and two frantic traffic officers in white hats were trying to lay down a flare pattern to divert east and westbound traffic. Every eastbound lane was blocked by the wreckage of a spectacular four car collision.

Roscoe pulled on his red lights, crossed the center divider and parked the wrong way on Venice Boulevard.

"Glad you got here," said a heavy middle aged traffic policeman who came running up with a handful of flares and spots of ash on his uniform. "Worst goddamn crash I seen in a long time. Drag race. Two cars laid down sixty feet of skids before they plowed into a northbound station wagon and knocked it clear back into the eastbound lanes."

"What station wagon?" Dean asked, adjusting his hat, getting his flashlight ready as he and Roscoe jogged back toward the wreckage where several souvenir hunters were already starting to prowl.

"Get the hell out of here or you're going to jail!" the traffic officer shouted to the unkempt teenagers.

"Everybody gone to the hospital?" Roscoe asked, waving his flashlight violently at a car which was trying to get past the wreckage to go south on Ridgely Drive.

"Two ambulances been here," the traffic officer said. "You're the only radio car to show up. The fucking fire department hasn't even been here yet and there's two dead bodies jammed inside that station wagon!"

"Will someone tell me where the hell the station wagon is?" Dean asked, holding a handful of flares, preparing to lay a pattern fifty feet south of the corner and divert the horn blowing cars through an east-west alley.

"That's it! That's the station wagon!" the traffic officer said, pointing to a small heap of mangled steel which had knocked down the light standard, plunging the intersection into darkness. "It was cut in half!"

"Blow it out your ass, pizza face!" Roscoe shouted to a sputtering acned man in a white Cadillac who was honking his horn and yelling as though he thought the policemen could magically sweep away ten tons of scrap metal and let him continue about his business which was to get to a west Hollywood bar before it closed and try to pick up a thirty-five dollar prostitute.

By now a dozen of the trapped cars were flashing their high beams in the policemen's faces and blowing their horns while Roscoe violently waved them toward the alley where Dean Pratt was laying flares.

"Terrible wreck," the traffic policeman muttered. "A woman in the station wagon was decapitated. She's one of the ones still inside."

"Yeah?" Roscoe said. He crossed the street, flashed his light at the heaps of debris in his path and stood beside the half of the station wagon, trying to make sense of the pile of mutilated flesh which had been a young couple. The tin cans and "Just Married" sign were still tied to the bumper.

And then Roscoe Rules was reminded of one of the two hilarious photographs he carried in his wallet from his Vietnam days.

"Oh yeah!" said Roscoe Rules excitedly. "Move the flares, partner!" he shouted to Dean, who was angrily waving his flashlight at the string of cars to get them moving through the alley, as at last the fire engines' sirens could be heard.

"What for?"

"I want them to pass by the wreck here across the gas station parking lot."

"What for?"

"I think it'll be easier to divert them down the alley."

"Okay." Dean shrugged, moving the line of flares, and then Roscoe Rules stood quietly on the far side of the station wagon, hoping the fire trucks or another ambulance wouldn't get there too quickly and spoil things.

The first car to pass Roscoe was not suitable. The driver was well dressed, prosperous, just the kind of prick who'd call in and make a complaint, Roscoe thought. Neither was the second car. The traffic was crawling by, most of the drivers gawking hungrily for a glimpse of blood.

The twelfth car in the line was perfect. It was a late model Dodge containing a man and two women. The bulging luggage rack, travel stickers and Ohio license said they were tourists passing through and not likely to take time to stop and complain about a policeman, no matter the outrage.

When the station wagon crawled by, Roscoe, still standing half hidden beside the wreckage, smiled encouragingly at the pudgy woman on the passenger side. Her window was down and she said, "Quite a wreck, eh, officer?"

"Yes, ma'am," Roscoe answered, and he knew this was the one.

"Over here, partner!" he called to Whaddayamean Dean, since every legend needs a Boswell.

The woman shook her head sadly and clucked. As her husband was revving the engine and the creeping traffic was starting, she said to Roscoe, "Anyone hurt bad?"

Then Roscoe Rules came from behind the wreckage and stepped to her window, lifting the dripping, severed head of the young bride, and said, "Yeah, this one got banged up a bit."

The woman from Ohio drowned out the fire engines' sirens with her screams as her husband drove into the flow of traffic.

Dean Pratt told the story to at least thirty policemen before going home that night. Roscoe Rules had achieved a place in police folklore, and was a Legend in His Own Time.

6

7-A-33: Spencer Van Moot and Father Willie Wright

Willie Wright was also destined to become a police celebrity. It happened four months before the choir practice killing. On the night he met a brother in the basement.

Of course he could not have dreamed of the bizarre turns this tour of duty would take when he sat in the rollcall room late that afternoon and wished he could grow a moustache like the one belonging to Sam Niles of 7-A-29, or Calvin Potts of 7-A-77 who had a heavy one which made the muscular black policeman look even more formidable.

Willie was sure that if he grew one it would look like Francis Tanaguchi's sparse and sad one, which many old women could duplicate.

It was a peaceful, untraumatic rollcall that afternoon. Lieutenant Finque was on a day off and Sergeant Yanov sat before them alone at his table on the platform.

"Got an unusual one last night," Sergeant Yanov said, trying to look through the crimes to find one that might amuse the watch. "Guy tried to shove a Pepsi bottle in his wife's giz after he caught her stepping out on him."

"I took that report," said Sam Niles. "It was nothing. The bottle didn't have the cap on it."

"Reminds me of the guy stuck a screwdriver up his ass to scratch his prostate. Remember that, partner?" Roscoe asked Whaddayamean Dean. "Couldn't get it out and the wife called the police. That was funny!" Rules chuckled as he pulled at his crotch and made Harold Bloomguard sick.

Then Roscoe blushed and got angry when Sergeant Yanov said, "By the way, an unnamed officer turned in a report last night where he wrote a pursesnatcher was l-e-r-k-i-n-g and p-r-a-y-i-n-g on his victims. Check the dictionary if you're not sure. These reports end up in courts of law. Makes us look dumb."

"I told you to check my spelling, goddamnit," Roscoe whispered to Dean Pratt who smiled weakly and said, "Sorry, partner."

"One word of advice," Sergeant Yanov said. "The captain is uptight about the pissy wino they found sleeping in the back of Sergeant Sneed's car. They suspect one of you guys put him there."

"Me? Why me all the time?" Francis Tanaguchi cried when all eyes turned to him.

"Gee, rollcalls are quiet without the lieutenant here," observed Spermwhale Whalen, who then turned to Willie Wright and said, "Hey, kid, how about comin in the bathroom with me? My back's hurt and I ain't supposed to lift nothin heavy."

Spencer Van Moot was happy when rollcall ended early. It gave him more time to shop. Spencer was, at forty, the second oldest choirboy, next to fifty-two year old Spermwhale Whalen, the two of them the only choirboys over thirty. Spencer Van Moot had convinced Harold Bloomguard that he should be accepted as a MacArthur Park choirboy because he was only temporarily married, was hated by his wife Tootie and her three kids and would probably soon be thrice divorced like Spermwhale Whalen.

Harold welcomed the complainer Spencer Van Moot for the same reason he welcomed Roscoe Rules. He invited Spencer Van Moot because he was the most artistic scrounger and promoter at Wilshire Station.

Spencer knew every retail store within a mile of his beat. His "police discounts" had furnished his house princely. He wore the finest Italian imports from the racks of the Miracle Mile clothing stores. He dined superbly in one of three expensive restaurants near Wilshire and Catalina which were actually in Rampart Division. Retailers became convinced that Spencer Van Moot could ward off burglars, shoplifters, fire and vandalism. That somehow this tall blond recruiting poster policeman with the confident jaw and the small foppish moustache could even forestall economic reversal.

Despite his natural morose nature and his self pitying complaints about his unhappy marriage, he was accepted at once by the choirboys. He arrived with a dowry of three cases of cold beer and four bottles of Chivas Regal Scotch. And he brought his partner, Willie Wright.

Willie was one of the smallest choirboys, along with Francis Tanaguchi and Harold Bloomguard, under five feet nine inches tall. Willie in fact had stretched to make five feet eight and was almost disqualified when he took his first police physical. He was a devoutly religious young man, raised as a Baptist, converted to Jehovah's Witnesses when he married Geneva Smythe, his high school sweetheart. Willie was now twenty-four and Geneva twenty-five. She, like Willie, was short and chubby. She took *Watchtower* magazines door to door three times a week. Willie accompanied her on his days off.

Spencer Van Moot loved him as a partner because Willie thought it was crooked to accept gifts or wholesale prices from retail stores, thereby leaving Spencer a double share of everything he could promote. The only concession Willie would make was a nightly free meal in one of Spencer Van Moot's gourmet restaurants.

After being practically dragged to the first choir practice by Spencer, Willie Wright discovered something totally extraordinary: that choir practice was fun, more fun in fact than anything he had ever done in his young life. He was accepted by the other choirboys almost from the start because he entertained them by preaching squeaky sermons. He told them how wrong it was to drink and lust after the two camp followers, Ora Lee Tingle and Carolina Moon, who often turned up at choir practice. But then when drunk he turned into an evil eyed little mustang.

Harold Bloomguard dubbed him official chaplain of the MacArthur Park choirboys. He was thereafter known as The Padre, *Father* Willie Wright.

The night that Father Willie Wright personally called for choir practice was the night he found the brother in the basement. It had begun much like every other night, with Spencer Van Moot driving the radio car madly to all of his various stops before the stores closed. First he had to make three cigarette stops where he picked up two packs of cigarettes for each of them, which Father Willie didn't use. Father Willie suspected quite rightly that Spencer wholesaled the cigarettes to his neighbors.

And then there was the dairy stop where Spencer got his daily allotment of buttermilk and yogurt, one quart for each partner, which Willie likewise refused. Each night at 10:00 P.M. the manager walked swiftly to his car under the protective beam of Spencer's spotlight. Then there were other stops, if he could get them in, at various men's shops on Wilshire Boulevard where Spencer and salesmen tossed around Italian names like Brioni and Valentino and which invariably ended in Spencer's trying on something in a fine cabretta leather jacket over his blue police uniform. Father Willie sat bored in the dressing room holding his partner's Sam Browne, gun and hat while Spencer preened.

Sometimes a new salesman would make the mistake of quoting the retail price to the tall policeman and would find himself cowering before an indignant stare, a twitching toothbrush moustache and a withering piece of advice to "Check with the manager about my police discount."

Father Willie often thought about asking for a new partner but he didn't want to hurt Spencer's feelings. Spencer had tried for years to find a partner like Father Willie, who would not accept his rightful share of free cigarettes, wholesale merchandise and free liquor. It had gotten to be tedious for Spencer breaking in new partners:

"You smoke?"

"No, Spencer."

"Today you do. I'll take both packs if you don't want them."

And inevitably a partner would become greedy. "I'll take a pack today, Spencer."

"What for? You don't smoke."

"I'll give them to my brother. What the hell, three packs a day I'm entitled to."

Spencer got to keep Willie's share of petty booty in every case. And Father Willie never complained when Spencer scrounged up some liquor for choir practices.

"We're having a retirement party for one of our detective lieutenants," Spencer would inevitably lie to a long suffering liquor store proprietor who would take two bottles of Scotch from the shelf behind him.

"We're having a big big party." Spencer would smile benignly until the proprietor would get the message and bring up another two bottles.

But Spencer was considerate about spreading it around and rarely went to the same liquor store more than once a month for anything but cigarettes. The cigarette shop however was a relentless daily ritual. It was said that during the Watts riot of 1965, Spencer drove a half burned black and white with every window shot out ten miles to Beverly Boulevard, his face streaked with soot and sweat, and managed to make all three cigarette stops before the stores closed at 2:00 A.M.

Spencer Van Moot had accepted a thousand packs of cigarettes and as many free meals in his time. And though he had bought enough clothing at wholesale prices to dress a dozen movie stars, he had never even considered taking a five dollar bill nor was one ever offered except once when he stopped a Chicago grocer in Los Angeles on vacation. The police department and its members made an exact distinction between petty gratuities and cash offerings, which were considered money bribes no matter how slight and would result in a merciless dismissal as well as criminal prosecution.

It was not that the citizens and police of Los Angeles were inherently less debased than their Eastern counterparts, it was that the West, being a network of sprawling young towns and cities, did not lend itself to the old intimate teeming ward or ghetto where political patronage and organized crime bedded down together. The numbers racket, for instance, had been a dismal failure in western America. The average citizen of Los Angeles hadn't the faintest idea how it worked. Yet in the Pennsylvania steel town where Spencer Van Moot was born, every living soul had played numbers and consulted dream books for winners and contributed to organized crime's greatest source of revenue in that region. The bookies came door to door. They even accepted children's penny bets. Western criminals had found it impossible to organize a crazy quilt collection of several communities which existed inside the 460 square mile limits of the city, where there was an automobile for every adult. The city had geography and history going for it.

So it was that Spencer Van Moot's supplication provided about half of the beverage consumed at choir practice, the rest provided by Roscoe Rules who bullied the free booze from cowering liquor store owners on his beat.

After making his various stops and depositing his treasures in the back of his camper truck in the station parking lot, Spencer began whining again about his unhappy domestic life.

"I mean how can you understand a woman, Padre?" Spencer complained as the setting sun filtered through the smog and burned Father Willie's sensitive, bulging blue eyes.

"I don't know, Spencer," Father Willie sighed, and wondered how long Spencer would use him as a sounding board tonight. Sometimes when he was lucky the complaining would stop after the first two hours of their tour of duty.

"I'm forty years old, Father Willie," Spencer griped, touching his twenty dollar haircut which he got free in a Wilshire Boulevard styling parlor. "Look at my hair, it's getting gray. Why should I live in such misery."

"I'm twenty-four," Father Willie reminded him, "and you have more hair than I do. Who cares if it's gray."

"She's a bitch, Padre. It's hell, believe me," Spencer whined. "She's worse by far than my first two wives put together. And she's turned her kids against me. They hate me more than she does because she tells them lies about me, that I drink a lot and run around with other women."

"That's not a lie, Spencer," Father Willie reminded him. "You *do* drink a lot and run around with other women."

"It's nothing to tell teenagers, for god's sake!" Spencer answered. "I never shoulda married an older broad with kids. Damn, forty-two years old and her legs're turning green. Green, I tell you! And here I am with only four years to go until I can pull the pin and retire. And what happens, she gets knocked up!"

"Maybe it'll work out, Spencer," Father Willie offered as his partner drove east on Eighth Street away from the sun's dying harsh rays.

"Work out? Work out? Four years to my pension and she's gonna foal, and then how can I retire with a little rug rat crawling around?"

"Oh well," Father Willie shrugged. "Oh well."

"A man gets drunk and careless and screws himself into another ten years on the job. It ain't fair."

"Oh well," said Father Willie.

"Everything happens to me!" Spencer said.

Spencer Van Moot was interrupted for a moment by catching a glimpse of a seventy year old pensioner who lived in a Seventh Street fleabag called the Restful Arms Motel. He pushed his wheelchair down the sidewalk backward with his *foot* as he held his useless arthritic hands in his lap. The pensioner was trying to get to the mom-and-pop market one block west where he could buy two cans of nutritious dog food for his dinner.

"Things could always be worse, Spencer."

"Oh sure, I'm gonna be unloading shitty diapers at forty years old and . . ."

"You've got a new camper. You can get away with your wife sometimes and go fishing."

"Oh sure. I got a new camper. I'm so thrilled, so happy! I'm in debt again. I was getting insecure not owing money."

"It'll work out."

"Yeah, it will. I'll be dead soon. No one in my family lives very long. I got an uncle that died of old age at forty-five. That's what the doctor said. Every organ in the man's body was old, dissipated. I won't last long. At least then I'll be rid of my old lady. I tell you, Padre, she's got a tongue so sharp it's a wonder she don't cut her mouth to pieces and bleed to death."

"You want to come to church with Geneva and me?" Father Willie offered. "Some of the best Witnesses I know came to God later in life. And what with the early deaths in your family . . ."

"Goddamnit, I ain't dead yet!" Spencer cried, suddenly frightened. "Padre, gimme a chance! I ain't lived yet!"

"Well, I only meant with poor health and all . . ."

"Poor health? Poor health? I'm too young to be thinking about dying. Jesus, partner, you're getting morbid!"

It was almost an hour befere Spencer fully recovered from the suggestion of his imminent demise. He had the worst sick record on the nightwatch. He was tall and strong, in the prime of life, and had seen vats of spilled blood and acres of mutilated flesh in his sixteen years of police work, but he became faint when he'd scratch his finger. He could bear any pain but his own.

Just before dark they passed the Mary Sinclair Adams Home for Girls, a funded institution where young women who were pregnant and indigent could be cared for. It was a converted two story home two blocks east of Hancock Park and had once been a palatial residence of an eighty year old virgin who died envying young girls the fun they had growing round bellies.

There was a teenage girl with an eight month stomach standing in front of the house: cigarette dangling, eyebrows plucked to nothing, eyes shadowed to three inch black orbs, talking to three young men on chopper motorcycles.

"The Stork Club," Spencer remarked, shaking his head disgustedly. "They go in there, drop a frog and cut out."

"I hear the county's okayed the installation of interuterine devices in some of these girls they place in foster homes," Father Willie said.

"Someone shoulda plugged my old lady's birdbath and I wouldn't be in this fix," Spencer answered, blowing a cloud of smoke out the window. "Old dried up sponge, I don't know how she ever got knocked up. I'll just have to cut down on expenses, live like a goddamn Trappist monk. I won't be able to eat like a human being anymore, that's all."

"It'll work out all right," Father Willie said. Then, "Spencer, we'll still be able to eat roast duckling with orange sauce, won't we?"

"Oh sure."

"With glazed carrots and shallots?"

"Oh, we'll still eat at our restaurants for free just like we always have," said Spencer, allaying Father Willie's fears. "I meant *at home* I'll have to starve. My wife and kids'll have to go without and maybe wear old clothes with patches."

Father Willie felt like suggesting Spencer could make patches with some of the fourteen Italian suits which hung in his closet, when he spotted a Lincoln blow the red light on Wilshire and Western. The Lincoln pulled over the moment Father Willie tooted his horn.

"You just have to learn to budget," Spencer sighed as they gathered up hats and ticket book and flashlights now that dusk had settled. "Mail your check for the telephone bill to the gas company and theirs to the electric company. By the time they send them back and forth you can balance your checkbook."

Father Willie nodded as they got out of the black and white Matador and walked forward, crisscrossing so that Father Willie, whose turn it was, could approach the driver's side while Spencer went to the other side and shined the light in the window to protect Father Willie's approach.

The driver, a balding fat man about Spencer's age, smiled and said, "What's the problem, boys?" He offered Father Willie his driver's license without being asked.

"You were a full second late on that red light, sir," Father Willie said, his light on the license, checking that it was not expired, noting the Beverly Hills address in Trousdale Estates.

"That doesn't seem possible," the man said, getting out of the car and following the little officer to the police car where Spencer waited in the headlight beam between the two cars.

"Careful, sir," Father Willie warned, as a car sped by very close to the Matador which was stopped behind the Lincoln, three feet farther into the traffic lane to protect the approaching officer from being picked off by a motorist who might be driving HUA which meant: Head Up Ass.

"Officer!" the fat man appealed to Spencer as Father Willie began to write the ticket on the hood of the radio car. "Surely I wasn't late on the red light, and if I was I didn't mean it."

He offered Spencer his business card which said, "Murray Fern's Stereo Emporium."

Spencer Van Moot's eyes brightened with visions of a new stereo system in his barroom at home. At wholesale, of course. He was about to suggest to his partner that Mr. Fern probably deserved some professional courtesy when he saw that it was too late. The ticket was already started, and since they were numbered it was impossible to cancel one without a report and explanation. So Spencer shrugged sadly and handed the business card back to the man.

"You gonna write me a ticket?" Murray Fern asked Father Willie.

"Yes sir," Father Willie said, never looking up as he wrote.

"Why me? Why me?" Murray Fern demanded, reminding Father Willie of Spencer.

"You ran a red light, sir," Father Willie said, looking up for the first time then continuing with the citation.

"But I can't get another ticket. One more and they'll suspend my license. Christ, gimme a break!"

Father Willie did not answer but continued to write in embarrassed silence.

"Just my luck to get stopped by a couple of pricks," the fat man said as he paced in a tight circle. "A couple of ticket hungry, heartless pricks."

Now Spencer Van Moot no longer cared about a cut rate stereo set and looked around the rear of the car for a taillight violation that Willie could add to the ticket.

"A couple of two bit, ticket happy, stupid fucking pricks!" Murray Fern said as Father Willie continued his writing without comment.

"Sign on the line," Spencer said coldly, speaking for the first time.

"Fuck you," said Murray Fern. "I'm innocent and I'm not signing."

"You're not admitting guilt," Father Willie said quietly. "If you don't sign, thereby promising to appear, we'll have to take you in and book you on the violation."

"Prick!" the fat man said, brushing Father Willie's ballpoint aside, taking a gold plated fountain pen from his inside coat pocket and leaning on the hood to study the ticket.

"It's only a promise . . ."

"I know what the fuck it is!" the man interrupted. "What I'd like to know is why you tinhorns aren't out catching criminals instead of harassing honest citizens, that's what I'd like to know."

The fat man scrawled his name across the ticket and turned his back on the two officers while Father Willie tore off the violator's copy and handed it to him along with his driver's license.

"I'll see you in court!" Murray Fern sputtered as he snatched his copy and license from Father Willie's hand. "I'll have a lawyer. I'll beat you. I'll make you go to court on your day off and I'll make you look like the dumb shit you are!"

He spun around and jammed the ticket, pen and license into his coat pocket. But when he jerked his hand out, a tiny .25 caliber automatic clattered to the pavement.

"Oh shit," said Murray Fern bleakly as Spencer Van Moot quickly pulled and pointed his .38 at the fat man's eyes.

"Who says there's no God?" Father Willie grinned happily.

"I only carry a gun when I make bank deposits," croaked Murray Fern. "I know it's against the law but I'm a businessman! You're not gonna put me in jail for something as petty as this?"

"Who *says* there's no God?" Father Willie repeated as he drew his handcuffs.

By the time the two policemen obtained the booking approval and ran a record check on Murray Fern who had three drunk driving arrests, but no other criminal record, the fat man had threatened every officer at Wilshire Station with a lawsuit. It was 8:30 P.M. when they stood with Murray Fern in front of the booking officer, Elwood Banks, a fifty-year old black man and former partner of Spencer Van Moot.

"How's the retail trade in Los Angeles holdin up?" he asked Spencer when they brought the prisoner inside the lockup.

"Fair to middling, Elwood," Spencer answered. "Booking this guy for CCW."

"Kinda old to be playin with guns, ain't you, Dad?" commented Elwood Banks, looking up from his typewriter as he inserted a booking form.

"I'll sue you too, you bastard," Murray Fern warned. "Just one more smart remark and I'll put you on the lawsuit."

Sitting on a bench to the side of the booking cage, waiting to be fingerprinted, was a tall, once powerful derelict with a bloody wet bandage over one eye. He was forty-eight years old, looked sixty-five, and had fought with the officers who had arrested him for plain drunk. The assault on the officers made him a felon now, but his fourteen page rap sheet included fifty-four arrests for only plain drunk and vagrancy, so now he would be tried and sentenced as a misdemeanant.

Elwood Banks knew the derelict as Timothy "Clickety-clack" Reilly, so called because his ill-fitting false teeth clicked together when he talked. Elwood Banks had booked Clickety-clack three times in the past, had never known him to be violent and rightly guessed that the young arresting officer, Roscoe Rules, had antagonized the derelict. His smashed nose and scarred eyes should have been a tip-off to Roscoe. Clickety-clack had once been a ranked heavyweight.

When Clickety-clack was brought inside the station by Roscoe he had merely said what he said to every arresting officer from Boston to Los Angeles: "I could whip you, Officer. In a fair fight I could whip you from here to East Fifth Street, know that?"

And most arresting officers answered something like: "Yeah, Clickety-clack, I know you could—in a fair fight. But if you try it, it ain't gonna be a fair fight cause my partner and me and half the nightwatch are gonna work out on your gourd with our sticks and do the fandango on your kisser. But in a fair fight you'd kick my ass, that's for sure."

And Clickety-clack would be satisfied. But on this night when he made the same speech to Roscoe Rules, Roscoe replied, "Oh yeah, you're gonna whip me, old man?"

And then in the corridor of Wilshire Station by the front desk in the presence of luscious Officer Reba Hadley whom he was trying to impress, Roscoe Rules took off his hat, slammed it on the desk, stood on the balls of his feet in front of the hulking derelict, put on his black gloves dramatically, both fists on his hips and said, "You think you can whip my ass, you wrinkled wart? You stinking tub a puke. Think you can whip me in a fair fight, huh?"

And Clickety-clack just said, "Yeah." And from a corner of his all but destroyed brain, he found a memory, a rhythm, an instinct and sent a picture left hook whistling through the air. Roscoe Rules woke up three minutes later in the lap of luscious Officer Reba Hadley who said to him, "You dumb shit."

Clickety-clack Reilly was of course buried by five of six blue uniforms and ended up with a badly cut lip and three more stitches in his eyes which made no difference at all to that caved in, monstrous face.

But now he sat, calm and secure and happy in the jail of Elwood Banks who knew exactly how to pacify him, thereby eliminating the possibility of further problems for himself.

"You okay, Mister Reilly?" he asked when Spencer and Father Willie entered the jail with Murray Fern. "Mind if I book this prisoner for these officers so they can get back out on the street?"

"No, Officer, I don't mind," the derelict smiled painfully to the black jailor. He looked as though he would love to hear it again, that word applied to him so seldom in his bitter lonely life.

"Thanks a lot, *Mister* Reilly," Elwood Banks said. "We'll just be a minute."

"Glad to hear you quit eatin in those greasy spoons down on Jefferson," Elwood Banks said to Spencer without even looking at Murray Fern. Then to Father Willie, "Once we was eatin in this soul kitchen and we caught a momma cockroach and three babies crawlin on his plate. Spencer just told them to fry it. It was free."

"My tastes've changed since those days," Spencer remarked.

"I knew you wasn't the soul food type at heart, Spencer," Elwood Banks said. Then he turned to Murray Fern and said, "Name?"

"Go to hell," the arrestee answered.

"Man, your face is red as a bucket a blood," Elwood Banks said. "Calm down, make it easy on yourself."

"I'm including *you* in the lawsuit," said Murray Fern.

"You're sure lucky you got these easygoin officers here," Elwood Banks said. "You was busted by an officer named Roscoe Rules he'd a been up side your head long ago. They'd a needed a sewing machine to put in the stitches."

"I demand an attorney."

"After you're booked you can call one," said Elwood Banks.

"I demand an MD. I'm on medication for a serious allergy."

"Ain't none here," Elwood Banks said. "Boys can take you to the hospital if you want, right now before they book you."

"That'll take too long. I'm bailing out of here at once."

"Then why do you want a doctor?"

"Because I do. I demand an MD be brought here."

"Well there ain't none here."

"Then I demand an RN."

"You keep this shit up and you're gonna get an RIN," the black jailor informed him.

"What's that?" asked Murray Fern.

"A rap in the nuts. Now gimme your full name and address."

"I refuse to answer."

"That does it," Elwood Banks said, his lip curling as he came out from behind the counter. "I usually search *after* booking but I'm gonna make an exception. Strip down."

"What?" Murray Fern asked nervously. "What are you gonna do?"

"Nothin. *If* you do like I say." Elwood Banks wore crisp jail khakis, his LAPD badge was highly polished, his feet were spread as he stood before the fat white man whose courage and insolence were in direct proportion to what was on his body and in his pockets. Or as Elwood Banks often put it, "Strip em down and show em what they are: nothin!"

"You want me to take off *all* my clothes?" Murray Fern asked, looking from one policeman to another as Elwood Banks reached roughly into his pockets, removing his wallet, keys, handkerchief, cigarettes and chewing gum.

"Turn em inside out," Elwood Banks said, and Murray Fern obeyed, trying to beat the jailor to the pockets, fearing he would rip them.

"Satisfied?" Murray Fern asked, when everything including his Patek Philippe wristwatch was on the counter.

"No way, baby," said Elwood Banks. "Get them fancy threads off that chubby body and on the counter. I mean strip and do it now!"

Thirty seconds later, Murray Fern stood before the three policemen wearing only ninety dollar boots of imported Swiss leather, knee length blue silk socks, and silk boxer shorts dotted with tiny hearts.

"Satisfied?" he asked again, but now his authoritative baritone was a tenuous rasp and his eyes darted past the men to the corridor outside.

"I said strip, damnit!" Elwood Banks ordered. "Now get them boots and britches off before I rip em off!"

In a moment Murray Fern stood utterly naked before them, turning his body to one side and another, his composure breaking to pieces before their eyes, the rolls of textured fat shaking as he squirmed and wriggled with nowhere to hide.

"Turn around and bend over and spread your cheeks, Murray," Elwood Banks said for the first time using the fat man's name.

"Bend over?"

"Bend over and show me that round brown," Elwood Banks said. "I gotta see if you're hiding a machine gun in there."

When Murray Fern timidly did as he was told Elwood Banks said, "Humph, my kid's basset hound got better makins than that. Okay, boy, lift your feet up one at a time and show me the bottoms."

Murray Fern obeyed quickly and quietly.

When he was finished, Elwood Banks said, "Okay, Murray, now turn around and face me and open your mouth and lift up your balls. We don't want you rat-holin twenty bucks in some little crease down there. You can't be no better off than Mr. Reilly when we lock you in the tank together."

As Murray Fern opened his mouth for inspection he unconsciously held his hands over his shriveled penis, which was lost in the hair and layers of overhanging fat.

Elwood Banks then delivered the coup de grace. "Okay, Murray, now take your hands away and skin your wee wee back. I once knew a bookie kept bettin markers hid under his foreskin."

When the search and booking were finished, Murray Fern was docile, tamed by the jailor who knew that this soft wealthy white man could be subdued as easily as a black pimp could be mastered by the threat to book his flash money as evidence. As easily as a fighting derelict could be pacified simply by calling him "sir" and "mister." Elwood Banks had never set foot in a college classroom, but life had made him a psychologist.

"Wanna use the phone now, Murray?" Elwood Banks asked when he finished the fingerprinting and offered Murray Fern a cigarette.

"Yes sir," said Murray Fern, who was ever so grateful to the black jailor for giving him his silk underwear with the little hearts, a cigarette and a dime for a phone call.

After booking Murray Fern, Spencer longed to get up to Wilshire Boulevard and eat liver pâté and poached turbot with sautéed cucumbers. But Father Willie made the mistake of clearing on the radio and they were given a call at once. "Seven-A-Thirty-three, Seven-Adam-Thirty-three, see the woman, Eleventh and Ardmore, possible DB."

"A dead body, at eleven fifteen! Goddamnit, Padre, how many times I told you about picking up that frigging mike and clearing?"

"I know, Spencer, I know," Willie answered.

"You're too goddamn conscientious!"

"I know."

"Wait'll you been on the job awhile. You think the sergeants care we bust our balls? You think that cunt Lieutenant Finque cares?"

"I know, Spencer, I know."

"Christ, I got a headache already. All that jawing from that fat prick, Murray Fern. My head aches and I'm sick to my stomach."

"I know."

"I didn't get my vichyssoise tonight, for chrissake."

"I'm sorry."

"I didn't get my veau à la crème."

"There's nothing I can do . . ."

"And I had my heart set on maybe some Coquilles St. Jacques Parisienne!" Spencer cried.

"Is that the one with scallops, garlic and herbs?"

"No that's Provençale. This is the one with scallops and mushrooms."

"In a white wine sauce?"

"Yeah."

"I like that one."

"And I had my heart set on some artichoke hearts and truffles!" Spencer continued. "Oh God!"

"I'm really awful sorry, Spencer," Father Willie said.

"When you started working with me you thought all menus were printed on the wall. I trained you!" reminded Spencer Van Moot.

"I know, Spencer, I know."

"And this is the thanks I get. All because you're so goddamn gung ho and have to pick up the mike and clear. Now I gotta smell a dead body instead of a soufflé au chocolat! Oh God!"

"I'll make it up to you, Spencer," promised Father Willie, wondering when he was going to learn to act like a veteran.

A wizened crone in a black dress and dirty sweatsocks was drinking beer on the porch of a two story frame house just south of the corner. She waved as Spencer flashed their spotlight around, hoping not to find the caller.

Spencer lagged behind disgustedly as they parked, and gathered up his flashlight and hat slowly. He always put the hat on while looking in the rearview mirror so as not to disturb the hairstyle.

"Yes, ma'am?" Father Willie turned his light on the porch steps as the old woman drained the can without getting out of her rocking chair. She steamed like dank mulching weeds.

"Think my tenant's dead in the basement," the old woman grinned in triumph.

"What makes you think . . . uh, oh," said Spencer as he got to the top step of the porch and smelled the tenant who made them forget the old woman's putrescence.

"When did you discover him?" Father Willie asked, as Spencer sneered, thinking he would have to endure this instead of peach Melba.

"Ain't seen him in about three days. Thought he moved out without paying the rent. Sort of discovered him, you might say, about an hour ago when the wind started stirring things around."

Spencer sighed and nodded and led Father Willie through the musty hallway of the boardinghouse which was partitioned off to accommodate seven single men. They found the basement door slightly ajar.

"Wonder if that witch is drinking beer or bat milk?" Spencer remarked.

"He's down there all right," Father Willie said, almost retching as they tried the stairs.

Then Spencer found the light switch and led Father Willie down the ancient wooden stairway where next to a gravity-heat furnace they found the tenant hanging from the ceiling joists, his knees almost dragging the ground.

"Kee-rist!" Spencer said, forgetting the overpowering smell for a moment.

The neck of the hanging man was almost ten inches long and the dragging legs formed a bridge for a column of ants which trooped up his legs to his face and ears and nose where they nested and fed with a velvety spider. And there were wounds on the man's neck which Father Willie realized were rat bites after he saw the mounds of droppings on the floor beneath the hanging man.

"Wonder how long he's been hanging around here?" Spencer quipped to his little partner who had a handkerchief pressed to his nose.

"He probably reached the end of his rope," Spencer said, but Father Willie didn't hear Spencer's gags.

Willie Wright had not seen that many dead men in his three year police career and he was struck by the youth of this man and by the swollen hands darkened by draining blood and by the gray face which looked as if it belonged in a wax cabinet. And though the elongated neck shocked him, because he did not dream it could happen like this, he was almost shocked because for the first time in twenty-four years Father Willie Wright realized something. He looked at that one dull eye open and truly believed that he would join the waxen hanging man. That they were brothers going somewhere. Or nowhere.

It was just a young man consciously coming to a basic truth for the first time. But Father Willie, not knowing the source of his fear, became very frightened by the hunk of fat in his belly and had a hard time keeping Spencer Van Moot from noticing.

This was the night that Father Willie Wright encouraged the others to go to choir practice. It was the first time Father Willie had been the prime mover.

And later that very night, perhaps because of the hanging man, Father Willie Wright was to become a beloved MacArthur Park choirboy for what he did to put that hoity toity bitch, Officer Reba Hadley, in her place.

There were two Officer Hadleys, no relation, in Wilshire Division: Phillip Hadley, a policeman on the daywatch, and Reba Hadley, the policewoman on the nightwatch. So as to know which Hadley one was talking about, the other officers referred to them as Balls Hadley and No-Balls Hadley.

No-Balls Hadley was on the nightwatch desk. She had been in the department two years, had an M.A. in Business Administration from UCLA, and believed that the brass of the department was discriminating against women by not promoting them past the rank of sergeant. And by humiliating women in forcing them to undergo the same police training as the men. She felt it was degrading and ludicrous that women in patrol assignments had to wear short hair and a man's uniform complete to the trousers and hat, obviously an attempt by the brass to discourage those women who had been forced on them. Of course she was right.

She also vociferously proclaimed that it took little or no brains or administrative ability to wrestle a pukey drunk into a radio car, to chase and subdue a burglar in an alley or to drive a high speed chase after some joyriding bubblegummer. She was again right.

No-Balls Hadley, who was sometimes called Dickless Tracy, was also right when she declared fearlessly at a policewomen's meeting attended by chauvinist spies for Commander Moss that he, as well as most high ranking officers of the department, had little or no street experience and had advanced quickly through the ranks because they could pass exams, not because they were street cops.

So No-Balls Hadley was considered a rabble-rouser and troublemaker by those high ranking members of the Los Angeles Police Department who believed that women had *some* value in rape cases, juvenile investigations and public relations. But otherwise should keep their big fat insecure libber mouths shut because they were probably bull dykes at heart and were out to steal men's jobs. No-Balls Hadley knew that the brass was not about to give up those jobs since they had kissed so many asses to get them.

In short, No-Balls Hadley was intelligent, articulate, courageous and correct most of the time. She was utterly feminine, with long shapely legs, tapering fingers, honey colored bobbed hair, naturally jutting young breasts. She was also discriminating in the men she dated, preferring professional men of breeding and affluence, thus dashing the hopes of every policeman on the Wilshire nightwatch. For this reason she was considered an insufferable bitch and it took the person who loved her more than anyone on earth to put her in her place.

It happened after work at 2:00 A.M. on the night Father Willie found the brother in the basement. Father Willie was dozing drunkenly at choir practice in MacArthur Park when Spencer Van Moot grabbed the little man by the jaws.

"Leave me alone, Spencer," Willie squeaked while his partner held him by the chin, saying, "Get up, Padre. Goddamnit, wake up!"

"The hanging man!" Father Willie cried in confusion as the earth heaved. "The hanging man!"

"Never mind the hanging man," Spencer said. "Bloomguard and Niles just showed up. They been at a party at Sergeant Yanov's apartment. We're all going over there."

"No, no," Father Willie moaned, and tried to lie back down on his blanket but Spencer wouldn't have it.

Father Willie was the last choirboy to arise. The others were already gunning their car motors, turning on lights, driving toward the apartment near Fourth and Bronson where the bachelor sergeant resided. Though Yanov wisely declined choir practice invitations, he occasionally threw an impromptu party of his own.

"Come on, Padre," Spencer said, dragging the little man to his feet, careful not to get any of the duck slime from Willie's checkered bermuda shorts on his fifty-five dollar tie dyed jeans with the needlepoint patches which he had bought at a police discount from a men's store on Beverly Boulevard. "Father Willie, listen! No-Balls Hadley's there!"

And Father Willie's swollen eyelids cracked apart. The little man shook his thin wheat-colored hair out of his eyes, shot a hopeful grin at his partner and took his arm as Spencer led him to the car on Parkview Street just south of Wilshire.

"You sobering up?" Spencer asked as he drove them in Father Willie's station wagon, a five year old Dodge with a "God Is Love" bumper sticker on front and back.

"Yes," said Father Willie who was getting drunker with each bump and rumble, catching fire with a consuming passionate gut wrenching love for No-Balls Hadley whom he never discussed while sober.

He had succeeded in driving away his sweet obsessive fantasies except for those infrequent moments when his Jehovah's Witness wife would consent to a five minute straight lay without too much annoying foreplay. At those times it was not the plump little Witness he was mounting, but Officer Reba Hadley, No-Balls Hadley of the splendid breasts, elegant legs and caustic tongue who never so much as glanced at little Father Willie Wright when he passed the desk and screwed up enough courage to say, "Good afternoon" or "Good evening" or "The desk pretty busy tonight?"

She would sometimes mumble a perfunctory reply when not busy with a ringing phone or routine report which she felt beneath her to write in the first place. But once, as she leaned on the counter chatting into the telephone, dressed in the tailored blue long sleeved blouse and fitted skirt of a desk officer, instead of a man's uniform like a female patrol officer, she asked Father Willie if he would mind getting her a soft drink from the machine because she had three crime reports going and couldn't leave the phone.

Father Willie Wright dropped his pocket change all over the floor in his haste to get the coins in the machine and was careful not to spill a single drop as he set it before No-Balls Hadley as reverently as any real priest ever offered a chalice at the altar.

No-Balls Hadley said into the phone, "Look, Madge, we have to have the nerve to walk into the chief's office and say what we think. Of course he hates our guts but he's afraid of us now. We've got the media with us. Damn it, Madge, what've we got to lose? You think I want to spend a career standing at this desk writing bike reports and making inane small talk to a bunch of semiliterate slobs?"

One of the semiliterate slobs of whom she spoke stood shyly across the counter, the large gap in his front teeth bared to No-Balls Hadley who had forgotten he was there until she saw the dime still on the counter in front of her.

"Just a minute, Madge," she said testily into the mouthpiece, then held her hand over it and said, "Officer . . ."

"Wright," Father Willie said. "Willie Wright's my name!"

"Yes, of course," she said impatiently. "You think I don't know every man on the nightwatch? I've only been chained to this desk six months. I ought to know."

"Oh sure," said Father Willie, who was so plain, so small, so unassuming that she could never remember his name.

"Listen, Wright, did you want something?"

"Oh no," Father Willie said to the tall girl while his mad impetuous young heart longed to say, "Oh yes! Oh yes, Reba! Oh yes!"

He had never called her "Reba," never once in the six months she had been in Wilshire Division after being transferred from Parker Center where she tried to stage a policewomen's work slowdown.

"Well, what do you want then, Wright? How about taking your dime and excusing me? I have this important call."

"Sure, Officer Hadley." Father Willie reddened and turned awkwardly.
"Just a minute, Wright. Take your dime for the drink."
"Oh no," Willie mumbled. "It's my pleasure. Honestly, I . . ."
"Take the dime," said No-Balls Hadley, her eyes narrowing as she momentarily forgot the phone she held pressed in her hands.
"Really, it's my . . ."
"Look, buster," No-Balls Hadley said, "I pay my own way just like every officer in this station. I don't need you to buy my Bubble-up. Now you take this dime!"
Father Willie snatched the dime in his sweaty hand, scurried down the steps to the parking lot, got in the radio car and roared out onto Venice Boulevard.
"What's the matter with you?" Spencer had asked, seeing Father Willie's brick red face.
"Nothing. Nothing."
Father Willie had vowed to forget No-Balls Hadley but found to his shame and dismay that she was even more desirable.

When Spencer and Father Willie arrived at the party at Sergeant Yanov's apartment, Willie had not been thinking of his previous unsuccessful encounter with No-Balls Hadley. His gin ravaged brain would not admit those warnings and fears which keep most men from achieving celebrity.
When Father Willie Wright set foot in that raucous smoke filled steamy apartment he was roaring drunk. He squirmed past sweaty bodies which danced wall to wall in the suffocating rooms. The party spilled out onto the balcony and even extended to the pool where at least a dozen clerks from Wilshire and Rampart and Hollywood stations swam bikini clad while goatish policemen swam naked until the apartment house manager threatened to call the police—the ones with clothes on. The men then swam in their underwear or trousers until the manager scurried back inside then stripped again.
Father Willie's protuberant blue eyes were red and raw by the time he bumped his way through the crowd. The smoke was making him slightly sick and defeated when he heard it coming from the bedroom. Her voice!
"Listen, Sheila," she was saying to Officer Sheila Franklin, a personable brunette who worked Juvenile at Central, "I want to leave right this minute and I don't care if you *are* worried about Nick Yanov's feelings. Damn it, he should control these stupid disgusting drunks if he expects people to stay at the party. Of course I got out of the pool! I'm not staying there while these pea brained chest beaters swim around nude! I'm not interested in Sergeant Nick Yanov or any of these creeps and I only came here because you . . ."
And as Father Willie strained to hear the voice of his secret love, Francis Tanaguchi abruptly changed the tape from Elton John to The Carpenters because he had finally managed to get a dance with Ida Keely, a cute communications operator with eyes like a deer. He had a blue veiner even before the song began.

Lookin back on how it was in years
gone by and the
good times that I had
Makes today seem rather sad
so much has changed.

Officer Sheila Franklin sighed, stood and made her way out of the cluttered bedroom where most of the living room furniture had been pushed to make room for the dancers. She stopped before opening the door and said, "All right, Reba, I've asked you to be sociable and stay a little while because you know how I feel about Nick Yanov. But if you have to go . . ."
"I can call a cab. You stay."

"Damn it, Reba, I brought you here. I'll take you back to your car. But you know something? It's *not* a rough party. They're just dancing and . . ."

"I was practically mauled in the swimming pool!"

"One drunk grabbed your ass. Come on, Reba, you're a cop too, for God's sake. They're just a little drunk."

"I'll call a cab."

"No, no, no, I'll tell Nick we're leaving. Go ahead and change."

And then as Father Willie ducked into the bathroom the partially opened bedroom door swung open and Sheila Franklin, still wearing her wet bikini under a blue terry cloth robe, crossed the hallway and went out a side door which opened onto a terrace where Sergeant Nick Yanov sat playing nickel and dime poker with five other policemen.

It was songs of love that I would sing to them
And I'd memorize each word.
Those old melodies still sound so good to me
As they melt the years away.

No-Balls Hadley still sat where Sheila Franklin had left her. On a large glass coffee table. In her wet bathing suit. A short robe she had borrowed from Nick Yanov covered her sleek flesh as Father Willie Wright quietly pushed open the door behind her.

The sound of No-Balls Hadley's voice. The heart searing voice of Karen Carpenter. The unbearable nostalgia of his high school days. Twelve ounces of gin fermenting in his young bloodstream. Father Willie Wright had very little to do with what happened next. Seldom has a legend been born more spontaneously.

All my best memories come back clearly to me,
Some can even make me cry—just like before.
It's yesterday once more.

First, Father Willie tried to formulate a perfect sentence: something tender, loving, endearing but he could not. He leaned against the wall, unseen behind No-Balls Hadley. Breathing became labored. Nostrils flared. Bulging eyes rolled back in unbearable ecstasy and passion. Like Byron on the Acropolis.

Ev'ry sha-la-la-la, ev'ry wo-oh-wo-oh still shines
Ev'ry shing-a-ling-ling that they're startin'
to sing so fine.

He knew instinctively that this was his moment. His life had led him here. Behind her where she sat perched on the glass table, pissed off at her friend Sheila Franklin and these swinish policemen and men in general. And no man could have stopped what happened next when, still wearing the short robe, she slipped off her bikini bottom and kicked it against the wall in a wet and angry plop.

The coffee table was suddenly cold on the bare buttocks of No-Balls Hadley and she tried to tuck the robe under her as she thought again of that fat hairy ugly pig, Spermwhale Whalen, and how he had tried to dive under the water and grab her by the ass. As she sat fuming on the glass coffee table, Father Willie Wright knew he was not worthy to touch this exquisite golden girl who had filled his young life with torment and guilt.

Ev'ry sha-la-la-la, ev'ry wo-oh-wo-oh still shines
Ev'ry shing-a-ling-ling that they're startin'
to sing so fine . . .

Father Willie Wright found himself on his knees crawling across the red carpet. Without willing it he was on his back worming forward under the glass table.

Then No-Balls Hadley thought she heard something. A sound, wet and sticky. But with the noise in the living room she dismissed it and smoldered and waited for her friend, determined not even to go in the other room to get her clothes. She would let Sheila bring them to her. She wouldn't risk an encounter with another drunken cop.

She heard the sound again. Louder. A smacking sound, close but somehow distant. Then she heard it directly beneath her! She uncrossed her legs and spread them and looked down in horror at the white and bloodless nose and lips of Father Willie Wright pressed against the underside of the glass table, smearing the glass directly beneath her bare bottom with wet and loving kisses while his blue eyes crossed and bulged from the meticulous maddening scrutiny of the golden twat of his beloved.

No-Balls Hadley screamed. She shrieked in consummate disgust as Father Willie Wright, unaware that she was gone from the glass, still slurped tenderly and vaguely wondered what someone was yelling about.

No-Balls Hadley screamed. And screamed.

Before the first three policemen had burst through the door Father Willie realized that something was wrong, his face pressed like a fish against the smeary wet glass, eyes popping. Then Father Willie understood that he was discovered.

"God love ya!" Father Willie whispered reverently just before No-Balls Hadley picked up a huge ceramic lamp and smashed it down on the tempered glass while all hell broke loose around the confused and troubled choirboy chaplain.

Then someone pulled him out from under the table to save him while No-Balls Hadley grabbed a three iron from the golf bag of Sergeant Nick Yanov and began breaking chunks from the glass. Father Willie went skidding across the floor, Spencer Van Moot dragging him by the heels.

Someone wrestled the three iron from No-Balls Hadley who yelled, "You filthy disgusting obscene little motherfucker! I'll kill you!"

She tore a picture from the wall and threw it crashing through the bedroom window to the terrace outside where it thudded against the side of the head of a poker player, sending him to the emergency ward for five stitches.

No-Balls Hadley, minus her robe which had been pulled away by a policeman trying to restrain her, clad only in a green bikini top, began beating Father Willie Wright back against the sliding closet door and kicking him in the soft belly.

Then she was sitting on top of Father Willie, pummeling him with both fists as he covered his little face with both arms saying, "But I love you, Officer Hadley. Don't you see?"

Finally, Sergeant Nick Yanov, one of the few sober policemen at the party, ovepowered the spitting kicking cursing policewoman and dragged her still naked into the other bedroom where Officer Sheila Franklin got her in a wristlock until she fell exhausted, blurting what Father Willie had done.

As the bleeding bewildered Father Willie Wright was being carried to his car by Spencer Van Moot and Harold Bloomguard, he turned his battered face to Harold Bloomguard and said, "What'd I do wrong, Harold? What'd I do?"

"I'll tell you what you did, Padre! You put that hoity-toity bitch No-Balls Hadley in her place, is all!" Harold Bloomguard cried proudly as they carried Father Willie down the sidewalk. "You just became a Legend in Your Own Time!"

From that day on, in choirboy folklore, the episode of No-Balls Hadley became known as The Night the Padre Tried to Eat Pressed Ham Through the Wrapper.

7

7-A-77: Calvin Potts and Francis Tanaguchi

A choir practice was certainly in order and was called for by Francis Tanaguchi on The Night the U-Boat Was Decommissioned. It was three months before the killing in MacArthur Park.

The night was bound to be an extraordinary one, beginning as it did with a noisy argument in which the nightwatch ganged up on Lieutenant Finque who was trying to defend the department's disciplinary policies to the rebellious assembly of bluesuited young men who thought he was full of shit.

''Look,'' the exasperated watch commander argued, ''that West Los Angeles officer *deserved* thirty days off for what he did.''

''Deserved? Deserved?'' Spermwhale Whalen thundered. ''His old man and his old man's old man owned that fuckin bar for thirty years. He grew up behind the bar.''

''Department policy forbids policemen to engage in off-duty employment in places where alcoholic beverages . . .''

''What would *you* do if your old man was pressed for a bartender for a couple weeks?''

''He *only* got thirty days.'

''Only? *Only!* Take thirty days' pay off me and I'd starve to death. So would my ex-wives and my ex-kids and my turtle. Where the fuck else does a guy get fined for somethin he does during nonworkin hours that don't violate no laws?''

''Professional sports,'' said Lieutenant Finque.

''They can afford it, we can't,'' Spermwhale shot back. ''All I can say is I'm glad I got my twenty in next January. I'm gonna start speakin my mind then.''

''The lieutenant needs that like a dose of clap,'' said Sergeant Nick Yanov, who winked at Spermwhale.

''Fuckin pussies run this outfit,'' Spermwhale growled, settling down a little under the placating grin of Sergeant Yanov. ''I know why all the brass downtown go up to Chinatown for lunch. They operate this fuckin department from the fortune cookies.''

''Well, what say we read the crimes?'' Sergeant Yanov asked, much to the relief of Lieutenant Finque who feared gross and ugly and dangerous old cops like Spermwhale Whalen. Lieutenant Finque could never seem to reason with them.

''Here's one on Virginia Road where a housewife invented a do it yourself antiburglary kit,'' Nick Yanov said, rubbing his bristling chin as he read. ''She's an invalid who stays in bed all day with a Colt .38 under her pillow. Blew up a burglar the other day when he opened the kitchen window and tippy-toed in. Her *second.''*

After everyone finished cheering, Sergeant Yanov looked at the clock and said, ''Not much time left. Here's a mug shot of that dude the dicks want for shanking his old lady. Cut her long, deep and continuous. Hangs around the poolroom on Adams.''

''Hey, Sarge,'' Spencer Van Moot said, ''I'm getting tired of all these station calls to the old broad lives on West Boulevard. Doesn't the desk officer know she's a dingaling? She always wants to know things like where does she buy a crash helmet big enough for her thirty-five year old epileptic son who keeps falling on his head.''

''Only takes a minute,'' Sergeant Yanov said. ''Her boy's been dead for five years. Makes the old woman feel good talking to a big good looking blond like you, Spencer. You probably remind her of him.''

"Well she's not my type and I got better things to do," Spencer answered, and then he got mad as the assembly room exploded into hoots and laughter because everyone but Lieutenant Finque knew that Spencer's better things to do were bargain hunting on Wilshire Boulevard.

"It's time we hit the streets," Lieutenant Finque repeated, since he believed that a lieutenant should never let a sergeant, especially one as lenient as Nick Yanov, take over the rollcall.

Unquestionably, the biggest pain in the ass on the nightwatch at Wilshire Station was Francis Tanaguchi. He was twenty-five years old, a third generation Japanese-American who grew up in the barrio of East Los Angeles and spoke good street Spanish but not a word of Japanese. He adored guacamole, chile relleno, barbacoa, menudo, albondigas soup and tequila with anything. He hated sushi, tempura, teriyani steak, sake and could not operate a pair of chopsticks to save his life.

As a teenage member of a Chicano youth gang he had spray painted "Peewee Raiders" on more walls than any other gang member. Still, he was never totally accepted by Mexican boys who lumped all Orientals together by invariably nicknaming them "Chino" or "Chink." Francis fought to be called "Francisco" or at least "Pancho" but settled for "Chink-ano." It stayed with him until he joined the Los Angeles Police Department at the age of twenty-one.

Gradually he found it was advantageous to be Japanese. There were many Mexican-American policemen but there were few Japanese-American policemen, even though Los Angeles has the largest Japanese-American population in California.

Sometimes Francis and his black partner, Calvin Potts, had profound philosophical discussions about their ethnic roots.

"So now if I wanna get somewhere in the department I gotta be a Buddhahead," Francis moaned to his partner.

"You think you got problems?" Calvin remarked. "How about me? How'd you like to be a brother in your paddy world, huh?"

"Who said I'm a paddy for chrissake?" Francis answered. "Goddamnit, I'm a Mexican."

"You're a Nip, Francis," Calvin reminded him.

"So quit calling me a paddy."

"You all look alike."

"It's goddamn hard becoming a Jap when you're my age. I been at it four years now and I still can't take a picture or mow a lawn straight."

"You think you got it rough," Calvin said. "How'd you like to have other policemen put you down when you date a white chick. How'd you like that, Francis?"

"I ain't seen it stop you yet, Calvin."

"That's because I'm drunk when I date a white chick. I get drunk to stop the hurt."

"You get drunk when you date *any* chick. In fact, everybody knows you're an alcoholic, for chrissake."

"I'm only an alcoholic because it dulls the hurtin," said Calvin.

"How'd you like to get sick to your stomach every time you look a fish head in the eye?"

"I *do* get sick to my stomach every time I look a fish head in the eye."

"Yeah, but that asshole Lieutenant Finque ain't trying to duke you into the Oriental community by using you as a part time community relations officer at Japanese luncheons where you force down three raw squid and puke all the way to Daniel Freeman Hospital afterward."

"That's all in your head, that reaction to Nip soul food."

"That's the worst place to be sick—in the head. And that prick Lieutenant Finque is doing it to me."

"We'll talk to the guys at the next choir practice. Roscoe or one a those whackos'll think up some way to fix his ass."

Calvin Potts, at twenty-eight, was three years older than Francis Tanaguchi and had been a policeman two years longer. He was tall, athletic, divorced, the son of a Los Angeles bail bondsman. He had been raised in Baldwin Hills when there were only a few black families on the hill. He had dated girls and women of all colors all his life. In truth he seldom had any trouble with racial slur. It wouldn't have bothered him much if he had. He was an alcoholic because his father was an alcoholic, as was a brother, a sister, two uncles and numerous cousins. He came from a hard drinking family. He had been a Scotch drinker at sixteen. He was also an alcoholic because he was insane about his ex-wife, Martha Twogood Potts, whose father was one of the most successful black trial lawyers in Los Angeles.

Martha Twogood Potts had decided in the second year of their marriage, after several reasonably successful sexual encounters with more marriageable men, that she had been goofy to marry a no-account cop. She scooped Calvin Jr. out of the crib and called her daddy who convinced a Superior Court judge that it would not be unreasonable for Officer Calvin Potts to pay child support and alimony equal to thirty-five percent of his net pay. This left fifteen percent for the car payment, twenty-five percent for food, twenty percent for gas and car repairs, and forty percent for an enormous personal loan he incurred getting started lavishly in married life. Since the total outlay was 135 percent, Calvin remedied the situation by letting the Mercedes be repossessed and buying a second-hand gearless Schwinn bicycle which he rode back and forth to work. He then divided the twenty-five percent food allowance into two equal parts, half for food and half for booze, and discovered that twelve and a half percent of a policeman's net salary would not buy enough booze for even an average alcoholic. So he moved in with a girl known as Lottie LaFarb, a part time telephone operator who made certain calls on company time which earned her up to two hundred dollars a night when she got home.

Calvin Potts had been working with Francis Tanaguchi for six months and they had become inseparable. Calvin could not begin to understand this since he hated people in general and Francis Tanaguchi was by all odds the biggest pain in the ass at Wilshire Station. But there it was. They were always together. Everyone called them The Gook and The Spook.

There were several very good reasons why Francis Tanaguchi was such an enormous pain in the ass. He did annoying things, some of which were cyclical, some more or less permanent. One of the permanent annoying things he was accused of doing was arranging calls to the other choirboys' residences at 4:00 A.M. A mysterious woman with a lasciviously voluptuous voice would begin to talk as the sleepy choirboy was coming awake in the darkness. The listener would be treated to a low crooning lush sexual litany which could transform almost any old three ounce cylinder of flesh, vein and muscle into a diamond cutter. Though it was generally suspected that Francis Tanaguchi was responsible for these bizarre calls, it was never proved and he never admitted it. Drunk and sober, Calvin Potts had begged, threatened and bribed him to no avail.

No one had ever seen the Dragon Lady, as they had come to call the owner of the voice. And no one had ever been able to hang up once she was into her routine. All had wet dreams about her. The wife of Spencer Van Moot had left him for the third time when she, on another phone extension, heard the erotic, blood boiling promises.

Perhaps the greatest harm was done to Father Willie Wright one night as his fat dumpling of a wife lay snoring beside him. Father Willie answered the phone and sat galvanized in the darkness while the Dragon Lady promised to use her body and Willie's in a way that any reasonable man should have known was physically impossible. But Father Willie was not reasonable at this moment. He was gulping, dizzy, disoriented. He was speechless and frenzied. The Dragon Lady began making incredibly luxurious, unwholesome, juicy noises. Then she hung up.

Father Willie lay there for a moment then fell on the sleeping Jehovah's Witness who only tolerated sex when she was awake and prepared for it.

The next afternoon before rollcall, Father Willie Wright, his left eye blood red from a desperate blow by a chubby little fist in the night, waited at Francis Tanaguchi's locker and challenged him to a fight to the death in the basement of Wilshire Police Station. Calvin Potts and several other officers interceded while Francis professed total innocence. Father Willie was led into the rollcall room swallowing tears of rage, swearing for the very first time in anyone's memory.

"Ya fuck, ya!" yelled Father Willie. "Ya dirty slant-eyed heathen godless little fuck, ya!"

Francis Tanaguchi had other annoying habits, not the least of which was biting people on the neck. It started when Francis went to a shabby Melrose Boulevard movie house where they were offering a Bela Lugosi Film Festival to a college crowd which hooted and yelled and smoked pot and ate popcorn.

Francis was with a chilly clerk typist named Daphne Simon who worked the morning watch at Wilshire Records and seldom dated policemen because she felt they were too horny. Francis had won her heart by sending a thirty dollar floral arrangement which he had gotten free by stopping at a Japanese nursery near Crenshaw Boulevard and thrilling the immigrant proprietors with his blue clad Oriental body. Francis had only planned to try to get them to bounce for a handful of violets, but when he saw how delighted they were with him, he promoted the assorted multicolored carnations.

As he sat in the smoke filled movie house, Daphne Simon roughly pulled his hand out from between her legs every time he let it accidentally fall there. It made him wish he had saved the flowers for Ora Lee Tingle at choir practice. Francis Tanaguchi came to dislike Daphne Simon who was in some exotic way giving him a blue veiner by squeezing his hand saucily before she slammed it down on the wooden armrest between the seats. But if he was starting to dislike Daphne Simon he was falling in love with Bela Lugosi.

"You wanna go where, Francis?" Calvin Potts squinted, when Francis settled into the black and white the next afternoon.

"To that big costume store on Western," Francis repeated.

"You goin to a masquerade?"

'No."

"I know, you're gonna buy a polar bear suit for you and Ora Lee to wear while you flog each other with dead baby ducks at the next choir practice."

"I'm gonna buy some fangs," Francis said simply.

For three weeks, which was about as long as one of Francis' whims lasted, he was called the Nisei Nipper by the policemen at Wilshire Station. He skulked around the station with two blood dripping fangs slipped over his incisors, attacking the throat of everyone below the rank of sergeant.

"It was okay for a while," Spencer Van Moot complained to Calvin Potts one day. "But those frigging teeth hurt. And it starts to get really depressing having Francis draped around your neck all the time."

And even as he spoke Francis leaped from behind a wall and onto Spencer's back, nipping him on the neck with the gory plastic fangs.

Sam Niles finally came to work with a bullet painted silver and let Francis see him putting it in his gun.

Harold Bloomguard hung parsley over his locker and told Francis it was wolfsbane. Then Whaddayamean Dean, and finally everyone else, started carrying crosses to ward off the Oriental vampire who would hiss and snarl when a cross was produced and slink back to his locker until he spotted someone with his back turned.

Spermwhale Whalen finally grabbed Francis by the collar and said, "There's so fuckin many crosses around this locker room it looks like a platoon a nuns' dresses here. Francis, I'm gonna stick those goofy teeth right up your skinny ass if you don't knock it off!''

''Okay. I'm getting sick and tired of tasting all these crummy necks anyway,'' Francis said, and the vampire returned to earth permanently.

The night that Francis got bloody hands and decommissioned the U-boat was a smoggy evening in late spring. It started as usual with Calvin complaining that he always drove.

''Looky here, Francis, I been on the job longer than you, and I been on this miserable earth longer and I don't know why the fuck I let you jive me around like this.''

''Like what?''

''Like drivin you around like a fuckin chauffeur every night.''

''I write better English than you so you should drive while I should keep books.''

''You what? You write half the time like some ignorant wetback. You didn't learn no English in those Chicano East L.A. schools.''

''Well you drive better than me.''

''Bullshit. You ever seen a brother drivin at Indianapolis?''

''You ever seen a Buddhahead driving? Every cop knows a Buddhahead is a worse driver even than a brother.''

''Tomorrow you drive.''

''I can't. I don't want nobody to see me with glasses on. They make me look like an Iwo Jima sniper. It embarrasses me.''

''I never seen you with glasses.''

''I only wear them when I wanna see.''

''And we been partners all this time and you never wanted to see?''

''There's nothing on this job I wanna see, Calvin. The only time I put em on is when other guys take em off. I put em on to get laid. That's all I wanna see anymore.''

''Do you put em on at choir practice when you ball Ora Lee Tingle or Carolina Moon?''

''No, that's another thing I don't wanna see.''

Then Calvin started getting sullen. It came over him more frequently of late and he was drinking more than ever before. He had been forcing himself lately to stop thinking of that bitch, Martha Twogood Potts and her sleek caramel flesh. But he could not repress his thoughts of Calvin Jr. and how the toddler hardly knew him now and did not even want to be with his father on weekends. And how he truly *didn't* want the boy with him in the apartment of Lottie LaFarb, even though she was a kind-hearted telephone operator and barely a prostitute and lavished him with pussy and what money she had and loved Calvin Jr. unequivocally.

Sometimes he wanted to beat the shit out of Lottie LaFarb and Francis Tanaguchi, the only two people in the world who, he felt, gave a damn whether or not he stuck that Smith K-38 in his mouth and blew the top of his skull all over the tobacco stained plastic headliner in that black and white Matador which at the moment smelled of urine and vomit from the drunk the daywatch had booked near end-of-watch.

Calvin Potts' surging anger was broken when the honey voice the choirboys had come to love said, ''Seven-A-Seventy-seven, Seven-A-Seventy-seven, see the woman, family dispute at the bar, Adams and Cloverdale.''

''That's us, Calvin,'' Francis said jauntily, jotting the call on the pad attached to the hotsheet holder on the dashboard.

''Well, roger it then, goddamnit,'' Calvin said viciously.

''Seven-A-Seventy-seven, roger,'' Francis said, looking at his partner whose coffee face was polished by the dipping hazy sunlight as they drove west at dusk. ''What're you pissed off at, Calvin?''

''Nothin. I'm just gettin sick and tired a workin this car. Why can't we go back up to the north end next month?''

"We can, I thought you wanted action."

"I'm sick a action. I'm sick a these eastside trashy niggers that've took over this area down here. I'd rather work the Fairfax beat. I could easier put up with all the Hebes in Kosher Canyon chippin their teeth every time you give them a ticket."

"Okay. We'll talk to the boss about working a north end car next month. I know what you need."

"What?"

"A little trim."

"Oh yeah, just what I need," said Calvin looking skyward for a disgusted instant.

"I know Lottie's taking care of your everyday needs but I got a special one just moved in my apartment building. Meant to tell you about her."

"The Dragon Lady?" Calvin said suddenly, and for a moment he felt the depression subside a bit.

"Now, Calvin, you know I don't know any more about the Dragon Lady than you guys," said Francis, with his attempt at an inscrutable mysterious Oriental grin.

"Well, what's she like?"

"Better than that lanky one we met at the party in the Hollywood Hills."

"She better be."

"Too bad you didn't score with that one."

"Yeah, well she woulda came on in if it wasn't for that lawyer throwin his wallet open every two minutes showin all that bread. People just wear me down when they start that bullshit."

"It's all he has going for him," Francis observed.

"I bet she woulda got up off some pussy if I coulda showed a few fifty dollar bills."

"If you gotta buy it it ain't worth it."

"I *woulda* bought it that night. I was hurtin for certain. She had me by the joint, you know."

"Sure."

"I told you that, didn't I?"

"Another alcoholic fantasy, Calvin. You better come down off that Johnnie Walker bottle you're living in."

"Listen, you slant eyed little fenderhead, I'm tellin you she was lopin my mule under the table."

"Calvin, you were so bombed that night even the Dragon Lady couldn't've given you a blue veiner. I mean a black veiner."

"Now *you're* wearin me down, Francis."

"I just ain't going for it, Calvin."

Calvin Potts was glaring at Francis and almost failed to stand on the brakes in time to keep from broadsiding a dilapidated ten year old Pontiac which had limped onto Adams Boulevard from the driveway of Elmer's Barbeque Kitchen which was one half block from the family dispute call.

"Gud-damn!" Calvin yelled to the driver of the Pontiac who managed a frightened smile and gripped the steering wheel nervously with big dusty work-hard hands, his knuckles like walnuts.

"Whooo-eee!" the driver said and stopped in the traffic lane to wait a command from the black and white which pulled up on his right in the number two lane.

"A gud-damn, Mississippi-transplanted, chittlin eatin nigger," Calvin moaned as he switched on his red light and debated going to the call or writing a ticket first.

Francis settled it for him. "I'm up, Calvin."

"Okay, write him then."

"I don't wanna write him, Calvin. He doesn't look like he can afford it."

"I'll write him then."

"I'm up. I'm going up my turn on him. You write the next one."

"Sorry, Officer," the driver said as the black policeman glared at him. "I ain't used to Los Angeles traffic. I'm jist a country boy."

"Drive a tractor then, asshole!" Calvin yelled, switching off the red light and speeding to the call at Adams and Cloverdale where they found two bleary-eyed black women in print housedresses and shower shoes arguing in front of the bar.

"You call?" Francis asked, putting on his hat while Calvin merely shook his head and, cap in hand, followed the two women and Francis inside.

The two policemen found four other combatants all more or less allied against a thirtyish buxom mulatto woman who sat in a corner booth sipping a milkball and tearing at a fat stick of beef jerky.

"There's the bitch that's causin all this ruckus, Officer," said the bigger of the two women who had led them inside.

"Yeah, you hussy," said the other one before the beefeater could speak. "She been livin wif my uncle. My uncle jist up and passed away and she wanna do the funeral, and she think she be gittin the house and the car because this old man wif a brain like pigfeet made some kinda raggedy ass agreement she think is a legal will!"

"She spend all my uncle's bread on wine and beer," said a bony customer at the bar.

"Whadda you spend your old woman's bread on, bastard?" the buxom young woman answered. And then to Francis, "We was livin common law."

"They ain't no common law in this state, bitch," said the smaller of the two women who stepped toward the booth but was stopped by Calvin who walked in front of her.

"Lemme talk to you private," Calvin said and only then did she stop chewing beef jerky and follow the tall black policeman toward the silent jukebox in the corner of the bar.

"What's happenin here, baby?" Calvin asked when they were alone.

"Well see, I was this funky ol man's main momma. I give that man two a the best years he ever had. Ever time I turn aroun he was wantin some face scoldin. Baby, I got calluses on the inside of my mouth from that evil old fool. I woulda went steppin when he died but these people got on my case heavy the first day the ol man was dead. Shoot, I jist decided I was gonna stay and fight for what's mine."

"That all there is?"

"Nothin to it, baby," the woman said and smiled at Calvin for the first time, stepping in close and touching his chest with her swooping breasts.

Just then the man at the bar lurched forward drunkenly saying, "Don't you believe nothin this hussy says about my uncle. It's all a shuck. He was senile and she was usin that old man."

The man was holding something in his arms pressed tightly against his ribs and in the gloom of the bar room it looked like a rusty bath towel. Then Calvin noticed it was leaking down onto the man's cracked leather wing tips and then to the grimy floor.

"Man, you're bleedin!"

"Yeah," the man said. "I is." And as though embarrassed, he pulled the filthy towel away and a mucous trickle spurted out of the puncture in his chest and ran down his rib cage to the floor. The wound bubbled and gaped a bit larger with every breath he took. "That bitch done it to me."

"Okay, bastard!" said the buxom heiress. "Now I'm gonna show em what you done to me!"

As she spoke she squirmed and wriggled and hiked her tight dress over her wobbly buttocks and displayed a soppy Kotex which had been pressed inside her blue panties to stem the flow of blood from an eight inch knife wound across the hip and stomach which peeled back flesh and fat and bared a sliver of gleaming hipbone.

"What the fuck is goin on?" Calvin exploded, waving Francis over and pointing at both ugly wounds.

"You said you wasn't gonna say nothin if I didn't say nothin, you funky ol devil!" the heiress complained.

"Well, he ast me, bitch. What was I gonna say, that I was holdin a pack a bloody meat in this here towel?"

"Did you get cut in the fracas?" Francis asked, shocked at the slash across her belly.

"No, bout five inches above it," the woman answered.

"So, who cut who?" Calvin demanded, disgusted because now they would have to make crime reports and likely book both antagonists in a "mutual combat" situation so common to ghetto policemen.

"I fell on a ice pick," the man said.

"Who cut *you*?" Francis asked the heiress.

"I fell on a butcher knife," she answered.

"Tell me somethin," the man said as Francis squinted in the bleak dusty light at the chest hole and finally stepped forward to watch the sinister little orifice blow and foam as the man breathed. "If somebody was to attack somebody with a ice pick, and this here other somebody was to defend hisself wif a butcher knife, would this somebody wif a butcher knife go to jail?"

Before the policemen could answer, the heiress added, "And if this motherfuckin *dawg* of a lyin wino was really the one to attack a *woman* with a butcher knife and she had to defend *herself* with a ice pick, wouldn't this *woman* be a righteous victim of this other evil ol motherfucker? She wouldn't go to jail, would she?"

"Anybody else see this?" Francis asked, but everyone suddenly turned to his beer for some serious drinking.

"The detectives would book em both and let em hassle it out in court," Calvin scowled contemptuously. "And before it got to a court trial there'd be three continuances by the two defendants and in the end they'd both agree not to prosecute each other and it'd be a big motherfuckin waste of *my* time and the taxpayers' money."

"Kin you give me a ride to the hospital?" asked the heiress.

"You wanna make a crime report against him?"

"No."

"Take the bus," Calvin said. "The doctor'll sew you up for free. It's an emergency."

"Don't they send you a bill?" she asked, and finally tamped the Kotex compress back into place and squirmed the dress back down.

"Sure, but jist put it with the rest of your bills inside the hole in your shoe."

"Calvin, we better take *him* anyway," Francis said. "That's a chest puncture. This man's hurt bad."

"You wanna make a crime report against her?" asked Calvin.

"No," the man said and the breath made a rattling bubble on his chest and a soft pop when it burst.

"Groovy," Calvin said, heading for the door. "Jist take two aspirin and stay in bed tomorrow."

"He's hurt bad, Calvin." Francis had to run to catch his long striding partner outside on the sidewalk.

"Hey, jump back, Jack! I made my decision. I ain't fuckin with no more a these people. If they wanna rip each other from the lips to the hips, let em go head on!"

"He could die. His lung could collapse."

"You can't kill these niggers, Francis. I was broke in on the job by a cracker named Dixie Suggs who hated black people like you hate squid. He taught me you gotta practically cut off their heads and shrink em to kill the motherfuckers. Damn, let's work a north end car next month. I can take those big-mouth kikes better than niggers."

"Okay, Calvin, okay." Francis watched his partner for a moment before raising the hand mike to clear from the call.

They cruised, Calvin smoking quietly, until darkness settled. Then Calvin patted the breast pocket of his uniform and said, "Let's stop by Easy's and get some smokes."

Francis, who had been drinking heavily the night before, was dozing in his seat, his head bobbing on his chest every few seconds, his long black hair hanging over his thin face as small as a boy's.

"We get a call?" Francis asked, fumbling for the pencil in his shirt pocket.

"Go back to sleep, Francis. We didn't get no call."

Calvin made a lazy turn onto Venice Boulevard to the liquor store run by Easy Willis, a jolly black man who supplied two packs of cigarettes a day to each of the three cars patrolling the district around the clock. Easy felt that this would promote the reputation that cops came into Easy's at any time, thus discouraging the robbers and potential robbers who lived in the area.

The packs of cigarettes ensured that not only would the officers walk in once on each watch, but they would make it a point to shine the spotlight in the window every time they passed. In truth, a pack of cigarettes did make them drive by a bit more than they would have normally and a policeman's spotlight is most reassuring to liquor store and gas station proprietors in the ghettos. Many of whom have faced a gun and been slugged and attacked more than a squad of policemen and in fact have a far more physically dangerous occupation.

"Say, Calvin, what's shakin?" Easy grinned, as Calvin walked hatless into the store which was stocked wall to wall with beer, hard liquor and cheap wine. The ghetto dwellers were not dilettante drinkers.

"Aw right, aw right, Easy, my man," Calvin said, leaning on the counter while Easy slid three fifths of Scotch into a paper bag for a boozy black woman who had a child in her arms and another hanging from her dress.

Calvin looked around the store at the sagging liquor counters and the display shelves. Like most ghetto establishments the shelves held *no* candy bars or cigarettes because of juvenile shoplifting. Calvin glanced at the rows of skin magazines and then at the elaborate sprinkler system which the white owner of the store had installed in case there was ever another black riot in Los Angeles.

The proprietor, Lolly Herman, had owned a store in Watts which had been looted and fire-bombed in 1965. He feared another black rebellion more than any antebellum plantation owner. The proprietor had all windows barred and a silent robbery alarm button situated in five stategic locations in the store: behind the counter, in the restroom in case a thief would force him in there, in the cold storage locker if that should be where he was forced to go, near the back door of the store which led out into the yard, that was enclosed by a ten foot chain link fence with five strands of barbed wire around the top, and finally in the money room which was just to the side of the counter and enclosed by ceiling high sheets of bullet-proof glass. The door to the money room was electrically controlled as was the swinging wrought iron gate which protected the front door when the premises were secured at 2:00 A.M.

Perhaps more formidable than the lonely vicious Doberman which prowled the service yard at the rear and lay flea bitten in the blazing sunshine was the carbine that Mr. Herman had displayed on the wall inside the bulletproof money room to dissuade any thief who thought his protection was merely preventative.

Three weeks after he had finished every elaborate antirobbery and antiburglary device, he was sapped by a ninety pound teenager on roller skates when he was getting into his car after closing. Three thousand dollars were stolen from his socks and underwear.

After that, Lolly Herman, with eighteen sutures in his skull, stopped working at the liquor store, retired to his Beverly Hills home and let Easy Willis take over management of the store.

Of course, business was not as good. Easy and the other six employees could not be made to hustle without Lolly Herman watching them. They stole about a thousand a month among them to supplement their incomes, but the liquor store was still a gold mine and Mrs. Herman secretly thanked God that the ninety pound teenager, called Chipmunk Grimes, had coldcocked the old man and driven him into retirement.

"Momma made some souse and head cheese, Calvin," Easy said when the customer left. Then Easy flipped two packs of Camels on the counter without asking.

"Thanks but I don't eat much soul these days." Calvin put both packs in his pockets, glad that Francis didn't smoke.

Of course Easy knew that Francis didn't smoke but went along with the charade since they first came in the store together and Calvin said, "This is my new partner, Easy. His name's Francis and he smokes Camels just like me."

Two packs to a car is what Lolly Herman said to give, and Easy didn't give a damn whether it was to one cop or two. In fact, now that Lolly Herman had retired, Easy often popped for two *extra* packs, and knowing Calvin's drinking problem was reaching an acute stage, bounced for a fifth of Johnnie Walker Black Label once a week.

"Officer!" yelled a young black man in yellow knits as he burst into the store. "Some dude jist stole a radio out of a car there on La Brea!"

"How long ago?"

"Bout twenny minutes."

"How bout jist skatin on out to the car and waking up my little partner. He'll take a report."

"Ain't you gonna try and catch him?"

"Man, twenty minutes? Sucker's halfway to Compton by now."

"He ain't from Compton. Wasn't no brother. He was a paddy long hair blondey like dude. I think he was one a them cats what works at that place down the street where they talks to you about a job but the oniest ones that's makin any money is the one talkin about the jobs, and they get it from the gov'ment."

"Yeah, well we'll take a report," Calvin said blandly, "and since that job place is closed tonight the detectives'll check it out tomorrow."

"Oughtta keep the jiveass honkies outta our neighborhoods," said Easy. "Most a these young jitterbug social workers don't look like they got all their shit in one bag anyhow. And they be tryin to tell us how to do it. I think most a them is Comminists or some other off brand types."

"Nother thing," the young man said to Calvin. "The brother what owned the radio is bleedin around the eye. This paddy started talkin some crazy shit when the dude owned the car caught him stealin the radio. Then this honky jist fired on the brother and took the box."

"What he look like when he swung?" Easy asked.

"Baaaaad motherfucker. Fast hands. Punched like Ali."

"Wasn't none a them do-gooders then," said Easy. "They all sissies. Musta been a righteous paddy crook jist passin through."

After penciling out the brief theft report, Francis was fully awake and the moment they drove away from Easy's liquor store he said, "How about code seven?"

"Too early to eat."

"How about just stopping for a taco at Bennie's?"

"Aw right." Calvin lit another cigarette, grimacing at the thought of one of Bennie's salty guacamole filled drippy tacos which sent Francis Tanaguchi into fits of joy.

"Driver of the pimpmobile looks hinky," Francis said as they crossed Pico Boulevard on La Brea, slowly passing a red and white Cadillac convertible driven by a lanky black man in an orange wide brimmed hat with matching ascot.

"Let's bring him down. Might have a warrant," Calvin said. "Anything to keep from smellin those greasy tacos."

The driver pretended not to see the red light nor hear the honking black and white which followed him for a block until Calvin angrily blasted him to the curb with the siren.

"Watch him say 'who me?' " said Calvin as he got out of the car and approached from the driver's side while Francis advanced on the passenger side, shining his light, distracting the driver to protect his vulnerable partner on the street.

"You got a driver's license?" Calvin asked, right hand on his gun, three cell light in his left hand, searching for the right hand of the driver which was hidden from view.

He relaxed when the driver brought his hand up to the steering wheel and said, "Who me?"

"You know, I once shot a player like you," Calvin lied. "Dude laid there with two magnums in his belly and when I said, 'Leroy, you got any last words?' he said, 'Who me?' and fell over dead. Now break out somethin with your name on it since I know you ain't got a driver's license."

"Sure, Officer," the man said, stepping out onto the street without being told after Calvin jerked open the door of the Cadillac.

Calvin shined his light over the alligators and crab apple green knicker suit with silky orange knee length socks while the man fumbled in the kangaroo wallet nervously.

"Here it is, Officer," he smiled, as Calvin admired the five inch hammered medallion on the bare chest of the young man.

Calvin took the slip of paper which was a speeding ticket issued one week earlier by an LAPD motor officer.

"This all you got with your name on it?" Calvin asked.

"That was gave me by one of your PO-licemen. It's official, ain't it?"

"Shit," Calvin said. "Fuckin motor cops only care about writin a ticket. Bet he took your word about who you are. Bet you keep this ticket for ID until it's time to go to warrant and then get another ticket and use that for a while. Bet every fuckin one is in a different name. What's your *real* name?"

"Jist like it say there, James Holiday."

"Why you sweatin, James?" Calvin asked, flashlight in his sap pocket now, both fists on his hips, stretching so that he could be taller than the pimp and look down on him.

"You makin me nervous cause you don't believe me." The man licked his lips when they popped dryly.

"Gimme that wallet," Calvin said suddenly.

"Ain't that illegal search and seizure, Officer?" asked the pimp.

"Gimme that wallet, chump, or it's gonna be a search and *squeez-ure* of your fuckin neck!"

"Okay, okay," the young man said, handing Calvin the wallet. "Looky here, I ain't no crook or nothin. I owns two or three bars in San Diego."

"Two or three," Francis observed.

"Three, probably," said Calvin, pulling a bail receipt out of an inner compartment of the wallet.

"Uh oh," said the man.

"Uh huh," said Calvin.

"What's his real name?" Francis asked, stepping to the open door of the radio car and pulling the hand mike outside to run a make.

"Omar Wellington," Calvin said. "How about savin us a little time, Omar? You got warrants out or what?"

"Uh-huh," said Omar Wellington. "Couple traffic warrants."

"Well that ain't so bad," said Calvin.

"Oh man, I don't wanna go to jail tonight!"

"No big thing," Calvin said, touching his handcuffs. "We don't have to hook you up, do we?"

"Handcuffs? Naw, I ain't gonna give nobody no trouble. I'm nonviolent. How come you stopped me? It's them fuckin license plates, ain't it?"

Calvin looked at the personalized license plate and replied, "Didn't even notice em, Omar."

"Then how'd you tumble? They's lots a players around here in Cadillacs. It was my orange hat, wasn't it? You wouldn't even a saw me if it wasn't for that motherfuckin hat."

"Yeah, it was the hat, Omar," Francis said to pacify the pimp, who like most street people believed superstitiously that there was one explainable reason for being singled out.

"What do your friends call you, Omar?"

"They jist calls me Omar."

"Okay, Omar, get in the black and white. Let's get goin so you can bail out tonight."

"I only got a hundred bucks on me. The mother fuckin warrants are for more than that. And a bailbondsman don't work on traffic cases. And I ain't got no one I can get hold of for four hours. Ain't this some bullshit?"

"Tell me, Omar," Francis said, sliding in beside the pimp in the back seat. "Why don't you just pay the tickets when you get them?"

"Shee-it! You don't give The Man your money till you *has* to!" Omar Wellington looked at Francis as though he were a cretin. "Y'unnerstan?"

After booking the pimp Calvin repeated that he wasn't hungry. Nothing Francis said seemed to help Calvin out of his depression this night and Francis was constrained to try his last resort.

"Calvin, is the periscope still in the trunk?" he asked innocently.

"Now jist a minute, Francis. Jist one fuckin minute!"

"Pull over, Calvin. Lemme just see it."

"Gud-damn you, Francis, you promised."

"Wolfgang's working alone tonight in a report car. He's all alone!" Francis said, trying his inscrutable smile on Calvin Potts.

Wolfgang Werner, a twenty-four year old formidable specimen in tailored blue, had been in America from Stuttgart ten years before joining the police department. Francis and Wolfgang had shared a radio car the month before Calvin Potts and Francis formed their partnership. Francis didn't mind working with Wolfgang. At first he found Wolfgang hilarious. "If you dundt sign zat traffic ticket we must luck you in ze slummer!" He only began to hate Wolfgang when the huge German went to Lieutenant Finque and asked to be assigned to another partner because of a personality conflict.

Francis thought it reprehensible of the German. It was customary on the Los Angeles force for police supervisors to leave unquestioned the ambiguous phrase "personality conflict" which masked a plethora of problems. Often it simply meant that two cops hated each other's guts and would be venting their feelings on the citizens if left together for a protracted period in the incredibly gritty intimate world of the radio car. Francis was furious because too many "personality conflicts" would result in a policeman's receiving a reputation of "not being able to get along."

The department was still controlled by men who wanted subordinates who could "get along" and who firmly believed that "a good follower makes a good leader."

Francis Tanaguchi never believed in following since there was no one to follow when you were making life and death decisions on the street at night. So Francis said that Wolfgang Werner was a schmuck. He said he knew the real reason that Wolfgang had dumped him. It was because he couldn't abide what Harold Bloomguard named them, which was quickly picked up by the other officers. Harold called them The Axis Partners.

One night, after Francis had stopped being an Axis Partner and had become half of the Gook and the Spook team, they were cruising Crenshaw Boulevard on a quiet Wednesday when Francis spotted Wolfgang talking with a red haired motorist whom he had stopped near Rodeo Road ostensibly to write a ticket for a burned out taillight.

"Vell, I dunt sink ve neet to write ze ticket zis time, miss," Wolfgang lisped, standing tall in the street next to the lime Mustang, staring at the driver's license, memorizing the address, eyes hidden under the brim of his hat which was always pulled too far forward à la Roscoe Rules.

"Thank you, Officer," the girl giggled, measuring the massive shoulders and chest of this young Hercules who dripped with Freudian symbolism. There were the phallic objects: the gun, the badge. Not to mention the oversized sap hanging from the sap pocket. And in Wolfgang's case (he was the only nightwatch officer who *never* got out of his car without it) there was the nightstick. The obtuse girl had not the slightest understanding of the siege these accouterments lay to her libido.

When Wolfgang handed her back the license with a practiced Teutonic grin, Francis knew that Wolfgang would now say, "Vut say ve meedt ufter vork for a little chin and tunick?"

"That phony krauthead," Francis complained as he watched the pantomime from his passenger seat in the radio car.

He ordered Calvin to park near the opposite corner, saying, "I'm gonna sink that sausage eating Aryan son of a bitch," Later that night he bought a plastic periscope at a five-and-dime. Francis knew Wolfgang Werner could not abide an assault on his dignity. The U-boat attacks began.

On the evening of the first attack Wolfgang was working solo taking reports. Francis turned his police hat around backward, scooted down in his seat with Calvin Potts driving and brought his new toy slowly up over the window ledge.

"Do you have a mirror in your periscope?" Calvin asked.

"No."

"Then you can't see a fuckin thing?"

"No, you gotta tell me when I'm sighted in on Wolfgang."

"Is that all you're gonna do, sight in on Wolfgang?"

"No, that ain't all. We're gonna sink that *pendejo,*" Francis replied, lapsing into Spanish. "Bring her alongside."

Wolfgang was stopped on Wilshire Boulevard between Western and Muirfield. This time his quarry was out of the Mercedes. She was brunette, leggy, bejeweled and pissed off because she rightly suspected that Wolfgang didn't really give a shit about the burned out light over her license plate. It was ten o'clock. A starless night. The traffic was light on Wilshire and Francis was afraid Wolfgang would see them cruising in.

"Turn out your lights," Francis commanded.

Calvin shrugged and did so, bringing the black and white into the curb behind Wolfgang's radio car when Francis suddenly said, "Not behind them, turkey! Pull up *next* to them. And slow."

Then Francis Tanaguchi took a breath and said, "Ssssswwwwwoooooooooooosh," causing Wolfgang to turn and stare at them quizzically.

"A miss!" Francis said suddenly. "Dive! Dive! Dive!"

"What?"

"Get the fuck outta here!" Francis yelled and Calvin pulled away, leaving Wolfgang and the baffled brunette staring after them in wonder.

It took them more than an hour to find Wolfgang Werner the next night they attacked. They finally located him by listening for his calls given by a new radio voice which Calvin suspiciously thought almost as sexy as the Dragon Lady's.

"Seven-X-L-Five, Seven-X-L-Five, see the woman, prowler complaint, Crescent Heights and Colgate."

"He'll drop everything to roll on that one," said Francis. "I know how his mind works. He'll figure it's a peeping tom complaint and that she might be good enough to deserve the peeping. All ahead full!"

Francis turned his hat around backward and brought the periscope out from under the seat as they glided toward Wolfgang's car.

The big German was getting out of the car, flashlight in one hand and report notebook in the other. He didn't see them as they cruised closer, their engine cut by Calvin Potts.

Then Francis yelled, "Achtung! Fire one! Fire two!"

Wolfgang whirled, the flashlight clattered and broke on the asphalt and the German had his clamshell holster open and was halfway into a draw when Francis Tanaguchi said, "Ssssswwwwwoooooosh."

"Francis, did we get him?" Calvin asked as he switched on the engine and lights and dropped a yard and a half of smoking LAPD rubber on the asphalt

"Banzai! Banzai!" Francis giggled mysteriously.

They didn't see Wolfgang until end-of-watch in the locker room when he came to Francis' locker before changing and said with a tight grin "Okay, Francis, you sunk me vunce. Vut say ve meg a truce?"

Francis only smiled inscrutably and left with Calvin to choir practice to brag to Harold Bloomguard that he was driving Wolfgang crackers. He called his U-boat the S.S. *Chorizo* after the spicy Mexican sausage.

The very last time Francis' boat went to sea was the night he had blood on his hands, when Wolfgang Werner was standing in front of Wilshire Police Station talking to his newest girlfriend: a big rosy lusty girl named Olga who waited tables at a La Brea drive-in which fed the car in the area for free.

"Let it go, baby," Calvin said as they pulled out of the station parking lot onto Venice Boulevard and Francis Tanaguchi leered at Olga and turned his cap around.

"Go back," Francis said grimly and pulled the periscope from under the seat.

"That dude is gonna kick your little ass and I ain't woofin."

"Go back, Calvin."

"That cat is gonna tear your head off and piss in the hole, Francis."

"You scared of him?"

"You gud-damn right."

"If you take me on one more attack I promise I'll throw away my periscope."

"Okay, but why now?"

"I'm in love with Olga. She's so *big*! Go back and I swear I'll never fire another torpedo."

"You swear?"

"Yes."

"You swear to Buddha?"

"Knock off that Jap stuff, goddamnit. That fuckin Lieutenant Finque made me go to another Nip luncheon today. How'd you like a shirt full of vomity squid, asshole?"

"Okay, I'm goin back. But that storm trooper is gonna burn you down."

"Let's go!" Francis said as Calvin wheeled the radio car around and headed back toward Venice Boulevard.

Wolfgang was turned away from them as they drove in from the west, this time in a fast glide and with lights on because of the westbound traffic.

"This is the last fuckin time I go to sea, Francis," Calvin warned.

"Okay, okay, now you're making me nervous," said the commander, as he sighted in, peeking up over the window ledge because the eyehole of the periscope revealed nothing but a three inch color photograph of a hairy vagina which Calvin had cut from a *Playboy* magazine and glued inside the plastic tube to amuse Francis.

"Steer an evasive course afterward," Francis ordered as Wolfgang turned from Olga who was dressed in the sheerest tightest hiphugging bellbottoms Francis

Tanaguchi had ever seen. She was pantyless and her crotch was dark beneath the sheer yellow bells.

Francis leaned out the window, periscope extended, and aimed it not at Wolfgang but at Olga's bulging fluff.

"Sssswwwwwoooosh," cried Francis Tanaguchi and Calvin Potts sped away, fearfully stealing a glance at the grim face of Wolfgang Werner.

That night in the locker room Wolfgang grabbed Francis by the throat without warning and said, "If you efen tink uf putting your lousy torpedo vere you pudt it tonight, I vill tvist you neg off. You vood be smart to decommission your U-boat, Francis."

Wolfgang made Francis promise by squeezing and encouraging him to bob his head. Then he left Francis gasping in front of the locker while Calvin Potts pretended to need another trip to the urinal, away from Wolfgang Werner.

When Calvin returned he said, "I think we better put the S.S. *Chorizo* in dry dock for good, Francis."

That last dangerous attack on the German came after the call which would awaken Francis sweating in the night with red in the crevices of his knuckles and under his nails.

"Seven-A-Seventy-seven, see the woman, unknown trouble, Pico and Ogden."

"Seven-A-Seventy-seven, roger," Francis muttered and threw the hand mike on the seat. "Damn it, I'm drooling for a guacamole taco!"

"This must be it," Calvin said five minutes later and Francis looked up as Calvin hit the high beam, lighting a man and woman who stood in front of a seedy apartment house which was still located in a predominantly white neighborhood, but which was experiencing a high vacancy factor because blacks were getting more numerous.

"Hope this is a quickie," Francis said as they gathered up their flashlights, hats and notebook. The smog hung over the streets and the building like airbrushed, painted smoke.

"I'm the one that called," said a woman in a quilted bathrobe, her orange hair frizzing beneath a hairnet.

A balding man with a sloppy grin sat on the steps beside her. There were six empty beer cans between them.

"What's the problem?" Francis asked, slightly uneasy over an "unknown trouble" call, which can mean anything but sometimes means only that the communications officer who took the call could not think of a convenient category in which to classify it.

"I'm the manager," said the woman, bunching the robe at the bosom as though she were not twenty years past the age when most policemen would look. "I got a tenant up there in number twelve. Name's Mrs. Stafford. She got three little kids and I shouldn't oughtta have rented to her cause we don't want no more than one kid per apartment."

"So what happened?" Calvin asked impatiently, wondering if Francis would object too strongly if he were to stop by McGoon's Saloon and have a little taste. Just maybe one little Johnnie Walker on the rocks . . .

"Well, see don't you think it's unusual? I hear this noise about two hours ago just when it was getting dark. Then I don't hear nothing. They go to bed awful early, her and her kids. I feel so sorry for them I loaned them an old TV. She just got here from Arkansas and ain't eligible for welfare or nothing yet so she's trying to find work as a waitress. But it's hard."

"The noise," Calvin said. "The noise."

"Yeah, so then I thought I heard screaming. Not too loud, but a scream. But kids always holler. And then, then about twenty minutes ago I see a man go out and then nothing. There ain't no lights on in there. Just nothing. I went up and knocked but nothing."

"So?"

"They're home. They didn't go out. I woulda saw them if they went out."

"So they're asleep."

"The TV's on."

"They just forgot . . ."

"Look sir," the woman said, turning to Francis, "it's an old TV but it works good. I can hear the station. It's the same channel as I'm watching. And I peek in through the drapes and I can see the screen and it's all white and sparkly. You can't hardly make out the picture."

"What's that mean?"

"I don't know, sir." The woman turned to Calvin again. "She don't have many friends. Poor little woman stays with her kids all day and all night. Just trying to find work is only time she leaves them and then I keep an eye on them."

"Why don't you use your passkey and go on in?"

"That's the problem, I ain't got one. Last tenant didn't turn his in and I gave her my passkey. Can you just go in and see if everything's all right?"

"Don't suppose you want us to break the door down?" Calvin muttered as the two policemen started up the steps.

"Can't you just slip the lock like all the cops in the movies?"

"No, and I can't open a safe by listenin to the tumblers either," Calvin said as Francis reached the landing first and knocked loudly on the door of number twelve.

"I don't want you to break the door." The landlady stood at the foot of the stairs helplessly.

Francis began fiddling with the sliding window beside the front door and said, "Hold this," to Calvin, giving his tall partner the notebook. Then he pushed hard on the window with the tips of the fingers of one hand while he pried at the frame with a coin from his pocket. There was a meallic snap and the window slid to the left.

"Oughtta be a burglar, Francis," Calvin observed.

"Too respectable. I'd rather be a cop." Francis pushed back the faded draperies and lifted himself up and into the dark room, lit only from the snow filled screen of the TV set whose volume was barely audible.

"Calvin!" Francis suddenly whispered.

"What is it?" His partner instinctively grabbed his gun and stepped to the side of the window.

"Calvin!" Francis repeated, weakly this time, and Calvin Potts dropped the notebook, convinced that his partner was in danger. Calvin crouched, looked for cover, considered the distance to the steps.

"Calvin!" Francis said again, and Calvin Potts drew his gun while the landlady below shrieked and ran to her apartment to escape a gun battle.

The door opened slowly and Calvin flattened himself against the wall, adrenalin jetting. Francis stepped woodenly across the theshold.

"Calvin!" he said as softly as a child.

"What is it? What the fuck *is* it?" Calvin demanded, his gun pointed directly at Francis who did not seem to notice.

"There's some people murdered in there!"

"Gud-damn it, Francis!" Calvin pushed his partner aside and entered the apartment, gun still drawn, flashlight sweeping the room until he found the light switch.

The first one Calvin saw was the woman. She was unbelievably thin and pale with huge eye sockets. She lay on the couch on her back, the nightgown gathered around her hips. Her legs were spread, knees up, head thrown back in agony. The classic pose of a victim raped and murdered.

The TV antenna wire was knotted around her neck and her eyes and mouth were open. The dead eyes, still clear and unclouded, stared at the top of the doorway which led to the two bedrooms. Hanging from the doorway was a blonde baby doll. The doll wore a red party dress trimmed in white. The dress had been washed many times and the painted face of the doll was chipped and worn. The doll was hanging by the neck, dangling from the doorjamb by a bathrobe sash which was taped to the jamb with adhesive tape. The tape roll was on the floor in the doorway to the bathroom.

As Calvin made a mental note to put the tape roll aside for prints, Francis startled him by walking up behind him and saying, "The kitchen!"

Calvin took two steps to his left into a tiny kitchen with a small yellow refrigerator and apartment stove. On the floor by the sink lay a sandy haired boy of seven. The telephone cord was spiraled around his neck and his face rested on a pillow as though the killer wanted him comfortable. The green velvet pillow was wet from the fluids which ran from the child's mouth while he was strangling. His pajama top was pulled up and there were two cigarette burns on his back and another on his neck. His eyes were closed, more tightly than Calvin had ever before seen in death. As though he had died crying hopelessly for his mother, his face pressed into the velvet pillow.

"The bathroom!" Francis said and Calvin nodded mechanically and followed his partner aeross the little room, pausing to look at the baby doll hanging in the doorway. It turned gently as Francis' hat touched the fat rubber foot when he passed.

Francis looked in the bathroom to verify what he had already seen before he opened the door for his partner. Then he looked at the pink baby doll and back to Calvin.

Calvin Potts knew for certain what he would find in the bathroom and his heart was banging in his ears when Francis switched on the light and stepped aside to let his partner see the child dangling from the bar over the shower stall.

She was the youngest, four, clad in animal cracker pajamas. She was hanging by two pair of panty hose knotted together. The coroner was to say later it probably took her longest to die. Calvin did not want to see if she had been burned. He did not want to touch her. Her eyes were open like her mother's. Her mouth was closed because the head hung forward on her chest. She turned slowly when Francis touched her foot.

"What the fuck you doin?"

"Huh?" Francis said dumbly.

"Keep your hands off them!"

"Huh?" Francis said, not knowing he had reached out and consolingly patted the tiny feet which were strapped together at the ankles with a brown belt and were pointed toes downward like a ballerina's.

"Let's go outside and get the dicks down here right now!"

Calvin wiped his dripping forehead with the back of his hand. "Wait a minute! How many kids she say there was?"

"I'm not sure."

"Three, wasn't it?"

"Yeah, it was three," Francis said, sounding very sick.

"The bedrooms!" Calvin switched on the light in the main bedroom which contained a double bed where the woman slept with the youngest child. He was breathing heavily as he looked in the closet and behind a box of old toys.

"Calvin!" Francis said from the other bedroom where there were twin beds and colorful plastic gimcracks on an old dresser and a painted Formica shelf covered with pictures of daisies, apparently to make the dreary bedroom look as though a child slept there.

Francis was on his knees between the beds, his hat and flashlight on the floor beside him, the beam shining under the bed lighting the body of the five year old boy.

Calvin dropped to his knees, removed his hat and using Francis' flashlight, looked under. The bundle was drenched in blood, the pajamas shredded around the tiny huddled body unrecognizable as a child except for some short blond hair not blood soaked.

"Musta crawled under there to get away from him," Calvin said hoarsely. "The killer musta crawled after him and cut the kid up there under the bed. Just laid there under that bed slashin and slashin. Musta been that way. It's clean all around the outside a the bed. The little thing hidin under the bed and the killer crawlin under after him with the knife. There ain't no God, Francis! I swear there *ain't*!"

Then Francis was on his feet, throwing the bed aside and pulling at the little form, dragging it through the viscous red puddle until Calvin stopped him.

"Don't touch that body!"

"I think I saw him move, Calvin! I think maybe he's still alive!"

"Francis!" Calvin shouted, jerking his partner up as the little body thudded softly to the floor, splashing heavy drops onto the dirty wallpaper. "His insides are all over the fuckin floor! Look!" And he pointed at the ominous red blossoms. "Look at the blood! Look at the face! That child's dead, Francis."

Francis Tanaguchi looked at his partner for a moment, looked at his own bloody hands, then said, "Oh. I can't see too good without my glasses. I guess I should wear my glasses."

"Let's go call the dicks," Calvin said, gently leading his partner out of the apartment which in twenty minutes was swarming with detectives, fingerprint specialists, photographers, deputy coroners and high ranking police admimistrators who had nothing to do with the investigation but who were always the ones who acted as spokesmen on the television news.

Deputy Chief Lynch was there, his hairpiece a little askew because he had just been in a motel with Theda Gunther.

Commander Moss was there, waving and grinning until he finally persuaded a newsman to take his picture. He pretended that he was examining a lift of a latent fingerprint found on the side of the television set. He held the lift upside down as he scrutinized it. Then he waved with both arms at the newsmen as he was leaving, his blond wavy hair gleaming under the lights. One journalist said he acted like a Rose Queen on a flower float.

There were few clues left by the killer. The latent print was found to have belonged to the victim, Mrs. Mary Stafford. An old boyfriend of hers was ultimately arrested for the murders but the evidence was not sufficient for a complaint. Commander Moss' picture never appeared in the newspapers.

It was later that night, with a child's blood still lodged in the creases of his fingers, that Francis Tanaguchi raised a plastic periscope and began that last obsessive U-boat attack on Wolfgang Werner and big Olga. Then he called for a choir practice and drank and worried about the nightmares sure to come.

8

7-A-1: Spermwhale Whalen and Baxter Slate

At first, Spermwhale Whalen was uncommonly quiet at rollcall on a smoggy June afternoon, just two months before the choir practice killing. Spermwhale was not over the death of a son who claimed to despise him as much as he loved the son. Actually, they hardly knew each other.

Baxter Slate, his partner, was never a boisterous young man so it was not unusual that he said very little while half the nightwatch hooted and jeered at Roscoe Rules and Lieutenant Finque.

"Damn it, Lieutenant, I resent the investigators showing my picture all the time to rape victims," Roscoe Rules complained. "I didn't know they were doing it till last month."

"Apparently they just noticed that your picture mixes well with white sex suspects," Lieutenant Finque replied, getting a migraine as he always did at rollcall these days.

"Yeah, well I shoulda got suspicious when that pussy kiddy cop caught me in civvies and asked to let her snap a Polaroid a me to test out the new camera."

"No harm, Roscoe," Sergeant Yanov grinned.

"No? That cunt's been using my picture in a mug shot showup every fucking time a paddy rapes somebody around here!"

"She can't help it you look like such a deviate," Spermwhale said, as his partner Baxter Slate grinned. "I think she'll stop, Roscoe, by the time two or three victims pick *you* out of the lineup."

"They'd probably have the right guy," said Harold Bloomguard.

"Naw, he can't even get a blue veiner, let alone a diamond cutter," said Calvin Potts. "We ever get a limp dick bandit around here he'll be a prime suspect."

"Very funny, Potts, very fucking funny," Roscoe Rules said murderously as he unconsciously pulled on his limp dick.

"Well, I'll see what I can do, Rules," the lieutenant said. "Now onto the next subject of our supervisors' meeting. That is : excessive force complaints. The captain says he had an awful lot of paper work to do because an officer on the morning watch broke a suspect's arm with a wristlock. Just be careful in the future. Remember, a wristlock is very hard to put on if a man resists, so don't get carried away."

"Question, Lieutenant," Baxter Slate said.

"Yes?"

"If a man *didn't* resist, why would you ever put it on in the first place?"

Sergeant Yanov saved his superior officer by taking control of the rollcall and saying, "How about my reading the crimes. Here's a sex story. Might perk up your evening."

And as Sergeant Yanov rescued his lieutenant from further embarrassing faux pas, Lieutenant Finque smoldered. Yanov related so easily with men, was so obviously well liked, that Finque knew he had to be a rotten supervisor. This belief was bolstered in that Yanov had been working for him three months and had never yet been capable of catching a policeman with his hat off or smoking in public view. Lieutenant Finque made a note to mention to Captain Drobeck that Yanov, at thirty-four just a few months younger than Lieutenant Finque, was probably too young and inexperienced to be an effective field sergeant and should be encouraged to go into the detective bureau.

Captain Drobeck would be the first to agree with such a proposal because he had hated Yanov ever since the sergeant openly disagreed with the captain at a meeting of all the Wilshire Division supervisors. Yanov refuted an "administrative suggestion" from the captain and argued that he would willingly fool the chief of police and lie to the mayor, and to his own wife if he still had one, but never to his men. Because he never asked his chief, mayor or wife to fight for him or save his ass.

Captain Drobeck wrote on Sergeant Yanov's rating report: "Is yet too young and immature to grasp the fundamentals of supervision."

To get even with the troops Lieutenant Finque interrupted Sergeant Yanov's reading of the noteworthy crimes. Lieutenant Finque decided to inform them of what he had just heard prior to rollcall: that a Superior Court jury had acquitted a man charged with the murder of a Los Angeles police officer.

"Acquitted?" thundered Spermwhale Whalen when the lieutenant announced it, but even Spermwhale's bellow was lost in the deafening clamor which went up in that room.

The accused was thought to be a narcotic dealer. He went to a hotel with an undercover officer who posed as a buyer, and a third man, a police informant. The officer was prepared to make a large buy but as it turned out the accused had no drugs. He *did* have a small caliber pistol with which he shot and killed the officer who returned fire ineffectively before his death. The accused stole the suitcase full of money and ran out the door but was arrested immediately by other officers hiding outside.

The police called the shooting a straight ripoff operation in which the plan was to steal the money. The informant testified that the defendant grabbed the suitcase and fired without warning. The defendant's testimony was that the slain officer unaccountably drew his gun and the defendant, thinking *he* was to be ripped off, fired first to protect himself. The investigating officers scoffed. They said it was a "dead bang" case. A cinch. The evidence was overwhelming. There was an eyewitness. The defendant's story was desperate and ludicrous. He was acquitted.

The judge, upon hearing the verdict, proclaimed that he was shocked. But he was not nearly as shocked as the twenty-eight men in Lieutenant Finque's rollcall who would never become accustomed to shocking jury verdicts. It took five minutes to quiet them down and get several questions answered. But they weren't questions. They were statements of indignation and disbelief. Outcries. Then threats. Then a violent obscene danming of the jury system.

Baxter Slate, perhaps the most articulate choirboy, said grimly that this bulwark of democracy was actually a crap game in which twelve telephone operators, mailmen, public utilities employees, pensioners and middle aged housewives, with no knowledge of the law and less of the sociopath, make irrevocable decisions based upon their exposure to movies like *Twelve Angry Men* and television shows like *Perry Mason*.

Lieutenant Finque let them rail until he was sure their stomachs were as sour as his always was because of them. He beamed contentedly. He wasn't even afraid of them at the moment.

Their outrage was so complete that they quickly talked themselves out. One moment shrill trembling voices. Questions unanswered and unanswerable. Then silence. Defeat. Depression. And smoldering fury.

Lieutenant Finque sent them out to do police work with one further blandishment: "You men take with you the captain's last warning from the supervisors' meeting. Any wetfoot hotdogs who like to put a shoe in the carburetor better stand by. The next preventable traffic accident is going to mean the commander comes down on the captain, who's going to come down hard on me and I'm going to have to come down hard on you!"

Finally Spermwhale Whalen spoke. He said, "I know shit rolls downhill. But why am I *always* livin in the valley?"

Herbert "Spermwhale" Whalen despised the new station Wilshire Division had moved to in early 1974. Daily he would drive by the dilapidated, inadequate old building on Pico Boulevard which, by God, *looked* like a police station. He longed for the old days.

Spermwhale, at 260 pounds with the pig eyes of a whale, was aptly named. He was of Irish Catholic stock, divorced three times, considering himself thus excommunicated. "It's just too bad I ain't rich enough to've got a fancy annulment approved by the Pope like all these rich cunts and cocksuckers you read about. Then I coulda stayed in the church."

It was a refrain often heard at MacArthur Park choir practice when Spermwhale was almost in the tank, a fifth of bourbon or Scotch in the huge red hand. "Now I gotta go to hell cause I'm excommunicated!"

And if Father Willie Wright was drunk enough and suffering from his frequent attacks of overwhelming guilt for having just dismounted Ora Lee Tingle or Carolina Moon, claiming his plump little wife would only ball him dispassionately twice a month, he would say softly, "I'll be with you, Spermwhale. I'm afraid I'll be with you!"

Baxter Slate was a good partner for Spermwhale Whalen because he didn't talk too much and give Spermwhale a headache. Also he had almost five years on the job, having been sworn in on his twenty-second birthday. Spermwhale, a nineteen year veteran, considered anyone with less time a fuzz nutted rookie and couldn't stand to work with rookie partners.

Also Baxter didn't complain when Spermwhale would occasionally pick up a streetwalking prostitute whom Spermwhale knew from his old days on the vice squad, saying, "It's time for a little skull." Were he to be caught it would mean their jobs, and Spermwhale Whalen was just months away from a pension. It was a calculated risk and Spermwhale sweated it out each time because the LAPD brass definitely did not approve of uniformed officers in black and whites getting a little skull.

It was surprising that Spermwhale would take such a risk. He often said that a sergeant who caught him doing something for which he could be fired would never get back to the station alive, because he, Spermwhale Whalen, would kill any cocksucker who tried to keep him from making his twenty years and getting that irretrievable pension. Anyone Spermwhale didn't like was either a "cunt," a "gelding," a "eunuch," or a "cocksucker," and that included almost all civilians, certainly all police brass and station supervisors (except Sergeant Nick Yanov) and all employees of the Civil Service Department who had designed nitpicking promotional exams which had frustrated him all these years and kept him from advancing past the basic policeman rank.

It was especially galling in that Spermwhale Whalen was a major in the Air Force Reserve and often ran into LAPD lieutenants and captains, also military reservists, who, during summer military exercises, had to salute him.

Spermwhale was proof positive that polish was not necessary to achieve staff rank in the United States Air Force Reserve, just as Commander Moss was proof positive that common sense was not needed to achieve staff rank in the Los Angeles Police Department.

But Spermwhale Whalen was just possibly one of the coolest most competent transport pilots in the 452nd Wing. He had flown in World War II and later in Korea until he left the Air Force and joined the police department. He was the only Los Angeles police officer in history to engage in one of his country's wars while still an active member of the department. His remarkable feat was accomplished by flying C-124 Globemasters on three and four day missions from March Air Force Base to Danang in 1966 and 1967, almost being shot down twice by Communist surface to air missiles. Spermwhale was, for this reason, a minor legend in the department. In those years it had been fun for the Wilshire policemen to play straight man for Spermwhale among police officers from other stations, saying things like:

"Oh, Marvin, where'd you go on your days off?"

"Disneyland with my sister's kids, how about you?"

"Fishing with Simon and his girlfriend up to Big Bear Lake, and how about *you*, Spermwhale?"

"Danang. Wasn't much happenin. Few rocket attacks is all."

Spermwhale seldom took two days off a week in those years. Like many policemen, he preferred to work nine and ten days straight to string his days off together. But his were for combat missions for which he was paid a bonus by the government of the United States to give to his three wives, each of whom had borne him a child before the divorce. When Spermwhale was off flying and the nightwatch sat bored in the assembly room, someone would always say when a low-flying aircraft roared over making an approach to LA International:

"Well, sounds like Spermwhale's late for rollcall again."

Spermwhale bore a Z-shaped scar which began in the fur of one black tufted eyebrow, crossed the flattened bridge of his nose, swooped under his right eye and came back onto the nose showing white in the swatch of red veins. Once at choir practice Carolina Moon asked him how he had gotten that scar.

"Landin in the rain with half my tail shot away."

"Where, Spermy? Where'd it happen?"

An extraordinary thing happened: Spermwhale could not remember. Not for almost a full minute. The alcohol had temporarily debilitated his brain but it was more than that. He had flown so many missions for his government in which he had been asked to kill or cause the deaths of Oriental people that they had started to run together: Japanese, Korean, Vietnamese. He truly couldn't answer. Not immediately.

"Oh yeah," he said finally. "Korea. Jesus Christ! Korea. Jesus Christ! I couldn't remember which war!"

After the Vietnam War ended, Spermwhale still flew but of course lost a good deal of his military pay and had a difficult time paying off the three wives and keeping enough to drink and take out a broad when he got lucky. It was for economic reasons more than anything else that he became a faithful choirboy and put up with the younger policemen who gave him such a headache. At choir practice there was always free booze supplied by Roscoe Rules and Spencer Van Moot. And there was sometimes Carolina Moon whom Spermwhale fell in love with at every single choir practice. The fat girl and the fat policeman would go off hand in hand for a stagger around the duck pond, sucking at a bottle of Scotch and cooing like doves. The other choirboys called them the campus couple.

Both Spermwhale Whalen and Baxter Slate were in a foul mood after rollcall. What had them generally pissed off was that they were both just now feeling the loss of pay from a four days' suspension.

The suspension had resulted from Lieutenant Elliott "Hardass" Grimsley's deciding to celebrate his fortieth birthday by going out in the field for the evening and showing the station commander, Captain Drobeck, that he could be as big a prick as Captain Drobeck any old day, and that even though he had only been a lieutenant eight months, his nine years as a field sergeant had given him plenty of experience at being a prick.

Captain Drobeck on the other hand had recently tried to demonstrate he was not a prick but a prince, during a formal inspection conducted by Deputy Chief Lynch himself. Every patrol officer in Wilshire Station wore lintless blue and polished black leather for that inspection. They were formed into three sweating platoons.

Captain Drobeck, with his plumy white mane freshly done, was resplendent in his blues, wearing all the campaign ribbons he earned in Patton's Third Army. The Wilshire policemen knew that he had only been a clerk typist in that army and not a tank commander as he hinted and they often whispered that Captain Drobeck never retreated but backspaced lots of times.

Deputy Chief Lynch always showed up for ceremonies after a twenty minute wait, just as he answered the phone after a three minute wait. Captain Drobeck fussed nervously with his trouser creases and hoped his shoes were spit shined well enough by his adjutant, Sergeant Sneed, who learned such things while a trombone player in the U.S. Army band. The captain waved to Ardella Grimsley, the wife of Lieutenant Elliott "Hardass" Grimsley. She stood on the sidewalk by the parking lot where a dozen other spectators waited with cameras.

During one of the anxious moments, Lieutenant Grimsley nodded and winked at his wife of twenty years who wore a hat, gloves, and incredibly enough, a corsage for the occasion. Ardella Grimsley beamed and blew her husband a sweeping kiss which was answered by a horrendous fart in the rear ranks and a voice saying, "And here's a kiss for *you!*"

"WHO DID THAT?" Lieutenant Grimsley screamed, almost literally scaring the crap out of the already nervous Captain Drobeck.

"What the hell's going on, Grimsley?" demanded the captain.

"Somebody farted!"

"Is that so terrible?"

"At my wife!"

"I don't understand you, Grimsley."

Just then, Sergeant Sneed, called Suckass Sneed by the men, came running forward from his place at the rear of the first platoon.

"I think it was a colored voice, sir," he whispered breathlessly to the captain. "I mean a black voice."

"If I may," said Officer Baxter Slate, who stood in the front rank, "a voice may have timbre, resonance, even pitch but it is singularly without color." He said it with a wide easy grin at Captain Drobeck which Lieutenant Grimsley knew was phony but which was so well done it was impossible to accuse him of insubordination.

Captain Drobeck, sure of the affection of his men, smiled benevolently and said, "Please, gentlemen, let's calm ourselves. This is perfectly silly."

"It's *not* silly, Captain. Somebody insulted *my* wife," Lieutenant Grimsley answered.

"Please, Lieutenant, please!" Captain Drobeck whispered. "The deputy chief is going to be here any minute and you're acting like a child. My god, I can't believe this."

"It was personal, sir. It was vicious!"

"All right, all right, will you settle for an apology? It was undoubtedly some young policeman's idea of a joke. Christ, most of these men here are closer to twenty than thirty. They're kids! I'll have the boy apologize and we can forget it." Captain Drobeck turned to the platoon of men and showed his toothy paternal grin and said, "Okay, fellas. Let's fess up. Who farted?"

And he laughed uproariously with the men as he waited for the culprit to reply so he could show the men how silly Hardass Grimsley was and how magnanimously he could forgive the insult to Ardella Grimsley who was one of those garrulous bitches Captain Drobeck couldn't stand in the first place.

But a funny thing happened: nobody fessed up.

"Come on now, boys," Captain Drobeck laughed, but the laughter was a little strained. "Just cop out whoever you are. Tell Lieutenant Grimsley it was an accident and it's all forgotten."

And the laughter continued but was not joined in this time by Captain Drobeck who smiled patiently and waited for the guilty party to show Lieutenant Grimsley how he, Captain Drobeck, could relate with his men.

Still, nobody fessed up.

"I just can't understand this," Captain Drobeck said. "I've given you every opportunity to show some maturity here and I think Lieutenant Grimsley deserves it. Now, by God, I'd like the young man to just apologize to the lieutenant and it'll all be forgotten. But we can't wait all day and I expect it to be done immediately."

But nobody copped out.

Captain Drobeck was suddenly not laughing nor was he smiling. He was fidgeting with the crease in his uniform pants and nodding angrily. "All right, that's the way it's going to be, huh? By god, you wanna act like kids I can treat you like kids. You want the field sergeant to start coming down on you, huh? Well that can be arranged, I assure you. Now this is your last chance. If the man that farted isn't man enough to admit it I want the man next to him to do it."

And the man next to him obediently did it. His fart was louder than the first.

"ATTEN-HUT!" screamed Captain Drobeck and the platoon snapped to attention. The captain began pacing the rear ranks like a lion, muttering viciously as he looked each man in the eye and tried to apply some detective techniques he had learned from reading books on investigation when he studied for the captain's exam. He looked for nervous twitches, telltale blinking. The trouble was he was so nervous waiting for Deputy Chief Lynch and now so angry himself that his own eyes were winking like semaphores.

After he paced the entire platoon he strode angrily to the front and whispered to Suckass Sneed, "You find out who did it, hear me?"

"Yes sir. The first or the second fart?"

"I *want* that man! The *first* one!"

"It was a colored voice, I mean a black voice, I'm sure of it," said Sneed. "That narrows it down to six."

Just then Deputy Chief Lynch's car arrived. The incident was set aside temporarily. The inspection was conducted and it was a great success. Captain Drobeck thanked the chief for his gracious compliments and assured him the credit was due to the loyalty of the men.

Thirty minutes after the inspection, Captain Drobeck was in a cubicle in the restroom relieving his rumbling bowels from the tension of the day. He had the morning paper there and was grunting happily and smoking his pipe. Suddenly the door to the restroom burst open and someone released a terrible, vengeful fart. Before the footsteps ran back out a voice said, "Take that, you jive turkey!"

Captain Drobeck never solved the mystery. But one thing was certain: it was a colored voice.

On one of his weekly evenings out on the streets, Lieutenant Grimsley caught eight officers with their hats off, one smoking in public and three others drinking coffee which proved to have been gratuitously received. Just before calling it a night, he added to his score by bagging Spermwhale Whalen and Baxter Slate staked out on a stop sign at 11:00 P.M. on a residential street where a car didn't pass more often than once every half hour. Both officers were slumped in their seats, heads resting against the windows. But like any veteran policemen, they could rely on years of experience to trigger signals in deep slumber when 7-A-1 was mentioned among the ceaseless garbled almost unintelligible radio messages.

Legally speaking, Lieutenant Hardass Grimsley was a strict constructionist. He could not prove his suspicions that Spermwhale and Baxter were asleep, so their suspension papers said:

> Officers failed to remain alert in that officers assumed a position of repose in a parked police vehicle with eyelids pressed together, breathing heavily and regularly. Four days.

In addition, through diligent police work, Lieutenant Grimsley found a bag of avocados in the trunk of the black and white, which he traced to Francis Tanaguchi, who, it turned out, accepted them gratuitously from a Japanese produce market wherein the owner was proud of Francis' being a Japanese policeman, not knowing that Francis was Mexican at heart and would use the avocados in making guacamole which he would ladle into his tacos. Spermwhale and Baxter were given an additional punishment of a divisional admonishment which read:

> I hereby admonish you in that you accepted some avocados from another officer who received them from a private party who was not, in fact, morally correct in giving the avocados without recompense. Moreover, the other officer was guilty of moral turpitude for accepting the free avocados. The acceptance of gratuities is against Department regulations and you were aware of this regulation at the time you imprudently accepted the avocados from the officer who was also aware when he imprudently accepted the avocados from the man who should have been more prudent.

Francis Tanaguchi was not given an admonishment or any other penalty because the community relations officer, Lieutenant Gay, was trying to make public relations inroads with the Oriental community by putting Officer Tanaguchi up as a model policeman. He persuaded Captain Drobeck not to let Lieutenant Grimsley reprimand Francis officially. Lieutenant Grimsley acceded to the decision since it came from the station captain but he was frustrated because there wasn't something he could get on the old Japanese who gave Francis the avocados. He asked the vice squad to keep an eye on the market in case the old man should sell beer to minors. And he certainly put Lieutenant Gay and Francis on his list.

But if Lieutenant Gay, Francis Tanaguchi and the old Japanese were on Lieutenant Grimsley's list, Lieutenant Grimsley was certainly on Spermwhale Whalen's list.

"His dance card's all filled up," Spermwhale vowed at choir practice when the whole night had been spent on plotting revenge.

"I get the first waltz," said Francis Tanaguchi, who sat in the dark on a blanket under a tree.

The choirboys began various subtle attacks on Lieutenant Grimsley which ultimately ended up in his transfer from Wilshire Station because according to the station captain he was getting too chummy with certain officers.

The officers he was apparently getting so chummy with were two of the MacArthur Park choirboys, namely Spermwhale Whalen and Baxter Slate, who when they were finished with him could actually walk into Lieutenant Grimsley's office and muss up his lint covered, thinning hair and say things like, "How about a day off tomorrow, Hardass?" When no one else under the rank of lieutenant ever dared to address him even by his first name, Elliott.

This remarkable familiarity was accomplished by some groundwork supplied by Francis Tanaguchi which included shimming the door of the lieutenant's private car and putting three MacArthur ducks in the back seat.

It was entertaining for the choirboys to stake out the police parking lot after end-of-watch and see Lieutenant Grimsley trudge through the dark, sleepy after a hard night of paper work, and get into his car only to come flying out five seconds later and fall on his ass from the duck excrement on his shoes. It was said that his wife nagged him for months about the green slime she would find stubbornly clinging to the creases of the leather upholstery.

The choirboys also put a particularly fierce black gander in Lieutenant Grimsley's locker at the station which resulted in an investigation by officers of Internal Affairs Division which lasted a week.

Harold Bloomguard, the protector of ducks and all animals, in each case volunteered to take the hissing, squawking birds and get rid of them after the duck shit hit the fan. This should have made him a logical suspect since he mysteriously showed up after each duck attack but Lieutenant Grimsley was too outraged to put two and two together. Besides, it was extremely hard to add two and two when your personal belongings were dripping and foul smelling and an enraged loathsome creature had been banging on your head with its bill.

There were minor attacks wherein the siren on the Lieutenant's police car was fixed so that it wailed and could not be shut off when he started the engine. And his baton, which he kept in the door holder, was removed, carefully sawed in half and replaced.

But the coup which utterly demolished Lieutenant Grimsley and made him a slave to Spermwhale Whalen and precipitated his transfer occurred when Spermwhale bribed a black whore named Fanny Forbes, who was tall and curvy and slender despite her years, to entertain Lieutenant Grimsley. Spermwhale Whalen told her in which restaurant the lieutenant ate on Thursday nights when he could break away from his duties which consisted of signing routine reports and trying to catch policemen loafing in the station when they should be handling their calls.

It took Fanny Forbes, who posed as a tourist from Philadelphia, exactly twenty-five minutes to talk Lieutenant Grimsley into driving her and her bogus suitcase, containing the dirty laundry of Spermwhale Whalen, to a motel on La Brea. He parked his black and white on a side street and insisted on carrying her bag up the back stairs while she registered alone.

Eight minutes after she registered, and while Lieutenant Grimsley, naked except for his black police socks, was hotly kissing the well worn source of her income and whispering endearments like, "Oh baby, you don't seem like a Negro. You look like a Samoan!" Spermwhale Whalen and Baxter Slate crept up the same back stairway and opened the door which the whore had left unlocked.

The two choirboys waited a few minutes more, their ears to the door, and heard Lieutenant Grimsley panting so loudly they were afraid they'd miss the prearranged signal from Fanny Forbes.

"She's really got him sucking wind."

"Yeah!" Spermwhale whispered, his hat in hand, ear pressed to the door, waiting, waiting.

And then they heard it, the signal: "Oh honey!" cried the whore. "You got balls like a elephant and a whang like a ox!"

Just as Spermwhale burst through the door Lieutenant Grimsley was in the throes of blissful agony. When he withdrew and jumped from the bed his face was like a dead man's.

"Okay, who called the pol . . . Lieutenant Grimsley! " cried Spermwhale Whalen.

"What're you men doing here?" cried Lieutenant Grimsley.

"We got a call a woman was being raped in this room! We had no idea!" cried Baxter Slate.

"Musta been some cop hating neighbor saw you come in with the young lady!" cried Spermwhale Whalen.

"How humiliatin!" cried the whore.

"Let's keep our voices down," whispered Lieutenant Grimsley, still motionless and pale.

"Sir, there's some dew on the lily," offered Spermwhale Whalen.

"Oh," said Lieutenant Grimsley, coming to his senses and wiping his whang with his jockey shorts while Fanny Forbes lay nude on the bed and winked at Spermwhale Whalen who was possibly enjoying the sweetest moment of his life.

"Well, we better be goin . . . Hardass," Spermwhale grinned, as Lieutenant Grimsley toppled clumsily over on the bed trying to get his pants on two legs at a time.

"Yes, well, meet me at Pop's coffee shop, will you, fellas? I'd like to buy you a cup of coffee and talk over a few things before we go back in."

"Sure . . . Hardass," Spermwhale grinned, playfully mussing up Lieutenant Grimsley's hair.

Lieutenant Grimsley was actually glad when, three weeks later, Captain Drobeck suggested that he was getting too chummy with certain officers and perhaps should think about a transfer. Lieutenant Grimsley was glad because he was sick and tired of Spermwhale Whalen sitting on his desk and winking and mussing up his hair every time he came in to have a report approved.

Fanny Forbes complained when Spermwhale only slipped her a ten dollar bill, but when he reminded her that it was ten bucks more than she had gotten for similar activity with himself, she shrugged and accepted the stipend.

But on the night they caught the Regretful Rapist, both Spermwhale and Baxter were still mightily pissed off from receiving the four days' suspension for sleeping with the avocados. Lieutenant Grimsley had by then been transferred to Internal Affairs Division where he could catch lots of errant policemen.

The arrest of the Regretful Rapist was possibly the best pinch Baxter Slate had ever made. The rapist had sexually attacked more than thirty women at knifepoint on the streets of Los Angeles and got his name from apologizing profusely after each act and sometimes giving the women cab fare when the attack was finished. The rapist had been fortunate in that not one of his victims had violently resisted and it was unknown how far he would have gone with his eight inch dagger if he had met a real fighter. Nevertheless, he was rightly considered an extremely dangerous man, not only to the female citizens he preyed upon, but to any potential arresting officer.

The night they caught the rapist had been a fairly uneventful night. The first call of the evening was to warn a resident of a twenty-three room house in Hancock Park that he should not go outside to swat flies in the afternoon, particularly when he had to climb a ladder to get them, and especially when his next door neighbor's daughter, a nineteen year old blonde, just happened to be washing her Mercedes 450 SL and couldn't help seeing that he was stark naked beneath his bathrobe, which kept flapping open.

The second call of the evening had been to take a burglary report at an air conditioning manufacturer's whose company had been closed for three days. They heard the burglary victim's opinion which Spermwhale had heard perhaps a thousand times in his police career:

"It must've been kids who did it," said the victim, since burglary victims of both residential and commercial burglaries hate to consider the prospect of a grown man viciously and dangerously violating the sanctity of their premises by his presence. If there is nothing taken, or if property of any value whatsoever is left behind, the victims invariably allay their fear of prowling deadly men with the refrain, "It must've been kids."

Spermwhale just nodded and said, "Yeah, kids," and noted that the burglar went through the file cabinet by opening the drawers bottom to top so that he would not have to push the drawers shut thus taking a chance of leaving a fingerprint. That he had carefully ransacked all file boxes, drawers and logical places where money is hidden. That he had pocketed only easy to carry items. That he had stolen fifteen rolls of postage stamps which could be sold for eighty cents on the dollar and had left, closing the self-latching door behind him so that any doorshaking watchman would find nothing amiss during the evening rounds.

"All the good stuff he didn't even touch," the vice president of the company said. "The typewriter, the calculator. Anyone but kids would've taken something besides stamps, wouldn't he, Officer?"

"Oh sure. Had to've been kids," Spermwhale agreed as the vice president managed a relieved smile. Spermwhale wrote "Stamp and money burglar" in the MO box of his report.

Spermwhale had lapsed into a very bad mood when they took the burglary report to the station that night. He had just been turned down by Lieutenant Finque on his request to hang a picture of his old friend Knuckles Garrity in the coffee room. Garrity had been a Central beat cop for fifteen years and finished out his twenty-five year career at Wilshire Station where he and Spermwhale were radio car partners. Just before Garrity was to have retired on a service pension he became involved in his third divorce and was found shot to death in his car in the station parking lot.

The car was locked from the inside with the keys in the ignition and his service revolver was on the seat beside him. Yet, despite all logic, Spermwhale refused to believe that his partner had not been murdered. He had to be given three special days off to get his thoughts together. Finally he accepted Knuckles Garrity's obvious suicide and became the partner of Baxter Slate and eventually a MacArthur Park choirboy.

Spermwhale Whalen had been broken in on a Central beat by Knuckles Garrity who told his rookie partners that a policeman only needed three things to succeed: common sense, a sense of humor and compassion. That none of these could be taught in a college classroom and that most men could succeed without one of the three, but a policeman never could. Spermwhale shivered for an instant, wondering how Knuckles had lost his sense of humor.

Spermwhale obtained the last picture ever taken of Knuckles in his police uniform and had it enlarged and framed with a brass plate on the bottom of the picture which said simply:

Thomas ''Knuckles'' Garrity
E.O.W. 4–29–74

It was on a lovely April afternoon with arrows of sunlight darting through the smog that Knuckles Garrity went End-of-Watch forever in the old police station parking lot on Pico Boulevard.

But the lieutenant said the picture would have to come down from the coffee room wall and that Spermwhale Whalen should take it home because Knuckles Garrity was not killed on duty like the other dead officers in the pictures which hung in the station.

''He was!'' Spermwhale growled to the lieutenant who handed him the picture and turned away from the burning little eyes of the fat policeman.

''Listen, Whalen,'' Lieutenant Finque explained. ''It's the captain's decision. Garrity shot himself, for God's sake.''

Spermwhale Whalen very quietly said, ''Knuckles Garrity died as a direct result of his police duties. As sure as any cop who was ever blown up in a shootout. Knuckles Garrity was the best fuckin cop we ever had in this station and that cunt of a captain should be *proud* to have his picture on the wall.''

''I'm sorry,'' the lieutenant said, turning and walking back to his office, leaving Spermwhale with the picture in his enormous red hands.

''I could shoot somebody,'' said Spermwhale Whalen when he got back in the radio car after the incident.

Baxter Slate fired up the engine and turned on the lights as darkness settled in. ''Anybody in particular?''

''The captain. The lieutenant maybe. Anybody,'' Spermwhale said, not knowing that in exactly two hours he *would* shoot somebody and that it would give him almost as much pleasure as if it had been the captain or the lieutenant.

But before Spermwhale had that pleasure he and Baxter received a call in 7-A-85's area because Roscoe Rules and Whaddayamean Dean were handling a call in 7-A-33's area because Spencer Van Moot and Father Willie had received a fateful call which almost made them the only team in LAPD history to get beaten up by a man three feet tall:

''Seven-A-Thirty-three, Seven-A-Thirty-three, see the woman, three-eleven suspect, First and Harvard.''

''Seven-A-Thirty-three, roger on the call,'' Father Willie automatically answered and then turned suddenly to Spencer. ''She say First and Harvard?''

''Yeah,'' Spencer replied absently.

''A wienie wagger at First and Harvard!'' said Father Willie.

Spencer was puzzled for a moment and then said, ''Oh.''

''Filthy Herman!'' they both cried at once and then a noisy string of obscenities from the black and white startled a woman pedestrian waiting for the light to change on Beverly Boulevard.

''Niles and Bloomguard are out fucking off again!'' Spencer whined. ''Why aren't they handling the call? It's their area!''

''Darn it!'' Father Willie said. ''No, wait a minute, I saw them in the station penciling out an arrest report.''

''Filthy Herman!'' Spencer groaned as the black and white came to a stop in some heavy evening traffic near the Wilshire Country Club, which further angered the policeman.

"Just put your mind in neutral with the car, partner," Father Willie advised. "We aren't going anywhere in this traffic for a while."

"Goddamnit!" snapped Spencer, yelling to any motorist within earshot. "If you're gonna camp here, pitch a fucking tent!"

The reason that Spencer Van Moot was so angry and Father Willie so apprehensive was Filthy Herman. He was a legless wienie wagger who lived in a boardinghouse near First and Harvard owned by his daughter Rosie Muldoon who struck it rich by marrying an extremely successful anesthesiologist and now could afford to keep her father, Filthy Herman, in a piece of rental property across town from her.

It was ordinarily a good arrangement. The house was large and Herman often had it filled with other alcoholics who congregated in the Eighth Street bars, a half mile from Herman's home. Filthy Herman was somewhat of a celebrity on Eighth Street, partly because of his grotesque physical presence. He was a torso in a wheelchair. Both legs had been amputated at the buttocks when he was thirty-seven years old, a powerful ironworker until a steel beam crushed him. He was also a celebrity because, with the monthly allowance from the daughter who visited him once a year on Christmas, Herman would buy drinks for every man who could not afford to buy his own. This meant that Filthy Herman had a group of some thirty to forty admirers and hangers-on among his Eighth Street entourage. What he didn't spend on drinks for the house he gambled away in gin rummy games or with the many bookies who frequented the area.

About twice a year, for no apparent reason, Filthy Herman would live up to his name and his normal alcoholic binge would end with his standing on two inch stumps on the wooden porch of his home, naked except for a Dodger baseball cap, screaming, "My cock's dragging the ground, how about yours?" Which indeed it was, what with the absence of legs.

Then the unfortunate radio car officers who got the call would be subjected to a barrage of incredible obscenities, empty bottles, beer cans, spitting, bites on the leg and surprisingly painful punches from the gnarled fists of Filthy Herman, who at fifty was not devoid of the strength acquired while an ironworker.

Any officer who had worked the division long enough had seen the legless torso of Filthy Herman bouncing across the asphalt as he was dragged cursing into the station by two disheveled policemen. Because of his physical impairment he was a pathetic sight when cleaned up and no judge had ever given him more than sixty days in the county jail for battery on a police officer.

The outraged victim of Filthy Herman was standing with her husband on the northwest corner of First and Harvard when the policemen arrived. Spencer sighed, parked on the east side of Harvard, slowly set the brake and turned off the headlights. He grabbed his flashlight and baton and followed Father Willie across the street.

"You call?" Father Willie asked the fortyish mousy woman who held a white toy poodle to her face and deferred to her tight lipped husband, a big man in a loose golf sweater and checkered pants.

"My wife was walking the dog," the man sputtered. "Just out walking our dog and she passed a house up there on Harvard and this filthy little *animal*, this *creature*, exposed himself to her!"

"Where'd it happen?" Father Willie asked, opening his report book and leaning against a car at the curb, his hat tipped back as he wrote.

"Back up the street," the man said. "The third or fourth house."

"You see it, sir?" Father Willie asked.

"No, my wife ran home and got me, and I came back here with her and she pointed out the house, but there was nobody on the porch. I was going to kill him." And the man put his arm around the skinny woman who clutched the toy poodle more tightly, lip quivering.

"What'd he do, ma'am?" asked Willie as he filled in the blanks for type of crime and location.

"He exposed himself! I told you!" said the man.

"Have to hear it from the witness," Spencer said.

"He yelled something horrible to me as I walked by," the woman answered brokenly. "And he showed himself. Oh, he was a horrible creature!"

"What'd he look like?" asked Father Willie, writing a cursory narrative.

"He . . . he had no legs!" cried the woman. "He was a horrible ugly little creature with, oh, I don't know, grayish hair and a horribly twisted body. And he had no legs! And he was naked! Except for a blue baseball cap!"

"I see," said Father Willie and then, unable to resist, "Did you notice anything *unusual* about him?"

And the woman answered, "Well, he had a tattoo on his chest, a woman or something. His porch light was on and I could see him very well."

"What'd he say to you when you passed?"

"Oh, God!" the woman said and the poodle yapped when she squeezed it to her face.

"Do we have to?" the man asked. "I'd like to go back and kick that little freak clear off the porch."

"You could," shrugged Spencer, "but he's a wiry little guy. Probably bite you in the knee and give you lockjaw."

"He said . . . he said . . . God!" the woman sobbed.

"Yeah," Spencer encouraged her.

"He said, 'I ain't got no left knee and no right knee, but look at my wienie!' Oh, God!"

"Yeah, that's our man all right," said Father Willie grimly. "Filthy Herman!"

After taking the complaining party's name, address and other routine information, the two policemen told them to go home and let the law deal with the little criminal. And they knew they stood a good chance of being punched in the balls or bitten on the thigh if they weren't careful. In that Filthy Herman was a legless man, not one team of policemen had ever had the good sense to call for assistance when arresting him. It was a matter of pride that two policemen with four legs between them should not have to call brother officers to help with this recurring problem.

"I'd like to punt the little prick six yards," Spencer said nervously as they climbed the steps to the darkened house of Filthy Herman.

"Wish we had a gunnysack to put him in. I hear he bites like a crocodile," said Father Willie, leading the way with his flashlight beam trained on the doorway.

The officers banged on the door and rang the bell several times until Spencer finally said, "Let's cut out. We tried. He's probably in there hiding. Let the dicks get a warrant and go down on Eighth Street during the day and pluck him off the bar at one of those gin mills where he plays the horses."

"Fine by me," Father Willie breathed, starting to imagine he heard a ghostly dragging chain above him in the dark old house. He looked up and saw dust falling from the porch roof which was sagging and full of holes and patched in several places with plywood and canvas.

Then they heard canvas tear and shingles fell on their heads as Filthy Herman sprung his surprise which put Spencer in Central Receiving Hospital for observation.

Spencer Van Moot was jolted forward almost out of his shoes, leaving his hat and flashlight behind as he flew crashing through Filthy Herman's front door while Father Willie stared in shock.

Father Willie slowly and incredulously realized what had happened when Filthy Herman came swinging back out the door, suspended by a heavy chain, and spit as he passed. Then he swung back in toward the doorway screaming, "C'mon and fight, you big sissy!" and spit again.

Detectives who filed felony charges against Filthy Herman for the violent assault against Spencer Van Moot were to piece together the story the next day. The self-confessed attacker said he had become tired of being dragged off to jail every time he got a little bit drunk and flogged his dummy on the porch. Filthy Herman had decided to frustrate the next arrest by chaining himself to an ancient steel and porcelain freestanding bathtub in the second story bathroom of his home. He had acquired a fifty foot piece of chain from a fellow horse player on Eighth Street who worked at a wrecking yard, and with a tempered steel lock supplied by the same friend, had crisscrossed his torso, using the chain like the bandolier of a Mexican bandit. Then he encircled his waist and locked it in the front.

After his crime against the woman with the poodle, Filthy Herman had been in the bathroom on the second floor when he saw the officers arrive. He had planned to fight it out there in the bathroom but suddenly the swashbuckling plan burst forth. He crawled out on the porch roof, dragging his chain, until he was just over the unsuspecting officers at the front door beneath him. And without anticipating the consequences, he yelled, "Geronimo!" and pitched forward through a hole in the porch roof, swinging down and in, striking Spencer Van Moot behind the neck with 150 pounds of beefy torso and propelling the policeman through the front door, splitting it in two and knocking the doorjamb ten feet across the room. Then he was swinging back and forth, screaming obscenities, spitting, snapping and challenging the bewildered Father Willie.

When Father Willie eventually came to his senses with Filthy Herman swaying dizzily in front of his eyes, the choirboy began yelling, "You *dirty* little bugger!" and swinging the nightstick wildly until he broke it on Filthy Herman's head.

Then by the time the neighbors, who were sick and tired of the crashing and screaming, called for additional police, Father Willie had Filthy Herman punched silly.

It took an hour and a half to get Filthy Herman dragged back up on the roof by his chain, pulled into the bathroom and covered with a bathrobe until an officer from Central Property could arrive with bolt cutters large enough to handle the heavy links.

Spencer Van Moot was in the hospital for three days with neck and back spasms. Father Willie was on light duty for a week with two broken bones in his right hand. Filthy Herman had one tooth knocked loose, two black eyes and a broken nose.

Both Filthy Herman and his daughter wept in each other's arms in court three weeks later and Herman was eventually put on probation for one year with the stipulation that he drink no alcoholic beverage. One week after the sentence Filthy Herman got drunk again, masturbated from the step of a fire truck and threw a fire extinguisher at an amazed fireman. Filthy Herman got six months in jail for that one, which proved what all policemen already knew: it's more risky to beat up firemen because they're popular.

So, while Spencer was meeting his Waterloo at the hands of Filthy Herman, Spermwhale Whalen and Baxter Slate had to meander south into the ghetto of Wilshire Division, which would probably not be called a ghetto in any other large city in the world, to answer a call that ended up being just another attempt by Clyde Percy to get into Camarillo State Hospital.

Clyde Percy was a seventy year old black man who lived in the vicinity of the Baldwin Hills reservoir. Because in the great flood of 1963 he had plunged into the raging water and rescued a drowning woman who was trapped in her overturned car, Clyde Percy was presented with a commendation by the City of Los Angeles, the first official praise he had ever been given in his entire life. Now he simply couldn't wander too far from the scene of his triumph and was the object of numerous radio calls. People would find Clyde Percy asleep in their unlocked cars or in the storage sheds of small businesses, and once, in a pièce de résistance, he slept all night on a posture perfect mattress in the window of a department store in the Crenshaw shopping district. The next morning he was discovered by passing shoppers still in the store window, fully clothed, muddy shoes and all. He was snoring peacefully, slobbering out the side of his toothless mouth, dreaming of some woman far far back in his memory, holding onto an erection which only came in sleep. Clyde got ninety days that time.

"Wonder why Spencer Van Moot and Father Willie weren't assigned the call," Spermwhale grumbled to Baxter Slate. "I'll bet they're off in some fuckin clothin store buyin some Lord Fauntleroy bow tie for Spencer or some tooty fruity boots. Man's forty years old and he dresses like an interior decorator or somethin."

The radio call which Spermwhale and Baxter Slate received concerned an open door a tremulous security guard had found while making his rounds at a furniture store on the east side of Crenshaw. The security officer had heard ghostly sounds coming from within the store and though the sun had not yet set, it was dim and shadow filled inside. The guard was seventy-five years old and didn't really want to be a security guard but if he relied on Social Security to support him and his seventy-three year old wife they'd have to eat dog food five days a week instead of two.

"Go on about your rounds," Spermwhale told the old man. "We'll check it out."

"I'll be right over there across the street by my car if you need me," the guard promised. "I'll be close to my radio in case you need help."

"Sure," Spermwhale said, "stay there in case we need you."

And he patted the guard on the shoulder and pointed him toward his car which was not across the street as he thought but in the parking lot back of the building. The old man lost his car at least once a night.

When they were alone and dusk was deepening, Baxter said, "We're calling for another car, aren't we?"

"Nope," said Spermwhale, "it's just old Clyde Percy."

"Who?"

"Clyde the lifeguard. The old dingaling that pulled the broad outta the sewer back in the flood. Ain't you heard a him? He's always gettin busted for somethin or other."

"How do you know it's him?"

"His MO. He breaks into places right after they close and he eats up whatever's around and goes to sleep. I know it's him because a the noises the doorshaker said he made. Like a ghost. They always say that, people who call in."

"What's the noise?"

"He cries. Sits in there and cries. He sounds like a mournful moose. I tell you it's Clyde Percy in there."

But just in case, Baxter Slate unlocked the Ithaca shotgun from the rack and jacked one in the chamber when they walked single file into the darkened store looking for the mournful moose.

It was a small furniture store which advertised entire living room sets for six hundred dollars. Clyde Percy would have none of the cheap furniture. They found him in the rear on the second floor by the manager's office sprawled out on a nine hundred dollar tufted Chesterfield, eating a half empty bag of potato chips and a banana, which one of the clerks had left behind. He wore his regular attire, which was two dirty undershirts and three outer shirts with a ragged colorless turtleneck sweater over all, a pair of stout flannel pants over longjohn underwear, run over combat boots and a World War II flier's hat without the goggles.

"H'lo, Clyde," Spermwhale said as Baxter lowered the riot gun and ejected the live round from the chamber.

"Aw right, Officer, aw right," said Clyde Percy, grinning happily and standing at attention, his purple lips smeared with banana, his skin blue-black in the shadows. "Y'all caught me fair an square. Don't need no handcuffs. I'm gonna come peaceable. Course if you wanna use handcuffs it's okay too."

"Ain't seen you around for a while, Clyde," Spermwhale said as they walked the old man down the stairs, each policeman holding an elbow because he reeked of wine and staggered on the landing.

"Got locked up last November. Jist in time for Thanksgivin. Ain't missed a Thanksgivin at Central Jail in twenny-eight years."

''You've been in jail since November?'' Baxter asked as he navigated down the steep stairs gingerly, holding Clyde and the shotgun and now needing a flashlight in the gloom.

''No suh,'' Clyde Percy said. ''This time a wunnuful thing happened to ol Clyde. I was sent to Camarilla State Hospital. The public defender say ol Clyde's crazy. An first I din't wanna go cause I likes your jail. I likes the sheriff's jail even better, no offense to you officers. He tell me, Clyde, we gonna get you sent to this crazy hospital and you gonna like it even better'n jail. So I say okay, and off I go up to Camarilla, and know what? They gives me a job up there teachin.''

''Teaching?'' Baxter said and stumbled with Clyde at the bottom of the stairs, dropping his riot gun and flashlight, kicking the light under a counter in the dark.

While the two policemen got down on their knees to look for the last flashlight, Clyde Percy picked up the riot gun helpfully and was holding it cradled in his arms like a baby when Sergeant Nick Yanov came through the front door.

''Holy shit!'' yelled Nick Yanov, drawing, crouching, throwing his flashlight beam on Clyde Percy who had lifted the gun to his shoulder upside down and started eating potato chips over the prone bodies of the two policemen.

''Drop the fucking gun or I'll blow you away!'' Nick Yanov screamed.

The next few minutes involved several panic stricken shouts after which Spermwhale sat the sergeant down on a display couch, gave him a cigarette and convinced him they were alive, that Baxter had unloaded the magazine when he ejected the live round, that Clyde Percy was a harmless old acquaintance of Spermwhale Whalen's and that Sergeant Yanov should remain on the couch until his legs steadied.

''Sure glad it was you, Sarge,'' Spermwhale Whalen said to the chesty, bristle jawed sergeant. ''If it was one a them other cunt supervisors he'd a probably cut old Clyde in half and we'd a ended up with another suspension for lettin Clyde get wasted.''

''Why do you do things like this to me,'' Nick Yanov said, drawing heavily on the cigarette as some color returned to his face.

Then the two policemen and Clyde Percy helped the weak kneed Sergeant Yanov out of the store and to his car, Clyde Percy apologizing profusely for scaring him to death.

''Where's the nearest gas station?'' Sergeant Yanov asked as he got back in his black and white and threw his hat and light on the seat, running both hands through his heavy black hair.

''Why, you gotta take a crap?'' Spermwhale grinned.

''No, I just did! I gotta clean up!'' said Nick Yanov as he fired up the radio car and roared away.

''Good fuckin sergeant,'' Spermwhale Whalen mused in an extremely rare moment, and then reverted to his old self. ''Not like that eunuch lieutenant and that gelding captain and all the other cocksuckin sergeants on the nightwatch.''

''So what's with the teaching you say you did at Camarillo?'' Baxter asked when they got Clyde safely in the radio car and were on their way to jail to book him for drunk.

''I tell you, Officer,'' said Clyde Percy, munching toothlessly on potato chips, ''it was *such* a fine place. They was all these kids, retarded, you know? Ain't nobody come to visit em most a the time. They gives em jobs to keep em busy, like makin these little balloon toys. You puts the balloons on the little blow-up stems like. So they gives me the job a helpin watch over all the kids. So I does things like make sure they kin attach balloons right and that they don't fight too much and don't fall on their heads and bite their tongues and so forth like that. And then one day I made a invention. I drills holes in this board to put the stems in and then the kids kin attach three balloons at once and makes it easier to hold em. One a the bosses there says to me, 'Clyde, you jist about the best we ever have workin here.' So I tells him bout the time I save the lady in the flood and he say, 'Clyde, you kin stay here if you wants to.' ''

"Why're you out then?" asked Spermwhale, driving the black and white west on Venice Boulevard.

"They say one day they jist ain't no more room, jist room for real crazy people and I ain't that crazy. So that night I start sayin I'm the President and mayor, and like that. But they say it ain't no good, Clyde, we know you ain't really crazy like some folks, leastways you ain't so crazy you gonna hurt somebody. And then I thought bout hurtin one a the technicians, punchin em or somethin, but they all so nice to me I couldn't. So they put me out and here I is, back home agin."

"That's a goddamn shame," Spermwhale said angrily, turning in his seat toward Baxter. "I seen fifty dollar a trick whores, and dopers and pimps, and thieves and assholes for three generations all on welfare and we can't even afford a fuckin bed and three squares at a state hospital for Clyde. That pisses me off!"

"Think you kin do somethin to git me back there?" asked the old man, his blue lips flaked with potato chips, the left earflap of his flier's cap turned up from the scuffle with Sergeant Yanov.

"By God, if there's any justice in this miserable world, which there ain't, somebody oughtta help you. Tell you what, you plead not guilty at your arraignment tomorrow. Then I'll be in court on trial day. I'll talk to the city attorney and tell him that you're always walkin around the street threatenin everybody and sayin you're the Easter Bunny and wavin your dong at housewives and stuffin dog shit in mailboxes and settin trash fires and in general bein a bigger pain in the ass than Francis Tanaguchi."

"Francis who?"

"Oh, never mind," Spermwhale said as they parked in the station parking lot and got out of the car. "Anyways, I'm gonna tell him you're the Wilshire Division whacko and a horrible asshole and you shouldn't be put away for ninety days for drunk like you usually are because you're a dingaling. And then I'll say I think you should get a sanity hearin and shipped off to Camarillo again."

"Oh, Officer," said Clyde, and the tears welled in the old man's eyes and he even stopped eating potato chips. "Oh, I'll be crazier than you say I is, I kin stand on my head . . ."

"No, don't go too far," Spermwhale said. "Just stare off in space and say somethin goofy every time somebody asks you somethin."

"I'll shoo skeeters that ain't there," said Clyde as they shuffled toward the steps of the station.

"Yeah, like that," Spermwhale said as they half lifted the old man up the steps.

"I'll punch a policeman right in the mouf," said Clyde.

"No, don't do that," said Spermwhale.

"A public defender?" Baxter Slate suggested.

"No, no," Spermwhale said as they opened the side door and took Clyde inside.

"A judge? How about a judge?" Baxter offered.

"No," Spermwhale said, "let's not overdo it. Just swat invisible mosquitoes or beat off at the jury or somethin."

Then Clyde Percy came to a limping halt in front of the barred jail doors and looked up at Spermwhale, and Clyde's face, dust covered, but charcoal black in places, was streaked and wet.

"I appreciates it, Officer," he said to the fat policeman. "I wants to go back to the chirruns, back to Camarilla. I appreciates what you doin for me." And then he took Spermwhale's big hand in his and wept.

"Jesus, Clyde! Okay! Okay!" Spermwhale said, pulling his hand away and looking around to see if other policemen were looking. "It's okay. You don't have to . . . it's gonna be all right. I don't mind bein there in court. I ain't got nothin to do anyways. Jesus, it's okay. Quit cryin, will ya?"

Spermwhale Whalen *did* go to the court trial of Clyde Percy, and *did* succeed in getting a sanity hearing for the old man. But Clyde Percy was deemed not to be a hazard to himself or others and sane enough to be released. He *was* released, after which he walked one mile downtown, shoplifted a short dog of wine, poured it over his head and lay down in the middle of the intersection at First and Los Angeles streets, having to wait only ninety seconds until a police car heading into the police building was forced to stop, pick up the Baldwin Hills lifeguard and book him into Central Jail on a plain drunk charge. He was given ninety days in the county jail, which was better than nothing but a far cry from Camarillo State Hospital where he invented the device to help retarded children blow up balloons.

When Whaddayamean Dean broke into one of his numerous drunken crying jags at choir practice after hearing of the ultimate fate of Clyde Percy, Roscoe Rules called him a nigger lover and said the old cocksucker probably wanted to go back to Camarillo in the first place just to molest the little dummies.

Spermwhale Whalen was in a foul mood after they booked Clyde Percy. The mail drop had arrived at Wilshire Station and contained an eight by ten glossy photo sent to Spermwhale by his classmate, Sergeant Harry Bragg of the police department photo lab. The picture was a mug shot of Spermwhale Whalen's eldest son, Patrick, who had died thirteen months earlier of a drug overdose. It was the only picture the boy had taken in the last two years of his life, this one when he was arrested for car theft in Van Nuys.

Spermwhale, the veteran of three failed marriages, had not seen much of the boy after adolescence, and he studied the photo carefully, appreciating the skill of Sergeant Harry Bragg who had removed the booking number and profile shot, and blown up the full face part of the double mug shot until probably only a policeman would suspect from whence it had come.

Technically it was a successful picture, artistically a dismal failure. He could detect none of the boy's considerable intelligence in the arrogant eyes and narrow mouth. The shoulder length hair was totally unfamiliar, as was a small fresh scar over the right eye. It was not the son he wanted to remember, not if he wished to keep the guilt from overtaking him.

Spermwhale was scowling and chewing a cigar to shreds when he and Baxter went back to the radio car. The night had become exceptionally black.

"What's wrong with you?" Baxter asked.

"Nothin."

"Look a little mad."

"I ain't mad. Why should I be mad? I make seventeen grand a year, don't I? Course after income tax and pension contribution and Police Relief and Police Protective League and the credit union and three wives and rent, I have about a dollar thirty cents to eat on between paydays. And I just come off a four day suspension so I gotta stop eatin for about two weeks. So what've I got to be pissed off about?"

"That it? Money?"

"Money, who needs money? Just because I been cuffed around a little bit by the heavy hand a justice? Just because I lost four days' pay? Shit, that ain't nothin. I only got three ex-wives to support, and three ex-kids . . . no, *two* ex-kids to feed. And an ex-dog and my turtle. Course the turtle's sometimes in hibernation so he don't eat too much. It's only fair that I got four days' suspension for keepin those avocados Francis gave me. But the thing bothers me. I wonder if Lieutenant Grimsley and all them IAD headhunters get a finder's fee when they nail a cop? Maybe they get a percentage of what the city saves off our paycheck when we get suspended. Ever think a that?"

"I could loan you twenty bucks till payday."

"Fuck it, I don't need money. Old Clyde Percy gets along without it, don't he?"

"It's pretty decent what you're going to do for him," Baxter Slate said. "The way you're going to bat to get the old man back in the laughing academy."

"Listen, partner," Spermwhale said, and now the cigar was almost eaten and he was spitting black leafy tobacco out the window of the radio car, "just because

I *seem* to care about people once in a while, don't make no mistakes about me. Nineteen plus years a workin these streets has taught me that people are shit. They're scum. Only reason I don't treat em like Roscoe Rules or some a those black glove hotdogs is what's that do for you? Gets you fired for brutality or an ulcer or somethin. For what? The human race is no fuckin good but workin with these rotten bastards is all we got, right? It's the only game in town so you gotta play like you're still *in* the game. If you don't, if you drop out, you take your fuckin six inch Colt and see can you pull the trigger twice while you're eatin it. I just don't wanna off myself like so many cops do. So once in a while I do somethin that might look to you like I give a fuck about some of these scumbags. But there's nothin more rotten than people."

And the very next call of the night did nothing to change Spermwhale's mind.

"Think I'll go see my ex-wife tomorrow," Spermwhale said to Baxter who had just suggested taking code seven at the half price restaurant north of Wilshire on Western.

"Which one?" asked Baxter.

"The second ex-wife," Spermwhale said. "I like her best in some ways. She had the most balls. Took every dime I had. I like to see her once in a while and visit my ex-dog and my ex-car."

"She still give you a little?"

"Wouldn't want it. Her ass is so big she has to sit down in shifts. And she's as old as runnin water. I like them young animals like Carolina Moon. Her fat's all smooth and bouncy. I like em with enough strength to fight!"

"Gonna have to call a choir practice one of these nights," said Baxter Slate, as the Regretful Rapist was pulling a black woman out of her Ford sedan just two blocks ahead and trying to drag her off behind a large trash dumpster in the darkness.

She screamed at two men passing by who just kept walking, observing the golden rule of city dwellers: Do unto others if you want to risk getting your fucking head blown off.

"I'm getting awfully hungry," Baxter Slate said as the Regretful Rapist was discovering that the black woman was almost as strong as he and was not going to submit, knife or no knife. The rapist was furiously trying to find the dagger she had knocked from his hand to plunge it into her throat.

"You know, there's somethin about Nick Yanov reminds me a my youngest kid," Spermwhale said as he lit a fresh cigar and Baxter glided slowly around the traffic consisting of diners looking for parking off La Cienega's Restaurant Row, to avoid tipping valet parking lot attendants.

"Your kid isn't that old," Baxter said.

"No," said Spermwhale, "but he just looks somethin like Yanov. You know, I'm afraid he's gonna get in trouble like the others. Last time he came to see me he wouldn't even accept some clothes I bought him. Only wants to hang around Venice Beach with the hippies. Don't even want some clean underwear. You see, he can't stand ownin *anything*. He only wants the clothes on his back. Can't even stand the responsibility of changin his skivvies. I'm afraid if he ever went to jail and had someone make all his decisions for him, he might like it."

Baxter Slate tried to think of something to change the subject because he didn't want Spermwhale to start thinking of the oldest boy.

And the Regretful Rapist, not a bit regretful at the moment, grabbed the black woman by the throat and almost choked the life out of her before she succeeded in burying her teeth in his bicep and squirming free just long enough to manage a chilling scream which was nearly her very last.

"Jesus Christ, what was that?" Spermwhale jerked upright in his seat and grabbed the flashlight as Baxter wheeled the car around and screeched into the darkened parking lot, catching the screaming woman and the raging rapist full in the headlight beams as they fought on the ground.

Then Spermwhale, moving like a younger, slimmer man, was out of the car before it stopped, chasing the fleeing rapist across the parking lot shouting, "Stop, you motherfucker, or you're maggot meat!"

Baxter Slate, finally getting his flashlight to work by banging it on his hip as he ran, caught up with Spermwhale who was standing motionless and aiming two handed at a running shadow eighty feet away. Then there were three explosions in Baxter's ear and the Regretful Rapist dropped to the asphalt shrieking in terror from a slight wound which entered his lower back, broke two ribs, ricocheted around the rib cage, following the path of least resistance, and exited in the front, causing, aside from the broken ribs, little more than a flesh wound. And this caused Roscoe Rules at the next afternoon's rollcall to scream loudly for the hundredth time that they should be permitted to carry dumdums and high velocity ammo.

When the two policemen got to the wounded suspect and stood over him, he shook his mop of sweaty hair out of his face and yelled in panic and shock, "You shot me in the back, you chickenshit!"

Spermwhale, panting heavily from excitement and exhaustion, yelled back, "There ain't no rules out here, you cocksucker! The Marquis of Queensberry's just some fag over on Eighth Street!"

And the Regretful Rapist was caught. Spermwhale Whalen and Baxter Slate each received a Class A commendation which was worth exactly nothing in terms of promotion, prestige or economic remuneration. They both offered to trade it for the four days' pay which had been taken away for accepting the imprudent avocados, but the watch commander told them he didn't think that was very funny.

Perhaps Spermwhale Whalen's greatest contribution was the rapport he established with the rapist in the five hours they were together at the emergency hospital, the detective bureau and finally the General Hospital jail ward where they booked him.

It started when Spermwhale bought two candy bars for himself and his starving partner and discovered that he had punched the wrong button and got one full of caramel which he never ate because it stuck to his partial plate.

"Here, want some candy?" he asked the rapist as the young man was sitting handcuffed to a chair in the emergency ward.

"Thanks," the rapist said, and Spermwhale noticed that his eyes were glassy and shining from tears, and though he had refused to speak to detectives, the fat policeman said, "Pretty good candy, ain't it? You like candy?"

"It's okay," the rapist said, his large blue eyes moving around the room.

Then Spermwhale said, "I did you a favor by shootin you."

The rapist turned, wiped his face on the shoulder of his torn jacket and said, "How's that?"

"You woulda been booked in an LAPD jail. We wake our prisoners up at five A.M. and serve them meals of red death, Gainesburgers and donkey dicks. This way you're gonna be in the hospital jail ward and then in the county jail when you heal up. Chow's a hundred percent better. Same with the bed and cell. I did you a favor."

"Thanks."

"You know, I don't blame you for what you done. I get the urge sometimes myself. Ugly guy like me and all the pussy around just teasin a guy with this no bra stuff and tight pants. Shit, they ask for it."

"You think so?"

"Sure. We all got our bad habits. Hell, I can't quit smokin and drinkin, how can I criticize you?"

The Regretful Rapist smiled at the fat policeman and eventually accepted two more candy bars with caramel and almonds and confessed to more than thirty rapes, including twelve which had never been reported to the police but were verified through a detective follow-up.

Spermwhale Whalen was given his usual subpar score the very next time he went before a board on a promotional exam. He had for years been wasting his off-duty time flying 200,000 pounds of mechanized and human cargo for his country instead of taking police science classes at night school.

As Captain Drobeck said at a private staff meeting, who in the hell wants supervisors and executives who were only good for flying airplanes and catching dangerous crooks like the Regretful Rapist? Besides, Spermwhale Whalen was unpolished and fat and had ridiculous feet. He wore a wide triple E shoe but his feet were an abnormally short size 7 1/2. It looked like he was walking on waffles.

9

Tommy Rivers

''Kudos to Roscoe Rules!'' Sergeant Nick Yanov announced at rollcall on the night Baxter Slate shot the ordinary guy. ''Roscoe just had his annual physical, and the medical report here says his *Phthirius pubis* count is very low this year. I looked that up and it means body crabs.''

After the nightwatch stopped applauding the scowling Roscoe Rules, Lieutenant Finque tried to get everyone in really good spirits by showing them photos he had borrowed from homicide detectives of the monstrously bloody corpse of Nathan Zelinski, a seventy-two year old janitor who had been stomped to death by two sixteen year old boys during a burglary at a junior high school three years earlier.

''Drove his nose bones right down his throat,'' Lieutenant Finque said. ''Old man actually drowned on his own blood. Took him almost forty-five minutes to die. According to their confessions they kept coming over and looking at him every once in a while.''

''They have a fascination for such things,'' Baxter Slate whispered to no one in particular.

''Who?'' Spermwhale asked.

''Kids.''

''Reason I showed you,'' the lieutenant continued, ''is that the second boy was just released from camp and is back in our division. The first got out four months ago.''

And while the nightwatch passed the pictures around and cursed the courts and penal authorities and their lot in general, Sergeant Nick Yanov asked under his breath, ''Lieutenant, did you have to do this?''

''Of course,'' the lieutenant answered. ''I want them to know what kind of idiots we have to fight within the system.''

''Don't you think they know? Why keep reminding them they're shoveling shit against the tide? Why?''

''We'll talk about it later,'' Lieutenant Finque said.

But they never did. On Nick Yanov's next rating report Lieutenant Finque wrote, ''Sergeant Yanov needs a lot of seasoning before he can hope to be a top supervisor. Lacks maturity.''

And to continue to show Sergeant Yanov who was boss, Lieutenant Finque said to the assembly, ''Oh, and by the way, did you hear about the other young kids the Youth Opportunity folks placed at General Hospital for summer employment. They had *lengthy* drug records so they put them in the *pharmacy* washing bottles. You can guess the rest. And a couple of things we discussed at the supervisors' meeting,'' the lieutenant went on, now that he was getting warmed up. ''We have some local businessmen who make frequent burglary and theft reports and don't want uniformed officers coming in the front door to take reports. Gives the place a bad name.''

The lieutenant smiled smugly when he heard the roar this tidbit aroused. ''Of course the captain gave them what for. You would've been proud of him.''

''I always knew he was behind us,'' said Spermwhale Whalen. ''I felt him there many times.''

The lieutenant didn't know how to interpret Spermwhale's observation so he continued with the good news. ''And you can all just quit grousing about how long you have to wait in court until your case is called. I've talked it over with the captain and he talked it over with the commander and he talked it over with the deputy chief . . .''

''And he talked it over with Dear Abby who's runnin this fuckin department,'' said Spermwhale Whalen.

''And he talked it over with his counterpart at the courts,'' said Lieutenant Finque ignoring the laughter. ''Private counsel simply has priority at court trials over defendants with public defenders.''

''Yeah,'' Spermwhale said, ''most a the people we bust have public defenders who don't have to get out quick to make a few more bucks from some other client, so us cops and our civilian witnesses and victims have to cool our heels while these black-robed pussies take care a their fuckin fraternity brothers. If they ain't got a monopoly I don't know who does. Who worries about cops?''

''Who worries about victims?'' Baxter Slate observed.

''Them too,'' Spermwhale nodded.

''Well, it's good to get these things off our chests at rollcall,'' Lieutenant Finque said jauntily now that he had turned twenty-eight cheerful men into seething blue avengers. Then Lieutenant Finque said, ''Sergeant Yanov's going to hold a gun inspection while I keep an appointment with the captain. There've been some dirty guns in recent inspections and the captain says he's going to start coming down hard on you men. You may not appreciate it but you work a damned good division. Even the people we serve are the best. Our citizens show a geat interest in the Basic Car Plan meetings and they purchase lots of whistles.''

''Hey, Lieutenant,'' Spermwhale said. ''Is it true the station buys those whistles for seven cents?''

''I don't know the details,'' said Lieutenant Finque.

''That's a forty-three cent profit on each whistle,'' said Spermwhale.

''I don't know the details.''

''Jesus, we musta made thousands a bucks with this caper,'' Spermwhale observed.

''I don't know, but it's for our Youth Services Fund so it's a worthy cause.''

''Is is true there's some civilian whistle maker flyin all over the goddamn country tryin to sell the idea to other departments?''

''I'm not familiar.''

''What a scam. You gotta hand it to some a the eunuchs in this department. Once in a while they come up with an idea. Why didn't I think a that? I coulda made enough in one year to pay off all my ex-wives!''

''Enough on whistles,'' Lieutenant Finque smiled nervously, since he was the eunuch who thought of it or at least who stole the idea from the senile old lady who thought crime could be stamped out if there were thousands of other old ladies running around blowing whistles at bad guys.

''Maybe I could get in on the action, Lieutenant,'' Spermwhale persisted. ''I got this idea for sellin one to every broad in the city. See, we design a whistle shaped like a cock and the part you hold is shaped like a pair a balls with two LAPD badges pinned to them. Our sales motto could be 'Blow for your local policeman.' ''

''It might work, Lieutenant!'' cried Francis Tanaguchi.

''That's a swell idea, Spermwhale!'' cried Spencer Van Moot.

''I know a guy could design the whistles!'' cried Harold Bloomguard.

Lieutenant Finque felt like crying. It always happened like this. He'd discuss a serious subject with the men and they'd end up making fun of him. Supervisor or not, he would have given anything to punch Spermwhale Whalen right in his big, red, scarred up nose. And he'd have done it too if he weren't petrified of the fat policeman and if he weren't absolutely sure Spermwhale would break his back.

"I think you better hurry if you're going to make your appointment," Sergeant Yanov suggested, to save his superior officer from further trauma.

But before Lieutenant Finque walked out the door he said, "I'll tell you men one thing. Because of our whistles we've developed excellent rapport with the people we serve. If you should get in a fight with a suspect out there on these streets you don't have to worry. Our good people won't stand by and let you get kicked in the head!"

"No, they'll cut it off and shrink it," Roscoe Rules said dryly as Lieutenant Finque exited trembling.

Sergeant Yanov tried to make the gun inspection palatable by taking Harold Bloomguard's gun, looking down the barrel and saying, "Kee-rist, Harold, when was the last time you cleaned this thing? There's a spider been down there so long he has three hash marks on his sleeve."

Baxter Slate was one of three college graduates among the choirboys, the others being Sam Niles and Harold Bloomguard, both of whom obtained degrees while police officers. Two of the others were upperclassmen in part time studies, and all but Spermwhale Whalen had some college units. Baxter Slate not only had his baccalaureate in the classics, but had been a graduate student and honors candidate when he dropped out of college in disgust and impulsively joined the Los Angeles Police Department five years earlier. He was an unusually handsome young man, almost twenty-seven years old. He lived alone in a one bedroom apartment. He had no plans for marrying and no ambition to advance in rank. He said he liked working uniform patrol, that it gave him a chance to live more intensely, that sometimes he seemed to live a week or a month in a single night.

Whereas Calvin Potts read every new book in the police library which he thought might help him pass the coming sergeant's examination, Baxter Slate read no books in the police library since they invariably dealt with law, crime and police. Though Baxter Slate enjoyed doing police work he hated reading about it. And though Baxter Slate firmly believed that his extensive education in the classics had been the most colossal waste of money his mother had ever squandered and that his degree would never at any time in his life be worth more than the surprisingly cheap paper it was printed on, he nevertheless could not break old habits. He would occasionally, for the fun of it, struggle with Virgil and Pliny the Elder to see if he could apply their admonitions to the sensual, self-contained, alcoholic microcosm of choir practice which to Baxter Slate made more sense than the larger world outside.

Most of the choirboys had worked with Baxter as a partner at one time or another. He had been in the division three years and had worked Juvenile for nine months until he discovered he was a lousy Juvenile officer. Baxter thought he was also a lousy patrol officer. No one else said that Baxter was a lousy anything, except Roscoe Rules, who disliked Baxter for having ideas which confused Roscoe. At choir practice Roscoe often drunkenly accused Baxter of using ten dollar words just to show off in front of Ora Lee Tingle who was so bombed out on gin and vodka she wouldn't have known the difference if Baxter had spoken Latin. And as a matter of fact, Baxter *could* tell dirty jokes in Latin which amused the choirboys except for Roscoe.

"You and your faggy big words," Roscoe shouted one night as he soaked his feet in the MacArthur Park duck pond, watching warily that the ducks did not swim by and attack his toes.

"Baxter don't use big words," Spermwhale Whalen said, looking as though he would like to pulverize Roscoe Rules, who feared and hated Spermwhale even more than he feared and hated the little ducks.

"Well I think he does, goddamnit," Roscoe said but was careful to smile at Spermwhale when he said it.

Baxter was some forty feet away in the darkness, lying on a blanket and shaking his head in wonder that even here in the idyllic tranquilized and totally artificial world of choir practice, it was not entirely possible to escape hostility and violence.

"I think it's faggy and uppity to talk like that," Roscoe Rules said, while the other choirboys drank and teased Ora Lee Tingle or played mumbletypeg in the grass with confiscated and illegal ten inch stilettos or, like Spermwhale Whalen, tossed little stones on the water to watch the ripples, and to neck with Carolina Moon.

Finally Baxter uncoiled his lean body, brushed back his heavy umber hair, longer than anyone's but Spencer Van Moot's, who was constantly under fire from the watch commander to get a haircut, and said, "Roscoe, I sincerely try not to use any big words."

"There! See, you did it again!" Roscoe pointed, banging on the arm of his partner Whaddayamean Dean Pratt who was dozing on his blanket. "See, you said 'sincerely.' Shit. Faggy word. Faggy is what it is."

"I simply asked the fellows if . . ."

"See! You did it again!" shouted the mean and drunken Roscoe Rules as he punched on Dean to arouse him, but his partner only whispered drunkenly. " 'Fellows.' How many cops you ever hear say 'fellows'? Cops say 'guys' or 'dudes' or 'studs' or 'cats,' but *no* cop in the history of LAPD ever said 'fellows.' Nobody but you, Baxter Slate."

"He didn't say nothin faggy I heard," Calvin Potts said, and the tall black policeman was suddenly standing behind Roscoe Rules who was thinking that the only thing worse than a fag is a nigger and how much fun it would be to kneedrop Calvin Potts and puncture his kidney and smash his spleen like a rotten peach.

"For chrissake, Baxter, tell Roscoe what you said so I can relax," said Francis Tanaguchi who was lost in the expansive bosom of Ora Lee Tingle, trying to persuade her to pull the train for a few of the choirboys. She was now wearing only Spermwhale's T-shirt and her own skintight black flares as she held Francis Tanaguchi in her arms saying how fucking cute Nips are.

"Roscoe," Baxter said patiently, "I only said that policemen see the worst of people and people at their worst. I was simply trying to explain to you and me and all of us our premature cynicism. That's all I said and I wish I'd keep my big mouth shut."

"So do I," muttered Roscoe. "Fucking ten dollar words. A policeman only needs about a hundred words in his whole vocabulary."

"The only big words I use were taught me in the police academy, Roscoe," said Baxter. "Words like hemorrhage and defecation." Baxter took a drink of cold vodka and said, "You know, Roscoe, even you use euphemisms, police euphemisms, like calling your nightstick a baton because the LAPD says to call it that. I refuse to call it that. A baton is a plaything for young girls. There's no phallic connotation whatsoever. If I'm going to carry something to beat people over the head with I insist it have Freudian implications. I learned that in graduate school. Everything must have Freudian implications."

"You making fun a me, Slate?" Roscoe demanded, trying to stagger to his feet.

"You know, a graduate student would love to use a big faggy word like 'emasculated' on you, Roscoe. That's a favorite word of all graduate students. And they would say of your baton that the true symbol of your sexual identity is the wooden appendage you store at the station. In other words, your cock's in your locker."

"Oh, I don't like you, Slate, I never liked you," said Roscoe Rules who really didn't like Baxter Slate any less than he liked Harold Bloomguard, Francis Tanaguchi,

Calvin Potts and Spermwhale Whalen, not necessarily in that order. He only just tolerated his partner, Dean Pratt, who was starting to get on his nerves, and Father Willie Wright who seemed to be afraid of him.

"Let's talk economics instead of philosophy, Roscoe," Baxter Slate said, deciding to test the meanest choirboy. "I think that the inflationary period follows the prediction of the deficit meanders of corollary Harry, that Roscoes cannot breed in captivity and that Chandu the Magician is a cousin of the condor at Santa Barbara."

"I don't buy that faggy idea any more than the last one," Roscoe Rules said, passing the test.

"Whaddaya mean, Baxter? Whaddaya mean?" asked Whaddayamean Dean who had crawled across the grass into the conversation area.

"What do I mean, Dean, my friend?" said Baxter Slate. "I mean that I was a lousy Juvenile officer, that's what I mean. I mean that a battered child has a marvelous capacity to adjust to his torture and will ceaselessly love his battering parents. I mean that the mother of a sexually molested child will not leave nor truly protect the child from the father as long as the man has a good job or otherwise preserves that mother from an economic life which is more horrifying to her than the molestation of her child. I mean that the weakness of the human race is stupefying and that it's not the capacity for evil which astounds young policemen like you and me, Dean. Rather it's the mind boggling worthlessness of human beings. There's not enough dignity in mankind for evil and *that's* the most terrifying thing a policeman learns."

"Whaddaya trying to say, Baxter? Whaddaya trying to say?" pleaded Whaddayamean Dean drunkenly.

"I mean that twelve good men and true are a gaggle of nonprofessional neophytes conditioned by the heroics of cinema juries which inevitably free the defendant who is inevitably innocent. I mean that they can never really believe that a natural father could do such an unnatural thing to his child."

"I don't get it! I don't get it!" cried Whaddayamean Dean.

"I mean that doctors and professional men are the most arrogant and incompetent witnesses at any criminal proceedings and that they'll screw up your case for sure.

"I mean that the weak and inept parents will always refuse to surrender their neglected children to the authorities because they want to atone for failures with older children and the cycle inevitably repeats itself.

"I mean that perhaps economics, not morality, is our last consideration, and that the judge has a point when you plead with him to put a man away to save that man's family and the judge says, 'Swell, but who do you want me to let out?' "

"What's he mean? What's he mean?" yelled Whaddayamean Dean to the drunken choirboys. Dean was boozy enough for a crying jag now, the tears welling as he bobbed and weaved and almost fell over backward.

"And I mean that when policemen have to deal with small inflexible men in their own ranks, perhaps it becomes too much. And perhaps part of the reason that Roscoe Rules is small and inflexible and insensitive is because traditional police administrators—men like Captain Drobeck, and Commander Moss and Chief Lynch—are small and inflexible and insensitive and . . ."

"I heard that faggy remark, Slate, you scrote!" said Roscoe Rules, still unable to stand.

"I mean that cops chase society's devils as well as their own, which becomes unbearably terrifying since the devil is at last only the mirror image of a creature utterly without worth or dignity. And that the physical dangers of police work are grossly overrated but the emotional dangers make it the most hazardous job on earth."

"Oh, Baxter, oh, Baxter," moaned the bewildered Whaddayamean Dean who was starting to get sick.

"I mean that I carry only two memories from my childhood in Dominican boarding schools where I was placed by my beautiful, well traveled mother: if you touch the communion wafer with your teeth it's not so good and should be avoided. And the only unforgivable sin is to murder yourself because there is absolutely no possibility of absolution and redemption, and . . ."

"What the fuck're you babblin about, Baxter?" asked Spermwhale Whalen who was suddenly behind Baxter, having slept long enough to be more or less capable of driving home before dawn.

"Spermwhale! Thought you were stacking those Z's." Baxter Slate offered his partner a quick wide grin and a drink of vodka.

"Baxter, you sound like a silly pseudointellectual horse's ass. You're gettin embarrassin. C'mon, I'll drive you to your pad." Spermwhale felt a stab of pain across the front of his skull when he lifted his young partner to his feet and helped steady him.

Actually, Baxter Slate was rarely such a silly pseudointellectual horse's ass, but he had been undergoing a prolonged period of despondency brought about partly because he thought he had been such an unsuccessful Juvenile officer.

The murder of Tommy Rivers was the final blow to his career as a Juvenile officer because Baxter Slate had foreseen the imminent demise of Tommy Rivers and had been powerless, or rationalized that he was powerless, to prevent it.

It was three months to the day after Tommy Rivers' death and almost two months before the choir practice shooting that Baxter Slate became the only one of the ten choirboys to kill a man on duty.

Contrary to film and fiction, policemen rarely fire their guns in combat, and even Spermwhale Whalen with nineteen and a half years service and Spencer Van Moot with sixteen years had never killed a man on duty. The flesh wound to the Regretful Rapist was the only time Spermwhale had ever fired his revolver outside of monthly qualification shooting, even including the Watts Riot. So it naturally became a topic of conversation during choir practice when Baxter Slate killed a man.

The night Baxter Slate killed a man started out a busy one. Ten minutes after they hit the bricks and cleared at 3:45 in the afternoon, Roscoe Rules and Dean Pratt put out an "officers need assistance" call on Chesapeake Avenue in the vicinity of Dorsey High School.

A call for either help or assistance demands all-out coverage, and every car on the nightwatch made a squealing turn and headed south through the heavy afternoon traffic, figuring that Roscoe Rules had probably caused a riot at the school.

As it turned out the call was indeed put out by Roscoe Rules. He and Dean had been driving by the campus so Roscoe could show off by parading his tailored blue body and gleaming badge in front of the high school girls, when they spotted a young black car stripper struggling with the bucket seats of a Porsche which was parked in the faculty parking lot.

Whaddayamean Dean had dropped his baton getting out of the radio car and the clatter of wood on asphalt caused the sweating car stripper to look back and see the "Mickey Mouse ears" on the roof of the police car, which is what students call the siren lights. The car stripper was off in a 9.5 hundred yard dash which left Dean far behind and Roscoe radioing for assistance.

During the chase, the car stripper ran right into the arms of a pretty, twenty-five year old, white history teacher named Pamela Brockington who saw the exhausted policeman hotfooting after the boy. She pushed the boy into the gymnasium and was standing in front of the door when the lanky redhead came panting up to her.

"That boy go in there?" Dean gasped.

"I know that boy, Officer," Pamela Brockington said. "Whatever happened we can settle it without your running through the school grounds and starting a problem."

"Out . . . out of the way, lady," Dean puffed.

"Listen, you're on Board of Education property," the teacher said, planting her feet and spreading her legs, which wasn't easy, her blue jersey skirt being so tightly fitted.

"You know him, okay, it's no problem," Dean said, catching his breath. "Just give us his name and we'll pick him up at home."

"Well, what did he do?" For the first time the teacher looked unsure of herself.

"Tried to rip off the bucket seats from a white Porsche in the parking lot. What's the kid's name?"

"Oh," the teacher said in a small voice.

"Your car?"

"No, Mr. Krump's car. Oh."

"What's his name?"

"Well, I don't actually know his name but he's always around." Pamela Brockington moved aside to let Dean into the gym. But it was far too late and the car stripper had gone out the other door.

"He goes to school here, doesn't he? You can pick his picture out of your school mug shots," Dean said, removing his hat and wiping the sweat from his freckled brow.

"Well, I don't think he actually goes to school here, but . . ." and the young woman started to wither under the outraged scowl Dean was working up to. "He's . . . he's always hanging around the streets after school and I'm sure you could find him again tomorrow or the next day."

When Dean returned to the radio car without the car stripper and with the tale of Pamela Brockington, Roscoe Rules smiled ironically and in a very soft voice said, "Now ain't that typical, partner? I mean that's just so typical of some bleeding heart, left wing social science teacher, now ain't it?"

"I don't know if she teaches social science," Dean offered as Roscoe's voice rose an octave.

"Yes, well it certainly is typical and now our little motherfucking car stripper is halfway to Watts or wherever the hell."

"You broadcast a description?" Dean asked as he saw the familiar mad glint working its way into Roscoe's blue eyes as his hairless brows knitted and unknitted, making Dean terribly nervous because he didn't know if Roscoe would suddenly turn on him. Which he did.

"And *you* . . . partner," Roscoe said, his voice getting louder still as he revved the black and white, ready to leave half a tire on the pavement. "*You,* partner, let this little pinko, scum eating, shit sucking cunt keep you from hot pursuit? It's hard to believe!"

"Well . . . partner," Dean gulped. "We'll get him some other time. Maybe."

"And now you're sounding just like what this nigger loving split tail must've sounded like, partner. If I'd been there I'd a grabbed that come licking, do-gooder little cunt and CHOKED HER OUT AND MADE HER DO THE FUCKING CHICKEN! YOU HEAR ME?"

It was quite an ordinary Roscoe Rules incident, interesting later to Baxter because the car stripper ran across Exposition Boulevard and up Palmgrove Avenue where he made the almost fatal error of crossing through the fenced yard of Yolanda Gutierrez, aged sixty-two, and her niece, Rosario Apodaca, aged fifty-one, who, unlike Pamela Brockington, spoke no English but understood immediately what it meant when this young boy leaped their fence and crouched behind a hibiscus as a black and white cruised by with the officers craning their necks.

Yolanda Gutierrez calmly opened a trunk belonging to her son who had been killed in Korea twenty-three years earlier, removed his Colt .45 automatic and drew down on the boy.

The young car stripper laughed like hell at the old woman holding the heavy gun until Yolanda Gutierrez fired one for effect and blew out the window of the car parked in front of the house. The car stripper fell shrieking to the ground, not knowing the old lady had lost the bucking gun and her glasses and was crawling around the porch trying to find both when two black and whites attracted by the explosion came roaring down the street and arrested the car stripper.

"Something to be learned here," Baxter Slate remarked later to Spermwhale. "How two social classes perceive reality. The educated schoolteacher and the simple old woman."

"Who gives a fuck about reality anyway?" Spermwhale mumbled.

"Not me," Baxter grinned cheerfully. "I prefer choir practice to reality any old day."

Then Baxter's wide grin vanished as he watched a yellow gangrenous dog being dragged down the street by a larger bitch who had him locked inside her, his passion having turned to agony and howling terror. A gang of black kindergarteners, as guileless as a bunch of plums, laughed and pelted both muddy animals with rocks and tin cans.

"Maybe I'll fly another raid with some a the guys my next day off," Spermwhale suddenly said. "Need some excitement around here."

"Don't start that nonsense again," Baxter said, putting on his sunglasses and driving back toward their beat.

Spermwhale began to think about the mission he had flown three weeks earlier. It had started innocently enough with some alcoholic conversation at choir practice about how the white men of Palm Springs had cheated the Indians out of their birthright by stealing the desert spa from the Indians. Roscoe Rules had corrected them by pointing out that Jews and not white men had done it and that he wished the tribe would rise up and massacre every one of those kike bastards and cut off their scalps and kneedrop them.

Then, at precisely fifteen minutes before dawn, Francis Tanaguchi slapped Spermwhale Whalen awake where he slept entwined in the chubby arms of Carolina Moon.

"I'd love to see those two in a lewd movie," Francis Tanaguchi remarked as they threw dirty pond water in Spermwhale's face until he gagged and choked for air.

"Why bother?" Calvin said. "You can see them in real life anytime you want just by sneakin behind the bushes where they usually mate."

"Yeah, but it'd be different in a movie," Francis answered. "You know, a red sexy room with a red silky bedspread and Carolina and Spermwhale all fat and white and oiled and sliding around!"

"You'd need a cinemascope lens," Baxter Slate offered. "A wide wide angle to take all that flesh."

"Wall to Wall Meat! What a title! Outta sight!" cried Francis Tanaguchi.

An hour later, Francis, Calvin, Dean and Spermwhale, who were all off duty the next night, were in Spermwhale's rented orange and white Cessna 172 at Burbank Airport where Spermwhale often flew if he could get someone to pay for the rental and gasoline. Spermwhale had taken off without a flight plan, but with three hungover choirboys, two fifths of Scotch and one of gin, on a mission to recapture Palm Springs by way of Ontario Airport where Spermwhale reluctantly agreed to land because Whaddayamean Dean wanted some potato chips. They were reprimanded at Ontario by a man in the tower for landing without using the radio, but Spermwhale told him to fuck off and decided to hire a taxi to the Ontario Motor Speedway to watch some motorcycles qualifying for a race.

It was a long hot day at the racetrack spent sleeping shirtless in the bleachers, drinking the two fifths of Scotch and a case of beer and eating all the potato chips Whaddayamean Dean could hold.

Nothing eventful happened at the speedway until late in the afternoon when the choirboys wandered down to the track and a bearded racer told Spermwhale to get his fat ass off his bike. Spermwhale replied that he could fix it so the bearded racer could equal Evel Knievel's record for broken bones on a motor track.

The racer then called for track security officers and after being threatened with arrest the four choirboys put on their tank tops and basketball jerseys and scuttled off, moaning about never being able to find a cop when you want one. Whaddayamean

Dean was so drunk he had to be helped into his filthy yellow sweatshirt and they got it on backward with the picture of Bugs Bunny on the back and "What's Up, Doc?" on the front.

The choirboys discovered something extraordinary during the flight from Ontario to Palm Springs: that flying with a blood alcohol reading of .20 was actually invigorating. They celebrated by breaking open the fifth of gin almost immediately after takeoff and cruising at a carefree five thousand feet.

"I hate gin," Spermwhale said, tipping the bottle and drinking a quarter of a pint without taking it from his lips, flying the airplane as steady as a rock.

"It's what the brothers drink when they can't get Scotch," remarked Calvin Potts, who rode behind the self styled navigator, Francis Tanaguchi, who had never flown in any aircraft except once in the Army on the way to Fort Ord.

"But you people can drink airplane fuel," Francis said, grimacing from the burning gin.

"Yeah, and you Chicanos are models of sobriety," said Calvin.

"He's not a Chicano, you fuckin idiot. He's a Jap." Spermwhale said.

"That's right," said Calvin Potts, shaking his head. "Guddamn. I better start layin off the booze. I'm gettin simple!"

"It's confusin workin with a madman like Francis, is all," said Spermwhale, belching wetly.

"Gin! Gin!" cried Whaddayamean Dean, taking the bottle from Calvin and after three long swallows dropping into complete obliterating drunkenness.

Twenty minutes from the Palm Springs Airport, Spermwhale discovered he was well off the course through Banning Pass and was coming in dangerously low over the San Jacinto Mountains. "Aw shit!" he said and took the plane up seven thousand feet.

"Dynamite!" chuckled Calvin Potts as they climbed.

"My ears hurt! My ears hurt!" Whaddayamean Dean moaned.

"Far out!" Francis exclalmed as they soared through a cloud and came in like a Ping-Pong ball in the turbulence over the mountains.

"Hey, I can see that guy's eyeballs down there!" Calvin Potts said.

"What guy?" Spermwhale asked.

"The guy in the brown uniform. Looks like a forest ranger or somethin. The guy that jumped off the rock and fell on his ass when we buzzed him."

"We didn't buzz nobody," Spermwhale said. "Not on purpose."

"Well, ain't we flying a little low to the mountaintop?" asked Calvin.

"Whaddaya mean? Whaddaya mean?" asked Whaddayamean Dean.

"You know, there's somethin wrong. Somethin's fucked up," Spermwhale said. "We ain't comin in on the airport. We're comin in on somethin else looks a little different. I think maybe I'm a little more off course than I thought."

Then Calvin Potts was suddenly draped around Spermwhale's neck screaming, "Are we gonna crash?"

"Whaddaya mean? Whaddaya mean?" yelled Whaddayamean Dean.

"Get off my fuckin neck, Calvin, goddamnit!" Spermwhale ordered, prying Calvin's fingers loose. "Damn! You remind me a that vampire partner of yours. Jumpin around people's necks!"

"We are most certainly *not* going to crash," said Francis Tanaguchi, who was giggling idiotically as the airplane swooped down and up again. "As long as I am navigator we shall not crash!"

"Crash? Crash?" said Whaddayamean Dean.

"Give Dean another drink and take one yourself, Calvin," Spermwhale said as they dropped down toward the business district of Palm Springs and the airplane's engine started to attract attention below.

Then they were buzzing the Canyon Country Club. Calvin Potts, his red tank top soaked and plastered to him, cinnamon shoulders gleaming, said, "That's a *green* motherfuckin airport, Spermwhale. That's a . . . GUD-DAMN! THAT'S A GOLF COURSE!''

And Spermwhale jerked the wheel and the airplane pulled out and up, throwing them all back against their seats.

''We're gonna be all right,'' Spermwhale assured everybody. ''I'm just a little lost is all.''

''Lost? Lost?'' cried Whaddayamean Dean. ''What's he mean, Calvin? What's he mean, Calvin?''

''Here,'' said Francis Tanaguchi and Whaddayamean Dean accepted the bottle and was happy again.

As often happened when the choirboys would get drunk with the simpering redhead, they would find themselves unconsciously talking rapid fire and double action after hearing Whaddayamean Dean for a time.

Spermwhale was next to do it when he said, ''I could use a drink. I could use a drink.''

''Here. Here. Drink. Drink,'' said Francis.

''You had enough. You had enough,'' said Calvin Potts.

''What're you trying to say? What're you trying to say?'' said Whaddayamean Dean.

Francis played with the gauge and pretended he was a real pilot while Spermwhale turned around for a second pass over what he thought had to be the airport but was another golf course.

''Motherfucker's shootin at us!'' screamed Calvin Potts as Spermwhale Whalen swooped down over the fifteenth fairway and then up toward the mountaintop.

''Who is?'' demanded Spermwhale Whalen, deliberately turning the roaring little airplane around and diving belligerently toward the golf course.

''It was nothing,'' said Francis disgustedly. ''Some guy pointing a golf club is all it was. He jumped into the sand trap that time down.''

Then Spermwhale circled downtown Palm Springs for another few minutes as the police department sent two cars to sight and identify the aircraft.

Francis suddenly turned surly to the chagrin of Calvin Potts who had stopped drinking fifteen minutes ago.

''Rotten paleface assholes!'' screamed Francis. ''Steal the Indians' land! I wish Roscoe Rules was here, you lousy scrotes. Roscoe'd fix you. He'd make you do the fucking chicken!''

''Whaddayamean, Francis? Whaddayamean, Francis?'' asked Whaddayamean Dean.

''They stole the land!'' said Frandis, and the sadness in his voice was all that Whaddayamean Dean understood but it was enough to make him cry and wail, ''They stole the land! They stole the land!''

''Shut up, Dean, goddamm-it!'' growled Spermwhale. ''That's all we need now, for you to start bawlin.''

''Have a drink, Dean,'' Calvin Potts said, shakily handing Whaddayamean Dean the bottle as Spermwhale circled the town and Francis raged against all white men.

''Thank you, Calvin. Thank you, Calvin,'' Whaddayamean Dean said, smiling bravely. Then he wiped his moist eyes on his sleeve and sat back sucking up the gin, wondering what everything meant.

''Dive! Dive! Dive!'' commanded the angry navigator, but Calvin Potts said, ''Don't you motherfuckers be talkin that crazy shit now! You sound like when we sunk ol Wolfgang. But this ain't no play submarine. THIS IS A REAL MOTHERFUCKIN AIRPLANE!''

''Dive! Dive! Dive!'' Francis repeated, staring saucer eyed at the reeling pilot who said, ''I want gin!'' causing Calvin Potts' heart to stop and making him want to weep with Whaddayamean Dean, who actually wasn't weeping but was giggling at Calvin as he held the almost empty gin bottle in front of his face, playing peekaboo, enjoying Calvin's hilariously distorted black moustache through the glass.

"Where should I dive to?" Spermwhale asked finally and Francis said, "That fucking golf course. We're landing and claiming this whole town for the tribe. If you don't you're chickenshit!"

"Me, chickenshit? Me, chickenshit?" Spermwhale yelled, and as Calvin screamed the airplane dove in a gut-erupting 190 mph dive which threatened the design limitations of the little aircraft, and Whaddayamean Dean shouted, "I just wanna know: What's it all mean? What's it all mean?" which Calvin Potts decided was the most intelligent remark he had heard lately, as the airplane leveled out and climbed with Whaddayamean Dean throwing up all over everybody.

"Goddamn you, Dean! " Spermwhale yelled.

"That does it!" Francis raged. "I hate *all* thieving white men, even the ones in this airplane. I feel like crashing just to kill all you pukey pricks!"

"How about me? How about me?" Calvin Potts pleaded. "I ain't a white man. Why kill *me*?"

"You're all alike," Francis said.

"Whaddayamean Dean puked. I didn't puke," Calvin pleaded, and then Calvin realized that Whaddayamean Dean was vomiting in Calvin's lap so Calvin did too, in his own lap.

"See, you're all alike," said Francis disgustedly. "All a bunch of pukey white men. I wish Roscoe Rules was here to rupture your spleens!"

"I swear I'm not a white man," said Calvin Potts as he upchucked a second time.

"Okay, I dived. What the fuck else can I do?" Spermwhale Whalen challenged. "Want some aerobatics? Might as well spread all this vomit around."

"Buzz that golf course one more time," the exultant navigator commanded, while both Whaddayamean Dean and Calvin moaned and rolled their heads and craved sweet cool air.

"Where is it?" asked Spermwhale.

"Jesus Christ, Spermwhale, it's green, ain't it? Just go straight ahead only down lower. We can't miss something that big!"

But they could. They just missed the, mountains, barely.

Spermwhale obeyed the navigator and dived down toward the golf course again, though he was starting to come to his senses from the concentrated effort of flying. He was beginning to realize that someone might not like Francis' little prank of landing on a golf course claiming it for the Cahuilla Tribe. He was flying so low he made Calvin Potts scream in terror when he got over the golf course and Francis flapped the windows open and threw the empty gin bottle which shattered on the patio of the clubhouse, ending the attack on Palm Springs Indian land.

Ten minutes later, Spermwhale Whalen was heading in the general direction of Los Angeles, starting to think of mundane things like whether or not they would be arrested upon landing at Burbank. But within an hour he had stopped worrying about being arrested at Burbank. Night had fallen and brought with it dense fog, and he was glancing at his fuel gauge and wondering why he could not see the Burbank Airport. For the first time that day he made the concession of turning on his radio and he said to the other choirboys, "You guys see anything through all this soup? I mean in the last five minutes or so?"

"I saw somethin about fifteen minutes ago," Calvin Potts said, the only one of the passengers sober enough and frightened enough to be completely awake. "I saw a string a lights."

"Whaddaya mean lights? Whaddaya mean?" asked Spermwhale. "Jesus, I'm startin to sound like Dean."

"Well, it looked like a ribbon a lights. Coulda been street lights or headlights."

'Headlights?" murmured Spermwhale, straining his eyes but seeing nothing below them. Nothing but fog and darkness. "Hold on, I'm goin down."

"Down, you're goin down?" yelled Calvin Potts.

"Who's going down?" Francis asked, waking with a smile. "Ora Lee?"

"You sober now?" Calvin asked. "You're gettin sober, ain't you, Spermwhale?"

"Yeah, I'm gettin . . . Oh, mother! Oh, mother! I think I know where we are!"

"I see somethin. I see somethin," said Calvin Potts when they were at a hundred feet.

"What is it? What the fuck is it?" Francis demanded, awake and sober enough to share Calvin's sweaty terror.

"The ocean!" yelled the horrified choirboy. "That's the fuckin ocean down there! Oh, Lord!"

"The ocean!" screamed Francis.

"The ocean! The ocean! Which ocean?" yelled Whaddayamean Dean, waking from his deep alcoholic sleep.

"Keep the fuck off my back, Calvin," shouted Spermwhale shoving Calvin back and making the black policeman jump on Francis' back instead.

"We gonna go down, Spermwhale? We gonna go down?" Francis croaked, unaware that Calvin was choking him.

"We ain't goin nowhere but back to Burbank. Now shut the fuck up!" Spermwhale yelled.

But he looked at his fuel gauge and believed deep in his heart that this was his last flight. He hoped that somehow he could get in close to the coast when he was forced to put her down in the water, probably killing them all on impact. But he still flew as calmly as he had flown into Ontario Airport that morning.

"I see it! I see it!" shouted Calvin suddenly. "The ribbon a light!"

"Okay, that's the coast highway," Spermwhale said, sighing imperceptibly. "Santa Monica Airport's probably really socked in." He turned on his Burbank VOR, watched the dial and said, "Come on needle, come on needle."

Then he took the plane up over the Santa Monica mountains, and ten minutes later with less than two gallons of gasoline in each tank the choirboys landed at Burbank Airport, dragged Whaddayamean Dean out of the plane and drove home together.

"That old bastard ain't got a nerve in his body. He ain't afraid a nothin," Calvin said to Francis Tanaguchi the next night on patrol.

"Nobody got our airplane numbers?"

"Guess not. Nothin's happened," said Calvin.

"Outta sight!" cried Francis Tanaguchi, shaking his black hair off his thin little face, as he started making airplane noises behind the wheel of the radio car, pretending he was Spermwhale Whalen flying a fearless mission into downtown Palm Springs. "*Too* much!" Francis exclaimed, now that he had a real hero. "I just *gotta* see Spermwhale and Carolina Moon in a lewd movie if I have to produce it myself!"

And at the next choir practice, Francis tried to convince her that she should star with Spermwhale Whalen in the dirty movie he was going to produce. Spermwhale said okay, but next year after he had his twenty years' service and a pension locked up. Carolina Moon said she wasn't that kind of a girl.

Spermwhale was joking when he mentioned another mission like the Palm Springs raid to Baxter Slate on the night Baxter killed the ordinary guy, but Baxter Slate, not knowing the full extent of their terror that night over the dark lonely water, wondered if he meant it. Baxter was about to ask him if he was serious when they received a radio call to meet the officers at Ninth Street and Hudson.

Baxter drove easily to the location since there was no code on the call and met Sergeant Nick Yanov and 7-A-33. Spencer Van Moot was laughing while Father Willie stood glumly, hands in the pockets of his uniform pants, pushing out his gun on one side and baton on the other, making him look shorter and chubbier than he was.

When they got out of the car Spencer said to Baxter, "Ever hear of somebody lipping off to you?" And he held up a clean mayonnaise jar which contained a ragged pink object something like a sliver of veal.

"It's a piece of a woman's lip." Father Willie grimaced while Spencer Van Moot laughed uproariously.

"There was a fight here half an hour ago," Sergeant Yanov explained. "Two neighborhood women got in a hassle over the husband of one of them. There was kicking and gouging and biting and one broad ran home with her eyeball half torn out. When she recovered from the shock fifteen minutes later she found her neighbor's lip in her mouth. She must've bit off half of it. At least it looks like a lip."

Baxter Slate examined the raw meat in the jar and said, "It's a lip."

"The lipless lady, Mrs. Dooley, was taken to the hospital by a friend," Nick Yanov said. "So we're gonna take the biter on down to the hospital for an MT too. After that, we'll bring them both to the dick's bureau. Meantime, how about taking the lip in and seeing if they have to book it in any special way to preserve it. I really don't know. I never had a lip to take care of before."

So Baxter and Spermwhale drove part of Mrs. Dooley to the detective bureau in Wilshire Station while Spencer and Father Willie located the rest of her at Daniel Freeman Hospital. The detective just smiled when Baxter showed him the lip and said it would require no special handling because undoubtedly both ladies would make up before the case ever went to trial and it would be dismissed in the interest of justice after four court continuances.

When Spencer Van Moot and Father Willie found the rest of Mrs. Dooley at the emergency ward and arrested her for mayhem, she objected and they had a row with her. She had to be handcuffed and Spencer received a handcuff cut on the finger, a common injury for policemen who wrestle with slippery arms and sharp steel ratchets. The cut was not deep enough to require sutures and Spencer sat on a stool in the same emergency ward, no longer weak from laughing at the lip in the jar but from seeing his blood running down his hand.

He was white and dizzy when the crusty old nurse applied disinfectant and a butterfly bandage to the one inch wound. Father Willie helped support him on the right side while Spencer stood shakily. He was too nauseated to get mad when the nurse said, "Why don't you bite a bullet?"

When Baxter Slate and Spermwhale left Wilshire Station without Mrs. Dooley's lip, Baxter turned south on La Brea, causing Spermwhale to ask, "Where we goin, kid? Our area's east."

"Just felt like driving around the ghetto for a while," Baxter smiled. The slim policeman had an extraordinarily wide mouth which made his smile infectious and convincing even when he didn't mean it. And he didn't mean it now.

"Suit yourself," Spermwhale shrugged. "I just wanna take it easy tonight."

Suddenly Baxter said: "You know what I think is the best a cop can hope for?"

"Tell me, professor."

"The very best, most optimistic hope we can cling to is that we're tic birds who ride the rhino's back and eat the parasites out of the flesh and keep the beast from disease and hope we're not parasites too. In the end we suspect it's all vanity and delusion. Parasites, all of us."

"Yeah," Spermwhale said, trying to think of where they could get a free or half price meal tonight now that greedy Roscoe Rules had burned up their eating spot at Sam's by not only demanding free food for himself and Dean, but wanting four hamburgers to go after they finished. Roscoe Rules could fuck up a wet dream, Spermwhale said.

"Do you know how sad it would be to live in a place where a woman couldn't walk on the street after certain hours because she would either be robbed, raped or taken for a prostitute?"

"I don't think about it," Spermwhale answered.

"See that pedestrian underpass? When I worked Juvenile I met with some black mothers who said that six children were hit by cars at this intersection in one school year and yet the underpass had to be fenced off and locked up because juvenile muggers made it dangerous to use. The city couldn't keep lights in the tunnel. They were broken twice a day. So it's locked up and the children get hit by cars."

"What can we do about that kind a bullshit? It's not our problem."

"It's somebody's problem. I caught two of the muggers down there one day waiting to rip off the smaller kids for their lunch money. They were loaded from sniffing paint and had felony records from when they were ten years old. At the hearing the judge went along with the defense contention that I should've had the paint analyzed in the lab to determine if the kids really were under the influence of paint. I told them we were talking about the health of these boys. They were staggering when I busted them. But the case got kicked and . . ."

"Look, the whole juvenile justice system is a fuckin joke. Everybody knows that, so what's new?"

"It's just that it used to be an equity proceeding. It was supposedly for the good of the child. Now every kid has the public defender representing him and it's just as adversary as adult court. Kids are taught early on to get a mouthpiece and keep their mouths shut."

"That's the way it should be, you want my opinion. Give every five year old a shyster. Then send em to the joint if you convict em."

"But at sentencing it reverts to an equity court or a burlesque on one, and a kid who should be taken away from his miserable home is left on the streets after the fifth serious felony. It's crazy. Juvenile court is a revolving door, and then suddenly the kid turns eighteen, goes out and commits a strong arm robbery just like always but ends up in *adult* jail for six months. Then he's crying for his mother and saying, 'But you always sent me home before. You always gave me another chance.' And he can't understand it and why should he?"

"Baxter, I'm startin to worry about where your head is. I mean if you're gonna start frettin about injustice in the system . . ."

"I just hated being a kiddy cop. I'm glad I'm out. Today's street warriors were yesterday's hoodlums but now they're government funded. Do you have any idea how many ineffectual parents with whiskey voices and unconcerned delinquent kids I've counseled? Hundreds. Thousands, maybe."

As Baxter talked, a black child about five years old stood at the corner and waited for the police car to drive off from the stop sign.

"Go ahead, kid," Spermwhale said, waving at the boy to cross.

But the child walked up to the car on the driver's side and grinned and said, "Who you lookin for?"

"I'm looking for a little guy in a blue shirt with two teeth missing in front," Baxter said. "Seen him around?"

The boy giggled toothlessly and said, "You really be lookin for Ladybug, ain't you?"

"Maybe, what's she doing wrong?" Baxter asked.

"She round behind the house right now wif her head in a glue bag," said the child.

"Well, we'd sure like to bust her, sonny," Spermwhale said. "But we got this big murder case to work on. Now you tell Ladybug to get her dumb head outta that glue bag, okay?'

"Okay, Mr. PO-lice."

The boy waved as Baxter drove away saying, "Bet Ladybug's mother runs off and leaves her in a county foster home. And I'll bet the county just places her right back with her when she comes off her little spree because the taxpayers can't afford to *keep* Ladybug in a foster home. And what the hell, if we supported every little black kid that's neglected . . ."

"I am *really* startin to worry about you, Baxter," Spermwhale said. "You are *really* startin to worry me with all this crybaby social worker bullshit. Man, you never shoulda left patrol and went to Juvenile. I don't know what happened to you workin with those kiddy cops but whatever it was you better get your mind together. Shine it on, baby."

"Okay," Baxter grinned, pushing his umber hair back from his forehead. "I'm just going to shine it on."

But Baxter Slate wasn't sure what in his life he should shine on, unless it was Foxy Farrell. And anyone with an ounce of sense should know that. But the more despondent he had become lately, the more he wanted Foxy Farrell. The five foot two inch, ninety-eight pound, copper haired nude dancer somehow scratched deep and bewildering itches in Baxter's soul.

And no other girl would do though there were many possibilities. Baxter Slate's imposing figure, penetrating green eyes, heavy lashes and wide boyish grin made him quite popular with the clerk typists around the station as well as with the single girls in his apartment building. He tried to enjoy other women and made it a point to stay away from Foxy for days at a time. But he would always go back and despise her as she laughed and talked obscenely about what she didn't do to other men in his absence, while she did it to him. And afterward she would chatter about a flashy boyfriend of one of the dancers and talk of how cute and sexy he was and why didn't Baxter dress in a white jump suit with a fur collar instead of a stupid woolly herringbone sport coat and a dumb striped necktie like a fucking schoolteacher.

Spermwhale had persuaded Baxter to take him to the Sunset Strip once after work to meet Foxy and the two policemen were taken backstage by a burly assistant manager. Foxy was standing nude in her dressing room combing her pubic hair and pushing the vaginal lips back inside before the second show.

"Flops out once in a while," she smiled, upon seeing the two men standing there. "Hi, you must be Spermwhale. I'm Foxy."

"Yes, you are! You are!" cried Spermwhale Whalen. Spermwhale found that Foxy Farrell made him itch all over—to throw her down and bury his face in the burnished thatch of pubic hair which had been shaved to the shape of a heart, and dyed by squatting in a dish of hair color twice a month and brushing it carefully.

"Jesus, Foxy," Baxter said, "can't you occasionally act like a . . . oh what's the use?"

"He's a prude," Foxy laughed, throwing her coppery hair over her shoulder and slipping into a sheer peignoir. "Baxter's such a prude. That's why we love each other."

And she stepped over to the disgusted young policeman and rubbed her naked body against him and pulled his face down to hers, holding him by the ears.

Spermwhale watched and swallowed twice and developed a diamond cutter which delighted Foxy Farrell.

Baxter Slate despised Foxy Farrell. Which was why he wanted to be with her every moment he was off duty and even dared to drive the black and white up to the Sunset Strip in full uniform and leave Spermwhale in the car while he sneaked in the back door of the nightclub and listened at the door, catching Foxy Farrell blowing some fat cat in the dressing room.

Baxter had actually done this twice and each time he had the presence of mind to leave without being seen and wait to deal with Foxy Farrell when he was off duty. The way he dealt with her the last time was to accuse and rage and finally slap her, which she didn't mind as long as he didn't raise lumps or make her so black and blue that it would show on the stage.

When his anger was spent and he fell in her arms she smiled. Peppermint breath. Perfumed. Overripe. "Baxter, sweetie, it's okay, it's okay. Mama *understands* her baby. Honest, honey, I didn't do nothing to that guy. Only fooled around with him a little. I wasn't Frenching him. It sounded like that because you were all upset and playing vice cop and your imagination ran away with you."

Baxter smiled grimly and said, "You disgusting bitch. You're worthless, you know that? Irredeemably worthless. Without honor. Without humanity. And someday somebody'll kill you. But really, what good would that do?"

Foxy smiled slant eyed and licked Baxter on the cheek. "Honest, honey," she purred, "I wouldn't go down there and kiss that rich man's cock and suck his balls like I'm gonna do to you right now. You know I wouldn't do that to no other man, don't you, honey?"

And while she did it, Baxter Slate clenched his teeth and whispered, "You worthless slut. You worthless slut. I hate you."

He whispered it again and again. She gave him the most sensual and agonizing moments of his entire life and this time even *she* enjoyed it and laughed excitedly all the way, her cheek throbbing where he had struck her.

Baxter seldom talked to Foxy Farrell cruelly. Usually he treated her like a perfect lady which she hated. And took her to intimate French restaurants which bored her. And brought her bottles of Bordeaux wines he really couldn't afford, which she served to other friends over icecubes. In fact she rather disliked everything about Baxter except that he was unquestionably good looking, and being a cop could get her out of minor scrapes with the law or at least might help if she were ever picked up by vice cops for going too far during her nude dancing routine. She sometimes did go too far and once was taken from the stage by a vice officer for pulling a customer's face into her bumping groin. A phone call to Baxter Slate saved Foxy from going to jail because the vice cop was an academy classmate of Baxter's and liked him very much, as did all other policemen with the exception of Roscoe Rules.

Eventually, Foxy Farrell found Baxter Slate a terrible bore and was starting to hate him as much as Spermwhale found Foxy Farrell exciting and was starting to love her. But she found a twenty-five year old pimp named Goldie Grant irresistible. He saw her whenever she could ditch Baxter and eventually he became her real old man instead of her play old man and moved in with her and let her support him and go down on lots of fat cats and high rollers for lots of money and beat her up maybe twice a month whether she needed it or not. They were very happy together and everyone said made a handsome couple.

When Baxter did not appear unhappy enough one night Foxy told a story of how a cute and sexy player had taken her out for a drink after work and tried to give her a hundred dollars just to let him push her face in his lap and only stopped when she told him how her boyfriend was a cop. And what a hard on the player had!

Then Foxy feigned hurt and shock when Baxter grinned crookedly and said, "What a cheap stupid little animal you are."

She pouted and said, "Honest, Baxter, I didn't do *this* to him." And she began the little charade which would end in his passionate moaning and her excited laughter.

But no matter how much she despised Baxter Slate, Foxy Farrell could not have begun to fathom how much he was starting to despise the same young man.

The relationship with Foxy Farrell had begun after Baxter's tour of duty at Wilshire Juvenile where he felt he failed miserably as a kiddy cop and had not prevented the demise of Tommy Rivers, age six and a half.

Of course no one guessed that Baxter Slate somehow felt responsible for the fate of Tommy Rivers.

What made Baxter think he could have prevented Tommy Rivers' death was that he had, before transferring to Juvenile, received the very first radio call to the home of Lena Rivers shortly after she was reunited with her then five year old son Tommy who in his blue sailor suit looked like little Shirley Temple with a haircut.

Lena Rivers had three children by the husband who preceded Tommy's father who was a petty officer in the U.S. Navy. Lena had farmed the boy out to her mother six months after his birth when the sailor shipped out for good and never returned. Lena Rivers had undergone shock treatments after that and had hated the sailor relentlessly and never wanted the child he spawned. Now, five years later, with Lena's mother ill, Lena had been forced to drive to the Greyhound Depot in downtown Los Angeles and pick up the little sailor who had traveled several hundred miles alone without a whimper, the darling of the bus.

The first thing Lena Rivers did, according to later statements from her other children, was to take Tommy home and tear the sailor suit from his body. Some weeks later Baxter Slate received a radio call to the Rivers house from a neighbor who reported that several older neighborhood children had begun hanging around the Rivers home and that some behaved as though they had been drinking. And that the new arrival, Tommy, seldom came outside and looked very sick when he did.

Baxter Slate, working alone on the daywatch at that time, had gone to the Rivers house and met Lena Rivers. She was drunk and dirty and her house was a mess. He had asked to see her youngest child and held his ground when she protested that he was taking a nap.

Finally, Lena Rivers did admit Baxter Slate to the child's room and he did in fact find the child: unwashed, fully clothed, in a crib too small for him. When Baxter later became a Juvenile officer and saw many neglected children he was to remember that Tommy Rivers' pants looked almost as though they were pressed flat on the bed but he did not realize at the time that starving children can often be distinguished from very thin children by the absence of buttocks.

But at that time Baxter Slate knew very little about starving children, never having been in war like some of the other choirboys. So he had retreated when Mrs. Rivers ordered him out of her house. Baxter had often retreated, especially when working alone, if he felt he was on shaky constitutional grounds. Baxter Slate had aways believed implicitly in limited police power, due process, the jury system. And even now though his years on the street had eroded his beliefs he still insisted on not overstepping his authority. This caused many partners to say, "Baxter's a good partner to work with, goes along with most anything you want to do, but he's so naive I think he was brought up in a bottle."

The Wilburn Military Academy was not exactly a bottle, but it was a hothouse for upper middle class children, which Baxter was until his mother foolishly lost her fat alimony-check by impetuously marrying an alarm clock manufacturer who lost most of his money by diversifying into offshore oil drilling. Then the years at the authoritarian Dominican boarding school taught the boy what pansies the teachers at Wilburn were as they *played* at being soldiers. God's army had much more dedicated generals. It was surprising that a boy who had been cuffed around and dealt with so strictly and splendidly educated in the traditional sense—virtually without parents unless one counted holidays and summers with Mom—would be the kind of policeman who would worry about human rights and due process. After all, they had always been denied him. But he *did* worry about such things. Fiercely. Even after he concluded that he had been a fool to entertain such notions.

Once, Baxter Slate, working alone in the West Adams district, saw a car driving by with two young white children waving frantically from the rear window and then dropping out of sight on the seat. The driver was a black man in a stingy brim hat. Baxter followed the car two miles for another glimpse of the white children, asking himself if he would be doing this had the driver been white, wondering if it were just a children's prank. Finally, Baxter turned on his red lights and stopped the car. The white children were crouched down on the seat in the rear, giggling. The man, a boyfriend of the children's mother, asked angrily, "Would you have stopped me if those kids had been black?" And Baxter Slate lied and said he would, but he never forgot.

Two weeks before Tommy Rivers died Baxter Slate received the second radio call to the Rivers home. This one from a neighbor on the other side of the street who reported that there was definitely something wrong. Tommy had come to live with his mother nine months before but had been seen only occasionally as he sat with a brother or sister in the front yard.

"I believe he's a sick boy," the woman had said to Baxter Slate when he responded to the radio call.

And this time Baxter Slate did overstep his authority a bit in demanding to see Tommy Rivers and scaring Lena Rivers with an implied threat to call in Juvenile officers if she refused.

Lena Rivers finally consented, and the gaunt young woman with bright darting eyes went to the bedroom and returned with a dirty but obviously fat and healthy child of seven who smiled at the policeman and asked to touch his gun.

"Satisfied?" Lena Rivers said. "Meddling neighbors oughtta mind their own business."

Baxter Slate looked at Lena Rivers, at her scraggly colorless ponytail and dark rimmed blinking eyes, at the face already starting to bloat from alcohol despite her skinny build and relative youthfulness.

"That little boy looks different from when I saw him last," said Baxter.

"When did you see him?" the woman slurred as Baxter smelled the booze.

"I was called here once before," Baxter said, still standing in the doorway. "I was the one you let into the bedroom to look at Tommy, remember?"

"Oh yeah. You're gonna spend your career hassling me, is that it?"

"No, I guess not," Baxter said.

Every skill he had picked up during his four years as a policeman told him that this woman was lying. As with most policemen the hardest thing to learn was what consummate liars people are, and it was even more difficult for Baxter because he had been brought up to believe there is such a thing as unvarnished truth and that most people speak it.

"Is that the same boy I saw before?" Baxter asked and he believed it was a lie when she said, "Of course it is!"

"What's your name, son?" Baxter asked, stooping and smiling at the child.

"Tommy Rivers," the boy said and looked up at his mother.

"I don't believe that's the same child I saw. He was thin, very very thin."

"So he's gained a few pounds. He was sick. Did my nosy neighbor tell you he was sick?"

And Baxter Slate nodded because the neighbor *had* said that, and yet . . .

"Look," Baxter said, trying his broad, winning smile on Lena Rivers, "this is my second call here. Tell you what, I'll just come in for a look around and then everybody'll be satisfied and you won't see me again. Okay?"

And then the woman stepped out on the porch in the sunlight and Baxter was no longer looking at her through the screen door and could see the yellow pouches around her sparkling demented eyes.

"You been cooperated with all you're gonna be. You got no right here and I want you outta my face and off my property. So I don't keep a spic and span house, so what? My kids're cared for and here's the one you're so goddamn worried about. Now tell that bitch she got any more complaints I'll go over there and kick her ass all over the neighborhood!"

Lena Rivers went inside and slammed the door, leaving Baxter Slate standing indecisively on the front porch.

For months after that Baxter wondered how much of his hesitancy would be attributed to his boarding school politeness and whether perhaps the more obtrusive working class produced the best cops after all, that perhaps police departments were foolish to recruit from any other social group.

But no matter how many times he postulated a hypothetical situation to other policemen, never daring to admit to them he had contact with Tommy Rivers, he had to come to the inescapable conclusion that very few would have stood on that porch. As tentative as Hamlet. Only to wipe sweat from his hat brim and drive away to another call.

The answers to his hypothetical question varied slightly:

"I think I'd have called for a backup unit and maybe a supervisor or Juvenile officer and gone on in. I mean if I really suspected she had switched kids on me." That from Father Willie Wright.

"I'da walked over the cunt and looked for the little whelp." That from Roscoe Rules.

Not one of the choirboys, and he asked each privately, had suggested that he would consider that there was not enough probable cause to enter the woman's home or cause her further discomfiture. Most agreed with Francis Tanaguchi who shrugged and said, "I don't worry about it when a little kid's safety's at stake. If the court wants to kick the case out, groovy, but I'll see that the kid's okay."

They thought it absurd even to consider constitutional questions which get in the way of police work. "We'll worry about the United States Supreme Court when we're writing our arrest reports," as Spencer Van Moot succinctly put it.

And Baxter Slate believed that was the general attitude of all policemen, not just the choirboys. It was absurdly easy for any high school graduate with a year's police experience to skirt the most sophisticated and intricate edict arrived at by nine aging men who could never guard against the fact that restrictive rules of law simply produced facile liars among policemen. There wasn't a choirboy who had not lied in probable cause situations to ensure a prosecution of a guilty defendant.

Not a choirboy except Baxter Slate who had heard too much about Truth and Honor and Sin in Dominican schools. Even Father Willie Wright lied but when he did it from the witness stand he always held his hands under his legs, fingers crossed.

And in the case of Tommy Rivers Baxter Slate need not have lied. He simply had to open the unlocked door and enter Lena Rivers' home and walk through her house ignoring her drunken threats and search for the real Tommy Rivers. But since he had only a suspicion, since he was not sure, since he could never be convinced that people lied so outrageously, since it was too bizarre to suspect foul play when Mrs. Rivers had several other healthy children, since he was Baxter Slate and not Roscoe Rules, he threw in his hand and lost to a bluff. And Lena Rivers was free to continue with her gradual murder of Tommy Rivers.

When Baxter Slate read Bruce Simpson's arrest report the first time, his heart was banging so loud he actually believed the man next to him could hear it, and he foolishly cleared his throat and shuffled his feet on the asphalt tile in the squadroom. The second time through the report he believed his heart had stopped, so shallow was his breathing. The third time through he didn't think about his heart at all.

Bruce Simpson's arrest report was a minor classic in kiddy cop circles because he did not write like most policemen in the bald vernacular: "Person reporting stated . . ."

Arresting officer Simpson composed a horror story which included every tiny fragment of gruesome detail—when it was necessary and when it was not. Simpson did it because there was a policewoman named Doris Guber, whose pants Simpson was trying to penetrate, who loved to work the sex detail and always asked teenage runaways about their illicit sex lives and included in her reports exactly how many times an illicit penis was inserted and withdrawn from an illicit vagina. Which wasn't all that important to the prosecution of delinquent youngsters.

Doris always loved to find out about the orgasm, whether it occurred, and if so how big it was and of what duration. She'd get Simpson hot just talking about it so he started doing his reports the same way.

"Did you have an orgasm with the girl?" Doris once asked a surly eighteen year old black boy she wanted to prosecute for banging his neighbor.

"Did I have a what?"

"Did you come?" asked Doris Guber, eyes shining.

"Oh yeah. Like a hound dog."

Bruce Simpson's inimitably colorful prose left nothing out. The pages reeked of agony and death. He described how Lena Rivers had shredded the little sailor suit from Tommy Rivers the first day. He hypothesized how Tommy had resembled the long gone, fair haired sailor who had shattered the romantic dreams of Lena Rivers by taking his discharge from the Navy and heading for parts unknown. Bruce Simpson delineated in the sharpest detail how Tommy Rivers entered hell that day and was not released from torment until he died ten months later.

Lena Rivers had begun by subjecting Tommy to a sustained barrage of verbal abuse which was unrelenting up to and including the period when daily beatings gave way to starvation and torture. But as cruel as Lena Rivers was to Tommy she was kinder than ever before to her other three children who ranged in age from seven to ten. And she was exceptionally kind to the older children of the neighborhood and frequently entertained the teenage boys by supplying beer and gambling money from her bimonthly checks from the Bureau of Public Assistance and finally by deflowering three of them after a game of strip poker.

It became gossip among the adolescents of the block that Lena Rivers was awfully tough on the new arrival, her six year old son Tommy. Then later it was positively established that at least two of the lads, who were learning more than poker from Lena Rivers, had seen acts amounting to felony crimes committed on Tommy Rivers. Lena had been observed on two occasions thrusting the boy's hand into the flame of the gas stove for bedwetting. On another occasion she had ordered the child to copulate orally one of her poker playing sixteen year old lovers but the older boy claimed he declined, during his testimony at Lena's trial. Finally, no less than three teenage boys who were ordinary products of the ordinary neighborhood saw Lena Rivers carrying the naked, screaming, twenty-eight pound child through the house by a pair of pliers clamped to his penis.

Lena Rivers had less exotic punishment for Tommy Rivers during that ten month siege of terror, such as locking him in a kitchen broom closet every time he cried for his grandmother whom he would never see again. The broom closet eventually became a refuge for Tommy, and Lena Rivers would often forget he was there and leave him alone in the peaceful darkness for hours at a time. His older siblings sometimes brought food to him beyond his daily ration but never enough to sustain him in health, and eventually the broom closet became his permanent bedroom. He built himself a nest of rags and newspapers next to a water heater which was warm in the night.

Baxter Slate was always to rationalize that even if he had been less indecisive that day he might never have found the little figure cowering in the corner of the broom closet, might never have verified his suspicions that Lena Rivers had shown him the wrong son.

Baxter was to question more experienced Juvenile officers at a later time and consult texts on abnormal psychology and ask again and again: "But *how* could the other children, especially the older neighborhood children, have failed to report it to the police? They *knew* what was going on. Even the little ones knew how wrong it was!"

But the most frequent explanation was: "Kids are awfully curious and have a morbid fascination for the bizarre. She was supplying booze and sex for the older ones and her own could see by Tommy what could happen to them if Mama stopped loving them, so . . ."

Later as a kiddy cop Baxter encountered case after case of witnesses who ignored flagrant acts of brutality, not just youngsters, but adults: neighbors and family. Then Baxter Slate, former Roman Catholic, age twenty-six, learned how tenuous is the life of the soul. And realized that his soul, if he truly had one, was starting to die.

Baxter asked for and received a transfer back to patrol for "personal reasons" and decided to quit police work. But he made inquiries and discovered how valueless was his education in the classics. He had an offer to teach elementary school but that job was conditional since Baxter did not have a teaching credential and had not the ambition to get one. And actually, policemen received a better wage.

So he became satisfied with working uniform patrol again and did not aspire to a more exalted position. He never again tried to borrow money from his mother who was now divorced for the fourth time, and most of all he was very cautious never to let anyone know he was intelligent and educated since it could offend people like Roscoe Rules who assumed that Baxter had studied police science in college.

Baxter always made it a point to throw a few "don'ts" in place of "doesn'ts" in his conversation with other policemen and unless he was drunk at choir practice he never used adverbs in the presence of Roscoe Rules who became infuriated because it sounded so faggy.

Tommy Rivers, reduced to a shroud of flesh on a little skeleton, eventually died from the blow of a hammer that a healthy child could probably have survived. Lena Rivers was arrested, giving Bruce Simpson the opportunity to titillate Doris Guber with his purple prose. And Baxter Slate quit being a Juvenile officer because he thought he was the worst one in history and intensified his relationship with Foxy Farrell. He only broke it off when during their mating she bit into his chest so savagely she tore the skin and kissed him with a bloody mouth crooning, "You liked it, Baxter! You *liked* it, you bastard! Admit it, you pig motherfucker! Want me to do it again? Or do you want me to tell you what I did to Goldie last night after I left you? Goldie's cock is so . . ."

And then Baxter was weeping for shame and fury and was backhanding Foxy Farrell and more blood was on her mouth mixing with his blood. Then her eyes glassed over and she held his wrists and the words dripped like blood from thin dark lips: "That's enough. I know what you like, honey. It's okay. Mama knows. Mama *knows*."

So after he stopped being a kiddy cop and after he stopped thinking so much about the things Foxy Farrell had taught him about himself which he never should have learned and after he started dating other women and trying to enjoy a more ordinary sex life, Baxter Slate became the only choirboy to kill a man in the line of duty. He killed the ordinary guy.

Baxter and Spermwhale liked to meet for coffee with the other north end cars, particularly 7-A-29, manned by Sam Niles and Harold Bloomguard. They would meet at about 7:00 P.M. on week nights at the drive-in on Olympic Boulevard when the air wasn't too busy.

Policemen always asked, "How's the air?" or "The air busy?" referring to the radio airwaves which directed their working lives. "Quiet air" was what the policemen longed for so that they could be free to cruise and look for real crooks instead of being twenty-five year old marriage counselors to fifty-five year old unhappily married couples.

To Baxter Slate quiet air meant only a prolonged coffee break at the drive-in, where they might meet one or two other radio cars and hope an angry citizen didn't call the station and report them for bunching up and wasting taxpayers' money by swilling coffee instead of catching burglars and thieves.

It was usually the same outraged citizen who, when getting a traffic ticket by a policeman who was *not* drinking coffee, would demand to know why he was writing tickets instead of catching burglars and thieves. The same question about burglars and thieves was asked of narcotics officers by dopers and of vice cops by whores, tricks and gamblers. And of motor cops by drunk drivers.

Burglars and thieves sometimes complained that they only committed crimes against property, not like muggers and rapists. Muggers and rapists never faulted policemen at all, which caused the choirboys to comment that as a rule muggers and rapists were the most appreciative people they contacted.

But Baxter just wanted to drink coffee on the night he killed the ordinary guy. He was content to sit at the drive-in with Spermwhale and joke with the carhops.

While Baxter and Spermwhale drank their coffee a Porsche pulled in beside them and Spermwhale remarked to the lone driver that her blonde hair was complemented by the canary yellow Porsche.

The girl laughed and said, "How many girls do you stop for tickets because their hair coordinates with their paint jobs?"

"None that I ever wrote a ticket to," Spermwhale leered as Baxter automatically put his hand on his gun because a man shuffled over to the left side of the car with his hand inside a topcoat.

It was seventy-five degrees that night but the man wore his tan trench coat turned up. He also wore a black hat with a wide brim that had been out of style for twenty years but was now coming back. His face was round and cleft like putty smashed by a fist.

He reached inside his coat, and while Spermwhale talked to the girl with canary hair, he flipped out toy handcuffs and a plastic wallet with a dime store badge pinned inside. He said, "I'm working this neighborhood. Any tips for me? Anybody you're after? Be glad to help out."

Baxter relaxed his gun hand and still sitting behind the wheel of the radio car, looked up at the man, at the vacant blue eyes peering out from under the hat brim, with a hint of a mongoloid fault in those eyes. Baxter guessed the man's mental age to be about ten.

Spermwhale just shook his head and said, "Partner, you're a born blood donor," because Baxter Slate dug through their notebook and found some old mug shots of suspects long since in jail and gave them to the retardee who could hardly believe his good fortune.

"Gosh, thanks!" said the play detective. "I'll get right on the case! I'll find these guys! I'll help you make the pinch!"

"Okay, just give us a call when you find them," Baxter smiled as the young man shuffled away, beaming at the mug shots.

After being unable to entice a telephone number from the laughing girl in the yellow Porsche, Spermwhale looked at her license number and ran a DMV check over the radio, writing down her name and address. Then he leaned out the window of the police car and said, "You know, you remind me of a girl used to live up in Hollywood on Fountain, next to where I used to live."

The girl looked stunned and said, "You lived on Fountain?"

"Yeah," Spermwhale said convincingly. "There was this girl, lived in the six thousand block. I used to see her coming out her apartment. I fell in love with her but I never met her. Once I asked the manager of her building what her name was and he said, Norma. You sure look like her."

"I look . . . but that's me! My name's Norma!"

And then she saw Baxter grinning and she reddened and said, "Okay, how'd you know? Oh yeah, my license plate. Your radio. Oh yeah."

"But it coulda happened like that," Spermwhale said, his scarred furry eyebrows pulled down contritely.

"Well, since you have my name and address, I might as well give you my phone number," said the girl with the canary hair who was impressed with the powers of the law and by Baxter's good looks.

While Spermwhale flirted, Baxter sipped coffee and thought of how the smog had been at twilight. How blue it was and even purple in the deep shadows. Poison can be lovely, thought Baxter Slate.

Then another radio car pulled into the drive-in and parked in the last stall near the darkened alley and Baxter decided he'd leave Spermwhale to romance the blonde. Baxter left his hat and flashlight but took his coffee and strolled over to talk with the other choirboys.

And at that moment the rear door window on the passenger side of 7-A-77's car shattered before his eyes! Then the front fender went THUNK!

Calvin Potts screamed, "SOMEBODY'S SHOOTIN AT US!"

Baxter Slate dove to the pavement as the doors to the black and white burst open. Calvin and Francis were down with him crawling on their bellies and no one else, not even Spermwhale who had a blue veiner, even noticed.

Then Spermwhale turned down the police radio which had begun to get noisy and looked across the parking lot at the three choirboys on their bellies just as his windshield shattered and he went flying out the passenger door even faster than Lieutenant Grimsley when they put the angry ducks in his car.

"Did you see the flash?" yelled Baxter, who was on his knees scrambling for the protection of his black and white as business went on around them as usual. Car radios blared cacophonously. Dishes clattered. Trays clanged. People slurped creamy milkshakes. Chewed blissfully on fat hamburgers. Gossiped. No one perceived a threat. No one noticed four blue suited men crawling on their bellies. Finally, a miniskirted carhop stopped and said to Baxter, "Lose your contact lens or something, honey?"

Then all four policemen were on their feet running for a fence which separated the parking lot from the alley where the shots had to have come from.

Baxter got his wits about him and yelled, "Spermwhale, go call for help!"

Then gingerly shining his light through the darkness, Francis Tanaguchi shouted, "There's a rifle in the alley!"

Calvin Potts crawled forward out of sight for a few minutes, then, crouching, ran back out of the alley carrying a modified .22 caliber rifle with a tommy gun grip and an infrared scope lovingly mounted on the stock. The gun could fire hollow points almost as fast as you could pull the trigger, and what possibly saved the policemen was that the sniper had jammed the gun in his excitement.

Baxter Slate was the first to suggest driving around to the street on the west, and while Francis and Calvin quickly cleared glass from the seat, Baxter was squealing out, knocking coffee cups all over the parking lot as the siren of the nearest help car could already be heard in the distance.

Spermwhale asked to be dropped near the mouth of the alley on the next residential block west while Baxter circled one block farther on the theory that a man could run very far and fast after just having tried to ambush some policemen.

On St. Andrew's Place, Baxter Slate saw a dark running shadow. He jammed down the accelerator and the next sixty seconds became a fragmented impression as he screeched to a stop beside the running figure and jumped out in the darkness, gun drawn. He was met by a fanatical screaming charge by what turned out to be a weaponless man, and for once Baxter Slate did not intellectualize. He simply obeyed his instinct and training and emptied his gun at point blank range, hitting the man three times out of six, one bullet cracking through the left frontal lobe killing him almost at once. He discovered that unlike choreographed slow motion movie violence the real thing is swift and oblique and incoherent.

After intensive interrogation by the Robbery-Homicide Division shooting team and after his own reports were written, a pale and tense Baxter Slate met the other nine choirboys at MacArthur Park and tried to fill them in as best he could on the details. The trouble was there weren't any.

The young man's name was Brian Greene, and luckily for Baxter his fingerprints *were* found on the rifle. He was twenty-two years old. He was white. He had no arrest record. He had no history of mental illness. The Vietnam War was long over and he was not a veteran. He was not a student. He cared nothing about politics. He was a garage mechanic. He had a wife and baby.

Francis was beside himself that night at choir practice, not so much in fear but rage. And finally despair.

"So quit talkin about it," Calvin said. "I'm sick a hearin about it. The asshole tried to shoot us and it's over and that's it."

"But Calvin, don't you see? He didn't even *know* us. We're just . . . just . . . blue symbols!"

"Okay, so we're blue," Calvin reminded him. "You only see black and blue around the ghetto when the sun goes down."

"But we were on Olympic Boulevard. That's not a ghetto. He was white. Why'd he shoot? Who *was* he? Doesn't he know we're more than bluecoats and badges? It's weird. I don't know where these people are coming from. I dunno."

"I dunno where *you're* comin from," Calvin said angrily.

"I dunno where I'm coming from either," Francis said. "I don't know where my head is."

"What fuckin Establishment did we represent to him?" Spermwhale demanded to know. "I'm tired a bein a symbol! I'm not a symbol to my ex-wives and ex-kids. Why does an ordinary guy wanna shoot me?"

And all the choirboys looked at each other in the moonlight but there were no answers forthcoming.

"I didn't want to kill him," Baxter Slate said quietly. "I never wanted to kill anybody."

It was suddenly cold in the park. They were ecstatic when Ora Lee Tingle showed up and hinted she might pull that train.

10

7-A-29: Sam Niles and Harold Bloomguard

Lieutenant Finque had a splitting migraine at rollcall on the night Sam Niles and Harold Bloomguard met the Moaning Man and called for choir practice.

The migraine was brought about by his defense of the Police Protective League, the bargaining agent manned by Los Angeles police officers for the department.

"How the fuck can the Protective League do anything for us?" Spermwhale demanded. "As long as brass're members of the league. Don't you see, the league gotta be more like a real union. It's management against labor. You people are management. Only the policeman rank and maybe sergeants should be in the league. The rest of the brass are the *enemy*, for chrissake!"

"That's not true!" Lieutenant Finque said. "The commanders and the deputy chiefs are just as much police officers as . . ."

"My ass, Lieutenant!" Spermwhale roared. "When did you last hear of a deputy chief gettin TB or a hernia or whiplash or pneumonia or shot or beat up or stabbed? Only cop's disease they ever get is heart trouble and that's not cause they have to jump outta radio cars and run down or fight some fuckin animal who wants to make garbage outta them, it's cause they eat and drink so much at all those sex orgies where they think up ways to fuck and rape the troops!"

"How many deputy chiefs or commanders ever get suicidal?" Baxter Slate asked suddenly, and for a moment the room was quiet as each man thought of that most dangerous of policemen's diseases.

"Yeah, it's usually the workin cop who eats his gun," Spermwhale said as he unconsciously thought of at least ten men he had served with who had done it.

"I'd hate to be a member of this department if we ever go from the Protective League to a labor union," Lieutenant Finque solemnly announced with the consuming hatred and distrust of labor unions that was prevalent in those police officers who had sprung from the middle class and whose only collective bargaining experiences had been as Establishment representatives facing angry sign wavers on picket lines.

"Protective League my ass!" Spermwhale Whalen said. "They take our dues and wine and dine politicians while I eat okra and gumbo at Fat Ass Charlie's Soul Kitchen."

"I thought you like eatin like a home boy, Spermwhale," Calvin Potts grinned.

"We gotta sue the fuckin city for nearly every raise we get," Spermwhale continued. "I'm sick a payin dues to the Protective League. I get more protection from a two year old box a rubbers!"

"Anyone for changing the subject?" Sergeant Nick Yanov suggested, as the lieutenant held his throbbing head and vowed to check Spermwhale Whalen's personnel package to see how many more months he had to go before retirement. And to ask the captain if there weren't a place they could transfer him until then. Like West Valley Station which was twenty-five miles away.

Lieutenant Finque's eyes were starting to get as red and glassy as Roscoe Rules' always were. Of late the lieutenant always had drops of grainy white saliva glued to the corners of his mouth from his incessant sucking of antacid tablets.

"I'm going to change the subject, change the subject," Lieutenant Finque announced strangely. "The captain inspected the shotgun locker and found a gun with cigars stuffed down the barrel! If that happens again somebody's going to pay!"

No one had to turn toward Spermwhale who was the only cigar smoker on the watch. "Young coppers they hire these days'll rip you off for anything," said Spermwhale. "Gotta hide your goods, Lieutenant."

Lieutenant Finque had begun losing weight of late what with his migraines and acid stomach and inability to relate with Captain Drobeck who had turned down three dinner invitations this month despite the fact that Lieutenant Finque had done everything he could think of to woo the captain, including joining his American Legion Police Post. The lieutenant knew he should be clear headed what with the ordeal of studying for the captain's exam three hours a day when his wife and children would leave him alone. And here at the job he had to deal with recalcitrant uglies like Spermwhale Whalen.

"Let's read some crimes," the watch commander said, picking up a sheaf of papers. "There was an ADW on a teacher at the high school. Says here a thirty-four year old schoolteacher had just started her third period when . . ."

"Kind of late in life, ain't it?" Francis Tanaguchi giggled and Lieutenant Finque jerked spasmodically and tore the report.

Lieutenant Finque blinked several times and simply could not regain the thread. "This report's terrible. It's sloppy. Who did it?" And his eyes were so watery he couldn't read the name.

"Just a few pencigraphical errors, sir," said the culprit, Harold Bloomguard.

"Uh . . . Intelligence has a rumor," Lieutenant Finque said, forgetting the crimes and going on disjointedly to a note in the rotating folder. "We may have a riot in the vicinity of Dorsey High School between four and four-thirty this afternoon. Some militant . . ."

"A half hour riot?" said Calvin Potts and Lieutenant Finque's thread came totally unraveled. He began talking to Sergeant Yanov on his right as though they were alone in the room.

"You know, Yanov, there's a rumor that these young Vietnam vets they're hiring these days are smoking pot. You see how hard it is to make them keep their hair off their collars and their moustaches trimmed? And there's a rumor about *fragging!* Someone heard some policemen talking about bombing a watch commander!"

"I'll read the crimes," Sergeant Yanov said abruptly, putting a steadying hand on Lieutenant Finque's arm while the assembly of policemen looked at one another in growing realization. "Let's see, here's one to perk up your evening. A rapist stuck his automatic down in his belt while he made the victim blow him and he got so excited he shot his balls off right in the middle of the headjob!"

The explosion of cheers startled the shit out of Lieutenant Finque who thought he was being fragged. He only kept from jumping up because Sergent Yanov's strong left hand held his arm pressed to the table top as the sergeant regained control of the rollcall.

"Keep an eyeball out for Melvin Barnes," Sergeant Yanov continued. "His picture's on the board. Local boy and he's running from his parole officer. He'll be around Western Avenue. He likes to run because he's a celebrity on the avenue when the cops're looking for him. But he'll be around because he doesn't mind getting busted. He's an institutional man. There're thousands like him."

"Amen," Spermwhale Whalen said. "Ask me, I think half the fuckin population craves some kind of institution or other. They can't get it, they'll get taken care of some other way. If we just made our jails comfortable, gave the boys some pussy and all, shit, we couldn't blast em out on the streets. Be a lot cheaper makin em happy and keepin em inside the rest a their lives than runnin them through the fuckin system over and over again while a few people get hurt along the way."

"You got lots of ideas, Spermwhale," said Harold Bloomguard. "Ever consider getting perverted to sergeant?"

As Sergeant Yanov got everyone in a better frame of mind to go out into the streets, Lieutenant Finque sat going through some envelopes which came to him through department mail. The voice of Yanov and the others seemed far away. He never noticed Francis Tanaguchi grin at his partner Calvin Potts when the lieutenant tore open the last envelope. It was a crime lab photo of a ninety year old black woman who had been dead for three weeks when her body was found and the picture taken. Her white hair was electric. Her silver eyes were open and her blackened tongue protruded. The note attached to the photo said, "Dear Lieutenant Finque, how come you don't come to see me no more now that you transferred to the westside? You cute little blue eyed devil!"

The lieutenant blinked and twitched and hoped he could get out of the station this night alive without being either framed or fragged. He stood up suddenly and said something unintelligible to Sergeant Yanov before walking out the door.

That night someone put a taped roll of freeway flares attached to a cheap alarm clock under the watch commander's desk when Lieutenant Finque was having coffee. At 10:00 P.M. the bomb squad was at Wilshire Station assuring the captain by telephone that it was not dynamite but only a prank evidently played by some member of the nightwatch. At 11:00 P.M. Lieutenant Finque left Daniel Freeman Hospital severely tranquilized. He was off sick for seven days with something not unlike combat fatigue. Due to his splendid record as a whistle salesman he was taken downtown and made the adjutant of Chief Lynch. He was definitely an up-and-comer.

At six feet two inches and 185 pounds Sam Niles was not a particularly big man but next to Harold Bloomguard he felt like Gulliver. Harold Bloomguard was, at 149 pounds on a delicate frame, the smallest choirboy of them all. He had gorged himself with a banana-soybean mixture for three days to pass his original police department physical.

The choirboys always said that what Harold lacked in physical stature he made up for in physical weakness. Both Ora Lee Tingle and Caroline Moon had beaten him in arm wrestling on the same night at choir practice, and Harold, who usually loved fun and frolic, waded off in his underwear and sulked with the ducks on Duck Island. He wouldn't come back until all of the choirboys had either gotten drunk or gone home.

"What's it all about, Harold? What's it all about, Harold?" cried Whaddayamean Dean to the lonely white figure huddled in the darkness of Duck Island which was a thirty by thirty mound of dirt and shrubbery in the middle of the large duck pond they called MacArthur Lake.

"What'd he say, Dean?" asked Harold Bloomguard's partner, Sam Niles, as Whaddayamean Dean rejoined the choirboys who were trying to persuade Carolina

Moon to pull that train even if she *was* tired from being on her feet all night hustling drinks at the Peppermint Club in Hollywood.

"What'd who say?"

"Harold! Who the hell were you just off yelling at, for chrissake!"

"I don't know," said Whaddayamean Dean, his brow screwed in confusion.

"Harold Bloomguard, goddamnit!" said Spermwhale, who got more pissed off at Whaddayamean Dean than anyone since Spermwhale more or less looked after him when he was drunk like this.

"You were yelling at Harold over on Duck Island, weren't you?" asked Ora Lee Tingle patiently as Francis Tanaguchi crawled around behind her on the grass in his LAPD baseball shirt with number 69 on the back and pinched her ample buttocks and yelled when she punched him in the shoulder and knocked him over the cushiony Carolina Moon who grabbed him and smothered him in her enormous breasts and chubby arms and said, "Ya cute little fuckin Nip, ya!"

"I admit I was yelling but I don't remember at who," said Whaddayamean Dean, wishing everyone would stop picking on him and just let him drink and lie down on top of Ora Lee Tingle and rest his brain for a while. "I think I heard someone answer."

"Well, you simple asshole, what'd he say?" demanded Spermwhale.

"I think he said, 'Quack quack.' "

As all the choirboys moaned and fell over and rolled their eyes disgustedly, Spermwhale grabbed Whaddayamean Dean by the back of the Bugs Bunny sweatshirt and said, "That was a fuckin duck! Ducks say quack quack. Harold don't say quack quack. You was talkin to a duck!"

"At least he didn't yell at me," Whaddayamean Dean sniffled and a large salty globular tear rolled out his left eye. "I don't know what you mean. What're you trying to say? Why is everybody picking on me? Huh? Huh?"

And so they gave up and left Whaddayamean Dean to finish his vodka and within three minutes he forgot that everyone had been picking on him and that Harold Bloomguard was almost naked and alone with the ducks on Duck Island. As a matter of fact, everyone forgot Harold Bloomguard but Sam Niles, and he would like to have forgotten.

At 5:00 A.M., when only the two girls and three of the choirboys were left sprawled on their blankets, Sam Niles stripped down and waded through the sludge to Duck Island, knocked the sleeping ducklings off Harold Bloomguard's shivering body, shook him awake and dragged him through the cold dirty water to his blanket and clothes. But Sam decided that Harold was too covered with filth to put him in Sam's Ferrari so he broke the lock on the park gardening shed with a rock and found a hose with a strong nozzle. Then he forced the protesting Harold Bloomguard to stand shivering on the grass and be sprayed down from head to foot before drying in the blankets and dressing.

"I'd never do this to you, Sam!" Harold screamed as the merciless jet of water stung and pounded him and shriveled his balls to acorns.

"You're not getting in my Ferrari covered with that green slimy duck shit," said Sam Niles who had a thundering headache.

"I loaned you part of the down payment!" reminded Harold and shrieked as the spray hit him in the acorns, waking up Roscoe Rules who saw two nearly nude men by the gardening shack and figured it was a pair of park fairies.

Roscoe belched and shouted, "All you faggy bastards in this park better keep the noise down or I'll make you do the chicken!" And then he went back to sleep.

When Harold was relatively clean Sam Niles vowed that somehow, someday, he would rid himself of Harold Bloomguard who was by his own admission a borderline mental case.

Sometimes Sam Niles felt that he had always been burdened with Harold Bloomguard, that there had never been a time in his life when there was not a little figure beside him, blinking his large hazel eyes, cracking his knuckles, scratching an ever-present pimply rash on the back of his neck with a penknife and worst of all unconsciously rolling his tongue in a tube and blowing spit bubbles through the channel into the air.

"It's sickening!" Sam Niles had informed Harold Bloomguard a thousand times in the seven years he had known him. "Sickening!"

And Harold would agree and swear never to do it again, and whenever he would get nervous or bewildered or frightened by one of the several hundred neurotic fears he lived with, he would sit and worry and his tongue would fold in two and little shiny spit bubbles would drop from his little pink mouth.

Sam Niles realized that at twenty-six, just four months older than Harold Bloomguard, he was a father figure. It had been that way since Vietnam where Harold Bloomguard more or less attempted to attach himself to Sam Niles for life, taking his discharge two months later than Sam and following him into the Los Angeles Police Department after returning to his family home in Pomona, California, where Harold's father practiced law and his mother was confined in a mental hospital.

It was always the same, with Harold begging Sam to sit quietly and help him interpret his latest dream full of intricate symbols, Sam always protesting that if Harold were really worried about joining his mother in the funny place, he should see a psychiatrist. The problem was that Harold Bloomguard always believed that it was her weekly session with a shrink that put his mother in the hospital in the first place, and until she went into psychotherapy when Harold was overseas, she was more or less an ordinary neurotic. So Sam Niles became the only psychiatrist Harold Bloomguard ever had and it had been this way since Sam took pity on the skinny weak little marine.

"Sam, I gotta tell you about the dream I had last night," Harold said as they left Wilshire Station at change of watch and drove into the gritty personal night world of police partners, most intimate perhaps because they might have to depend upon each other for their very lives.

"Yes, Harold yes," Sam sighed and pushed his fashionable, heavy, steel rimmed goggles up on his nose and promised himself to get his eyes examined because he was becoming more nearsighted than ever.

He cruised steadily through the traffic as Harold said, "There was this black cat that crossed my path and I was very afraid and couldn't understand it and I reached in my pocket and pulled out an eight inch switchblade to defend myself from I don't know what as I walked down this dark street with apartments on both sides. God, it was awful!"

"So what happened then?"

"I can't remember. I think I woke up."

"That's it?"

"Sure. It's horrible! Makes my hands sweat to think about it."

"What's so horrible?"

"Don't you see? The knife is phallic. The cat is a pussy. It's black. Black pussy. I'm unconsciously wanting to rape a black woman! Just before I crack up like my mother that's what I'll probably do, rape a black woman. Watch me very carefully around black women, Sam. As a friend I want you to watch me."

"Harold, I've watched you around black women and white women. You're perfectly normal with women. For God's sake, Harold . . ."

"I know, I know, Sam. You think it's my imagination, these deep stirrings in my twisted psyche. I know. But remember my mother. My mother is mad, Sam. The poor woman is mad!"

And Sam Niles would push up his slipping glasses, finger his brown moustache, light a cigarette and search for something else for Harold to worry about, which was generally the way to shut him up when any particular obsession was getting too obsessive.

"Harold, you know you're losing some hair lately? You noticed that?"

"Of course I've noticed," Harold sighed, touching his ginger colored sideburns. He admired Sam Niles' deep brown hair and his several premature gray ones in the front. Harold admired everything about Sam Niles, always had from the days when Sam was his fire team leader at the spider holes, and though they were in the same police academy recruit class, Harold always treated him with the deference due a senior partner and let him be the boss of the radio car. Harold even admired Sam's steel rimmed goggles and wished he was nearsighted so he could wear them.

Sam Niles admired almost nothing about Harold Bloomguard and especially did not admire his annoying habit of amusing himself with doubletalk.

Harold would tell about a traffic accident that befell 7-A-77 the night before which resulted in a "collusion at the interjection" of Venice and La Brea. Or when Sam asked where he would like to take their code seven lunch break Harold might say, "It's invenereal to me."

Or in court Harold would ask the DA if he had any "exterminating evidence." And then ask if the DA wanted him to "draw a diaphragm." On and on it went and became almost as unbearable as the plinking spit bubbles.

But none of that was as bad as Harold Bloomguard's relentlessly sore teeth. He claimed he was a sufferer of bruxism and that he ground his teeth mercilessly in his sleep. If the nightmares were memorable the night before Harold would eat soup and soppy crackers during code seven.

But as with Harold's other maladies, Sam Niles suspected it was imaginary. He had once demanded to see Harold Bloomguard's teeth at choir practice and Ora Lee held Harold's head in her comfy lap while Father Willie struck matches for all the choirboys to examine Harold's molars which were not flat and worn down but were as sharp and serviceable as anyone's.

"They *are* worn down, I tell you," Harold said that night in the park. And he opened his mouth wider as Sam struck matches and everyone looked at his teeth.

"Let's see yours to compare, Roscoe," said Father Willie who was already very drunk.

Roscoe Rules only agreed because he wanted to take Harold's place on Ora Lee's lap and cop a feel. But while they were comparing, Father Willie accidentally dropped a match down Roscoe's throat.

Then everyone started yelling frantically with Roscoe who got up and began jumping around.

"Gimme a drink!" Roscoe shrieked.

"Give him some bourbon!" shouted Spermwhale.

"No, it'll start a fire in his tummy!" yelled Ora Lee Tingle.

"Give him the fuckin bourbon then!" yelled Spermwhale.

But Roscoe had panicked and run for the duck pond and was on his belly drinking pond water.

"He'll get typhoid!" shouted Ora Lee Tingle.

"He might at that!" yelled Spermwhale hopefully.

"Stop, Roscoe, you'll get typhoid!" Carolina Moon yelled.

"Do what feels best, Roscoe!" shouted Spencer Van Moot.

A few minutes later, Roscoe walked back to the blankets very calmly and frightened everybody because, though he had a blister on his tonsils, he was actually smiling.

"Gee, I'm sorry, Roscoe!" said the terrified Father Willie as he sat down next to Roscoe and punched Roscoe's arm playfully. "You're not mad at me, are ya?"

And Roscoe still smiled as he said, "Heavens, no, Padre! Let's have a drink."

"Sure!" said the choirboy chaplain. "Here, have a shot of vodka."

"No," Roscoe smiled, pointing at his throat. "No thank you. Think I'd prefer beer."

"Oh sure, Roscoe," Father Willie said eagerly. "I'll get it."

Roscoe said quietly, "I think there's a full six-pack down by the water."

"There is? I'll get it for you," Father Willie said.

"I'll help you," Roscoe said, putting his arm around Father Willie's shoulder and strolling with him toward the duck pond.

Thirty seconds later the other choirboys were running headlong toward the pond to rescue the screaming padre whose neck was in the arm of Roscoe Rules who was trying his best to make Father Willie do the chicken. It took four choirboys to overpower Roscoe and pin him until he promised not to choke or kneedrop the chaplain. He only relented when Ora Lee Tingle promised him she'd let him be engineer the next time she pulled the choo choo.

Ironically it was Harold Bloomguard who got Sam Niles the temporary duty assignment to the vice squad which he had been hoping for. When asked by the vice lieutenant to work the squad for two weeks because they needed some new faces to use on the street whores, Harold had surprised the lieutenant by saying, "I know I don't look like a cop, I'm so little and all, but why don't you take my partner, Sam Niles, too? He doesn't look like a cop either."

"You kidding?" Lieutenant Handy said. "He's the dark haired kid with a moustache, isn't he?"

"Yeah."

"Got cop written all over him."

"He wears glasses," offered Harold. "Not too many policemen wear glasses, sir."

"No way. The girls'd make him for a cop in a minute. You're the one I want. We'll dress you up in a Brooks Brothers suit and they'll swarm all over you."

"Well sir," Harold said shyly. "I sure do appreciate it. You're the first one in the four and a half years I've been on the job who offered to put me in plainclothes. And I really do appreciate it. But . . ."

"Yeah?"

"You see, Sam and I were in the same outfit in Nam. And we've been radio car partners here at Wilshire for . . ."

"Okay. Look, I can bring in two more of you bluesuits for the two weeks. I'd already decided on Baxter Slate because he seems like a heads-up guy, and I'd decided on some morning watch kid. But if you just gotta have Niles, okay. I'll bring him along instead of the morning watch rookie."

"That's great, Lieutenant," Harold said. "You won't be sorry. Sam's the greatest cop I've ever worked with. And the greatest guy."

"Yeah, yeah, okay. We'll use you till the middle of August. Gonna have a little crusade against the whores. Let you know more about it later."

Sam Niles never knew about Harold's meeting with the vice squad lieutenant and was a little nonplussed when he heard that Harold Bloomguard was also being brought in.

"I've been trying for thirteen months to get a crack at vice," Sam Niles said to his partner on the night he was told. "What made them ask you, I wonder?"

"I dunno, Sam," Harold said. "Tagging along on your coattails, I guess."

But before they took their temporary vice assignment, Sam Niles and Harold Bloomguard were to have an experience which prompted Sam Niles to call for choir practice. It was before they worked vice, and before the August killing in MacArthur Park. Sam and Harold were to meet the Moaning Man.

They made a pretty good pinch, or almost did, five minutes out of the station that evening. It was four o'clock in the afternoon. Without question, the skinny hype in a long sleeved dress shirt at the corner of Fourth and Ardmore had to be suffering. And he had to be a hype, standing there on the sidewalk so weak and sick he didn't see the black and white gliding down the street against the late afternoon sun with Sam Niles behind the wheel and Harold Bloomguard writing in the log.

The hype was a Mexican: tall, emaciated, eyes like muddy water. He had recently recovered from hepatitis gotten from a piece of community artillery passed from junkie to junkie in an East Los Angeles shooting gallery.

"There's one that's hurtin for certain," Sam Niles said as he pulled the black and white into the curb, going the wrong way on the street.

Harold jumped out the door before the addict saw them. The addict spun and tried to walk away from Harold but Sam trotted up, grabbed him by the shirt and spun him easily into Harold's arms.

"Just freeze and let my partner pat you down," Sam Niles said and the hype responded with the inevitable, "Who me?"

"Oh shit," said Sam Niles.

As Harold finished the pat down on the front, neck to knee, and moved his hands around to the back, the hype made what he thought was a quick move for his belt but was grabbed in a wristlock by Sam Niles who lifted him up, up on his tippy toes and made him forget the other hurts plaguing him.

"Easy, goddamnit, easy!" yelped the hype.

"I told you not to make any sudden moves, baby." Sam crooked his arm around the hype's throat and applied just enough of a vise to the carotid artery to show him that the colorless odorless gas he breathed could be even more sweet and precious than the white crystalline chemical he had for twenty years buried in his arms and hands and legs and neck and penis.

"I got it, Sam." Harold stripped a paper bindle from the inside of the hype's belt where it had been taped.

"Pretty makeshift bindle, man," Sam Niles said, removing the pressure from the neck but keeping a wristlock which made the Mexican stand tall, sweating in the sunlight.

"Okay, okay, you got it," the hype said and Sam released the pressure.

"You sick?" Harold Bloomguard asked.

"Lightweight, lightweight," the hype said, wiping his eyes and nose on his shoulder while Sam Niles handcuffed his hands behind his back. "Listen, man, you don't wanna book me for that little bit a junk. I shoulda fixed. That'll teach me."

"Sick as you are, how come you *didn't* shoot it up?" Sam Niles asked when the hype was safely cuffed.

"This broad. Fucking broad. She was gonna pick me up here. Take me home. I was supposed to score and she was supposed to meet me here. She had the outfit and she digs on me. Oh Christ . . ." And he looked lovingly at the bindle in Harold's hand and said, "Look, I'll work for you. Gimme a break and I'll tell you where you can bring down a guy that deals in ounces. Just gimme a chance. I don't want no money, just a break. I'll be your main man for free. You can leave a little geez for me hidden away sometimes when you rip off a doper's pad. Just stash a dime bag or two in a corner and after you're gone with the guys I roll over on, I'll skate on in and pick it up. We can work like partners. You guys'll make more busts than the narcs! How about it?"

"Let's go," Sam Niles said, shoving the hype toward the police car but Harold's eyes widened as he envisioned the sick addict having international dope connections.

He said, "Sam, let's hear him out."

"Harold, for God's sake, this junkie'd say anything . . ."

"And burglars, Christ, I know a million of them!" the hype said, still handcuffed, talking desperately to Harold as Sam Niles tried to aim him toward the open door of the police car. "Mostly daytime burglars. All dopers. Lazy broads lay around in bed so long these days it's pretty hard to rip off the pads in the morning like we used to, but I still know lots and lots of burglars. Want a burglar, Officer . . . ?"

"Bloomguard."

"Officer Bloomguard, yeah. Want a burglar, Mr. Bloomguard?"

"Why not listen to him, Sam?" Harold asked as Sam Niles tried to push the addict down into the back seat of the police car.

"And tricks. Man, I can teach you a few tricks. You could learn something from me, Mr. Bloomguard. I been around this world over forty years. Been shooting dope since I was fifteen and I'm still alive. Listen, you know how to tell a hype even if he's healthy? Look for burn holes in his clothes and blisters on his fingers. When he's geezing and on the nod, he'll burn himself half to death when he's smoking cigarettes. That ain't a bad tip, is it?''

''Not bad,'' said Harold Bloomguard. ''Sam, lemme just talk to him for a minute.''

Sam Niles dropped his hands in disgust, threw his hat in the radio car, sat on the front fender of the black and white while the hype told Harold Bloomguard of his miserable life and his jealous rage at a girlfriend who had been cheating on him.

''. . . and I got me some plans for that bitch, Mr. Bloomguard. I'm gonna wait down the hall in her apartment house and when her new boy comes sneaking in, I'm gonna creep up behind him, see? I'm gonna hit him over the gourd with a wrench then I'm gonna drag him into the broom closet and pull down his pants and fuck him! Yeah! And then I'm gonna drag his beat-up, fucked over ass to my old lady's door and ring the bell and say, ''Here, bitch! Here's your girlfriend!''

''This guy's got style!'' Harold Bloomguard said to Sam Niles who replied, ''Oh yes. Real panache. Let's invite him to choir practice, Harold.''

''And listen, Officer, because you been nice enough to listen to me I'm gonna save you from embarrassment. Guess what? You want the real truth? I ain't even sure you can get me booked. Know why?''

''Why?'' asked Harold Bloomguard while Sam Niles was ready to throw the hype *and* Harold into the car.

''Because I think I mighta got burned on this score. This rotten motherfucker I bought the dope from sometimes tries to sell you pure milk sugar and hope you don't catch him for a few days. He's so strung out he'll do anything to make a little bread.''

''You think this is milk sugar?'' Harold asked and took the bindle out of the pocket of his uniform shirt as Sam Niles got off the car, stepped on his cigarette, adjusted his steel rimmed glasses and said, ''Harold, let's go.''

''I think it's probably milk sugar,'' the hype nodded, ''and you're gonna have to let me go soon as you run one of those funny little tests at the station. Taste it. I think it's pure sugar.''

''Harold!'' Sam Niles said as Harold opened the bindle curiously, making sure that the hype's hands were securely cuffed behind him.

''Harold!'' Sam Niles said, stepping forward just as Harold licked his finger to touch the sugar and just as the hype made good his promise to teach Harold a few tricks.

The addict blew the gram of heroin out of the bindle into the air and Sam Niles watched the powder fall to the Bermuda grass at his feet and disappear.

''Oh God,'' said Harold Bloomguard, dropping to his knees, pulling up grass, looking for the evidence the hype had just blown away.

The addict held his breath for a moment as Sam Niles stepped forward towering over him, gray eyes smoldering. But then Sam Niles wordlessly unlocked the addict's handcuffs, put them in his handcuff case, returned the key to his key ring, took the car keys from the belt of his Sam Browne and got behind the steering wheel while Harold Bloomguard crawled around the grass searching for a few granules of powder.

''I don't think you could even pick it up with a vacuum,'' the hype said sympathetically. ''It's very powdery. And there was only a gram.''

''Guess you're right,'' said Harold Bloomguard, getting in the police car beside the silent Sam Niles just in time to keep from losing a leg as Sam squealed from the curb heading for the drive-in for a badly needed cup of coffee.

''Sorry, Sam,'' Harold smiled weakly, not looking at his grim partner.

The junkie waved bye-bye and decided that Harold was a very nice boy. The addict hoped that all five of the sons he had fathered to various welfare mothers would turn out that nice.

It was almost ten minutes before Harold Bloomguard spoke to Sam Niles which was probably a record for Harold Bloomguard who sat and tried to think of something conciliatory to say.

Unable to think of something he decided to entertain Sam.

"It was consti-pa-tion, I know," sang Harold Bloomguard to the melody of "Fascination," watching Sam Niles who did not smile, which forced Harold to sing, "I'll be loving you, maternally. With a love that's true . . ."

Getting only a languid sigh from Sam Niles he switched to a livelier melody and sang, "Gee, but it's great after eating my date, walking my baby back home."

Finally Sam Niles spoke. He said, "Harold, I don't mind your dumb songs but if you don't stop scratching those pimples on your neck with that penknife, I'm gonna stick it up your ass."

And then Harold tried to forget about losing the heroin by remembering a disturbing dream he had last Thursday and had not yet discussed with his partner. And as he concentrated he folded his tongue into a long pink tube and blew little spit bubbles which plinked wetly on the dashboard and made Sam Niles grind his teeth.

"Sam, there's something I'd like your advice about."

"Yes, yes, yes. What the hell is it this time?"

"I think I'm getting impotent."

"Uh huh."

"I haven't awakened one morning in the past week with a diamond cutter. Or even a blue veiner."

"You're not impotent."

"How do you know that, Sam? I mean how do you know it's not happening to me? I was reading about impotency recently and . . ."

"Stop reading, Harold. That's part of your problem. You read about these diseases and then you've got the symptoms."

"You think it's hypochondria but . . ."

"You're going to choir practice too often. Cool it for a while. Too much booze makes a limp noodle. Also you're getting old. Twenty-six. You're over the hill. At your age you should drink Vano starch instead of booze."

"It's not funny, Sam. It's serious."

"Really scares you, huh, Harold?"

"Indeed," said Harold and Sam Niles gritted his teeth again. He had come to hate the word "indeed" because it was one of Harold's favorite expressions.

"Well, I'll tell you, Harold. Being impotent wouldn't be too bad for you because Carolina Moon and Ora Lee Tingle are just about the only broads you ever ball lately and I think you only do that to be a respectable member of an unrespectable group that gets drunk once a week and gangbangs two fat cocktail waitresses."

"That's not fair of you to say that, Sam. You know some of us don't approve of more than one guy mounting the same girl the same night. You and Baxter and Dean never do it. You know *I* don't."

"You did it last week!"

"I didn't!"

"Then what the hell were you and Ora Lee doing off in the bushes?"

"Only fooling around. I just can't board the train like horny old Spencer or that pig Roscoe Rules."

"Did you have a blue veiner?"

"A diamond cutter as a matter of fact."

"Then what makes you think you're impotent?"

"Because I haven't woke up for a week with anything but a limp noodle!"

"So you'll be low man on the scrotum pole at the next choir practice," said Sam Niles, turning a Bloomguardism against him.

"God, that's cruel, Sam."

"Harold, you're not impotent. Take my word. And you're not going to end up in a rubber room like your mother. But *I* might end up there if you keep using *me* for your shrink. Now if you only wanna wake up with a hard on, then ask the captain to put you on the morning watch. When you're out there at about sunrise, waking up in a radio car, after trying to sleep with an upset stomach from the crazy hours and the greasy eggs you ate at two A.M., and the nervous sleep in some alley where you're worrying about a sergeant catching you and you're longing for all the normal things people do at that hour like being flaked out in a warm bed with a warm friendly body, you know what? You'll wake up with the hardest diamond cutter you ever had. Try it if you don't believe me."

"Morning watch, huh? Don't think I'd mind that. How about it, will you go with me?"

"No, I think you'd be better off going it alone with a new partner. Who knows? Maybe you'll catch one with an MS in abnormal psych."

Harold Bloomguard thought it over for five seconds and said, "I think I'll stick with you, Sam. We'll just have to come up with another solution for my impotency."

Then they received a routine radio call to the south end where a black man had thrown a pot of hot soup on his teenage daughter and beaten the mother over the head with the pot lid. But since he was gone and the girl had already been removed to the hospital by ambulance there wasn't much to do but take the report from the mother and phone the hospital for the treatment information on the child.

After dark they received another routine call, this time on the north end to a small house inhabited by a disheveled white woman, who was barefoot in a torn dress, with three small children literally hanging on her clothing. She lurched from dragging the weight but also from the pint of bourbon she had consumed that afternoon.

Sam Niles let Harold Bloomguard handle it since somehow Harold always did anyway, excitedly jumping into a conversation with a distraught married couple or the victim of a burglary with every sort of advice, wanted or otherwise. Harold's notebook bulged with the addresses of referral agencies that ostensibly provided a remedy for any malaise Los Angeles had to offer.

The tired eyed woman had called them to report that her teenage daughter had threatened to run off with a forty-nine year old piano tuner who lived next door. Harold Bloomguard promised to arrange an appointment with juvenile officers at Wilshire Station the next morning, then he advised the mother to try to help police ascertain if she had been taken advantage of by the older man.

"If she been what?" the woman asked as Sam Niles turned on his flashlight and prepared to descend the porch steps.

"Taken advantage of," Harold said as Sam was halfway down the walk heading for the radio car.

The woman nodded dumbly and Harold said, "Well, I'm very glad we could be of service. I certainly hope we can help the young lady get back on the track tomorrow, ma'am, and if there's any way we can expedite matters prior to your appointment, you just call us back and we'll be here at once."

"Ex-pee-dite?" mumbled the woman as the lassitudinous Sam Niles, hands in his pockets, hoped the little bubblegummer's keys had been well pounded by the piano tuner so she could get out of this house, even to go to the home for unwed mothers.

"So long, ma'am," Harold said cheerfully as he took off his hat and opened the door of the radio car, turning back to wave at the stooped woman who now had no less than seven children flocked around her on the sagging wooden porch in the dim light of a naked bulb. "By the way, wherever did all these children come from?"

"From fuckin," yelled the woman, wondering how the little policeman could be so stupid as not to know that.

"Now you know where they came from, Harold," Sam said as he drove away.

It was always like this with Harold Bloomguard and always had been. Yet for reasons impossible to explain Sam could not rid himself of the clinging little man any more than the weary woman could rid herself of the clinging children.

But I didn't fuck to *get* him, thought Sam Niles. I just *got* fucked the day I accepted him into my fire team in Nam. And then Sam Niles felt the fear sweep over him as he thought of Vietnam and for a second he actually hated Harold Bloomguard. It always came this way: first fear at the memory and then a split second of incredible hatred which he assumed was for Harold Bloomguard who knew the secret of the cave. And relief for Harold's never having revealed the secret to anyone, for never having mentioned the secret even to Sam Niles.

If he'd just bring it up once, thought Sam Niles, but he never did. And that was perhaps the reason he could never rid himself of Harold Bloomguard.

"You know, Sam, I think it's time I got married," Harold suddenly announced, interrupting Sam's fearful reverie.

"Anybody I know? Ora Lee maybe? Or Carolina?"

"Don't be silly, Sam."

"If it's Ora Lee be sure to rent her out to us once a week for choir practice."

"I'm serious, Sam," Harold said as Sam Niles winked his headlights at an oncoming car and cruised west on Beverly Boulevard, glancing in store windows, most of which were darkened by now.

"So who're you going to marry?" Sam asked, not truly interested.

"I dunno. I haven't met her yet. I wonder what she'll be like?"

"Just like the girl that married dear old dad," said Sam Niles, thinking it would be rather difficult to find one like the mother Harold described to him, who up until the day he went overseas had twisted the tops off the catsup bottles and pried the lids from the cottage cheese containers, replacing them gently so that Harold would not strain himself when getting something to eat.

But she was never there to care for him again, after a certain summer afternoon when Harold was in Vietnam and her psychiatrist was on vacation in Martinique and Mrs. Bloomguard decided she was Ann Miller and did a naked tap dance in front of the Pomona courthouse and had to be taken to the screw factory to get rethreaded.

As they patrolled the nighttime streets and Harold complained that perhaps he should never get married because his mother's insanity might be congenital, Sam Niles was reminded of his own fifteen month marriage which had just been finally dissolved last year.

His ex-wife, Kimberly Cutler Niles, was a tall athletic student he had met in a college night class. She was a blonde tawny cat of a girl with daring amber eyes that looked inquisitively and boldly at you. She was bright, articulate, personable. She said Harold Bloomguard was a doll and asked Sam to invite him home to dinner often. And incredibly enough she could cook. Not like a twenty-two year old student wife can cook but like a cook can cook. She was tidy and their little apartment was always immaculate. Harold Bloomguard loved her like a sister. He was ecstatically happy for his best friend, Sam Niles. Kimberly was darling. Sam Niles hated her guts.

But he didn't hate her at first, that came later. They were probably married three weeks before he started to hate her. But he didn't *know* that he hated her after three weeks, he just knew that she made him terribly uncomfortable. She was as terrific in the sack as he knew she would be the first night they met in class. She had introduced herself by shaking hands smoothly and firmly and saying, "I knew you were a Taurus. I just love bulls."

And moments later she was chatting glibly about tennis which interested Sam, saying, "You're a pretty good sized boy, but I'll bet you could get into size thirty-three tennis shorts. My brother left some at my place when he went away to school. Want them?''

''Sure, I'd like to play with you,'' Sam said with a hint of a smile so he could withdraw gracefully but she delighted him by saying, ''You could probably get into much smaller tennis shorts given the opportunity, couldn't you, Sam?''

And Sam Niles had a blue veiner going on a diamond cutter and was impulsively married within four months, wondering, as did Kimberly Cutler, how the hell it all happened.

The first thing Sam Niles didn't like about being married to Kimberly Cutler was having to sleep in the same bed with another human being. It wasn't that Kimberly wasn't carnal and syrupy, she certainly was. But prior to marriage he had seldom had to spend a whole night in a bed with anybody. And early on, Kimberly's doubts were heightened by Sam's saying that he'd like to trade their king size bed for twins.

''That's unnatural,'' Kimberly told him as they lay in their king size bed unable to sleep.

''What's unnatural about it?''

''Newlyweds should sleep in the same bed, for God's sake.''

''Where does it say that?''

''Sam, don't you enjoy me in bed?''

''That's dumb. Do I act like I enjoy you?''

''As a matter of fact you act like a man who does a pretty good act of making love. Oh, I don't mean fucking. You like *that* all right. I mean *loving*. You don't really give yourself. You hold lots and lots back from me. It's purely physical, your lovemaking.''

''All this because I want twin beds. Kim, it's just that my old man and old lady were drunks and we were so goddamn poor I grew up on the floor. Or when we could rent a pad with a bed I always had to share it with two brothers. And I'm talking about a *little* bed, an army surplus cot. Christ, I felt like a married man at seven years old, always crowded into bed with one or both brothers. I just can't bear it anymore to be . . .''

''Close?''

''Yeah, close.''

''You never want to get close to anybody.''

''What're you talking about?''

''I'm saying that you won't let yourself get close to anyone. I can't understand how you could be friends with Harold so long. He's a sweet little guy but he's like glue. How do you stand it?''

''Whaddaya mean?'' Sam asked, then added, ''Jesus, I'm starting to sound like Dean.''

''There's something about Harold. You've yelled his name in your sleep.''

''So maybe I'm fruit for Harold.''

''You don't like people, Sam. You've had a mean rough life with weak parents and you hate them even though they're dead. You won't even see your brothers and sisters unless you have to. It's very sad. You don't really want to be close to anyone. Not even me.''

''There oughtta be a law against people taking Psych 1b,'' Sam Niles said.

''But *why* do you stay friends with Harold, Sam? You're so different. You've both been in war and police work, yet he still sees honey where you see slime. He's always enthusiastic, you're always bored. Why do you let *him* crowd you? There's something, something in the marines. In Vietnam . . .''

''My mother always told us it cost a nickel a minute to burn a light,'' Sam Niles said as he switched off the lamp, leaving Kimberly Cutler Niles to wonder in the darkness. ''Of course it doesn't cost a nickel but I'm a creature of habit. It was just another thing that lousy drunken bitch lied about.''

And Sam rolled over, wishing the king sized bed was a twin, and went to sleep, yelling in the night about a spider hole and a cave, which Kimberly Cutler knew would never be explained, not to her.

From then on the marriage deteriorated very quickly, especially after Sam Niles began to attend various choir practices with various groups of choirboys, much to the disapproval of Harold Bloomguard who tried to hint that he should go home to Kimberly.

Three months later two bitter young people lay side by side in their twin beds, both doing poorly in their college classes because of their miserable relationship. They seethed over an argument they had about one watching television when the other was trying to study.

"So I'll just quit school in my senior year," Sam said. "Why's a cop need an education anyway? No more than a trash collector. That's all we do, clean up garbage."

"The garbage is in your mind, Sam."

"Fine, I'll just feed on it. That's what pigs do, isn't it?"

And then bitter silence until Kimberly made a gambit. "Sam, do you wanna come over here and make love to me?"

"No, I'd rather have a wet dream."

"Well then go up on Hollywood Boulevard and pick yourself up a queer if I can't turn you on, you cocksucker!"

"Just like a woman. Never tell a man to go out and get some pussy. Too vain to think another woman might be able to do what you can't. It's go get a fag, never a broad."

"Fuck you!"

"Tennis, anyone?" said Sam Niles, and that was the last word spoken that night.

Two nights later, after they had not seen each other except as she came and went to class and he to the police station, Sam came in after getting off the nightwatch. He found Kimberly sleeping soundly, but as he looked at her long tan body, the blue veiner he brought with him became a diamond cutter. He quickly stripped and got in her bed, nudging her.

"Hi, Kim," he whispered.

"Oh Christ, what time is it?"

"Two thirty, maybe. I wake you up?"

"Oh no, Sam, I've been lying here worrying about you getting shot like those idiotic cops' wives on television. Where were you? Out drinking with the boys again?"

Then Sam was up close, breathing in her ear, touching her with a diamond cutter, saying, "This'll keep you awake."

"Only if you stick it in my eye," replied Kimberly and she didn't mind at all when Sam slammed out the door, half dressed.

The next night was perhaps the worst since they were both thinking about sex, hoping they could bring some of the drama back into their lives, neither wanting to make the move across the two feet of carpet to the other's bed.

"You wanna come to my bed?" Kimberly finally asked pugnaciously.

"What do you have in mind, a prizefight?"

"Goddamnit, do you or don't you?"

"Aren't you too tired tonight?"

"I'm too tired every night after I've been studying for four hours and you come tripping in at some godawful time."

"Well I'm a policeman and I work godawful hours!"

"You wanna get in bed with me?"

"Sure, but I'm tired too. Just for once, why don't you come to my bed?"

"If we had one bed we wouldn't have to be walking a beat across the goddamn carpet."

"All right, I'll come to your bed."

"Not if it's too much trouble."

"You want me to or not?"

"All right, all right."

Sam Niles pulled himself up and walked two steps and lay down beside Kimberly Cutler Niles, and after three minutes of silence wherein neither of the stubborn young people stirred, Sam finally said, "Shall we *both* put it in and toss a coin to see who has to move?"

Five minutes later it was Kimberly who was half dressed and slamming out the door.

The honeymoon was definitely over, but like so many people, Sam and Kimberly needed a dramatic moment to convince them of what they should have known. Six days later they got it.

It started with Sam Niles deciding to drive Kimberly bananas much as Celeste Holm tried to drive Ronald Colman bananas on a movie Sam had seen on "The Late Show." He felt a little silly that night as he lay in his twin bed, knowing that he had made enough noise coming home from work to wake up the landlady down stairs. He knew that Kimberly could not possibly sleep through his drawer banging, toilet flushing, door slamming, shoe dropping, and would have to respond as Sam lay in the darkness with his back to her and forced out a muffled hilarious laugh guaranteed to drive her wild.

After the third stream of laughter he heard Kimberly stir in her bed and say, "Sam, are you drunk or what?"

"No."

"Then what's so damn funny at three A.M.?"

"Nothing."

"Then please let me sleep."

"Okay."

And moments later Sam Niles was giggling more hilariously than before, because, by God, it worked! He knew she would soon be beside herself with jealousy, curiosity and debilitating rage. Then Sam began chuckling in earnest, his body and bed shaking.

Finally Kimberly spoke again. "Sam, honey."

"Yes?"

"No offense, but any guy who won't screw his wife and giggles a lot really should try to get himself together on Hollywood Boulevard. Why don't you put on my yellow miniskirt and go out strolling. You might get lucky."

So Sam Niles angrily decided that what worked for Celeste Holm would not work on Kimberly Cutler Niles. He was not yet convinced that Oscar Wilde was right and Aristotle was wrong: that life imitates art. So he went back to television for an answer to his domestic misery. And he found it on "The Late, Late Show."

It was John Wayne telling Maureen O'Hara that there'd be no locked doors in their marriage as he broke down a three inch oak door and threw the stunning redhead onto their four-poster, breaking it to the ground.

Like so many policemen, Sam Niles was a John Wayne fan, though he had never fallen prey to the malaise the Los Angeles police psychologist called the "John Wayne Syndrome," wherein a young hotdog responds with independence, assurance and violence to all of life's problems and comes to believe his four inch oval shield is as large as Gawain's ever was. Roscoe Rules, who swaggered and talked police work every waking moment and wore black gloves and figuratively shot from the hip and literally from the lip, was surely suffering from the syndrome. But though Sam Niles had never been a hotdog or black glove cop, he admired the direct, forceful, simplistic approach to life found in a John Wayne film. And he was given the chance to be the Duke that very week.

It started over Sam's bitching about Kimberly's cooking which like everything else in their marriage had deteriorated to the point that even she could hardly eat it. It ended with her in angry tears, which was not unusual, and running into the bathroom and locking the door, which was extremely unusual.

"Goddamn women," Sam Niles muttered in consummate frustration, hurling his half-eaten plate of food against the wall, his stomach afire from the poisons he was manufacturing.

Sam found himself standing in front of the bathroom door, making a fist and shouting, "There'll be no locked doors in our marriage, Kimberly Cutler Niles!"

And when there was no answer he John Wayned the door, kicking it right next to the lock and sending it crashing across the bathroom to smash into the wall and crack the porcelain toilet.

The door exploded. It made a loud boom. But nothing like the boom his Smith and Wesson .38 made in the hands of Kimberly Cutler Niles as she stood inside the bathroom, half out of her mind, watching the door sailing past.

Then Sam Niles was lying flat on his stomach from his feet trying to run backward. Then he was kneeling on his broken glasses pleading, "Please Kimberly! Please don't kill me! Oh, God!" And then there was another explosion and a third, and Sam Niles was up and crashing through the aluminum screen door and running down the walk and across the street to a vacant lot where he lay trembling in the knee-high weeds, watching the front of the apartment building, waiting for a wrathful figure to emerge from the darkness. Ready to run like a turpentined cat as far as his legs could carry him from the maniacal Kimberly Cutler Niles.

The police were called by three neighbors that night, but the walls and concrete walks of the apartment building had played tricks with the sound of gunfire and no one knew the shots had come from the Niles' apartment. It was finally thought that someone had driven by and shot up the place. Two detectives worked for three weeks on the theory that an unknown assailant had a grudge against the apartment house manager who sweated off ten pounds during the investigation. Kimberly bought a new door and toilet and had the interior bullet holes patched before she moved out and filed for her divorce.

When he was sure Kimberly was in class Sam Niles came back and got his clothes, ready to bolt out the door any second. He found his belongings on the living room floor. There was a note beside his gun which read, "Who's got the biggest balls now, hero?"

Sam Niles never fully appreciated a John Wayne film after that night.

But he wasn't thinking too much about Kimberly Cutler or John Wayne the night the hype blew their case away and they arrested the man who painted himself red.

Both Sam Niles and Harold Bloomguard had heard of the man who painted himself red. But prior to the contact with him he was known only as the man who painted his *car* red. His name was Oscar Mobley and he was fifty-eight years old, white, unmarried, lived alone, was unemployed and liked to paint his car red. It would never have been called to the attention of the Los Angeles Police Department if it weren't for the fact that Oscar Mobley did it with a paintbrush and bucket and did it perhaps once a month. The policemen who knew him said that his fifteen year old Ford outweighed a Cadillac limousine, so thick were the coats of peeling red enamel.

And yet Oscar Mobley would probably never have become the subject of rollcall gossip if it weren't that he would occasionally paint his headlights red and drive along Wilshire Boulevard at night, making cars pull over. Oscar Mobley had many warnings and traffic tickets over painting his headlights red, but just as it appeared that he would give up painting his headlights red, Oscar Mobley suddenly for no apparent reason painted all the windows of his car red, and unable to see through a red opaque windshield, got himself into a traffic accident on Washington Boulevard. He was ordered by a traffic court judge never ever to paint his headlights or windshield red again.

Oscar Mobley had not been heard from for several months, apparently content to have a car with red body, red bumpers, red tires, red hubcaps and red grille, but with unpainted windows and headlights. Then something happened on the night Sam and Harold met Oscar Mobley.

''Seven-A-Twenty-nine, see the woman, male mental case, Eleventh and Irolo, code two.''

''Seven-Adam-Twenty-nine, roger,'' Harold responded as Sam picked up speed a little and drove through the nighttime traffic to the residential neighborhood of Oscar Mobley.

''It's about time you got here,'' said the caller, Mrs. Jasper, the next door neighbor of Oscar Mobley. Her hair was wet with red paint and a blue cotton dress she held in her hands was covered with the stuff. ''I just asked that crazy nut Oscar why he was painting his headlights and windshield red, that's all I did . . .''

''Wait a minute,'' Sam Niles said as he and Harold stood in the street with Mrs. Jasper, her husband, her brother and eight other neighborhood men and women who had almost decided to lynch the frail Oscar Mobley until someone had the presence of mind to call the police.

''Oscar started to paint his car again tonight,'' said Mr. Jasper, a man with receding hair and a parrot's face, who was even more frail than Oscar Mobley and who had no stomach for fighting for Mrs. Jasper who could have licked Oscar Mobley and Mr. Jasper at the same time on her worst day.

''Yeah, we know about Oscar,'' Sam Niles said.

''Well he started to paint again,'' Mr. Jasper continued. ''He ain't done that for three, four months now. He won't ever tell anyone on the street why he paints his car red and we asked him a thousand times, maybe a million. He just smiles and keeps painting and won't answer you. Well tonight he done what the judge told him *not* to do, he started painting the headlights and the windows red, and my wife just came out on the front porch and asked him why.''

''That's all I done and that crazy little . . .''

''Please, ma'am, one at a time,'' Harold said.

''Well, my little woman just comes out and sees him there under the streetlight, painting everything red and she asks him why he's doing it and he says something she can't hear and she thinks at last maybe she's gonna learn the secret of why Oscar Mobley paints his car red and she just walks over . . .''

''Out of curiosity,'' added Mrs. Jasper.

''Out of curiosity,'' said Mr. Jasper, ''and when she gets close she says, 'Oscar, why do you paint your car red?' And he don't say a word. Then he done it.''

''Done . . . did what?'' asked Harold.

''Painted *me* red!'' Mrs. Jasper shouted. ''The little son of a bitch started painting *me*. I got the paintbrush in my mouth and I couldn't breathe. He was painting my hair and neck and arms. If he hadn't a surprised me I'd a knocked the little bastard down the sewer, but pretty soon I couldn't even see for the paint in my eyes. And I turn and run for the house and he chases me painting my . . .''

''Her ass,'' said Mr. Jasper.

''Yes, the dirty beggar even did that to me and I've been scrubbing with paint thinner till my skin's almost wore off. Look at me!''

Harold shined the flashlight past Mrs. Jasper's face so as not to hit her eyes with the beam and it was true, her face and neck were a splotched and faded red like a pomegranate.

''Well, it's time someone did something about Oscar,'' Sam Niles sighed and he and Harold got their batons and put them in the rings on their Sam Brownes and went to find Oscar Mobley and let Mrs. Jasper make a citizen's arrest on him for painting her red.

As Sam expected, Oscar Mobley did not open the door when he pounded and rang the bell.

"It's unlocked, Sam," Harold said when he turned the knob of the front door of the little three room house where Oscar lived with two cats and a goldfish.

Sam shrugged and readied his revolver and Harold Bloomguard also fingered his gun, ready to touch the spring on the clamshell holster. Both men entered the darkened kitchen and tiptoed toward the narrow hallway to the tiny bedroom where a lamp burned.

Sam went in first, his gun out in front and he said quietly, "Mr. Mobley, if you're in here I want you to come out. We're police officers and we want to talk to you. We won't hurt you. Come out."

There was no answer and Sam entered the room, seeing nothing but an unmade bed, a box of cat litter, a broken down nightstand with an old radio on it, a pile of dirty clothing on the floor and a napless overstuffed chair.

Sam was about to check under the bed when he and Harold were scared half out of their wits by the naked Oscar Mobley who suddenly leaped out from behind the overstuffed chair, painted red from head to foot, arms outstretched.

"Up popped the devil!" yelled Oscar Mobley cheerfully.

It was miraculous that neither officer shot him. Both were exerting at least a pound of trigger pull on their guns which like all department issued guns had been altered to fire only double action. They stood, shoulders pressed together, backs to the wall, gaping at Oscar Mobley who posed, arms extended, grinning proudly, the paint hardly dry on his small naked body.

Everything had been painted: the palms of his hands, the soles of his feet, his hair, face, body, genitals. He had managed with a roller to get the center of his back. He had neglected his teeth only because he forgot them. He had not painted his eyeballs only because he started to and it hurt.

As Sam Niles later stood in Oscar Mobley's kitchen and smoked to steady his nerves, the equally shaken Harold Bloomguard patiently persuaded Oscar Mobley that despite the beautiful paint job he should wear a bathrobe to go where they were going because it was a nippy evening and he might catch cold.

After agreeing that Elwood Banks, the jailor at Wilshire Station, might object to their bringing in a man who painted himself red since it would be messy to try to roll fingerprints over the coat of red enamel, Sam and Harold took Oscar Mobley where he belonged: Unit Three, Psychiatric Admitting, of the Los Angeles County General Hospital. The hospital now had a grander name: Los Angeles County, University of Southern California Medical Center. But it would forever be General Hospital to the indigent people it served.

Oscar Mobley was admitted, later had a sanity hearing wherein he steadfastly refused to tell anyone why he painted his car, himself and Mrs. Jasper red, and went to a state hospital for six months where he refused to tell anyone else his secret.

After his release he moved to a new neighborhood, took a job delivering throwaway circulars, did it beautifully for eight days, then painted his boss and his boss' wife red and was recommitted to the state hospital. But all this happened long after Sam Niles and Harold Bloomguard took him to Unit Three, in time to miss code seven though they were starving, and just in time to meet the Moaning Man.

The call came just after 11:00 P.M. "Seven-Adam-Twenty-nine, shot fired vicinity of Ninth and New Hampshire."

"Rampart Division," Sam Niles said to Harold Bloomguard who nodded, picked up the mike and said, "Seven-A-Twenty-nine reporting that the call is in Rampart Division."

"Seven-Adam-Twenty-nine, stand by," said the radio operator as she checked with one of the policemen who supervise the girls and assign the call tickets.

"Goddamn Rampart cars've been pulling this shit too often lately," Sam said to Harold who didn't mind handling the call in someone else's division because Sam had been exceedingly quiet and Harold was getting as bored as Sam always was.

''If we have to handle this one, next time a Rampart car gets a call in our area we'll just let the bastards handle it,'' Sam said.

''Seven-Adam-Twenty-nine, handle the call in Rampart Division,'' said the radio operator. ''No Rampart units available.''

''Seven-Adam-Twenty-nine, roger on the call,'' Harold Bloomguard said as Sam Niles pushed up his drooping steel rimmed glasses and threw a cigarette out the window saying, ''They're probably all over on Alvarado eating hamburgers, the lazy pricks.''

Sam drove slowly on the seedy residential streets, mostly a white Anglo district, but with some black and Latin residents. He shined the spotlights on the front of homes and apartments, hoping not to find anyone who may have phoned about shots being fired. Sam Niles wanted to go to an east Hollywood drive-in and eat cherry pie and drink coffee and try to score with a waitress he knew.

''There it is,'' Harold said as Sam's spotlight beam lighted a chinless withered man in a bathrobe who waited in front of a two story stucco apartment house. The door glass had been broken so many times the panes were replaced by plywood and cardboard.

Sam took his time parking, and Harold was already across the narrow street by the time Sam gathered up his flashlight and put his cigarette pack in his pocket and locked the car door so someone didn't have fun slashing the upholstery or stealing the shotgun from the rack.

''Heard a shot,'' the old man said. His eyes were a quiet brown like a dog's.

''You live here?''

''Yep.''

''You the manager?''

''Nope, but I got a passkey. I help out Charlie Bates. He's the manager.''

''Why do we need a key?'' Harold asked.

''Shot came from up there.''

And the man in the bathrobe pointed a yellow bony finger up to the front window on the second floor where a gray muslin drape flapped rhythmically as the gusts of wind blew and sucked through the black hole of an open window on what had become a chilled and cloudy night.

''Give us the passkey, we'll have a look,'' Sam Niles said and later he wondered if he felt something then.

It seemed he did. He was to recall distinctly wishing that a Rampart unit would feel guilty that Wilshire was handling their calls and perhaps come driving down Ninth Street to relieve them.

The stairs creaked as they climbed and the whole building reeked, dank and sour from urine and moldy wool carpet on the stairs. They stood one on each side of the door and Sam knocked.

The dying tree outside, the last on the block, rattled in the wind which rushed through the narrow hallway upstairs. The building was surprisingly quiet for one housing eighty-five souls. Sam reached up and unscrewed the only bulb at their end of the hall, and said, ''We better be in the dark.''

''Might be some drunk sitting in there playing with a gun,'' Harold nodded and both policemen drew their service revolvers.

Sam knocked again and the sound echoed through the empty hall which had no floor carpet, only old wooden floors caked with grime which could never be removed short of sanding the wood a quarter of an inch down. A mustard colored cat, displaying the indifference Sam Niles usually feigned, watched from the windowsill.

The wind blew and it was a cold wind, yet Sam was to remember later that he was sweating. He tasted the salt running through his moustache into the dimple of his upper lip. Then they heard it.

At first Sam Niles thought it was the wind. Then he saw the look on Harold Bloomguard's face in the dark hallway when he moved into a patch of moonlight. He knew that Harold heard it and that it wasn't the wind.

Then they heard it again. The Moaning Man was saying:

"Mmmmmm. Mmmmmmm. Mmmmmuuuuuuuhhhhhhhh."

Then Sam was sweating in earnest and Harold's pale little face was glistening in the swatch of moonlight as he pressed himself against the wall, gun in his left hand. Sam Niles turned the key slowly and then kicked the door open with his toe and jumped back against the wall.

"Mmmmm," said the Moaning Man. "Uuuuhhhhh. Mmmmmuuuuuhhhhh."

"Jesus Christ motherfucker son of a bitch!" Sam Niles, like many men, swore incoherently when he was frightened.

The moans sounded like cattle lowing. They came from inside. Inside in the darkness.

Finally Sam Niles moved. He dropped to his knees and with his flashlight in his left hand and gun in the right, crawled into the tiny apartment ready to switch on the flashlight and ready to shoot. He crept toward the bedroom which was just behind the cluttered kitchen.

Sam Niles smelled blood. And he felt the flesh wriggling on his rib cage and on his back and up the sides of his dripping neck into his temple when the Moaning Man said it again. But it was loud this time and plaintive:

"Mmmmm. Uuuuuhhhhh. Mmmmmuuuuuhhhhh!"

Then Harold Bloomguard, tiptoeing through the kitchen behind Sam who was on his knees, accidentally dropped his flashlight and the beam switched on when it hit the floor and Sam Niles cursed and jumped to his feet and leaped to the doorway, his gun following the beam from his own flashlight in the darkness. And he met the Moaning Man.

He was sitting up in bed, his back pressed to the wall. He was naked except for undershorts. Every few seconds the wind would snap the dirty ragged drapes and the moonlight would wash his chalky body which otherwise lay in the slash of light. He held a 9mm. Luger in his left hand and had used it for the first and last time by placing it under his chin, gouging the soft flesh between the throat and the jawbone and pulling the trigger.

The top of the head of the Moaning Man was on the bed and on the floor beside the bed. The wall he leaned against was spotted with sticky bits of brain and drops of blood. Most of his face was intact, except it was crisscrossed with rivulets of blood in the moonlight, filling his eyes with blood. The most incredible thing of all was not that the Moaning Man was able to make sounds, it was that the gun he had killed himself with was clenched tightly in a fist across his body at port arms. He moved it back and forth in rhythm with the moans.

"Oh my God oh my God oh my God," Sam Niles said as Harold Bloomguard gaped slackjawed at the Moaning Man whose gun hand was swaying, swaying, back and forth with the snapping of the drapes in the wind as he said:

"Mmmmmm. Uuuuuhhhhhhh Mmmmmuuuuuhhhhh."

And Sam Niles knew that he *never* would have done what the terrified Harold Bloomguard did next, which was to walk slowly across that room, watching the Luger swaying in the hand of the Moaning Man, the pieces of skull crackling under his leather soles, crackling with each step, until he stood beside the bed.

Sam Niles would forever smell the blood and hear the wind and the snapping drapes and Harold's shoes crackling on the fragments of bone and Harold's teeth clicking together frightfully as he moved a trembling hand toward the Luger which the Moaning Man held in front, swaying to and fro as he said:

"Mmmmmm. Uuuuu. Mmmmmuuuuuhhhtherr."

And then Harold Bloomguard spoke to the Moaning Man. He said, "Now now now. Hush now, I'm right here. You're not alone."

Harold Bloomguard gripped the wrist and hand of the Moaning Man and the moaning stopped instantly. The fist relaxed, dropping the pistol on the bed. The bloody eyes slid shut and overflowed. The Moaning Man died without a sound.

Both policemen remained motionless for a long moment before Harold Bloomguard controlled his shaking and said, "He was calling his mother, is all. Why do so many call their mother?"

"He was dead!" Sam Niles said. "He was dead before we saw him!"

"He only needed the touch of a human being," said Harold Bloomguard. "I was so scared. *So* scared!"

Sam Niles turned and left Harold in the darkness with the Moaning Man and called for a detective to take the death report and he did not speak to Harold for the remainder of the watch and demanded a choir practice when they changed into civilian clothes later that night. It was a bitter night for choir practice and only half the choirboys showed up. But Carolina Moon was there so it wasn't too bad.

11

Sergeant Dominic Scuzzi

With a galloping heartbeat Harold Bloomguard entered the opened door of the vice squad office on the first night of his vice assignment. Harold was twenty-five minutes early. He wore a conservative gray suit, white button-down shirt, a paisley tie and traditional wing tip brogues.

The office was open but empty when Harold arrived. It looked different from the detective squad room. It was much smaller. And more cluttered. Covering one wall were three large street maps dotted with multicolored pins. Certain streets were covered with green pins signifying prostitution activity. Other streets were sporadically dotted with pins marking suspected bookmaking locations: cashrooms in the southerly black neighborhoods, phone spots in the northerly white neighborhoods. Cocktail lounges were marked where handbooks and agents operated.

There was a painted motto over the door. It said: "What you say here, What you see here, What you hear here, Let it stay here, When you leave here."

Harold Bloomguard read that motto with shining eyes. He shook back his thin, ginger-colored hair and smiled enchantedly. For a dreamy moment he sipped from a frothy goblet in Bombay, Macao, Port Said: white linen suits, narrow teeming passages, mingled aromas of spice, rich dried fruit, dusky succulent women, clawing danger. The mystique of the secret agent enveloped this room.

Just then a swarthy unshaven overweight man of fifty in a dirty short sleeve dress shirt shuffled through the door in run over sneakers. He looked Harold up and down and said, "You don't look big enough to fight, fuck or run a footrace. You one a the new kids on the block?"

"I'm . . . I'm . . . are *you* a policeman?"

"I'm a sergeant. I run the nightwatch." The man shambled to a desk, rummaged through piles of papers until he found a cigar, belched three times before he offered his hand and said, "Name's Dom Scuzzi. You can call me Scuz. You Slate, Niles or Bloomguard?"

"Bloomguard . . . Sergeant."

"I said call me Scuz. Ain't no formality in the vice squad. Not since I got rid a that prick, Lieutenant Cotton-Balls Klingham. I'll never understand how he got on the squad. Cotton-Balls. One hundred percent sterile like they say on the box. Everything about him was sterile, especially his conversation."

Sergeant Scuzzi paused long enough to puff on the cigar and belch once or twice before continuing. "Anyways, we got rid a him. Can't tell you how I did it. But

I'll always be beholding to one a your nightwatch bluesuits, name a Spermwhale Whalen, for giving me the idea. How long you been at Wilshire?''

''Almost two years. You know, Sarge . . . Scuz, I've seen you around but . . .''

''That's Scuz. Don't rhyme with fuzz. Rhymes with loose. That's Scooose. As in scuse a me.''

''Scooose.''

''That's it! I ain't been here at this station too long.''

''Yeah, I've seen you around, but I always thought you were . . .''

''A janitor?''

''Yeah, I guess so.''

''I don't mind. My old man's a janitor. Supported nine kids pushing a broom. Never talked a word a English, hardly. I don't mind looking like a janitor. The other two loaners look good as you?''

''What do you mean?''

''You look good. I mean *good*. How tall're you?''

''Five eight.''

''Weigh about a hundred fifty?''

''Just about.''

''How the hell you get on the department?''

''I stretched and ate bananas and stuff.''

''You look *good*. Here.'' Scuz pulled open the drawer of his desk, propped his tennis shoes up in front of him, leaned back, puffed his cigar and said, ''Try em on.''

Harold picked up the horn rimmed glasses, held them to his eyes and said, ''They're clear glass.''

''Sure. Makes you look even less like a cop if that's possible. You're gonna be a real whore operator, my boy. Glad you wore a suit tonight. You're definitely the suit and tie type. Tell em you're an accountant. Here.''

And Scuz reached back in the drawer, rummaged through it for a few seconds and found a packet of business cards which said, ''Krump, Krump and Leekly, Certified Public Accountants.''

''Any broads get cute with you trying to guess if you're a cop, just lay a card on her. Tell her it's your private business phone and she can call you during business hours. That's our straight-in line here. We got a girl works here on the daywatch who's good at conning callers. If a whore won't go for you tonight she'll go for you tomorrow night after she checks you out with our girl.''

''I don't know anything about vice, Scuz,'' Harold said, relaxing in the chair in front of the unshaven sergeant who reached inside his shirt and scratched his belly which was almost as big as Spermwhale's, and puffed the cigar blissfully with his eyes closed.

''Now don't go worrying . . . what's your first name?''

''Harold.''

''Harold, don't worry about nothing. I never let my coppers get hurt, specially not a loanee like you who I gotta return to the patrol lieutenant in a couple weeks in as good a shape as I borrowed him. There ain't nothing to working whores. They offer you a sex act for money. Got it? Sex, money. You in the service?''

''Marines.''

''Overseas?''

''Vietnam.''

''All right,'' Scuz nodded, chewing his cigar, leaning back in the chair, hands behind his head. ''Overseas the broads got it made. Fucky sucky, five bucks. See, they saw what every whore said in war or peace for five thousand years. Sex, money. Now, these whores today know that there's a thing called entrapment, which means you can't plant an evil idea in their heads, as if that was possible. So in effect they're gonna wanna say sucky fucky and let *you* say the price. Or they're gonna say the price and let *you* say sucky fucky. Get it?''

"I think so."

"It's just a game but I don't wanna see you perjure yourself for a shitty little whore pinch so you play it straight. Figure out a way to make her say the whole thing: Sucky fucky, five bucks. But of course it ain't five bucks, it's twenty on the street. And she ain't gonna say sucky fucky usually. She's gonna say French or half and half or party, and all these words been construed by the black robed pussies that sit on the bench to be words with sexual connotations. So soon as she says one a these words and she mentions money, Boom! Bring her down. Hook her up. You got a legal pinch. Got it?"

"God, I hope so," said Harold.

"Well, just don't entrap them. Course you're gonna run into guys who say, bullshit, she says sucky fucky and gets cute about the price, I pull out the iron and zoom her. I say no. Nice and legal."

"Sucky fucky, five bucks," said Harold.

"You got it, kid, I knew you was smart!" Scuz said, moving the cigar from the right side of his mouth to the left. "Course she might throw you a curve."

"Like how?"

"She might say, 'I think you look like a cop. If you ain't a cop, take out a twenty dollar bill and wrap it around your cock and wave it at me.' One did that to me once."

"What'd you do?"

"I only had a ten," said Scuz, closing his eyes, enveloping himself in a shroud of cigar smoke which was starting to choke Harold Bloomguard. "But don't worry about these brain teasers. Don't happen too much. Most girls're just gonna say . . ."

"Sucky fucky, five bucks."

"I like you, kid," said Scuz. "Wanna cigar?"

"No thanks, Scuz," Harold said, thinking about inviting the vice sergeant to choir practice, just as Sam Niles and Baxter Slate came through the door.

Scuz opened his eyes, peeked through the cloud of smoke which hung over him and shook his head disapprovingly at the two strapping six footers, at their hair styled just over the ears, but not long enough to offend the station captain totally. Baxter wore tie dyed jeans, a denim jacket and a red velvet shirt. Sam Niles wore a buckskin shirt over a tank top, brushed demins and Wallabees. His neat brown moustache did not drop down around the lip far enough to anger the same station captain and his sideburns did not quite flare out into muttonchops. The steel rimmed goggles did not help mitigate the whole picture.

"Shit!" Scuz said, fanning the smoke away from his face. "You look just like two healthy, clean cut, twenty-six year old studs, which is what you are. You look like young *cops*. Why can't you look sick and puny like him?" And Scuz pointed to Harold Bloomguard who decided not to invite him to choir practice.

"This is a sergeant," said Harold Bloomguard to Sam and Baxter in case they wouldn't believe it.

"Just call me Scuz," said Scuz.

"Anything wrong with the way we look?" Sam Niles asked.

"No, you can't help it," Scuz said. "It wouldn't even help if I made you funky. You just got copper written all over you. It's okay, you guys can work in the trap."

"Trap?" said Baxter Slate.

"Fruits," Scuz said, dropping his feet to the floor and remembering they had not shaken hands, offering his hairy paw to both policemen. "What's your first names?"

"Sam, Sam Niles."

"Baxter Slate."

"Okay, guys, glad to have you. Hope you enjoy the two weeks here. Anyways, you can work fruits with the regular team tonight and maybe tomorrow, then you can have some fun on the weekend working a Wilshire Boulevard bar. We got a complaint there's a big game going on in the back room a this cocktail lounge after closing time. Gotta check it out. Give you some front money maybe. See how you operate. Call it Secret Service money. The department is cheap. Cheapest fucking outfit you ever saw. The money's just for flash. You spend as little as you have to and bring the rest back. You lose it or somebody burns you for it, I gotta shoot myself like a Jap general. You don't wanna see old Scuz fall on his sword, do you, Sam?''

''No, Sergeant.''

''Scuz.''

''Scuz.''

''You, Baxter?''

''No, Scuz.''

''Okay, boys, then when your partners get here and start your teaching, pay attention to what they tell you. They'll tell you better than me. Just remember a couple things. One is that we work a misdemeanor detail and I don't want any man hurt for a shitty little misdemeanor. *Don't get hurt*. Got it, boys?''

And as Harold Bloomguard gulped nervously all three young men nodded at Scuz. ''And another thing, I'm sorry I gotta give you some a the shitty jobs but we get a vice complaint we gotta investigate it. I wish I could just let you work fun things like gambling and call girls and bookmaking back offices and fancy bars with good drinks, but that usually ain't what we gotta do. So try to have fun but don't get hurt. That's the only rule I got. You let yourself get hurt and I'll break your arm!''

For the next fifteen minutes six regular vice officers straggled into the squad room and said hello to Scuz who continued to befoul the entire room with the cheap cigar. The vice cops introduced themselves all around and worked in their logbooks and vice complaints.

The regular vice cops looked like Hollywood's version of Tripoli buccaneers, Turkish brigands or Viking warriors. One, a black, looked like a Sudanese caravan raider. All were young men, fiercely moustachioed and bearded with enough hair to stuff a mattress. They wore stylishly funky clothes like most young people. Yet beneath it all they were carefully washed and sprayed and powdered. They were so baroque and theatrical they *had* to be cops. Only Dominic Scuzzi could fool the street people.

''This one here's Harold Bloomguard,'' Scuz said to his troops. ''Look at him. This is what I been trying to tell you guys about how you should look. Ain't nobody gonna make him for the heat, right?''

''Right,'' answered the Viking.

''Then why don't you guys try to look like him? Why do you wanna look like you walk a beat for Attila the Hun?''

''Scuz, I ain't looked like Harold since I was twelve years old,'' said a Turkish brigand while Harold blushed at the laughter.

The three loanees were given a further briefing and within an hour they were heading for their vice cars.

''One more thing I almost forgot,'' Sergeant Scuzzi said, stopping the squad of men in the doorway. He sat back down, lit a new cigar and said, ''You new kids listen. If you go sneaking and peeking and prowling around backyards, you gotta *always* pay attention to the *size* a the dog shit. Got me?''

Then Scuz put his tennis shoes up on the desk and leaned back and puffed while a persistent fly who wanted desperately to light on the vice sergeant's pungent flesh decided to fly from the choking polluted clouds. Fleeing for his very life.

The three new kids on the block found themselves standing in the parking lot just before dark, each with a tiny flashlight the other vice cops lent them since their three and five cell lights were unwieldy on the vice detail. They waited for each of the three teams to pick one of them and were totally bewildered when no one did.

As Pete Zoony, a loose limbed vice cop with a woolly dust colored hairdo and a Fu Manchu moustache, got in his car he turned to the three loanees and said, ''We're not being unfriendly, it's just that Scuz is gonna come slipping and sliding out the door in a couple seconds. He can't relax when there's new guys around. Thinks you'll get killed if he don't break you in personally. Tomorrow night you'll work with us and we'll get better acquainted. Oh, oh. Here he comes.''

And the three choirboys turned to see Scuz shuffling through the door, stepping on the frayed ends of his shoelaces and scratching his balls, which was easy to do given the shiny baggy gabardine pants ready to wear through. Then he banged his little flashlight on the heel of his hairy hand, puffed a cloud of smoke into the summer breeze and scuttled across the parking lot, just stepping back in time to keep a black and white from running over him.

The officer driving, who was Roscoe Rules, said to Whaddayamean Dean, ''Fucking janitors they like these days look like goat shit! Oughtta make that prick clean up or fire him!''

As Scuz reached the three choirboys and his teams of regular vice cops who sat grinning in their cars, he said to Pete Zoony, ''Don't mind if I take the new kids out, do you, Pete? Just for tonight. I ain't got nothing to do anyways except the progress report for our psycho captain. Can't seem to think a any good lies to put in there tonight.''

''No, we don't mind, Scuz,'' Pete Zoony said. ''Just tell us where you're gonna take em so we don't bunch up in the same place.''

''Well, we got that three-eighteen about the shithouse up there in the department store.''

''Yeah.''

''And I might try this wimpy little kid here out on the whores on Western. Don't he look terrific?'' And Scuz threw a heavy arm around the wimpy little kid and hugged him.

Five minutes later, Sergeant Scuzzi was driving north on La Brea in a four door, five year old Plymouth which looked every bit like a detective car and disappointed the choirboys.

Sam Niles sat in the back seat with Baxter Slate and Harold sat in front, nervously blowing spit bubbles off his tongue which plinked on the dashboard as he scratched the strawberry rash on the back of his neck with a little penknife. Sam Niles decided then that Harold and Scuz would make perfect partners.

''This ain't much of an undercover car, is it, boys?'' Scuz remarked as they bumped and pounded over dips in the asphalt.

''Not much,'' Baxter Slate said. He looked at Scuz in disbelief but not without affection from time to time.

''Cheap outfit, boys. I mean we work for a cheap outfit. Be amazed how little Secret Service money I get. End up spending my own bread more often than not. Think we can go in the bar and nurse one drink for three hours? Shit, they *know* we're cops when they see how fucking stingy we are.''

''Where we going first, Scuz?'' Harold asked, perspiring because the sun had not yet set and it was muggy for Los Angeles. And because he was very nervous.

''Boys, I gotta take you to a trap first off tonight. And I gotta apologize which I don't like to do cause I always feel a cop shouldn't have to apologize for doing his job. But the truth is—and don't tell your lieutenant old Scuz told you this when you go back to patrol—but the truth is that most of a vice cop's job is just public relations. See, we can say we're protecting the city's morals and point to statistics to prove it, but fact is we ain't doing much a anything. So you might say, Scuz, what the hell we doing it for? And I say, boys, it's part a the game. Every business has its PR department where they manufacture bullshit, right? General Motors got it. U.S. Steel got it. AT&T got it. For sure the White House got it and City Hall. We can tell all the folks who pay our salary that we're guarding the morals a the citizens from the degenerates that wanna pay money to suck, fuck or gamble with someone they ain't married to outta the privacy a their own bedroom. You only work this vice detail for eighteen months and then you're out. I say it's a little break from routine for me so I work it but I ain't got no illusions about cleaning up maggots. In the first place how do I know I ain't just a maggot myself, you stand back and look at the whole picture in general?''

The choirboys glanced at one another and gave Scuz no argument.

''So anyways that's my philosophy about vice work. And you kids're gonna work for me for a couple weeks. And since you're doing a job that ain't gonna help nobody anyways, I just don't want you to get hurt, see? So let's say you run into some six foot six fruit with nineteen inch arms who's a foot fetishist. And he buys a pair a black satin shoes from the shoe department a this store I'm taking you to, and takes the shoes into the shitter where he pulls out a can a whipped cream which he shoots all over the shoes. And then he stands there and licks the whipped cream off. Whadda you do about it, seeing as how you're gonna be behind a wall looking through a screen into the john and protecting the public morals?''

''Huh?'' said Harold Bloomguard.

''I asked, whaddaya gonna do about this weird guy?''

''Well, I dunno, Scuz,'' Harold said, blowing a spit bubble while Sam Niles toyed with his moustache and shook his head disgustedly, as Baxter Slate's wide smile grew wider with affection for Scuz.

''Harold, my boy,'' Scuz said. ''First place, I gave you a hint. I said the weirdo has nineteen inch arms!''

''Oh, I see!'' said Harold. ''Shine him on. Pass him by.''

''You got it!'' Scuz said, driving only fifteen miles per hour which was driving Sam Niles to distraction. ''Course there ain't no misdemeanor here in the first place. So happens that some guys like to eat whipped cream off black satin shoes. Just wish they'd do it home and we wouldn't get no calls about it but thing is they like to do it in public. Anyways there ain't no law against it I know, so you just hope he gets full a whipped cream in a hurry and gets the hell out before someone calls the station and the station turns the problem over to the vice squad. Ready for another hypothetical?''

''Sure, Scuz,'' grinned Baxter Slate, accepting a cigarette from the lethargic Sam Niles who was wondering how it was he had wanted to work vice.

''Okay, you're in the trap, peeking through the screen and some dude walks in the john and he pulls down his jeans and there inside the underwear he carries a toothbrush and a feather. And his dick's all wrapped in rubber bands and rags to make it bulge outta his tight pants. And he sits down on the pot and reaches down in the toilet water and after he unwraps it he starts splashing cold water up on his dong. And he brushes it off with the toothbrush. Then he pulls out the feather and tickles his balls and when all this is done he's able to take a leak, which he does sitting down, and then he leaves. Any violation there?''

''None,'' Baxter Slate said.

''Okay, what if there ain't no door on any a the toilets, which there ain't because the manager a this department store is trying to discourage the fruits who like to meet here and poke their cocks through glory holes and all that. Now there he is, no door, just side walls around the toilet and everybody walks in can see him, including little kids.''

''Well . . .'' Baxter hesitated.

''And just to mix you boys up a little, let's say that our vice complaint which brought us here in the first place is from some lady lives near here and her kids always come use this rest room on the way home from school, and she says they got propositioned by some grown up fruits and don't her kids got no rights?''

''Well . . .'' Baxter Slate hesitated.

''Sure, if the fruits didn't get a naughty kick outta doing it in public johns because it's guilt and sin and fun and anal obsession and everything all mixed up and it ain't the same in a private room, well then we wouldn't have to come here at all.

But that ain't the case and it's pretty hard to tell the lady her kids just have to put up with some dude propositioning them or blowing some other dude in front a them in the shithouse, ain't it, Harold?''

''I guess so, Scuz.''

''Agree, Baxter?''

''I guess. Seems as though there should be some other solution.''

''Seems like,'' Scuz said, ''but there ain't. Not for us. We got the problem and the complaint. We gotta do something and that something is to make at least one arrest so when the lady calls back because some other fruit tried to grope her kid, we can show her that we took action on her last complaint. See, boys, there's just a million problems in this world that there ain't no solutions to and cops get most of those kind.''

''So how would you handle the guy who doesn't bother any children and just does his number with the toothbrush and feather?'' asked Sam Niles whose pose was always boredom whether or not he was bored.

''I shoot him,'' Scuz answered.

''You what?'' Harold exclaimed.

''I shoot him. With this,'' Scuz said, pulling a pink plastic water pistol from the pocket of his baggy gabardines. ''I just shoot him through the screen where I'm peeking. First it confuses him, then it scares him soon's he realizes where it's coming from. See, I don't add to his thrill by bracing him and threatening him or any a that shit. Just makes him wanna come back some more. Remember, guilt and punishment and stuff from his kiddy days is partly the reason he has to do all this in a public place. So I just shoot him with my gun. Pretty soon he don't know who or what's behind that wall. Sometimes he yells, 'Who're you? You store security? You a cop? Who's shooting me?' ''

''What do you say?'' asked Harold.

''Nothing. I just shoot him again. It's humiliating. It degrades him in a way he can't stand. See, he might wanna degrade himself with the stuff he does in a public shitter but he can't take the kind of humiliation I give him. I'm saying to him with my water gun that his little act ain't worth no more than a few squirts a water. *That* he can't stand. I've seen em go out in tears and never come back. At least not to *that* rest room and that's all I can worry about at the moment. Make any sense?''

''Maybe it does at that,'' Baxter Slate said as Scuz lit another cigar and turned on Wilshire Boulevard.

''See, I don't wanna get in a big fight with these guys. I don't wanna hurt them but I sure don't wanna have them hurt me or my boys. So I spend most of my time figuring out how I can satisfy the citizens that make the vice complaints and keep my boys from getting hurt at the same time. I know most vice supervisors wouldn't agree with me but I don't think it's too bad a way to run a vice squad.''

''Not bad at all, Scuz,'' grinned Baxter Slate, rolling down the window to let out some of the smoke.

''Reason we gotta work this department store tonight is they stay open till nine, and some fruit picks up some cat in the rest room couple weeks ago and offers him ten bucks to let him give the guy a headjob which is okay except he don't have no money after he does it. And to keep from getting his skull caved in he agrees to let the guy buy ten dollars worth a merchandise on his credit card. And the butch guy goes out and buys a hundred dollar suit and tells the fruit if he don't sign for it he'll do a fandango on his gourd with his boots. So then the fruit comes and complains about the cowboy. So I say to the guys in the dicks' bureau, you got an extortion, maybe a credit card hustle, you ain't got no vice squad case. But our captain says, 'I think you better take a three-eighteen, Sergeant, and let your vice boys make an arrest there.' See, he always calls me 'Sergeant' when he's on the rag which is most a the time. So anyways we gotta work the trap in the john and

I hope we make a pinch tonight so I can put this vice complaint to bed. I don't like to make my guys sit around smelling shit."

A few minutes later the battered vice car bumped into the parking lot at the rear of the large Wilshire Boulevard department store where shoppers were carrying bundles and fighting each other for parking places and stealing packages out of each other's cars, as smoggy summer darkness finally fell on Los Angeles.

As Scuz led the three choirboys into the building and to the storage room which was attached to the rest room on the second floor, Baxter Slate spotted a man sitting on the floor of the corridor leading from the rest room. A stack of ten newspapers was on the floor beside him. His legs were folded under him like hinged sticks. His right hand was a claw, his left was worse. He scratched at the wall like a mutilated insect, unable to gain his feet. He was a forty year old newspaper vendor and several times a day he had to leave his newsstand to use the rest room in the department store. He had cerebral palsy but could usually get to the rest room and back to his chair quite easily, often selling a paper or two along the way. Tonight he was suffering from a summer cold which weakened him like an attack of pneumonia would disable a healthy man.

Scuz turned around and saw two of the choirboys looking down the hallway at the man. Sam Niles wanted to help the man stand up but hated to attract attention to himself and make the other policemen think he was a do-gooder. Baxter Slate wanted to help the man stand up but was afraid the man would interpret his gesture as patronizing and snarl him away with righteous indignation. So both Sam and Baxter pretended not to see the man lolling on the floor and averted their eyes self-consciously. And felt guilt because they were unable to help.

Just then Harold Bloomguard saw the man. He didn't think much of anything. He just said, "Oh," walked down the corridor, took the palsied newspaper vendor by the arm and started to raise him up.

Then Scuz, who wondered why his parade had slowed, turned and saw Harold Bloomguard. He didn't intellectualize either. He walked past Sam and Baxter and joined Harold who almost had the man to his feet.

"Stumbled, huh?" Scuz said, bending over and picking up the fallen man with one arm as easily as a doll, while he gathered up the stack of newspapers with the other. "Slippery goddamn floors in this store. Someone always going on their ass."

He half carried the man to a bench near the rear door and seated him there with the stack of papers beside him as the man perspired and panted, unable to speak.

"Got the late edition?" Scuz asked, taking a coin from his pocket and putting it in the lap of the man as he took a paper from the stack and folded it into the back pocket of his gabardines. "Feel okay, partner? Want me to take you anywheres?"

The man managed a twisted smile and shook his head, and Scuz nodded, saying, "See you around, partner." Then he shuffled off down the hall with Harold Bloomguard at his side and the other choirboys trailing.

As Scuz passed an old man people-watching on a bench by the elevator, he said, "Here you go, Dad," dropping the paper beside the threadbare pensioner. "It's a late edition. I ain't got time to read it."

"Well, thanks," said the old man as Scuz opened the door of the storage room and led the three choirboys to the platform.

Two men could stand and look through a heavily screened one by two foot opening into the lighted rest room where shoplifters hid merchandise under their clothing and where men publicly masturbated and buggered each other, forcing Sergeant Dominic Scuzzi to force the choirboys to peek and smell shit.

They weren't in the trap ten minutes before a man in a candy striped shirt and double breasted blue blazer walked in, looked nervously in each toilet stall and, finding himself alone, withdrew his penis and wrote a lazy S on the rest room floor from wall to wall.

''That deserves a shot,'' whispered Scuz from the platform in the darkened room. ''See if I remembered to load it. Yeah, I did.'' And he put his pink plastic water pistol up to the screen and gave the man two bursts.

The man looked up at the ceiling for leaky pipes, saw none and tried to write some more. Scuz gave him two more bursts which caused him to cry out and walk around the rest room for another puzzled look into each toilet stall. Then Scuz gave him another burst and the man screamed and ran outside.

''He was easy,'' Scuz said, stepping down from the platform to let Sam Niles have a look. ''Reason I ran him off is I suspect he's one a these pissy pork pullers. Takes a leak and beats off and cuts out. Guy can do most anything legally long as he's alone. Gotta catch one that does his number with somebody else. Then we can make a pinch and close the vice complaint and get the fuck outta here and say we protected the people's morality. Until somebody else makes another vice complaint. Some fun, hey, boys?''

''Yeah,'' muttered Baxter Slate as Sam Niles grimaced disgustedly and longed for a cigarette because he couldn't have one in the close dark room.

''Tell you what,'' Scuz said. ''I'm gonna leave you two guys here and take Harold with me for a pass down Western Avenue. See if we can catch ourselves a whore. Now I don't like leaving two new guys here like this so I'll be sending a team to come and sit with you. You two guys just hang loose and wait here and don't go busting nobody unless a murder is being committed before your eyes, got me?''

''Uh huh,'' Sam Niles said.

Scuz opened the door to the outside corridor and let Harold out into the light. Then Scuz turned and said, ''You get bored you might amuse yourselves by betting quarters whether the next guy in will be a helmet or a anteater.''

''What's that mean?'' Baxter Slate asked.

''Circumcised or uncircumcised,'' said Scuz as he shoved another cigar between his teeth. Then he threw his pink water pistol to Sam Niles saying, ''Careful, it's loaded.''

The first man into the rest room stepped up to the urinal and emptied his bladder. The two choirboys looked at each other and wondered how they had gotten here. He was an anteater.

The second man was also an anteater. However, the third, fourth and fifth were helmets. The sixth was an anteater and cost Baxter Slate twenty-five cents. The seventh was a helmet and Baxter won the money back. Neither man cared what the eighth one was. The ninth was an anteater but he soon turned into a helmet because he sat down on the toilet and began playing with himself after looking at a picture of Raquel Welch in a movie magazine. But then he looked at a picture of Warren Beatty and seemed just as excited.

Sam Niles gave him four bursts with the pistol and he ran out cursing, wiping the wet pages of the magazine on his shirt.

Baxter Slate said, ''I can't take two weeks of this.''

Sam Niles offered Baxter a cigarette, opened the door for ventilation and nodded.

Meanwhile Sergeant Dominic Scuzzi was sitting in the parking lot of a food market near Pico and Western briefing an exceedingly nervous Harold Bloomguard.

''So I'm gonna be right here in the parking lot,'' Scuz said as Harold nodded and compulsively blew spit bubbles and cleaned the bogus horn rimmed glasses for the third time and made ready to get in his own car, a three year old Dodge Charger which they had picked up at the station parking lot after leaving Sam and Baxter.

''I don't want you roaming too far, Harold, got me? Just go a block or so down Western and no more than a couple blocks east on Pico. You get a broad in the car, you get your offer like I told you, then badge her and bring her back here quick. She wants to jump out, let the bitch do it. You drive here to me and we'll just cruise on back and scrape her off the street. You don't go roaming more than a couple blocks from me, right?''

''Right,'' said Harold.

''You nervous, Harold?''

''No. Not too much,'' he lied.

''Got a comb?''

''Yeah.''

''Comb you hair back off your forehead. You goddamn kids all gotta look like rock singers. Comb it back. Show your high forehead. Makes you look even more square than you already look.''

Scuz turned the rearview mirror for Harold who parted his ginger hair and combed it back.

''Help if you had some greasy kid stuff,'' said Scuz, who put the glasses on Harold when he was finished.

''I look okay?''

''Shit, ain't nobody gonna make you, Harold. Nobody.''

''Guess I'm ready then.''

''Okay, try going east on Pico there, circle south on Oxford, maybe, then back to Western. I want you close to me.''

As Harold fired up the Charger, Scuz fired up a fresh cigar and swatted at a swarm of gnats which had discovered him.

Meanwhile, as Harold Bloomguard began his maiden voyage into the land of vice, things were happening in the store where two revolted choirboys sat smelling human defecation in a dark and stuffy room.

First, Pete Zoony, the veteran vice cop with the woolly hair and the Fu Manchu strolled into the rest room, grinned up at the screened hole on the wall and said, ''Don't bother making a bet. I'm a Jew.''

''How long we have to stay in here?'' asked Sam Niles, whose voice boomed through the vent hole and echoed off the tile of the rest room.

''Scuz called us on the radio,'' Pete Zoony said, examining his teeth in the mirror. ''Told my partner to drop me here to sit with you. Said to give it an hour, no more. We wanna close this complaint bad. Wish we had a drunk wagon like Central. I'd have them carry two sleeping winos inside and leave them in the same toilet stall, then call the store manager to witness the orgy we discovered. After that we could close the complaint.''

''Well, nothing's happened since we've been here,'' Baxter said. ''Maybe the fruits stopped coming here.''

''Maybe so. Think I'll mosey outside and see there's any new broads I haven't met. When you come out for a break take a look at the set of tits works the perfume counter right across from junior miss clothes. I hear a policeman from North Hollywood's balling her. Dynamite! Catch you later.''

And Pete Zoony was out the door looking for willing young clerks when he spotted two uniformed policemen entering the office of store security. Out of curiosity he sauntered across the floor and caught one of the three night security officers coming out.

''What's happening?'' Pete Zoony asked the plainclothes security officer who knew all the vice cops from the rest room watch.

''Shoplifter. No big thing. Second time we caught her. Gonna put her in the slammer this time to see if it discourages her. Make her steal from Sears instead of us.''

Pete Zoony nodded and decided to go leer at the girl who balled the North Hollywood policeman but had been coyly resisting Zoony's persistent advances.

Then one of the uniformed policemen came out of the security office and headed straight for the rest room. Pete Zoony, who generally worked daywatch vice, was not known by many bluesuits on the nightwatch. He made a regrettable error in judgment by deciding to have a little fun and entertain the two new kids on the block. He followed the uniformed cop into the rest room.

"Roscoe Rules!" whispered Sam and Baxter simultaneously when the door to the rest room opened.

Then it was a matter of trying to suppress giggles as Roscoe, a helmet, relieved himself at the urinal and afterward stepped to the sink singing some Stevie Wonder.

He took off his cap carefully and teased his mousy hair, making it fall over the ears as much as possible without offending the lieutenant. Then he squeezed a watery pimple on his nose, straightened his tie and smiled with satisfaction while Baxter and Sam leaned on each other, smothering back the laughter. Their fellow choirboy stepped from the mirror, put the hat squarely on his head, held both fists against his hips and stood spraddle legged and broad shouldered, admiring the whole picture. And Sam Niles almost fell off the platform in muffled hysterics just as the rest room door flew open again and Pete Zoony came swishing in.

"Sam! Sam!" Baxter whispered, pulling his friend back to the screen as Pete minced past Roscoe Rules singing, "I Got a Crush on You, Sweetie Pie!"

He stepped to the urinal, peeked coyly over his shoulder at the unbelieving policeman and pretended to be taking a leak while he batted his eyelashes at the choirboy.

"Well I'll be a motherfucker!" said the outraged Roscoe Rules.

"Oh, I hope you're not!" Pete Zoony squealed as he zipped up his pants and swished across the room to the washbasin where he put a few drops of water on his fingers and patted his cheeks.

He dabbed daintily with a paper towel, singing, "Couldja coo, couldja care . . ."

"You got a lot a guts, you know that?" Roscoe Rules said as Pete Zoony peeked at him from time to time and giggled.

"Why whatever do you mean, Officer?" Pete lisped.

"You . . . you, you come in here and act like . . . like I'm a civilian!"

"Well I don't care what you are. You're just cute as can be, is all you are," said Pete Zoony, primping in the mirror as the choirboys behind the wall desperately tried to see through their tears.

"Goddamn you! How dare you talk to a police officer like this! Gimme some identification!" Roscoe sputtered.

"Gosh, don't get so upset," Pete Zoony lisped. "I mean just because a person pays you a compliment."

"You break out some ID right now," Roscoe demanded and Pete Zoony was preparing to pull his police badge from his back pocket when he erred, not knowing Roscoe Rules.

"Now, I'm gonna show you my driver's license, see, but I want you to promise you won't ask for my phone number cause I don't know you that well yet."

"You fag! You insolent fucking sissy!" screamed Roscoe Rules.

"Well!" said Pete Zoony huffily, so carried away with his role that he underestimated the light in Roscoe's close set eyes. "You wouldn't make fun of a person because he's crippled, wouldja? Huh?"

"You bastard!" Roscoe shrieked.

Pete Zoony pursed his lips and smacked a little kiss and said, "Oh, you're so cute when you're all mad! You blue meanie!"

Then Roscoe Rules reared back and slapped Pete Zoony across the moustache with the heel of his hand, catching him flush on the jaw and the vice cop was skidding across the slippery floor and banging against the metal trash can.

The two choirboys in the trap yelled, "No, Roscoe!" and jumped down from the platform and out the door, running down the corridor to the rest room.

They entered in time to intercept Pete Zoony who was growling and cursing and sliding on the floor attempting to get his feet under him as the bewildered Roscoe Rules looked up at the walls and ceiling, certain that he had heard ghostly voices shout his name.

"Niles! Slate!" Roscoe exclaimed as his fellow choirboys jumped on Pete Zoony to keep something terrible from happening which could get them all in trouble.

"You cocksucker!" shouted the outraged Pete Zoony, desperate to play catchup with Roscoe.

"*Me,* cocksucker? *Me,* cocksucker? You got a lotta guts, ya fag!" said Roscoe Rules.

It took a full five minutes to get Pete Zoony calmed down and Roscoe filled in on the prank that backfired. Finally the glassy eyed Pete Zoony smiled tightly and said, "No hard feelings, Rules," and swung a roundhouse left which caught Roscoe on the right cheekbone and dumped him into a toilet stall, wherein both choirboys switched their attack to the cursing, raging Roscoe Rules who might have shot Pete Zoony to death were it not for Sam Niles keeping a wristlock on his gun hand.

The toilet stakeout was called off for the night then and there. Sam Niles would not release his wristlock on Roscoe until Baxter Slate had taken Pete Zoony out of the rest room to the parking lot in the rear. They found a pay phone and had Pete's partner pick them all up to rendezvous with Scuz and Harold Bloomguard.

When Spermwhale Whalen heard about the incident later that night at choir practice, he shook his head and said, "Someone's always punchin Roscoe Rules. Kid, you oughtta wear a catcher's mask."

"Greetings and hallucinations!" cried frightened Harold Bloomguard to the first street whore he spotted after cruising the streets for twenty minutes.

"Say what?" the tawny black girl said as she stopped on the sidewalk and cautiously approached the Charger which was parked under the streetlight in the red zone at Pico and Western.

She wore mint green pants, skin tight to the ankles where they flared out over patent green clogs. Her stomach was bare and she wore a green halter top which tied at the neck. Harold was sure he had seen her several times before but Scuz had assured him that the girls have a difficult time recognizing uniform cops when they see them in plainclothes. To whores, as to most people, the patrol cop is a badge and blue suit and little more.

"Hello hello!" said Harold Bloomguard, turning off his headlights and bravado as the girl approached the car, walking with the traffic so that customers could pull to the curb without making an illegal U-turn that might draw a police car.

"Well, hi there, baby," smiled the whore when she saw how "good" Harold looked.

But just then a set of headlights behind them flashed a high beam and a black and white pulled up beside him, preparing to write a parking ticket, thus doing its bit to combat prostitution. It was Spencer Van Moot and Father Willie.

"Okay, sir," Spencer said as the radio car double parked. "Let's . . ."

And then Spencer found himself looking into the tense, bespectacled face of his fellow choirboy, Harold Bloomguard, whom he knew was on temporary vice loan.

"Yes, Officer?" Harold Bloomguard winked.

Father Willie, thinking faster than his partner, said loud enough for the whore to hear, "Partner! We just got a hot call!" and he dropped the car into low.

"You're in a red zone, buster!" yelled Spencer Van Moot as Father Willie pulled out. "Don't be here when I come back!"

"Now don't be scared, honey," said the girl as the radio car sped away. "They jist love to scare off our tricks. Got nothin else to do, jist hassle people."

"And they're never around when you need them," Harold added.

"Tha's right."

Then the girl looked up as a white Lincoln pulled in behind Harold and a big suntanned man waved to the girl. She looked him over but opened Harold's door and got inside.

"Motherfucker looks like a cop to me," she said. "They borry these big shiny cars and try to fool us sometimes."

"Cop?" cried Harold Bloomguard, trying his hand at acting now that the attractive, sweet smelling whore was sitting next to him, looking much less exotic and threatening.

"Now, you jist calm down, honey. Ain't no cause to git scared."

"Cop?" repeated Harold Bloomguard, speaking in dry monosyllables, trying to remember the good opening lines Scuz had fed him as he drove east on Pico.

The whore pretended to be fixing her lipstick in the rearview mirror but was actually watching for a vice car.

"Now jist calm right down. Ain't no worry about cops. Those two told you bout the parkin ticket? I got a friend pays them off. Fact he pays off all the black and whites and all the vice in this district for me. So see, we kin jist have us a nice party and don't have to worry bout nothin."

"Party?" Harold wanted a more explicit word for a better case. His hands were sweating and slipping on the steering wheel.

"Party. You know? Love. Half and half. French. Whatever you wants."

"Oh yeah, I want!" Harold turned south on Oxford, hoping she would hurry and mention the money, too nervous to appreciate her billowy breasts as she dabbed at her lipstick and making sure there was no vice car slipping behind them with lights out.

"You got twenny-five dollars, sweetie?"

"Sure."

"That's the tariff. And it's cheap for all you get."

Then Harold turned west on Fourteenth Street and the girl said to turn left on Western but Harold turned right.

"Hey!" she said suspiciously but Harold pressed the accelerator to the floor, sped north for half a block, screeched across the southbound traffic lanes and skidded into the market parking lot while the whore yelled, "Gud-damn!" and bounced around in the car. Then Harold saw Scuz in the vice car sitting in the dark at the rear of the market. Only then did he feel heady and elated.

He pulled off his glasses, the triumphant unmasking of an undercover man, and said, "You're under arrest!"

"Oh shit," she replied.

Then for effect Harold put the glasses back on, skidded to a stop beside Scuz, pulled them off again and said, "You're under arrest, young lady!"

"You already said that. I got ears, stupid," said the whore.

Scuz shuffled around the car and opened the door for the whore as Harold decided he should show her his badge.

"Don't bother, Harold. She knows who you are—now. I'll baby-sit Bonnie here. We're old pals. You go out and see you can get another one."

The girl stalked gloomily to the back door of the vice car and said, "Sergeant, where'd you get this little devil? He don't look nothin like a cop."

"See? See, Harold?" grinned Scuz, puffing happily on his cigar, delighted with the professional accolade.

"You're so young," Harold said to the girl as she slid across the seat of Scuz's car. Harold noticed her smooth brown legs for the first time and her pretty mouth and shapely natural hairdo.

"She's even younger than you, kid," Scuz said, closing the door and getting in the front seat where he could blow cigar smoke out the window and not suffocate the whore. "See you can get us another one that easy, Harold."

"You're so young and pretty," said the saddened choirboy. "How'd you get started in this business?"

"Oh no!" the whore cried, slumping back in the seat, appealing to Scuz.

"Harold, just go on back out, see you can get another one," Scuz said. "Let Bonnie here rest her sore feet."

Harold Bloomguard emptied his gas tank driving and made himself dizzy circling around and around the block looking for another whore so Sergeant Dominic Scuzzi could write a good progress report for that psycho of a captain, while a sullen young whore named Bonnie Benson got sick from the air befouled by Dominic Scuzzi's ten cent cigar.

While this was happening Sam Niles and Baxter Slate were sitting in a cozy dark cocktail lounge much farther north on Western Avenue where there was obviously little chance for a vice arrest but lots of chances for free drinks which the management gladly supplied Pete Zoony and his fellow vice cops.

Pete sat in the booth with Baxter and Sam and sipped a Scotch on the rocks, using the ice to rub on the bruise which Roscoe Rules had put on his jawbone before he put a much larger one on Roscoe.

Finally Pete said, "Mind if my partner and me disappear for a while? We gotta check out an answering service supposed to be taking call girl action. More than one or two guys'd look suspicious. Be back in an hour. We'll raise Scuz on the radio and tell him where you are, so either he'll pick you up or we will. Meantime, drink all you want and get a beef dip, they're pretty good. It's all on the house."

"Sure, Pete," Baxter said.

After the vice cop left, Sam said, "Wonder how big her tits are? Wish she had a couple friends."

Baxter Slate downed his bourbon and ordered a double. "Just as well drink like a vice cop," he grinned as they sat on tufted seats and felt fortunate to be out of the toilet. "Guess you might say we had a fruitless night."

"That sounds like something Harold would say," Sam yawned, starting to look bored. "Just like everything else. It'll start to be a drag."

"What?"

"Vice work. Jesus, what a way to make a living."

"Did you feel embarrassed, like we were peeping toms or something?"

"Christ, yes. You see enough shit on the streets without going to rest rooms to look for more."

And then Baxter, who was getting a glow from the bourbon, said, "There're worse jobs than vice."

"What for instance?"

"Juvenile."

"Oh yeah. I always wondered what made you leave so soon."

"Just didn't like it," Baxter said, draining his glass and signaling to the waitress.

She looked even more bored than Sam Niles as she padded across the carpet in a silly tight costume which was supposed to push her breasts up and out and make her look like a sexy tavern wench instead of what she was: a blowsy divorcée with three young children who were running wild because she worked nights and wasn't supervising them.

"Don't think I'd like Juvenile either," Sam Niles said, ordering a double Scotch. "Bad enough working with adults without taking crap from bubblegummers."

"You handle some dangerous little criminals over and over again and you can't get them off the streets because of their tender age. Despite the fact that they're more predatory and lack an adult's inhibitions. But I could live with that. It was the other things that bothered me. The children as victims."

"Can't let it bother you," Sam Niles said as he drained his glass. "Must water their drinks here. Oh well, the price is right." And he was ready to signal for another round.

"You know, you expect certain dreadful cases," Baxter continued, "like the child molester who loved to see little girls tied up and screaming. Or the four year old I saw on my first day in court when her mother's boyfriend was brought in and she started crying and a policewoman said to me, 'He stuck it in one day and gave her gonorrhea.' "

Sam Niles wished a couple of unattached girls would come in and end Baxter's stories.

"What I wasn't prepared for were the other things." Baxter's speech was beginning to slur as he stared at the glass, for the first time failing to smile and thank the waitress who put a fresh one in front of him. "You should see what the generic term 'unfit home' can mean. The broken toilet so full of human excrement that it's slopping over the top. And a kitten running through the crap and then up onto the table and across the dirty dishes. Brown footprints on the dishes which won't even be washed."

"Can't we change the subject? I've literally smelled enough shit for one night."

"And a boy who's a man at nine years of age. And wants to bathe his filthy little brothers and sisters and tries to, except that he accidentally scalds the infant to death."

"Baxter . . ."

"And a simple thing like a bike theft," Baxter Slate continued, looking Sam Niles in the eyes now. "Do you know how *sad* a bike theft can be when there's only one broken down bike in a family of eight children?"

"That kind of thing doesn't phase me, Baxter, you know that?" Sam Niles said angrily, and *his* speech was thick and boozy. "I have only two words of advice for guys like you and Harold Bloomguard. *Change jobs*. If you can't face the fact that the world is a garbage dump, you'll jump off the City Hall Tower. Christ, when I was a kid we never had *any* bikes, broken or not. My brother and I made a tether ball out of a bag of rags and I tied it to a street sign. That's the only toy I remember. Baxter, you can't save the world."

"But you see, Sam, I thought I could!" Baxter said, spilling some bourbon on his velvet shirt as he drank excitedly. "I thought it *was* possible to save the world—the world of the one specific child I was dealing with. Sometimes I would work as hard as I could to get a kid out of his environment and into a foster home. And he would run back to his degradation. Once I handled a case of child abuse at a county licensed foster home where I'd placed a little child. She'd been beaten up by the foster mother and I had the job of arresting the foster mother and taking the child out of the very home I had placed her in."

"So what?"

"The child had marks on her stomach. Strange cuts, almost healed. She was only three years old, Sam, and she wouldn't talk to me. She got hysterical around policewomen too. Finally I was the one to find out what the marks were. They were letters: L.D.B., which turned out to be the initials of an old boyfriend of the foster mother. *She* put them on the little girl with a paring knife. I'd placed the kid in that foster home to save the world of that one specific child. I was the worst Juvenile officer the department's ever had!"

"Hey, miss," yelled Sam and held up two fingers and sighed languorously as the waitress brought another round while Baxter Slate held his empty drink in both hands and stared at rings on the table.

"Listen, Baxter," Sam said. "We have crime in direct proportion to freedom. Lots of freedom, lots of crime. All I know for sure is something I've believed all my life. And it was verified for me in Vietnam and certified in the four and a half years I've been a cop. It's that people are never more pathetic than when they're asking themselves that absurd, ridiculous, laughable question, 'Who am I?' "

And then it was Sam's turn to spill several drops as he tipped his glass. He paused, wiped off his moustache, pressed the nosepiece of his glasses and said, "If most people ever let themselves find the answer to *that* question they'd go into the toilet and slash their wrists. Because they're nothing! The sooner you understand that, the sooner you can do police work without torturing yourself."

"I wouldn't be telling you this, Sam, if it weren't for this," Baxter Slate apologized, holding up the glass. "Sometimes I try to tell my partner but Spermwhale's only interested in paying off his ex-wives." And Baxter tried a broad Baxter Slate smile which did not work because there was fear in his bourbon-clouded green eyes. "After I left Juvenile I started experiencing strange flashes in the middle of the night. I could almost see glimpses of what it is *not* to be, to have life go on without you. It happens in a half sleep. It's happened a lot since I killed that man. Have you ever experienced it?''

And then Sam Niles touched his moustache and said, ''No.'' And Baxter Slate, who always believed his friends, did not know that Sam Niles was lying. ''I wish some broads'd come in. I wish the drinks weren't so watered down,'' Sam Niles said.

''Sam, I know you're right about people being nothing. All my life, all my religious training in Dominican schools was built on an explicit belief in evil. But there is none. Man hasn't the diginty for evil. And if there's no evil there's very likely no goodness! There're only accidents!''

''Please, Baxter,'' Sam Niles said, ''I'm just a cop. I don't . . . I'm not . . .''

''Sorry, Sam,'' said Baxter Slate, draining the bourbon and turning green watery eyes to his friend. ''I don't always go on like this. I'm not usually such a silly pseudointellectual horse's ass. Ask Spermwhale.''

And then he managed a real Baxter Slate grin, candid, disarming and tried to make light of it. ''It's that I know you just got your degree in political science. I love to talk to someone who won't get mad at me for using an adverb or two.''

Then Sam Niles managed an embarrassed chuckle because it was over. ''Okay, Baxter, it *is* nice not having to move your lips when you read so as not to offend a Philistine like Roscoe Rules.''

Sam Niles was starting to like his friend Baxter Slate so much he never wanted to see him again.

And while Baxter and Sam were getting drunk and being horses' asses, and while Baxter secretly thought of the ordinary guy he killed and the tortured child he let die, Harold Bloomguard finally found another whore.

The Cadillac Eldorado had not been there on his last pass, Harold was sure of it. Then he saw the white girl saunter out of the bar and head for the car. Harold tried to get over to the number two lane but the car behind him began hitting his headlight dimmer switch and blowing his horn. Harold drove two blocks east of Western Avenue, turned his Dodge around and came back. The white girl was gone. But in her place was a black girl who opened the door of the silver Eldorado, had an afterthought, turned and went into the bar.

Harold started to head for the vice car to ask Scuz if he could go in the bar. But he thought about it a moment and knew what the answer would be. Then he thought about getting a two-banger on his first night as a vice cop and he parked the car on Western Avenue, put his gun, handcuffs and badge under the seat, locked the car, wiped his moist hands on his handkerchief and entered.

The tavern was not a white man's cocktail lounge. It poured an extraordinary amount of hard liquor and the bartender didn't like to be troubled with fancy drinks. There was a jukebox playing Tina Turner, the volume turned five decibels higher than Harold could bear. There was a pool table on the side crowded with men playing nine ball at a dollar a ball and filling the room with blue tobacco smoke. There was a back room where nightly crap games attracted dozens of customers and occasional vice cops. As with most black men's crap games there was always a set of crooked dice in use and sometimes two sets, with one crooked gambler using shaved cubes against another.

But there was a vitality in the bar and Harold was excited as well as frightened when he saw that aside from the white girl, he was the only paddy in the place. Then he got a good look at the brassy blonde in the open red satin coat who sat on a bar stool holding an eight month pregnancy against the vinyl-covered cushioned railing.

It was ambition and curiosity, but mostly youth, which drove Harold Bloomguard to one of the empty stools on the near side of the bar as several black men at the pool table stopped the game and slipped any money from the table into their pockets until they were satisfied that Harold was a trick and not a cop.

The black girl who had almost gotten into the Eldorado was sitting next to the white girl and she, like the bartender, looked Harold over carefully and became satisfied that he could not possibly be The Man.

Then she smiled and said, "Why don't you sit over here?" And she moved to the right and gave Harold the bar stool between the two of them.

"Why not? It's invenereal to me where I sit," said Harold, using a Bloomguardism they didn't seem to understand or appreciate.

"What'll you have, chief?" asked the bartender, a graying black man with a bass voice that could drown out Tina Turner any old day.

"A Bombay martini straight up, very dry, with a twist, please."

The bartender just leaned on the bar and stared at Harold while the two girls edged closer. Then the bartender said, "I been workin hard all night, chief. Can't you make it easy on me?"

"Give him what the fuck he wants," said the black girl, who was taller than Harold and outweighed him but who was solidly proportioned, buxom and attractive.

"Look, I ain't trickin with him," the bartender said. "Besides, I ain't got no more Bombay."

"J&B and water?" offered Harold Bloomguard, rightly assuming from the number of black bandits who asked for J&B Scotch before sticking up a liquor store that the bartender would have no problem filling that order.

"Comin up," the bartender said. "You buyin for the ladies?"

"Indeed," said Harold Bloomguard, and he immediately thought of Roscoe Rules who disapproved of Harold's saying "indeed" because it made him sound like a fag.

After the three of them had their drink, the blonde with the eight month pregnancy put her hand on Harold's thigh and said, "Got a match?"

Harold picked up the match pack from the bar and found that he couldn't get it working. He was crestfallen when the blonde took the pack from his hand and lit her own cigarette. The choirboy feared that his nerves might give him away, but it had the opposite effect in that most inexperienced tricks were every bit as frightened as Harold Bloomguard.

"My name's Sabrina," said the big black girl who had a sensual glistening mouth.

"My name's Tammy," the pregnant blonde said. She had terrible teeth she was going to have pulled as soon as she dropped her frog and adopted it out and could hustle enough money to see a dentist, which she was having trouble doing what with her grotesque shape.

"My name's Harold Leekly. I'm a certified public accountant."

"Nobody asked you what you did," said Sabrina. "Why'd you say that? Maybe you're a cop."

"A cop!" cried Harold. "Ha ha! A cop!"

The bartender put the three drinks in front of them and said, "If this sucker's a cop, I'm a astronaut."

Then the blonde put her hand on Harold's thigh again and moved it up his leg. The leg began to tremble as Harold realized that Sabrina had her hand around his waist and both girls were smiling and making incoherent small talk and patting him down caressingly, expertly, just to reassure themselves. Then Sabrina put her hand on his right leg, the quiet one. It began to shake worse than the other.

"You shakin like a paint mixer," Sabrina said. "But we gettin outta here in a minute. We goin somewheres to quiet you down."

"Where we going?" Harold asked, thinking that if he swallowed the Scotch it might help relax him.

"Maybe to our pad, baby," Tammy smiled, showing her decaying fangs.

"That'll be eight dollars, chief," the bartender said as the girls gathered up their cigarettes and purses.

"For three little drinks?" Harold said. The bartender straightened up and glared down at him and Harold added, "Oh yes indeed, very good drinks, too, I must say!"

Harold tipped the bartender fifty cents which drew a sneer and a grumble and he followed the girls outside, remembering that Scuz had warned him that under no circumstance was he to go into a room with a whore because of the danger involved. He was hoping the girls would have given the offer before now and since they hadn't he decided to push it.

"By the way, what am I gonna get when we get where we're going?"

"Don't be in such a hurry, you cute little blue eyed jitterbug," Sabrina smiled as she fished the Cadillac keys out of a red leather handbag.

"Am I going with you?" Harold asked, thinking frantically for an excuse not to.

Sabrina answered, "No, you follow us in your car."

"Okay," Harold said, much relieved. "But I wanna know what's gonna happen. How do I know I'm gonna like it?"

"Oh, you gonna like it," Sabrina said, and she stepped over to him, there on the corner of Pico and Western, under the streetlights in full view of passing cars, and gave his genitals a squeeze.

"Woooo," said Harold Bloomguard, pulling back in embarrassment. "Woooo."

"I was just gonna tell you what you're getting," Sabrina said, as Harold stood off a few steps and blushed and swung his arms around, wondering if anyone had seen that.

He knew that he had just been "honked," as the vice cops called it, in a public place and that Scuz had said something about honking being a misdemeanor. But he couldn't remember if it applied only to fruit cases or whores as well. And he couldn't remember if the honking precluded the need for a money offer.

And as he stood there considering the next move, Tammy bounced over to him, grabbed his arm and said, "Let's go, cutie," and she gave him two more toots with a thumb and forefinger.

"Wooooo," said Harold Bloomguard, honked again.

"Gud-damn, man!" Sabrina said testily. "We ain't got time to stand around here all night and listen to you woo woo. Follow us down the street there where it's dark. We gonna talk about money."

"Money," said Harold Bloomguard, grateful to Sabrina for solving his problem.

He ran across Pico to his car, made a U-turn in a gas station and pulled back onto Pico facing east, following the slow moving Cadillac which turned right onto Oxford where it was residential. And very dark. The Cadillac pulled into the first available parking space on the right. Harold pushed his borrowed glasses up on his nose like his partner Sam Niles and found a parking space fifty feet farther south.

Then Harold carefully reached down, found his two inch off-duty gun, which he had decided to carry working undercover, and his badge and handcuffs. He shoved the gun and cuffs inside his belt in the back, put the badge in his back pocket and affected a jauntiness he did not feel as he quickly walked back to the Cadillac, to the whores waiting in the darkness.

Harold stepped up on the sidewalk, leaned in the passenger window, looked at Tammy's pathetic teeth and said, "Well, girls, let's bring this pimple to a head. Get down to business. How . . ."

"Git in," said Sabrina.

"Well before . . ."

"Get in," Tammy said, pushing the Cadillac's door open.

"Shouldn't we . . ."

"We gonna talk business *after* you inside," Sabrina said. Then she purred, "We want you here between us where we can feel your hot little body so maybe we kin git you to give us another dollar or two for our work."

"Slide over me, honey," Tammy said as Sabrina pushed the electric switches which took the white leather seats back and down.

As he was gingerly lifting himself across Tammy's enormous belly, he worried that she might feel the gun, but she didn't. And he thought how sad it was that a pregnant girl should be doing this kind of work, and while he was feeling sad she reached up between his legs and squeezed, making him say, "Woo woo," and sit down on her hand.

"Ouch!" she cried, pulling her hand out. "You fucking near broke my wrist!"

"Sorry," said Harold.

Then he began to wonder if he was doing the right thing by getting in the car. But he knew he was very close to bringing in a two-banger and he just couldn't stop now.

"You got fifty dollars, sweetie?" Sabrina asked abruptly.

"Sure."

"Well let's see it."

"Later, after we get where we're going."

"Ain't goin nowhere. We gonna do it right here."

"We are?"

Then it occurred to Harold that he had been honked and he had been solicited for money, but no one had specifically mentioned a sex act and he wondered if the arrest would be legal without it and just then Tammy honked him again and he grabbed her hand.

"Wait a minute, wait a minute," Harold said, desperately trying to remember the phrases Scuz had told him which would not be construed as entrapment.

"Why you just sittin there blowin bubbles off your tongue?" Sabrina asked.

The air was close in the darkness of the Cadillac with both big women pressing him. Then Harold remembered a word: "I'm looking for *excitement!*" he cried.

"Well, no shit!" said Tammy, and she honked him again but harder this time because she was getting sick and tired of dicking around with the little creep.

"What the fuck's wrong with you?" Sabrina demanded and she leaned back against the driver's door and pulled her dress midway up her thigh.

"I just wanna know what I'm gonna get," Harold said, and now his voice was hoarse and parched and he feared he was going to lose it all.

"We tryin to show you!" said Sabrina. "You wanna do it or talk about it, man?"

"Talk about what?" asked Harold Bloomguard who was oh so close to his arrest.

"Ballin! Frenchin! What the fuck you think?" shouted Sabrina.

"Sucky fucky, five bucks, oh thank you," whispered Harold Bloomguard who felt he had his case at last.

"What?"

"Sabrina!" said Tammy as she adroitly unzipped Harold's pants and shoved her hand inside. "He's hung like a hummingbird. He don't wanna ball. He's some kinda freak! Probably wants to beat on us with his shoe or something!"

"No, I don't," said Harold Bloomguard, pulling her hand from his pants and trying to rezip, but getting caught on the shirttail of his white dress shirt which protruded six inches from his fly.

"What's goin on here?" Sabrina demanded.

"Yeah!" said Tammy.

"Nothing," said Harold Bloomguard, struggling with the zipper.

"Feel my pussy if you ain't a freak!" Sabrina ordered and took Harold's hand and dropped it on her thigh.

"Let's get in my car and go to some romantic place," said Harold Bloomguard as his cold wet hand slipped off Sabrina's warm dry flesh.

"Shit," said Sabrina.

"Crapsake," said Tammy.

"You a freak," said Sabrina.

"I'm not!" said Harold.

"You a freak!" Sabrina shouted.

"Like hell!" Harold Bloomguard answered indignantly.

Then he pulled free from Sabrina, reached over Tammy's belly, opened her door and crawled over her lap until he was on the street.

"You a freak!" screamed Sabrina, thinking they had lost the fifty dollar trick.

"I not a freak!" shouted Harold Bloomguard, reaching in his back pocket and exultantly pulling his shield. "I a cop!"

And while the two whores stared dumbstruck, Harold reached inside the car and grabbed both purses and the car keys from the ignition.

"Hey!" Sabrina gathered her wits too late to stop him. "Now I've got your keys and I've got your purses so you're not going anywhere but with me!" said Harold Bloomguard, ripping off the horned rimmed glasses to show them the real man beneath the disguise. "Just don't try anything funny!"

"Well I'll be gud-damned," said Sabrina to Tammy who was about to cry. "PO-lice Department got to be mighty hard up these days to be hirin little cock-a-roaches like this!"

"Out of the car!" demanded the little cock-a-roach, reaching back for his handcuffs, remembering that Scuz had said that in vice cases you *always* handcuff two suspects and sometimes one if there's any doubt at all.

"We goin with you, man, but you ain't gonna be puttin those things on no pregnant lady, hear me?" Sabrina said as the three were standing on the sidewalk beside the Cadillac.

Harold Bloomguard thought it over, decided not to force the issue now that they were obeying so nicely, and put the handcuffs back in his belt, saying, "All right, but behave yourselves."

As they walked slowly to Harold's car on the dark sidewalk, Harold Bloomguard started to feel a little sad once again.

"You're both so young," said Harold. "Bet you're not over twenty-five, are you?"

When the miserable whores failed to reply, Harold said, "Ever been arrested before?"

"Bout thirty times," said Sabrina.

"Bout forty times," said Tammy.

"Oh," said Harold. And he tried to cheer them up by saying something funny, "I have no altourniquet but to do my job." Then he added, "I'm sorry about you and your baby and all."

"Why?" snapped Tammy, dabbing at her tears. "You didn't put it in my belly. You couldn't even get it up when I was playing with your dick, for chrissake."

"Well, it's not that I find either of you unattractive," Harold explained, "it's just that I'm a vice off . . ."

And then Sabrina started to groan and the groan quickly turned into a wail and then to a deathless shriek.

"RRRRRRRAAAAAAAAAAAAAPE!"

Sabrina grabbed Tammy's hand and then Tammy started to do it:

"RRRRRRRAAAAAAAAAAAAAPE!"

"Don't do that," said Harold Bloomguard but they didn't listen to him. Harold looked around at the darkness and the houses and said, "You're resisting arrest, you know."

"RRRRRRRAAAAAAAAAAAAAPE!" screamed the two whores in unison, and then, Sabrina leading, they started to run north on Oxford, hand in hand. Lights began coming on. Doors opened. A woman put her head out a window.

"I'm a policeman," said Harold Bloomguard. She closed the window.

Then Harold slung his purses over his arm and began jogging after the two whores, finding it easy to keep up at first, not particularly frightened now, just confused and embarrassed, wondering what the next move should be, wishing he had never presumed to catch a two-banger.

A strange thing happened. The two whores began to outdistance him as they turned west on Fourteenth Street and crossed over to the north sidewalk still screaming for help. Now Harold's heart began working a bit hard and he sprinted to catch up. Tammy turned and saw him closing in and dashed for the porch of the nearest house on the north side of the street where the front yards were small and the old houses were bunched together.

"Help! Help!" Tammy screamed as she banged on the door with one hand and held her belly with the other.

It was a sixty-five year old white man who came to the door, pulling his pants up and struggling with a bathrobe.

"What's going on here?" he said, switching on the light and squinting through the darkness.

"Help us!" Sabrina pleaded, standing on the porch next to Tammy, catching her breath.

Harold blocked the steps, holding his badge in his hand. "I'm a police officer!" he panted. "Go to your phone and call for help! Give your address!"

"Don't believe him!" Tammy said, leaning against the porch railing. "Please help me. I'm gonna have a baby!"

"I order you to call the police right now!" said Harold Bloomguard.

"But you say *you're* the police," the old man said, scratching his gray jaw stubble and looking from one to the other.

"I *order* you!" said Harold Bloomguard.

"Now just a minute, young fella, this's my house!" the old man said.

"Fred, you come in here and leave those lunatics be!" said a shrill voice inside.

Then Sabrina grabbed Tammy's hand and both girls pushed past Harold and began running back down the sidewalk the way they had come.

"I order you to get me some help, Fred!" Harold Bloomguard yelled as he turned and pursued the girls.

"Maybe you're a cop and maybe not. I wish you'd all stay for a while so I can find out what's happening!" the disappointed old man answered, but Harold Bloomguard had to concentrate on the prostitutes who had now passed a house where five young black men had been playing cards in the kitchen and were now attracted to the commotion out front.

The young men laughed as the girls ran past and the tallest one blocked the sidewalk and drained a bottle of beer and then tapped the bottle on his hand. Harold Bloomguard stopped.

"What for you chasin those little girls, man?" the youth demanded.

Harold Bloomguard puffed and panted and stood his ground. He reached for his badge and said, "I'm a police officer. Let me pass."

Then the others laughed and the tall one said, "That ain't no real badge. How I know who you be? I think you better jam off, baby. Leave those little girls alone."

Suddenly Harold Bloomguard was gripped by strangely exhilarating rage. "Okay, asshole, I'm *not* a cop," he said, pulling his gun and pointing it at the mouth of the young black man. "I'm a rapist! What the hell you gonna do about it?"

"No, I think maybe you *are* the PO-lice," the youth grinned, dropping the bottle to the sidewalk and stepping back for Harold to pass, as all the young men hooted and whistled while the chase continued.

The girls were plodding down Pico Boulevard now, trying to reach Western Avenue. Harold had to run hard to catch them, his purses still over the left arm, the gun in his right hand, the shirttail still protruding from his fly.

Sabrina ran into the street making a desperate lunge toward a car which had slowed on Pico at the sight of the two frantic women. She jerked the door open and was pleading with the man behind the wheel when Harold came running up behind, grabbed her hair and jerked her flat on her back as he fell, taking her with him.

Two women passing in a green Oldsmobile began to scream hysterically and the car screeched to a stop as Harold fumbled with his gun and purses.

"I'm a policeman!" Harold yelled to them, thinking that all a vice cop ever did was tell people he's a policeman.

As Sabrina limped to her feet, Tammy teetered on the curb, puffing, blowing, staring vacantly into space. Then Sabrina was running toward Tammy and pulling her coat sleeve, and miraculously the pregnant girl began to run.

Harold still pursued, catching misty glimpses of people driving and walking by, shaggy blurs. And he heard disconnected sounds as he wiped the sweat from his eyes and caught the two whores at the busy intersection.

Sabrina spun around and swung desperately at Harold but missed, and her hand slammed into the wooden wall of a vacant newsstand. She cried out and turned, but Harold grabbed her hair again and his neck was burning as Sabrina broke loose and fell into the street, crawling twenty feet into the center of the intersection where she sprawled on her stomach, her dress pulled up over her plump pantyless behind.

Tammy then limped frantically into the street, arms dangling, coat half torn from her back, belly bulging dangerously. She skidded while yet fifteen feet from her partner and toppled over slowly to her knees. Then she leaned forward, almost in slow motion, until her distended belly touched the asphalt. Harold knelt on the pavement and panted and stared for many seconds as she tottered on the enormous mound. Then she rolled over slowly and deliberately and floundered there belly up like a harpooned walrus. Tammy blocked two lanes of traffic and Sabrina one and a half.

The air was still razor sharp when Harold Bloomguard, taking large gulps of it, dragged Sabrina bumping and crying out of the traffic lane across the asphalt until her foot lay next to the hand of Tammy who was all but unconscious, lying there, panting softly, eyes closed, pink tongue protruding.

Harold finally had the chance to put his gun back in his waistband, and he handcuffed Sabrina's ankle to Tammy's wrist with no resistance whatever. Then he sat down in the traffic lane, in the glow of many headlights, as motorists yelled and blew horns and made every guess but the right one as to what the hell was going on.

Finally he heard the siren and instinctively behaved like a policeman trying to clear the intersection. He waved his purses at the motorists who became frightened and ran from their cars, leaving them abandoned and making things worse.

They came from all directions, painting the streets with rubber: radio cars, motorcycles, plainclothes units. Five separate hotshot calls had gone out. Neighbors complained of a man with a gun, a woman screaming, a purse snatch in progress, a man assaulting women and a mental case exposing himself. A code four, that suspects were in custody, was broadcast and still they came. Their emergency lights bathing Pico Boulevard in a crimson glow, lining up on both sides of the street, making the traffic jam more impossible.

Sergeant Yanov specifically put out an order for units to resume patrol. And yet they came. For policemen are by nature and training inquisitive and obtrusive. Twenty-one police units ultimately responded and a huge crowd gathered after Harold, Sabrina and Tammy had been whisked away. Officers and citizens asked many questions of each other which none could answer.

The prostitutes were treated at the emergency hospital for contusions and abrasions prior to being booked and Harold Bloomguard was surprised to discover a seven inch cut that began at his left earlobe, crossed the jawbone and ended on the neck. It was not a deep cut and only required a disinfectant.

"Must've gotten it from Sabrina's fingernails," Harold told Scuz when the girls were booked and they were back at the station composing a complicated arrest report.

"Harold, I thought you was smart," Scuz said. "I told you these're fucking misdemeanors. They ain't worth nothing, these vice cases. Who told you to go out and get hurt?"

"Sorry, Scuz, I just . . . I just wanted to win the game."

"I oughtta kick your ass for gettin hurt."

"I didn't get hurt, just this scratch on my neck."

"You coulda got killed! For what? A game? I ask you don't get hurt. That asking too much?"

"Sorry, Scuz."

"There's lots a vice sergeants in this town that'd pat you on the ass and write you an attaboy for bringing down the whores. But I ain't one a them. Risking your life for a shitty vice pinch! I thought you was smart!"

Then Sergeant Scuzzi paced around the vice office stepping on his shoestrings, and Harold sat quietly with the other two new kids on the block. Sam Niles and Baxter Slate were falling down drunk after having sat in the bar for three hours waiting for Scuz and Harold Bloomguard who were busy with other things. The two choirboys had swilled free drinks all evening.

"You kicking me off the squad?" Harold asked sheepishly.

"I oughtta kick you all off. Christ, you almost get killed and these other two twenty-six year old rummies get swacked sucking up bourbon."

"I was drinking Scotch, Scuz," said Sam Niles who held his head in both hands.

"Shut up, Niles!" Scuz said, relighting his cigar which was so badly chewed there were soppy flakes of tobacco stuck all over his lips and chin.

"Okay, you three just watch it from now on. Bloomguard, you need a keeper. I'm gonna supervise you personal. Make sure you stay alive the weeks you're here. Slate, you and Niles better keep your boozing under control, hear me?"

"Yes, Sergeant," Baxter Slate said. He was sitting woodenly, trying to convince Sergeant Scuzzi that he was cold sober.

"Fucking kids," Scuz said, shaking his head at the three repentant choirboys. "And another thing, Slate and Niles, I'd like to know how Pete Zoony got that knot on his face tonight. He was working fruits with you two a little earlier, wasn't he?"

"Yes, Sergeant," Baxter Slate said.

"Don't call me sergeant."

"Yes, Scuz," said Baxter Slate, who was trying to keep from vomiting.

"Lotta fucking mysteries around here," said Scuz. "Okay, you three go home and get some sleep. I want you in good shape tomorrow night. Gonna try to take a big poker game. And I'll be along to make sure you don't get killed!"

The three choirboys left then. Baxter vomited in the parking lot and felt much better. Sam said his headache was going away. Harold was buoyant from getting three whores his first night on vice. They wanted to go to choir practice but thought they better heed Scuz's advice. Then they decided to stop at the park just to see if any of the choirboys were still there.

"Drive by Pico and Western on our way," Harold said as Baxter aimed his Volkswagen in an easterly direction, not as sober as he thought he was.

"What for?"

"Wanna show you guys how far we ran," Harold said.

"Who gives a shit?" Sam Niles said, already sorry he had decided to come along to choir practice.

"Come on, lemme just show you," Harold pleaded, and Baxter smiled understandingly and said, "Sure, Harold."

When they got to the intersection, Harold insisted they circle the block and told the interested Baxter Slate and the disinterested Sam Niles how the chase began. He showed them Fred's house and the house where he drew down on the young black man.

"You know it's sad working vice," Harold said. "Those girls were young. All the girls I busted tonight were young."

"Their job demands the hope and vigor of youth," Baxter Slate said. He was beginning to feel better, reviving in the night air.

"Maybe so," Harold said. "Maybe so."

"Just like our job," Baxter added.

"If we're going to choir practice, let's go," Sam Niles said, sitting in the back seat of the Volkswagen with his long legs turned sideways, not enjoying his cigarette because his body wanted more oxygen than he was giving it.

"Right here is where she swung at me and scratched me," Harold said as Baxter stopped, ready to make a right turn on the red.

Then Harold said, "Wait a minute, Baxter. Pull over, will you?"

"Now what, Harold?" Sam Niles sighed, taking off his steel rims and wiping his eyes.

But Harold had hopped out of the Volkswagen as soon as Baxter parked and he stooped, picking up something from the gutter.

"What the hell're you doing, Harold?" Sam asked.

"Look!" Harold Bloomguard said, stepping over to the car.

It was a springblade knife: four inches of steel with a sequined handle. A woman's knife, feminine, well honed. The point had been broken off and Harold felt his heart make light hollow thuds as he walked to the vacant newsstand. He used the broken blade of the knife to dig the tiny triangle of steel out of the wooden wall. It was throat high and deeply imbedded.

"What're you doing, Harold?" Sam Niles demanded and was surprised when Harold snarled, "Shut up, Sam!"

Then the ugly chip of steel popped out and fell into Harold's palm and he looked at it for a moment. Harold Bloomguard propped the knife against the curb and disposed of it cop style with a sharp blade-snapping heel kick.

Baxter Slate figured it out first. "Any chance of getting a lift off the knife, Harold?"

"Rough fancy surface on the handle," Harold said. "No chance for prints. No chance."

Sam Niles started to ask Harold if he still felt sorry for the whores, but when Harold turned toward Baxter, Sam saw how tired and bitter Harold Bloomguard's mouth looked.

There were still a few dogged choirboys in the park when they arrived at 4:00 A.M., but Carolina Moon had gone home and Ora Lee Tingle had not been able to make it. Harold thought the night air was strangely chilled for the end of July. They adjourned when Francis Tanaguchi said that tonight's choir practice was a bummer.

12

Alexander Blaney

Alexander Blaney was not a choirboy but he had witnessed his share of choir practices. He had even come to know some of the choirboys by name as he sat alone two hundred feet across the grass in the darkness of MacArthur Park and listened to the lusty voices carry over the water.

Alexander Blaney often wished he could meet the choirboys, at least some of them. He knew of course that they were off-duty policemen. He wondered what

Father Willie looked like and the one called Dean who cried a lot when he was drunk. And he would have liked to meet Harold Bloomguard who was always protecting the ducks of MacArthur Park. There was one he didn't want to meet, not under any circumstances. He didn't want to meet Roscoe Rules whose talk was full of threats and violence. He didn't know what it meant to do the chicken but he was certain he wouldn't like it if Roscoe Rules made him do the chicken.

Alexander Blaney had grown up less than three blocks from MacArthur Park and was well known by some of the Juvenile officers at nearby Rampart Police Station. He was not known to the choirboys of Wilshire Station. Alexander was a handsome boy, even more handsome than Baxter Slate. He had dark curls and bright blue eyes, and though he was six feet tall, he hardly ate, weighing only 130 pounds.

Alexander Blaney was known by Rampart Juvenile officers because since the age of fourteen he had come to them with complaints about men who allegedly accosted him in MacArthur Park where he had played as long as he could remember. Alexander, an only child, had usually played alone. Since the neighborhood around Alvarado Street was predominantly white with a sprinkling of Cubans and Indians, it was not considered a ghetto. His parents never knew about the halfway houses nearby or of the number of men frequenting MacArthur Park who had spent years behind bars buggering young men who were not half as handsome and vulnerable as Alexander Blaney.

This is not to say that the neighborhood made Alexander Blaney what he was. No one, not even Alexander Blaney, knew what made him what he was. What he was *not* was the golden young conqueror his father had read about in his salad days when he dreamed of being more than a semi-invalid elevator operator. But if the lad had never acquired his namesake's taste for battle and glory, he had developed the sexual preference of the Greek warrior. For Alexander Blaney was, at eighteen and a half, a rubber wristed, lisping, mincing faggot.

While Alexander Blaney began getting accustomed to being gay and could not fool anyone by trying to hide the fact, Harold Bloomguard, nearing the end of his two weeks of vice duty, got drunk and came to the same conclusion.

"You're what?" Sam Niles asked as he and Sam sat alone in a vice car on a nighttime whore stakeout after having drunk six pitchers of beer in a beer bar they failed to operate effectively.

"I'm afraid I'm turning homosexual, Sam," said the beery choirboy. "And I'm terrified. I'm probably going to shoot myself or go to live with my mom in the funny place!"

"Oh please! Why me? Why me?" cried Sam Niles, slumping down in the car seat and pushing up his steel rims, so he could look to a heaven he did not believe in, to a God he knew did not exist. "All right, let's get this over with. When did you discover you were gay?"

"Just this week working the traps. You see, I started to wonder if a guy couldn't begin to identify, what with seeing that all the time, and with identifying comes acceptance and then . . . well, once I wondered if I might get a blue veiner watching that stuff sometime, and if I did it would mean I'm turning. And I'd have to kill myself."

"And did you get a blue veiner?"

"Well no, but maybe it's only my straight inhibitions stopping it. See what I mean?"

"I see," said Sam, lighting a cigarette. "And what's your next move? Gonna shoot yourself over on Duck Island?"

"I don't know," Harold belched. "You know how insanity runs in my family. I'll probably end up with Mom no matter what."

"You know, Harold, I think having you around might be more effective than electroshock. Your mother'll probably cure herself just to get away from you."

"Don't get testy with me, Sam. You're the only real friend I've got. I'm a sick man."

"You've been a sick man since you joined my fire team in Nam! You've been a sick man all your life, I'm sure. But somehow you survive all this by telling *me* all the screwy loony goofy neurotic fears you have THAT I DON'T WANNA HEAR ABOUT! I tell you *I'll* be the one doing the nudie tap dance with your mom in the state hospital!"

"Sam, you can tell your problems to me. I'd love to hear about *your* fears and . . ."

"I don't *want* you to be my confessor. I don't *need* a confessor, Harold."

"Everybody should tell his problems to someone, Sam, and you're my best . . ."

"Don't say it, Harold," Sam interrupted, trying to calm himself. "Please don't say I'm your best anything. We've been together a long time, I know. God, how I know."

"I'm sorry, I'll never burden you again," Harold said boozily.

"Oh yes you will. In a day or two you'll tell me you've discovered you're a sadist and you want me to keep an eye on you in case you start sticking pencils in somebody's eyeballs."

"I'm sorry, Sam. I never meant to be a burden."

They sat quietly for a moment and then Sam said, "Harold, did you ball Carolina Moon Tuesday night at choir practice?"

"Sort of, but only because I was drunk. And first."

"Well anyone who likes pussy enough to screw *that* fat bitch *can't* be a fruit, okay?"

"You know I never thought of that!" said Harold Bloomguard, brightening. "I never thought of that! Thanks, Sam. You always come through for me. If it weren't for you . . ."

"Yeah, yeah, I know," said the bored and disgusted Sam Niles.

Then Harold Bloomguard thought a moment and said, "How do I know I'm not bisexual?"

Harold Bloomguard's fears of being a bisexual were soon displaced by a more pressing fear when he decided he had cancer. Harold's discovery of the cancer came as a result of Scuz giving them the vice complaint against the Gypsy fortune teller, Margarita Palmara, who lived in back of a modest wood frame cottage near Twelfth and Irolo. The tiny building had been painted a garish yellow but was otherwise not unlike other homes in the area. The residence of Margarita Palmara was a garage apartment which had been converted from a chicken coop. The husband of Margarita Palmara literally flew the coop one day and left Mrs. Palmara to fend for her five children which she did in Gypsy fashion by con games, shoplifting and fortune-telling to supplement the welfare check. But then she had the good luck to tell a woman thought to be dying of a radium treated cancer that she would soon get well, and lo, she did. From then on Margarita Palmara was called upon by neighborhood women, who hailed from a dozen Latin countries, to cure anything from acne to leukemia. Just prior to the Wilshire vice detail's receiving a complaint from a disgruntled patient, Mrs. Palmara had quickly earned more than ten thousand dollars from the Spanish speaking women of the neighborhood. Never one to overdo a good thing she was thinking it was time she flew the coop herself before the cops heard about her.

But she waited a bit too long and the cops *did* hear about her. A middle aged Mexican-American policewoman named Nena Santos was ordered to pose as a neighborhood housewife and attempt to operate Margarita Palmara to get a violation of law.

"I see you will soon be cured of that which you believe to be cancer in your breast," the Gypsy said in Spanish to the undercover policewoman. "And this thing which is not a cancer, but an evil visitation, will leave your body. And you will feel twenty years old again and enjoy your man in bed as you have never enjoyed him before. And your luck will change. Your husband will find a better job that will pay as much as twelve thousand dollars a year. All this will happen if you keep the charm I am going to give you and if you faithfully say the words I am going to teach you and if you donate three hundred dollars to me which I shall use to support the orphans of my native land.''

But instead of crossing the Gypsy's palm with three hundred scoots, Nena Santos crossed the Gypsy's wrists with sixteen bucks worth of steel, and Margarita Palmara was busted.

Harold Bloomguard and Sam Niles were only two of the vice cops detailed to the stakeout across the street, and after getting the signal from Nena Santos, they went inside to meet the Gypsy and drive her to jail where she would be booked and released on bail that afternoon. Ultimately she was made to come to court and pay a fine of 150 dollars before she moved to El Monte, California, where she was able to make fourteen thousand dollars telling fortunes before being arrested again. It kept her and her children in fine style even after an angry judge then fined her 250 dollars to teach her a lesson.

But before she was taken from the house that day she left a curse or two behind.

Harold Bloomguard, along with Sergeant Scuzzi, Sam Niles and Baxter Slate, was roaming around the Gypsy's chicken coop waiting for the woman to make arrangements with a neighbor to take care of the children until she could bail out. In a little bedroom of the chicken coop the officers found a frightened seven year old Gypsy girl in a Communion dress.

She was a husky child, with a broad peasant face and black hair which grew too far down her forehead. Her skin was so dark it made the antique Communion dress look marshmallow white to Harold Bloomguard.

''*Cómo se llama?*'' Harold Bloomguard asked with an atrocious accent which embarrassed Sam Niles and made him snort in disgust.

In fact every time Harold made a good natured attempt to speak Spanish to people it embarrassed Sam Niles who said he knew enough Spanish to keep his mouth shut by not trying to speak it.

Sam argued with Harold Bloomguard later when Harold claimed the homely little girl was beautiful and that her dress was charming, when Sam could see it was a hand-me-down and almost gray from so many washings. Sam said that she was nothing but an ugly little thief who would grow up to be an ugly big thief like her mother.

As they were leaving the house the angry Gypsy turned a sagging chamois face to the gathering of vice cops and said in English, ''You believe I not have power? That I cheat people? Very well than. I prove you are wrong. I can cure. I can make sick. You!'' And the golden bracelets clanged as she pointed a scrawny finger at Harold Bloomguard. ''*You* shall get the sickness!''

It was a terrified and bleary eyed Harold Bloomguard who was in the district attorney's office the next day nervously blowing spit bubbles as he filed a complaint against the Gypsy for grand theft. He was absolutely certain that the prosecution of the Gypsy would seal his fate.

It was actually weeks before Harold stopped asking other choirboys to feel his breasts for suspicious lumps he knew lurked beneath the flesh. He only desisted when one night at choir practice Spermwhale Whalen agreed to feel the left one and got Harold in a headlock and stroked his tiny nipple lasciviously and said, ''Harold, this's givin me a blue veiner!'' And threw Harold down on the grass, dropping on top of him, making the little choirboy scream for help. After that Harold suffered in silence and never asked anyone to feel his breasts.

Alexander Blaney didn't know he was going to be an admitted homosexual and arrested at age eighteen and a half, when at the age of fourteen he started noticing the cruel looking men with pasty jailhouse complexions who would stare at him in the park rest rooms. But he became aware early on that MacArthur Park was more than a place for old men to play at lawn bowling or for immigrants to kick a soccer ball or city dwellers to sit on the grass and picnic, throwing crumbs to the ubiquitous ducks in the large pond.

Alexander saw and understood the eye signals, the furtive smiles, the men who met and paired off to disappear in the bushes at night or to meet and join inside the rest room where vice officers often arrested them and sometimes got in bloody fights before the eyes of the boy.

The lad was once reading a book on the grass by a park rest room when he was startled by the noise inside and saw a huge ex-convict they called The Hippo crashing through the door, beaten to a bloody pulp by a cursing, burly vice cop whose lip was split and hanging loose and who was playing catchup on The Hippo with a sixteen ounce sap.

Alexander Blaney saw far more than that in the same park rest room. He once saw a young man masturbating at a urinal and watched in fascination until the young man stepped away and ejaculated against the dirty tile wall between the urinals and toilets only to have a white haired man with flesh like onionskin and arms like pencils get up off the toilet and wipe the semen off the wall with his fingers and put it in his mouth. He smiled at Alexander Blaney and sickened the boy.

And it was about that time that Alexander Blaney became known to Rampart Juvenile officers. The boy would come in at least once a month to report a lurid sex act he had observed in MacArthur Park. Once he claimed to have seen a big man sitting on the toilet with his trousers at his ankles stuffing his penis in his own rectum. And then there was the hermaphrodite who found Alexander Blaney lying on the grass composing madrigals to his music teacher. Alexander was fifteen and the busty hermaphrodite showed the boy her undeveloped penis and said she liked women not men, having been given male hormone shots since birth. And when darkness fell proved it was a lie by attempting to rape Alexander.

And all of the lad's stories were more or less taken with a grain of salt until at sixteen he finally came to the Juvenile sergeant and said that a handsome young man had dragged him away into the bushes and made Alexander Blaney orally copulate him and in turn forcibly performed the same act on Alexander. When he was finished with his account, the Juvenile sergeant said, "Is this the first time, Alexander?"

And Alexander Blaney cried and said yes and he wanted the police to arrest the young man but didn't know his name. The Juvenile sergeant bought the boy an ice cream bar and walked him to the door and told Alexander he wanted to talk to his parents.

When the boy was gone the sergeant said, "Well, Alexander finally turned himself out. We won't be seeing him anymore."

And the sergeant was right. Alexander Blaney came out of the closet at that time and was promptly beaten bloody by a high school friend whom he made the mistake of propositioning and who had hitherto liked and befriended him.

Alexander, who had always been a sensitive, nervous lad, then began getting even thinner than usual and suffered from insomnia as well as weight loss and spent many tearful evenings with his mother and father saying over and over, "But I don't *know* why I'm gay, I just am."

His mother wept and his father pleaded with him not to be what he could not help being. Finally, after many homosexual encounters, most of them in MacArthur Park, which terrified, excited, degraded and confused the boy, he was arrested by a Rampart Division vice officer.

The vice officer was to Alexander Blaney not unlike the first young man whom he had reported to the police for dragging him unwillingly into the bushes. The vice officer was tall and clean, and Alexander, not knowing he was a vice officer, was unable to control the tremble in his voice when their eyes met. They sat not far apart on the grass where Alexander tossed popcorn to the ducks, some of which he actually knew one from the other.

But the vice officer was not anxious to work fruits and wanted Alexander Blaney to get on with an offer so he could bust him and go to a favorite bar to shoot snooker for the remainder of his tour of duty.

Therefore when Alexander said shyly, ''I don't meet too many people here,'' the vice cop replied, ''Do you have something in mind or not?''

And Alexander, startled by the young man's boldness, almost decided to say, ''No, no I have nothing in mind,'' but he was afraid to lose the young man who looked so clean and decent.

Alexander said, ''Well, I thought we might go to a movie and get to know each other.''

The vice cop sighed impatiently and said, ''Look, do you suck or not?''

Alexander felt like crying because this one would be no better than most and probably even more cruel than some. Alexander arrogantly replied, ''Yes, I'll do that. If that's all you want. I guess I can do that all right.''

The vice officer whistled for his partner who was hiding behind the trees and showed his badge to Alexander Blaney and looked disgusted when the boy lowered his head to weep.

The vice cop later wrote in his arrest report: ''Defendant stated : 'I'll suck you or do anything you want. I guess I can do that all right.' ''

Alexander pled guilty to a lesser misdemeanor after the city attorney dropped the lewd conduct violation in the plea bargaining session, and Alexander Blaney had a police record. But the thing which he could not forget, and which made him burn with humiliation, was that the vice cop didn't seem to care one way or the other what happened to him. If he had hated homosexuais and beaten him up Alexander would have found it more tolerable. It's just that he was *nothing* to the policeman, and even in court the vice officer didn't seem to recognize him and just shrugged when the city attorney asked him if he had any objection to Alexander's lawyer getting the charge reduced and pleading him guilty.

The tour on vice for the three choirboys ended on an unsuccessful note in that a call girl they had been staking out never took the bait which was a phone call from Baxter Slate who was given a duke-in name of Gaylord Bottomley. A snitch said Bottomley was a savings and loan executive who had introduced certain circumspect friends to the exotic call gril.

The snitch was a paid cofidential informant who belonged to Pete Zoony and the moustachioed vice cop jealously guarded his informant's identity. Real policemen, unlike movie cops, actually cherish and protect a good informant as they would a sibling. Informants are people to be bribed, threatened, cajoled, but above all protected. It was not uncommon for a policeman to guard the identity of a good snitch even from a partner he rode with nightly.

As Pete Zoony said, ''I never gave a snitch's righteous name since I been on the job. Once we ripped off some dopers and some stupid cop calls me on the radio and gives the snitch's name right over the air! But we always used a code name and he didn't get a rat jacket behind it. Nobody knows my snitch's name, not even my lieutenant. Nobody.''

Pete's informant told them about Gina Summers who lived in a thousand-a-month apartment near Wilshire Boulevard. Allegedly she was a specialist in applying just the required amount of imaginative punishment to genteel but eager customers who paid from fifty to five hundred dollars for her unique services.

Sam and Baxter had watched one man and sometimes two a night come and go and often saw the voluptuous brunette herself leaving and entering the apartment. None of the vice cops had been able to operate her successfully. The informant had told them that the vivacious girl had a chamber of horrors in her bedroom closet which included ancient thumbscrews, brands, scourges and other collector's items. Actually most were seldom needed. Customers could usually be satisfied by less painful acts of degradation such as a urine shower. And often an ordinary spanking with a leather belt would do them just fine.

Because she was such an extraordinary hooker the vice cops naturally wanted to arrest her badly but the hours of stakeouts were to no avail.

On a sultry August night Baxter Slate watched through binoculars as she undressed before an open window on the sixth floor of her apartment house, and said to Sam, "If that bitch weren't a brunette she'd remind me a lot of a nude dancer I used to know."

"Yeah?" Sam answered, totally bored with the stakeout and his two weeks of vice duty. "The other one that good looking?"

"Oh, I guess they don't exactly look alike. But they're both sisters at heart."

Sam Niles never bothered to ask Baxter to explain the allusion. He was just glad it was their last night on vice and that the choir practice they had planned should be a memorable one.

The choir practice which celebrated the return of the three choirboys from the tour of vice squad duty was *bound* to be a memorable one. After all Roscoe Rules outdid himself when he scrounged fifteen bottles of booze from the liquor stores of Wilshire Division in a single night.

"I tell you the captain's throwing a big *big* party, godamnit," he informed some of the more reluctant proprietors who were offering only one fifth to Roscoe, wearing his black gloves, standing tall and menacing.

And what Roscoe couldn't scrounge with intimidation Spencer Van Moot obtained by his incredible rapport with the merchants on his beat. They said they couldn't wait for his retirement from the police department when he would open a retail store on the Miracle Mile and implement his merchandising genius for the mutual benefit of all.

Therefore there was enough liquor, wine and beer to kill them all, and trays of foil covered barbecue, salami, pastrami, roast beef and turkey, not to mention German potato salad, bean salad, sourdough rolls and condiments.

Strangely enough, despite the humiliation of his arrest, or perhaps because of it and the overwhelming guilt it engendered, Alexander Blaney was back in MacArthur Park for every homosexual contact from then on. It had never been more enticing now that he was aware of the possibility of vice officers and the courts and the impersonal retribution of the law.

So at eighteen and a half, with a genuine affection for policemen which was a remnant of his numerous trips to Rampart Juvenile Division and which was not vitiated by his single arrest by the Rampart vice officer, Alexander Blaney loved to sit across the water at night in the cool enveloping darkness and feed the ducks and listen to the antics of the choirboys and wonder if Calvin Potts was the only black man among them and if Francis Tanaguchi was as comical to look at as he was to listen to and to hope that Whaddayamean Dean would never become like his partner Roscoe Rules.

He had never let the choirboys see him, but on this night, when gunfire would shatter the sylvan stillness, he revealed himself to the two roommates, Ora Lee Tingle and Carolina Moon. The plump cocktail waitresses trotted across the grass from the yellow Buick which they always left on Park View Street when they got off work.

Alexander had been lying very still listening to the crickets chirp and watching Jupiter, the only star one could see in the Los Angeles summer sky when it was very smoggy. Alexander watched for it ever since he heard the policeman called Baxter telling the others that it was reassuring to at least have one great star pierce the smog and that Baxter would find the sky unbearably lonely without it.

As the laughing, chattering girls approached, Alexander was afraid he might frighten them sitting there in the dark, so when they got within thirty feet the boy called out, "Hi, nice evening isn't it?"

"Real nice," Carolina said, slowing a bit until she saw the slender harmless boy lying in the grass with three ducklings.

"Whatcha doing out here in the dark, honey?" asked Ora Lee Tingle as Alexander looked at her massive bustline and wide hips and sticky upswept blonde hair and thought she looked exactly as he pictured her.

"Just feeding the ducks," said Alexander.

"Watch yourself, honey," Carolina said. "There's rapists around here."

"Yeah," Ora Lee giggled, "and we're gonna go join a bunch of em."

They hurried off across the grass and Alexander heard Carolina say, "Feeding the ducks. Sure."

All ten choirboys were there that night and already half drunk an hour after arriving. They wore their usual summertime choir practice garb: safari jackets, sweatshirts, tank tops, LAPD baseball or basketball shirts, faded jeans and denim, Nike and Adidas athletic shoes, or Wallabees. They wore nothing which would be ruined if someone fell or was pushed in the duck pond when a choir practice got rough. They were absolutely delighted when Ora Lee Tingle and Carolina Moon surprised them by bouncing across the grass at 1:00 A.M. The girls were still wearing their mesh stockings and short skirts which barely covered their red ruffled panties. They wore peasant blouses with laced midriffs which forced their enormous breasts up and out, guaranteed to drive bar patrons wild and keep them swilling booze at $1.85 a throw.

"Surprise! The boss let us off early!" yelled Carolina as both fat girls literally threw themselves into the festivities by bouncing on the blanket of their favorite, Francis Tanaguchi, burying the little choirboy under a total of three hundred and ten pounds of young willing flesh as he joyfully screamed, "You girls just gotta do a part in my dirty movie! Now part your legs and let's see how you act!"

The choir practice had officially begun. As usual, they first had to ventilate with a gripe session. Spermwhale began it by complaining about Lieutenant Finque who had brought charges of Conduct Unbecoming an Officer against the nightwatch desk officer, Lard Logan, resulting in a five day suspension.

"That eunuch, Finque!" Spermwhale growled. "Snuck around like a spy and nailed Lard for remarks to citizens which he decides are unprofessional. I can't wait till I get my twenty in so I can tell that gelding what I think a him!"

"What happened to old Lard?" Roscoe beamed, thrilled that Spermwhale was actually talking to him.

"First one, this dingaling came in off the street and told Lard she wants to see the captain. Naturally he tries to shine her on. Finally she starts tellin him her problem which is that her sixteen year old girl got knocked up from swimmin in the L.A. High School pool. And her little girl's a virgin and she read that spermatozoa can swim and she wants the crime lab to go make a sperm count in the pool so she can sue the Board of Education. And all Lard did was listen patiently and say, 'Lady, if the water done it it musta been awful hard water.' And boom! The lieutenant writes him up for cue-bow."

"Well that ain't enough to get five days for," Roscoe observed.

"No, but then the lieutenant adds another count when Lard takes this theft report from some rich broad in the Towers who had her two Persian cats ripped off. Just for a gag he writes in the MO box: 'Suspect deals in hot pussy.' "

"I'd say fuck that lieutenant," Roscoe said. "Probably be a good one at that. He's enough of a cunt!"

"Then poor Lard gets shanked in the back by the lieutenant for making his press statement, hear about that, Sam?"

"Haven't heard anything," Sam Niles yawned, bored by all the talk of Lieutenant Finque.

"You remember the slut roamed into Sears and had the baby in the rest room?"

"What about her?"

"She cut the cord with her fingernails and just dumped the little toad in the trash can and left it for the janitor to find next day. And the dicks couldn't prove the baby ever drew breath and she cried all over the courtroom and they couldn't find her guilty of manslaughter or nothin. Anyways, some dude from one a these Right to Life groups comes into the station to interview the detectives on how they felt about it and the dicks kissed him off down to the desk officer who happened to be Lard. And Lard says, 'You want my opinion, the little third-generation welfare pig shoulda been sterilized when she turned fourteen so she wouldn't be runnin around foalin in every shithouse in town. Far as a crime's concerned she did the taxpayers a favor. Only crime she should be found guilty of is litterbug.' "

"So what happened?" Roscoe asked. "I suppose the Catholic bishop reported Lard to the captain?"

"The very same day."

"You gotta learn not to tell the truth in this world. Some guys never learn," Roscoe said. "I got two days off once when I had to make a notification in Watts to this bitch. Her old man got his ass killed in a poolroom knife fight. I knocked on the door and when she answered I said, 'You the widow Brown?' She said, 'No, I ain't a widow.' I said, 'The hell you ain't.' "

"Hey, Spermwhale," said Father Willie, "is it true one time your neighbors complained and the captain got you for cue-bow and gave you two days off for refusing to mow your lawn?"

When Spermwhale muttered something unintelligible, Whaddayamean Dean said, "I heard your lawn was four feet high just before you left your third old lady."

Roscoe Rules, now near the beer cooler, decided it was time to gripe about the headhunters of Internal Affairs Division whom they all naturally despised.

"Yeah, I remember a few years back when I worked Central they get a rumor me and my partner was rolling drunks," said Roscoe. "You imagine? Rolling drunks in the B-wagon? How many pissy ass winos have more'n a dollar fifty anytime? So one a those headhunters gets himself all dirtied up, thinks he looks like a drunk and lays down on the corner of Fifth and Stanford and pretends he's passed out. With a wallet sticking outta his pocket no less. So we drive up and see the asshole but my partner recognizes the bastard from when he worked Foothill traffic. So he winks at me and gives me a note saying this drunk's a cop and probably working IAD. So we pick the cocksucker up and throw him in the wagon just like any wino and then we go down East Fifth Street and prowl the alleys till we find three old smelly shitters. You know, with the skin rotting off them and the piss and vomit all over them? And just for good measure we scoop up some dog crap and put it in their pockets and we throw them in the wagon with the headhunter. Then we ride around for an hour and a half before we make the Central Jail booking run. And *that's* what I think a headhunters!"

"You know, Roscoe, maybe I been misjudgin you," said Spermwhale. "You're startin to sound like a class guy after all."

And as smoky clouds crossed the moon and shadows deepened and a summer breeze rippled over the duck pond, the choirboys settled back to eat and drink and unwind. Baxter Slate looked skyward, reassured to see that the light from the great star slithered easily through the smog tonight.

Spermwhale's rare praise had put Roscoe in good enough spirits to turn storyteller. He scratched his head and leered at the two fat girls who were still making over Francis Tanaguchi, feeding him beef like a shogun in a geisha house.

Roscoe said, "I just loved working that B-wagon. Only thing I liked about Central in fact. Never forget the night we got the old fag wino in back a the wagon. I turn around and see him through the cage going down on some young drunk that's passed out. So I stop the wagon and me and my partner open the back door and know what? He won't stop. Said later it was the first taste he had in a year and he just wouldn't give it up. I took out my sap and hit him upside the gourd every time he went down on the guy. His head was like a clump a grapes when I finished sapping him. Goddamn it was fun working that wagon!''

Baxter Slate then said, ''Tell you what, Roscoe. For our next choir practice we'll go to a hatchery and buy a gross of rabbits. Then we'll get a yard of piano wire and all come to the park and sit around the whole night watching you garroting baby bunnies.''

And Roscoe, who was getting very drunk very early, said, ''You know, Slate, I *never* liked you.''

Spermwhale Whalen said, ''Roscoe, you got class all right and it's all low. You got the class of a hyena.''

Since Roscoe Rules was scared to death of Spermwhale Whalen he merely pouted and said, ''All right. See if I come to choir practice, that's the way you feel. How would you like to start *buying* your booze instead of me bringing it?''

''Now wait a minute,'' said Calvin Potts, jumping off his blanket, ''don't let's get hasty, Roscoe!''

And Spermwhale quickly added, ''Right. I was only kiddin, Roscoe.''

''You're a hell of a guy, Roscoe,'' Sam Niles said, patting Roscoe on the cheek as Roscoe smiled and accepted it all magnanimously.

Whaddayamean Dean, whose mind was not yet obliterated from the bourbon, was trying to console Father Willie Wright who had begun to pine for No-Balls Hadley. The chaplain had seen her that night driving by the station on her way to meet a neurosurgeon she was dating.

Father Willie had waved hopefully, but No-Balls Hadley, now working Central daywatch, merely curled her lip and mouthed an obscenity and flipped Father Willie the middle digit.

''God she's so beautiful, Dean!'' said Father Willie. ''I swear I'd leave my wife for her.''

''I know how it is, Padre,'' said Whaddayamean Dean sadly. ''You'd eat the peanuts out of her shit. I know how it is.''

''She's *so* beautiful!''

''Cofidentially, what'd her poon look like, Father?''

''Dean, it was *all* perfect,'' said Father Willie who really didn't remember.

''Wow! Even her asshole?''

''It was a pearl,'' said the choirboy chaplain as he gulped down the Scotch.

''Imagine that!'' said Whaddayamean Dean, visibly impressed. ''An asshole like a pearl!''

And as the choir practice gained momentum, a slender boy sat across the water quietly feeding the ducks from a sack of breadcrumbs he carried. Alexander Blaney sensed that this was going to be a memorable choir practice since at 2:00 A.M. six choirboys were roaring drunk and four others were not far behind.

Arguments began raging all over the grass there by the duck pond.

''You can't prove it was me who had the Dragon Lady call you up that time,'' said Francis Tanaguchi who had his head in Carolina's lap and his feet in Ora Lee's.

''I can't prove it but I *know* it was you,'' said Father Willie Wright who was in an extremely rare mood of belligerence thinking of No-Balls Hadley's upraised finger.

''Well you should have proof before you accuse somebody,'' Francis said, his little eyes glowing wildly in the moonlight.

''You sound like a hype on the street,'' Calvin Potts said, turning on his partner. ''Prove it. Prove it. Shit!''

''And you sound like Roscoe Rules the time he tried to choke me because the Dragon Lady called him. Fine partner you are!''

''I think you're guilty is what I think. And I'd like to meet the Dragon Lady to prove it,'' Calvin Potts challenged. And then Calvin lay back on the grass, savoring the Scotch, fantasizing about the Dragon Lady, who in his thoughts greatly resembled that bitch, Martha Twogood Potts.

"That was a filthy thing to say, Spencer! I heard that!" Carolina Moon suddenly yelled to Spencer Van Moot who was drinking with Harold Bloomguard.

"I wasn't talking about you."

"Yes you was. I heard you say fat!"

"My wife's got an ass twice as wide as yours. I wasn't talking about you!"

"What'd he say?" asked Ora Lee who was drinking champagne out of Francis Tanaguchi's tennis shoe.

"He said he'd like to rebush somebody by sticking a picnic ham in her unit and pulling the bone out, is what he said!"

"I swear I wasn't talking about you! It was my wife!" Spencer pleaded, fearing that Carolina might pull that train tonight and leave him off. "Why is everybody so sensitive tonight?"

"Oh stop it," Francis said. "Carolina, want some Japanese food?"

"You cute little shitbird," she giggled, pounding Francis on the head. "Is it like Chinese food?"

"Better," said Francis lasciviously.

"That Chinese food," Ora Lee giggled. "You know a half hour later . . ."

"Way she accuses me," Spencer pouted. "And I like her so much I balled her on the same night my first wife was delivering our last kid."

"You *both* had a baby on the same night!" Harold Bloomguard observed.

"Hey, munchkin!" yelled Roscoe Rules to Harold Bloomguard. "You're the littlest guy around here. Settle this argument. Do you think there's anything immoral about screwing a midget?"

"I didn't say immoral," protested Father Willie. "I just said it seemed a little perverted."

"Well I'm not sorry," said Roscoe, sneering at Carolina Moon. "She was a lot better than some big girls I could name."

"Roscoe'd screw the crack of dawn," said Father Willie who was creeping closer to Carolina Moon who was sick of playing with Francis' bare feet while he sang Spanish songs.

"You're bilingual, ain't you, Francis?" asked Carolina Moon.

"Does that mean he licks girls *and* boys?" asked Spermwhale.

"I'm just afraid my marriage isn't going to work," Father Willie said to Carolina Moon who was suddenly holding *his* head in her lap.

"Why do you say that?" asked Carolina.

"My wife just doesn't like sex. She'd rather hand out Watchtowers than . . ."

"She ever catch you coming home with a slight odor of vagina on your breath, Padre?" Calvin Potts giggled as he tried to decide at what point Carolina Moon would become more exciting than the fifth of Johnnie Walker he was demolishing.

"Gosh no," blushed Father Willie as Carolina Moon groped him good naturedly under his blanket.

"Oughtta be glad she wasn't like that bitch I was married to," grumbled Calvin. "I hadda check to see if the toilet seat was up or down every time I came home."

"Why don't you get a hair transplant, Spermy?" asked Ora Lee Tingle, waddling past the fat policeman who was sprawled back on his elbows. She bumped him on the side of the head with her enormous ass saying, "Make it pubic hair. Stands up when a girl walks past."

Then Ora Lee squealed as he rolled over and made a grab for her. She eluded him and jumped over Whaddayamean Dean and fell on Sam Niles, slapping him on the side of the face with one gigantic tit which knocked his glasses into the bushes.

"Where's my glasses? Where's my glasses?" yelled Sam Niles, crawling around Calvin Potts who decided the Johnnie Walker was preferable to Carolina Moon for the moment.

"Calvin probably stole your glasses," said Spencer Van Moot. "You know you shouldn't leave nothing around these people."

"Your daddy had three dollars stead a two dollars you'd be black too, chump," said Calvin Potts as Sam Niles found the glasses and cleaned them on his shirttail.

"Where'd Roscoe go?" asked Father Willie who staggered around several sprawling choirboys. "Roscoe! Where are you? Roscoe!"

"Hey, Roscoe! Roscoe!" yelled Francis.

"Roscoe!" yelled several choirboys who didn't give a shit where Roscoe was.

"Roscoe, you there?" yelled Spermwhale Whalen unzipping his fly and looking inside at which time Carolina Moon made a grab for him.

"Ain't time yet, me beauty," said Spermwhale, zipping up and kissing the girl in a quivering fleshy embrace.

"I'll pay you two *anything* to do a dirty movie for me!" screamed Francis Tanaguchi.

"You looked like a blue eyed home boy," said Calvin Potts to Whaddayamean Dean who was leaning against a tree gnawing on spareribs with barbecue sauce all over his face.

"Whaddaya mean? Whaddaya mean?" asked Whaddayamean Dean, and all the choirboys looked knowingly at each other, silently agreeing that Whaddayamean Dean had done it again.

"You gonna slip old Carolina a roll of tarpaper tonight, Calvin?" Francis whispered.

"Not if I ain't first. I ain't drunk enough for that," said Calvin Potts.

"I feel like a construction engineer," Spencer Van Moot said, overhearing the conversation. "Gonna lay some pipe, six inches at a time!"

"Stealing a girl's cherry is cock robbin," said Carolina Moon to Whaddayamean Dean who looked at her blankly.

"Darn it, did you fart?" Father Willie suddenly asked Sam Niles.

"No, was I supposed to?" replied the weary choirboy.

"So I can't take you away from Carolina, huh?" said Ora Lee Tingle to Spermwhale Whalen after she won a two dollar bet by finishing a half bottle of champagne without taking it from her mouth.

"I said you can't get me there right *now,*" Spermwhale corrected her and gave one of her huge thighs a playful pinch, tearing her mesh stocking.

"Well it's easier to . . . let's see. Padre! Father Willie!" Ora Lee yelled. "How's it go? In the Bible about the camel and the eye of a needle?"

"I dunno, something about a humping hype," said Father Willie, reaching the stage of drunkenness wherein he was revolted by his uncontrollable sinfulness, yet not to the point where he goatishly succumbed.

"Mothers, brothers and others, lend me your ears," said Harold Bloomguard, staggering to his feet. "Hear about Calvin and Francis almost blowing up some dude tonight?"

"No, what happened?" asked Baxter Slate as the choirboys quieted down for a cops 'n' robbers story.

"No big thing," Calvin said. "Cat on a family dispute almost draws down on Francis when he tried to lay the iron on his wrists after the dude had went upside Momma's head."

"It was nothing," Francis said. "He was drunk. Makes a grab for what I thought was a gun. Was his wallet. All I did is whack him across the arm with my flashlight."

"I almost blew the sucker away," Calvin said. "Thought it was a piece the way he went to the drawer. Was ready to bust a cap between his fuckin horns."

"Be glad you didn't," said Baxter Slate soberly.

"Could you live with yourself if you blew up a guy by mistake that way?" asked Father Willie Wright.

"I could a blowed him up and lived with his foxy old lady," said Calvin Potts.

"Remember that time you busted your flashlight on the black belt guy, Spermwhale?" Spencer Van Moot asked. "This hamburger they were busting thinks he's

Kung Fu and tries to drop Baxter. He says, 'Yaaa!' and kicks Baxter and Spermwhale yells, 'Ever-ready!' and hits him with his flashlight. Then Spermwhale gave him nine from the sky with his stick.''

Spencer Van Moot then stumbled over Spermwhale's feet and fell against Calvin Potts.

''What's a matter? Fall off your wallet?'' Calvin asked the richest choirboy.

''Must give you a hernia carrying that money belt around,'' said Sam Niles.

''Careful a your head when you fall,'' Spermwhale said. ''All that fuckin hair spray you use could cause brain damage.''

''With your money why don't you hire a coolie to pull you around the park so you won't be tripping all over everybody?'' said Harold Bloomguard.

And Spencer Van Moot, the best dressed and richest choirboy, lay back on the grass and laughed uproariously when Carolina Moon fell on him lovingly and smothered him in kisses while she felt his body up and down to see if he really *did* have a money belt.

Roscoe Rules looked at his comrades and now thought they weren't such bad guys. He was even able to tolerate the Gook and the Spook tonight.

Roscoe had met Francis and Calvin at the first choir practice months before when Francis was going through his vampire period.

When they met, both Calvin and Francis were drunk and sullen and sat together in the shadows examining the new choirboy.

''Are you the two they call the Gook and the Spook?'' Roscoe had asked with a big smile that was met with stony silence.

''Yeah,'' said Calvin Potts finally, glaring at Roscoe since Calvin didn't yet know that Roscoe had brought three fifths of Scotch with him.

''Uh, what do your friends call you?'' Roscoe asked, having a hard time seeing their faces in the dark.

''You can call me the Gook,'' said the Gook.

''You can call me the Spook,'' said the Spook. ''But if you do I'll kick your face off.''

And after that Roscoe had sat furious and quiet and wondered why people didn't like him. After all he had been willing to treat them all the same, even niggers and slopeheads. Then he started looking hard at the Gook. And it looked as if his teeth had grown grotesquely. Roscoe was sure it was the drink because there in the darkness of MacArthur Park it looked as if the Gook had fangs! But of course that was silly. Yet five minutes later when Roscoe got up to walk off into the trees to relieve himself, he was bushwhacked by a hissing demon which leaped on his back and bit him on the neck while Roscoe screamed in terror and tried to reach for his gun as he wet all over his shoes.

It had taken Spermwhale Whalen to pry Francis Tanaguchi from Roscoe Rules' throat that first night, and as Roscoe threatened to kill Francis, it was Harold Bloomguard who explained to Calvin and Francis that the new kid on the block had brought *three fifths* of Scotch to choir practice which they could expect at any future choir practice Roscoe might attend.

Ater hearing that, Francis and Calvin became very tolerant of the insufferable prick and Roscoe Rules was an accepted choirboy. He was able to sit now at this memorable choir practice and not think that nobody liked him. And he could pinch Ora Lee and Carolina just like the other guys.

While Roscoe remembered his first choir practice and felt all cozy and secure because now he belonged, he started talking to Sam Niles who was already mightily pissed off because one of the lenses on his glasses got scratched when Ora Lee slapped him in the face with a tit.

''Niles, we just gotta get the department to give us good ammo,'' Roscoe began. ''You see, high velocity shock waves're like sonic booms and they burst the veins and arteries. But they don't stop like the hollow points and the blunt nose. A copper casing holds the lead together. Centrifugal force breaks up the lead. You only need a pointed projectile for accuracy. Get it?''

''I get it,'' Sam sighed.

Then Roscoe said, ''I ever tell you what I used to do to all the pricks in the juvie gangs when they turned eighteen? I used to send them a Xerox of the page of the LAPD manual which tells about shooting at adults only. With the page I'd enclose a dumdum bullet and a greeting card. On the card I'd write, 'You are now, by law, an adult. Have a nice eighteenth birthday, asshole.' ''

''That's about as interesting as a night in the drunk tank,'' said Sam Niles, who lay back smoking, looking at the great star while the bourbon went to work on his entire body, turning it to rock.

''Looky here, Ora Lee,'' said Calvin Potts as he was starting to think that the fat girls weren't so repulsive after all. In fact, depending on how you looked at her, Ora Lee was starting to get downright gorgeous.

''Looky here, what?'' asked Ora Lee. ''You boys aren't interested in us girls tonight. You're all sitting around like that bunch of fruits hangs around the other side of the duck pond.''

''Well you know, consenting adults!'' said Francis Tanaguchi, kissing his partner Calvin Potts who pushed him away.

''. . . and I been thinking about buying this baby falcon,'' said Roscoe Rules to Harold Bloomguard. ''I live out in the country with decent people. Room for an eagle even. I could train him to kill on command. Shit, how many guys own a hunting hawk?''

''Last guy I know of was William the Conqueror,'' said Baxter Slate.

''Would really be great!'' Roscoe mused. ''Your own killing bird!''

''You could feed him raw meat right out of your hand,'' said Baxter.

''Sure!'' said Roscoe.

''And to save feed money you could train him to fly over the kindergarten and carry off kids,'' Baxter Slate said.

''You know, I never liked you, Slate,'' said Roscoe Rules, turning sullen.

''Roscoe needs his steel plate buffed!'' Spencer said gleefully.

''Are you trying to incinerate that Roscoe belongs in the funny place?'' asked Harold Bloomguard, taking pleasure in the thought that someone else might be going there with him someday.

''What're you trying to say? What're you trying to say?'' Whaddayamean Dean blurted, still propped against the same tree, a pile of rib bones on his lap, a half empty bourbon bottle resting on his chest.

''I don't think it's fair,'' said Father Willie, arguing a point of law with Spencer Van Moot. ''In these unlawful sex cases a boy of thirteen *can* be booked as opposed to the old statutory rape charge where he couldn't. Who enjoys it more, the ear being scratched or the finger scratching?''

''If they're doing it in the ear they deserve to be booked, the perverts!'' said Carolina Moon as Spermwhale Whalen threw her down and kissed her again.

''I'd give anything to direct this scene!'' cried Francis Tanaguchi.

''You know she wouldn't do nothing in front of everybody. They're just kissing,'' said Ora Lee Tingle as Spermwhale kneaded and squeezed every inch of Carolina's ample body.

''Why doesn't a Jap have a camera anyway, I'd like to know?'' Roscoe remarked suspiciously. ''Maybe Francis is really a Chinaman. A Commie, no doubt.''

''I'm a Mexican and you can go scratch your ass,'' said Francis Tanaguchi.

''I'm gonna have you defrocked, Padre,'' Ora Lee giggled when Father Willie groped her.

''Anybody gets frocked it better be me!'' Carolina whooped when Spermwhale let her breathe.

Just then Harold Bloomguard staggered a few paces away and threw up. He was the first. Everybody jeered and hooted and he walked ashamedly down to the duck pond and washed his face in dirty water.

". . . so this guy demands his rights when I arrest him," said Roscoe Rules to Whaddayamean Dean who hadn't the foggiest idea what Roscoe was talking about. "And I say, 'You'll get your rights and a few lefts too, asshole! Bang! Pow! Splat!' "

Whereas Spencer Van Moot only whined to Father Willie Wright when he was sober, he was now whining to as many assembled choirboys as would listen now that he was drunk.

"This dirty scummy rotten bitch that lives next door . . ."

"Watch that fuckin language," said Spermwhale Whalen who was passionately kissing Carolina Moon a few feet away in the shadows while Francis Tanaguchi knelt beside them, grinning.

"Sorry, Spermwhale. Sorry, girls," said Spencer who belched sourly and quickly took a few sips of beer. "Anyway, this bitch always wears these short shorts and comes out by the fence when I'm down on my knees trimming the grass. So finally after three months of this I kneel there and look right at her bird and up it goes!"

"A blue veiner?" asked Father Willie.

"A goddamn diamond cutter!" said Spencer and Ora Lee said, "Ooooooohhhhhhh, Spencer, that's sexy!" and fell over backward as Francis Tanaguchi pounced on her and smothered her with kisses.

"Why do you wear those sissy faggy mod clothes, Spencer?" asked Roscoe, beginning to turn mean. "And why does a man your age have one of those kiss-me-quick haircuts?"

"Lemme finish my story, goddamnit."

"Spencer's so mod he wears flared jockey shorts," said Harold Bloomguard who was trying to stand with the aid of a broken willow branch.

"Why do we need a motel?" Ora Lee said to Roscoe who whispered something in her ear. "You can beat off in a nickel toilet, you cheap little fuck, ya."

"Anyway," Spencer continued, "my neighbor sees my diamond cutter and she runs into her house. Runs. And I mean after she'd done everything but rub my face in it. She runs in and calls my wife and tells her that I'm going around the yard looking at her with a big hard on."

"Probably a libber," said Roscoe Rules. "All these cunts're like that these days. Wanna be truck drivers. I say back em up and give em a load, they wanna be truck drivers."

"You ain't got a load, Roscoe, you dirty mouthed chauvinist pig!" said Carolina Moon, coming up for air, while Spermwhale Whalen looked around, saw double, got dizzy and had to stagger away to relieve himself.

"Who asked you? You a libber or something?" Roscoe challenged.

"I *know* you ain't got a load," said Carolina, taking a drink from Calvin's bottle. "You walk into a wall with your little hard on and you'll break your nose."

To keep Roscoe and Carolina from fighting, Harold Bloomguard began to sing a soothing song he just made up called "She'll not puncture your kidney, Sidney. And he shan't rupture your spleen, Kathleen."

But Spermwhale Whalen hobbled back in their midst and his enormous presence looming over Roscoe quieted down the meanest choirboy. Especially when Spermwhale said, "You look like a ruptured rectum sittin there with your mean little mouth all scrunched up. Why don't you quit pickin on the ladies?"

"Yeah, it makes you ugly, Roscoe," said Ora Lee. "You get drunk you get uglier than usual."

"I don't have to take this," Roscoe Rules said, struggling to his feet and heading toward the duck pond, hoping to find a duck he could kneedrop.

"He gets so ugly he looks like something carved off the back of Quasimodo," Spencer Van Moot observed.

"Hey, stick around, Roscoe!" Carolina yelled. "Every choir practice needs a soprano."

"Don't get nasty now," Spermwhale whispered as he bit the fat girl on the neck and sent her into paroxysms of passion. They resumed their interminable kiss and rolled around on the ground, making the earth shake under the ear of Francis Tanaguchi, who said, "Dynamite!" and lay next to them hoping the behemoths would couple before his very eyes.

Just then a park homosexual with sandals, long hair and beard walked by the group curiously.

The choirboys looked at this Biblical apparition and Sam Niles said, "Think he'll take us to heaven?"

"I can use *my* ticket validated by somebody," said Father Willie who was furiously trying to think of a way to steal Carolina Moon from Spermwhale Whalen.

"All I can say is I get treated like a dog at home," Spencer Van Moot whined, returning to his favorite subject.

"Anytime they wanna teach you a lesson they just hold back the sex," Father Willie agreed, suddenly having a miserable vision of the chubby Jehovah's Witness seeing him drunk and playing with the thigh of Ora Lee Tingle.

"Well who cares?" said Spencer. "The three most overrated things in the world are: home cooking, home pussy and the FBI."

"You know, Spermy, you got more hair in your nose than on your head," Carolina Moon said from the shadows where she and Spermwhale and Francis Tanaguchi rolled around.

"What dialogue! What dialogue! I could make you a star, girl!" cried Francis. "Say something back to her, Spermwhale! Something romantic!"

"Okay. I adore you, my darling," Spermwhale crooned to the sighing fat girl. "Your ass is springy as a life raft."

"And I love *you,* Ora Lee," Francis Tanaguchi blurted suddenly, running to the other cocktail waitress, dragging his fingers through her upswept hairdo, which was no mean task given the half can of hair spray that was on it.

"That's just whiskey talking, you cute little shit."

"No it ain't! I love! I love you!" Francis proclaimed. "If you had a hysterectomy and took your teeth out and owned a liquor store, I swear I'd marry you!"

"Thanks, Junior," said the disgusted waitress as she pushed Francis away. "You handled that love scene like a real pro—a prophylactic!"

Just then the bearded park fairy with the ascetic face, shoulder-length hair and sandals encountered Roscoe Rules down by the duck pond trying to entice a black duck out of the water so he could hit it with a rock and drown it.

"Hello," said the Jesus fairy.

"Holy Christ!" said Roscoe Rules and the remark was not that inappropriate.

"Are you with those others?" asked the bearded man, stooping to scoop some water in both hands.

"Yeah. Who the fuck're you, John the Baptist?"

Ignoring the remark the man said, "Do you men actually screw those women in the park?"

"No, in the cunt," said Roscoe. "Now take a walk, John, before I bring your fucking head to Salome."

Meanwhile, back at the choir practice Father Willie was going to hell in a hurry. He had stripped off his shirt and shoes and was asking Ora Lee if she dared him to streak through the park as Harold Bloomguard composed a song called "I Left My Heart in Titty City."

"Put your shirt back on, Padre," said his partner Spencer Van Moot. "I gotta quit feeding you all the cherries jubilee. You're getting to look like a basketball."

"How's your *como se llama* these days, Ora Lee?" asked Francis as he tried to squeeze a finger inside the leg of Ora Lee's ruffled pants, causing her to honk him severely, making him cry out in pain.

"How do *you* like being a sex object, huh?" the fat girl grinned.

"See, you're not a *real* Mexican!" yelled shirtless Father Willie who was staggering around looking for trouble. "You're not even a Jap! A real Mexican like General Zapata could take a little hurt without whimpering!"

"How'd you like to get your nuts crushed by this big moose?" said the injured choirboy, holding himself.

"Who's a moose?" demanded Ora Lee Tingle, glowering at Francis. "You call me names I'll hit you so hard and fast you'll think you was in a gang fight!"

"Carolina's putting on a little more weight," Baxter Slate observed as he sat next to Sam Niles and the two quietly tried to drink themselves into unconsciousness.

"Maybe she's pregnant," Sam observed.

"What're you trying to say, what're you trying to say, Sam?" Whaddayamean Dean cried out but quieted down when Baxter handed him a full bottle of bourbon.

"If she's pregnant I'll take her soon as her milk comes in," said Spencer Van Moot. "I can't feed my wife and kids no more on a policeman's pay what with the inflation and all."

"That's cause you spend all your money on faggy clothes! A man your age!" said a voice from the darkness as Roscoe Rules got tired of waiting for someone to coax him back to the flock.

Then Francis Tanaguchi staggered away from the other choirboys and they heard him retching on the grass.

"Booo! Booo! Zapata my rear end!" giggled Father Willie Wright.

And while the party entered its final phase, Alexander Blaney slept on the grass not a hundred feet away beside two friendly ducklings while his mother wept at home and imagined him locked in the cruel embrace of a tattooed merchant seaman in some skid row flophouse.

At the end of that memorable choir practice some ordinary and extraordinary things started to happen.

An ordinary thing was that Whaddayamean Dean broke out in several crying jags and sobbed, "What're you trying to say?" every time a choirboy was foolish enough to send a remark in his direction.

An extraordinary thing was that Spermwhale Whalen lost his diamond cutter and in fact lost the use of all his muscles. He could only sit against an elm tree and snarl at anyone who came near him. Spermwhale, the biggest strongest and bravest choirboy, was so drunk he was as helpless as the baby ducks out of water.

Another ordinary thing was that Roscoe Rules became as mean as a rabid dog, and with Sam Niles drunk and Spermwhale Whalen helpless, it seemed for a time that no one was around who could tame the young policeman. He was going around jealously insulting Ora Lee and Carolina because they didn't feel like pulling that train and in any event wouldn't let anyone as mean as Roscoe have a ride.

"Pig fuckers!" Roscoe Rules sneered. "If you don't oink they won't touch you! Gotta lead you up to a trough first to see if you're worthwhile, huh?"

Sam Niles looked up from where he lay on his stomach groaning, and said, "Roscoe, this just might be the night I get you in a lip lock and shut you up for good."

"Yeah, go ahead and try it, Niles," Roscoe said. "You and your friend Slate together couldn't handle me. Don't think I don't know you dopeheads go over there by Duck Island and smoke grass. You ain't fooling nobody, you two."

"Who's got grass?" piped Harold Bloomguard.

"Better knock off that talk about grass, Harold," Father Willie advised as he tried in vain to slap Spermwhale Whalen alive so he could scare Roscoe Rules and make him quit throwing his weight around.

"I told you about smokin grass, Harold!" the paralyzed Spermwhale growled. "I got nineteen and a half years on the job and that don't ring the bell. You bring any pot here and get me fired and lose my pension with only six months to go and I'll buy a whole kilo a grass. And I'll pound it right up your ass and bury your head in the dirt and let the fuckin ducks get loaded by eatin the seeds outta your shit! YOU GOT ME?''

''I was just kidding, Spermwhale,'' Harold gulped.

''Well I know Slate and Niles smoke grass, the fucking degenerates,'' said Roscoe Rules.

Actually Roscoe was partly right. Baxter and Sam *did* go down by the duck pond occasionally for an illicit drug. But it wasn't marijuana. Baxter had been dating a nurse who lived in his apartment building who was an inveterate pill popper and kept Baxter supplied with sedatives and hypnotics. So it was red capsules and yellow ones which Baxter and Sam swallowed with their booze down by the duck pond, both knowing the risks involved when they mixed the drugs with heavy drinking. In fact, Baxter Slate only seemed to want the barbiturates when he *had* been drinking excessively.

Roscoe walked over to Father Willie Wright who was telling Ora Lee Tingle how cute she was as the fat girl's head started to drop on her shoulder.

Roscoe sniffed and said, ''Padre, fucking that pig without a rubber is like playing the Rams without a helmet. Hope you got protection.''

''Well I like her!'' shouted Father Willie, lurching to his feet combatively. ''She's better'n Frank Buck any old day. She really brings em back alive!''

''Siddown, you drunken little prick,'' Roscoe Rules said, shoving the chaplain to the ground, making Father Willie yell, ''Darn you, Roscoe! Gosh darn you, you bully!''

''Hey, Tanaguchi!'' the jealous Roscoe yelled as he saw Francis stroking Carolina's quaking buttocks. ''I hear when Carolina was living with that Greek bartender he used to butt-fuck her all the time.''

''Never on Sunday!'' Carolina answered and Francis' giggles made Roscoe angrier.

''Her box is so big she wouldn't even feel your hand unless you wore a wristwatch,'' Roscoe grumbled.

''You can bet you ain't gonna know, Roscoe!'' said Carolina, throwing Francis off her as she sat up and rearranged her clothing. ''Cause Father Willie told me you got clap!''

''I didn't say that!'' Father Willie protested. ''I just told how when we were at Daniel Freeman Hospital that time you talked to the doctor about the strain you were having down there. And he said, 'Do you have a discharge, Officer?' and you said, 'Yes, Honorable.' And then you turned red when the doc and me cracked up. Oh God, that was funny!''

The chaplain rolled up in a little ball and cackled hilariously until Roscoe Rules was standing over him saying dangerously, ''Padre, I thought I warned you not to tell anyone that story.''

Then Father Willie sobered up and said, ''Gosh I forgot, Roscoe. I'm sorry.''

''I oughtta punch your lights out,'' Roscoe said, eyes like a cobra.

''I'm sorry, Roscoe.''

''I oughtta kneedrop you right now.''

''What a cunt!'' Spermwhale Whalen said to Roscoe, stirring around against the tree, trying to get control of his legs so he could come over and throw Roscoe Rules in the duck pond.

Father Willie started sniveling and said, ''I'm really sorry, Roscoe.''

Spermwhale Whalen got disgusted with the chaplain and glared at him, saying, ''What a cunt!''

And Carolina Moon squatted by the liquor case and found the Scotch all gone and thought Roscoe Rules was ruining the choir practice. She started to cry great drunken tears.

Spermwhale Whalen looked at her and said, ''What a cunt!''

Carolina sniffed and said, ''Thank you, Spermy. At least somebody appreciates me.''

Whaddayamean Dean suddenly said, "What's it all about, Roscoe? What's it all about?"

"Oh the hell with all a you," said Roscoe Rules. "You're all a bunch a scrotes!"

The meanest choirboy took a full bottle of bourbon, the last in fact, and stalked off into the darkness to think about what he'd like to do to all of them and drink bourbon and absently pull on his whang while he fantasized.

"Gimme Scotch," said Ora Lee Tingle suddenly as her head stopped lolling.

"Ain't none," said Carolina who stopped crying and got happy again now that Roscoe was gone.

"Gimme beer," said Ora Lee Tingle as Francis Tanaguchi lurched toward the duck pond to soak his head so that he wouldn't miss the rest of the choir practice by passing out like his partner Calvin Potts who dozed next to one of Ora Lee Tingle's big legs.

"I wish we had a stereo," said Spencer Van Moot, mummified on the grass, his blanket wrapped tightly around him until only his face was exposed. "I'm older than you kids. I'd like some old music."

"I'm older than Christ Almighty," groaned Spermwhale Whalen, at last able to wiggle his fingers and toes.

"I'm old," Spencer continued, "so I remember things you kids only saw in movies. Like the big bands. They were still around when I was young. Great times. Christ, I graduated high school in 1952. Imagine that."

"I was killin gooks in 1952," Spermwhale muttered. "No offense, Francis. And that was my *second* war."

"If we had a stereo we could dance on the grass," said Spencer nostalgically.

"God, you can get sweet sometimes, Spencer," croaked Ora Lee Tingle as she crawled over and lay on top of the blanket-wrapped choirboy, making him gasp for air.

"I've got a portable stereo," offered Harold Bloomguard. "But my tweeter and woofer aren't very big."

"Get some hormone shots," offered Father Willie Wright, scrounging desperately through the debris of boxes and packages for some more beer.

"Oh, that's funny!" Carolina Moon screamed suddenly. "Francis just says he told this waitress he wanted to be a counterspy and so he leans over the counter and spies up her dress. Oh, you horny little Nip!" and she honked him so clumsily he fell to his knees groaning in pain.

"Boooo!" cried Father Willie. "Booooo! Mexican my rear end!"

"Knock it off, Padre!" said Calvin Potts. "You jist woke me up."

"Well he oughtta be able to take a little pain, he's Pancho Villa or somebody," said the choirboy chaplain, belching up some beer on his bare chest and making them all boo *him*.

The weight of Ora Lee Tingle on the blanketed Spencer Van Moot caused the choirboy to gag violently and the fat girl leaped off him surprisingly fast.

"My cop runneth over!" whooped Ora Lee Tingle, causing Harold Bloomguard to collapse in hysterical laughter in her great pink arms.

Just then Roscoe Rules, still holding his bourbon bottle which was only two thirds full, came staggering back among them. "Yeah? I'll tell you what *you* are, you big titted scrote. You're just a camp follower! A station house groupie! A cop sucker!"

Then Roscoe wheeled and headed back toward the duck pond where Spencer Van Moot was already washing his vomity blanket. Roscoe paused only for an instant by Baxter Slate's blanket and quickly grabbed a set of car keys and when he was sure no one was watching, threw them into the middle of the pond.

Then Carolina Moon started showing off. The big girl quickly overpowered Francis Tanaguchi and got him in a wristlock Spermwhale had taught her, which came in handy with rowdy customers at the cocktail lounge where she worked. As the other choirboys cheered, Carolina played rough by forcing the groaning choirboy forward until his head was on the ground and his LAPD basketball jersey was falling down over his face. Then she picked him up by the belled bottoms of his faded white jeans and started bouncing him off the grass.

"Yea, Carolina! Yea!" shouted Father Willie Wright who was still shirtless and barefoot, pacing around the wrestlers.

Then while the puffing fat girl was shaking the upside-down choirboy against her plump dimpled belly, some coins, keys, a comb and a package of prophylactics fell out of Francis' pocket causing Carolina Moon to drop him abruptly on his head.

"Rubbers!" exclaimed Carolina in sweaty disbelief, her stiff lacquered hair stuck to her face. "Rubbers! Ora Lee, this chickenshit is carrying rubbers!"

"Pancho Villa, my rear end!" said Father Willie. "Booooo ! Booooo !"

"A cundrum!" cried Carolina Moon. "This is what you think of us! I oughtta pull it over your head, you little prick!"

"Black Jack Pershing woulda whipped faggy Mexicans like Francis!" yelled Roscoe Rules from his exile in the darkness.

"I'll never forget the first time I met Carolina Moon," said Spencer Van Moot romantically as he limped back from the duck pond, smelling of vomit and rancid water, causing Carolina to scurry away from him.

"She was younger then and *so* lovely," Spencer said with a liquid burp that scared everyone. "It was before your time, guys, and I was a younger buck and this gorgeous blonde girl with bazooms like volleyballs walks up to my radio car when we're parked in the drive-in on La Brea, and she looks me right in the eyeball and says, 'Gee, I thought I blew every cop in Wilshire.' I just loved that girl from then on!"

Carolina smiled shyly and said, "Spence, honey, you're a doll. But why don't you think about going home to your wife and kiddies now? You smell awful ripe."

Spencer wrapped his blanket around him like a toga and downed a can of warm beer he found in the grass and belched perilously again. His pinky ring glittered and his little blond toothbrush moustache twitched as he breathed the night air and looked at the smog filled night sky for the great star and yearned for his lost youth.

"Gud-damn, Spencer stinks," Calvin Potts complained. "I think we better call the coroner."

"It's all right, Spencer. You look like Marcus Aurelius," Baxter Slate grinned, raising his head surprisingly well from where he had dozed for over an hour. "You long for those days when we didn't think we would fail. When we didn't think we would die! When we were *young*."

"I heard you, Slate," a slurred gravel voice shouted from the darkness. "So don't start that faggy talk. And don't think you and Niles can sneak off and smoke pot. I'm watching you!"

"But who guards the guards, Roscoe?" Baxter yelled.

"Who said that?" Roscoe suddenly confused the voices.

"Juvenal," Baxter Slate said.

"Who you calling a juvenile?" snapped Roscoe Rules.

"Now's the time for drinking! Horace said that, Roscoe," Baxter Slate yelled.

"Horace! Horace!" answered Roscoe. "Never catch a cop with a name like that. Some faggy friend a yours, huh?"

And with his bottle of bourbon three quarters gone Roscoe Rules decided to punch Baxter Slate's faggy lights out once and for all. But he found his legs didn't work and he fell heavily on his chest and panted quietly for a moment and went to sleep.

"Yeah I remember the good old days, Spencer," said Carolina Moon who also felt nostalgic. "We was wild young kids then, Ora Lee and me. Remember how we used to say we did more to relieve policemen than the whole Los Angeles Police Relief Association?" she asked her slightly older roommate who had fallen fast asleep and was snoring noisily.

Carolina shrugged and said, "When they put that slogan 'To Protect and To Serve' on all police cars we had one made for our Pontiac saying, 'To Protect and To Service.' One time Ora Lee and me figured we sucked off more cops than the whole police wives' association."

"Impossible!" cried Harold Bloomguard.

"Well it's true," said Carolina. "We got seven thousand cops in this town, right? And I bet there ain't five hundred whose wives belong to that group. Am I right Spencer?"

"Right," said Spencer starting to be offended by his own smelly toga.

"Most of em are ladies, ain't they, Spencer? Probably only blew one, two policemen?" Carolina asked.

"No more than that," said Spencer Van Moot.

"My wife never even did one," Father Willie Wright noted. "That's my trouble."

"See," said Carolina to the assembly. "That means they couldn't a did more than eight hundred at most. Christ, Ora Lee and me done more than that *one* summer when we were hanging around Seventy-seventh Station!"

"They *do* have a lot of guys working down there," Spencer had to admit.

And it was finally conceded that the two girls had easily outfaced the entire police wives' association. But just as the girls were thinking about pulling that train for a couple of their favorites Francis Tanaguchi came charging into their midst from the direction of the duck pond.

"Come see what I did!" giggled the choirboy prankster.

"Whaddaya mean? Whaddaya mean?" asked Whaddayamean Dean.

"Not now, not now," said Spencer Van Moot, leering at Carolina Moon.

"Now! Now!" said Francis Tanaguchi, shaking all the drunken choirboys.

"What's it all about? What's it all about?" cried Whaddayamean Dean.

"Oh shit, oh shit," said Calvin Potts as Whaddayamean Dean had them all talking double action.

Carolina Moon got up and stumbled after Francis. And all the choirboys, even Spermwhale Whalen, walked or crawled toward the duck pond where Roscoe Rules slept soundly on his back with a large white duck hanging out his fly.

"My word!" said Baxter Slate.

"How'd you manage that, Francis?" asked Sam Niles, impressed out of his ennui.

"Now that's class!" mumbled Spermwhale Whalen gravely as he was finally able to stand up shakily like an enormous toddler.

"I just took some bread and sprinkled it from the water to Roscoe's crotch," giggled Francis Tanaguchi. "Then I unzipped his pants and dropped some inside!"

"He'd a caught you he'd a said it was a faggy thing to do," Father Willie remarked.

"Boy, that duck's really working out on old Roscoe," Carolina Moon said admiringly as the fat white body worked itself between Roscoe's legs and the greedy head burrowed and ate.

"Roscoe was never one to duck a fuck, but to fuck a duck?" said Spencer Van Moot.

"Wake up, Roscoe, you cunt!" growled Spermwhale, throwing an empty beer can at Roscoe which startled the duck and made it flap and jump around.

"Don't throw things! You might hit the duck!" said Harold Bloomguard.

"Hey!" Calvin Potts said. "That sucker can't get his pecker outta Roscoe's pants!"

"They got bills not peckers," said Francis.

The choirboys watched in fascination as the duck thrashed and flapped and squawked with his head entangled in the fly of Roscoe's jockey shorts. Suddenly the meanest choirboy, who had always hated and feared the loathsome creatures, awakened to see one attacking his balls.

"YAAAAAA!" screamed Roscoe Rules, awakening Alexander Blaney who had been sleeping peacefully on the grass across the water.

Then there was pandemonium as the hopelessly drunk Roscoe Rules lurched to his feet and began running in circles, screaming and pulling at the duck who was panicked and quacking in rage and terror.

"Don't hurt the duck!" yelled Harold Bloomguard as several choirboys rushed to aid the creature before Roscoe broke its neck as he ran shrieking and fell headlong into the pond.

"He'll drown it!" Harold Bloomguard cried as Father Willie and Francis plunged into the water to rescue the bird.

Roscoe Rules pitched wildly in the slime and choked on filthy water and shouted for Spencer who didn't want to get his eighty dollar shoes wet.

They grabbed Roscoe and dragged him and the duck onto shore just as the bird got a death grip on the sac containing Roscoe's left testicle. Roscoe shrieked again and broke through the drunken ranks and ran bellowing toward the blankets where he had left his gun, wallet, and keys. He fell over the body of Ora Lee Tingle who woke up to blink sleepily at the dripping man standing six feet away with a fat white object swaying wildly between his legs. She said, "I don't know who *you* are, honey, but welcome to choir practice!"

"He'll break its neck!" yelled Harold Bloomguard who led the charge toward the horror stricken Roscoe Rules who was pitching wildly side to side, the duck swinging like a pendulum.

Harold tackled Roscoe at the ankles and several choirboys pulled off Roscoe's pants and extricated the bird from his shorts. Then there was more pandemonium as Roscoe Rules, naked from the waist down except for wet shoes and socks, made a screaming lunge for the gun. But by then they were crawling all over him. Sam Niles jumped on Roscoe's gun and Father Willie yelled, "Handcuffs! Anybody got some cuffs?"

"I do!" yelled Baxter Slate and ran to his gunbelt which he had wrapped in his blanket.

"Over there! Over there to the tree!" commanded Spermwhale Whalen as they dragged the kicking biting Roscoe Rules to the elm tree where he snapped and snarled like a rabid dog.

"Put his arms around the tree!" Spermwhale ordered, and then Roscoe found himself hugging the elm, his wrists locked together in front.

"I'll kill you for this!" Roscoe screamed. "I'll kill you all!"

"Don't kill me, Roscoe, I'm your pal," Father Willie belched but the half naked policeman kicked out at him with a drippy shoe.

"Did the duck hurt your dick, Roscoe?" asked Carolina Moon solicitously.

"I'll kill you for sure, you scrotes!" Roscoe howled, now kneeling against the tree, the bark rough against his wounded genitals.

"Let's just leave him alone for a few minutes," Spermwhale Whalen said. "Just leave him be."

"I think he's really mad at us this time," said Father Willie as they went back to the blankets to suck the last few drops of booze out of the empty bottles.

"I think we should make a rule, no guns at choir practice," said Harold Bloomguard.

While the handcuffed Roscoe Rules raged and cursed around the elm tree, the choirboys returned to their places because Carolina Moon announced that she was going to take her blanket off into the bushes and pull that train.

"I'm first! I'm the engineer!" cried Harold Bloomguard.

"I'm second! I'm conductor!" cried Spencer Van Moot.

"I know who rides the caboose," Father Willie pouted.

But Carolina Moon put Spermwhale Whalen's big arm around her shoulder and helped the hulking choirboy off to her nest while Calvin Potts yelled grumpily, "You're gonna die in the push-up position, Spermwhale. You oughtta slow down, man your age."

By now it was after 4:00 A.M. Alexander Blaney had gone home and was at this moment trying to explain to his bawling mother that he had been asleep alone in MacArthur Park and hadn't been bedded by a tattooed merchant seaman.

And by now Ora Lee Tingle had decided to pull her own choo choo and made public her choice of engineer.

"I want Whaddayamean Dean," she said.

"Why him? He can't even understand what we're talking about," Spencer Van Moot whined.

"Him first or nobody," said Ora Lee Tingle.

"What're you trying to say? What're you trying to say?" asked Whaddayamean Dean blankly and the choirboys cursed and swore and walked in nervous circles.

"Well I'm taking my blankets and going to the bushes in private," announced Ora Lee Tingle, "and if there's gonna be a choo choo, I better see Whaddayamean Dean first."

So then the choirboys squatted and began lightly slapping Whaddayamean Dean on the cheeks and rubbing his wrists and ankles as he stared vacantly from one to the other with a drunken, sincere, idiotic smile that chilled their hearts.

Especially when Spermwhale Whalen stepped out of the brush and said, "Train jumped the track."

"Whaddayamean? Whaddayamean?" asked Father Willie, not Whaddayamean Dean.

"I mean Carolina passed out. I guess I ain't so old after all, boys. Just wear em out is what I do."

"Well passed out or not, I'm next," whined Spencer Van Moot.

"No you ain't," said the glowering Spermwhale Whalen. "We ain't animals to take advantage of a passed-out girl!"

Then there was wailing and gnashing of teeth in MacArthur Park as several choirboys pleaded in vain with Spermwhale Whalen who of course dominated them all by his age, seniority, courage and ability to kick the living shit out of them.

"What's the matter with Ora Lee? She's conscious, ain't she?" asked Spermwhale.

"Yeah, but she wants Dean first or nobody," Father Willie whined, starting to sound like his partner Spencer Van Moot.

"I see," said Spermwhale, shaking his head sadly as he looked over at the simpering choirboy sitting on the grass, red hair tousled by Harold Bloomguard who still worked frantically massaging his wrists and neck.

Then Francis Tanaguchi sat by Whaddayamean Dean, telling him exaggerated lascivious impossible things that Ora Lee Tingle was going to do to him, and Father Willie shouted, "That's exactly what the Dragon Lady promised to do to *me* the night she phoned and made my wife punch me in the eye! Now I *know* who the Dragon Lady works for, ya dirty Godless heathen little fuck, ya!"

And temporarily everyone forgot Ora Lee and looked at Father Willie in astonishment because he had uttered the second vulgarity of his life.

"I can't help it," Father Willie said sheepishly. "That was the dirtiest trick anyone ever played on me."

"Lemme try," said Calvin Potts. "Since Dean can't understand regular English I think you should talk to him like we talked to the whores in Vietnam. We always managed to communicate and they couldn't talk no English."

Several choirboys agreed that it was worth a try, so Calvin knelt in front of the placid redhead whose face from eyebrows to chin was caked with dried barbecue sauce and tried pidgin. "Ora Lee like bang bang. Her plenty good. All time bang bang. Plenty good. You sabby?"

And Whaddayamean Dean clapped his hands happily and chuckled.

"Jesus, you're just entertaining him," said Spencer Van Moot. "That ain't getting us nowhere. He ain't a gook. That rice paddy talk ain't the answer."

"You got a better idea?" Calvin asked.

"Yeah I do," said Spencer. "I been analyzing this. He's sitting there now with the mind of a three year old, right?"

"Approximately," nodded Harold Bloomguard.

"Okay," said Spencer. "We couldn't tell a three year old to go screw in the bushes, could we? You have to talk to a three year old *like* a three year old."

Spencer Van Moot elbowed Calvin out of the way and squatted in front of Whaddayamean Dean. "Spencer has secret for Deanie," Spencer said desperately. "Ora Lee loves Deanie. Ora Lee take Deanie and blow up like biiiiiig balloon!" And Spencer Van Moot drew a biiiiiig sausage-shaped balloon in the air before the watery eyes of Whaddayamean Dean who sat cross legged in his barbecue-stained Bugs Bunny sweatshirt and clapped his hands like an infant. And squealed.

"My God, he's regressing," said Harold Bloomguard grimly.

"He'll be spitting up in a minute," Father Willie observed.

"We'll have to burp him, for chrissake," said Francis Tanaguchi.

"All right, all right, outta the way!" said Spermwhale Whalen, staggering forward and sitting on the grass next to the simpering redhead who now had his hands folded uselessly in his lap, his brain marinated.

"Gimme a can a beer," Spermwhale said and Baxter Slate flipped him one.

While the other choirboys watched, Spermwhale popped it open and soaked a paper napkin in beer and sat in front of Dean and washed all the barbecue from his face and plastered down the tangle of hair as Whaddayamean Dean sat unprotesting.

When the young man was cleaned up Spermwhale said, "Listen, Dean. Listen, son. It's me, your da da. It's Spermwhale. You know me, don't ya?"

And Whaddayamean Dean licked his chops happily and cried, "Beer! Beer!"

"No no," said Spermwhale Whalen. "First you listen. Then beer beer. Get it?"

Whaddayamean Dean eyed them all craftily and chuckled at some private joke.

"Now, Dean, my boy, we been pals awhile and I know you trust old Spermwhale. So listen careful. This thing that booze does to you, turnin you into a carrot, this ain't a good thing for you. You gotta master the effect a that booze. I been doin it for years. Remember when I flew us on that Palm Springs raid, dead drunk?"

And Whaddayamean Dean filled their hearts with hope, for he nodded at all of them.

"That's right!" Spermwhale said. "You *do* remember! See, I *know* you understand. Just concentrate. Okay, so here's what's happened tonight. Old Spermwhale's just too much man and screwed old Carolina Moon till she went fast asleep. Now that means there's only Ora Lee Tingle to pull that train for a few a the boys. And guess what? She picked *you* first. And *that* means you gotta go over there behind those bushes and show Ora Lee what a sport you are. And then maybe a couple a other fellas can get on the track. Get it?"

But Whaddayamean Dean cocked his head and wrinkled his brow in confusion and filled their hearts with dread.

"I'll make it simpler, son," said Spermwhale. "You just gotta go over there and do a number on Ora Lee, that's all you gotta do. So I want you to stand up now and show these fellas that my boy ain't no radish. Now you just listen to old Spermwhale and go over there and fuck old Ora Lee's socks off. Get it?"

The eager ring of faces shone sweatily in the moonlight and no one breathed as the grinning simpering redhead struggled valiantly with the words. They came and went from his consciousness and at times almost hung together coherently.

Finally he looked Spermwhale Whalen dead in the eye and raised a hand to the oldest choirboy's pink jowls and said sincerely, "Whaddayamean, Spermwhale? Just tell me what you *mean*."

And then eight choirboys—minus Roscoe Rules who was handcuffed to a tree and Whaddayamean Dean who sat and flashed a bewildered smile—beat their own heads with their fists or strangled phantoms in the air or showed white eyeballs and groaned pitifully.

Suddenly Spermwhale Whalen roared to his feet and grabbed Dean by the belt and the back of the shirt and lifted him four feet in the air as Harold Bloomguard yelled, "Don't hurt him, Spermwhale!"

And Baxter Slate shouted, "He can't help it, Spermwhale!"

And Spencer Van Moot yelled, "Kill the fucking idiot!"

And Whaddayamean Dean broke into tears and bawled, "Why's everyone picking on me? I don't get it! I don't get it!"

Spermwhale Whalen carried the weeping choirboy toward the bushes, toward Ora Lee Tingle and threw the redhead on top of the snoozing fat girl. "There!" Spermwhale bellowed. "You stupid goofy simple minded idiotic fuckin moron! Is exactly WHAT I MEAN!"

"Oh hi, Dean honey," said Ora Lee Tingle, waking up and pulling him down on her bulk.

The whimpering choirboy wiped his eyes on his sweatshirt and sniffed and looked back at Spermwhale and the others and then down to the fat girl he was sitting on as she licked her lips seductively.

"Oh!" said Whaddayamean Dean. "Oh! Why didn't you say so? Now I get it! Now I get it!"

And the choirboys sighed in unison and staggered back to their blankets and fell to the ground in relief.

Meanwhile, a fifty-one year old insomniac hairdresser who lived in an Alvarado Street hotel had come for a very early morning stroll through the cool invigorating darkness of MacArthur Park and found a man nude from the waist down sitting beside an elm tree with his arms enveloping the trunk. The hairdresser's name was Luther Quigly and it was the most carnal erotic sight he had ever seen. It was his wildest libidinous fantasy come true.

"My God! My God!" Luther Quigly whispered.

"Who's there?" Roscoe exclaimed.

"Oh!" said Luther Quigly. "Oh!" And the tiny balding hairdresser leaned back against a eucalyptus and tried to calm his pounding heart.

"Who're you?" Roscoe demanded, suffering terrible pain in his shoulders and back from having been totally forgotten by the drunken choirboys.

"Anyone you want me to be," answered Luther Quigly.

"Listen, goddamnit, go over by the duck pond. There's some drunks there. Go get one of em!"

"Who needs anyone else?" gasped Luther Quigly. "Three's a crowd!"

"I do! I'm chained to this tree!"

"Chained!" cried Luther Quigly. It was truly a mad salacious fantasy! It just couldn't be! A man naked except for his shirt and shoes! *Chained* to a tree!

"Oh, my lord!" cried Luther Quigly, getting faint.

Roscoe scurried around the elm, keeping it between himself and Luther Quigly, saying, "Stay away from me! I'll kill you you touch me, you faggy son of a bitch! I'll kneedrop you, so help me! I'll puncture your kidneys! I'll rupture your spleen! SPERMWHALE!"

Then Luther Quigly heard running footsteps across the grass. He jumped up and fled toward Seventh Street and ran all the way home to sit shakily in his room and wonder if it had all been a fantasy after all. He decided it had and called his psychiatrist later that morning.

The choirboys were full of apologies when they took the handcuffs off Roscoe Rules and brought him his wet underwear and pants.

"We forgot, Roscoe," said Harold Bloomguard.

"Real sorry, fella," said Spermwhale Whalen.

"Forgive us, Roscoe, forgive us," said Father Willie.

"It was that goddamn Dean," said Spencer. "We got preoccupied and forgot."

"You okay, man? How's your wrists?" said Calvin Potts.

Roscoe betrayed nothing in his manner as he put on his underwear and wrung out his pants, stepping into each soppy leg, and walked slowly and deliberately back toward his blanket.

"Roscoe, wait up a minute, will ya?" Spermwhale said, the first to get suspicious. He tried to trot past Roscoe who was heading directly toward his belongings.

But he was too late. Roscoe broke into a mad thirty yard sprint as Spermwhale screamed, "THE GUN!"

Seconds later Roscoe Rules was running back toward the ducking diving fleeing choirboys with his four inch magnum in his hand. Sphincter muscles and bladders were loosening all around and Francis Tanaguchi thought he was dead for sure as three explosions deafened the closest choirboys.

Harold Bloomguard was the first to look up and see Roscoe Rules insanely wading into the duck pond blasting away at the birds whose bills had been tucked securely under their wings but now squawked and flapped and swam for their lives from the orange fireballs and the terrifying explosions. Then when he clicked three times on empty cylinders Roscoe caught a hapless duck by the throat and tried to pistol-whip it and punch its lights out and drag it to shore where he could kneedrop it, rupturing its spleen.

"Stop him!" screamed Francis Tanaguchi.

"Get the gun!" yelled Spermwhale Whalen.

"Save the ducks!" yelled Harold Bloomguard while five frightened choirboys jumped on Roscoe and took away his gun and held his head under water for twenty seconds.

Then they dragged him and the duck onto the shore as Roscoe bellowed, "Lemme go! Lemme go! I'll strangle that cocksucker! I'll make that fuckin duck do the chicken!"

And as they pried the duck's neck from Roscoe's fist he swung a left and a right, the first of which socked the hissing bird on the bill, the second of which caught Spermwhale Whalen in the eye. There was yet a third punch thrown, this by Spermwhale, and it knocked the rabies right out of Roscoe.

The choir practice ended in a hurry with everyone running to his car to get away in case someone heard the shots and was calling the police. Unfortunately Roscoe could not leave, not after he discovered it was his own set of keys he had thrown into the middle of the pond. He waded in the buttery mud and dove in the mucky water until daybreak.

The quietus was uttered by Ora Lee Tingle as she and Carolina Moon were bouncing half dressed across the grass toward Park View Street at 5:00 A.M.

She turned and yelled, "It was a swell choir practice, fellas! And don't worry, Roscoe, we ain't gonna start calling you a duck socker!"

13

Catullus

It was two weeks after that memorable choir practice before there was talk of going to MacArthur Park. Roscoe's shootout with the ducks had unnerved everyone and had caused ten choirboys and two cocktall waitresses to study the newspapers the next day for any mention of persons hit with stray bullets in the vicinity of the park. There was none. They were ready to try again. It was scheduled for a Thursday night near the end of August. Harold Bloomguard intended to make sure all the choirboys left their guns in their cars.

"We can't have any more shooting at ducks," Harold had informed the others.

"How about shooting at fags?" Roscoe Rules had remarked.

"Believe it or not it's kind of nice to get back in a radio car after two weeks on vice," said Sam Niles to Harold Bloomguard the Tuesday night before.

"I was getting tired of those smelly rest rooms," Harold agreed as he blew a spit bubble against the steering wheel.

Sam slouched in the black and white and glanced languidly at the traffic which was light at this time of night. He didn't mind when Harold drove toward the Miracle Mile for a change of scenery.

"Remember the whore who lived there?" asked Sam as they passed a freshly painted lemon and white townhouse apartment building.

"Yeah, sometimes vice was fun," said Harold.

Then Sam Niles said something he would profoundly regret: "Just for kicks, drive by Gina Summers' apartment, right off Wilshire."

"Who?"

"That sadist whore, the one who takes those special tricks and does a number on them in her little torture chamber."

"Oh yeah," Harold said. "I never did see her. I remember you and Baxter talking about her."

"Wanna see if she's undressing up by her window tonight?" Sam asked. "Then you can see her. Tits like avocados."

"All *right!*" Harold said.

When Harold pulled to the curb beside Gina Summers' apartment and turned the lights out, Sam Niles said, "Yeah, she's home. See the light up there in the sixth floor corner apartment? Just sit for a minute, see if she parades in front of the window naked."

"Got lots of time." Harold had his eyes glued to the light.

But after they sat for five minutes Harold got antsy and said, "Well?"

"No action tonight. Let's split," said Sam.

Just then Gina Summers walked in front of the window, a long piece of leather draped around her neck. She unbuttoned her blouse and stood naked to the waist, the leather resting on one breast as she lowered the shade.

"Outta sight!" Harold Bloomguard exclaimed.

"Harold, that was a man's belt, wasn't it?" Sam Niles asked.

"It was a long fat leather belt. Mighta been a whip!"

"Goddamn. She's got a trick up there."

"So what?"

"So what? Do you know that Scuz and Baxter and I stake out four nights straight trying to close the vice complaint on this bitch? We never got close. Now she's got a trick up there. And she's got her whip!"

"So? We're not working vice anymore."

"It's police work, isn't it? Besides, Scuz'd get his rocks off if a couple of bluesuits brought in Gina Summers on a vice pinch when his squad's been working on her so long."

"Come on, Sam," Harold said. "It's only a lousy misdemeanor like Scuz always said. Besides we can't sneak and peek in full uniform."

"Let's try. You might get to see her bare ass, Harold."

"That's different. Let's go," Harold Bloomguard said, and the partners gathered up their hats and flashlights and locked the radio car.

"But how the hell we gonna get a violation?" Harold asked.

They crossed the street, looking up at the lighted window, entered the unlocked apartment building, took the carpeted stairs two at a time, clear to the fourth floor.

"We have to be able to hear the offer and the action," Sam said.

"That's impossible," Harold answered, puffing up the stairs.

"I've got good ears."

''Scuz said never to perjure yourself for a chickenshit vice arrest, remember?''

''Don't worry. Did you see the fire escape by her window? Baxter and I always had it planned if we saw a trick inside we'd go out on the fire escape. It's only three feet from her bedroom. I'm positive I could hear anything that was happening from there.''

''Well,'' Harold shrugged and then they stopped and rested on the fifth landing.

Harold longed for the elevator. But he knew why Sam disliked the confinement.

At last they reached the sixth floor, and while Harold Bloomguard had second and third thoughts about doing vice work in uniform, Sam Niles climbed out on the fire escape and was squatting in the darkness catching his breath. Then Sam heard female laughter and a muffled male voice in Gina Summers' bedroom.

He took off his hat and glasses and wiped his forehead on his blue woolen shirtsleeve and cleaned his glasses with his handkerchief, catching a breeze near the rooftops.

He listened. The voices were low but after three minutes he heard a woman's voice say, ''Is *this* what you want?''

And then the crack of leather and a man's gasp of pain.

''I can do better, honey. This isn't much,'' said the woman's voice again, followed by another crack and a man's cry and then another crack and a groan.

Then the woman's voice got more husky and guttural. She said, ''You feel like you belong to me now, don't you, baby? Well you do, you bastard! You worthless son of a bitch! Right now Gina *owns* you! You're not a man. You're an animal! Gina's animal!''

Then there were three cracks of leather and unbroken groaning. Sam Niles was chilled from the rib cage to the top of his head and furiously beckoned for Harold to climb out on the fire escape.

''But I can do better.'' The woman's laugh was like a bark. ''I can *really* hurt, baby, you give me a chance. There's no extra charge. Same price.''

And the man whimpered and moaned. Then there were three quick sharp cracks. And silence.

Harold Bloomguard crawled through the window and huddled next to his partner during the quiet moments.

''We've got it,'' Sam whispered. ''Goddamnit, we've got it. I heard it. The money offer. The act.''

Sam crawled back through the window into the hallway and Harold followed him down the hall where they ducked into an alcove.

''I heard her saying something about no extra charge,'' Sam said. ''I heard the act. It's a good legal pinch!''

''What act? Screwing?''

''No. She's whipping some guy!''

''Far out!'' whistled Harold Bloomguard. ''I sure never made a bust like this. Sex, money. We got her for prostitution. And him. Wait, is whipping considered a sex act?''

''I think so,'' Sam Nlies said, putting his hat on and pushing his glasses up on his nose. ''Isn't it?''

''You got me. I haven't had that fantasy yet,'' said Harold Bloomguard who thought he probably would by the time he got in bed tonight.

''Let's go. I say we've got her,'' Sam said. ''We'll just wait until he comes out . . .''

''Can't we knock? I don't wanna waste the whole night here. I haven't eaten all day.''

''Okay, let's go. They're probably through by now. Unless he's gonna let her beat him to death.''

While Harold stood back against the wall Sam Niles knocked at the door. There was no response so he knocked again, saying, ''Miss Summers !''

Then they heard frantic footsteps and a woman's voice, soft and sultry now. ''Who is it?''

''Assistant manager, Miss Summers. There's a gas leak on this floor, ma'am. We're evacuating the building.''

The door opened a few inches, but before she could slam it, Sam Niles shouldered it wide open and the naked girl was thrown back against the wall saying, ''Hey, what's the big idea?'' as both policemen rushed into the apartment past the naked brunette.

''Just go in the room there with my partner while I have a talk with your friend,'' Sam Niles said as he rushed down the hall to arrest the other party to the prostitution.

Then he was in the bedroom face to face with the customer who was putting on his pants. Shivering. Sweat soaked. Face like alabaster.

''Baxter!'' Sam Niles gasped. Freezing in his tracks. Face to face with Baxter Slate who was naked to the waist, his body wet and gleaming.

Then Sam heard Gina Summers threatening Harold Bloomguard with false arrest while Harold nodded placatingly and leered at her naked breasts.

Sam Niles closed the bedroom door and Baxter Slate went to the window and looked out and choked off a sob. Sam Niles stared at the ugly raw welts and stripes on Baxter's body which already were swelling and said, ''Why, Baxter?''

Then Sam went to a chair and sat. And disbelieved. He removed his hat and ran his hand through his hair and looked at his friend who wiped his pale sweating face with a shirt but never turned from the window.

''Why?'' groaned Sam Niles who couldn't take his eyes from Baxter's welted flesh.

''What's happening, Sam?'' called Harold Bloomguard from the hall outside where Gina Summers was demanding to call her lawyer.

Yet she made no move to the phone nor to the closet where her robes hung with the whips and boots and exotic underwear. Harold Bloomguard went on explaining the arrest to her while she stood nude, hands on her hips.

''I thought we didn't work vice anymore, Sam,'' Baxter said finally with a quivering smile which was nothing, *nothing* like a Baxter Slate smile. He went to the bed and sat, his wounded back still turned to his friend.

''Why?'' Sam Niles asked. ''Why?''

''I don't know for sure, Sam.''

''Does she know you're a cop?''

''No, of course not.''

Sam Niles lit a cigarette and sighed and turned from the sight of Baxter's tortured flesh and said, ''I'll tell her it was a mistake. She'll be damn glad not to be hitting the slammer so she won't ask any questions of me.''

''And Harold?''

''I'll tell Harold the guy in the room was a deputy from the sheriff's department and I decided to give him a break. I can take care of Harold. You tell that fucking whore you bought me off for fifty bucks. Then everybody's happy.''

When Sam stood and turned to go out the door, Baxter Slate called desperately, ''Sam!''

''What is it, Baxter?'' Sam answered without looking at his friend.

''It's . . . it's just that I was afraid to park my own car near here. I took a cab from Pico and La Brea. And I gave her every dime. Well . . . ,'' and then he tried another twisted smile which was so unlike Baxter Slate's easy grin it made Sam Niles want to turn and run. ''Could you maybe drop Harold at the station and think of some excuse to come back? I could use the ride. I'm too weak to walk, Sam.''

Then Sam dug in his pockets and found seven dollars and some change. ''Here!'' he said, throwing the money on the bed. ''Catch a cab!''

''You . . . you couldn't . . . I wouldn't mind waiting if you could drive me, Sam. I could wait out front. . . . I'd really appreciate . . . I could maybe meet you after you get off work and talk . . . explain . . .''

"Goddamnit, I gave you my last dollar for a cab! What the fuck do you want from me?"

"Nothing, Sam. Nothing. Thanks for the money," said Baxter Slate.

And as Sam Niles jerked the bedroom door open he heard Baxter Slate say, "It's not evil, Sam. I haven't enough dignity to be evil."

Then Sam was stalking down the hall to the living room where Gina Summers was sidling up to Harold Bloomguard and trying to convince him that his partner could not possibly have heard what he thought he heard and why doesn't everyone just forget the whole thing?

"Come on, let's go, Harold," Sam said.

"Go?"

"Yeah, go. We made a mistake."

"A mistake?"

"Goddamnit, let's go! We made a mistake!"

As Sam started for the front door with his bewildered partner trailing behind, Gina Summers then made the mistake of saying, "Well I coulda told you that. You'll be lucky if I don't sue over this. You'll be lucky . . ."

She was astonished by how quickly Sam Niles moved as he whirled and grabbed her by the throat and pinched off the carotid artery with his powerful right hand. Gina Summers came up off the floor, naked, clinging to his wrist with both hands, fighting for breath, gaping at Sam Niles' unblinking iron gray eyes, slightly magnified by his steel rimmed glasses.

"If I *ever* hear you complain about *anything,*" he whispered, "I'll be back here. And if you're not here I'll be where you are, baby. You groove on handing out pain? Well maybe you don't know what it is to *feel* pain. I'll show you. Can you dig it?"

And as Gina Summers nodded and gripped his wrist and gurgled, Sam Niles released her throat and she fell to her knees, gasping. The two policemen burst out the door quicker than they had come in.

Sam Niles literally hurtled down those six flights, leaving Harold half a landing behind. He hated Harold Bloomguard like he never had before. As he hated Baxter Slate. They were weaklings. They were bleeders. They were sick, wretched, disgusting.

Sam Niles got dizzy as he flew down those stairs and swung past the landings holding the handrails. Hating them. They bleed. They need. Like the Moaning Man as he lay there bleeding and needing past the grave. Hands reaching out. They never let you alone. Reaching past death. Until someone touched them. He despised them all. He hated them as he had hated his weak sick disgusting parents. Sam Niles had never needed anyone. Except for one minute, sixty seconds in his life.

He stopped on the last landing and waited for the puffing little man who had seen him need that one time. And he feared that if Harold had *ever* mentioned that moment in the suffocating blackness of that cave, he would now, at this moment, draw his revolver and shoot him dead on the staircase. But Harold had never talked about it. Not even to Sam. Sam hoped that Harold had somehow forgotten it in his own terrible fear. Sometimes Sam Niles even believed that it never had happened.

"What's the hurry, Sam?" Harold stammered, trying to catch his breath before the last flight of steps. Never once suggesting they use the elevator because he understood his partner better than his partner dreamed. "What's the rush?"

"Nothing," Sam said viciously. "There's no rush. None at all."

Five minutes later in the car Sam Niles shouted, "Goddamnit, he was a deputy sheriff I know from court! You don't know him. Never mind his fucking name. I wanted to give him a break. He told me he had a wife and kids and was going to a psychiatrist. I made a decision and I DON'T WANT TO EVER TALK ABOUT IT AGAIN!"

And though they never did, Harold Bloomguard scratched his neck with a penknife and blew spit bubbles not only that night but the next afternoon when Baxter Slate suddenly called off sick, saying he had the flu. Harold heard Sam Niles question

Baxter's partner Spermwhale Whalen as to whether he had heard from Baxter. Harold saw that Sam seemed troubled that Spermwhale had not.

When Baxter Slate did not come to work the Thursday of choir practice and Sam Niles was jumpy as a cat while putting on his uniform, Harold Bloomguard developed a brand new rash all over his neck and began to suspect that Gina Summers' trick was not a deputy sheriff after all.

The choirboys were happy that Thursday afternoon in the assembly room because Sergeant Nick Yanov was conducting the rollcall alone. But Nick Yanov entered the room grimly and didn't seem to hear a few jokes directed his way from men in the front row. Though his jaws were as dark and fierce as always from his incredibly thick whiskers which he had shaved only three hours earlier, his forehead and Baltic cheekbones were white. He was white around the eyes. His hands were unsteady when he lit a cigarette. The men quieted down. Something was very wrong with Nick Yanov.

He took a deep puff on the cigarette, sucked it into his lungs and said, "Baxter Slate's dead. They just found him in his apartment. Shot himself. Spermwhale, you'll be working a report car tonight. Seven-U-One is your unit. Would you like to go down now and get your car?"

The rollcall room was deathly still for a moment. No one moved or spoke as Nick Yanov waited for Spermwhale. One could hear the hum of the wall clock. Spermwhale Whalen finally said to the sergeant, "Are you *sure?*"

"Go on down and get your car, Spermwhale," said Nick Yanov quietly. But as shaky as Spermwhale looked when he gathered his things and walked through the door, Harold Bloomguard looked even shakier when he looked at Sam Niles who had broken out in a violent sweat and had ripped open his collar and was having trouble getting enough air.

Then Sam jumped up and burst through the door behind Spermwhale Whalen. Harold Bloomguard started up, thought better of it and sat back down.

Nick Yanov called the roll and dismissed the watch without another word.

There was speculation and many rumors in the parking lot about Baxter Slate's suicide, and several members of the Wilshire nightwatch spent a lingering fearful evening handling calls, cruising, smoking silently, trying to avoid thinking of that most terminal of all policeman's diseases. Wondering how one catches it and how one avoids it.

None of the choirboys took the initiative to do police work that night. It was as though a monotonous routine would be somehow comforting, reassuring. The only thing out of the ordinary done by a nightwatch radio car was that 7-A-29 drove to West Los Angeles Police Station, the area in which Baxter Slate had resided because he loved Westwood Village and the cultural activities at UCLA and the theater which showed foreign films and a small unpretentious French restaurant with wonderful wines.

"I'd like to see the homicide team. Whoever's handling Officer Slate's suicide," Sam Niles said to the lone detective in the squad room.

"All gone home, Officer. Can you come back tomorrow?"

The detective wasn't much older than Sam and like Sam he had a moustache. His suit coat was thrown over a chair. He wore an uncomfortable looking shoulder holster.

"I'd like to see the death report on Baxter Slate," Sam Niles said.

"I can't go into homicide's cases. Come back tomorrow. You can talk to . . ."

"Please," said Sam Niles. "I only want to see the report. Please."

And the detective was about to refuse, but he looked at Harold Bloomguard who turned and walked out of the office, and he looked at Sam Niles who did not walk away. He looked at Sam's face and asked, "Was he a friend?"

"Please let me see the report. I have to see it. I don't know why."

"Have a seat," the detective said and walked to a filing cabinet drawer marked "Suicides—1974" and pulled out a manila folder, removed the pictures in the file which Sam Niles definitely did not want to see and gave the file to the choirboy.

Sam read the perfunctory death report which listed the landlady as the person discovering the body. The person hearing the shot was a neighbor, Mrs. Flynn. He saw that Baxter's mother who was in Hawaii had not been contacted as yet. His married sister in San Diego was the nearest relative notified. The speckled pup which Baxter had been caring for since he found her on the street outside Wilshire Station was taken to the animal shelter where she would soon be as dead as her master. The narrative told him nothing except that Baxter had fired one shot into his mouth at 11:00 A.M. that morning on a sunny smogless delightful day.

In the file was a note to the milkman which Baxter had written asking that two quarts of skim milk be left. The handwriting was scratchy, halting, not the sure flowing stroke of Baxter Slate. No more than that horrible grimace of consummate humiliation in Gina Summers' apartment had been a Baxter Slate grin.

The report said that several books were scattered around the table where the body was found. Baxer Slate had gone to his classics at the end. Disjointedly. Desperately. The detective had torn several pages from the clothbound texts. He had thought the pages marked by that same spidery crawl might prove enlightening.

One marked passage from Socrates read: "No evil can happen to a good man, either in life or after death."

Another from Euripides said: "When good men die their goodness does not perish, but lives though they are gone. As for the bad, all that was theirs dies and is buried with them."

Baxter had marked a passage from Cicero, the only one not specifically mentioning good and evil and death. It made Sam Niles moan aloud which startled the nightwatch detective. It said: "He removes the greatest ornament of friendship who takes away from it respect."

Sam removed his glasses and cleaned them before reading the last page. The page was powdery from dried blood. Sam's hands were shaking so badly the nightwatch detective was alarmed. Sam read it and left the squad room without thanking the detective for his help. The passage was underlined. It simply said: "What is it, Catullus? Why do you not make haste to die?"

14

The Moaning Man

At the end of that tour of duty on the day Baxter Slate died, the choirboys were more anxious for a choir practice than they had ever been. When Father Willie asked quietly, "Are we still going to have choir practice?" Spencer Van Moot said angrily, "Of *course* we're having choir practice. What the fuck's wrong with you?"

Never had the choirboys drunk so obsessively in MacArthur Park. They were snarling at each other and guzzling sullenly, all except Roscoe who had gotten a station call to transfer an overflow of five drunks from Wilshire to Central Jail and had not yet shown up at choir practice by 1:00 A.M.

Before they could be too thankful for the absence of Roscoe a blue panel truck appeared from nowhere, grinding and rumbling across the grass in MacArthur Park with its lights out, clanking to a stop under the trees in the darkest shadows.

"I was hopin I could get drunk painlessly," Calvin Potts said as Roscoe Rules, still in uniform, jumped out of the drunk wagon and came trotting across the grass.

"Hey!" yelled Roscoe *cheerfully,* which was enough to make everyone mad to begin with, "I was on my way back to the station but I couldn't wait to tell you!"

"Tell us what, Roscoe?" Spermwhale grumbled. He was lying on his blanket, a can of beer on his huge stomach, looking up at the moonless, smog-filled summer sky which even hid Baxter Slate's great star.

"Down at Central Jail after I transported the drunks I ran into a guy I know. Works homicide downtown. Guess what they found when the coroner posted Baxter Slate's body? Whip marks! All over his back! Whip marks! They think he musta been a pervert. I always said he was weird, but whip marks!"

"What? What did you say?" Sam Niles said as he sat in the darkness on the cool grass and cut his hands when he suddenly tore an empty beer can in half.

"Well I liked him as much as the next guy," said Roscoe, "but kee-rist, whip marks on his back! The dicks think he was some kind a freak or pervert. You know how faggy he always talked . . ."

Then Roscoe Rules was even more astonished than Gina Summers had been at how quickly Sam Niles could move. Roscoe was hit twice with each of Sam's fists before he fell heavily on his back. Sam lifted him by the front of his uniform and hit him so hard the third time that Sam's glasses flew farther than the chip from Roscoe's tooth.

Spermwhale Whalen overpowered Sam and several others restrained Roscoe who tried to kneedrop Sam as he lay pinned to the ground by Spermwhale, and the park was alive with shouting choirboys and quacking ducks, and four park fairies came running to the sounds of fighting.

Father Willie Wright staggered drunkenly over to examine the body of Roscoe Rules who fell in the bushes just as a park fairy said, "A policeman! What happened to him?"

"Stand back, give him room to breathe," commanded Father Willie. "Lemme work on him."

"Are you a doctor?" asked the second fairy.

"I'm a priest," answered Father Willie as Spermwhale roared the fairies away.

"People like you killed him!" Sam Niles yelled as Spermwhale Whalen enveloped him in his enormous arms and pinned him to the ground saying, "Calm down, kid. Calm down."

"I'll kill *you,* you scrote!" screamed the revived Roscoe Rules as three choirboys held him and took away his gun.

"Shut up, Roscoe!" Spermwhale barked as Sam Niles began to weep for the first time since the spider holes. But only Spermwhale saw and he said softly, "Listen, son, Roscoe's an asshole but he didn't kill Baxter."

"I'll puncture your kidneys and rupture your spleen, Niles !" screamed the thrashing Roscoe Rules.

Now that Spermwhale was sure he could release his grip on Sam Niles he did so. Spermwhale then stood up and walked across the grass to the pile of bodies on the ground and said, "Roscoe, if you don't get your mind together and relax, I'm gonna relax you."

And he held up a big red fist which Roscoe Rules remembered.

After that it was only a matter of everyone dusting Roscoe's uniform off and apologies all around except from Sam Niles who stalked off to the duck pond to sit and drink and try not to think of Baxter Slate.

Roscoe Rules rubbed his lumpy jaw and touched the broken tooth with his tongue and became appeased by everyone apologizing for Sam Niles and patting him on the shoulder and being nice which he was totally unused to. And Roscoe said, "I'm already long past end-of-watch. I'll just have a beer before I drive the wagon back in."

With the police drunk wagon parked on the grass in MacArthur Park under the trees, Roscoe sat there in uniform and had a beer which led to three while Sam Niles drank Scotch without mercy to his flaming throat and stomach. He relentlessly sought the intellectual oblivion which alcohol brought to Whaddayamean Dean Pratt.

At 2:00 A.M. Harold Bloomguard walked quietly up behind his brooding partner and startled him by saying, "Sam, let's talk."

"I've got nothing to talk about, Harold. Leave me alone."

"We have to talk."

"Look, goddamn you. You got problems? A new neurosis that's bothering you? Eat your fucking gun. Like Baxter. But leave me alone."

"I don't wanna talk, Sam. I wanna listen. Please talk to me. About Baxter. About anything you want."

But Sam Niles cursed and struggled to his knees and pushed up his drooping glasses and held up a fist bloodied by Roscoe's teeth and said: "I don't need you. I've *never* needed you. Or anybody. Now you get away from me. YOU LEAVE ME ALONE!"

Harold Bloomguard nodded and trudged back to his blanket, back to the others, and drank silently.

At 2:30 A.M. Spencer Van Moot said, "Hey, Roscoe, don't start on that hard stuff. You're sitting here in uniform, case you did't know. And that funny blue wagon over there is a police vehicle."

"So bust me for drunk driving," Roscoe giggled, the pain in his jaw almost anesthetized by now. "Besides, Ora Lee and Carolina might be here soon and they ain't never seen how good looking I am in uniform."

"I wish he'd just walk toward Duck Island till his hat floats," said Calvin Potts.

The choirboys drank quietly and speculated about Baxter Slate and felt the closeness of death and stole glances at Roscoe's gun and thought how near and familiar the instrument always was to men who somehow contract this policeman's disease. They wondered if the closeness and familiarity of the instrument had something to do with it or was it the nature of the work which Baxter always called emotionally perilous? Or was it a clutch of other things? And since they didn't know they drank. And drank.

It was a miserable choir practice. All attempts at jokes fell flat. Harold often looked toward the duck pond where Sam was drinking himself into paralysis but did not go to him. Whaddayamean Dean got on a usual crying jag but this time he cried without respite. Spermwhale took him away from the others and put him down on his blanket and gave him a pint of bourbon.

"Spermwhale! Spermwhale!" Dean cried. "Baxter's dead! Baxter's dead!"

"I know, son. I know," said Spermwhale Whalen, leaving Dean to drink alone on the grass on a gloomy night under a very black sky.

They were grateful that Ora Lee and Carolina didn't show up that night. Finally as the moon misted over, Spermwhale looked at the glowing Roscoe Rules and said, "Roscoe, you better get that fuckin wagon back to the station. You're gettin swacked."

"You guys gonna be here when I come back?"

"I'm going home," said the miserable Francis Tanaguchi.

"Gimme that fuckin Scotch," said Calvin Potts as he raised himself up on an elbow.

"I'm going home too," said Father Willie Wright who was sitting quietly by the trees.

Then Spencer Van Moot stood and tried to walk toward the pond but fell flat on his face.

"Jesus!" said Spermwhale as three choirboys struggled to their feet dizzily and tried to pick up their groaning comrade.

"He can't drive home," Father Willie said.

"Somebody drive him home," said Spermwhale. "Padre, why don't you drive his car to the station parking lot and one of us'll take him home?"

But then the body of Spencer Van Moot reacted logically to the abuse being done to it. Spencer sat up and retched and vomited all over himself in enormous bilious waves as the choirboys cursed and scattered.

And that normal physical reaction sealed the fate of a human being in that park.

"Oh shit, he's *covered* with puke!" Francis Tanaguchi said.

"Oh gross !" said Harold Bloomguard.

"I ain't taking him in *my* car," said Calvin Potts who strangely enough could not get drunk while thinking of the suicide of Baxter Slate.

"Okay, okay," said Spermwhale. "Put him in the back of the wagon. Roscoe, you drive him to the station parking lot. Padre, you drive his car there and put him in it and let him sleep it off for a few hours. I'll get up at six o'clock or so and go down to the station and wake him up so he can get cleaned up before anybody notices him."

"Can't he sleep in the wagon all night?" offered Roscoe.

"Fuck no, stupid!" said Spermwhale. "A sergeant finds him there tomorrow he'll get racked. Do like I say."

"Well who's gonna put him in the wagon now? I don't wanna touch him!"

"Goddamnit, get outta the way," Spermwhale said. He grabbed the semiconscious Spencer by the feet and dragged him across the grass and rolled him over on his stomach and back to wipe off some of the vomit. Then he and Calvin Potts took his wrists and ankles and flipped him up to the floor of the wagon and got inside and lifted him up on the bench.

"Better put him on the floor," Father Willie said. "He'll fall off the way Roscoe drives."

As Spencer Van Moot was being ministered to and as Sam Niles was finding himself too drunk to get to his feet and was searching in vain for Baxter Slate's great star Jupiter, an eighteen year old boy was strolling toward Sam on the other side of the pond, tossing bread crumbs to the ducks, making hopeful plans about his life, how he would make a career for himself and care for his parents.

When Alexander Blaney approached the staggering figure by the pond he stopped in the shadows. He saw that it was a drunken man and he heard the voices off by the trees and saw a blue panel truck parked between the drunken man on the grass and the others. He knew it was the group of policemen again and he debated about whether to try to help the drunken one or to mind his own business. For all he knew the drunken policeman might be the one called Roscoe who raged about fags and might kneedrop him, whatever that meant.

Then Sam Niles, who did not see Alexander Blaney, managed to get to his feet and swayed toward the subdued choir practice. But he made it only as far as the panel truck where he found the doors open and saw a pair of feet and a body on the floor.

"That you, Harold?" mumbled Sam as he leaned into the foul and shadowy truck and tugged on the sleeve of the snoring figure.

"That you, Dean?" asked Sam Niles who crawled into the truck and collapsed on the floor next to Spencer Van Moot.

"That you, Padre?" he asked, and tried to help the sleeping figure up to the bench in the truck but got dizzy and sat down on the opposite bench. Then Sam Niles became nauseated and violently light-headed and he had to lie down on the bench while the earth spun madly. Within seconds he was dozing.

Alexander Blaney watched all this and saw that the policeman was safely inside the blue truck and he sat down on the grass closer to the choir practice than he had ever been before and listened to the voices which were not loud and funny tonight. But quiet and bitter.

Then Alexander backed into the shadow of the trees when he saw a uniformed policeman and another man walking toward the truck.

"Hey, look at this, Padre," Roscoe Rules said when he got to the back of the wagon.

"Sam!" said Father Willie.

"Spencer's got another drunk for company. Fuckin scrote, probably been smoking pot and passed out. Just like that dopehead friend of his, Baxter Slate."

"Baxter's dead," Father Willie reminded, thinking Roscoe didn't look sober enough to drive.

"I liked him as much as the next guy," Roscoe said. "I just didn't like his pervert ways."

"What'll we do about Sam?"

"Take him with Spencer, I guess," said Roscoe.

"So somebody's gonna have to drive two cars to the station."

"Let's get it over with before we have the whole fucking bunch back here," Roscoe Rules said, pushing Spencer's feet inside and slamming the door to the wagon.

After the wagon was closed Roscoe urinated on the grass and Alexander Blaney heard him laughing as he rejoined the dying choir practice.

Then when they were out of sight Alexander Blaney heard a muffled scream from inside the wagon.

It was less the clanging wagon door and the snapping of the lock than it was the feel of the body on the floor beside him, but Sam Niles' eyes popped open. It was black. There was no light. He didn't know where he was. For a brief instant he didn't know *who* he was. Then he felt the body. He leaped to his feet in the darkness and slammed his head against the metal roof. He screamed and turned to his right, smashing his glasses on the wall of the wagon. He clawed at those unyielding walls.

He walked on the body and his alcohol weakened legs slipped and his ankle turned and he fell on the body. He screamed again.

"Harold! Harold!" Sam screamed. And he smelled fish sauce and garlic and pressed his face to the slimey wall and awaited the molten horror from the flame thrower.

Then he wept and screamed, "Harold! Harold!" But instead of saying, "Now now now. Hush now, I'm with you. You're not alone," the body said nothing. Because it was dead. It was Baxter Slate!

While Roscoe was laughingly reporting to Spermwhale Whalen that he found Sam Niles asleep in the wagon, Sam Niles was pleading, "Baxter! Baxter! Baxter!"

But the body beside him did not answer. Not in a human tongue. It only said, "Mmmmmmmmmm. Uuuuuuuuhh."

The top of Baxter's head was gone and crackled under Sam Niles' shoes as he backed against the doors of the wagon, his head bent from the low roof, his face bleeding from the broken glasses. He screamed. He couldn't breathe. He was hyperventilating.

But the only one who could hear those dreadful cries was a boy named Alexander Blaney who summoned enough courage and came out of the shadows and hurried to the back of the truck to open the doors for the screaming policeman.

Back at the blankets Harold Bloomguard said, "You what!"

"We left him in the back of the wagon," said Roscoe.

"Did you close the doors?"

"Yeah, why?"

"Sam doesn't like to be closed in. I better go have a look!"

But before he could get there Alexander Blaney was standing at the back door of the wagon trying to get the rusty bolt slid to the right as Sam Niles was hiding his bloody face in his hands, screaming like a woman, trying hopelessly to escape the body that was Baxter Slate. And the Moaning Man. Trying to breathe.

Then Sam reached for the M-14 which wasn't there. He instinctively went for his waistband for his off-duty Smith and Wesson .38 caliber two-inch revolver which *was* there. The thundering explosions commenced just as the right door flew open. The first two fireballs missed Alexander Blaney by a foot. The third splattered into his throat, throwing out a pocket of blood. The fourth and fifth would have hit him except that he dropped and lay on the grass grabbing his throat, gasping for the oxygen that was always there for Sam. Spencer Van Moot scrambled through the door, covering his ears and screaming louder than Sam Niles.

Then Sam found himself being pulled from the wagon by Harold Bloomguard who sat him on the ground holding him in his arms. Roscoe Rules stood over the convulsive body of Alexander Blaney saying, "It's a park fairy! He shot a park fairy!"

Then Roscoe was on his ass so fast it didn't even surpise him anymore. Spermwhale Whalen, who had hurled him aside, was on the ground reaching inside Alexander Blaney's mouth, pulling the swallowed tongue free.

Then Spermwhale was sitting on the grass holding the boy like a baby, blowing his hot lusty lion's breath into the lad's mouth, pausing every so often to hammer on the thin chest and say, "Come on, boy! Come on, son! Breathe !"

Alexander Blaney had given up very easily. When death offered, the lonely boy accepted, and his life leaked away. Still Spermwhale stubbornly tried to force his brawny vigorous life into Alexander. Most of it bellowed into the chest of the boy, some foamed out the hole in his throat.

It was a full five minutes before Spermwhale Whalen looked up, his face and arms and hands smeared with blood, his balding head wet and shining, his white eyes glimmering in the moonlight. Had that indolent moon appeared when Sam Niles was clawing at the blackness, it might have shined in the window of the truck and reassured the drunk and panic stricken choirboy, bringing him to his senses.

As Spermwhale got to his feet, leaving the sprawling body, several choirboys started walking in circles babbling incoherently. A dozen plans were made while Spermwhale Whalen wiped the blood of Alexander Blaney, shining black in the moonlight, from his own face and hands.

But finally it was a strange and stern and determined Harold Bloomguard standing next to Sam Niles whose face was bleeding and lowered. Sam shivered and smoked silently and was content to let others think and do for him.

"I'm taking Sam to Wilshire dicks," Harold said evenly. "I'm telling them that we bought some booze and were on our way to my pad to have a few drinks when we decided to stop in the park and have a beer. While we were here we both got a little drunk. Sam dropped his gun. When he picked it up he fell on his face and broke his glasses."

"I'll sweep the broken glass outta the truck!" Roscoe jabbered frantically, "in case they . . ."

"Shut up!" Spermwhale said. "Go on, Harold."

"That's it. He fell and must've pulled the trigger and this boy was walking by and . . . that's it."

"That fucking gun was fired five times!" Calvin Potts said.

"I'm replacing four of the rounds," Harold said. "It's a dirty gun. It's been fired several times between cleaning."

"I dunno, Harold," Spencer said.

"The rest of you can go home," Harold said. "Only Sam and I are involved. Sam's career is finished. And I'm not staying on the job without him so I've got nothing to lose anyway."

"I don't know, Harold," Father Willie said. "Maybe we should . . ."

"No sense anybody else riding this beef," Harold said stubbornly. "Spermwhale, you've got *almost* twenty years to protect. It's too late for you to be involved in something like this."

Spermwhale Whalen sighed and the others waited for him. He walked over to Sam Niles and put his hand on Sam's shoulder without looking at him. He patted Sam's shoulder and walked wearily to his blanket to gather up his belongings. Choir practice was over.

Within ten minutes Roscoe was pushing the blue truck for all it was worth down Venice Boulevard.

Within fifteen minutes hasty plans were made after several violent arguments as to whether they should lie, but finally Harold Bloomguard replaced four of the empty shells in Sam's gun with four live rounds.

Within thirty minutes Sam Niles and Harold Bloomguard were sitting in the detective bureau at Wilshire Station and a homicide team was on the way, as was Captain Drobeck, as was a team of officers from Internal Affairs Division.

Since the killing was officer-involved, the homicide team that showed up at Wilshire Station that night were strangers. There was an old one with bifocals who was even more near-sighted than Sam Niles. There was a young one with a hair style longer than was permitted at Wilshire station.

Harold Bloomguard had swabbed most of the blood from around the eyes of Sam Niles before they were separated. When the detectives entered the interrogation room Sam's right eye was puffy and cut at the corner. He squinted myopically at the detectives until they sat down in front of him.

''Lost your glasses, huh, Sam?'' the older detective asked.

''Yes.''

''Wanna talk about it now? Tell us how it happened.''

''Yes. We went to the park just like Harold said. We drank some b-b-b-beer. W-w-w-we . . .''

''Wanna smoke, Sam?''

''Th-th-th-thank you,'' Sam Niles said, accepting the cigarette from the detective.

''Internal Affairs will be here real soon,'' the younger detective said. ''Let's get the story now before you have to tell the headhunters.''

''Sure,'' said Sam Niles, looking blankly at both detectives. ''W-w-w-well, I d-d-d-dropped my gun and p-p-p-p . . .''

''You picked it up?''

''Sure,'' Sam nodded, looking from one face to the other.

He sat perfectly still, did not sweat, did not tremble, looked normal, except more earnest than laconic. It was only the stutter which was different.

''Did the gun go off, Sam?'' the younger detective asked impatiently as the older detective sat back and studied the choirboy.

''Y-y-y-y . . .''

''All right, that's enough for the moment,'' the older detective said.

As the two detectives started out the door Sam Niles made his last statement on the subject of the shooting at MacArthur Park. He said, ''The h-h-h-head was all shot off. The b-b-b-blood was everywhere!''

''Whose?'' the young detective asked as they turned in the doorway.

''Th-th-th-the Moaning Man!'' cried Sam Niles. ''He said, 'Mmmmmmmmm. Uuuuuuuuuh.' ''

''Who?'' the younger detective asked.

''Baxter! He said, 'Mmmmmmmmm. Uuuuuuuhhhh!' I couldn't touch him! He was too . . . revolting! How could I take his hand? How *could* I?''

''Who?'' the younger detective asked.

''Baxter Slate!'' Sam Niles sobbed.

''Holy mother,'' said the younger detective.

''Okay, Sam,'' the older detective said. ''You just relax and finish your smoke. We're gonna let you go to bed soon.''

The older detective came out of the interrogation room and walked straight to Sergeant Nick Yanov and said, ''I want a radio car to take this boy to the Hospital Detail for immediate commitment to the psycho ward at General Hospital.''

''But the headhunters're on the way,'' said Nick Yanov.

''It's *my* case and I'll take the responsibility,'' the old detective answered. ''This boy isn't fit to be interrogated by *anyone,* especially not the headhunters.''

"They won't be able to get to him in the hospital," Nick Yanov said with a grim smile. "They're not gonna like it."

"Too goddamn bad," the old detective said, making a decision which would cost him a suspension and ten days' pay.

By the time the black and white arrived at Unit Three, Psychiatric Admitting, Sam Niles was described by a young intern as catatonic.

15

Dr. Emil Moody

"Niles and Bloomguard!" said Lieutenant Elliott "Hardass" Grimsley, formerly of Wilshire nightwatch, now of Internal Affairs Division, when he was telephoned at home that morning by his investigators who could not break Harold Bloomguard's spurious story. Nor could they gain admission to General Hospital Psychiatric Ward to talk to Sam Niles, who by now could not even have told them his name.

"I remember them," Lieutenant Grimsley said. "Troublemakers. Friends of that slob, Spermwhale Whalen. Listen, I heard rumors they used to go to choir practice with several other officers from the nightwatch. MacArthur Park? Maybe that's where they go. Get to Whalen's house. Roust the fat pig outta bed and bring him down to IAD. Let's sweat him."

At 9:00 A.M. the two headhunters sat with Spermwhale Whalen in an interrogation room on the fifth floor of the police building. They looked at his bristling red jowls and huge stomach and fierce little eyes filled with contempt and rebellion.

"You don't expect us to believe that you know *nothing* about this shooting?" the unsmiling investigator said. "We have reliable information that you were there."

Spermwhale Whalen looked at both young plainclothes sergeants and said, "You know so much, what're you fuckin with me for?"

"Listen, Whalen." The other plainclothes sergeant leaned over the table. "We found empty booze bottles not far from the body. You boys didn't clean up everything well enough. And we found tire tracks and casts've been made. One of you had a car parked there."

"I told you I went home after work last night. I don't know what this's all about and I resent the shit outta you two bringin me here."

The investigator who played bad guy stood up disgustedly and stormed out of the door so his partner could play good guy which of course Spermwhale wasn't buying.

"He say anything?" asked Lieutenant Grimsley who was waiting in the corridor outside with Commander Hector Moss and Deputy Chief Adrian Lynch who had spent the night in a motel with his passionate secretary, Theda Gunther, and predictably had his toupee twisted.

"Whalen's a good actor, Lieutenant," the investigator said. "Unless it's the truth. Maybe Bloomguard isn't lying. He's sticking to the original story right down the line."

"Bullshit!" Lieutenant Grimsley interrupted. "I know Bloomguard's lying. Those beer cans and bottles . . ."

"We can't prove they put them there," the investigator said.

"How about that bra you found?" Lieutenant Grimsley asked.

"Looked like it'd been there several days. Covered with leaves and debris."

"What size was it?"

"Enormous. Forty-four, D cup."

"Any station groupies with tits that big?" pondered Lieutenant Grimsley, unconsciously glancing at the amorous deputy chief.

"What're you looking at me for, Lieutenant?"

"Oh. Sorry, sir," Hardass Grimsley blanched.

"Why don't you have a try at him, Lieutenant?" asked Commander Moss, and Lieutenant Grimsley smiled nervously as he visualized a scene with Spermwhale Whalen telling about the black woman from Philadelphia he had caught Grimsley going down on when he was the Wilshire watch commander.

"I don't like to interfere with my men's investigations," Lieutenant Grimsley said, hoping that Spermwhale Whalen wouldn't see him and wink and muss up his hair.

"Well I took the liberty of going through his personnel package in your office, Lieutenant," Chief Lynch said. "Do you mind if I have a try?"

"Not at all, sir," Lieutenant Grimsley said, enormously relieved. "After all, you're an old IAD man."

And it was true that Chief Lynch was an old IAD man, it being pretty much agreed upon that Internal Affairs Division experience was the best springboard for promotion. Headhunters made rank consistently better than other investigators, the regular detective bureau being a dead end for the ambitious.

His three years as a headhunter were the most pleasurable in Chief Lynch's entire career. He understood certain things about policemen. He knew the polygraph worked extremely well on them because of their job-induced guilt feelings, whereas it was almost useless on guiltless sociopathic criminals. Also he knew that all men fear something and he guessed what a fifty-two year old patrol cop like Spermwhale Whalen probably feared most.

Five minutes later Deputy Chief Lynch was sitting across from Spermwhale, drinking coffee, offering Spermwhale none. Chief Lynch was smiling. "I'm not going to waste time on you, Whalen."

"That's good, Chief, because I got nothin to say and I don't know what this is all about."

"You're a goddamn liar!" Chief Lynch suddenly said and Spermwhale's little eyes narrowed. The furry eyebrows dipped dangerously and the Z-shaped scar showed very white through the eyebrow and across his red nose. Chief Lynch, despite himself, glanced anxiously toward the door and wished he'd have let one of the investigators sit with him here in the stark room, with the table and wooden chairs and tape machine hissing.

"I'm not going to try to fool an old veteran like you, Whalen," Chief Lynch said, continuing more amiably. "Of course we're going to tape your statement. I'm not going to try to fool you about anything."

"That's good," said Spermwhale, "because I got nothin . . ."

"Quite a record you have," Chief Lynch interrupted. "You have quite a history of being insubordinate. I see why you've remained in uniform patrol for twenty years."

"I *like* uniform patrol," Spermwhale said, sitting motionless, his big hands on his knees, wishing for a cup of coffee, his mouth dry as ashes.

"Did I say twenty years? Well not quite. You only have nineteen and a half years, don't you? Less some bad time you have to make up. My, my, you were so close to that twenty year pension. Now you'll get nothing."

"Listen, Chief . . ."

"*You* listen, Whalen," Chief Lynch snapped. "You listen good. Maybe Niles wasted that fruit practicing a quick draw. Or shooting at beer bottles. I don't know how he did it and I don't really care. But I'm going to get the truth from every man who was there. You can cooperate or I'll push for at least involuntary manslaughter against Niles and I guarantee you'll find your ass on trial as an accessory after the fact. Ever hear of the crime of harboring and concealing after a felony's been committed?"

"Listen, Chief . . ."

"*You* listen, Whalen," said Chief Lynch, warming up, leaning across the table, his breath smelling lemony from Theda Gunther's douche powder. "You're fifty-two years old. Fifty-two. Think of that. Look at you. You're a crude, fat, aging man. You going to go out and get a job? Doing what? Flying airplanes? No chance. You aren't going to be able to get a job cleaning out shithouses after you're *fired* from the police department. How're you going to live? I'll bet after you serve your six months in *jail,* and after your whole career's down the drain, without a *dime* of pension money, that you end up on skidrow with the other bums. I'll bet you're begging for nickles or selling your blood for a few bucks. Know some of the other things the old winos do to make a few bucks, Whalen? Want me to tell you? Think it could never happen to you?"

And then Chief Lynch tried the inquisitor's device of lie and half lie to get truth and half truth. "We found a very interesting fingerprint on a bourbon bottle there in the park. You have five minutes to make up your mind. I'm walking out this door right now. You either give us the full story on this killing or you're on your way to a trial board and criminal prosecution. Then it'll be too late to make a deal. Nineteen and a half years, huh? You almost made the pension, baby."

Spermwhale Whalen found himself staring at a vacant chair. He didn't move for three minutes. He had never felt more alone. He listened to the muffled voices outside. He listened to his heart and to the hissing tape machine. Sweat studded his upper lip. He heard it patting to the floor. Then the bravest and strongest choirboy, the veteran of three wars, the only Los Angeles policeman to fly combat missions while an active member of the department, the winner of a Silver Star, six Air Medals and two Purple Hearts, who feared no man, nor even death from any hand but his own, the bravest and strongest and *oldest* choirboy, found that he feared life. The horrifying life described by Chief Lynch. He feared it dreadfully. He felt the fear sweep over him. His throat constricted and his scalp tingled from fear. The tape recorder was unbearable. Hissing. His big red hand almost slipped off the doorknob when he rushed to open the door. He stepped tentatively into the hallway where five men waited.

Deputy Chief Lynch looked into Spermwhale's little eyes. Chief Lynch smoothed his toupee, his own scraggly hair curling behind his ears. He stepped back into the room smiling confidently. Spermwhale held the door for him.

By 11:00 A.M. that day eight choirboys were separately sitting in various offices on the fifth floor of Parker Center. By 4:00 P.M. that day Sergeant Nick Yanov, who by now knew the story from Captain Drobeck, who had gotten it from Commander Moss, was on the phone calling Lieutenant Rudy Ortiz who often defended accused officers at department trial boards.

Nick Yanov was raging into the telephone, hurting the ears of the defender. "The stupid goddamn idiots cooked up a story and stuck to it except Whalen who informed on himself and the others!"

"Christ!" Lieutenant Ortiz said. "All they had the others for was maybe cue-bow for getting drunk in the park. They just should've called the dicks and told the whole story at the scene. Niles was the only one in *serious* trouble, except for the dummy who was in uniform."

"I know. I know. The idiots!" said Nick Yanov. "Now they've got them *all* for withholding evidence and lying to the investigators and insubordination."

"They can fire their young asses behind this caper," Lieutenant Ortiz said. "They could even prosecute them in criminal court."

"I know. Can't you help them?" Nick Yanov pleaded.

By 5:00 P.M., Deputy Chief Lynch was on the phone, chatting good naturedly with Assistant Chief Buster Llewellyn.

"Right, Buster, I wish we could fire them too. And throw them in the slammer. But that would attract attention. As it is we've got it under control."

"Thank God the victim was just some fag. Imagine if it'd been someone decent," said Assistant Chief Buster Llewellyn, sipping on his coffee, wondering for the hundredth time about the mysterious stain on his hand tooled blotter.

"Nobody decent would be in MacArthur Park at that time of night. Nobody *except* fruits. And this group of policemen."

"Talk to the victim's mother, Adrian?"

"Personally," smiled Chief Lynch. "She took it pretty hard. But you know, I think his old man was actually kind of relieved."

"Better off," Chief Llewellyn nodded. "Woulda got his throat cut in some fruit hustle sooner or later anyway. If he didn't die of syphilis."

"So we came out all right. Mr. and Mrs. Blaney know there were some policemen in the park and that one of them dropped his gun and it went off and that the perpetrator went nuts after the accident and is now in the squirrel tank getting his head shocked. The newspapers know basically the same information except I had to level with them that the officers had a beer or two. And that nine were involved and that there was some withholding of all the facts at first but that it was an accident pure and simple."

"Thank God that officer went crazy afterward."

"Well actually he went nuts before, Buster. When they locked him in the wagon."

"No one know about that?"

"Not necessary to tell all the details. Doesn't change the facts. We've got it effectively stonewalled."

"Blast it, Adrian, don't use that word!"

"Sorry, Buster."

"What're we going to give them?"

"The maximum, short of firing, which we can't very well do if we don't want too many rumors about choir practice to come out. Of course I'd be happy if we could scare all of them into voluntarily resigning under the threat of criminal prosecution."

"Think they will?"

"Maybe. One of them already has: Bloomguard. Of course, Niles is really batty they tell me and if he doesn't come around that's two down right away. Not to mention that Officer Slate who killed himself the other night. He was one of the gang, I'm told. But he had the good grace to blow his brains out before this shooting in the park."

"It's these young policemen we're getting these days," said Assistant Chief Llewellyn. "No morality in the country anymore. The young policemen reflect it. Imagine them trying to withhold the facts and cover up something like that!"

"Yes, sir, it's pathetic. Honesty is a rare commodity nowadays."

"Well you did a fine job, Adrian. You should be commended. There was hardly a mention in the papers and nothing on television."

"Thank you, Buster," said Deputy Chief Lynch, hoping this would be only the start of his praise and recognition for the coverup.

Dr. Emil Moody, the police department psychologist, was sick and tired of being nothing but a marriage counselor. And he was sick and tired of writing his monthly column in the police magazine. He rarely had the opportunity to examine psychotic officers like Sam Niles. The department and the city got great public relations mileage from the infrequent knifing, slugging and shooting of policemen but hated to admit that something as unglamorous and *expensive* as mental illness should be added to heart disease, tuberculosis, hernia and whiplash, the more common job-induced police cripplers.

Lacking the information for a psychological workup, he did a brief profile on the MacArthur Park choirboys for his own education. He found that unlike policemen from other generations these were not of the working class and not of foreign born parents. Bloomguard, Slate, Pratt, Potts, Wright, Tanaguchi and Van Moot had solid middle class upbringing. Whalen and Rules were of working class families and only one, Sam Niles, had a childhood history of poverty and parental neglect.

Only three were married: Van Moot, Wright and Rules. Three had been divorced: Potts, Whalen, and Niles, Whalen having been thrice divorced, Van Moot divorced and remarried.

Van Moot was a veteran of the Korean War. Niles, Bloomguard, Rules and Potts were Vietnam vets. Tanaguchi had seen service but not combat. Slate, Wright and Pratt had not been in the military. Whalen had, incredibly enough, seen combat in World War II, Korea and even in Vietnam on weekend flights from March Air Force Base.

Nine had college training and most were still making efforts to obtain a degree. Three had bachelor's degrees: Bloomguard in business administration, Niles in political science, Slate in classical literature. Most were pursuing degrees in police science or prelaw. Whalen had never gone to college.

With the exception of fifty-two year old Herbert Whalen and forty year old Spencer Van Moot, they were all young men in their twenties, all apparently in good physical health.

In short the brief profile proved exactly nothing. Dr. Moody wrote it, read it and threw it in the wastebasket. He had hoped to promote a thesis that policemen are entitled to effective preventive medicine for job-induced mental illness.

He wanted very much to contact Officer Niles' best friend, Officer Bloomguard, who had resigned on the morning of the shooting. He wanted to consult with psychiatrists at General Hospital where Niles was committed. He wanted most to visit Niles himself. He suspected there was more to the incident than the administration knew. He suspected that the suicide of Officer Baxter Slate contributed to the deadly episode in the park.

But Dr. Moody went back to his innocuous writing of an innocuous column for the innocuous police magazine. The police department liked people who could get along. He had a nice steady job and wanted to keep it.

Just as Chief Lynch thought everything was going to work out smoothly Spencer Van Moot got stubborn. Since he was unconscious during the shooting he didn't think he deserved a six month suspension. He pleaded not guilty at his trial board. Father Willie Wright, hearing Spencer plead not guilty and thinking what six months loss of pay would do to him did the same thing.

Some said theirs were the quickest trial boards anyone ever had for a firing offense. The witnesses were heard in two hours. Spermwhale Whalen was the chief witness for the department advocate. He was gray and trembling when he testified against his fellow choirboys. He had lost twenty pounds since the shooting. His fat had lost its ferocious tone. He looked soft. And old.

Theoretically the trial boards are unbiased hearings before superior officers of the rank of captain or higher. But like any hierarchy, particularly a hierarchy of quasi-military persuasion, the captains knew exactly the wishes of Assistant Chief Buster Llewellyn who answered only to the big chief and to God. And they also knew the wishes of Deputy Chief Adrian Lynch who answered only to Assistant Chief Llewellyn and to Theda Gunther, who was so impressed and thrilled with Chief Lynch's masterful subjugation of Spermwhale Whalen and the subsequent uncovery of the disgusting orgy that she banged him in his office one afternoon putting a stain on *his* blotter and tearing his toupee to shreds. His hairpiece looked moth-eaten. It lay on his head like a dead squirrel. When it was time to go home to his wife he had to leave the police building in a golf cap.

Spencer was found guilty of insubordination, lying to investigators and withholding evidence. His defender, Lieutenant Rudy Ortiz, pleaded for leniency. Sergeant Nick Yanov testified to Spencer's good character and work performance. But there were examples to be made. The custom of choir practice was to be discouraged. He was fired in record time. Sixteen years went up in smoke.

Lieutenant Rudy Ortiz angrily accused the trial board, Internal Affairs Division and the department brass of being ruthless and cavalier. He admitted that for some time he had been in favor of civilian review boards. Not to protect citizens from overzealous street cops since there were legal remedies for that. But to protect street cops from overzealous disciplinarians within the ranks. He denounced forced polygraphs and their admission as evidence, the acceptance of hearsay, investigator's opinion as to truth and lie, the arbitrary searches of person and locker, private cars and officers' homes under threat of insubordination, a firing offense.

Lieutenant Rudy Ortiz finally had his say about internal investigations and the constitutional rights of policemen all right. And so did Assistant Chief Adrian Lynch. He said privately that the only way that dumpy little greaseball Ortiz would ever make captain was by joining the Mexican Army.

Father Willie Wright's trial board was even quicker. Unlike Spencer, who went out shakily but defiant, Father Willie openly wept at the penalty.

When Spencer and Father Willie were fired the other choirboys stopped complaining. They all freely admitted their guilt at their own trial boards. They gladly accepted the six months' suspension. Spermwhale Whalen was given only a thirty day suspension as a reward for helping Internal Affairs crack the case by informing on all of them.

Sam Niles was still hospitalized and was quietly released by the police department. Since he had less than five years' service, the city did not have to pay him a pension for the incapacitating illness which the city said did not happen as a result of police service. Sam Niles was confined for a time at the Veterans Hospital and was later transferred to Camarillo State Hospital.

Harold Bloomguard was asked to stop visiting him because his visits seemed to upset the patient.

Epilogue

It was somehow eerie to be standing there in MacArthur Park on a cold and damp and shadowy winter night in February. Sergeant Nick Yanov was looking at a place he had never cared to visit, satisfying the curiosity of his new boss, Lieutenant Willard Woodcock, a recently promoted thirty-one year old whiz kid who they said was going places in the department. They said he had lots of top spin.

"So this is where it happened?" Lieutenant Woodcock observed, his brand new hat with the gold lieutenant's badge a bit too large. It slid down to his ears over the fresh haircut.

"Yes, right here from what they tell me," Sergeant Nick Yanov said, his hands in the pockets of his blue jacket, a cigarette dangling from his lips, white against his glowering jaw. Since he had only shaved once today his lower jaws were dark and fierce.

"Been about six months now, hasn't it?"

"Just about."

"They'll be back to work very soon then. I think we should make plans."

"Plans."

"We can't let them bunch up again."

"Aren't many in the bunch anymore," Nick Yanov said, pushing his hands deeper into the pockets and pulling up the collar of the old wool jacket with the frayed sergeant's chevrons ripping from one sleeve.

"There're enough to cause trouble."

"Slate's dead. Niles is mutilating himself from time to time in the state hospital. Bloomguard resigned . . ."

"Where's the big one now? The one who became a witness for the department?"

"Whalen, he's retired. Took his pension last month. I hear they're sending his checks to some remote little town in Utah. Wright's fired. Van Moot's fired. That only leaves four, Lieutenant: Rules, Dean Pratt, Tanaguchi and Potts. After six months without pay I'll just bet they're pretty well pacified."

"I still think it was a bad idea to leave them in Wilshire Division. They should've been scattered to hell and gone after their six months' suspension."

"But this way the department can show that discipline works on troublemakers. They'll be tame ex-troublemakers, isn't that it."

"Yes, I suppose that's the theory," said Lieutenant Woodcock.

"Except that they *weren't* troublemakers."

"What do you mean by that?" the lieutenant said, trying to examine the face of the sergeant who had his cigarette half smoked, not touching it with his hands.

Nick Yanov stared at the sleeping ducks in the peaceful pond and said, "They were just policemen. Rather ordinary young guys, I thought. Maybe a little lonelier than some. Maybe they banded together when they were especially lonely. Or scared.''

''*Ordinary!* How can you say that, Yanov? I've heard they were animals. They brought sluts here for orgies. One of them was possibly a pillhead and a pervert. The one that killed himself. What was his name?''

''Baxter Slate. I liked him.''

''Christ, Yanov, there's a lesson to be learned here for policemen everywhere!''

''What lesson have *you* learned, Lieutenant.''

Lieutenant Woodcock glared at the big chested sergeant who never took his eyes off the shimmering water. The lieutenant made a mental note to keep tabs on this field sergeant and mention the incident to Captain Drobeck and perhaps cancel the special day off which Nick Yanov had requested. Finally the lieutenant said, ''Suicidal degenerates. Drunken killers. Whoremongers. Probably dopeheads. Sergeant, these guys would try to seduce an eighty year old nun. Or break her arm.''

''Maybe,'' Nick Yanov said, blowing a cloud of smoke through his nose, the cigarette glowing in the darkness. ''But they wouldn't steal her purse.''

''Is that the test of a policeman, Yanov? Is that all there is to making a good policeman?''

''I don't know, Lieutenant. I truly don't know what makes a good policeman. Or a good anything.''

''Let's go back to the station,'' said the disgusted watch commander. ''It's cold out here.''

But for a moment Sergeant Nick Yanov stood there alone on the wet grass, his weight pressing footprints in the black spongy earth. The grass smelled washed and fresh and the rows of trees crouched like huge quail. The duck pond was silver and black sapphire. The treetops shivered and rustled in the cold wind and loosened the white blossoms of a flowering pear.

Nick Yanov looked up at the brooding darkness, at the tarnished misty moon. There were no stars. Not even the great star could pierce that black sky. Nick Yanov stood where they had put their blankets down, close enough to the water to pretend they were with nature, here in the bowels of the violent city. He felt some light mocking rain, yet longed to stay in the solitude, while dead leaves scraped at his feet like perishing brown parchment.

Then he flipped the cigarette into the pond and heard the hiss and watched it float. He was immediately sorry he did it. Yet there was other debris on the still water and in the bushes if one used the moonlight to look closely.

He didn't want to look closely. He preferred to think it was lovely and clean and pastoral here by the silent lagoon and the slumbering ducks in the icy water. Where the choirboys frolicked in the duck shit.